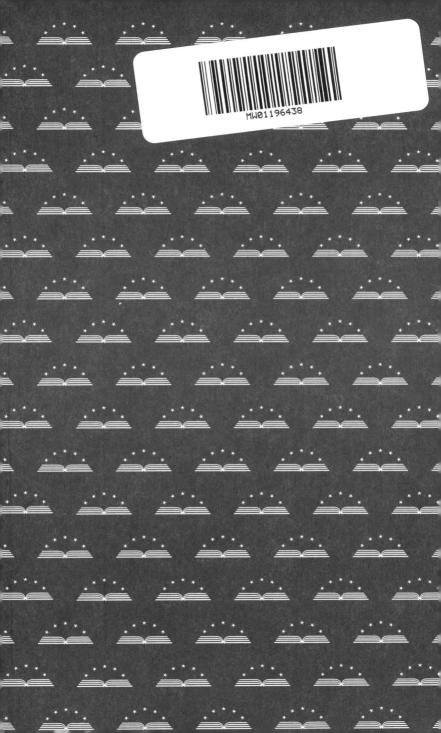

EDITH WHARTON

EDITH WHARTON

FOUR NOVELS OF THE 1920s

The Glimpses of the Moon
A Son at the Front
Twilight Sleep
The Children

Hermione Lee, *editor*

THE LIBRARY OF AMERICA

Contents

THE GLIMPSES
OF THE MOON

Chapter I

I T rose for them—their honey-moon—over the waters of a lake so famed as the scene of romantic raptures that they were rather proud of not having been afraid to choose it as the setting of their own.

"It required a total lack of humour, or as great a gift for it as ours, to risk the experiment," Susy Lansing opined, as they hung over the inevitable marble balustrade and watched their tutelary orb roll its magic carpet across the waters to their feet.

"Yes—or the loan of Strefford's villa," her husband emended, glancing upward through the branches at a long low patch of paleness to which the moonlight was beginning to give the form of a white house-front.

"Oh, come—when we'd five to choose from. At least if you count the Chicago flat."

"So we had—you wonder!" He laid his hand on hers, and his touch renewed the sense of marvelling exultation which the deliberate survey of their adventure always roused in her. . . . It was characteristic that she merely added, in her steady laughing tone: "Or, not counting the flat—for I hate to brag—just consider the others: Violet Melrose's place at Versailles, your aunt's villa at Monte Carlo—*and* a moor!"

She was conscious of throwing in the moor tentatively, and yet with a somewhat exaggerated emphasis, as if to make sure that he shouldn't accuse her of slurring it over. But he seemed to have no desire to do so. "Poor old Fred!" he merely remarked; and she breathed out carelessly: "Oh, well—"

His hand still lay on hers, and for a long interval, while they stood silent in the enveloping loveliness of the night, she was aware only of the warm current running from palm to palm, as the moonlight below them drew its line of magic from shore to shore.

Nick Lansing spoke at last. "Versailles in May would have been impossible: all our Paris crowd would have run us down within twenty-four hours. And Monte Carlo is ruled out because it's exactly the kind of place everybody expected us to go. So—with all respect to you—it wasn't much of a mental strain to decide on Como."

His wife instantly challenged this belittling of her capacity. "It took a good deal of argument to convince you that we could face the ridicule of Como!"

"Well, I should have preferred something in a lower key; at least I thought I should till we got here. Now I see that this place is idiotic unless one is perfectly happy; and that then it's— as good as any other."

She sighed out a blissful assent. "And I must say that Streffy has done things to a turn. Even the cigars—*who* do you suppose gave him those cigars?" She added thoughtfully: "You'll miss them when we have to go."

"Oh, I say, don't let's talk to-night about going. Aren't we outside of time and space . . . ? Smell that guinea-a-bottle stuff over there: what is it? Stephanotis?"

"Y-yes. . . . I suppose so. Or gardenias. . . . Oh, the fire-flies! Look . . . there, against that splash of moonlight on the water. Apples of silver in a net-work of gold. . . ." They leaned together, one flesh from shoulder to finger-tips, their eyes held by the snared glitter of the ripples.

"I could bear," Lansing remarked, "even a nightingale at this moment. . . ."

A faint gurgle shook the magnolias behind them, and a long liquid whisper answered it from the thicket of laurel above their heads.

"It's a little late in the year for them: they're ending just as we begin."

Susy laughed. "I hope when our turn comes we shall say good-bye to each other as sweetly."

It was in her husband's mind to answer: "They're not saying good-bye, but only settling down to family cares." But as this did not happen to be in his plan, or in Susy's, he merely echoed her laugh and pressed her closer.

The spring night drew them into its deepening embrace. The ripples of the lake had gradually widened and faded into a silken smoothness, and high above the mountains the moon was turning from gold to white in a sky powdered with vanishing stars.

Across the lake the lights of a little town went out, one after another, and the distant shore became a floating blackness. A breeze that rose and sank brushed their faces with the scents of the garden; once it blew out over the water a great white moth like a drifting magnolia petal. The nightingales had paused and the trickle of the fountain behind the house grew suddenly insistent.

When Susy spoke it was in a voice languid with visions. "I have been thinking," she said, "that we ought to be able to make it last at least a year longer."

Her husband received the remark without any sign of surprise or disapprobation; his answer showed that he not only understood her, but had been inwardly following the same train of thought.

"You mean," he enquired after a pause, "without counting your grandmother's pearls?"

"Yes—without the pearls."

He pondered a while, and then rejoined in a tender whisper: "Tell me again just how."

"Let's sit down, then. No, I like the cushions best."

He stretched himself in a long willow chair, and she curled up on a heap of boat-cushions and leaned her head against his knee. Just above her, when she lifted her lids, she saw bits of moon-flooded sky incrusted like silver in a sharp black patterning of plane-boughs. All about them breathed of peace and beauty and stability, and her happiness was so acute that it was almost a relief to remember the stormy background of bills and borrowing against which its frail structure had been reared. "People with a balance can't be as happy as all this," Susy mused, letting the moonlight filter through her lazy lashes.

People with a balance had always been Susy Branch's bugbear; they were still, and more dangerously, to be Susy Lansing's. She detested them, detested them doubly, as the natural enemies of mankind and as the people one always had to put one's self out for. The greater part of her life having been passed among them, she knew nearly all that there was to know about them, and judged them with the contemptuous lucidity of nearly twenty years of dependence. But at the present moment her animosity was diminished not only by the softening effect of love but by the fact that she had got out of those very people more—yes,

ever so much more—than she and Nick, in their hours of most
reckless planning, had ever dared to hope for.

"After all, we owe them *this*!" she mused.

Her husband, lost in the drowsy beatitude of the hour, had
not repeated his question; but she was still on the trail of the
thought he had started. A year—yes, she was sure now that with
a little management they could have a whole year of it! "It"
was their marriage, their being together, and away from bores
and bothers, in a comradeship of which both of them had long
ago guessed the immediate pleasure, but she at least had never
imagined the deeper harmony.

It was at one of their earliest meetings—at one of the heterogeneous dinners that the Fred Gillows tried to think
"literary"—that the young man who chanced to sit next to her,
and of whom it was vaguely rumoured that he had "written,"
had presented himself to her imagination as the sort of luxury
to which Susy Branch, heiress, might conceivably have treated
herself as a crowning folly. Susy Branch, pauper, was fond of
picturing how this fancied double would employ her millions:
it was one of her chief grievances against her rich friends that
they disposed of theirs so unimaginatively.

"I'd rather have a husband like that than a steam-yacht!" she
had thought at the end of her talk with the young man who had
written, and as to whom it had at once been clear to her that
nothing his pen had produced, or might hereafter set down,
would put him in a position to offer his wife anything more
costly than a row-boat.

"His wife—! As if he could ever have one! For he's not the
kind to marry for a yacht either." In spite of her past, Susy had
preserved enough inner independence to detect the latent signs
of it in others, and also to ascribe it impulsively to those of the
opposite sex who happened to interest her. She had a natural
contempt for people who gloried in what they need only have
endured. She herself meant eventually to marry, because one
couldn't forever hang on to rich people; but she was going to
wait till she found some one who combined the maximum of
wealth with at least a minimum of companionableness.

She had at once perceived young Lansing's case to be exactly
the opposite: he was as poor as he could be, and as companionable as it was possible to imagine. She therefore decided to see

as much of him as her hurried and entangled life permitted; and this, thanks to a series of adroit adjustments, turned out to be a good deal. They met frequently all the rest of that winter; so frequently that Mrs. Fred Gillow one day abruptly and sharply gave Susy to understand that she was "making herself ridiculous."

"Ah—" said Susy with a long breath, looking her friend and patroness straight in the painted eyes.

"Yes," cried Ursula Gillow in a sob, "before you interfered Nick liked me awfully . . . and, of course, I don't want to reproach you . . . but when I think. . . ."

Susy made no anwer. How could she, when *she* thought? The dress she had on had been given her by Ursula; Ursula's motor had carried her to the feast from which they were both returning. She counted on spending the following August with the Gillows at Newport . . . and the only alternative was to go to California with the Bockheimers, whom she had hitherto refused even to dine with.

"Of course, what you fancy is perfect nonsense, Ursula; and as to my interfering—" Susy hesitated, and then murmured: "But if it will make you any happier I'll arrange to see him less often. . . ." She sounded the lowest depths of subservience in returning Ursula's tearful kiss. . . .

Susy Branch had a masculine respect for her word; and the next day she put on her most becoming hat and sought out young Mr. Lansing in his lodgings. She was determined to keep her promise to Ursula; but she meant to look her best when she did it.

She knew at what time the young man was likely to be found, for he was doing a dreary job on a popular encyclopædia (V to X), and had told her what hours were dedicated to the hateful task. "Oh, if only it were a novel!" she thought as she mounted his dingy stairs; but immediately reflected that, if it were the kind that she could bear to read, it probably wouldn't bring him in much more than his encyclopædia. Miss Branch had her standards in literature. . . .

The apartment to which Mr. Lansing admitted her was a good deal cleaner, but hardly less dingy, than his staircase. Susy, knowing him to be addicted to Oriental archæology, had pictured him in a bare room adorned by a single Chinese bronze of flawless shape, or by some precious fragment of Asiatic pottery.

But such redeeming features were conspicuously absent, and no attempt had been made to disguise the decent indigence of the bed-sitting-room.

Lansing welcomed his visitor with every sign of pleasure, and with apparent indifference as to what she thought of his furniture. He seemed to be conscious only of his luck in seeing her on a day when they had not expected to meet. This made Susy all the sorrier to execute her promise, and the gladder that she had put on her prettiest hat; and for a moment or two she looked at him in silence from under its conniving brim.

Warm as their mutual liking was, Lansing had never said a word of love to her; but this was no deterrent to his visitor, whose habit it was to speak her meaning clearly when there were no reasons, worldly or pecuniary, for its concealment. After a moment, therefore, she told him why she had come; it was a nuisance, of course, but he would understand. Ursula Gillow was jealous, and they would have to give up seeing each other.

The young man's burst of laughter was music to her; for, after all, she had been rather afraid that being devoted to Ursula might be as much in his day's work as doing the encyclopædia.

"But I give you my word it's a raving-mad mistake! And I don't believe she ever meant *me*, to begin with—" he protested; but Susy, her common-sense returning with her reassurance, promptly cut short his denial.

"You can trust Ursula to make herself clear on such occasions. And it doesn't make any difference what *you* think. All that matters is what *she* believes."

"Oh, come! I've got a word to say about that too, haven't I?"

Susy looked slowly and consideringly about the room. There was nothing in it, absolutely nothing, to show that he had ever possessed a spare dollar—or accepted a present.

"Not as far as I'm concerned," she finally pronounced.

"How do you mean? If I'm as free as air—?"

"I'm not."

He grew thoughtful. "Oh, then, of course—. It only seems a little odd," he added drily, "that in that case, the protest should have come from Mrs. Gillow."

"Instead of coming from my millionaire bridegroom? Oh, I haven't any; in that respect I'm as free as you."

"Well, then—? Haven't we only got to stay free?"

Susy drew her brows together anxiously. It was going to be rather more difficult than she had supposed.

"I said I was as free in that respect. I'm not going to marry—and I don't suppose you are?"

"God, no!" he ejaculated fervently.

"But that doesn't always imply complete freedom. . . ."

He stood just above her, leaning his elbow against the hideous black marble arch that framed his fireless grate. As she glanced up she saw his face harden, and the colour flew to hers.

"Was that what you came to tell me?" he asked.

"Oh, you don't understand—and I don't see why you don't, since we've knocked about so long among exactly the same kind of people." She stood up impulsively and laid her hand on his arm. "I do wish you'd help me—!"

He remained motionless, letting the hand lie untouched.

"Help you to tell me that poor Ursula was a pretext, but that there *is* someone who—for one reason or another—really has a right to object to your seeing me too often?"

Susy laughed impatiently. "You talk like the hero of a novel—the kind my governess used to read. In the first place I should never recognize that kind of right, as you call it—never!"

"Then what kind do you?" he asked with a clearing brow.

"Why—the kind I suppose you recognize on the part of your publisher." This evoked a hollow laugh from him. "A business claim, call it," she pursued. "Ursula does a lot for me: I live on her for half the year. This dress I've got on now is one she gave me. Her motor is going to take me to a dinner to-night. I'm going to spend next summer with her at Newport. . . . If I don't, I've got to go to California with the Bockheimers—so good-bye."

Suddenly in tears, she was out of the door and down his steep three flights before he could stop her—though, in thinking it over, she didn't even remember if he had tried to. She only recalled having stood a long time on the corner of Fifth Avenue, in the harsh winter radiance, waiting till a break in the torrent of motors laden with fashionable women should let her cross, and saying to herself: "After all, I might have promised Ursula . . . and kept on seeing him. . . ."

Instead of which, when Lansing wrote the next day entreating a word with her, she had sent back a friendly but firm refusal;

and had managed soon afterward to get taken to Canada for a fortnight's ski-ing, and then to Florida for six weeks in a house-boat. . . .

As she reached this point in her retrospect the remembrance of Florida called up a vision of moonlit waters, magnolia fragrance and balmy airs; merging with the circumambient sweetness, it laid a drowsy spell upon her lids. Yes, there had been a bad moment: but it was over; and she was here, safe and blissful, and with Nick; and this was his knee her head rested on, and they had a year ahead of them . . . a whole year. . . . "Not counting the pearls," she murmured, shutting her eyes. . . .

Chapter II

Lansing threw the end of Strefford's expensive cigar into the lake, and bent over his wife. Poor child! She had fallen asleep. . . . He leaned back and stared up again at the silver-flooded sky. How queer—how inexpressibly queer—it was to think that that light was shed by his honey-moon! A year ago, if anyone had predicted his risking such an adventure, he would have replied by asking to be locked up at the first symptoms. . . .

There was still no doubt in his mind that the adventure was a mad one. It was all very well for Susy to remind him twenty times a day that they had pulled it off—and so why should he worry? Even in the light of her far-seeing cleverness, and of his own present bliss, he knew the future would not bear the examination of sober thought. And as he sat there in the summer moonlight, with her head on his knee, he tried to recapitulate the successive steps that had landed them on Streffy's lake-front.

On Lansing's side, no doubt, it dated back to his leaving Harvard with the large resolve not to miss anything. There stood the evergreen Tree of Life, the Four Rivers flowing from its foot; and on every one of the four currents he meant to launch his little skiff. On two of them he had not gone very far, on the third he had nearly stuck in the mud; but the fourth had carried him to the very heart of wonder. It was the stream of his lively imagination, of his inexhaustible interest in every form of beauty and strangeness and folly. On this stream, sitting in the stout little craft of his poverty, his insignificance and his independence, he had made some notable voyages. . . . And so, when Susy Branch, whom he had sought out through a New York season as the prettiest and most amusing girl in sight, had surprised him with the contradictory revelation of her modern sense of expediency and her old-fashioned standard of good faith, he had felt an irresistible desire to put off on one more cruise into the unknown.

It was of the essence of the adventure that, after her one brief visit to his lodgings, he should have kept his promise and not tried to see her again. Even if her straightforwardness had not roused his emulation, his understanding of her difficulties would have moved his pity. He knew on how frail a thread the popularity of the penniless hangs, and how miserably a girl like Susy was the sport of other people's moods and whims. It was a part of his difficulty and of hers that to get what they liked they so often had to do what they disliked. But the keeping of his promise was a greater bore than he had expected. Susy Branch had become a delightful habit in a life where most of the fixed things were dull, and her disappearance had made it suddenly clear to him that his resources were growing more and more limited. Much that had once amused him hugely now amused him less, or not at all: a good part of his world of wonder had shrunk to a village peep-show. And the things which had kept their stimulating power—distant journeys, the enjoyment of art, the contact with new scenes and strange societies—were becoming less and less attainable. Lansing had never had more than a pittance; he had spent rather too much of it in his first plunge into life, and the best he could look forward to was a middle-age of poorly-paid hackwork, mitigated by brief and frugal holidays. He knew that he was more intelligent than the average, but he had long since concluded that his talents were not marketable. Of the thin volume of sonnets which a friendly publisher had launched for him, just seventy copies had been sold; and though his essay on "Chinese Influences in Greek Art" had created a passing stir, it had resulted in controversial correspondence and dinner invitations rather than in more substantial benefits. There seemed, in short, no prospect of his ever earning money, and his restricted future made him attach an increasing value to the kind of friendship that Susy Branch had given him. Apart from the pleasure of looking at her and listening to her—of enjoying in her what others less discriminatingly but as liberally appreciated—he had the sense, between himself and her, of a kind of free-masonry of precocious tolerance and irony. They had both, in early youth, taken the measure of the world they happened to live in: they knew just what it was worth to them and for what reasons, and the community of these reasons lent to their intimacy its last exquisite touch. And now, because of some jealous whim of a dissatisfied fool of a woman, as to whom he felt himself no more to blame than any young man who has paid for good dinners by good manners, he was to be deprived of the one complete companionship he had ever known. . . .

His thoughts travelled on. He recalled the long dull spring in New York after his break with Susy, the weary grind on his last articles, his listless speculations as to the cheapest and least boring way of disposing of the summer; and then the amazing luck of going, reluctantly and at the last minute, to spend a Sunday with the poor Nat Fulmers, in the wilds of New Hampshire, and of finding Susy there—Susy, whom he had never even suspected of knowing anybody in the Fulmers' set!

She had behaved perfectly—and so had he—but they were obviously much too glad to see each other. And then it was unsettling to be with her in such a house as the Fulmers', away from the large setting of luxury they were both used to, in the cramped cottage where their host had his studio in the verandah, their hostess practised her violin in the dining-room, and five ubiquitous children sprawled and shouted and blew trumpets and put tadpoles in the water-jugs, and the mid-day dinner was two hours late—and proportionately bad—because the Italian cook was posing for Fulmer.

Lansing's first thought had been that meeting Susy in such circumstances would be the quickest way to cure them both of their regrets. The case of the Fulmers was an awful object-lesson in what happened to young people who lost their heads; poor Nat, whose pictures nobody bought, had gone to seed so terribly—and Grace, at twenty-nine, would never again be anything but the woman of whom people say, "I can remember her when she was lovely."

But the devil of it was that Nat had never been such good company, or Grace so free from care and so full of music; and that, in spite of their disorder and dishevelment, and the bad food and general crazy discomfort, there was more amusement to be got out of their society than out of the most opulently staged house-party through which Susy and Lansing had ever yawned their way.

It was almost a relief to the young man when, on the second afternoon, Miss Branch drew him into the narrow hall to say: "I really can't stand the combination of Grace's violin and little Nat's motor-horn any longer. Do let us slip out till the duet is over."

"How do *they* stand it, I wonder?" he basely echoed, as he followed her up the wooded path behind the house.

"It might be worth finding out," she rejoined with a musing smile.

But he remained resolutely sceptical. "Oh, give them a year or two more and they'll collapse—! His pictures will never sell, you know. He'll never even get them into a show."

"I suppose not. And she'll never have time to do anything worth while with her music."

They had reached a piny knoll high above the ledge on which the house was perched. All about them stretched an empty landscape of endless featureless wooded hills. "Think of sticking here all the year round!" Lansing groaned.

"I know. But then think of wandering over the world with some people!"

"Oh, Lord, yes. For instance, my trip to India with the Mortimer Hickses. But it was my only chance—and what the deuce is one to do?"

"I wish I knew!" she sighed, thinking of the Bockheimers; and he turned and looked at her.

"Knew what?"

"The answer to your question. What *is* one to do—when one sees both sides of the problem? Or every possible side of it, indeed?"

They had seated themselves on a commanding rock under the pines, but Lansing could not see the view at their feet for the stir of the brown lashes on her cheek.

"You mean: Nat and Grace may after all be having the best of it?"

"How can I say, when I've told you I see all the sides? Of course," Susy added hastily, "*I* couldn't live as they do for a week. But it's wonderful how little it's dimmed them."

"Certainly Nat was never more coruscating. And she keeps it up even better." He reflected. "We do them good, I daresay."

"Yes—or they us. I wonder which?"

After that, he seemed to remember that they sat a long time silent, and that his next utterance was a boyish outburst against the tyranny of the existing order of things, abruptly followed by the passionate query why, since he and she couldn't alter it, and since they both had the habit of looking at facts as they were, they wouldn't be utter fools not to take their chance of being happy in the only way that was open to them? To this challenge he did not recall Susy's making any definite answer; but after another interval, in which all the world seemed framed in a sudden kiss, he heard her murmur to herself in a brooding tone: "I don't suppose it's ever been tried before; but we might—." And then and there she had laid before him the very experiment they had since hazarded. . . .

She would have none of surreptitious bliss, she began by declaring; and she set forth her reasons with her usual lucid impartiality. In the first place, she should have to marry some day, and when she made the bargain she meant it to be an honest one; and secondly, in the matter of love, she would never give herself to anyone she did not really care for, and if such happiness ever came to her she did not want it shorn of half its brightness by the need of fibbing and plotting and dodging.

"I've seen too much of that kind of thing. Half the women I know who've had lovers have had them for the fun of sneaking and lying about it; but the other half have been miserable. And I should be miserable."

It was at this point that she unfolded her plan. Why shouldn't they marry; belong to each other openly and honourably, if for ever so short a time, and with the definite understanding that whenever either of them got the chance to do better he or she should be immediately released? The law of their country facilitated such exchanges, and society was beginning to view them as indulgently as the law. As Susy talked, she warmed to her theme and began to develop its endless possibilities.

"We should really, in a way, help more than we should hamper each other," she ardently explained. "We both know the ropes so well; what one of us didn't see the other might—in the way of opportunities, I mean. And then we should be a novelty as married people. We're both rather unusually popular—why not be frank?—and it's such a blessing for dinner-givers to be able to count on a couple of whom neither one is a blank. Yes, I really believe we should be more than twice the success we are now; at least," she added with a smile, "if there's that amount of room for improvement. I don't know how you feel; a man's popularity is so much less precarious than a girl's—but I know it would furbish me up tremendously to reappear as a married woman." She glanced away from him down the long valley at their feet, and added in a lower tone: "And I should like, just for a little while, to feel I had something in life of my very own—something that nobody had lent me, like a fancy-dress or a motor or an opera cloak."

The suggestion, at first, had seemed to Lansing as mad as it was enchanting: it had thoroughly frightened him. But Susy's arguments were irrefutable, her ingenuities inexhaustible. Had he ever thought it all out? She asked. No. Well, she had; and would he kindly not interrupt? In the first place, there would be all the wedding-presents. Jewels, and a motor, and a silver dinner service, did she mean? Not a bit of it! She could see he'd never given the question proper thought. Cheques, my dear, nothing but cheques—she undertook to manage that on her side: she really thought she could count on about fifty, and she supposed he could rake up a few more? Well, all that would simply represent pocket-money! For they would have plenty of houses to live in: he'd see. People were always glad to lend their house to a newly-married couple. It was such fun to pop down and see them: it made one feel romantic and jolly. All they need do was to accept the houses in turn: go on honey-mooning for a year! What was he afraid of? Didn't he think they'd be happy enough to want to keep it up? And why not at least try—get engaged, and then see what would happen? Even if she was all wrong, and her plan failed, wouldn't it have been rather nice, just for a month or two, to fancy they were going to be happy? "I've often fancied it all by myself," she concluded; "but fancying it with you would somehow be so awfully different. . . ."

That was how it began: and this lakeside dream was what it had led up to. Fantastically improbable as they had seemed, all her previsions had come true. If there were certain links in the chain that Lansing had never been able to put his hand on, certain arrangements and contrivances that still needed further elucidation, why, he was lazily resolved to clear them up with her some day; and meanwhile it was worth all the past might have cost, and every penalty the future might exact of him, just to be sitting here in the silence and sweetness, her sleeping head on his knee, clasped in his joy as the hushed world was clasped in moonlight.

He stooped down and kissed her. "Wake up," he whispered, "it's bed-time."

Chapter III

THEIR month of Como was within a few hours of ending. Till the last moment they had hoped for a reprieve; but the accommodating Streffy had been unable to put the villa at their disposal for a longer time, since he had had the luck to let it for a thumping price to some beastly bounders who insisted on taking possession at the date agreed on.

Lansing, leaving Susy's side at dawn, had gone down to the lake for a last plunge; and swimming homeward through the crystal light he looked up at the garden brimming with flowers, the long low house with the cypress wood above it, and the window behind which his wife still slept. The month had been exquisite, and their happiness as rare, as fantastically complete, as the scene before him. He sank his chin into the sunlit ripples and sighed for sheer content. . . .

It was a bore to be leaving the scene of such complete well-being, but the next stage in their progress promised to be hardly less delightful. Susy was a magician: everything she predicted came true. Houses were being showered on them; on all sides he seemed to see beneficent spirits winging toward them, laden with everything from a *piano nobile* in Venice to a camp in the Adirondacks. For the present, they had decided on the former. Other considerations apart, they dared not risk the expense of a journey across the Atlantic; so they were heading instead for the Nelson Vanderlyns' palace on the Giudecca. They were agreed that, for reasons of expediency, it might be wise to return to New York for the coming winter. It would keep them in view, and probably lead to fresh opportunities; indeed, Susy already had in mind the convenient flat that she was sure a migratory cousin (if tactfully handled, and assured that they would not overwork her cook) could certainly be induced to lend them. Meanwhile the need of making plans was still remote; and if there was one art in which young Lansing's twenty-eight years of existence had perfected him it was that of living completely and unconcernedly in the present. . . .

If of late he had tried to look into the future more insistently than was his habit, it was only because of Susy. He had meant, when they married, to be as philosophic for her as for himself; and he knew she would have resented above everything his regarding their partnership as a reason for anxious thought. But since they had been together she had given him glimpses of her past that made him angrily long to shelter and defend her future. It was intolerable that a spirit as fine as hers should be ever so little dulled or diminished by the kind of compromises out of which their wretched lives were made. For himself, he didn't care a hang: he had composed for his own guidance a rough-and-ready code, a short set of "mays" and "mustn'ts" which immensely simplified his course. There were things a fellow put up with for the sake of certain definite and otherwise unattainable advantages; there were other things he wouldn't traffic with at any price. But for a woman, he began to see, it might be different. The temptations might be greater, the cost considerably higher, the dividing line between the "mays" and "mustn'ts" more fluctuating and less sharply drawn. Susy, thrown on the world at seventeen, with only a weak wastrel of a father to define that treacherous line for her, and with every circumstance soliciting her to overstep it, seemed to have been preserved chiefly by an innate scorn of most of the objects of human folly. "Such trash as he went to pieces for," was her curt comment on her parent's premature demise: as though she accepted in advance the necessity of ruining one's self for something, but was resolved to discriminate firmly between what was worth it and what wasn't.

This philosophy had at first enchanted Lansing; but now it began to rouse vague fears. The fine armour of her fastidiousness had preserved her from the kind of risks she had hitherto been exposed to; but what if others, more subtle, found a joint in it? Was there, among her delicate discriminations, any equivalent to his own rules? Might not her taste for the best and rarest be the very instrument of her undoing; and if something that wasn't "trash" came her way, would she hesitate a second to go to pieces for it?

He was determined to stick to the compact that they should do nothing to interfere with what each referred to as the other's "chance"; but what if, when hers came, he couldn't agree with her in recognizing it? He wanted for her, oh, so passionately, the best; but his conception of that best had so insensibly, so subtly been transformed in the light of their first month together!

His lazy strokes were carrying him slowly shoreward; but the hour was so exquisite that a few yards from the landing he laid hold of the mooring rope of Streffy's boat and floated there, following his dream. . . . It was a bore to be leaving; no doubt that was what made him turn things inside-out so uselessly. Venice would be delicious, of course; but nothing would ever again be as sweet as this. And then they had only a year of security before them; and of that year a month was gone.

Reluctantly he swam ashore, walked up to the house, and pushed open a window of the cool painted drawing-room. Signs of departure were already visible. There were trunks in the hall, tennis rackets on the stairs; on the landing, the cook Giulietta had both arms around a slippery hold-all that refused to let itself be strapped. It all gave him a chill sense of unreality, as if the past month had been an act on the stage, and its setting were being folded away and rolled into the wings to make room for another play in which he and Susy had no part.

By the time he came down again, dressed and hungry, to the terrace where coffee awaited him, he had recovered his usual pleasant sense of security. Susy was there, fresh and gay, a rose in her breast and the sun in her hair: her head was bowed over Bradshaw, but she waved a fond hand across the breakfast things, and presently looked up to say: "Yes, I believe we can just manage it."

"Manage what?"

"To catch the train at Milan—if we start in the motor at ten sharp."

He stared. "The motor? What motor?"

"Why, the new people's—Streffy's tenants. He's never told me their name, and the chauffeur says he can't pronounce it. The chauffeur's is Ottaviano, anyhow; I've been making friends with him. He arrived last night, and he says they're not due at Como till this evening. He simply jumped at the idea of running us over to Milan."

"Good Lord—" said Lansing, when she stopped.

She sprang up from the table with a laugh. "It will be a scramble; but I'll manage it, if you'll go up at once and pitch the last things into your trunk."

"Yes; but look here—have you any idea what it's going to cost?"

She raised her eyebrows gaily. "Why, a good deal less than our railway tickets. Ottaviano's got a sweetheart in Milan, and hasn't seen her for six months. When I found that out I knew he'd be going there anyhow."

It was clever of her, and he laughed. But why was it that he had grown to shrink from even such harmless evidence of her always knowing how to "manage"? "Oh, well," he said to himself, "she's right: the fellow would be sure to be going to Milan."

Upstairs, on the way to his dressing room, he found her in a cloud of finery which her skilful hands were forcibly compressing into a last portmanteau. He had never seen anyone pack as cleverly as Susy: the way she coaxed reluctant things into a trunk was a symbol of the way she fitted discordant facts into her life. "When I'm rich," she often said, "the thing I shall hate most will be to see an idiot maid at my trunks."

As he passed, she glanced over her shoulder, her face pink with the struggle, and drew a cigar-box from the depths. "Dearest, do put a couple of cigars into your pocket as a tip for Ottaviano."

Lansing stared. "Why, what on earth are you doing with Streffy's cigars?"

"Packing them, of course. . . . You don't suppose he meant them for those other people?" She gave him a look of honest wonder.

"I don't know whom he meant them for—but they're not ours. . . ."

She continued to look at him wonderingly. "I don't see what there is to be solemn about. The cigars are not Streffy's either . . . you may be sure he got them out of some bounder. And there's nothing he'd hate more than to have them passed on to another."

"Nonsense. If they're not Streffy's they're much less mine. Hand them over, please, dear."

"Just as you like. But it does seem a waste; and, of course, the other people will never have one of them. . . . The gardener and Giulietta's lover will see to that!"

Lansing looked away from her at the waves of lace and muslin from which she emerged like a rosy Nereid. "How many boxes of them are left?"

"Only four."

"Unpack them, please."

Before she moved there was a pause so full of challenge that Lansing had time for an exasperated sense of the disproportion between his anger and its cause. And this made him still angrier.

She held out a box. "The others are in your suit-case downstairs. It's locked and strapped."

"Give me the key, then."

"We might send them back from Venice, mightn't we? That lock is so nasty: it will take you half an hour."

"Give me the key, please." She gave it.

He went downstairs and battled with the lock, for the allotted half-hour, under the puzzled eyes of Giulietta and the sardonic grin of the chauffeur, who now and then, from the threshold, politely reminded him how long it would take to get to Milan. Finally the key turned, and Lansing, broken-nailed and perspiring, extracted the cigars and stalked with them into the deserted drawing-room. The great bunches of golden roses that he and Susy had gathered the day before were dropping their petals on the marble embroidery of the floor, pale camellias floated in the alabaster *tazzas* between the windows, haunting scents of the garden blew in on him with the breeze from the lake. Never had Streffy's little house seemed so like a nest of pleasures. Lansing laid the cigar boxes on a console and ran upstairs to collect his last possessions. When he came down again, his wife, her eyes brilliant with achievement, was seated in their borrowed chariot, the luggage cleverly stowed away, and Giulietta and the gardener kissing her hand and weeping out inconsolable farewells.

"I wonder what she's given *them*?" he thought, as he jumped in beside her and the motor whirled them through the nightingale-thickets to the gate.

Chapter IV

CHARLIE STREFFORD'S villa was like a nest in a rose-bush;
the Nelson Vanderlyns' palace called for loftier analogies.
Its vastness and splendour seemed, in comparison, oppressive
to Susy. Their landing, after dark, at the foot of the great shadowy staircase, their dinner at a dimly-lit table under a ceiling
weighed down with Olympians, their chilly evening in a corner
of a drawing-room where minuets should have been danced
before a throne, contrasted with the happy intimacies of Como
as their sudden sense of disaccord contrasted with the mutual
confidence of the day before.

The journey had been particularly jolly: both Susy and Lansing had had too long a discipline in the art of smoothing things
over not to make a special effort to hide from each other the ravages of their first disagreement. But, deep down and invisible,
the disagreement remained; and compunction for having been
its cause gnawed at Susy's bosom as she sat in her tapestried and
vaulted bedroom, brushing her hair before a tarnished mirror.

"I thought I liked grandeur; but this place is really out of
scale," she mused, watching the reflection of a pale hand move
back and forward in the dim recesses of the mirror.

"And yet," she continued, "Ellie Vanderlyn's hardly half an
inch taller than I am; and she certainly isn't a bit more digni-
fied. . . . I wonder if it's because I feel so horribly small to-night
that the place seems so horribly big."

She loved luxury: splendid things always made her feel handsome and high ceilings arrogant; she did not remember having
ever before been oppressed by the evidences of wealth.

She laid down the brush and leaned her chin on her clasped
hands. . . . Even now she could not understand what had made
her take the cigars. She had always been alive to the value of
her inherited scruples: her reasoned opinions were unusually
free, but with regard to the things one couldn't reason about
she was oddly tenacious. And yet she had taken Streffy's cigars!
She had taken them—yes, that was the point—she had taken
them for Nick, because the desire to please him, to make the
smallest details of his life easy and agreeable and luxurious, had

become her absorbing preoccupation. She had committed, for him, precisely the kind of little baseness she would most have scorned to commit for herself; and, since he hadn't instantly felt the difference, she would never be able to explain it to him.

She stood up with a sigh, shook out her loosened hair, and glanced around the great frescoed room. The maid-servant had said something about the Signora's having left a letter for her; and there it lay on the writing-table, with her mail and Nick's; a thick envelope addressed in Ellie's childish scrawl, with a glaring "Private" dashed across the corner.

"What on earth can she have to say, when she hates writing so?" Susy mused.

She broke open the envelope, and four or five stamped and sealed letters fell from it. All were addressed, in Ellie's hand, to Nelson Vanderlyn Esqre; and in the corner of each was faintly pencilled a number and a date: one, two, three, four—with a week's interval between the dates.

"Goodness—" gasped Susy, understanding.

She had dropped into an armchair near the table, and for a long time she sat staring at the numbered letters. A sheet of paper covered with Ellie's writing had fluttered out among them, but she let it lie; she knew so well what it would say! She knew all about her friend, of course; except poor old Nelson, who didn't? But she had never imagined that Ellie would dare to use her in this way. It was unbelievable . . . she had never pictured anything so vile. . . . The blood rushed to her face, and she sprang up angrily, half minded to tear the letters in bits and throw them all into the fire.

She heard her husband's knock on the door between their rooms, and swept the dangerous packet under the blotting-book.

"Oh, go away, please, there's a dear," she called out; "I haven't finished unpacking, and everything's in such a mess." Gathering up Nick's papers and letters, she ran across the room and thrust them through the door. "Here's something to keep you quiet," she laughed, shining in on him an instant from the threshold.

She turned back feeling weak with shame. Ellie's letter lay on the floor: reluctantly she stooped to pick it up, and one by one the expected phrases sprang out at her.

"One good turn deserves another. . . . Of course you and Nick are welcome to stay all summer. . . . There won't be a particle of

so lived themselves into the vision of indolent summer days on
the lagoon, of flaming hours on the beach of the Lido, and
evenings of music and dreams on their broad balcony above
the Giudecca, that the idea of having to renounce these joys,
and deprive her Nick of them, filled Susy with a wrath intensi-
fied by his having confided in her that when they were quietly
settled in Venice he "meant to write." Already nascent in her
breast was the fierce resolve of the author's wife to defend her
husband's privacy and facilitate his encounters with the Muse.
It was abominable, simply abominable, that Ellie Vanderlyn
should have drawn her into such a trap!

Well—there was nothing for it but to make a clean breast of
the whole thing to Nick. The trivial incident of the cigars—how
trivial it now seemed!—showed her the kind of stand he would
take, and communicated to her something of his own uncom-
promising energy. She would tell him the whole story in the
morning, and try to find a way out with him: Susy's faith in her
power of finding a way out was inexhaustible. But suddenly she
remembered the adjuration at the end of Mrs. Vanderlyn's letter:
"If you're ever owed me anything in the way of kindness, you
won't, on your sacred honour, say a word to Nick. . . ."

It was, of course, exactly what no one had the right to ask of
her: if indeed the word "right" could be used in any conceivable
relation to this coil of wrongs. But the fact remained that, in the
way of kindness, she did owe much to Ellie; and that this was
the first payment her friend had ever exacted. She found herself,
in fact, in exactly the same position as when Ursula Gillow,
using the same argument, had appealed to her to give up Nick
Lansing. Yes, Susy reflected; but then Nelson Vanderlyn had
been kind to her too; and the money Ellie had been so kind
with was Nelson's. . . . The queer edifice of Susy's standards tottered on its base—she honestly didn't know where fairness lay,
as between so much that was foul.

The very depth of her perplexity puzzled her. She had been in
"tight places" before; had indeed been in so few that were not,
in one way or another, constricting! As she looked back on her
past it lay before her as a very network of perpetual concessions
and contrivings. But never before had she had such a sense of
being tripped up, gagged and pinioned. The little misery of the

expense for you—the servants have orders. . . . If you'll just be an angel and post these letters yourself. . . . It's been my only chance for such an age; when we meet I'll explain everything. And in a month at latest I'll be back to fetch Clarissa. . . ."

Susy lifted the letter to the lamp to be sure she had read aright. To fetch Clarissa! Then Ellie's child was here? Here, under the roof with them, left to their care? She read on, raging. "She's so delighted, poor darling, to know you're coming. I've had to sack her beastly governess for impertinence, and if it weren't for you she'd be all alone with a lot of servants I don't much trust. So for pity's sake be good to my child, and forgive me for leaving her. She thinks I've gone to take a cure; and she knows she's not to tell her Daddy that I'm away, because it would only worry him if he thought I was ill. She's perfectly to be trusted; you'll see what a clever angel she is. . ." And then, at the bottom of the page, in a last slanting postscript: "Susy darling, if you've ever owed me anything in the way of kindness, you won't, on your sacred honour, say a word of this to any one, even to Nick. And *I know I can count on you to rub out the numbers.*"

Susy sprang up and tossed Mrs. Vanderlyn's letter into the fire: then she came slowly back to the chair. There, at her elbow, lay the four fatal envelopes; and her next affair was to make up her mind what to do with them.

To destroy them on the spot had seemed, at first thought, inevitable: it might be saving Ellie as well as herself. But such a step seemed to Susy to involve departure on the morrow, and this in turn involved notifying Ellie, whose letter she had vainly scanned for an address. Well—perhaps Clarissa's nurse would know where one could write to her mother; it was unlikely that even Ellie would go off without assuring some means of communication with her child. At any rate, there was nothing to be done that night: nothing but to work out the details of their flight on the morrow, and rack her brains to find a substitute for the hospitality they were rejecting. Susy did not disguise from herself how much she had counted on the Vanderlyn apartment for the summer: to be able to do so had singularly simplified the future. She knew Ellie's largeness of hand, and had been sure in advance that as long as they were her guests their only expense would be an occasional present to the servants. And what would the alternative be? She and Lansing, in their endless talks, had cigars still galled her, and now this big humiliation superposed itself on the raw wound. Decidedly, the second month of their honey-moon was beginning cloudily. . . .

She glanced at the enamelled travelling-clock on her dressing table—one of the few wedding-presents she had consented to accept in kind—and was startled at the lateness of the hour. In a moment Nick would be coming; and an uncomfortable sensation in her throat warned her that through sheer nervousness and exasperation she might blurt out something ill-advised. The old habit of being always on her guard made her turn once more to the looking-glass. Her face was pale and haggard; and having, by a swift and skilful application of cosmetics, increased its appearance of fatigue, she crossed the room and softly opened her husband's door.

He too sat by a lamp, reading a letter which he put aside as she entered. His face was grave, and she said to herself that he was certainly still thinking about the cigars.

"I'm very tired, dearest, and my head aches so horribly that I've come to bid you good-night." Bending over the back of his chair, she laid her arms on his shoulders. He lifted his hands to clasp hers, but, as he threw his head back to smile up at her she noticed that his look was still serious, almost remote. It was as if, for the first time, a faint veil hung between his eyes and hers.

"I'm so sorry: it's been a long day for you," he said absently, pressing his lips to her hands.

She felt the dreaded twitch in her throat.

"Nick!" she burst out, tightening her embrace, "before I go, you've got to swear to me on your honour that you *know* I should never have taken those cigars for myself!"

For a moment he stared at her, and she stared back at him with equal gravity; then the same irresistible mirth welled up in both, and Susy's compunctions were swept away on a gale of laughter.

When she woke the next morning the sun was pouring in between her curtains of old brocade, and its refraction from the ripples of the Canal was drawing a network of golden scales across the vaulted ceiling. The maid had just placed a tray on a slim marquetry table near the bed, and over the edge of the tray

Susy discovered the small serious face of Clarissa Vanderlyn. At the sight of the little girl all her dormant qualms awoke.

Clarissa was just eight, and small for her age: her little round chin was barely on a level with the tea-service, and her clear brown eyes gazed at Susy between the ribs of the toast-rack and the single tea-rose in an old Murano glass. Susy had not seen her for two years, and she seemed, in the interval, to have passed from a thoughtful infancy to complete ripeness of feminine experience. She was looking with approval at her mother's guest.

"I'm so glad you've come," she said in a small sweet voice. "I like you so very much. I know I'm not to be often with you; but at least you'll have an eye on me, won't you?"

"An eye on you! I shall never want to have it off you, if you say such nice things to me!" Susy laughed, leaning from her pillows to draw the little girl up to her side.

Clarissa smiled and settled herself down comfortably on the silken bedspread. "Oh, I know I'm not to be always about, because you're just married; but *could* you see to it that I have my meals regularly?"

"Why, you poor darling! Don't you always?"

"Not when mother's away on these cures. The servants don't always obey me: you see I'm so little for my age. In a few years, of course, they'll have to—even if I don't grow much," she added judiciously. She put out her hand and touched the string of pearls about Susy's throat. "They're small, but they're very good. I suppose you don't take the others when you travel?"

"The others? Bless you! I haven't any others—and never shall have, probably."

"No other pearls?"

"No other jewels at all."

Clarissa stared. "Is that *really* true?" she asked, as if in the presence of the unprecedented.

"Awfully true," Susy confessed. "But I think I can make the servants obey me all the same."

This point seemed to have lost its interest for Clarissa, who was still gravely scrutinizing her companion. After a while she brought forth another question.

"Did you have to give up all your jewels when you were divorced?"

"Divorced—?" Susy threw her head back against the pillows and laughed. "Why, what are you thinking of? Don't you remember that I wasn't even married the last time you saw me?"

"Yes; I do. But that was two years ago." The little girl wound her arms about Susy's neck and leaned against her caressingly. "Are you going to be soon, then? I'll promise not to tell if you don't want me to."

"Going to be divorced? Of course not! What in the world made you think so?"

"Because you look so awfully happy," said Clarissa Vanderlyn simply.

Chapter V

I T was a trifling enough sign, but it had remained in Susy's mind: that first morning in Venice Nick had gone out without first coming in to see her. She had stayed in bed late, chatting with Clarissa, and expecting to see the door open and her husband appear; and when the child left, and she had jumped up and looked into Nick's room, she found it empty, and a line on his dressing table informed her that he had gone out to send a telegram.

It was lover-like, and even boyish, of him to think it necessary to explain his absence; but why had he not simply come in and told her? She instinctively connected the little fact with the shade of preoccupation she had noticed on his face the night before, when she had gone to his room and found him absorbed in a letter; and while she dressed she had continued to wonder what was in the letter, and whether the telegram he had hurried out to send was an answer to it.

She had never found out. When he reappeared, handsome and happy as the morning, he proffered no explanation; and it was part of her life-long policy not to put uncalled-for questions. It was not only that her jealous regard for her own freedom was matched by an equal respect for that of others; she had steered too long among the social reefs and shoals not to know how narrow is the passage that leads to peace of mind, and she was determined to keep her little craft in mid-channel. But the incident had lodged itself in her memory, acquiring a sort of symbolic significance, as of a turning-point in her relations with her husband. Not that these were less happy, but that she now beheld them, as she had always formerly beheld such joys, as an unstable islet in a sea of storms. Her present bliss was as complete as ever, but it was ringed by the perpetual menace of all she knew she was hiding from Nick, and of all she suspected him of hiding from her. . . .

She was thinking of these things one afternoon about three weeks after their arrival in Venice. It was near sunset, and she sat alone on the balcony, watching the cross-lights on the water weave their pattern above the flushed reflection of old palace-basements. She was almost always alone at that hour. Nick had taken to writing in the afternoons—he had been as good as his word, and so, apparently, had the Muse—and it was his habit to join his wife only at sunset, for a late row on the lagoon. She had taken Clarissa, as usual, to the Giardino Pubblico, where that obliging child had politely but indifferently "played"—Clarissa joined in the diversions of her age as if conforming to an obsolete tradition—and had brought her back for a music lesson, echoes of which now drifted down from a distant window.

Susy had come to be extremely thankful for Clarissa. But for the little girl, her pride in her husband's industry might have been tinged with a faint sense of being at times left out and forgotten; and as Nick's industry was the completest justification for their being where they were, and for her having done what she had, she was grateful to Clarissa for helping her to feel less alone. Clarissa, indeed, represented the other half of her justification: it was as much on the child's account as on Nick's that Susy had held her tongue, remained in Venice, and slipped out once a week to post one of Ellie's numbered letters. A day's experience of the Palazzo Vanderlyn had convinced Susy of the impossibility of deserting Clarissa. Long experience had shown her that the most crowded households often contain the loneliest nurseries, and that the rich child is exposed to evils unknown to less pampered infancy; but hitherto such things had merely been to her one of the uglier bits in the big muddled pattern of life. Now she found herself feeling where before she had only judged: her precarious bliss came to her charged with a new weight of pity.

She was thinking of these things, and of the approaching date of Ellie Vanderlyn's return, and of the searching truths she was storing up for that lady's private ear, when she noticed a gondola turning its prow toward the steps below the balcony. She leaned over, and a tall gentleman in shabby clothes, glancing up at her as he jumped out, waved a mouldy Panama in joyful greeting.

"Streffy!" she exclaimed as joyfully; and she was half-way down the stairs when he ran up them followed by his luggage-laden boatman.

"It's all right, I suppose?—Ellie said I might come," he explained in a shrill cheerful voice; "and I'm to have my same green room with the parrot-panels, because its furniture is already so frightfully stained with my hair-wash."

Susy was beaming on him with the deep sense of satisfaction which his presence always produced in his friends. There was no one in the world, they all agreed, half as ugly and untidy and delightful as Streffy; no one who combined such outspoken selfishness with such imperturbable good humour; no one who knew so well how to make you believe he was being charming to you when it was you who were being charming to him.

In addition to these seductions, of which none estimated the value more accurately than their possessor, Strefford had for Susy another attraction of which he was probably unconscious. It was that of being the one rooted and stable being among the fluid and shifting figures that composed her world. Susy had always lived among people so denationalized that those one took for Russians generally turned out to be American, and those one was inclined to ascribe to New York proved to have originated in Rome or Bucharest. These cosmopolitan people, who, in countries not their own, lived in houses as big as hotels, or in hotels where the guests were as international as the waiters, had inter-married, inter-loved and inter-divorced each other over the whole face of Europe, and according to every code that attempts to regulate human ties. Strefford, too, had his home in this world, but only one of his homes. The other, the one he spoke of, and probably thought of, least often, was a great dull English country-house in a northern county, where a life as monotonous and self-contained as his own was chequered and dispersed had gone on for generation after generation; and it was the sense of that house, and of all it typified even to his vagrancy and irreverence, which, coming out now and then in his talk, or in his attitude toward something or somebody, gave him a firmer outline and a steadier footing than the other marionettes in the dance. Superficially so like them all, and so eager to outdo them in detachment and adaptability, ridiculing the prejudices he had shaken off, and the people to whom he belonged, he still kept, under his easy pliancy, the skeleton of old faiths and old fashions. "He talks every language as well as the rest of us," Susy had once said of him, "but at least he talks one language better than the others"; and Strefford, told of the remark, had laughed, called her an idiot, and been pleased.

As he shambled up the stairs with her, arm in arm, she was thinking of this quality with a new appreciation of its value. Even she and Lansing, in spite of their unmixed American-ism, their substantial background of old-fashioned cousinships in New York and Philadelphia, were as mentally detached, as universally at home, as touts at an International Exhibition. If they were usually recognized as Americans it was only because they spoke French so well, and because Nick was too fair to be "foreign," and too sharp-featured to be English. But Charlie Strefford was English with all the strength of an inveterate habit; and something in Susy was slowly waking to a sense of the beauty of habit.

Lounging on the balcony, whither he had followed her with-out pausing to remove the stains of travel, Strefford showed himself immensely interested in the last chapter of her history, greatly pleased at its having been enacted under his roof, and hugely and flippantly amused at the firmness with which she refused to let him see Nick till the latter's daily task was over.

"Writing? Rot! What's he writing? He's breaking you in, my dear; that's what he's doing: establishing an alibi. What'll you bet he's just sitting there smoking and reading *Le Rire*? Let's go and see."

But Susy was firm. "He's read me his first chapter: it's wonder-ful. It's a philosophic romance—rather like *Marius*, you know."

"Oh, yes—I *do*!" said Strefford, with a laugh that she thought idiotic.

She flushed up like a child. "You're stupid, Streffy. You forget that Nick and I don't need alibis. We've got rid of all that hyprocrisy by agreeing that each will give the other a hand up when either of us wants a change. We've not married to spy and lie, and nag each other; we've formed a partnership for our mutual advantage."

"I see; that's capital. But how can you be sure that, when Nick wants a change, you'll consider it for his advantage to have one?"

It was the point that had always secretly tormented Susy; she often wondered if it equally tormented Nick.

"I hope I shall have enough common sense—" she began.

"Oh, of course: common sense is what you're both bound to base your argument on, whichever way you argue."

This flash of insight disconcerted her, and she said, a little irritably: "What should *you* do then, if you married?—Hush, Streffy! I forbid you to shout like that—all the gondolas are stopping to look!"

"How can I help it?" He rocked backward and forward in his chair. " 'If you marry,' she says: 'Streffy, what have you decided to do if you suddenly become a raving maniac?' "

"I said no such thing. If your uncle and your cousin died, you'd marry to-morrow; you know you would."

"Oh, now you're talking business." He folded his long arms and leaned over the balcony, looking down at the dusky ripples streaked with fire. "In that case I should say: 'Susan, my dear—Susan—now that by the merciful intervention of Providence you have become Countess of Altringham in the peerage of Great Britain, and Baroness Dunsterville and d'Amblay in the peerages of Ireland and Scotland, I'll thank you to remember that you are a member of one of the most ancient houses in the United Kingdom—and not to get found out.' "

Susy laughed. "We know what those warnings mean! I pity my namesake."

He swung about and gave her a quick look out of his small ugly twinkling eyes. "Is there any other woman in the world named Susan?"

"I hope so, if the name's an essential. Even if Nick chucks me, don't count on *me* to carry out that programme. I've seen it in practice too often."

"Oh, well: as far as I know, everybody's in perfect health at Altringham." He fumbled in his pocket and drew out a fountain-pen, a handkerchief over which it had leaked, and a packet of dishevelled cigarettes. Lighting one, and restoring the other objects to his pocket, he continued calmly: "Tell me—how did you manage to smooth things over with the Gillows? Ursula was running amuck when I was in Newport last Summer; it was just when people were beginning to say that you were going to marry Nick. I was afraid she'd put a spoke in your wheel; and I hear she put a big cheque in your hand instead."

Susy was silent. From the first moment of Strefford's appearance she had known that in the course of time he would put that question. He was as inquisitive as a monkey, and when he had made up his mind to find out anything it was useless to try to divert his attention. After a moment's hesitation she said: "I flirted with Fred. It was a bore—but he was very decent."

"He would be—poor Fred. And you got Ursula thoroughly frightened!"

"Well—enough. And then luckily that young Nerone Altineri turned up from Rome: he went over to New York to look for a job as an engineer, and Ursula made Fred put him in their iron works." She paused again, and then added abruptly: "Streffy! If you knew how I hate that kind of thing. I'd rather have Nick come in now and tell me frankly, as I know he would, that he's going off with—"

"With Coral Hicks?" Strefford suggested.

She laughed. "Poor Coral Hicks! What on earth made you think of the Hickses?"

"Because I caught a glimpse of them the other day at Capri. They're cruising about: they said they were coming in here."

"What a nuisance! I do hope they won't find us out. They were awfully kind to Nick when he went to India with them, and they're so simpleminded that they would expect him to be glad to see them."

Strefford aimed his cigarette-end at a tourist in a puggaree who was gazing up from his guidebook at the palace. "Ah," he murmured with satisfaction, seeing the shot take effect; then he added: "Coral Hicks is growing up rather pretty."

"Oh, Streff—you're dreaming! That lump of a girl with spectacles and thick ankles! Poor Mrs. Hicks used to say to Nick: 'When Mr. Hicks and I had Coral educated we presumed culture was in greater demand in Europe than it appears to be.' "

"Well, you'll see: that girl's education won't interfere with her, once she's started. So then: if Nick came in and told you he was going off—"

"I should be so thankful if it was with a fright like Coral! But you know," she added with a smile, "we've agreed that it's not to happen for a year."

Chapter VI

SUSY found Strefford, after his first burst of nonsense, unusually kind and responsive. The interest he showed in her future and Nick's seemed to proceed not so much from his habitual spirit of scientific curiosity as from simple friendliness. He was privileged to see Nick's first chapter, of which he formed so favourable an impression that he spoke sternly to Susy on the importance of respecting her husband's working hours; and he even carried his general benevolence to the length of showing a fatherly interest in Clarissa Vanderlyn. He was always charming to children, but fitfully and warily, with an eye on his independence, and on the possibility of being suddenly bored by them; Susy had never seen him abandon these precautions so completely as he did with Clarissa.

"Poor little devil! Who looks after her when you and Nick are off together? Do you mean to tell me Ellie sacked the governess and went away without having anyone to take her place?"

"I think she expected me to do it," said Susy with a touch of asperity. There were moments when her duty to Clarissa weighed on her somewhat heavily; whenever she went off alone with Nick she was pursued by the vision of a little figure waving wistful farewells from the balcony.

"Ah, that's like Ellie: you might have known she'd get an equivalent when she lent you all this. But I don't believe she thought you'd be so conscientious about it."

Susy considered. "I don't suppose she did; and perhaps I shouldn't have been, a year ago. But you see"—she hesitated—"Nick's so awfully good: it's made me look at a lot of things differently. . . ."

"Oh, hang Nick's goodness! It's happiness that's done it, my dear. You're just one of the people with whom it happens to agree."

Susy, leaning back, scrutinized between her lashes his crooked ironic face.

"What is it that's agreeing with you, Streffy? I've never seen you so human. You must be getting an outrageous price for the villa."

Strefford laughed and clapped his hand on his breast-pocket. "I should be an ass not to: I've got a wire here saying they must have it for another month at any price."

"What luck! I'm so glad. Who are they, by the way?"

He drew himself up out of the long chair in which he was disjointedly lounging, and looked down at her with a smile. "Another couple of love-sick idiots like you and Nick. . . . I say, before I spend it all let's go out and buy something ripping for Clarissa."

The days passed so quickly and radiantly that, but for her concern for Clarissa, Susy would hardly have been conscious of her hostess's protracted absence. Mrs. Vanderlyn had said: "Four weeks at the latest," and the four weeks were over, and she had neither arrived nor written to explain her non-appearance. She had, in fact, given no sign of life since her departure, save in the shape of a post-card which had reached Clarissa the day after the Lansings' arrival, and in which Mrs. Vanderlyn instructed her child to be awfully good, and not to forget to feed the mongoose. Susy noticed that this missive had been posted in Milan.

She communicated her apprehensions to Strefford. "I don't trust that green-eyed nurse. She's forever with the younger gondolier; and Clarissa's so awfully sharp. I don't see why Ellie hasn't come: she was due last Monday."

Her companion laughed, and something in the sound of his laugh suggested that he probably knew as much of Ellie's movements as she did, if not more. The sense of disgust which the subject always roused in her made her look away quickly from his tolerant smile. She would have given the world, at that moment, to have been free to tell Nick what she had learned on the night of their arrival, and then to have gone away with him, no matter where. But there was Clarissa—!

To fortify herself against the temptation, she resolutely fixed her thoughts on her husband. Of Nick's beatitude there could be no doubt. He adored her, he revelled in Venice, he rejoiced in his work; and concerning the quality of that work her judgment was as confident as her heart. She still doubted if he would ever earn a living by what he wrote, but she no longer doubted that he would write something remarkable. The mere fact that he was engaged on a philosophic romance, and not a mere novel, seemed the proof of an intrinsic superiority. And if she had mistrusted her impartiality Strefford's approval would have reassured her. Among their friends Strefford passed as an authority on such matters: in summing him up his eulogists always added: "And you know he writes." As a matter of fact, the paying public had remained cold to his few published pages; but he lived among the kind of people who confuse taste with talent, and are impressed by the most artless attempts at literary expression; and though he affected to disdain their judgment, and his own efforts, Susy knew he was not sorry to have it said of him: "Oh, if only Streffy had chosen—!"

Strefford's approval of the philosophic romance convinced her that it had been worth while staying in Venice for Nick's sake; and if only Ellie would come back, and carry off Clarissa to St. Moritz or Deauville, the disagreeable episode on which their happiness was based would vanish like a cloud, and leave them to complete enjoyment.

Ellie did not come; but the Mortimer Hickses did, and Nick Lansing was assailed by the scruples his wife had foreseen. Strefford, coming back one evening from the Lido, reported having recognized the huge outline of the *Ibis* among the pleasure craft of the outer harbour; and the very next evening, as the guests of Palazzo Vanderlyn were sipping their ices at Florian's, the Hickses loomed up across the Piazza.

Susy pleaded in vain with her husband in defence of his privacy. "Remember you're here to write, dearest; it's your duty not to let any one interfere with that. Why shouldn't we tell them we're just leaving?"

"Because it's no use: we're sure to be always meeting them. And besides, I'll be hanged if I'm going to shirk the Hickses. I spent five whole months on the *Ibis*, and if they bored me occasionally, India didn't."

"We'll make them take us to Aquileia anyhow," said Strefford philosophically; and the next moment the Hickses were bearing down on the defenceless trio.

They presented a formidable front, not only because of their mere physical bulk—Mr. and Mrs. Hicks were equally and majestically three-dimensional—but because they never moved abroad without the escort of two private secretaries (one for the foreign languages), Mr. Hicks's doctor, a maiden lady known as

Eldoradder Tooker, who was Mrs. Hicks's cousin and stenographer, and finally their daughter, Coral Hicks.

Coral Hicks, when Susy had last encountered the party, had been a fat spectacled school-girl, always lagging behind her parents, with a reluctant poodle in her wake. Now the poodle had gone, and his mistress led the procession. The fat school-girl had changed into a young lady of compact if not graceful outline; a long-handled eye-glass had replaced the spectacles, and through it, instead of a sullen glare, Miss Coral Hicks projected on the world a glance at once confident and critical. She looked so strong and so assured that Susy, taking her measure in a flash, saw that her position at the head of the procession was not fortuitous, and murmured inwardly: "Thank goodness she's not pretty too!"

If she was not pretty, she was well-dressed; and if she was overeducated, she seemed capable, as Strefford had suggested, of carrying off even this crowning disadvantage. At any rate, she was above disguising it; and before the whole party had been seated five minutes in front of a fresh supply of ices (with Eldorada and the secretaries at a table slightly in the background) she had taken up with Nick the question of exploration in Mesopotamia.

"Queer child, Coral," he said to Susy that night as they smoked a last cigarette on their balcony. "She told me this afternoon that she'd remembered lots of things she heard me say in India. I thought at the time that she cared only for caramels and picture-puzzles, but it seems she was listening to everything, and reading all the books she could lay her hands on; and she got so bitten with Oriental archæology that she took a course last year at Bryn Mawr. She means to go to Bagdad next spring, and back by the Persian plateau and Turkestan."

Susy laughed luxuriously: she was sitting with her hand in Nick's, while the late moon—theirs again—rounded its orange-coloured glory above the belfry of San Giorgio.

"Poor Coral! How dreary—" Susy murmured.

"Dreary? Why? A trip like that is about as well worth doing as anything I know."

"Oh, I meant: dreary to do it without you or me," she laughed, getting up lazily to go indoors. A broad band of moonlight,

dividing her room into two shadowy halves, lay on the painted
Venetian bed with its folded-back sheet, its old damask coverlet
and lace-edged pillows. She felt the warmth of Nick's enfolding
arm and lifted her face to his.

The Hickses retained the most tender memory of Nick's
sojourn on the *Ibis*, and Susy, moved by their artless pleasure in
meeting him again, was glad he had not followed her advice and
tried to elude them. She had always admired Strefford's ruthless
talent for using and discarding the human material in his path,
but now she began to hope that Nick would not remember her
suggestion that he should mete out that measure to the Hickses.
Even if it had been less pleasant to have a big yacht at their door
during the long golden days and the nights of silver fire, the
Hickses' admiration for Nick would have made Susy suffer them
gladly. She even began to be aware of a growing liking for them,
a liking inspired by the very characteristics that would once have
provoked her disapproval. Susy had had plenty of training in
liking common people with big purses; in such cases her stock
of allowances and extenuations was inexhaustible. But they had
to be successful common people; and the trouble was that the
Hickses, judged by her standards, were failures. It was not only
that they were ridiculous; so, heaven knew, were many of their
rivals. But the Hickses were both ridiculous and unsuccessful.
They had consistently resisted the efforts of the experienced
advisers who had first descried them on the horizon and tried
to help them upward. They were always taking up the wrong
people, giving the wrong kind of party, and spending millions
on things that nobody who mattered cared about. They all
believed passionately in "movements" and "causes" and "ideals,"
and were always attended by the exponents of their latest beliefs,
always asking you to hear lectures by haggard women in pep-
lums, and having their portraits painted by wild people who
never turned out to be the fashion.

All this would formerly have increased Susy's contempt; now
she found herself liking the Hickses most for their failings. She
was touched by their simple good faith, their isolation in the
midst of all their queer apostles and parasites, their way of
drifting about an alien and indifferent world in a compactly
clinging group of which Eldorada Tooker, the doctor and the
two secretaries formed the outer fringe, and by their view of

themselves as a kind of collective re-incarnation of some past state of princely culture, symbolised for Mrs. Hicks in what she called "the court of the Renaissance." Eldorada, of course, was their chief prophetess; but even the intensely "bright" and modern young secretaries, Mr. Beck and Mr. Buttles, showed a touching tendency to share her view, and spoke of Mr. Hicks as "promoting art," in the spirit of Pandolfino celebrating the munificence of the Medicis.

"I'm getting really fond of the Hickses; I believe I should be nice to them even if they were staying at Danieli's," Susy said to Strefford.

"And even if *you* owned the yacht?" he answered; and for once his banter struck her as beside the point.

The *Ibis* carried them, during the endless June days, far and wide along the enchanted shores; they roamed among the Euganeans, they saw Aquileia and Pomposa and Ravenna. Their hosts would gladly have taken them farther, across the Adriatic and on into the golden network of the Aegean; but Susy resisted this infraction of Nick's rules, and he himself preferred to stick to his task. Only now he wrote in the early mornings, so that on most days they could set out before noon and steam back late to the low fringe of lights on the lagoon. His work continued to progress, and as page was added to page Susy obscurely but surely perceived that each one corresponded with a hidden secretion of energy, the gradual forming within him of something that might eventually alter both their lives. In what sense she could not conjecture: she merely felt that the fact of his having chosen a job and stuck to it, if only through a few rosy summer weeks, had already given him a new way of saying "Yes" and "No."

Chapter VII

O F some new ferment at work in him Nick Lansing himself
was equally aware. He was a better judge of the book he
was trying to write than either Susy or Strefford; he knew its
weaknesses, its treacheries, its tendency to slip through his fingers just as he thought his grasp tightest; but he knew also that
at the very moment when it seemed to have failed him it would
suddenly be back, beating its loud wings in his face.

He had no delusions as to its commercial value, and had
winced more than he triumphed when Susy produced her
allusion to *Marius*. His book was to be called *The Pageant of
Alexander*. His imagination had been enchanted by the idea of
picturing the young conqueror's advance through the fabulous
landscapes of Asia: he liked writing descriptions, and vaguely
felt that under the guise of fiction he could develop his theory
of Oriental influences in Western art at the expense of less learning than if he had tried to put his ideas into an essay. He knew
enough of his subject to know that he did not know enough to
write about it; but he consoled himself by remembering that
Wilhelm Meister has survived many weighty volumes on æsthetics; and between his moments of self-distrust he took himself at
Susy's valuation, and found an unmixed joy in his task.

Never—no, never!—had he been so boundlessly, so confi-
dently happy. His hack-work had given him the habit of application, and now habit wore the glow of inspiration. His previous
literary ventures had been timid and tentative: if this one was
growing and strengthening on his hands, it must be because the
conditions were so different. He was at ease, he was secure, he
was satisfied; and he had also, for the first time since his early
youth, before his mother's death, the sense of having some one
to look after, some one who was his own particular care, and
to whom he was answerable for himself and his actions, as he
had never felt himself answerable to the hurried and indifferent
people among whom he had chosen to live.

Susy had the same standards as these people: she spoke their
language, though she understood others, she required their

42

pleasures if she did not revere their gods. But from the moment that she had become his property he had built up in himself a conception of her answering to some deep-seated need of veneration. She was his, he had chosen her, she had taken her place in the long line of Lansing women who had been loved, honoured, and probably deceived, by bygone Lansing men. He didn't pretend to understand the logic of it; but the fact that she was his wife gave purpose and continuity to his scattered impulses, and a mysterious glow of consecration to his task.

Once or twice, in the first days of his marriage, he had asked himself with a slight shiver what would happen if Susy should begin to bore him. The thing had happened to him with other women as to whom his first emotions had not differed in intensity from those she inspired. The part he had played in his previous love-affairs might indeed have been summed up in the memorable line: "I am the hunter and the prey," for he had invariably ceased to be the first only to regard himself as the second. This experience had never ceased to cause him the liveliest pain, since his sympathy for his pursuer was only less keen than his commiseration for himself; but as he was always a little sorrier for himself, he had always ended by distancing the pursuer.

All these pre-natal experiences now seemed utterly inapplicable to the new man he had become. He could not imagine being bored by Susy—or trying to escape from her if he were. He could not think of her as an enemy, or even as an accomplice, since accomplices are potential enemies: she was some one with whom, by some unheard-of miracle, joys above the joys of friendship were to be tasted, but who, even through these fleeting ecstasies, remained simply and securely his friend.

These new feelings did not affect his general attitude toward life: they merely confirmed his faith in its ultimate "jolliness." Never had he more thoroughly enjoyed the things he had always enjoyed. A good dinner had never been as good to him, a beautiful sunset as beautiful; he still rejoiced in the fact that he appreciated both with an equal acuity. He was as proud as ever of Susy's cleverness and freedom from prejudice: she couldn't be too "modern" for him now that she was his. He shared to the full her passionate enjoyment of the present, and all her feverish eagerness to make it last. He knew when she was thinking of ways of extending their golden opportunity, and he secretly thought with her, wondering what new means they could devise. He was thankful that Ellie Vanderlyn was still absent, and began to hope they might have the palace to themselves for the remainder of the summer. If they did, he would have time to finish his book, and Susy to lay up a little interest on their wedding cheques; and thus their enchanted year might conceivably be prolonged to two.

Late as the season was, their presence and Strefford's in Venice had already drawn thither several wandering members of their set. It was characteristic of these indifferent but agglutinative people that they could never remain long parted from each other without a dim sense of uneasiness. Lansing was familiar with the feeling. He had known slight twinges of it himself, and had often ministered to its qualms in others. It was hardly stronger than the faint gnawing which recalls the tea-hour to one who has lunched well and is sure of dining as abundantly; but it gave a purpose to the purposeless, and helped many hesitating spirits over the annual difficulty of deciding between Deauville and St. Moritz, Biarritz and Capri.

Nick was not surprised to learn that it was becoming the fashion, that summer, to pop down to Venice and take a look at the Lansings. Streffy had set the example, and Streffy's example was always followed. And then Susy's marriage was still a subject of sympathetic speculation. People knew the story of the wedding cheques, and were interested in seeing how long they could be made to last. It was going to be the thing, that year, to help prolong the honey-moon by pressing houses on the adventurous couple. Before June was over a band of friends were basking with the Lansings on the Lido.

Nick found himself unexpectedly disturbed by their arrival. To avoid comment and banter he put his book aside and forbade Susy to speak of it, explaining to her that he needed an interval of rest. His wife instantly and exaggeratedly adopted this view, guarding him from the temptation to work as jealously as she had discouraged him from idling; and he was careful not to let her find out that the change in his habits coincided with his having reached a difficult point in his book. But though he was not sorry to stop writing he found himself unexpectedly oppressed by the weight of his leisure. For the first time communal dawdling had lost its charm for him; not because his fellow dawdlers were less congenial than of old, but because in the interval he had known something so immeasurably better. He had always felt himself to be the superior of his habitual associates, but now the advantage was too great: really, in a sense, it was hardly fair to them.

He had flattered himself that Susy would share this feeling; but he perceived with annoyance that the arrival of their friends heightened her animation. It was as if the inward glow which had given her a new beauty were now refracted upon her by the presence of the very people they had come to Venice to avoid.

Lansing was vaguely irritated; and when he asked her how she liked being with their old crowd again his irritation was increased by her answering with a laugh that she only hoped the poor dears didn't see too plainly how they bored her. The patent insincerity of the reply was a shock to Lansing. He knew that Susy was not really bored, and he understood that she had simply guessed his feelings and instinctively adopted them: that henceforth she was always going to think as he thought. To confirm this fear he said carelessly: "Oh, all the same, it's rather jolly knocking about with them again for a bit"; and she answered at once, and with equal conviction: "Yes, isn't it? The old darlings—all the same!"

A fear of the future again laid its cold touch on Lansing. Susy's independence and self-sufficiency had been among her chief attractions; if she were to turn into an echo their delicious duet ran the risk of becoming the dullest of monologues. He forgot that five minutes earlier he had resented her being glad to see their friends, and for a moment he found himself leaning dizzily over that insoluble riddle of the sentimental life: that to be differed with is exasperating, and to be agreed with monotonous.

Once more he began to wonder if he were not fundamentally unfitted for the married state; and was saved from despair only by remembering that Susy's subjection to his moods was not likely to last. But even then it never occurred to him to reflect that his apprehensions were superfluous, since their tie was avowedly a temporary one. Of the special understanding on which their marriage had been based not a trace remained in his thoughts of her; the idea that he or she might ever renounce each other for their mutual good had long since dwindled to the ghost of an old joke.

It was borne in on him, after a week or two of unbroken sociability, that of all his old friends it was the Mortimer Hickses who bored him the least. The Hickses had left the *Ibis* for an apartment in a vast dilapidated palace near the Canareggio. They had hired the apartment from a painter (one of their newest discoveries), and they put up philosophically with the absence of modern conveniences in order to secure the inestimable advantage of "atmosphere." In this privileged air they gathered about them their usual mixed company of quiet studious people and noisy exponents of new theories, themselves totally unconscious of the disparity between their different guests, and beamingly convinced that at last they were seated at the source of wisdom.

In old days Lansing would have got half an hour's amusement, followed by a long evening of boredom, from the sight of Mrs. Hicks, vast and jewelled, seated between a quiet-looking professor of archæology and a large-browed composer, or the high priest of a new dance-step, while Mr. Hicks, beaming above his vast white waistcoat, saw to it that the champagne flowed more abundantly than the talk, and the bright young secretaries industriously "kept up" with the dizzy cross-current of prophecy and erudition. But a change had come over Lansing. Hitherto it was in contrast to his own friends that the Hickses had seemed most insufferable; now it was as an escape from these same friends that they had become not only sympathetic but even interesting. It was something, after all, to be with people who did not regard Venice simply as affording exceptional opportunities for bathing and adultery, but who were reverently if confusedly aware that they were in the presence of something unique and ineffable, and determined to make the utmost of their privilege.

"After all," he said to himself one evening, as his eyes wandered, with somewhat of a convalescent's simple joy, from one to another of their large confiding faces, "after all, they've got a religion. . . ." The phrase struck him, in the moment of using it, as indicating a new element in his own state of mind, and as being, in fact, the key to his new feeling about the Hickses. Their muddled ardour for great things was related to his own new view of the universe: the people who felt, however dimly, the wonder and weight of life must ever after be nearer to him than those to whom it was estimated solely by one's balance at the bank. He supposed, on reflexion, that that was what he meant when he thought of the Hickses as having "a religion." . . .

A few days later, his well-being was unexpectedly disturbed by the arrival of Fred Gillow. Lansing had always felt a tolerant liking for Gillow, a large smiling silent young man with an intense and serious desire to miss nothing attainable by one of his fortune and standing. What use he made of his experiences, Lansing, who had always gone into his own modest adventures rather thoroughly, had never been able to guess; but he had always suspected the prodigal Fred of being no more than a well-disguised looker-on. Now for the first time he began to view him with another eye. The Gillows were, in fact, the one uneasy point in Nick's conscience. He and Susy, from the first, had talked of them less than of any other members of their group: they had tacitly avoided the name from the day on which Susy had come to Lansing's lodgings to say that Ursula Gillow had asked her to renounce him, till that other day, just before their marriage, when she had met him with the rapturous cry: "Here's our first wedding present! Such a thumping big cheque from Fred and Ursula!"

Plenty of sympathizing people were ready, Lansing knew, to tell him just what had happened in the interval between those two dates; but he had taken care not to ask. He had even affected an initiation so complete that the friends who burned to enlighten him were discouraged by his so obviously knowing more than they; and gradually he had worked himself around to their view, and had taken it for granted that he really did.

Now he perceived that he knew nothing at all, and that the "Hullo, old Fred!" with which Susy hailed Gillow's arrival might be either the usual tribal welcome—since they were all "old," and all nick-named, in their private jargon—or a greeting that concealed inscrutable depths of complicity.

Susy was visibly glad to see Gillow; but she was glad of everything just then, and so glad to show her gladness! The fact disarmed her husband and made him ashamed of his uneasiness. "You ought to have thought this all out sooner, or else you ought to chuck thinking of it at all," was the sound but ineffectual advice he gave himself on the day after Gillow's arrival; and immediately set to work to rethink the whole matter.

Fred Gillow showed no consciousness of disturbing any one's peace of mind. Day after day he sprawled for hours on the Lido sands, his arms folded under his head, listening to Streffy's nonsense and watching Susy between sleepy lids; but he betrayed no desire to see her alone, or to draw her into talk apart from the others. More than ever he seemed content to be the gratified spectator of a costly show got up for his private entertainment. It was not until he heard her, one morning, grumble a little at the increasing heat and the menace of mosquitoes, that he said, quite as if they had talked the matter over long before, and finally settled it: "The moor will be ready any time after the first of August."

Nick fancied that Susy coloured a little, and drew herself up more defiantly than usual as she sent a pebble skimming across the dying ripples at their feet.

"You'll be a lot cooler in Scotland," Fred added, with what, for him, was an unusual effort at explicitness.

"Oh, shall we?" she retorted gaily; and added with an air of mystery and importance, pivoting about on her high heels: "Nick's got work to do here. It will probably keep us all summer."

"Work? Rot! You'll die of the smells." Gillow stared perplexedly skyward from under his tilted hat-brim; and then brought out, as from the depth of a rankling grievance: "I thought it was all understood."

"Why," Nick asked his wife that night, as they re-entered Ellie's cool drawing-room after a late dinner at the Lido, "did Gillow think it was understood that we were going to his moor in August?" He was conscious of the oddness of speaking of their friend by his surname, and reddened at his blunder.

Susy had let her lace cloak slide to her feet, and stood before him in the faintly-lit room, slim and shimmering-white through black transparencies.

She raised her eyebrows carelessly. "I told you long ago he'd asked us there for August."

"You didn't tell me you'd accepted."

She smiled as if he had said something as simple as Fred. "I accepted everything—from everybody!"

What could he answer? It was the very principle on which their bargain had been struck. And if he were to say: "Ah, but this is different, because I'm jealous of Gillow," what light would such an answer shed on his past? The time for being jealous—if so antiquated an attitude were on any ground defensible—would have been before his marriage, and before the acceptance of the bounties which had helped to make it possible. He wondered a little now that in those days such scruples had not troubled him. His inconsistency irritated him, and increased his irritation against Gillow. "I suppose he thinks he owns us!" he grumbled inwardly.

He had thrown himself into an armchair, and Susy, advancing across the shining arabesques of the floor, slid down at his feet, pressed her slender length against him, and whispered with lifted face and lips close to his: "We needn't ever go anywhere you don't want to." For once her submission was sweet, and folding her close he whispered back through his kiss: "Not there, then."

In her response to his embrace he felt the acquiescence of her whole happy self in whatever future he decided on, if only it gave them enough of such moments as this; and as they held each other fast in silence his doubts and distrust began to seem like a silly injustice.

"Let us stay here as long as ever Ellie will let us," he said, as if the shadowy walls and shining floors were a magic boundary drawn about his happiness.

She murmured her assent and stood up, stretching her sleepy arm above her shoulders. "How dreadfully late it is. . . . Will you unhook me? . . . Oh, there's a telegram."

She picked it up from the table, and tearing it open stared a moment at the message. "It's from Ellie. She's coming to-morrow."

She turned to the window and strayed out onto the balcony. Nick followed her with enlacing arm. The canal below them lay in moonless shadow, barred with a few lingering lights. A last snatch of gondola-music came from far off, carried upward on a sultry gust.

"Dear old Ellie. All the same . . . I wish all this belonged to you and me." Susy sighed.

Chapter VIII

IT was not Mrs. Vanderlyn's fault if, after her arrival, her palace seemed to belong any less to the Lansings.

She arrived in a mood of such general benevolence that it was impossible for Susy, when they finally found themselves alone, to make her view even her own recent conduct in any but the most benevolent light.

"I knew you'd be the veriest angel about it all, darling, because I knew you'd understand me—especially *now*," she declared, her slim hands in Susy's, her big eyes (so like Clarissa's) resplendent with past pleasures and future plans.

The expression of her confidence was unexpectedly distasteful to Susy Lansing, who had never lent so cold an ear to such warm avowals. She had always imagined that being happy one's self made one—as Mrs. Vanderlyn appeared to assume—more tolerant of the happiness of others, of however doubtful elements composed; and she was almost ashamed of responding so languidly to her friend's outpourings. But she herself had no desire to confide her bliss to Ellie; and why should not Ellie observe a similar reticence?

"It was all so perfect—you see, dearest, *I was meant to be happy*," that lady continued, as if the possession of so unusual a characteristic singled her out for special privileges.

Susy, with a certain sharpness, responded that she had always supposed we all were.

"Oh, no, dearest: not governesses and mothers-in-law and companions, and that sort of people. They wouldn't know how if they tried. But you and I, darling—"

"Oh, I don't consider myself in any way exceptional," Susy intervened. She longed to add: "Not in *your* way, at any rate—" but a few minutes earlier Mrs. Vanderlyn had told her that the palace was at her disposal for the rest of the summer, and that she herself was only going to perch there—if they'd let her?—long enough to gather up her things and start for St. Moritz. The memory of this announcement had the effect of curbing Susy's irony, and of making her shift the conversation to the safer if scarcely less absorbing topic of the number of day and evening dresses required for a season at St. Moritz.

As she listened to Mrs. Vanderlyn—no less eloquent on this theme than on the other—Susy began to measure the gulf between her past and present. "This is the life I used to lead; these are the things I used to live for," she thought, as she stood before the outspread glories of Mrs. Vanderlyn's wardrobe. Not that she did not still care: she could not look at Ellie's laces and silks and furs without picturing herself in them, and wondering by what new miracle of management she could give herself the air of being dressed by the same consummate artists. But these had become minor interests: the past few months had given her a new perspective, and the thing that most puzzled and disconcerted her about Ellie was the fact that love and finery and bridge and dining-out were seemingly all on the same plane to her.

The inspection of the dresses lasted a long time, and was marked by many fluctuations of mood on the part of Mrs. Vanderlyn, who passed from comparative hopefulness to despair at the total inadequacy of her wardrobe. It wouldn't do to go to St. Moritz looking like a frump, and yet there was no time to get anything sent from Paris, and, whatever she did, she wasn't going to show herself in any dowdy re-arrangements done at home. But suddenly light broke on her, and she clasped her hands for joy. "Why, Nelson'll bring them—I'd forgotten all about Nelson! There'll be just time if I wire to him at once."

"Is Nelson going to join you at St. Moritz?" Susy asked, surprised.

"Heavens, no! He's coming here to pick up Clarissa and take her to some stuffy cure in Austria with his mother. It's too lucky: there's just time to telegraph him to bring my things. I didn't mean to wait for him; but it won't delay me more than a day or two."

Susy's heart sank. She was not much afraid of Ellie alone, but Ellie and Nelson together formed an incalculable menace. No one could tell what spark of truth might flash from their collision. Susy felt that she could deal with the two dangers separately and successively, but not together and simultaneously.

"But, Ellie, why should you wait for Nelson? I'm certain to find someone here who's going to St. Moritz and will take your things if he brings them. It's a pity to risk losing your rooms."

This argument appealed for a moment to Mrs. Vanderlyn. "That's true; they say all the hotels are jammed. You dear, you're always so practical!" She clasped Susy to her scented bosom. "And you know, darling, I'm sure you'll be glad to get rid of me—you and Nick! Oh, don't be hypocritical and say 'Nonsense!' You see, I understand . . . I used to think of you so often, you two . . . during those blessed weeks when *we* two were alone. . . ."

The sudden tears, brimming over Ellie's lovely eyes, and threatening to make the blue circles below them run into the adjoining carmine, filled Susy with compunction.

"Poor thing—oh, poor thing!" she thought; and hearing herself called by Nick, who was waiting to take her out for their usual sunset on the lagoon, she felt a wave of pity for the deluded creature who would never taste that highest of imaginable joys. "But all the same," Susy reflected, as she hurried down to her husband, "I'm glad I persuaded her not to wait for Nelson."

Some days had elapsed since Susy and Nick had had a sunset to themselves, and in the interval Susy had once again learned the superior quality of the sympathy that held them together. She now viewed all the rest of life as no more than a show: a jolly show which it would have been a thousand pities to miss, but which, if the need arose, they could get up and leave at any moment—provided that they left it together.

In the dusk, while their prow slid over inverted palaces, and through the scent of hidden gardens, she leaned against him and murmured, her mind returning to the recent scene with Ellie: "Nick, should you hate me dreadfully if I had no clothes?"

Her husband was kindling a cigarette, and the match lit up the grin with which he answered: "But, my dear, have I ever shown the slightest symptom—?"

"Oh, rubbish! When a woman says: 'No clothes,' she means: 'Not the right clothes.'"

He took a meditative puff. "Ah, you've been going over Ellie's finery with her."

"Yes: all those trunks and trunks full. And she finds she's got nothing for St. Moritz!"

"Of course," he murmured, drowsy with content, and manifesting but a languid interest in the subject of Mrs. Vanderlyn's wardrobe.

"Only fancy—she very nearly decided to stop over for Nelson's arrival next week, so that he might bring her two or three more trunkfuls from Paris. But mercifully I've managed to persuade her that it would be foolish to wait."

Susy felt a hardly perceptible shifting of her husband's lounging body, and was aware, through all her watchful tentacles, of a widening of his half-closed lids.

"You 'managed'—?" She fancied he paused on the word ironically. "But why?"

"Why—what?"

"Why on earth should you try to prevent Ellie's waiting for Nelson, if for once in her life she wants to?"

Susy, conscious of reddening suddenly, drew back as though the leap of her tell-tale heart might have penetrated the blue flannel shoulder against which she leaned.

"Really, dearest—!" she murmured; but with a sudden doggedness he renewed his "Why?"

"Because she's in such a fever to get to St. Moritz—and in such a funk lest the hotel shouldn't keep her rooms," Susy somewhat breathlessly produced.

"Ah—I see." Nick paused again. "You're a devoted friend, aren't you?"

"What an odd question! There's hardly anyone I've reason to be more devoted to than Ellie," his wife answered; and she felt his contrite clasp on her hand.

"Darling! No; nor I—. Or more grateful to for leaving us alone in this heaven."

Dimness had fallen on the waters, and her lifted lips met his bending ones.

Trailing late into dinner that evening, Ellie announced that, after all, she had decided it was safest to wait for Nelson.

"I should simply worry myself ill if I weren't sure of getting my things," she said, in the tone of tender solicitude with which she always discussed her own difficulties. "After all, people who deny themselves *everything* do get warped and bitter, don't they?" she argued plaintively, her lovely eyes wandering from one to the other of her assembled friends.

Strefford remarked gravely that it was the complaint which had fatally undermined his own health; and in the laugh that followed the party drifted into the great vaulted dining-room.

"Oh, I don't mind *your* laughing at me, Streffy darling," his hostess retorted, pressing his arm against her own; and Susy, receiving the shock of their rapidly exchanged glance, said to herself, with a sharp twinge of apprehension: "Of course Streffy knows everything; he showed no surprise at finding Ellie away when he arrived. And if he knows, what's to prevent Nelson's finding out?" For Strefford, in a mood of mischief, was no more to be trusted than a malicious child. Susy instantly resolved to risk speaking to him, if need be even betraying to him the secret of the letters. Only by revealing the depth of her own danger could she hope to secure his silence.

On the balcony, late in the evening, while the others were listening indoors to the low modulations of a young composer who had embroidered his fancies on Browning's "Toccata," Susy found her chance. Strefford, unsummoned, had followed her out, and stood silently smoking at her side.

"You see, Streff—oh, why should you and I make mysteries to each other?" she suddenly began.

"Why, indeed: but do we?"

Susy glanced back at the group around the piano. "About Ellie, I mean—and Nelson."

"Lord! Ellie and Nelson? You call *that* a mystery? I should as soon apply the term to one of the million-candle-power advertisements that adorn your native thoroughfares."

"Well, yes. But—" She stopped again. Had she not tacitly promised Ellie not to speak?

"My Susan, what's wrong?" Strefford asked.

"I don't know. . . ."

"Well, I do, then: you're afraid that, if Ellie and Nelson meet here, she'll blurt out something—injudicious."

"Oh, *she* won't!" Susy cried with conviction.

"Well, then—who will? I trust that superhuman child not to. And you and I and Nick——"

"Oh," she gasped, interrupting him, "that's just it. Nick doesn't know . . . doesn't even suspect. And if he did. . . ."

Strefford flung away his cigar and turned to scrutinize her. "I don't see—hanged if I do. What business is it of any of us, after all?"

That, of course, was the old view that cloaked connivance in an air of decency. But to Susy it no longer carried conviction, and she hesitated.

"If Nick should find out that I know. . . ."

"Good Lord—doesn't he know that you know? After all, I suppose it's not the first time—"

She remained silent.

"The first time you've received confidences—from married friends. Does Nick suppose you've lived even to your tender age without. . . . Hang it, what's come over you, child?"

What had, indeed, that she could make clear to him? And yet more than ever she felt the need of having him securely on her side. Once his word was pledged, he was safe: otherwise there was no limit to his capacity for wilful harmfulness.

"Look here, Streff, you and I know that Ellie hasn't been away for a cure; and that if poor Clarissa was sworn to secrecy it was not because it 'worries father' to think that mother needs to take care of her health." She paused, hating herself for the ironic note she had tried to sound.

"Well—?" he questioned, from the depths of the chair into which he had sunk.

"Well, Nick doesn't . . . doesn't dream of it. If he knew that we owed our summer here to . . . to my knowing. . . ."

Strefford sat silent: she felt his astonished stare through the darkness. "Jove!" he said at last, with a low whistle. Susy bent over the balustrade, her heart thumping against the stone rail.

"*What of soul was left, I wonder—?*" the young composer's voice shrilled through the open windows.

Strefford sank into another silence, from which he roused himself only as Susy turned back toward the lighted threshold.

"Well, my dear, we'll see it through between us; you and I—and Clarissa," he said with his rasping laugh, rising to follow her. He caught her hand and gave it a short pressure as they re-entered the drawing-room, where Ellie was saying plaintively to Fred Gillow: "I can never hear that thing sung without wanting to cry like a baby."

Chapter IX

M R. NELSON VANDERLYN, still in his travelling clothes, paused on the threshold of his own dining-room and surveyed the scene with pardonable satisfaction.

He was a short round man, with a grizzled head, small facetious eyes and a large and credulous smile.

At the luncheon table sat his wife, between Charlie Strefford and Nick Lansing. Next to Strefford, perched on her high chair, Clarissa throned in infant beauty, while Susy Lansing cut up a peach for her. Through wide orange awnings the sun slanted in upon the white-clad group.

"Well—well—well! So I've caught you at it!" cried the happy father, whose inveterate habit it was to address his wife and friends as if he had surprised them at an inopportune moment. Stealing up from behind, he lifted his daughter into the air, while a chorus of "Hullo, old Nelson," hailed his appearance.

It was two or three years since Nick Lansing had seen Mr. Vanderlyn, who was now the London representative of the big New York bank of Vanderlyn & Co., and had exchanged his sumptuous house in Fifth Avenue for another, more sumptuous still, in Mayfair; and the young man looked curiously and attentively at his host.

Mr. Vanderlyn had grown older and stouter, but his face still kept its look of somewhat worn optimism. He embraced his wife, greeted Susy affectionately, and distributed cordial handgrasps to the two men.

"Hullo," he exclaimed, suddenly noticing a pearl and coral trinket hanging from Clarissa's neck. "Who's been giving my daughter jewellery, I'd like to know?"

"Oh, Streffy did—just think, father! Because I said I'd rather have it than a book, you know," Clarissa lucidly explained, her arms tight about her father's neck, her beaming eyes on Strefford.

Nelson Vanderlyn's own eyes took on the look of shrewdness which came into them whenever there was a question of material values.

"What, Streffy? Caught you at it, eh? Upon my soul—spoiling the brat like that! You'd no business to, my dear chap—a lovely baroque pearl—" he protested, with the half-apologetic tone of the rich man embarrassed by too costly a gift from an impecunious friend.

"Oh, hadn't I? Why? Because it's too good for Clarissa, or too expensive for me? Of course you daren't imply the first; and as for me—I've had a windfall, and am blowing it in on the ladies."

Strefford, Lansing had noticed, always used American slang when he was slightly at a loss, and wished to divert attention from the main point. But why was he embarrassed, whose attention did he wish to divert? It was plain that Vanderlyn's protest had been merely formal: like most of the wealthy, he had only the dimmest notion of what money represented to the poor. But it was unusual for Strefford to give any one a present, and especially an expensive one: perhaps that was what had fixed Vanderlyn's attention.

"A windfall?" he gaily repeated.

"Oh, a tiny one: I was offered a thumping rent for my little place at Como, and dashed over here to squander my millions with the rest of you," said Strefford imperturbably.

Vanderlyn's look immediately became interested and sympathetic. "What—the scene of the honey-moon?" He included Nick and Susy in his friendly smile.

"Just so: the reward of virtue. I say, give me a cigar, will you, old man? I left some awfully good ones at Como, worse luck—and I don't mind telling you that Ellie's no judge of tobacco, and that Nick's too far gone in bliss to care what he smokes," Strefford grumbled, stretching a hand toward his host's cigar-case.

"I *do* like jewellery best," Clarissa murmured, hugging her father.

Nelson Vanderlyn's first word to his wife had been that he had brought her all her toggery; and she had welcomed him with appropriate enthusiasm. In fact, to the lookers-on her joy at seeing him seemed rather too patently in proportion to her satisfaction at getting her clothes. But no such suspicion appeared to mar Mr. Vanderlyn's happiness in being, for once, and for nearly twenty-four hours, under the same roof with his wife and child. He did not conceal his regret at having promised his mother to join her the next day; and added, with a wistful glance at Ellie: "If only I'd known you meant to wait for me—!"

But being a man of duty, in domestic as well as business affairs, he did not even consider the possibility of disappointing the exacting old lady to whom he owed his being. "Mother cares for so few people," he used to say, not without a touch of filial pride in the parental exclusiveness, "that I have to be with her rather more than if she were more sociable"; and with smiling resignation he gave orders that Clarissa should be ready to start the next evening.

"And meanwhile," he concluded, "we'll have all the good time that's going."

The ladies of the party seemed united in the desire to further this resolve; and it was settled that as soon as Mr. Vanderlyn had despatched a hasty luncheon, his wife, Clarissa and Susy should carry him off for a tea-picnic at Torcello. They did not even suggest that Strefford or Nick should be of the party, or that any of the other young men of the group should be summoned; as Susy said, Nelson wanted to go off alone with his harem. And Lansing and Strefford were left to watch the departure of the happy Pasha ensconced between attentive beauties.

"Well—that's what you call being married!" Strefford commented, waving his battered Panama at Clarissa.

"Oh, no, I don't!" Lansing laughed.

"*He* does. But do you know—" Strefford paused and swung about on his companion— "do you know, when the Rude Awakening comes, I don't care to be there. I believe there'll be some crockery broken."

"Shouldn't wonder," Lansing answered indifferently. He wandered away to his own room, leaving Strefford to philosophize to his pipe.

Lansing had always known about poor old Nelson: who hadn't, except poor old Nelson? The case had once seemed amusing because so typical; now, it rather irritated Nick that Vanderlyn should be so complete an ass. But he would be off the next day, and so would Ellie, and then, for many enchanted weeks, the palace would once more be the property of Nick and Susy. Of all the people who came and went in it, they were the only ones who appreciated it, or knew how it was meant to be lived in; and that made it theirs in the only valid sense. In this light it became easy to regard the Vanderlyns as mere transient intruders.

Having relegated them to this convenient distance, Lansing shut himself up with his book. He had returned to it with fresh energy after his few weeks of holiday-making, and was determined to finish it quickly. He did not expect that it would bring in much money; but if it were moderately successful it might give him an opening in the reviews and magazines, and in that case he meant to abandon archæology for novels, since it was only as a purveyor of fiction that he could count on earning a living for himself and Susy.

Late in the afternoon he laid down his pen and wandered out of doors. He loved the increasing heat of the Venetian summer, the bruised peach-tints of worn house-fronts, the enamelling of sunlight on dark green canals, the smell of half-decayed fruits and flowers thickening the languid air. What visions he could build, if he dared, of being tucked away with Susy in the attic of some tumble-down palace, above a jade-green waterway, with a terrace overhanging a scrap of neglected garden—and cheques from the publishers dropping in at convenient intervals! Why should they not settle in Venice if he pulled it off?

He found himself before the church of the Scalzi, and pushing open the leathern door wandered up the nave under the whirl of rose-and-lemon angels in Tiepolo's great vault. It was not a church in which one was likely to run across sight-seers; but he presently remarked a young lady standing alone near the choir, and assiduously applying her field-glass to the celestial vortex, from which she occasionally glanced down at an open manual.

As Lansing's step sounded on the pavement, the young lady, turning, revealed herself as Miss Hicks.

"Ah—you like this too? It's several centuries out of your line, though, isn't it?" Nick asked as they shook hands.

She gazed at him gravely. "Why shouldn't one like things that are out of one's line?" she answered; and he agreed, with a laugh, that it was often an incentive.

She continued to fix her grave eyes on him, and after one or two remarks about the Tiepolos he perceived that she was feeling her way toward a subject of more personal interest.

"I'm glad to see you alone," she said at length, with an abruptness that might have seemed awkward had it not been so completely unconscious. She turned toward a cluster of straw chairs, and signed to Nick to seat himself beside her.

"I seldom do," she added, with the serious smile that made her heavy face almost handsome; and she went on, giving him no time to protest: "I wanted to speak to you—to explain about father's invitation to go with us to Persia and Turkestan."

"To explain?"

"Yes. You found the letter when you arrived here just after your marriage, didn't you? You must have thought it odd, our asking you just then; but we hadn't heard that you were married."

"Oh, I guessed as much: it happened very quietly, and I was remiss about announcing it, even to old friends."

Lansing frowned. His thoughts had wandered away to the evening when he had found Mrs. Hicks's letter in the mail awaiting him at Venice. The day was associated in his mind with the ridiculous and mortifying episode of the cigars—the expensive cigars that Susy had wanted to carry away from Strefford's villa. Their brief exchange of views on the subject had left the first blur on the perfect surface of his happiness, and he still felt an uncomfortable heat at the remembrance. For a few hours the prospect of life with Susy had seemed unendurable; and it was just at that moment that he had found the letter from Mrs. Hicks, with its almost irresistible invitation. If only her daughter had known how nearly he had accepted it!

"It was a dreadful temptation," he said, smiling.

"To go with us? Then why—?"

"Oh, everything's different now: I've got to stick to my writing."

Miss Hicks still bent on him the same unblinking scrutiny. "Does that mean that you're going to give up your real work?"

"My real work—archæology?" He smiled again to hide a twitch of regret. "Why, I'm afraid it hardly produces a living wage; and I've got to think of that." He coloured suddenly, as if suspecting that Miss Hicks might consider the avowal an opening for he hardly knew what ponderous offer of aid. The Hicks munificence was too uncalculating not to be occasionally oppressive. But looking at her again he saw that her eyes were full of tears.

"I thought it was your vocation," she said.

"So did I. But life comes along, and upsets things."

"Oh, I understand. There may be things—worth giving up all other things for."

"There *are*!" cried Nick with beaming emphasis.

He was conscious that Miss Hicks's eyes demanded of him even more than this sweeping affirmation.

"But your novel may fail," she said with her odd harshness.

"It may—it probably will," he agreed. "But if one stopped to consider such possibilities—"

"Don't you have to, with a wife?"

"Oh, my dear Coral—how old are you? Not twenty?" he questioned, laying a brotherly hand on hers.

She stared at him a moment, and sprang up clumsily from her chair. "I was never young . . . if that's what you mean. It's lucky, isn't it, that my parents gave me such a grand education? Because, you see, art's a wonderful resource." (She pronounced it *re*-source.)

He continued to look at her kindly. "You won't need it—or any other—when you grow young, as you will some day," he assured her.

"Do you mean, when I fall in love? But I *am* in love— Oh, there's Eldorada and Mr. Beck!" She broke off with a jerk, signalling with her field-glass to the pair who had just appeared at the farther end of the nave. "I told them that if they'd meet me here to-day I'd try to make them understand Tiepolo. Because, you see, at home we never really *have* understood Tiepolo; and Mr. Beck and Eldorada are the only ones to realize it. Mr. Buttles simply won't." She turned to Lansing and held out her hand. "I *am* in love," she repeated earnestly, "and that's the reason why I find art such a *re*-source."

She restored her eye-glasses, opened her manual, and strode across the church to the expectant neophytes.

Lansing, looking after her, wondered for half a moment whether Mr. Beck were the object of this apparently unrequited sentiment; then, with a queer start of introspection, abruptly decided that, no, he certainly was not. But then—but then—.

Well, there was no use in following up such conjectures. . . .
He turned homeward, wondering if the picnickers had already
reached Palazzo Vanderlyn.

They got back only in time for a late dinner, full of chaff and
laughter, and apparently still enchanted with each other's society. Nelson Vanderlyn beamed on his wife, sent his daughter
off to bed with a kiss, and leaning back in his armchair before
the fruit-and-flower-laden table, declared that he'd never spent
a jollier day in his life. Susy seemed to come in for a full share
of his approbation, and Lansing thought that Ellie was unusually demonstrative to her friend. Strefford, from his hostess's
side, glanced across now and then at young Mrs. Lansing, and
his glance seemed to Lansing a confidential comment on the
Vanderlyn raptures. But then Strefford was always having private jokes with people or about them; and Lansing was irritated
with himself for perpetually suspecting his best friends of vague
complicities at his expense. "If I'm going to be jealous of Streffy
now—!" he concluded with a grimace of self-derision.

Certainly Susy looked lovely enough to justify the most irrational pangs. As a girl she had been, for some people's taste, a
trifle fine-drawn and sharp-edged; now, to her old lightness of
line was added a shadowy bloom, a sort of star-reflecting depth.
Her movements were slower, less angular; her mouth had a
nestling droop, her lids seemed weighed down by their lashes;
and then suddenly the old spirit would reveal itself through the
new languor, like the tartness at the core of a sweet fruit. As her
husband looked at her across the flowers and lights he laughed
inwardly at the nothingness of all things else.

Vanderlyn and Clarissa left betimes the next morning; and
Mrs. Vanderlyn, who was to start for St. Moritz in the afternoon, devoted her last hours to anxious conferences with her
maid and Susy. Strefford, with Fred Gillow and the others, had
gone for a swim at the Lido, and Lansing seized the opportunity to get back to his book.

The quietness of the great echoing place gave him a foretaste
of the solitude to come. By mid-August all their party would be
scattered: the Hickses off on a cruise to Crete and the Ægean,
Fred Gillow on the way to his moor, Strefford to stay with

friends in Capri till his annual visit to Northumberland in September. One by one the others would follow, and Lansing and Susy be left alone in the great sun-proof palace, alone under the star-laden skies, alone with the great orange moons—still theirs!—above the bell-tower of San Giorgio. The novel, in that blessed quiet, would unfold itself as harmoniously as his dreams.

He wrote on, forgetful of the passing hours, till the door opened and he heard a step behind him. The next moment two hands were clasped over his eyes, and the air was full of Mrs. Vanderlyn's last new scent.

"You dear thing—I'm just off, you know," she said. "Susy told me you were working, and I forbade her to call you down. She and Streffy are waiting to take me to the station, and I've run up to say good-bye."

"Ellie, dear!" Full of compunction, Lansing pushed aside his writing and started up; but she pressed him back into his seat.

"No, no! I should never forgive myself if I'd interrupted you. I oughtn't to have come up; Susy didn't want me to. But I had to tell you, you dear. . . . I had to thank you. . . ."

In her dark travelling dress and hat, so discreetly conspicuous, so negligent and so studied, with a veil masking her paint, and gloves hiding her rings, she looked younger, simpler, more natural than he had ever seen her. Poor Ellie—such a good fellow, after all!

"To thank me? For what? For being so happy here?" he laughed, taking her hands.

She looked at him, laughed back, and flung her arms about his neck.

"For helping *me* to be so happy elsewhere—you and Susy, you two blessed darlings!" she cried, with a kiss on his cheek.

Their eyes met for a second; then her arms slipped slowly downward, dropping to her sides. Lansing sat before her like a stone.

"Oh," she gasped, "why do you stare so? Didn't you know . . . ?"

They heard Strefford's shrill voice on the stairs. "Ellie, where the deuce are you? Susy's in the gondola. You'll miss the train!"

Lansing stood up and caught Mrs. Vanderlyn by the wrist. "What do you mean? What are you talking about?"

"Oh, nothing. . . . But you were both such bricks about the letters. . . . And when Nelson was here, too. . . . Nick, don't hurt my wrist so! I must run!"

He dropped her hand and stood motionless, staring after her and listening to the click of her high heels as she fled across the room and along the echoing corridor.

When he turned back to the table he noticed that a small morocco case had fallen among his papers. In falling it had opened, and before him, on the pale velvet lining, lay a scarf-pin set with a perfect pearl. He picked the box up, and was about to hasten after Mrs. Vanderlyn—it was so like her to shed jewels on her path!—when he noticed his own initials on the cover.

He dropped the box as if it had been a hot coal, and sat for a long while gazing at the gold N. L., which seemed to have burnt itself into his flesh.

At last he roused himself and stood up.

Chapter X

WITH a sigh of relief Susy drew the pins from her hat and
threw herself down on the lounge.

The ordeal she had dreaded was over, and Mr. and Mrs.
Vanderlyn had safely gone their several ways. Poor Ellie was not
noted for prudence, and when life smiled on her she was given
to betraying her gratitude too openly; but thanks to Susy's
vigilance (and, no doubt, to Strefford's tacit co-operation), the
dreaded twenty-four hours were happily over. Nelson Vanderlyn had departed without a shadow on his brow, and though
Ellie's, when she came down from bidding Nick good-bye, had
seemed to Susy less serene than usual, she became her normal
self as soon as it was discovered that the red morocco bag with
her jewel-box was missing. Before it had been discovered in the
depths of the gondola they had reached the station, and there
was just time to thrust her into her "sleeper," from which she
was seen to wave an unperturbed farewell to her friends.

"Well, my dear, we've seen it through," Strefford remarked
with a deep breath as the St. Moritz express rolled away.

"Oh," Susy sighed in mute complicity; then, as if to cover her
self-betrayal: "Poor darling, she does so like what she likes!"

"Yes—even if it's a rotten bounder," Strefford agreed.

"A rotten bounder? Why, I thought—"

"That it was still young Davenant? Lord, no—not for the last
six months. Didn't she tell you—?"

Susy felt herself redden. "I didn't ask her—"

"Ask her? You mean you didn't let her!"

"I didn't let her. And I don't let you," Susy added sharply, as
he helped her into the gondola.

"Oh, all right: I daresay you're right. It simplifies things,"
Strefford placidly acquiesced.

She made no answer, and in silence they glided homeward.

Now, in the quiet of her own room, Susy lay and pondered on
the distance she had travelled during the last year. Strefford had
read her mind with his usual penetration. It was true that there
had been a time when she would have thought it perfectly natural that Ellie should tell her everything; that the name of young

Davenant's successor should be confided to her as a matter of course. Apparently even Ellie had been obscurely aware of the change, for after a first attempt to force her confidences on Susy she had contented herself with vague expressions of gratitude, allusive smiles and sighs, and the pretty "surprise" of the sapphire bangle slipped onto her friend's wrist in the act of their farewell embrace.

The bangle was extremely handsome. Susy, who had an auctioneer's eye for values, knew to a fraction the worth of those deep convex stones alternating with small emeralds and brilliants. She was glad to own the bracelet, and enchanted with the effect it produced on her slim wrist; yet, even while admiring it, and rejoicing that it was hers, she had already transmuted it into specie, and reckoned just how far it would go toward the paying of domestic necessities. For whatever came to her now interested her only as something more to be offered up to Nick.

The door opened and Nick came in. Dusk had fallen, and she could not see his face; but something in the jerk of the door-handle roused her ever-wakeful apprehension. She hurried toward him with outstretched wrist.

"Look, dearest—wasn't it too darling of Ellie?"

She pressed the button of the lamp that lit her dressing-table, and her husband's face started unfamiliarly out of the twilight. She slipped off the bracelet and held it up to him.

"Oh, I can go you one better," he said with a laugh; and pulling a morocco case from his pocket he flung it down among the scent-bottles.

Susy opened the case automatically, staring at the pearl because she was afraid to look again at Nick.

"Ellie—gave you this?" she asked at length.

"Yes. She gave me this." There was a pause. "Would you mind telling me," Lansing continued in the same dead-level tone, "exactly for what services we've both been so handsomely paid?"

"The pearl *is* beautiful," Susy murmured, to gain time, while her head spun round with unimaginable terrors.

"So are your sapphires; though, on closer examination, my services would appear to have been valued rather higher than yours. Would you be kind enough to tell me just what they were?"

Susy threw her head back and looked at him. "What on earth are you talking about, Nick? Why shouldn't Ellie have given us these things? Do you forget that it's like our giving her a penwiper or a button-hook? What is it you are trying to suggest?"

It had cost her a considerable effort to hold his eyes while she put the questions. Something had happened between him and Ellie, that was evident—one of those hideous unforeseeable blunders that may cause one's cleverest plans to crumble at a stroke; and again Susy shuddered at the frailty of her bliss. But her old training stood her in good stead. There had been more than one moment in her past when everything—somebody else's everything—had depended on her keeping a cool head and a clear glance. It would have been a wonder if now, when she felt her own everything at stake, she had not been able to put up as good a defence.

"What is it?" she repeated impatiently, as Lansing continued to remain silent.

"That's what I'm here to ask," he returned, keeping his eyes as steady as she kept hers. "There's no reason on earth, as you say, why Ellie shouldn't give us presents—as expensive presents as she likes; and the pearl *is* a beauty. All I ask is: for what specific services were they given? For, allowing for all the absence of scruple that marks the intercourse of truly civilized people, you'll probably agree that there are limits; at least up to now there have been limits. . . ."

"I really don't know what you mean. I suppose Ellie wanted to show that she was grateful to us for looking after Clarissa."

"But she gave us all this in exchange for that, didn't she?" he suggested, with a sweep of the hand around the beautiful shadowy room. "A whole summer of it if we choose."

Susy smiled. "Apparently she didn't think that enough."

"What a doting mother! It shows the store she sets upon her child."

"Well, don't you set store upon Clarissa?"

"Clarissa is exquisite; but her mother didn't mention her in offering me this recompense."

Susy lifted her head again. "Whom *did* she mention?"

"Vanderlyn," said Lansing.

"Vanderlyn? Nelson?"

"Yes—and some letters . . . something about letters. . . . What is it, my dear, that you and I have been hired to hide from Vanderlyn? Because I should like to know," Nick broke out savagely, "if we've been adequately paid."

Susy was silent: she needed time to reckon up her forces, and study her next move; and her brain was in such a whirl of fear that she could at last only retort: "What is it that Ellie said to you?"

Lansing laughed again. "That's just what you'd like to find out—isn't it?—in order to know the line to take in making your explanation."

The sneer had an effect that he could not have foreseen, and that Susy herself had not expected.

"Oh, don't—don't let us speak to each other like that!" she cried; and sinking down by the dressing-table she hid her face in her hands.

It seemed to her, now, that nothing mattered except that their love for each other, their faith in each other, should be saved from some unhealable hurt. She was willing to tell Nick everything—she wanted to tell him everything—if only she could be sure of reaching a responsive chord in him. But the scene of the cigars came back to her, and benumbed her. If only she could make him see that nothing was of any account as long as they continued to love each other!

His touch fell compassionately on her shoulder. "Poor child—don't," he said.

Their eyes met, but his expression checked the smile breaking through her tears. "Don't you see," he continued, "that we've got to have this thing out?"

She continued to stare at him through a prism of tears. "I can't—while you stand up like that," she stammered, childishly.

She had cowered down again into a corner of the lounge; but Lansing did not seat himself at her side. He took a chair facing her, like a caller on the farther side of a stately tea-tray. "Will that do?" he asked with a stiff smile, as if to humour her.

"Nothing will do—as long as you're not you!"

"Not me?"

She shook her head wearily. "What's the use? You accept things theoretically—and then when they happen. . . ."

"What things? What *has* happened?"

A sudden impatience mastered her. What did he suppose, after all—? "But you know all about Ellie. We used to talk about her often enough in old times," she said.

"Ellie and young Davenant?"

"Young Davenant; or the others. . . ."

"Or the others. But what business was it of ours?"

"Ah, that's just what I think!" she cried, springing up with an explosion of relief. Lansing stood up also, but there was no answering light in his face.

"We're outside of all that; we've nothing to do with it, have we?" he pursued.

"Nothing whatever."

"Then what on earth is the meaning of Ellie's gratitude? Gratitude for what we've done about some letters—and about Vanderlyn?"

"Oh, not *you*," Susy cried, involuntarily.

"Not I? Then you?" He came close and took her by the wrist. "Answer me. Have you been mixed up in some dirty business of Ellie's?"

There was a pause. She found it impossible to speak, with that burning grasp on the wrist where the bangle had been. At length he let her go and moved away. "Answer," he repeated.

"I've told you it was my business and not yours."

He received this in silence; then he questioned: "You've been sending letters for her, I suppose? To whom?"

"Oh, why do you torment me? Nelson was not supposed to know that she'd been away. She left me the letters to post to him once a week. I found them here the night we arrived. . . . It was the price—for *this*. Oh, Nick, say it's been worth it—say at least that it's been worth it!" she implored him.

He stood motionless, unresponding. One hand drummed on the corner of her dressing-table, making the jewelled bangle dance.

"How many letters?"

"I don't know . . . four . . . five . . . What does it matter?"

"And once a week, for six weeks—?"

"Yes."

"And you took it all as a matter of course?"

"No: I hated it. But what could I do?"

"What could you do?"

"When our being together depended on it? Oh, Nick, how could you think I'd give you up?"

"Give me up?" he echoed.

"Well—doesn't our being together depend on—on what we can get out of people? And hasn't there always got to be some give-and-take? Did you ever in your life get anything for nothing?" she cried with sudden exasperation. "You've lived among these people as long as I have; I suppose it's not the first time—"

"By God, but it is," he exclaimed, flushing. "And that's the difference—the fundamental difference."

"The difference?"

"Between you and me. I've never in my life done people's dirty work for them—least of all for favours in return. I suppose you guessed it, or you wouldn't have hidden this beastly business from me."

The blood rose to Susy's temples also. Yes, she had guessed it; instinctively, from the day she had first visited him in his bare lodgings, she had been aware of his stricter standard. But how could she tell him that under his influence her standard had become stricter too, and that it was as much to hide her humiliation from herself as to escape his anger that she had held her tongue?

"You knew I wouldn't have stayed here another day if I'd known," he continued.

"Yes: and then where in the world should we have gone?"

"You mean that—in one way or another—what you call give-and-take is the price of our remaining together?"

"Well—isn't it?" she faltered.

"Then we'd better part, hadn't we?"

He spoke in a low tone, thoughtfully and deliberately, as if this had been the inevitable conclusion to which their passionate argument had led.

Susy made no answer. For a moment she ceased to be conscious of the causes of what had happened; the thing itself seemed to have smothered her under its ruins.

Nick wandered away from the dressing-table and stood gazing out of the window at the darkening canal flecked with lights. She looked at his back, and wondered what would happen if she were to go up to him and fling her arms about him. But even if her touch could have broken the spell, she was not sure she would have chosen that way of breaking it. Beneath her speech-less anguish there burned the half-conscious sense of having been unfairly treated. When they had entered into their queer compact, Nick had known as well as she on what compromises and concessions the life they were to live together must be based. That he should have forgotten it seemed so unbelievable that she wondered, with a new leap of fear, if he were using the wretched Ellie's indiscretion as a means of escape from a tie already wearied of. Suddenly she raised her head with a laugh.

"After all—you were right when you wanted me to be your mistress."

He turned on her with an astonished stare. "You—my mistress?"

Through all her pain she thrilled with pride at the discovery that such a possibility had long since become unthinkable to him. But she insisted. "That day at the Fulmers'—have you forgotten? When you said it would be sheer madness for us to marry."

Lansing stood leaning in the embrasure of the window, his eyes fixed on the mosaic volutes of the floor.

"I was right enough when I said it would be sheer madness for us to marry," he rejoined at length.

She sprang up trembling. "Well, that's easily settled. Our compact—"

"Oh, that compact—" he interrupted her with an impatient laugh.

"Aren't you asking me to carry it out now?"

"Because I said we'd better part?" He paused. "But the compact—I'd almost forgotten it—was to the effect, wasn't it, that we were to give each other a helping hand if either of us had a better chance? The thing was absurd, of course; a mere joke; from my point of view, at least. I shall never want any better chance . . . any other chance. . . ."

"Oh, Nick, oh, Nick . . . but then. . . ." She was close to him, his face looming down through her tears; but he put her back.

"It would have been easy enough, wouldn't it," he rejoined, "if we'd been as detachable as all that? As it is, it's going to hurt horribly. But talking it over won't help. You were right just now when you asked how else we were going to live. We're born parasites, both, I suppose, or we'd have found out some way long ago. But I find there are things I might put up with for myself, at a pinch—and should, probably, in time—that I can't let you put up with for me . . . ever. . . . Those cigars at Como: do you suppose I didn't know it was for me? And this too? Well, it won't do . . . it won't do. . . ."

He stopped, as if his courage failed him; and she moaned out: "But your writing—if your book's a success. . . ."

"My poor Susy—that's all part of the humbug. We both know that my sort of writing will never pay. And what's the alternative—except more of the same kind of baseness? And getting more and more blunted to it? At least, till now, I've minded certain things; I don't want to go on till I find myself taking them for granted."

She reached out a timid hand. "But you needn't ever, dear . . . if you'd only leave it to me. . . ."

He drew back sharply. "That seems simple to you, I suppose? Well, men are different." He walked toward the dressing-table and glanced at the little enamelled clock which had been one of her wedding-presents.

"Time to dress, isn't it? Shall you mind if I leave you to dine with Streffy, and whoever else is coming? I'd rather like a long tramp, and no more talking just at present—except with myself."

He passed her by and walked rapidly out of the room. Susy stood motionless, unable to lift a detaining hand or to find a final word of appeal. On her disordered dressing-table Mrs. Vanderlyn's gifts glittered in the rosy lamp-light.

Yes: men were different, as he said.

Chapter XI

B UT there were necessary accommodations, there always had been; Nick in old times, had been the first to own it. . . . How they had laughed at the Perpendicular People, the people who went by on the other side (since you couldn't be a good Samaritan without stooping over and poking into heaps of you didn't know what)! And now Nick had suddenly become perpendicular. . . .

Susy, that evening, at the head of the dinner table, saw—in the breaks between her scudding thoughts—the nauseatingly familiar faces of the people she called her friends: Strefford, Fred Gillow, a giggling fool of a young Breckenridge, of their New York group, who had arrived that day, and Prince Nerone Altineri, Ursula's Prince, who, in Ursula's absence at a tiresome cure, had, quite simply and naturally, preferred to join her husband at Venice. Susy looked from one to the other of them, as if with newly-opened eyes, and wondered what life would be like with no faces but such as theirs to furnish it. . . .

Ah, Nick had become perpendicular! . . . After all, most people went through life making a given set of gestures, like dance-steps learned in advance. If your dancing manual told you at a given time to be perpendicular, you had to be, automatically—and that was Nick!

"But what on earth, Susy," Gillow's puzzled voice suddenly came to her as from immeasurable distances, "*are* you going to do in this beastly stifling hole for the rest of the summer?"

"Ask Nick, my dear fellow," Strefford answered for her; and: "By the way, where *is* Nick—if one may ask?" young Breckenridge interposed, glancing up to take belated note of his host's absence.

"Dining out," said Susy glibly. "People turned up: blighting bores that I wouldn't have dared to inflict on you." How easily the old familiar fibbing came to her!

"The kind to whom you say, 'Now *mind* you look me up'; and then spend the rest of your life dodging—like our good Hickses," Strefford amplified.

The Hickses—but, of course, Nick was with the Hickses! It went through Susy like a knife, and the dinner she had so lightly fibbed became a hateful truth. She said to herself feverishly: "I'll call him up there after dinner—and then he *will* feel silly"—but only to remember that the Hickses, in their mediæval setting, had of course sternly denied themselves a telephone.

The fact of Nick's temporary inaccessibility—since she was now convinced that he was really at the Hickses'—turned her distress to a mocking irritation. Ah, that was where he carried his principles, his standards, or whatever he called the new set of rules he had suddenly begun to apply to the old game! It was stupid of her not to have guessed it at once.

"Oh, the Hickses—Nick adores them, you know. He's going to marry Coral next," she laughed out, flashing the joke around the table with all her practised flippancy.

"Lord!" gasped Gillow, inarticulate: while the Prince displayed the unsurprised smile which Susy accused him of practising every morning with his Mueller exercises.

Suddenly Susy felt Strefford's eyes upon her.

"What's the matter with me? Too much rouge?" she asked, passing her arm in his as they left the table.

"No: too little. Look at yourself," he answered in a low tone.

"Oh, in these cadaverous old looking-glasses—everybody looks fished up from the canal!"

She jerked away from him to spin down the long floor of the *sala*, hands on hips, whistling a rag-time tune. The Prince and young Breckenridge caught her up, and she spun back with the latter, while Gillow—it was believed to be his sole accomplishment—snapped his fingers in simulation of bones, and shuffled after the couple on stamping feet.

Susy sank down on a sofa near the window, fanning herself with a floating scarf, and the men foraged for cigarettes, and rang for the gondoliers, who came in with trays of cooling drinks.

"Well, what next—this ain't all, is it?" Gillow presently queried, from the divan where he lolled half-asleep with dripping brow. Fred Gillow, like Nature, abhorred a void, and it was inconceivable to him that every hour of man's rational existence should not furnish a motive for getting up and going somewhere else. Young Breckenridge, who took the same view, and the Prince, who earnestly desired to, reminded the company that somebody they knew was giving a dance that night at the Lido.

Strefford vetoed the Lido, on the ground that he'd just come back from there, and proposed that they should go out on foot for a change.

"Why not? What fun!" Susy was up in an instant. "Let's pay somebody a surprise visit—I don't know who! Streffy, Prince, can't you think of somebody who'd be particularly annoyed by our arrival?"

"Oh, the list's too long. Let's start, and choose our victim on the way," Strefford suggested.

Susy ran to her room for a light cloak, and without changing her high-heeled satin slippers went out with the four men. There was no moon—thank heaven there was no moon!—but the stars hung over them as close as fruit, and secret fragrances dropped on them from garden-walls. Susy's heart tightened with memories of Como.

They wandered on, laughing and dawdling, and yielding to the drifting whims of aimless people. Presently someone proposed taking a nearer look at the façade of San Giorgio Maggiore, and they hailed a gondola and were rowed out through the bobbing lanterns and twanging guitar-strings. When they landed again, Gillow, always acutely bored by scenery, and particularly resentful of midnight æsthetics, suggested a night club near at hand, which was said to be jolly. The Prince warmly supported this proposal; but on Susy's curt refusal they started their rambling again, circuitously threading the vague dark lanes and making for the Piazza and Florian's ices. Suddenly, at a *calle*-corner, unfamiliar and yet somehow known to her, Susy paused to stare about her with a laugh.

"But the Hickses—surely that's their palace? And the windows all lit up! They must be giving a party! Oh, do let's go up and surprise them!" The idea struck her as one of the drollest that she had ever originated, and she wondered that her companions should respond so languidly.

"I can't see anything very thrilling in surprising the Hickses," Gillow protested, defrauded of possible excitements; and Strefford added: "It would surprise *me* more than them if I went."

But Susy insisted feverishly: "You don't know. It may be awfully exciting! I have an idea that Coral's announcing her engagement—her engagement to Nick! Come, give me a hand, Streff—and you the other, Fred—" she began to hum the first bars of Donna Anna's entrance in *Don Giovanni*. "Pity I haven't got a black cloak and a mask. . . ."

"Oh, your face will do," said Strefford, laying his hand on her arm.

She drew back, flushing crimson. Breckenridge and the Prince had sprung on ahead, and Gillow, lumbering after them, was already halfway up the stairs.

"My face? My face? What's the matter with my face? Do you know any reason why I shouldn't go to the Hickses to-night?" Susy broke out in sudden wrath.

"None whatever; except that if you do it will bore me to death," Strefford returned, with serenity.

"Oh, in that case—!"

"No; come on. I hear those fools banging on the door already." He caught her by the hand, and they started up the stairway. But on the first landing she paused, twisted her hand out of his, and without a word, without a conscious thought, dashed down the long flight, across the great resounding vestibule and out into the darkness of the *calle*.

Strefford caught up with her, and they stood a moment silent in the night.

"Susy—what the devil's the matter?"

"The matter? Can't you see? That I'm tired, that I've got a splitting headache—that you bore me to death, one and all of you!" She turned and laid a deprecating hand on his arm. "Streffy, old dear, don't mind me: but for God's sake find a gondola and send me home."

"Alone?"

"Alone."

It was never any concern of Streff's if people wanted to do things he did not understand, and she knew that she could count on his obedience. They walked on in silence to the next canal, and he picked up a passing gondola and put her in it.

"Now go and amuse yourself," she called after him, as the boat shot under the nearest bridge. Anything, anything, to be alone, away from the folly and futility that would be all she had left if Nick were to drop out of her life. . . .

"But perhaps he has dropped already—dropped for good," she thought as she set her foot on the Vanderlyn threshold.

The short summer night was already growing transparent: a new-born breeze stirred the soiled surface of the water and sent it lapping freshly against the old palace doorways. Nearly two o'clock! Nick had no doubt come back long ago. Susy hurried up the stairs, reassured by the mere thought of his nearness. She knew that when their eyes and their lips met it would be impossible for anything to keep them apart.

The gondolier dozing on the landing roused himself to receive her, and to proffer two envelopes. The upper one was a telegram for Strefford: she threw it down again and paused under the lantern hanging from the painted vault, the other envelope in her hand. The address it bore was in Nick's writing.

"When did the signore leave this for me? Has he gone out again?"

Gone out again? But the signore had not come in since dinner: of that the gondolier was positive, as he had been on duty all the evening. A boy had brought the letter—an unknown boy: he had left it without waiting. It must have been about half an hour after the signora had herself gone out with her guests.

Susy, hardly hearing him, fled on to her own room, and there, beside the very lamp which, two months before, had illuminated Ellie Vanderlyn's fatal letter, she opened Nick's.

"Don't think me hard on you, dear; but I've got to work this thing out by myself. The sooner the better—don't you agree? So I'm taking the express to Milan presently. You'll get a proper letter in a day or two. I wish I could think, now, of something to say that would show you I'm not a brute—but I can't. N. L."

There was not much of the night left in which to sleep, even had a semblance of sleep been achievable. The letter fell from Susy's hands, and she crept out onto the balcony and cowered there, her forehead pressed against the balustrade, the dawn-wind stirring in her thin laces. Through her closed eyelids and the tightly-clenched fingers pressed against them, she felt the penetration of the growing light, the relentless advance of another day—a day without purpose and without meaning—a day without Nick. At length she dropped her hands, and staring from dry lids saw a rim of fire above the roofs across the Grand

Canal. She sprang up, ran back into her room, and dragging the heavy curtains shut across the windows, stumbled over in the darkness to the lounge and fell among its pillows—face downward—groping, delving for a deeper night. . . .

She started up, stiff and aching, to see a golden wedge of sun on the floor at her feet. She had slept, then—was it possible?—it must be eight or nine o'clock already! She had slept—slept like a drunkard—with that letter on the table at her elbow! Ah, now she remembered—she had dreamed that the letter was a dream! But there, inexorably, it lay; and she picked it up, and slowly, painfully re-read it. Then she tore it into shreds, hunted for a match, and kneeling before the empty hearth, as though she were accomplishing some funeral rite, she burnt every shred of it to ashes. Nick would thank her for that some day!

After a bath and a hurried toilet she began to be aware of feeling younger and more hopeful. After all, Nick had merely said that he was going away for "a day or two." And the letter was not cruel: there were tender things in it, showing through the curt words. She smiled at herself a little stiffly in the glass, put a dash of red on her colourless lips, and rang for the maid.

"Coffee, Giovanna, please; and will you tell Mr. Strefford that I should like to see him presently."

If Nick really kept to his intention of staying away for a few days she must trump up some explanation of his absence; but her mind refused to work, and the only thing she could think of was to take Strefford into her confidence. She knew that he could be trusted in a real difficulty; his impish malice transformed itself into a resourceful ingenuity when his friends required it.

The maid stood looking at her with a puzzled gaze, and Susy somewhat sharply repeated her order. "But don't wake him on purpose," she added, foreseeing the probable effect on Strefford's temper.

"But, signora, the gentleman is already out."

"Already out?" Strefford, who could hardly be routed from his bed before luncheon-time! "Is it so late?" Susy cried, incredulous.

"After nine. And the gentleman took the eight o'clock train for England. Gervaso said he had received a telegram. He left word that he would write to the signora."

The door closed upon the maid, and Susy continued to gaze at her painted image in the glass, as if she had been trying to outstare an importunate stranger. There was no one left for her to take counsel of, then—no one but poor Fred Gillow! She made a grimace at the idea. . . . But what on earth could have summoned Strefford back to England?

Chapter XII

N ICK LANSING, in the Milan express, was roused by the same bar of sunshine lying across his knees. He yawned, looked with disgust at his stolidly sleeping neighbours, and wondered why he had decided to go to Milan, and what on earth he should do when he got there. The difficulty about trenchant decisions was that the next morning they generally left one facing a void. . . .

When the train drew into the station at Milan, he scrambled out, got some coffee, and having drunk it decided to continue his journey to Genoa. The state of being carried passively onward postponed action and dulled thought; and after twelve hours of furious mental activity that was exactly what he wanted.

He fell into a doze again, waking now and then to haggard intervals of more thinking, and then dropping off to the clank and rattle of the train. Inside his head, in his waking intervals, the same clanking and grinding of wheels and chains went on unremittingly. He had done all his lucid thinking within an hour of leaving the Palazzo Vanderlyn the night before; since then, his brain had simply continued to revolve indefatigably about the same old problem. His cup of coffee, instead of clearing his thoughts, had merely accelerated their pace.

At Genoa he wandered about in the hot streets, bought a cheap suit-case and some underclothes, and then went down to the port in search of a little hotel he remembered there. An hour later he was sitting in the coffee-room, smoking and glancing vacantly over the papers while he waited for dinner, when he became aware of being timidly but intently examined by a small round-faced gentleman with eyeglasses who sat alone at the adjoining table.

"Hullo—Buttles!" Lansing exclaimed, recognising with surprise the recalcitrant secretary who had resisted Miss Hicks's endeavour to convert him to Tiepolo.

Mr. Buttles, blushing to the roots of his scant hair, half rose and bowed ceremoniously.

Nick Lansing's first feeling was of annoyance at being disturbed in his solitary broodings; his next, of relief at having to postpone them even to converse with Mr. Buttles.

"No idea you were here: is the yacht in harbour?" he asked, remembering that the *Ibis* must be just about to spread her wings.

Mr. Buttles, at salute behind his chair, signed a mute negation: for the moment he seemed too embarrassed to speak.

"Ah—you're here as an advance guard? I remember now—I saw Miss Hicks in Venice the day before yesterday," Lansing continued, dazed at the thought that hardly forty-eight hours had passed since his encounter with Coral in the Scalzi.

Mr. Buttles, instead of speaking, had tentatively approached his table. "May I take this seat for a moment, Mr. Lansing? Thank you. No, I am not here as an advance guard—though I believe the *Ibis* is due some time to-morrow." He cleared his throat, wiped his eyeglasses on a silk handkerchief, replaced them on his nose, and went on solemnly: "Perhaps, to clear up any possible misunderstanding, I ought to say that I am no longer in the employ of Mr. Hicks."

Lansing glanced at him sympathetically. It was clear that he suffered horribly in imparting this information, though his compact face did not lend itself to any dramatic display of emotion.

"Really?" Nick smiled, and then ventured: "I hope it's not owing to conscientious objections to Tiepolo?"

Mr. Buttles's blush became a smouldering agony. "Ah, Miss Hicks mentioned to you . . . told you . . . ? No, Mr. Lansing. I am principled against the effete art of Tiepolo, and of all his contemporaries, I confess; but if Miss Hicks chooses to surrender herself momentarily to the unwholesome spell of the Italian decadence it is not for me to protest or to criticize. Her intellectual and æsthetic range so far exceeds my humble capacity that it would be ridiculous, unbecoming. . . ."

He broke off, and once more wiped a faint moisture from his eyeglasses. It was evident that he was suffering from a distress which he longed and yet dreaded to communicate. But Nick made no farther effort to bridge the gulf of his own preoccupations; and Mr. Buttles, after an expectant pause, went on:

"If you see me here to-day it is only because, after a somewhat abrupt departure, I find myself unable to take leave of our friends without a last look at the *Ibis*—the scene of so many stimulating hours. But I must beg you," he added earnestly, "should you see Miss Hicks—or any other member of the party—to make no allusion to my presence in Genoa. I wish," said Mr. Buttles with simplicity, "to preserve the strictest incognito."

Lansing glanced at him kindly. "Oh, but—isn't that a little unfriendly?"

"No other course is possible, Mr. Lansing," said the ex-secretary, "and I commit myself to your discretion. The truth is, if I am here it is not to look once more at the *Ibis*, but at Miss Hicks: once only. You will understand me, and appreciate what I am suffering."

He bowed again, and trotted away on his small, tightly-booted feet; pausing on the threshold to say: "From the first it was hopeless," before he disappeared through the glass doors.

A gleam of commiseration flashed through Nick's mind: there was something quaintly poignant in the sight of the brisk and efficient Mr. Buttles reduced to a limp image of unrequited passion. And what a painful surprise to the Hickses to be thus suddenly deprived of the secretary who possessed "the foreign languages"! Mr. Beck kept the accounts and settled with the hotel-keepers; but it was Mr. Buttles's loftier task to entertain in their own tongues the unknown geniuses who flocked about the Hickses, and Nick could imagine how disconcerting his departure must be on the eve of their Grecian cruise—which Mrs. Hicks would certainly call an Odyssey.

The next moment the vision of Coral's hopeless suitor had faded, and Nick was once more spinning around on the wheel of his own woes. The night before, when he had sent his note to Susy, from a little restaurant close to Palazzo Vanderlyn that they often patronized, he had done so with the firm intention of going away for a day or two in order to collect his wits and think over the situation. But after his letter had been entrusted to the landlord's little son, who was a particular friend of Susy's, Nick had decided to await the lad's return. The messenger had not been bidden to ask for an answer; but Nick, knowing the friendly and inquisitive Italian mind, was almost sure that the boy, in the hope of catching a glimpse of Susy, would linger about while the letter was carried up. And he pictured the maid knocking at his wife's darkened room, and Susy dashing some powder on her tear-stained face before she turned on the light—poor foolish child!

The boy had returned rather sooner than Nick expected, and he had brought no answer, but merely the statement that the signora was out: that everybody was out.

"Everybody?"

"The signora and the four gentlemen who were dining at the palace. They all went out together on foot soon after dinner. There was no one to whom I could give the note but the gondolier on the landing, for the signora had said she would be very late, and had sent the maid to bed; and the maid had, of course, gone out immediately with her *innamorato*."

"Ah—" said Nick, slipping his reward into the boy's hand, and walking out of the restaurant.

Susy had gone out—gone out with their usual band, as she did every night in these sultry summer weeks, gone out after her talk with Nick, as if nothing had happened, as if his whole world and hers had not crashed in ruins at their feet. Ah, poor Susy! After all, she had merely obeyed the instinct of self-preservation, the old hard habit of keeping up, going ahead and hiding her troubles; unless indeed the habit had already engendered indifference, and it had become as easy for her as for most of her friends to pass from drama to dancing, from sorrow to the cinema. What of soul was left, he wondered—?

His train did not start till midnight, and after leaving the restaurant Nick tramped the sultry by-ways till his tired legs brought him to a standstill under the vine-covered pergola of a gondolier's wine-shop at a landing close to the Piazzetta. There he could absorb cooling drinks until it was time to go to the station.

It was after eleven, and he was beginning to look about for a boat, when a black prow pushed up to the steps, and with much chaff and laughter a party of young people in evening dress jumped out. Nick, from under the darkness of the vine, saw that there was only one lady among them, and it did not need the lamp above the landing to reveal her identity. Susy, bareheaded and laughing, a light scarf slipping from her bare shoulders, a cigarette between her fingers, took Strefford's arm and turned in the direction of Florian's, with Gillow, the Prince and young Breckenridge in her wake. . . .

Nick had relived this rapid scene hundreds of times during his hours in the train and his aimless trampings through the streets of Genoa. In that squirrel-wheel of a world of his and Susy's you had to keep going or drop out—and Susy, it was evident, had chosen to keep going. Under the lamp-flare on the landing he had had a good look at her face, and had seen that the mask of paint and powder was carefully enough adjusted to hide any ravages the scene between them might have left. He even fancied that she had dropped a little atropine into her eyes. . . .

There was no time to spare if he meant to catch the midnight train, and no gondola in sight but that which his wife had just left. He sprang into it, and bade the gondolier carry him to the station. The cushions, as he leaned back, gave out a breath of her scent; and in the glare of electric light at the station he saw at his feet a rose which had fallen from her dress. He ground his heel into it as he got out.

There it was, then; that was the last picture he was to have of her. For he knew now that he was not going back; at least not to take up their life together. He supposed he should have to see her once, to talk things over, settle something for their future. He had been sincere in saying that he bore her no ill-will; only he could never go back into that slough again. If he did, he knew he would inevitably be drawn under, slipping downward from concession to concession. . . .

The noises of a hot summer night in the port of Genoa would have kept the most care-free from slumber; but though Nick lay awake he did not notice them, for the tumult in his brain was more deafening. Dawn brought a negative relief, and out of sheer weariness he dropped into a heavy sleep. When he woke it was nearly noon, and from his window he saw the well-known outline of the *Ibis* standing up dark against the glitter of the harbour. He had no fear of meeting her owners, who had doubtless long since landed and betaken themselves to cooler and more fashionable regions: oddly enough, the fact seemed to accentuate his loneliness, his sense of having no one on earth to turn to.

He dressed, and wandered out disconsolately to pick up a cup of coffee in some shady corner.

As he drank his coffee his thoughts gradually cleared. It became obvious to him that he had behaved like a madman or a petulant child—he preferred to think it was like a madman. If he and Susy were to separate there was no reason why it should not be done decently and quietly, as such transactions were habitually managed among people of their kind. It seemed grotesque to introduce melodrama into their little world of unruffled Sybarites, and he felt inclined, now, to smile at the incongruity of his gesture. . . . But suddenly his eyes filled with tears. The future without Susy was unbearable, inconceivable. Why, after all, should they separate? At the question, her soft face seemed close to his, and that slight lift of the upper lip that made her smile so exquisite. Well—he would go back. But not with any pretence of going to talk things over, come to an agreement, wind up their joint life like a business association. No—if he went back he would go without conditions, for good, forever. . . .

Only, what about the future? What about the not far-distant day when the wedding cheques would have been spent, and Granny's pearls sold, and nothing left except unconcealed and unconditional dependence on rich friends, the rôle of the acknowledged hangers-on? Was there no other possible solution, no new way of ordering their lives? No—there was none: he could not picture Susy out of her setting of luxury and leisure, could not picture either of them living such a life as the Nat Fulmers, for instance! He remembered the shabby untidy bungalow in New Hampshire, the slatternly servants, uneatable food and ubiquitous children. How could he ask Susy to share such a life with him? If he did, she would probably have the sense to refuse. Their alliance had been based on a moment's midsummer madness; now the score must be paid. . . .

He decided to write. If they were to part he could not trust himself to see her. He called a waiter, asked for pen and paper, and pushed aside a pile of unread newspapers on the corner of the table where his coffee had been served. As he did so, his eye lit on a *Daily Mail* of two days before. As a pretext for postponing his letter, he took up the paper and glanced down the first page. He read:

"Tragic Yachting Accident in the Solent. The Earl of Altringham and his son Viscount d'Amblay drowned in midnight collision. Both bodies recovered."

He read on. He grasped the fact that the disaster had happened the night before he had left Venice—and that, as the result of a fog in the Solent, their old friend Strefford was now Earl of Altringham, and possessor of one of the largest private fortunes in England. It was vertiginous to think of their old impecunious Streff as the hero of such an adventure. And what irony in that double turn of the wheel which, in one day, had plunged him, Nick Lansing, into nethermost misery, while it tossed the other to the stars!

With an intenser precision he saw again Susy's descent from the gondola at the *calle* steps, the sound of her laughter and of Strefford's chaff, the way she had caught his arm and clung to it, sweeping the other men on in her train. Strefford—Susy and Strefford! . . . More than once, Nick had noticed the softer inflections of his friend's voice when he spoke to Susy, the brooding look in his lazy eyes when they rested on her. In the security of his wedded bliss Nick had made light of those signs. The only real jealousy he had felt had been of Fred Gillow, because of his unlimited power to satisfy a woman's whims. Yet Nick knew that such material advantages would never again suffice for Susy. With Strefford it was different. She had delighted in his society while he was notoriously ineligible; might not she find him irresistible now?

The forgotten terms of their bridal compact came back to Nick: the absurd agreement on which he and Susy had solemnly pledged their faith. But was it so absurd, after all? It had been Susy's suggestion (not his, thank God!); and perhaps in making it she had been more serious than he imagined. Perhaps, even if their rupture had not occurred, Strefford's sudden honours might have caused her to ask for her freedom. . . .

Money, luxury, fashion, pleasure: those were the four cornerstones of her existence. He had always known it—she herself had always acknowledged it, even in their last dreadful talk together; and once he had gloried in her frankness. How could he ever have imagined that, to have her fill of these things, she would not in time stoop lower than she had yet stooped? Perhaps in giving her up to Strefford he might be saving her. At any rate, the taste of the past was now so bitter to him that he was moved to thank whatever gods there were for pushing that mortuary paragraph under his eye. . . .

"Susy, dear [he wrote], the fates seem to have taken our future in hand, and spared us the trouble of unravelling it. If I have sometimes been selfish enough to forget the conditions on which you agreed to marry me, they have come back to me during these two days of solitude. You've given me the best a man can have, and nothing else will ever be worth much to me. But since I haven't the ability to provide you with what you want, I recognize that I've no right to stand in your way. We must owe no more Venetian palaces to underhand services. I see by the newspapers that Streff can now give you as many palaces as you want. Let him have the chance—I fancy he'll jump at it, and he's the best man in sight. I wish I were in his shoes.

"I'll write again in a day or two, when I've collected my wits, and can give you an address. NICK."

He added a line on the subject of their modest funds, put the letter into an envelope, and addressed it to Mrs. Nicholas Lansing. As he did so, he reflected that it was the first time he had ever written his wife's married name.

"Well—by God, no other woman shall have it after her," he vowed, as he groped in his pocket-book for a stamp.

He stood up with a stretch of weariness—the heat was stifling!—and put the letter in his pocket.

"I'll post it myself, it's safer," he thought; "and then what in the name of goodness shall I do next, I wonder?" He jammed his hat down on his head and walked out into the sun-blaze.

As he was turning away from the square by the general Post Office, a white parasol waved from a passing cab, and Coral Hicks leaned forward with outstretched hand.

"I knew I'd find you," she triumphed. "I've been driving up and down in this broiling sun for hours, shopping and watching for you at the same time."

He stared at her blankly, too bewildered even to wonder how she knew he was in Genoa; and she continued, with the kind of shy imperiousness that always made him feel, in her presence, like a member of an orchestra under a masterful *bâton*; "Now please get right into this carriage, and don't keep me roasting here another minute." To the cab-driver she called out: "*Al porto.*"

Nick Lansing sank down beside her. As he did so he noticed a heap of bundles at her feet, and felt that he had simply added one more to the number. He supposed that she was taking her spoils to the *Ibis*, and that he would be carried up to the deck-house to be displayed with the others. Well, it would all help to pass the day—and by night he would have reached some kind of a decision about his future.

On the third day after Nick's departure the post brought to the Palazzo Vanderlyn three letters for Mrs. Lansing.

The first to arrive was a word from Strefford, scribbled in the train and posted at Turin. In it he briefly said that he had been called home by the dreadful accident of which Susy had probably read in the daily papers. He added that he would write again from England, and then—in a blotted postscript—: "I wanted uncommonly badly to see you for good-bye, but the hour was impossible. Regards to Nick. Do write me just a word to Altringham."

The other two letters, which came together in the afternoon, were both from Genoa. Susy scanned the addresses and fell upon the one in her husband's writing. Her hand trembled so much that for a moment she could not open the envelope. When she had done so, she devoured the letter in a flash, and then sat and brooded over the outspread page as it lay on her knee. It might mean so many things—she could read into it so many harrowing alternatives of indifference and despair, of irony and tenderness! Was he suffering tortures when he wrote it, or seeking only to inflict them upon her? Or did the words represent his actual feelings, no more and no less, and did he really intend her to understand that he considered it his duty to abide by the letter of their preposterous compact? He had left her in wrath and indignation, yet, as a closer scrutiny revealed, there was not a word of reproach in his brief lines. Perhaps that was why, in the last issue, they seemed so cold to her . . . She shivered and turned to the other envelope.

The large stilted characters, though half-familiar, called up no definite image. She opened the envelope and discovered a post-card of the *Ibis*, canvas spread, bounding over a rippled sea. On the back was written:

"So awfully dear of you to lend us Mr. Lansing for a little cruise. You may count on our taking the best of care of him. CORAL."

PART II

Chapter XIII

WHEN Violet Melrose had said to Susy Branch, the winter before in New York: "But why on earth don't you and Nick go to my little place at Versailles for the honey-moon? I'm off to China, and you could have it to yourselves all summer," the offer had been tempting enough to make the lovers waver.

It was such an artless ingenuous little house, so full of the demoralizing simplicity of great wealth, that it seemed to Susy just the kind of place in which to take the first steps in renunciation. But Nick had objected that Paris, at that time of year, would be swarming with acquaintances who would hunt them down at all hours; and Susy's own experience had led her to remark that there was nothing the very rich enjoyed more than taking pot-luck with the very poor. They therefore gave Strefford's villa the preference, with an inward proviso (on Susy's part) that Violet's house might very conveniently serve their purpose at another season.

These thoughts were in her mind as she drove up to Mrs. Melrose's door on a rainy afternoon late in August, her boxes piled high on the roof of the cab she had taken at the station. She had travelled straight through from Venice, stopping in Milan just long enough to pick up a reply to the telegram she had despatched to the perfect house-keeper whose permanent presence enabled Mrs. Melrose to say: "Oh, when I'm sick of everything I just rush off without warning to my little shanty at Versailles, and live there all alone on scrambled eggs."

The perfect house-keeper had replied to Susy's enquiry: "Am sure Mrs. Melrose most happy"; and Susy, without further thought, had jumped into a Versailles train, and now stood in the thin rain before the sphinx-guarded threshold of the pavilion.

The revolving year had brought around the season at which Mrs. Melrose's house might be convenient: no visitors were to be feared at Versailles at the end of August, and though Susy's reasons for seeking solitude were so remote from those she had once prefigured, they were none the less cogent. To be alone—alone! After those first exposed days when, in the persistent presence of Fred Gillow and his satellites, and in the mocking radiance of late summer on the lagoons, she had turned and turned about in her agony like a trapped animal in a cramping cage, to be alone had seemed the only respite, the one craving: to be alone somewhere in a setting as unlike as possible to the sensual splendours of Venice, under skies as unlike its azure roof. If she could have chosen she would have crawled away into a dingy inn in a rainy northern town, where she had never been and no one knew her. Failing that unobtainable luxury, here she was on the threshold of an empty house, in a deserted place, under lowering skies. She had shaken off Fred Gillow, sulkily departing for his moor (where she had half-promised to join him in September); the Prince, young Breckenridge, and the few remaining survivors of the Venetian group, had dispersed in the direction of the Engadine or Biarritz; and now she could at least collect her wits, take stock of herself, and prepare the countenance with which she was to face the next stage in her career. Thank God it was raining at Versailles!

The door opened, she heard voices in the drawing-room, and a slender languishing figure appeared on the threshold.

"Darling!" Violet Melrose cried in an embrace, drawing her into the dusky perfumed room.

"But I thought you were in China!" Susy stammered.

"In China . . . in China?" Mrs. Melrose stared with dreamy eyes, and Susy remembered her drifting disorganised life, a life more planless, more inexplicable than that of any of the other ephemeral beings blown about upon the same winds of pleasure.

"Well, Madam, I thought so myself till I got a wire from Mrs. Melrose last evening," remarked the perfect house-keeper, following with Susy's hand-bag.

Mrs. Melrose clutched her cavernous temples in her attenuated hands. "Of course, of course! I *had* meant to go to China—no, India. . . . But I've discovered a genius . . . and Genius, you know. . . ." Unable to complete her thought, she sank down upon a pillowy divan, stretched out an arm, cried: "Fulmer! Fulmer!" and, while Susy Lansing stood in the middle of the room with widening eyes, a man emerged from the more deeply cushioned and scented twilight of some inner apartment, and she saw with surprise Nat Fulmer, the good Nat Fulmer of the New Hampshire bungalow and the ubiquitous progeny, standing before her in lordly ease, his hands in his pockets, a cigarette between his lips, his feet solidly planted in the insidious depths of one of Violet Melrose's white leopard skins.

"Susy!" he shouted with open arms; and Mrs. Melrose murmured: "You didn't know, then? You hadn't heard of his masterpieces?"

In spite of herself, Susy burst into a laugh. "Is Nat your genius?"

Mrs. Melrose looked at her reproachfully.

Fulmer laughed. "No; I'm Grace's. But Mrs. Melrose has been our Providence, and. . . ."

"Providence?" his hostess interrupted. "Don't talk as if you were at a prayer-meeting! He had an exhibition in New York . . . it was the most fabulous success. He's come abroad to make studies for the decoration of my music-room in New York. Ursula Gillow has given him her garden-house at Roslyn to do. And Mrs. Bockheimer's ball-room—oh, Fulmer, where *are* the cartoons?" She sprang up, tossed about some fashion-papers heaped on a lacquer table, and sank back exhausted by the effort. "I'd got as far as Brindisi. I've travelled day and night to be here to meet him," she declared. "But, you darling," and she held out a caressing hand to Susy, "I'm forgetting to ask if you've had tea?"

An hour later, over the tea-table, Susy already felt herself mysteriously reabsorbed into what had so long been her native element. Ellie Vanderlyn had brought a breath of it to Venice; but Susy was then nourished on another air, the air of Nick's presence and personality; now that she was abandoned, left again to her own devices, she felt herself suddenly at the mercy of the influences from which she thought she had escaped.

In the queer social whirligig from which she had so lately fled, it seemed natural enough that a shake of the box should have tossed Nat Fulmer into celebrity, and sent Violet Melrose chasing back from the ends of the earth to bask in his success. Susy knew that Mrs. Melrose belonged to the class of moral parasites; for in that strange world the parts were sometimes reversed, and

the wealthy preyed upon the pauper. Wherever there was a reputation to batten on, there poor Violet appeared, a harmless vam-
pire in pearls who sought only to feed on the notoriety which all
her millions could not create for her. Any one less versed than
Susy in the shallow mysteries of her little world would have seen
in Violet Melrose a baleful enchantress, in Nat Fulmer her helpless victim. Susy knew better. Violet, poor Violet, was not even
that. The insignificant Ellie Vanderlyn, with her brief trivial
passions, her artless mixture of amorous and social interests,
was a woman with a purpose, a creature who fulfilled herself;
but Violet was only a drifting interrogation.

And what of Fulmer? Mustering with new eyes his short
sturdily-built figure, his nondescript bearded face, and the eyes
that dreamed and wandered, and then suddenly sank into you
like claws, Susy seemed to have found the key to all his years of
dogged toil, his indifference to neglect, indifference to poverty,
indifference to the needs of his growing family. . . . Yes: for the
first time she saw that he looked commonplace enough to be a
genius—*was* a genius, perhaps, even though it was Violet Melrose who affirmed it! Susy looked steadily at Fulmer, their eyes
met, and he smiled at her faintly through his beard.

"Yes, I did discover him—I *did*," Mrs. Melrose was insisting,
from the depths of the black velvet divan in which she lay sunk
like a wan Nereid in a midnight sea. "You mustn't believe a
word that Ursula Gillow tells you about having pounced on
his 'Spring Snow Storm' in a dark corner of the American Artists' exhibition—*skied*, if you please! They *skied* him less than a
year ago! And naturally Ursula never in her life looked higher
than the first line at a picture-show. And now she actually pretends . . . oh, for pity's sake don't say it doesn't matter, Fulmer!
Your saying that just encourages her, and makes people think
she *did*. When, in reality, any one who saw me at the exhibition on varnishing-day. . . . Who? Well, Eddy Breckenridge,
for instance. He was in Egypt, you say? Perhaps he was! As if
one could remember the people about one, when suddenly one
comes upon a great work of art, as St. Paul did—didn't he?—and
the scales fell from his eyes. Well . . . that's exactly what happened to me that day . . . and Ursula, everybody knows, was
down at Roslyn at the time, and didn't come up for the opening

of the exhibition at all. And Fulmer sits there and laughs, and says it doesn't matter, and that he'll paint another picture any day for me to discover!"

Susy had rung the door-bell with a hand trembling with eagerness—eagerness to be alone, to be quiet, to stare her situation in the face, and collect herself before she came out again among her kind. She had stood on the door-step, cowering among her bags, counting the instants till a step sounded and the door-knob turned, letting her in from the searching glare of the outer world. . . . And now she had sat for an hour in Violet's drawing-room, in the very house where her honey-moon might have been spent; and no one had asked her where she had come from, or why she was alone, or what was the key to the tragedy written on her shrinking face. . . .

That was the way of the world they lived in. Nobody questioned, nobody wondered any more—because nobody had time to remember. The old risk of prying curiosity, of malicious gossip, was virtually over: one was left with one's drama, one's disaster, on one's hands, because there was nobody to stop and notice the little shrouded object one was carrying. As Susy watched the two people before her, each so frankly unaffected by her presence, Violet Melrose so engrossed in her feverish pursuit of notoriety, Fulmer so plunged in the golden sea of his success, she felt like a ghost making inaudible and imperceptible appeals to the grosser senses of the living.

"If I wanted to be alone," she thought, "I'm alone enough, in all conscience." There was a deathly chill in such security. She turned to Fulmer.

"And Grace?"

He beamed back without sign of embarrassment. "Oh, she's here, naturally—we're in Paris, kids and all. In a *pension*, where we can polish up the lingo. But I hardly ever lay eyes on her, because she's as deep in music as I am in paint; it was as big a chance for her as for me, you see, and she's making the most of it, fiddling and listening to the fiddlers. Well, it's a considerable change from New Hampshire." He looked at her dreamily, as if making an intense effort to detach himself from his dream, and situate her in the fading past. "Remember the bungalow? And Nick—ah, how's Nick?" he brought out triumphantly.

"Oh, yes—darling Nick?" Mrs. Melrose chimed in; and Susy, her head erect, her cheeks aflame, declared with resonance: "Most awfully well—splendidly!"

"He's not here, though?" from Fulmer.

"No. He's off travelling—cruising."

Mrs. Melrose's attention was faintly roused. "With anybody interesting?"

"No; you wouldn't know them. People we met. . . ." She did not have to continue, for her hostess's gaze had again strayed.

"And you've come for your clothes, I suppose, darling? Don't listen to people who say that skirts are to be wider. I've discovered a new woman—a Genius—and she absolutely *swathes* you. . . . Her name's my secret; but we'll go to her together."

Susy rose from her engulfing armchair. "Do you mind if I go up to my room? I'm rather tired—coming straight through."

"Of course, dear. I think there are some people coming to dinner . . . Mrs. Match will tell you. She has such a memory . . . Fulmer, where on *earth* are those cartoons of the music-room?"

Their voices pursued Susy upstairs, as, in Mrs. Match's perpendicular wake, she mounted to the white-panelled room with its gay linen hangings and the low bed heaped with more cushions.

"If we'd come here," she thought, "everything might have been different." And she shuddered at the sumptuous memories of the Palazzo Vanderlyn, and the great painted bedroom where she had met her doom.

Mrs. Match, hoping she would find everything, and mentioning that dinner was not till nine, shut her softly in among her terrors.

"Find everything?" Susy echoed the phrase. Oh, yes, she would always find everything: every time the door shut on her now, and the sound of voices ceased, her memories would be there waiting for her, every one of them, waiting quietly, patiently, obstinately, like poor people in a doctor's office, the people who are always last to be attended to, but whom nothing will discourage or drive away, people to whom time is nothing, fatigue nothing, hunger nothing, other engagements nothing: who just wait. . . . Thank heaven, after all, that she had not found the house empty, if, whenever she returned to her room, she was to meet her memories there!

It was just a week since Nick had left her. During that week, crammed with people, questions, packing, explaining, evading, she had believed that in solitude lay her salvation. Now she understood that there was nothing she was so unprepared for, so unfitted for. When, in all her life, had she ever been alone? And how was she to bear it now, with all these ravening memories besetting her?

Dinner not till nine? What on earth was she to do till nine o'clock? She knelt before her boxes, and feverishly began to unpack. . . .

Gradually, imperceptibly, the subtle influences of her old life were stealing into her. As she pulled out her tossed and crumpled dresses she remembered Violet's emphatic warning: "Don't believe the people who tell you that skirts are going to be wider." Were hers, perhaps, too wide as it was? She looked at her limp raiment, piling itself up on bed and sofa, and understood that, according to Violet's standards, and that of all her set, those dresses, which Nick had thought so original and exquisite, were already commonplace and dowdy, fit only to be passed on to poor relations or given to one's maid. And Susy would have to go on wearing them till they fell to bits—or else. . . . Well, or else begin the old life again in some new form. . . .

She laughed aloud at the turn of her thoughts. Dresses? How little they had mattered a few short weeks ago! And now, perhaps, they would again be one of the foremost considerations in her life. How could it be otherwise, if she were to return again to her old dependence on Ellie Vanderlyn, Ursula Gillow, Violet Melrose? And beyond that, only the Bockheimers and their kind awaited her. . . .

A knock on the door—what a relief! It was Mrs. Match again, with a telegram. To whom had Susy given her new address? With a throbbing heart she tore open the envelope and read:

"Shall be in Paris Friday for twenty-four hours where can I see you write Nouveau Luxe."

Ah, yes—she remembered now: she had written to Strefford! And this was his answer: he was coming. She dropped into a chair, and tried to think. What on earth had she said in her letter? It had been mainly, of course, one of condolence; but now she remembered having added, in a precipitate postscript:

"I can't give your message to Nick, for he's gone off with the Hickses—I don't know where, or for how long. It's all right, of course: it was in our bargain."

She had not meant to put in that last phrase; but as she sealed her letter to Strefford her eye had fallen on Nick's missive, which lay beside it. Nothing in her husband's brief lines had embittered her as much as the allusion to Strefford. It seemed to imply that Nick's own plans were made, that his own future was secure, and that he could therefore freely and handsomely take thought for hers, and give her a pointer in the right direction. Sudden rage had possessed her at the thought: where she had at first read jealousy she now saw only a cold providence, and in a blur of tears she had scrawled her postscript to Strefford. She remembered that she had not even asked him to keep her secret. Well—after all, what would it matter if people should already know that Nick had left her? Their parting could not long remain a mystery, and the fact that it was known might help her to keep up a pretence of indifference.

"It was in the bargain—in the bargain," rang through her brain as she re-read Strefford's telegram. She understood that he had snatched the time for this hasty trip solely in the hope of seeing her, and her eyes filled. The more bitterly she thought of Nick the more this proof of Strefford's friendship moved her.

The clock, to her relief, reminded her that it was time to dress for dinner. She would go down presently, chat with Violet and Fulmer, and with Violet's other guests, who would probably be odd and amusing, and too much out of her world to embarrass her by awkward questions. She would sit at a softly-lit table, breathe delicate scents, eat exquisite food (trust Mrs. Match!), and be gradually drawn again under the spell of her old associations. Anything, anything but to be alone. . . .

She dressed with even more than her habitual care, reddened her lips attentively, brushed the faintest bloom of pink over her drawn cheeks, and went down—to meet Mrs. Match coming up with a tray.

"Oh, Madam, I thought you were too tired. . . . I was bringing it up to you myself—just a little morsel of chicken."

Susy, glancing past her, saw, through the open door, that the lamps were not lit in the drawing-room.

"Oh, no, I'm not tired, thank you. I thought Mrs. Melrose expected friends at dinner?"

"Friends at dinner—*to-night*?" Mrs. Match heaved a despairing sigh. Sometimes, the sigh seemed to say, her mistress put too great a strain upon her. "Why, Mrs. Melrose and Mr. Fulmer were engaged to dine in Paris. They left an hour ago. Mrs. Melrose told me she'd told you," the house-keeper wailed.

Susy kept her little fixed smile. "I must have misunderstood. In that case . . . well, yes, if it's no trouble, I believe I *will* have my tray upstairs."

Slowly she turned, and followed the house-keeper up into the dread solitude she had just left.

Chapter XIV

THE next day a lot of people turned up unannounced for luncheon. They were not of the far-fetched and the exotic, in whom Mrs. Melrose now specialized, but merely commonplace fashionable people belonging to Susy's own group, people familiar with the amusing romance of her penniless marriage, and to whom she had to explain (though none of them really listened to the explanation) that Nick was not with her just now, but had gone off cruising . . . cruising in the Ægean with friends . . . getting up material for his book (this detail had occurred to her in the night).

It was the kind of encounter she had most dreaded; but it proved, after all, easy enough to go through compared with those endless hours of turning to and fro, the night before, in the cage of her lonely room. Anything, anything, but to be alone. . . .

Gradually, from the force of habit, she found herself actually in tune with the talk of the luncheon table, interested in the references to absent friends, the light allusions to last year's loves and quarrels, scandals and absurdities. The women, in their pale summer dresses, were so graceful, indolent and sure of themselves, the men so easy and good-humoured! Perhaps, after all, Susy reflected, it was the world she was meant for, since the other, the brief Paradise of her dreams, had already shut its golden doors upon her. And then, as they sat on the terrace after luncheon, looking across at the yellow tree-tops of the park, one of the women said something—made just an allusion—that Susy would have let pass unnoticed in the old days, but that now filled her with a sudden deep disgust. . . . She stood up and wandered away, away from them all through the fading garden.

Two days later Susy and Strefford sat on the terrace of the Tuileries above the Seine. She had asked him to meet her there, with the desire to avoid the crowded halls and drawing-room of the Nouveau Luxe where, even at that supposedly "dead" season, people one knew were always drifting to and fro; and they sat on a bench in the pale sunlight, the discoloured leaves heaped at their feet, and no one to share their solitude but a lame working-man and a haggard woman who were lunching together mournfully at the other end of the majestic vista.

Strefford, in his new mourning, looked unnaturally prosperous and well-valeted; but his ugly untidy features remained as undisciplined, his smile as whimsical, as of old. He had been on cool though friendly terms with the pompous uncle and the poor sickly cousin whose joint disappearance had so abruptly transformed his future; and it was his way to understate his feelings rather than to pretend more than he felt. Nevertheless, beneath his habitual bantering tone Susy discerned a change. The disaster had shocked him profoundly; already, in his brief sojourn among his people and among the great possessions so tragically acquired, old instincts had awakened, forgotten associations had spoken in him. Susy listened to him wistfully, silenced by her imaginative perception of the distance that these things had put between them.

"It was horrible . . . seeing them both there together, laid out in that hideous Pugin chapel at Altringham . . . the poor boy especially . . . I suppose that's really what's cutting me up now," he murmured, almost apologetically.

"Oh, it's more than that—more than you know," she insisted; but he jerked back: "Now, my dear, don't be edifying, please," and fumbled for a cigarette in the pocket which was already beginning to bulge with his miscellaneous properties.

"And now about you—for that's what I came for," he continued, turning to her with one of his sudden movements. "I couldn't make head or tail of your letter."

She paused a moment to steady her voice. "Couldn't you? I suppose you'd forgotten my bargain with Nick. *He* hadn't—and he's asked me to fulfil it."

Strefford stared. "What—that nonsense about your setting each other free if either of you had the chance to make a good match?"

She signed "Yes."

"And he's actually asked you—?"

"Well: practically. He's gone off with the Hickses. Before going he wrote me that we'd better both consider ourselves free. And Coral sent me a post-card to say that she would take the best of care of him."

Strefford mused, his eyes upon his cigarette. "But what the deuce led up to all this? It can't have happened like that, out of a clear sky."

Susy flushed, hesitated, looked away. She had meant to tell Strefford the whole story; it had been one of her chief reasons for wishing to see him again, and half-unconsciously, perhaps, she had hoped, in his laxer atmosphere, to recover something of her shattered self-esteem. But now she suddenly felt the impossibility of confessing to anyone the depths to which Nick's wife had stooped. She fancied that her companion guessed the nature of her hesitation.

"Don't tell me anything you don't want to, you know, my dear."

"No; I *do* want to; only it's difficult. You see—we had so very little money. . . ."

"Yes?"

"And Nick—who was thinking of his book, and of all sorts of big things, fine things—didn't realise . . . left it all to me . . . to manage. . . ."

She stumbled over the word, remembering how Nick had always winced at it. But Strefford did not seem to notice her, and she hurried on, unfolding in short awkward sentences the avowal of their pecuniary difficulties, and of Nick's inability to understand that, to keep on with the kind of life they were leading, one had to put up with things . . . accept favours. . . .

"Borrow money, you mean?"

"Well—yes; and all the rest." No—decidedly she could not reveal to Strefford the episode of Ellie's letters. "Nick suddenly felt, I suppose, that he couldn't stand it," she continued; "and instead of asking me to try—to try to live differently, go off somewhere with him and live like work-people, in two rooms, without a servant, as I was ready to do; well, instead he wrote me that it had all been a mistake from the beginning, that we couldn't keep it up, and had better recognize the fact; and he went off on the Hickses' yacht. The last evening that you were in Venice—the day he didn't come back to dinner—he had gone off to Genoa to meet them. I suppose he intends to marry Coral."

Strefford received this in silence. "Well—it *was* your bargain, wasn't it?" he said at length.

"Yes; but—"

"Exactly: I always told you so. You weren't ready to have him go yet—that's all."

She flushed to the forehead. "Oh, Streff—is it really all?"

"A question of time? If you doubt it, I'd like to see you try, for a while, in those two rooms without a servant; and then let me hear from you. Why, my dear, it's only a question of time in a palace, with a steam-yacht lying off the door-step, and a flock of motors in the garage; look around you and see. And did you ever imagine that you and Nick, of all people, were going to escape the common doom, and survive like Mr. and Mrs. Tithonus, while all about you the eternal passions were crumbling to pieces, and your native Divorce-states piling up their revenues?"

She sat with bent head, the weight of the long years to come pressing like a leaden load on her shoulders.

"But I'm so young . . . life's so long. What does last, then?"

"Ah, you're too young to believe me, if I were to tell you; though you're intelligent enough to understand."

"What does, then?"

"Why, the hold of the things we all think we could do without. Habits—they outstand the Pyramids. Comforts, luxuries, the atmosphere of ease . . . above all, the power to get away from dulness and monotony, from constraints and uglinesses. You chose that power, instinctively, before you were even grown up; and so did Nick. And the only difference between you is that he's had the sense to see sooner than you that those *are* the things that last, the prime necessities."

"I don't believe it!"

"Of course you don't: at your age one doesn't reason one's materialism. And besides you're mortally hurt that Nick has found out sooner than you, and hasn't disguised his discovery under any hypocritical phrases."

"But surely there are people—"

"Yes—saints and geniuses and heroes: all the fanatics! To which of their categories do you suppose we soft people belong? And the heroes and the geniuses—haven't they their enormous frailties and their giant appetites? And how should we escape being the victims of our little ones?"

She sat for a while without speaking. "But, Streff, how can you say such things, when I know you care: care for me, for instance?"

"Care?" He put his hand on hers. "But, my dear, it's just the fugitiveness of mortal caring that makes it so exquisite! It's because we *know* we can't hold fast to it, or to each other, or to anything. . . ."

"Yes . . . yes . . . but hush, please! Oh, don't say it!" She stood up, the tears in her throat, and he rose also.

"Come along, then; where do we lunch?" he said with a smile, slipping his hand through her arm.

"Oh, I don't know. Nowhere. I think I'm going back to Versailles."

"Because I've disgusted you so deeply? Just my luck—when I came over to ask you to marry me!"

She laughed, but he had become suddenly grave. "Upon my soul, I did."

"Dear Streff! As if—now—"

"Oh, not now—I know. I'm aware that even with your accelerated divorce methods—"

"It's not that. I told you it was no use, Streff—I told you long ago, in Venice."

He shrugged ironically. "It's not Streff who's asking you now. Streff was not a marrying man: he was only trifling with you. The present offer comes from an elderly peer of independent means. Think it over, my dear: as many days out as you like, and five footmen kept. There's not the least hurry, of course; but I rather think Nick himself would advise it."

She flushed to the temples, remembering that Nick had; and the remembrance made Strefford's sneering philosophy seem less unbearable. Why should she not lunch with him, after all? In the first days of his mourning he had come to Paris expressly to see her, and to offer her one of the oldest names and one of the greatest fortunes in England. She thought of Ursula Gillow, Ellie Vanderlyn, Violet Melrose, of their condescending kindnesses, their last year's dresses, their Christmas cheques, and all the careless bounties that were so easy to bestow and so hard to accept. "I should rather enjoy paying them back," something in her maliciously murmured.

She did not mean to marry Strefford—she had not even got as far as contemplating the possibility of a divorce—but it was undeniable that this sudden prospect of wealth and freedom was like fresh air in her lungs. She laughed again, but now without bitterness.

"Very good, then; we'll lunch together. But it's Streff I want to lunch with to-day."

"Ah, well," her companion agreed, "I rather think that for a *tête-à-tête* he's better company."

During their repast in a little restaurant over the Seine, where she insisted on the cheapest dishes because she was lunching with "Streff," he became again his old whimsical companionable self. Once or twice she tried to turn the talk to his altered future, and the obligations and interests that lay before him; but he shrugged away from the subject, questioning her instead about the motley company at Violet Melrose's, and fitting a droll or malicious anecdote to each of the people she named.

It was not till they had finished their coffee, and she was glancing at her watch with a vague notion of taking the next train, that he asked abruptly: "But what are you going to do? You can't stay forever at Violet's."

"Oh, no!" she cried with a shiver.

"Well, then—you've got some plan, I suppose?"

"Have I?" she wondered, jerked back into grim reality from the soothing interlude of their hour together.

"You can't drift indefinitely, can you? Unless you mean to go back to the old sort of life once for all."

She reddened and her eyes filled. "I can't do that, Streff—I know I can't!"

"Then what—?"

She hesitated, and brought out with lowered head: "Nick said he would write again—in a few days. I must wait—"

"Oh, naturally. Don't do anything in a hurry." Strefford also glanced at his watch. "*Garçon, l'addition!* I'm taking the train back to-night, and I've a lot of things left to do. But look here, my dear—when you come to a decision one way or the other let me know, will you? Oh, I don't mean in the matter I've most at heart; we'll consider that closed for the present. But at least

I can be of use in other ways—hang it, you know, I can even lend you money. There's a new sensation for our jaded palates!"

"Oh, Streff . . . Streff!" she could only falter; and he pressed on gaily: "Try it, now do try it—I assure you there'll be no interest to pay, and no conditions attached. And promise to let me know when you've decided anything."

She looked into his humorously puckered eyes, answering their friendly smile with hers.

"I promise!" she said.

Chapter XV

THAT hour with Strefford had altered her whole perspective. Instead of possible dependence, an enforced return to the old life of connivances and concessions, she saw before her—whenever she chose to take them—freedom, power and dignity. Dignity! It was odd what weight that word had come to have for her. She had dimly felt its significance, felt the need of its presence in her inmost soul, even in the young thoughtless days when she had seemed to sacrifice so little to the austere divinities. And since she had been Nick Lansing's wife she had consciously acknowledged it, had suffered and agonized when she fell beneath its standard. Yes: to marry Strefford would give her that sense of self-respect which, in such a world as theirs, only wealth and position could ensure. If she had not the mental or moral training to attain independence in any other way, was she to blame for seeking it on such terms?

Of course there was always the chance that Nick would come back, would find life without her as intolerable as she was finding it without him. If that happened—ah, if that happened! Then she would cease to strain her eyes into the future, would seize upon the present moment and plunge into it to the very bottom of oblivion. Nothing on earth would matter then—money or freedom or pride, or her precious moral dignity, if only she were in Nick's arms again!

But there was Nick's icy letter, there was Coral Hicks's insolent post-card, to show how little chance there was of such a solution. Susy understood that, even before the discovery of her transaction with Ellie Vanderlyn, Nick had secretly wearied, if not of his wife, at least of the life that their marriage compelled him to lead. His passion was not strong enough—had never been strong enough—to outweigh his prejudices, scruples, principles, or whatever one chose to call them. Susy's dignity might go up like tinder in the blaze of her love; but his was made of a less combustible substance. She had felt, in their last talk together, that she had forever destroyed the inner harmony between them.

Well—there it was, and the fault was doubtless neither hers nor his, but that of the world they had grown up in, of their own moral contempt for it and physical dependence on it, of his half-talents and her half-principles, of the something in them both that was not stout enough to resist nor yet pliant enough to yield. She stared at the fact on the journey back to Versailles, and all that sleepless night in her room; and the next morning, when the housemaid came in with her breakfast tray, she felt the factitious energy that comes from having decided, however half-heartedly, on a definite course.

She had said to herself: "If there's no letter from Nick this time next week I'll write to Streff—" and the week had passed, and there was no letter.

It was now three weeks since he had left her, and she had had no word but his note from Genoa. She had concluded that, foreseeing the probability of her leaving Venice, he would write to her in care of their Paris bank. But though she had immediately notified the bank of her change of address no communication from Nick had reached her; and she smiled with a touch of bitterness at the difficulty he was doubtless finding in the composition of the promised letter. Her own scrap-basket, for the first days, had been heaped with the fragments of the letters she had begun; and she told herself that, since they both found it so hard to write, it was probably because they had nothing left to say to each other.

Meanwhile the days at Mrs. Melrose's drifted by as they had been wont to drift when, under the roofs of the rich, Susy Branch had marked time between one episode and the next of her precarious existence. Her experience of such sojourns was varied enough to make her acutely conscious of their effect on her temporary hosts; and in the present case she knew that Violet was hardly aware of her presence. But if no more than tolerated she was at least not felt to be an inconvenience; when your hostess forgot about you it proved that at least you were not in her way.

Violet, as usual, was perpetually on the wing, for her profound indolence expressed itself in a disordered activity. Nat Fulmer had returned to Paris; but Susy guessed that his benefactress was still constantly in his company, and that when Mrs. Melrose was whirled away in her noiseless motor it was generally toward the scene of some new encounter between Fulmer and the arts. On these occasions she sometimes offered to carry Susy to Paris, and they devoted several long and hectic mornings to the dress-makers, where Susy felt herself gradually succumbing to the familiar spell of heaped-up finery. It seemed impossible, as furs and laces and brocades were tossed aside, brought back, and at last carelessly selected from, that anything but the whim of the moment need count in deciding whether one should take all or none, or that any woman could be worth looking at who did not possess the means to make her choice regardless of cost.

Once alone, and in the street again, the evil fumes would evaporate, and daylight re-enter Susy's soul; yet she felt that the old poison was slowly insinuating itself into her system. To dispel it she decided one day to look up Grace Fulmer. She was curious to know how the happy-go-lucky companion of Fulmer's evil days was bearing the weight of his prosperity, and she vaguely felt that it would be refreshing to see some one who had never been afraid of poverty.

The airless *pension* sitting-room, where she waited while a reluctant maid-servant screamed about the house for Mrs. Fulmer, did not have the hoped-for effect. It was one thing for Grace to put up with such quarters when she shared them with Fulmer; but to live there while he basked in the lingering radiance of Versailles, or rolled from *château* to picture gallery in Mrs. Melrose's motor, showed a courage that Susy felt unable to emulate.

"My dear! I knew you'd look me up," Grace's joyous voice rang down the stairway; and in another moment she was clasping Susy to her tumbled person.

"Nat couldn't remember if he'd given you our address, though he promised me he would, the last time he was here." She held Susy at arms' length, beaming upon her with blinking short-sighted eyes: the same old dishevelled Grace, so careless of her neglected beauty and her squandered youth, so amused and absent-minded and improvident, that the boisterous air of the New Hampshire bungalow seemed to enter with her into the little air-tight *salon*.

While she poured out the tale of Nat's sudden celebrity, and its unexpected consequences, Susy marvelled and dreamed. Was the secret of his triumph perhaps due to those long hard unrewarded years, the steadfast scorn of popularity, the indifference to every kind of material ease in which his wife had so gaily abetted him? Had it been bought at the cost of her own freshness and her own talent, of the children's "advantages," of everything except the closeness of the tie between husband and wife? Well—it was worth the price, no doubt; but what if, now that honours and prosperity had come, the tie were snapped, and Grace were left alone among the ruins?

There was nothing in her tone or words to suggest such a possibility. Susy noticed that her ill-assorted raiment was costlier in quality and more professional in cut than the home-made garments which had draped her growing bulk at the bungalow: it was clear that she was trying to dress up to Nat's new situation. But, above all, she was rejoicing in it, filling her hungry lungs with the strong air of his success. It had evidently not occurred to her as yet that those who consent to share the bread of adversity may want the whole cake of prosperity for themselves.

"My dear, it's too wonderful! He's told me to take as many concert and opera tickets as I like; he lets me take all the children with me. The big concerts don't begin till later; but of course the Opera is always going. And there are little things—there's music in Paris at all seasons. And later it's just possible we may get to Munich for a week—oh, Susy!" Her hands clasped, her eyes brimming, she drank the new wine of life almost sacramentally.

"Do you remember, Susy, when you and Nick came to stay at the bungalow? Nat said you'd be horrified by our primitiveness—but I knew better! And I was right, wasn't I? Seeing us so happy made you and Nick decide to follow our example, didn't it?" She glowed with the remembrance. "And now, what are your plans? Is Nick's book nearly done? I suppose you'll have to live very economically till he finds a publisher. And the baby, darling—when is *that* to be? If you're coming home soon I could let you have a lot of the children's little old things."

"You're always so dear, Grace. But we haven't any special plans as yet—not even for a baby. And I wish you'd tell me all of yours instead."

Mrs. Fulmer asked nothing better: Susy perceived that, so far, the greater part of her European experience had consisted in talking about what it was to be. "Well, you see, Nat is so taken up all day with sight-seeing and galleries and meeting important people that he hasn't had time to go about with us; and as so few theatres are open, and there's so little music, I've taken the opportunity to catch up with my mending. Junie helps me with it now—she's our eldest, you remember? She's grown into a big girl since you saw her. And later, perhaps, we're to travel. And the most wonderful thing of all—next to Nat's recognition, I mean—is not having to contrive and skimp, and give up something every single minute. Just think—Nat has even made special arrangements here in the *pension*, so that the children all have second helpings to everything. And when I go up to bed I can think of my music, instead of lying awake calculating and wondering how I can make things come out at the end of the month. Oh, Susy, that's simply *heaven!*"

Susy's heart contracted. She had come to her friend to be taught again the lesson of indifference to material things, and instead she was hearing from Grace Fulmer's lips the long-repressed avowal of their tyranny. After all, that battle with poverty on the New Hampshire hillside had not been the easy smiling business that Grace and Nat had made it appear. And yet . . . and yet. . . .

Susy stood up abruptly, and straightened the expensive hat which hung irresponsibly over Grace's left ear.

"What's wrong with it? Junie helped me choose it, and she generally knows," Mrs. Fulmer wailed with helpless hands.

"It's the way you wear it, dearest—and the bow is rather top-heavy. Let me have it a minute, please." Susy lifted the hat from her friend's head and began to manipulate its trimming. "This is the way Maria Guy or Suzanne would do it. . . . And now go on about Nat. . . ."

She listened musingly while Grace poured forth the tale of her husband's triumph, of the notices in the papers, the demand for his work, the fine ladies' battles over their priority in discovering him, and the multiplied orders that had resulted from their rivalry.

"Of course they're simply furious with each other—Mrs. Melrose and Mrs. Gillow especially—because each one pretends to have been the first to notice his 'Spring Snow-Storm,' and in reality it wasn't either of them, but only poor Bill Haslett, an art-critic we've known for years, who chanced on the picture, and rushed off to tell a dealer who was looking for a new painter to push." Grace suddenly raised her soft myopic eyes to Susy's face. "But, do you know, the funny thing is that I believe Nat is beginning to forget this, and to believe that it *was* Mrs. Melrose who stopped short in front of his picture on the opening day, and screamed out: 'This is genius!' It seems funny he should care so much, when I've always known he had genius—and *he* has known it too. But they're all so kind to him; and Mrs. Melrose especially. And I suppose it makes a thing sound new to hear it said in a new voice."

Susy looked at her meditatively. "And how should you feel if Nat liked too much to hear Mrs. Melrose say it? Too much, I mean, to care any longer what you felt or thought?"

Her friend's worn face flushed quickly, and then paled: Susy almost repented the question. But Mrs. Fulmer met it with a tranquil dignity. "You haven't been married long enough, dear, to understand . . . how people like Nat and me feel about such things . . . or how trifling they seem, in the balance . . . the balance of one's memories."

Susy stood up again, and flung her arms about her friend. "Oh, Grace," she laughed with wet eyes, "how can you be as wise as that, and yet not have sense enough to buy a decent hat?" She gave Mrs. Fulmer a quick embrace and hurried away. She had learned her lesson after all; but it was not exactly the one she had come to seek.

The week she had allowed herself had passed, and still there was no word from Nick. She allowed herself yet another day, and that too went by without a letter. She then decided on a step from which her pride had hitherto recoiled; she would call at the bank and ask for Nick's address. She called, embarrassed and hesitating; and was told, after enquiries in the post-office department, that Mr. Nicholas Lansing had given no address since that of the Palazzo Vanderlyn, three months previously. She went back to Versailles that afternoon with the definite intention of writing to Strefford unless the next morning's post brought a letter.

The next morning brought nothing from Nick, but a scribbled message from Mrs. Melrose: would Susy, as soon as possible, come into her room for a word? Susy jumped up, hurried through her bath, and knocked at her hostess's door. In the immense low bed that faced the rich umbrage of the park Mrs. Melrose lay smoking cigarettes and glancing over her letters. She looked up with her vague smile, and said dreamily: "Susy darling, have you any particular plans—for the next few months, I mean?"

Susy coloured: she knew the intonation of old, and fancied she understood what it implied.

"Plans, dearest? Any number . . . I'm tearing myself away the day after to-morrow . . . to the Gillows' moor, very probably," she hastened to announce.

Instead of the relief she had expected to read on Mrs. Melrose's dramatic countenance she discovered there the blankest disappointment.

"Oh, really? That's too bad. Is it absolutely settled—?"

"As far as I'm concerned," said Susy crisply.

The other sighed. "I'm too sorry. You see, dear, I'd meant to ask you to stay on here quietly and look after the Fulmer children. Fulmer and I are going to Spain next week—I want to be with him when he makes his studies, receives his first impressions; such a marvellous experience, to be there when he and Velázquez meet!" She broke off, lost in prospective ecstasy. "And, you see, as Grace Fulmer insists on coming with us—"

"Ah, I see."

"Well, there are the five children—such a problem," sighed the benefactress. "If you *were* at a loose end, you know, dear, while Nick's away with his friends, I could really make it worth your while. . . ."

"So awfully good of you, Violet; only I'm not, as it happens."

Oh the relief of being able to say that, gaily, firmly and even truthfully! Take charge of the Fulmer children, indeed! Susy remembered how Nick and she had fled from them that autumn afternoon in New Hampshire. The offer gave her a salutary glimpse of the way in which, as the years passed, and she lost her freshness and novelty, she would more and more be used as a convenience, a stop-gap, writer of notes, runner of errands, nursery governess or companion. She called to mind several elderly women of her acquaintance, pensioners of her own group, who still wore its livery, struck its attitudes and

chattered its jargon, but had long since been ruthlessly relegated
to these slave-ant offices. Never in the world would she join their
numbers.

Mrs. Melrose's face fell, and she looked at Susy with the plaintive bewilderment of the wielder of millions to whom everything that cannot be bought is imperceptible.

"But I can't see why you can't change your plans," she murmured with a soft persistency.

"Ah, well, you know"—Susy paused on a slow inward smile—
"they're not mine only, as it happens."

Mrs. Melrose's brow clouded. The unforeseen complication
of Mrs. Fulmer's presence on the journey had evidently tried
her nerves, and this new obstacle to her arrangements shook her
faith in the divine order of things.

"Your plans are not yours only? But surely you won't let
Ursula Gillow dictate to you? . . . There's my jade pendant; the
one you said you liked the other day. . . . The Fulmers won't
go with me, you understand, unless they're satisfied about the
children; the whole plan will fall through. Susy darling, you
were always too unselfish; I hate to see you sacrificed to Ursula."

Susy's smile lingered. Time was when she might have been
glad to add the jade pendant to the collection already enriched
by Ellie Vanderlyn's sapphires; more recently, she would have
resented the offer as an insult to her newly-found principles. But
already the mere fact that she might henceforth, if she chose, be
utterly out of reach of such bribes, enabled her to look down on
them with tolerance. Oh, the blessed moral freedom that wealth
conferred! She recalled Mrs. Fulmer's uncontrollable cry: "The
most wonderful thing of all is not having to contrive and skimp,
and give up something every single minute!" Yes; it was only on
such terms that one could call one's soul one's own. The sense of
it gave Susy the grace to answer amicably: "If I could possibly
help you out, Violet, I shouldn't want a present to persuade
me. And, as you say, there's no reason why I should sacrifice
myself to Ursula—or to anybody else. Only, as it happens"—she
paused and took the plunge—"I'm going to England because
I've promised to see a friend."

That night she wrote to Strefford.

Chapter XVI

S TRETCHED out under an awning on the deck of the *Ibis* Nick Lansing looked up for a moment at the vanishing cliffs of Malta and then plunged again into his book.

He had had nearly three weeks of drug-taking on the *Ibis*. The drugs he had absorbed were of two kinds: visions of fleeing landscapes, looming up from the blue sea to vanish into it again, and visions of study absorbed from the volumes piled up day and night at his elbow. For the first time in months he was in reach of a real library, just the kind of scholarly yet miscellaneous library that his restless and impatient spirit craved. He was aware that the books he read, like the fugitive scenes on which he gazed, were merely a form of anæsthetic: he swallowed them with the careless greed of the sufferer who seeks only to still pain and deaden memory. But they were beginning to produce in him a moral languor that was not disagreeable, that, indeed, compared with the fierce pain of the first days, was almost pleasurable. It was exactly the kind of drug that he needed.

There is probably no point on which the average man has more definite views than on the uselessness of writing a letter that is hard to write. In the line he had sent to Susy from Genoa Nick had told her that she would hear from him again in a few days; but when the few days had passed, and he began to consider setting himself to the task, he found fifty reasons for postponing it.

Had there been any practical questions to write about it would have been different; he could not have borne for twenty-four hours the idea that she was in uncertainty as to money. But that had all been settled long ago. From the first she had had the administering of their modest fortune. On their marriage Nick's own meagre income, paid in, none too regularly, by the agent who had managed for years the dwindling family properties, had been transferred to her: it was the only wedding present he could make. And the wedding cheques had of course all been deposited in her name. There were therefore no "business" reasons for communicating with her; and when it came to reasons of another order the mere thought of them benumbed him.

For the first few days he reproached himself for his inertia; then he began to seek reasons for justifying it. After all, for both their sakes a waiting policy might be the wisest he could pursue. He had left Susy because he could not tolerate the conditions on which he had discovered their life together to be based; and he had told her so. What more was there to say?

Nothing was changed in their respective situations; if they came together it could be only to resume the same life; and that, as the days went by, seemed to him more and more impossible. He had not yet reached the point of facing a definite separation; but whenever his thoughts travelled back over their past life he recoiled from any attempt to return to it. As long as this state of mind continued there seemed nothing to add to the letter he had already written, except indeed the statement that he was cruising with the Hickses. And he saw no pressing reason for communicating that.

To the Hickses he had given no hint of his situation. When Coral Hicks, a fortnight earlier, had picked him up in the broiling streets of Genoa, and carried him off to the *Ibis*, he had thought only of a cool dinner and perhaps a moonlight sail. Then, in reply to their friendly urging, he had confessed that he had not been well—had indeed gone off hurriedly for a few days' change of air—and that left him without defence against the immediate proposal that he should take his change of air on the *Ibis*. They were just off to Corsica and Sardinia, and from there to Sicily: he could rejoin the railway at Naples, and be back at Venice in ten days.

Ten days of respite—the temptation was irresistible. And he really liked the kind uncomplicated Hickses. A wholesome honesty and simplicity breathed through all their opulence, as if the rich trappings of their present life still exhaled the fragrance of their native prairies. The mere fact of being with such people was like a purifying bath. When the yacht touched at Naples he agreed—since they were so awfully kind—to go on to Sicily. And when the chief steward, going ashore at Naples for the last time before they got up steam, said: "Any letters for the post, sir?" he answered, as he had answered at each previous halt: "No, thank you: none."

Now they were heading for Rhodes and Crete—Crete, where he had never been, where he had so often longed to go. In spite of the lateness of the season the weather was still miraculously fine: the short waves danced ahead under a sky without a cloud, and the strong bows of the *Ibis* hardly swayed as she flew forward over the flying crests.

Only his hosts and their daughter were on the yacht—of course with Eldorada Tooker and Mr. Beck in attendance. An eminent archæologist, who was to have joined them at Naples, had telegraphed an excuse at the last moment; and Nick noticed that, while Mrs. Hicks was perpetually apologizing for the great man's absence, Coral merely smiled and said nothing.

As a matter of fact, Mr. and Mrs. Hicks were never as pleasant as when one had them to one's self. In company, Mr. Hicks ran the risk of appearing over-hospitable, and Mrs. Hicks confused dates and names in the desire to embrace all culture in her conversation. But alone with Nick, their old travelling-companion, they shone out in their native simplicity, and Mr. Hicks talked soundly of investments, and Mrs. Hicks recalled her early married days in Apex City, when, on being brought home to her new house in Aeschylus Avenue, her first thought had been: "How on earth shall I get all those windows washed?"

The loss of Mr. Buttles had been as serious to them as Nick had supposed: Mr. Beck could never hope to replace him. Apart from his mysterious gift of languages, and his almost superhuman faculty for knowing how to address letters to eminent people, and in what terms to conclude them, he had a smattering of archæology and general culture on which Mrs. Hicks had learned to depend—her own memory being, alas, so inadequate to the range of her interests.

Her daughter might perhaps have helped her; but it was not Miss Hicks's way to mother her parents. She was exceedingly kind to them, but left them, as it were, to bring themselves up as best they could, while she pursued her own course of self-development. A sombre zeal for knowledge filled the mind of this strange girl: she appeared interested only in fresh opportunities of adding to her store of facts. They were illuminated by little imagination and less poetry; but, carefully catalogued and neatly sorted in her large cool brain, they were always as accessible as the volumes in an up-to-date public library.

To Nick there was something reposeful in this lucid intellectual curiosity. He wanted above all things to get away from sentiment, from seduction, from the moods and impulses and flashing contradictions that were Susy. Susy was not a great reader: her store of facts was small, and she had grown up among people who dreaded ideas as much as if they had been a contagious disease. But, in the early days especially, when Nick had put a book in her hand, or read a poem to her, her swift intelligence had instantly shed a new light on the subject, and, penetrating to its depths, had extracted from them whatever belonged to her. What a pity that this exquisite insight, this intuitive discrimination, should for the most part have been spent upon reading the thoughts of vulgar people, and extracting a profit from them—should have been wasted, since her childhood, on all the hideous intricacies of "managing"!

And visible beauty—how she cared for that too! He had not guessed it, or rather he had not been sure of it, till the day when, on their way through Paris, he had taken her to the Louvre, and they had stood before the little Crucifixion of Mantegna. He had not been looking at the picture, or watching to see what impression it produced on Susy. His own momentary mood was for Correggio and Fragonard, the laughter of the Music Lesson and the bold pagan joys of the Antiope; and then he had missed her from his side, and when he came to where she stood, forgetting him, forgetting everything, had seen the glare of that tragic sky in her face, her trembling lip, the tears on her lashes. That was Susy. . . .

Closing his book he stole a glance at Coral Hicks's profile, thrown back against the cushions of the deck-chair at his side. There was something harsh and bracing in her blunt primitive build, in the projection of the black eyebrows that nearly met over her thick straight nose, and the faint barely visible black down on her upper lip. Some miracle of will-power, combined with all the artifices that wealth can buy, had turned the fat sallow girl he remembered into this commanding young woman, almost handsome—at times indisputably handsome— in her big authoritative way. Watching the arrogant lines of her profile against the blue sea, he remembered, with a thrill that was sweet to his vanity, how twice—under the dome of the Scalzi and in the streets of Genoa—he had seen those same lines soften at his approach, turn womanly, pleading and almost humble. That was Coral. . . .

Suddenly she said, without turning toward him: "You've had no letters since you've been on board."

He looked at her, surprised. "No—thank the Lord!" he laughed.

"And you haven't written one either," she continued in her hard statistical tone.

"No," he again agreed, with the same laugh.

"That means that you really *are* free—"

"Free?"

He saw the cheek nearest him redden. "Really off on a holiday, I mean; not tied down."

After a pause he rejoined: "No, I'm not particularly tied down."

"And your book?"

"Oh, my book—" He stopped and considered. He had thrust *The Pageant of Alexander* into his hand-bag on the night of his flight from Venice; but since then he had never looked at it. Too many memories and illusions were pressed between its pages; and he knew just at what page he had felt Ellie Vanderlyn bending over him from behind, caught a whiff of her scent, and heard her breathless "I *had* to thank you!"

"My book's hung up," he said impatiently, annoyed with Miss Hicks's lack of tact. *There* was a girl who never put out feelers. . . .

"Yes; I thought it was," she went on quietly, and he gave her a startled glance. What the devil else did she think, he wondered? He had never supposed her capable of getting far enough out of her own thick carapace of self-sufficiency to penetrate into any one else's feelings.

"The truth is," he continued, embarrassed, "I suppose I dug away at it rather too continuously; that's probably why I felt the need of a change. You see I'm only a beginner."

She still continued her relentless questioning. "But later—you'll go on with it, of course?"

"Oh, I don't know." He paused, glanced down the glittering deck, and then out across the glittering water. "I've been dreaming dreams, you see. I rather think I shall have to drop the book altogether, and try to look out for a job that will pay. To indulge in my kind of literature one must first have an assured income."

He was instantly annoyed with himself for having spoken. Hitherto in his relations with the Hickses he had carefully avoided the least allusion that might make him feel the heavy hand of their beneficence. But the idle procrastinating weeks had weakened him and he had yielded to the need of putting into words his vague intentions. To do so would perhaps help to make them more definite.

To his relief Miss Hicks made no immediate reply; and when she spoke it was in a softer voice, and with an unwonted hesitation.

"It seems a shame that with gifts like yours you shouldn't find some kind of employment that would leave you leisure enough to do your real work. . . ."

He shrugged ironically. "Yes—there are a goodish number of us hunting for that particular kind of employment."

Her tone became more business-like. "I know it's hard to find—almost impossible. But would you take it, I wonder, if it were offered to you—?"

She turned her head slightly, and their eyes met. For an instant blank terror loomed upon him; but before he had time to face it she continued, in the same untroubled voice: "Mr. Buttles's place, I mean. My parents must absolutely have some one they can count on. You know what an easy place it is. . . . I think you would find the salary satisfactory."

Nick drew a deep breath of relief. For a moment her eyes had looked as they had in the Scalzi—and he liked the girl too much not to shrink from re-awakening that look. But Mr. Buttles's place: why not?

"Poor Buttles!" he murmured, to gain time.

"Oh," she said, "you won't find the same reasons as he did for throwing up the job. He was the martyr of his artistic convictions."

He glanced at her sideways, wondering. After all she did not know of his meeting with Mr. Buttles in Genoa, nor of the latter's confidences; perhaps she did not even know of Mr. Buttles's hopeless passion. At any rate her face remained calm.

"Why not consider it—at least just for a few months? Till after our expedition to Mesopotamia?" she pressed on, a little breathlessly.

"You're awfully kind: but I don't know—"

She stood up with one of her abrupt movements. "You needn't, all at once. Take time—think it over. Father wanted me to ask you," she appended.

He felt the inadequacy of his response. "It tempts me awfully, of course. But I must wait, at any rate—wait for letters. The fact is I shall have to wire from Rhodes to have them sent. I had chucked everything, even letters, for a few weeks."

"Ah, you *are* tired," she murmured, giving him a last downward glance as she turned away.

From Rhodes Nick Lansing telegraphed to his Paris bank to send his letters to Candia; but when the *Ibis* reached Candia, and the mail was brought on board, the thick envelope handed to him contained no letter from Susy.

Why should it, since he had not yet written to her?

He had not written, no: but in sending his address to the bank he knew he had given her the opportunity of reaching him if she wished to. And she had made no sign.

Late that afternoon, when they returned to the yacht from their first expedition, a packet of newspapers lay on the deck-house table. Nick picked up one of the London journals, and his eye ran absently down the list of social events.

He read:

"Among the visitors expected next week at Ruan Castle (let for the season to Mr. Frederick J. Gillow of New York) are Prince Altineri of Rome, the Earl of Altringham and Mrs. Nicholas Lansing, who arrived in London last week from Paris."

Nick threw down the paper. It was just a month since he had left the Palazzo Vanderlyn and flung himself into the night express for Milan. A whole month—and Susy had not written. Only a month—and Susy and Strefford were already together!

Chapter XVII

S USY had decided to wait for Strefford in London.

The new Lord Altringham was with his family in the north, and though she found a telegram on arriving, saying that he would join her in town the following week, she had still an interval of several days to fill.

London was a desert; the rain fell without ceasing, and alone in the shabby family hotel which, even out of season, was the best she could afford, she sat at last face to face with herself.

From the moment when Violet Melrose had failed to carry out her plan for the Fulmer children her interest in Susy had visibly waned. Often before, in the old days, Susy Branch had felt the same abrupt change of temperature in the manner of the hostess of the moment; and often—how often!—had yielded, and performed the required service, rather than risk the consequences of estrangement. To that, at least, thank heaven, she need never stoop again.

But as she hurriedly packed her trunks at Versailles, scraped together an adequate tip for Mrs. Match, and bade good-bye to Violet (grown suddenly fond and demonstrative as she saw her visitor safely headed for the station)—as Susy went through the old familiar mummery of the enforced leave-taking, there rose in her so deep a disgust for the life of makeshifts and accommodations, that if at that moment Nick had reappeared and held out his arms to her, she was not sure she would have had the courage to return to them.

In her London solitude the thirst for independence grew fiercer. Independence with ease, of course. Oh, her hateful useless love of beauty . . . the curse it had always been to her, the blessing it might have been if only she had had the material means to gratify and to express it! And instead, it only gave her a morbid loathing of that hideous hotel bedroom drowned in yellow rain-light, of the smell of soot and cabbage through the window, the blistered wall-paper, the dusty wax bouquets under glass globes, and the electric lighting so contrived that as you turned on the feeble globe hanging from the middle of the ceiling the feebler one beside the bed went out!

What a sham world she and Nick had lived in during their few months together! What right had either of them to those exquisite settings of the life of leisure: the long white house hidden in camellias and cypresses above the lake, or the great rooms on the Giudecca with the shimmer of the canal always playing over their frescoed ceilings? Yet she had come to imagine that these places really belonged to them, that they would always go on living, fondly and irreproachably, in the frame of other people's wealth. . . . That, again, was the curse of her love of beauty, the way she always took to it as if it belonged to her!

Well, the awakening was bound to come, and it was perhaps better that it should have come so soon. At any rate there was no use in letting her thoughts wander back to that shattered fool's paradise of theirs. Only, as she sat there and reckoned up the days till Strefford arrived, what else in the world was there to think of?

Her future and his?

But she knew that future by heart already! She had not spent her life among the rich and fashionable without having learned every detail of the trappings of a rich and fashionable marriage. She had calculated long ago just how many dinner-dresses, how many tea-gowns and how much lacy *lingerie* would go to make up the outfit of the future Countess of Altringham. She had even decided to which dress-maker she would go for her chinchilla cloak—for she meant to have one, and down to her feet, and softer and more voluminous and more extravagantly sumptuous than Violet's or Ursula's . . . not to speak of silver foxes and sables . . . nor yet of the Altringham jewels.

She knew all this by heart; had always known it. It all belonged to the make-up of the life of elegance: there was nothing new about it. What had been new to her was just that short interval with Nick—a life unreal indeed in its setting, but so real in its essentials: the one reality she had ever known. As she looked back on it she saw how much it had given her besides the golden flush of her happiness, the sudden flowering of sensuous joy in heart and body. Yes—there had been the flowering too, in pain like birth-pangs, of something graver, stronger, fuller of future power, something she had hardly heeded in her first light rapture, but that always came back and possessed her stilled soul when the rapture sank: the deep disquieting sense of something that Nick and love had taught her, but that reached out even beyond love and beyond Nick.

Her nerves were racked by the ceaseless swish-swish of the rain on the dirty panes and the smell of cabbage and coal that came in under the door when she shut the window. This nauseating foretaste of the luncheon she must presently go down to was more than she could bear. It brought with it a vision of the dank coffee-room below, the sooty Smyrna rug, the rain on the sky-light, the listless waitresses handing about food that tasted as if it had been rained on too. There was really no reason why she should let such material miseries add to her depression. . . .

She sprang up, put on her hat and jacket, and calling for a taxi drove to the London branch of the Nouveau Luxe hotel. It was just one o'clock and she was sure to pick up a luncheon, for though London was empty that great establishment was not. It never was. Along those sultry velvet-carpeted halls, in that great flowered and scented dining-room, there was always a come-and-go of rich aimless people, the busy people who, having nothing to do, perpetually pursue their inexorable task from one end of the earth to the other.

Oh, the monotony of those faces—the faces one always knew, whether one knew the people they belonged to or not! A fresh disgust seized her at the sight of them: she wavered, and then turned and fled. But on the threshold a still more familiar figure met her: that of a lady in exaggerated pearls and sables, descending from an exaggerated motor, like the motors in magazine advertisements, the huge arks in which jewelled beauties and slender youths pause to gaze at snow-peaks from an Alpine summit.

It was Ursula Gillow—dear old Ursula, on her way to Scotland—and she and Susy fell on each other's necks. It appeared that Ursula, detained till the next evening by a dress-maker's delay, was also out of a job and killing time, and the two were soon smiling at each other over the exquisite preliminaries of a luncheon which the head-waiter had authoritatively asked Mrs. Gillow to "leave to him, as usual."

Ursula was in a good humour. It did not often happen; but when it did her benevolence knew no bounds.

Like Mrs. Melrose, like all her tribe in fact, she was too much absorbed in her own affairs to give more than a passing thought to any one else's; but she was delighted at the meeting with Susy, as her wandering kind always were when they ran across fellow-wanderers, unless the meeting happened to interfere with choicer pleasures. Not to be alone was the urgent thing; and Ursula, who had been forty-eight hours alone in London, at once exacted from her friend a promise that they should spend the rest of the day together. But once the bargain struck her mind turned again to her own affairs, and she poured out her confidences to Susy over a succession of dishes that manifested the head-waiter's understanding of the case.

Ursula's confidences were always the same, though they were usually about a different person. She demolished and rebuilt her sentimental life with the same frequency and impetuosity as that with which she changed her dress-makers, did over her drawing-rooms, ordered new motors, altered the mounting of her jewels, and generally renewed the setting of her life. Susy knew in advance what the tale would be; but to listen to it over perfect coffee, an amber-scented cigarette at her lips, was pleas-anter than consuming cold mutton alone in a mouldy coffee-room. The contrast was so soothing that she even began to take a languid interest in her friend's narrative.

After luncheon they got into the motor together and began a systematic round of the West End shops: furriers, jewellers and dealers in old furniture. Nothing could be more unlike Violet Melrose's long hesitating sessions before the things she thought she wanted till the moment came to decide. Ursula pounced on silver foxes and old lacquer as promptly and decisively as on the objects of her surplus sentimentality: she knew at once what she wanted, and valued it more after it was hers.

"And now—I wonder if you couldn't help me choose a grand piano?" she suggested, as the last antiquarian bowed them out.

"A piano?"

"Yes: for Ruan. I'm sending one down for Grace Fulmer. She's coming to stay . . . did I tell you? I want people to hear her. I want her to get engagements in London. My dear, she's a Genius."

"A Genius—Grace?" Susy gasped. "I thought it was Nat. . . ."

"Nat—Nat Fulmer?" Ursula laughed derisively. "Ah, of course—you've been staying with that silly Violet! The poor thing is off her head about Nat—it's really pitiful. Of course he has talent: *I* saw that long before Violet had ever heard of him. Why, on the opening day of the American Artists' exhibition, last winter, I stopped short before his 'Spring Snow-Storm' (which nobody else had noticed till that moment), and said to the Prince, who was with me: 'The man has *talent*.' But genius— why, it's his wife who has genius! Have you never heard Grace play the violin? Poor Violet, as usual, is off on the wrong tack. I've given Fulmer my garden-house to do—no doubt Violet told you—because I wanted to help him. But Grace is *my* discovery, and I'm determined to make her known, and to have every one understand that *she* is the genius of the two. I've told her she simply must come to Ruan, and bring the best accompanyist she can find. You know poor Nerone is dreadfully bored by sport, though of course he goes out with the guns. And if one didn't have a little art in the evening. . . . Oh, Susy, do you mean to tell me you don't know how to choose a piano? I thought you were so fond of music!"

"I am fond of it; but without knowing anything about it—in the way we're all of us fond of the worth-while things in our stupid set," she added to herself—since it was obviously useless to impart such reflections to Ursula.

"But are you sure Grace is coming?" she questioned aloud.

"Quite sure. Why shouldn't she? I wired to her yesterday. I'm giving her a thousand dollars and all her expenses."

It was not till they were having tea in a Piccadilly tea-room that Mrs. Gillow began to manifest some interest in her companion's plans. The thought of losing Susy became suddenly intolerable to her. The Prince, who did not see why he should be expected to linger in London out of season, was already at Ruan, and Ursula could not face the evening and the whole of the next day by herself.

"But what are you doing in town, darling? I don't remember if I've asked you," she said, resting her firm elbows on the tea-table while she took a light from Susy's cigarette.

Susy hesitated. She had foreseen that the time must soon come when she should have to give some account of herself; and why should she not begin by telling Ursula?

But telling her what?

Her silence appeared to strike Mrs. Gillow as a reproach, and she continued with compunction: "And Nick? Nick's with you? How is he? I thought you and he still were in Venice with Ellie Vanderlyn."

"We were, for a few weeks." She steadied her voice. "It was delightful. But now we're both on our own again—for a while."

Mrs. Gillow scrutinized her more searchingly. "Oh, you're alone here, then; quite alone?"

"Yes: Nick's cruising with some friends in the Mediterranean."

Ursula's shallow gaze deepened singularly. "But, Susy darling, then if you're alone—and out of a job, just for the moment?"

Susy smiled. "Well, I'm not sure."

"Oh, but if you *are*, darling, and you would come to Ruan! I know Fred asked you—didn't he? And he told me that both you and Nick had refused. He was awfully huffed at your not coming; but I suppose that was because Nick had other plans. We couldn't have him *now*, because there's no room for another gun; but since he's not here, and you're free, why you know, dearest, don't you, how we'd love to have you? Fred would be too glad—too outrageously glad—but you don't much mind Fred's love-making, do you? And you'd be such a help to me— if *that's* any argument! With that big house full of men, and people flocking over every night to dine, and Fred caring only for sport, and Nerone simply loathing it and ridiculing it, and not a minute to myself to try to keep him in a good humour. . . . Oh, Susy darling, don't say no, but let me telephone at once for a place in the train to-morrow night!"

Susy leaned back, letting the ash lengthen on her cigarette. How familiar, how hatefully familiar, was that old appeal! Ursula felt the pressing need of someone to flirt with Fred for a few weeks . . . and here was the very person she needed. Susy shivered at the thought. She had never really meant to go to Ruan. She had simply used the moor as a pretext when Violet Melrose had gently put her out of doors. Rather than do what Ursula asked she would borrow a few hundred pounds of Strefford, as he had suggested, and then look about for some temporary occupation until—

Until she became Lady Altringham? Well, perhaps. At any rate, she was not going back to slave for Ursula.

She shook her head with a faint smile. "I'm so sorry, Ursula: of course I want awfully to oblige you—"

Mrs. Gillow's gaze grew reproachful. "I should have supposed you would," she murmured. Susy, meeting her eyes, looked into them down a long vista of favours bestowed, and perceived that Ursula was not the woman to forget on which side the obligation lay between them.

Susy hesitated: she remembered the weeks of ecstasy she had owed to the Gillows' wedding cheque, and it hurt her to appear ungrateful.

"If I could, Ursula . . . but really . . . I'm not free at the moment." She paused, and then took an abrupt decision. "The fact is, I'm waiting here to see Strefford."

"Strefford? Lord Altringham?" Ursula stared. "Ah, yes—I remember. You and he used to be great friends, didn't you?" Her roving attention deepened. . . . But if Susy were waiting to see Lord Altringham—one of the richest men in England? Suddenly Ursula opened her gold-meshed bag and snatched a miniature diary from it.

"But wait a moment—yes, it *is* next week! I knew it was next week he's coming to Ruan! But, you darling, that makes everything all right. You'll send him a wire at once, and come with me to-morrow, and meet him there instead of in this nasty sloppy desert. . . . Oh, Susy, if you knew how hard life is for me in Scotland between the Prince and Fred you couldn't possibly say no!"

Susy still wavered; but, after all, if Strefford were really bound for Ruan, why not see him there, agreeably and at leisure, instead of spending a dreary day with him in roaming the wet London streets, or screaming at him through the rattle of a restaurant orchestra? She knew he would not be likely to postpone his visit to Ruan in order to linger in London with her: such concessions had never been his way, and were less than ever likely to be, now that he could do so thoroughly and completely as he pleased.

For the first time she fully understood how different his destiny had become. Now of course all his days and hours were mapped out in advance: invitations assailed him, opportunities pressed on him, he had only to choose. . . . And the women! She had never before thought of the women. All the girls in England would be wanting to marry him, not to mention her own enterprising compatriots. And there were the married women, who were even more to be feared. Streff might, for the time, escape marriage; though she could guess the power of persuasion, family pressure, all the converging traditional influences he had so often ridiculed, yet, as she knew, had never completely thrown off. . . . Yes, those quiet invisible women at Altringham—his uncle's widow, his mother, the spinster sisters—it was not impossible that, with tact and patience—and the stupidest women could be tactful and patient on such occasions—they might eventually persuade him that it was his duty, they might put just the right young loveliness in his way. . . . But meanwhile, now, at once, there were the married women. Ah, *they* wouldn't wait, *they* were doubtless laying their traps already! Susy shivered at the thought. She knew too much about the way the trick was done, had followed, too often, all the sinuosities of such approaches. Not that they were very sinuous nowadays: more often there was just a swoop and a pounce when the time came; but she knew all the arts and the wiles that led up to it. She knew them, oh, how she knew them—though with Streff, thank heaven, she had never been called upon to exercise them! His love was there for the asking: would she not be a fool to refuse it?

Perhaps; though on that point her mind still wavered. But at any rate she saw that, decidedly, it would be better to yield to Ursula's pressure; better to meet him at Ruan, in a congenial setting, where she would have time to get her bearings, observe what dangers threatened him, and make up her mind whether, after all, it was to be her mission to save him from the other women. . . .

"Well, if you like, then, Ursula. . . ."

"Oh, you angel, you! I'm so glad! We'll go to the nearest post office, and send off the wire ourselves."

As they got into the motor Mrs. Gillow seized Susy's arm with a pleading pressure. "And you *will* let Fred make love to you a little, won't you, darling?"

Chapter XVIII

"BUT I can't think," said Ellie Vanderlyn earnestly, "why you don't announce your engagement before waiting for your divorce. People are beginning to do it, I assure you—it's so much safer!"

Mrs. Vanderlyn, on the way back from St. Moritz to England, had paused in Paris to renew the depleted wardrobe which, only two months earlier, had filled so many trunks to bursting. Other ladies, flocking there from all points of the globe for the same purpose, disputed with her the Louis XVI suites of the Nouveau Luxe, the pink-candled tables in the restaurant, the hours for trying-on at the dress-makers'; and just because they were so many, and all feverishly fighting to get the same things at the same time, they were all excited, happy and at ease. It was the most momentous period of the year: the height of the "dress-makers' season."

Mrs. Vanderlyn had run across Susy Lansing at one of the Rue de la Paix openings, where rows of ladies wan with heat and emotion sat for hours in rapt attention while spectral apparitions in incredible raiment tottered endlessly past them on aching feet.

Distracted from the regal splendours of a chinchilla cloak by the sense that another lady was also examining it, Mrs. Vanderlyn turned in surprise at sight of Susy, whose head was critically bent above the fur.

"Susy! I'd no idea you were here! I saw in the papers that you were with the Gillows." The customary embraces followed; then Mrs. Vanderlyn, her eyes pursuing the matchless cloak as it disappeared down a vista of receding *mannequins*, interrogated sharply: "Are you shopping for Ursula? If you mean to order that cloak for *her* I'd rather know."

Susy smiled, and paused a moment before answering. During the pause she took in all the exquisite details of Ellie Vanderlyn's perpetually youthful person, from the plumed crown of her head to the perfect arch of her patent-leather shoes. At last she said quietly: "No—to-day I'm shopping for myself."

"Yourself? Yourself?" Mrs. Vanderlyn echoed with a stare of incredulity.

"Yes; just for a change," Susy serenely acknowledged.

"But the cloak—I meant the chinchilla cloak . . . the one with the ermine lining. . . ."

"Yes; it *is* awfully good, isn't it? But I mean to look elsewhere before I decide."

Ah, how often she had heard her friends use that phrase; and how amusing it was, now, to see Ellie's amazement as she heard it tossed off in her own tone of contemptuous satiety! Susy was becoming more and more dependent on such diversions; without them her days, crowded as they were, would nevertheless have dragged by heavily. But it still amused her to go to the big dress-makers', watch the *mannequins* sweep by, and be seen by her friends superciliously examining all the most expensive dresses in the procession. She knew the rumour was abroad that she and Nick were to be divorced, and that Lord Altringham was "devoted" to her. She neither confirmed nor denied the report: she just let herself be luxuriously carried forward on its easy tide. But although it was now three months since Nick had left the Palazzo Vanderlyn she had not yet written to him—nor he to her.

Meanwhile, in spite of all that she packed into them, the days passed more and more slowly, and the excitements she had counted on no longer excited her. Strefford was hers: she knew that he would marry her as soon as she was free. They had been together at Ruan for ten days, and after that she had motored south with him, stopping on the way to see Altringham, from which, at the moment, his mourning relatives were absent.

At Altringham they had parted; and after one or two more visits in England she had come back to Paris, where he was now about to join her. After her few hours at Altringham she had understood that he would wait for her as long as was necessary: the fear of the "other women" had ceased to trouble her. But, perhaps for that very reason, the future seemed less exciting than she had expected. Sometimes she thought it was the sight of that great house which had overwhelmed her: it was too vast, too venerable, too like a huge monument built of ancient territorial traditions and obligations. Perhaps it had been lived

in for too long by too many serious-minded and conscientious
women: somehow she could not picture it invaded by bridge
and debts and adultery. And yet that was what would have to be,
of course . . . she could hardly picture either Strefford or herself
continuing there the life of heavy county responsibilities, dull
parties, laborious duties, weekly church-going, and presiding
over local committees. . . . What a pity they couldn't sell it and
have a little house on the Thames!

Nevertheless she was not sorry to let it be known that Altringham was hers when she chose to take it. At times she wondered
whether Nick knew . . . whether rumours had reached him. If
they had, he had only his own letter to thank for it. He had told
her what course to pursue; and she was pursuing it.

For a moment the meeting with Ellie Vanderlyn had been a
shock to her; she had hoped never to see Ellie again. But now
that they were actually face to face Susy perceived how dulled
her sensibilities were. In a few moments she had grown used
to Ellie, as she was growing used to everybody and to everything in the old life she had returned to. What was the use of
making such a fuss about things? She and Mrs. Vanderlyn left
the dress-maker's together, and after an absorbing session at a
new milliner's were now taking tea in Ellie's drawing-room at
the Nouveau Luxe.

Ellie, with her spoiled child's persistency, had come back to
the question of the chinchilla cloak. It was the only one she had
seen that she fancied in the very least, and as she hadn't a decent
fur garment left to her name she was naturally in somewhat of a
hurry . . . but, of course, if Susy *had* been choosing that model
for a friend. . . .

Susy, leaning back against her cushions, examined through
half-closed lids Mrs. Vanderlyn's small delicately-restored countenance, which wore the same expression of childish eagerness
as when she discoursed of the young Davenant of the moment.
Once again Susy remarked that, in Ellie's agitated existence,
every interest appeared to be on exactly the same plane.

"The poor shivering dear," she answered laughing, "of course
it shall have its nice warm winter cloak, and I'll choose another
one instead."

"Oh, you darling, you! If you would! Of course, whoever you
were ordering it for need never know. . . ."

"Ah, you can't comfort yourself with that, I'm afraid. I've already told you that I was ordering it for myself." Susy paused to savour to the full Ellie's look of blank bewilderment; then her amusement was checked by an indefinable change in her friend's expression.

"Oh, dearest—seriously? I didn't know there was someone. . . ."

Susy flushed to the forehead. A horror of humiliation overwhelmed her. That Ellie should dare to think that of her—that anyone should dare to!

"Someone buying chinchilla cloaks for me? Thanks!" she flared out. "I suppose I ought to be glad that the idea didn't immediately occur to you. At least there was a decent interval of doubt. . . ." She stood up, laughing again, and began to wander about the room. In the mirror above the mantel she caught sight of her flushed angry face, and of Mrs. Vanderlyn's disconcerted stare. She turned toward her friend.

"I suppose everybody else will think it if you do; so perhaps I'd better explain." She paused, and drew a quick breath. "Nick and I mean to part—have parted, in fact. He's decided that the whole thing was a mistake. He will probably marry again soon—and so shall I."

She flung the avowal out breathlessly, in her nervous dread of letting Ellie Vanderlyn think for an instant longer that any other explanation was conceivable. She had not meant to be so explicit; but once the words were spoken she was not altogether sorry. Of course people would soon begin to wonder why she was again straying about the world alone; and since it was by Nick's choice, why should she not say so? Remembering the burning anguish of those last hours in Venice she asked herself what possible consideration she owed to the man who had so humbled her.

Ellie Vanderlyn glanced at her in astonishment. "You? You and Nick—are going to part?" A light appeared to dawn on her. "Ah—then that's why he sent me back my pin, I suppose?"

"Your pin?" Susy wondered, not at once remembering.

"The poor little scarf-pin I gave him before I left Venice. He sent it back almost at once, with the oddest note—just: 'I haven't earned it, really.' I couldn't think why he didn't care for the pin. But, now I suppose it was because you and he had

quarrelled; though really, even so, I can't see why he should bear
me a grudge. . . ."

Susy's quick blood surged up. Nick had sent back the pin—
the fatal pin! And she, Susy, had kept the bracelet—locked it up
out of sight, shrunk away from the little packet whenever her
hand touched it in packing or unpacking—but never thought of
returning it, no, not once! Which of the two, she wondered, had
been right? Was it not an indirect slight to her that Nick should
fling back the gift to poor uncomprehending Ellie? Or was it
not rather another proof of his finer moral sensitiveness? . . .
And how could one tell, in their bewildering world?

"It was not because we've quarrelled; we haven't quarrelled,"
she said slowly, moved by the sudden desire to defend her
privacy and Nick's, to screen from every eye their last bitter
hour together. "We've simply decided that our experiment was
impossible—for two paupers."

"Ah, well—of course we all felt that at the time. And now
somebody else wants to marry you? And it's your *trousseau* you
were choosing that cloak for?" Ellie cried in incredulous rapture; then she flung her arms about Susy's shrinking shoulders.
"You lucky lucky girl! You clever clever darling! But who on
earth can he be?"

And it was then that Susy, for the first time, had pronounced
the name of Lord Altringham.

"Streff—Streff? Our dear old Streff? You mean to say he
wants to *marry* you?" As the news took possession of her mind
Ellie became dithyrambic. "But, my dearest, what a miracle of
luck! Of course I always knew he was awfully gone on you:
Fred Davenant used to say so, I remember . . . and even Nelson,
who's so stupid about such things, noticed it in Venice. . . . But
then it was so different. No one could possibly have thought
of marrying him then; whereas now of course every woman
is trying for him. Oh, Susy, whatever you do, don't miss your
chance! You can't conceive of the wicked plotting and intriguing
there will be to get him—on all sides, and even where one least
suspects it. You don't know what horrors women will do—and
even girls!" A shudder ran through her at the thought, and she
caught Susy's wrists in vehement fingers. "But I can't think, my
dear, why you don't announce your engagement at once. People
are beginning to do it, I assure you—it's so much safer!"

Susy looked at her, wondering. Not a word of sympathy for the ruin of her brief bliss, not even a gleam of curiosity as to its cause! No doubt Ellie Vanderlyn, like all Susy's other friends, had long since "discounted" the brevity of her dream, and perhaps planned a sequel to it before she herself had seen the glory fading. She and Nick had spent the greater part of their few weeks together under Ellie Vanderlyn's roof; but to Ellie, obviously, the fact meant no more than her own escapade, at the same moment, with young Davenant's supplanter—the "bounder" whom Strefford had never named. Her one thought for her friend was that Susy should at last secure her prize—her incredible prize. And therein at any rate Ellie showed the kind of cold disinterestedness that raised her above the smiling perfidy of the majority of her kind. At least her advice was sincere; and perhaps it was wise. Why should Susy not let every one know that she meant to marry Strefford as soon as the "formalities" were fulfilled?

She did not immediately answer Mrs. Vanderlyn's question; and the latter, repeating it, added impatiently: "I don't understand you; if Nick agrees—"

"Oh, he agrees," said Susy.

"Then what more do you want? Oh, Susy, if you'd only follow my example!"

"Your example?" Susy paused, weighed the word, was struck by something embarrassed, arch yet half-apologetic in her friend's expression. "Your example?" she repeated. "Why, Ellie, what on earth do you mean? Not that you're going to part from poor Nelson?"

Mrs. Vanderlyn met her reproachful gaze with a crystalline glance. "I don't want to, heaven knows—poor dear Nelson! I assure you I simply *hate* it. He's always such an angel to Clarissa . . . and then we're used to each other. But what in the world am I to do? Algie's so rich, so appallingly rich, that I have to be perpetually on the watch to keep other women away from him—and it's too exhausting. . . ."

"Algie?"

Mrs. Vanderlyn's lovely eyebrows rose. "Algie: Algie Bockheimer. Didn't you know? I think he said you've dined with his parents. Nobody else in the world is as rich as the Bockheimers; and Algie's their only child. Yes, it was with him . . . with him

I was so dreadfully happy last spring . . . and now I'm in mortal terror of losing him. And I do assure you there's no other way of keeping them, when they're as hideously rich as that!"

Susy rose to her feet. A little shudder ran over her. She remembered, now, having seen Algie Bockheimer at one of his parents' first entertainments, in their newly-inaugurated marble halls in Fifth Avenue. She recalled his too faultless clothes and his small glossy furtive countenance. She looked at Ellie Vanderlyn with sudden scorn.

"I think you're abominable," she exclaimed.

The other's perfect little face collapsed. "A-bo-mi-nable? A-bo-mi-nable? Susy!"

"Yes . . . with Nelson . . . and Clarissa . . . and your past together . . . and all the money you can possibly want . . . and *that* man! Abominable."

Ellie stood up trembling: she was not used to scenes, and they disarranged her thoughts as much as her complexion.

"You're very cruel, Susy—so cruel and dreadful that I hardly know how to answer you," she stammered. "But you simply don't know what you're talking about. *As if anybody ever had all the money they wanted!*" She wiped her dark-rimmed eyes with a cautious handkerchief, glanced at herself in the mirror, and added magnanimously: "But I shall try to forget what you've said."

Chapter XIX

JUST such a revolt as she had felt as a girl, such a disgusted recoil from the standards and ideals of everybody about her as had flung her into her mad marriage with Nick, now flamed in Susy Lansing's bosom.

How could she ever go back into that world again? How echo its appraisals of life and bow down to its judgments? Alas, it was only by marrying according to its standards that she could escape such subjection. Perhaps the same thought had actuated Nick: perhaps he had understood sooner than she that to attain moral freedom they must both be above material cares. Perhaps . . .

Her talk with Ellie Vanderlyn had left Susy so oppressed and humiliated that she almost shrank from her meeting with Altringham the next day. She knew that he was coming to Paris for his final answer; he would wait as long as was necessary if only she would consent to take immediate steps for a divorce. She was staying at a modest hotel in the Faubourg St. Germain, and had once more refused his suggestion that they should lunch at the Nouveau Luxe, or at some fashionable restaurant of the Boulevards. As before, she insisted on going to an out-of-the-way place near the Luxembourg, where the prices were moderate enough for her own purse.

"I can't understand," Strefford objected, as they turned from her hotel door toward this obscure retreat, "why you insist on giving me bad food, and depriving me of the satisfaction of being seen with you. Why must we be so dreadfully clandestine? Don't people know by this time that we're to be married?"

Susy winced a little: she wondered if the word would always sound so unnatural on his lips.

"No," she said, with a laugh, "they simply think, for the present, that you're giving me pearls and chinchilla cloaks."

He wrinkled his brows good-humouredly. "Well, so I would, with joy—at this particular minute. Don't you think perhaps you'd better take advantage of it? I don't wish to insist—but I foresee that I'm much too rich not to become stingy."

She gave a slight shrug. "At present there's nothing I loathe more than pearls and chinchilla . . . or anything else in the world that's expensive and enviable. . . ."

Suddenly she broke off, colouring with the consciousness that she had said exactly the kind of thing that all the women who were trying for him (except the very cleverest) would be sure to say; and that he would certainly suspect her of attempting the conventional comedy of disinterestedness, than which nothing was less likely to deceive or to flatter him.

His twinkling eyes played curiously over her face, and she went on, meeting them with a smile: "But don't imagine, all the same, that if I should . . . decide . . . it would be altogether for your *beaux yeux*. . . ."

He laughed, she thought, rather drily. "No," he said, "I don't suppose that's ever likely to happen to me again."

"Oh, Streff—" she faltered with compunction. It was odd— once upon a time she had known exactly what to say to the man of the moment, whoever he was, and whatever kind of talk he required; she had even, in the difficult days before her marriage, reeled off glibly enough the sort of lime-light sentimentality that plunged poor Fred Gillow into such speechless beatitude. But since then she had spoken the language of real love, looked with its eyes, embraced with its hands; and now the other trumpery art had failed her, and she was conscious of bungling and groping like a beginner under Strefford's ironic scrutiny.

They had reached their obscure destination and he opened the door and glanced in.

"It's jammed—not a table. And stifling! Where shall we go? Perhaps they could give us a room to ourselves—" he suggested.

She assented, and they were led up a cork-screw staircase to a squat-ceilinged closet lit by the arched top of a high window, the lower panes of which served for the floor below. Strefford opened the window, and Susy, throwing her cloak on the divan, leaned on the balcony while he ordered luncheon.

On the whole she was glad they were to be alone. Just because she felt so sure of Strefford it seemed ungenerous to keep him longer in suspense. The moment had come when they must have a decisive talk, and in the crowded rooms below it would have been impossible.

Strefford, when the waiter had brought the first course and left them to themselves, made no effort to revert to personal matters. He turned instead to the topic always most congenial to him: the humours and ironies of the human comedy, as presented by his own particular group. His malicious commentary on life had always amused Susy because of the shrewd flashes of philosophy he shed on the social antics they had so often watched together. He was in fact the one person she knew (excepting Nick) who was in the show and yet outside of it; and she was surprised, as the talk proceeded, to find herself so little interested in his scraps of gossip, and so little amused by his comments on them.

With an inward shrug of discouragement she said to herself that probably nothing would ever really amuse her again; then, as she listened, she began to understand that her disappointment arose from the fact that Strefford, in reality, could not live without these people whom he saw through and satirized, and that the rather commonplace scandals he narrated interested him as much as his own racy considerations on them; and she was filled with terror at the thought that the inmost core of the richly-decorated life of the Countess of Altringham would be just as poor and low-ceilinged a place as the little room in which he and she now sat, elbow to elbow yet so unapproachably apart.

If Strefford could not live without these people, neither could she and Nick; but for reasons how different! And if his opportunities had been theirs, what a world they would have created for themselves! Such imaginings were vain, and she shrank back from them into the present. After all, as Lady Altringham she would have the power to create that world which she and Nick had dreamed . . . only she must create it alone. Well, that was probably the law of things. All human happiness was thus conditioned and circumscribed, and hers, no doubt, must always be of the lonely kind, since material things did not suffice for it, even though it depended on them as Grace Fulmer's, for instance, never had. Yet even Grace Fulmer had succumbed to Ursula's offer, and had arrived at Ruan the day before Susy left, instead of going to Spain with her husband and Violet Melrose. But then Grace was making the sacrifice for her children, and somehow one had the feeling that in giving up her liberty she was not surrendering a tittle of herself. All the difference was there. . . .

"How I do bore you!" Susy heard Strefford exclaim. She became aware that she had not been listening: stray echoes of names of places and people—Violet Melrose, Ursula, Prince Altineri, others of their group and persuasion—had vainly knocked at her barricaded brain; what had he been telling her about them? She turned to him and their eyes met; his were full of a melancholy irony.

"Susy, old girl, what's wrong?"

She pulled herself together. "I was thinking, Streff, just now—when I said I hated the very sound of pearls and chinchilla—how impossible it was that you should believe me; in fact, what a blunder I'd made in saying it."

He smiled. "Because it was what so many other women might be likely to say—so awfully unoriginal, in fact?"

She laughed for sheer joy at his insight. "It's going to be easier than I imagined," she thought. Aloud she rejoined: "Oh, Streff—how you're always going to find me out! Where on earth shall I ever hide from you?"

"Where?" He echoed her laugh, laying his hand lightly on hers. "In my heart, I'm afraid."

In spite of the laugh his accent shook her: something about it took all the mockery from his retort, checked on her lips the: "What? A valentine!" and made her suddenly feel that, if he were afraid, so was she. Yet she was touched also, and wondered half exultingly if any other woman had ever caught that particular deep inflexion of his shrill voice. She had never liked him as much as at that moment; and she said to herself, with an odd sense of detachment, as if she had been rather breathlessly observing the vacillations of someone whom she longed to persuade but dared not: "Now—*now*, if he speaks, I shall say yes!"

He did not speak; but abruptly, and as startlingly to her as if she had just dropped from a sphere whose inhabitants had other methods of expressing their sympathy, he slipped his arm around her and bent his keen ugly melting face to hers. . . .

It was the lightest touch—in an instant she was free again. But something within her gasped and resisted long after his arm and his lips were gone, and he was proceeding, with a too-studied ease, to light a cigarette and sweeten his coffee.

He had kissed her. . . . Well, naturally: why not? It was not the first time she had been kissed. It was true that one didn't habitually associate Streff with such demonstrations; but she had not that excuse for surprise, for even in Venice she had begun to notice that he looked at her differently, and avoided her hand when he used to seek it.

No—she ought not to have been surprised; nor ought a kiss to have been so disturbing. Such incidents had punctuated the career of Susy Branch: there had been, in particular, in far-off discarded times, Fred Gillow's large but artless embraces. Well—nothing of that kind had seemed of any more account than the flick of a leaf in a woodland walk. It had all been merely epidermal, ephemeral, part of the trivial accepted "business" of the social comedy. But this kiss of Strefford's was what Nick's had been, under the New Hampshire pines, on the day that had decided their fate. It was a kiss with a future in it: like a ring slipped upon her soul. And now, in the dreadful pause that followed—while Strefford fidgeted with his cigarette-case and rattled the spoon in his cup—Susy remembered what she had seen through the circle of Nick's kiss: that blue illimitable distance which was at once the landscape at their feet and the future in their souls. . . .

Perhaps that was what Strefford's sharply narrowed eyes were seeing now, that same illimitable distance that she had lost forever—perhaps he was saying to himself, as she had said to herself when her lips left Nick's: "Each time we kiss we shall see it all again. . . ." Whereas all she herself had felt was the gasping recoil from Strefford's touch, and an intenser vision of the sordid room in which he and she sat, and of their two selves, more distant from each other than if their embrace had been a sudden thrusting apart. . . .

The moment prolonged itself, and they sat numb. How long had it lasted? How long ago was it that she had thought: "It's going to be easier than I imagined"? Suddenly she felt Strefford's queer smile upon her, and saw in his eyes a look, not of reproach or disappointment, but of deep and anxious comprehension. Instead of being angry or hurt, he had seen, he had understood, he was sorry for her!

Impulsively she slipped her hand into his, and they sat silent for another moment. Then he stood up and took her cloak from the divan. "Shall we go now? I've got cards for the private view of the Reynolds exhibition at the Petit Palais. There are some portraits from Altringham. It might amuse you."

In the taxi she had time, through their light rattle of talk, to readjust herself and drop back into her usual feeling of friendly ease with him. He had been extraordinarily considerate, for anyone who always so undisguisedly sought his own satisfaction above all things; and if his considerateness were just an indirect way of seeking that satisfaction now, well, that proved how much he cared for her, how necessary to his happiness she had become. The sense of power was undeniably pleasant; pleasanter still was the feeling that someone really needed her, that the happiness of the man at her side depended on her yes or no. She abandoned herself to the feeling, forgetting the abysmal interval of his caress, or at least saying to herself that in time she would forget it, that really there was nothing to make a fuss about in being kissed by anyone she liked as much as Streff. . . .

She had guessed at once why he was taking her to see the Reynoldses. Fashionable and artistic Paris had recently discovered English eighteenth century art. The principal collections of England had yielded up their best examples of the great portrait painter's work, and the private view at the Petit Palais was to be the social event of the afternoon. Everybody—Strefford's everybody and Susy's—was sure to be there; and these, as she knew, were the occasions that revived Strefford's intermittent interest in art. He really liked picture shows as much as the races, if one could be sure of seeing as many people there. With Nick how different it would have been! Nick hated openings and varnishing days, and worldly æsthetics in general; he would have waited till the tide of fashion had ebbed, and slipped off with Susy to see the pictures some morning when they were sure to have the place to themselves.

But Susy divined that there was another reason for Strefford's suggestion. She had never yet shown herself with him publicly, among their own group of people: now he had determined that she should do so, and she knew why. She had humbled his pride; he had understood, and forgiven her. But she still continued to treat him as she had always treated the Strefford of old, Charlie Strefford, dear old negligible impecunious Streff; and he wanted to show her, ever so casually and adroitly, that the man who had asked her to marry him was no longer Strefford, but Lord Altringham.

At the very threshold, his Ambassador's greeting marked the difference: it was followed, wherever they turned, by ejaculations of welcome from the rulers of the world they moved in. Everybody rich enough or titled enough, or clever enough or stupid enough, to have forced a way into the social citadel, was there, waving and flag-flying from the battlements; and to all of them Lord Altringham had become a marked figure. During their slow progress through the dense mass of important people who made the approach to the pictures so well worth fighting for, he never left Susy's side, or failed to make her feel herself a part of his triumphal advance. She heard her name mentioned: "Lansing—a Mrs. Lansing—an American . . . Susy Lansing? Yes, of course. . . . You remember her? At Newport? At St. Moritz? Exactly. . . . Divorced already? They say so . . . Susy darling! I'd no idea you were here . . . and Lord Altringham! You've forgotten me, I know, Lord Altringham. . . . Yes, last year, in Cairo . . . or at Newport . . . or in Scotland . . . Susy, dearest, when will you bring Lord Altringham to dine? Any night that you and he are free I'll arrange to be. . . ."

"You and he": they were "you and he" already!

"Ah, there's one of them—of my great-grandmothers," Strefford explained, giving a last push that drew him and Susy to the front rank, before a tall isolated portrait which, by sheer majesty of presentment, sat in its great carved golden frame as on a throne above the other pictures.

Susy read on the scroll beneath it: "The Honble Diana Lefanu, fifteenth Countess of Altringham"—and heard Strefford say: "Do you remember? It hangs where you noticed the empty space above the mantel-piece, in the Vandyke room. They say Reynolds stipulated that it should be put with the Vandykes."

She had never before heard him speak of his possessions, whether ancestral or merely material, in just that full and satisfied tone of voice: the rich man's voice. She saw that he was already feeling the influence of his surroundings, that he was glad the portrait of a Countess of Altringham should occupy the central place in the principal room of the exhibition, that the crowd about it should be denser there than before any of the other pictures, and that he should be standing there with Susy, letting her feel, and letting all the people about them guess, that the day she chose she could wear the same name as his pictured ancestress.

On the way back to her hotel, Strefford made no farther allusion to their future; they chatted like old comrades in their respective corners of the taxi. But as the carriage stopped at her door he said: "I must go back to England the day after to-morrow, worse luck! Why not dine with me to-night at the Nouveau Luxe? I've got to have the Ambassador and Lady Ascot, with their youngest girl and my old Dunes aunt, the Dowager Duchess, who's over here hiding from her creditors; but I'll try to get two or three amusing men to leaven the lump. We might go on to a *boîte* afterward, if you're bored. Unless the dancing amuses you more. . . ."

She understood that he had decided to hasten his departure rather than linger on in uncertainty; she also remembered having heard the Ascots' youngest daughter, Lady Joan Senechal, spoken of as one of the prettiest girls of the season; and she recalled the almost exaggerated warmth of the Ambassador's greeting at the private view.

"Of course I'll come, Streff dear!" she cried, with an effort at gaiety that sounded successful to her own strained ears, and reflected itself in the sudden lighting up of his face.

She waved a good-bye from the step, saying to herself, as she looked after him: "He'll drive me home to-night, and I shall say 'yes'; and then he'll kiss me again. But the next time it won't be nearly as disagreeable."

She turned into the hotel, glanced automatically at the empty pigeon-hole for letters under her key-hook, and mounted the stairs following the same train of images. "Yes, I shall say 'yes' to-night," she repeated firmly, her hand on the door of her room. "That is, unless, they've brought up a letter. . . ." She never re-entered the hotel without imagining that the letter she had not found below had already been brought up.

Opening the door, she turned on the light and sprang to the table on which her correspondence sometimes awaited her.

There was no letter; but the morning papers, still unread, lay at hand, and glancing listlessly down the column which chronicles the doings of society, she read:

"After an extended cruise in the Ægean and the Black Sea on their steam-yacht *Ibis*, Mr. and Mrs. Mortimer Hicks and their daughter are established at the Nouveau Luxe in Rome. They have lately had the honour of entertaining at dinner the Reigning Prince of Teutoburger-Waldhain and his mother the Princess Dowager, with their suite. Among those invited to meet their Serene Highnesses were the French and Spanish Ambassadors, the Duchesse de Vichy, Prince and Princess Bagnidilucca, Lady Penelope Pantiles—" Susy's eye flew impatiently on over the long list of titles—"and Mr. Nicholas Lansing of New York, who has been cruising with Mr. and Mrs. Hicks on the *Ibis* for the last few months."

Chapter XX

THE Mortimer Hickses were in Rome; not, as they would in former times have been, in one of the antiquated hostelries of the Piazza di Spagna or the Porta del Popolo, where of old they had so gaily defied fever and nourished themselves on local colour; but spread out, with all the ostentation of philistine millionaires, under the *piano nobile* ceilings of one of the high-perched "Palaces," where, as Mrs. Hicks shamelessly declared, they could "rely on the plumbing," and "have the privilege of over-looking the Queen Mother's Gardens."

It was that speech, uttered with beaming aplomb at a dinner-table surrounded by the cosmopolitan nobility of the Eternal City, that had suddenly revealed to Lansing the profound change in the Hicks point of view.

As he looked back over the four months since he had so unexpectedly joined the *Ibis* at Genoa, he saw that the change, at first insidious and unperceived, dated from the ill-fated day when the Hickses had run across a Reigning Prince on his travels.

Hitherto they had been proof against such perils: both Mr. and Mrs. Hicks had often declared that the aristocracy of the intellect was the only one which attracted them. But in this case the Prince possessed an intellect, in addition to his few square miles of territory, and to one of the most beautiful Field Marshal's uniforms that had ever encased a royal warrior. The Prince was not a warrior, however; he was stooping, pacific and spectacled, and his possession of the uniform had been revealed to Mrs. Hicks only by the gift of a full-length photograph in a Bond Street frame, with *Anastasius* written slantingly across its legs. The Prince—and herein lay the Hickses' undoing—the Prince was an archæologist: an earnest anxious enquiring and scrupulous archæologist. Delicate health (so his suite hinted) banished him for a part of each year from his cold and foggy principality; and in the company of his mother, the active and enthusiastic Dowager Princess, he wandered from one Mediter-ranean shore to another, now assisting at the exhumation of Ptolemaic mummies, now at the excavation of Delphic temples or of North African basilicas. The beginning of winter usually brought the Prince and his mother to Rome or Nice, unless indeed they were summoned by family duties to Berlin, Vienna or Madrid; for an extended connection with the principal royal houses of Europe compelled them, as the Princess Mother said, to be always burying or marrying a cousin. At other moments they were seldom seen in the glacial atmosphere of courts, preferring to royal palaces those of the other, and more modern type, in one of which the Hickses were now lodged.

Yes: the Prince and his mother (they gaily avowed it) revelled in Palace Hotels; and, being unable to afford the luxury of inhabiting them, they liked, as often as possible, to be invited to dine there by their friends—"or even to tea, my dear," the Princess laughingly avowed, "for I'm so awfully fond of buttered scones; and Anastasius gives me so little to eat in the desert."

The encounter with these ambulant Highnesses had been fatal—Lansing now perceived it—to Mrs. Hicks's principles. She had known a great many archæologists, but never one as agreeable as the Prince, and above all never one who had left a throne to camp in the desert and delve in Libyan tombs. And it seemed to her infinitely pathetic that these two gifted beings, who grumbled when they had to go to "marry a cousin" at the Palace of St. James or of Madrid, and hastened back breathlessly to the far-off point where, metaphorically speaking, pick-axe and spade had dropped from their royal hands—that these heirs of the ages should be unable to offer themselves the comforts of up-to-date hotel life, and should enjoy themselves "like babies" when they were invited to the other kind of "Palace," to feast on buttered scones and watch the tango.

She simply could not bear the thought of their privations; and neither, after a time, could Mr. Hicks, who found the Prince more democratic than anyone he had ever known at Apex City, and was immensely interested by the fact that their spectacles came from the same optician.

But it was, above all, the artistic tendencies of the Prince and his mother which had conquered the Hickses. There was fascination in the thought that, among the rabble of vulgar uneducated royalties who overran Europe from Biarritz to the Engadine, gambling, tangoing, and sponging on no less vulgar plebeians, they, the unobtrusive and self-respecting Hickses, should have had the luck to meet this cultivated pair, who joined them in gentle ridicule of their own frivolous kinsfolk, and whose tastes were exactly those of the eccentric, unreliable and sometimes money-borrowing persons who had hitherto represented the higher life to the Hickses.

Now at last Mrs. Hicks saw the possibility of being at once artistic and luxurious, of surrendering herself to the joys of modern plumbing and yet keeping the talk on the highest level. "If the poor dear Princess *wants* to dine at the Nouveau Luxe why shouldn't we give her that pleasure?" Mrs. Hicks smilingly enquired; "and as for enjoying her buttered scones like a baby, as she says, I think it's the sweetest thing about her."

Coral Hicks did not join in this chorus; but she accepted, with her curious air of impartiality, the change in her parents' manner of life, and for the first time (as Nick observed) occupied herself with her mother's toilet, with the result that Mrs. Hicks's outline became firmer, her garments soberer in hue and finer in material; so that, should anyone chance to detect the daughter's likeness to her mother, the result was less likely to be disturbing.

Such precautions were the more needful—Lansing could not but note—because of the different standards of the society in which the Hickses now moved. For it was a curious fact that admission to the intimacy of the Prince and his mother—who continually declared themselves to be the pariahs, the outlaws, the Bohemians among crowned heads—nevertheless involved not only living in Palace Hotels but mixing with those who frequented them. The Prince's aide-de-camp—an agreeable young man of easy manners—had smilingly hinted that their Serene Highnesses, though so thoroughly democratic and unceremonious, were yet accustomed to inspecting in advance the names of the persons whom their hosts wished to invite with them; and Lansing noticed that Mrs. Hicks's lists, having been "submitted," usually came back lengthened by the addition of numerous wealthy and titled guests. Their Highnesses never struck out a name; they welcomed with enthusiasm and curiosity the Hickses' oddest and most inexplicable friends, at most putting off some of them to a later day on the plea that it would be "cosier" to meet them on a more private occasion; but they invariably added to the list many friends of their own, with the gracious hint that they wished these latter (though socially so well-provided for) to have the "immense privilege" of knowing the Hickses. And thus it happened that when October gales necessitated laying up the *Ibis*, the Hickses, finding again in Rome the august travellers from whom they had parted the previous month in Athens, also found their visiting-list enlarged by all that the capital contained of fashion.

It was true enough, as Lansing had not failed to note, that the Princess Mother adored prehistoric art, and Russian music, and the paintings of Gauguin and Matisse; but she also, and with a beaming unconsciousness of perspective, adored large pearls and powerful motors, caravan tea and modern plumbing, perfumed cigarettes and society scandals; and her son, while apparently less sensible to these forms of luxury, adored his mother, and was charmed to gratify her inclinations without cost to himself—"Since poor Mamma," as he observed, "is so courageous when we are roughing it in the desert."

The smiling aide-de-camp, who explained these things to Lansing, added with an intenser smile that the Prince and his mother were under obligations, either social or cousinly, to most of the titled persons whom they begged Mrs. Hicks to invite; "and it seems to their Serene Highnesses," he added, "the most flattering return they can make for the hospitality of their friends to give them such an intellectual opportunity."

The dinner-table at which their Highnesses' friends were seated on the evening in question represented, numerically, one of the greatest intellectual opportunities yet afforded them. Thirty guests were grouped about the flower-wreathed board, from which Eldorada and Mr. Beck had been excluded on the plea that the Princess Mother liked cosy parties and begged her hosts that there should never be more than thirty at table. Such, at least, was the reason given by Mrs. Hicks to her faithful followers; but Lansing had observed that, of late, the same skilled hand which had refashioned the Hickses' social circle usually managed to exclude from it the timid presences of the two secretaries. Their banishment was the more displeasing to Lansing from the fact that, for the last three months, he had filled Mr. Buttles's place, and was himself their salaried companion. But since he had accepted the post, his obvious duty was to fill it in accordance with his employers' requirements;

and it was clear even to Eldorada and Mr. Beck that he had, as Eldorada ungrudgingly said, "Something of Mr. Buttles's marvellous social gifts."

During the cruise his task had not been distasteful to him. He was glad of any definite duties, however trivial, he felt more independent as the Hickses' secretary than as their pampered guest, and the large cheque which Mr. Hicks handed over to him on the first of each month refreshed his languishing sense of self-respect.

He considered himself absurdly over-paid, but that was the Hickses' affair; and he saw nothing humiliating in being in the employ of people he liked and respected. But from the moment of the ill-fated encounter with the wandering Princes, his position had changed as much as that of his employers. He was no longer, to Mr. and Mrs. Hicks, a useful and estimable assistant, on the same level as Eldorada and Mr. Beck; he had become a social asset of unsuspected value, equalling Mr. Buttles in his capacity for dealing with the mysteries of foreign etiquette, and surpassing him in the art of personal attraction. Nick Lansing, the Hickses found, already knew most of the Princess Mother's rich and aristocratic friends. Many of them hailed him with enthusiastic "Old Nicks," and he was almost as familiar as His Highness's own aide-de-camp with all those secret ramifications of love and hate that made dinner-giving so much more of a science in Rome than at Apex City.

Mrs. Hicks, at first, had hopelessly lost her way in this labyrinth of subterranean scandals, rivalries and jealousies; and finding Lansing's hand within reach she clung to it with pathetic tenacity. But if the young man's value had risen in the eyes of his employers it had deteriorated in his own. He was condemned to play a part he had not bargained for, and it seemed to him more degrading when paid in bank-notes than if his retribution had consisted merely in good dinners and luxurious lodgings. The first time the smiling aide-de-camp had caught his eye over a verbal slip of Mrs. Hicks's, Nick had flushed to the forehead and gone to bed swearing that he would chuck his job the next day.

Two months had passed since then, and he was still the paid secretary. He had contrived to let the aide-de-camp feel that he was too deficient in humour to be worth exchanging glances with; but even this had not restored his self-respect, and on the evening in question, as he looked about the long table, he said to himself for the hundredth time that he would give up his position on the morrow.

Only—what was the alternative? The alternative, apparently, was Coral Hicks. He glanced down the line of diners, beginning with the tall lean countenance of the Princess Mother, with its small inquisitive eyes perched as high as attic windows under a frizzled thatch of hair and a pediment of uncleaned diamonds; passed on to the vacuous and overfed or fashionably haggard masks of the ladies next in rank; and finally caught, between branching orchids, a distant glimpse of Miss Hicks.

In contrast with the others, he thought, she looked surprisingly noble. Her large grave features made her appear like an old monument in a street of Palace Hotels; and he marvelled at the mysterious law which had brought this archaic face out of Apex City, and given to the oldest society of Europe a look of such mixed modernity.

Lansing perceived that the aide-de-camp, who was his neighbour, was also looking at Miss Hicks. His expression was serious, and even thoughtful; but, as his eyes met Lansing's he readjusted his official smile.

"I was admiring our hostess's daughter. Her absence of jewels is—er—an inspiration," he remarked in the confidential tone which Lansing had come to dread.

"Oh, Miss Hicks is full of inspirations," he returned curtly, and the aide-de-camp bowed with an admiring air, as if inspirations were rarer than pearls, as in his *milieu* they undoubtedly were. "She is the equal of any situation, I am sure," he replied; and then abandoned the subject with one of his automatic transitions.

After dinner, in the embrasure of a drawing-room window, he surprised Nick by returning to the same topic, and this time without thinking it needful to readjust his smile. His face remained serious, though his manner was studiously informal.

"I was admiring, at dinner, Miss Hicks's invariable sense of appropriateness. It must permit her friends to foresee for her almost any future, however exalted."

Lansing hesitated, and controlled his annoyance. Decidedly he wanted to know what was in his companion's mind.

"What do you mean by exalted?" he asked, with a smile of faint amusement.

"Well—equal to her marvellous capacity for shining in the public eye."

Lansing still smiled. "The question is, I suppose, whether her desire to shine equals her capacity."

The aide-de-camp stared. "You mean, she's not ambitious?"

"On the contrary; I believe her to be immeasurably ambitious."

"Immeasurably?" The aide-de-camp seemed to try to measure it. "But not, surely, beyond—" "*Beyond what we can offer*," his eyes completed the sentence; and it was Lansing's turn to stare. The aide-de-camp faced the stare. "*Yes*," his eyes concluded in a flash, while his lips let fall: "The Princess Mother admires her immensely." But at that moment a wave of Mrs. Hicks's fan drew them hurriedly from their embrasure.

"Professor Darchivio had promised to explain to us the difference between the Sassanian and Byzantine motives in Carolingian art; but the Manager has sent up word that the two new Creole dancers from Paris have arrived, and her Serene Highness wants to pop down to the ball-room and take a peep at them. . . . She's sure the Professor will understand. . . ."

"And accompany us, of course," the Princess irresistibly added.

Lansing's brief colloquy in the Nouveau Luxe window had lifted the scales from his eyes. Innumerable dim corners of memory had been flooded with light by that one quick glance of the aide-de-camp's: things he had heard, hints he had let pass, smiles, insinuations, cordialities, rumours of the improbability of the Prince's founding a family, suggestions as to the urgent need of replenishing the Teutoburger treasury. . . .

Miss Hicks, perforce, had accompanied her parents and their princely guests to the ballroom; but, as she did not dance, and took little interest in the sight of others so engaged, she remained aloof from the party, absorbed in an archæological discussion with the baffled but smiling *savant* who was to have enlightened the party on the difference between Sassanian and Byzantine ornament.

Lansing, also aloof, had picked out a post from which he could observe the girl: she wore a new look to him since he had seen her as the centre of all these scattered threads of intrigue. Yes; decidedly she was growing handsomer; or else she had learned how to set off her massive lines instead of trying to disguise them. As she held up her long eye-glass to glance absently at the dancers he was struck by the large beauty of her arm and the careless assurance of the gesture. There was nothing nervous or fussy about Coral Hicks; and he was not surprised that, plastically at least, the Princess Mother had discerned her possibilities.

Nick Lansing, all that night, sat up and stared at his future. He knew enough of the society into which the Hickses had drifted to guess that, within a very short time, the hint of the Prince's aide-de-camp would reappear in the form of a direct proposal. Lansing himself would probably—as the one person in the Hicks entourage with whom one could intelligibly commune—be entrusted with the next step in the negotiations: he would be asked, as the aide-de-camp would have said, "to feel the ground." It was clearly part of the state policy of Teutoburg to offer Miss Hicks, with the hand of its sovereign, an opportunity to replenish its treasury.

What would the girl do? Lansing could not guess; yet he dimly felt that her attitude would depend in a great degree upon his own. And he knew no more what his own was going to be than on the night, four months earlier, when he had flung out of his wife's room in Venice to take the midnight express for Genoa.

The whole of his past, and above all the tendency, on which he had once prided himself, to live in the present and take whatever chances it offered, now made it harder for him to act. He began to see that he had never, even in the closest relations of life, looked ahead of his immediate satisfaction. He had thought it rather fine to be able to give himself so intensely to the fullness of each moment instead of hurrying past it in pursuit of something more, or something else, in the manner of the over-scrupulous or the under-imaginative, whom he had always grouped together and equally pitied. It was not till he had linked his life with Susy's that he had begun to feel it reaching forward into a future he longed to make sure of, to fasten upon and shape to his own wants and purposes, till, by an imperceptible substitution, that future had become his real present, his all-absorbing moment of time.

Now the moment was shattered, and the power to rebuild it failed him. He had never before thought about putting together broken bits: he felt like a man whose house has been wrecked by an earthquake, and who, for lack of skilled labour, is called upon for the first time to wield a trowel and carry bricks. He simply did not know how.

Will-power, he saw, was not a thing one could suddenly decree oneself to possess. It must be built up imperceptibly and laboriously out of a succession of small efforts to meet definite objects, out of the facing of daily difficulties instead of cleverly eluding them, or shifting their burden on others. The making of the substance called character was a process about as slow and arduous as the building of the Pyramids; and the thing itself, like those awful edifices, was mainly useful to lodge one's descendants in, after they too were dust. Yet the Pyramid-instinct was the one which had made the world, made man, and caused his fugitive joys to linger like fading frescoes on imperishable walls. . . .

Chapter XXI

O N the drive back from her dinner at the Nouveau Luxe, events had followed the course foreseen by Susy.

She had promised Strefford to seek legal advice about her divorce, and he had kissed her; and the promise had been easier to make than she had expected, the kiss less difficult to receive.

She had gone to the dinner a-quiver with the mortification of learning that her husband was still with the Hickses. Morally sure of it though she had been, the discovery was a shock, and she measured for the first time the abyss between fearing and knowing. No wonder he had not written—the modern husband did not have to: he had only to leave it to time and the newspapers to make known his intentions. Susy could imagine Nick's saying to himself, as he sometimes used to say when she reminded him of an unanswered letter: "But there are lots of ways of answering a letter—and writing doesn't happen to be mine."

Well—he had done it in his way, and she was answered. For a minute, as she laid aside the paper, darkness submerged her, and she felt herself dropping down into the bottomless anguish of her dreadful vigil in the Palazzo Vanderlyn. But she was weary of anguish: her healthy body and nerves instinctively rejected it. The wave was spent, and she felt herself irresistibly struggling back to light and life and youth. He didn't want her? Well, she would try not to want him! There lay all the old expedients at her hand—the rouge for her white lips, the atropine for her blurred eyes, the new dress on her bed, the thought of Strefford and his guests awaiting her, and of the conclusions that the diners of the Nouveau Luxe would draw from seeing them together. Thank heaven no one would say: "Poor old Susy—did you know Nick had chucked her?" They would all say: "Poor old Nick! Yes, I daresay she was sorry to chuck him; but Altringham's mad to marry her, and what could she do?"

And once again events had followed the course she had foreseen. Seeing her at Lord Altringham's table, with the Ascots and the old Duchess of Dunes, the interested spectators could not but regard the dinner as confirming the rumour of her marriage. As Ellie said, people didn't wait nowadays to announce their "engagements" till the tiresome divorce proceedings were over. Ellie herself, prodigally pearled and ermined, had floated in late with Algie Bockheimer in her wake, and sat, in conspicuous *tête-à-tête*, nodding and signalling her sympathy to Susy. Approval beamed from every eye: it was awfully exciting, they all seemed to say, seeing Susy Lansing pull it off! As the party, after dinner, drifted from the restaurant back into the hall, she caught, in the smiles and hand-pressures crowding about her, the scarcely-repressed hint of official congratulations; and Violet Melrose, seated in a corner with Fulmer, drew her down with a wan jade-circled arm, to whisper tenderly: "It's most awfully clever of you, darling, not to be wearing any jewels."

In all the women's eyes she read the reflected lustre of the jewels she could wear when she chose: it was as though their glitter reached her from the far-off bank where they lay sealed up in the Altringham strong-box. What a fool she had been to think that Strefford would ever believe she didn't care for them!

The Ambassadress, a blank perpendicular person, had been a shade less affable than Susy could have wished; but then there was Lady Joan—and the girl was handsome, alarmingly handsome—to account for that: probably every one in the room had guessed it. And the old Duchess of Dunes was delightful. She looked rather like Strefford in a wig and false pearls (Susy was sure they were as false as her teeth); and her cordiality was so demonstrative that the future bride found it more difficult to account for than Lady Ascot's coldness, till she heard the old lady, as they passed into the hall, breathe in a hissing whisper to her nephew: "Streff, dearest, when you have a minute's time, and can drop in at my wretched little *pension*, I know you can explain in two words what I ought to do to pacify those awful money-lenders. . . . And you'll bring your exquisite American to see me, won't you? . . . No, Joan Senechal's too fair for my taste. . . . Insipid . . ."

Yes: the taste of it all was again sweet on her lips. A few days later she began to wonder how the thought of Strefford's endearments could have been so alarming. To be sure he was not lavish of them; but when he did touch her, even when he kissed her, it no longer seemed to matter. An almost complete absence of sensation had mercifully succeeded to the first wild flurry of her nerves.

And so it would be, no doubt, with everything else in her new life. If it failed to provoke any acute reactions, whether of pain or pleasure, the very absence of sensation would make for peace. And in the meanwhile she was tasting what, she had begun to suspect, was the maximum of bliss to most of the women she knew: days packed with engagements, the exhilaration of fashionable crowds, the thrill of snapping up a jewel or a *bibelot* or a new "model" that one's best friend wanted, or of being invited to some private show, or some exclusive entertainment, that one's best friend couldn't get to. There was nothing, now, that she couldn't buy, nowhere that she couldn't go: she had only to choose and to triumph. And for a while the surface-excitement of her life gave her the illusion of enjoyment.

Strefford, as she had expected, had postponed his return to England, and they had now been for nearly three weeks together in their new, and virtually avowed, relation. She had fancied that, after all, the easiest part of it would be just the being with Strefford—the falling back on their old tried friendship to efface the sense of strangeness. But, though she had so soon grown used to his caresses, he himself remained curiously unfamiliar: she was hardly sure, at times, that it was the old Strefford she was talking to. It was not that his point of view had changed, but that new things occupied and absorbed him. In all the small sides of his great situation he took an almost childish satisfaction; and though he still laughed at both its privileges and its obligations, it was now with a jealous laughter.

It amused him inexhaustibly, for instance, to be made up to by all the people who had always disapproved of him, and to unite at the same table persons who had to dissemble their annoyance at being invited together lest they should not be invited at all. Equally exhilarating was the capricious favouring of the dull and dowdy on occasions when the brilliant and disreputable expected his notice. It enchanted him, for example, to ask the old Duchess of Dunes and Violet Melrose to dine with the Vicar of Altringham, on his way to Switzerland for a month's holiday, and to watch the face of the Vicar's wife while the Duchess narrated her last difficulties with book-makers and money-lenders, and Violet proclaimed the rights of Love and Genius to all that had once been supposed to belong exclusively to Respectability and Dulness.

Susy had to confess that her own amusements were hardly of a higher order; but then she put up with them for lack of better, whereas Strefford, who might have had what he pleased, was completely satisfied with such triumphs.

Somehow, in spite of his honours and his opportunities, he seemed to have shrunk. The old Strefford had certainly been a larger person, and she wondered if material prosperity were always a beginning of ossification. Strefford had been much more fun when he lived by his wits. Sometimes, now, when he tried to talk of politics, or assert himself on some question of public interest, she was startled by his limitations. Formerly, when he was not sure of his ground, it had been his way to turn the difficulty by glib nonsense or easy irony; now he was actually dull, at times almost pompous. She noticed too, for the first time, that he did not always hear clearly when several people were talking at once, or when he was at the theatre; and he developed a habit of saying over and over again: "Does so-and-so speak indistinctly? Or am I getting deaf, I wonder?" which wore on her nerves by its suggestion of a corresponding mental infirmity.

These thoughts did not always trouble her. The current of idle activity on which they were both gliding was her native element as well as his; and never had its tide been as swift, its waves as buoyant. In his relation to her, too, he was full of tact and consideration. She saw that he still remembered their frightened exchange of glances after their first kiss; and the sense of this little hidden spring of imagination in him was sometimes enough for her thirst.

She had always had a rather masculine punctuality in keeping her word, and after she had promised Strefford to take steps toward a divorce she had promptly set about doing it. A sudden reluctance prevented her asking the advice of friends like Ellie Vanderlyn, whom she knew to be in the thick of the same negotiations, and all she could think of was to consult a young American lawyer practising in Paris, with whom she felt she could talk the more easily because he was not from New York, and probably unacquainted with her history.

She was so ignorant of the procedure in such matters that she was surprised and relieved at his asking few personal questions; but it was a shock to learn that a divorce could not be obtained, either in New York or Paris, merely on the ground of desertion or incompatibility.

"I thought nowadays . . . if people preferred to live apart . . . it could always be managed," she stammered, wondering at her own ignorance, after the many conjugal ruptures she had assisted at.

The young lawyer smiled, and coloured slightly. His lovely client evidently intimidated him by her grace, and still more by her inexperience.

"It can be—generally," he admitted; "and especially so if . . . as I gather is the case . . . your husband is equally anxious. . . ."

"Oh, quite!" she exclaimed, suddenly humiliated by having to admit it.

"Well, then—may I suggest that, to bring matters to a point, the best way would be for you to write to him?"

She recoiled slightly. It had never occurred to her that the lawyers would not "manage it" without her intervention.

"Write to him . . . but what about?"

"Well, expressing your wish . . . to recover your freedom. . . . The rest, I assume," said the young lawyer, "may be left to Mr. Lansing."

She did not know exactly what he meant, and was too much perturbed by the idea of having to communicate with Nick to follow any other train of thought. How could she write such a letter? And yet how could she confess to the lawyer that she had not the courage to do so? He would, of course, tell her to go home and be reconciled. She hesitated perplexedly.

"Wouldn't it be better," she suggested, "if the letter were to come from—from your office?"

He considered this politely. "On the whole: no. If, as I take it, an amicable arrangement is necessary—to secure the requisite evidence—then a line from you, suggesting an interview, seems to me more advisable."

"An interview? Is an interview necessary?" She was ashamed to show her agitation to this cautiously smiling young man, who must wonder at her childish lack of understanding; but the break in her voice was uncontrollable.

"Oh, please write to him—I can't! And I can't see him! Oh, can't you arrange it for me?" she pleaded.

She saw now that her idea of a divorce had been that it was something one went out—or sent out—to buy in a shop: something concrete and portable, that Strefford's money could pay for, and that it required no personal participation to obtain. What a fool the lawyer must think her! Stiffening herself, she rose from her seat.

"My husband and I don't wish to see each other again. . . . I'm sure it would be useless . . . and very painful."

"You are the best judge, of course. But in any case, a letter from you, a friendly letter, seems wiser . . . considering the apparent lack of evidence. . . ."

"Very well, then; I'll write," she agreed, and hurried away, scarcely hearing his parting injunction that she should take a copy of her letter.

That night she wrote. At the last moment it might have been impossible, if at the theatre little Breckenridge had not bobbed into her box. He was just back from Rome, where he had dined with the Hickses ("a bang-up show—they're really *lancés*—you wouldn't know them!"), and had met there Lansing, whom he reported as intending to marry Coral "as soon as things were settled." "You were dead right, weren't you, Susy," he snickered, "that night in Venice last summer, when we all thought you were joking about their engagement? Pity now you chucked our surprise visit to the Hickses, and sent Streff up to drag us back just as we were breaking in! You remember?"

He flung off the "Streff" airily, in the old way, but with a tentative side-glance at his host; and Lord Altringham, leaning toward Susy, said coldly: "Was Breckenridge speaking about me? I didn't catch what he said. Does he speak indistinctly—or am I getting deaf, I wonder?"

After that it seemed comparatively easy, when Strefford had dropped her at her hotel, to go upstairs and write. She dashed off the date and her address, and then stopped; but suddenly she remembered Breckenridge's snicker, and the words rushed from her. "Nick dear, it was July when you left Venice, and I have had no word from you since the note in which you said you had gone for a few days, and that I should hear soon again.

"You haven't written yet, and it is five months since you left me. That means, I suppose, that you want to take back your freedom and give me mine. Wouldn't it be kinder, in that case, to tell me so? It is worse than anything to go on as we are now. I don't know how to put these things—but since you seem unwilling to write to me perhaps you would prefer to send your answer to Mr. Frederic Spearman, the American lawyer here. His address is 100, Boulevard Haussmann. I hope—"

She broke off on the last word. Hope? What did she hope, either for him or for herself? Wishes for his welfare would sound like a mockery—and she would rather her letter should seem bitter than unfeeling. Above all, she wanted to get it done. To have to re-write even those few lines would be torture. So she left "I hope," and simply added: "to hear before long what you have decided."

She read it over, and shivered. Not one word of the past—not one allusion to that mysterious interweaving of their lives which had enclosed them one in the other like the flower in its sheath! What place had such memories in such a letter? She had the feeling that she wanted to hide that other Nick away in her own bosom, and with him the other Susy, the Susy he had once imagined her to be. . . . Neither of them seemed concerned with the present business.

The letter done, she stared at the sealed envelope till its presence in the room became intolerable, and she understood that she must either tear it up or post it immediately. She went down to the hall of the sleeping hotel, and bribed the night-porter to carry the letter to the nearest post office, though he objected that, at that hour, no time would be gained. "I want it out of the house," she insisted: and waited sternly by the desk, in her dressing-gown, till he had performed the errand.

As she re-entered her room, the disordered writing-table struck her; and she remembered the lawyer's injunction to take a copy of her letter. A copy to be filed away with the documents in "Lansing *versus* Lansing!" She burst out laughing at the idea. What were lawyers made of, she wondered? Didn't the man guess, by the mere look in her eyes and the sound of her voice, that she would never, as long as she lived, forget a word of that letter—that night after night she would lie down, as she was lying down to-night, to stare wide-eyed for hours into the darkness, while a voice in her brain monotonously hammered out: "Nick dear, it was July when you left me . . ." and so on, word after word, down to the last fatal syllable?

Chapter XXII

S TREFFORD was leaving for England.

Once assured that Susy had taken the first step toward freeing herself, he frankly regarded her as his affianced wife, and could see no reason for further mystery. She understood his impatience to have their plans settled; it would protect him from the formidable menace of the marriageable, and cause people, as he said, to stop meddling. Now that the novelty of his situation was wearing off, his natural indolence reasserted itself, and there was nothing he dreaded more than having to be on his guard against the innumerable plans that his well-wishers were perpetually making for him. Sometimes Susy fancied he was marrying her because to do so was to follow the line of least resistance.

"To marry me is the easiest way of not marrying all the others," she laughed, as he stood before her one day in a quiet alley of the Bois de Boulogne, insisting on the settlement of various preliminaries. "I believe I'm only a protection to you."

An odd gleam passed behind his eyes, and she instantly guessed that he was thinking: "And what else am I to you?"

She changed colour, and he rejoined, laughing also: "Well, you're that at any rate, thank the Lord!"

She pondered, and then questioned: "But in the interval— how are you going to defend yourself for another year?"

"Ah, you've got to see to that; you've got to take a little house in London. You've got to look after me, you know."

It was on the tip of her tongue to flash back: "Oh, if that's all you care—!" But caring was exactly the factor she wanted, as much as possible, to keep out of their talk and their thoughts. She could not ask him how much he cared without laying herself open to the same question; and that way terror lay. As a matter of fact, though Strefford was not an ardent wooer—perhaps from tact, perhaps from temperament, perhaps merely from the long habit of belittling and disintegrating every sentiment and every conviction—yet she knew he did care for her as much as he was capable of caring for anyone. If the element of habit entered largely into the feeling—if he liked her, above all, because he was

163

used to her, knew her views, her indulgences, her allowances, knew he was never likely to be bored, and almost certain to be amused, by her; why, such ingredients, though not of the fieriest, were perhaps those most likely to keep his feeling for her at a pleasant temperature. She had had a taste of the tropics, and wanted more equable weather; but the idea of having to fan his flame gently for a year was unspeakably depressing to her. Yet all this was precisely what she could not say. The long period of probation, during which, as she knew, she would have to amuse him, to guard him, to hold him, and to keep off the other women, was a necessary part of their situation. She was sure that, as little Breckenridge would have said, she could "pull it off"; but she did not want to think about it. What she would have preferred would have been to go away—no matter where—and not see Strefford again till they were married. But she dared not tell him that either.

"A little house in London—?" She wondered.

"Well, I suppose you've got to have some sort of a roof over your head."

"I suppose so."

He sat down beside her. "If you like me well enough to live at Altringham some day, won't you, in the meantime, let me provide you with a smaller and more convenient establishment?"

Still she hesitated. The alternative, she knew, would be to live on Ursula Gillow, Violet Melrose, or some other of her rich friends, any one of whom would be ready to lavish the largest hospitality on the prospective Lady Altringham. Such an arrangement, in the long run, would be no less humiliating to her pride, no less destructive to her independence, than Altringham's little establishment. But she temporized. "I shall go over to London in December, and stay for a while with various people—then we can look about."

"All right; as you like." He obviously considered her hesitation ridiculous, but was too full of satisfaction at her having started divorce proceedings to be chilled by her reply.

"And now, look here, my dear; couldn't I give you some sort of a ring?"

"A ring?" She flushed at the suggestion. "What's the use, Streff, dear? With all those jewels locked away in London—"

"Oh, I daresay you'll think them old-fashioned. And, hang it, why shouldn't I give you something new? I ran across Ellie and Bockheimer yesterday, in the rue de la Paix, picking out sapphires. Do you like sapphires, or emeralds? Or just a diamond? I've seen a thumping one. . . . I'd like you to have it."

Ellie and Bockheimer! How she hated the conjunction of the names! Their case always seemed to her like a caricature of her own, and she felt an unreasoning resentment against Ellie for having selected the same season for her unmating and re-mating.

"I wish you wouldn't speak of them, Streff . . . as if they were like us! I can hardly bear to sit in the same room with Ellie Vanderlyn."

"Hullo? What's wrong? You mean because of her giving up Clarissa?"

"Not that only. . . . You don't know. . . . I can't tell you. . . ." She shivered at the memory, and rose restlessly from the bench where they had been sitting.

Strefford gave his careless shrug. "Well, my dear, you can hardly expect me to agree, for after all it was to Ellie I owed the luck of being so long alone with you in Venice. If she and Algie hadn't prolonged their honeymoon at the villa—"

He stopped abruptly, and looked at Susy. She was conscious that every drop of blood had left her face. She felt it ebbing away from her heart, flowing out of her as if from all her severed arteries, till it seemed as though nothing were left of life in her but one point of irreducible pain.

"Ellie—at your villa? What do you mean? Was it Ellie and Bockheimer who—?"

Strefford still stared. "You mean to say you didn't know?"

"Who came after Nick and me . . . ?" she insisted.

"Why, do you suppose I'd have turned you out otherwise? That beastly Bockheimer simply smothered me with gold. Ah, well, there's one good thing: I shall never have to let the villa again! I rather like the little place myself, and I daresay once in a while we might go there for a day or two. . . . Susy, what's the matter?" he exclaimed.

She returned his stare, but without seeing him. Everything swam and danced before her eyes.

"Then she was *there* while I was posting all those letters for her—?"

"Letters—what letters? What makes you look so frightfully upset?"

She pursued her thought as if he had not spoken. "She and Algie Bockheimer arrived there the very day that Nick and I left?"

"I suppose so. I thought she'd told you. Ellie always tells everybody everything."

"She would have told me, I daresay—but I wouldn't let her."

"Well, my dear, that was hardly my fault, was it? Though I really don't see—"

But Susy, still blind to everything but the dance of dizzy sparks before her eyes, pressed on as if she had not heard him. "It was their motor, then, that took us to Milan! It was Algie Bockheimer's motor!" She did not know why, but this seemed to her the most humiliating incident in the whole hateful business. She remembered Nick's reluctance to use the motor—she remembered his look when she had boasted of her "managing." The nausea mounted to her throat.

Strefford burst out laughing. "I say—you borrowed their motor? And you didn't know whose it was?"

"How could I know? I persuaded the chauffeur . . . for a little tip. . . . It was to save our railway fares to Milan . . . extra luggage costs so frightfully in Italy. . . ."

"Good old Susy! Well done! I can see you doing it—"

"Oh, how horrible—how horrible!" she groaned.

"Horrible? What's horrible?"

"Why, your not seeing . . . not feeling . . ." she began impetuously; and then stopped. How could she explain to him that what revolted her was not so much the fact of his having given the little house, as soon as she and Nick had left it, to those two people of all others—though the vision of them in the sweet secret house, and under the plane-trees of the terrace, drew such a trail of slime across her golden hours? No, it was not that from which she most recoiled, but from the fact that Strefford, living in luxury in Nelson Vanderlyn's house, should at the same time have secretly abetted Ellie Vanderlyn's love-affairs, and allowed her—for a handsome price—to shelter them under his own roof. The reproach trembled on her lip—but she remembered her own part in the wretched business, and the impossibility of avowing it to Strefford, and of revealing to him that Nick had left her for that very reason. She was not afraid that the discovery would diminish her in Strefford's eyes: he was untroubled by moral problems, and would laugh away her avowal, with a sneer at Nick in his new part of moralist. But that was just what she could not bear: that anyone should cast a doubt on the genuineness of Nick's standards, or should know how far below them she had fallen.

She remained silent, and Strefford, after a moment, drew her gently down to the seat beside him. "Susy, upon my soul I don't know what you're driving at. Is it me you're angry with—or yourself? And what's it all about? Are you disgusted because I let the villa to a couple who weren't married? But, hang it, they're the kind that pay the highest price—and I had to earn my living somehow! One doesn't run across a bridal pair every day. . . ."

She lifted her eyes to his puzzled incredulous face. Poor Streff! No, it was not with him that she was angry. Why should she be? Even that ill-advised disclosure had told her nothing she had not already known about him. It had simply revealed to her once more the real point of view of the people he and she lived among, had shown her that, in spite of the superficial difference, he felt as they felt, judged as they judged, was blind as they were—and as she would be expected to be, should she once again become one of them. What was the use of being placed by fortune above such shifts and compromises, if in one's heart one still condoned them? And she would have to—she would catch the general note, grow blunted as those other people were blunted, and gradually come to wonder at her own revolt, as Strefford now honestly wondered at it. She felt as though she were on the point of losing some new-found treasure, a treasure precious only to herself, but beside which all he offered her was nothing, the triumph of her wounded pride nothing, the security of her future nothing.

"What is it, Susy?" he asked, with the same puzzled gentleness.

Ah, the loneliness of never being able to make him understand! She had felt lonely enough when the flaming sword of Nick's indignation had shut her out from their Paradise; but there had been a cruel bliss in the pain. Nick had not opened her eyes to new truths, but had waked in her again something which had lain unconscious under years of accumulated indifference. And that re-awakened sense had never left her since, and had somehow kept her from utter loneliness because it was a secret shared with Nick, a gift she owed to Nick, and which, in leaving her, he could not take from her. It was almost, she suddenly felt, as if he had left her with a child.

"My dear girl," Strefford said, with a resigned glance at his watch, "you know we're dining at the Embassy. . . ."

At the Embassy? She looked at him vaguely: then she remembered. Yes, they were dining that night at the Ascots', with Strefford's cousin, the Duke of Dunes, and his wife, the handsome irreproachable young Duchess; with the old gambling Dowager Duchess, whom her son and daughter-in-law had come over from England to see; and with other English and French guests of a rank and standing worthy of the Duneses. Susy knew that her inclusion in such a dinner could mean but one thing: it was her definite recognition as Altringham's future wife. She was "the little American" whom one had to ask when one invited him, even on ceremonial occasions. The family had accepted her; the Embassy could but follow suit.

"It's late, dear; and I've got to see someone on business first," Strefford reminded her patiently.

"Oh, Streff—I can't, I can't!" The words broke from her without her knowing what she was saying. "I can't go with you—I can't go to the Embassy. I can't go on any longer like this. . . ." She lifted her eyes to his in desperate appeal. "Oh, understand— do please understand!" she wailed, knowing, while she spoke, the utter impossibility of what she asked.

Strefford's face had gradually paled and hardened. From sallow it turned to a dusky white, and lines of obstinacy deepened between the ironic eyebrows and about the weak amused mouth.

"Understand? What do you want me to understand?" He laughed. "That you're trying to chuck me—already?"

She shrank at the sneer of the "already," but instantly remembered that it was the only thing he could be expected to say, since it was just because he couldn't understand that she was flying from him.

"Oh, Streff—if I knew how to tell you!"

"It doesn't so much matter about the how. *Is* that what you're trying to say?"

Her head drooped, and she saw the dead leaves whirling across the path at her feet, lifted on a sudden wintry gust.

"The reason," he continued, clearing his throat with a stiff smile, "is not quite as important to me as the fact."

She stood speechless, agonized by his pain. But still, she thought, he had remembered the dinner at the Embassy! The thought gave her courage to go on.

"It wouldn't do, Streff. I'm not a bit the kind of person to make you happy."

"Oh, leave that to me, please, won't you?"

"No, I can't. Because I should be unhappy too."

He flicked at the leaves as they whirled past. "You've taken a rather long time to find it out." She saw that his new-born sense of his own consequence was making him suffer even more than his wounded affection; and that again gave her courage.

"If I've taken long it's all the more reason why I shouldn't take longer. If I've made a mistake it's you who would have suffered from it. . . ."

"Thanks," he said, "for your extreme solicitude."

She looked at him helplessly, penetrated by the despairing sense of their inaccessibility to each other. Then she remembered that Nick, during their last talk together, had seemed as inaccessible, and wondered if, when human souls try to get too near each other, they do not inevitably become mere blurs to each other's vision. She would have liked to say this to Streff—but he would not have understood it either. The sense of loneliness once more enveloped her, and she groped in vain for a word that should reach him.

"Let me go home alone, won't you?" she appealed to him.

"Alone?"

She nodded. "To-morrow—to-morrow. . . ."

He tried, rather valiantly, to smile. "Hang to-morrow! Whatever is wrong, it needn't prevent my seeing you home." He glanced toward the taxi that awaited them at the end of the deserted drive.

"No, please. You're in a hurry; take the taxi. I want immensely a long long walk by myself . . . through the streets, with the lights coming out. . . ."

He laid his hand on her arm. "I say, my dear, you're not ill?"

"No; I'm not ill. But you may say I am, to-night at the Embassy."

He released her and drew back. "Oh, very well," he answered coldly; and she understood by his tone that the knot was cut, and that at that moment he almost hated her. She turned away, hastening down the deserted alley, flying from him, and knowing, as she fled, that he was still standing there motionless, staring after her, wounded, humiliated, uncomprehending. It was neither her fault nor his. . . .

Chapter XXIII

As she fled on toward the lights of the streets a breath of freedom seemed to blow into her face.

Like a weary load the accumulated hypocrisies of the last months had dropped from her: she was herself again, Nick's Susy, and no one else's. She sped on, staring with bright bewildered eyes at the stately façades of the La Muette quarter, the perspectives of bare trees, the awakening glitter of shop-windows holding out to her all the things she would never again be able to buy. . . .

In an avenue of shops she paused before a milliner's window, and said to herself: "Why shouldn't I earn my living by trimming hats?" She met work-girls streaming out under a doorway, and scattering to catch trams and omnibuses; and she looked with newly-wakened interest at their tired independent faces. "Why shouldn't I earn my living as well as they do?" she thought. A little farther on she passed a Sister of Charity with softly trotting feet, a calm anonymous glance, and hands hidden in her capacious sleeves. Susy looked at her and thought: "Why shouldn't I be a Sister, and have no money to worry about, and trot about under a white coif helping poor people?"

All these strangers on whom she smiled in passing, and glanced back at enviously, were free from the necessities that enslaved her, and would not have known what she meant if she had told them that she must have so much money for her dresses, so much for her cigarettes, so much for bridge and cabs and tips, and all kinds of extras, and that at that moment she ought to be hurrying back to a dinner at the British Embassy, where her permanent right to such luxuries was to be solemnly recognized and ratified.

The artificiality and unreality of her life overcame her as with stifling fumes. She stopped at a street-corner, drawing long panting breaths as if she had been running a race. Then, slowly and aimlessly, she began to saunter along a street of small private houses in damp gardens that led to the Avenue du Bois. She sat down on a bench. Not far off, the Arc de Triomphe raised its august bulk, and beyond it a river of lights streamed down toward Paris, and the stir of the city's heart-beats troubled the quiet in her bosom. But not for long. She seemed to be looking at it all from the other side of the grave; and as she got up and wandered down the Champs Elysées, half empty in the evening lull between dusk and dinner, she felt as if the glittering avenue were really changed into the Field of Shadows from which it takes its name, and as if she were a ghost among ghosts.

Halfway home, a weakness of loneliness overcame her, and she seated herself under the trees near the Bond Point. Lines of motors and carriages were beginning to animate the converging thoroughfares, streaming abreast, crossing, winding in and out of each other in a tangle of hurried pleasure-seeking. She caught the light on jewels and shirt-fronts and hard bored eyes emerging from dim billows of fur and velvet. She seemed to hear what the couples were saying to each other, she pictured the drawing-rooms, restaurants, dance-halls they were hastening to, the breathless routine that was hurrying them along, as Time, the old vacuum-cleaner, swept them away with the dust of their carriage-wheels. And again the loneliness vanished in a sense of release. . . .

At the corner of the Place de la Concorde she stopped, recognizing a man in evening dress who was hailing a taxi. Their eyes met, and Nelson Vanderlyn came forward. He was the last person she cared to run across, and she shrank back involuntarily. What did he know, what had he guessed, of her complicity in his wife's affairs? No doubt Ellie had blabbed it all out by this time; she was just as likely to confide her love-affairs to Nelson as to anyone else, now that the Bockheimer prize was landed.

"Well—well—well—so I've caught you at it! Glad to see you, Susy, my dear." She found her hand cordially clasped in Vanderlyn's, and his round pink face bent on her with all its old urbanity. Did nothing matter, then, in this world she was fleeing from, did no one love or hate or remember?

"No idea you were in Paris—just got here myself," Vanderlyn continued, visibly delighted at the meeting. "Look here, don't suppose you're out of a job this evening by any chance, and would come and cheer up a lone bachelor, eh? No? You are? Well, that's luck for once! I say, where shall we go? One of the places where they dance, I suppose? Yes, I twirl the light fantastic once in a while myself. Got to keep up with the times! Hold on, taxi! Here—I'll drive you home first, and wait while you jump into your toggery. Lots of time." As he steered her toward the carriage she noticed that he had a gouty limp, and pulled himself in after her with difficulty.

"Mayn't I come as I am, Nelson? I don't feel like dancing. Let's go and dine in one of those nice smoky little restaurants by the Place de la Bourse."

He seemed surprised but relieved at the suggestion, and they rolled off together. In a corner at Baugé's they found a quiet table, screened from the other diners, and while Vanderlyn adjusted his eyeglasses to study the *carte* Susy stole a long look at him. He was dressed with even more than his usual formal trimness, and she detected, in an ultra-flat wrist-watch and discreetly expensive waistcoat buttons, an attempt at smartness altogether new. His face had undergone the same change: its familiar look of worn optimism had been, as it were, done up to match his clothes, as though a sort of moral cosmetic had made him pinker, shinier and sprightlier without really rejuvenating him. A thin veil of high spirits had merely been drawn over his face, as the shining strands of hair were skilfully brushed over his baldness.

"Here! *Carte des vins*, waiter! What champagne, Susy?" He chose, fastidiously, the best the cellar could produce, grumbling a little at the *bourgeois* character of the dishes. "Capital food of its kind, no doubt, but coarsish, don't you think? Well, I don't mind . . . it's rather a jolly change from the Luxe cooking. A new sensation—I'm all for new sensations, ain't you, my dear?" He re-filled their champagne glasses, flung an arm sideways over his chair, and smiled at her with a foggy benevolence.

As the champagne flowed his confidences flowed with it.

"Suppose you know what I'm here for—this divorce business? We wanted to settle it quietly, without a fuss, and of course Paris is the best place for that sort of job. Live and let live; no questions asked. None of your dirty newspapers. Great country, this. No hypocrisy . . . they understand Life over here!"

Susy gazed and listened. She remembered that people had thought Nelson would make a row when he found out. He had always been addicted to truculent anecdotes about unfaithful

wives, and the very formula of his perpetual ejaculation—
"Caught you at it, eh?"—seemed to hint at a constant preoccupation with such ideas. But now it was evident that, as the
saying was, he had "swallowed his dose" like all the others. No
strong blast of indignation had momentarily lifted him above
his normal stature: he remained a little man among little men,
and his eagerness to rebuild his life with all the old smiling optimism reminded Susy of the patient industry of an ant remaking
its ruined ant-heap.

"Tell you what, great thing, this liberty! Everything's changed
nowadays; why shouldn't marriage be too? A man can get out
of a business partnership when he wants to; but the parsons
want to keep us noosed up to each other for life because we've
blundered into a church one day and said 'Yes' before one of
'em. No, no—that's too easy. We've got beyond *that*. Science,
and all these new discoveries. . . . I say the Ten Commandments
were made for man, and not man for the Commandments; and
there ain't a word against divorce in 'em, anyhow! That's what
I tell my poor old mother, who builds everything on her Bible.
'Find me the place where it says: *Thou shalt not sue for divorce.*' It
makes her wild, poor old lady, because she can't; and she doesn't
know how they happen to have left it out. . . . I rather think
Moses left it out because he knew more about human nature
than these snivelling modern parsons do. Not that they'll always
bear investigating either; but I don't care about that. Live and
let live, eh, Susy? Haven't we all got a right to our Affinities?
I hear you're following our example yourself. First-rate idea:
I don't mind telling you I saw it coming on last summer at
Venice. Caught you at it, so to speak! Old Nelson ain't as blind
as people think. Here, let's open another bottle to the health of
Streff and Mrs. Streff!"

She caught the hand with which he was signalling to the
sommelier. This flushed and garrulous Nelson moved her more
poignantly than a more heroic figure. "No more champagne,
please, Nelson. Besides," she suddenly added, "it's not true."

He stared. "Not true that you're going to marry Altringham?"
"No."

"By George—then what on earth did you chuck Nick for?
Ain't you got an Affinity, my dear?"

She laughed and shook her head.

"Do you mean to tell me it's all Nick's doing, then?"

"I don't know. Let's talk of you instead, Nelson. I'm glad you're in such good spirits. I rather thought—"

He interrupted her quickly. "Thought I'd cut up a rumpus— do some shooting? I know—people did." He twisted his moustache, evidently proud of his reputation. "Well, maybe I did see red for a day or two—but I'm a philosopher, first and last. Before I went into banking I'd made and lost two fortunes out West. Well, how did I build 'em up again? Not by shooting anybody— even myself. By just buckling to, and beginning all over again. That's how . . . and that's what I am doing now. Beginning all over again. . . ." His voice dropped from boastfulness to a note of wistful melancholy, the look of strained jauntiness fell from his face like a mask, and for an instant she saw the real man, old, ruined, lonely. Yes, that was it: he was lonely, desperately lonely, foundering in such deep seas of solitude that any presence out of the past was like a spar to which he clung. Whatever he knew or guessed of the part she had played in his disaster, it was not callousness that had made him greet her with such forgiving warmth, but the same sense of smallness, insignificance and isolation which perpetually hung like a cold fog on her own horizon. Suddenly she too felt old—old and unspeakably tired.

"It's been nice seeing you, Nelson. But now I must be getting home."

He offered no objection, but asked for the bill, resumed his jaunty air while he scattered *largesse* among the waiters, and sauntered out behind her after calling for a taxi.

They drove off in silence. Susy was thinking: "And Clarissa?" but dared not ask. Vanderlyn lit a cigarette, hummed a dance-tune, and stared out of the window. Suddenly she felt his hand on hers.

"Susy—do you ever see her?"

"See—Ellie?"

He nodded, without turning toward her.

"Not often . . . sometimes. . . ."

"If you do, for God's sake tell her I'm happy . . . happy as a king . . . tell her you could see for yourself that I was. . . ." His voice broke in a little gasp. "I . . . I'll be damned if . . . if she shall ever be unhappy about me . . . if I can help it. . . ." The cigarette dropped from his fingers, and with a sob he covered his face.

"Oh, poor Nelson—poor Nelson," Susy breathed. While their cab rattled across the Place du Carrousel, and over the bridge, he continued to sit beside her with hidden face. At last he pulled out a scented handkerchief, rubbed his eyes with it, and groped for another cigarette.

"*I'm all right*! Tell her that, will you, Susy? There are some of our old times I don't suppose I shall ever forget; but they make me feel kindly to her, and not angry. I didn't know it would be so, beforehand—but it is . . . And now the thing's settled I'm as right as a trivet, and you can tell her so. . . . Look here, Susy . . ." he caught her by the arm as the taxi drew up at her hotel. . . . "Tell her I *understand*, will you? I'd rather like her to know that. . . ."

"I'll tell her, Nelson," she promised; and climbed the stairs alone to her dreary room.

Susy's one fear was that Strefford, when he returned the next day, should treat their talk of the previous evening as a fit of "nerves" to be jested away. He might, indeed, resent her behaviour too deeply to seek to see her at once; but his easy-going modern attitude toward conduct and convictions made that improbable. She had an idea that what he had most minded was her dropping so unceremoniously out of the Embassy Dinner.

But, after all, why should she see him again? She had had enough of explanations during the last months to have learned how seldom they explain anything. If the other person did not understand at the first word, at the first glance even, subsequent elucidations served only to deepen the obscurity. And she wanted above all—and especially since her hour with Nelson Vanderlyn—to keep herself free, aloof, to retain her hold on her precariously recovered self. She sat down and wrote to Strefford—and the letter was only a little less painful to write than the one she had despatched to Nick. It was not that her own feelings were in any like measure engaged; but because, as the decision to give up Strefford affirmed itself, she remembered only his kindness, his forbearance, his good humour, and all the other qualities she had always liked in him; and because she felt ashamed of the hesitations which must cause him so much pain and humiliation. Yes: humiliation chiefly. She knew that what she had to say would hurt his pride, in whatever way she framed her renunciation; and her pen wavered, hating its task. Then she remembered Vanderlyn's words about his wife: "There are some of our old times I don't suppose I shall ever forget—" and a phrase of Grace Fulmer's that she had but half grasped at the time: "You haven't been married long enough to understand how trifling such things seem in the balance of one's memories."

Here were two people who had penetrated farther than she into the labyrinth of the wedded state, and struggled through some of its thorniest passages; and yet both, one consciously, the other half-unaware, testified to the mysterious fact which was already dawning on her: that the influence of a marriage begun in mutual understanding is too deep not to reassert itself even in the moment of flight and denial.

"The real reason is that you're not Nick" was what she would have said to Strefford if she had dared to set down the bare truth; and she knew that, whatever she wrote, he was too acute not to read that into it.

"He'll think it's because I'm still in love with Nick . . . and perhaps I am. But even if I were, the difference doesn't seem to lie there, after all, but deeper, in things we've shared that seem to be meant to outlast love, or to change it into something different." If she could have hoped to make Strefford understand that, the letter would have been easy enough to write—but she knew just at what point his imagination would fail, in what obvious and superficial inferences it would rest.

"Poor Streff—poor me!" she thought as she sealed the letter.

After she had despatched it a sense of blankness descended on her. She had succeeded in driving from her mind all vain hesitations, doubts, returns upon herself: her healthy system naturally rejected them. But they left a queer emptiness in which her thoughts rattled about as thoughts might, she supposed, in the first moments after death—before one got used to it. To get used to being dead: that seemed to be her immediate business. And she felt such a novice at it—felt so horribly alive! How had those others learned to do without living? Nelson—well, he was still in the throes; and probably never would understand, or be able to communicate, the lesson when he had mastered it. But Grace Fulmer—she suddenly remembered that Grace was in Paris, and set forth to find her.

Chapter XXIV

NICK LANSING had walked out a long way into the Campagna. His hours were seldom his own, for both Mr. and Mrs. Hicks were becoming more and more addicted to sudden and somewhat imperious demands upon his time; but on this occasion he had simply slipped away after luncheon, and taking the tram to the Porta Salaria, had wandered on thence in the direction of the Ponte Nomentano.

He wanted to get away and think; but now that he had done it the business proved as unfruitful as everything he had put his hand to since he had left Venice. Think—think about what? His future seemed to him a negligible matter since he had received, two months earlier, the few lines in which Susy had asked him for her freedom.

The letter had been a shock—though he had fancied himself so prepared for it—yet it had also, in another sense, been a relief, since, now that at last circumstances compelled him to write to her, they also told him what to say. And he had said it as briefly and simply as possible, telling her that he would put no obstacle in the way of her release, that he held himself at her lawyer's disposal to answer any further communication—and that he would never forget their days together, or cease to bless her for them.

That was all. He gave his Roman banker's address, and waited for another letter; but none came. Probably the "formalities," whatever they were, took longer than he had supposed; and being in no haste to recover his own liberty, he did not try to learn the cause of the delay. From that moment, however, he considered himself virtually free, and ceased, by the same token, to take any interest in his own future. His life seemed as flat as a convalescent's first days after the fever has dropped.

The only thing he was sure of was that he was not going to remain in the Hickses' employ: when they left Rome for Central Asia he had no intention of accompanying them. The part of Mr. Buttles's successor was becoming daily more intolerable to him, for the very reasons that had probably made it most gratifying to Mr. Buttles. To be treated by Mr. and Mrs. Hicks as a paid oracle, a paraded and petted piece of property, was a good deal more distasteful than he could have imagined any relation with these kindly people could be. And since their aspirations had become frankly social he found his task, if easier, yet far less congenial than during his first months with them. He preferred patiently explaining to Mrs. Hicks, for the hundredth time, that Sassanian and Saracenic were not interchangeable terms, to unravelling for her the genealogies of her titled guests, and reminding her, when she "seated" her dinner-parties, that Dukes ranked higher than Princes. No—the job was decidedly intolerable; and he would have to look out for another means of earning his living. But that was not what he had really got away to think about. He knew he should never starve; he had even begun to believe again in his book. What he wanted to think of was Susy—or rather, it was Susy that he could not help thinking of, on whatever train of thought he set out.

Again and again he fancied he had established a truce with the past: had come to terms—the terms of defeat and failure— with that bright enemy called happiness. And, in truth, he had reached the point of definitely knowing that he could never return to the kind of life that he and Susy had embarked on. It had been the tragedy of their relation that loving her roused in him ideals she could never satisfy. He had fallen in love with her because she was, like himself, amused, unprejudiced and disenchanted; and he could not go on loving her unless she ceased to be all these things. From that circle there was no issue, and in it he desperately revolved.

If he had not heard such persistent rumours of her re-marriage to Lord Altringham he might have tried to see her again; but, aware of the danger and the hopelessness of a meeting, he was, on the whole, glad to have a reason for avoiding it. Such, at least, he honestly supposed to be his state of mind until he found himself, as on this occasion, free to follow out his thought to its end. That end, invariably, was Susy; not the bundle of qualities and defects into which his critical spirit had tried to sort her out, but the soft blur of identity, of personality, of eyes, hair, mouth, laugh, tricks of speech and gesture, that were all so solely and profoundly her own, and yet so mysteriously independent of what she might do, say, think, in crucial circumstances. He remembered her once saying to him: "After all, you were right when you wanted me to be your mistress," and the indignant stare of incredulity with which he had answered her. Yet in these hours it was the palpable image of her that clung closest, till, as invariably happened, his vision came full circle, and feeling her on his breast he wanted her also in his soul.

Well—such all-encompassing loves were the rarest of human experiences; he smiled at his presumption in wanting no other. Wearily he turned, and tramped homeward through the winter twilight. . . .

At the door of the hotel he ran across the Prince of Teutoburg's aide-de-camp. They had not met for some days, and Nick had a vague feeling that if the Prince's matrimonial designs took definite shape he himself was not likely, after all, to be their chosen exponent. He had surprised, now and then, a certain distrustful coldness under the Princess Mother's cordial glance, and had concluded that she perhaps suspected him of being an obstacle to her son's aspirations. He had no idea of playing that part, but was not sorry to appear to; for he was sincerely attached to Coral Hicks, and hoped for her a more human fate than that of becoming Prince Anastasius's consort.

This evening, however, he was struck by the beaming alacrity of the aide-de-camp's greeting. Whatever cloud had hung between them had lifted: the Teutoburg clan, for one reason or another, no longer feared or distrusted him. The change was conveyed in a mere hand-pressure, a brief exchange of words, for the aide-de-camp was hastening after a well-known dowager of the old Roman world, whom he helped into a large coronetted brougham which looked as if it had been extracted, for some ceremonial purpose, from a museum of historic vehicles. And in an instant it flashed on Lansing that this lady had been the person chosen to lay the Prince's offer at Miss Hicks's feet.

The discovery piqued him; and instead of making straight for his own room he went up to Mrs. Hicks's drawing-room.

The room was empty, but traces of elaborate tea pervaded it, and an immense bouquet of stiff roses lay on the centre table. As he turned away, Eldorada Tooker flushed and tear-stained, abruptly entered.

"Oh, Mr. Lansing—we were looking everywhere for you."

"Looking for me?"

"Yes. Coral especially . . . she wants to see you. She wants you to come to her own sitting-room."

She led him across the ante-chamber and down the passage to the separate suite which Miss Hicks inhabited. On the threshold Eldorada gasped out emotionally: "You'll find her looking lovely—" and jerked away with a sob as he entered.

Coral Hicks was never lovely: but she certainly looked unusually handsome. Perhaps it was the long dress of black velvet which, outlined against a shaded lamp, made her strong build seem slenderer, or perhaps the slight flush on her dusky cheek: a bloom of womanhood hung upon her which she made no effort to dissemble. Indeed, it was one of her originalities that she always gravely and courageously revealed the utmost of whatever mood possessed her.

"How splendid you look!" he said, smiling at her.

She threw her head back and gazed him straight in the eyes. "That's going to be my future job."

"To look splendid?"

"Yes."

"And wear a crown?"

"And wear a crown. . . ."

They continued to consider each other without speaking. Nick's heart contracted with pity and perplexity.

"Oh, Coral—it's not decided?"

She scrutinized him for a last penetrating moment; then she looked away. "I'm never long deciding."

He hesitated, choking with contradictory impulses, and afraid to formulate any, lest they should either mislead or pain her.

"Why didn't you tell me?" he questioned lamely; and instantly perceived his blunder.

She sat down, and looked up at him under brooding lashes—had he ever noticed the thickness of her lashes before?

"Would it have made any difference if I had told you?"

"Any difference—?"

"Sit down by me," she commanded. "I want to talk to you. You can say now whatever you might have said sooner. I'm not married yet: I'm still free."

"You haven't given your answer?"

"It doesn't matter if I have."

The retort frightened him with the glimpse of what she still expected of him, and what he was still so unable to give.

"That means you've said yes?" he pursued, to gain time.

"Yes or no—it doesn't matter. I had to say something. What I want is your advice."

"At the eleventh hour?"

"Or the twelfth." She paused. "What shall I do?" she questioned, with a sudden accent of helplessness.

He looked at her as helplessly. He could not say: "Ask yourself—ask your parents." Her next word would sweep away such frail hypocrisies. Her "What shall I do?" meant "What are *you* going to do?" and he knew it, and knew that she knew it.

"I'm a bad person to give any one matrimonial advice," he began, with a strained smile; "but I had such a different vision for you."

"What kind of a vision?" She was merciless.

"Merely what people call happiness, dear."

" 'People call'—you see you don't believe in it yourself! Well, neither do I—in that form, at any rate."

He considered. "I believe in trying for it—even if the trying's the best of it."

"Well, I've tried, and failed. And I'm twenty-two, and I never was young. I suppose I haven't enough imagination." She drew a deep breath. "Now I want something different." She appeared to search for the word. "I want to be—prominent," she declared.

"Prominent?"

She reddened swarthily. "Oh, you smile—you think it's ridiculous: it doesn't seem worth while to you. That's because you've always had all those things. But I haven't. I know what father pushed up from, and I want to push up as high again—higher. No, I haven't got much imagination. I've always liked Facts. And I find I shall like the fact of being a Princess—choosing the people I associate with, and being up above all these European grandees that father and mother bow down to, though they think they despise them. You can be up above these people by just being yourself; you know how. But I need a platform—a sky-scraper. Father and mother slaved to give me my education. They thought education was the important thing; but, since we've all three of us got mediocre minds, it has just landed us among mediocre people. Don't you suppose I see through all the sham science and sham art and sham everything we're surrounded with? That's why I want to buy a place at the very top, where I shall be powerful enough to get about me the people I want, the big people, the right people, and to help them. I want to promote culture, like those Renaissance women you're always talking about. I want to do it for Apex City; do you understand? And for father and mother too. I want all those titles carved on my tombstone. *They're* facts, anyhow! Don't laugh at me. . . ." She broke off with one of her clumsy smiles, and moved away from him to the other end of the room.

He sat looking at her with a curious feeling of admiration. Her harsh positivism was like a tonic to his disenchanted mood, and he thought: "What a pity!"

Aloud he said: "I don't feel like laughing at you. You're a great woman."

"Then I shall be a great Princess."

"Oh—but you might have been something so much greater!"

Her face flamed again. "Don't say that!"

He stood up involuntarily, and drew near her.

"Why not?"

"Because you're the only man with whom I can imagine the other kind of greatness."

It moved him—moved him unexpectedly. He got as far as saying to himself: "Good God, if she were not so hideously rich—" and then of yielding for a moment to the persuasive vision of all that he and she might do with those very riches which he dreaded. After all, there was nothing mean in her ideals—they were hard and material, in keeping with her primitive and massive person; but they had a certain grim nobility. And when she spoke of "the other kind of greatness" he knew that she understood what she was talking of, and was not merely saying something to draw him on, to get him to commit himself. There was not a drop of guile in her, except that which her very honesty distilled.

"The other kind of greatness?" he repeated.

"Well, isn't that what you said happiness was? I wanted to be happy . . . but one can't choose."

He went up to her. "No, one can't choose. And how can anyone give you happiness who hasn't got it himself?" He took her hands, feeling how large, muscular and voluntary they were, even as they melted in his palms.

"My poor Coral, of what use can I ever be to you? What you need is to be loved."

She drew back and gave him one of her straight strong glances: "No," she said gallantly, "but just to love."

PART III

Chapter XXV

I N the persistent drizzle of a Paris winter morning Susy Lansing walked back alone from the school at which she had just deposited the four eldest Fulmers to the little house in Passy where, for the last two months, she had been living with them.

She had on ready-made boots, an old waterproof and a last year's hat; but none of these facts disturbed her, though she took no particular pride in them. The truth was that she was too busy to think much about them. Since she had assumed the charge of the Fulmer children, in the absence of both their parents in Italy, she had had to pass through such an arduous apprenticeship of motherhood that every moment of her waking hours was packed with things to do at once, and other things to remember to do later. There were only five Fulmers; but at times they were like an army with banners, and their power of self-multiplication was equalled only by the manner in which they could dwindle, vanish, grow mute, and become as it were a single tumbled brown head bent over a book in some corner of the house in which nobody would ever have thought of hunting for them—and which, of course, were it the *bonne's* room in the attic, or the subterranean closet where the trunks were kept, had been singled out by them for that very reason.

These changes from ubiquity to invisibility would have seemed to Susy, a few months earlier, one of the most maddening of many characteristics not calculated to promote repose. But now she felt differently. She had grown interested in her charges, and the search for a clue to their methods, whether tribal or individual, was as exciting to her as the development of a detective story.

What interested her most in the whole stirring business was the discovery that they *had* a method. These little creatures, pitched upward into experience on the tossing waves of their parents' agitated lives, had managed to establish a rough-and-ready system of self-government. Junie, the eldest (the one who already chose her mother's hats, and tried to put order in her wardrobe) was the recognized head of the state. At twelve she knew lots of things which her mother had never thoroughly learned, and Susy, her temporary mother, had never even guessed at: she spoke with authority on all vital subjects, from castor-oil to flannel under-clothes, from the fair sharing of stamps or marbles to the number of helpings of rice-pudding or jam which each child was entitled to.

There was hardly any appeal from her verdict; yet each of her subjects revolved in his or her own orbit of independence, according to laws which Junie acknowledged and respected; and the interpreting of this mysterious charter of rights and privileges had not been without difficulty for Susy.

Besides this, there were material difficulties to deal with. The six of them, and the breathless *bonne* who cooked and slaved for them all, had but a slim budget to live on; and, as Junie remarked, you'd have thought the boys ate their shoes, the way they vanished. They ate, certainly, a great deal else, and mostly of a nourishing and expensive kind. They had definite views about the amount and quality of their food, and were capable of concerted rebellion when Susy's catering fell beneath their standard. All this made her life a hurried and harassing business, but never—what she had most feared it would be—a dull or depressing one.

It was not, she owned to herself, that the society of the Fulmer children had roused in her any abstract passion for the human young. She knew—had known since Nick's first kiss—how she would love any child of his and hers; and she had cherished poor little Clarissa Vanderlyn with a shrinking and wistful solicitude. But in these rough young Fulmers she took a positive delight, and for reasons that were increasingly clear to her. It was because, in the first place, they were all intelligent; and because their intelligence had been fed only on things worth caring for. However inadequate Grace Fulmer's bringing-up of her increasing tribe had been, they had heard in her company nothing trivial or dull: good music, good books and good talk had been their daily food, and if at times they stamped and roared and crashed about like children unblessed by such privileges, at others they shone with the light of poetry and spoke with the voice of wisdom.

That had been Susy's discovery: for the first time she was among awakening minds which had been wakened only to beauty. From their cramped and uncomfortable household Grace and Nat Fulmer had managed to keep out mean envies, vulgar admirations, shabby discontents; above all the din and confusion the great images of beauty had brooded, like those ancestral figures that stood apart on their shelf in the poorest Roman households.

No, the task she had undertaken for want of a better gave Susy no sense of a missed vocation: "mothering" on a large scale would never, she perceived, be her job. Rather it gave her, in odd ways, the sense of being herself mothered, of taking her first steps in the life of immaterial values which had begun to seem so much more substantial than any she had known.

On the day when she had gone to Grace Fulmer for counsel and comfort she had little guessed that they would come to her in this form. She had found her friend, more than ever distracted and yet buoyant, riding the large untidy waves of her life with the splashed ease of an amphibian. Grace was probably the only person among Susy's friends who could have understood why she could not make up her mind to marry Altringham; but at the moment Grace was too much absorbed in her own problems to pay much attention to her friend's, and, according to her wont, she immediately "unpacked" her difficulties.

Nat was not getting what she had hoped out of his European opportunity. Oh, she was enough of an artist herself to know that there must be fallow periods—that the impact of new impressions seldom produced immediate results. She had allowed for all that. But her past experience of Nat's moods had taught her to know just when he was assimilating, when impressions were fructifying in him. And now they were not, and he knew it as well as she did. There had been too much rushing about, too much excitement and sterile flattery . . . Mrs. Melrose? Well, yes, for a while . . . the trip to Spain had been a love-journey, no doubt. Grace spoke calmly, but the lines of her face sharpened: she had suffered, oh horribly, at his going to Spain without her. Yet she couldn't, for the children's sake, afford to miss the big sum that Ursula Gillow had given her for her fortnight at Ruan. And her playing had struck people, and led, on the way back, to two or three profitable engagements in private houses in London. Fashionable society had made "a little fuss" about her, and it had surprised and pleased Nat, and given her a new importance in his eyes. "He was beginning to forget that I wasn't only a nursery-maid, and it's been a good thing for him to be reminded . . . but the great thing is that with what I've earned he and I can go off to southern Italy and Sicily for three months. You know I know how to manage . . . and, alone with me, Nat will settle down to work: to observing, feeling, soaking things in. It's the only way. Mrs. Melrose wants to take him, to pay all the expenses again—well she shan't. *I'll* pay them." Her worn cheek flushed with triumph. "And you'll see what wonders will come of it. . . . Only there's the problem of the children. Junie quite agrees that we can't take them. . . ."

Thereupon she had unfolded her idea. If Susy was at a loose end, and hard up, why shouldn't she take charge of the children while their parents were in Italy? For three months at most—Grace could promise it shouldn't be longer. They couldn't pay her much, of course, but at least she would be lodged and fed. "And, you know, it will end by interesting you—I'm sure it will," the mother concluded, her irrepressible hopefulness rising even to this height, while Susy stood before her with a hesitating smile.

Take care of five Fulmers for three months! The prospect cowed her. If there had been only Junie and Geordie, the oldest and youngest of the band, she might have felt less hesitation. But there was Nat, the second in age, whose motor-horn had driven her and Nick out to the hill-side on their fatal day at the Fulmers' and there were the twins, Jack and Peggy, of whom she had kept memories almost equally disquieting. To rule this uproarious tribe would be a sterner business than trying to beguile Clarissa Vanderlyn's ladylike leisure; and she would have refused on the spot, as she had refused once before, if the only possible alternatives had not come to seem so much less bearable, and if Junie, called in for advice, and standing there, small, plain and competent, had not said in her quiet grown-up voice: "Oh, yes, I'm sure Mrs. Lansing and I can manage while you're away—especially if she reads aloud well."

Reads aloud well! The stipulation had enchanted Susy. She had never before known children who cared to be read aloud to;

she remembered with a shiver her attempts to interest Clarissa in anything but gossip and the fashions, and the tone in which the child had said, showing Strefford's trinket to her father: "Because I said I'd rather have it than a book."

And here were children who consented to be left for three months by their parents, but on condition that a good reader was provided for them!

"Very well—I will! But what shall I be expected to read to you?" she had gaily questioned; and Junie had answered, after one of her sober pauses of reflection: "The little ones like nearly everything; but Nat and I want poetry particularly, because if we read it to ourselves we so often pronounce the puzzling words wrong, and then it sounds so horrid."

"Oh, I hope I shall pronounce them right," Susy murmured, stricken with self-distrust and humility.

Apparently she did; for her reading was a success, and even the twins and Geordie, once they had grown used to her, seemed to prefer a ringing page of Henry V, or the fairy scenes from the Midsummer Night's Dream, to their own more specialized literature, though that had also at times to be provided.

There were, in fact, no lulls in her life with the Fulmers; but its commotions seemed to Susy less meaningless, and therefore less fatiguing, than those that punctuated the existence of people like Altringham, Ursula Gillow, Ellie Vanderlyn and their train; and the noisy uncomfortable little house at Passy was beginning to greet her with the eyes of home when she returned there after her tramps to and from the children's classes. At any rate she had the sense of doing something useful and even necessary, and of earning her own keep, though on so modest a scale; and when the children were in their quiet mood, and demanded books or music (or, even, on one occasion, at the surprising Junie's instigation, a collective visit to the Louvre, where they recognized the most unlikely pictures, and the two elders emitted startling technical judgments, and called their companion's attention to details she had not observed); on these occasions, Susy had a surprised sense of being drawn back into her brief life with Nick, or even still farther and deeper, into those visions of Nick's own childhood on which the trivial later years had heaped their dust.

It was curious to think that if he and she had remained together, and she had had a child—the vision used to come to her, in her sleepless hours, when she looked at little Geordie, in his cot by her bed—their life together might have been very much like the life she was now leading, a small obscure business to the outer world, but to themselves how wide and deep and crowded!

She could not bear, at that moment, the thought of giving up this mystic relation to the life she had missed. In spite of the hurry and fatigue of her days, the shabbiness and discomfort of everything, and the hours when the children were as "horrid" as any other children, and turned a conspiracy of hostile faces to all her appeals; in spite of all this she did not want to give them up, and had decided, when their parents returned, to ask to go back to America with them. Perhaps, if Nat's success continued, and Grace was able to work at her music, they would need a kind of governess-companion. At any rate, she could picture no future less distasteful.

She had not sent to Mr. Spearman Nick's answer to her letter. In the interval between writing to him and receiving his reply she had broken with Strefford; she had therefore no object in seeking her freedom. If Nick wanted his, he knew he had only to ask for it; and his silence, as the weeks passed, woke a faint hope in her. The hope flamed high when she read one day in the newspapers a vague but evidently "inspired" allusion to the possibility of an alliance between his Serene Highness the reigning Prince of Teutoburg-Waldhain and Miss Coral Hicks of Apex City; it sank to ashes when, a few days later, her eye lit on a paragraph wherein Mr. and Mrs. Mortimer Hicks "requested to state" that there was no truth in the report.

On the foundation of these two statements Susy raised one watch-tower of hope after another, feverish edifices demolished or rebuilt by every chance hint from the outer world wherein Nick's name figured with the Hickses'. And still, as the days passed and she heard nothing, either from him or from her lawyer, her flag continued to fly from the quaking structures.

Apart from the custody of the children there was indeed little to distract her mind from these persistent broodings. She winced sometimes at the thought of the ease with which her fashionable friends had let her drop out of sight. In the perpetual purposeless rush of their days, the feverish making of winter plans, hurrying off to the Riviera or St. Moritz, Egypt or New York, there was no time to hunt up the vanished or to wait for the laggard. Had they learned that she had broken her "engagement" (how she hated the word!) to Strefford, and had the fact gone about that she was once more only a poor hanger-on, to be taken up when it was convenient, and ignored in the intervals? She did not know; though she fancied Strefford's newly-developed pride would prevent his revealing to any one what had passed between them. For several days after her abrupt flight he had made no sign; and though she longed to write and ask his forgiveness she could not find the words. Finally it was he who wrote: a short note, from Altringham, typical of all that was best in the old Strefford. He had gone down to Altringham, he told her, to think quietly over their last talk, and try to understand what she had been driving at. He had to own that he couldn't; but that, he supposed, was the very head and front of his offending. Whatever he had done to displease her, he was sorry for; but he asked, in view of his invincible ignorance, to be allowed not to regard his offence as a cause for a final break. The possibility of that, he found, would make him even more unhappy than he had foreseen; as she knew, his own happiness had always been his first object in life, and he therefore begged her to suspend her decision a little longer. He expected to be in Paris within another two months, and before arriving he would write again, and ask her to see him.

The letter moved her but did not make her waver. She simply wrote that she was touched by his kindness, and would willingly see him if he came to Paris later; though she was bound to tell him that she had not yet changed her mind, and did not believe it would promote his happiness to have her try to do so.

He did not reply to this, and there was nothing further to keep her thoughts from revolving endlessly about her inmost hopes and fears.

On the rainy afternoon in question, tramping home from the "*cours*" (to which she was to return at six), she had said to herself that it was two months that very day since Nick had known she was ready to release him—and that after such a delay he was not likely to take any further steps. The thought filled her with a vague ecstasy. She had had to fix an arbitrary date as the term of her anguish, and she had fixed that one; and behold she was justified. For what could his silence mean but that he too. . . .

On the hall-table lay a typed envelope with the Paris postage-mark. She opened it carelessly, and saw that the letter-head bore Mr. Spearman's office address. The words beneath spun round before her eyes. . . . "Has notified us that he is at your disposal . . . carry out your wishes . . . arriving in Paris . . . fix an appointment with his lawyers . . ."

Nick—it was Nick the words were talking of! It was the fact of Nick's return to Paris that was being described in those prepos-terous terms! She sank down on the bench beside the dripping umbrella-stand and stared vacantly before her. It had fallen at last—this blow in which she now saw that she had never really believed! And yet she had imagined she was prepared for it, had expected it, was already planning her future life in view of it—an effaced impersonal life in the service of somebody else's children—when, in reality, under that thin surface of abnega-tion and acceptance, all the old hopes had been smouldering red-hot in their ashes! What was the use of any self-discipline, any philosophy, any experience, if the lawless self underneath could in an instant consume them like tinder?

She tried to collect herself—to understand what had hap-pened. Nick was coming to Paris—coming not to see her but to consult his lawyer! It meant, of course, that he had definitely resolved to claim his freedom; and that, if he had made up his mind to this final step, after more than six months of inaction and seeming indifference, it could be only because something unforeseen and decisive had happened to him. Feverishly, she put together again the stray scraps of gossip and the news-paper paragraphs that had reached her in the last months. It was evident that Miss Hicks's projected marriage with the Prince of Teutoburg-Waldhain had been broken off at the last moment; and broken off because she intended to marry Nick. The announcement of his arrival in Paris and the publication of Mr. and Mrs. Hicks's formal denial of their daughter's betrothal coincided too closely to admit of any other inference. Susy tried to grasp the reality of these assembled facts, to picture to herself their actual tangible results. She thought of Coral Hicks bearing the name of Mrs. Nick Lansing—*her* name, Susy's own!—and entering drawing-rooms with Nick in her wake, gaily welcomed by the very people who, a few months before, had welcomed Susy with the same warmth. In spite of Nick's growing dislike of society, and Coral's attitude of intellectual superiority, their wealth would fatally draw them back into the world to which Nick was attached by all his habits and associations. And no doubt it would amuse him to re-enter that world as a dispenser of hospitality, to play the part of host where he had so long been a guest; just as Susy had once fancied it would amuse her to re-enter it as Lady Altringham. . . . But, try as she would, now that the reality was so close on her, she could not visualize it or relate it to herself. The mere juxtaposition of the two names—Coral, Nick—which in old times she had so often laughingly coupled, now produced a blur in her brain.

She continued to sit helplessly beside the hall-table, the tears running down her cheeks. The appearance of the *bonne* aroused her. Her youngest charge, Geordie, had been feverish for a day or two; he was better, but still confined to the nursery, and he had heard Susy unlock the house-door, and could not imagine why she had not come straight up to him. He now began to manifest his indignation in a series of racking howls, and Susy, shaken out of her trance, dropped her cloak and umbrella and hurried up.

"Oh, that child!" she groaned.

Under the Fulmer roof there was little time or space for the indulgence of private sorrows. From morning till night there was always some immediate practical demand on one's attention; and Susy was beginning to see how, in contracted households, children may play a part less romantic but not less useful than that assigned to them in fiction, through the mere fact of giving their parents no leisure to dwell on irremediable grievances. Though her own apprenticeship to family life had been so short, she had already acquired the knack of rapid mental readjustment, and as she hurried up to the nursery her private cares were dispelled by a dozen problems of temperature, diet and medicine.

Such readjustment was of course only momentary; yet each time it happened it seemed to give her more firmness and flexibility of temper. "What a child I was myself six months ago!"

she thought, wondering that Nick's influence, and the tragedy of their parting, should have done less to mature and steady her than these few weeks in a house full of children.

Pacifying Geordie was not easy, for he had long since learned to use his grievances as a pretext for keeping the offender at his beck with a continuous supply of stories, songs and games. "You'd better be careful never to put yourself in the wrong with Geordie," the astute Junie had warned Susy at the outset, "because he's got such a memory, and he won't make it up with you till you've told him every fairy-tale he's ever heard before."

But on this occasion, as soon as he saw her, Geordie's indignation melted. She was still in the doorway, compunctious, abject and racking her dazed brain for his favourite stories, when she saw, by the smoothing out of his mouth and the sudden serenity of his eyes, that he was going to give her the delicious but not wholly reassuring shock of being a good boy.

Thoughtfully he examined her face as she knelt down beside the cot; then he poked out a finger and pressed it on her tearful cheek.

"Poor Susy got a pain too," he said, putting his arms about her; and as she hugged him close, he added philosophically: "Tell Geordie a new story, darling, and 'oo'll forget all about it."

Chapter XXVI

N ICK LANSING arrived in Paris two days after his lawyer had announced his coming to Mr. Spearman.

He had left Rome with the definite purpose of freeing himself and Susy; and though he was not pledged to Coral Hicks he had not concealed from her the object of his journey. In vain had he tried to rouse in himself any sense of interest in his own future. Beyond the need of reaching a definite point in his relation to Susy his imagination could not travel. But he had been moved by Coral's confession, and his reason told him that he and she would probably be happy together, with the temperate happiness based on a community of tastes and an enlargement of opportunities. He meant, on his return to Rome, to ask her to marry him; and he knew that she knew it. Indeed, if he had not spoken before leaving it was with no idea of evading his fate, or keeping her longer in suspense, but simply because of the strange apathy that had fallen on him since he had received Susy's letter. In his incessant self-communings he dressed up this apathy as a discretion which forbade his engaging Coral's future till his own was assured. But in truth he knew that Coral's future was already engaged, and his with it: in Rome the fact had seemed natural and even inevitable.

In Paris, it instantly became the thinnest of unrealities. Not because Paris was not Rome, nor because it was Paris; but because hidden away somewhere in that vast unheeding labyrinth was the half-forgotten part of himself that was Susy. . . . For weeks, for months past, his mind had been saturated with Susy: she had never seemed more insistently near him than as their separation lengthened, and the chance of reunion became less probable. It was as if a sickness long smouldering in him had broken out and become acute, enveloping him in the Nessus-shirt of his memories. There were moments when, to his memory, their actual embraces seemed perfunctory, accidental, compared with this deep deliberate imprint of her soul on his.

Yet now it had become suddenly different. Now that he was in the same place with her, and might at any moment run across her, meet her eyes, hear her voice, avoid her hand—now that

penetrating ghost of her with which he had been living was
sucked back into the shadows, and he seemed, for the first time
since their parting, to be again in her actual presence. He woke
to the fact on the morning of his arrival, staring down from his
hotel window on a street she would perhaps walk through that
very day, and over a limitless huddle of roofs, one of which covered her at that hour. The abruptness of the transition startled
him; he had not known that her mere geographical nearness
would take him by the throat in that way. What would it be,
then, if she were to walk into the room?

Thank heaven that need never happen! He was sufficiently
informed as to French divorce proceedings to know that they
would not necessitate a confrontation with his wife; and with
ordinary luck, and some precautions, he might escape even
a distant glimpse of her. He did not mean to remain in Paris
more than a few days; and during that time it would be easy—
knowing, as he did, her tastes and Altringham's—to avoid the
places where she was likely to be met. He did not know where
she was living, but imagined her to be staying with Mrs. Melrose, or some other rich friend, or else lodged, in prospective
affluence, at the Nouveau Luxe, or in a pretty flat of her own.
Trust Susy—ah, the pang of it—to "manage"!

His first visit was to his lawyer's; and as he walked through
the familiar streets each approaching face, each distant figure
seemed hers. The obsession was intolerable. It would not last,
of course; but meanwhile he had the exposed sense of a fugitive
in a nightmare, who feels himself the only creature visible in
a ghostly and besetting multitude. The eye of the metropolis
seemed fixed on him in an immense unblinking stare.

At the lawyer's he was told that, as a first step to freedom, he
must secure a domicile in Paris. He had of course known of this
necessity: he had seen too many friends through the Divorce
Court, in one country or another, not to be fairly familiar with
the procedure. But the fact presented a different aspect as soon
as he tried to relate it to himself and Susy: it was as though Susy's
personality were a medium through which events still took on a
transfiguring colour. He found the "domicile" that very day: a
tawdrily furnished *rez-de-chaussée*, obviously destined to far different uses. And as he sat there, after the *concierge* had discreetly
withdrawn with the first quarter's payment in her pocket, and

stared about him at the vulgar plushy place, he burst out laughing at what it was about to figure in the eyes of the law: a Home, and a Home desecrated by his own act! The Home in which he and Susy had reared their precarious bliss, and seen it crumble at the brutal touch of his unfaithfulness and his cruelty—for he had been told that he must be cruel to her as well as unfaithful! He looked at the walls hung with sentimental photogravures, at the shiny bronze "nudes," the moth-eaten animal-skins and the bedizened bed—and once more the unreality, the impossibility, of all that was happening to him entered like a drug into his veins.

To rouse himself he stood up, turned the key on the hideous place, and returned to his lawyer's. He knew that in the hard dry atmosphere of the office the act of giving the address of the flat would restore some kind of reality to the phantasmal transaction. And with wonder he watched the lawyer, as a matter of course, pencil the street and the number on one of the papers enclosed in a folder on which his own name was elaborately engrossed.

As he took leave it occurred to him to ask where Susy was living. At least he imagined that it had just occurred to him, and that he was making the enquiry merely as a measure of precaution, in order to know what quarter of Paris to avoid; but in reality the question had been on his lips since he had first entered the office, and lurking in his mind since he had emerged from the railway station that morning. The fact of not knowing where she lived made the whole of Paris a meaningless unintelligible place, as useless to him as the face of a huge clock that has lost its hour hand.

The address in Passy surprised him: he had imagined that she would be somewhere in the neighborhood of the Champs Elysées or the Place de l'Etoile. But probably either Mrs. Melrose or Ellie Vanderlyn had taken a house at Passy. Well—it was something of a relief to know that she was so far off. No business called him to that almost suburban region beyond the Trocadéro, and there was much less chance of meeting her than if she had been in the centre of Paris.

All day he wandered, avoiding the fashionable quarters, the streets in which private motors glittered five deep, and furred and feathered silhouettes glided from them into tea-rooms, picture-galleries and jewellers' shops. In some such scenes Susy was no doubt figuring: slenderer, finer, vivider, than the other images of clay, but imitating their gestures, chattering their jargon, winding her hand among the same pearls and sables. He struck away across the Seine, along the quays to the Cité, the net-work of old Paris, the great grey vaults of St. Eustache, the swarming streets of the Marais. He gazed at monuments, dawdled before shop windows, sat in squares and on quays, watching people bargain, argue, philander, quarrel, work-girls stroll past in linked bands, beggars whine on the bridges, derelicts doze in the pale winter sun, mothers in mourning hasten by taking children to school, and street-walkers beat their weary rounds before the cafés.

The day drifted on. Toward evening he began to grow afraid of his solitude, and to think of dining at the Nouveau Luxe, or some other fashionable restaurant where he would be fairly sure to meet acquaintances, and be carried off to a theatre, a *boîte* or a dancing-hall. Anything, anything now, to get away from the maddening round of his thoughts. He felt the same blank fear of solitude as months ago in Genoa. . . . Even if he were to run across Susy and Altringham, what of it? Better get the job over. People had long since ceased to take on tragedy airs about divorce: dividing couples dined together to the last, and met afterward in each other's houses, happy in the consciousness that their respective remarriages had provided two new centres of entertainment. Yet most of the couples who took their re-matings so philosophically had doubtless had their hour of enchantment, of belief in the immortality of loving; whereas he and Susy had simply and frankly entered into a business contract for their mutual advantage. The fact gave the last touch of incongruity to his agonies and exaltations, and made him appear to himself as grotesque and superannuated as the hero of a romantic novel.

He stood up from a bench on which he had been lounging in the Luxembourg gardens, and hailed a taxi. Dusk had fallen, and he meant to go back to his hotel, take a rest, and then go out to dine. But instead, he threw Susy's address to the driver, and settled down in the cab, resting both hands on the knob of his umbrella and staring straight ahead of him as if he were accomplishing some tiresome duty that had to be got through with before he could turn his mind to more important things.

"It's the easiest way," he heard himself say.

At the street-corner—her street-corner—he stopped the cab, and stood motionless while it rattled away. It was a short vague street, much farther off than he had expected, and fading away at the farther end in a dusky blur of hoardings overhung by trees. A thin rain was beginning to fall, and it was already night in this inadequately lit suburban quarter. Lansing walked down the empty street. The houses stood a few yards apart, with bare-twigged shrubs between, and gates and railings dividing them from the pavement. He could not, at first, distinguish their numbers; but presently, coming abreast of a street-lamp, he discovered that the small shabby façade it illuminated was precisely the one he sought. The discovery surprised him. He had imagined that, as frequently happened in the outlying quarters of Passy and La Muette, the mean street would lead to a stately private hotel, built upon some bowery fragment of an old country-place. It was the latest whim of the wealthy to establish themselves on these outskirts of Paris, where there was still space for verdure; and he had pictured Susy behind some pillared house-front, with lights pouring across glossy turf to sculptured gateposts. Instead, he saw a six-windowed house, huddled among neighbours of its kind, with the family wash fluttering between meagre bushes. The arc-light beat ironically on its front, which had the worn look of a tired workwoman's face; and Lansing, as he leaned against the opposite railing, vainly tried to fit his vision of Susy into so humble a setting.

The probable explanation was that his lawyer had given him the wrong address; not only the wrong number but the wrong street. He pulled out the slip of paper, and was crossing over to decipher it under the lamp, when an errand-boy appeared out of the obscurity, and approached the house. Nick drew back, and the boy, unlatching the gate, ran up the steps and gave the bell a pull.

Almost immediately the door opened; and there stood Susy, the light full upon her, and upon a red-cheeked child against her shoulder. The space behind them was dark, or so dimly lit that it formed a black background to her vivid figure. She looked

at the errand-boy without surprise, took his parcel, and after
he had turned away, lingered a moment in the door, glancing
down the empty street.

That moment, to her watcher, seemed quicker than a flash yet
as long as a life-time. There she was, a stone's throw away, but
utterly unconscious of his presence: his Susy, the old Susy, and
yet a new Susy, curiously transformed, transfigured almost, by
the new attitude in which he beheld her.

In the first shock of the vision he forgot his surprise at her
being in such a place, forgot to wonder whose house she was
in, or whose was the sleepy child in her arms. For an instant she
stood out from the blackness behind her, and through the veil
of the winter night, a thing apart, an unconditioned vision, the
eternal image of the woman and the child; and in that instant
everything within him was changed and renewed. His eyes
were still absorbing her, finding again the familiar curves of her
light body, noting the thinness of the lifted arm that upheld the
little boy, the droop of the shoulder he weighed on, the brooding way in which her cheek leaned to his even while she looked
away; then she drew back, the door closed, and the street-lamp
again shone on blankness.

"But she's mine!" Nick cried, in a fierce triumph of
recovery. . . .

His eyes were so full of her that he shut them to hold in the
crowding vision.

It remained with him, at first, as a complete picture; then
gradually it broke up into its component parts, the child
vanished, the strange house vanished, and Susy alone stood
before him, his own Susy, only his Susy, yet changed, worn,
tempered—older, even—with sharper shadows under the cheek-
bones, the brows drawn, the joint of the slim wrist more prominent. It was not thus that his memory had evoked her, and he
recalled, with a remorseful pang, the fact that something in
her look, her dress, her tired and drooping attitude, suggested
poverty, dependence, seemed to make her after all a part of the
shabby house in which, at first sight, her presence had seemed
so incongruous.

"But she looks *poor*!" he thought, his heart tightening. And
instantly it occurred to him that these must be the Fulmer children whom she was living with while their parents travelled in

Italy. Rumours of Nat Fulmer's sudden ascension had reached him, and he had heard that the couple had lately been seen in Naples and Palermo. No one had mentioned Susy's name in connection with them, and he could hardly tell why he had arrived at this conclusion, except perhaps because it seemed natural that, if Susy were in trouble, she should turn to her old friend Grace.

But why in trouble? What trouble? What could have happened to check her triumphant career?

"That's what I mean to find out!" he exclaimed.

His heart was beating with a tumult of new hopes and old memories. The sight of his wife, so remote in mien and manner from the world in which he had imagined her to be re-absorbed, changed in a flash his own relation to life, and flung a mist of unreality over all that he had been trying to think most solid and tangible. Nothing now was substantial to him but the stones of the street in which he stood, the front of the house which hid her, the bell-handle he already felt in his grasp. He started forward, and was halfway to the threshold when a private motor turned the corner, the twin glitter of its lamps carpeting the wet street with gold to Susy's door.

Lansing drew back into the shadow as the motor swept up to the house. A man jumped out, and the light fell on Strefford's shambling figure, its lazy disjointed movements so unmistakably the same under his fur coat, and in the new setting of prosperity.

Lansing stood motionless, staring at the door. Strefford rang, and waited. Would Susy appear again? Perhaps she had done so before only because she had been on the watch. . . .

But no: after a slight delay a *bonne* appeared—the breathless maid-of-all-work of a busy household—and at once effaced herself, letting the visitor in. Lansing was sure that not a word passed between the two, of enquiry on Lord Altringham's part, or of acquiescence on the servant's. There could be no doubt that he was expected.

The door closed on him, and a light appeared behind the blind of the adjoining window. The maid had shown the visitor into the sitting-room and lit the lamp. Upstairs, meanwhile, Susy was no doubt running skilful fingers through her tumbled hair and daubing her pale lips with red. Ah, how Lansing knew every movement of that familiar rite, even to the pucker of the brow and the pouting thrust-out of the lower lip! He was seized with a sense of physical sickness as the succession of remembered gestures pressed upon his eyes. . . . And the other man? The other man, inside the house, was perhaps at that very instant smiling over the remembrance of the same scene!

At the thought, Lansing plunged away into the night.

Chapter XXVII

SUSY and Lord Altringham sat in the little drawing-room, divided from each other by a table carrying a smoky lamp and heaped with tattered school-books.

In another half hour the *bonne*, despatched to fetch the children from their classes, would be back with her flock; and at any moment Geordie's imperious cries might summon his slave up to the nursery. In the scant time allotted them, the two sat, and visibly wondered what to say.

Strefford, on entering, had glanced about the dreary room, with its piano laden with tattered music, the children's toys littering the lame sofa, the bunches of dyed grass and impaled butterflies flanking the cast-bronze clock. Then he had turned to Susy and asked simply: "Why on earth are you here?"

She had not tried to explain; from the first, she had understood the impossibility of doing so. And she would not betray her secret longing to return to Nick, now that she knew that Nick had taken definite steps for his release. In dread lest Strefford should have heard of this, and should announce it to her, coupling it with the news of Nick's projected marriage, and lest, hearing her fears thus substantiated, she should lose her self-control, she had preferred to say, in a voice that she tried to make indifferent: "The 'proceedings,' or whatever the lawyers call them, have begun. While they're going on I like to stay quite by myself. . . . I don't know why. . . ."

Strefford, at that, had looked at her keenly. "Ah," he murmured; and his lips were twisted into their old mocking smile. "Speaking of proceedings," he went on carelessly, "what stage have Ellie's reached, I wonder? I saw her and Vanderlyn and Bockheimer all lunching cheerfully together to-day at Larue's."

The blood rushed to Susy's forehead. She remembered her tragic evening with Nelson Vanderlyn, only two months earlier, and thought to herself: "In time, then, I suppose, Nick and I. . . ."

Aloud she said: "I can't imagine how Nelson and Ellie can ever want to see each other again. And in a restaurant, of all places!"

Strefford continued to smile. "My dear, you're incorrigibly old-fashioned. Why should two people who've done each other the best turn they could by getting out of each other's way at the right moment behave like sworn enemies ever afterward? It's too absurd; the humbug's too flagrant. Whatever our generation has failed to do, it's got rid of humbug; and that's enough to immortalize it. I daresay Nelson and Ellie never liked each other better than they do to-day. Twenty years ago, they'd have been afraid to confess it; but why shouldn't they now?"

Susy looked at Strefford, conscious that under his words was the ache of the disappointment she had caused him; and yet conscious also that that very ache was not the overwhelming penetrating emotion he perhaps wished it to be, but a pang on a par with a dozen others; and that even while he felt it he foresaw the day when he should cease to feel it. And she thought to herself that this certainty of oblivion must be bitterer than any certainty of pain.

A silence had fallen between them. He broke it by rising from his seat, and saying with a shrug: "You'll end by driving me to marry Joan Senechal."

Susy smiled. "Well, why not? She's lovely."

"Yes; but she'll bore me."

"Poor Streff! So should I—"

"Perhaps. But nothing like as soon—" He grinned sardonically. "There'd be more margin." He appeared to wait for her to speak. "And what else on earth are *you* going to do?" he concluded, as she still remained silent.

"Oh, Streff, I couldn't marry you for a reason like that!" she murmured at length.

"Then marry me, and find your reason afterward."

Her lips made a movement of denial, and still in silence she held out her hand for good-bye. He clasped it, and then turned away; but on the threshold he paused, his screwed-up eyes fixed on her wistfully.

The look moved her, and she added hurriedly: "The only reason I can find is one for *not* marrying you. It's because I can't yet feel unmarried enough."

"Unmarried enough? But I thought Nick was doing his best to make you feel that."

"Yes. But even when he has—sometimes I think even that won't make any difference."

He still scrutinized her hesitatingly, with the gravest eyes she had ever seen in his careless face.

"My dear, that's rather the way I feel about you," he said simply as he turned to go.

That evening after the children had gone to bed Susy sat up late in the cheerless sitting-room. She was not thinking of Strefford but of Nick. He was coming to Paris—perhaps he had already arrived. The idea that he might be in the same place with her at that very moment, and without her knowing it, was so strange and painful that she felt a violent revolt of all her strong and joy-loving youth. Why should she go on suffering so unbearably, so abjectly, so miserably? If only she could see him, hear his voice, even hear him say again such cruel and humiliating words as he had spoken on that dreadful day in Venice—even that would be better than this blankness, this utter and final exclusion from his life! He had been cruel to her, unimaginably cruel: hard, arrogant, unjust; and had been so, perhaps, deliberately, because he already wanted to be free. But she was ready to face even that possibility, to humble herself still farther than he had humbled her—she was ready to do anything, if only she might see him once again.

She leaned her aching head on her hands and pondered. Do anything? But what could she do? Nothing that should hurt him, interfere with his liberty, be false to the spirit of their pact: on that she was more than ever resolved. She had made a bargain, and she meant to stick to it, not for any abstract reason, but simply because she happened to love him in that way. Yes—but to see him again, only once!

Suddenly she remembered what Strefford had said about Nelson Vanderlyn and his wife. "Why should two people who've just done each other the best turn they could behave like sworn enemies ever after?" If in offering Nick his freedom she had indeed done him such a service as that, perhaps he no longer hated her, would no longer be unwilling to see her. . . . At any rate, why should she not write to him on that assumption, write in a spirit of simple friendliness, suggesting that they should meet and "settle things"? The business-like word "settle" (how she hated it) would prove to him that she had no secret designs upon his liberty; and besides he was too unprejudiced, too modern, too free from what Strefford called humbug, not to understand and accept such a suggestion. After all, perhaps Strefford was right; it was something to have rid human relations of hypocrisy, even if, in the process, so many exquisite things seemed somehow to have been torn away with it. . . .

She ran up to her room, scribbled a note, and hurried with it through the rain and darkness to the post-box at the corner. As she returned through the empty street she had an odd feeling that it was not empty—that perhaps Nick was already there, somewhere near her in the night, about to follow her to the door, enter the house, go up with her to her bedroom in the old way. It was strange how close he had been brought by the mere fact of her having written that little note to him!

In the bedroom, Geordie lay in his crib in ruddy slumber, and she blew out the candle and undressed softly for fear of waking him.

Nick Lansing, the next day, received Susy's letter, transmitted to his hotel from the lawyer's office.

He read it carefully, two or three times over, weighing and scrutinizing the guarded words. She proposed that they should meet to "settle things." What things? And why should he accede to such a request? What secret purpose had prompted her? It was horrible that nowadays, in thinking of Susy, he should always suspect ulterior motives, be meanly on the watch for some hidden tortuousness. What on earth was she trying to "manage" now, he wondered?

A few hours ago, at the sight of her, all his hardness had melted, and he had charged himself with cruelty, with injustice, with every sin of pride against himself and her; but the appearance of Strefford, arriving at that late hour, and so evidently expected and welcomed, had driven back the rising tide of tenderness.

Yet, after all, what was there to wonder at? Nothing was changed in their respective situations. He had left his wife, deliberately, and for reasons which no subsequent experience had caused him to modify. She had apparently acquiesced in his decision, and had utilized it, as she was justified in doing, to assure her own future.

In all this, what was there to wail or knock the breast between two people who prided themselves on looking facts in the face, and making their grim best of them, without vain repinings? He had been right in thinking their marriage an act of madness. Her charms had overruled his judgment, and they had had their year . . . their mad year . . . or at least all but two or three months of it. But his first intuition had been right; and now they must both pay for their madness. The Fates seldom forget the bargains made with them, or fail to ask for compound interest. Why not, then, now that the time had come, pay up gallantly, and remember of the episode only what had made it seem so supremely worth the cost?

He sent a pneumatic telegram to Mrs. Nicholas Lansing to say that he would call on her that afternoon at four. "That ought to give us time," he reflected drily, "to 'settle things,' as she calls it, without interfering with Strefford's afternoon visit."

Chapter XXVIII

H ER husband's note had briefly said:
"To-day at four o'clock. N. L."

All day she pored over the words in an agony of longing,
trying to read into them regret, emotion, memories, some echo
of the tumult in her own bosom. But she had signed "Susy," and
he signed "N. L." That seemed to put an abyss between them.
After all, she was free and he was not. Perhaps, in view of his
situation, she had only increased the distance between them by
her unconventional request for a meeting.

She sat in the little drawing-room, and the cast-bronze clock
ticked out the minutes. She would not look out of the window:
it might bring bad luck to watch for him. And it seemed to
her that a thousand invisible spirits, hidden demons of good
and evil, pressed about her, spying out her thoughts, counting
her heart-beats, ready to pounce upon the least symptom of
over-confidence and turn it deftly to derision. Oh, for an altar
on which to pour out propitiatory offerings! But what sweeter
could they have than her smothered heart-beats, her choked-
back tears?

The bell rang, and she stood up as if a spring had jerked her to
her feet. In the mirror between the dried grasses her face looked
long pale inanimate. Ah, if he should find her too changed—!
If there were but time to dash upstairs and put on a touch of
red. . . .

The door opened; it shut on him; he was there.

He said: "You wanted to see me—"

She answered: "Yes." And her heart seemed to stop beating.

At first she could not make out what mysterious change
had come over him, and why it was that in looking at him she
seemed to be looking at a stranger; then she perceived that his
voice sounded as it used to sound when he was talking to other
people; and she said to herself, with a sick shiver of understanding, that she had become an "other person" to him.

There was a deathly pause; then she faltered out, not knowing
what she said: "Nick—you'll sit down?"

He said: "Thanks," but did not seem to have heard her, for he continued to stand motionless, half the room between them. And slowly the uselessness, the hopelessness of his being there overcame her. A wall of granite seemed to have built itself up between them. She felt as if it hid her from him, as if with those remote new eyes of his he were staring into the wall and not at her. Suddenly she said to herself: "He's suffering more than I am, because he pities me, and is afraid to tell me that he is going to be married."

The thought stung her pride, and she lifted her head and met his eyes with a smile.

"Don't you think," she said, "it's more sensible—with everything so changed in our lives—that we should meet as friends, in this way? I wanted to tell you that you needn't feel—feel in the least unhappy about me."

A deep flush rose to his forehead. "Oh, I know—I know that—" he declared hastily; and added, with a factitious animation: "But thank you for telling me."

"There's nothing, is there," she continued, "to make our meeting in this way in the least embarrassing or painful to either of us, when both have found. . . ." She broke off, and held her hand out to him. "I've heard about you and Coral," she ended.

He just touched her hand with cold fingers, and let it drop. "Thank you," he said for the third time.

"You won't sit down?"

He sat down.

"Don't you think," she continued, "that the new way of . . . of meeting as friends . . . and talking things over without ill-will . . . is much pleasanter and more sensible, after all?"

He smiled. "It's immensely kind of you—to feel that."

"Oh, I do feel it!" She stopped short, and wondered what on earth she had meant to say next, and why she had so abruptly lost the thread of her discourse.

In the pause she heard him cough slightly and clear his throat. "Let me say, then," he began, "that I'm glad too—immensely glad that your own future is so satisfactorily settled."

She lifted her glance again to his walled face, in which not a muscle stirred.

"Yes: it—it makes everything easier for you, doesn't it?"

"For you too, I hope." He paused, and then went on: "I want also to tell you that I perfectly understand—"

"Oh," she interrupted, "so do I; your point of view, I mean." They were again silent.

"Nick, why can't we be friends—real friends? Won't it be easier?" she broke out at last with twitching lips.

"Easier—?"

"I mean, about talking things over—arrangements. There are arrangements to be made, I suppose?"

"I suppose so." He hesitated. "I'm doing what I'm told— simply following out instructions. The business is easy enough, apparently. I'm taking the necessary steps—"

She reddened a little, and drew a gasping breath. "The necessary steps: what are they? Everything the lawyers tell one is so confusing. . . . I don't yet understand—how it's done."

"My share, you mean? Oh, it's very simple." He paused, and added in a tone of laboured ease: "I'm going down to Fontainebleau to-morrow—"

She stared, not understanding. "To Fontainebleau—?"

Her bewilderment drew from him his first frank smile. "Well—I chose Fontainebleau—I don't know why . . . except that we've never been there together."

At that she suddenly understood, and the blood rushed to her forehead. She stood up without knowing what she was doing, her heart in her throat. "How grotesque—how utterly disgusting!"

He gave a slight shrug. "I didn't make the laws. . . ."

"But isn't it too stupid and degrading that such things should be necessary when two people want to part—?" She broke off again, silenced by the echo of that fatal "*want to part*." . . .

He seemed to prefer not to dwell farther on the legal obligations involved.

"You haven't yet told me," he suggested, "how you happen to be living here."

"Here—with the Fulmer children?" She roused herself, trying to catch his easier note. "Oh, I've simply been governessing them for a few weeks, while Nat and Grace are in Sicily." She did not say: "It's because I've parted with Strefford." Somehow it helped her wounded pride a little to keep from him the secret of her precarious independence.

He looked his wonder. "All alone with that bewildered *bonne*? But how many of them are there? Five? Good Lord!" He contemplated the clock with unseeing eyes, and then turned them again on her face.

"I should have thought a lot of children would rather get on your nerves."

"Oh, not *these* children. They're so good to me."

"Ah, well, I suppose it won't be for long."

He sent his eyes again about the room, which his absent-minded gaze seemed to reduce to its dismal constituent elements, and added, with an obvious effort at small talk: "I hear the Fulmers are not hitting it off very well since his success. Is it true that he's going to marry Violet Melrose?"

The blood rose to Susy's face. "Oh, never, never! He and Grace are travelling together now."

"Oh, I didn't know. People say things. . . ." He was visibly embarrassed with the subject, and sorry that he had broached it.

"Some of the things that people say are true. But Grace doesn't mind. She says she and Nat belong to each other. They can't help it, she thinks, after having been through such a lot together."

"Dear old Grace!"

He had risen from his chair, and this time she made no effort to detain him. He seemed to have recovered his self-composure, and it struck her painfully, humiliatingly almost, that he should have spoken in that light way of the expedition to Fontainebleau on the morrow. . . . Well, men were different, she supposed; she remembered having felt that once before about Nick.

It was on the tip of her tongue to cry out: "But wait—wait! I'm not going to marry Strefford after all!"—but to do so would seem like an appeal to his compassion, to his indulgence; and that was not what she wanted. She could never forget that he had left her because he had not been able to forgive her for "managing"—and not for the world would she have him think that this meeting had been planned for such a purpose.

"If he doesn't see that I *am* different, in spite of appearances . . . and that I never was what he said I was that day—if in all these months it hasn't come over him, what's the use of trying to make him see it now?" she mused. And then, her thoughts hurrying on: "Perhaps he's suffering too—I believe he *is* suffering—at any rate, he's suffering for me, if not for himself. But if he's pledged to Coral, what can he do? What would he think of me if I tried to make him break his word to her?"

There he stood—the man who was "going to Fontainebleau to-morrow"; who called it "taking the necessary steps!" Who could smile as he made the careless statement! A world seemed to divide them already: it was as if their parting were already over. All the words, cries, arguments beating loud wings in her dropped back into silence. The only thought left was: "How much longer does he mean to go on standing there?"

He may have read the question in her face, for turning back from an absorbed contemplation of the window curtains he said: "There's nothing else—?"

"Nothing else?"

"I mean: you spoke of things to be settled—" She flushed, suddenly remembering the pretext she had used to summon him.

"Oh," she faltered, "I didn't know . . . I thought there might be. . . . But the lawyers, I suppose. . . ."

She saw the relief on his contracted face. "Exactly. I've always thought it was best to leave it to them. I assure you"—again for a moment the smile strained his lips—"I shall do nothing to interfere with a quick settlement."

She stood motionless, feeling herself turn to stone. He appeared already a long way off, like a figure vanishing down a remote perspective.

"Then—good-bye," she heard him say from its farther end.

"Oh—good-bye," she faltered, as if she had not had the word ready, and was relieved to have him supply it.

He stopped again on the threshold, looked back at her, began to speak. "I've—" he said; then he repeated "Good-bye," as though to make sure he had not forgotten to say it; and the door closed on him.

It was over; she had had her last chance and missed it. Now, whatever happened, the one thing she had lived and longed for would never be. He had come, and she had let him go again. . . .

How had it come about? Would she ever be able to explain it to herself? How was it that she, so fertile in strategy, so practised in feminine arts, had stood there before him, helpless, inarticulate, like a school-girl a-choke with her first love-longing? If he was gone, and gone never to return, it was her own fault, and none but hers. What had she done to move him, detain him, make his heart beat and his head swim as hers were beating and swimming? She stood aghast at her own inadequacy, her stony inexpressiveness. . . .

And suddenly she lifted her hands to her throbbing forehead and cried out: "But this is love! This must be love!"

She had loved him before, she supposed; for what else was she to call the impulse that had drawn her to him, taught her how to overcome his scruples, and whirled him away with her on their mad adventure? Well, if that was love, this was something so much larger and deeper that the other feeling seemed the mere dancing of her blood in tune with his. . . .

But, no! Real love, great love, the love that poets sang, and privileged and tortured beings lived and died of, that love had its own superior expressiveness, and the sure command of its means. The petty arts of coquetry were no farther from it than the numbness of the untaught girl. Great love was wise, strong, powerful, like genius, like any other dominant form of human power. It knew itself, and what it wanted, and how to attain its ends.

Not great love, then . . . but just the common humble average of human love was hers. And it had come to her so newly, so overwhelmingly, with a face so grave, a touch so startling, that she had stood there petrified, humbled at the first look of its eyes, recognizing that what she had once taken for love was merely pleasure and spring-time, and the flavour of youth.

"But how was I to know? And now it's too late!" she wailed.

Chapter XXIX

THE inhabitants of the little house in Passy were of necessity early risers; but when Susy jumped out of bed the next morning no one else was astir, and it lacked nearly an hour of the call of the *bonne's* alarm-clock.

For a moment Susy leaned out of her dark room into the darker night. A cold drizzle fell on her face, and she shivered and drew back. Then, lighting a candle, and shading it, as her habit was, from the sleeping child, she slipped on her dressing-gown and opened the door. On the threshold she paused to look at her watch. Only half-past five! She thought with compunction of the unkindness of breaking in on Junie Fulmer's slumbers; but such scruples did not weigh an ounce in the balance of her purpose. Poor Junie would have to oversleep herself on Sunday, that was all.

Susy stole into the passage, opened a door, and cast her light on the girl's face.

"Junie! Dearest Junie, you must wake up!"

Junie lay in the abandonment of youthful sleep; but at the sound of her name she sat up with the promptness of a grown person on whom domestic burdens have long weighed.

"Which one of them is it?" she asked, one foot already out of bed.

"Oh, Junie dear, no . . . it's nothing wrong with the children . . . or with anybody," Susy stammered, on her knees by the bed.

In the candlelight, she saw Junie's anxious brow darken reproachfully.

"Oh, Susy, then why—? I was just dreaming we were all driving about Rome in a great big motor-car with father and mother!"

"I'm so sorry, dear. What a lovely dream! I'm a brute to have interrupted it—"

She felt the little girl's awakening scrutiny. "If there's nothing wrong with anybody, why are you crying, Susy? Is it *you* there's something wrong with? What has happened?"

"Am I crying?" Susy rose from her knees and sat down on the counterpane. "Yes, it *is* me. And I had to disturb you."

"Oh, Susy, darling, what is it?" Junie's arms were about her in a flash, and Susy grasped them in burning fingers.

"Junie, listen! I've got to go away at once—to leave you all for the whole day. I may not be back till late this evening; late to-night; I can't tell. I promised your mother I'd never leave you; but I've got to—I've got to."

Junie considered her agitated face with fully awakened eyes. "Oh, I won't tell, you know, you old brick," she said with simplicity.

Susy hugged her. "Junie, Junie, you darling! But that wasn't what I meant. Of course you may tell—you *must* tell. I shall write to your mother myself. But what worries me is the idea of having to go away—away from Paris—for the whole day, with Geordie still coughing a little, and no one but that silly Angèle to stay with him while you're out—and no one but you to take yourself and the others to school. But Junie, Junie, I've *got* to do it!" she sobbed out, clutching the child tighter.

Junie Fulmer, with her strangely mature perception of the case, and seemingly of every case that fate might call on her to deal with, sat for a moment motionless in Susy's hold. Then she freed her wrists with an adroit twist, and leaning back against the pillows said judiciously: "You'll never in the world bring up a family of your own if you take on like this over other people's children."

Through all her turmoil of spirit the observation drew a laugh from Susy. "Oh, a family of my own—I don't deserve one, the way I'm behaving to *you*!"

Junie still considered her. "My dear, a change will do you good: you need it," she pronounced.

Susy rose with a laughing sigh. "I'm not at all sure it will! But I've got to have it, all the same. Only I *do* feel anxious—and I can't even leave you my address!"

Junie still seemed to examine the case.

"Can't you even tell me where you're going?" she ventured, as if not quite sure of the delicacy of asking.

"Well—no, I don't think I can; not till I get back. Besides, even if I could it wouldn't be much use, because I couldn't give you my address there. I don't know what it will be."

"But what does it matter, if you're coming back to-night?"

"Of course I'm coming back! How could you possibly imagine I should think of leaving you for more than a day?"

"Oh, I shouldn't be afraid—not much, that is, with the poker, and Nat's water-pistol," emended Junie, still judicious.

Susy again enfolded her vehemently, and then turned to more practical matters. She explained that she wished if possible to catch an eight-thirty train from the Gare de Lyon, and that there was not a moment to lose if the children were to be dressed and fed, and full instructions written out for Junie and Angèle, before she rushed for the underground.

While she bathed Geordie, and then hurried into her own clothes, she could not help wondering at her own extreme solicitude for her charges. She remembered, with a pang, how often she had deserted Clarissa Vanderlyn for the whole day, and even for two or three in succession—poor little Clarissa, whom she knew to be so unprotected, so exposed to evil influences. She had been too much absorbed in her own greedy bliss to be more than intermittently aware of the child; but now, she felt, no sorrow however ravaging, no happiness however absorbing, would ever again isolate her from her kind.

And then these children were so different! The exquisite Clarissa was already the predestined victim of her surroundings: her budding soul was divided from Susy's by the same barrier of incomprehension that separated the latter from Mrs. Vanderlyn. Clarissa had nothing to teach Susy but the horror of her own hard little appetites; whereas the company of the noisy argumentative Fulmers had been a school of wisdom and abnegation.

As she applied the brush to Geordie's shining head and the handkerchief to his snuffling nose, the sense of what she owed him was so borne in on Susy that she interrupted the process to catch him to her bosom.

"I'll have *such* a story to tell you when I get back to-night, if you'll promise me to be good all day," she bargained with him; and Geordie, always astute, bargained back: "Before I promise, I'd like to know *what* story."

At length all was in order. Junie had been enlightened, and Angèle stunned, by the minuteness of Susy's instructions; and the latter, waterproofed and stoutly shod, descended the door-step, and paused to wave at the pyramid of heads yearning to her from an upper window.

It was hardly light, and still raining, when she turned into the dismal street. As usual, it was empty; but at the corner she perceived a hesitating taxi, with luggage piled beside the driver. Perhaps it was some early traveller, just arriving, who would release the carriage in time for her to catch it, and thus avoid the walk to the *métro*, and the subsequent strap-hanging; for it was the work-people's hour. Susy raced toward the vehicle, which, overcoming its hesitation, was beginning to move in her direction. Observing this, she stopped to see where it would discharge its load. Thereupon the taxi stopped also, and the load discharged itself in front of her in the shape of Nick Lansing.

The two stood staring at each other through the rain till Nick broke out: "Where are you going? I came to get you."

"To get me? To get me?" she repeated. Beside the driver she had suddenly remarked the old suit-case from which her husband had obliged her to extract Strefford's cigars as they were leaving Como; and everything that had happened since seemed to fall away and vanish in the pang and rapture of that memory.

"To get you; yes. Of course." He spoke the words peremptorily, almost as if they were an order. "Where were you going?" he repeated.

Without answering, she turned toward the house. He followed her, and the laden taxi closed the procession.

"Why are you out in such weather without an umbrella?" he continued, in the same severe tone, drawing her under the shelter of his.

"Oh, because Junie's umbrella is in tatters, and I had to leave her mine, as I was going away for the whole day." She spoke the words like a person in a trance.

"For the whole day? At this hour? Where?"

They were on the doorstep, and she fumbled automatically for her key, let herself in, and led the way to the sitting-room. It had not been tidied up since the night before. The children's school books lay scattered on the table and sofa, and the empty fireplace was grey with ashes. She turned to Nick in the pallid light.

"I was going to see you," she stammered, "I was going to follow you to Fontainebleau, if necessary, to tell you . . . to prevent you. . . ."

He repeated in the same aggressive tone: "Tell me what? Prevent what?"

"Tell you that there must be some other way . . . some decent way . . . of our separating . . . without that horror . . . that horror of your going off with a woman. . . ."

He stared, and then burst into a laugh. The blood rushed to her face. She had caught a familiar ring in his laugh, and it wounded her. What business had he, at such a time, to laugh in the old way?

"I'm sorry; but there *is* no other way, I'm afraid. No other way but one," he corrected himself.

She raised her head sharply. "Well?"

"That you should be the woman.—Oh, my dear!" He had dropped his mocking smile, and was at her side, her hands in his. "Oh, my dear, don't you see that we've both been feeling the same thing, and at the same hour? You lay awake thinking of it all night, didn't you? So did I. Whenever the clock struck, I said to myself: 'She's hearing it too.' And I was up before daylight, and packed my traps—for I never want to set foot again in that awful hotel where I've lived in hell for the last three days. And I swore to myself that I'd go off with a woman by the first train I could catch—and so I mean to, my dear."

She stood before him numb. Yes, numb: that was the worst of it! The violence of the reaction had been too great, and she could hardly understand what he was saying. Instead, she noticed that the tassel of the window-blind was torn off again (oh, those children!), and vaguely wondered if his luggage were safe on the waiting taxi. One heard such stories. . . .

His voice came back to her. "Susy! Listen!" he was entreating. "You must see yourself that it can't be. We're married—isn't that all that matters? Oh, I know—I've behaved like a brute: a cursed arrogant ass! You couldn't wish that ass a worse kicking than I've given him! But that's not the point, you see. The point is that we're *married*. . . . Married. . . . Doesn't it mean something to you, something—inexorable? It does to me. I didn't dream it would—in just that way. But all I can say is that I suppose the people who don't feel it aren't really married—and they'd better separate; much better. As for us—"

Through her tears she gasped out: "That's what I felt . . . that's what I said to Streff. . . ."

He was upon her with a great embrace. "My darling! My darling! You *have* told him?"

"Yes," she panted. "That's why I'm living here." She paused. "And you've told Coral?"

She felt his embrace relax. He drew away a little, still holding her, but with lowered head.

"No . . . I . . . haven't."

"Oh, Nick! Oh, Nick! But then—?"

He caught her to him again, resentfully. "Well—then what? What do you mean? What earthly difference does it make?"

"But if you've told her you were going to marry her—" (Try as she would, her voice was full of silver chimes.)

"Marry her? Marry her?" he echoed. "But how could I? What does marriage mean anyhow? If it means anything at all it means—*you*! And I can't ask Coral Hicks just to come and live with me, can I?"

Between crying and laughing she lay on his breast, and his hand passed over her hair.

They were silent for a while; then he began again: "You said it yourself yesterday, you know."

She strayed back from sunlit distances. "Yesterday?"

"Yes: that Grace Fulmer says you can't separate two people who've been through a lot of things—"

"Ah, been through them together—it's not the things, you see, it's the togetherness," she interrupted.

"The togetherness—that's it!" He seized on the word as if it had just been coined to express their case, and his mind could rest in it without farther labour.

The door-bell rang, and they started. Through the window they saw the taxi-driver gesticulating enquiries as to the fate of the luggage.

"He wants to know if he's to leave it here," Susy laughed.

"No—no! You're to come with me," her husband declared.

"Come with you?" She laughed again at the absurdity of the suggestion.

"Of course: this very instant. What did you suppose? That I was going away without you? Run up and pack your things," he commanded.

"My things? My things? But I can't leave the children!"

He stared, between indignation and amusement. "Can't leave the children? Nonsense! Why, you said yourself you were going to follow me to Fontainebleau—"

She reddened again, this time a little painfully. "I didn't know what I was doing. . . . I had to find you . . . but I should have come back this evening, no matter what happened."

"No matter what?"

She nodded, and met his gaze resolutely.

"No; but really—"

"Really, I can't leave the children till Nat and Grace come back. I promised I wouldn't."

"Yes; but you didn't know then. . . . Why on earth can't their nurse look after them?"

"There isn't any nurse but me."

"Good Lord!"

"But it's only for two weeks more," she pleaded.

"Two weeks! Do you know how long I've been without you?" He seized her by both wrists, and drew them against his breast. "Come with me at least for two days—*Susy!*" he entreated her.

"Oh," she cried, "that's the very first time you've said my name!"

"Susy, Susy, then—my Susy—Susy! And you've only said mine once, you know."

"Nick!" she sighed, at peace, as if the one syllable were a magic seed that flung out great branches to envelop them.

"Well, then, Susy, be reasonable. Come!"

"Reasonable—oh, reasonable!" she sobbed through laughter.

"Unreasonable, then! That's even better."

She freed herself, and drew back gently. "Nick, I swore I wouldn't leave them; and I can't. It's not only my promise to their mother—it's what they've been to me themselves. You don't know . . . You can't imagine the things they've taught me. They're awfully naughty at times, because they're so clever; but when they're good they're the wisest people I know." She paused, and a sudden inspiration illuminated her. "But why shouldn't we take them with us?" she exclaimed.

Her husband's arms fell away from her, and he stood dumfounded.

"*Take them with us?*"

"Why not?"

"All five of them?"

"Of course—I couldn't possibly separate them. And Junie and Nat will help us to look after the young ones."

"Help *us?*" he groaned.

"Oh, you'll see; they won't bother you. Just leave it to me; I'll manage—" The word stopped her short, and an agony of crimson suffused her from brow to throat. Their eyes met; and without a word he stooped and laid his lips gently on the stain of red on her neck.

"Nick," she breathed, her hands in his.

"But those children—"

Instead of answering, she questioned: "Where are we going?" His face lit up.

"Anywhere, dearest, that you choose."

"Well—I choose Fontainebleau!" she exulted.

"So do I! But we can't take all those children to an hotel at Fontainebleau, can we?" he questioned weakly. "You see, dear, there's the mere expense of it—"

Her eyes were already travelling far ahead of him. "The expense won't amount to much. I've just remembered that Angèle, the *bonne*, has a sister who is cook there in a nice old-fashioned *pension* which must be almost empty at this time of year. I'm sure I can ma—arrange easily," she hurried on, nearly tripping again over the fatal word. "And just think of the treat it will be to them! This is Friday, and I can get them let off from their afternoon classes, and keep them in the country till Monday. Poor darlings, they haven't been out of Paris for months! And I daresay the change will cure Geordie's cough—Geordie's the youngest," she explained, surprised to find herself, even in the rapture of reunion, so absorbed in the welfare of the Fulmers.

She was conscious that her husband was surprised also; but instead of prolonging the argument he simply questioned: "Was Geordie the chap you had in your arms when you opened the front door the night before last?"

She echoed: "I opened the front door the night before last?"

"To a boy with a parcel."

"Oh," she sobbed, "you were there? You were watching?"

He held her to him, and the currents flowed between them warm and full as on the night of their moon over Como.

In a trice, after that, she had the matter in hand and her forces marshalled. The taxi was paid, Nick's luggage deposited in the vestibule, and the children, just piling down to breakfast, were summoned in to hear the news.

It was apparent that, seasoned to surprises as they were, Nick's presence took them aback. But when, between laughter and embraces, his identity, and his right to be where he was, had been made clear to them, Junie dismissed the matter by asking him in her practical way: "Then I suppose we may talk about you to Susy now?"—and thereafter all five addressed themselves to the vision of their imminent holiday.

From that moment the little house became the centre of a whirlwind. Treats so unforeseen, and of such magnitude, were rare in the young Fulmers' experience, and had it not been for Junie's steadying influence Susy's charges would have got out of hand. But young Nat, appealed to by Nick on the ground of their common manhood, was induced to forego celebrating the event on his motor horn (the very same which had tortured the New Hampshire echoes), and to assert his authority over his juniors; and finally a plan began to emerge from the chaos, and each child to fit into it like a bit of a picture puzzle.

Susy, riding the whirlwind with her usual firmness, nevertheless felt an undercurrent of anxiety. There had been no time as yet, between her and Nick, to revert to money matters; and where there was so little money it could not, obviously, much matter. But that was the more reason for being secretly aghast at her intrepid resolve not to separate herself from her charges. A three days' honey-moon with five children in the party—and children with the Fulmer appetite—could not but be a costly business; and while she settled details, packed them off to school, and routed out such nondescript receptacles as the house contained in the way of luggage, her thoughts remained fixed on the familiar financial problem.

Yes—it was cruel to have it rear its hated head even through the bursting boughs of her new spring; but there it was, the perpetual serpent in her Eden, to be bribed, fed, sent to sleep with such scraps as she could beg, borrow or steal for it. And she supposed it was the price that fate meant her to pay for her blessedness, and was surer than ever that the blessedness was worth it. Only, how was she to compound the business with her new principles?

With the children's things to pack, luncheon to be got ready, and the Fontainebleau *pension* to be telephoned to, there was little time to waste on moral casuistry; and Susy asked herself with a certain irony if the chronic lack of time to deal with money difficulties had not been the chief cause of her previous lapses. There was no time to deal with this question either; no time, in short, to do anything but rush forward on a great gale of plans and preparations, in the course of which she whirled Nick forth to buy some *charcuterie* for luncheon, and telephone to Fontainebleau.

Once he was gone—and after watching him safely round the corner—she too got into her wraps, and transferring a small packet from her dressing-case to her pocket, hastened out in a different direction.

Chapter XXX

I T took two brimming taxi-cabs to carry the Nicholas Lansings to the station on their second honey-moon. In the first were Nick, Susy and the luggage of the whole party (little Nat's motor horn included, as a last concession, and because he had hitherto forborne to play on it); and in the second, the five Fulmers, the *bonne*, who at the eleventh hour had refused to be left, a cage-full of canaries, and a foundling kitten who had murderous designs on them; all of which had to be taken because, if the *bonne* came, there would be nobody left to look after them.

At the corner Susy tore herself from Nick's arms and held up the procession while she ran back to the second taxi to make sure that the *bonne* had brought the house-key. It was found of course that she hadn't but that Junie had; whereupon the caravan got under way again, and reached the station just as the train was starting; and there, by some miracle of good nature on the part of the guard, they were all packed together into an empty compartment—no doubt, as Susy remarked, because train officials never failed to spot a newly-married couple, and treat them kindly.

The children, sentinelled by Junie, at first gave promise of superhuman goodness; but presently their feelings overflowed, and they were not to be quieted till it had been agreed that Nat should blow his motor-horn at each halt, while the twins called out the names of the stations, and Geordie, with the canaries and kitten, affected to change trains.

Luckily the halts were few; but the excitement of travel, combined with over-indulgence in the chocolates imprudently provided by Nick, overwhelmed Geordie with a sudden melancholy that could be appeased only by Susy's telling him stories till they arrived at Fontainebleau.

The day was soft, with mild gleams of sunlight on decaying foliage; and after luggage and livestock had been dropped at the *pension* Susy confessed that she had promised the children a scamper in the forest, and buns in a tea-shop afterward. Nick placidly agreed, and darkness had long fallen, and a great many buns been consumed, when at length the procession turned down the street toward the *pension*, headed by Nick with the sleeping Geordie on his shoulder, while the others, speechless with fatigue and food, hung heavily on Susy.

It had been decided that, as the *bonne* was of the party, the children might be entrusted to her for the night, and Nick and Susy establish themselves in an adjacent hotel. Nick had flattered himself that they might remove their possessions there when they returned from the tea-room; but Susy, manifestly surprised at the idea, reminded him that her charges must first be given their supper and put to bed. She suggested that he should meanwhile take the bags to the hotel, and promised to join him as soon as Geordie was asleep.

She was a long time coming, but waiting for her was sweet, even in a deserted hotel reading-room insufficiently heated by a sulky stove; and after he had glanced through his morning's mail, hurriedly thrust into his pocket as he left Paris, he sank into a state of drowsy beatitude. It was all the maddest business in the world, yet it did not give him the sense of unreality that had made their first adventure a mere golden dream; and he sat and waited with the security of one in whom dear habits have struck deep roots. In this mood of acquiescence even the presence of the five Fulmers seemed a natural and necessary consequence of all the rest; and when Susy at length appeared, a little pale and tired, with the brooding inward look that busy mothers bring from the nursery, that too seemed natural and necessary, and part of the new order of things.

They had wandered out to a cheap restaurant for dinner; now, in the damp December night, they were walking back to the hotel under a sky full of rain-clouds. They seemed to have said everything to each other, and yet barely to have begun what they had to tell; and at each step they took, their heavy feet dragged a great load of bliss.

In the hotel almost all the lights were already out; and they groped their way to the third floor room which was the only one that Susy had found cheap enough. A ray from a street-lamp struck up through the unshuttered windows; and after Nick had revived the fire they drew their chairs close to it, and sat quietly for a while in the dark.

Their silence was so sweet that Nick could not make up his mind to break it; not to do so gave his tossing spirit such a sense of permanence, of having at last unlimited time before him in which to taste his joy and let its sweetness stream through him. But at length he roused himself to say: "It's queer how things coincide. I've had a little bit of good news in one of the letters I got this morning."

Susy took the announcement serenely. "Well, you *would*, you know," she commented, as if the day had been too obviously designed for bliss to escape the notice of its dispensers.

"Yes," he continued with a thrill of pardonable pride. "During the cruise I did a couple of articles on Crete—oh, just travel-impressions, of course; they couldn't be more. But the editor of the *New Review* has accepted them, and asks for others. And here's his cheque, if you please! So you see you might have let me take the jolly room downstairs with the pink curtains. And it makes me awfully hopeful about my book."

He had expected a rapturous outburst, and perhaps some reassertion of wifely faith in the glorious future that awaited *The Pageant of Alexander*; and deep down under the lover's well-being the author felt a faint twinge of mortified vanity when Susy, leaping to her feet, cried out, ravenously and without preamble: "Oh, Nick, Nick—let me see how much they've given you!"

He flourished the cheque before her in the firelight. "A couple of hundred, you mercenary wretch!"

"Oh, oh—" she gasped, as if the good news had been almost too much for her tense nerves; and then surprised him by dropping to the ground, and burying her face against his knees.

"Susy, my Susy," he whispered, his hand on her shaking shoulder. "Why, dear, what is it? You're not crying?"

"Oh, Nick, Nick—two hundred? Two hundred dollars? Then I've got to tell you—oh now, at once!"

A faint chill ran over him, and involuntarily his hand drew back from her bowed figure.

"Now? Oh, why now?" he protested. "What on earth does it matter now—whatever it is?"

"But it does matter—it matters more than you can think!"

She straightened herself, still kneeling before him, and lifted her head so that the firelight behind her turned her hair into a ruddy halo.

"Oh, Nick, the bracelet—Ellie's bracelet. . . . I've never returned it to her," she faltered out.

He felt himself recoiling under the hands with which she clutched his knees. For an instant he did not remember what she alluded to; it was the mere mention of Ellie Vanderlyn's name that had fallen between them like an icy shadow. What an incorrigible fool he had been to think they could ever shake off such memories, or cease to be the slaves of such a past!

"The bracelet?—Oh, yes," he said, suddenly understanding, and feeling the chill mount slowly to his lips.

"Yes, the bracelet . . . Oh, Nick, I meant to give it back at once; I did—I *did*; but the day you went away I forgot everything else. And when I found the thing, in the bottom of my bag, weeks afterward, I thought everything was over between you and me, and I had begun to see Ellie again, and she was kind to me—and how could I?" To save his life he could have found no answer, and she pressed on: "And so this morning, when I saw you were frightened by the expense of bringing all the children with us, and when I felt I couldn't leave them, and couldn't leave you either, I remembered the bracelet; and I sent you off to telephone while I rushed round the corner to a little jeweller's where I'd been before, and pawned it so that you shouldn't have to pay for the children. . . . But now, darling, you see, if you've got all that money, I can get it out of pawn at once, can't I, and send it back to her?"

She flung her arms about him, and he held her fast, wondering if the tears he felt were hers or his. Still he did not speak; but as he clasped her close she added, with an irrepressible flash of her old irony: "Not that Ellie will understand why I've done it. She's never yet been able to make out why you returned her scarf-pin."

For a long time she continued to lean against him, her head on his knees, as she had done on the terrace of Como on the last night of their honeymoon. She had ceased to talk, and he sat silent also, passing his hand quietly to and fro over her hair. The first rapture had been succeeded by soberer feelings. Her confession had broken up the frozen pride about his heart, and humbled him to the earth; but it had also roused forgotten things, memories and scruples swept aside in the first rush of their reunion. He and she belonged to each other for always: he understood that now. The impulse which had first drawn them together again, in spite of reason, in spite of themselves almost, that deep-seated instinctive need that each had of the other, would never again wholly let them go. Yet as he sat there he thought of Strefford, he thought of Coral Hicks. He had been a coward in regard to Coral, and Susy had been sincere and courageous in regard to Strefford. Yet his mind dwelt on Coral with tenderness, with compunction, with remorse; and he was almost sure that Susy had already put Strefford utterly out of her mind.

It was the old contrast between the two ways of loving, the man's way and the woman's; and after a moment it seemed to Nick natural enough that Susy, from the very moment of finding him again, should feel neither pity nor regret, and that Strefford should already be to her as if he had never been. After all, there was something Providential in such arrangements.

He stooped closer, pressed her dreaming head between his hands, and whispered: "Wake up; it's bedtime."

She rose; but as she moved away to turn on the light he caught her hand and drew her to the window. They leaned on the sill in the darkness, and through the clouds, from which a few drops were already falling, the moon, labouring upward, swam into a space of sky, cast her troubled glory on them, and was again hidden.

THE END

A SON AT THE FRONT

Something veil'd and abstracted is often a part of the manners of these beings.

—WALT WHITMAN

IN MEMORY

OF

RONALD SIMMONS

BOOK I

Chapter I

JOHN CAMPTON, the American portrait-painter, stood in his bare studio in Montmartre at the end of a summer afternoon contemplating a battered calendar that hung against the wall.

The calendar marked July 30, 1914.

Campton looked at this date with a gaze of unmixed satisfaction. His son, his only boy, who was coming from America, must have landed in England that morning, and after a brief halt in London would join him the next evening in Paris. To bring the moment nearer, Campton, smiling at his weakness, tore off the leaf and uncovered the 31. Then, leaning in the window, he looked out over his untidy scrap of garden at the silver-grey sea of Paris spreading mistily below him.

A number of visitors had passed through the studio that day. After years of obscurity Campton had been projected into the light—or perhaps only into the limelight—by his portrait of his son George, exhibited three years earlier at the spring show of the French Society of Painters and Sculptors. The picture seemed to its author to be exactly in the line of the unnoticed things he had been showing before, though perhaps nearer to what he was always trying for, because of the exceptional interest of his subject. But to the public he had appeared to take a new turn; or perhaps some critic had suddenly found the right phrase for him; or, that season, people wanted a new painter to talk about. Didn't he know by heart all the Paris reasons for success or failure?

The early years of his career had given him ample opportunity to learn them. Like other young students of his generation, he had come to Paris with an exaggerated reverence for the few conspicuous figures who made the old Salons of the 'eighties like bad plays written around a few stars. If he could get near enough to Beausite, the ruling light of the galaxy, he thought he might do things not unworthy of that great master; but

Beausite, who had ceased to receive pupils, saw no reason for making an exception in favour of an obscure youth without a backing. He was not kind; and on the only occasion when a painting of Campton's came under his eye he let fall an epigram which went the round of Paris, but shocked its victim by its revelation of the great man's ineptitude.

Campton, if he could have gone on admiring Beausite's work, would have forgotten his unkindness and even his critical incapacity; but as the young painter's personal convictions developed he discovered that his idol had none, and that the dazzling *maëstria* still enveloping his work was only the light from a dead star.

All these things were now nearly thirty years old. Beausite had vanished from the heavens, and the youth he had sneered at throned there in his stead. Most of the people who besieged Campton's studio were the lineal descendants of those who had echoed Beausite's sneer. They belonged to the types that Campton least cared to paint; but they were usually those who paid the highest prices, and he had lately had new and imperious reasons for wanting to earn all the money he could. So for two years he had let it be as difficult and expensive as possible to be "done by Campton"; and this oppressive July day had been crowded with the visits of suppliants of a sort unused to waiting on anybody's pleasure, people who had postponed St. Moritz and Deauville, Aix and Royat, because it was known that one had to accept the master's conditions or apply elsewhere.

The job bored him more than ever; the more of their fatuous faces he recorded the more he hated the task; but for the last two or three days the monotony of his toil had been relieved by a new element of interest. This was produced by what he called the "war-funk," and consisted in the effect on his sitters and their friends of the suggestion that something new, incomprehensible and uncomfortable might be about to threaten the ordered course of their pleasures.

Campton himself did not "believe in the war" (as the current phrase went); therefore he was able to note with perfect composure its agitating effect upon his sitters. On the whole the women behaved best: the idiotic Mme. de Dolmetsch had actually grown beautiful through fear for her lover, who turned out (in spite of a name as exotic as hers) to be a French subject of military age. The men had made a less creditable showing—especially the big banker and promoter, Jorgenstein, whose round red face had withered like a pricked balloon, and young Prince Demetrios Palamèdes, just married to the fabulously rich daughter of an Argentine wheat-grower, and so secure as to his bride's fortune that he could curse impartially all the disturbers of his summer plans. Even the great tuberculosis specialist, Fortin-Lescluze, whom Campton was painting in return for the physician's devoted care of George the previous year, had lost something of his professional composure, and no longer gave out the sense of tranquillizing strength which had been such a help in the boy's fight for health. Fortin-Lescluze, always in contact with the rulers of the earth, must surely have some hint of their councils. Whatever it was, he revealed nothing, but continued to talk frivolously and infatuatedly about a new Javanese dancer whom he wanted Campton to paint; but his large beaked face with its triumphant moustache had grown pinched and grey, and he had forgotten to renew the dye on the moustache.

Campton's one really imperturbable visitor was little Charlie Alicante, the Spanish secretary of Embassy at Berlin, who had dropped in on his way to St. Moritz, bringing the newest news from the Wilhelmstrasse, news that was all suavity and reassurance, with a touch of playful reproach for the irritability of French feeling, and a reminder of Imperial longanimity in regard to the foolish misunderstandings of Agadir and Saverne.

Now all the visitors had gone, and Campton, leaning in the window, looked out over Paris and mused on his summer plans. He meant to plunge straight down to Southern Italy and Sicily, perhaps even push over to North Africa. That at least was what he hoped for: no sun was too hot for him and no landscape too arid. But it all depended on George; for George was going with him, and if George preferred Spain they would postpone the desert.

It was almost impossible to Campton to picture what it would be like to have the boy with him. For so long he had seen his son only in snatches, hurriedly, incompletely, uncomprehendingly: it was only in the last three years that their intimacy had had a chance to develop. And they had never travelled together, except for hasty dashes, two or three times, to seashore or

mountains; had never gone off on a long solitary journey such
as this. Campton, tired, disenchanted, and nearing sixty, found
himself looking forward to the adventure with an eagerness as
great as the different sort of ardour with which, in his youth,
he had imagined flights of another kind with the woman who
was to fulfill every dream.

"Well—I suppose that's the stuff pictures are made of," he
thought, smiling at his inextinguishable belief in the complete-
ness of his next experience. Life had perpetually knocked him
down just as he had his hand on her gifts; nothing had ever
succeeded with him but his work. But he was as sure as ever that
peace of mind and contentment of heart were waiting for him
round the next corner; and this time, it was clear, they were to
come to him through his wonderful son.

The doorbell rang, and he listened for the maid-servant's step.
There was another impatient jingle, and he remembered that
his faithful Mariette had left for Lille, where she was to spend
her vacation with her family. Campton, reaching for his stick,
shuffled across the studio with his lame awkward stride.

At the door stood his old friend Paul Dastrey, one of the few
men with whom he had been unbrokenly intimate since the first
days of his disturbed and incoherent Parisian life. Dastrey came
in without speaking: his small dry face, seamed with premature
wrinkles of irony and sensitiveness, looked unusually grave. The
wrinkles seemed suddenly to have become those of an old man;
and how grey Dastrey had turned! He walked a little stiffly, with
a jauntiness obviously intended to conceal a growing tendency
to rheumatism.

In the middle of the floor he paused and tapped a varnished
boot-tip with his stick.

"Let's see what you've done to Daisy Dolmetsch."

"Oh, it's been done for me—you'll see!" Campton laughed.
He was enjoying the sight of Dastrey and thinking that this visit
was providentially timed to give him a chance of expatiating on
his coming journey. In his rare moments of expansiveness he
felt the need of some substitute for the background of domestic
sympathy which, as a rule, would have simply bored or exasperated him; and at such times he could always talk to Dastrey.

The little man screwed up his eyes and continued to tap his
varnished toes.

"But she's magnificent. She's seen the Medusa!"

Campton laughed again. "Just so. For days and days I'd been trying to do something with her; and suddenly the war-funk did it for me."

"The war-funk?"

"Who'd have thought it? She's frightened to death about Ladislas Isador—who is French, it turns out, and mobilisable. The poor soul thinks there's going to be war!"

"Well, there *is*," said Dastrey.

The two men looked at each other: Campton amused, incredulous, a shade impatient at the perpetual recurrence of the same theme, and aware of presenting a smile of irritating unresponsiveness to his friend's solemn gaze.

"Oh, come—you too? Why, the Duke of Alicante has just left here, fresh from Berlin. You ought to hear him laugh at us . . ."

"How about Berlin's laughing at *him*?" Dastrey sank into a wicker armchair, drew out a cigarette and forgot to light it. Campton returned to the window.

"There can't be war: I'm going to Sicily and Africa with George the day after to-morrow," he broke out.

"Ah, George——. To be sure . . ."

There was a silence; Dastrey had not even smiled. He turned the unlit cigarette in his dry fingers.

"Too young for 'seventy—and too old for this! Some men are born under a curse," he burst out.

"What on earth are you talking about?" Campton exclaimed, forcing his gaiety a little.

Dastrey stared at him with furious eyes. "But I shall get something, somewhere . . . they can't stop a man's enlisting . . . I had an old uncle who did it in 'seventy . . . he was older than I am now."

Campton looked at him compassionately. Poor little circumscribed Paul Dastrey, whose utmost adventure had been an occasional article in an art review, an occasional six weeks in the near East! It was pitiful to see him breathing fire and fury on an enemy one knew to be engaged, at that very moment, in meeting England and France more than half-way in the effort to smooth over diplomatic difficulties. But Campton could make allowances for the nerves of the tragic generation brought up in the shadow of Sedan.

"Look here," he said, "I'll tell you what. Come along with George and me—as far as Palermo, anyhow. You're a little stiff again in that left knee, and we can bake our lamenesses together in the good Sicilian oven."

Dastrey had found a match and lighted his cigarette.

"My poor Campton—there'll be war in three days."

Campton's incredulity was shot through with the deadly chill of conviction. There it was—there would be war! It was too like his cursed luck not to be true . . . He smiled inwardly, perceiving that he was viewing the question exactly as the despicable Jorgenstein and the fatuous Prince Demetrios had viewed it: as an unwarrantable interference with his private plans. Yes—but his case was different . . . Here was the son he had never seen enough of, never till lately seen at all as most fathers see their sons; and the boy was to be packed off to New York that winter, to go into a bank; and for the Lord knew how many months this was to be their last chance, as it was almost their first, of being together quietly, confidentially, uninterruptedly. These other men were whining at the interruption of their vile pleasures or their viler money-making; he, poor devil, was trembling for the chance to lay the foundation of a complete and lasting friendship with his only son, at the moment when such understandings do most to shape a youth's future . . . "And with what I've had to fight against!" he groaned, seeing victory in sight, and sickening at the idea that it might be snatched from him.

Then another thought came, and he felt the blood leaving his ruddy face and, as it seemed, receding from every vein of his heavy awkward body. He sat down opposite Dastrey, and the two looked at each other.

"There won't be war. But if there were—why shouldn't George and I go to Sicily? You don't see us sitting here making lint, do you?"

Dastrey smiled. "Lint is unhygienic; you won't have to do that. And I see no reason why *you* shouldn't go to Sicily—or to China." He paused. "But how about George—I thought he and you were both born in France?"

Campton reached for a cigarette. "We were, worse luck. He's subject to your preposterous military regulations. But it doesn't make any difference, as it happens. He's sure to be discharged after that touch of tuberculosis he had last year, when he had to be rushed up to the Engadine."

"Ah, I see. Then, as you say . . . Still, of course he wouldn't be allowed to leave the country."

A constrained silence fell between the two. Campton became aware that, for the first time since they had known each other, their points of view were the width of the poles apart. It was hopeless to try to bridge such a distance.

"Of course, you know," he said, trying for his easiest voice, "I still consider this discussion purely academic . . . But if it turns out that I'm wrong I shall do all I can—all I can, do you hear?— to get George discharged . . . You'd better know that . . ."

Dastrey, rising, held out his hand with his faithful smile. "My dear old Campton, I perfectly understand a foreigner's taking that view . . ." He walked toward the door and they parted without more words.

When he had gone Campton began to recover his reassurance. Who was Dastrey, poor chap, to behave as if he were in the councils of the powers? It was perfect nonsense to pretend that a diplomatist straight from Berlin didn't know more about what was happening there than the newsmongers of the Boulevards. One didn't have to be an Ambassador to see which way the wind was blowing; and men like Alicante, belonging to a country uninvolved in the affair, were the only people capable of a cool judgment at moments of international tension.

Campton took the portrait of Mme. de Dolmetsch and leaned it against the other canvases along the wall. Then he started clumsily to put the room to rights—without Mariette he was so helpless—and finally, abandoning the attempt, said to himself: "I'll come and wind things up to-morrow."

He was moving that day from the studio to the Hotel de Crillon, where George was to join him the next evening. It would be jolly to be with the boy from the moment he arrived; and, even if Mariette's departure had not paralyzed his primitive housekeeping, he could not have made room for his son at the studio. So, reluctantly, for he loathed luxury and conformity, but joyously, because he was to be with George, Campton threw some shabby clothes into a shapeless portmanteau, and prepared to despatch the concierge for a taxicab.

He was hobbling down the stairs when the old woman met him with a telegram. He tore it open and saw that it was dated Deauville, and was not, as he had feared, from his son.

"Very anxious. Must see you to-morrow. Please come to Avenue Marigny at five without fail. Julia Brant."

"Oh, damn," Campton growled, crumpling up the message. The concierge was looking at him with searching eyes.

"Is it war, sir?" she asked, pointing to the bit of blue paper. He supposed she was thinking of her grandsons.

"No—no—nonsense! War?" He smiled into her shrewd old face, every wrinkle of which seemed full of a deep human experience.

"War? Can you imagine anything more absurd? Can you, now? What should you say if they told you war was going to be declared, Mme. Lebel?"

She gave him back his look with profound earnestness; then she spoke in a voice of sudden resolution. "Why, I should say we don't want it, sir—I'd have four in it if it came—*but that this sort of thing has got to stop*."

Campton shrugged. "Oh, well—it's not going to come, so don't worry. And call me a taxi, will you? No, no, I'll carry the bags down myself."

Chapter II

"**B**UT even if they do mobilise: mobilisation is not war—*is* it?" Mrs. Anderson Brant repeated across the teacups.

Campton dragged himself up from the deep armchair he had inadvertently chosen. To escape from his hostess's troubled eyes he limped across to the window and stood gazing out at the thick turf and brilliant flower-borders of the garden which was so unlike his own. After a moment he turned and glanced about him, catching the reflection of his heavy figure in a mirror dividing two garlanded panels. He had not entered Mrs. Brant's drawing-room for nearly ten years; not since the period of the interminable discussions about the choice of a school for George; and in spite of the far graver preoccupations that now weighed on him, and of the huge menace with which the whole world was echoing, he paused for an instant to consider the contrast between his clumsy person and that expensive and irreproachable room.

"You've taken away Beausite's portrait of you," he said abruptly, looking up at the chimney-panel, which was filled with the blue and umber bloom of a Fragonard landscape.

A full-length of Mrs. Anderson Brant by Beausite had been one of Mr. Brant's wedding-presents to his bride; a Beausite portrait, at that time, was as much a part of such marriages as pearls and sables.

"Yes. Anderson thought . . . the dress had grown so dreadfully old-fashioned," she explained indifferently; and went on again: "You think it's *not* war: don't you?"

What was the use of telling her what he thought? For years and years he had not done that—about anything. But suddenly, now, a stringent necessity had drawn them together, confronting them like any two plain people caught in a common danger—like husband and wife, for example!

"It *is* war, this time, I believe," he said.

She set down her cup with a hand that had begun to tremble.

"I disagree with you entirely," she retorted, her voice shrill with anxiety. "I was frightfully upset when I sent you that

telegram yesterday; but I've been lunching to-day with the old
Duc de Montlhéry—you know he fought in 'seventy—and with
Lévi-Michel of the 'Jour,' who had just seen some of the govern-
ment people; and they both explained to me quite clearly——"

"That you'd made a mistake in coming up from Deauville?"

To save himself Campton could not restrain the sneer; on
the rare occasions when a crisis in their lives flung them on
each other's mercy, the first sensation he was always conscious
of was the degree to which she bored him. He remembered the
day, years ago, long before their divorce, when it had first come
home to him that she was always going to bore him. But he
was ashamed to think of that now, and went on more patiently:
"You see, the situation is rather different from anything we've
known before; and, after all, in 1870 all the wise people thought
till the last minute that there would be no war."

Her delicate face seemed to shrink and wither with
apprehension.

"Then—what about George?" she asked, the paint coming
out about her haggard eyes.

Campton paused a moment. "You may suppose I've thought
of *that*."

"Oh, of course . . ." He saw she was honestly trying to be
what a mother should be in talking of her only child to that
child's father. But the long habit of superficiality made her stammering and inarticulate when her one deep feeling tried to rise
to the surface.

Campton seated himself again, taking care to choose a
straight-backed chair. "I see nothing to worry about with regard
to George," he said.

"You mean——?"

"Why, they won't take him—they won't want him . . . with
his medical record."

"Are you sure? He's so much stronger . . . He's gained twenty
pounds . . ." It was terrible, really, to hear her avow it in a reluctant whisper! That was the view that war made mothers take of
the chief blessing they could ask for their children! Campton
understood her, and took the same view. George's wonderful
recovery, the one joy his parents had shared in the last twenty
years, was now a misfortune to be denied and dissembled. They
looked at each other like accomplices, the same thought in their

eyes: if only the boy had been born in America! It was grotesque that the whole of joy or anguish should suddenly be found to hang on a geographical accident.

"After all, we're Americans; this is not our job—" Campton began.

"No—" He saw she was waiting, and knew for what.

"So of course—if there were any trouble—but there won't be; if there were, though, I shouldn't hesitate to do what was necessary . . . use any influence . . ."

"Oh, then we agree!" broke from her in a cry of wonder.

The unconscious irony of the exclamation struck him, and increased his irritation. He remembered the tone—undefinably compassionate—in which Dastrey had said: "I perfectly understand a foreigner's taking that view" . . . But *was* he a foreigner, Campton asked himself? And what was the criterion of citizenship, if he, who owed to France everything that had made life worth while, could regard himself as owing her nothing, now that for the first time he might have something to give her? Well, for himself that argument was all right: preposterous as he thought war—any war—he would have offered himself to France on the instant if she had had any use for his lame carcass. But he had never bargained to give her his only son.

Mrs. Brant went on in excited argument.

"Of course you know how careful I always am to do nothing about him without consulting you; but since you feel about it as *we* do——" She blushed under her faint rouge. The "we" had slipped out accidentally, and Campton, aware of turning hard-lipped and grim, sat waiting for her to repair the blunder. Through the years of his poverty it had been impossible not to put up, on occasions, with that odious first person plural: as long as his wretched inability to make money had made it necessary that his wife's second husband should pay for his son's keep, such allusions had been part of Campton's long expiation. But even then he had tacitly made his former wife understand that, when they had to talk of the boy, he could bear her saying "I think," or "Anderson thinks," this or that, but not "*we* think it." And in the last few years, since Campton's unforeseen success had put him, to the astonishment of every one concerned, in a position of financial independence, "Anderson" had almost entirely dropped out of their talk about George's future. Mrs.

Brant was not a clever woman, but she had a social adroitness that sometimes took the place of intelligence.

On this occasion she saw her mistake so quickly, and blushed for it so painfully, that at any other time Campton would have smiled away her distress; but at the moment he could not stir a muscle to help her.

"Look here," he broke out, "there are things I've had to accept in the past, and shall have to accept in the future. The boy is to go into Bullard and Brant's—it's agreed; I'm not sure enough of being able to provide for him for the next few years to interfere with—with your plans in that respect. But I thought it was understood once for all——"

She interrupted him excitedly. "Oh, of course . . . of course. You must admit I've always respected your feeling . . ."

He acknowledged awkwardly: "Yes."

"Well, then—won't you see that this situation is different, terribly different, and that we ought all to work together? If Anderson's influence can be of use . . ."

"Anderson's influence——" Campton's gorge rose against the phrase! It was always Anderson's influence that had been invoked—and none knew better than Campton himself how justly—when the boy's future was under discussion. But in this particular case the suggestion was intolerable.

"Of course," he interrupted drily. "But, as it happens, I think I can attend to this job myself."

She looked down at her huge rings, hesitated visibly, and then flung tact to the winds. "What makes you think so? You don't know the right sort of people."

It was a long time since she had thrown that at him: not since the troubled days of their marriage, when it had been the cruellest taunt she could think of. Now it struck him simply as a particularly unpalatable truth. No, he didn't know "the right sort of people" . . . unless, for instance, among his new patrons, such a man as Jorgenstein answered to the description. But, if there were war, on what side would a cosmopolitan like Jorgenstein turn out to be?

"Anderson, you see," she persisted, losing sight of everything in the need to lull her fears, "Anderson knows all the political people. In a business way, of course, a big banker has to. If there's really any chance of George's being taken you've no right to refuse Anderson's help—none whatever!"

Campton was silent. He had meant to reassure her, to reaffirm his conviction that the boy was sure to be discharged. But as their eyes met he saw that she believed this no more than he did; and he felt the contagion of her incredulity.

"But if you're so sure there's not going to be war——" he began.

As he spoke he saw her face change, and was aware that the door behind him had opened and that a short man, bald and slim, was advancing at a sort of mincing trot across the pompous garlands of the Savonnerie carpet. Campton got to his feet. He had expected Anderson Brant to stop at sight of him, mumble a greeting, and then back out of the room—as usual. But Anderson Brant did nothing of the sort: he merely hastened his trot toward the tea-table. He made no attempt to shake hands with Campton, but bowing shyly and stiffly said: "I understood you were coming, and hurried back . . . on the chance . . . to consult . . ."

Campton gazed at him without speaking. They had not seen each other since the extraordinary occasion, two years before, when Mr. Brant, furtively one day at dusk, had come to his studio to offer to buy George's portrait; and, as their eyes met, the memory of that visit reddened both their faces.

Mr. Brant was a compact little man of about sixty. His sandy hair, just turning grey, was brushed forward over a baldness which was ivory-white at the crown and became brick-pink above the temples, before merging into the tanned and freckled surface of his face. He was always dressed in carefully cut clothes of a discreet grey, with a tie to match, in which even the plump pearl was grey, so that he reminded Campton of a dry perpendicular insect in protective tints; and the fancy was encouraged by his cautious manner, and the way he had of peering over his glasses as if they were part of his armour. His feet were small and pointed, and seemed to be made of patent leather; and shaking hands with him was like clasping a bunch of twigs.

It had been Campton's lot, on the rare occasions of his meeting Mr. Brant, always to see this perfectly balanced man in moments of disequilibrium, when the attempt to simulate poise probably made him more rigid than nature had created him. But to-day his perturbation betrayed itself in the gesture with which he drummed out a tune on the back of the gold and platinum cigar-case he had unconsciously drawn from his pocket.

After a moment he seemed to become aware of what he had in his hand, and pressing the sapphire spring held out the case with the remark: "Coronas."

Campton made a movement of refusal, and Mr. Brant, over-whelmed, thrust the cigar-case away.

"I ought to have taken one—I may need him," Campton thought; and Mrs. Brant said, addressing her husband: "He thinks as *we* do—exactly."

Campton winced. Thinking as the Brants did was, at all times, so foreign to his nature and his principles that his first impulse was to protest. But the sight of Mr. Brant, standing there helplessly, and trying to hide the twitching of his lip by stroking his lavender-scented moustache with a discreetly curved hand, moved the painter's imagination.

"Poor devil—he'd give all his millions if the boy were safe," he thought, "and he doesn't even dare to say so."

It satisfied Campton's sense of his rights that these two powerful people were hanging on his decision like frightened children, and he answered, looking at Mrs. Brant: "There's nothing to be done at present . . . absolutely nothing—— Except," he added abruptly, "to take care not to talk in this way to George."

Mrs. Brant lifted a startled gaze.

"What do you mean? If war is declared, you can't expect me not to speak of it to him."

"Speak of it as much as you like, but don't drag him in. Let him work out his own case for himself." He went on with an effort: "It's what I intend to do."

"But you said you'd use every influence!" she protested, obtusely.

"Well—I believe this is one of them."

She looked down resignedly at her clasped hands, and he saw her lips tighten. "My telling her that has been just enough to start her on the other tack," he groaned to himself, all her old stupidities rising up around him like a fog.

Mr. Brant gave a slight cough and removed his protecting hand from his lips.

"Mr. Campton is right," he said, quickly and timorously. "I take the same view—entirely. George must not know that we are thinking of using . . . any means . . ." He coughed again, and groped for the cigar-case.

As he spoke, there came over Campton a sense of their possessing a common ground of understanding that Campton had never found in his wife. He had had a hint of the same feeling, but had voluntarily stifled it, on the day when Mr. Brant, apologetic yet determined, had come to the studio to buy George's portrait. Campton had seen then how the man suffered from his failure, but had chosen to attribute his distress to the humiliation of finding there were things his money could not purchase. Now, that judgment seemed as unimaginative as he had once thought Mr. Brant's overture. Campton turned on the banker a look that was almost brotherly.

"We men know . . ." the look said; and Mr. Brant's parched cheek was suffused with a flush of understanding. Then, as if frightened at the consequences of such complicity, he repeated his bow and went out.

When Campton issued forth into the Avenue Marigny, it came to him as a surprise to see the old unheeding life of Paris still going on. In the golden decline of day the usual throng of idlers sat under the horse-chestnuts of the Champs Elysées, children scampered between turf and flowers, and the perpetual stream of motors rolled up the central avenue to the restaurants beyond the gates.

Under the last trees of the Avenue Gabriel the painter stood looking across the Place de la Concorde. No doubt the future was dark: he had guessed from Mr. Brant's precipitate arrival that the banks and the Stock Exchange feared the worst. But what could a man do, whose convictions were so largely formed by the play of things on his retina, when, in the setting sun, all that majesty of space and light and architecture was spread out before him undisturbed? Paris was too triumphant a fact not to argue down his fears. There she lay in the security of her beauty, and once more proclaimed herself eternal.

Chapter III

THE night was so lovely that, though the Boulogne express arrived late, George at once proposed dining in the Bois.

His luggage, of which, as usual, there was a good deal, was dropped at the Crillon, and they shot up the Champs Elysées as the summer dusk began to be pricked by lamps.

"How jolly the old place smells!" George cried, breathing in the scent of sun-warmed asphalt, of flower-beds and freshly-watered dust. He seemed as much alive to such impressions as if his first word at the station had not been: "Well, this time I suppose we're in for it." In for it they might be; but meanwhile he meant to enjoy the scents and scenes of Paris as acutely and unconcernedly as ever.

Campton had hoped that he would pick out one of the humble cyclists' restaurants near the Seine; but not he. "Madrid, is it?" he said gaily, as the taxi turned into the Bois; and there they sat under the illuminated trees, in the general glitter and expensiveness, with the Tziganes playing down their talk, and all around them the painted faces that seemed to the father so old and obvious, and to the son, no doubt, so full of novelty and mystery.

The music made conversation difficult; but Campton did not care. It was enough to sit and watch the face in which, after each absence, he noted a new and richer vivacity. He had often tried to make up his mind if his boy were handsome. Not that the father's eye influenced the painter's; but George's young head, with its thick blond thatch, the complexion ruddy to the golden eyebrows, and then abruptly white on the forehead, the short amused nose, the inquisitive eyes, the ears lying back flat to the skull against curly edges of fair hair, defied all rules and escaped all classifications by a mixture of romantic gaiety and shrewd plainness like that in certain eighteenth-century portraits.

As father and son faced each other over the piled-up peaches, while the last sparkle of champagne died down in their glasses, Campton's thoughts went back to the day when he had first discovered his son. George was a schoolboy of twelve, at home for the Christmas holidays. At home meant at the Brants', since it was always there he stayed: his father saw him only on certain days. Usually Mariette fetched him to the studio on one afternoon in the week; but this particular week George was ill, and it had been arranged that in case of illness his father was to visit him at his mother's. He had one of his frequent bad colds, and Campton recalled him, propped up in bed in his luxurious overheated room, a scarlet sweater over his nightshirt, a book on his thin knees, and his ugly little fever-flushed face bent over it in profound absorption. Till that moment George had never seemed to care for books: his father had resigned himself to the probability of seeing him grow up into the ordinary pleasant young fellow, with his mother's worldly tastes. But the boy was reading as only a bookworm reads—reading with his very finger-tips, and his inquisitive nose, and the perpetual dart ahead of a gaze that seemed to guess each phrase from its last word. He looked up with a smile, and said: "Oh, Dad . . ." but it was clear that he regarded the visit as an interruption. Campton, leaning over, saw that the book was a first edition of Lavengro.

"Where the deuce did you get that?"

George looked at him with shining eyes. "Didn't you know? Mr. Brant has started collecting first editions. There's a chap who comes over from London with things for him. He lets me have them to look at when I'm seedy. I say, isn't this topping? Do you remember the fight?" And, marvelling once more at the ways of Providence, Campton perceived that the millionaire's taste for owning books had awakened in his stepson a taste for reading them. "I couldn't have done that for him," the father had reflected with secret bitterness. It was not that a bibliophile's library was necessary to develop a taste for letters; but that Campton himself, being a small reader, had few books about him, and usually borrowed those few. If George had lived with him he might never have guessed the boy's latent hunger, for the need of books as part of one's daily food would scarcely have presented itself to him.

From that day he and George had understood each other. Initiation had come to them in different ways, but their ardour for beauty had the same root. The visible world, and its transposition in terms of one art or another, were thereafter the subject of their interminable talks; and Campton, with a passionate interest, watched his son absorbing through books what had mysteriously reached him through his paintbrush.

They had been parted often, and for long periods; first by George's schooling in England, next by his French military service, begun at eighteen to facilitate his entry into Harvard; finally, by his sojourn at the University. But whenever they were together they seemed to make up in the first ten minutes for the longest separation; and since George had come of age, and been his own master, he had given his father every moment he could spare.

His career at Harvard had been interrupted, after two years, by the symptoms of tuberculosis which had necessitated his being hurried off to the Engadine. He had returned completely cured, and at his own wish had gone back to Harvard; and having finished his course and taken his degree, he had now come out to join his father on a long holiday before entering the New York banking-house of Bullard and Brant.

Campton, looking at the boy's bright head across the lights and flowers, thought how incredibly stupid it was to sacrifice an hour of such a life to the routine of money-getting; but he had had that question out with himself once for all, and was not going to return to it. His own success, if it lasted, would eventually help him to make George independent; but meanwhile he had no right to interfere with the boy's business training. He had hoped that George would develop some marked talent, some irresistible tendency which would decide his future too definitely for interference; but George was twenty-five, and no such call had come to him. Apparently he was fated to be only a delighted spectator and commentator; to enjoy and interpret, not to create. And Campton knew that this absence of a special bent, with the strain and absorption it implies, gave the boy his peculiar charm. The trouble was that it made him the prey of other people's plans for him. And now all these plans—Campton's dreams for the future as well as the business arrangements which were Mr. Brant's contribution—might be wrecked by to-morrow's news from Berlin. The possibility still seemed unthinkable; but in spite of his incredulity the evil shadow hung on him as he and his son chatted of political issues.

George made no allusion to his own case: his whole attitude was so dispassionate that his father began to wonder if he had not solved the question by concluding that he would not pass the medical examination. The tone he took was that the whole affair, from the point of view of twentieth-century civilization, was too monstrous an incongruity for something not to put a stop to it at the eleventh hour. His easy optimism at first stimulated his father, and then began to jar on him.

"Dastrey doesn't think it can be stopped," Campton said at length.

The boy smiled.

"Dear old Dastrey! No, I suppose not. That after-Sedan generation have got the inevitability of war in their bones. They've never been able to get beyond it. *Our* whole view is different: we're internationals, whether we want to be or not."

"To begin with, if by 'our' view you mean yours and mine, you and I haven't a drop of French blood in us," his father interposed, "and we can never really know what the French feel on such matters."

George looked at him affectionately. "Oh, but I didn't—I meant 'we' in the sense of my generation, of whatever nationality. I know French chaps who feel as I do—Louis Dastrey, Paul's nephew, for one; and lots of English ones. They don't believe the world will ever stand for another war. It's too stupidly uneconomic, to begin with: I suppose you've read Angell? Then life's worth too much, and nowadays too many millions of people know it. That's the way we all feel. Think of everything that counts—art and science and poetry, and all the rest—going to smash at the nod of some doddering diplomatist! It was different in old times, when the best of life, for the immense majority, was never anything but plague, pestilence and famine. People are too healthy and well-fed now; they're not going off to die in a ditch to oblige anybody."

Campton looked away, and his eye, straying over the crowd, lit on the long heavy face of Fortin-Lescluze, seated with a group of men on the other side of the garden.

Why had it never occurred to him before that if there was one being in the world who could get George discharged it was the great specialist under whose care he had been?

"Suppose war does come," the father thought, "what if I were to go over and tell him I'll paint his dancer?" He stood up and made his way between the tables.

Fortin-Lescluze was dining with a party of jaded-looking politicians and journalists. To reach him Campton had to squeeze past another table, at which a fair worn-looking lady sat beside a handsome old man with a dazzling mane of white hair and a Grand Officer's rosette of the Legion of Honour. Campton bowed, and the lady whispered something to her companion, who returned a stately vacant salute. Poor old Beausite, dining alone with his much-wronged and all-forgiving wife, bowing to the people she told him to bow to, and placidly murmuring: "War—war," as he stuck his fork into the peach she had peeled!

At Fortin's table the faces were less placid. The men greeted Campton with a deference which was not lost on Mme. Beausite, and the painter bent close over Fortin, embarrassed at the idea that she might overhear him. "If I can make time for a sketch—will you bring your dancing lady to-morrow?"

The physician's eyes lit up under their puffy lids.

"My dear friend—will I? She's simply set her heart on it!" He drew out his watch and added: "But why not tell her the good news yourself? You told me, I think, you'd never seen her? This is her last night at the 'Posada,' and if you'll jump into my motor we shall be just in time to see her come on."

Campton beckoned to George, and father and son followed Fortin-Lescluze. None of the three men, on the way back to Paris, made any reference to the war. The physician asked George a few medical questions, and complimented him on his look of recovered health; then the talk strayed to studios and theatres, where Fortin-Lescluze firmly kept it.

The last faint rumours of the conflict died out on the threshold of the "Posada." It would have been hard to discern, in the crowded audience, any appearance but that of ordinary pleasure-seekers momentarily stirred by a new sensation. Collectively, fashionable Paris was already away, at the seashore or in the mountains, but not a few of its chief ornaments still lingered, as the procession through Campton's studio had proved; and others had returned drawn back by doubts about the future, the desire to be nearer the source of news, the irresistible French craving for the forum and the market when messengers are foaming in. The public of the "Posada," therefore, was still Parisian enough to flatter the new dancer; and on all the pleasure-tired faces, belonging to every type of money-getters and amusement-seekers, Campton saw only the old familiar music-hall look: the look of a house with lights blazing and windows wide, but nobody and nothing within.

The usualness of it all gave him a sense of ease which his boy's enjoyment confirmed. George, lounging on the edge of their box, and watching the yellow dancer with a clear-eyed interest refreshingly different from Fortin's tarnished gaze, George so fresh and cool and unafraid, seemed to prove that a world which could produce such youths would never again settle its differences by the bloody madness of war.

Gradually Campton became absorbed in the dancer and began to observe her with the concentration he brought to bear on any subject that attracted his brush. He saw that she was more paintable than he could have hoped, though not in the extravagant dress and attitude he was sure her eminent admirer would prefer; but rather as a little crouching animal against a sun-baked wall. He smiled at the struggle he should have when the question of costume came up.

"Well, I'll do her, if you like," he turned to say; and two tears of senile triumph glittered on the physician's cheeks.

"To-morrow, then—at two—may I bring her? She leaves as soon as possible for the south. She lives on sun, heat, radiance . . ."

"To-morrow—yes," Campton nodded.

His decision once reached, the whole subject bored him, and in spite of Fortin's entreaties he got up and signalled to George.

As they strolled home through the brilliant midnight streets, the boy said: "Did I hear you tell old Fortin you were going to do his dancer?"

"Yes—why not? She's very paintable," said Campton, abruptly shaken out of his security.

"Beginning to-morrow?"

"Why not?"

"Come, you know—*to-morrow*!" George laughed.

"We'll see," his father rejoined, with an obscure sense that if he went on steadily enough doing his usual job it might somehow divert the current of events.

On the threshold of the hotel they were waylaid by an elderly man with a round face and round eyes behind gold eye-glasses. His grey hair was cut in a fringe over his guileless forehead, and he was dressed in expensive evening clothes, and shone with soap and shaving; but the anxiety of a frightened child puckered his innocent brow and twitching cheeks.

"My dear Campton—the very man I've been hunting for! You remember me—your cousin Harvey Mayhew of Utica?"

Campton, with an effort, remembered, and asked what he could do, inwardly hoping it was not a portrait.

"Oh, the simplest thing in the world. You see, I'm here as a Delegate——" At Campton's look of enquiry, Mr. Mayhew interrupted himself to explain: "To the Peace Congress at The Hague——why, yes: naturally. I landed only this morning, and find myself in the middle of all this rather foolish excitement, and unable to make out just how I can reach my destination. My time is—er—valuable, and it is very unfortunate that all this commotion should be allowed to interfere with our work. It would be most annoying if, after having made the effort to break away from Utica, I should arrive too late for the opening of the Congress."

Campton looked at him wonderingly. "Then you're going anyhow?"

"Going? Why not? You surely don't think——?" Mr. Mayhew threw back his shoulders, pink and impressive. "I shouldn't, in any case, allow anything so opposed to my convictions as *war* to interfere with my carrying out my mandate. All I want is to find out the route least likely to be closed if—if this monstrous thing should happen."

Campton considered. "Well, if I were you, I should go round by Luxembourg—it's longer, but you'll be out of the way of trouble." He gave a nod of encouragement, and the Peace Delegate thanked him profusely.

Father and son were lodged on the top floor of the Crillon, in the little apartment which opens on the broad terraced roof. Campton had wanted to put before his boy one of the city's most perfect scenes; and when they reached their sitting-room George went straight out onto the terrace, and leaning on the parapet, called back: "Oh, don't go to bed yet—it's too jolly."

Campton followed, and the two stood looking down on the festal expanse of the Place de la Concorde strown with great flower-clusters of lights between its pearly distances. The sky was full of stars, pale, remote, half-drowned in the city's vast illumination; and the foliage of the Champs Elysées and the Tuileries made masses of mysterious darkness behind the statues and the flashing fountains.

For a long time neither father nor son spoke; then Campton said: "Are you game to start the day after to-morrow?"

George waited a moment. "For Africa?"

"Well—my idea would be to push straight through to the south—as far as Palermo, say. All this cloudy watery loveliness gives me a furious appetite for violent red earth and white houses crackling in the glare."

George again pondered; then he said: "It sounds first-rate. But if you're so sure we're going to start why did you tell Fortin to bring that girl to-morrow?"

Campton, reddening in the darkness, felt as if his son's clear eyes were following the motions of his blood. Had George suspected why he had wanted to ingratiate himself with the physician?

"It was stupid—I'll put her off," he muttered. He dropped into an armchair, and sat there, in his clumsy infirm attitude, his arms folded behind his head, while George continued to lean on the parapet.

The boy's question had put an end to their talk by baring the throbbing nerve of his father's anxiety. If war were declared the next day, what did George mean to do? There was every hope of his obtaining his discharge; but would he lend himself to the attempt? The deadly fear of crystallizing his son's refusal by forcing him to put it into words kept Campton from asking the question.

Chapter IV

T HE evening was too beautiful, and too full of the sense
  of fate, for sleep to be possible, and long after George had
finally said "All the same, I think I'll turn in," his father sat on,
listening to the gradual subsidence of the traffic, and watching
the night widen above Paris.

As he sat there, discouragement overcame him. His last plan,
his plan for getting George finally and completely over to his
side, was going to fail as all his other plans had failed. If there
were war there would be no more portraits to paint, and his
vision of wealth would vanish as visions of love and happiness
and comradeship had one by one faded away. Nothing had ever
succeeded with him but the thing he had in some moods set
least store by, the dogged achievement of his brush; and just as
that was about to assure his happiness, here was this horrible
world-catastrophe threatening to fall across his path.

His misfortune had been that he could neither get on easily
with people nor live without them; could never wholly isolate
himself in his art, nor yet resign himself to any permanent
human communion that left it out, or, worse still, dragged
it in irrelevantly. He had tried both kinds, and on the whole
preferred the first. His marriage, his stupid ill-fated marriage,
had after all not been the most disenchanting of his adventures,
because Julia Ambrose, when she married him, had made no
pretense of espousing his art.

He had seen her first in the tumble-down Venetian palace
where she lived with her bachelor uncle, old Horace Ambrose,
who dabbled in bric-a-brac and cultivated a guileless Bohemi-
anism. Campton, looking back, could still understand why,
to a youth fresh from Utica, at odds with his father, unwilling to go into the family business, and strangling with violent unexpressed ideas on art and the universe, marriage with
Julia Ambrose had seemed so perfect a solution. She had been
brought up abroad by her parents, a drifting and impecunious
American couple; and after their deaths, within a few months
of each other, her education had been completed, at her uncle's
expense, in a fashionable Parisian convent. Thence she had been

transplanted at nineteen to his Venetian household, and all the ideas that most terrified and scandalized Campton's family were part of the only air she had breathed. She had never intentionally feigned an exaggerated interest in his ambitions. But her bringing-up made her regard them as natural; she knew what he was aiming at, though she had never understood his reasons for trying. The jargon of art was merely one of her many languages; but she talked it so fluently that he had taken it for her mother-tongue.

The only other girls he had known well were his sisters—earnest eye-glassed young women, whose one answer to all his problems was that he ought to come home. The idea of Europe had always been terrifying to them, and indeed to his whole family, since the extraordinary misadventure whereby, as the result of a protracted diligence journey over bad roads, of a violent thunderstorm, and a delayed steamer, Campton had been born in Paris instead of Utica. Mrs. Campton the elder had taken the warning to heart, and never again left her native soil; but the sisters, safely and properly brought into the world in their own city and State, had always felt that Campton's persistent yearnings for Europe, and his inexplicable detachment from Utica and the Mangle, were mysteriously due to the accident of their mother's premature confinement.

Compared with the admonitions of these domestic censors, Miss Ambrose's innocent conversation was as seductive as the tangles of Neæra's hair, and it used to be a joke between them (one of the few he had ever been able to make her see) that he, the raw up-Stater, was Parisian born, while she, the glass and pattern of worldly knowledge, had seen the light in the pure atmosphere of Madison Avenue.

Through her, in due course, he came to know another girl, a queer abrupt young American, already an old maid at twenty-two, and in open revolt against her family for reasons not unlike his own. Adele Anthony had come abroad to keep house for a worthless "artistic" brother, who was preparing to be a sculptor by prolonged sessions in Anglo-American bars and the lobbies of music-halls. When he finally went under, and was shipped home, Miss Anthony stayed on in Paris, ashamed, as she told Campton, to go back and face the righteous triumph of a family connection who had unanimously disbelieved in the possibility

of making Bill Anthony into a sculptor, and in the wisdom of
his sister's staking her small means on the venture.

"Somehow, behind it all, I was right, and they were wrong;
but to do anything with poor Bill I ought to have been able to
begin two or three generations back," she confessed.

Miss Anthony had many friends in Paris, of whom Julia
Ambrose was the most admired; and she had assisted sympa-
thizingly (if not enthusiastically) at Campton's wooing of Julia,
and their hasty marriage. Her only note of warning had been
the reminder that Julia had always been poor, and had always
lived as if she were rich; and that was silenced by Campton's
rejoinder that the Magic Mangle, to which the Campton prosperity was due, was some day going to make him rich, though
he had always lived as if he were poor.

"Well—you'd better not, any longer," Adele sharply advised;
and he laughed, and promised to go out and buy a new hat.
In truth, careless of comfort as he was, he adored luxury in
women, and was resolved to let his wife ruin him if she did it
handsomely enough. Doubtless she might have, had fate given
her time; but soon after their marriage old Mr. Campton died,
and it was found that a trusted manager had so invested the
profits of the Mangle that the heirs inherited only a series of
law-suits.

John Campton, henceforth, was merely the unsuccessful son
of a ruined manufacturer; painting became a luxury he could no
longer afford, and his mother and sisters besought him to come
back and take over what was left of the business. It seemed so
clearly his duty that, with anguish of soul, he prepared to go;
but Julia, on being consulted, developed a sudden passion for
art and poverty.

"We'd have to live in Utica—for some years at any rate?"

"Well, yes, no doubt——" They faced the fact desolately.

"They'd much better look out for another manager. What do
you know about business? Since you've taken up painting you'd
better try to make a success of that," she advised him; and he
was too much of the same mind not to agree.

It was not long before George's birth, and they were fully
resolved to go home for the event, and thus spare their hoped-
for heir the inconvenience of coming into the world, like his

father, in a foreign country. But now this was not to be thought of, and the eventual inconvenience to George was lost sight of by his progenitors in the contemplation of nearer problems.

For a few years their life dragged along shabbily and depressingly. Now that Campton's painting was no longer an amateur's hobby but a domestic obligation, Julia thought it her duty to interest herself in it; and her only idea of doing so was by means of what she called "relations," using the word in its French and diplomatic sense.

She was convinced that her husband's lack of success was due to Beausite's blighting epigram, and to Campton's subsequent resolve to strike out for himself. "It's a great mistake to try to be original till people have got used to you," she said, with the shrewdness that sometimes startled him. "If you'd only been civil to Beausite he would have ended by taking you up, and then you could have painted as queerly as you liked."

Beausite, by this time, had succumbed to the honours which lie in wait for such talents, and in his starred and titled maturity his earlier dread of rivals had given way to a prudent benevolence. Young artists were always welcome at the receptions he gave in his sumptuous hotel of the Avenue du Bois. Those who threatened to be rivals were even invited to dine; and Julia was justified in triumphing when such an invitation finally rewarded her efforts.

Campton, with a laugh, threw the card into the stove.

"If you'd only understand that that's not the way," he said.

"What is, then?"

"Why, letting all that lot see what unutterable rubbish one thinks them!"

"I should have thought you'd tried that long enough," she said with pale lips; but he answered jovially that it never palled on him.

She was bitterly offended; but she knew Campton by this time, and was not a woman to waste herself in vain resentment. She simply suggested that since he would not profit by Beausite's advance the only alternative was to try to get orders for portraits; and though at that stage he was not in the mood for portrait-painting, he made an honest attempt to satisfy her. She began, of course, by sitting for him. She sat again and again; but, lovely as she was, he was not inspired, and one day, in sheer self-defence, he blurted out that she was not paintable. She never forgot the epithet, and it loomed large in their subsequent recriminations.

Adele Anthony—it was just like her—gave him his first order, and she did prove paintable. Campton made a success of her long crooked pink-nosed face; but she didn't perceive it (she had wanted something oval, with tulle, and a rose in a taper hand), and after heroically facing the picture for six months she hid it away in an attic, whence, a year or so before the date of the artist's present musings, it had been fished out as an "early Campton," to be exhibited half a dozen times, and have articles written about it in the leading art reviews.

Adele's picture acted as an awful warning to intending patrons, and after one or two attempts at depicting mistrustful friends Campton refused to constrain his muse, and no more was said of portrait-painting. But life in Paris was growing too expensive. He persuaded Julia to try Spain, and they wandered about there for a year. She was not fault-finding, she did not complain, but she hated travelling, she could not eat things cooked in oil, and his pictures seemed to her to be growing more and more ugly and unsalable.

Finally they came one day to Ronda, after a trying sojourn at Cordova. In the train Julia had moaned a little at the mosquitoes of the previous night, and at the heat and dirt of the second-class compartment; then, always conscious of the ill-breeding of fretfulness, she had bent her lovely head above her Tauchnitz. And it was then that Campton, looking out of the window to avoid her fatally familiar profile, had suddenly discovered another. It was that of a peasant girl in front of a small whitewashed house, under a white pergola hung with bunches of big red peppers. The house, which was close to the railway, was propped against an orange-coloured rock, and in the glare cast up from the red earth its walls looked as blue as snow in shadow. The girl was all blue-white too, from her cotton skirt to the kerchief knotted turbanwise above two folds of blue-black hair. Her round forehead and merry nose were relieved like a bronze medallion against the wall; and she stood with her hands on her hips, laughing at a little pig asleep under a cork-tree, who lay on his side like a dog.

The vision filled the carriage-window and then vanished; but it remained so sharply impressed on Campton that even then he knew what was going to happen. He leaned back with a sense of relief, and forgot everything else.

The next morning he said to his wife: "There's a little place up the line that I want to go back and paint. You don't mind staying here a day or two, do you?"

She said she did not mind; it was what she always said; but he was somehow aware that this was the particular grievance she had always been waiting for. He did not care for that, or for anything but getting a seat in the diligence which started every morning for the village nearest the white house. On the way he remembered that he had left Julia only forty pesetas, but he did not care about that either . . . He stayed a month, and when he returned to Ronda his wife had gone back to Paris, leaving a letter to say that the matter was in the hands of her lawyers.

"What did you do it for—I mean in that particular way? For goodness knows I understand all the rest," Adele Anthony had once asked him, while the divorce proceedings were going on; and he had shaken his head, conscious that he could not explain.

It was a year or two later that he met the first person who *did* understand: a Russian lady who had heard the story, was curious to know him, and asked, one day, when their friendship had progressed, to see the sketches he had brought back from his *fugue*.

"*Comme je vous comprends!*" she had murmured, her grey eyes deep in his; but perceiving that she did not allude to the sketches, but to his sentimental adventure, Campton pushed the drawings out of sight, vexed with himself for having shown them.

He forgave the Russian lady her artistic obtuseness for the sake of her human comprehension. They had met at the loneliest moment of his life, when his art seemed to have failed him like everything else, and when the struggle to get possession of his son, which had been going on in the courts ever since the break with Julia, had finally been decided against him. His Russian friend consoled, amused and agitated him, and after a few years drifted out of his life as irresponsibly as she had drifted into it; and he found himself, at forty-five, a lonely thwarted man, as full as ever of faith in his own powers, but with little left in

human nature or in opportunity. It was about this time that
he heard that Julia was to marry again, and that his boy would
have a stepfather.

He knew that even his own family thought it "the best thing
that could happen." They were tired of clubbing together to
pay Julia's alimony, and heaved a united sigh of relief when they
learned that her second choice had fallen, not on the bankrupt
"foreign Count" they had always dreaded, but on the Paris partner of the famous bank of Bullard and Brant. Mr. Brant's request
that his wife's alimony should be discontinued gave him a moral
superiority which even Campton's recent successes could not
shake. It was felt that the request expressed the contempt of an
income easily counted in seven figures for a pittance painfully
screwed up to four; and the Camptons admired Mr. Brant much
more for not needing their money than for refusing it.

Their attitude left John Campton without support in his
struggle to keep a hold on his boy. His family sincerely thought
George safer with the Brants than with his own father, and
the father could advance to the contrary no arguments they
would have understood. All the forces of order seemed leagued
against him; and it was perhaps this fact that suddenly drove
him into conformity with them. At any rate, from the day of
Julia's remarriage no other woman shared her former husband's
life. Campton settled down to the solitude of his dusty studio at
Montmartre, and painted doggedly, all his thoughts on George.

At this point in his reminiscences the bells of Sainte Clotilde
rang out the half-hour after midnight, and Campton rose and
went into the darkened sitting-room.

The door into George's room was open, and in the silence the
father heard the boy's calm breathing. A light from the bathroom cast its ray on the dressing-table, which was scattered with
the contents of George's pockets. Campton, dwelling with a
new tenderness on everything that belonged to his son, noticed
a smart antelope card-case (George had his mother's weakness
for Bond Street novelties), a wrist-watch, his studs, a bundle of
bank-notes; and beside these a thumbed and dirty red book, the
size of a large pocket diary.

The father wondered what it was; then of a sudden he knew.
He had once seen Mme. Lebel's grandson pull just such a red

book from his pocket as he was leaving for his "twenty-eight days" of military service; it was the *livret militaire* that every French citizen under forty-eight carries about with him.

Campton had never paid much attention to French military regulations: George's service over, he had dismissed the matter from his mind, forgetting that his son was still a member of the French army, and as closely linked to the fortunes of France as the grandson of the concierge of Montmartre. Now it occurred to him that that little red book would answer the questions he had not dared to put; and stealing in, he possessed himself of it and carried it back to the sitting-room. There he sat down by the lamp and read.

First George's name, his domicile, his rank as a *maréchal des logis* of dragoons, the number of his regiment and its base: all that was already familiar. But what was this on the next page?

"In case of general mobilisation announced to the populations of France by public proclamations, or by notices posted in the streets, the bearer of this order is to rejoin his regiment at —— .

"He is to take with him provisions for one day.

"He is to present himself at the station of —— on the third day of mobilisation at 6 o'clock, and to take the train indicated by the station-master.

"The days of mobilisation are counted from o o'clock to 24 o'clock. The first day is that on which the order of mobilisation is published."

Campton dropped the book and pressed his hands to his temples. "The days of mobilisation are counted from o o'clock to 24 o'clock. The first day is that on which the order of mobilisation is published." Then, if France mobilised that day, George would start the second day after, at six in the morning. George might be going to leave him within forty-eight hours from that very moment!

Campton had always vaguely supposed that, some day or other, if war came, a telegram would call George to his base; it had never occurred to him that every detail of the boy's military life had long since been regulated by the dread power which had him in its grasp.

He read the next paragraph: "The bearer will travel free of charge——" and thought with a grin how it would annoy

Anderson Brant that the French government should presume to treat his stepson as if he could not pay his way. The plump bundle of bank-notes on the dressing-table seemed to look with ineffectual scorn at the red book that sojourned so democratically in the same pocket. And Campton, picturing George jammed into an overcrowded military train, on the plebeian wooden seat of a third-class compartment, grinned again, forgetful of his own anxiety in the vision of Brant's exasperation.

Ah, well, it wasn't war yet, whatever they said!

He carried the red book back to the dressing-table. The light falling across the bed drew his eye to the young face on the pillow. George lay on his side, one arm above his head, the other laxly stretched along the bed. He had thrown off the blankets, and the sheet, clinging to his body, modelled his slim flank and legs as he lay in dreamless rest.

For a long time Campton stood gazing; then he stole back to the sitting-room, picked up a sketch-book and pencil and returned. He knew there was no danger of waking George, and he began to draw, eagerly but deliberately, fascinated by the happy accident of the lighting, and of the boy's position.

"Like a statue of a young knight I've seen somewhere," he said to himself, vexed and surprised that he, whose plastic memories were always so precise, should not remember where; and then his pencil stopped. What he had really thought was: "Like the *effigy* of a young knight"—though he had instinctively changed the word as it formed itself. He leaned in the doorway, the sketch-book in hand, and continued to gaze at his son. It was the clinging sheet, no doubt, that gave him that look . . . and the white glare of the electric burner.

If war came, that was just the way a boy might lie on a battlefield—or afterward in a hospital bed. Not *his* boy, thank heaven; but very probably his boy's friends: hundreds and thousands of boys like his boy, the age of his boy, with a laugh like his boy's . . . The wicked waste of it! Well, that was what war meant . . . what to-morrow might bring to millions of parents like himself.

He stiffened his shoulders, and opened the sketch-book again. What watery stuff was he made of, he wondered? Just because the boy lay as if he were posing for a tombstone! . . .

What of Signorelli, who had sat at his dead son's side and drawn him, tenderly, minutely, while the coffin waited?

Well, damn Signorelli—that was all! Campton threw down his book, turned out the sitting-room lights, and limped away to bed.

Chapter V

THE next morning he said to George, over coffee on the terrace: "I think I'll drop in at Cook's about our tickets."

George nodded, munching his golden roll.

"Right. I'll run up to see mother, then."

His father was silent. Inwardly he was saying to himself: "The chances are she'll be going back to Deauville this afternoon."

There had not been much to gather from the newspapers heaped at their feet. Austria had ordered general mobilisation; but while the tone of the despatches was nervous and contradictory that of the leading articles remained almost ominously reassuring. Campton absorbed the reassurance without heeding its quality: it was a drug he had to have at any price.

He expected the Javanese dancer to sit to him that afternoon, but he had not proposed to George to be present. On the chance that things might eventually take a wrong turn he meant to say a word to Fortin-Lescluze; and the presence of his son would have been embarrassing.

"You'll be back for lunch?" he called to George, who still lounged on the terrace in pyjamas.

"Rather.—That is, unless mother makes a point . . . in case she's leaving."

"Oh, of course," said Campton with grim cordiality.

"You see, dear old boy, I've got to see Uncle Andy some time . . ." It was the grotesque name that George, in his babyhood, had given to Mr. Brant, and when he grew up it had been difficult to substitute another. "Especially now——" George added, pulling himself up out of his chair.

"Now?"

They looked at each other in silence, irritation in the father's eye, indulgent amusement in the son's.

"Why, if you and I are really off on this long trek——"

"Oh, of course," agreed Campton, relieved. "You'd much better lunch with them. I always want you to do what's decent." He paused on the threshold to add: "By the way, don't forget Adele."

"Well, rather not," his son responded. "And we'll keep the evening free for something awful."

As he left the room he heard George rapping on the telephone and calling out Miss Anthony's number.

Campton had to have reassurance at any price; and he got it, as usual, irrationally but irresistibly, through his eyes. The mere fact that the midsummer sun lay so tenderly on Paris, that the bronze dolphins of the fountains in the square were spraying the Nereids' Louis Philippe chignons as playfully as ever; that the sleepy Cities of France dozed as heavily on their thrones, and the Horses of Marly pranced as fractiously on their pedestals; that the glorious central setting of the city lay there in its usual mellow pomp—all this gave him a sense of security that no crisscrossing of Reuters and Havases could shake.

Nevertheless, he reflected that there was no use in battling with the silly hysterical crowd he would be sure to encounter at Cook's; and having left word with the hotel-porter to secure two "sleepings" on the Naples express, he drove to the studio.

On the way, as his habit was, he thought hard of his model: everything else disappeared like a rolled-up curtain, and his inner vision centred itself on the little yellow face he was to paint.

Peering through her cobwebby window, he saw old Mme. Lebel on the watch. He knew she wanted to pounce out and ask if there would be war; and composing his most taciturn countenance he gave her a preoccupied nod and hurried by.

The studio looked grimy and disordered, and he remembered that he had intended, the evening before, to come back and set it to rights. In pursuance of this plan, he got out a canvas, fussed with his brushes and colours, and then tried once more to make the place tidy. But his attempts at order always resulted in worse confusion; the fact had been one of Julia's grievances against him, and he had often thought that a reaction from his ways probably explained the lifeless neatness of the Anderson Brant drawing-room.

Campton had fled to Montmartre to escape a number of things: first of all, the possibility of meeting people who would want to talk about the European situation, then of being called up by Mrs. Brant, and lastly of having to lunch alone in a fashionable restaurant. In his morbid dread of seeing people he would have preferred an omelette in the studio, if only Mariette had been at hand to make it; and he decided, after a vain struggle with his muddled "properties," to cross over to the Luxembourg quarter and pick up a meal in a wine-shop.

He did not own to himself his secret reason for this decision; but it caused him, after a glance at his watch, to hasten his steps down the rue Montmartre and bribe a passing taxi to carry him to the Museum of the Luxembourg. He reached it ten minutes before the midday closing, and hastening past the serried statues, turned into a room half-way down the gallery. Whistler's Mother and the Carmencita of Sargent wondered at each other from its walls; and on the same wall with the Whistler hung the picture Campton had come for: his portrait of his son. He had given it to the Luxembourg the day after Mr. Brant had tried to buy it, with the object of inflicting the most cruel slight he could think of on the banker.

In the generous summer light the picture shone out on him with a communicative warmth: never had he seen so far into its depths. "No wonder," he thought, "it opened people's eyes to what I was trying for."

He stood and stared his own eyes full, mentally comparing the features before him with those of the firmer harder George he had left on the terrace of the Crillon, and noting how time, while fulfilling the rich promise of the younger face, had yet taken something from its brightness.

Campton, at that moment, found more satisfaction than ever in thinking how it must have humiliated Brant to have the picture given to France. "He could have understood my keeping it myself—or holding it for a bigger price—but *giving it*——!" The satisfaction was worth the sacrifice of the best record he would ever have of that phase of his son's youth. At various times afterward he had tried for the same George, but not one of his later studies had that magic light on it. Still, he was glad he had given the picture. It was safe, safer than it would have been with him. His great dread had always been that if his will were mislaid (and his things were always getting mislaid) the picture might be sold, and fall into Brant's hands after his death.

The closing signal drove him out of the Museum, and he turned into the first wine-shop. He had advised George to lunch with the Brants, but there was disappointment in his heart. Seeing the turn things were taking, he had hoped the boy would feel the impulse to remain with him. But, after all, at such a time a son could not refuse to go to his mother. Campton pictured the little party of three grouped about the luncheon-table in the high cool dining-room of the Avenue Marigny, with the famous Hubert Robert panels, and the Louis XV silver and Sèvres; while he, the father, George's father, sat alone at the soiled table of a frowsy wine-shop.

Well—it was he who had so willed it. Life was too crazy a muddle—and who could have foreseen that he might have been repaid for twenty-six years with such a wife by keeping an undivided claim on such a son?

His meal over, he hastened back to the studio, hoping to find the dancer there. Fortin-Lescluze had sworn to bring her at two, and Campton was known to exact absolute punctuality. He had put the final touch to his fame by refusing to paint the mad young Duchesse de la Tour Crenelée—who was exceptionally paintable—because she had kept him waiting three-quarters of an hour. But now, though it was nearly three, and the dancer and her friend had not come, Campton dared not move, lest he should miss Fortin-Lescluze.

"Sent for by a rich patient in a war-funk; or else hanging about in the girl's dressing-room while she polishes her toe-nails," Campton reflected; and sulkily sat down to wait.

He had never been willing to have a telephone. To him it was a live thing, a kind of Laocoön-serpent that caught one in its coils and dragged one struggling to the receiver. His friends had spent all their logic in trying to argue away this belief; but he answered obstinately: "Every one would be sure to call me up when Mariette was out." Even the Russian lady, during her brief reign, had pleaded in vain on this point.

He would have given a good deal now if he had listened to her. The terror of having to cope with small material difficulties, always strongest in him in moments of artistic inspiration—when the hushed universe seemed hardly big enough to hold him and his model—this dread anchored him to his seat while he tried to make up his mind to send Mme. Lebel to the nearest telephone-station.

If he called to her, she would instantly begin: "And the war, sir?" And he would have to settle that first. Besides, if he did not

telephone himself he could not make sure of another appointment with Fortin-Lescluze. But the idea of battling alone with
the telephone in a public place covered his large body with a
damp distress. If only George had been in reach!

He waited till four, and then, furious, locked the studio and
went down. Mme. Lebel still sat in her spidery den. She looked
at him gravely, their eyes met, they exchanged a bow, but she
did not move or speak. She was busy as usual with some rusty
sewing—he thought it odd that she should not rush out to
waylay him. Everything that day was odd.

He found all the telephone-booths besieged. The people waiting were certainly bad cases of war-funk, to judge from their
looks; after scrutinizing them for a while he decided to return
to his hotel, and try to communicate with Fortin-Lescluze from
there.

To his annoyance there was not a taxi to be seen. He limped
down the slope of Montmartre to the nearest métro-station, and
just as he was preparing to force his lame bulk into a crowded
train, caught sight of a solitary horse-cab: a vehicle he had not
risked himself in for years.

The cab-driver, for gastronomic reasons, declined to take him
farther than the Madeleine; and getting out there, Campton
walked along the rue Royale. Everything still looked wonderfully as usual; and the fountains in the Place sparkled gloriously.

Comparatively few people were about: he was surprised to see
how few. A small group of them, he noticed, had paused near
the doorway of the Ministry of Marine, and were looking—
without visible excitement—at a white paper pasted on the wall.

He crossed the street and looked too. In the middle of the
paper, in queer Gothic-looking characters, he saw the words

"*Les Armées de Terre et de Mer. . . .*"

War had come——
He knew now that he had never for an instant believed it possible. Even when he had had that white-lipped interview with
the Brants, even when he had planned to take Fortin-Lescluze
by his senile infatuation, and secure a medical certificate for
George; even then, he had simply been obeying the superstitious

impulse which makes a man carry his umbrella when he goes out on a cloudless morning.

War had come.

He stood on the edge of the sidewalk, and tried to think—now that it was here—what it really meant: that is, what it meant to him. Beyond that he had no intention of venturing. "This is not our job anyhow," he muttered, repeating the phrase with which he had bolstered up his talk with Julia.

But abstract thinking was impossible: his confused mind could only snatch at a few drifting scraps of purpose. "Let's be practical," he said to himself.

The first thing to do was to get back to the hotel and call up the physician. He strode along at his fastest limp, suddenly contemptuous of the people who got in his way.

"War—and they've nothing to do but dawdle and gape! How like the French!" He found himself hating the French.

He remembered that he had asked to have his sleepings engaged for the following night. But even if he managed to secure his son's discharge, there could be no thought, now, of George's leaving the country; and he stopped at the desk to cancel the order.

There was no one behind the desk: one would have said that confusion prevailed in the hall, if its emptiness had not made the word incongruous. At last a waiter with rumpled hair strayed out of the restaurant, and of him, imperiously, Campton demanded the concierge.

"The concierge? He's gone."

"To get my places for Naples?"

The waiter looked blank. "Gone: mobilised—to join his regiment. It's the war."

"But look here, some one must have attended to getting my places, I suppose," cried Campton wrathfully. He invaded the inner office and challenged a secretary who was trying to deal with several unmanageable travellers, but who explained to him, patiently, that his sleepings had certainly not been engaged, as no trains were leaving Paris for the present. "Not for civilian travel," he added, still more patiently.

Campton had a sudden sense of suffocation. No trains leaving Paris "for the present"? But then people like himself—people who had nothing on earth to do with the war—had been caught like rats in a trap! He reflected with a shiver that Mrs. Brant would not be able to return to Deauville, and would probably insist on his coming to see her every day. He asked: "How long is this preposterous state of things to last?"—but no one answered, and he stalked to the lift and had himself carried up-stairs.

He was confident that George would be there waiting; but the sitting-room was empty. He felt as if he were on a desert island, with the last sail disappearing over the dark rim of the world.

After much vain ringing he got into communication with Fortin's house, and heard a confused voice saying that the physician had already left Paris.

"Left—for where? For how long?"

And then the eternal answer: "The doctor is mobilised. *It's the war.*"

Mobilised—already? Within the first twenty-four hours? A man of Fortin's age and authority? Campton was terrified by the uncanny rapidity with which events were moving, he whom haste had always confused and disconcerted, as if there were a secret link between his lameness and the movements of his will. He rang up Dastrey, but no one answered. Evidently his friend was out, and his friend's *bonne* also. "I suppose *she's* mobilised: they'll be mobilising the women next."

At last, from sheer over-agitation, his fatigued mind began to move more deliberately: he collected his wits, laboured with his more immediate difficulties, and decided that he would go to Fortin-Lescluze's house, on the chance that the physician had not, after all, really started.

"Ten to one he won't go till to-morrow," Campton reasoned.

The hall of the hotel was emptier than ever, and no taxi was in sight down the whole length of the rue Royale, or the rue Boissy d'Anglas, or the rue de Rivoli: not even a horse-cab showed against the deserted distances. He crossed to the métro, and painfully descended its many stairs.

Chapter VI

CAMPTON, proffering twenty francs to an astonished maid-servant, learned that, yes, to his intimates—and of course Monsieur was one?—the doctor *was* in, was in fact dining, and did not leave till the next morning.

"Dining—at six o'clock?"

"Monsieur's son, Monsieur Jean, is starting at once for his depot. That's the reason."

Campton sent in his card. He expected to be received in the so-called "studio," a lofty room with Chinese hangings, Renaissance choir-stalls, organ, grand piano, and post-impressionist paintings, where Fortin-Lescluze received the celebrities of the hour. Mme. Fortin never appeared there, and Campton associated the studio with amusing talk, hot-house flowers, and ladies lolling on black velvet divans. He supposed that the physician was separated from his wife, and that she had a home of her own.

When the maid reappeared she did not lead him to the studio, but into a small dining-room with the traditional Henri II sideboard of waxed walnut, a hanging table-lamp under a beaded shade, an India-rubber plant on a plush pedestal, and napkins that were just being restored to their bone rings by the four persons seated about the red-and-white checkered table-cloth.

These were: the great man himself, a tall large woman with grey hair, a tiny old lady, her face framed in a peasant's fluted cap, and a plain young man wearing a private's uniform, who had a nose like the doctor's and simple light blue eyes.

The two ladies and the young man—so much more interesting to the painter's eye than the sprawling beauties of the studio—were introduced by Fortin-Lescluze as his wife, his mother and his son. Mme. Fortin said, in a deep alto, a word or two about the privilege of meeting the famous painter who had portrayed her husband, and the old mother, in a piping voice, exclaimed: "Monsieur, I was at Sedan in 1870. I saw the Germans. I saw the Emperor sitting on a bench. He was crying."

"My mother's heard everything, she's seen everything. There's no one in the world like my mother!" the physician said, laying his hand on hers.

"You won't see the Germans again, *ma bonne mère*!" her daughter-in-law added, smiling.

Campton took coffee with them, bore with a little inevitable talk about the war, and then eagerly questioned the son. The young man was a chemist, a *préparateur* in the laboratory of the Institut Pasteur. He was also, it appeared, given to prehistoric archæology, and had written a "thesis" on the painted caves of the Dordogne. He seemed extremely serious, and absorbed in questions of science and letters. But it appeared to him perfectly simple to be leaving it all in a few hours to join his regiment. "The war had to come. This sort of thing couldn't go on," he said, in the words of Mme. Lebel.

He was to start in an hour, and Campton excused himself for intruding on the family, who seemed as happily united, as harmonious in their deeper interests, as if no musical studio-parties and exotic dancers had ever absorbed the master of the house.

Campton, looking at the group, felt a pang of envy, and thought, for the thousandth time, how frail a screen of activity divided him from depths of loneliness he dared not sound. "'For every man hath business and desire,'" he muttered as he followed the physician.

In the consulting-room he explained: "It's about my son——"

He had not been able to bring the phrase out in the presence of the young man who must have been just George's age, and who was leaving in an hour for his regiment. But between Campton and the father there were complicities, and there might therefore be accommodations. In the consulting-room one breathed a lower air.

It was not that Campton wanted to do anything underhand. He was genuinely anxious about George's health. After all, tuberculosis did not disappear in a month or even a year: his anxiety was justified. And then George, but for the stupid accident of his birth, would never have been mixed up in the war. Campton felt that he could make his request with his head high.

Fortin-Lescluze seemed to think so too; at any rate he expressed no surprise. But could anything on earth have surprised him, after thirty years in that confessional of a room?

The difficulty was that he did not see his way to doing anything—not immediately, at any rate.

"You must let the boy join his base. He leaves to-morrow? Give me the number of his regiment and the name of the town, and trust me to do what I can."

"But you're off yourself?"

"Yes: I'm being sent to a hospital at Lyons. But I'll leave you my address."

Campton lingered, unable to take this as final. He looked about him uneasily, and then, for a moment, straight into the physician's eyes.

"You must know how I feel; your boy is an only son, too."

"Yes, yes," the father assented, in the absent-minded tone of professional sympathy. But Campton felt that he felt the deep difference.

"Well, goodbye—and thanks."

As Campton turned to go the physician laid a hand on his shoulder and spoke with sudden fierce emotion. "Yes: Jean is an only son—an only child. For his mother and myself it's not a trifle—having our only son in the war."

There was no allusion to the dancer, no hint that Fortin remembered her; it was Campton who lowered his gaze before the look in the other father's eyes.

Chapter VII

" A son in the war——"
      The words followed Campton down the stairs.

What did it mean, and what must it feel like, for parents in this safe denationalized modern world to be suddenly saying to each other with white lips: A son in the war?

He stood on the kerbstone, staring ahead of him and forgetting whither he was bound. The world seemed to lie under a spell, and its weight was on his limbs and brain. Usually any deep inward trouble made him more than ever alive to the outward aspect of things; but this new world in which people talked glibly of sons in the war had suddenly become invisible to him, and he did not know where he was, or what he was staring at. He noted the fact, and remembered a story of St. Bernard—he thought it was—walking beside a beautiful lake in supersensual ecstasy, and saying afterward: "Was there a lake? I didn't see it."

On the way back to the hotel he passed the American Embassy, and had a vague idea of trying to see the Ambassador and find out if the United States were not going to devise some way of evading the tyrannous regulation that bound young Americans to France. "And they call this a free country!" he heard himself exclaiming.

The remark sounded exactly like one of Julia's, and this reminded him that the Ambassador frequently dined at the Brants'. They had certainly not left his door untried; and since, to the Brant circles, Campton was still a shaggy Bohemian, his appeal was not likely to fortify theirs.

His mind turned to Jorgenstein, and the vast web of the speculator's financial relations. But, after all, France was on the verge of war, if not in it; and following up the threads of the Jorgenstein web was likely to land one in Frankfort or Vienna.

At the hotel he found his sitting-room empty; but presently the door opened and George came in laden with books, fresh yellow and grey ones in Flammarion wrappers.

"Hullo, Dad," he said; and added: "So the silly show is on."

"Mobilisation is not war——," said Campton.

"No——"

"What on earth are all those books?"

"Provender. It appears we may rot at the depot for weeks. I've just seen a chap who's in my regiment."

Campton felt a sudden relief. The purchase of the books proved that George was fairly sure he would not be sent to the front. His father went up to him and tapped him on the chest.

"How about this——?" He wanted to add: "I've just seen Fortin, who says he'll get you off"; but though George's eye was cool and unenthusiastic it did not encourage such confidences.

"Oh—lungs? I imagine I'm sound again." He paused, and stooped to turn over the books. Carelessly, he added: "But then the stethoscope may think differently. Nothing to do but wait and see."

"Of course," Campton agreed.

It was clear that the boy hated what was ahead of him; and what more could his father ask? Of course he was not going to confess to a desire to shirk his duty; but it was easy to see that his whole lucid intelligence repudiated any sympathy with the ruinous adventure.

"Have you seen Adele?" Campton enquired, and George replied that he had dropped in for five minutes, and that Miss Anthony wanted to see his father.

"Is she—nervous?"

"Old Adele? I should say not: she's fighting mad. *La Revanche* and all the rest of it. She doesn't realize—*sancta simplicitas!*"

"Oh, I can see Adele throwing on the faggots!"

Father and son were silent, both busy lighting cigarettes. When George's was lit he remarked: "Well, if we're not called at once it'll be a good chance to read 'The Golden Bough' right through."

Campton stared, not knowing the book even by name. What a queer changeling the boy was! But George's composure, his deep and genuine indifference to the whole political turmoil, once more fortified his father.

"Have they any news—?" he ventured. "They," in their private language, meant the Brants.

"Oh, yes, lots: Uncle Andy was stiff with it. But not really amounting to anything. Of course there's no doubt there'll be war."

"How about England?"

"Nobody knows; but the bankers seem to think England's all right." George paused, and finally added: "Look here, dear old boy—before she leaves I think mother wants to see you."

Campton hardened instantly. "She *has* seen me—yesterday."

"I know; she told me."

The son began to cut the pages of one of his books with a visiting-card he had picked up, and the father stood looking out on the Place de la Concorde through the leafy curtain of the terrace.

Campton knew that he could not refuse his son's request; in his heart of hearts he was glad it had been made, since it might mean that "they" had found a way—perhaps through the Ambassador.

But he could never prevent a stiffening of his whole self at any summons or suggestion from the Brants. He thought of the seeming unity of the Fortin-Lescluze couple, and of the background of peaceful family life revealed by the scene about the checkered table-cloth. Perhaps that was one of the advantages of a social organization which still, as a whole, ignored divorce, and thought any private condonation better than the open breaking-up of the family.

"All right; I'll go——" he agreed. "Where are we dining?"

"Oh, I forgot—an awful orgy. Dastrey wants us at the Union. Louis Dastrey is dining with him, and he let me ask Boylston——"

"Boylston——?"

"You don't know him. A chap who was at Harvard with me. He's out here studying painting at the Beaux-Arts. He's an awfully good sort, and he wanted to see me before I go."

The father's heart sank. Only one whole day more with his boy, and this last evening but one was to be spent with poor embittered Dastrey, and two youths, one unknown to Campton, who would drown them in stupid war-chatter! But it was what George wanted; and there must not be a shade, for George, on these last hours.

"All right! You promised me something awful for to-night," Campton grinned sardonically.

"Do you mind? I'm sorry."

"It's only Dastrey's damned chauvinism that I mind. Why don't you ask Adele to join the chorus?"

"Well—you'll like Boylston," said George.

Dastrey, after all, turned out less tragic and aggressive than Campton had feared. His irritability had vanished, and though he was very grave he seemed preoccupied only with the fate of Europe, and not with his personal stake in the affair.

But the older men said little. The youngsters had the floor, and Campton, as he listened to George and young Louis Dastrey, was overcome by a sense of such dizzy unreality that he had to grasp the arms of his ponderous leather armchair to assure himself that he was really in the flesh and in the world.

What! Two days ago they were still in the old easy Europe, a Europe in which one could make plans, engage passages on trains and steamers, argue about pictures, books, theatres, ideas, draw as much money as one chose out of the bank, and say: "The day after to-morrow I'll be in Berlin or Vienna or Belgrade." And here they sat in their same evening clothes, about the same shining mahogany writing-table, apparently the same group of free and independent youths and elderly men, and in reality prisoners, every one of them, hand-cuffed to this hideous masked bully of "War"!

The young men were sure that the conflict was inevitable—the evening papers left no doubt of it—and there was much animated discussion between young Dastrey and George.

Already their views diverged; the French youth, theoretically at one with his friend as to the senselessness of war in general, had at once resolutely disengaged from the mist of doctrine the fatal necessity of this particular war.

"It's the old festering wound of Alsace-Lorraine: Bismarck foresaw it and feared it—or perhaps planned it and welcomed it: who knows? But as long as the wound was there, Germany believed that France would try to avenge it, and as long as Germany believed that, she had to keep up her own war-strength; and she's kept it up to the toppling-over point, ruining herself and us. That's the whole thing, as I see it. War's rot; but to get rid of war forever we've got to fight this one first."

It was wonderful to Campton that this slender learned youth should already have grasped the necessity of the conflict and its deep causes. While his own head was still spinning with wrath and bewilderment at the bottomless perversity of mankind, Louis Dastrey had analyzed and accepted the situation and his own part in it. And he was not simply resigned; he was trembling with eagerness to get the thing over. "If only England is with us we're safe—it's a matter of weeks," he declared.

"Wait a bit—wait a bit; I want to know more about a whole lot of things before I fix a date for the fall of Berlin," his uncle interposed; but Louis flung him a radiant look. "We've been there before, my uncle!"

"But there's Russia too——" said Boylston explosively. He had not spoken before.

" '*Nous l'avons eu, votre Rhin allemand,*' " quoted George, as he poured a golden Hock into his glass.

He was keenly interested, that was evident; but interested as a looker-on, a dilettante. He had neither Valmy nor Sedan in his blood, and it was as a sympathizing spectator that he ought by rights to have been sharing his friend's enthusiasm, not as a combatant compelled to obey the same summons. Campton, glancing from one to another of their brilliant faces, felt his determination harden to save George from the consequences of his parents' stupid blunder.

After dinner young Dastrey proposed a music-hall. The audience would be a curious sight: there would be wild enthusiasm, and singing of the Marseillaise. The other young men agreed, but their elders, after a tacitly exchanged glance, decided to remain at the club, on the plea that some one at the Ministry of War had promised to telephone if there were fresh news.

Campton and Dastrey, left alone, stood on the balcony watching the Boulevards. The streets, so deserted during the day, had become suddenly and densely populated. Hardly any vehicles were in sight: the motor omnibuses were already carrying troops to the stations, there was a report abroad that private motors were to be requisitioned, and only a few taxis and horse-cabs, packed to the driver's box with young men in spick-and-span uniforms, broke through the mass of pedestrians which filled the whole width of the Boulevards. This mass moved slowly and vaguely, swaying this way and that, as though it awaited a portent from the heavens. In the glare of electric lamps and glittering theatre-fronts the innumerable faces stood out vividly, grave, intent, slightly bewildered. Except when the soldiers passed no cries or songs came from the crowd, but only the deep inarticulate rumour which any vast body of people gives forth.

"Queer——! How silent they are: how do you think they're taking it?" Campton questioned.

But Dastrey had grown belligerent again. He saw the throngs before him bounding toward the frontier like the unchained furies of Rude's "Marseillaise"; whereas to Campton they seemed full of the dumb wrath of an orderly and laborious people upon whom an unrighteous quarrel has been forced. He knew that the thought of Alsace-Lorraine still stirred in French hearts; but all Dastrey's eloquence could not convince him that these people wanted war, or would have sought it had it not been thrust on them. The whole monstrous injustice seemed to take shape before him, and to brood like a huge sky-filling dragon of the northern darknesses over his light-loving, pleasure-loving, labour-loving France.

George came home late.

It was two in the morning of his last day with his boy when Campton heard the door open, and saw a flash of turned-on light.

All night he had lain staring into the darkness, and thinking, thinking: thinking of George's future, George's friends, George and women, of that unknown side of his boy's life which, in this great upheaval of things, had suddenly lifted its face to the surface. If war came, if George were not discharged, if George were sent to the front, if George were killed, how strange to think that things the father did not know of might turn out to have been the central things of his son's life!

The young man came in, and Campton looked at him as though he were a stranger.

"Hullo, Dad—any news from the Ministry?" George, tossing aside his hat and stick, sat down on the bed. He had a crumpled rose in his button-hole, and looked gay and fresh, with the indestructible freshness of youth.

"What do I really know of him?" the father asked himself.

Yes: Dastrey had had news. Germany had already committed acts of overt hostility on the frontier: telegraph and telephone communications had been cut, French locomotives seized, troops massed along the border on the specious pretext of the "*Kriegsgefahrzustand*." It was war.

"Oh, well," George shrugged. He lit a cigarette, and asked: "What did you think of Boylston?"

"Boylston——?"

"The fat brown chap at dinner."

"Yes—yes—of course." Campton became aware that he had not thought of Boylston at all, had hardly been aware of his presence. But the painter's registering faculty was always latently at work, and in an instant he called up a round face, shyly jovial, with short-sighted brown eyes as sharp as needles, and dark hair curling tightly over a wide watchful forehead.

"Why—I liked him."

"I'm glad, because it was a tremendous event for him, seeing you. He paints, and he's been keen on your things for years."

"I wish I'd known . . . Why didn't he say so? He didn't say anything, did he?"

"No: he doesn't, much, when he's pleased. He's the very best chap I know," George concluded.

Chapter VIII

THAT morning the irrevocable stared at him from the headlines of the papers. The German Ambassador was recalled. Germany had declared war on France at 6.40 the previous evening; there was an unintelligible allusion, in the declaration, to French aeroplanes throwing bombs on Nuremberg and Wesel. Campton read that part of the message over two or three times.

Aeroplanes throwing bombs? Aeroplanes as engines of destruction? He had always thought of them as a kind of giant kite that fools went up in when they were tired of breaking their necks in other ways. But aeroplane bombardment as a cause for declaring war? The bad faith of it was so manifest that he threw down the papers half relieved. Of course there would be a protest on the part of the allies; a great country like France would not allow herself to be bullied into war on such a pretext.

The ultimatum to Belgium was more serious; but Belgium's gallant reply would no doubt check Germany on that side. After all, there was such a thing as international law, and Germany herself had recognized it . . . So his mind spun on in vain circles, while under the frail web of his casuistry gloomed the obstinate fact that George was mobilised, that George was to leave the next morning.

The day wore on: it was the shortest and yet most interminable that Campton had ever known. Paris, when he went out into it, was more dazzlingly empty than ever. In the hotel, in the hall, on the stairs, he was waylaid by flustered compatriots—"Oh, Mr. Campton, you don't know me, but of course all Americans know *you*!"—who appealed to him for the very information he was trying to obtain for himself: how one could get money, how one could get hold of the concierge, how one could send cables, if there was any restaurant where the waiters had not all been mobilised, if he had any "pull" at the Embassy, or at any of the steamship offices, or any of the banks. One disordered beauty blurted out: "Of course, with your connection with Bullard and Brant"—and was only waked to her mistake by Campton's indignant stare, and his plunge past her while she called out excuses.

But the name acted as a reminder of his promise to go and see Mrs. Brant, and he decided to make his visit after lunch, when George would be off collecting last things. Visiting the Brants with George would have been beyond his capacity.

The great drawing-rooms, their awnings spread against the sun, their tall windows wide to the glow of the garden, were empty when he entered; but in a moment he was joined by a tall angular woman with a veil pushed up untidily above her pink nose. Campton reflected that he had never seen Adele Anthony in the daytime without a veil pushed up above a flushed nose, and dangling in irregular wisps from the back of a small hard hat of which the shape never varied.

"Julia will be here in a minute. When she told me you were coming I waited."

He was glad to have a word with her before meeting Mrs. Brant, though his impulse had been almost as strong to avoid the one as the other. He dreaded belligerent bluster as much as vain whimpering, and in the depths of his soul he had to own that it would have been easier to talk to Mr. Brant than to either of the women.

"Julia is powdering her nose," Miss Anthony continued. "She has an idea that if you see she's been crying you'll be awfully angry."

Campton made an impatient gesture. "If I were—much it would matter!"

"Ah, but you might tell George; and George is not to know." She paused, and then bounced round on him abruptly. She always moved and spoke in explosions, as if the wires that agitated her got tangled, and then were too suddenly jerked loose.

"*Does* George know?"

"About his mother's tears?"

"About this plan you're all hatching to have him discharged?"

Campton reddened under her lashless blue gaze, and the consciousness of doing so made his answer all the curter.

"Probably not—unless you've told him!"

The shot appeared to reach the mark, for an answering blush suffused her sallow complexion. "You'd better not put ideas into my head!" she laughed. Something in her tone reminded him of all her old dogged loyalties, and made him ashamed of his taunt.

"Anyhow," he grumbled, "his place is not in the French army."

"That was for you and Julia to decide twenty-six years ago, wasn't it? Now it's up to him."

Her capricious adoption of American slang, fitted anyhow into her old-fashioned and punctilious English, sometimes amused but oftener exasperated Campton.

"If you're going to talk modern slang you ought to give up those ridiculous stays, and not wear a fringe like a mid-Victorian royalty," he jeered, trying to laugh off his exasperation.

She let this pass with a smile. "Well, I wish I could find the language to make you understand how much better it would be to leave George alone. This war will be the making of him."

"He's made quite to my satisfaction as it is, thanks. But what's the use of talking? You always get your phrases out of books."

The door opened, and Mrs. Brant came in.

Her appearance answered to Miss Anthony's description. A pearly mist covered her face, and some reviving liquid had cleared her congested eyes. Her poor hands had suddenly grown so thin and dry that the heavy rings, slipping down to the joints, slid back into place as she shook hands with Campton.

"Thank you for coming," she said.

"Oh——" he protested, helpless, and disturbed by Miss Anthony's presence. At the moment his former wife's feelings were more intelligible to him than his friend's: the maternal fibre stirred in her, and made her more appealing than any elderly virgin on the war-path.

"I'm off, my dears," said the elderly virgin, as if guessing his thought. Her queer shallow eyes included them both in a sweeping glance, and she flung back from the threshold: "Be careful of what you say to George."

What they had to say to each other did not last many minutes. The Brants had made various efforts, but had been baffled on all sides by the general agitation and confusion. In high quarters the people they wanted to see were inaccessible; and those who could be reached lent but a distracted ear. The Ambassador had at once declared that he could do nothing; others vaguely promised they "would see"—but hardly seemed to hear what they were being asked.

"And meanwhile time is passing—and he's going!" Mrs. Brant lamented.

The reassurance that Campton brought from Fortin-Lescluze, vague though it was, came to her as a miraculous promise, and raised Campton suddenly in her estimation. She looked at him with a new confidence, and he could almost hear her saying to Brant, as he had so often heard her say to himself: "You never seem able to get anything done. I don't know how other people manage."

Her gratitude gave him the feeling of having been engaged in something underhand and pusillanimous. He made haste to take leave, after promising to pass on any word he might receive from the physician; but he reminded her that he was not likely to hear anything till George had been for some days at his base.

She acknowledged the probability of this, and clung to him with trustful eyes. She was much disturbed by the preposterous fact that the Government had already requisitioned two of the Brant motors, and Campton had an idea that, dazzled by his newly-developed capacity to "manage," she was about to implore him to rescue from the clutches of the authorities her Rolls-Royce and Anderson's Delaunay.

He was hastening to leave when the door again opened. A rumpled-looking maid peered in, evidently perplexed, and giving way doubtfully to a young woman who entered with a rush, and then paused as if she too were doubtful. She was pretty in an odd dishevelled way, and with her elaborate clothes and bewildered look she reminded Campton of a fashion-plate torn from its page and helplessly blown about the world. He had seen the same type among his compatriots any number of times in the last days.

"Oh, Mrs. Brant—yes, I *know* you gave orders that you were not in to anybody, but I just wouldn't listen, and it's not that poor woman's fault," the visitor began, in a plaintive staccato which matched her sad eyes and her fluttered veils.

"You see, I simply had to get hold of Mr. Brant, because I'm here without a penny—literally!" She dangled before them a bejewelled mesh-bag. "And in a hotel where they don't know me. And at the bank they wouldn't listen to me, and they said Mr. Brant wasn't there, though of course I suppose he was; so I said to the cashier: 'Very well, then, I'll simply go to the Avenue Marigny and batter in his door—unless you'd rather I jumped into the Seine?' "

"Oh, Mrs. Talkett——" murmured Mrs. Brant.

"Really: it's a case of my money or my life!" the young lady continued with a studied laugh. She stood between them, artificial and yet so artless, conscious of intruding but evidently used to having her intrusions pardoned; and her large eyes turned interrogatively to Campton.

"Of course my husband will do all he can for you. I'll telephone," said Mrs. Brant; then, perceiving that her visitor continued to gaze at Campton, she added: "Oh, no, *this* is not . . . this is Mr. Campton."

"John Campton? I knew it!" Mrs. Talkett's eyes became devouring and brilliant. "Of course I ought to have recognised you at once—from your photographs. I have one pinned up in my room. But I was so flurried when I came in." She detained the painter's hand. "Do forgive me! For *years* I've dreamed of your doing me . . . you see, I paint a little myself . . . but it's ridiculous to speak of such things now." She added, as if she were risking something: "I knew your son at St. Moritz. We saw a great deal of him there, and in New York last winter."

"Ah——" said Campton, bowing awkwardly.

"Cursèd fools—all women," he anathematized her on the way downstairs.

In the street, however, he felt grateful to her for reducing Mrs. Brant to such confusion that she had made no attempt to detain him. His way of life lay so far apart from his former wife's that they had hardly ever been exposed to accidents of the kind, and he saw that Julia's embarrassment kept all its freshness.

The fact set him thinking curiously of what her existence had been since they had parted. She had long since forgotten her youthful art-jargon to learn others more consonant to her tastes. As the wife of the powerful American banker she dispensed the costliest hospitality with the simple air of one who has never learnt that human life may be sustained without the aid of orchids and champagne. With guests either brought up in the same convictions or bent on acquiring them she conversed earnestly and unweariedly about motors, clothes and morals; but perhaps her most stimulating hours were those brightened by the weekly visit of the Rector of her parish. With happy untrammelled hands she was now free to rebuild to her own measure a corner of the huge wicked welter of Paris; and immediately it became as neat, as empty, as air-tight as her own immaculate drawing-room. There he seemed to see her, throning year after year in an awful emptiness of wealth and luxury and respectability, seeing only dull people, doing only dull things, and fighting feverishly to defend the last traces of a beauty which had never given her anything but the tamest and most unprofitable material prosperity.

"She's never even had the silly kind of success she wanted—poor Julia!" he mused, wondering that she had been able to put into her life so few of the sensations which can be bought by wealth and beauty. "And now what will be left—how on earth will she fit into a war?"

He was sure all her plans had been made for the coming six months: her week-end sets of heavy millionaires secured for Deauville, and after that for the shooting at the big château near Compiègne, and three weeks reserved for Biarritz before the return to Paris in January. One of the luxuries Julia had most enjoyed after her separation from Campton (Adele had told him) had been that of planning things ahead: Mr. Brant, thank heaven, was not impulsive. And now here was this black bolt of war falling among all her carefully balanced arrangements with a crash more violent than any of Campton's inconsequences!

As he reached the Place de la Concorde a newsboy passed with the three o'clock papers, and he bought one and read of the crossing of Luxembourg and the invasion of Belgium. The Germans were arrogantly acting up to their menace: heedless of international law, they were driving straight for France and England by the road they thought the most accessible . . .

In the hotel he found George, red with rage, devouring the same paper: the boy's whole look was changed.

"The howling blackguards! The brigands! This isn't war—it's simple murder!"

The two men stood and stared at each other. "Will England stand it?" sprang to their lips at the same moment.

Never—never! England would never permit such a violation of the laws regulating the relations between civilized peoples. They began to say both together that after all perhaps it was the best thing that could have happened, since, if there had been the least hesitation or reluctance in any section of English opinion, this abominable outrage would instantly sweep it away.

"They've been too damned clever for once!" George exulted. "France is saved—that's certain anyhow!"

Yes; France was saved if England could put her army into the field at once. But could she? Oh, for the Channel tunnel at this hour! Would this lesson at last cure England of her obstinate insularity? Belgium had announced her intention of resisting; but what was that gallant declaration worth in face of Germany's brutal assault? A poor little country pledged to a guaranteed neutrality could hardly be expected to hold her frontiers more than forty-eight hours against the most powerful army in Europe. And what a narrow strip Belgium was, viewed as an outpost of France!

These thoughts, racing through Campton's mind, were swept out of it again by his absorbing preoccupation. What effect would the Belgian affair have on George's view of his own participation in the war? For the first time the boy's feelings were visibly engaged; his voice shook as he burst out: "Louis Dastrey's right: this kind of thing has got to stop. We shall go straight back to cannibalism if it doesn't.—God, what hounds!"

Yes, but—Campton pondered, tried to think up Pacifist arguments, remembered his own discussion with Paul Dastrey three days before. "My dear chap, hasn't France perhaps gone about with a chip on her shoulder? Saverne, for instance: some people think——"

"Damn Saverne! Haven't the Germans shown us what they are now? Belgium sheds all the light *I* want on Saverne. They're not fit to live with white people, and the sooner they're shown it the better."

"Well, France and Russia and England are here to show them."

George laughed. "Yes, and double quick."

Both were silent again, each thinking his own thoughts. They were apparently the same, for just as Campton was about to ask where George had decided that they should take their last dinner, the young man said abruptly: "Look here, Dad; I'd planned a little tête-à-tête for us this evening."

"Yes——?"

"Well—I can't. I'm going to chuck you." He smiled a little, his colour rising nervously. "For some people I've just run across—who were awfully kind to me at St. Moritz—and in New York last winter. I didn't know they were here till . . . till just now. I'm awfully sorry; but I've simply got to dine with them."

There was a silence. Campton stared out over his son's shoulder at the great sunlit square. "Oh, all right," he said briskly.

This—on George's last night!

"You don't mind *much*, do you? I'll be back early, for a last pow-wow on the terrace." George paused, and finally brought out: "You see, it really wouldn't have done to tell mother that I was deserting her on my last evening because I was dining with you!"

A weight was lifted from Campton's heart, and he felt ashamed of having failed to guess the boy's real motive.

"My dear fellow, naturally . . . quite right. And you can stop in and see your mother on the way home. You'll find me here whenever you turn up."

George looked relieved. "Thanks a lot—you always know. And now for my adieux to Adele."

He went off whistling the waltz from the Rosenkavalier, and Campton returned to his own thoughts.

He was still revolving them when he went upstairs after a solitary repast in the confused and servantless dining-room. Adele Anthony had telephoned to him to come and dine—after seeing George, he supposed; but he had declined. He wanted to be with his boy, or alone.

As he left the dining-room he ran across Adamson, the American newspaper correspondent, who had lived for years in Paris and was reputed to have "inside information." Adamson was grave but confident. In his opinion Russia would probably not get to Berlin before November (he smiled at Campton's astonished outcry); but if England—oh, they were sure of England!— could get her army over without delay, the whole business would very likely be settled before that, in one big battle in Belgium. (Yes—poor Belgium, indeed!) Anyhow, in the opinion of the military experts the war was not likely to last more than three or four months; and of course, even if things went badly on the western front, which was highly unlikely, there was Russia to clench the business as soon as her huge forces got in motion. Campton drew much comfort from this sober view of the situation, midway between that of the optimists who knew Russia would be in Berlin in three weeks, and of those who saw the Germans in Calais even sooner. Adamson was a level-headed fellow, who weighed what he said and pinned his faith to facts.

Campton managed to evade several people whom he saw lurking for him, and mounted to his room. On the terrace, alone with the serene city, his confidence grew, and he began to feel more and more sure that, whatever happened, George was likely to be kept out of the fighting till the whole thing was over. With such formidable forces closing in on her it was fairly obvious that Germany must succumb before half or even a quarter of the allied reserves had been engaged. Sustained by the thought, he let his mind hover tenderly over George's future, and the effect on his character of this brief and harmless plunge into a military career.

Chapter IX

G EORGE was gone.

When, with a last whistle and scream, his train had ploughed its way out of the clanging station; when the last young figures clinging to the rear of the last carriage had vanished, and the bare rails again glittered up from the cindery tracks, Campton turned and looked about him.

All the platforms of the station were crowded as he had seldom seen any place crowded, and to his surprise he found himself taking in every detail of the scene with a morbid accuracy of observation. He had discovered, during these last days, that his artist's vision had been strangely unsettled. Sometimes, as when he had left Fortin's house, he saw nothing: the material world, which had always tugged at him with a thousand hands, vanished and left him in the void. Then again, as at present, he saw everything, saw it too clearly, in all its superfluous and negligible reality, instead of instinctively selecting, and disregarding what was not to his purpose.

Faces, faces—they swarmed about him, and his overwrought vision registered them one by one. Especially he noticed the faces of the women, women of all ages, all classes. These were the wives, mothers, grandmothers, sisters, mistresses of all those heavily laden trainfuls of French youth. He was struck with the same strong cheerfulness in all: some pale, some flushed, some serious, but all firmly and calmly smiling.

One young woman in particular his look dwelt on—a dark girl in a becoming dress—both because she was so pleasant to see, and because there was such assurance in her serenity that she did not have to constrain her lips and eyes, but could trust them to be what she wished. Yet he saw by the way she clung to the young artilleryman from whom she was parting that hers were no sisterly farewells.

An immense hum of voices filled the vast glazed enclosure. Campton caught the phrases flung up to the young faces piled one above another in the windows—words of motherly admonishment, little jokes, tender names, mirthful allusions, last callings out: "Write often! Don't forget to wrap up your throat . . .

Remember to send a line to Annette . . . Bring home a Prussian helmet for the children! *On les aura, pas, mon vieux*?" It was all bright, brave and confident. "If Berlin could only see it!" Campton thought.

He tried to remember what his own last words to George had been, but could not; yet his throat felt dry and thirsty, as if he had talked a great deal. The train vanished in a roar, and he leaned against a pier to let the crowd flood by, not daring to risk his lameness in such a turmoil.

Suddenly he heard loud sobs behind him. He turned, and recognized the hat and hair of the girl whose eyes had struck him. He could not see them now, for they were buried in her hands and her whole body shook with woe. An elderly man was trying to draw her away—her father, probably.

"Come, come, my child——"

"Oh—oh—oh," she hiccoughed, following blindly.

The people nearest stared at her, and the faces of other women grew pale. Campton saw tears on the cheeks of an old body in a black bonnet who might have been his own Mme. Lebel. A pale lad went away weeping.

But they were all afraid, then, all in immediate deadly fear for the lives of their beloved! The same fear grasped Campton's heart, a very present terror, such as he had hardly before imagined. Compared to it, all that he had felt hitherto seemed as faint as the sensations of a looker-on. His knees failed him, and he grasped a transverse bar of the pier.

People were leaving the station in groups of two or three who seemed to belong to each other; only he was alone. George's mother had not come to bid her son goodbye; she had declared that she would rather take leave of him quietly in her own house than in a crowd of dirty people at the station. But then it was impossible to conceive of her being up and dressed and at the Gare de l'Est at five in the morning—and how could she have got there without her motor? So Campton was alone, in that crowd which seemed all made up of families.

But no—not all. Ahead of him he saw one woman moving away alone, and recognized, across the welter of heads, Adele Anthony's adamantine hat and tight knob of hair.

Poor Adele! So she had come too—and had evidently failed in her quest, not been able to fend a way through the crowd, and perhaps not even had a glimpse of her hero. The thought smote Campton with compunction: he regretted his sneering words when they had last met, regretted refusing to dine with her. He wished the barrier of people between them had been less impenetrable; but for the moment it was useless to try to force a way through it. He had to wait till the crowd shifted to other platforms, whence other trains were starting, and by that time she was lost to sight.

At last he was able to make his way through the throng, and as he came out of a side entrance he saw her. She appeared to be looking for a taxi—she waved her sunshade aimlessly. But no one who knew the Gare de l'Est would have gone around that corner to look for a taxi; least of all the practical Adele. Besides, Adele never took taxis: she travelled in the bowels of the earth or on the dizziest omnibus tops.

Campton knew at once that she was waiting for him. He went up to her and a guilty pink suffused her nose.

"You missed him after all——?" he said.

"I—oh, no, I didn't."

"You didn't? But I was with him all the time. We didn't see you——"

"No, but *I* saw—distinctly. That was all I went for," she jerked back.

He slipped his arm through hers. "This crowd terrifies me. I'm glad you waited for me," he said.

He saw her pleasure, but she merely answered: "I'm dying of thirst, aren't you?"

"Yes—or hunger, or something. Could we find a *laiterie?*"

They found one, and sat down among early clerks and shop-girls, and a few dishevelled women with swollen faces whom Campton had noticed in the station. One of them, who sat opposite an elderly man, had drawn out a pocket mirror and was powdering her nose.

Campton hated to see women powder their noses—one of the few merits with which he credited Julia Brant was that of never having adopted these dirty modern fashions, of continuing to make her toilet in private "like a lady," as people used to say when he was young. But now the gesture charmed him, for he had recognized the girl who had been sobbing in the station.

"How game she is! I like that. But why is she so frightened?" he wondered. For he saw that her chocolate was untouched, and that the smile had stiffened on her lips.

Since his talk with Adamson he could not bring himself to be seriously alarmed. Fear had taken him by the throat for a moment in the station, at the sound of the girl's sobs; but already he had thrown it off. Everybody agreed that the war was sure to be over in a few weeks; even Dastrey had come round to that view; and with Fortin's protection, and the influences Anderson Brant could put in motion, George was surely safe—as safe at his depot as anywhere else in this precarious world. Campton poured out Adele's coffee, and drank off his own as if it had been champagne.

"Do you know anything about the people George was dining with last night?" he enquired abruptly.

Miss Anthony knew everything and everybody in the American circle in Paris; she was a clearing-house of Franco-American gossip, and it was likely enough that if George had special reasons for wishing to spend his last evening away from his family she would know why. But the chance of her knowing what had been kept from him made Campton's question, as soon as it was put, seem indiscreet, and he added hastily: "Not that I want——"

She looked surprised. "No: he didn't tell me. Some young man's affair, I suppose . . ." She smirked absurdly, her lashless eyes blinking under the pushed-back veil.

Campton's mind had already strayed from the question. Nothing bored him more than Adele doing the "sad dog," and he was vexed at having given her such a chance to be silly. What he wanted to know was whether George had spoken to his old friend about his future—about his own idea of his situation, and his intentions and wishes in view of the grim chance which people, with propitiatory vagueness, call "anything happening." Had the boy left any word, any message with her for any one? But it was useless to speculate, for if he had, the old goose, true as steel, would never betray it by as much as a twitch of her lids. She could look, when it was a question of keeping a secret, like such an impenetrable idiot that one could not imagine any one's having trusted a secret to her.

Campton had no wish to surprise George's secrets, if the boy had any. But their parting had been so hopelessly Anglo-Saxon, so curt and casual, that he would have liked to think his son had left, somewhere, a message for him, a word, a letter, in case . . . in case there was anything premonitory in the sobbing of that girl at the next table.

But Adele's pink nose confronted him, as guileless as a rabbit's, and he went out with her unsatisfied. They parted at the door of the restaurant, and Campton went to the studio to see if there were any news of his maid-servant Mariette. He meant to return to sleep there that night, and even his simple housekeeping was likely to be troublesome if Mariette should not arrive.

On the way it occurred to him that he had not yet seen the morning papers, and he stopped and bought a handful.

Negotiations, hopes, fears, conjectures—but nothing new or definite, except the insolent fact of Germany's aggression, and the almost-certainty of England's intervention. When he reached the studio he found Mme. Lebel in her usual place, paler than usual, but with firm lips and bright eyes. Her three grandsons had left for their depots the day before: one was in the *Chasseurs Alpins*, and probably already on his way to Alsace, another in the infantry, the third in the heavy artillery; she did not know where the two latter were likely to be sent. Her eldest son, their father, was dead; the second, a man of fifty, and a cabinetmaker by trade, was in the territorials, and was not to report for another week. He hoped, before leaving, to see the return of his wife and little girl, who were in the Ardennes with the wife's people. Mme. Lebel's mind was made up and her philosophy ready for immediate application.

"It's terribly hard for the younger people; but it had to be. I come from Nancy, Monsieur: I remember the German occupation. I understand better than my daughter-in-law . . ."

There was no news of Mariette, and small chance of having any for some days, much less of seeing her. No one could tell how long civilian travel would be interrupted. Mme. Lebel, moved by her lodger's plight, promised to "find some one"; and Campton mounted to the studio.

He had left it only two days before, on the day when he had vainly waited for Fortin and his dancer; and an abyss already divided him from that vanished time. Then his little world still hung like a straw above an eddy; now it was spinning about in the central vortex.

The pictures stood about untidily, and he looked curiously at all those faces which belonged to the other life. Each bore the mark of its own immediate passions and interests; not one betrayed the least consciousness of coming disaster except the face of poor Madame de Dolmetsch, whose love had enlightened her. Campton began to think of the future from the painter's point of view. What a modeller of faces a great war must be! What would the people who came through it look like, he wondered.

His bell tinkled, and he turned to answer it. Dastrey, he supposed . . . he had caught a glimpse of his friend across the crowd at the Gare de l'Est, seeing off his nephew, but had purposely made no sign. He still wanted to be alone, and above all not to hear war-talk. Mme. Lebel, however, had no doubt revealed his presence in the studio, and he could not risk offending Dastrey.

When he opened the door it was a surprise to see there, instead of Dastrey's anxious face, the round rosy countenance of a well-dressed youth with a shock of fair hair above eyes of childish candour.

"Oh—come in," Campton said, surprised, but divining a compatriot in a difficulty.

The youth obeyed, blushing his apologies.

"I'm Benny Upsher, sir," he said, in a tone modest yet confident, as if the name were an introduction.

"Oh——" Campton stammered, cursing his absent-mindedness and his unfailing faculty for forgetting names.

"You're a friend of George's, aren't you?" he risked.

"Yes—tremendous. We were at Harvard together—he was two years ahead of me."

"Ah—then you're still there?"

Mr. Upsher's blush became a mask of crimson. "Well—I thought I was, till this thing happened."

"What thing?"

The youth stared at the older man with a look of celestial wonder.

"This war.—George has started already, hasn't he?"

"Yes. Two hours ago."

"So they said—I looked him up at the Crillon. I wanted most awfully to see him; if I had, of course I shouldn't have bothered you."

"My dear young man, you're not bothering me. But what can I do?"

Mr. Upsher's composure seemed to be returning as the necessary preliminaries were cleared away. "Thanks a lot," he said. "Of course what I'd like best is to join his regiment."

"Join his regiment—*you*!" Campton exclaimed.

"Oh, I know it's difficult; I raced up from Biarritz quick as I could to catch him." He seemed still to be panting with the effort. "I want to be in this," he concluded.

Campton contemplated him with helpless perplexity. "But I don't understand—there's no reason, in your case. With George it was obligatory—on account of his being born here. But I suppose you were born in America?"

"Well, I guess so: in Utica. My mother was Madeline Mayhew. I think we're a sort of cousins, sir, aren't we?"

"Of course—of course. Excuse my not recalling it—just at first. But, my dear boy, I still don't see——"

Mr. Upsher's powers of stating his case were plainly limited. He pushed back his rumpled hair, looked hard again at his cousin, and repeated doggedly: "I want to be *in* this."

"This war?"

He nodded.

Campton groaned. What did the boy mean, and why come to him with such tomfoolery? At that moment he felt even more unfitted than usual to deal with practical problems, and in spite of the forgotten cousinship it was no affair of his what Madeline Mayhew's son wanted to be in.

But there was the boy himself, stolid, immovable, impenetrable to hints, and with something in his wide blue eyes like George—and yet so childishly different.

"Sit down—have a cigarette, won't you?—You know, of course," Campton began, "that what you propose is almost insuperably difficult?"

"Getting into George's regiment?"

"Getting into the French army at all—for a foreigner, a neutral . . . I'm afraid there's really nothing I can do."

Benny Upsher smiled indulgently. "I can fix that up all right; getting into the army, I mean. The only thing that might be hard would be getting into his regiment."

"Oh, as to that—out of the question, I should think." Campton was conscious of speaking curtly: the boy's bland determination was beginning to get on his nerves.

"Thank you no end," said Benny Upsher, getting up. "Sorry to have butted in," he added, holding out a large brown hand.

Campton followed him to the door perplexedly. He knew that something ought to be done—but what? On the threshold he laid his hand impulsively on the youth's shoulder. "Look here, my boy, we're cousins, as you say, and if you're Madeline Mayhew's boy you're an only son. Moreover you're George's friend—which matters still more to me. I can't let you go like this. Just let me say a word to you before——"

A gleam of shrewdness flashed through Benny Upsher's inarticulate blue eyes. "A word or two *against*, you mean? Why, it's awfully kind, but not the least earthly use. I guess I've heard all the arguments. But all I see is that hulking bully trying to do Belgium in. England's coming in, ain't she? Well, then why ain't we?"

"England? Why—why, there's no analogy——"

The young man groped for the right word. "I don't know. Maybe not. Only in tight places we always *do* seem to stand together."

"You're mad—this is not our war. Do you really want to go out and butcher people?"

"Yes—this kind of people," said Benny Upsher cheerfully. "You see, I've had all this talk from Uncle Harvey Mayhew a good many times on the way over. We came out on the same boat: he wanted me to be his private secretary at the Hague Congress. But I was pretty sure I'd have a job of my own to attend to."

Campton still contemplated him hopelessly. "Where is your uncle?" he wondered.

Benny grinned. "On his way to the Hague, I suppose."

"He ought to be here to look after you—some one ought to!"

"Then you don't see your way to getting me into George's regiment?" Benny simply replied.

An hour later Campton still seemed to see him standing there, with obstinate soft eyes repeating the same senseless question. It cost him an effort to shake off the vision.

He returned to the Crillon to collect his possessions. On his table was a telegram, and he seized it eagerly, wondering if by some mad chance George's plans were changed, if he were being sent back, if Fortin had already arranged something . . .

He tore open the message, and read: "Utica July thirty-first. No news from Benny please do all you can to facilitate his immediate return to America dreadfully anxious your cousin Madeline Upsher."

"Good Lord!" Campton groaned—"and I never even asked the boy's address!"

BOOK II

Chapter X

THE war was three months old—three centuries. By virtue of some gift of adaptation which seemed forever to discredit human sensibility, people were already beginning to live into the monstrous idea of it, acquire its ways, speak its language, regard it as a thinkable, endurable, arrangeable fact; to eat it by day, and sleep on it—yes, and soundly—at night.

The war went on; life went on; Paris went on. She had had her great hour of resistance, when, alone, exposed and defenceless, she had held back the enemy and broken his strength. She had had, afterward, her hour of triumph, the hour of the Marne; then her hour of passionate and prayerful hope, when it seemed to the watching nations that the enemy was not only held back but thrust back, and victory finally in reach. That hour had passed in its turn, giving way to the grey reality of the trenches. A new speech was growing up in this new world. There were trenches now, there was a "Front"—people were beginning to talk of their sons at the front.

The first time John Campton heard the phrase it sent a shudder through him. Winter was coming on, and he was haunted by the vision of the youths out there, boys of George's age, thousands and thousands of them, exposed by day in reeking wet ditches and sleeping at night under the rain and snow. People were talking calmly of victory in the spring—the spring that was still six long months away! And meanwhile, what cold and wet, what blood and agony, what shattered bodies out on that hideous front, what shattered homes in all the lands it guarded!

Campton could bear to think of these things now. *His* son was not at the front—was safe, thank God, and likely to remain so!

During the first awful weeks of silence and uncertainty, when every morning brought news of a fresh disaster, when no letters came from the army and no private messages could reach it—during those weeks, while Campton, like other fathers, was without news of his son, the war had been to him simply a huge featureless mass crushing him earthward, blinding him, letting him neither think nor move nor breathe.

But at last he had got permission to go to Chalons, whither Fortin, who chanced to have begun his career as a surgeon, had been hastily transferred. The physician, called from his incessant labours in a roughly-improvised operating-room, to which Campton was led between rows of stretchers laden with livid blood-splashed men, had said kindly, but with a shade of impatience, that he had not forgotten, had done what he could; that George's health did not warrant his being discharged from the army, but that he was temporarily on a staff-job at the rear, and would probably be kept there if such and such influences were brought to bear. Then, calling for hot water and fresh towels, the surgeon vanished and Campton made his way back with lowered eyes between the stretchers.

The "influences" in question were brought to bear—not without Anderson Brant's assistance—and now that George was fairly certain to be kept at clerical work a good many miles from the danger-zone Campton felt less like an ant under a landslide, and was able for the first time to think of the war as he might have thought of any other war: objectively, intellectually, almost dispassionately, as of history in the making.

It was not that he had any doubt as to the rights and wrongs of the case. The painfully preserved equilibrium of the neutrals made a pitiful show now that the monstrous facts of the first weeks were known: Germany's diplomatic perfidy, her savagery in the field, her premeditated and systematized terrorizing of the civil populations. Nothing could efface what had been done in Belgium and Luxembourg, the burning of Louvain, the bombardment of Rheims. These successive outrages had roused in Campton the same incredulous wrath as in the rest of mankind; but being of a speculative mind—and fairly sure now that George would never lie in the mud and snow with the others—he had begun to consider the landslide in its universal relations, as well as in its effects on his private ant-heap.

His son's situation, however, was still his central thought. That this lad, who was meant to have been born three thousand miles away in his own safe warless country, and who was regarded by the government of that country as having been born there, as subject to her laws and entitled to her protection—that this lad, by the most idiotic of blunders, a blunder perpetrated before he was born, should have been dragged into a conflict in which he was totally unconcerned, should become temporarily and arbitrarily the subject of a foreign state, exposed to whatever catastrophes that state might draw upon itself, this fact still seemed to Campton as unjust as when it first dawned on him that his boy's very life might hang on some tortuous secret negotiation between the cabinets of Europe.

He still refused to admit that France had any claim on George, any right to his time, to his suffering or to his life. He had argued it out a hundred times with Adele Anthony. "You say Julia and I were to blame for not going home before the boy was born—and God knows I agree with you! But suppose we'd meant to go? Suppose we'd made every arrangement, taken every precaution, as my parents did in my own case, got to Havre or Cherbourg, say, and been told the steamer had broken her screw—or been prevented ourselves, at the last moment, by illness or accident, or any sudden grab of the Hand of God? You'll admit we shouldn't have been to blame for that; yet the law would have recognized no difference. George would still have found himself a French soldier on the second of last August because, by the same kind of unlucky accident, he and I were born on the wrong side of the Atlantic. And I say that's enough to prove it's an iniquitous law, a travesty of justice. Nobody's going to convince me that, because a steamer may happen to break a phlange of her screw at the wrong time, or a poor woman be frightened by a thunderstorm, France has the right to force an American boy to go and rot in the trenches."

"In the trenches—is George in the trenches?" Adele Anthony asked, raising her pale eyebrows.

"No," Campton thundered, his fist crashing down among her tea things; "and all your word-juggling isn't going to convince me that he ought to be there." He paused and stared furiously about the little lady-like drawing-room into which Miss Anthony's sharp angles were so incongruously squeezed. She made no answer, and he went on: "George looks at the thing exactly as I do."

"Has he told you so?" Miss Anthony enquired, rescuing his teacup and putting sugar into her own.

"He has told me nothing to the contrary. You don't seem to be aware that military correspondence is censored, and that a soldier can't always blurt out everything he thinks."

Miss Anthony followed his glance about the room, and her eyes paused with his on her own portrait, now in the place of honour over the mantelpiece, where it hung incongruously above a menagerie of china animals and a collection of trophies from the Marne.

"I dropped in at the Luxembourg yesterday," she said. "Do you know whom I saw there? Anderson Brant. He was looking at George's portrait, and turned as red as a beet. You ought to do him a sketch of George some day—after this."

Campton's face darkened. He knew it was partly through Brant's influence that George had been detached from his regiment and given a staff job in the Argonne; but Miss Anthony's reminder annoyed him. The Brants had acted through sheer selfish cowardice, the desire to safeguard something which belonged to them, something they valued as they valued their pictures and tapestries, though of course in a greater degree; whereas he, Campton, was sustained by a principle which he could openly avow, and was ready to discuss with any one who had the leisure to listen.

He had explained all this so often to Miss Anthony that the words rose again to his lips without an effort. "If it had been a national issue I should have wanted him to be among the first: such as our having to fight Mexico, for instance——"

"Yes; or the moon. For my part, I understand Julia and Anderson better. They don't care a fig for national issues; they're just animals defending their cub."

"*Their*—thank you!" Campton exclaimed.

"Well, poor Anderson really *was* a dry-nurse to the boy. Who else was there to look after him? You were painting Spanish beauties at the time." She frowned. "Life's a puzzle. I see perfectly that if you'd let everything else go to keep George you'd never have become the great John Campton: the *real* John Campton you were meant to be. And it wouldn't have been half as satisfactory for you—or for George either. Only, in the meanwhile, somebody had to blow the child's nose, and pay his dentist and doctor; and you ought to be grateful to Anderson for doing it. Aren't there bees or ants, or something, that are kept for such purposes?"

Campton's lips were opened to reply when her face changed, and he saw that he had ceased to exist for her. He knew the reason. That look came over everybody's face nowadays at the hour when the evening paper came. The old maid-servant brought it in, and lingered to hear the *communiqué*. At that hour, everywhere over the globe, business and labour and pleasure (if it still existed) were suspended for a moment while the hearts of all men gathered themselves up in a question and a prayer.

Miss Anthony sought for her *lorgnon* and failed to find it. With a shaking hand she passed the newspaper over to Campton.

"Violent enemy attacks in the region of Dixmude, Ypres, Armentières, Arras, in the Argonne, and on the advanced slopes of the Grand Couronné de Nancy, have been successfully repulsed. We have taken back the village of Soupir, near Vailly (Aisne); we have taken Maucourt and Mogeville, to the northeast of Verdun. Progress has been made in the region of Vermelles (Pas-de-Calais), south of Aix Noulette. Enemy attacks in the Hauts-de-Meuse and southeast of Saint-Mihiel have also been repulsed.

"In Poland the Austrian retreat is becoming general. The Russians are still advancing in the direction of Kielce-Sandomir and have progressed beyond the San in Galicia. Mlawa has been reoccupied, and the whole railway system of Poland is now controlled by the Russian forces."

A good day—oh, decidedly a good day. At this rate, what became of the gloomy forecasts of the people who talked of a winter in the trenches, to be followed by a spring campaign? True, the Serbian army was still retreating before superior Austrian forces—but there too the scales would soon be turned if the Russians continued to progress. That day there was hope everywhere: the old maid-servant went away smiling, and Miss Anthony poured out another cup of tea.

Campton had not lifted his eyes from the paper. Suddenly they lit on a short paragraph: "Fallen on the Field of Honour." One had got used to that with the rest; used even to the pang of reading names one knew, evoking familiar features, young faces blotted out in blood, young limbs convulsed in the fires of that hell called "the Front." But this time Campton turned pale and the paper fell to his knee.

"Fortin-Lescluze; Jean-Jacques-Marie, lieutenant of *Chasseurs à Pied*, gloriously fallen for France . . ." There followed a ringing citation.

Fortin's son, his only son, was dead.

Campton saw before him the honest *bourgeois* dining-room, so strangely out of keeping with the rest of the establishment; he saw the late August sun slanting in on the group about the table, on the ambitious and unscrupulous great man, the two quiet women hidden under his illustrious roof, and the youth who had held together these three dissimilar people, making an invisible home in the heart of all that publicity. Campton remembered his brief exchange of words with Fortin on the threshold, and the father's uncontrollable outburst: "For his mother and myself it's not a trifle—having our only son in the war."

Campton shut his eyes and leaned back, sick with the memory. This man had had a share in saving George; but his own son he could not save.

"What's the matter?" Miss Anthony asked, her hand on his arm.

Campton could not bring the name to his lips. "Nothing —nothing. Only this room's rather hot—and I must be off anyhow." He got up, escaping from her solicitude, and made his way out. He must go at once to Fortin's for news. The physician was still at Chalons; but there would surely be some one at the house, and Campton could at least leave a message and ask where to write.

Dusk had fallen. His eyes usually feasted on the beauty of the new Paris, the secret mysterious Paris of veiled lights and deserted streets; but to-night he was blind to it. He could see nothing but Fortin's face, hear nothing but his voice when he said: "Our only son in the war."

He groped along the pitch-black street for the remembered outline of the house (since no house-numbers were visible), and rang several times without result. He was just turning away when a big mud-splashed motor drove up. He noticed a soldier at the steering-wheel, then three people got out stiffly: two women smothered in crape and a haggard man in a dirty uniform. Campton stopped, and Fortin-Lescluze recognized him by the light of the motor-lamp. The four stood and looked at each other. The old mother, under her crape, appeared no bigger than a child.

"Ah—you know?" the doctor said. Campton nodded.

The father spoke in a firm voice. "It happened three days ago—at Suippes. You've seen his citation? They brought him in to me at Chalons without a warning—and too late. I took off both legs, but gangrene had set in. Ah—if I could have got hold of one of our big surgeons . . . Yes, we're just back from the funeral . . . My mother and my wife . . . they had that comfort . . ."

The two women stood beside him like shrouded statues. Suddenly Mme. Fortin's deep voice came through the crape: "You saw him, Monsieur, that last day . . . the day you came about your own son, I think?"

"I . . . yes . . ." Campton stammered in anguish.

The physician intervened. "And, now, *ma bonne mère*, you're not to be kept standing. You're to go straight in and take your *tisane* and go to bed." He kissed his mother and pushed her into his wife's arms. "Good-bye, my dear. Take care of her."

The women vanished under the porte-cochère, and Fortin turned to the painter.

"Thank you for coming. I can't ask you in—I must go back immediately."

"Back?"

"To my work. Thank God. If it were not for that——"

He jumped into the motor, called out "*En route*," and was absorbed into the night.

Chapter XI

CAMPTON went home to his studio.

He still lived there, shiftlessly and uncomfortably—for Mariette had never come back from Lille. She had not come back, and there was no news of her. Lille had become a part of the "occupied provinces," from which there was no escape; and people were beginning to find out what that living burial meant.

Adele Anthony had urged Campton to go back to the hotel, but he obstinately refused. What business had he to be living in expensive hotels when, for the Lord knew how long, his means of earning a livelihood were gone, and when it was his duty to save up for George—George, who was safe, who was definitely out of danger, and whom he longed more than ever, when the war was over, to withdraw from the stifling atmosphere of his stepfather's millions?

He had been so near to having the boy to himself when the war broke out! He had almost had in sight the proud day when he should be able to say: "Look here: this is your own bank-account. Now you're independent—for God's sake stop and consider what you want to do with your life."

The war had put an end to that—but only for a time. If victory came before long, Campton's reputation would survive the eclipse, his chances of money-making would be as great as ever, and the new George, the George matured and disciplined by war, would come back with a finer sense of values, and a soul steeled against the vulgar opportunities of wealth.

Meanwhile, it behoved his father to save every penny. And the simplest way of saving was to go on camping in the studio, taking his meals at the nearest wine-shop, and entrusting his bed-making and dusting to old Mme. Lebel. In that way he could live for a long time without appreciably reducing his savings.

Mme. Lebel's daughter-in-law, Mme. Jules, who was in the Ardennes with the little girl when the war broke out, was to have replaced Mariette. But, like Mariette, Mme. Jules never arrived, and no word came from her or the child. They too were in an occupied province. So Campton jogged on without a servant. It was very uncomfortable, even for his lax standards; but the dread of letting a stranger loose in the studio made him prefer to put up with Mme. Lebel's intermittent services.

So far she had borne up bravely. Her orphan grandsons were all at the front (how that word had insinuated itself into the language!) but she continued to have fairly frequent reassuring news of them. The *Chasseur Alpin*, slightly wounded in Alsace, was safe in hospital; and the others were well, and wrote cheerfully. Her son Jules, the cabinetmaker, was guarding a bridge at St. Cloud, and came in regularly to see her; but Campton noticed that it was about him that she seemed most anxious.

He was a silent industrious man, who had worked hard to support his orphaned nephews and his mother, and had married in middle age, only four or five years before the war, when the lads could shift for themselves, and his own situation was secure enough to permit the luxury of a wife and baby.

Mme. Jules had waited patiently for him, though she had other chances; and finally they had married and the baby had been born, and blossomed into one of those finished little Frenchwomen who, at four or five, seem already to be musing on the great central problems of love and thrift. The parents used to bring the child to see Campton, and he had made a celebrated sketch of her, in her Sunday bonnet, with little earrings and a wise smile. And these two, mother and child, had disappeared on the second of August as completely as if the earth had opened and swallowed them.

As Campton entered he glanced at the old woman's den, saw that it was empty, and said to himself: "She's at St. Cloud again." For he knew that she seized every chance of being with her eldest.

He unlocked his door and felt his way into the dark studio. Mme. Lebel might at least have made up the fire! Campton lit the lamp, found some wood, and knelt down stiffly by the stove. Really, life was getting too uncomfortable . . .

He was trying to coax a flame when the door opened and he heard Mme. Lebel.

"Really, you know——" he turned to rebuke her; but the words died on his lips. She stood before him, taking no notice;

then her shapeless black figure doubled up, and she sank down into his own armchair. Mme. Lebel, who, even when he offered her a seat, never did more than rest respectful knuckles on its back!

"What's the matter? What's wrong?" he exclaimed.

She lifted her aged face. "Monsieur, I came about your fire; but I am too unhappy. I have more than I can bear." She fumbled vainly for a handkerchief, and wiped away her tears with the back of her old laborious hand.

"Jules has enlisted, Monsieur; enlisted in the infantry. He has left for the front without telling me."

"Good Lord. Enlisted? At his age—is he crazy?"

"No, Monsieur. But the little girl—he's had news——"

She waited to steady her voice, and then fishing in another slit of her multiple skirts, pulled out a letter. "I got that at midday. I hurried to St. Cloud—but he left yesterday."

The letter was grim reading. The poor father had accidentally run across an escaped prisoner who had regained the French lines near the village where Mme. Jules and the child were staying. The man, who knew the wife's family, had been charged by them with a message to the effect that Mme. Jules, who was a proud woman, had got into trouble with the authorities, and been sent off to a German prison on the charge of spying. The poor little girl had cried and clung to her mother, and had been so savagely pushed aside by the officer who made the arrest that she had fallen on the stone steps of the "Kommandantur" and fractured her skull. The fugitive reported her as still alive, but unconscious, and dying.

Jules Lebel had received this news the previous day; and within twenty-four hours he was at the front. Guard a bridge at St. Cloud after that? All he asked was to kill and be killed. He knew the name and the regiment of the officer who had denounced his wife. "If I live long enough I shall run the swine down," he wrote. "If not, I'll kill as many of his kind as God lets me."

Mme. Lebel sat silent, her head bowed on her hands; and Campton stood and watched her. Presently she got up, passed the back of her hand across her eyes, and said: "The room is cold. I'll fetch some coal."

Campton protested. "No, no, Mme. Lebel. Don't worry about me. Make yourself something warm to drink, and try to sleep——"

"Oh, Monsieur, thank God for the work! If it were not for that——" she said, in the same words as the physician.

She hobbled away, and presently he heard her bumping up again with the coal.

When his fire was started, and the curtains drawn, and she had left him, the painter sat down and looked about the studio. Bare and untidy as it was, he did not find the sight unpleasant: he was used to it, and being used to things seemed to him the first requisite of comfort. But to-night his thoughts were elsewhere: he saw neither the tattered tapestries with their huge heroes and kings, nor the blotched walls hung with pictures, nor the canvases stacked against the chair-legs, nor the long littered table at which he wrote and ate and mixed his colours. At one moment he was with Fortin-Lescluze, speeding through the night toward fresh scenes of death; at another, in the *loge* downstairs, where Mme. Lebel, her day's work done, would no doubt sit down as usual by her smoky lamp and go on with her sewing. "Thank God for the work——" they had both said.

And here Campton sat with idle hands, and did nothing——

It was not exactly his fault. What was there for a portrait-painter to do? He was not a portrait-painter only, and on his brief trip to Chalons some of the scenes by the way—gaunt unshorn faces of territorials at railway bridges, soldiers grouped about a provision-lorry, a mud-splashed company returning to the rear, a long grey train of "seventy-fives" ploughing forward through the rain—at these sights the old graphic instinct had stirred in him. But the approaches of the front were sternly forbidden to civilians, and especially to neutrals (Campton was beginning to wince at the word); he himself, who had been taken to Chalons by a high official of the Army Medical Board, had been given only time enough for his interview with Fortin, and brought back to Paris the same night. If ever there came a time for art to interpret the war, as Raffet, for instance, had interpreted Napoleon's campaigns, the day was not yet; the world in which men lived at present was one in which the word "art" had lost its meaning.

And what was Campton, what had he ever been, but an artist? . . . A father; yes, he had waked up to the practice of that other art, he was learning to be a father. And now, at a stroke, his only two reasons for living were gone: since the second of August he had had no portraits to paint, no son to guide and to companion.

Other people, he knew, had found jobs: most of his friends had been drawn into some form of war-work. Dastrey, after vain attempts to enlist, thwarted by an untimely sciatica, had found a post near the front, on the staff of a Red Cross Ambulance. Adele Anthony was working eight or nine hours a day in a Depot which distributed food and clothing to refugees from the invaded provinces; and Mrs. Brant's name figured on the committees of most of the newly-organized war charities. Among Campton's other friends many had accepted humbler tasks. Some devoted their time to listing and packing hospital supplies, keeping accounts in ambulance offices, sorting out refugees at the railway-stations, and telling them where to go for food and help; still others spent their days, and sometimes their nights, at the bitter-cold suburban sidings where the long train-loads of wounded stopped on the way to the hospitals of the interior. There was enough misery and confusion at the rear for every civilian volunteer to find his task.

Among them all, Campton could not see his place. His lameness put him at a disadvantage, since taxicabs were few, and it was difficult for him to travel in the crowded métro. He had no head for figures, and would have thrown the best-kept accounts into confusion; he could not climb steep stairs to seek out refugees, nor should he have known what to say to them when he reached their attics. And so it would have been at the railway canteens; he choked with rage and commiseration at all the suffering about him, but found no word to cheer the sufferers.

Secretly, too, he feared the demands that would be made on him if he once let himself be drawn into the network of war charities. Tiresome women would come and beg for money, or for pictures for bazaars: they were already getting up bazaars.

Money he could not spare, since it was his duty to save it for George; and as for pictures—why, there were a few sketches he might give, but here again he was checked by his fear of establishing a precedent. He had seen in the papers that the

English painters were already giving blank canvases to be sold by auction to millionaires in quest of a portrait. But that form of philanthropy would lead to his having to paint all the unpaintable people who had been trying to bribe a picture out of him since his sudden celebrity. No artist had a right to cheapen his art in that way: it could only result in his turning out work that would injure his reputation and reduce his sales after the war.

So far, Campton had not been troubled by many appeals for help; but that was probably because he had kept out of sight, and thrown into the fire the letters of the few ladies who had begged a sketch for their sales, or his name for their committees.

One appeal, however, he had not been able to avoid. About two months earlier he had had a visit from George's friend Boylston, the youth he had met at Dastrey's dinner the night before war was declared. In the interval he had entirely forgotten Boylston; but as soon as he saw the fat brown young man with a twinkle in his eyes and his hair, Campton recalled him, and held out a cordial hand. Had not George said that Boylston was the best fellow he knew?

Boylston seemed much impressed by the honour of waiting on the great man. In spite of his cool twinkling air he was evidently full of reverence for the things and people he esteemed, and Campton's welcome sent the blood up to the edge of his tight curls. It also gave him courage to explain his visit.

He had come to beg Campton to accept the chairmanship of the American Committee of "The Friends of French Art," an international group of painters who proposed to raise funds for the families of mobilised artists. The American group would naturally be the most active, since Americans had, in larger numbers than any other foreigners, sought artistic training in France; and all the members agreed that Campton's name must figure at their head. But Campton was known to be inaccessible, and the committee, aware that Boylston was a friend of George's, had asked him to transmit their request.

"You see, sir, nobody else represents . . ."

Campton thought as seldom as possible of what followed: he hated the part he had played. But, after all, what else could he have done? Everything in him recoiled from what acceptance would bring with it: publicity, committee meetings, speechifying, writing letters, seeing troublesome visitors, hearing

harrowing stories, asking people for money—above all, having
to give his own; a great deal of his own.

He stood before the young man, abject, irresolute, chink-
ing a bunch of keys in his trouser-pocket, and remembering
afterward that the chink must have sounded as if it were full
of money. He remembered too, oddly enough, that as his own
embarrassment increased Boylston's vanished. It was as though
the modest youth, taking his host's measure, had reluctantly
found him wanting, and from that moment had felt less in awe
of his genius. Illogical, of course, and unfair—but there it was.

The talk had ended by Campton's refusing the chairmanship, but agreeing to let his name figure on the list of honorary
members, where he hoped it would be overshadowed by rival
glories. And, having reached this conclusion, he had limped to
his desk, produced a handful of notes, and after a moment's
hesitation held out two hundred francs with the stereotyped:
"Sorry I can't make it more . . ."

He had meant it to be two hundred and fifty; but, with his
usual luck, all his fumbling had failed to produce a fifty-franc
note; and he could hardly ask Boylston to "make the change."

On the threshold the young man paused to ask for the last
news of George; and on Campton's assuring him that it was
excellent, added, with evident sincerity: "Still hung up on that
beastly staff-job? I do call that hard luck——" And now, of all the
unpleasant memories of the visit, that phrase kept the sharpest
sting.

Was it in fact hard luck? And did George himself think so?
There was nothing in his letters to show it. He seemed to have
undergone no change of view as to his own relation to the war;
he had shown no desire to "be in it," as that mad young Upsher
said.

For the first time since he had seen George's train pull out
of the Gare de l'Est Campton found himself wondering at the
perfection of his son's moral balance. So many things had happened since; war had turned out to be so immeasurably more
hideous and abominable than those who most abhorred war
had dreamed it could be; the issues at stake had become so glar-
ingly plain, right and wrong, honour and dishonour, humanity
and savagery faced each other so squarely across the trenches,
that it seemed strange to Campton that his boy, so eager, so

impressionable, so quick on the uptake, should not have felt some such burst of wrath as had driven even poor Jules Lebel into the conflict.

The comparison, of course, was absurd. Lebel had been parted from his dearest, his wife dragged to prison, his child virtually murdered: any man, in his place, must have felt the blind impulse to kill. But what was Lebel's private plight but a symbol of the larger wrong? This war could no longer be compared to other wars: Germany was conducting it on methods that civilization had made men forget. The occupation of Luxembourg; the systematic destruction of Belgium; the savage treatment of the people of the invaded regions; the outrages of Louvain and Rheims and Ypres; the voice with which these offences cried to heaven had waked the indignation of humanity. Yet George, in daily contact with all this woe and ruin, seemed as unmoved as though he had been behind a desk in the New York office of Bullard and Brant.

If there were any change in his letters it was rather that they were more indifferent. His reports of himself became drier, more stereotyped, his comments on the situation fewer: he seemed to have been subdued to the hideous business he worked in. It was true that his letters had never been expressive: his individuality seemed to dry up in contact with pen and paper. It was true also that letters from the front were severely censored, and that it would have been foolish to put in them anything likely to prevent their delivery. But George had managed to send several notes by hand, and these were as colourless as the others; and so were his letters to his mother, which Mrs. Brant always sent to Miss Anthony, who privately passed them on to Campton.

Besides, there were other means of comparison. People with sons at the front were beginning to hand about copies of their letters; a few passages, strangely moving and beautiful, had found their way into the papers. George, God be praised, was not at the front; but he was in the war zone, far nearer the sights and sounds of death than his father, and he had comrades and friends in the trenches. Strange that what he wrote was still so cold to the touch . . .

"It's the scientific mind, I suppose," Campton reflected. "These youngsters are all rather like beautifully made machines . . ." Yet it had never before struck him that his son was like a beautifully made machine.

He remembered that he had not dined, and got up wearily. As he passed out he noticed on a pile of letters and papers a brand-new card: he could always tell the new cards by their whiteness, which twenty-four hours of studio-dust turned to grey.

Campton held the card to the light. It was large and glossy, a beautiful thick pre-war card; and on it was engraved:

HARVEY MAYHEW

Délégué des Etats Unis au Congrès de la Paix

with a pen-stroke through the lower line. Beneath was written an imperative "p.t.o."; and reversing the card, Campton read, in an agitated hand: "Must see you at once. Call up Nouveau Luxe"; and, lower down: "Excuse ridiculous card. Impossible get others under six weeks."

So Mayhew had turned up! Well, it was a good thing: perhaps he might bring news of that mad Benny Upsher whose doings had caused Campton so much trouble in the early days that he could never recall the boy's obstinate rosy face without a stir of irritation.

"I want to be *in* this thing——" Well, young Upsher had apparently been in it with a vengeance; but what he had cost Campton in cables to his distracted family, and in weary pilgrimages to the War Office, the American Embassy, the Consulate, the Prefecture of Police, and divers other supposed sources of information, the painter meant some day to tell his young relative in no measured terms. That is, if the chance ever presented itself; for, since he had left the studio that morning four months ago, Benny had so completely vanished that Campton sometimes wondered, with a little shiver, if they were ever likely to exchange words again in this world.

"Mayhew will know; he wants to tell me about the boy, I suppose," he mused.

Harvey Mayhew—Harvey Mayhew with a pen-stroke through the title which, so short a time since, it had been his chief ambition to display on his cards! No wonder it embarrassed him now. But where on earth had he been all this time? As Campton pondered on the card a memory flashed out.

Mayhew? Mayhew? Why, wasn't it Mayhew who had waylaid him in the Crillon a few hours before war was declared, to ask his advice about the safest way of travelling to the Hague? And hadn't he, Campton, in all good faith, counselled him to go by Luxembourg "in order to be out of the way of trouble"?

The remembrance swept away the painter's sombre thoughts, and he burst into a laugh that woke the echoes of the studio.

Chapter XII

Not having it in his power to call up his cousin on the telephone, Campton went the next morning to the Nouveau Luxe.

It was the first time that he had entered the famous hotel since the beginning of the war; and at sight of the long hall his heart sank as it used to whenever some untoward necessity forced him to run its deadly blockade.

But the hall was empty when he entered, empty not only of the brilliant beings who filled his soul with such dismay, but also of the porters, footmen and lift-boys who, even in its unfrequented hours, lent it the lustre of their liveries.

A tired concierge sat at the desk, and near the door a boy scout, coiling his bare legs about a high stool, raised his head languidly from his book. But for these two, the world of the Nouveau Luxe had disappeared.

As the lift was not running there was nothing to disturb their meditations; and when Campton had learned that Mr. Mayhew would receive him he started alone up the deserted stairs.

Only a few dusty trunks remained in the corridors where luggage used to be piled as high as in the passages of the great liners on sailing-day; and instead of the murmur of ladies'-maids' skirts, and explosions of laughter behind glazed service-doors, the swish of a charwoman's mop alone broke the silence.

"After all," Campton thought, "if war didn't kill people how much pleasanter it might make the world!"

This was evidently not the opinion of Mr. Harvey Mayhew, whom he found agitatedly pacing a large room hung in shrimp-pink brocade, which opened on a vista of turquoise tiling and porcelain tub.

Mr. Mayhew's round countenance, composed of the same simple curves as his nephew's, had undergone a remarkable change. He was still round, but he was ravaged. His fringe of hair had grown greyer, and there were crow's-feet about his blue eyes, and wrathful corrugations in his benignant forehead.

He seized Campton's hands and glared at him through indignant eye-glasses.

"My dear fellow, I looked you up as soon as I arrived. I need you—we all need you—we need your powerful influence and your world-wide celebrity. Campton, the day for words has gone by. We must *act*!"

Campton let himself down into an armchair. No verb in the language terrified him as much as that which his cousin had flung at him. He gazed at the ex-Delegate with dismay. "I didn't know you were here. Where have you come from?" he asked.

Mr. Mayhew, resting a manicured hand on the edge of a gilt table, looked down awfully on him.

"I come," he said, "from a German prison."

"Good Lord—*you*?" Campton gasped.

He continued to gaze at his cousin with terror, but of a new kind. Here at last was someone who had actually been in the jaws of the monster, who had seen, heard, suffered—a witness who could speak of that which he knew! No wonder Mr. Mayhew took himself seriously—at last he had something to be serious about! Campton stared at him as if he had risen from the dead.

Mr. Mayhew cleared his throat and went on: "You may remember our meeting at the Crillon—on the 31st of last July it was—and my asking you the best way of getting to the Hague, in view of impending events. At that time" (his voice took a note of irony) "I was a Delegate to the Peace Congress at the Hague, and conceived it to be my duty to carry out my mandate at whatever personal risk. You advised me—as you may also remember—in order to be out of the way of trouble, to travel by Luxembourg," (Campton stirred uneasily). "I followed your advice; and, not being able to go by train, I managed, with considerable difficulty, to get permission to travel by motor. I reached Luxembourg as the German army entered it—the next day I was in a German prison."

The next day! Then this pink-and-white man who stood there with his rimless eye-glasses and neatly trimmed hair, and his shining nails reflected in the plate glass of the table-top, this perfectly typical, usual sort of harmless rich American, had been for four months in the depths of the abyss that men were beginning to sound with fearful hearts!

"It is a simple miracle," said Mr. Mayhew, "that I was not shot as a spy."

Campton's voice choked in his throat. "Where were you imprisoned?"

"The first night, in the Police commissariat, with common thieves and vagabonds—with—" Mr. Mayhew lowered his voice and his eyes: "With prostitutes, Campton . . ."

He waited for this to take effect, and continued: "The next day, in consequence of the energetic intervention of our consul—who behaved extremely well, as I have taken care to let them know in Washington—I was sent back to my hotel on parole, and kept there, kept there, Campton—*I*, the official representative of a friendly country—under strict police surveillance, like . . . like an unfortunate woman . . . for eight days: a week and one day over!"

Mr. Mayhew sank into a chair and passed a scented handkerchief across his forehead. "When I was finally released I was without money, without luggage, without my motor or my wretched chauffeur—a Frenchman, who had been instantly carried off to Germany. In this state of destitution, and without an apology, I was shipped to Rotterdam and put on a steamer sailing for America." He wiped his forehead again, and the corners of his agitated lips. "Peace, Campton—*Peace*? When I think that I believed in a thing called Peace! That I left Utica—always a difficult undertaking for me—because I deemed it my duty, in the interests of *Peace*," (the word became a hiss) "to travel to the other side of the world, and use the weight of my influence and my experience in such a cause!"

He clenched his fist and shook it in the face of an invisible foe.

"My influence, if I have any; my experience—ha, I *have* had experience now, Campton! And, my God, sir, they shall both be used till my last breath to show up these people, to proclaim to the world what they really are, to rouse public opinion in America against a nation of savages who ought to be hunted off the face of the globe like vermin—like the vermin in their own prison cells! Campton—if I may say so without profanity—I come to bring not Peace but a Sword!"

It was some time before the flood of Mr. Mayhew's wrath subsided, or before there floated up from its agitated depths some fragments of his subsequent history and present intentions. Eventually, however, Campton gathered that after a short sojourn in America, where he found opinion too lukewarm for him, he had come back to Europe to collect the experiences of other victims of German savagery. Mr. Mayhew, in short, meant to devote himself to Atrocities; and he had sought out Campton to ask his help, and especially to be put in contact with persons engaged in refugee-work, and likely to have come across flagrant offences against the law of nations.

It was easy to comply with the latter request. Campton scribbled a message to Adele Anthony at her refugee Depot; and he undertook also to find out from what officials Mr. Mayhew might obtain leave to visit the front.

"I know it's difficult——" he began; but Mr. Mayhew laughed. "I am here to surmount difficulties—after what I've been through!"

It was not until then that Mr. Mayhew found time to answer an enquiry about his nephew.

"Benny Upsher? Ha—I'm proud of Benny! He's a hero, that nephew of mine—he was always my favourite."

He went on to say that the youth, having failed to enlist in the French army, had managed to get back to England, and there, passing himself off as a Canadian ("Born at Murray Bay, sir— wasn't it lucky?") had joined an English regiment, and, after three months' training, was now on his way to the front. His parents had made a great outcry—moved heaven and earth for news of him—but the boy had covered up his tracks so cleverly that they had had no word till he was starting for Boulogne with his draft. Rather high-handed—and poor Madeline had nearly gone out of her mind; but Mr. Mayhew confessed he had no patience with such feminine weakness. "Benny's a man, and must act as a man. That boy, Campton, saw things as they were from the first."

Campton took leave, dazed and crushed by the conversation. It was all one to him if Harvey Mayhew chose to call on America to avenge his wrongs; Campton himself was beginning to wish that his country would wake up to what was going on in the world; but that he, Campton, should be drawn into the affair, should have to write letters, accompany the ex-Delegate to Embassies and Red Crosses, languish with him in ministerial antechambers, and be deafened with appeals to his own celebrity and efficiency; that he should have ascribed to himself that mysterious gift of "knowing the ropes" in which his whole blundering career had proved him to be cruelly lacking: this was so dreadful to him as to obscure every other question.

"Thank the Lord," he muttered, "I haven't got the telephone anyhow!"

He glanced cautiously down the wide stairs of the hotel to assure himself of a safe retreat; but in the hall an appealing voice detained him.

"Dear Master! Dear great Master! I've been lying in wait for you!"

A Red Cross nurse advanced: not the majestic figure of the Crimean legend, but the new version evolved in the rue de la Paix: short skirts, long ankles, pearls and curls. The face under the coif was young, wistful, haggard with the perpetual hurry of the aimless. Where had he seen those tragic eyes, so full of questions and so invariably uninterested in the answers?

"I'm Madge Talkett—I saw you at—I saw you the day war was declared," the young lady corrected herself. Campton remembered their meeting at Mrs. Brant's, and was grateful for her evident embarrassment. So few of the new generation seemed aware that there were any privacies left to respect! He looked at Mrs. Talkett more kindly.

"You *must* come," she continued, laying her hand on his arm (her imperatives were always in italics). "Just a step from here—to my hospital. There's someone asking for you."

"For me? Someone wounded?" What if it were Benny Upsher? A cold fear broke over Campton.

"Someone dying," Mrs. Talkett said. "Oh, nobody you know—a poor young French soldier. He was brought here two days ago . . . and he keeps on repeating your name . . ."

"My name? Why my name?"

"We don't know. We don't think he knows you . . . but he's shot to pieces and half delirious. He's a painter, and he's seen pictures of yours, and keeps talking about them, and saying he wants you to look at his . . . You *will* come? It's just next door, you know."

He did not know—having carefully avoided all knowledge of hospitals in his dread of being drawn into war-work, and his horror of coming as a mere spectator to gaze on agony he could neither comfort nor relieve. Hospitals were for surgeons and women; if he had been rich he would have given big sums to aid them; being unable to do even that, he preferred to keep aloof.

He followed Mrs. Talkett out of the hotel and around the corner. The door of another hotel, with a big Red Cross above it, admitted them to a marble vestibule full of the cold smell of disinfectants. An orderly sat reading a newspaper behind the desk, and nurses whisked backward and forward with trays and pails. A lady with a bunch of flowers came down the stairs drying her eyes.

Campton's whole being recoiled from what awaited him. Since the poor youth was delirious, what was the use of seeing him? But women took a morbid pleasure in making one do things that were useless!

On an upper floor they paused at a door where there was a moment's parleying.

"Come," Mrs. Talkett said; "he's a little better."

The room contained two beds. In one lay a haggard elderly man with closed eyes and lips drawn back from his clenched teeth. His legs stirred restlessly, and one of his arms was in a lifted sling attached to a horrible kind of gallows above the bed. It reminded Campton of Juan de Borgoña's pictures of the Inquisition, in the Prado.

"Oh, *he's* all right; he'll get well. It's the other . . ."

The other lay quietly in his bed. No gallows overhung him, no visible bandaging showed his wound. There was a flush on his young cheeks and his eyes looked out, large and steady, from their hollow brows. But he was the one who would not get well.

Mrs. Talkett bent over him: her voice was sweet when it was lowered.

"I've kept my promise. Here he is."

The eyes turned in the lad's immovable head, and he and Campton looked at each other. The painter had never seen the face before him: a sharp irregular face, prematurely hollowed by pain, with thick chestnut hair tumbled above the forehead.

"It's you, Master!" the boy said.

Campton sat down beside him. "How did you know? Have you seen me before?"

"Once—at one of your exhibitions." He paused and drew a hard breath. "But the first thing was the portrait at the Luxembourg . . . your son . . ."

"Ah, you look like him!" Campton broke out.

The eyes of the young soldier lit up. "Do I? . . . Someone told me he was your son. I went home from seeing that and began to paint. After the war, would you let me come and work with you? My things . . . wait . . . I'll show you my things first." He tried to raise himself. Mrs. Talkett slipped her arm under his shoulders, and resting against her he lifted his hand and pointed to the bare wall facing him.

"There—there; you see? Look for yourself. The brushwork . . . not too bad, eh? I was . . . getting it . . . There, that head of my grandfather, eh? And my lame sister . . . Oh, I'm young . . ." he smiled . . . "never had any models . . . But after the war you'll see . . ."

Mrs. Talkett let him down again, and feverishly, vehemently, he began to describe, one by one, and over and over again, the pictures he saw on the naked wall in front of him.

A nurse had slipped in, and Mrs. Talkett signed to Campton to follow her out. The boy seemed aware that the painter was going, and interrupted his enumeration to say: "As soon as the war's over you'll let me come?"

"Of course I will," Campton promised.

In the passage he asked: "Can nothing save him? Has everything possible been done?"

"Everything. We're all so fond of him—the biggest surgeons have seen him. It seems he has great talent—but he never could afford models, so he has painted his family over and over again." Mrs. Talkett looked at Campton with a good deal of feeling in her changing eyes. "You see, it *did* help, your coming. I know you thought it tiresome of me to insist." She led him downstairs and into the office, where a lame officer with the Croix de Guerre sat at the desk. The officer wrote out the young soldier's name—René Davril—and his family's address.

"They're quite destitute, Monsieur. An old infirm grandfather, a lame sister who taught music, a widowed mother and several younger children . . ."

"I'll come back, I'll come back," Campton again promised as he parted from Mrs. Talkett.

He had not thought it possible that he would ever feel so kindly toward her as at that moment. And then, a second later, she nearly spoiled it by saying: "Dear Master—you see the penalty of greatness!"

The name of René Davril was with Campton all day. The boy had believed in him—his eyes had been opened by the sight of George's portrait! And now, in a day or two more, he would be filling a three-by-six ditch in a crowded graveyard. At twenty— and with eyes like George's.

What could Campton do? No one was less visited by happy inspirations; the "little acts of kindness" recommended to his pious infancy had always seemed to him far harder to think of than to perform. But now some instinct carried him straight to the corner of his studio where he remembered having shoved out of sight a half-finished study for George's portrait. He found it, examined it critically, scribbled his signature in one corner, and set out with it for the hospital. On the way he had to stop at the Ministry of War on Mayhew's tiresome business, and was delayed there till too late to proceed with his errand before luncheon. But in the afternoon he passed in again through the revolving plate glass, and sent up his name. Mrs. Talkett was not there, but a nurse came down, to whom, with embarrassment, he explained himself.

"Poor little Davril? Yes—he's still alive. Will you come up? His family are with him."

Campton shook his head and held out the parcel. "It's a picture he wanted——"

The nurse promised it should be given. She looked at Campton with a vague benevolence, having evidently never heard his name; and the painter turned away with a cowardly sense that he ought to have taken the picture up himself. But to see the death-change on a face so like his son's, and its look reflected in other anguished faces, was more than he could endure. He turned away.

The next morning Mrs. Talkett wrote that René Davril was better, that the fever had dropped, and that he was lying quietly looking at the sketch. "The only thing that troubles him is that he realizes now that you have not seen his pictures. But he is very happy, and blesses you for your goodness."

His goodness! Campton, staring at the letter, could only curse himself for his stupidity. He saw now that the one thing which might have comforted the poor lad would have been to have his own pictures seen and judged; and that one thing, he, Campton, so many years vainly athirst for the approbation of the men he revered—that one thing he had never thought of doing! The only way of atoning for his negligence was instantly to go out to the suburb where the Davril family lived. Campton, without a scruple, abandoned Mr. Mayhew, with whom he had an appointment at the Embassy and another at the War Office, and devoted the rest of the day to the expedition. It was after six when he reached the hospital again; and when Mrs. Talkett came down he went up to her impetuously.

"Well—I've seen them; I've seen his pictures, and he's right. They're astonishing! Awkward, still, and hesitating; but with such a sense of air and mass. He'll do things—May I go up and tell him?"

He broke off and looked at her.

"He died an hour ago. If only you'd seen them yesterday!" she said.

Chapter XIII

THE killing of René Davril seemed to Campton one of the most senseless crimes the war had yet perpetrated. It brought home to him, far more vividly than the distant death of poor Jean Fortin, what an incalculable sum of gifts and virtues went to make up the monster's daily meal.

"Ah, you want genius, do you? Mere youth's not enough . . . and health and gaiety and courage; you want brains in the bud, imagination and poetry, ideas all folded up in their sheath! It takes that, does it, to tempt your jaded appetite?" He was reminded of the rich vulgarians who will eat only things out of season. "That's what war is like," he muttered savagely to himself.

The next morning he went to the funeral with Mrs. Talkett —between whom and himself the tragic episode had created a sort of improvised intimacy—walking at her side through the November rain, behind the poor hearse with the tricolour over it.

At the church, while the few mourners shivered in a damp side chapel, he had time to study the family: a poor sobbing mother, two anæmic little girls, and the lame sister who was musical—a piteous group, smelling of poverty and tears. Behind them, to his surprise, he saw the curly brown head and short-sighted eyes of Boylston. Campton wondered at the latter's presence; then he remembered "The Friends of French Art," and concluded that the association had probably been interested in poor Davril.

With some difficulty he escaped from the thanks of the mother and sisters, and picked up a taxi to take Mrs. Talkett home.

"No—back to the hospital," she said. "A lot of bad cases have come in, and I'm on duty again all day." She spoke as if it were the most natural thing in the world; and he shuddered at the serenity with which women endure the unendurable.

At the hospital he followed her in. The Davril family, she told him, had insisted that they had no claim on his picture, and that it must be returned to him. Mrs. Talkett went up to fetch

it; and Campton waited in one of the drawing-rooms. A step
sounded behind him, and another nurse came in—but was it a
nurse, or some haloed nun from an Umbrian triptych, her pure
oval framed in white, her long fingers clasping a book and lily?

"Mme. de Dolmetsch!" he cried; and thought: "A new face
again—what an artist!"

She seized his hands.

"I heard from dear Madge Talkett that you were here, and
I've asked her to leave us together." She looked at him with
ravaged eyes, as if just risen from a penitential vigil.

"Come, please, into my little office: you didn't know that I
was the *Infirmière-Major*? My dear friend, what upheavals, what
cataclysms! I see no one now: all my days and nights are given
to my soldiers."

She glided ahead on noiseless sandals to a little room where
a bowl of jade filled with gardenias, and a tortoise-shell box of
gold-tipped cigarettes, stood on a desk among torn and discoloured *livrets militaires*. The room was empty, and Mme. de
Dolmetsch, closing the door, drew Campton to a seat at her
side. So close to her, he saw that the perfect lines of her face
were flawed by marks of suffering. "The woman really has a
heart," he thought, "or the war couldn't have made her so much
handsomer."

Mme. de Dolmetsch leaned closer: a breath of incense floated
from her conventual draperies.

"I know why you came," she continued; "you were good
to that poor little Davril." She clutched Campton suddenly
with a blue-veined hand. "My dear friend, can anything justify
such horrors? Isn't it abominable that boys like that should be
murdered? That some senile old beast of a diplomatist should
decree, after a good dinner, that all we love best must be offered
up?" She caught his hands again, her liturgical scent enveloping
him. "Campton, I know you feel as I do." She paused, pressing
his fingers hard, her beautiful mouth trembling. "For God's
sake tell me," she implored, "how you've managed to keep your
son from the front!"

Campton drew away, red and inarticulate. "I—my son?
Those things depend on the authorities. My boy's health . . ."
he stammered.

"Yes, yes; I know. Your George is delicate. But so is my Ladislas
—dreadfully. The lungs too. I've trembled for him for so long;
and now, at any moment . . ." Two tears gathered on her long
lashes and rolled down . . . "at any moment he may be taken
from the War Office, where he's doing invaluable work, and
forced into all that blood and horror; he may be brought back
to me like those poor creatures up-stairs, who are hardly men
any longer . . . mere vivisected animals, without eyes, without
faces." She lowered her voice and drew her lids together, so that
her very eyes seemed to be whispering. "Ladislas has enemies
who are jealous of him (I could give you their names); at this
moment someone who ought to be at the front is intriguing to
turn him out and get his place. Oh, Campton, you've known
this terror—you know what one's nights are like! Have pity—tell
me how you managed!"

He had no idea of what he answered, or how he finally got
away. Everything that was dearest to him, the thought of
George, the vision of the lad dying upstairs, was defiled by
this monstrous coupling of their names with that of the supple
middle-aged adventurer safe in his spotless uniform at the War
Office. And beneath the boiling-up of Campton's disgust a new
fear lifted its head. How did Mme. de Dolmetsch know about
George? And what did she know? Evidently there had been
foolish talk somewhere. Perhaps it was Mrs. Brant—or perhaps
Fortin himself. All these great doctors forgot the professional
secret with some one woman, if not with many. Had not Fortin
revealed to his own wife the reason of Campton's precipitate
visit? The painter escaped from Mme. de Dolmetsch's scented
lair, and from the sights and sounds of the hospital, in a state of
such perturbation that for a while he stood in the street wondering where he had meant to go next.

He had his own reasons for agreeing to the Davrils' suggestion that the picture should be returned to him; and presently
these reasons came back. "They'd never dare to sell it themselves; but why shouldn't I sell it for them?" he had thought,
remembering their denuded rooms, and the rusty smell of the
women's mourning. It cost him a pang to part with a study of
his boy; but he was in a superstitious and expiatory mood, and
eager to act on it.

He remembered having been told by Boylston that "The Friends of French Art" had their office in the Palais Royal, and he made his way through the deserted arcades to the door of a once-famous restaurant.

Behind the plate-glass windows young women with rolled-up sleeves and straw in their hair were delving in packing-cases, while, divided from them by an improvised partition, another group were busy piling on the cloak-room shelves garments such as had never before dishonoured them.

Campton stood fascinated by the sight of the things these young women were sorting: pink silk combinations, sporting ulsters in glaring black and white checks, straw hats wreathed with last summer's sunburnt flowers, high-heeled satin shoes split on the instep, and fringed and bugled garments that suggested obsolete names like "dolman" and "mantle," and looked like the costumes dug out of a country-house attic by amateurs preparing to play "Caste." Was it possible that "The Friends of French Art" proposed to clothe the families of fallen artists in these prehistoric properties?

Boylston appeared, flushed and delighted (and with straw in his hair also), and led his visitor up a cork-screw stair. They passed a room where a row of people in shabby mourning like that of the Davril family sat on restaurant chairs before a *caissière's* desk; and at the desk Campton saw Miss Anthony, her veil pushed back and a card-catalogue at her elbow, listening to a young woman who was dramatically stating her case.

Boylston saw Campton's surprise, and said: "Yes, we're desperately short-handed, and Miss Anthony has deserted her refugees for a day or two to help me to straighten things out."

His own office was in a faded *cabinet particulier* where the dinner-table had been turned into a desk, and the weak-springed divan was weighed down under suits of ready-made clothes bearing the label of a wholesale clothier.

"These are the things we really give them; but they cost a lot of money to buy," Boylston explained. On the divan sat a handsomely dressed elderly lady with a long emaciated face and red eyes, who rose as they entered. Boylston spoke to her in an undertone and led her into another *cabinet*, where Campton saw her tragic figure sink down on the sofa, under a glass scrawled with amorous couplets.

"That was Mme. Beausite . . . You didn't recognize her? Poor thing! Her youngest boy is blind: his eyes were put out by a shell. She is very unhappy, and she comes here and helps now and then. Beausite? Oh no, we never see *him*. He's only our Honorary President."

Boylston, obviously spoke without afterthought; but Campton felt the sting. He too was on the honorary committee.

"Poor woman! What? The young fellow who did Cubist things? I hadn't heard . . ." He remembered the cruel rumour that Beausite, when his glory began to wane, had encouraged his three sons in three different lines of art, so that there might always be a Beausite in the fashion . . . "You must have to listen to pretty ghastly stories here," he said.

The young man nodded, and Campton, with less embarrassment than he had expected, set forth his errand. In that atmosphere it seemed natural to be planning ways of relieving misery, and Boylston at once put him at his ease by looking pleased but not surprised.

"You mean to sell the sketch, sir? That will put the Davrils out of anxiety for a long time; and they're in a bad way, as you saw." Boylston undid the parcel, with a respectful: "May I?" and put the canvas on a chair. He gazed at it for a few moments, the blood rising sensitively over his face till it reached his tight ridge of hair. Campton remembered what George had said of his friend's silent admirations; he was glad the young man did not speak.

When he did, it was to say with a businesslike accent: "We're trying to get up an auction of pictures and sketches—and if we could lead off with this . . ."

It was Campton's turn to redden. The possibility was one he had not thought of. If the picture were sold at auction, Anderson Brant would be sure to buy it! But he could not say this to Boylston. He hesitated, and the other, who seemed quick at feeling his way, added at once: "But perhaps you'd rather sell it privately? In that case we should get the money sooner."

It was just the right thing to say: and Campton thanked him and picked up his sketch. At the door he hesitated, feeling that it became a member of the honorary committee to add something more.

"How are you getting on? Getting all the help you need?"

Boylston smiled. "We need such a lot. People have been very generous: we've had several big sums. But look at those ridiculous clothes down-stairs—we get boxes and boxes of such rubbish! And there are so many applicants, and such hard cases. Take those poor Davrils, for instance. The lame Davril girl has a talent for music: plays the violin. Well, what good does it do her now? The artists are having an awful time. If this war goes on much longer, it won't be only at the front that they'll die."

"Ah——" said Campton. "Well, I'll take this to a dealer——"

On the way down he turned in to greet Miss Anthony. She looked up in surprise, her tired face haloed in tumbling hair-pins; but she was too busy to do more than nod across the group about her desk.

At his offer to take her home she shook her head. "I'm here till after seven. Mr. Boylston and I are nearly snowed under. We've got to go down presently and help unpack; and after that I'm due at my refugee canteen at the Nord. It's my night shift."

Campton, on the way back to Montmartre, fell to wondering if such excesses of altruism were necessary, or a mere vain overflow of energy. He was terrified by his first close glimpse of the ravages of war, and the efforts of the little band struggling to heal them seemed pitifully ineffectual. No doubt they did good here and there, made a few lives less intolerable; but how the insatiable monster must laugh at them as he spread his red havoc wider!

On reaching home, Campton forgot everything at sight of a letter from George. He had not had one for two weeks, and this interruption, just as the military mails were growing more regular, had made him anxious. But it was the usual letter: brief, cheerful, inexpressive. Apparently there was no change in George's situation, nor any wish on his part that there should be. He grumbled humorously at the dulness of his work and the monotony of life in a war-zone town; and wondered whether, if this sort of thing went on, there might not soon be some talk of leave. And just at the end of his affectionate and unsatisfactory two pages, Campton lit on a name that roused him.

"I saw a fellow who'd seen Benny Upsher yesterday on his way to the English front. The young lunatic looked very fit. You know he volunteered in the English army when he found he couldn't get into the French. He's likely to get all the fighting he wants." It was a relief to know that someone had seen Benny Upsher lately. The letter was but four days old, and he was then on his way to the front. Probably he was not yet in the fighting he wanted, and one could, without remorse, call up an unmutilated face and clear blue eyes.

Campton, re-reading the postscript, was struck by a small thing. George had originally written: "I saw Benny Upsher yesterday," and had then altered the phrase to: "I saw a fellow who'd seen Benny Upsher." There was nothing out of the way in that: it simply showed that he had written in haste and revised the sentence. But he added: "The young lunatic looked very fit." Well: that too was natural. It was "the fellow" who reported Benny as looking fit; the phrase was rather elliptic, but Campton could hardly have said why it gave him the impression that it was George himself who had seen Upsher. The idea was manifestly absurd, since there was the length of the front between George's staff-town and the fiery pit yawning for his cousin. Campton laid aside the letter with the distinct wish that his son had not called Benny Upsher a young lunatic.

Chapter XIV

WHEN Campton took his sketch of George to Léonce Black, the dealer who specialized in "Camptons," he was surprised at the magnitude of the sum which the great picture-broker, lounging in a glossy War Office uniform among his Gauguins and Vuillards, immediately offered.

Léonce Black noted his surprise and smiled. "You think there's nothing doing nowadays? Don't you believe it, Mr. Campton. Now that the big men have stopped painting, the collectors are all the keener to snap up what's left in their port-folios." He placed the cheque in Campton's hand, and drew back to study the effect of the sketch, which he had slipped into a frame against a velvet curtain. "Ah——" he said, as if he were tasting an old wine.

As Campton turned to go the dealer's enthusiasm bubbled over. "Haven't you got anything more? Remember me if you have."

"I don't sell my sketches," said Campton. "This was excep-tional—for a charity . . ."

"I know, I know. Well, you're likely to have a good many more calls of the same sort before we get *this* war over," the dealer remarked philosophically. "Anyhow, remember I can place anything you'll give me. When people want a Campton it's to me they come. I've got standing orders from two clients . . . both given before the war, and both good to-day."

Campton paused in the doorway, seized by his old fear of the painting's passing into Anderson Brant's possession.

"Look here: where is this one going?"

The dealer cocked his handsome grey head and glanced archly through plump eyelids. "Violation of professional secrecy? Well . . . Well . . . under constraint I'll confess it's to a young lady: great admirer, artist herself. Had her order by cable from New York a year ago. Been on the lookout ever since."

"Oh, all right," Campton answered, repocketing the money.

He set out at once for "The Friends of French Art," and Léonce Black, bound for the Ministry of War, walked by his side, regaling him alternately with the gossip of the Ministry and with racy anecdotes of the dealers' world. In M. Black's opinion the war was an inexcusable blunder, since Germany was getting to be the best market for the kind of freak painters out of whom the dealers who "know how to make a man 'foam' " can make a big turn-over. "I don't know what on earth will become of all those poor devils now: Paris cared for them only because she knew Germany would give any money for their things. Personally, as you know, I've always preferred sounder goods: I'm a classic, my dear Campton, and I can feel only classic art," said the dealer, swelling out his uniformed breast and stroking his Assyrian nose as though its handsome curve followed the pure Delphic line. "But, as long as things go on as they are at present in *my* department of the administration, the war's not going to end in a hurry," he continued. "And now we're in for it, we've got to see the thing through."

Campton found Boylston, as usual, in his melancholy *cabinet particulier*. He was listening to the tale of a young woman with streaming eyes and an extravagant hat. She was so absorbed in her trouble that she did not notice Campton's entrance, and behind her back the painter made a sign to say that she was not to be interrupted.

He was as much interested in the suppliant's tale as in watching Boylston's way of listening. That modest and commonplace-looking young man was beginning to excite a lively curiosity in Campton. It was not only that he remembered George's commendation, for he knew that the generous enthusiasms of youth may be inspired by trifles imperceptible to the older. It was Boylston himself who interested the painter. He knew no more of the young man than the scant details Miss Anthony could give. Boylston, it appeared, was the oldest hope of a well-to-do Connecticut family. On his leaving college a place had been reserved for him in the paternal business; but he had announced good-humouredly that he did not mean to spend his life in an office, and one day, after a ten minutes' conversation with his father, as to which details were lacking, he had packed a suitcase and sailed for France. There he had lived ever since, in shabby rooms in the rue de Verneuil, on the scant allowance remitted by an irate parent: apparently never running into debt, yet always ready to help a friend.

All the American art-students in Paris knew Boylston; and though he was still in the early thirties, they all looked up to him. For Boylston had one quality which always impresses youth: Boylston knew everybody. Whether you went with him to a smart restaurant in the rue Royale, or to a wine-shop of the Left Bank, the *patron* welcomed him with the same cordiality, and sent the same emphatic instructions to the cook. The first fresh peas and the tenderest spring chicken were always for this quiet youth, who, when he was alone, dined cheerfully on veal and *vin ordinaire*. If you wanted to know where to get the best Burgundy, Boylston could tell you; he could also tell you where to buy an engagement ring for your girl, a Ford runabout going at half-price, or the *papier timbré* on which to address a summons to a recalcitrant laundress.

If you got into a row with your landlady you found that Boylston knew her, and that at sight of him she melted and withdrew her claim; or, failing this, he knew the solicitor in whose office her son was a clerk, or had other means of reducing her to reason. Boylston also knew a man who could make old clocks go, another who could clean flannels without their shrinking, and a third who could get you old picture-frames for a song; and, best of all, when any inexperienced American youth was caught in the dark Parisian cobweb (and the people at home were on no account to hear about it) Boylston was found to be the friend and familiar of certain occult authorities who, with a smile and a word of warning, could break the mesh and free the victim.

The mystery was, how and why all these people did what Boylston wanted; but the reason began to dawn on Campton as he watched the young woman in the foolish hat deliver herself of her grievance. Boylston was simply a perfect listener—and most of his life was spent in listening. Everything about him listened: his round forehead and peering screwed-up eyes, his lips twitching responsively under the close-clipped moustache, and every crease and dimple of his sagacious and humorous young countenance; even the attitude of his short fat body, with elbows comfortably bedded in heaped-up papers, and fingers plunged into his crinkled hair. There was never a hint of hurry or impatience about him: having once asserted his right to do what he liked with his life, he was apparently content to let all his friends prey on it. You never caught his eye on the clock, or his lips shaping an answer before you had turned the last corner of your story. Yet when the story was told, and he had surveyed it in all its bearings, you could be sure he would do what he could for you, and do it before the day was over.

"Very well, Mademoiselle," he said, when the young woman had finished. "I promise you I'll see Mme. Beausite, and try to get her to recognize your claim."

"Mind you, I don't ask charity—I won't *take* charity from your committee!" the young lady hissed, gathering up a tawdry hand-bag.

"Oh, we're not forcing it on any one," smiled Boylston, opening the door for her.

When he turned back to Campton his face was flushed and frowning. "Poor thing! She's a nuisance, but I'll fight to the last ditch for her. The chap she lives with was Beausite's secretary and understudy, and devilled for him before the war. The poor fellow has come back from the front a complete wreck, and can't even collect the salary Beausite owes him for the last three months before the war. Beausite's plea is that he's too poor, and that the war lets him out of paying. Of course he counts on our doing it for him."

"And you're not going to?"

"Well," said Boylston humorously, "I shouldn't wonder if he beat us in the long run. But I'll have a try first; and anyhow the poor girl needn't know. She used to earn a little money doing fashion-articles, but of course there's no market for that now, and I don't see how the pair can live. They have a little boy, and there's an infirm mother, and they're waiting to get married till the girl can find a job."

"Good Lord!" Campton groaned, with a sudden vision of the countless little trades and traffics arrested by the war, and all the industrious thousands reduced to querulous pauperism or slow death.

"How *do* they live—all these people?"

"They don't—always. I could tell you——"

"Don't, for God's sake; I can't stand it." Campton drew out the cheque. "Here: this is what I've got for the Davrils."

"Good Lord!" said Boylston, staring with round eyes.

"It will pull them through, anyhow, won't it?" Campton triumphed.

"Well——" said Boylston. "It will if you'll endorse it," he added, smiling. Campton laughed and took up a pen.

A day or two later Campton, returning home one afternoon, overtook a small black-veiled figure with a limp like his own. He guessed at once that it was the lame Davril girl, come to thank him; and his dislike of such ceremonies caused him to glance about for a way of escape. But as he did so the girl turned with a smile that put him to shame. He remembered Adele Anthony's saying, one day when he had found her in her refugee office patiently undergoing a like ordeal: "We've no right to refuse the only coin they can repay us in."

The Davril girl was a plain likeness of her brother, with the same hungry flame in her eyes. She wore the nondescript black that Campton had remarked at the funeral; and knowing the importance which the French attach to every detail of conventional mourning, he wondered that mother and daughter had not laid out part of his gift in crape. But doubtless the equally strong instinct of thrift had caused Mme. Davril to put away the whole sum.

Mlle. Davril greeted Campton pleasantly, and assured him that she had not found the long way from Villejuif to Montmartre too difficult.

"I would have gone to you," the painter protested; but she answered that she wanted to see with her own eyes where her brother's friend lived.

In the studio she looked about her with a quick searching glance, said "Oh, a piano——" as if the fact were connected with the object of her errand—and then, settling herself in an armchair, unclasped her shabby hand-bag.

"Monsieur, there has been a misunderstanding; this money is not ours." She laid Campton's cheque on the table.

A flush of annoyance rose to the painter's face. What on earth had Boylston let him in for? If the Davrils were as proud as all that it was not worth while to have sold a sketch it had cost him such a pang to part with. He felt the exasperation of the would-be philanthropist when he first discovers that nothing complicates life as much as doing good.

"But, Mademoiselle——"

"This money is not ours. If René had lived he would never have sold your picture; and we would starve rather than betray his trust."

When stout ladies in velvet declare that they would starve rather than sacrifice this or that principle, the statement has only the cold beauty of rhetoric; but on the drawn lips of a thinly-clad young woman evidently acquainted with the process, it becomes a fiery reality.

"Starve—nonsense! My dear young lady, you betray him when you talk like that," said Campton, moved.

She shook her head. "It depends, Monsieur, which things matter most to one. We shall never—my mother and I—do anything that René would not have done. The picture was not ours: we brought it back to you——"

"But if the picture's not yours it's mine," Campton interrupted; "and I'd a right to sell it, and a right to do what I choose with the money."

His visitor smiled. "That's what we feel; it was what I was coming to." And clasping her threadbare glove-tips about the arms of the chair Mlle. Davril set forth with extreme precision the object of her visit.

It was to propose that Campton should hand over the cheque to "The Friends of French Art," devoting one-third to the aid of the families of combatant painters, the rest to young musicians and authors. "It doesn't seem right that only the painters' families should benefit by what your committee are doing. And René would have thought so too. He knew so many young men of letters and journalists who, before the war, just managed to keep their families alive; and in my profession I could tell you of poor music-teachers and accompanists whose work stopped the day war broke out, and who have been living ever since on the crusts their luckier comrades could spare them. René would have let us accept from you help that was shared with others: he would have been so glad, often, of a few francs to relieve the misery we see about us. And this great sum might be the beginning of a co-operative work for artists ruined by the war."

She went on to explain that in the families of almost all the young artists at the front there was at least one member at home who practised one of the arts, or who was capable of doing some kind of useful work. The value of Campton's gift, Mlle. Davril argued, would be tripled if it were so employed as to give the artists and their families occupation: producing at least the illusion that those who could were earning their living, or helping their less fortunate comrades. "It's not only a question of saving their dignity: I don't believe much in that. You have dignity or you haven't—and if you have, it doesn't need any saving," this clear-toned young woman remarked. "The real question, for all of us artists, is that of keeping our hands in, and our interest in our work alive; sometimes, too, of giving a new talent its first chance. At any rate, it would mean work and not stagnation; which is all that most charity produces."

She developed her plan: for the musicians, concerts in private houses (hence her glance at the piano); for the painters, small exhibitions in the rooms of the committee, where their pictures would be sold with the deduction of a percentage, to be returned to the general fund; and for the writers—well, their lot was perhaps the hardest to deal with; but an employment agency might be opened, where those who chose could put their names down and take such work as was offered. Above all, Mlle. Davril again insisted, the fund created by Campton's gift was to be spent only in giving employment, not for mere relief.

Campton listened with growing attention. Nothing hitherto had been less in the line of his interests than the large schemes of general amelioration which were coming to be classed under the transatlantic term of "Social Welfare." If questioned on the subject a few months earlier he would probably have concealed his fundamental indifference under the profession of an extreme individualism, and the assertion of every man's right to suffer and starve in his own way. Even since René Davril's death had brought home to him the boundless havoc of the war, he had felt no more than the impulse to ease his own pain by putting his hand in his pocket when a particular case was too poignant to be ignored.

Yet here were people who had already offered their dearest to France, and were now pleading to be allowed to give all the rest; and who had had the courage and wisdom to think out in advance the form in which their gift would do most good. Campton had the awe of the unpractical man for anyone who knows how to apply his ideas. He felt that there was no use in disputing Mlle. Davril's plan: he must either agree to it or repocket his cheque.

"I'll do as you want, of course; but I'm not much good about details. Hadn't you better consult some one else?" he suggested.

Oh, that was already done: she had outlined her project to Miss Anthony and Mr. Boylston, who approved. All she wanted was Campton's consent; and this he gave the more cordially when he learned that, for the present at least, nothing more was expected of him. First steps in beneficence, he felt, were unspeakably terrifying; yet he was already aware that, resist as he might, he would never be able to keep his footing on the brink of that abyss.

Into it, as the days went by, his gaze was oftener and oftener plunged. He had begun to feel that pity was his only remaining link with his kind, the one barrier between himself and the dreadful solitude which awaited him when he returned to his studio. What would there have been to think of there, alone among his unfinished pictures and his broken memories, if not the wants and woes of people more bereft than himself? His own future was not a thing to dwell on. George was safe: but what George and he were likely to make of each other after the ordeal was over was a question he preferred to put aside. He was more and more taking George and his safety for granted, as a solid standing-ground from which to reach out a hand to the thousands struggling in the depths. As long as the world's fate was in the balance it was every man's duty to throw into that balance his last ounce of brain and muscle. Campton wondered how he had ever thought that an accident of birth, a remoteness merely geographical, could justify, or even make possible, an attitude of moral aloofness. Harvey Mayhew's reasons for wishing to annihilate Germany began to seem less grotesque than his own for standing aside.

In the heat of his conversion he no longer grudged the hours given to Mr. Mayhew. He patiently led his truculent relative from one government office to another, everywhere laying stress on Mr. Mayhew's sympathy with France and his desire to advocate her cause in the United States, and trying to curtail his enumeration of his grievances by a glance at the clock, and the reminder that they had another Minister to see. Mr. Mayhew was not very manageable. His adventure had grown with repetition, and he was increasingly disposed to feel that the retaliation he called down on Germany could best be justified by telling every one what he had suffered from her. Intensely aware of the value of time in Utica, he was less sensible of it in Paris, and seemed to think that, since he had left a flourishing business to preach the Holy War, other people ought to leave their affairs to give him a hearing. But his zeal and persistence were irresistible, and doors which Campton had seen barred against the most reasonable appeals flew open at the sound of Mr. Mayhew's trumpet. His pink face and silvery hair gave him an apostolic air, and circles to which America had hitherto been a mere speck in space suddenly discovered that he represented that legendary character, the Typical American.

The keen Boylston, prompt to note and utilize the fact, urged Campton to interest Mr. Mayhew in "The Friends of French Art," and with considerable flourish the former Peace Delegate was produced at a committee meeting and given his head. But his interest flagged when he found that the "Friends" concerned themselves with Atrocities only in so far as any act of war is one, and that their immediate task was the humdrum one of feeding and clothing the families of the combatants and sending "comforts" to the trenches. He served up, with a somewhat dog-eared eloquence, the usual account of his own experiences, and pressed a modest gift upon the treasurer; but when he departed, after wringing everybody's hands, and leaving the French members bedewed with emotion, Campton had the conviction that their quiet weekly meetings would not often be fluttered by his presence.

Campton was spending an increasing amount of time in the Palais Royal restaurant, where he performed any drudgery for which no initiative was required. Once or twice, when Miss Anthony was submerged by a fresh influx of refugees, he lent her a hand too; and on most days he dropped in late at her office, waited for her to sift and dismiss the last applicants, and saw her home through the incessant rain. It interested him to note that the altruism she had so long wasted on pampered friends was developing into a wise and orderly beneficence. He had always thought of her as an eternal schoolgirl; now she had grown into a woman. Sometimes he fancied the change dated from the moment when their eyes had met across the station, the day they had seen George off. He wondered whether it might not be interesting to paint her new face, if ever painting became again thinkable.

"Passion—I suppose the great thing is a capacity for passion," he mused.

In himself he imagined the capacity to be quite dead. He loved his son: yes—but he was beginning to see that he loved him for certain qualities he had read into him, and that perhaps after all——. Well, perhaps after all the sin for which he was now atoning in loneliness was that of having been too exclusively an artist, of having cherished George too egotistically and self-indulgently, too much as his own most beautiful creation. If he had loved him more humanly, more tenderly and recklessly, might he have not put into his son the tenderness and reckless-ness which were beginning to seem to him the qualities most supremely human?

Chapter XV

A WEEK or two later, coming home late from a long day's work at the office, Campton saw Mme. Lebel awaiting him. He always stopped for a word now; fearing each time that there was bad news of Jules Lebel, but not wishing to seem to avoid her.

To-day, however, Mme. Lebel, though mysterious, was not anxious.

"Monsieur will find the studio open. There's a lady: she insisted on going up."

"A lady? Why did you let her in? What kind of a lady?"

"A lady—well, a lady with such magnificent furs that one couldn't keep her out in the cold," Mme. Lebel answered with simplicity.

Campton went up apprehensively. The idea of unknown persons in possession of his studio always made him nervous. Whoever they were, whatever errands they came on, they always—especially women—disturbed the tranquil course of things, faced him with unexpected problems, unsettled him in one way or another. Bouncing in on people suddenly was like dynamiting fish: it left him with his mind full of fragments of dismembered thoughts.

As he entered he perceived from the temperate atmosphere that Mme. Lebel had not only opened the studio but made up the fire. The lady's furs must indeed be magnificent.

She sat at the farther end of the room, in a high-backed chair near the stove, and when she rose he recognized his former wife. The long sable cloak, which had slipped back over the chair, justified Mme. Lebel's description, but the dress beneath it appeared to Campton simpler than Mrs. Brant's habitual raiment. The lamplight, striking up into her powdered face, puffed out her underlids and made harsh hollows in her cheeks. She looked frightened, ill and yet determined.

"John——" she began, laying her hand on his sleeve.

It was the first time she had ever set foot in his shabby quarters, and in his astonishment he could only stammer out: "Julia——"

But as he looked at her he saw that her face was wet with tears. "Not—bad news?" he broke out.

She shook her head and, drawing a handkerchief from a diamond-monogrammed bag, wiped away the tears and the powder. Then she pressed the handkerchief to her lips, gazing at him with eyes as helpless as a child's.

"Sit down," said Campton.

As they faced each other across the long table, with papers and paint-rags and writing materials pushed aside to make room for the threadbare napkin on which his plate and glass, and bottle of *vin ordinaire*, were set out, he wondered if the scene woke in her any memory of their first days of gaiety and poverty, or if she merely pitied him for still living in such squalor. And suddenly it occurred to him that when the war was over, and George came back, it would be pleasant to hunt out a little apartment in an old house in the Faubourg St. Germain, put some good furniture in it, and oppose the discreeter charm of such an interior to the heavy splendours of the Avenue Marigny. How could he expect to hold a luxury-loving youth if he had only this dingy studio to receive him in?

Mrs. Brant began to speak.

"I came here to see you because I didn't wish any one to know; not Adele, nor even Anderson." Leaning toward him she went on in short breathless sentences: "I've just left Madge Talkett: you know her, I think? She's at Mme. de Dolmetsch's hospital. Something dreadful has happened . . . too dreadful. It seems that Mme. de Dolmetsch was very much in love with Ladislas Isador; a writer, wasn't he? I don't know his books, but Madge tells me they're wonderful . . . and of course men like that ought not to be sent to the front . . ."

"Men like what?"

"Geniuses," said Mrs. Brant. "He was dreadfully delicate besides, and was doing admirable work on some military commission in Paris; I believe he knew any number of languages. And poor Mme. de Dolmetsch—you know I've never approved of her; but things are so changed nowadays, and at any rate she was madly attached to him, and had done everything to keep him in Paris: medical certificates, people at Headquarters working for her, and all the rest. But it seems there are no end of officers always intriguing to get staff-jobs: strong able-bodied young men who ought to be in the trenches, and are fit for nothing else, but who are jealous of the others. And last week, in spite of all she could do, poor Isador was ordered to the front."

Campton made an impatient movement. It was even more distasteful to him to be appealed to by Mrs. Brant in Isador's name than by Mme. de Dolmetsch in George's. His gorge rose at the thought that people should associate in their minds cases as different as those of his son and Mme. de Dolmetsch's lover.

"I'm sorry," he said. "But if you've come to ask me to do something more about George—take any new steps—it's no use. I can't do the sort of thing to keep my son safe that Mme. de Dolmetsch would do for her lover."

Mrs. Brant stared. "Safe? He was killed the day after he got to the front."

"Good Lord—Isador?"

Ladislas Isador killed at the front! The words remained unmeaning; by no effort could Campton relate them to the fat middle-aged philanderer with his Jewish eyes, his Slav eloquence, his Levantine gift for getting on, and for getting out from under. Campton tried to picture the clever contriving devil drawn in his turn into that merciless red eddy, and gulped down the Monster's throat with the rest. What a mad world it was, in which the same horrible and magnificent doom awaited the coward and the hero!

"Poor Mme. de Dolmetsch!" he muttered, remembering with a sense of remorse her desperate appeal and his curt rebuff. Once again the poor creature's love had enlightened her, and she had foreseen what no one else in the world would have believed: that her lover was to die like a hero.

"Isador was nearly forty, and had a weak heart; and she'd left nothing, literally nothing, undone to save him." Campton read in his wife's eyes what was coming. "It's impossible *now* that George should not be taken," Mrs. Brant went on.

The same thought had tightened Campton's own heart-strings; but he had hoped she would not say it.

"It may be George's turn any day," she insisted.

They sat and looked at each other without speaking; then she began again imploringly: "I tell you there's not a moment to be lost!"

Campton picked up a palette-knife and began absently to rub it with an oily rag. Mrs. Brant's anguished voice still sounded on. "Unless something is done immediately . . . It appears there's a regular hunt for *embusqués*, as they're called. As if it was everybody's business to be killed! How's the staff-work to be carried on if they're all taken? But it's certain that if we don't act at once . . . act energetically . . ."

He fixed his eyes on hers. "Why do you come to *me*?" he asked.

Her lids opened wide. "But he's our child."

"Your husband knows more people—he has ways, you've often told me——"

She reddened faintly and seemed about to speak; but the reply died on her lips.

"Why did you say," Campton pursued, "that you had come here because you wanted to see me without Brant's knowing it?"

She lowered her eyes and fixed them on the knife he was still automatically rubbing.

"Because Anderson thinks . . . Anderson won't . . . He says he's done all he can."

"Ah——" cried Campton, drawing a deep breath. He threw back his shoulders, as if to shake off a weight. "I—feel exactly as Brant does," he declared.

"You—you feel as he does? You, George's father? But a father has never done all he can for his son! There's always something more that he can do!"

The words, breaking from her in a cry, seemed suddenly to change her from an ageing doll into a living and agonized woman. Campton had never before felt as near to her, as moved to the depths by her. For the length of a heart-beat he saw her again with a red-haired baby in her arms, the light of morning on her face.

"My dear—I'm sorry." He laid his hand on hers.

"Sorry—sorry? I don't want you to be sorry. I want you to do something—I want you to save him!"

He faced her with bent head, gazing absently at their interwoven fingers: each hand had forgotten to release the other.

"I can't do anything more," he repeated.

She started up with a despairing exclamation. "What's happened to you? Who has influenced you? What has changed you?"

How could he answer her? He hardly knew himself: had hardly been conscious of the change till she suddenly flung it in his face. If blind animal passion be the profoundest as well as the fiercest form of attachment, his love for his boy was at that moment as nothing to hers. Yet his feeling for George, in spite of all the phrases he dressed it in, had formerly in its essence been no other. That his boy should survive—survive at any price—that had been all he cared for or sought to achieve. It had been convenient to justify himself by arguing that George was not bound to fight for France; but Campton now knew that he would have made the same effort to protect his son if the country engaged had been his own.

In the careless pre-war world, as George himself had once said, it had seemed unbelievable that people should ever again go off and die in a ditch to oblige anybody. Even now, the automatic obedience of the millions of the untaught and the unthinking, though it had its deep pathetic significance, did not move Campton like the clear-eyed sacrifice of the few who knew why they were dying. Jean Fortin, René Davril, and such lads as young Louis Dastrey, with his reasoned horror of butchery and waste in general, and his instant grasp of the necessity of this particular sacrifice: it was they who had first shed light on the dark problem.

Campton had never before, at least consciously, thought of himself and the few beings he cared for as part of a greater whole, component elements of the immense amazing spectacle. But the last four months had shown him man as a defenceless animal suddenly torn from his shell, stripped of all the interwoven tendrils of association, habit, background, daily ways and words, daily sights and sounds, and flung out of the human habitable world into naked ether, where nothing breathes or lives. That was what war did; that was why those who best understood it in all its farthest-reaching abomination willingly gave their lives to put an end to it.

He heard Mrs. Brant crying.

"Julia," he said, "Julia, I wish you'd try to see . . ."

She dashed away her tears. "See what? All I see is *you*, sitting here safe and saying you can do nothing to save him! But to have the right to say that you ought to be in the trenches yourself! What do you suppose those young men out there think of their fathers, safe at home, who are too high-minded and conscientious to protect them?"

He looked at her compassionately. "Yes," he said, "that's the bitterest part of it. But for that, there would hardly be anything in the worst war for us old people to lie awake about."

Mrs. Brant had stood up and was feverishly pulling on her gloves: he saw that she no longer heard him. He helped her to draw her furs about her, and stood waiting while she straightened her veil and tapped the waves of hair into place, her eyes blindly seeking for a mirror. There was nothing more that either could say.

He lifted the lamp, and went out of the door ahead of her.

"You needn't come down," she said in a sob; but leaning over the rail into the darkness he answered: "I'll give you a light: the concierge has forgotten the lamp on the stairs."

He went ahead of her down the long greasy flights, and as they reached the ground floor he heard a noise of feet coming and going, and frightened voices exclaiming. In the doorway of the porter's lodge Mrs. Brant's splendid chauffeur stood looking on compassionately at a group of women gathered about Mme. Lebel.

The old woman sat in her den, her arms stretched across the table, her sewing fallen at her feet. On the table lay an open letter. The grocer's wife from the corner stood by, sobbing.

Mrs. Brant stopped, and Campton, sure now of what was coming, pushed his way through the neighbours about the door. Mme. Lebel's eyes met his with the mute reproach of a tortured animal. "Jules," she said, "last Wednesday . . . through the heart."

Campton took her old withered hand. The women ceased sobbing and a hush fell upon the stifling little room. When Campton looked up again he saw Julia Brant, pale and bewildered, hurrying toward her motor, and the vault of the porte-cochère sent back the chauffeur's answer to her startled question: "Poor old lady—yes, her only son's been killed at the front."

Chapter XVI

C AMPTON sat with his friend Dastrey in the latter's pleasant little *entresol* full of Chinese lacquer and Venetian furniture. Dastrey, in the last days of January, had been sent home from his ambulance with an attack of rheumatism; and when it became clear that he could no longer be of use in the mud and cold of the army zone he had reluctantly taken his place behind a desk at the Ministry of War. The friends had dined early, so that he might get back to his night-shift; and they sat over coffee and liqueurs, the mist of their cigars floating across lustrous cabinet-fronts and the worn gilding of slender consoles.

On the other side of the hearth young Boylston, sunk in an armchair, smoked and listened.

"It always comes back to the same thing," Campton was saying nervously. "What right have useless old men like me, sitting here with my cigar by this good fire, to preach blood and butchery to boys like George and your nephew?"

Again and again, during the days since Mrs. Brant's visit, he had turned over in his mind the same torturing question. How was he to answer that last taunt of hers?

Not long ago, Paul Dastrey would have seemed the last person to whom he could have submitted such a problem. Dastrey, in the black August days, starting for the front in such a frenzy of baffled blood-lust, had remained for Campton the type of man with whom it was impossible to discuss the war. But three months of hard service in *Postes de Secours* and along the awful battle-edge had sent him home with a mind no longer befogged by personal problems. He had done his utmost, and knew it; and the fact gave him the professional calm which keeps surgeons and nurses steady through all the horrors they are compelled to live among. Those few months had matured and mellowed him more than a lifetime of Paris.

He leaned back with half-closed lids, quietly considering his friend's difficulty.

"I see. Your idea is that, being unable to do even the humble kind of job that I've been assigned to, you've no right *not* to try to keep your boy out of it if you can?"

"Well—by any honourable means."

Dastrey laughed faintly, and Campton reddened. "The word's not happy, I admit."

"I wasn't thinking of that: I was considering how the meaning had evaporated out of lots of our old words, as if the general smash-up had broken their stoppers. So many of them, you see," said Dastrey smiling, "we'd taken good care not to uncork for centuries. Since I've been on the edge of what's going on fifty miles from here a good many of my own words have lost their meaning, and I'm not prepared to say where honour lies in a case like yours." He mused a moment, and then went on: "What would George's view be?"

Campton did not immediately reply. Not so many weeks ago he would have welcomed the chance of explaining that George's view, thank God, had remained perfectly detached and objective, and that the cheerful acceptance of duties forcibly imposed on him had not in the least obscured his sense of the fundamental injustice of his being mixed up in the thing at all.

But how could he say this now? If George's view were still what his father had been in the habit of saying it was, then he held that view alone: Campton himself no longer thought that any civilized man could afford to stand aside from such a conflict.

"As far as I know," he said, "George hasn't changed his mind."

Boylston stirred in his armchair, knocked the ash from his cigar, and looked up at the ceiling.

"Whereas *you*——" Dastrey suggested.

"Yes," said Campton. "I feel differently. You speak of the difference of having been in contact with what's going on out there. But how can anybody *not* be in contact, who has any imagination, any sense of right and wrong? Do these pictures and hangings ever shut it out from you—or those books over there, when you turn to them after your day's work? Perhaps they do, because you've got a real job, a job you've been ordered to do, and can't not do. But for a useless drifting devil like me— my God, the sights and the sounds of it are always with me!"

"There are a good many people who wouldn't call you useless, Mr. Campton," said Boylston.

Campton shook his head. "I wish there were any healing in the kind of thing I'm doing; perhaps there is to you, to whom it appears to come naturally to love your kind." (Boylston laughed.) "Service is of no use without conviction: that's one of the uncomfortable truths this stir-up has brought to the surface. I was meant to paint pictures in a world at peace, and I should have more respect for myself if I could go on unconcernedly doing it, instead of pining to be in all the places where I'm not wanted, and should be of no earthly use. That's why——" he paused, looked about him, and sought understanding in Dastrey's friendly gaze: "That's why I respect George's opinion, which really consists in not having any, and simply doing without comment the work assigned to him. The whole thing is so far beyond human measure that one's individual rage and revolt seem of no more use than a woman's scream at an accident she isn't in."

Even while he spoke, Campton knew he was arguing only against himself. He did not in the least believe that any individual sentiment counted for nothing at such a time, and Dastrey really spoke for him in rejoining: "Every one can at least contribute an attitude: as you have, my dear fellow. Boylston's here to confirm it."

Boylston grunted his assent.

"An attitude—an attitude?" Campton retorted. "The word is revolting to me! Anything a man like me can do is too easy to be worth doing. And as for anything one can *say*: how dare one say anything, in the face of what is being done out there to keep this room and this fire, and this ragged end of life, safe for such survivals as you and me?" He crossed to the table to take another cigar. As he did so he laid an apologetic pressure on his host's shoulder. "Men of our age are the chorus of the tragedy, Dastrey; we can't help ourselves. As soon as I open my lips to blame or praise I see myself in white petticoats, with a long beard held on by an elastic, goading on the combatants in a cracked voice from a safe corner of the ramparts. On the whole I'd sooner be spinning among the women."

"Well," said Dastrey, getting up, "I've got to get back to my spinning at the Ministry; where, by the way, there are some very pretty young women at the distaff. It's extraordinary how much better pretty girls type than plain ones; I see now why they get all the jobs."

The three went out into the winter blackness. They were used by this time to the new Paris: to extinguished lamps, shuttered windows, deserted streets, the almost total cessation of wheeled traffic. All through the winter, life had seemed in suspense everywhere, as much on the battle-front as in the rear. Day after day, week after week, of rain and sleet and mud; day after day, week after week, of vague non-committal news from west and east; everywhere the enemy baffled but still menacing, everywhere death, suffering, destruction, without any perceptible oscillation of the scales, any compensating hope of good to come out of the long slow endless waste. The benumbed and darkened Paris of those February days seemed the visible image of a benumbed and darkened world.

Down the empty asphalt sheeted with rain the rare street lights stretched interminable reflections. The three men crossed the bridge and stood watching the rush of the Seine. Below them gloomed the vague bulk of deserted bath-houses, unlit barges, river-steamers out of commission. The Seine too had ceased to live: only a single orange gleam, low on the water's edge, undulated on the jetty waves like a streamer of seaweed.

The two Americans left Dastrey at his Ministry, and the painter strolled on to Boylston's lodging before descending to the underground railway. He, whom his lameness had made so heavy and indolent, now limped about for hours at a time over wet pavements and under streaming skies: these midnight tramps had become a sort of expiatory need to him. "Out there—out there, if they had these wet stones under them they'd think it was the floor of heaven," he used to muse, driving on obstinately through rain and darkness.

The thought of "Out there" besieged him day and night, the phrase was always in his ears. Wherever he went he was pursued by visions of that land of doom: visions of fathomless mud, rat-haunted trenches, freezing nights under the sleety sky, men dying in the barbed wire between the lines or crawling out to save a comrade and being shattered to death on the return. His collaboration with Boylston had brought Campton into close contact with these things. He knew by heart the history of scores and scores of young men of George's age who were doggedly suffering and dying a few hours away from the Palais

Royal office where their records were kept. Some of these histories were so heroically simple that the sense of pain was lost in beauty, as though one were looking at suffering transmuted into poetry. But others were abominable, unendurable, in their long-drawn useless horror: stories of cold and filth and hunger, of ineffectual effort, of hideous mutilation, of men perishing of thirst in a shell-hole, and half-dismembered bodies dragging themselves back to shelter only to die as they reached it. Worst of all were the perpetually recurring reports of military blunders, medical neglect, carelessness in high places: the torturing knowledge of the lives that might have been saved if this or that officer's brain, this or that surgeon's hand, had acted more promptly. An impression of waste, confusion, ignorance, obstinacy, prejudice, and the indifference of selfishness or of mortal fatigue, emanated from these narratives written home from the front, or faltered out by white lips on hospital pillows.

"The Friends of French Art," especially since they had enlarged their range, had to do with young men accustomed to the freest exercise of thought and criticism. A nation in arms does not judge a war as simply as an army of professional soldiers. All these young intelligences were so many subtly-adjusted instruments for the testing of the machinery of which they formed a part; and not one accepted the results passively. Yet in one respect all were agreed: the "had to be" of the first day was still on every lip. The German menace must be met: chance willed that theirs should be the generation to meet it; on that point speculation was vain and discussion useless. The question that stirred them all was how the country they were defending was helping them to carry on the struggle. There the evidence was cruelly clear, the comment often scathingly explicit; and Campton, bending still lower over the abyss, caught a shuddering glimpse of what might be—must be—if political blunders, inertia, tolerance, perhaps even evil ambitions and connivances, should at last outweigh the effort of the front. There was no logical argument against such a possibility. All civilizations had their orbit; all societies rose and fell. Some day, no doubt, by the action of that law, everything that made the world livable to Campton and his kind would crumble in new ruins above the old. Yes—but woe to them by whom such things came; woe to the generation that bowed to such a law!

The Powers of Darkness were always watching and seeking their hour; but the past was a record of their failures as well as of their triumphs. Campton, brushing up his history, remembered the great turning-points of progress, saw how the liberties of England had been born of the ruthless discipline of the Norman conquest, and how even out of the hideous welter of the French Revolution and the Napoleonic wars had come more freedom and a wiser order. The point was to remember that the efficacy of the sacrifice was always in proportion to the worth of the victims; and there at least his faith was sure.

He could not, he felt, leave his former wife's appeal unnoticed; after a day or two he wrote to George, telling him of Mrs. Brant's anxiety, and asking in vague terms if George himself thought any change in his situation probable. His letter ended abruptly: "I suppose it's hardly time yet to ask for leave——"

Chapter XVII

Not long after his midnight tramp with Boylston and Dastrey the post brought Campton two letters. One was postmarked Paris, the other bore the military frank and was addressed in his son's hand: he laid it aside while he glanced at the first. It contained an engraved card:

Mrs. Anderson Brant

At Home on February 20th at 4 o'clock

Mr. Harvey Mayhew will give an account of his captivity in Germany
Mme. de Dolmetsch will sing

For the benefit of the "Friends of French Art Committee"

Tickets 100 francs

Enclosed was the circular of the sub-committee in aid of Musicians at the Front, with which Campton was not directly associated. It bore the names of Mrs. Talkett, Mme. Beausite and a number of other French and American ladies.

Campton tossed the card away. He was not annoyed by the invitation: he knew that Miss Anthony and Mlle. Davril were getting up a series of drawing-room entertainments for that branch of the charity, and that the card had been sent to him as a member of the Honorary Committee. But any reminder of the sort always gave a sharp twitch to the Brant nerve in him. He turned to George's letter.

It was no longer than usual; but in other respects it was unlike his son's previous communications. Campton read it over two or three times.

"Dear Dad, thanks for yours of the tenth, which must have come to me on skis, the snow here is so deep." (There had, in fact, been a heavy snow-fall in the Argonne). "Sorry mother is bothering about things again; as you've often reminded me, they always have a way of 'being as they will be,' and even war doesn't seem to change it. Nothing to worry her in my case—but you can't expect her to believe that, can you? Neither you nor I can help it, I suppose.

"There's one thing that might help, though; and that is, your letting her feel that you're a little nearer to her. War makes a lot of things look differently, especially this sedentary kind of war: it's rather like going over all the old odds-and-ends in one's cupboards. And some of them do look so foolish.

"I wish you'd see her now and then—just naturally, as if it had happened. You know you've got one Inexhaustible Topic between you. The said I. T. is doing well, and has nothing new to communicate up to now except a change of address. Hereafter please write to my Base instead of directing here, as there's some chance of a shift of H. Q. The precaution is probably just a new twist of the old red tape, signifying nothing; but Base will always reach me if we *are* shifted. Let mother know, and explain, please; otherwise she'll think the unthinkable.

"Interrupted by big drive—quill-drive, of course!
                                    "As ever
                                            "GEORGIUS SCRIBLERIUS.

"P. S. Don't be too savage to Uncle Andy either.

"No. 2.—I *had* thought of leave; but perhaps you're right about that."

It was the first time George had written in that way of his mother. His smiling policy had always been to let things alone, and go on impartially dividing his devotion between his parents, since they refused to share even that common blessing. But war gave everything a new look; and he had evidently, as he put it, been turning over the old things in his cupboards. How was it possible, Campton wondered, that after such a turning-over he was still content to write "Nothing new to communicate," and to make jokes about another big quill-drive? Glancing at the date of the letter, Campton saw that it had been written on the day after the first ineffectual infantry assault on Vauquois. And George was sitting a few miles off, safe in headquarters at Sainte Menehould, with a stout roof over his head and a beautiful brown gloss on his boots, scribbling punning letters while his comrades fell back from that bloody summit . . .

Suddenly Campton's eyes filled. No; George had not written that letter for the sake of the joke: the joke was meant to cover what went before it. Ah, how young the boy was to imagine that his father would not see! Yes, as he said, war made so many of the old things look foolish . . .

Campton set out for the Palais Royal. He felt happier than for a long time past: the tone of his boy's letter seemed to correspond with his own secret change of spirit. He knew the futility of attempting to bring the Brants and himself together, but was glad that George had made the suggestion. He resolved to see Julia that afternoon.

At the Palais Royal he found the indefatigable Boylston busy with an exhibition of paintings sent home from the front, and Mlle. Davril helping to catalogue them. Lamentable pensioners came and went, bringing fresh tales of death, fresh details of savagery; the air was dark with poverty and sorrow. In the background Mme. Beausite flitted about, tragic and ineffectual. Boylston had not been able to extract a penny from Beausite for his secretary and the latter's left-handed family; but Mme. Beausite had discovered a newly-organized charity which lent money to "temporarily embarrassed" war-victims; and with an artless self-satisfaction she had contrived to obtain a small loan for the victim of her own thrift. "For what other purpose are such charities founded?" she said, gently disclaiming in advance the praise which Miss Anthony and Boylston had no thought of offering her. Whenever Campton came in she effaced herself behind a desk, where she bent her beautiful white head over a card-catalogue without any perceptible results.

The telephone rang. Boylston, after a moment, looked up from the receiver.

"Mr. Campton!"

The painter glanced apprehensively at the instrument, which still seemed to him charged with explosives.

"Take the message, do. The thing always snaps at me."

There was a listening pause: then Boylston said: "It's about Upsher——"

Campton started up. "Killed——?"

"Not sure. It's Mr. Brant. The news was wired to the bank; they want you to break it to Mr. Mayhew."

"Oh, Lord," the painter groaned, the boy's face suddenly rising before his blurred eyes. Miss Anthony was not at the office that morning, or he would have turned to her; at least she might have gone with him on his quest. He could not ask Boylston to leave the office, and he felt that curious incapacity to deal with the raw fact of sorrow which had often given an elfin unreality to the most poignant moments of his life. It was as though experience had to enter into the very substance of his soul before he could even feel it.

"Other people," he thought, "would know what to say, and I shan't . . ."

Some one, meanwhile, had fetched a cab, and he drove to the Nouveau Luxe, though with little hope of finding Mr. Mayhew. But Mr. Mayhew had grown two secretaries, and turned the shrimp-pink drawing-room into an office. One of the secretaries was there, hammering at a typewriter. She was a competent young woman, who instantly extracted from her pocket-diary the fact that her chief was at Mrs. Anderson Brant's, rehearsing.

"Rehearsing——?"

"Why, yes; he's to speak at Mrs. Brant's next week on Atrocities," she said, surprised at Campton's ignorance.

She suggested telephoning; but in the shrunken households of the rich, where but one or two servants remained, telephoning had become as difficult as in the under-staffed hotels; and after one or two vain attempts Campton decided to go to the Avenue Marigny. He felt that to get hold of Mayhew as soon as possible might still in some vague way help poor Benny—since it was not yet sure that he was dead. "Or else it's just the need to rush about," he thought, conscious that the only way he had yet found of dealing with calamity was a kind of ant-like agitation.

On the way the round pink face of Benny Upsher continued to float before him in its very substance, with the tangibility that only a painter's visions wear. "I want to be *in* this thing," he heard the boy repeating, as if impelled by some blind instinct flowing down through centuries and centuries of persistent childish minds.

"If he or his forebears had ever thought things out he probably would have been alive and safe to-day," Campton mused, "like George . . . The average person is always just obeying impulses stored up thousands of years ago, and never re-examined since." But this consideration, though drawn from George's own philosophy, did not greatly comfort his father.

At the Brants' a bewildered concierge admitted him and rang a bell which no one answered. The vestibule and the stairs were piled with bales of sheeting, bulging jute-bags, stacked-up hospital supplies. A boy in scout's uniform swung inadequate legs from the lofty porter's arm-chair beside the table with its monumental bronze inkstand. Finally, from above, a maid called to Campton to ascend.

In the drawing-room pictures and tapestries, bronzes and *pâtes tendres*, had vanished, and a plain moquette replaced the priceless Savonnerie across whose pompous garlands Campton had walked on the day of his last visit.

The maid led him to the ball-room. Through double doors of glass Mr. Mayhew's oratorical accents, accompanied by faint chords on the piano, reached Campton's ears: he paused and looked. At the far end of the great gilded room, on a platform backed by velvet draperies, stood Mr. Mayhew, a perfect pearl in his tie and a perfect crease in his trousers. Beside him was a stage-property tripod surmounted by a classical perfume-burner; and on it Mme. de Dolmetsch, swathed in black, leaned in an attitude of affliction.

Beneath the platform a bushy-headed pianist struck an occasional chord from Chopin's Dead March; and near the door three or four Red Cross nurses perched on bales of blankets and listened. Under one of their coifs Campton recognized Mrs. Talkett. She saw him and made a sign to the lady nearest her; and the latter, turning, revealed the astonished eyes of Julia Brant.

Campton's first impression, while they shook hands under cover of Mr. Mayhew's rolling periods, was of his former wife's

gift of adaptation. She had made herself a nurse's face; not a theatrical imitation of it like Mme. de Dolmetsch's, nor yet the face
of a nurse on a war-poster, like Mrs. Talkett's. Her lovely hair
smoothed away under her strict coif, her chin devoutly framed
in linen, Mrs. Brant looked serious, tender and efficient. Was it
possible that she had found her vocation?

She gave him a glance of alarm, but his eyes must have told
her that he had not come about George, for with a reassured
smile she laid a finger on her lip and pointed to the platform;
Campton noticed that her nails were as beautifully polished as
ever.

Mr. Mayhew was saying: "All that I have to give, yes, all that
is most precious to me, I am ready to surrender, to offer up,
to lay down in the Great Struggle which is to save the world
from barbarism. I, who was one of the first Victims of that
barbarism . . ."

He paused and looked impressively at the bales of blankets.
The piano filled in the pause, and Mme. de Dolmetsch, without
changing her attitude, almost without moving her lips, sang a
few notes of lamentation.

"Of that hideous barbarism——" Mr. Mayhew began again.
"I repeat that I stand here ready to give up everything I hold
most dear——"

"Do stop him," Campton whispered to Mrs. Brant.

Little Mrs. Talkett, with the quick intuition he had noted
in her, sprang up and threaded her way to the stage. Mme. de
Dolmetsch flowed from one widowed pose into another, and
Mr. Mayhew, majestically descending, approached Mrs. Brant.

"You agree with me, I hope? You feel that anything more
than Mme. de Dolmetsch's beautiful voice—anything in the
way of a choral accompaniment—would only weaken my effect?
Where the facts are so overwhelming it is enough to state them;
that is," Mr. Mayhew added modestly, "if they are stated vigor-
ously and tersely—as I hope they are."

Mme. de Dolmetsch, with the gesture of a marble mourner
torn from her cenotaph, glided up behind him and laid her hand
in Campton's.

"Dear friend, you've heard? . . . You remember our talk? I am
Cassandra, cursed with the hideous gift of divination." Tears

rained down her cheeks, washing off the paint like mud swept by a shower. "My only comfort," she added, fixing her perfect eyes on Mr. Mayhew, "is to help our great good friend in this crusade against the assassins of my Ladislas."

Mrs. Talkett had said a word to Mr. Mayhew. Campton saw his complacent face go to pieces as if it had been vitrioled.

"Benny—Benny——" he screamed, "Benny hurt? My Benny? It's some mistake! What makes you think——?" His eyes met Campton's. "Oh, my God! Why, he's my sister's child!" he cried, plunging his face into his soft manicured hands.

In the cab to which Campton led him, he continued to sob with the full-throated sobs of a large invertebrate distress, beating his breast for an unfindable handkerchief, and, when he found it, immediately weeping it into pulp.

Campton had meant to leave him at the bank; but when the taxi stopped Mr. Mayhew was in too pitiful a plight for the painter to resist his entreaty.

"It was you who saw Benny last—you can't leave me!" the poor man implored; and Campton followed him up the majestic stairway.

Their names were taken in to Mr. Brant, and with a motion of wonder at the unaccountable humours of fate, Campton found himself for the first time entering the banker's private office.

Mr. Brant was elsewhere in the great glazed labyrinth, and while the visitors waited, the painter's registering eye took in the details of the room, from the Barye *cire-perdue* on a peach-coloured marble mantel to the blue morocco armchairs about a giant writing-table. On the table was an electric lamp in a celadon vase, and just the right number of neatly folded papers lay under a paper-weight of Chinese crystal. The room was as tidy as an expensive stage-setting or the cage of a well-kept canary: the only object marring its order was a telegram lying open on the desk.

Mr. Brant, grey and glossy, slipped in on noiseless patent leather. He shook hands with Mr. Mayhew, bowed stiffly but deprecatingly to Campton, gave his usual cough, and said: "This is terrible."

And suddenly, as the three men sat there, so impressive and important and powerless, with that fatal telegram marring the tidiness of the desk, Campton murmured to himself: "If this thing were to happen to me I couldn't bear it . . . I simply couldn't bear it . . ."

Benny Upsher was not dead—at least his death was not certain. He had been seen to fall in a surprise attack near Neuve Chapelle; the telegram, from his commanding officer, reported him as "wounded and missing."

The words had taken on a hideous significance in the last months. Freezing to death between the lines, mutilation and torture, or weeks of slow agony in German hospitals: these were the alternative visions associated with the now familiar formula. Mr. Mayhew had spent a part of his time collecting details about the treatment of those who had fallen, alive but wounded, into German hands; and Campton guessed that as he sat there every one of these details, cruel, sanguinary, remorseless, had started to life, and that all their victims wore the face of Benny.

The wretched man sat speechless, so unhinged and swinging loose in his grief that Mr. Brant and Campton could only look on, following the thoughts he was thinking, seeing the sights he was seeing, and each avoiding the other's eye lest they should betray to one another the secret of their shared exultation at George's safety.

Finally Mr. Mayhew was put in charge of a confidential clerk, who was to go with him to the English Military Mission in the hope of getting further information. He went away, small and shrunken, with the deprecating smile of a man who seeks to ward off a blow; as he left the room Campton heard him say timidly to the clerk: "No doubt you speak French, sir? The words I want don't seem to come to me."

Campton had meant to leave at the same time; but some vague impulse held him back. He remembered George's postscript: "Don't be too savage to Uncle Andy," and wished he could think of some friendly phrase to ease off his leave-taking. Mr. Brant seemed to have the same wish. He stood, erect and tightly buttoned, one small hand resting on the arm of his desk-chair, as though he were posing for a cabinet size, with the photographer telling him to look natural. His lids twitched behind his protective glasses, and his upper lip, which was as straight as a ruler, detached itself by a hair's breadth from the lower; but no word came.

Campton glanced up and down the white-panelled walls, and spoke abruptly.

"There was no reason on earth," he said, "why poor young Upsher should ever have been in this thing."

Mr. Brant bowed.

"This sort of crazy impulse to rush into other people's rows," Campton continued with rising vehemence, "is of no more use to a civilized state than any other unreasoned instinct. At bottom it's nothing but what George calls the baseball spirit: just an ignorant passion for fisticuffs."

Mr. Brant looked at him intently. "When did—George say that?" he asked, with his usual cough before the name.

Campton coloured. "Oh—er—some time ago: in the very beginning, I think. It was the view of most thoughtful young fellows at that time."

"Quite so," said Mr. Brant, cautiously stroking his moustache.

Campton's eyes again wandered about the room.

"*Now*, of course——"

"Ah—*now* . . ."

The two men looked at each other, and Campton held out his hand. Mr. Brant, growing pink about the forehead, extended his dry fingers, and they shook hands in silence.

Chapter XVIII

IN the street Campton looked about him with the same confused sense as when he had watched Fortin-Lescluze driving away to Chalons, his dead son's image in his eyes.

Each time that Campton came in contact with people on whom this calamity had fallen he grew more acutely aware of his own inadequacy. If he had been Fortin-Lescluze it would have been impossible for him to go back to Chalons and resume his task. If he had been Harvey Mayhew, still less could he have accommodated himself to the intolerable, the really inconceivable, thought that Benny Upsher had vanished into that fiery furnace like a crumpled letter tossed into a grate. Young Fortin was defending his country—but Upsher, in God's name what was Benny Upsher of Connecticut doing in a war between the continental powers?

Suddenly Campton remembered that he had George's letter in his pocket, and that he had meant to go back with it to Mrs. Brant's. He had started out that morning full of the good intentions the letter had inspired; but now he had no heart to carry them out. Yet George had said: "Let mother know, and explain, please"; and such an injunction could not be disregarded.

He was still hesitating on a street corner when he remembered that Miss Anthony was probably on her way home for luncheon, and that if he made haste he might find her despatching her hurried meal. It was instinctive with him, in difficult hours, to turn to her, less for counsel than for shelter; her simple unperplexed view of things was as comforting as his mother's solution of the dark riddles he used to propound in the nursery.

He found her in her little dining-room, with Delft plates askew on imitation Cordova leather, and a Death's Head Pennon and a Prussian helmet surmounting the nymph in cast bronze on the mantelpiece. In entering he faced the relentless light of a ground-glass window opening on an air-shaft; and Miss Anthony, flinging him a look, dropped her fork and sprang up crying: "George——"

"George—why George?" Campton recovered his presence of mind under the shock of her agitation. "What made you think of George?"

"Your—your face," she stammered, sitting down again. "So absurd of me . . . But you looked . . . A seat for monsieur, Jeanne," she cried over her shoulder to the pantry.

"Ah—my face? Yes, I suppose so. Benny Upsher has disappeared—I've just had to break it to Mayhew."

"Oh, that poor young Upsher? How dreadful!" Her own face grew instantly serene. "I'm so sorry—so very sorry . . . Yes, yes, you *shall* lunch with me—I know there's another cutlet," she insisted.

He shook his head. "I couldn't."

"Well, then, I've finished." She led the way into the drawing-room. There it was her turn to face the light, and he saw that her own features were as perturbed as she had apparently discovered his to be.

"Poor Benny, poor boy!" she repeated, in the happy voice she might have had if she had been congratulating Campton on the lad's escape. He saw that she was still thinking not of Upsher but of George, and her inability to fit her intonation to her words betrayed the violence of her relief. But why had she imagined George to be in danger?

Campton recounted the scene at which he had just assisted, and while she continued to murmur her sympathy he asked abruptly: "Why on earth should you have been afraid for George?"

Miss Anthony had taken her usual armchair. It was placed, as the armchairs of elderly ladies usually are, with its high back to the light, and Campton could no longer observe the discrepancy between her words and her looks. This probably gave her laugh its note of confidence. "My dear, if you were to cut me open George's name would run out of every vein," she said.

"But in that tone—it was your tone. You thought he'd been— that something had happened," Campton insisted. "How could it, where he is?"

She shrugged her shoulders in the "foreign" way she had picked up in her youth. The gesture was as incongruous as her slang, but it had become part of her physical self, which lay in a loose mosaic of incongruities over the solid crystal block of her character.

"Why, indeed? I suppose there are risks everywhere, aren't there?"

"I don't know." He pulled out the letter he had received that morning. A sudden light had illuminated it, and his hand shook. "I don't even know where George is any longer."

She seemed to hesitate for a moment, and then asked calmly: "What do you mean?"

"Here—look at this. We're to write to his base. I'm to tell his mother of the change." He waited, cursing the faint winter light, and the protecting back of her chair. "What can it mean," he broke out, "except that he's left Sainte-Menehould, that he's been sent elsewhere, and that he doesn't want us to find out where?"

Miss Anthony bent her long nose over the page. Her hand held the letter steadily, and he guessed, as she perused it, that she had had one of the same kind, and had already drawn her own conclusions. What they were, that first startled "George!" seemed to say. But would she ever let Campton see as far into her thoughts again? He continued to watch her hands patiently, since nothing was to be discovered of her face. The hands folded the letter with precision, and handed it back to him.

"Yes: I see why you thought that—one might have," she surprised him by conceding. Then, darting at his unprotected face a gaze he seemed to feel though he could not see it: "If it had meant that George had been ordered to the front, how would you have felt?" she demanded.

He had not expected the question, and though in the last weeks he had so often propounded it to himself, it caught him in the chest like a blow. A sense of humiliation, a longing to lay his weakness bare, suddenly rose in him, and he bowed his head. "I couldn't . . . I couldn't bear it," he stammered.

She was silent for an interval; then she stood up, and laying her hand on his shaking shoulder crossed the room to a desk in which he knew she kept her private papers. Her keys clinked, and a moment later she handed him a letter. It was in George's writing, and dated on the same day as his own.

"Dearest old girl, nothing new but my address. Hereafter please write to our Base. This order has just been lowered from the empyrean at the end of an endless reel of red tape. What it means nobody knows. It does not appear to imply an immediate change of Headquarters; but even if such a change comes, my job is likely to remain the same. I'm getting used to it, and no wonder, for one day differeth not from another, and I've had many of them now. Take care of Dad and mother, and of your matchless self. I'm writing to father to-day. Your George the First—and Last (or I'll know why)."

The two letters bore one another out in a way which carried conviction. Campton saw that his sudden doubts must have been produced (since he had not felt them that morning) by the agonizing experience he had undergone: the vision of Benny Upsher had unmanned him. George was safe, and asked only to remain so: that was evident from both letters. And as the certainty of his son's acquiescence once more penetrated Campton it brought with it a fresh reaction of shame. Ashamed—yes, he had begun to be ashamed of George as well as of himself. Under the touch of Adele Anthony's implacable honesty his last pretenses shrivelled up, and he longed to abase himself. He lifted his head and looked at her, remembering all she would be able to read in his eyes.

"You're satisfied?" she enquired.

"Yes. If that's the word." He stretched his hand toward her, and then drew it back. "But it's *not*: it's not the word any longer." He laboured with the need of self-expression, and the opposing instinct of concealing feelings too complex for Miss Anthony's simple gaze. How could he say: "I'm satisfied; but I wish to God that George were not"? And was he satisfied, after all? And how could he define, or even be sure that he was actually experiencing, a feeling so contradictory that it seemed to be made up of anxiety for his son's safety, shame at that anxiety, shame at George's own complacent acceptance of his lot, and terror of a possible change in that lot? There were hours when it seemed to Campton that the Furies were listening, and ready to fling their awful answer to him if he as much as whispered to himself: "Would to God that George were not satisfied!"

The sense of their haunting presence laid its clutch on him, and caused him, after a pause, to finish his phrase in another tone. "No; satisfied's not the word; I'm *glad* George is out of it!" he exclaimed.

Miss Anthony was folding away the letter as calmly as if it had been a refugee record. She did not appear to notice the change in Campton's voice.

"I don't pretend to your sublime detachment: you've never had a child," he sneered. (Certainly, if the Furies were listening, they would put that down to his credit!)

"Oh, my poor John," she said; then she locked the desk, took her hat from the lamp-chimney on which it had been hanging, jammed it down on her head like a helmet, and remarked: "We'll go together, shall we? It's time I got back to the office."

On the way downstairs both were silent. Campton's ears echoed with his stupid taunt, and he glanced at her without daring to speak. On the last landing she paused and said: "I'll see Julia this evening about George's change of address. She may be worried; and I can explain—I can take her my letter."

"Oh, do," he assented. "And tell her—tell her—if she needs me——"

It was as much of a message as he found courage for. Miss Anthony nodded.

Chapter XIX

O NE day Mme. Lebel said: "The first horse-chestnuts are in bloom. And monsieur must really buy himself some new shirts."

Campton looked at her in surprise. She spoke in a different voice; he wondered if she had had good news of her grandchildren. Then he saw that the furrows in her old face were as deep as ever, and that the change in her voice was simply an unconscious response to the general stirring of sap, the spring need to go on living, through everything and in spite of everything.

On se fait une raison, as Mme. Lebel would have said. Life had to go on, and new shirts had to be bought. No one knew why it was necessary, but every one felt that it was; and here were the horse-chestnuts once more actively confirming it. Habit laid its compelling grasp on the wires of the poor broken marionettes with which the Furies had been playing, and they responded, though with feebler flappings, to the accustomed jerk.

In Campton the stirring of the sap had been a cold and languid process, chiefly felt in his reluctance to go on with his relief work. He had tried to close his ears to the whispers of his own lassitude, vexed, after the first impulse of self-dedication, to find that no vocation declared itself, that his task became each day more tedious as well as more painful. Theoretically, the pain ought to have stimulated him: perpetual immersion in that sea of anguish should have quickened his effort to help the poor creatures sinking under its waves. The woe of the war had had that effect on Adele Anthony, on young Boylston, on Mlle. Davril, on the greater number of his friends. But their ardour left him cold. He wanted to help, he wanted it, he was sure, as earnestly as they; but the longing was not an inspiration to him, and he felt more and more that to work listlessly was to work ineffectually.

"I give the poor devils so many boots and money-orders a day; you give them yourself, and so does Boylston," he complained to Miss Anthony; who murmured: "Ah, *Boylston*——" as if that point of the remark were alone worth noticing.

"At his age too; it's extraordinary, the way the boy's got out of himself."

"Or into himself, rather. He *was* a pottering boy before—now he's a man, with a man's sense of things."

"Yes; but his patience, his way of getting into their minds, their prejudices, their meannesses, their miseries! He doesn't seem to me like the kind who was meant to be a missionary."

"Not a bit of it . . . But he's burnt up with shame at our not being in the war—as all the young Americans are."

Campton made an impatient movement. "Benny Upsher again——! Can't we let our government decide all that for us? What else did we elect it for, I wonder?"

"I wonder," echoed Miss Anthony.

Talks of this kind were irritating and unprofitable, and Campton did not again raise the question. Miss Anthony's vision was too simplifying to penetrate far into his doubts, and after nearly a year's incessant contact with the most savage realities her mind still seemed at ease in its old formulas.

Simplicity, after all, was the best safeguard in such hours. Mrs. Brant was as absorbed in her task as Adele Anthony. Since the Brant villa at Deauville had been turned into a hospital she was always on the road, in a refulgent new motor emblazoned with a Red Cross, carrying supplies, rushing down with great surgeons, hurrying back to committee meetings and conferences with the Service de Santé (for she and Mr. Brant were now among the leaders in American relief work in Paris), and throwing open the Avenue Marigny drawing-rooms for concerts, lectures and such sober philanthropic gaieties as society was beginning to countenance.

On the day when Mme. Lebel told Campton that the horse-chestnuts were in blossom and he must buy some new shirts he was particularly in need of such incentives. He had made up his mind to go to see Mrs. Brant about a concert for "The Friends of French Art" which was to be held in her house. Ever since George had asked him to see something of his mother Campton had used the pretext of charitable collaboration as the best way of getting over their fundamental lack of anything to say to each other.

The appearance of the Champs Elysées confirmed Mme. Lebel's announcement. Everywhere the punctual rosy spikes were rising above unfolding green; and Campton, looking up at them, remembered once thinking how Nature had adapted herself to the scene in overhanging with her own pink lamps and green fans the lamps and fans of the *cafés chantants* beneath. The latter lights had long since been extinguished, the fans folded up; and as he passed the bent and broken arches of electric light, the iron chairs and dead plants in paintless boxes, all heaped up like the scenery of a bankrupt theatre, he felt the pang of Nature's obstinate renewal in a world of death. Yet he also felt the stir of the blossoming trees in the form of a more restless discontent, a duller despair, a new sense of inadequacy. How could war go on when spring had come?

Mrs. Brant, having reduced her household and given over her drawing-rooms to charity, received in her boudoir, a small room contrived by a clever upholsterer to simulate a seclusion of which she had never felt the need. Photographs strewed the low tables; and facing the door Campton saw George's last portrait, in uniform, enclosed in an expensive frame. Campton had received the same photograph, and thrust it into a drawer; he thought a young man on a safe staff job rather ridiculous in uniform, and at the same time the sight filled him with a secret dread.

Mrs. Brant was bidding good-bye to a lady in mourning whom Campton did not know. His approach through the carpeted antechamber had been unnoticed, and as he entered the room he heard Mrs. Brant say in French, apparently in reply to a remark of her visitor: "Bridge, *chère Madame*? No; not yet. I confess I haven't the courage to take up my old life. We mothers with sons at the front . . ."

"Ah," exclaimed the other lady, "there I don't agree with you. I think one owes it to them to go on as if one were as little afraid as *they* are. That is what all my sons prefer . . . Even," she added, lowering her voice but lifting her head higher, "even, I'm sure, the one who is buried by the Marne." With a flush on her handsome face she pressed Mrs. Brant's hand and passed out.

Mrs. Brant had caught sight of Campton as she received the rebuke. Her colour rose slightly, and she said with a smile: "So many women can't get on without amusement."

"No," he agreed. There was a pause, and then he asked: "Who was it?"

"The Marquise de Tranlay—the widow."

"Where are the sons she spoke of?"

"There are three left: one in the *Chasseurs à Pied*; the youngest, who volunteered at seventeen, in the artillery in the Argonne; the third, badly wounded, in hospital at Compiègne. And the eldest killed. I simply can't understand . . ."

"Why," Campton interrupted, "did you speak as if George were at the front? Do you usually speak of him in that way?"

Her silence and her deepening flush made him feel the unkindness of the question. "I didn't mean . . . forgive me," he said. "Only sometimes, when I see women like that I'm——"

"Well?" she questioned.

He was silent in his turn, and she did not insist. They sat facing each other, each forgetting the purpose of their meeting. For the hundredth time he felt the uselessness of trying to carry out George's filial injunction: between himself and George's mother these months of fiery trial seemed to have loosed instead of tightening the links.

He wandered back to Montmartre through the bereft and beautiful city. The light lay on it in wide silvery washes, harmonizing the grey stone, the pale foliage, and a sky piled with clouds which seemed to rebuild in translucid masses the monuments below. He caught himself once more viewing the details of the scene in the terms of his trade. River, pavements, terraces heavy with trees, the whole crowded sky-line from Notre Dame to the Panthéon, instead of presenting themselves in their bare reality, were transposed into a painter's vision. And the faces around him became again the starting-point of rapid incessant combinations of line and colour, as if the visible world were once more at its old trick of weaving itself into magic designs. The reawakening of this instinct deepened Campton's sense of unrest, and made him feel more than ever unfitted for a life in which such things were no longer of account, in which it seemed a disloyalty even to think of them.

He returned to the studio, having promised to deal with some office work which he had carried home the night before. The papers lay on the table; but he turned to the window and looked out over his budding lilacs at the new strange Paris. He remembered that it was almost a year since he had leaned in the same place, gazing down on the wise and frivolous old city in her summer dishabille while he planned his journey to

Africa with George; and something George had once quoted from Faust came drifting through his mind: "Take care! You've broken my beautiful world! There'll be splinters . . ." Ah, yes, splinters, splinters . . . everybody's hands were red with them! What retribution devised by man could be commensurate with the crime of destroying his beautiful world? Campton sat down to the task of collating office files.

His bell rang, and he started up, as much surprised as if the simplest events had become unusual. It would be natural enough that Dastrey or Boylston should drop in—or even Adele Anthony—but his heart beat as if it might be George. He limped to the door, and found Mrs. Talkett.

She said: "May I come in?" and did so without waiting for his answer. The rapidity of her entrance surprised him less than the change in her appearance. But for the one glimpse of her dishevelled elegance, when she had rushed into Mrs. Brant's drawing-room on the day after war was declared, he had seen her only in a nursing uniform, as absorbed in her work as if it had been a long-thwarted vocation. Now she stood before him in raiment so delicately springlike that it seemed an emanation of the day. Care had dropped from her with her professional garb, and she smiled as though he must guess the reason.

In ordinary times he would have thought: "She's in love——" but that explanation was one which seemed to belong to other days. It reminded him, however, how little he knew of Mrs. Talkett, who, after René Davril's death, had vanished from his life as abruptly as she had entered it. Allusions to "the Talketts," picked up now and again at Adele Anthony's, led him to conjecture an invisible husband in the background; but all he knew of Mrs. Talkett was what she had told him of her "artistic" yearnings, and what he had been able to divine from her empty questioning eyes, from certain sweet inflections when she spoke of her wounded soldiers, and from the precise and finished language with which she clothed her unfinished and unprecise thoughts. All these indications made up an image not unlike that of the fashion-plate torn from its context of which she had reminded him at their first meeting; and he looked at her with indifference, wondering why she had come.

With an abrupt gesture she pulled the pin from her heavily-plumed hat, tossed it on the divan, and said: "Dear Master, I just want to sit with you and have you talk to me." She dropped down beside her hat, clasped her thin hands about her thin knee, and broke out, as if she had already forgotten that she wanted him to talk to her: "Do you know, I've made up my mind to begin to live again—to live my own life, I mean, to be my real *me*, after all these dreadful months of exile from myself. I see now that *that* is my real duty—just as it is yours, just as it is that of every artist and every creator. Don't you feel as I do? Don't you agree with me? We *must* save Beauty for the world; before it is too late we must save it out of this awful wreck and ruin. It sounds ridiculously presumptuous, doesn't it, to say 'we' in talking of a great genius like you and a poor little speck of dust like me? But after all there is the same instinct in us, the same craving, the same desire to realize Beauty, though you do it so magnificently and so—so objectively, and I . . ." she paused, unclasped her hands, and lifted her lovely bewildered eyes, "I do it only by a ribbon in my hair, a flower in a vase, a way of looping a curtain, or placing a lacquer screen in the right light. But I oughtn't to be ashamed of my limitations, do you think I ought? Surely every one ought to be helping to save Beauty; every one is needed, even the humblest and most ignorant of us, or else the world will be all death and ugliness. And after all, ugliness is the only *real* death, isn't it?" She drew a deep breath and added: "It has done me good already to sit here and listen to you."

Campton, a few weeks previously, would have been amused, or perhaps merely irritated. But in the interval he had become aware in himself of the same irresistible craving to "live," as she put it, and as he had heard it formulated, that very day, by the mourning mother who had so sharply rebuked Mrs. Brant. The spring was stirring them all in their different ways, secreting in them the sap which craved to burst into bridge-parties, or the painting of masterpieces, or a consciousness of the need for new shirts.

"But what am I in all this?" Mrs. Talkett rushed on, sparing him the trouble of a reply. "Nothing but the match that lights the flame! Sometimes I imagine that I might put what I mean into poetry . . . I *have* scribbled a few things, you know . . . but that's not what I was going to tell you. It's you, dear Master, who must set us the example of getting back to our work, our real work, whatever it is. What have you done in all these dreadful months—the real You? Nothing! And the world will be the poorer for it ever after. Master, you must paint again—you must begin today!"

Campton gave an uneasy laugh. "Oh—paint!" He waved his hand toward the office files of "The Friends of French Art." "There's my work."

"Not the real you. It's your dummy's work—just as my nursing has been mine. Oh, one did one's best—but all the while beauty and art and the eternal things were perishing! And what will the world be like without them?"

"I shan't be here," Campton growled.

"But your son will." She looked at him profoundly. "You know I know your son—we're friends. And I'm sure he would feel as I feel—he would tell you to go back to your painting."

For months past any allusion to George had put Campton on his guard, stiffening him with improvised defences. But this appeal of Mrs. Talkett's found him unprepared, demoralized by the spring sweetness, and by his secret sense of his son's connivance with it. What was war—any war—but an old European disease, an ancestral blood-madness seizing on the first pretext to slake its frenzy? Campton reminded himself again that he was the son of free institutions, of a country in no way responsible for the centuries of sinister diplomacy which had brought Europe to ruin, and was now trying to drag down America. George was right, the Brants were right, this young woman through whose lips Campton's own secret instinct spoke was right.

He was silent so long that she rose with the anxious frown that appeared to be her way of blushing, and faltered out: "I'm boring you—I'd better go."

She picked up her hat and held its cataract of feathers poised above her slanted head.

"Wait—let me do you like that!" Campton cried. It had never before occurred to him that she was paintable; but as she stood there with uplifted arm the long line flowing from her wrist to her hip suddenly wound itself about him like a net.

"Me?" she stammered, standing motionless, as if frightened by the excess of her triumph.

"Do you mind?" he queried; and hardly hearing her faltered-out: "Mind? When it was what I came for!" he dragged forth an easel, flung on it the first canvas he could lay hands on (though he knew it was the wrong shape and size), and found himself instantly transported into the lost world which was the only real one.

Chapter XX

F OR a month Campton painted on in transcendent bliss.
His first stroke carried him out of space and time, into a
region where all that had become numbed and atrophied in him
could expand and breathe. Lines, images, colours were again the
sole facts: he plunged into their whirling circles like a stranded
sea-creature into the sea. Once more every face was not a vague
hieroglyph, a curtain drawn before an invisible aggregate of
wants and woes, but a work of art, a flower in a pattern, to be
dealt with on its own merits, like a bronze or a jewel. During the
first day or two his hand halted; but the sense of insufficiency
was a goad, and he fought with his subject till he felt a strange
ease in every renovated muscle, and his model became like a
musical instrument on which he played with careless mastery.

He had transferred his easel to Mrs. Talkett's apartment. It
was an odd patchwork place, full of bold beginnings and doubtful pauses, rash surrenders to the newest fashions and abrupt
insurrections against them, where Louis-Philippe mahogany
had entrenched itself against the aggression of *art nouveau*
hangings, and the frail grace of eighteenth-century armchairs
shed derision on lumpy modern furniture painted like hobby-
horses at a fair. It amused Campton to do Mrs. Talkett against
such a background: her thin personality needed to be filled out
by the visible results of its many quests and cravings. There
were people one could sit down before a blank wall, and all
their world was there, in the curves of their faces and the way
their hands lay in their laps; others, like Mrs. Talkett, seemed
to be made out of the reflection of what surrounded them, as if
they had been born of a tricky grouping of looking-glasses, and
would vanish if it were changed.

At first Campton was steeped in the mere sensual joy of his
art; but after a few days the play of the mirrors began to interest him. Mrs. Talkett had abandoned her hospital work, and
was trying, as she said, to "recreate herself." In this she was
aided by a number of people who struck Campton as rather
too young not to have found some other job, or too old to care
any longer for that particular one. But all this did not trouble

his newly recovered serenity. He seemed to himself, somehow, like a drowned body—but drowned in a toy aquarium—still staring about with living eyes, but aware of the other people only as shapes swimming by with a flash of exotic fins. They were enclosed together, all of them, in an unreal luminous sphere, mercifully screened against the reality from which a common impulse of horror had driven them; and since he was among them it was not his business to wonder at the others. So, through the cloud of his art, he looked out on them impartially.

The high priestess of the group was Mme. de Dolmetsch, with Harvey Mayhew as her acolyte. Mr. Mayhew was still in pursuit of Atrocities: he was in fact almost the only member of the group who did not rather ostentatiously disavow the obligation to "carry on." But he had discovered that to discharge this sacred task he must vary it by frequent intervals of relaxation. He explained to Campton that he had found it to be "his duty to rest"; and he was indefatigable in the performance of duty. He had therefore, with an expenditure of eloquence which Campton thought surprisingly slight, persuaded Boylston to become his understudy, and devote several hours a day to the whirling activities of the shrimp-pink Bureau of Atrocities at the Nouveau Luxe. Campton, at first, could not understand how the astute Boylston had allowed himself to be drawn into the eddy; but it turned out that Boylston's astuteness had drawn him in. "You see, there's an awful lot of money to be got out of it, one way and another, and I know a use for every penny—that is, Miss Anthony and I do," the young man modestly explained; adding, in response to the painter's puzzled stare, that Mr. Mayhew's harrowing appeals were beginning to bring from America immense sums for the Victims, and that Mr. Mayhew, while immensely gratified by the effect of his eloquence, and the prestige it was bringing him in French social and governmental circles, had not the cloudiest notion how the funds should be used, and had begged Boylston to advise him. It was owing to this that the ex-Delegate to the Hague was able, with a light conscience, to seek the repose of Mrs. Talkett's company and, with a smile of the widest initiation, to listen to the subversive conversation of her familiars.

"Subversive" was the motto of the group. Every one was engaged in attacking some theory of art or life or letters which nobody in particular defended. Even Mr. Talkett—a kindly young man with eye-glasses and glossy hair, who roamed about straightening the furniture, like a gentlemanly detective watching the presents at a wedding—owned to Campton that *he* was subversive; and on the painter's pressing for a definition, added: "Why, I don't believe in anything *she* doesn't believe in," while his eye-glasses shyly followed his wife's course among the teacups.

Mme. de Dolmetsch, though obviously anxious to retain her hold on Mr. Mayhew, did not restrict herself to such mild fare, but exercised her matchless eyes on a troop of followers: the shock-haired pianist who accompanied her recitations, a straight-backed young American diplomatist whose collars seemed a part of his career, a lustrous South American millionaire, and a short squat Sicilian who designed the costumes for the pianist's unproduced ballets.

All these people appeared to believe intensely in each other's reality and importance; but it gradually came over Campton that all of them, excepting their host and hostess, knew that they were merely masquerading.

To Campton, used to the hard-working world of art, this playing at Bohemia seemed a nursery-game; but the scene acquired an unexpected solidity from the appearance in it, one day, of the banker Jorgenstein, who strolled in as naturally as if he had been dropping into Campton's studio to enquire into the progress of his own portrait.

"I must come and look you up, Campton—get you to finish me," he said jovially, tapping his fat boot with a malacca stick as he looked over the painter's head at the canvas on which Mrs. Talkett's restless image seemed to flutter like a butterfly impaled.

"You'll owe it to *me* if he does you," the sitter declared, smiling back at the leer which Campton divined behind his shoulder; and he felt a sudden pity for her innocence.

"My wife made Campton come back to his real work—doing his bit, you know," said Mr. Talkett, straightening a curtain and disappearing again, like a diving animal; and Mrs. Talkett turned her plaintive eyes on Campton. "That kind of idiocy is all I've ever had," they seemed to say; and he nearly cried back to her: "But, you poor child, it's the only honest thing anywhere near you!"

Absorbed in his picture, he hardly stopped to wonder at Jorgenstein's reappearance, at his air of bloated satisfaction or his easy allusions to Cabinet Ministers and eminent statesmen. The atmosphere of the Talkett house was so mirage-like that even the big red bulk of the international financier became imponderable in it.

But one day Campton, on his way home, ran across Dastrey, and remembered that they had not met for weeks. The ministerial drudge looked worn and preoccupied, and Campton was abruptly recalled to the world he had been trying to escape from.

"You seem rather knocked-up—what's wrong with you?"

Dastrey stared. "Wrong with me? Well—did you like the communiqué this morning?"

"I didn't read it," said Campton curtly. They walked along a few steps in silence.

"You see," the painter continued, "I've gone back to my job—my painting. I suddenly found I had to."

Dastrey glanced at him with surprising kindliness. "Ah, that's good news, my dear fellow!"

"You think so?" Campton half-sneered.

"Of course—why not? What are you painting? May I come and see?"

"Naturally." Campton paused. "The fact is, I was bitten the other day with a desire to depict that little will-o'-the-wisp of a Mrs. Talkett. Come to her house any afternoon and I'll show you the thing."

"To her house?" Dastrey paused with a frown. "Then the picture's finished?"

"No—not by a long way. I'm doing it there—in her *milieu*, among her crowd. It amuses me; they amuse me. When will you come?" He shot out the sentences like challenges; and his friend took them up in the same tone.

"To Mrs. Talkett's—to meet her crowd? Thanks—I'm too much tied down by my job."

"No; you're not. You're too disapproving," said Campton quarrelsomely. "You think we're all a lot of shirks, of drones, of international loafers—I don't know what you call us. But I'm one of them, so whatever name you give them I must answer to. Well, I'll tell you what they are, my dear fellow—and I'm not ashamed to be among them: they're people who've resolutely, unanimously, unshakeably decided, for a certain number of hours each day, to forget the war, to ignore it, to live as if it were not and never had been, so that——"

"So that?"

"So that beauty shall not perish from the earth!" Campton shouted, bringing his stick down with a whack on the pavement.

Dastrey broke into a laugh. *"Allons donc*! Decided to forget the war? Why, bless your heart, they've never, not one of 'em, ever been able to remember it for an hour together; no, not from the first day, except as it interfered with their plans or cut down their amusements or increased their fortunes. You're the only one of them, my dear chap, (since you class yourself among them) of whom what you've just said is true; and if you can forget the war while you're at your work, so much the better for you and for us and for posterity; and I hope you'll paint all Mrs. Talkett's crowd, one after another. Though I doubt if they're as good subjects now as when you caught them last July with the war-funk on." He held out his hand with a dry smile. "Goodbye. I'm off to meet my nephew, who's here on leave."

He hastened away, leaving Campton in a crumbled world. Louis Dastrey on leave? But that was because he was at the front, the real front, in the trenches, had already had a slight wound and a fine citation. Staff-officers, as George had wisely felt, were not asking for leave just yet . . .

The thoughts excited by this encounter left Campton more than ever resolved to drug himself with work and frivolity. It was none of his business to pry into the consciences of the people about him, not even into Jorgenstein's—into which one would presumably have had to be let down in a diver's suit, with oxygen pumping at top pressure. If the government tolerated Jorgenstein's presence in France, probably on the ground that he could be useful—so the banker himself let it be known—it was silly of people like Adele Anthony and Dastrey to wince at the mere mention of his name. There woke in Campton all the old spirit of aimless random defiance—revolt for revolt's sake—which had marked the first period of his life after his separation from his wife. He had long since come to regard it as a crude and juvenile phase—yet here he was reliving it.

Though he knew of the intimacy between Mrs. Talkett and the Brants he had no fear of meeting Julia: it was impossible to picture her neat head battling with the blasts of that dishevelled drawing-room. But though she did not appear there, he heard her more and more often alluded to, in terms of startling familiarity, by Mrs. Talkett's visitors. It was clear that they all saw her, chiefly in her own house, that they thought her, according to their respective vocabularies, "a perfect dear," "*une femme exquise*" or "*une bonne vieille*" (ah, poor Julia!); and that their sudden enthusiasm for her was not uninspired by the fact that she had got her marvellous *chef* demobilised, and was giving little "war-dinners" followed by a quiet turn at bridge.

Campton remembered Mme. de Tranlay's rebuke to Mrs. Brant on the day when he had last called in the Avenue Marigny; then he remembered also that it was on that very day that he had returned to his painting.

"After all, she held out longer than I did—poor Julia!" he mused, annoyed at the idea of her being the complacent victim of all the voracities he saw about him, and yet reflecting that she was at last living her life, as they called it at Mrs. Talkett's. After all, the fact that George was not at the front seemed to exonerate his parents—unless, indeed, it did just the opposite.

One day, coming earlier than usual to Mrs. Talkett's to put in a last afternoon's work on her portrait, Campton, to his surprise, found his wife in front of it. Equally to his surprise he noticed that she was dressed with a juvenility quite new to her; and for the first time he thought she looked old-fashioned and also old. She met him with her usual embarrassment.

"I didn't know you came as early as this. Madge told me I might just run in——" She waved her hand toward the portrait.

"I hope you like it," he said, suddenly finding that he didn't.

"It's marvellous—marvellous." She looked at him timidly. "It's extraordinary, how you've caught her rhythm, her *tempo*," she ventured in the jargon of the place. Campton, to hide a smile, turned away to get his brushes. "I'm so glad," she continued hastily, "that you've begun to paint again. We all need to . . . to . . ."

"Oh, not you and I, do we?" he rejoined with a scornful laugh.

She evidently caught the allusion, for she blushed all over her uncovered neck, up through the faintly wrinkled cheeks to the roots of her newly dyed hair; then he saw her eyes fill.

"What's she crying for? Because George is *not* in danger?" he wondered, busying himself with his palette.

Mrs. Talkett hurried in with surprise and apologies; and one by one the habitués followed, with cheery greetings for Mrs. Brant and a moment of constraint as they noted Campton's presence, and the relation between the two was mutely passed about. Then the bridge-tables were brought, Mr. Talkett began to straighten the cards nervously, and the guests broke up into groups, forgetting everything but their own affairs. As Campton turned back to his work he was aware of a last surprise in the sight of Mrs. Brant serene and almost sparkling, waving her adieux to the bridge-tables, and going out followed by Jorgenstein, with whom she seemed on terms of playful friendliness. Of all strange war promiscuities, Campton thought this the strangest.

Chapter XXI

THE next time Campton saw Mrs. Brant was in his own studio.

He was preparing, one morning, to leave the melancholy place, when the bell rang and his *bonne* let her in. Her dress was less frivolous than at Mrs. Talkett's, and she wore a densely patterned veil, like the ladies in cinema plays when they visit their seducers or their accomplices.

Through the veil she looked at him agitatedly, and said: "George is not at Sainte Menehould."

He stared.

"No. Anderson was there the day before yesterday."

"Brant? At Sainte Menehould?" Campton felt the blood rush to his temples. What! He, the boy's father, had not so much as dared to ask for the almost unattainable permission to go into the war-zone; and this other man, who was nothing to George, absolutely nothing, who had no right whatever to ask for leave to visit him, had somehow obtained the priceless favour, and instead of passing it on, instead of offering at least to share it with the boy's father, had sneaked off secretly to feast on the other's lawful privilege!

"How the devil——?" Campton burst out.

"Oh, he got a Red Cross mission; it was arranged very suddenly—through a friend . . ."

"Yes—well?" Campton stammered, sitting down lest his legs should fail him, and signing to her to take a chair.

"Well—he was not there!" she repeated excitedly. "It's what we might have known—since he's changed his address."

"Then he didn't see him?" Campton interrupted, the ferocious joy of the discovery crowding out his wrath and wonder.

"Anderson didn't? No. He wasn't there, I tell you!"

"The H. Q. has been moved?"

"No, it hasn't. Anderson saw one of the officers. He said George had been sent on a mission."

"To another H. Q.?"

"That's what they said. I don't believe it."

"What do you believe?"

"I don't know. Anderson's sure they told him the truth. The officer he saw is a friend of George's, and he said George was expected back that very evening."

Campton sat looking at her uncertainly. Did she dread, or did she rather wish, to disbelieve the officer's statement? Where did she hope or fear that George had gone? And what were Campton's own emotions? As confused, no doubt, as hers—as undefinable. The insecurity of his feelings moved him to a momentary compassion for hers, which were surely pitiable, whatever else they were. Then a savage impulse swept away every other, and he said: "Wherever George was, Brant's visit will have done him no good."

She grew pale. "What do you mean?"

"I wonder it never occurred to you—or to your husband, since he's so solicitous," Campton went on, prolonging her distress.

"Please tell me what you mean," she pleaded with frightened eyes.

"Why, in God's name, couldn't you both let well enough alone? Didn't you guess why George never asked for leave—why I've always advised him not to? Don't you know that nothing is as likely to get a young fellow into trouble as having his family force their way through to see him, use influence, seem to ask favours? I dare say that's how that fool of a Dolmetsch woman got Isador killed. No one would have noticed where he was if she hadn't gone on so about him. They *had* to send him to the front finally. And now the chances are——"

"Oh, no, no, no—don't say it!" She held her hands before her face as if he had flung something flaming at her. "It was I who made Anderson go!"

"Well—Brant ought to have thought of that—*I* did," he pursued sardonically.

Her answer disarmed him. "You're his father."

"I don't mean," he went on hastily, "that Brant's not right: of course there's nothing to be afraid of. I can't imagine why you thought there was."

She hung her head. "Sometimes when I hear the other women—other mothers—I feel as if our turn must come too. Even at Sainte Menehould a shell might hit the house. Anderson said the artillery fire seemed so near."

He made no answer, and she sat silent, without apparent thought of leaving. Finally he said: "I was just going out——"

She stood up. "Oh, yes—that reminds me. I came to ask you to come with me."

"With you——?"

"The motor's waiting—you must." She laid her hand on his arm. "To see Olida, the new *clairvoyante*. Everybody goes to her—everybody who's anxious about anyone. Even the scientific people believe in her. She's told people the most extraordinary things—it seems she warned Daisy de Dolmetsch . . . Well, I'd *rather* know!" she burst out passionately.

Campton smiled. "She'll tell you that George is back at his desk."

"Well, then—isn't that worth it? Please don't refuse me!"

He disengaged himself gently. "My poor Julia, go by all means if it will reassure you."

"Ah, but you've got to come too. You can't say no: Madge Talkett tells me that if *the two nearest* go together Olida sees so much more clearly—especially a father and mother," she added hastily, as if conscious of the inopportune "nearest." After a moment she went on: "Even Mme. de Tranlay's been; Daisy de Dolmetsch met her on the stairs. Olida told her that her youngest boy, from whom she'd had no news for weeks, was all right, and coming home on leave. Mme. de Tranlay didn't know Daisy, except by sight, but she stopped her to tell her. Only fancy—the last person she would have spoken to in ordinary times! But she was so excited and happy! And two days afterward the boy turned up safe and sound. You must come!" she insisted.

Campton was seized with a sudden deep compassion for all these women groping for a ray of light in the blackness. It moved him to think of Mme. de Tranlay's proud figure climbing a *clairvoyante's* stairs.

"I'll come if you want me to," he said.

They drove to the Batignolles quarter. Mrs. Brant's lips were twitching under her veil, and as the motor stopped she said childishly: "I've never been to this kind of place before."

"I should hope not," Campton rejoined. He himself, during the Russian lady's rule, had served an apprenticeship among the soothsayers, and come away disgusted with the hours wasted in their company. He suddenly remembered the Spanish girl in the little white house near the railway, who had told his fortune in the hot afternoons with cards and olive-stones, and had found, by irrefutable signs, that he and she would "come together" again. "Well, it was better than this pseudo-scientific humbug," he mused, "because it was picturesque—and so was she—and she believed in it."

Mrs. Brant rang, and Campton followed her into a narrow hall. A servant-woman showed them into a *salon* which was as commonplace as a doctor's waiting-room. On the mantelpiece were vases of Pampas grass, and a stuffed monkey swung from the electrolier. Evidently Mme. Olida was superior to the class of fortune-tellers who prepare a special stage-setting, and no astrologer's robe or witch's kitchen was to be feared.

The maid led them across a plain dining-room into an inner room. The shutters were partly closed, and the blinds down. A voluminous woman in loose black rose from a sofa. Gold ear-rings gleamed under her oiled black hair—and suddenly, through the billows of flesh, and behind the large pale mask, Campton recognized the Spanish girl who used to read his fortune in the house by the railway. Her eyes rested a moment on Mrs. Brant; then they met his with the same heavy stare. But he noticed that her hands, which were small and fat, trembled a little as she pointed to two chairs.

"Sit down, please," she said in a low rough voice, speaking in French. The door opened again, and a young man with Levantine eyes and a showy necktie looked in. She said sharply: "No," and he disappeared. Campton noticed that a large emerald flashed on his manicured hand. Mme. Olida continued to look at her visitors.

Mrs. Brant wiped her dry lips and stammered: "We're his parents—a son at the front . . ."

Mme. Olida fell back in a trance-like attitude, let her lids droop over her magnificent eyes, and rested her head against a soiled sofa-pillow. Presently she held out both hands.

"You are his parents? Yes? Give me each a hand, please." As her cushioned palm touched Campton's he thought he felt a tremor of recognition, and saw, in the half-light, the tremor communicate itself to her lids. He grasped her hand firmly, and she lifted her eyes, looked straight into his with her heavy velvety stare, and said: "You should hold my hand more loosely; the currents must not be compressed." She turned her palm upward, so that his finger-tips rested on it as if on a keyboard; he noticed that she did not do the same with the hand she had placed in Mrs. Brant's.

Suddenly he remembered that one sultry noon, lying under the olives, she had taught him, by signals tapped on his own knee, how to say what he chose to her without her brothers' knowing it. He looked at the huge woman, seeking the curve of the bowed upper lip on which what used to be a faint blue shadow had now become a line as thick as her eyebrows, and recalling how her laugh used to lift the lip above her little round teeth while she threw back her head, showing the Agnus Dei in her neck. Now her mouth was like a withered flower, and in a crease of her neck a string of pearls was embedded.

"Take hands, please," she commanded. Julia gave Campton her ungloved hand, and he sat between the two women.

"You are the parents? You want news of your son—ah, like so many!" Mme. Olida closed her eyes again.

"To know where he is—whereabouts—that is what we want," Mrs. Brant whispered.

Mme. Olida sat as if labouring with difficult visions. The noises of the street came faintly through the closed windows and a smell of garlic and cheap scent oppressed Campton's lungs and awakened old associations. With a final effort of memory he fixed his eyes on the *clairvoyante's* darkened mask, and tapped her palm once or twice. She neither stirred nor looked at him.

"I see—I see——" she began in the consecrated phrase. "A veil—a thick veil of smoke between me and a face which is young and fair, with a short nose and reddish hair: thick, thick, thick hair, exactly like this gentleman's when he was young . . ."

Mrs. Brant's hand trembled in Campton's. "It's true," she whispered, "before your hair turned grey it used to be as red as Georgie's."

"The veil grows denser—there are awful noises; there's a face with blood—but not that first face. This is a very young man, as innocent as when he was born, with blue eyes like flax-flowers, but blood, blood . . . why do I see that face? Ah, now it is on a hospital pillow—not your son's face, the other; there is no one near, no one but some German soldiers laughing and drinking;

the lips move, the hands are stretched out in agony; but no one notices. It is a face that has something to say to the gentleman; not to you, Madame. The uniform is different—is it an English uniform? . . . Ah, now the face turns grey; the eyes shut, there is foam on the lips. Now it is gone—there's another man's head on the pillow . . . Now, now your son's face comes back; but not near those others. The smoke has cleared . . . I see a desk and papers; your son is writing . . ."

"Oh," gasped Mrs. Brant.

"If you squeeze my hands you arrest the current," Mme. Olida reminded her. There was another interval; Campton felt his wife's fingers beating between his like trapped birds. The heat and darkness oppressed him; beads of sweat came out on his forehead. Did the woman really see things, and was that face with the blood on it Benny Upsher's?

Mme. Olida droned on. "It is your son who is writing—the young man with the very thick hair. He is writing to you—trying to explain something. Perhaps you have hoped to see him lately? That is it; he is telling you why it could not be. He is sitting quietly in a room. There is no smoke." She released Mrs. Brant's hand and Campton's. "Go home, Madame. You are fortunate. Perhaps his letter will reach you tomorrow."

Mrs. Brant stood up sobbing. She found her gold bag and pushed it toward Campton. He had been feeling in his own pocket for money; but as he drew it forth Mme. Olida put back his hand. "No. I am superstitious; it's so seldom that I can give good news. *Bonjour, madame, bonjour, monsieur.* I commend your son to the blessed Virgin and to all the saints and angels."

Campton put Julia into the motor. She was still crying, but her tears were radiant. "Isn't she wonderful? Didn't you see how she seemed to *recognize* George? There's no mistaking his hair! How could she have known what it was like? Don't think me foolish—I feel so comforted!"

"Of course; you'll hear from him to-morrow," Campton said. He was touched by her maternal passion, and ashamed of having allowed her so small a share in his jealous worship of his son. He walked away, thinking of the young man dying in a German hospital, and of the other man's face succeeding his on the pillow.

Chapter XXII

Two days later, to Campton's surprise, Anderson Brant appeared in the morning at the studio.

Campton, finishing a late breakfast in careless studio-garb, saw his visitor peer cautiously about, as though fearing undressed models behind the screens or empty beer-bottles under the tables. It was the first time that Mr. Brant had entered the studio since his attempt to buy George's portrait, and Campton guessed at once that he had come again about George.

He looked at the painter shyly, as if oppressed by the indiscretion of intruding at that hour.

"It was my—Mrs. Brant who insisted—when she got this letter," he brought out between precautionary coughs.

Campton looked at him tolerantly: a barrier seemed to have fallen between them since their brief exchange of words about Benny Upsher. The letter, as Campton had expected, was a line from George to his mother, written two days after Mr. Brant's visit to Sainte Menehould. It expressed, in George's usual staccato style, his regret at having been away. "Hard luck, when one is riveted to the same square yard of earth for weeks on end, to have just happened to be somewhere else the day Uncle Andy broke through." It was always the same tone of fluent banter, in which Campton fancied he detected a lurking stridency, like the scrape of an overworked gramophone containing only comic disks.

"Ah, well—his mother must be satisfied," Campton said as he gave the letter back.

"Oh, completely. So much so that I've induced her to go off for a while to Biarritz. The doctor finds her overdone; she'd got it into her head that George had been sent to the front; I couldn't convince her to the contrary."

Campton looked at him. "You yourself never believed it?"

Mr. Brant, who had half risen, as though feeling that his errand was done, slid back into his seat and clasped his small hands on his agate-headed stick.

"Oh, never."

"It was not," Campton pursued, "with that idea that you went to Sainte Menehould?"

Mr. Brant glanced at him in surprise. "No. On the contrary——"

"On the contrary?"

"I understood from—from his mother that, in the circumstances, you were opposed to his asking for leave; thought it unadvisable, that is. So, as it was such a long time since we'd seen him——" The "we," pulling him up short, spread a brick-red blush over his baldness.

"Not longer than since I have—but then I've not your opportunities," Campton retorted, the sneer breaking out in spite of him. Though he had grown kindly disposed toward Mr. Brant when they were apart, the old resentments still broke out in his presence.

Mr. Brant clasped and unclasped the knob of his stick. "I took the first chance that offered; I had his mother to think of." Campton made no answer, and he continued: "I was sorry to hear you thought I'd perhaps been imprudent."

"There's no perhaps about it," Campton retorted. "Since you say you were not anxious about the boy I can't imagine why you made the attempt."

Mr. Brant was silent. He seemed overwhelmed by the other's disapprobation, and unable to find any argument in his own defence. "I never dreamed it could cause any trouble," he said at length.

"That's the ground you've always taken in your interference with my son!" Campton had risen, pushing back his chair, and Mr. Brant stood up also. They faced each other without speaking.

"I'm sorry," Mr. Brant began, "that you should take such a view. It seemed to me natural . . . , when Mr. Jorgenstein gave me the chance——"

"Jorgenstein! It was Jorgenstein who took you to the front? Took you to see my son?" Campton threw his head back and laughed. "That's complete—that's really complete!"

Mr. Brant reddened as if the laugh had been a blow. He stood very erect, his lips as tightly closed as a shut penknife. He had the attitude of a civilian under fire, considerably perturbed, but obliged to set the example of fortitude.

Campton looked at him. At last he had Mr. Brant at a disadvantage. Their respective situations were reversed, and he saw that the banker was aware of it, and oppressed by the fear that he might have done harm to George. He evidently wanted to say all this and did not know how.

His distress moved Campton, in whose ears the sound of his own outburst still echoed unpleasantly. If only Mr. Brant would have kept out of his way he would have found it so easy to be fair to him!

"I'm sorry," he began in a quieter tone. "I dare say I'm unjust—perhaps it's in the nature of our relation. Can't you understand how I've felt, looking on helplessly all these years, while you've done for the boy everything I wanted to do for him myself? Haven't you guessed why I jumped at my first success, and nursed my celebrity till I'd got half the fools in Europe lining up to be painted?" His excitement was mastering him again, and he went on hurriedly: "Do you suppose I'd have wasted all these precious years over their stupid faces if I hadn't wanted to make my son independent of you? And he *would* have been, if the war hadn't come; been my own son again and nobody else's, leading his own life, whatever he chose it to be, instead of having to waste his youth in your bank, learning how to multiply your millions."

The futility of this retrospect, and the inconsistency of his whole attitude, exasperated Campton more than anything his visitor could do or say, and he stopped, embarrassed by the sound of his own words, yet seeing no escape save to bury them under more and more. But Mr. Brant had opened his lips.

"They'll be *his*, you know: the millions," he said.

Campton's anger dropped: he felt Mr. Brant at last too completely at his mercy. He waited for a moment before speaking.

"You tried to buy his portrait once—you remember I told you it was not for sale," he then said.

Mr. Brant stood motionless, grasping his stick in one hand and stroking his moustache with the other. For a while he seemed to be considering Campton's words without feeling their sting. "It was not the money . . ." he stammered out at length, from the depth of some unutterable plea for understanding; then he added: "I wish you a good morning," and walked out with his little stiff steps.

Chapter XXIII

CAMPTON was thoroughly ashamed of what he had said to Mr. Brant, or rather of his manner of saying it. If he could have put the same facts quietly, ironically, without forfeiting his dignity, and with the added emphasis which deliberateness and composure give, he would scarcely have regretted the opportunity. He had always secretly accused himself of a lack of courage in accepting Mr. Brant's heavy benefactions for George when the boy was too young to know what they might pledge him to; and it had been a disappointment that George, on reaching the age of discrimination, had not appeared to find the burden heavy, or the obligations unpleasant.

Campton, having accepted Mr. Brant's help, could hardly reproach his son for feeling grateful for it, and had therefore thought it "more decent" to postpone disparagement of their common benefactor till his own efforts had set them both free. Even then, it would be impossible to pay off the past—but the past might have been left to bury itself. Now his own wrath had dug it up, and he had paid for the brief joy of casting its bones in Mr. Brant's face by a deep disgust at his own weakness.

All these things would have weighed on him even more if the outer weight of events had not been so much heavier. He had not returned to Mrs. Talkett's since the banker's visit; he did not wish to meet Jorgenstein, and his talk with the banker, and his visit to the *clairvoyante*, had somehow combined to send that whole factitious world tumbling about his ears. It was absurd to attach any importance to poor Olida's vaticinations; but the vividness of her description of the baby-faced boy dying in a German hospital haunted Campton's nights. If it were not the portrait of Benny Upsher it was at least that of hundreds and thousands of lads like him, who were thus groping and agonizing and stretching out vain hands, while in Mrs. Talkett's drawing-room well-fed men and expensive women heroically "forgot the war." Campton, seeking to expiate his own brief forgetfulness by a passion of renewed activity, announced to Boylston the next afternoon that he was coming back to the office.

Boylston hardly responded: he looked up from his desk with a face so strange that Campton broke off to cry out: "What's happened?"

The young man held out a newspaper. "They've done it—they've done it!" he shouted. Across the page the name of the *Lusitania* blazed out like the writing on the wall.

The Berserker light on Boylston's placid features transformed him into an avenging cherub. "Ah, now we're in it—we're in it at last!" he exulted, as if the horror of the catastrophe were already swallowed up in its result. The two looked at each other without further words; but the older man's first thought had been for his son. Now, indeed, America was "in it": the gross tangible proof for which her government had forced her to wait was there in all its unimagined horror. Cant and cowardice in high places had drugged and stupefied her into the strange belief that she was too proud to fight for others; and here she was brutally forced to fight for herself. Campton waited with a straining heart for his son's first comment on the new fact that they were "in it."

But his excitement and Boylston's exultation were short-lived. Before many days it became apparent that the proud nation which had flamed up overnight at the unproved outrage of the *Maine* was lying supine under the flagrant provocation of the *Lusitania*. The days which followed were, to many Americans, the bitterest of the war: to Campton they seemed the ironic justification of the phase of indifference and self-absorption through which he had just passed. He could not go back to Mrs. Talkett and her group; but neither could he take up his work with even his former zeal. The bitter taste of the national humiliation was perpetually on his lips: he went about like a man dishonoured.

He wondered, as the days and the weeks passed, at having no word from George. Had he refrained from writing because he too felt the national humiliation too deeply either to speak of it or to leave it unmentioned? Or was he so sunk in security that he felt only a mean thankfulness that nothing was changed? From such thoughts Campton's soul recoiled; but they lay close under the surface of his tenderness, and reared their evil heads whenever they caught him alone.

As the summer dragged itself out he was more and more alone. Dastrey, cured of his rheumatism, had left the Ministry to resume his ambulance work. Miss Anthony was submerged under the ever-mounting tide of refugees. Mrs. Brant had taken a small house at Deauville (on the pretext of being near her hospital), and Campton heard of the Talketts' being with her, and others of their set. Mr. Mayhew appeared at the studio one day, in tennis flannels and a new straw hat, announcing that he "needed rest," and rather sheepishly adding that Mrs. Brant had suggested his spending "a quiet fortnight" with her. "I've *got* to do it, if I'm to see this thing through," Mr. Mayhew added in a stern voice, as if commanding himself not to waver.

A few days later, glancing over the *Herald*, Campton read that Mme. de Dolmetsch, "the celebrated *artiste*," was staying with Mr. and Mrs. Anderson Brant at Deauville, where she had gone to give recitations for the wounded in hospital. Campton smiled, and then thought with a tightening heart of Benny Upsher and Ladislas Isador, so incredibly unlike in their lives, so strangely one in their death. Finally, not long afterward, he read that the celebrated financier, Sir Cyril Jorgenstein (recently knighted by the British Government) had bestowed a gift of a hundred thousand francs upon Mrs. Brant's hospital. It was rumoured, the paragraph ended, that Sir Cyril would soon receive the Legion of Honour for his magnificent liberalities to France.

And still the flood of war rolled on. Success here, failure there, the menace of disaster elsewhere—Russia retreating to the San, Italy declaring war on Austria and preparing to cross the Isonzo, the British advance at Anzac, and from the near East news of the new landing at Suvla. Through all this alternating of tragedy and triumph ran the million and million individual threads of hope, fear, fortitude, resolve, with which the fortune of the war was obscurely but fatally interwoven. Campton remembered his sneer at Dastrey's phrase: "One can at least contribute an attitude." He had begun to feel the force of that, to understand the need of every human being's "pulling his weight" in the struggle, had begun to scan every face in the street in the passionate effort to distinguish between the stones in the wall of resistance and the cracks through which discouragement might filter.

The shabby office of the Palais Royal again became his only haven. His portrait of Mrs. Talkett had brought him many new orders; but he refused them all, and declined even to finish the pictures interrupted by the war. One of his abrupt revulsions of feeling had flung him back, heart and brain, into the horror he had tried to escape from. "If thou ascend up into heaven I am there; if thou make thy bed in hell, behold I am there," the war said to him; and as the daily head-lines shrieked out the names of new battle-fields, from the Arctic shore to the Pacific, he groaned back like the Psalmist: "Whither shall I go from thee?"

The people about him—Miss Anthony, Boylston, Mlle. Davril, and all their band of tired resolute workers—plodded ahead, their eyes on their task, seeming to find in its fulfillment a partial escape from the intolerable oppression. The women especially, with their gift of living in the particular, appeared hardly aware of the appalling development of the catastrophe; and Campton felt himself almost as lonely among these people who thought of nothing but the war as among those who hardly thought of it at all. It was only when he and Boylston, after a hard morning's work, went out to lunch together, that what he called the *Lusitania look*, suddenly darkening the younger man's face, moved the painter with an anguish like his own.

Boylston, breaking through his habitual shyness, had one day remonstrated with Campton for not going on with his painting: but the latter had merely rejoined: "We've each of us got to worry through this thing in our own way—" and the subject was not again raised between them.

The intervals between George's letters were growing longer. Campton, who noted in his pocket-diary the dates of all that he received, as well as those addressed to Mrs. Brant and Miss Anthony, had not had one to record since the middle of June. And in that there was no allusion to the *Lusitania*.

"It's queer," he said to Boylston, one day toward the end of July; "I don't know yet what George thinks about the *Lusitania*."

"Oh, yes, you do, sir!" Boylston returned, laughing; "but all the mails from the war-zone," he added, "have been very much delayed lately. When there's a big attack on anywhere they hold up everything along the line. And besides, no end of letters are lost."

"I suppose so," said Campton, pocketing the diary, and trying for the millionth time to call up a vision of his boy, seated at a desk in some still unvisualized place, his rumpled fair head bent above columns of figures or files of correspondence, while day after day the roof above him shook with the roar of the attacks which held up his letters.

BOOK III

Chapter XXIV

THE gates of Paris were behind them, and they were rushing through an icy twilight between long lines of houses, factory chimneys and city-girt fields, when Campton at last roused himself and understood.

It was he, John Campton, who sat in that car—that noiseless swiftly-sliding car, so cushioned and commodious, so ingeniously fitted for all the exigencies and emergencies of travel, that it might have been a section of the Nouveau Luxe on wheels; and the figure next to him, on the extreme other side of the deeply upholstered seat, was that of Anderson Brant. This, for the moment, was as far as Campton's dazed perceptions carried him . . .

The motor was among real fields and orchards, and the icy half-light which might just as well have been dusk was turning definitely to dawn, when at last, disentangling his mind from a tight coil of passport and permit problems, he thought: "But this is the road north of Paris—that must have been St. Denis."

Among all the multiplied strangenesses of the last strange hours it had hardly struck him before that, now he was finally on his way to George, it was not to the Argonne that he was going, but in the opposite direction. The discovery held his floating mind for a moment, but for a moment only, before it drifted away again, to be caught on some other projecting strangeness.

Chief among these was Mr. Brant's presence at his side, and the fact that the motor they were sitting in was Mr. Brant's. But Campton felt that such enormities were not to be dealt with yet. He had neither slept nor eaten since the morning before, and whenever he tried to grasp the situation in its entirety his spirit fainted away again into outer darkness . . .

His companion presently coughed, and said, in a voice even more than usually colourless and expressionless: "We are at Luzarches already."

It was the first time, Campton was sure, that Mr. Brant had spoken since they had got into the car together, hours earlier as it seemed to him, in the dark street before the studio in Montmartre; the first, at least, except to ask, as the chauffeur touched the self-starter: "Will you have the rug over you?"

The two travellers did not share a rug: a separate one, soft as fur and light as down, lay neatly folded on the grey carpet before each seat; but Campton, though the early air was biting, had left his where it lay, and had not answered.

Now he was beginning to feel that he could not decently remain silent any longer; and with an effort which seemed as mechanical and external as the movements of the chauffeur whose back he viewed through the wide single sheet of plate-glass, he brought out, like a far-off echo: "Luzarches . . . ?"

It was not that there lingered in him any of his old sense of antipathy toward Mr. Brant. In the new world into which he had been abruptly hurled, the previous morning, by the coming of that letter which looked so exactly like any other letter—in this new world Mr. Brant was nothing more than the possessor of the motor and of the "pull" that were to get him, Campton, in the shortest possible time, to the spot of earth where his son lay dying. Once assured of this, Campton had promptly and indifferently acquiesced in Miss Anthony's hurried suggestion that it would be only decent to let Mr. Brant go to Doullens with him.

But the exchange of speech with any one, whether Mr. Brant or another, was for the time being manifestly impossible. The effort, to Campton, to rise out of his grief, was like that of a dying person struggling back from regions too remote for his voice to reach the ears of the living. He shrank into his corner, and tried once more to fix his attention on the flying landscape.

All that he saw in it, speeding ahead of him even faster than their own flight, was the ghostly vision of another motor, carrying a figure bowed like his, mute like his: the figure of Fortin-Lescluze, as he had seen it plunge away into the winter darkness after the physician's son had been killed. Campton remembered asking himself then, as he had asked himself so often since: "How should I bear it if it happened to me?"

He knew the answer to that now, as he knew everything else a man could know: so it had seemed to his astonished soul since the truth had flashed at him out of that fatal letter. Ever since then he had been turning about and about in a vast glare of initiation: of all the old crowded misty world which the letter had emptied at a stroke, nothing remained but a few memories of George's boyhood, like a closet of toys in a house knocked down by an earthquake.

The vision of Fortin-Lescluze's motor vanished, and in its place Campton suddenly saw Boylston's screwed-up eyes staring out at him under furrows of anguish. Campton remembered, the evening before, pushing the letter over to him across the office table, and stammering: "Read it—read it to me. I can't——" and Boylston's sudden sobbing explosion: "But I *knew*, sir—I've known all along . . ." and then the endless pause before Campton gathered himself up to falter out (like a child deciphering the words in a primer): "You *knew*—knew that George was wounded?"

"No, no, not that; but that he might be—oh, at any minute! Forgive me—oh, do forgive me! He wouldn't let me tell you that he was at the front," Boylston had faltered through his sobs.

"Let you tell me——?"

"You and his mother: he refused a citation last March so that you shouldn't find out that he'd exchanged into an infantry regiment. He was determined to from the first. He's been fighting for months; he's been magnificent; he got away from the Argonne last February; but you were none of you to know."

"But why—why—why?" Campton had flashed out; then his heart stood still, and he awaited the answer with lowered head.

"Well, you see, he was afraid: afraid you might prevent . . . use your influence . . . you and Mrs. Brant . . ."

Campton looked up again, challenging the other. "He imagined perhaps that we *had*—in the beginning?"

"Oh, yes"—Boylston was perfectly calm about it—"he knew all about that. And he made us swear not to speak; Miss Anthony and me. Miss Anthony knew . . . If this thing happened," Boylston ended in a stricken voice, "you were not to be unfair to her, he said."

Over and over again that short dialogue distilled itself syllable by syllable, pang by pang, into Campton's cowering soul. He had had to learn all this, this overwhelming unbelievable truth about his son; and at the same instant to learn that that son was grievously wounded, perhaps dying (what else, in such circumstances, did the giving of the Legion of Honour ever mean?); and to deal with it all in the wild minutes of preparation for departure, of intercession with the authorities, sittings at the photographer's, and a crisscross of confused telephone-calls from the Embassy, the Préfecture and the War Office.

From this welter of images Miss Anthony's face next detached itself: white and withered, yet with a look which triumphed over its own ruin, and over Campton's wrath.

"Ah—you knew too, did you? You were his other confidant? How you all kept it up—how you all lied to us!" Campton had burst out at her.

She took it firmly. "I showed you his letters."

"Yes: the letters he wrote to you to be shown."

She received this in silence, and he followed it up. "It was you who drove him to the front—it was you who sent my son to his death!"

Without flinching, she gazed back at him. "Oh, John—it was you!"

"I—I? What do you mean? I never as much as lifted a finger——"

"No?" She gave him a wan smile. "Then it must have been the old man who invented the Mangle!" she cried, and cast herself on Campton's breast. He held her there for a long moment, stroking her lank hair, and saying "Adele—Adele," because in that rush of understanding he could not think of anything else to say. At length he stooped and laid on her lips the strangest kiss he had ever given or taken; and it was then that, drawing back, she exclaimed: "That's for George, when you get to him. Remember!"

The image of George's mother rose last on the whirling ground of Campton's thoughts: an uncertain image, blurred by distance, indistinct as some wraith of Mme. Olida's evoking.

Mrs. Brant was still at Biarritz; there had been no possibility of her getting back in time to share the journey to the front. Even Mr. Brant's power in high places must have fallen short of such an attempt; and it was not made. Boylston, despatched in haste to bear the news of George's wounding to the banker, had reported that the utmost Mr. Brant could do was to write at once to his wife, and arrange for her return to Paris, since telegrams to the frontier departments travelled more slowly than letters, and in nine cases out of ten were delayed indefinitely. Campton had asked no more at the time; but in the last moment before leaving Paris he remembered having said to Adele Anthony: "You'll be there when Julia comes?" and Miss Anthony had nodded back: "At the station."

The word, it appeared, roused the same memory in both of them; meeting her eyes, he saw there the Gare de l'Est in the summer morning, the noisily manœuvring trains jammed with bright young heads, the flowers, the waving handkerchiefs, and everybody on the platform smiling fixedly till some particular carriage-window slid out of sight. The scene, at the time, had been a vast blur to Campton: would he ever again, he wondered, see anything as clearly as he saw it now, in all its unmerciful distinctness? He heard the sobs of the girl who had said such a blithe goodbye to the young *Chasseur Alpin*, he saw her going away, led by her elderly companion, and powdering her nose at the *laiterie* over the cup of coffee she could not swallow. And this was what her sobs had meant . . .

"This place," said Mr. Brant, with his usual preliminary cough, "must be——" He bent over a motor-map, trying to decipher the name; but after fumbling for his eye-glasses, and rubbing them with a beautifully monogrammed cambric handkerchief, he folded the map up again and slipped it into one of the many pockets which honeycombed the interior of the car. Campton recalled the deathlike neatness of the banker's private office on the day when the one spot of disorder in it had been the torn telegram announcing Benny Upsher's disappearance.

The motor lowered its speed to make way for a long train of army lorries. Close upon them clattered a file of gun-wagons, with unshaven soldiers bestriding the gaunt horses. Torpedo-cars carrying officers slipped cleverly in and out of the tangle, and motor-cycles, incessantly rushing by, peppered the air with their explosions.

"This is the sort of thing he's been living in—living in for months and months," Campton mused.

He himself had seen something of the same kind when he had gone to Châlons in the early days to appeal to Fortin-Lescluze; but at that time the dread significance of the machinery of war had passed almost unnoticed in his preoccupation about his boy. Now he realized that for a year that machinery had been the setting of his boy's life; for months past such sights and sounds as these had formed the whole of George's world; and Campton's eyes took in every detail with an agonized avidity.

"What's that?" he exclaimed.

A huge continuous roar, seeming to fall from the low clouds above them, silenced the puny rumble and clatter of the road. On and on it went, in a slow pulsating rhythm, like the boom of waves driven by a gale on some far-distant coast.

"That? The guns——" said Mr. Brant.

"At the front?"

"Oh, sometimes they seem much nearer. Depends on the wind."

Campton sat bewildered. Had he ever before heard that sinister roar? At Châlons? He could not be sure. But the sound had assuredly not been the same; now it overwhelmed him like the crash of the sea over a drowning head. He cowered back in his corner. Would it ever stop, he asked himself? Or was it always like this, day and night, in the hell of hells that they were bound for? Was that merciless thud forever in the ears of the dying?

A sentinel stopped the motor and asked for their pass. He turned it about and about, holding it upside-down in his horny hands, and wrinkling his brows in the effort to decipher the inverted characters.

"How can I tell——?" he grumbled doubtfully, looking from the faces of the two travellers to their unrecognizable photographs.

Mr. Brant was already feeling for his pocket, and furtively extracting a bank-note.

"For God's sake—not that!" Campton cried, bringing his hand down on the banker's. Leaning over, he spoke to the sentinel. "My son's dying at the front. Can't you see it when you look at me?"

The man looked, and slowly gave back the paper. "You can pass," he said, shouldering his rifle.

The motor shot on, and the two men drew back into their corners. Mr. Brant fidgeted with his eye-glasses, and after an interval coughed again. "I must thank you," he began, "for—for saving me just now from an inexcusable blunder. It was done mechanically . . . one gets into the habit . . ."

"Quite so," said Campton drily. "But there are cases——"

"Of course—of course."

Silence fell once more. Mr. Brant sat bolt upright, his profile detached against the wintry fields. Campton, sunk into his corner, glanced now and then at the neat grey silhouette, in which the perpendicular glint of the eye-glass nearest him was the only point of light. He said to himself that the man was no doubt suffering horribly; but he was not conscious of any impulse of compassion. He and Mr. Brant were like two strangers pinned down together in a railway-smash: the shared agony did not bring them nearer. On the contrary, Campton, as the hours passed, felt himself more and more exasperated by the mute anguish at his side. What right had this man to be suffering as he himself was suffering, what right to be here with him at all? It was simply in the exercise of what the banker called his "habit"—the habit of paying, of buying everything, people and privileges and possessions—that he had acquired this ghastly claim to share in an agony which was not his.

"I shan't even have my boy to myself on his deathbed," the father thought in desperation; and the mute presence at his side became once more the symbol of his own failure.

The motor, with frequent halts, continued to crawl slowly on between lorries, field-kitchens, artillery wagons, companies of haggard infantry returning to their cantonments, and more and more vanloads of troops pressing forward; it seemed to Campton that hours elapsed before Mr. Brant again spoke.

"This must be Amiens," he said, in a voice even lower than usual.

The father roused himself and looked out. They were passing through the streets of a town swarming with troops—but he was still barely conscious of what he looked at. He perceived that he had been half-asleep, and dreaming of George as a little boy, when he used to have such bad colds. Campton remembered in particular the day he had found the lad in bed, in a scarlet sweater, in his luxurious overheated room, reading the first edition of Lavengro. It was on that day that he and his son had first really got to know each other; but what was it that had marked the date to George? The fact that Mr. Brant, learning of his joy in the book, had instantly presented it to him—with the price-label left inside the cover.

"And it'll be worth a lot more than that by the time you're grown up," Mr. Brant had told his step-son; to which George was recorded to have answered sturdily: "No, it won't, if I find other stories I like better."

Miss Anthony had assisted at the conversation and reported it triumphantly to Campton; but the painter, who had to save up to give his boy even a simple present, could see in the incident only one more attempt to rob him of his rights. "They won't succeed, though, they won't succeed: they don't know how to go about it, thank the Lord," he had said.

But they had succeeded after all; what better proof of it was there than Mr. Brant's tacit right to be sitting here beside him to-day; than the fact that but for Mr. Brant it might have been impossible for Campton to get to his boy's side in time?

Oh, that pitiless incessant hammering of the guns! As the travellers advanced the noise grew louder, fiercer, more unbroken; the closely-fitted panes of the car rattled and danced like those of an old omnibus. Sentinels stopped the chauffeur more frequently; Mr. Brant had to produce the blue paper again and again. The day was wearing on—Campton began again to be aware of a sick weariness, a growing remoteness and confusion of mind. Through it he perceived that Mr. Brant, diving into deeper recesses of upholstery, had brought out a silver sandwich-box, a flask and glasses. As by magic they stood on a shiny shelf which slid out of another recess, and Mr. Brant was proffering the box. "It's a long way yet; you'll need all your strength," he said.

Campton, who had half turned from the invitation, seized a sandwich and emptied one of the glasses. Mr. Brant was right; he must not let himself float away into the void, seductive as its drowsy shimmer was.

His wits returned, and with them a more intolerable sense of reality. He was all alive now. Every crash of the guns seemed to tear a piece of flesh from his body; and it was always the piece nearest the heart. The nurse's few lines had said: "A shell wound: the right arm fractured, fear for the lungs." And one of these awful crashes had done it: bursting in mystery from that innocent-looking sky, and rushing inoffensively over hundreds of other young men till it reached its destined prey, found George, and dug a red grave for him. Campton was convinced

now that his son was dead. It was not only that he had received
the Legion of Honour; it was the appalling all-destroying thun-
der of the shells as they went on crashing and bursting. What
could they leave behind them but mismated fragments? Gathering up all his strength in the effort not to recoil from the vision,
Campton saw his son's beautiful body like a carcass tumbled out
of a butcher's cart . . .

"Doullens," said Mr. Brant.

They were in a town, and the motor had turned into the
court of a great barrack-like building. Before them stood a line
of empty stretchers such as Campton had seen at Châlons. A
young doctor in a cotton blouse was lighting a cigarette and
laughing with a nurse—laughing! At regular intervals the can-
nonade shook the windows; it seemed the heart-beat of the
place. Campton noticed that many of the window-panes had
been broken, and patched with paper.

Inside they found another official, who called to another
nurse as she passed by laden with fresh towels. She disappeared
into a room where heaps of bloody linen were being stacked into
baskets, returned, looked at Campton and nodded. He looked
back at her blunt tired features and kindly eyes, and said to
himself that they had perhaps been his son's last sight on earth.

The nurse smiled.

"It's three flights up," she said; "he'll be glad."

Glad! He was not dead, then; he could even be glad! In the
staggering rush of relief the father turned instinctively to Mr.
Brant; he felt that there was enough joy to be shared. But Mr.
Brant, though he must have heard what the nurse had said, was
moving away; he did not seem to understand.

"This way——" Campton called after him, pointing to the
nurse, who was already on the first step of the stairs.

Mr. Brant looked slightly puzzled; then, as the other's meaning reached him, he coloured a little, bent his head stiffly, and
waved his stick toward the door.

"Thanks," he said, "I think I'll take a stroll first . . . stretch my
legs . . ." and Campton, with a rush of gratitude, understood
that he was to be left alone with his son.

Chapter XXV

H E followed his guide up the steep flights, which seemed to become buoyant and lift him like waves. It was as if the muscle that always dragged back his lame leg had suddenly regained its elasticity. He floated up as one mounts stairs in a dream. A smell of disinfectants hung in the cold air, and once, through a half-open door, a sickening odour came: he remembered it at Châlons, and Fortin's murmured: "Gangrene—ah, if only we could get them sooner!"

How soon had they got *his* boy, Campton wondered? The letter, mercifully sent by hand to Paris, had reached him on the third day after George's arrival at the Doullens hospital; but he did not yet know how long before that the shell-splinter had done its work. The nurse did not know either. How could she remember? They had so many! The administrator would look up the files and tell him. Only there was no time for that now.

On a landing Campton heard a babble and scream: a nauseating scream in a queer bleached voice that might have been man, woman or monkey's. Perhaps that was what the French meant by "a white voice": this voice which was as featureless as some of the poor men's obliterated faces! Campton shot an anguished look at his companion, and she understood and shook her head. "Oh, no: that's in the big ward. It's the way they scream after a dressing . . ."

She opened a door, and he was in a room with three beds in it, wooden pallets hastily knocked together and spread with rough grey blankets. In spite of the cold, flies still swarmed on the unwashed panes, and there were big holes in the fly-net over the bed nearest the window. Under the net lay a middle-aged bearded man, heavily bandaged about the chest and left arm: he was snoring, his mouth open, his gaunt cheeks drawn in with the fight for breath. Campton said to himself that if his own boy lived he should like some day to do something for this poor devil who was his roommate. Then he looked about him and saw that the two other beds were empty.

He drew back.

The nurse was bending over the bearded man. "He'll wake presently—I'll leave you"; and she slipped out. Campton looked again at the stranger; then his glance travelled to the scarred brown hand on the sheet, a hand with broken nails and blackened finger-tips. It was George's hand, his son's, swollen, disfigured but unmistakable. The father knelt down and laid his lips on it.

"What was the first thing you felt?" Adele Anthony asked him afterward: and he answered: "Nothing."

"Yes—at the very first, I know: it's always like that. But the first thing *after* you began to feel anything?"

He considered, and then said slowly: "The difference."

"The difference in *him*?"

"In him—in life—in everything."

Miss Anthony, who understood as a rule, was evidently puzzled. "What kind of a difference?"

"Oh, a complete difference." With that she had to be content.

The sense of it had first come to Campton when the bearded man, raising his lids, looked at him from far off with George's eyes, and touched him, very feebly, with George's hand. It was in the moment of identifying his son that he felt the son he had known to be lost to him forever.

George's lips were moving, and the father laid his ear to them; perhaps these were last words that his boy was saying.

"Old Dad—in a motor?"

Campton nodded.

The fact seemed faintly to interest George, who continued to examine him with those distant eyes.

"Uncle Andy's?"

Campton nodded again.

"Mother——?"

"She's coming too—very soon."

George's lips were screwed into a whimsical smile. "I must have a shave first," he said, and drowsed off again, his hand in Campton's . . .

"The other gentleman—?" the nurse questioned the next morning.

Campton had spent the night in the hospital, stretched on the floor at his son's threshold. It was a breach of rules, but for once the major had condoned it. As for Mr. Brant, Campton had forgotten all about him, and at first did not know what the nurse meant. Then he woke with a start to the consciousness of his fellow-traveller's nearness. Mr. Brant, the nurse explained, had come to the hospital early, and had been waiting below for the last two hours. Campton, almost as gaunt and unshorn as his son, pulled himself to his feet and went down. In the hall the banker, very white, but smooth and trim as ever, was patiently measuring the muddy flags.

"Less temperature this morning," Campton called from the last flight.

"Oh," stammered Mr. Brant, red and pale by turns.

Campton smiled haggardly and pulled himself together in an effort of communicativeness. "Look here—he's asked for you; you'd better go up. Only for a few minutes, please; he's awfully weak."

Mr. Brant, speechless, stood stiffly waiting to be conducted. Campton noticed the mist in his eyes, and took pity on him.

"I say—where's the hotel? Just a step away? I'll go around, then, and get a shave and a wash while you're with him," the father said, with a magnanimity which he somehow felt the powers might take account of in their subsequent dealings with George. If the boy was to live Campton could afford to be generous; and he had decided to assume that the boy would live, and to order his behaviour accordingly.

"I—thank you," said Mr. Brant, turning toward the stairs.

"Five minutes at the outside!" Campton cautioned him, and hurried out into the morning air through which the guns still crashed methodically.

When he got back to the hospital, refreshed and decent, he was surprised, and for a moment alarmed, to find that Mr. Brant had not come down.

"Sending up his temperature, of course—damn him!" Campton raged, scrambling up the stairs as fast as his stiff leg permitted. But outside of George's door he saw a small figure patiently mounting guard.

"I stayed with him less than five minutes; I was merely waiting to thank you."

"Oh, that's all right." Campton paused, and then made his supreme effort. "How does he strike you?"

"Hopefully—hopefully. He had his joke as usual," Mr. Brant said with a twitching smile.

"Oh, *that*——! But his temperature's decidedly lower. Of course they may have to take the ball out of the lung; but perhaps before they do it he can be moved from this hell."

The two men were silent, the same passion of anxiety consuming them, and no means left of communicating it to each other.

"I'll look in again later. Shall I have something to eat sent round to you from the hotel?" Mr. Brant suggested.

"Oh, thanks—if you would."

Campton put out his hand and crushed Mr. Brant's dry fingers. But for this man he might not have got to his son in time; and this man had not once made use of the fact to press his own claim on George. With pity in his heart, the father, privileged to remain at his son's bedside, watched Mr. Brant's small figure retreating alone. How ghastly to sit all day in that squalid hotel, his eyes on his watch, with nothing to do but to wonder and wonder about the temperature of another man's son!

The next day was worse; so much worse that everything disappeared from Campton's view but the present agony of watching, hovering, hanging helplessly on the words of nurse and doctor, and spying on the glances they exchanged behind his back.

There could be no thought yet of extracting the bullet; a great surgeon, passing through the wards on a hasty tour of inspection, had confirmed this verdict. Oh, to have kept the surgeon there—to have had him at hand to watch for the propitious moment and seize it without an instant's delay! Suddenly the vision which to Campton had been among the most hideous of all his crowding nightmares—that of George stretched naked on an operating-table, his face hidden by a chloroform mask, and an orderly hurrying away with a pile of red towels like those perpetually carried through the passages below—this vision became to the father's fevered mind as soothing as a glimpse of Paradise. If only George's temperature would go down—if only the doctors would pronounce him strong enough to have the bullet taken out! What would anything else matter then? Campton would feel as safe as he used to years ago, when after the recurring months of separation the boy came back from school, and he could take him in his arms and make sure that he was the same Geordie, only bigger, browner, with thicker curlier hair, and tougher muscles under his jacket.

What if the great surgeon, on his way back from the front, were to pass through the town again that evening, reverse his verdict, and perhaps even perform the operation then and there? Was there no way of prevailing on him to stop and take another look at George on the return? The idea took immediate possession of Campton, crowding out his intolerable anguish, and bringing such relief that for a few seconds he felt as if some life-saving operation had been performed on himself. As he stood watching the great man's retreat, followed by doctors and nurses, Mr. Brant suddenly touched his arm, and the eyes of the two met. Campton understood and gasped out: "Yes, yes; we must manage to get him back."

Mr. Brant nodded. "At all costs." He paused, again interrogated Campton's eyes, and stammered: "You authorize——?"

"Oh, God—anything!"

"He's dined at my house in Paris," Mr. Brant threw in, as if trying to justify himself.

"Oh, go—*go!*" Campton almost pushed him down the stairs. Ten minutes later he reappeared, modest but exultant.

"Well?"

"He wouldn't commit himself, before the others——"

"Oh——"

"But to me, as he was getting into the motor——"

"Well?"

"Yes: if possible. Somewhere about midnight."

Campton turned away, choking, and stumped off toward the tall window at the end of the passage. Below him lay the court. A line of stretchers was being carried across it, not empty this time, but each one with a bloody burden. Doctors, nurses, orderlies hurried to and fro. Drub, drub, drub, went the guns, shaking the windows, rolling their fierce din along the cloudy sky, down the corridors of the hospital and the pavement of the streets, like huge bowls crashing through story above story of a kind of sky-scraping bowling alley.

"Even the dead underground must hear them!" Campton muttered.

The word made him shudder superstitiously, and he crept back to George's door and opened it; but the nurse, within, shook her head.

"He must sleep after the examination. Better go."

Campton turned and saw Mr. Brant waiting. A bell rang twelve. The two, in silence, walked down the stairs, crossed the court (averting their eyes from the stretchers) and went to the hotel to get something to eat.

Midnight came. It passed. No one in the hurried confused world of the hospital had heard of the possibility of the surgeon's returning. When Campton mentioned it to the nurse she smiled her tired smile, and said: "He could have done nothing."

Done nothing! How could she know? How could any one, but the surgeon himself? Would he have promised if he had not thought there was some chance? Campton, stretched out on a blanket and his rolled-up coat, lay through the long restless hours staring at the moonlit sky framed by the window of the corridor. Great clouds swept over that cold indifferent vault: they seemed like the smoke from the guns which had not once ceased through the night. At last he got up, turned his back on the window, and lay down again facing the stairs. The moonlight unrolled a white strip along the stone floor. A church-bell rang one . . . two . . . there were noises and movements below. Campton raised himself, his heart beating all over his body. Steps came echoing up.

"Careful!" some one called. A stretcher rounded the stair-rail; another, and then another. An orderly with a lantern preceded them, followed by one of the doctors, an old bunched-up man in a muddy uniform, who stopped furtively to take a pinch of snuff. Campton could not believe his eyes; didn't the hospital people know that every bed on that floor was full? Every bed, that is, but the two in George's room; and the nurse had given Campton the hope, the promise almost, that as long as his boy was so ill she would keep those empty. "I'll manage somehow," she had said.

For a mad moment Campton was on the point of throwing himself in the way of the tragic procession, barring the

threshold with his arms. "What does this mean?" he stammered
to the nurse, who had appeared from another room with her
little lamp.

She gave a shrug. "More casualties—every hospital is like
this."

He stood aside, wrathful, impotent. At least if Brant had been
there, perhaps by some offer of money—but how, to whom?
Of what earthly use, after all, was Brant's boasted "influence"?
These people would only laugh at him—perhaps put them both
out of the hospital!

He turned despairingly to the nurse. "You might as well have
left him in the trenches."

"Don't say that, sir," she answered; and the echo of his own
words horrified him like a sacrilege.

Two of the stretchers were carried into George's room.
Campton caught a glimpse of George, muttering and tossing;
the moonlight lay in the hollows of his bearded face, and again
the father had the sense of utter alienation from that dark delirious man who for brief intervals suddenly became his son, and
then as suddenly wandered off into strangeness.

The nurse slipped out of the room and signed to him.

"Both nearly gone . . . they won't trouble him long," she
whispered.

The man on the third stretcher was taken to a room at the
other end of the corridor. Campton watched him being lifted
in. He was to lie on the floor, then? For in that room there
was certainly no vacancy. But presently he had the answer. The
bearers did not come out empty-handed; they carried another
man whom they laid on the empty stretcher. Lucky, lucky devil;
going, no doubt, to a hospital at the rear! As the procession
reached the stairs the lantern swung above the lucky devil's face:
his eyes stared ceilingward from black orbits. One arm, swinging loose, dangled down, the hand stealthily counting the steps
as he descended—and no one troubled, for he was dead.

At dawn Campton, who must have been asleep, started up,
again hearing steps. The surgeon? Oh, if this time it were the
surgeon! But only Mr. Brant detached himself from the shadows accumulated in the long corridor: Mr. Brant, crumpled and
unshorn, with blood-shot eyes, and gloves on his unconscious
hands.

Campton glared at him resentfully.

"Well—how about your surgeon? I don't see him!" he exclaimed.

Mr. Brant shook his head despondently. "No—I've been waiting all night in the court. I thought if he came back I should be the first to catch him. But he has just sent his orderly for instruments; he's not coming. There's been terrible fighting——"

Campton saw two tears running down Mr. Brant's face: they did not move him.

The banker glanced toward George's door, full of the question he dared not put.

Campton answered it. "You want to know how he is? Well, how should he be, with that bullet in him, and the fever eating him inch by inch, and two more wounded men in his room? *That's* how he is!" Campton almost shouted.

Mr. Brant was trembling all over.

"Two more men—in his room?" he echoed shrilly.

"Yes—bad cases; dying." Campton drew a deep breath. "You see there are times when your money and your influence and your knowing everybody are no more use than so much sawdust——"

The nurse opened the door and looked out. "You're talking too loudly," she said.

She shut the door, and the two men stood silent, abashed; finally Mr. Brant turned away. "I'll go and try again. There must be other surgeons . . . other ways . . ." he whispered.

"Oh, your surgeons . . . oh, your ways!" Campton sneered after him, in the same whisper.

Chapter XXVI

From the room where he sat at the foot of George's glossy white bed, Campton, through the open door, could watch the November sun slanting down a white ward where, in the lane between other white beds, pots of chrysanthemums stood on white-covered tables.

Through the window his eyes rested incredulously on a court enclosed in monastic arches of grey stone, with squares of turf bordered by box hedges, and a fountain playing. Beyond the court sloped the faded foliage of a park not yet entirely stripped by Channel gales; and on days without wind, instead of the boom of the guns, the roar of the sea came faintly over intervening heights and hollows.

Campton's ears were even more incredulous than his eyes. He was gradually coming to believe in George's white room, the ward beyond, the flowers between the beds, the fountain in the court; but the sound of the sea still came to him, intolerably but unescapably, as the crash of guns. When the impression was too overwhelming he would turn away from the window and cast his glance on the bed; but only to find that the smooth young face on the pillow had suddenly changed into that of the haggard bearded stranger on the wooden pallet at Doullens. And Campton would have to get up, lean over, and catch the twinkle in George's eyes before the evil spell was broken.

Few words passed between them. George, after all these days, was still too weak for much talk; and silence had always been Campton's escape from feeling. He never had the need to speak in times of inward stress, unless it were to vent his anger—as in that hateful scene at Doullens between himself and Mr. Brant. But he was sure that George always knew what was passing through his mind; that when the sea boomed their thoughts flew back together to that other scene, but a few miles and a few days distant, yet already as far off, as much an affair they were both rid of, as a nightmare to a wakened sleeper; and that for a moment the same vision clutched them both, mocking their attempts at indifference.

Not that the sound, to Campton at any rate, suggested any abstract conception of war. Looking back afterward at this phase of his life he perceived that at no time had he thought so little of the war. The noise of the sea was to him simply the voice of the engine which had so nearly destroyed his son: that association, deeply imbedded in his half-dazed consciousness, left no room for others.

The general impression of unreality was enhanced by his not having yet been able to learn the details of George's wounding. After a week during which the boy had hung near death, the great surgeon—returning to Doullens just as Campton had finally ceased to hope for him—had announced that, though George's state was still grave, he might be moved to a hospital at the rear. So one day, miraculously, the perilous transfer had been made, in one of Mrs. Brant's own motor-ambulances; and for a week now George had lain in his white bed, hung over by white-gowned Sisters, in an atmosphere of sweetness and order which almost made it seem as if he were a child recovering from illness in his own nursery, or a red-haired baby sparring with dimpled fists at a new world.

In truth, Campton found his son as hard to get at as a baby; he looked at his father with eyes as void of experience, or at least of any means of conveying it. Campton, at first, could only marvel and wait; and the isolation in which the two were enclosed by George's weakness, and by his father's inability to learn from others what the boy was not yet able to tell him, gave a strange remoteness to everything but the things which count in an infant's world: food, warmth, sleep. Campton's nearest approach to reality was his daily scrutiny of the temperature-chart. He studied it as he used to study the *communiqués* which he now no longer even thought of.

Sometimes when George was asleep Campton would sit pondering on the days at Doullens. There was an exquisite joy in silently building up, on that foundation of darkness and anguish, the walls of peace that now surrounded him, a structure so transparent that one could peer through it at the routed Furies, yet so impenetrable that he sat there in a kind of god-like aloofness. For one thing he was especially thankful—and that was the conclusion of his unseemly wrangle with Mr. Brant; thankful that, almost at once, he had hurried after the banker, caught up with him, and stammered out, clutching his hand: "I know—I know how you feel."

Mr. Brant's reactions were never rapid, and the events of the preceding days had called upon faculties that were almost atrophied. He had merely looked at Campton in mute distress, returned his pressure, and silently remounted the hospital stairs with him.

Campton hated himself for his ill-temper, but was glad, even at the time, that no interested motive had prompted his apology. He should have hated himself even more if he had asked the banker's pardon because of Mr. Brant's "pull," and the uses to which it might be put; or even if he had associated his excuses with any past motives of gratitude, such as the fact that but for Mr. Brant he might never have reached George's side. Instead of that, he simply felt that once more his senseless violence had got the better of him, and he was sorry that he had behaved like a brute to a man who loved George, and was suffering almost as much as he was at the thought that George might die . . .

After that episode, and Campton's apology, the relations of the two men became so easy that each gradually came to take the other for granted; and Mr. Brant, relieved of a perpetual hostile scrutiny, was free to exercise his ingenuity in planning and managing. It was owing to him—Campton no longer minded admitting it—that the famous surgeon had hastened his return to Doullens, that George's translation to the sweet monastic building near the sea had been so rapidly effected, and that the great man, appearing there soon afterward, had extracted the bullet with his own hand. But for Mr. Brant's persistence even the leave to bring one of Mrs. Brant's motor-ambulances to Doullens would never have been given; and it might have been fatal to George to make the journey in a slow and jolting military train. But for Mr. Brant, again, he would have been sent to a crowded military hospital instead of being brought to this white heaven of rest. "And all that just because I overtook him in time to prevent his jumping into his motor and going back to Paris in order to get out of my way!" Campton, at the thought, lowered his spirit into new depths of contrition.

George, who had been asleep, opened his eyes and looked at his father.

"Where's Uncle Andy?"

"Gone to Paris to get your mother."

"Yes. Of course. He told me——"

George smiled, and withdrew once more into his secret world.

But Campton's state of mind was less happy. As the time of Julia's arrival approached he began to ask himself with increasing apprehension how she would fit into the situation. Mr. Brant *had* fitted into it—perfectly. Campton had actually begun to feel a secret dependence on him, a fidgety uneasiness since he had left for Paris, sweet though it was to be alone with George. But Julia—what might she not do and say to unsettle things, break the spell, agitate and unnerve them all? Campton did not question her love for her son; but he was not sure what form it would take in conditions to which she was so unsuited. How could she ever penetrate into the mystery of peace which enclosed him and his boy? And if she felt them thus mysteriously shut off would she not dimly resent her exclusion? If only Adele Anthony had been coming too! Campton had urged Mr. Brant to bring her; but the banker had failed to obtain a permit for any one but the boy's mother. He had even found it difficult to get his own leave renewed; it was only after a first trip to Paris, and repeated efforts at the War Office, that he had been allowed to go to Paris and fetch his wife, who was just arriving from Biarritz.

Well—for the moment, at any rate, Campton had the boy to himself. As he sat there, trying to picture the gradual resurrection of George's pre-war face out of the delicately pencilled white mask on the pillow, he noted the curious change of planes produced by suffering and emaciation, and the altered relation of lights and shadows. Materially speaking, the new George looked like the old one seen in the bowl of a spoon, and through blue spectacles: peaked, narrow, livid, with elongated nose and sunken eye-sockets. But these altered proportions were not what had really changed him. There was something in the curve of the mouth that fever and emaciation could not account for. In that new line, and in the look of his eyes—the look travelling slowly outward through a long blue tunnel, like some mysterious creature rising from the depths of the sea—that was where the new George lurked, the George to be watched and lain in wait for, patiently and slowly puzzled out . . .

He reopened his eyes.

"Adele too?"

Campton had learned to bridge over the spaces between the questions. "No; not this time. We tried, but it couldn't be managed. A little later, I hope——"

"She's all right?"

"Rather! Blooming."

"And Boylston?"

"Blooming too."

George's lids closed contentedly, like doors shutting him away from the world.

It was the first time since his operation that he had asked about any of his friends, or had appeared to think they might come to see him. But his mind, like his stomach, could receive very little nutriment at a time; he liked to have one mouthful given to him, and then to lie ruminating it in the lengthening intervals between his attacks of pain.

Each time he asked for news of any one his father wondered what name would next come to his lips. Even during his delirium he had mentioned no one but his parents, Mr. Brant, Adele Anthony and Boylston; yet it was not possible, Campton thought, that these formed the circumference of his life, that some contracted fold of memory did not hold a nearer image, a more secret name . . . The father's heart beat faster, half from curiosity, half from a kind of shy delicacy, at the thought that at any moment that name might wake in George and utter itself.

Campton's thoughts again turned to his wife. With Julia there was never any knowing. Ten to one she would send the boy's temperature up. He was thankful that, owing to the difficulty of getting the news to her, and then of bringing her back from a frontier department, so many days had had to elapse.

But when she arrived, nothing, after all, happened as he had expected. She had put on her nurse's dress for the journey (he thought it rather theatrical of her, till he remembered how much easier it was to get about in any sort of uniform); but there was not a trace of coquetry in her appearance. As a frame for her haggard unpowdered face the white coif looked harsh and unbecoming; she reminded him, as she got out of the motor, of some mortified Jansenist nun from one of Philippe de Champaigne's canvases.

Campton led her to George's door, but left her there; she did not appear to notice whether or not he was following her. He whispered: "Careful about his temperature; he's very weak," and she bent her profile silently as she went in.

Chapter XXVII

G EORGE, that evening, seemed rather better, and his temperature had not gone up: Campton had to repress a movement of jealousy at Julia's having done her son no harm. Her experience as a nurse, disciplining a vague gift for the sickroom, had developed in her the faculty of self-command: before the war, if George had met with a dangerous accident, she would have been more encumbering than helpful.

Campton had to admit the change, but it did not draw them any nearer. Her manner of loving their son was too different. Nowadays, when he and Anderson Brant were together, he felt that they were thinking of the same things in the same way; but Julia's face, even aged and humanized by grief, was still a mere mask to him. He could never tell what form her thoughts about George might be taking.

Mr. Brant, on his wife's arrival, had judged it discreet to efface himself. Campton hunted for him in vain in the park, and under the cloister; he remained invisible till they met at the early dinner which they shared with the staff. But the meal did not last long, and when it was over, and nurses and doctors scattered, Mr. Brant again slipped away, leaving his wife and Campton alone.

Campton glanced after him, surprised. "Why does he go?"

Mrs. Brant pursed her lips, evidently as much surprised by his question as he by her husband's withdrawal.

"I suppose he's going to bed—to be ready for his early start to-morrow."

"A start?"

She stared. "He's going back to Paris."

Campton was genuinely astonished. "Is he? I'm sorry."

"Oh——" She seemed unprepared for this. "After all, you must see—we can't very well . . . all three of us . . . especially with these nuns . . ."

"Oh, if it's only *that*——"

She did not take this up, and one of their usual silences followed. Campton was thinking that it was all nonsense about the nuns, and meditating on the advisability of going in pursuit of Mr. Brant to tell him so. He dreaded the prospect of a long succession of days alone between George and George's mother.

Mrs. Brant spoke again. "I was sorry to find that the Sisters have been kept on here. Are they much with George?"

"The Sisters? I don't know. The upper nurses are Red Cross, as you saw. But of course the others are about a good deal. What's wrong? They seem to me perfect."

She hesitated and coloured a little. "I don't want them to find out—about the Extreme Unction," she finally said.

Campton repeated her words blankly. He began to think that anxiety and fatigue had confused her mind.

She coloured more deeply. "Oh, I forgot—you don't know. I couldn't think of anything but George at first . . . and the whole thing is so painful to me . . . Where's my bag?"

She groped for her reticule, found it in the folds of the cloak she had kept about her shoulders, and fumbled in it with wrinkled jewelled fingers.

"Anderson hasn't spoken to you, then—spoken about Mrs. Talkett?" she asked suddenly.

"About Mrs. Talkett? Why should he? What on earth has happened?"

"Oh, I wouldn't see her myself . . . I couldn't . . . so he had to. She had to be thanked, of course . . . but it seems to me so dreadful, so very dreadful . . . *our* boy . . . that woman . . ."

Campton did not press her further. He sat dumbfounded, trying to take in what she was so obviously trying to communicate, and yet instinctively resisting the approach of the revelation he foresaw.

"George—*Mrs. Talkett*?" He forced himself to couple the two names, unnatural as their union seemed.

"I supposed you knew. Isn't it dreadful? A woman old enough——" She drew a letter from her bag.

He interrupted her. "Is that letter what you want to show me?"

"Yes. She insisted on Anderson's keeping it—for you. She said it belonged to us, I believe . . . It seems there was a promise—made the night before he was mobilised—that if anything happened he would get word to her . . . No thought of *us*!" She began to whimper.

Campton reached out for the letter. Mrs. Talkett—Madge Talkett and George! That was where the boy had gone then, that last night when his father, left alone at the Crillon, had been so hurt by his desertion! That was the name which, in his hours of vigil in the little white room, Campton had watched for on his son's lips, the name which, one day, sooner or later, he would have to hear them pronounce . . . How little he had thought, as he sat studying the mysterious beauty of George's face, what a commonplace secret it concealed!

The writing was not George's, but that of an unlettered French soldier. Campton, glancing at the signature, recalled it as that of his son's orderly, who had been slightly wounded in the same attack as George, and sent for twenty-four hours to the same hospital at Doullens. He had been at George's side when he fell, and with the simple directness often natural to his class in France he told the tale of his lieutenant's wounding, in circumstances which appeared to have given George great glory in the eyes of his men. They thought the wound mortal; but the orderly and a stretcher-bearer had managed to get the young man into the shelter of a little wood. The stretcher-bearer, it turned out, was a priest. He had at once applied the consecrated oil, and George, still conscious, had received it "with a beautiful smile"; then the orderly, thinking all was over, had hurried back to the fighting, and been wounded. The next day he too had been carried to Doullens; and there, after many enquiries, he had found his lieutenant in the same hospital, alive, but too ill to see him.

He had contrived, however, to see the nurse, and had learned from her that the doctors had not given up hope. With that he had to be content; but before returning to his base he had hastened to fulfill his lieutenant's instructions (given "many months earlier") by writing to tell "his lady" that he was severely wounded, but still alive—"which is a good deal in itself," the orderly hopefully ended, "not to mention his receiving the Legion of Honour."

Campton laid the letter down. There was too much to be taken in all at once; and, as usual in moments of deep disturbance, he wanted to be alone, above all wanted to be away from Julia. But Julia held him with insistent eyes.

"Do you want this?" he asked finally, pushing the letter toward her.

She recoiled. "Want it? A letter written to that woman? No! I should have returned it at once—but Anderson wouldn't let me . . . Think of her forcing herself upon me as she did—and making you paint her portrait! I see it all now. Had you any idea this was going on?"

Campton shook his head, and perceived by her look of relief that what she had resented above all was the thought of his being in a secret of George's from which she herself was excluded.

"Adele didn't know either," she said, with evident satisfaction. Campton remembered that he had been struck by Miss Anthony's look of sincerity when he had asked her if she had any idea where George had spent his last evening, and she had answered negatively. This recollection made him understand Mrs. Brant's feeling of relief.

"Perhaps, after all, it's only a flirtation—a mere sentimental friendship," he hazarded.

"A flirtation?" Mrs. Brant's Mater Dolorosa face suddenly sharpened to worldly astuteness. "A sentimental friendship? Have you ever heard George mention her name—or make any sort of allusion to such a friendship?"

Campton considered. "No. I don't remember his ever speaking of her."

"Well, then——" Her eyes had the irritated look he had seen on the far-off day when he had thrown Beausite's dinner invitation into the fire. Once more, they seemed to say, she had taken the measure of his worldly wisdom.

George's silence—his care not even to mention that the Talketts were so much as known to him—certainly made it look as though the matter went deep with him. Campton, recalling the tone of the Talkett drawing-room and its familiars, had an even stronger recoil of indignation than Julia's; but he was silenced by a dread of tampering with his son's privacy, a sense of the sacredness of everything pertaining to that still-mysterious figure in the white bed upstairs.

Mrs. Brant's face had clouded again. "It's all so dreadful—and this Extreme Unction too! What is it exactly, do you know? A sort of baptism? Will the Roman Church try to get hold of him on the strength of it?"

Campton remembered with a faint inward amusement that, in spite of her foreign bringing-up, and all her continental affinities, Julia had remained as implacably and incuriously Protestant as if all her life she had heard the Scarlet Woman denounced from Presbyterian pulpits. At another time it would have amused him to ponder on this one streak in her of the ancestral iron; but now he wanted only to console her.

"Oh, no—it was just the accident of the priest's being there. One of our chaplains would have done the same kind of thing."

She looked at him mistrustfully. "The same kind of thing? It's never the same with them! Whatever they do reaches ahead. I've seen such advantage taken of the wounded when they were too weak to resist . . . didn't know what they were saying or doing . . ." Her eyes filled with tears. "A priest and a woman—I feel as if I'd lost my boy!"

The words went through Campton like a sword, and he sprang to his feet. "Oh, for God's sake be quiet—don't say it! What does anything matter but that he's alive?"

"Of course, of course . . . I didn't mean . . . But that he should think only of *her*, and not of us . . . that he should have deceived us . . . about everything . . . everything . . ."

"Ah, don't say that either! Don't tempt Providence! If he deceived us, as you call it, we've no one but ourselves to blame; you and I, and—well, and Brant. Didn't we all do our best to make him deceive us—with our intriguing and our wire-pulling and our cowardice? How he despised us for it—yes, thank God, how he despised us from the first! He didn't hide the truth from Boylston or Adele, because they were the only two on a level with him. And *they* knew why he'd deceived us; they understood him, they abetted him from the first." He stopped, checked by Mrs. Brant's pale bewildered face, and the eyes imploringly lifted, as if to ward off unintelligible words.

"Ah, well, all this is no use," he said; "we've got him safe, and it's more than we deserve." He laid his hand on her shoulder. "Go to bed; you're dead-beat. Only don't say things—things that might wake up the Furies . . ."

He pocketed the letter and went out in search of Mr. Brant, followed by her gaze of perplexity.

The latter was smoking a last cigar as he paced up and down the cloister with upturned coat-collar. Silence lay on the carefully darkened building, crouching low under an icy sea-fog; at intervals, through the hush, the waves continued to mimic the booming of the guns.

Campton drew out the orderly's letter. "I hear you're leaving to-morrow early, and I suppose I'd better give this back," he said.

Mr. Brant had evidently expected him. "Oh, thanks. But Mrs. Talkett says she has no right to it."

"No right to it? That's a queer thing to say."

"So I thought. I suppose she meant, till you'd seen it. She was dreadfully upset . . . till she saw me she'd supposed he was dead."

Campton shivered. "She sent this to your house?"

"Yes; the moment she got it. It was waiting there when my— when Julia arrived."

"And you went to thank her?"

"Yes." Mr. Brant hesitated. "Julia disliked to keep the letter. And I thought it only proper to take it back myself."

"Certainly. And—what was your impression?"

Mr. Brant hesitated again. He had already, Campton felt, reached the utmost limit of his power of communicativeness. It was against all his habits to "commit himself." Finally he said, in an unsteady voice: "It was impossible not to feel sorry for her."

"Did she say—er—anything special? Anything about herself and——"

"No; not a word. She was—well, all broken up, as they say."

"Poor thing!" Campton murmured.

"Yes—oh, yes!" Mr. Brant held the letter, turning it thoughtfully about. "It's a great thing," he began abruptly, as if the words were beyond his control, "to have such a beautiful account of the affair. George himself, of course, would never——"

"No, never." Campton considered. "You must take it back to her, naturally. But I should like to have a copy first."

Mr. Brant put a hand in his pocket. "I supposed you would. And I took the liberty of making two—oh, privately, of course. I hope you'll find my writing fairly legible." He drew two folded sheets from his note-case, and offered one to Campton.

"Oh, thank you." The two men grasped hands through the fog.

Mr. Brant turned to continue his round, and Campton went up to the white-washed cell in which he was lodged. Screening

his candle to keep the least light from leaking through the shutters, he re-read the story of George's wounding, copied out in
the cramped tremulous writing of a man who never took pen in
hand but to sign a daily batch of typed letters. The "hand-made"
copy of a letter by Mr. Brant represented something like the
pious toil expended by a monkish scribe on the page of a missal;
and Campton was moved by the little man's devotion.

As for the letter, Campton had no sooner begun to re-read it
than he entirely forgot that it was a message of love, addressed
at George's request to Mrs. Talkett, and saw in it only the record
of his son's bravery. And for the first time he understood that
from the moment of George's wounding until now he had never
really thought of him in relation to the war, never thought of
his judgment on the war, of all the unknown emotions, resolves
and actions which had drawn him so many months ago from his
safe shelter in the Argonne.

These things Campton, unconsciously, had put out of his
mind, or rather had lost out of his mind, from the moment
when he had heard of George's wounding. By-and-bye, he knew,
the sense of them, and of the questions they raised, would come
back and posses him; but meanwhile, emptied of all else, he
brimmed with the mere fact of George's bodily presence, with
the physical signs of him, his weakness, his temperature, the
pain in his arm, the oppression on his lung, all the daily insistent
details involved in coaxing him slowly back to life.

The father could bear no more; he put the letter away, as a
man might put away something of which his heart was too full
to measure it. Later—yes; now, all he knew was that his son
was alive.

But the hour of Campton's entering into glory came when,
two or three days later, George asked with a sudden smile:
"When I exchanged regiments I did what you'd always hoped
I would, eh, Dad?"

It was the first allusion, on the part of either, to the mystery
of George's transit from the Argonne to the front. At Doullens
he had been too weak to be questioned, and as he grew stronger,
and entered upon the successive stages of his convalescence, he
gave the impression of having travelled far beyond such matters,
and of living his real life in some inconceivable region from

which, with that new smile of his, he continued to look down unseeingly on his parents. "It's exactly as if he were dead," the father thought. "And if he were, he might go on watching us with just such a smile."

And then, one morning as they were taking a few steps on a sunny terrace, Campton had felt the pressure of the boy's sound arm, and caught the old George in his look.

"I . . . good Lord . . . at any rate I'm glad you felt sure of me," Campton could only stammer in reply.

George laughed. "Well—rather!"

There was a long silence full of sea-murmurs, too drowsy and indolent, for once, to simulate the horror of the guns.

"I—I only wish you'd felt you could trust me about it from the first, as you did Adele and Boylston," the father continued.

"But, my dear fellow, I did feel it! I swear I did! Only, you see, there was mother. I thought it all over, and decided it would be easier for you both if I said nothing. And, after all, I'm glad now that I didn't—that is, if you really do understand."

"Yes; I understand."

"That's jolly." George's eyes turned from his and rested with a joyful gravity on the little round-faced Sister who hurried up to say that he'd been out long enough. Campton often caught him fixing this look of serene benevolence on the people who were gradually repeopling his world, a look which seemed to say that they were new to him, yet dimly familiar. He was like a traveller returning after incommunicable adventures to the place where he had lived as a child; and, as happens with such wanderers, the trivial and insignificant things, the things a newcomer would not have noticed, seemed often to interest him most of all.

He said nothing more about himself, but with the look of recovered humanness which made him more lovable if less remotely beautiful, began to question his father.

"Boylston wrote that you'd begun to paint again. I'm glad."

"Oh, I only took it up for a while last spring."

"Portraits?"

"A few. But I chucked it. I couldn't stand the atmosphere."

"What atmosphere?"

"Of people who could want to be painted at such a time. People who wanted to 'secure a Campton.' Oh, and then the dealers—God!"

George seemed unimpressed. "After all, life's got to go on."

"Yes—that's what they say! And the only result is to make me doubt if *theirs* has."

His son laughed, and then threw off: "You did Mrs. Talkett?"

"Yes," Campton snapped, off his guard.

"She's a pretty creature," said George; and at that moment his eyes, resting again on the little nurse, who was waiting at his door with a cup of cocoa, lit up with celestial gratitude.

"The *communiqué's* good to-day," she cried; and he smiled at her boyishly. The war was beginning to interest him again: Campton was sure that every moment he could spare from that unimaginable region which his blue eyes guarded like a sword was spent among his comrades at the front.

As the day approached for the return to Paris, Campton began to penetrate more deeply into the meaning of George's remoteness. He himself, he discovered, had been all unawares in a far country, a country guarded by a wingèd sentry, as the old hymn had it: the region of silent incessant communion with his son. Just they two: everything else effaced; not discarded, destroyed, not disregarded even, but blotted out by a soft silver haze, as the brown slopes and distances were, on certain days, from the windows of the seaward-gazing hospital.

It was not that Campton had been unconscious of the presence of other suffering about them. As George grew stronger, and took his first steps in the wards, he and his father were inevitably brought into contact with the life of the hospital. George had even found a few friends, and two or three regimental comrades, among the officers perpetually coming and going, or enduring the long weeks of agony which led up to the end. But that was only toward the close of their sojourn, when George was about to yield his place to others, and be taken to Paris for the re-education of his shattered arm. And by that time the weeks of solitary communion had left such an imprint on Campton that, once the hospital was behind him, and no more than a phase of memory, it became to him as one of its own sea-mists, in which he and his son might have been peacefully shut away together from all the rest of the world.

Chapter XXVIII

"PREPAREDNESS!" cried Boylston in an exultant crow.

His round brown face with its curly crest and peering half-blind eyes beamed at Campton in the old way across the desk of the Palais Royal office; and from the corner where she had sunk down on one of the broken-springed divans, Adele Anthony echoed: "Preparedness!"

It was the first time that Campton had heard the word; but the sense of it had been in the air ever since he and George had got back to Paris. He remembered, on the very day of their arrival, noticing something different in both Boylston and Miss Anthony; and the change had shown itself in the same way: both seemed more vivid yet more remote. It had struck Campton in the moment of first meeting them, in the Paris hospital near the Bois de Boulogne—Fortin-Lescluze's old Nursing-Home transformed into a House of Re-education—to which George had been taken. In the little cell crowded with flowers—almost too many flowers, his father thought, for the patient's aching head and tired eyes—Campton, watching the entrance of the two visitors, the first to be admitted after Julia and Mr. Brant, had instantly remarked the air they had of sharing something so secret and important that their joy at seeing George seemed only the overflow of another deeper joy.

Their look had just such a vividness as George's own; as their glances crossed, Campton saw the same light in the eyes of all three. And now, a few weeks later, the clue to it came to him in Boylston's new word. *Preparedness*! America, it appeared, had caught it up from east to west, in that sudden incalculable way she had of flinging herself on a new idea; from a little group of discerning spirits the contagion had spread like a prairie fire, sweeping away all the other catchwords of the hour, devouring them in one great blaze of wrath and enthusiasm. America meant to be prepared! First had come the creation of the training camp at Plattsburg, for which, after long delays and much difficulty, permission had been wrung from a reluctant government; then, as candidates flocked to it, as the whole young manhood of the Eastern States rose to the call, other camps, rapidly planned, were springing up at Fort Oglethorpe in Georgia, at Fort Sheridan in Illinois, at The Presidio in California; for the idea was spreading through the West, and the torch kindled beside the Atlantic seaboard already flashed its light on the Pacific.

For hours at a time Campton heard Boylston talking about these training camps with the young Americans who helped him in his work, or dropped in to seek his counsel. More than ever, now, he was an authority and an oracle to these stray youths who were expending their enthusiasm for France in the humblest of philanthropic drudgery: students of the Beaux Arts or the University, or young men of leisure discouraged by the indifference of their country and the dilatoriness of their government, and fired by the desire to take part in a struggle in which they had instantly felt their own country to be involved in spite of geographical distance.

None of these young men had heard Benny Upsher's imperious call to be "in it" from the first, no matter how or at what cost. They were of the kind to wait for a lead—and now Boylston was giving it to them with his passionate variations on the great theme of Preparedness. George, meanwhile, lay there in his bed and smiled; and now and then Boylston brought one or two of the more privileged candidates to see him. One day Campton found young Louis Dastrey there, worn and haggard after a bad wound, and preparing to leave for America as instructor in one of the new camps. That seemed to bring the movement closer than ever, to bring it into their very lives. The thought flashed through Campton: "When George is up, we'll get him sent out too"; and once again a delicious sense of security crept through him.

George, as yet, was only sitting up for a few hours a day; the wound in the lung was slow in healing, and his fractured arm in recovering its flexibility. But in another fortnight he was to leave the hospital and complete his convalescence at his mother's.

The thought was bitter to Campton; he had had all kinds of wild plans—of taking George to the Crillon, or hiring an apartment for him, or even camping with him at the studio. But George had smiled all this away. He meant to return to the Avenue Marigny, where he always stayed when he came to Paris, and where it was natural that his mother should want him now. Adele Anthony pointed out to Campton how natural it was, one day as he and she left the Palais Royal together. They were going to lunch at a near-by restaurant, as they often did on leaving the office, and Campton had begun to speak of George's future arrangements. He would be well enough to leave the hospital in another week, and then no doubt a staff-job could be obtained for him in Paris—"with Brant's pull, you know," Campton concluded, hardly aware that he had uttered the detested phrase without even a tinge of irony. But Adele was aware, as he saw by the faint pucker of her thin lips.

He shrugged her smile away indifferently. "Oh, well—hang it, yes! Everything's changed now, isn't it? After what the boy's been through I consider that we're more than justified in using Brant's pull in his favour—or anybody else's."

Miss Anthony nodded and unfolded her napkin.

"Well, then," Campton continued his argument, "as he's likely to be in Paris now till the war is over—which means some time next year, they all say—why shouldn't I take a jolly apartment somewhere for the two of us? Those pictures I did last spring brought me in a lot of money, and there's no reason——" His face lit up. "Servants, you say? Why, my poor Mariette may be back from Lille any time now. They tell me there's sure to be a big push in the spring. They're saving up for that all along the line. Ask Dastrey . . . ask . . ."

"You'd better let George go to his mother," said Miss Anthony concisely.

"Why?"

"Because it's natural—it's human. *You're* not always, you know," she added with another pucker.

"Not human?"

"I don't mean that you're inhuman. But you see things differently."

"I don't want to see anything but one; and that's my own son. How shall I ever see George if he's at the Avenue Marigny?"

"He'll come to you."

"Yes—when he's not at Mrs. Talkett's!"

Miss Anthony frowned. The subject had been touched upon between them soon after Campton's return, but Miss Anthony had little light to throw on it: George had been as mute with her as with every one else, and she knew Mrs. Talkett but slightly, and seldom saw her. Yet Campton perceived that she could not hear the young woman named without an involuntary contraction of her brows.

"I wish I liked her!" she murmured.

"Mrs. Talkett?"

"Yes—I should think better of myself if I did. And it might be useful. But I can't—I can't!"

Campton said within himself: "Oh, women——!" For his own resentment had died out long ago. He could think of the affair now as one of hundreds such as happen to young men; he was even conscious of regarding it, in some unlit secret fold of himself, as a probable guarantee of George's wanting to remain in Paris, another subterranean way of keeping him, should such be needed. Perhaps that was what Miss Anthony meant by saying that her liking Mrs. Talkett might be "useful."

"Why shouldn't he be with me?" the father persisted. "He and I were going off together when the war begun. I was defrauded of that—why shouldn't I have him now?"

Miss Anthony smiled. "Well, for one thing, because of that very 'pull' you were speaking of."

"Oh, the Brants, the Brants!" Campton glanced impatiently at the bill-of-fare, grumbled: "*Déjeuner du jour*, I suppose?" and went on: "Yes; I might have known it—he belongs to them. From the minute we got back, and I saw them at the station, with their motor waiting, and everything arranged as only money can arrange it, I knew I'd lost my boy again." He stared moodily before him. "And yet if the war hadn't come I should have got him back—I almost had."

His companion still smiled, a little wistfully. She leaned over and laid her hand on his, under cover of the bill-of-fare. "You did get him back, John, forever and always, the day he exchanged into the infantry. Isn't that enough?"

Campton answered her smile. "You gallant old chap, you!" he said; and they began to lunch.

George was able to be up now, able to drive out, and to see more people; and Campton was not surprised, on approaching his door a day or two later, to hear several voices in animated argument.

The voices (and this did surprise him) were all men's. In one he recognized Boylston's deep round notes; but the answering voice, flat, toneless and yet eager, puzzled him with a sense of something familiar but forgotten. He opened the door, and saw, at the tea-tray between George and Boylston, the smoothly-brushed figure of Roger Talkett.

Campton had not seen Mrs. Talkett's husband for months, and in the interval so much had happened that the young man, always somewhat faintly-drawn, had become as dim as a daguerreotype held at the wrong angle.

The painter hung back, slightly embarrassed; but Mr. Talkett did not seem in the least disturbed by his appearance, or by the fact of himself being where he was. It was evident that, on whatever terms George might be with his wife, Mr. Talkett was determined to shed on him the same impartial beam as on all her other visitors.

His eye-glasses glinted blandly up at Campton. "Now I dare-say I *am* subversive," he began, going on with what he had been saying, but in a tone intended to include the newcomer. "I don't say I'm not. We *are* a subversive lot at home, all of us—you must have noticed that, haven't you, Mr. Campton?"

Boylston emitted a faint growl. "What's that got to do with it?" he asked.

Mr. Talkett's glasses slanted in his direction. "Why—every-thing! Resistance to the herd-instinct (to borrow one of my wife's expressions) is really innate in me. And the idea of giving in now, of sacrificing my convictions, just because of all this deafening noise about America's danger and America's duties—well, *no*," said Mr. Talkett, straightening his glasses, "Philis-tinism won't go down with me, in whatever form it tries to disguise itself." Instinctively, he stretched a neat hand toward the tea-cups, as if he had been rearranging the furniture at one of his wife's parties.

"But—but—but——" Boylston stuttered, red with rage.

George burst into a laugh. He seemed to take a boyish amuse-ment in the dispute. "Tea, father?" he suggested, reaching across the tray for a cigarette.

Talkett jerked himself to his feet. "Take my chair, now do, Mr. Campton. You'll be more comfortable. Here, let me shake up this cushion for you——" ("*Cushion!*" Boylston interjected scornfully.) "A light, George? Now don't move!—I don't say, of course, old chap," Talkett continued, as he held the match deferentially to George's cigarette, "that this sort of talk would be safe—or advisable—just now in public; subversive talk never is. But when two or three of the Elect are gathered together—well, your father sees my point, I know. The Hero," he nodded at George, "has his job, and the Artist," with a slant at Campton, "his. In Germany, for instance, as we're beginning to find out, the creative minds, the Intelligentsia (to use another of my wife's expressions), have been carefully protected from the beginning, given jobs, vitally important jobs of course, but where their lives were not exposed. The country needs them too much in other ways; they would probably be wretched fighters, and they're of colossal service in their own line. Whereas in France and England——" he suddenly seemed to see his chance——"Well, look here, Mr. Campton, I appeal to you, I appeal to the great creative Artist: in any country but France and England, would a fellow of George's brains have been *allowed*, even at this stage of the war, to chuck an important staff job, requiring intellect, tact and *savoir faire*, and try to get himself killed like any unbaked boy—like your poor cousin Benny Upsher, for instance? Would he?"

"Yes—in America!" shouted Boylston; and Mr. Talkett's tallowy cheeks turned pink.

"George knows how I feel about these things," he stammered.

George still laughed in his remote impartial way, and Boylston asked with a grin: "Why don't you get yourself naturalized—a neutral?"

Mr. Talkett's pinkness deepened. "I have lived too much among Artists——" he began; and George interrupted gaily: "There's a lot to be said on Talkett's side too. Going, Roger? Well, I shall be able to look in on you now in a few days. Remember me to Madge. Good-bye."

Boylston rose also, and Campton remained alone with his son.

"Remember me to Madge!" That was the way in which the modern young man spoke of his beloved to his beloved's proprietor. There had not been a shadow of constraint in George's tone; and now, glancing at the door which had closed on Mr. Talkett, he merely said, as if apostrophizing the latter's neat back: "Poor devil! He's torn to pieces with it."

"With what?" asked Campton, startled.

"Why, with Boylston's Preparedness. Wanting to do the proper thing—and never before having had to decide between anything more vital than straight or turned-down collars. It's playing the very deuce with him."

His eyes grew thoughtful. Was he going to pronounce Mrs. Talkett's name—at last? But no; he wandered back to her husband. "Poor little ass! Of course he'll decide against." He shrugged his shoulders. "And Boylston's just as badly torn in the other direction."

"Boylston?"

"Yes. Knowing that he wouldn't be taken himself, on account of his bad heart and his blind eyes, and wondering if, in spite of his disabilities, he's got the right to preach to all these young chaps here who hang on his words like the gospel. One of them taunted him with it the other day."

"The cur!"

"Yes. And ever since, of course, Boylston's been twice as fierce, and overworking himself to calm his frenzy. The men who can't go are all like that, when they know it's their proper work. It isn't everybody's billet out there—I've learnt that since I've had a look at it—but it would be Boylston's if he had the health, and he knows it, and that's what drives him wild." George looked at his father with a smile. "You don't know how I thank my stars that there weren't any 'problems' for me, but just a plain job that picked me up by the collar, and dropped me down where I belonged." He reached for another cigarette. "Old Adele's coming presently. Do you suppose we could rake up some fresh tea?" he asked.

Chapter XXIX

COMING out of the unlit rainy March night, it was agreeable but almost startling to Campton to enter Mrs. Talkett's drawing-room. In the softness of shaded lamplight, against curtains closely drawn, young women dressed with extravagant elegance chatted with much-decorated officers in the new "horizon" uniform, with here and there among them an elderly civilian head, such as Harvey Mayhew's silvery thatch and the square rapacious skull of the newly-knighted patriot, Sir Cyril Jorgenstein.

Campton had gone to Mrs. Talkett's that afternoon because she had lent her apartment to "The Friends of French Art," who were giving a concert organized by Miss Anthony and Mlle. Davril, with Mme. de Dolmetsch's pianist as their leading performer. It would have been ungracious to deprive the indefatigable group of the lustre they fancied Campton's presence would confer; and he was not altogether sorry to be there. He knew that George had promised Miss Anthony to come; and he wanted to see his son with Mrs. Talkett.

An abyss seemed to divide this careless throng of people, so obviously assembled for their own pleasure, the women to show their clothes, the men to admire them, from the worn preoccupied audiences of the first war-charity entertainments. The war still raged; wild hopes had given way to dogged resignation; each day added to the sum of public anguish and private woe. But the strain had been too long, the tragedy too awful. The idle and the useless had reached their emotional limit, and once more they dressed and painted, smiled, gossiped, flirted as though the long agony were over.

On a sofa stacked with orange-velvet cushions Mme. de Dolmetsch reclined in a sort of serpent-coil of flexible grey-green hung with strange amulets. Her eyes, in which fabulous islands seemed to dream, were fixed on the bushy-haired young man at the piano. Close by, upright and tight-waisted, sat the Marquise de Tranlay, her mourning veil thrown back from a helmet-like hat. She had planted herself in a Louis Philippe armchair, as if appealing to its sturdy frame to protect her from the anarchy of Mrs. Talkett's furniture; and beside her was the daughter for whose sake she had doubtless come—a frowning beauty who, in spite of her dowdy dress and ugly boots, somehow declared herself as having already broken away from the maternal tradition.

Mme. de Tranlay's presence in that drawing-room was characteristic enough. It meant—how often one heard it nowadays!—that mothers had to take their daughters wherever there was a chance of their meeting young men, and that such chances were found only in the few "foreign" houses where, discreetly, almost clandestinely, entertaining had been resumed. You had to take them there, Mme. de Tranlay's look seemed to say, because they had to be married (the sooner the better in these wild times, with all the old barriers down), and because the young men were growing so tragically few, and the competition was so fierce, and because in such emergencies a French mother, whose first thought is always for her children, must learn to accept, even to seek, propinquities from which her inmost soul, and all the ancestral souls within her, would normally recoil.

Campton remembered her gallant attitude on the day when, under her fresh crape, she had rebuked Mrs. Brant's despondency. "But how she hates it here—how she must loathe sitting next to that woman!" he thought; and just then he saw her turn toward Mme. de Dolmetsch with a stiff bend from the waist, and heard her say in her most conciliatory tone: "Your great friend, the rich American, *chère Madame*, the benefactor of France—we should so like to thank him, Claire and I, for all he is doing for our country."

Beckoned to by Mme. de Dolmetsch, Mr. Mayhew, all pink and silver and prominent pearl scarf-pin, bowed before the Tranlay ladies, while the Marquise deeply murmured: "We are grateful—we shall not forget—" and Mademoiselle de Tranlay, holding him with her rich gaze, added in fluent English: "Mamma hopes you'll come to tea on Sunday—with no one but my uncle the Duc de Montlhéry—so that we may thank you better than we can here."

"Great women—great women!" Campton mused. He was still watching Mme. de Tranlay's dauntless mask when her glance deserted the gratified Mayhew to seize on a younger figure. It was that of George, who had just entered. Mme. de Tranlay, with a quick turn, caught Campton's eye, greeted him with her trenchant cordiality, and asked, in a voice like the pounce of talons: "The young officer who has the Legion of Honour—the one you just nodded to—with reddish hair and his left arm in a sling? French, I suppose, from his uniform; and yet——? Yes, talking to Mrs. Talkett. Can you tell me——?"

"My son," said Campton with satisfaction.

The effect was instantaneous, though Mme. de Tranlay kept her radiant steadiness. "How charming—charming—charming!" And, after a proper interval: "But, Claire, my child, we've not yet spoken to Mrs. Brant, whom I see over there." And she steered her daughter swiftly toward Julia.

Campton's eyes returned to his son. George was still with Mrs. Talkett, but they had only had time for a word or two before she was called away to seat an important dowager. In that moment, however, the father noted many things. George, as usual nowadays, kept his air of guarded kindliness, though the blue of his eyes grew deeper; but Mrs. Talkett seemed bathed in light. It was such a self-revelation that Campton's curiosity was lost in the artist's abstract joy. "If I could have painted her like that!" he thought, reminded of having caught Mme. de Dolmetsch transfigured by fear for her lover; but an instant later he remembered. "Poor little thing!" he murmured. Mrs. Talkett turned her head, as if his thought had reached her. "Oh, yes—oh, yes; come and let me tell you all about it," her eyes entreated him. But Mayhew and Sir Cyril Jorgenstein were between them.

"George!" Mrs. Brant called; and across the intervening groups Campton saw his son bowing to the Marquise de Tranlay.

Mme. de Dolmetsch jumped up, her bracelets jangling like a prompter's call. "Silence!" she cried. The ladies squeezed into their seats, the men resigned themselves to door-posts and window-embrasures, and the pianist attacked Stravinsky . . .

"Dancing?" Campton heard his hostess answering some one. "N—no: not *quite* yet, I think. Though in London, already . . . oh, just for the officers on leave, of course. Poor darlings—why shouldn't they? But to-day, you see, it's for a charity." Her smile appealed to her hearer to acknowledge the distinction.

The music was over, and scanning the groups at the tea-tables, Campton saw Adele and Mlle. Davril squeezed away in the remotest corner of the room. He took a chair at their table, and Boylston presently blinked his way to them through the crowd.

They seemed, all four, more like unauthorized intruders on the brilliant scene than its laborious organizers. The entertainment, escaping from their control, had speedily reverted to its true purpose of feeding and amusing a crowd of bored and restless people; and the little group recognized the fact, and joked over it in their different ways. But Mlle. Davril was happy at the sale of tickets, which must have been immense to judge from the crowd (spying about the entrance, she had seen furious fine ladies turn away ticketless); and Adele Anthony was exhilarated by the nearness of people she did not know, or wish to know, but with whose names and private histories she was minutely and passionately familiar.

"That's the old Duchesse de Murols with Mrs. Talkett—there, she's put her at the Beausites' table! Well, of all places! Ah, but you're all too young to know about Beausite's early history. And now, of course, it makes no earthly difference to anybody. But there must be times when Mme. Beausite remembers, and grins. Now that she's begun to rouge again she looks twenty years younger than the Duchess.——Ah," she broke off, abruptly signing to Campton.

He followed her glance to a table at which Julia Brant was seating herself with the Tranlay ladies and George. Mayhew joined them, nobly deferential, and the elder ladies lent him their intensest attention, isolating George with the young girl.

"H'm," Adele murmured, "not such a bad thing! They say the girl will have half of old Montlhéry's money—he's her mother's uncle. And she's heaps handsomer than the other—not that *that* seems to count any more!"

Campton shrugged the subject away. Yes; it would be a good thing if George could be drawn from what his mother (with a retrospective pinching of the lips) called his "wretched infatuation." But the idea that the boy might be coaxed into a marriage—and a rich marriage—by the Brants, was even more distasteful to Campton. If he really loved Madge Talkett better stick to her than let himself be cajoled away for such reasons.

As the second part of the programme began, Campton and Boylston slipped out together. Campton was oppressed and disturbed. "It's queer," he said, taking Boylston's arm to steer him through the dense darkness of the streets; "all these people who've forgotten the war have suddenly made me remember it."

Boylston laughed. "Yes, I know." He seemed preoccupied and communicative, and the painter fancied he was going to lead the talk, as usual, to Preparedness and America's intervention; but after a pause he said: "You haven't been much at the office lately——"

"No," Campton interrupted. "I've shirked abominably since George got back. But now that he's gone to the Brants' you'll see——"

"Oh, I didn't mean it as a reproach, sir! How could you think it? We're running smoothly enough, as far as organization goes. That's not what bothers me——"

"You're bothered?"

Yes; he was—and so, he added, was Miss Anthony. The trouble was, he went on to explain, that Mr. Mayhew, after months of total indifference (except when asked to "represent" them on official platforms) had developed a disquieting interest in "The Friends of French Art." He had brought them, in the beginning, a certain amount of money (none of which came out of his own pocket), and in consequence had been imprudently put on the Financial Committee, so that he had a voice in the disposal of funds, though till lately he had never made it heard. But now, apparently, "Atrocities" were losing their novelty, and he was disposed to transfer his whole attention to "The Friends of French Art," with results which seemed incomprehensibly disturbing to Boylston, until he let drop the name of Mme. de Dolmetsch. Campton exclaimed at it.

"Well—yes. You must have noticed that she and Mr. Mayhew have been getting pretty chummy. You see, he's done such a lot of talking that people think he's at least an Oil King; and Mme. de Dolmetsch is dazzled. But she's got her musical prodigy to provide for——" and Boylston outlined the situation which his astuteness had detected while it developed unperceived under Campton's dreaming eyes. Mr. Mayhew was attending all their meetings now, finding fault, criticizing, asking to have the accounts investigated, though they had always been audited at regular intervals by expert accountants; and all this zeal originated in the desire to put Mme. de Dolmetsch in Miss

Anthony's place, on the plea that her greater social experience, her gift of attracting and interesting, would bring in immense sums of money—whereas, Boylston grimly hinted, they already had a large balance in the bank, and it was with an eye to that balance that Mme. de Dolmetsch was forcing Mayhew to press her claim.

"You see, sir, Mr. Mayhew never turns out to be as liberal as they expect when they first hear him talk; and though Mme. de Dolmetsch has him in her noose she's not getting what she wants—by a long way. And so they've cooked this up between them—she and Mme. Beausite—without his actually knowing what they're after."

Campton stopped short, releasing Boylston's arm. "But what you suggest is abominable," he exclaimed.

"Yes. I know it." But the young man's voice remained steady. "Well, I wish you'd come to our meetings, now you're back."

"I will—I will! But I'm no earthly use on financial questions. You're much stronger there."

He felt Boylston's grin through the darkness. "Oh, they'll have me out too before long."

"You? Nonsense! What do you mean?"

"I mean that lots of people are beginning to speculate in war charities—oh, in all sorts of ways. Sometimes I'm sick to the point of chucking it all. But Miss Anthony keeps me going."

"Ah, she would!" Campton agreed.

As he walked home his mind was burdened with Boylston's warning. It was not merely the affair itself, but all it symbolized, that made his gorge rise, made him, as Boylston said, sick to the point of wanting to chuck it all—to chuck everything connected with this hideous world that was dancing and flirting and money-making on the great red mounds of dead. He grinned at the thought that he had once believed in the regenerative power of war—the salutary shock of great moral and social upheavals. Yet he *had* believed in it, and never more intensely than at George's bedside at Doullens, in that air so cleansed by passion and pain that mere living seemed a meaningless gesture compared to the chosen surrender of life. But in the Paris to which he had returned after barely four months of absence the instinct of self-preservation seemed to have wiped all meaning from such words. Poor fatuous Mayhew dancing to Mme.

de Dolmetsch's piping, Jorgenstein sinking under the weight of his international honours, Mme. de Tranlay intriguing to push her daughter in such society, and Julia placidly abetting her—Campton hardly knew from which of these sorry visions he turned with a completer loathing . . .

There were still the others, to be sure, the huge obscure majority; out there in the night, the millions giving their lives for this handful of trivial puppets, and here in Paris, and everywhere, in every country, men and women toiling unweariedly to help and heal; but in Mrs. Talkett's drawing-room both fighters and toilers seemed to count as little in relation to the merry-makers as Miss Anthony and Mlle. Davril in relation to the brilliant people who had crowded their table into the obscurest corner of the room.

Chapter XXX

THESE thoughts continued to weigh on Campton; to shake them off he decided, with one of his habitual quick jerks of resolution, to get back to work. He knew that George would approve, and would perhaps be oftener with him if he had something interesting on his easel. Sir Cyril Jorgenstein had suggested that he would like to have his portrait finished—with the Legion of Honour added to his lapel, no doubt. And Harvey Mayhew, rosy and embarrassed, had dropped in to hint that, if Campton could find time to do a charcoal head—oh, just one of those brilliant sketches of his—of the young musical genius in whose career their friend Mme. de Dolmetsch was so much interested . . . But Campton had cut them both short. He was not working—he had no plans for the present. And in truth he had not thought even of attempting a portrait of George. The impulse had come to him, once, as he sat by the boy's bed; but the face was too incomprehensible. He should have to learn and unlearn too many things first——

At last, one day, it occurred to him to make a study of Mme. Lebel. He saw *her* in charcoal: her simple unquestioning anguish had turned her old face to sculpture. Campton set his canvas on the easel, and started to shout for her down the stairs; but as he opened the door he found himself face to face with Mrs. Talkett.

"Oh," she began at once, in her breathless way, "you're here? The old woman downstairs wasn't sure—and I couldn't leave all this money with her, could I?"

"Money? What money?" he echoed.

She was very simply dressed, and a veil, drooping low from her hat-brim, gave to her over-eager face a shadowy youthful calm.

"I *may* come in?" she questioned, almost timidly; and as Campton let her pass she added: "The money from the concert, of course—heaps and heaps of it! I'd no idea we'd made so much. And I wanted to give it to you myself."

She shook a bulging bag out of her immense muff, while Campton continued to stare at her.

"I didn't know you went out so early," he finally stammered, trying to push a newspaper over the disordered remains of his breakfast.

She lifted interrogative eye-brows. "That means that I'm in the way?"

"No. But why did you bring that money here?"

She looked surprised. "Why not? Aren't you the head—the real head of the committee? And wasn't the concert given in my house?" Her eyes rested on him with renewed timidity. "Is it—disagreeable to you to see me?" she asked.

"Disagreeable? My dear child, no." He paused, increasingly embarrassed. What did she expect him to say next? To thank her for having sent him the orderly's letter? It seemed to him impossible to plunge into the subject uninvited. Surely it was for her to give him the opening, if she wished to.

"Well, no!" she broke out. "I've never once pretended to you, have I? The money's a pretext. I wanted to see you—here, alone, with no one to disturb us."

Campton felt a confused stirring of relief and fear. All his old dread of scenes, commotions, disturbing emergencies—of anything that should upset his perpetually vibrating balance—was blent with the passionate desire to hear what his visitor had to say.

"You—it was good of you to think of sending us that letter," he faltered.

She frowned in her anxious way and looked away from him. "Afterward I was afraid you'd be angry."

"Angry? How could I?" He groped for a word. "Surprised—yes. I knew nothing . . . nothing about you and . . ."

"Not even that it was I who bought the sketch of him—the one that Léonce Black sold for you last year?"

The blood rushed to Campton's face. Suddenly he felt himself trapped and betrayed. "You—*you*? You've got that sketch?" The thought was somehow intolerable to him.

"Ah, now you *are* angry," Mrs. Talkett murmured.

"No, no; but I never imagined——"

"I know. That was what frightened me—your suspecting nothing." She glanced about her, dropped to a corner of the divan, and tossed off her hat with the old familiar gesture. "Oh, can I talk to you?" she pleaded.

Campton nodded.

"I wish you'd light your pipe, then, and sit down too." He reached for his pipe, struck a match, and slowly seated himself. "You always smoke a pipe in the morning, don't you? *He* told me that," she went on; then she paused again and drew a long anxious breath. "Oh, he's so changed! I feel as if I didn't know him any longer—do *you*?"

Campton looked at her with deepening wonder. This was more surprising than discovering her to be the possessor of the picture; he had not expected deep to call unto deep in their talk. "I'm not sure that I do," he confessed.

Her fidgeting eyes deepened and grew quieter. "Your saying so makes me feel less lonely," she sighed, half to herself. "But has he told you nothing since he came back—really nothing?"

"Nothing. After all—how could he? I mean, without indiscretion?"

"Indiscretion? Oh——" She shrugged the word away with half a smile, as though such considerations belonged to a pre-historic order of things. "Then he hasn't even told you that he wants me to get a divorce?"

"A divorce?" Campton exclaimed. He sat staring at her as if the weight of his gaze might pin her down, keep her from flut-tering away and breaking up into luminous splinters. George wanted her to get a divorce—wanted, therefore, to marry her! His passion went as deep for her as that—too deep, Campton conjectured, for the poor little ephemeral creature, who struck him as wriggling on it like a butterfly impaled.

"Please tell me," he said at length; and suddenly, in short inconsequent sentences, the confession poured from her.

George, it seemed, during the previous winter in New York, when they had seen so much of each other, had been deeply attracted, had wanted "everything," and at once—and there had been moments of tension and estrangement, when she had been held back by scruples she confessed she no longer understood (inherited prejudices, she supposed), and when her reluctance must have made her appear to be trifling, whereas, really it was just that she couldn't . . . couldn't . . . So they had gone on for several months, with the usual emotional ups-and-downs, till he had left for Europe to join his father; and when they had parted she had given him the half-promise that if they met abroad during the summer she would perhaps . . . after all . . .

Then came the war. George had been with her during those few last hours in Paris, and had dined with her and her husband (had Campton forgiven her?) the night before he was mobilised. And then, when he was gone, she had understood that only timidity, vanity, the phantom barriers of old terrors and traditions, had prevented her being to him all that he wanted . . .

She broke off abruptly, put in a few conventional words about an ill-assorted marriage, and never having been "really understood," and then, as if guessing that she was on the wrong tack, jumped up, walked to the other end of the studio, and turned back to Campton with the tears running down her ravaged face.

"And now—and now—he says he won't have me!" she lamented.

"Won't have you? But you tell me he wants you to be divorced."

She nodded, wiped away the tears, and in so doing stole an unconscious glance at the mirror above the divan. Then, seeing that the glance was detected, she burst into a sort of sobbing laugh. "My nose gets so dreadfully red when I cry," she stammered.

Campton took no notice, and she went on: "A divorce? Yes. And unless I do—unless I agree to marry him—we're never to be anything but friends."

"That's what he says?"

"Yes. Oh, we've been all in and out of it a hundred times."

She pulled out a gold-mesh bag and furtively restored her complexion, as Mrs. Brant had once done in the same place.

Campton sat still, considering. He had let his pipe go out. Nothing could have been farther from the revelation he had expected, and his own perplexity was hardly less great than his visitor's. Certainly it was not the way in which young men had behaved in his day—nor, evidently, had it been George's before the war.

Finally he made up his mind to put the question: "And Talkett?"

She burst out at once: "Ah, that's what I say—it's not so simple!"

"What isn't?"

"Breaking up—all one's life." She paused with a deepening embarrassment. "Of course Roger has made me utterly miserable—but then I know he really hasn't meant to."

"Have you told George that?"

"Yes. But he says we must first of all be aboveboard. He says he sees everything differently now. That's what I mean when I say that I don't understand him. He says love's not the same kind of feeling to him that it was. There's something of Meredith's that he quotes—I wish I could remember it—something about a mortal lease."

"Good Lord," Campton groaned, not so much at the hopelessness of the case as at the hopelessness of quoting Meredith to her. After a while he said abruptly: "You must forgive my asking: but things change sometimes—they change imperceptibly. Do you think he's as much in love with you as ever?"

He had been half afraid of offending her: but she appeared to consider the question impartially, and without a shadow of resentment. "Sometimes I think more—because in the beginning it wasn't meant to last. And now—if he wants to marry me? Oh, I wish I knew what to do!"

Campton continued to ponder. "There's one more question, since we're talking frankly: what does Talkett know of all this?"

She looked frightened. "Oh, nothing, nothing!"

"And you've no idea how he would take it?"

She examined the question with tortured eye-brows, and at length, to Campton's astonishment, brought out: "Magnificently——"

"He'd be generous, you mean? But it would go hard with him?"

"Oh, dreadfully, dreadfully!" She seemed to need the assurance to restore her shaken self-approval.

Campton rose with a movement of pity and laid his hand on her shoulder. "My dear child, if your husband cares for you, give up my son."

Her face fell, and she drew back. "Oh, but you don't understand—not in the least! It's not possible—it's not moral——. You know I'm all for the new morality. First of all, we must be true to self." She paused, and then broke out: "You tell me to give him up because you think he's tired of me. But he's not—I know he's not! It's his new ideas that you don't understand, any more than I do. It's the war that has changed him. He says he wants only things that last—that are permanent—things that hold a man fast. That sometimes he feels as if he were being swept away on a flood, and were trying to catch at things—at anything—as he's rushed along under the waves . . . He says he wants quiet, monotony . . . to be sure the same things will happen every day. When we go out together he sometimes stands for a quarter of an hour and stares at the same building, or at the Seine under the bridges. But he's happy, I'm sure . . . I've never seen him happier . . . only it's in a way I can't make out . . ."

"Ah, my dear, if it comes to that—I'm not sure that I can. Not sure enough to help you, I'm afraid."

She looked at him, disappointed. "You won't speak to him then?"

"Not unless he speaks to me."

"Ah, he frightens you—just as he does me!"

She pulled her hat down on her troubled brow, gathered up her furs, and took another sidelong peep at the glass. Then she turned toward the door. On the threshold she paused and looked back at Campton. "Don't you see," she cried, "that if I were to give George up he'd get himself sent straight back to the front?"

Campton's heart gave an angry leap; for a second he felt the impulse to strike her, to catch her by the shoulders and bundle her out of the room. With a great effort he controlled himself and opened the door.

"You don't understand—you don't understand!" she called back to him once again from the landing.

Madge Talkett had asked him to speak to his son: he had refused, and she had retaliated by planting that poisoned shaft in him. But what had retaliation to do with it? She had probably spoken the simple truth, and with the natural desire to enlighten him. If George wanted to marry her, it must be (since human nature, though it might change its vocabulary, kept its instincts), it must be that he was very much in love—and in that case her refusal would in truth go hard with him, and it would be natural that he should try to get himself sent away from Paris . . . From Paris, yes; but not necessarily to the front. After such wounds and such honours he had only to choose; a staff-appointment could easily be got. Or, no doubt, with his two languages, he might, if he preferred, have himself sent on a military mission to America. With all this propaganda talk, wasn't he the very type of officer they wanted for the neutral countries?

It was Campton's dearest wish that George should stay where he was; he knew his peace of mind would vanish the moment his son was out of sight. But he suspected that George would soon weary of staff-work, or of any form of soldiering at the rear, and try for the trenches if he left Paris; whereas, in Paris, Madge Talkett might hold him—as she had meant his father to see.

The first thing, then, was to make sure of a job at the War Office.

Campton turned and tossed like a sick man on the hard bed of his problem. To plan, to scheme, to plot and circumvent— nothing was more hateful to him, there was nothing in which he was less skilled. If only he dared to consult Adele Anthony! But Adele was still incorrigibly warlike, and her having been in George's secret while his parents were excluded from it left no doubt as to the side on which her influence would bear. She loved the boy, Campton sometimes thought, even more passionately than his mother did; but—how did the old song go?—she loved honour, or her queer conception of it, more. Ponder as he would, he could not picture her, even now, lifting a finger to keep George back.

Campton struggled all the morning with these questions. After lunch he pocketed Mrs. Talkett's money-bag and carried it to the Palais Royal, where he discovered Harvey Mayhew in confabulation with Mme. Beausite, who still trailed her ineffectual beauty about the office. The painter thought he detected a faint embarrassment in the glance with which they both greeted him.

"Hallo, Campton! Looking for our good friend Boylston? He's off duty this afternoon, Mme. Beausite tells me; as he is pretty often in these days, I've noticed," Mr. Mayhew sardonically added. "In fact, the office has rather been left to run itself lately—eh? Of course our good Miss Anthony is absorbed with her refugees—gives us but a divided allegiance. And Boylston— well, young men, young men! Of course it's been a weary pull for him. By the way, my dear fellow," Mr. Mayhew continued, as Campton appeared about to turn away, "I called at Mrs. Talkett's just now to ask for the money from the concert—a good round sum, I hear it is—and she told me she'd given it to you. Have you brought it with you? If so, Mme. Beausite here would take charge of it——"

Mme. Beausite turned her great resigned eyes on the painter. "Mr. Campton knows I'm very careful. I will lock it up till his friend's return. Now that Mr. Boylston is so much away I very often have such responsibilities."

Campton's eyes returned her glance; but he did not waver. "Thanks so much; but as the sum is rather large it seems to me the bank's the proper place. Will you please tell Boylston I've deposited it?"

Mr. Mayhew's benevolent pink turned to an angry red. For a moment Campton thought he was about to say something foolish. But he merely bent his head stiffly, muttered a vague phrase about "irregular proceedings," and returned to his seat by Mme. Beausite's desk.

As for Campton, his words had decided his course: he would take the money at once to Bullard and Brant's and seize the occasion to see the banker. Mr. Brant was the only person with whom, at this particular juncture, he cared to talk of George.

Chapter XXXI

M R. BRANT'S private office was as glitteringly neat as when Campton had entered it for the first time, and seen the fatal telegram about Benny Upsher marring the order of the desk.

Now he crossed the threshold with different feelings. To have Mr. Brant look up and smile, to shake hands with him, accept one of his cigars, and sink into one of the blue leather arm-chairs, seemed to be in the natural order of things. He felt only the relief of finding himself with the one person likely to understand.

"About George——" he began.

"Yes?" said Mr. Brant briskly. "It's curious—I was just thinking of looking you up. It's his birthday next Tuesday, you know."

"Oh——" said the father, slightly put off. He had not come to talk of birthdays; nor did he need to be reminded of his son's by Mr. Brant. He concluded that Mr. Brant would be less easy to get on with in Paris than at the front.

"And we thought of celebrating the day by a little party— a dinner, with perhaps the smallest kind of a dance: or just bridge—yes, probably just bridge," the banker added tentatively. "Opinions differ as to the suitability—it's for his mother to decide. But of course no evening clothes; and we hoped perhaps to persuade you. Our only object is to amuse him—to divert his mind from this wretched entanglement."

It was doubtful if Mr. Brant had ever before made so long a speech, except perhaps at a board meeting; and then only when he read the annual report. He turned pink and stared over Campton's shoulder at the panelled white wall, on which a false Reynolds hung.

Campton meditated. The blush was the blush of Mr. Brant, but the voice was the voice of Julia. Still, it was probable that neither husband nor wife was aware how far matters had gone with Mrs. Talkett.

"George is more involved than you think," Campton said.

Mr. Brant looked startled.

"In what way?"

"He means to marry her. He insists on her getting a divorce."

"A divorce? Good gracious," murmured Mr. Brant. He turned over a jade paper-cutter, trying its edge absently on his nail. "Does Julia——?" he began at length.

Campton shook his head. "No; I wanted to speak to you first."

Mr. Brant gave his quick bow. He was evidently gratified, and the sentiment stimulated his faculties, as it had when he found that Campton no longer resented his presence at the hospital. His small effaced features took on a business-like sharpness, and he readjusted his eye-glasses and straightened the paper-cutter, which he had put back on the desk a fraction of an inch out of its habitual place.

"You had this from George?" he asked.

"No; from her. She's been to see me. *She* doesn't want to divorce. She's in love with him; in her way, that is; but she's frightened."

"And that makes him the more eager?"

"The more determined, at any rate."

Mr. Brant appeared to seize the distinction. "George can be very determined."

"Yes. I think his mother ought to be made to understand that all this talk about a wretched entanglement isn't likely to make him any less so."

Mr. Brant's look seemed to say that making Julia understand had proved a no less onerous task for his maturity than for Campton's youth.

"If you don't object—perhaps the matter might, for the present, continue to be kept between you and me," he suggested.

"Oh, by all means. What I want," Campton pursued, "is to get him out of this business altogether. They wouldn't be happy—they couldn't be. She's too much like——" He broke off, frightened at what he had been about to say. "Too much," he emended, "like the usual fool of a woman that every boy of George's age thinks he wants simply because he can't get her."

"And you say she came to you for advice?"

"She came to me to persuade him to give up the idea of a divorce. Apparently she's ready for anything short of that. It's a queer business. She seems sorry for Talkett in a way."

Mr. Brant marked his sense of the weight of this by a succession of attentive nods. He put his hands in his pockets, leaned back, and tilted his dapper toes against the gold-trellised scrap-basket. The attitude seemed to change the pale panelling of his background into a glass-and-mahogany Wall Street office.

"Won't he be satisfied with—er—all the rest, so to speak; since you say she offers it?"

"No; he won't. There's the difficulty. It seems it's the new view. The way the young men feel since the war. He wants her for his wife. Nothing less."

"Ah, he respects her," murmured Mr. Brant, impressed; and Campton reflected that he had no doubt respected Julia.

"And what she wants is to get you to persuade him—to accept less?"

"Well—something of the sort."

Mr. Brant sat up and dropped his heels to the floor. "Well, then—*don't*!" he snapped.

"Don't——?"

"Persuade her, on the contrary, to keep him hoping—to make him think she means to marry him. Don't you see?" Mr. Brant exclaimed, almost impatiently. "Don't you see that if she turns him down definitely he'll be scheming to get away, to get back to the front, the minute his leave is over? Tell her that—appeal to her on that ground. Make her do it. She will if she's in love with him. And *we* can't stop him from going back—not one of us. He's restless here already—I know that. Always talking about his men, saying he's got to get back to them. The only way is to hold him by this girl. She's the very influence we need!"

He threw it all out in sharp terse phrases, as a business man might try to hammer facts about an investment into the bewildered brain of an unpractical client. Campton felt the blood rising to his forehead, not so much in anger at Mr. Brant as at the sense of his own inward complicity.

"There's no earthly reason why George should ever go back to the front," he said.

"None whatever. We can get him any staff-job he chooses. His mother's already got the half-promise of a post for him at the War Office. But you'll see, you'll see! We can't stop him. Did we before? There's only this woman who can do it!"

Campton looked over the banker's head at the reflection of the false Reynolds in the mirror. That any one should have been fool enough to pay a big price for such a patent fraud seemed to him as incomprehensible as his own present obtuseness seemed to the banker.

"You do see, don't you?" argued Mr. Brant anxiously.

"Oh, I suppose so." Campton slowly got to his feet. The adroit brush-work of the forged picture fascinated him, and he went up to look at it more closely. Mr. Brant pursued him with a gratified glance.

"Ah, you're admiring my Reynolds. I paid a thumping price for it—but that's always my principle. Pay high, but get the best. It's a better investment."

"Just so," Campton assented dully. Mr. Brant seemed suddenly divided from him by the whole width of the gulf between that daub on the wall and a real Reynolds. They had nothing more to say to each other—nothing whatever. "Well, good-bye." He held out his hand.

"Think it over—think it over," Mr. Brant called out after him as he enfiladed the sumptuous offices, a medalled veteran holding back each door.

It was not until Campton was back at Montmartre, and throwing off his coat to get into his old studio clothes, that he felt in his pocket the weight of the forgotten concert-money. It was too late in the day to take it back to the bank, even if he had had the energy to retrace his steps; and he decided to hand the bag over to Boylston, with whom he was dining that night to meet the elder Dastrey, home on a brief leave from his ambulance.

"Think it over!" Mr. Brant's adjuration continued to echo in Campton's ears. As if he needed to be told to think it over! Once again the war-worn world had vanished from his mind, and he saw only George, himself and George, George and safety, George and peace. They blamed women who were cowards about their husbands, mistresses who schemed to protect their lovers! Well—he was as bad as any one of them, if it came to that. His son had bought his freedom, had once offered his life and nearly lost it. Brant was right: at all costs they must keep him from rushing back into that hell.

That Mrs. Talkett should be the means of securing his safety was bitter enough. This trivial barren creature to be his all—it seemed the parody of Campton's own youth! And Julia, after all, had been only a girl when he had met her, inexperienced and still malleable. A man less absorbed in his art, less oblivious of the daily material details of life, might conceivably have made something of her. But this little creature, with her farrago of false ideas, her vanity, her restlessness, her undisguised desire to keep George and yet not lose her world, had probably reached the term of her development, and would trip on through an eternal infancy of fads and frenzies.

Luckily, as Mr. Brant said, they could use her for the time; use her better, no doubt, than had she been a more finely tempered instrument. Campton was still pondering on these things as he set out for the restaurant where he had agreed to meet Boylston and Dastrey. At the foot of his own stairs he was surprised to run against Boylston under the porte-cochère. They gave each other a quick questioning look, as men did when they encountered each other unexpectedly in those days.

"Anything up? Oh, the money—you've come for the money?" Campton remembered that he had left the bag upstairs.

"The money? Haven't you heard? Louis Dastrey's killed," said Boylston.

They stood side by side in the doorway, while Campton's darkened mind struggled anew with the mystery of fate. Almost every day now the same readjustment had to be gone through: the cowering averted mind dragged upward and forced to visualize a new gap in the ranks, and summon the remaining familiar figures to fill it up and blot it out. And today this cruel gymnastic was to be performed for George's best friend, the elder Dastrey's sole stake in life! Only a few days ago the lad had passed through Paris, just back from America, and in haste to rejoin his regiment; alive and eager, throbbing with ideas, with courage, mirth and irony—the very material France needed to rebuild her ruins and beget her sons! And now, struck down as George had been—not to rise like George . . .

Once more the inner voice in Campton questioned distinctly: "Could you bear it?" and again he answered: "Less than ever!"

Aloud he asked: "Paul?"

"Oh, he went off at once. To break the news to Louis' mother in the country."

"The boy was all Paul had left."

"Yes."

"What difference would it have made in the war, if he'd just stayed on at his job in America?"

Boylston did not answer, and the two stood silent, looking out unseeingly at the black empty street. There was nothing left to say, nowadays, when such blows fell; hardly anything left to feel, it sometimes seemed.

"Well, I suppose we must go and eat something," the older man said; and arm in arm they went out into the darkness.

When Campton returned home that night he sat down and, with the help of several pipes, wrote a note to Mrs. Talkett asking when she would receive him.

Thereafter he tried to go back to his painting and to continue his daily visits to the Palais Royal office. But for the time nothing seemed to succeed with him. He threw aside his study of Mme. Lebel—he hung about the office, confused and idle, and with the ever clearer sense that there also things were disintegrating.

George's birthday party had been given up on account of young Dastrey's death. Mrs. Brant evidently thought the postponement unnecessary; since George's return she had gone over heart and soul to the "business as usual" party. But Mr. Brant quietly sided with George; and Campton was glad to be spared the necessity of celebrating the day in such a setting.

It was some time since Campton had seen his son; but the fault was not his son's. The painter was aware of having voluntarily avoided George. He said to himself: "As long as I know he's safe why should I bother him?" But in reality he did not feel himself to be fit company for any one, and had even shunned poor Paul Dastrey on the latter's hurried passage through Paris, when he had come back from carrying the fatal news to young Dastrey's mother.

"What on earth could Paul and I have found to say to each other?" Campton argued with himself. "For men of our age there's nothing left to say nowadays. The only thing I can do is to try to work up one of my old studies of Louis. That might please him a little—later on."

But after one or two attempts he pushed away that canvas too.

At length one afternoon George came in. They had not met for over a week, and as George's blue uniform detached itself against the blurred tapestries of the studio, the north light modelling the fresh curves of his face, the father's heart gave a leap of pride. His son had never seemed to him so young and strong and vivid.

George, with a sudden blush, took his hand in a long pressure.

"I say, Dad—Madge has told me. Told me that you know about us and that you've persuaded her to see things as I do. She hadn't had a chance to speak to me of your visit till last night."

Campton felt his colour rising; but though his own part in the business still embarrassed him he was glad that the barriers were down.

"I didn't want," George continued, still flushed and slightly constrained, "to say anything to you about all this till I could say: 'Here's my wife.' And now she's promised."

"She's promised?"

"Thanks to you, you know. Your visit to her did it. She told me the whole thing yesterday. How she'd come here in desperation, to ask you to help her, to have her mind cleared up for her; and how you'd thought it all over, and then gone to see her, and how wise and perfect you'd been about it all. Poor child—if you knew the difference it's made to her!"

They were seated now, the littered table between them. Campton, his elbows on it, his chin on his hands, looked across at his son, who faced the light.

"The difference to you too?" he questioned.

George smiled: it was exactly the same detached smile which he used to shed on the little nurse who brought him his cocoa.

"Of course. Now I can go back without worrying." He let the words fall as carelessly as if there were nothing in them to challenge attention.

"Go back?" Campton stared at him with a blank countenance. Had he heard aright? The noise of a passing lorry suddenly roared in his ears like the guns of the front.

"Did you say: *go back*?"

George opened his blue eyes wide. "Why, of course; as soon as ever I'm patched up. You didn't think——?"

"I thought you had the sense to realize that you've done your share in one line, and that your business now is to do it in another."

The same detached smile again brushed George's lips. "But if I happen to have only one line?"

"Nonsense! You know they don't think that at the War Office."

"I don't believe the War Office will shut down if I leave it."

"What an argument! It sounds like——" Campton, breaking off on a sharp breath, closed his lids for a second. He had been gazing too steadily into George's eyes, and now at last he knew what that mysterious look in them meant. It was Benny Upsher's look, of course—inaccessible to reason, beyond reason, belonging to other spaces, other weights and measures, over the edge, somehow, of the tangible calculable world . . .

"A man can't do more than his duty: you've done that," he growled.

But George insisted with his gentle obstinacy: "You'll feel differently about it when America comes in."

Campton shook his head. "Never about your case."

"You will—when you see how we all feel. When we're all in it you wouldn't have me looking on, would you? And then there are my men—I've got to get back to my men."

"But you've no right to go now; no business," his father broke in violently. "Persuading that poor girl to wreck her life . . . and then leaving her, planting her there with her past ruined, and her future . . . George, you can't!"

George, in his long months of illness, had lost his old ruddiness of complexion. At his father's challenge the blood again rose the more visibly to his still-gaunt cheeks and white forehead: he was evidently struck.

"You'll kill her—and kill your mother!" Campton stormed.

"Oh, it's not for to-morrow. Not for a long time, perhaps. My shoulder's still too stiff. I was stupid," the young man haltingly added, "to put it as I did. Of course I've got to think of Madge now," he acknowledged, "as well as mother."

The blood flowed slowly back to Campton's heart. "You've got to think of—just the mere common-sense of the thing. That's all I ask. You've done your turn; you've done more. But never mind that. Now it's different. You're barely patched up: you're of use, immense use, for staff-work, and you know it. And you've asked a woman to tie up her future to yours—at what cost you know too. It's as much your duty to keep away from the front now as it was before—well, I admit it—to go there. You've done just what I should have wanted my son to do, up to this minute——"

George laid a hand on his a little wistfully. "Then just go on trusting me."

"I do—to see that I'm right! If I can't convince you, ask Boylston—ask Adele!"

George sat staring down at the table. For the first time since they had met at Doullens Campton was conscious of reaching his son's inner mind, and of influencing it.

"I wonder if you really love her?" he suddenly risked.

The question did not seem to offend George, scarcely to surprise him. "Of course," he said simply. "Only—well, everything's different nowadays, isn't it? So many of the old ideas have come to seem such humbug. That's what I want to drag her out of—the coils and coils of stale humbug. They were killing her."

"Well—take care *you* don't," Campton said, thinking that everything was different indeed, as he recalled the reasons young men had had for loving and marrying in his own time.

A faint look of amusement came into George's eyes. "Kill her? Oh, no. I'm gradually bringing her to life. But all this is hard to talk about—yet. By-and-bye you'll understand; she'll show you, we'll show you together. But at present nothing's to be said—to any one, please, not even to mother. Madge thinks this is no time for such things. There, of course, I don't agree; but I must be patient. The secrecy, the underhandedness, are hateful to me; but for her it's all a part of the sacred humbug."

He rose listlessly, as if the discussion had bled all the life out of him, and took himself away.

When he had gone his father drew a deep breath. Yes—the boy would stay in Paris; he would almost certainly stay; for the present, at any rate. And people were still prophesying that in the spring there would be a big push all along the line; and after that the nightmare might be over. Campton was glad he had gone to see Madge Talkett. He was glad, above all, that if the thing had to be done it was over, and that, by Madge's wish, no one was to know of what had passed between them. It was a distinct relief, in spite of what he had suggested to George, not to have to carry that particular problem to Adele Anthony or Boylston.

A few days later George accepted a staff-appointment in Paris.

BOOK IV

Chapter XXXII

H EAVILY the weeks went by.

The world continued to roar on through smoke and flame, and contrasted with that headlong race was the slow dragging lapse of hours and days to those who had to wait on events inactively.

When Campton met Paul Dastrey for the first time after the death of the latter's nephew, the two men exchanged a long hand-clasp and then sat silent. As Campton had felt from the first, there was nothing left for them to say to each other. If young men like Louis Dastrey must continue to be sacrificed by hundreds of thousands to save their country, for whom was the country being saved? Was it for the wasp-waisted youths in sham uniforms who haunted the reawakening hotels and restaurants, in the frequent intervals between their ambulance trips to safe distances from the front? Or for the elderly men like Dastrey and Campton, who could only sit facing each other with the spectre of the lost between them? Young Dastrey, young Fortin-Lescluze, René Davril, Benny Upsher—and how many hundreds more each day! And not even a child left by most of them, to carry on the faith they had died for . . .

"If we're giving all we care for so that those little worms can reopen their dance-halls on the ruins, what in God's name *is* left?" Campton questioned.

Dastrey sat looking at the ground, his grey head bent between his hands. "France," he said.

"What's France, with no men left?"

"Well—I suppose, an Idea."

"Yes. I suppose so." Campton stood up heavily.

An Idea: they must cling to that. If Dastrey, from the depths of his destitution, could still feel it and live by it, why did it not help Campton more? An Idea: that was what France, ever since she had existed, had always been in the story of civilization;

a luminous point about which striving visions and purposes could rally. And in that sense she had been as much Campton's spiritual home as Dastrey's; to thinkers, artists, to all creators, she had always been a second country. If France went, western civilization went with her; and then all they had believed in and been guided by would perish. That was what George had felt; it was what had driven him from the Argonne to the Aisne. Campton felt it too; but dully, through a fog. His son was safe; yes—but too many other men's sons were dying. There was no spot where his thoughts could rest: there were moments when the sight of George, intact and immaculate—his arm at last out of its sling—rose before his father like a reproach.

The feeling was senseless; but there it was. Whenever the young man entered the room Campton saw him attended by the invisible host of his comrades, the fevered, the maimed and the dying. The Germans had attacked at Verdun: horrible daily details of the struggle were pouring in. No one at the rear had really known, except in swift fitful flashes, about the individual suffering of the first months of the war; now such information was systematized and distributed everywhere, daily, with a cold impartial hand. And every night, when one laid one's old bones on one's bed, there were those others, the young in their thousands, lying down, perhaps never to rise again, in the mud and blood of the trenches.

Even Boylston's Preparedness was beginning to get on Campton's nerves. He tried to picture to himself how he should exult when his country at last fell into line; but he could realize only what his humiliation would be if she did not. It was almost a relief, at this time, to have his mind diverted to the dissensions among "The Friends of French Art," where, at a stormy meeting, Harvey Mayhew, as a member of the Finance Committee, had asked for an accounting of the money taken in at Mrs. Talkett's concert. This money, Mr. Mayhew stated, had passed through a number of hands. It should have been taken over by Mr. Boylston, as treasurer, at the close of the performance; but he had failed to claim it—had, in fact, been unfindable when the organizers of the concert brought their takings to Mrs. Talkett—and the money, knocking about from hand to hand, had finally been carried by Mrs. Talkett herself to Mr. Campton. The latter, when asked to entrust it to Mr. Mayhew, had refused on the ground that he had already deposited it in the bank; but a number of days later it was known to be still in his possession. All this time Mr. Boylston, treasurer, and chairman of the Financial Committee, appeared to think it quite in order that the funds should have been (as he assumed) deposited in the bank by a member who was not on that particular committee, and who, in reality, had forgotten that they were in his possession.

Mr. Mayhew delivered himself of this indictment amid an embarrassed silence. To Campton it had seemed as if a burst of protest must instantly clear the air. But after he himself had apologized for his negligence in not depositing the money, and Boylston had disengaged his responsibility in a few quiet words, there followed another blank interval. Then Mr. Mayhew suddenly suggested a complete reorganization of the work. He had something to criticize in every department. He, who so seldom showed himself at the office, now presented a list of omissions and commissions against which one after another of the active members rose to enter a mild denial. It was clear that some one belonging to the organization, and who was playing into his hands, had provided him with a series of cleverly falsified charges against the whole group of workers.

Presently Campton could stand it no longer, and, jumping up, suddenly articulate, he flung into his cousin's face a handful of home-truths under which he expected that glossy countenance to lose its lustre. But Mr. Mayhew bore the assault with urbanity. It did not behove him, he said, to take up the reproaches addressed to him by the most distinguished member of their committee—the most distinguished, he might surely say without offence to any of the others (a murmur of assent); it did not behove him, because one of the few occasions on which a great artist may be said to be at a disadvantage is when he is trying to discuss business matters with a man of business. He, Mr. Mayhew, was only that, nothing more; but he *was* that, and he had been trained to answer random abuse by hard facts. In no way did he intend to reflect on the devoted labours of certain ladies of the committee, nor on their sympathetic treasurer's gallant efforts to acquire, amid all his other pressing interests, the rudiments of business habits; but Miss Anthony had all along been dividing her time between two widely different charities, and Mr. Boylston, like his distinguished champion, was first of all an artist, with the habits of the studio rather than of the office. In the circumstances—

Campton jumped to his feet again. If he stayed a moment longer he felt he should knock Mayhew down. He jammed his hat on, shouted out "I resign," and limped out of the room.

It was the way in which his encounters with practical difficulties always ended. The consciousness of his inferiority in argument, the visionary's bewilderment when incomprehensible facts are thrust on him by fluent people, the helpless sense of not knowing what to answer, and of seeing his dream-world smashed in the rough-and-tumble of shabby motives—it all gave him the feeling that he was drowning, and must fight his way to the surface before they had him under.

In the street he stood in a cold sweat of remorse. He knew the charges of negligence against Miss Anthony and Boylston were trumped up. He knew there was an answer to be made, and that he was the man to make it; and his eyes filled with tears of rage and self-pity at his own incompetence. But then he took heart at the thought of Boylston's astuteness and Miss Anthony's courage. They would not let themselves be beaten—probably they would fight their battle better without him. He tried to protect his retreat with such arguments, and when he got back to the studio he called up Mme. Lebel, and plunged again into his charcoal study of her head. He did not remember having ever worked with such supernatural felicity: it was as if *that* were his victorious answer to all their lies and intrigues . . .

But the Mayhew party was victorious too. How it came about a mind like Campton's could not grasp. Mr. Mayhew, it appeared, had let fall that a very large gift of money from the world-renowned philanthropist, Sir Cyril Jorgenstein (obtained through the good offices of Mmes. de Dolmetsch and Beausite) was contingent on certain immediate changes in the organization ("drastic changes" was Mr. Mayhew's phrase); and thereupon several hitherto passive members had suddenly found voice to assert the duty of not losing this gift. After that the way was clear. Adele Anthony and Boylston were offered ornamental posts which they declined, and within a week the Palais Royal saw them no more, and Paris drawing-rooms echoed with the usual rumours of committee wrangles and dark discoveries.

The episode left Campton with a bitter taste in his soul. It seemed to him like an ugly little allegory of Germany's manœuvring the world into war. The speciousness of Mr. Mayhew's arguments, the sleight-of-hand by which he had dislodged the real workers and replaced them by his satellites, reminded the painter of the neutrals who were beginning to say that there were two sides to every question, that war was always cruel, and how about the Russian atrocities in Silesia? As the months dragged on a breath of lukewarmness had begun to blow through the world, damping men's souls, confusing plain issues, casting a doubt on the worth of everything. People were beginning to ask what one knew, after all, of the secret motives which had impelled half-a-dozen self-indulgent old men ensconced in Ministerial offices to plunge the world in ruin. No one seemed to feel any longer that life is something more than being alive; apparently the only people not tired of the thought of death were the young men still pouring out to it in their thousands.

Still those thousands poured; still the young died; still, wherever Campton went, he met elderly faces, known and unknown, disfigured by grief, shrunken with renunciation. And still the months wore on without result.

One day in crossing the Tuileries he felt the same soft sparkle which, just about a year earlier, had abruptly stirred the sap in him. Yes—it was nearly a year since the day when he had noticed the first horse-chestnut blossoms, and been reminded by Mme. Lebel that he ought to buy some new shirts; and though to-day the horse-chestnuts were still leafless they were already misty with buds, and the tall white clouds above them full-uddered with spring showers. It was spring again, spring with her deluding promises—her gilding of worn stones and chilly water, the mystery of her distances, the finish and brilliance of her nearer strokes. Campton, in spite of himself, drank down the life-giving draught and felt its murmur in his veins. And just then, across the width of the gardens he saw, beyond a stretch of turf and clipped shrubs, two people, also motionless, who seemed to have the same cup at their lips. He recognized his son and Mrs. Talkett.

Their backs were toward him, and they stood close together, looking with the same eyes at the same sight: an Apollo touched with flying sunlight. After a while they walked on again, slowly and close to each other. George, as they moved, seemed now and then to point out some beauty of sculpture, or the colour of a lichened urn; and once they turned and took their fill of the great perspective tapering to the Arch—the Arch on which Rude's Mænad-Marseillaise still yelled her battalions on to death.

Chapter XXXIII

C AMPTON finished his charcoal of Mme. Lebel; then he attacked her in oils. Now that his work at the Palais Royal was ended, painting was once more his only refuge.

Adele Anthony had returned to her refugees; Boylston, pale and obstinate, toiled on at Preparedness. But Campton found it impossible to take up any new form of work; his philanthropic ardour was exhausted. He could only shut himself up, for long solitary hours, in the empty and echoing temple of his art.

George emphatically approved of his course: George was as insistent as Mrs. Brant on the duty of "business as usual." But on the young man's lips the phrase had a different meaning; it seemed the result of that altered perspective which Campton was conscious of whenever, nowadays, he tried to see things as his son saw them. George was not indifferent, he was not callous; but he seemed to feel himself mysteriously set apart, destined to some other task for which he was passively waiting. Even the split among "The Friends of French Art" left him, despite of his admiration for Boylston, curiously unperturbed. He seemed to have taken the measure of all such ephemeral agitations, and to regard them with an indulgent pity which was worse than coldness.

"He feels that all we do is so useless," Campton said to Dastrey; "he's like a gardener watching ants rebuild their hill in the middle of a path, and knowing all the while that hill and path are going to be wiped out by his pick."

"Ah, they're all like that," Dastrey murmured.

Mme. Lebel came up to the studio every afternoon. The charcoal study had been only of her head; but for the painting Campton had seated her in her own horsehair arm-chair, her smoky lamp beside her, her sewing in her lap. More than ever he saw in the wise old face something typical of its race and class: the obstinate French gift, as some one had put it, of making one more effort after the last effort. The old woman could not imagine why he wanted to paint her; but when one day he told her it was for her grandsons, her eyes filled, and she said: "For which one, sir? For they're both at Verdun."

One autumn afternoon he was late in getting back to the studio, where he knew she was waiting for him. He pushed the door open, and there, in the beaten-down attitude in which he had once before seen her, she lay across the table, her cap awry, her hands clutching her sewing, and George kneeling at her side. The young man's arm was about her, his head pressed against her breast; and on the floor lay the letter, the fatal letter which was always, nowadays, the key to such scenes.

Neither George nor the old woman had heard Campton enter; and for a moment he stood and watched them. George's face, so fair and ruddy against Mme. Lebel's rusty black, wore a look of boyish compassion which Campton had never seen on it. Mme. Lebel had sunk into his hold as if it soothed and hushed her; and Campton said to himself: "These two are closer to each other than George and I, because they've both seen the horror face to face. He knows what to say to her ever so much better than he knows what to say to his mother or me."

But apparently there was no need to say much. George continued to kneel in silence; presently he bent and kissed the old woman's cheek; then he got to his feet and saw his father.

"The *Chasseur Alpin*," he merely said, picking up the letter and handing it to Campton. "It was the grandson she counted on most."

Mme. Lebel caught sight of Campton, smoothed herself and stood up also.

"I had found him a wife—a strong healthy girl with a good *dot*. There go my last great-grandchildren! For the other will be killed too. I don't understand any more, do you?" She made an automatic attempt to straighten the things on the table, but her hands beat the air and George had to lead her downstairs.

It was that day that Campton said to himself: "We shan't keep him in Paris much longer." But the heavy weeks of spring and summer passed, the inconclusive conflict at the front went on with its daily toll of dead, and George still stuck to his job. Campton, during this time, continued to avoid the Brants as much as possible. His wife's conversation was intolerable to him; her obtuse optimism, now that she had got her son back, was even harder to bear than the guiltily averted glance of Mr. Brant, between whom and Campton their last talk had hung a lasting shadow of complicity.

But most of all Campton dreaded to meet the Talketts; the wife with her flushed cheek-bones and fixed eyes, the husband still affably and continuously arguing against Philistinism. One afternoon the painter stumbled on them, taking tea with George in Boylston's little flat; but he went away again, unable to bear the interminable discussion between Talkett and Boylston, and the pacifist's reiterated phrase: "To borrow one of my wife's expressions"—while George, with a closed brooding face, sat silent, laughing drily now and then. What a different George from the one his father had found, in silence also, kneeling beside Mme. Lebel!

Once again Campton was vouchsafed a glimpse of that secret George. He had walked back with his son after the funeral mass for young Lebel; and in the porter's lodge of the Avenue Marigny they found a soldier waiting—a young square-built fellow, with a shock of straw-coloured hair above his sunburnt rural face. Campton was turning from the door when George dashed past him, caught the young man by both shoulders, and shouted out his name. It was that of the orderly who had carried him out of the firing-line and hunted him up the next day in the Doullens hospital. Campton saw the look the two exchanged: it lasted only for the taking of a breath; a moment later officer and soldier were laughing like boys, and the orderly was being drawn forth to shake hands with Campton. But again the glance was an illumination; it came straight from that far country, the Benny Upsher country, which Campton so feared to see in his son's eyes.

The orderly had been visiting his family, fugitives from the invaded regions who had taken shelter in one of Adele Anthony's suburban colonies. He had obtained permission to stop in Paris on his way back to the front; and for two joyful days he was lodged and feasted in the Avenue Marigny. Boylston provided him with an evening at Montmartre, George and Mrs. Brant took him to the theatre and the cinema, and on the last day of his leave Adele Anthony invited him to tea with Campton, Mr. Brant and Boylston. Mr. Brant, as they left this entertainment, hung back on the stairs to say in a whisper to Campton: "The family are provided for—amply. I've asked George to mention the fact to the young man; but not until just as he's starting."

Campton nodded. For George's sake he was glad; yet he could not repress a twinge of his dormant jealousy. Was it always to be Brant who thought first of the things to make George happy—always Brant who would alone have the power to carry them out?

"But he can't prevent that poor fellow's getting killed to-morrow," Campton thought almost savagely, as the young soldier beamed forth from the taxi in which George was hurrying him to the station.

It was not many days afterward that George looked in at the studio early one morning. Campton, over his breakfast, had been reading the *communiqué*. There was heavy news from Verdun; from east to west the air was dark with calamity; but George's face had the look it had worn when he greeted his orderly.

"Dad, I'm off," he said; and sitting down at the table, he unceremoniously poured himself some coffee into his father's empty cup.

"The battalion's been ordered back. I leave to-night. Let's lunch together somewhere presently, shall we?"

His eye was clear, his smile confident: a great weight seemed to have fallen from him, and he looked like the little boy sitting up in bed with his Lavengro. "After ten months of Paris——" he added, stretching his arms over his head with a great yawn.

"Yes—the routine——" stammered Campton, not knowing what he said. Yet he was glad too; yes, in his heart of hearts he knew he was glad; though, as always happened, his emotion took him by the throat and silenced him. But it did not matter, for George was talking.

"I shall have leave a good deal oftener nowadays," he said with animation. "And everything is ever so much better organized—letters and all that. I shan't seem so awfully far away. You'll see."

Campton still gazed at him, struggling for expression. Their hands met. Campton said—or imagined he said: "I see—I do see, already——" though afterward he was not even sure that he had spoken.

What he saw, with an almost blinding distinctness, was the extent to which his own feeling, during the long months, had imperceptibly changed, and how his inmost impulse, now that the blow had fallen, was not of resistance to it, but of acquiescence, since it made him once more one with his son.

He would have liked to tell that to George; but speech was impossible. And perhaps, after all, it didn't matter; it didn't matter, because George understood. Their hand-clasp had made that clear, and an hour or two later they were lunching together almost gaily.

Boylston joined them, and the three went on together to say goodbye to Adele Anthony. Adele, for once, was unprepared: it was almost a relief to Campton, who had winced in advance at the thought of her warlike attitude. The poor thing was far from warlike: her pale eyes clung to George's in a frightened stare, while her lips, a little stiffly, repeated the stock phrases of good cheer. "Such a relief . . . I congratulate you . . . getting out of all this *paperasserie* and red-tape . . . If I'd been you I couldn't have stood Paris another minute . . . The only hopeful people left are at the front . . ." It was the formula that sped every departing soldier.

The day wore on. To Campton its hours seemed as interminable yet as rapid as those before his son's first departure, nearly two years earlier. George had begged his father to come in the evening to the Avenue Marigny, where he was dining with the Brants. It was easier for Campton nowadays to fall in with such requests: during the months of George's sojourn in Paris a good many angles had had their edges rubbed off.

Besides, at that moment he would have done anything for his son—his son again at last! In their hand-clasp that morning the old George had come back to him, simple, boyish, just as he used to be; and Campton's dread of the future was lightened by a great glow of pride.

In the Avenue Marigny dining-room the Brants and George were still sitting together about the delicate silver and porcelain. There were no flowers: Julia, always correct, had long since banished them as a superfluity. But there was champagne for George's farewell, and a glimpse of rich fare being removed.

Mr. Brant rose to greet Campton. His concise features were drawn with anxiety, and with the effort to hide it; but his wife appeared to Campton curiously unperturbed, and the leave-taking was less painful and uselessly drawn out than he had expected.

George and his father were to be sent to the station in Mr. Brant's motor. Campton, as he got in, remembered with a shiver the grey morning, before daylight, when the same motor had stood at the studio door, waiting to carry him to Doullens; between himself and his son he seemed to see Mr. Brant's small suffering profile.

To shake off the memory he said: "Your mother's in wonder-fully good form. I was glad to see she wasn't nervous."

George laughed. "No. Madge met her this morning at the new *clairvoyante's.*—It does them all a lot of good," he added, with his all-embracing tolerance.

Campton shivered again. That universal smiling comprehension of George's always made him seem remoter than ever. "It makes him seem so old—a thousand years older than I am." But he forced an acquiescent laugh, and presently George went on: "About Madge—you'll be awfully good to her, won't you, if I get smashed?"

"My dear boy!"

There was another pause, and then Campton risked a question. "Just how do things stand? I know so little, after all."

For a moment George seemed to hesitate: his thick fair eye-brows were drawn into a puzzled frown. "I know—I've never explained it to you properly. I've tried to; but I was never sure that I could make you see." He paused and added quietly: "I know now that she'll never divorce Talkett."

"You know——?" Campton exclaimed with a great surge of relief.

"She thinks she will; but I see that the idea still frightens her. And I've kept on using the divorce argument only as a pretext."

The words thrust Campton back into new depths of perplexity. "A pretext?" he echoed.

"My dear old Dad—don't you guess? She's come to care for me awfully; if we'd gone all the lengths she wanted, and then I'd got killed, there would have been nothing on earth left for her. I hadn't the right, don't you see? We chaps haven't any futures to dispose of till this job we're in is finished. Of course, if I come back, and she can make up her mind to break with everything she's used to, we shall marry; but if things go wrong I'd rather leave her as she is, safe in her little old rut. So many people can't live out of one—and she's one of them, poor child, though she's so positive she isn't."

Campton sat chilled and speechless as the motor whirled them on through the hushed streets. It paralyzed his faculties to think that in a moment more they would be at the station.

"It's awfully fine: your idea," he stammered at length. "Awfully—magnanimous." But he still felt the chill down his spine.

"Oh, it's only that things look to us so different—so indescribably different—and always will, I suppose, even after this business is over. We seem to be sealed to it for life."

"Poor girl—poor girl!" Campton thought within himself. Aloud he said: "My dear chap, of course you can count on my being—my doing—"

"Of course, of course, old Dad."

They were at the station. Father and son got out and walked toward the train. Campton put both hands on George's shoulders.

"Look here," George broke out, "there's one thing more. I want to tell you that I know what a lot I owe to you and Adele. You've both been awfully fine: did you know it? You two first made me feel a lot of things I hadn't felt before. And you know this *is* my job; I've never been surer of it than at this minute."

They clasped hands in silence, each looking his fill of the other; then the crowd closed in, George exclaimed: "My kit-bag!" and somehow, in the confusion, the parting was over, and Campton, straining blurred eyes, saw his son's smile—the smile of the light-hearted lad of old days—flash out at him from the moving train. For an instant the father had the illusion that it was the goodbye look of the boy George, going back to school after the holidays.

Campton, as he came out of the station, stumbled, to his surprise, on Mr. Brant. The little man, as they met, flushed and paled, and sought the customary support from his eye-glasses.

"I followed you in the other motor," he said, looking away.

"Oh, I say——" Campton murmured; then, with an effort: "Shouldn't you like me to drive back with you?"

Mr. Brant shook his head. "Thank you. Thank you very much. But it's late and you'll want to be getting home. I'll be glad if you'll use my car." Together they strolled slowly across the station court to the place where the private motors waited; but there Campton held out his hand.

"Much obliged; I think I'll walk."

Mr. Brant nodded; then he said abruptly: "This *clairvoyante* business: is there anything in it, do you think? You saw how calm—er—Julia was just now: she wished me to tell you that that Spanish woman she goes to—her name is Olida, I think— had absolutely reassured her about . . . about the future. The woman says she knows that George will come back soon, and never be sent to the front again. Those were the exact words, I believe. *Never be sent to the front again.* Julia put every kind of question, and couldn't trip her up; she wanted me to tell you so. It does sound . . . ? Well, at any rate, it's a help to the mothers."

Chapter XXXIV

THE next morning Campton said to himself: "I can catch that goodbye look if I get it down at once——" and pulled out a canvas before Mme. Lebel came in with his coffee.

As sometimes happened to him, the violent emotions of the last twenty-four hours had almost immediately been clarified and transmuted into vision. He felt that he could think contentedly of George if he could sit down at once and paint him.

The picture grew under his feverish fingers—feverish, yet how firm! He always wondered anew at the way in which, at such hours, the inner flame and smoke issued in a clear guiding radiance. He saw—he saw; and the mere act of his seeing seemed to hold George safe in some pure impenetrable medium. His boy was there, sitting to him, the old George he knew and understood, essentially, vividly face to face with him.

He was interrupted by a ring. Mme. Lebel, tray in hand, opened the door, and a swathed and voluminous figure, sweeping in on a wave of musk, blotted her out. Campton, exasperated at the interruption, turned to face Mme. Olida.

So remote were his thoughts that he would hardly have recognized her had she not breathed, on the old familiar guttural: "Juanito!"

He was less surprised at her intrusion than annoyed at being torn from his picture. "Didn't you see a sign on the door? 'No admission before twelve'——" he growled.

"Oh, yes," she said; "that's how I knew you were in."

"But I'm *not* in; I'm working. I can't allow——"

Her large bosom rose. "I know, my heart! I remember how stern you always were. 'Work—work—my work!' It was always that, even in the first days. But I come to you on my knees: Juanito, imagine me there!" She sketched a plunging motion of her vast body, arrested it in time by supporting herself on the table, and threw back her head entreatingly, so that Campton caught a glint of the pearls in a crevasse of her quaking throat. He saw that her eyes were red with weeping.

"What can I do? You're in trouble?"

"Oh, such trouble, my heart—such trouble!" She leaned to him, absorbing his hands in her plump muscular grasp. "I must have news of my son; I must! The young man—you saw him that day you came with your wife? Yes—he looked in at the door: beautiful as a god, was he not? That was my son Pepito!" And with a deep breath of pride and anguish she unburdened herself of her tale.

Two or three years after her parting with Campton she had married a clever French barber from the Pyrenees. He had brought her to France, and they had opened a "Beauty Shop" at Biarritz and had prospered. Pepito was born there and soon afterward, alas, her clever husband, declaring that he "hated grease in cooking or in woman" ("and after my Pepito's birth I became as you now see me"), had gone off with the manicure and all their savings. Mme. Olida had had a struggle to bring up her boy; but she had kept on with the Beauty Shop, had made a success of it, and not long before the war had added fortune-telling to massage and hair-dressing.

"And my son, Juanito; was not my son an advertisement for a Beauty Shop, I ask you? Before he was out of petticoats he brought me customers; before he was sixteen all the ladies who came to me were quarrelling over him. Ah, there were moments when he crucified me . . . but lately he had grown more rea-sonable, had begun to see where his true interests lay, and we had become friends again, friends and business partners. When the war broke out I came to Paris; I knew that all the mothers would want news of their sons. I have made a great deal of money; and I have had wonderful results—wonderful! I could give you instances—names that you know—where I have fore-told everything! Oh, I have the gift, my heart, I have it!"

She pressed his hands with a smile of triumph; then her face clouded again.

"But six months ago my darling was called to his regiment—and for three months now I've had no news of him, none, none!" she sobbed, the tears making dark streaks through her purplish powder.

The upshot of it was that she had heard that Campton was "all-powerful"; that he knew Ministers and Generals, knew great financiers like Jorgenstein (who were so much more powerful than either Generals or Ministers), and could, if he chose, help her to trace her boy, who, from the day of his departure for the front, had vanished as utterly as if the earth had swallowed him.

"Not a word, not a sign—to me, his mother, who have slaved and slaved for him, who have made a fortune for him!"

Campton looked at her, marvelling. "But your gift as you call it . . . your powers . . . you can't use them for yourself?"

She returned his look with a tearful simplicity: she hardly seemed to comprehend what he was saying. "But my son! I want *news* of my son, real news; I want a letter; I want to see some one who has seen him! To touch a hand that has touched him! Oh, don't you understand?"

"Yes, I understand," he said; and she took up her desperate litany, clinging about him with soft palms like medusa-lips, till by dint of many promises he managed to detach himself and steer her gently to the door.

On the threshold she turned to him once more. "And your own son, Juanito—I know he's at the front again. His mother came the other day—she often comes. And I can promise you things if you'll help me. No, even if you don't help me—for the old days' sake, I will! I know secrets . . . magical secrets that will protect him. There's a Moorish salve, infallible against bullets . . . handed down from King Solomon . . . I can get it . . ."

Campton, guiding her across the sill, led her out and bolted the door on her; then he went back to his easel and stood gazing at the sketch of George. But the spell was broken: the old George was no longer there. The war had sucked him back into its awful whirlpool—once more he was that dark enigma, a son at the front . . .

In the heavy weeks which followed, a guarded allusion of Campton's showed him one day that Boylston was aware of there being "something between" George and Madge Talkett.

"Not that he's ever said anything—or even encouraged me to guess anything. But she's got a talking face, poor little thing; and not much gift of restraint. And I suppose it's fairly obvious to everybody—except perhaps to Talkett—that she's pretty hard hit."

"Yes. And George?"

Boylston's round face became remote and mysterious. "We don't really know—do we, sir?—exactly how any of them feel? Any more than if they were——" He drew up sharply on the word, but Campton faced it.

"Dead?"

"Transfigured, say; no, trans——what's the word in the theology books? A new substance . . . somehow . . ."

"Ah, you feel that too?" the father exclaimed.

"Yes. They don't know it themselves, though—how far they are from us. At least I don't think they do."

Campton nodded. "But George, in the beginning, was—frankly indifferent to the war, wasn't he?"

"Yes; intellectually he was. But he told me that when he saw the first men on their way back from the front—with the first mud on them—he knew he belonged where they'd come from. I tried hard to persuade him when he was here that his real job was on a military mission to America—and it *was*. Think what he might have done out there! But it was no use. His orderly's visit did the trick. It's the thought of their men that pulls them all back. Look at Louis Dastrey—they couldn't keep him in America. There's something in all their eyes: I don't know what. *Dulce et decorum*, perhaps——"

"Yes."

There was a pause before Campton questioned: "And Talkett?"

"Poor little ass—I don't know. He's here arguing with me nearly every day. She looks over his shoulder, and just shrugs at me with her eyebrows."

"Can you guess what she thinks of George's attitude?"

"Oh, something different every day. I don't believe she's ever really understood. But then she loves him, and nothing else counts."

Mrs. Brant continued to face life with apparent serenity. She had returned several times to Mme. Olida's, and had always brought away the same reassuring formula: she thought it striking, and so did her friends, that the *clairvoyante's* prediction never varied.

There was reason to believe that George's regiment had been sent to Verdun, and from Verdun the news was growing daily more hopeful. This seemed to Mrs. Brant a remarkable confirmation of Olida's prophecy. Apparently it did not occur to her that, in the matter of human life, victories may be as ruinous as defeats; and she triumphed in the fact—it had grown to be a fact to her—that her boy was at Verdun, when he might have been in the Somme, where things, though stagnant, were on the whole going less well. Mothers prayed for "a quiet sector"—and then, she argued, what happened? The men grew careless, the officers were oftener away; your son was ordered out to see to the repairs of a barbed-wire entanglement, and a sharpshooter picked him off while you were sitting reading one of his letters, and thinking: "Thank God he's out of the fighting." And besides, Olida was *sure*, and all her predictions had been so wonderful . . .

Campton began to dread his wife's discovering Mme. Olida's fears for her own son. Every endeavour to get news of Pepito had been fruitless; finally Campton and Boylston concluded that the young man must be a prisoner. The painter had a second visit from Mme. Olida, in the course of which he besought her (without naming Julia) to be careful not to betray her private anxiety to the poor women who came to her for consolation; and she fixed her tortured velvet eyes on him reproachfully.

"How could you think it of me, Juanito? The money I earn is for my boy! That gives me the strength to invent a new lie every morning."

He took her fraudulent hand and kissed it.

The next afternoon he met Mrs. Brant walking down the Champs Elysées with her light girlish step. She lifted a radiant face to his. "A letter from George this morning! And, do you know, Olida prophesied it? I was there again yesterday; and she told me that he would soon be back, and that at that very moment she could see him writing to me. You'll admit it's extraordinary? So many mothers depend on her—I couldn't live without her. And her messages from her own son are so beautiful——"

"From her own son?"

"Yes: didn't I tell you? He says such perfect things to her. And she confessed to me, poor woman, that before the war he hadn't always been kind: he used to take her money, and behave badly. But now every day he sends her a thought-message—such beautiful things! She says she wouldn't have the courage to keep us all up if it weren't for the way that she's kept up by her boy. And now," Julia added gaily, "I'm going to order the cakes for my bridge-tea this afternoon. You know I promised Georgie I wouldn't give up my bridge-teas."

Now and then Campton returned to his latest portrait of his son; but in spite of George's frequent letters, in spite of the sudden drawing together of father and son during their last moments at the station, the vision of the boy George, the careless happy George who had ridiculed the thought of war and pursued his millennial dreams of an enlightened world—that vision was gone. Sometimes Campton fancied that the letters themselves increased this effect of remoteness. They were necessarily more guarded than the ones written, before George's wounding, from an imaginary H. Q.; but that did not wholly account for the difference. Campton, in the last analysis, could only say that his vision of his boy was never quite in focus. Either—as in the moment when George had comforted Mme. Lebel, or greeted his orderly, or when he had said those last few broken words at the station—he seemed nearer than ever, seemed part and substance of his father; or else he became again that beautiful distant apparition, the wingèd sentry guarding the Unknown.

The weeks thus punctuated by private anxieties rolled on dark with doom. At last, in December, came the victory of Verdun. Men took it reverently but soberly. The price paid had been too heavy for rejoicing; and the horizon was too ominous in other quarters. Campton had hoped that the New Year would bring his son back on leave; but still George did not speak of coming. Meanwhile Boylston's face grew rounder and more beaming. At last America was stirring in her sleep. "Oh, if only George were out there!" Boylston used to cry, as if his friend had been an army. His faith in George's powers of persuasion was almost mystical. And not long afterward Campton had the surprise of a visit which seemed, in the most unforeseen way, to confirm this belief. Returning to his studio one afternoon he found it tenanted by Mr. Roger Talkett.

The young man, as carefully brushed and equipped as usual, but pale with emotion, clutched the painter's hand in a moist grasp.

"My dear Master, I had to see you—to see you alone and immediately."

Campton looked at him with apprehension. What was the meaning of his "alone"? Had Mrs. Talkett lost her head, and betrayed her secret—or had she committed some act of imprudence of which the report had come back to her husband?

"Do sit down," said the painter weakly.

But his visitor, remaining sternly upright, shook his head and glanced at his wrist-watch. "My moments," he said, "are numbered—literally; all I have time for is to implore you to look after my wife." He drew a handkerchief from his glossy cuff, and rubbed his eye-glasses.

"Your wife?" Campton echoed, dismayed.

"My dear sir, haven't you guessed? It's George's wonderful example . . . his inspiration . . . I've been converted! We men of culture can't stand by while the ignorant and illiterate are left to die for us. We must leave that attitude to the Barbarian. Our duty is to set an example. I'm off to-night for America—for Plattsburg."

"Oh——" gasped Campton, wringing his hand.

Boylston burst into the studio the next day. "What did I tell you, sir? George's influence—it wakes up everybody. But Talkett—I'll be hanged if I should have thought it! And have you seen his wife? She's a war-goddess! I went to the station with them: their farewells were harrowing. At that minute, you know, I believe she'd forgotten that George ever existed!"

"Well, thank God for that," Campton cried.

"Yes. Don't you feel how we're all being swept into it?" panted Boylston breathlessly. His face had caught the illumination. "Sealed, as George says—we're sealed to the job, every one of us! Even I feel that, sitting here at a stuffy desk . . ." He flushed crimson and his eyes filled. "We'll be in it, you know; America will—in a few weeks now, I believe! George was as sure of it as I am. And, of course, if the war goes on, our army will *have* to take short-sighted officers; won't they, sir? As England and France did from the first. They'll need the men; they'll need us all, sir!"

"They'll need *you*, my dear chap; and they'll have you, to the full, whatever your job is," Campton smiled; and Boylston, choking back a sob, dashed off again.

Yes, they were all being swept into it together—swept into the yawning whirlpool. Campton felt that as clearly as all these young men; he felt the triviality, the utter unimportance, of all their personal and private concerns, compared with this great headlong outpouring of life on the altar of conviction. And he understood why, for youths like George and Boylston, nothing, however close and personal to them, would matter till the job was over. "And not even for poor Talkett!" he reflected whimsically.

That afternoon, curiously appeased, he returned once more to his picture of his son. He had sketched the boy leaning out of the train window, smiling back, signalling, saying goodbye, while his destiny rushed him out into darkness as years ago the train used to rush him back to school. And while Campton worked he caught the glow again; it rested on brow and eyes, and spread in sure touches under his happy brush.

One day, as the picture progressed, he wavered over the remembrance of some little detail of the face, and went in search of an old portfolio into which, from time to time, he had been in the habit of thrusting his unfinished studies of George. He plunged his hand into the heap, and Georges of all ages looked forth at him: round baby-Georges, freckled schoolboys, a thoughtful long-faced youth (the delicate George of St. Moritz); but none seemed quite to serve his purpose and he rummaged on till he came to a page torn from an old sketch-book. It was the pencil study he had made of George as the lad lay asleep at the Crillon, the night before his mobilisation.

Campton threw the sketch down on the table; and as he sat staring at it he relived every phase of the emotion out of which it had been born. How little he had known then—how little he had understood! He could bear to look at the drawing now; could bear even to rethink the shuddering thoughts with which he had once flung it away from him. Was it only because the atmosphere was filled with a growing sense of hope? Because, in spite of everything, the victory of Verdun was there to show the inexhaustible strength of France, because people were more and more sure that America was beginning to waken . . . or just because, after too long and fierce a strain, human nature always instinctively contrives to get its necessary whiff of moral oxygen? Or was it that George's influence had really penetrated him, and that this strange renewed confidence in life and in ideals was his son's message of reassurance?

Certainly the old George was there, close to him, that morning; and somewhere else—in scenes how different—he was sure that the actual George, at that very moment, was giving out force and youth and hope to those about him.

"I couldn't be doing this if I didn't understand—at last," Campton thought as he turned back to the easel. The little pencil sketch had given him just the hint he needed, and he took up his palette with a happy sigh.

A knock broke in on his rapt labour, and without turning he called out: "Damn it, who are you? Can't you read the sign? *Not in!*"

The door opened and Mr. Brant entered.

He appeared not to have heard the painter's challenge; his eyes, from the threshold, sprang straight to the portrait, and remained vacantly fastened there. Campton, long afterward, remembered thinking, as he followed the glance: "He'll be trying to buy this one too!"

Mr. Brant moistened his lips, and his gaze, detaching itself from George's face, moved back in the same vacant way to Campton's. The two men looked at each other, and Campton jumped to his feet.

"Not—not——?"

Mr. Brant tried to speak, and the useless effort contracted his mouth in a pitiful grimace.

"*My son?*" Campton shrieked, catching him by the arm. The little man dropped into a chair.

"Not dead . . . not dead . . . Hope . . . hope . . ." was shaken out of him in jerks of anguish.

The door burst open again, and Boylston dashed in beaming. He waved aloft a handful of morning papers.

"America! You've seen? They've sacked Bernstorff! Broken off diplomatic——"

His face turned white, and he stood staring incredulously from one of the two bowed men to the other.

Chapter XXXV

CAMPTON once more stood leaning in the window of a Paris hospital.

Before him, but viewed at another angle, was spread that same great spectacle of the Place de la Concorde that he had looked down at from the Crillon on the eve of mobilisation; behind him, in a fresh white bed, George lay in the same attitude as when his father had stood in the door of his room and sketched him while he slept.

All day there had run through Campton's mind the *clairvoyante's* promise to Julia: "Your son will come back soon, and will never be sent to the front again."

Ah, this time it was true—never, never would he be sent to the front again! They had him fast now, had him safe. That was the one certainty. Fast how, safe how?—the answer to that had long hung in the balance. For two weeks or more after his return the surgeons had hesitated. Then youth had seemed to conquer, and the parents had been told to hope that after a long period of immobility George's shattered frame would slowly re-knit, and he would walk again—or at least hobble. A month had gone by since then; and Campton could at last trust himself to cast his mind back over the intervening days, so like in their anguish to those at Doullens, yet so different in all that material aid and organization could give.

Evacuation from the base, now so systematically and promptly effected, had become a matter of course in all but the gravest cases; and even the delicate undertaking of deflecting George's course from the hospital near the front to which he had been destined, and bringing him to Paris, had been accomplished by a word in the right quarter from Mr. Brant.

Campton, from the first, had been opposed to the attempt to bring George to Paris; partly perhaps because he felt that in the quiet provincial hospital near the front he would be able to have his son to himself. At any rate, the journey would have been shorter; though, as against that, Paris offered more possibilities of surgical aid. His opposition had been violent enough to check

485

his growing friendliness with the Brants; and at the hours when they came to see George, Campton now most often contrived to be absent.

Well, at any rate, George was alive, he was there under his father's eye, he was going to live: there seemed to be no doubt about it now. Campton could think it all over slowly and even calmly, marvelling at the miracle and taking it in . . . So at least he had imagined till he first made the attempt; then the old sense of unreality enveloped him again, and he struggled vainly to clutch at something tangible amid the swimming mists. "George—George—George——" He used to say the name over and over below his breath, as he sat and watched at his son's bedside; but it sounded far off and hollow, like the voice of a ghost calling to another.

Who was "George"? What did the name represent? The father left his post in the window and turned back to the bed, once more searching the boy's face for enlightenment. But George's eyes were closed: sleep lay on him like an impenetrable veil. The sleep of ordinary men was not like that: the light of their daily habits continued to shine through the chinks of their closed faces. But with these others, these who had been down into the lower circles of the pit, it was different: sleep instantly and completely sucked them back into the unknown. There were times when Campton, thus watching beside his son, used to say to himself: "If he were dead he could not be farther from me"—so deeply did George seem plunged in secret traffic with things unutterable.

Now and then Campton, sitting beside him, seemed to see a little way into those darknesses; but after a moment he always shuddered back to daylight, benumbed, inadequate, weighed down with the weakness of the flesh and the incapacity to reach beyond his habitual limit of sensation. "No wonder they don't talk to us," he mused.

By-and-bye, perhaps, when George was well again, and the war over, the father might penetrate into his son's mind, and find some new ground of communion with him: now the thing was not to be conceived.

He recalled again Adele Anthony's asking him, when he had come back from Doullens: "What was the first thing you felt?"

and his answering: "Nothing." . . . Well, it was like that now: every vibration had ceased in him. Between himself and George lay the unbridgeable abyss of his son's experiences.

As he sat there, the door was softly opened a few inches and Boylston's face showed through the crack: light shot from it like the rays around a chalice. At a sign from him Campton slipped out into the corridor and Boylston silently pushed a newspaper into his grasp. He bent over it, trying with dazzled eyes to read sense into the staring head-lines: but "America—America— America——" was all that he could see.

A nurse came gliding up on light feet: the tears were running down her face. "Yes—I know, I know, I know!" she exulted. Up the tall stairs and through the ramifying of long white passages rose an unwonted rumour of sound, checked, subdued, invisibly rebuked, but ever again breaking out, like the noise of ripples on a windless beach. In every direction nurses and orderlies were speeding from one room to another of the house of pain with the message: "America has declared war on Germany."

Campton and Boylston stole back into George's room. George lifted his eyelids and smiled at them, understanding before they spoke.

"The sixth of April! Remember the date!" Boylston cried over him in a gleeful whisper.

The wounded man, held fast in his splints, contrived to raise his head a little. His eyes laughed back into Boylston's. "You'll be in uniform within a week!" he said; and Boylston crimsoned.

Campton turned away again to the window. The day had come—had come; and his son had lived to see it. So many of George's comrades had gone down to death without hope; and in a few months more George, leaning from that same window—or perhaps well enough to be watching the spectacle with his father from the terrace of the Tuileries—would look out on the first brown battalions marching across the Place de la Concorde, where father and son, in the early days of the war, had seen the young recruits of the Foreign Legion patrolling under improvised flags.

At the thought Campton felt a loosening of the tightness about his heart. Something which had been confused and uncertain in his relation to the whole long anguish was abruptly lifted, giving him the same sense of buoyancy that danced in Boylston's glance. At last, random atoms that they were, they seemed all to have been shaken into their places, pressed into the huge mysterious design which was slowly curving a new firmament over a new earth . . .

There was another knock; and a jubilant nurse appeared, hardly visible above a great bunch of lilacs tied with a starred and striped ribbon. Campton, as he passed the flowers over to his son, noticed an envelope with Mrs. Talkett's perpendicular scrawl. George lay smiling, the lilacs close to his pillow, his free hand fingering the envelope; but he did not unseal the letter, and seemed to care less than ever to talk.

After an interval the door opened again, this time to show Mr. Brant's guarded face. He drew back slightly at the sight of Campton; but Boylston, jumping up, passed close to the painter to breathe: "To-day, sir, just to-day—you must!"

Campton went to the door and signed silently to Mr. Brant to enter. Julia Brant stood outside, flushed and tearful, carrying as many orchids as Mrs. Talkett had sent lilacs. Campton held out his hand, and with an embarrassed haste she stammered: "we couldn't wait——" Behind her he saw Adele Anthony hurriedly coming up the stairs.

For a few minutes they all stood or sat about George's bed, while their voices, beginning to speak low, rose uncontrollably, interrupting one another with tears and laughter. Mr. Brant and Boylston were both brimming with news, and George, though he listened more than he spoke, now and then put a brief question which loosened fresh floods. Suddenly Campton noticed that the young man's face, which had been too flushed, grew pale; but he continued to smile, and his eyes to move responsively from one illuminated face to the other. Campton, seeing that the others meant to linger, presently rose and slipping out quietly walked across the Rue de Rivoli to the deserted terrace of the Tuileries. There he sat for a long time, looking out on the vast glittering spaces of the Place de la Concorde, and calling up, with his painter's faculty of vivid and precise visualization, a future vision of interminable lines of brown battalions marching past.

When he returned to the hospital after dinner the night-nurse met him. She was not quite as well satisfied with her patient that evening: hadn't he perhaps had too many visitors? Yes, of course—she knew it had been a great day, a day of international rejoicing, above all a blessed day for France. But the doctors, from the beginning, must have warned Mr. Campton that his son ought to be kept quiet—very quiet. The last operation had been a great strain on his heart. Yes, certainly, Mr. Campton might go in; the patient had asked for him. Oh, there was no danger—no need for anxiety; only he must not stay too long; his son must try to sleep.

Campton nodded, and stole in.

George lay motionless in the shaded lamplight: his eyes were open, but they seemed to reflect his father's presence without any change of expression, like mirrors rather than like eyes. The room was doubly silent after the joyful hubbub of the afternoon. The nurse had put the orchids and lilacs where George's eyes could rest on them. But was it on the flowers that his gaze so tranquilly dwelt? Or did he see in their place the faces of their senders? Or was he again in that far country whither no other eyes could follow him?

Campton took his usual seat by the bed. Father and son looked at each other, and the old George glanced out for half a second between the wounded man's lids.

"There was too much talking to-day," Campton grumbled.

"Was there? I didn't notice," his son smiled.

No—he hadn't noticed; he didn't notice anything. He was a million miles away again, whirling into his place in the awful pattern of that new firmament . . .

"Tired, old man?" Campton asked under his breath.

"No; just glad," said George contentedly.

His father laid a hand on his and sat silently beside him while the spring night blew in upon them through the open window. The quiet streets grew quieter, the hush in their hearts seemed gradually to steal over the extinguished city. Campton kept saying to himself: "I must be off," and still not moving. The nurse was sure to come back presently—why should he not wait till she dismissed him?

After a while, seeing that George's eyes had closed, Campton rose, and crept across the room to darken the lamp with a news-paper. His movement must have roused his son, for he heard a slight struggle behind him and the low cry: "Father!"

Campton turned and reached the bed in a stride. George, ashy-white, had managed to lift himself a little on his free elbow. "Anything wrong?" the father cried.

"No; everything all right," George said. He dropped back, his lids closing again, and a single twitch ran through the hand that Campton had seized. After that he lay stiller than ever.

Chapter XXXVI

GEORGE'S prediction had come true. At his funeral, three days afterward, Boylston, a new-fledged member of the American Military Mission, was already in uniform . . .

But through what perversity of attention did the fact strike Campton, as he stood, a blank unfeeling automaton, in the front pew behind that coffin draped with flags and flanked with candle-glitter? Why did one thing rather than another reach to his deadened brain, and mostly the trivial things, such as Boylston's being already in uniform, and poor Julia's nose, under the harsh crape, looking so blue-red without its powder, and the chaplain's asking "O grave, where is thy victory?" in the querulous tone of a schoolmaster reproaching a pupil who mislaid things? It was always so with Campton: when sorrow fell it left him insensible and dumb. Not till long afterward did he begin to feel its birth-pangs . . .

They first came to him, those pangs, on a morning of the following July, as he sat once more on the terrace of the Tuileries. Most of his time, during the months since George's death, had been spent in endless aimless wanderings up and down the streets of Paris: and that day, descending early from Montmartre, he had noticed in his listless way that all the buildings on his way were fluttering with American flags. The fact left him indifferent: Paris was always decorating nowadays for one ally or another. Then he remembered that it must be the Fourth of July; but the idea of the Fourth of July came to him, through the same haze of indifference, as a mere far-off childish memory of surreptitious explosions and burnt fingers. He strolled on toward the Tuileries, where he had got into the way of sitting for hours at a time, looking across the square at what had once been George's window.

He was surprised to find the Rue de Rivoli packed with people; but his only thought was the instinctive one of turning away to avoid them, and he began to retrace his steps in the direction of the Louvre. Then at a corner he paused again and looked back at the Place de la Concorde. It was not curiosity that drew him, heaven knew—he would never again be curious about anything—but he suddenly remembered the day three months earlier when, leaning from George's window in the hospital, he had said to himself "By the time our first regiments arrive he'll be up and looking at them from here, or sitting with me over there on the terrace"; and that decided him to turn back. It was as if he had felt the pressure of George's hand on his arm.

Though it was still so early he had some difficulty in pushing his way through the throng. No seats were left on the terrace, but he managed to squeeze into a corner near one of the great vases of the balustrade; and leaning there, with the happy hubbub about him, he watched and waited.

Such a summer morning it was—and such a strange grave beauty had fallen on the place! He seemed to understand for the first time—he who had served Beauty all his days—how profoundly, at certain hours, it may become the symbol of things hoped for and things died for. All those stately spaces and raying distances, witnesses of so many memorable scenes, might have been called together just as the setting for this one event—the sight of a few brown battalions passing over them like a feeble trail of insects.

Campton, with a vague awakening of interest, glanced about him, studying the faces of the crowd. Old and young, infirm and healthy, civilians and soldiers—ah, the soldiers!—all were exultant, confident, alive. Alive! The word meant something new to him now—something so strange and unnatural that his mind still hung and brooded over it. For now that George was dead, by what mere blind propulsion did all these thousands of human beings keep on mechanically living?

He became aware that a boy, leaning over intervening shoulders, was trying to push a folded paper into his hand. On it was pencilled, in Mr. Brant's writing: "There will be a long time to wait. Will you take the seat I have kept next to mine?" Campton glanced down the terrace, saw where the little man sat at its farther end, and shook his head. Then some contradictory impulse made him decide to get up, laboriously work his halting frame through the crowd, and insert himself into the place next to Mr. Brant. The two men nodded without shaking hands; after that they sat silent, their eyes on the empty square. Campton noticed that Mr. Brant wore his usual gray clothes, but with a mourning band on the left sleeve. The sight of that little band irritated Campton . . .

There was, as Mr. Brant had predicted, a long interval of waiting; but at length a murmur of jubilation rose far off, and gathering depth and volume came bellowing and spraying up to where they sat. The square, the Champs Elysées and all the leafy distances were flooded with it; it was as though the voice of Paris had sprung up in fountains out of her stones. Then a military march broke shrilly on the tumult; and there they came at last, in a scant swaying line—so few, so new, so raw; so little, in comparison with the immense assemblages familiar to the place, so much in meaning and in promise.

"How badly they march—there hasn't even been time to drill them properly!" Campton thought; and at the thought he felt a choking in his throat, and his sorrow burst up in him in healing springs . . .

It was after that day that he first went back to his work. He had not touched paint or pencil since George's death; now he felt the inspiration and the power returning, and he began to spend his days among the young American officers and soldiers, studying them, talking to them, going about with them, and then hurrying home to jot down his impressions. He had not, as yet, looked at his last study of George, or opened the portfolio with the old sketches; if any one had asked him, he would probably have said that they no longer interested him. His whole creative faculty was curiously, mysteriously engrossed in the recording of the young faces for whose coming George had yearned.

"It's their marching so badly—it's their not even having had time to be drilled!" he said to Boylston, half-shamefacedly, as they sat together one August evening in the studio window.

Campton seldom saw Boylston nowadays. All the young man's time was taken up by his job with the understaffed and inexperienced Military Mission; but fagged as he was by continual overwork and heavy responsibilities, his blinking eyes had at last lost their unsatisfied look, and his whole busy person radiated hope and encouragement.

On the day in question he had turned up unexpectedly, inviting himself to dine with Campton and smoke a cigar afterward in the quiet window overhanging Paris. Campton was glad to have him there; no one could tell him more than Boylston about the American soldiers, their numbers, the accommodations prepared for their reception, their first contact with the other belligerents, and their own view of the business they were about. And the two chatted quietly in the twilight till the young man, rising, said it was time to be off.

"Back to your shop?"

"Rather! There's a night's work ahead. But I'm as good as new after our talk."

Campton looked at him wistfully. "You know I'd like to paint you some day."

"Oh——" cried Boylston, suffused with blushes; and added with a laugh: "It's my uniform, not me."

"Well, your uniform *is* you—it's all of you young men."

Boylston stood in the window twisting his cap about undecidedly. "Look here, sir—now that you've got back to work again——"

"Well?" Campton interrupted suspiciously.

The young man cleared his throat and spoke with a rush. "His mother wants most awfully that something should be decided about the monument."

"Monument? What monument? I don't want my son to have a monument," Campton exploded.

But Boylston stuck to his point. "It'll break her heart if something isn't put on the grave before long. It's five months now—and they fully recognize your right to decide——"

"Damn what they recognize! It was they who brought him to Paris; they made him travel when he wasn't fit; they killed him."

"Well—supposing they did: judge how much more they must be suffering!"

"Let 'em suffer. He's my son—my son. He isn't Brant's."

"Miss Anthony thinks——"

"And he's not hers either, that I know of!"

Boylston seemed to hesitate. "Well, that's just it, isn't it, sir? You've had him; you have him still. Nobody can touch that fact, or take it from you. Every hour of his life was yours. But they've never had anything, those two others, Mr. Brant and Miss Anthony; nothing but a reflected light. And so every outward sign means more to them. I'm putting it badly, I know——"

Campton held out his hand. "You don't mean to, I suppose. But better not put it at all. Good night," he said. And on the threshold he called out sardonically: "And who's going to pay for a monument, I'd like to know?"

A monument—they wanted a monument! Wanted him to decide about it, plan it, perhaps design it—good Lord, he didn't know! No doubt it all seemed simple enough to them: anything did, that money could buy . . . When he couldn't yet bear to turn that last canvas out from the wall, or look into the old portfolio even . . . Suffering, suffering! What did they any of them know about suffering? Going over old photographs, comparing studies, recalling scenes and sayings, discussing with some sculptor or other the shape of George's eyelids, the spring of his chest-muscles, the way his hair grew and his hands moved—why, it was like digging him up again out of that peaceful corner of the Neuilly cemetery where at last he was resting, like dragging him back to the fret and the fever, and the senseless roar of the guns that still went on.

And then: as he'd said to Boylston, who was to pay for their monument? Even if the making of it had struck him as a way of getting nearer to his boy, instead of building up a marble wall between them—even if the idea had appealed to him, he hadn't a penny to spare for such an undertaking. In the first place, he never intended to paint again for money; never intended to do anything but these gaunt and serious or round and baby-ish young American faces above their stiff military collars, and when their portraits were finished to put them away, locked up for his own pleasure; and what he had earned in the last years was to be partly for these young men—for their reading-rooms, clubs, recreation centres, whatever was likely to give them temporary rest and solace in the grim months to come; and partly for such of the protégés of "The Friends of French Art" as had been deprived of aid under the new management. Tales of private jealousy and petty retaliation came to Campton daily, now that Mme. Beausite administered the funds; Adele Anthony and Mlle. Davril, bursting with the wrongs of their pensioners, were always appealing to him for help. And then, hidden behind these more or less valid reasons, the old instinctive dread of spending had reasserted itself, he couldn't tell how or why, unless through some dim opposition to the Brants' perpetual outpouring: their hospitals, their motors, their bribes, their orchids, and now their monument—*their* monument!

He sought refuge from it all with his soldiers, haunting for hours every day one of the newly-opened Soldiers' and Sailors' Clubs. Adele Anthony had already found a job there, and was making a success of it. She looked twenty years older since George was gone, but she stuck to her work with the same humorous pertinacity; and with her mingled heartiness and ceremony, her funny resuscitation of obsolete American slang, and her ability to answer all their most disconcerting questions about Paris and France (Montmartre included), she easily eclipsed the ministering angels who twanged the home-town chord and called them "boys."

The young men appeared to return Campton's liking; it was as if they had guessed that he needed them, and wanted to offer him their shy help. He was conscious of something rather protecting in their attitude, of his being to them a vague unidentified figure, merely "the old gentleman" who was friendly to them; but he didn't mind. It was enough to sit and listen to their talk, to try and clear up a few of the countless puzzles which confronted them, to render them such fatherly services as he could, and in the interval to jot down notes of their faces—their inexhaustibly inspiring faces. Sometimes to talk with them was like being on the floor in George's nursery, among the blocks and the tin soldiers; sometimes like walking with young archangels in a cool empty heaven; but wherever he was he always had the sense of being among his own, the sense he had never had since George's death.

To think of them all as George's brothers, to study out the secret likeness to him in their young dedicated faces: that was now his one passion, his sustaining task; it was at such times that his son came back and sat among them . . .

Gradually, as the weeks passed, the first of his new friends, officers and soldiers, were dispersed throughout the training camps, and new faces succeeded to those he had tried to fix on his canvas; an endless line of Benny Upshers, baby-Georges, schoolboy Boylstons, they seemed to be. Campton saw each one go with a fresh pang, knowing that every move brought them so much nearer to the front, that ever-ravening and inexorable front. They were always happy to be gone; and that only increased his pain. Now and then he attached himself more particularly to one of the young men, because of some look of the eyes or some turn of the mind like George's; and then the parting became anguish.

One day a second lieutenant came to the studio to take leave. He had been an early recruit of Plattsburg, and his military training was so far advanced that he counted on being among the first officers sent to the fighting line. He was a fresh-coloured lad, with fair hair that stood up in a defiant crest.

"There are so few of us, and there's so little time to lose; they can't afford to be too particular," he laughed.

It was just the sort of thing that George would have said, and the laugh was like an echo of George's. At the sound Campton suddenly burst into tears, and was aware of his visitor's looking at him with eyes of dismay and compassion.

"Oh, don't, sir, *don't*," the young man pleaded, wringing the painter's hand, and making what decent haste he could to get out of the studio.

Campton, left alone, turned once more to his easel. He sat down before a canvas on which he had blocked out a group of soldiers playing cards at their club; but after a stroke or two he threw aside his brush, and remained with his head bowed on his hands, a lonely tired old man.

He had kept a cheerful front at his son's going; and now he could not say goodbye to one of these young fellows without crying. Well—it was because he had no one left of his own, he supposed. Loneliness like his took all a man's strength from him . . .

The bell rang, but he did not move. It rang again; then the door was pushed timidly open, and Mrs. Talkett came in. He had not seen her since the day of George's funeral, when he had fancied he detected her in a shrunken black-veiled figure hurrying past in the meaningless line of mourners.

In her usual abrupt fashion she began, without a greeting: "I've come to say goodbye; I'm going to America."

He looked at her remotely, hardly hearing what she said. "To America?"

"Yes; to join my husband."

He continued to consider her in silence, and she frowned in
her perplexed and fretful way. "He's at Plattsburg, you know."
Her eyes wandered unseeingly about the studio. "There's nothing else to do, is there—now—here or anywhere? So I sail to-
morrow; I mean to take a house somewhere near him. He's not
well, and he writes that he misses me. The life in camp is so
unsuited to him——"

Campton still listened absently. "Oh, you're right to go," he
agreed at length, supposing it was what she expected of him.

"Am I?" She half-smiled. "What's right and what's wrong? I
don't know any longer. I'm only trying to do what I suppose
George would have wanted." She stood uncertainly in front of
Campton. "All I *do* know," she cried, with a sharp break in her
voice, "is that I've never in my life been happy enough to be so
unhappy!" And she threw herself down on the divan in a storm
of desolate sobbing.

After he had comforted her as best he could, and she had
gone away, Campton continued to wander up and down the
studio forlornly. That cry of hers kept on echoing in his ears:
"I've never in my life been happy enough to be so unhappy!" It
associated itself suddenly with a phrase of Boylston's that he had
brushed away unheeding: "You've had your son—you have him
still; but those others have never had anything."

Yes; Campton saw now that it was true of poor Madge Talkett,
as it was of Adele Anthony and Mr. Brant, and even in a measure
of Julia. They had never—no, not even George's mother—had
anything, in the close inextricable sense in which Campton had
had his son. And it was only now, in his own hour of destitution, that he understood how much greater the depth of their
poverty had been. He recalled the frightened embarrassed look
of the young lieutenant whom he had discountenanced by his
tears; and he said to himself: "The only thing that helps is to be
able to do things for people. I suppose that's why Brant's always
trying——"

Julia too: it was strange that his thoughts should turn to her
with such peculiar pity. It was not because the boy had been
born of her body: Campton did not see her now, as he once had
in a brief moment of compassion, as the young mother bending
illumined above her baby. He saw her as an old empty-hearted

woman, and asked himself how such an unmanageable monster as grief was to fill the room up of her absent son.

What did such people as Julia do with grief, he wondered, how did they make room for it in their lives, get up and lie down every day with its taste on their lips? Its elemental quality, that awful sense it communicated of a whirling earth, a crumbling Time, and all the cold stellar spaces yawning to receive us— these feelings which he was beginning to discern and to come to terms with in his own way (and with the sense that it would have been George's way too), these feelings could never give their stern appeasement to Julia . . . Her religion? Yes, such as it was no doubt it would help; talking with the Rector would help; giving more time to her church-charities, her wounded soldiers, imagining that she was paying some kind of tax on her affliction. But the vacant evenings, at home, face to face with Brant! Campton had long since seen that the one thing which had held the two together was their shared love of George; and if Julia discovered, as she could hardly fail to do, how much more deeply Brant had loved her son than she had, and how much more inconsolably he mourned him, that would only increase her sense of isolation. And so, in sheer self-defence, she would gradually, stealthily, fill up the void with the old occupations, with bridge and visits and secret consultations at the dressmaker's about the width of crape on her dresses; and all the while the object of life would be gone for her. Yes; he pitied Julia most of all.

But Mr. Brant too—perhaps in a different way it was he who suffered most. For the stellar spaces were not exactly Mr. Brant's native climate, and yet voices would call to him from them, and he would not know . . .

There were moments when Campton looked about him with astonishment at the richness of his own denuded life; when George was in the sunset, in the voices of young people, or in any trivial joke that father and son would have shared; and other moments when he was nowhere, utterly lost, extinct and irrecoverable; and others again when the one thing which could have vitalized the dead business of living would have been to see him shove open the studio door, stalk in, pour out some coffee for himself in his father's cup, and diffuse through the air the warm sense of his bodily presence, the fresh smell of his clothes and his flesh and his hair. But through all these moods, Campton began to see, there ran the life-giving power of a reality embraced and accepted. George had been; George was; as long as his father's consciousness lasted, George would be as much a part of it as the closest, most actual of his immediate sensations. He had missed nothing of George, and here was his harvest, his golden harvest.

Such states of mind were not constant with Campton; but more and more often, when they came, they swept him on eagle wings over the next desert to the next oasis; and so, gradually, the meaningless days became linked to each other in some kind of intelligible sequence.

Boylston, after the talk which had so agitated Campton, did not turn up again at the studio for some time; but when he next appeared the painter, hardly pausing to greet him, began at once, as if they had just parted: "That monument you spoke about the other day . . . you know . . ."

Boylston glanced at him in surprise.

"If they want me to do it, I'll do it," Campton went on, jerking the words out abruptly and walking away toward the window. He had not known, till he began, that he had meant to utter them, or how difficult they would be to say; and he stood there a moment struggling with the unreasoning rebellious irritability which so often lay in wait for his better impulses. At length he turned back, his hands in his pockets, clinking his change as he had done the first time that Boylston had come to him for help. "But as I plan the thing," he began again, in a queer growling tone, "it's going to cost a lot—everything of the sort does nowadays, especially in marble. It's hard enough to get any one to do that kind of work at all. And prices have about tripled, you know."

Boylston's eyes filled, and he nodded, still without speaking.

"That's just what Brant'll like though, isn't it?" Campton said, with an irrepressible sneer in his voice. He saw Boylston redden and look away, and he too flushed to the forehead and broke off ashamed. Suddenly he had the vision of Mr. Brant effacing himself at the foot of the hospital-stairs when they had arrived at Doullens; Mr. Brant drawing forth the copy of the orderly's letter in the dark fog-swept cloister; Mr. Brant always yielding, always holding back, yet always remembering to do or to say the one thing the father's lacerated soul could bear.

"And he's had nothing—nothing—nothing!" Campton thought.

He turned again to Boylston, his face still flushed, his lips twitching. "Tell them—tell Brant—that I'll design the thing; I'll design it, and he shall pay for it. He'll want to—I understand that. Only, for God's sake, don't let him come here and thank me—at least not for a long time!"

Boylston again nodded silently, and turned to go.

After he had gone the painter moved back to his long table. He had always had a fancy for modelling—had always had lumps of clay lying about within reach. He pulled out all the sketches of his son from the old portfolio, spread them before him on the table, and began.

THE END

TWILIGHT SLEEP

FAUST.   *Und du, wer bist du?*
SORGE.   *Bin einmal da.*
FAUST.   *Entferne dich!*
SORGE.   *Ich bin am rechten Ort.*

                    Faust.   Teil II.   Akt V.

BOOK I

Chapter I

M ISS BRUSS, the perfect secretary, received Nona Manford at the door of her mother's boudoir ("the office," Mrs. Manford's children called it) with a gesture of the kindliest denial.

"She wants to, you know, dear—your mother always *wants* to see you," pleaded Maisie Bruss, in a voice which seemed to be thinned and sharpened by continuous telephoning. Miss Bruss, attached to Mrs. Manford's service since shortly after the latter's second marriage, had known Nona from her childhood, and was privileged, even now that she was "out," to treat her with a certain benevolent familiarity—benevolence being the note of the Manford household.

"But look at her list—just for this morning!" the secretary continued, handing over a tall morocco-framed tablet, on which was inscribed, in the colourless secretarial hand: "7.30 Mental uplift. 7.45 Breakfast. 8. Psycho-analysis. 8.15 See cook. 8.30 Silent Meditation. 8.45 Facial massage. 9. Man with Persian miniatures. 9.15 Correspondence. 9.30 Manicure. 9.45 Eurythmic exercises. 10. Hair waved. 10.15 Sit for bust. 10.30 Receive Mothers' Day deputation. 11. Dancing lesson. 11.30 Birth Control committee at Mrs.——"

"The manicure is there now, late as usual. That's what martyrizes your mother; everybody's being so unpunctual. This New York life is killing her."

"I'm not unpunctual," said Nona Manford, leaning in the doorway.

"No; and a miracle, too! The way you girls keep up your dancing all night. You and Lita—what times you two do have!" Miss Bruss was becoming almost maternal. "But just run your eye down that list—. You see your mother didn't *expect* to see you before lunch; now did she?"

Nona shook her head. "No; but you might perhaps squeeze me in."

It was said in a friendly, a reasonable tone; on both sides the matter was being examined with an evident desire for impartiality and good-will. Nona was used to her mother's engagements; used to being squeezed in between faith-healers, art-dealers, social service workers and manicures. When Mrs. Manford did see her children she was perfect to them; but in this killing New York life, with its ever-multiplying duties and responsibilities, if her family had been allowed to tumble in at all hours and devour her time, her nervous system simply couldn't have stood it—and how many duties would have been left undone!

Mrs. Manford's motto had always been: "There's a time for everything." But there were moments when this optimistic view failed her, and she began to think there wasn't. This morning, for instance, as Miss Bruss pointed out, she had had to tell the new French sculptor who had been all the rage in New York for the last month that she wouldn't be able to sit to him for more than fifteen minutes, on account of the Birth Control committee meeting at 11.30 at Mrs. ——

Nona seldom assisted at these meetings, her own time being—through force of habit rather than real inclination—so fully taken up with exercise, athletics and the ceaseless rush from thrill to thrill which was supposed to be the happy privilege of youth. But she had had glimpses enough of the scene: of the audience of bright elderly women, with snowy hair, eurythmic movements, and finely-wrinkled over-massaged faces on which a smile of glassy benevolence sat like their rimless *pince-nez*. They were all inexorably earnest, aimlessly kind and fathomlessly pure; and all rather too well-dressed, except the "prominent woman" of the occasion, who usually wore dowdy clothes, and had steel-rimmed spectacles and straggling wisps of hair. Whatever the question dealt with, these ladies always seemed to be the same, and always advocated with equal zeal Birth Control and unlimited maternity, free love or the return to the traditions of the American home; and neither they nor Mrs. Manford seemed aware that there was anything contradictory in these doctrines. All they knew was that they were determined to force certain persons to do things that those persons preferred not to do. Nona, glancing down the serried list, recalled a saying of her mother's former husband, Arthur

Wyant: "Your mother and her friends would like to teach the whole world how to say its prayers and brush its teeth."

The girl had laughed, as she could never help laughing at Wyant's sallies; but in reality she admired her mother's zeal, though she sometimes wondered if it were not a little too promiscuous. Nona was the daughter of Mrs. Manford's second marriage, and her own father, Dexter Manford, who had had to make his way in the world, had taught her to revere activity as a virtue in itself; his tone in speaking of Pauline's zeal was very different from Wyant's. He had been brought up to think there was a virtue in work *per se*, even if it served no more useful purpose than the revolving of a squirrel in a wheel. "Perhaps your mother tries to cover too much ground; but it's very fine of her, you know—she never spares herself."

"Nor us!" Nona sometimes felt tempted to add; but Manford's admiration was contagious. Yes; Nona did admire her mother's altruistic energy; but she knew well enough that neither she nor her brother's wife Lita would ever follow such an example—she no more than Lita. They belonged to another generation: to the bewildered disenchanted young people who had grown up since the Great War, whose energies were more spasmodic and less definitely directed, and who, above all, wanted a more personal outlet for them. "Bother earthquakes in Bolivia!" Lita had once whispered to Nona, when Mrs. Manford had convoked the bright elderly women to deal with a seismic disaster at the other end of the world, the repetition of which these ladies somehow felt could be avoided if they sent out a commission immediately to teach the Bolivians to do something they didn't want to do—not to *believe* in earthquakes, for instance.

The young people certainly felt no corresponding desire to set the houses of others in order. Why shouldn't the Bolivians have earthquakes if they chose to live in Bolivia? And why must Pauline Manford lie awake over it in New York, and have to learn a new set of Mahatma exercises to dispel the resulting wrinkles? "I suppose if we feel like that it's really because we're too lazy to care," Nona reflected, with her incorrigible honesty.

She turned from Miss Bruss with a slight shrug. "Oh, well," she murmured.

"You know, pet," Miss Bruss volunteered, "things always get worse as the season goes on; and the last fortnight in February is the worst of all, especially with Easter coming as early as it does this year. I never *could* see why they picked out such an awkward date for Easter: perhaps those Florida hotel people did it. Why, your poor mother wasn't even able to see your father this morning before he went down town, though she thinks it's *all wrong* to let him go off to his office like that, without finding time for a quiet little chat first . . . Just a cheery word to put him in the right mood for the day . . . Oh, by the way, my dear, I wonder if you happen to have heard him say if he's dining at home tonight? Because you know he never *does* remember to leave word about his plans, and if he hasn't, I'd better telephone to the office to remind him that it's the night of the big dinner for the Marchesa—"

"Well, I don't think father's dining at home," said the girl indifferently.

"Not—not—not? Oh, my gracious!" clucked Miss Bruss, dashing across the room to the telephone on her own private desk.

The engagement-list had slipped from her hands, and Nona Manford, picking it up, ran her glance over it. She read: "4 P.M. See A. — 4.30 P.M. Musical: Torfried Lobb."

"4 P.M. See A." Nona had been almost sure it was Mrs. Manford's day for going to see her divorced husband, Arthur Wyant, the effaced mysterious person always designated on Mrs. Manford's lists as "A," and hence known to her children as "Exhibit A." It was rather a bore, for Nona had meant to go and see him herself at about that hour, and she always timed her visits so that they should not clash with Mrs. Manford's, not because the latter disapproved of Nona's friendship with Arthur Wyant (she thought it "beautiful" of the girl to show him so much kindness), but because Wyant and Nona were agreed that on these occasions the presence of the former Mrs. Wyant spoilt their fun. But there was nothing to do about it. Mrs. Manford's plans were unchangeable. Even illness and death barely caused a ripple in them. One might as well have tried to bring down one of the Pyramids by poking it with a parasol as attempt to disarrange the close mosaic of Mrs. Manford's engagement-list.

Mrs. Manford herself couldn't have done it; not with the best
will in the world; and Mrs. Manford's will, as her children and
all her household knew, *was* the best in the world.

Nona Manford moved away with a final shrug. She had
wanted to speak to her mother about something rather important; something she had caught a startled glimpse of, the
evening before, in the queer little half-formed mind of her
sister-in-law Lita, the wife of her half-brother Jim Wyant—the
Lita with whom, as Miss Bruss remarked, she, Nona, danced
away the nights. There was nobody on earth as dear to Nona
as that same Jim, her elder by six or seven years, and who had
been brother, comrade, guardian, almost father to her—her
own father, Dexter Manford, who was so clever, capable and
kind, being almost always too busy at the office, or too firmly
requisitioned by Mrs. Manford, when he was at home, to be
able to spare much time for his daughter.

Jim, bless him, always had time; no doubt that was what his
mother meant when she called him lazy—as lazy as his father,
she had once added, with one of her rare flashes of impatience.
Nothing so conduced to impatience in Mrs. Manford as the
thought of anybody's having the least fraction of unapportioned
time and not immediately planning to do something with it. If
only they could have given it to *her*! And Jim, who loved and
admired her (as all her family did) was always conscientiously
trying to fill his days, or to conceal from her their occasional
vacuity. But he had a way of not being in a hurry, and this had
been all to the good for little Nona, who could always count on
him to ride or walk with her, to slip off with her to a concert or
a "movie," or, more pleasantly still, just to *be there*—idling in the
big untenanted library of Cedarledge, the place in the country,
or in his untidy study on the third floor of the town house, and
ready to answer questions, help her to look up hard words in
dictionaries, mend her golf-sticks, or get a thorn out of her Sealyham's paw. Jim was wonderful with his hands: he could repair
clocks, start up mechanical toys, make fascinating models of
houses or gardens, apply a tourniquet, scramble eggs, mimic his
mother's visitors—preferably the "earnest" ones who held forth
about "causes" or "messages" in her gilded drawing-rooms—
and make delicious coloured maps of imaginary continents,

concerning which Nona wrote interminable stories. And of all
these gifts he had, alas, made no particular use as yet—except
to enchant his little half-sister.

It had been just the same, Nona knew, with his father: poor
useless "Exhibit A"! Mrs. Manford said it was their "old New
York blood"—she spoke of them with mingled contempt and
pride, as if they were the last of the Capetians, exhausted by
a thousand years of sovereignty. Her own red corpuscles were
tinged with a more plebeian dye. Her progenitors had mined
in Pennsylvania and made bicycles at Exploit, and now gave
their name to one of the most popular automobiles in the
United States. Not that other ingredients were lacking in her
hereditary make-up: her mother was said to have contributed
southern gentility by being a Pascal of Tallahassee. Mrs. Manford, in certain moods, spoke of "The Pascals of Tallahassee"
as if they accounted for all that was noblest in her; but when
she was exhorting Jim to action it was her father's blood that
she invoked. "After all, in spite of the Pascal tradition, there
is no shame in being in trade. My father's father came over
from Scotland with two sixpences in his pocket . . ." and Mrs.
Manford would glance with pardonable pride at the glorious
Gainsborough over the dining-room mantelpiece (which she
sometimes almost mistook for an ancestral portrait), and at her
healthy handsome family sitting about the dinner-table laden
with Georgian silver and orchids from her own hot-houses.

From the threshold, Nona called back to Miss Bruss: "Please
tell mother I shall probably be lunching with Jim and Lita—"
but Miss Bruss was passionately saying to an unseen interlocutor: "Oh, but Mr. Rigley, but you *must* make Mr. Manford
understand that Mrs. Manford counts on him for dinner this
evening . . . The dinner-dance for the Marchesa, you know . . ."

The marriage of her half-brother had been Nona Manford's
first real sorrow. Not that she had disapproved of his choice:
how could any one take that funny irresponsible little Lita Cliffe
seriously enough to disapprove of her? The sisters-in-law were
soon the best of friends; if Nona had a fault to find with Lita, it
was that she didn't worship the incomparable Jim as blindly as
his sister did. But then Lita was made to be worshipped, not to
worship; that was manifest in the calm gaze of her long narrow

nut-coloured eyes, in the hieratic fixity of her lovely smile, in the very shape of her hands, so slim yet dimpled, hands which had never grown up, and which drooped from her wrists as if listlessly waiting to be kissed, or lay like rare shells or upcurved magnolia-petals on the cushions luxuriously piled about her indolent body.

The Jim Wyants had been married for nearly two years now; the baby was six months old; the pair were beginning to be regarded as one of the "old couples" of their set, one of the settled landmarks in the matrimonial quicksands of New York. Nona's love for her brother was too disinterested for her not to rejoice in this: above all things she wanted her old Jim to be happy, and happy she was sure he was—or had been until lately. The mere getting away from Mrs. Manford's iron rule had been a greater relief than he himself perhaps guessed. And then he was still the foremost of Lita's worshippers; still enchanted by the childish whims, the unpunctuality, the irresponsibility, which made life with her such a thrillingly unsettled business after the clock-work routine of his mother's perfect establishment.

All this Nona rejoiced in; but she ached at times with the loneliness of the perfect establishment, now that Jim, its one disturbing element, had left. Jim guessed her loneliness, she was sure: it was he who encouraged the growing intimacy between his wife and his half-sister, and tried to make the latter feel that his house was another home to her.

Lita had always been amiably disposed toward Nona. The two, though so fundamentally different, were nearly of an age, and united by the prevailing passion for every form of sport. Lita, in spite of her soft curled-up attitudes, was not only a tireless dancer but a brilliant if uncertain tennis-player, and an adventurous rider to hounds. Between her hours of lolling, and smoking amber-scented cigarettes, every moment of her life was crammed with dancing, riding or games. During the two or three months before the baby's birth, when Lita had been reduced to partial inactivity, Nona had rather feared that her perpetual craving for new "thrills" might lead to some insidious form of time-killing—some of the drinking or drugging that went on among the young women of their set; but Lita had sunk into a state of smiling animal patience, as if the mysterious work going on in her tender young body had a sacred significance for her, and it was enough to lie still and let it happen. All she asked was that nothing should "hurt" her: she had the blind dread of physical pain common also to most of the young women of her set. But all that was so easily managed nowadays: Mrs. Manford (who took charge of the business, Lita being an orphan) of course knew the most perfect "Twilight Sleep" establishment in the country, installed Lita in its most luxurious suite, and filled her rooms with spring flowers, hot-house fruits, new novels and all the latest picture-papers—and Lita drifted into motherhood as lightly and unperceivingly as if the wax doll which suddenly appeared in the cradle at her bedside had been brought there in one of the big bunches of hot-house roses that she found every morning on her pillow.

"Of course there ought to be no Pain . . . nothing but Beauty . . . It ought to be one of the loveliest, most poetic things in the world to have a baby," Mrs. Manford declared, in that bright efficient voice which made loveliness and poetry sound like the attributes of an advanced industrialism, and babies something to be turned out in series like Fords. And Jim's joy in his son had been unbounded; and Lita really hadn't minded in the least.

Chapter II

THE Marchesa was something which happened at irregular but inevitable moments in Mrs. Manford's life.

Most people would have regarded the Marchesa as a disturbance; some as a distinct inconvenience; the pessimistic as a misfortune. It was a matter of conscious pride to Mrs. Manford that, while recognizing these elements in the case, she had always contrived to make out of it something not only showy but even enviable.

For, after all, if your husband (even an ex-husband) has a first cousin called Amalasuntha degli Duchi di Lucera, who has married the Marchese Venturino di San Fedele, of one of the great Neapolitan families, it seems stupid and wasteful not to make some use of such a conjunction of names and situations, and to remember only (as the Wyants did) that when Amalasuntha came to New York it was always to get money, or to get her dreadful son out of a new scrape, or to consult the family lawyers as to some new way of guarding the remains of her fortune against Venturino's systematic depredations.

Mrs. Manford knew in advance the hopelessness of these quests—all of them, that is, except that which consisted in borrowing money from herself. She always lent Amalasuntha two or three thousand dollars (and put it down to the profit-and-loss column of her carefully-kept private accounts); she even gave the Marchesa her own last year's clothes, cleverly retouched; and in return she expected Amalasuntha to shed on the Manford entertainments that exotic lustre which the near relative of a Duke who is also a grandee of Spain and a great dignitary of the Papal Court trails with her through the dustiest by-ways, even if her mother has been a mere Mary Wyant of Albany.

Mrs. Manford had been successful. The Marchesa, without taking thought, fell naturally into the part assigned to her. In her stormy and uncertain life, New York, where her rich relations lived, and from which she always came back with a few thousand dollars, and clothes that could be made to last a year, and good advice about putting the screws on Venturino, was like a foretaste of heaven. "Live there? Carina, *no*! It is too—too uneventful. As heaven must be. But everybody is celestially kind . . . and Venturino has learnt that there are certain things my American relations will not tolerate . . ." Such was Amalasuntha's version of her visits to New York, when she recounted them in the drawing-rooms of Rome, Naples or St. Moritz; whereas in New York, quite carelessly and unthinkingly—for no one was simpler at heart than Amalasuntha—she pronounced names, and raised suggestions, which cast a romantic glow of unreality over a world bounded by Wall Street on the south and Long Island in most other directions; and in this glow Pauline Manford was always eager to sun her other guests.

"My husband's cousin" (become, since the divorce from Wyant "my son's cousin") was still, after twenty-seven years, a useful social card. The Marchesa di San Fedele, now a woman of fifty, was still, in Pauline's set, a pretext for dinners, a means of paying off social scores, a small but steady luminary in the uncertain New York heavens. Pauline could never see her rather forlorn wisp of a figure, always clothed in careless unnoticeable black (even when she wore Mrs. Manford's old dresses), without a vision of echoing Roman staircases, of the torchlit arrival of Cardinals at the Lucera receptions, of a great frescolike background of Popes, princes, dilapidated palaces, cypressguarded villas, scandals, tragedies, and interminable feuds about inheritances.

"It's all so dreadful—the wicked lives those great Roman families lead. After all, poor Amalasuntha has good American blood in her—her mother was a Wyant; yes—Mary Wyant married Prince Ottaviano di Lago Negro, the Duke of Lucera's son, who used to be at the Italian Legation in Washington; but what is Amalasuntha to do, in a country where there's no divorce, and a woman just has to put up with *everything*? The Pope has been most kind; he sides entirely with Amalasuntha. But Venturino's people are very powerful too—a great Neapolitan family—yes, Cardinal Ravello is Venturino's uncle . . . so that altogether it's been dreadful for Amalasuntha . . . and such an oasis to her, coming back to her own people . . ."

Pauline Manford was quite sincere in believing that it was dreadful for Amalasuntha. Pauline herself could conceive of nothing more shocking than a social organization which did not recognize divorce, and let all kinds of domestic evils fester undisturbed, instead of having people's lives disinfected and whitewashed at regular intervals, like the cellar. But while Mrs. Manford thought all this—in fact, in the very act of thinking it—she remembered that Cardinal Ravello, Venturino's uncle, had been mentioned as one of the probable delegates to the Roman Catholic Congress which was to meet at Baltimore that winter, and wondered whether an evening party for his Eminence could not be organized with Amalasuntha's help; even got as far as considering the effect of torch-bearing footmen (in silk stockings) lining the Manford staircase—which was of marble, thank goodness!—and of Dexter Manford and Jim receiving the Prince of the Church on the doorstep, and walking upstairs backward carrying silver candelabra; though Pauline wasn't sure she could persuade them to go as far as that.

Pauline felt no more inconsistency in this double train of thought than she did in shuddering at the crimes of the Roman Church and longing to receive one of its dignitaries with all the proper ceremonial. She was used to such rapid adjustments, and proud of the fact that whole categories of contradictory opinions lay down together in her mind as peacefully as the Happy Families exhibited by strolling circuses. And of course, if the Cardinal *did* come to her house, she would show her American independence by inviting also the Bishop of New York—her own Episcopal Bishop—and possibly the Chief Rabbi (also a friend of hers), and certainly that wonderful much-slandered "Mahatma" in whom she still so thoroughly believed . . .

But the word pulled her up short. Yes; certainly she believed in the "Mahatma." She had every reason to. Standing before the tall threefold mirror in her dressing-room, she glanced into the huge bathroom beyond—which looked like a biological laboratory, with its white tiles, polished pipes, weighing machines, mysterious appliances for douches, gymnastics and "physical culture"—and recalled with gratitude that it was certainly those eurythmic exercises of the Mahatma's ("holy ecstasy," he called them) which had reduced her hips after everything else had failed. And this gratitude for the reduction of her hips was exactly on the same plane, in her neat card-catalogued mind, with her enthusiastic faith in his wonderful mystical teachings about Self-Annihilation, Anterior Existence and Astral Affinities . . . all so incomprehensible and so pure . . . Yes; she would

certainly ask the Mahatma. It would do the Cardinal good
to have a talk with him. She could almost hear his Eminence
saying, in a voice shaken by emotion: "Mrs. Manford, I want
to thank you for making me know that Wonderful Man. If it
hadn't been for you—"

Ah, she did like people who said to her: "If it hadn't been for
you—!"

The telephone on her dressing-table rang. Miss Bruss had
switched on from the boudoir. Mrs. Manford, as she unhooked
the receiver, cast a nervous glance at the clock. She was already
seven minutes late for her Marcel-waving, and—

Ah: it was Dexter's voice! Automatically she composed her
face to a wifely smile, and her voice to a corresponding intonation. "Yes? Pauline, dear. Oh—about dinner tonight? Why,
you know, Amalasuntha . . . You say you're going to the theatre with Jim and Lita? But, Dexter, you can't! They're dining
here—Jim and Lita are. But *of course* . . . Yes, it must have been
a mistake; Lita's so flighty . . . I know . . ." (The smile grew a
little pinched; the voice echoed it. Then, patiently): "Yes; what
else? . . . *Oh* . . . oh, Dexter . . . what do you mean? . . . The
Mahatma? *What*? I don't understand!"

But she did. She was conscious of turning white under her
discreet cosmetics. Somewhere in the depths of her there had
lurked for the last weeks an unexpressed fear of this very thing:
a fear that the people who were opposed to the teaching of the
Hindu sage—New York's great "spiritual uplift" of the last two
years—were gaining power and beginning to be a menace. And
here was Dexter Manford actually saying something about
having been asked to conduct an investigation into the state
of things at the Mahatma's "School of Oriental Thought," in
which all sorts of unpleasantness might be involved. Of course
Dexter never said much about professional matters on the telephone; he did not, to his wife's thinking, say enough about
them when he got home. But what little she now gathered made
her feel positively ill.

"Oh, Dexter, but I must see you about this! At once! You
couldn't come back to lunch, I suppose? Not possibly? No—this
evening there'll be no chance. Why, the dinner for Amalasuntha—oh, please don't forget it *again*!"

With one hand on the receiver, she reached with the other for her engagement-list (the duplicate of Miss Bruss's), and ran a nervous unseeing eye over it. A scandal—another scandal! It mustn't be. She loathed scandals. And besides, she did believe in the Mahatma. He had "vision." From the moment when she had picked up that word in a magazine article she had felt she had a complete answer about him . . .

"But I must see you before this evening, Dexter. Wait! I'm looking over my engagements." She came to "4 P.M. See A. 4.30 Musical—Torfried Lobb." No; she couldn't give up Torfried Lobb: she was one of the fifty or sixty ladies who had "discovered" him the previous winter, and she knew he counted on her presence at his recital. Well, then—for once "A" must be sacrificed.

"Listen, Dexter; if I were to come to the office at 4? Yes; sharp. Is that right? And don't do anything till I see you—promise!"

She hung up with a sigh of relief. She would try to readjust things so as to see "A" the next day; though readjusting her list in the height of the season was as exhausting as a major operation.

In her momentary irritation she was almost inclined to feel as if it were Arthur's fault for figuring on that day's list, and thus unsettling all her arrangements. Poor Arthur—from the first he had been one of her failures. She had a little cemetery of them—a very small one—planted over with quick-growing things, so that you might have walked all through her life and not noticed there were any graves in it. To the inexperienced Pauline of thirty years ago, fresh from the factory-smoke of Exploit, Arthur Wyant had symbolized the tempting contrast between a city absorbed in making money and a society bent on enjoying it. Such a brilliant figure—and nothing to show for it! She didn't know exactly what she had expected, her own ideal of manly achievement being at that time solely based on the power of getting rich faster than your neighbours—which Arthur would certainly never do. His father-in-law at Exploit had seen at a glance that it was no use taking him into the motor-business, and had remarked philosophically to Pauline: "Better just regard him as a piece of jewellery: I guess we can afford it."

But jewellery must at least be brilliant; and Arthur had some-how—faded. At one time she had hoped he might play a part in state politics—with Washington and its enticing diplomatic society at the end of the vista—but he shrugged that away as contemptuously as what he called "trade." At Cedarledge he farmed a little, fussed over the accounts, and muddled away her money till she replaced him by a trained superintendent; and in town he spent hours playing bridge at his club, took an intermit-tent interest in racing, and went and sat every afternoon with his mother, old Mrs. Wyant, in the dreary house near Stuyvesant Square which had never been "done over," and was still lit by Carcel lamps.

An obstacle and a disappointment; that was what he had always been. Still, she would have borne with his inadequacy, his resultless planning, dreaming and dawdling, even his growing tendency to drink, as the wives of her generation were taught to bear with such failings, had it not been for the discovery that he was also "immoral." Immorality no high-minded woman could condone; and when, on her return from a rest-cure in Califor-nia, she found that he had drifted into a furtive love affair with the dependent cousin who lived with his mother, every law of self-respect known to Pauline decreed his repudiation. Old Mrs. Wyant, horror-struck, banished the cousin and pleaded for her son: Pauline was adamant. She addressed herself to the rising divorce-lawyer, Dexter Manford, and in his capable hands the affair was settled rapidly, discreetly, without scandal, wrangling or recrimination. Wyant withdrew to his mother's house, and Pauline went to Europe, a free woman.

In the early days of the new century divorce had not become a social institution in New York, and the blow to Wyant's pride was deeper than Pauline had foreseen. He lived in complete retirement at his mother's, saw his boy at the dates prescribed by the court, and sank into a sort of premature old age which contrasted painfully—even to Pauline herself—with her own recovered youth and elasticity. The contrast caused her a ret-rospective pang, and gradually, after her second marriage, and old Mrs. Wyant's death, she came to regard poor Arthur not as a grievance but as a responsibility. She prided herself on never neglecting her responsibilities, and therefore felt a not unnatural vexation with Arthur for having figured among her engagements that day, and thus obliged her to postpone him.

Moving back to the dressing-table she caught her reflection in the tall triple glass. Again those fine wrinkles about lids and lips, those vertical lines between the eyes! She would not permit it; no, not for a moment. She commanded herself: "Now, Pauline, *stop worrying*. You know perfectly well there's no such thing as worry; it's only dyspepsia or want of exercise, and everything's really all right—" in the insincere tone of a mother soothing a bruised baby.

She looked again, and fancied the wrinkles were really fainter, the vertical lines less deep. Once more she saw before her an erect athletic woman, with all her hair and all her teeth, and just a hint of rouge (because "people did it") brightening a still fresh complexion; saw her small symmetrical features, the black brows drawn with a light stroke over handsome directly-gazing gray eyes, the abundant whitening hair which still responded so crisply to the waver's wand, the firmly planted feet with arched insteps rising to slim ankles.

How absurd, how unlike herself, to be upset by that foolish news! She would look in on Dexter and settle the Mahatma business in five minutes. If there was to be a scandal she wasn't going to have Dexter mixed up in it—above all not against the Mahatma. She could never forget that it was the Mahatma who had first told her she was psychic.

The maid opened an inner door an inch or two to say rebukingly: "Madam, the hair-dresser; and Miss Bruss asked me to remind you—"

"Yes, yes, yes," Mrs. Manford responded hastily; repeating below her breath, as she flung herself into her kimono and settled down before her toilet-table: "Now, I forbid you to let yourself feel hurried! You *know* there's no such thing as hurry."

But her eye again turned anxiously to the little clock among her scent-bottles, and she wondered if she might not save time by dictating to Maisie Bruss while she was being waved and manicured. She envied women who had no sense of responsibility—like Jim's little Lita. As for herself, the only world she knew rested on her shoulders.

Chapter III

AT a quarter past one, when Nona arrived at her half-brother's house, she was told that Mrs. Wyant was not yet down. "And Mr. Wyant not yet up, I suppose? From his office, I mean," she added, as the young butler looked his surprise.

Pauline Manford had been very generous at the time of her son's marriage. She was relieved at his settling down, and at his seeming to understand that marriage connoted the choice of a profession, and the adoption of what people called regular habits. Not that Jim's irregularities had ever been such as the phrase habitually suggests. They had chiefly consisted in his not being able to make up his mind what to do with his life (so like his poor father, that!), in his always forgetting what time it was, or what engagements his mother had made for him, in his wanting a chemical laboratory fitted up for him at Cedarledge, and then, when it was all done, using it first as a kennel for breeding fox-terriers and then as a quiet place to practise the violin.

Nona knew how sorely these vacillations had tried her mother, and how reassured Mrs. Manford had been when the young man, in the heat of his infatuation for Lita, had vowed that if she would have him he would turn to and grind in an office like all the other husbands.

Lita have him! Lita Cliffe, a portionless orphan, with no one to guide her in the world but a harum-scarum and somewhat blown-upon aunt, the "impossible" Mrs. Percy Landish! Mrs. Manford smiled at her son's modesty while she applauded his good resolutions. "This experience has made a man of dear Jim," she said, mildly triumphing in the latest confirmation of her optimism. "If only it lasts—!" she added, relapsing into human uncertainty.

"Oh, it will, mother; you'll see; as long as Lita doesn't get tired of him," Nona had assured her.

"As long—? But, my dear child, why should Lita ever get tired of him? You seem to forget what a miracle it was that a girl like Lita, with no one but poor Kitty Landish to look after her, should ever have got such a husband!"

Nona held her ground. "Well—just look about you, mother! Don't they almost all get tired of each other? And when they do, will anything ever stop their having another try? Think of your big dinners! Doesn't Maisie always have to make out a list of previous marriages as long as a cross-word puzzle, to prevent your calling people by the wrong names?"

Mrs. Manford waved away the challenge. "Jim and Lita are not like that; and I don't like your way of speaking of divorce, Nona," she had added, rather weakly for her—since, as Nona might have reminded her, her own way of speaking of divorce varied disconcertingly with the time, the place and the divorce.

The young girl had leisure to recall this discussion while she sat and waited for her brother and his wife. In the freshly decorated and studiously empty house there seemed to be no one to welcome her. The baby (whom she had first enquired for) was asleep, his mother hardly awake, and the head of the house still "at the office." Nona looked about the drawing-room and wondered—the habit was growing on her.

The drawing-room (it suddenly occurred to her) was very expressive of the modern marriage state. It looked, for all its studied effects, its rather nervous attention to "values," complementary colours, and the things the modern decorator lies awake over, more like the waiting-room of a glorified railway station than the setting of an established way of life. Nothing in it seemed at home or at ease—from the early kakemono of a bearded sage, on walls of pale buff silk, to the three mourning irises isolated in a white Sung vase in the desert of an otherwise empty table. The only life in the room was contributed by the agitations of the exotic goldfish in a huge spherical aquarium; and they too were but transients, since Lita insisted on having the aquarium illuminated night and day with electric bulbs, and the sleepless fish were always dying off and having to be replaced.

Mrs. Manford had paid for the house and its decoration. It was not what she would have wished for herself—she had not yet quite caught up with the new bareness and selectiveness. But neither would she have wished the young couple to live in the opulent setting of tapestries and "period" furniture which she herself preferred. Above all she wanted them to keep up;

to do what the other young couples were doing; she had even digested—in one huge terrified gulp—Lita's black boudoir, with its welter of ebony velvet cushions overlooked by a statue as to which Mrs. Manford could only minimize the indecency by saying that she understood it was Cubist. But she did think it unkind—after all she had done—to have Nona suggest that Lita might get tired of Jim!

The idea had never really troubled Nona—at least not till lately. Even now she had nothing definite in her mind. Nothing beyond the vague question: what would a woman like Lita be likely to do if she suddenly grew tired of the life she was leading? But that question kept coming back so often that she had really wanted, that morning, to consult her mother about it; for who else was there to consult? Arthur Wyant? Why, poor Arthur had never been able to manage his own poor little concerns with any sort of common sense or consistency; and at the suggestion that any one might tire of Jim he would be as indignant as Mrs. Manford, and without her power of controlling her emotions.

Dexter Manford? Well—Dexter Manford's daughter had to admit that it really wasn't his business if his step-son's marriage threatened to be a failure; and besides, Nona knew how overwhelmed with work her father always was, and hesitated to lay this extra burden on him. For it would be a burden. Manford was very fond of Jim (as indeed they all were), and had been extremely kind to him. It was entirely owing to Manford's influence that Jim, who was regarded as vague and unreliable, had got such a good berth in the Amalgamated Trust Co.; and Manford had been much pleased at the way in which the boy had stuck to his job. Just like Jim, Nona thought tenderly—if ever you could induce him to do anything at all, he always did it with such marvellous neatness and persistency. And the incentive of working for Lita and the boy was enough to anchor him to his task for life.

A new scent—unrecognizable but exquisite. In its wake came Lita Wyant, half-dancing, half-drifting, fastening a necklace, humming a tune, her little round head, with the goldfish-coloured hair, the mother-of-pearl complexion and screwed-up auburn eyes, turning sideways like a bird's on her long throat. She was astonished but delighted to see Nona, indifferent to her husband's non-arrival, and utterly unaware that lunch had been waiting for half an hour.

"I had a sandwich and a cocktail after my exercises. I don't suppose it's time for me to be hungry again," she conjectured. "But perhaps you are, you poor child. Have you been waiting long?"

"Not much! I know you too well to be punctual," Nona laughed.

Lita widened her eyes. "Are you suggesting that I'm not? Well, then, how about your ideal brother?"

"He's down town working to keep a roof over your head and your son's."

Lita shrugged. "Oh, a roof—I don't care much for roofs, do you—or is it *rooves*? Not this one, at any rate." She caught Nona by the shoulders, held her at arm's-length, and with tilted head and persuasively narrowed eyes, demanded: "This room is *awful*, isn't it? Now acknowledge that it is! And Jim won't give me the money to do it over."

"Do it over? But, Lita, you did it exactly as you pleased two years ago!"

"Two years ago? Do you mean to say you like anything that you liked two years ago?"

"Yes—you!" Nona retorted: adding rather helplessly: "And, besides, everybody admires the room so much—" She stopped, feeling that she was talking exactly like her mother.

Lita's little hands dropped in a gesture of despair. "That's just it! *Everybody* admires it. Even Mrs. Manford does. And when you think what sort of things *Everybody* admires! What's the use of pretending, Nona? It's the typical *cliché* drawing-room. Every one of the couples who were married the year we were has one like it. The first time Tommy Ardwin saw it—you know he's the new decorator—he said: 'Gracious, how familiar all this seems!' and began to whistle '*Home, Sweet Home*'!"

"But of course he would, you simpleton! When what he wants is to be asked to do it over!"

Lita heaved a sigh. "If he only could! Perhaps he might reconcile me to this house. But I don't believe anybody could do that." She glanced about her with an air of ineffable disgust. "I'd like to throw everything in it into the street. I've been so bored here."

Nona laughed. "You'd be bored anywhere. I wish another Tommy Ardwin would come along and tell you what an old *cliché* being bored is."

"An old *cliché*? Why shouldn't it be? When life itself is such a bore? You can't redecorate life!"

"If you could, what would you begin by throwing into the street? The baby?"

Lita's eyes woke to fire. "Don't be an idiot! You know I adore my baby."

"Well—then Jim?"

"You know I adore my Jim!" echoed the young wife, mimicking her own emotion.

"Hullo—that sounds ominous!" Jim Wyant came in, clearing the air with his fresh good-humoured presence. "I fear my bride when she says she adores me," he said, taking Nona into a brotherly embrace.

As he stood there, sturdy and tawny, a trifle undersized, with his bright blue eyes and short blunt-nosed face, in which everything was so handsomely modelled and yet so safe and sober, Nona fell again to her dangerous wondering. Something had gone out of his face—all the wild uncertain things, the violin, model-making, inventing, dreaming, vacillating—everything she had best loved except the twinkle in his sobered eyes. Whatever else was left now was all plain utility. Well, better so, no doubt—when one looked at Lita! Her glance caught her sister-in-law's face in a mirror between two panels, and the reflection of her own beside it; she winced a little at the contrast. At her best she had none of that milky translucence, or of the long lines which made Lita seem in perpetual motion, as a tremor of air lives in certain trees. Though Nona was as tall and nearly as slim, she seemed to herself to be built, while Lita was spun of spray and sunlight. Perhaps it was Nona's general brownness— she had Dexter Manford's brown crinkled hair, his strong black lashes setting her rather usual-looking gray eyes; and the texture of her dusky healthy skin, compared to Lita's, seemed rough and opaque. The comparison added to her general vague sense of discouragement. "It's not one of my beauty days," she thought.

Jim was drawing her arm through his. "Come along, my girl. Is there going to be any lunch?" he queried, turning toward the dining-room.

"Oh, probably. In this house the same things always happen every day," Lita averred with a slight grimace.

"Well, I'm glad lunch does—on the days when I can make a dash up-town for it."

"On others Lita eats goldfish food," Nona laughed.

"Luncheon is served, madam," the butler announced.

The meal, as usual under Lita's roof, was one in which delicacies alternated with delays. Mrs. Manford would have been driven out of her mind by the uncertainties of the service and the incoherence of the *menu*; but she would have admitted that no one did a pilaff better than Lita's cook. Gastronomic refinements were wasted on Jim, whose indifference to the possession of the Wyant madeira was one of his father's severest trials. ("I shouldn't have been surprised if *you* hadn't cared, Nona; after all, you're a Manford; but that a Wyant shouldn't have a respect for old wine!" Arthur Wyant often lamented to her.) As for Lita, she either nibbled languidly at new health foods, or made ravenous inroads into the most indigestible dish presented to her. To-day she leaned back, dumb and indifferent, while Jim devoured what was put before him as if unaware that it was anything but canned beef; and Nona watched the two under guarded lids.

The telephone tinkled, and the butler announced: "Mr. Manford, madam."

Nona Manford looked up. "For me?"

"No, miss; Mrs. Wyant."

Lita was on her feet, suddenly animated. "Oh, all right . . . Don't wait for me," she flung over her shoulder as she made for the door.

"Have the receiver brought in here," Jim suggested; but she brushed by without heeding.

"That's something new—Lita sprinting for the telephone!" Jim laughed.

"And to talk to father!" For the life of her, Nona could not have told why she stopped short with a vague sense of embarrassment. Dexter Manford had always been very kind to his stepson's wife; but then everybody was kind to Lita.

Jim's head was bent over the pilaff; he took it down in quick undiscerning mouthfuls.

"Well, I hope he's saying something that will amuse her: nothing seems to, nowadays."

It was on the tip of Nona's tongue to rejoin: "Oh, yes; it amuses her to say that nothing amuses her." But she looked at her brother's face, faintly troubled under its surface serenity, and refrained.

Instead, she remarked on the beauty of the two yellow arums in a bronze jar reflected in the mahogany of the dining-table. "Lita has a genius for flowers."

"And for everything else—when she chooses!"

The door opened and Lita sauntered back and dropped into her seat. She shook her head disdainfully at the proffered pilaff. There was a pause.

"Well—what's the news?" Jim asked.

His wife arched her exquisite brows. "News? I expect you to provide that. I'm only just awake."

"I mean—" But he broke off, and signed to the butler to remove his plate. There was another pause; then Lita's little head turned on its long interrogative neck toward Nona. "It seems we're banqueting tonight at the Palazzo Manford. Did you know?"

"Did I know? Why, Lita! I've heard of nothing else for weeks. It's the annual feast for the Marchesa."

"I was never told," said Lita calmly. "I'm afraid I'm engaged."

Jim lifted his head with a jerk. "You were told a fortnight ago."

"Oh, a fortnight! That's too long to remember anything. It's like Nona's telling me that I ought to admire my drawing-room because I admired it two years ago."

Her husband reddened to the roots of his tawny hair. "Don't you admire it?" he asked, with a sort of juvenile dismay.

"There; Lita'll be happy now—she's produced her effect!" Nona laughed a little nervously.

Lita joined in the laugh. "Isn't he like his mother?" she shrugged.

Jim was silent, and his sister guessed that he was afraid to insist on the dinner engagement lest he should increase his wife's determination to ignore it. The same motive kept Nona from saying anything more; and the lunch ended in a clatter of talk about other things. But what puzzled Nona was that her father's communication to Lita should have concerned the fact that she was dining at his house that night. It was unlike Dexter

Manford to remember the fact himself (as Miss Bruss's frantic
telephoning had testified), and still more unlike him to remind
his wife's guests, even if he knew who they were to be—which
he seldom did. Nona pondered. "They must have been going
somewhere together—he told me he was engaged tonight—and
Lita's in a temper because they can't. But then she's in a temper
about everything today." Nona tried to make that cover all her
perplexities. She wondered if it did as much for Jim.

Chapter IV

I T would have been hard, Nona Manford thought, to find a greater contrast than between Lita Wyant's house and that at which, two hours later, she descended from Lita Wyant's smart Brewster.

"You won't come, Lita?" The girl paused, her hand on the motor door. "He'd like it awfully."

Lita shook off the suggestion. "I'm not in the humour."

"But he's such fun—he can be better company than anybody."

"Oh, for you he's a fad—for me he's a duty; and I don't happen to feel like duties." Lita waved one of her flower-hands and was off.

Nona mounted the pock-marked brown steps. The house was old Mrs. Wyant's, a faded derelict habitation in a street past which fashion and business had long since flowed. After his mother's death Wyant, from motives of economy, had divided it into small flats. He kept one for himself, and in the one overhead lived his mother's former companion, the dependent cousin who had been the cause of his divorce. Wyant had never married her; he had never deserted her; that, to Nona's mind, gave one a fair notion of his character. When he was ill—and he had developed, rather early, a queer sort of nervous hypochondria—the cousin came downstairs and nursed him; when he was well his visitors never saw her. But she was reported to attend to his mending, keep some sort of order in his accounts, and prevent his falling a prey to the unscrupulous. Pauline Manford said it was probably for the best. She herself would have thought it natural, and in fact proper, that her former husband should have married his cousin; as he had not, she preferred to decide that since the divorce they had been "only friends." The Wyant code was always a puzzle to her. She never met the cousin when she called on her former husband; but Jim, two or three times a year, made it a point to ring the bell of the upper flat, and at Christmas sent its invisible tenant an azalea.

Nona ran up the stairs to Wyant's door. On the threshold a thin gray-haired lady with a shadowy face awaited her.

"Come in, do. He's got the gout, and can't get up to open the door, and I had to send the cook out to get something tempting for his dinner."

"Oh, thank you, cousin Eleanor." The girl looked sympathetically into the other's dimly tragic eyes. "Poor Exhibit A! I'm sorry he's ill again."

"He's been—imprudent. But the worst of it's over. It will brighten him up to see you. Your cousin Stanley's there."

"Is he?" Nona half drew back, feeling herself faintly redden.

"He'll be going soon. Mr. Wyant will be disappointed if you don't go in."

"But of course I'm going in."

The older woman smiled a worn smile, and vanished upstairs while Nona slipped off her furs. The girl knew it would be useless to urge cousin Eleanor to stay. If one wished to see her one had to ring at her own door.

Arthur Wyant's shabby sitting-room was full of February sunshine, illustrated magazines, newspapers and cigar ashes. There were some books on shelves, shabby also: Wyant had apparently once cared for them, and his talk was still coloured by traces of early cultivation, especially when visitors like Nona or Stan Heuston were with him. But the range of his allusions suggested that he must have stopped reading years ago. Even novels were too great a strain on his attention. As far back as Nona could remember he had fared only on the popular magazines, picture-papers and the weekly purveyors of social scandal. He took an intense interest in the private affairs of the world he had ceased to frequent, though he always ridiculed this interest in talking to Nona or Heuston.

While he sat there, deep in his armchair, with bent shoulders, sunk head and clumsy bandaged foot, Nona saw him, as she always did, as taller, slimmer, more handsomely upstanding than any man she had ever known. He stooped now, even when he was on his feet; he was prematurely aged; and the fact perhaps helped to connect him with vanished institutions to which only his first youth could have belonged.

To Nona, at any rate, he would always be the Arthur Wyant of the race-meeting group in the yellowing photograph on his mantelpiece: clad in the gray frock-coat and topper of the early 'eighties, and tallest in a tall line of the similarly garbed, behind ladies with puffed sleeves and little hats tilting forward on elaborate hair. How peaceful, smiling and unhurried they all seemed! Nona never looked at them without a pang of regret that she had not been born in those spacious days of dog-carts, victorias, leisurely tennis and afternoon calls . . .

Wyant's face, even more than his figure, related him to that past: the small shapely head, the crisp hair grown thin on a narrow slanting forehead, the eyes in which a twinkle still lingered, eyes probably blue when the hair was brown, but now faded with the rest, and the slight fair moustache above an uncertain ironic mouth.

A romantic figure; or rather the faded photograph of one. Yes; perhaps Arthur Wyant had always been faded—like a charming reflection in a sallow mirror. And all that length of limb and beauty of port had been meant for some other man, a man to whom the things had really happened which Wyant had only dreamed.

His visitor, though of the same stock, could never have inspired such conjectures. Stanley Heuston was much younger—in the middle thirties—and most things about him were middling: height, complexion, features. But he had a strong forehead, his mouth was curved for power and mockery, and only his small quick eyes betrayed the uncertainty and lassitude inherited from a Wyant mother.

Wyant, at Nona's approach, held out a dry feverish hand. "Well, this is luck! Stan was just getting ready to fly at your mother's approach, and you turn up instead!"

Heuston got to his feet, and greeted Nona somewhat ceremoniously. "Perhaps I'd better fly all the same," he said in a singularly agreeable voice. His eyes were intent on the girl's.

She made a slight gesture, not so much to detain or dismiss as to signify her complete indifference. "Isn't mother coming presently?" she said, addressing the question to Wyant.

"No; I'm moved on till tomorrow. There must have been some big upheaval to make her change her plans at the last minute. Sit down and tell us all about it."

"I don't know of any upheaval. There's only the dinner-dance for Amalasuntha this evening."

"Oh, but that sort of thing is in your mother's stride. You underrate her capacity. Stan has been giving me a hint of something a good deal more volcanic."

Nona felt an inward tremor; was she going to hear Lita's name? She turned her glance on Heuston with a certain hostility.

"Oh, Stan's hints—."

"You see what Nona thinks of my views on cities and men," Heuston shrugged. He had remained on his feet, as though about to take leave; but once again the girl felt his eager eyes beseeching her.

"Are you waiting to walk home with me? You needn't. I'm going to stay for hours," she said, smiling across him at Wyant as she settled down into one of the chintz armchairs.

"Aren't you a little hard on him?" Wyant suggested, when the door had closed on their visitor. "It's not exactly a crime to want to walk home with you."

Nona made an impatient gesture. "Stan bores me."

"Ah, well, I suppose he's not enough of a novelty. Or not up-to-date enough; *your* dates. Some of his ideas seem to me pretty subversive; but I suppose in your set and Lita's a young man who doesn't jazz all day and drink all night—or vice versa—is a back number."

The girl did not take this up, and after a moment Wyant continued, in his half-mocking half-querulous voice: "Or is it that he isn't 'psychic' enough? That's the latest, isn't it? When you're not high-kicking you're all high-thinking; and that reminds me of Stan's news—"

"Yes?" Nona brought it out between parched lips. Her gaze turned from Wyant to the coals smouldering in the grate. She did not want to face any one just then.

"Well, it seems there's going to be a gigantic muck-raking—one of the worst we've had yet. Into this Mahatma business; you know, the nigger chap your mother's always talking about. There's a hint of it in the last number of the 'Looker-on'; here . . . where is it? Never mind, though. What it says isn't a patch on the real facts, Stan tells me. It seems the goings-on in that School of Oriental Thought—what does he call the place: Dawnside?—have reached such a point that the Grant Lindons, whose girl has been making a 'retreat' there, or whatever they call it, are out to have a thorough probing. They say the police don't want to move because so many people we know are mixed up in it; but Lindon's back is up, and he swears he won't rest till he gets the case before the Grand Jury . . ."

As Wyant talked, the weight lifted from Nona's breast. Much she cared for the Mahatma, or for the Grant Lindons! Stuffy old-fashioned people—she didn't wonder Bee Lindon had broken away from such parents—though she was a silly fool, no doubt. Besides, the Mahatma certainly had reduced Mrs. Manford's hips—and made her less nervous too: for Mrs. Manford sometimes *was* nervous, in spite of her breathless pursuit of repose. Not, of course, in the same querulous uncontrolled way as poor Arthur Wyant, who had never been taught poise, or mental uplift, or being in tune with the Infinite; but rather as one agitated by the incessant effort to be calm. And in that respect the Mahatma's rhythmic exercises had without doubt been helpful. No; Nona didn't care a fig for scandals about the School of Oriental Thought. And the relief of finding that the subject she had dreaded to hear broached had probably never even come to Wyant's ears, gave her a reaction of light-heartedness.

There were moments when Nona felt oppressed by responsibilities and anxieties not of her age, apprehensions that she could not shake off and yet had not enough experience of life to know how to meet. One or two of her girl friends—in the brief intervals between whirls and thrills—had confessed to the same vague disquietude. It was as if, in the beaming determination of the middle-aged, one and all of them, to ignore sorrow and evil, "think them away" as superannuated bogies, survivals of some obsolete European superstition unworthy of enlightened Americans, to whom plumbing and dentistry had given higher standards, and bi-focal glasses a clearer view of the universe—as if the demons the elder generation ignored, baulked of their natural prey, had cast their hungry shadow over the young. After all, somebody in every family had to remember now and then that such things as wickedness, suffering and death had not yet been banished from the earth; and with all those bright-complexioned white-haired mothers mailed in massage and optimism, and behaving as if they had never heard of anything but the Good and the Beautiful, perhaps their children had to serve as vicarious sacrifices. There were hours when Nona

Manford, bewildered little Iphigenia, uneasily argued in this way: others when youth and inexperience reasserted themselves, and the load slipped from her, and she wondered why she didn't always believe, like her elders, that one had only to be brisk, benevolent and fond to prevail against the powers of darkness.

She felt this relief now; but a vague restlessness remained with her, and to ease it, and prove to herself that she was not nervous, she mentioned to Wyant that she had just been lunching with Jim and Lita.

Wyant brightened, as he always did at his son's name. "Poor old Jim! He dropped in yesterday, and I thought he looked overworked! I sometimes wonder if that father of yours hasn't put more hustle into him than a Wyant can assimilate." Wyant spoke good-humouredly; his first bitterness against the man who had supplanted him (a sentiment regarded by Pauline as barbarous and mediæval) had gradually been swallowed up in gratitude for Dexter Manford's kindness to Jim. The oddly-assorted trio, Wyant, Pauline and her new husband, had been drawn into a kind of inarticulate understanding by their mutual tenderness for the progeny of the two marriages, and Manford loved Jim almost as much as Wyant loved Nona.

"Oh, well," the girl said, "Jim always does everything with all his might. And now that he's doing it for Lita and the baby, he's got to keep on, whether he wants to or not."

"I suppose so. But why do you say 'whether'?" Wyant questioned with one of his disconcerting flashes. "Doesn't he want to?"

Nona was vexed at her slip. "Of course. I only meant that he used to be rather changeable in his tastes, and that getting married has given him an object."

"How very old-fashioned! You *are* old-fashioned, you know, my child; in spite of the jazz. I suppose that's what I've done for *you*, in exchange for Manford's modernizing Jim. Not much of an exchange, I'm afraid. But how long do you suppose Lita will care about being an object to Jim?"

"Why shouldn't she care? She'd go on caring about the baby, even if . . . not that I mean . . ."

"Oh, I know. That's a great baby. Queer, you know—I can see he's going to have the Wyant nose and forehead. It's about all we've left to give. But look here—haven't you really heard anything more about the Mahatma? I thought that Lindon girl was a pal of yours. Now listen—"

When Nona Manford emerged into the street she was not surprised to meet Stanley Heuston strolling toward her across Stuyvesant Square. Neither surprised, nor altogether sorry; do what she would, she could never quite repress the sense of ease and well-being that his nearness gave. And yet half the time they were together she always spent in being angry with him and wishing him away. If only the relation between them had been as simple as that between herself and Jim! And it might have been—ought to have been—seeing that Heuston was Jim's cousin, and nearly twice her age; yes, and had been married before she left the schoolroom. Really, her exasperation was justified. Yet no one understood her as well as Stanley; not even Jim, who was so much dearer and more lovable. Life was a confusing business to Nona Manford.

"How absurd! I asked you not to wait. I suppose you think I'm not old enough to be out alone after dark."

"That hadn't occurred to me; and I'm not waiting to walk home with you," Heuston rejoined with some asperity. "But I do want to say two words," he added, his voice breaking into persuasion.

Nona stopped, her heels firmly set on the pavement. "The same old two?"

"No. Besides, there are three of those. You never *could* count." He hesitated: "This time it's only about Arthur—"

"Why; what's the matter?" The sense of apprehension woke in her again. What if Wyant really had begun to suspect that there was something, an imponderable something, wrong between Jim and Lita, and had been too shrewd to let Nona detect his suspicion?

"Haven't you noticed? He looks like the devil. He's been drinking again. Eleanor spoke to me—"

"Oh, dear." There it was—all the responsibilities and worries always closed in on Nona! But this one, after all, was relatively bearable.

"What can I do, Stan? I can't imagine why you come to *me*!"

He smiled a little, in his queer derisive way. "Doesn't everybody? The fact is—I didn't want to bother Jim."

She was silent. She understood; but she resented his knowing that she understood.

"Jim has got to be bothered. He's got to look after his father."

"Yes; but I— Oh, look here, Nona; won't you see?"

"See what?"

"Why—that if Jim is worried about his father now—Jim's a queer chap; he's tried his hand at fifty things, and never stuck to one; and if he gets a shock now, on top of everything else—"

Nona felt her lips grow hard: all her pride and tenderness for her brother stiffened into ice about her heart.

"I don't know what you mean. Jim's grown up—he's got to face things."

"Yes; I know. I've been told the same thing about myself. But there are things one doesn't ever have a chance to face in this slippery sliding modern world, because they don't come out into the open. They just lurk and peep and mouth. My case exactly. What on earth is there about Aggie that a fellow can *face*?"

Nona stopped short with a jerk. "We don't happen to be talking about you and Aggie," she said.

"Oh, well; I was merely using myself as an example. But there are plenty of others to choose from."

Her voice broke into anger. "I don't imagine you're comparing your married life to Jim's?"

"Lord, no. God forbid!" He burst into a dry laugh. "When I think of Aggie's life and Lita's—!"

"Never mind about Lita's life. What do you know about it, anyhow? Oh, Stan, why are we quarrelling again?" She felt the tears in her throat. "What you wanted was only to tell me about poor Arthur. And I'd guessed that myself—I know something ought to be done. But *what*? How on earth can I tell? I'm always being asked by everybody what ought to be done . . . and sometimes I feel too young to be always the one to judge, to decide . . ."

Heuston stood watching her in silence. Suddenly he took her hand and drew it through his arm. She did not resist, and thus linked they walked on slowly and without further speech through the cold deserted streets. As they approached more populous regions she freed her arm from his, and signalled to a taxi.

"May I come?"

"No. I'm going to meet Lita at the Cubist Cabaret. I promised to be there by four."

"Oh, all right." He looked at her irresolutely as the taxi drew up. "I wish to God I could always be on hand to help you when you're bothered!"

She shook her head.

"Never?"

"Not while Aggie—"

"That means never."

"Then never." She held out her hand, but he had turned and was already striding off in the opposite direction. She threw the address to the chauffeur and got in.

"Yes; I suppose it *is* never," she said to herself. After all, instead of helping her with the Wyant problem, Stan had only brought her another: his own—and hers. As long as Aggie Heuston, a sort of lay nun, absorbed in High Church practices and the exercise of a bleak but efficient philanthropy, continued to set her face against divorce, Nona would not admit that Heuston had any right to force it upon her. "It's her way of loving him," the girl said to herself for the hundredth time. "She wants to keep him for herself too—though she doesn't know it; but she does above all want to save him. And she thinks that's the way to do it. I rather admire her for thinking that there *is* a way to save people . . ." She pushed that problem once more into the back of her mind, and turned her thoughts toward the other and far more pressing one: that of poor Arthur Wyant's growing infirmity. Stanley was probably right in not wanting to speak to Jim about it at that particular moment—though how did Stanley know about Jim's troubles, and what did he know?—and she herself, after all, was perhaps the only person to deal with Arthur Wyant. Another interval of anxious consideration made her decide that the best way would be to seek her father's advice. After an hour's dancing she would feel better, more alive and competent, and there would still be time to dash down to Manford's office, the only place—as she knew by experience—where Manford was ever likely to have time for her.

Chapter V

THE door of his private office clicked on a withdrawing client, and Dexter Manford, giving his vigorous shoulders a shake, rose from his desk and stood irresolute.

"I must get out to Cedarledge for some golf on Saturday," he thought. He lived among people who regarded golf as a universal panacea, and in a world which believed in panaceas.

As he stood there, his glance lit on the looking-glass above the mantel and he mustered his image impatiently. Queer thing, for a man of his age to gape at himself in a looking-glass like a dago dancing-master! He saw a swarthy straight-nosed face, dark crinkling hair with a dash of gray on the temples, dark eyes under brows that were beginning to beetle across a deep vertical cleft. Complexion turning from ruddy to sallow; eyes heavy—would he put his tongue out next? The matter with him was . . .

He dropped back into his desk-chair and unhooked the telephone receiver.

"Mrs. James Wyant? Yes . . . Oh—*out*? You're sure? And you don't know when she'll be back? Who? Yes; Mr. Manford. I had a message for Mrs. Wyant. No matter."

He hung up and leaned back, stretching his legs under the table and staring moodily at the heap of letters and legal papers in the morocco-lined baskets set out before him.

"I look ten years older than my age," he thought. Yet that last new type-writer, Miss Vollard, or whatever her name was, really behaved as if . . . was always looking at him when she thought he wasn't looking . . . "Oh, what rot!" he exclaimed.

His day had been as all his days were now: a starting in with a great sense of pressure, importance and authority—and a drop at the close into staleness and futility.

The evening before, he had stopped to see his doctor and been told that he was over-working, and needed a nerve-tonic and a change of scene. "Cruise to the West Indies, or something of the sort. Couldn't you get away for three or four weeks? No? Well, more golf then, anyhow."

Getting away from things; the perpetual evasion, moral, mental, physical, which he heard preached, and saw practised, everywhere about him, except where money-making was concerned! He, Dexter Manford, who had been brought up on a Minnesota farm, paid his own way through the State College at Delos, and his subsequent course in the Harvard Law School; and who, ever since, had been working at the top of his pitch with no more sense of strain, no more desire for evasion (shirking, he called it) than a healthy able-bodied man of fifty had a right to feel! If his task had been mere money-getting he might have known—and acknowledged—weariness. But he gloried in his profession, in its labours and difficulties as well as its rewards, it satisfied him intellectually and gave him that calm sense of mastery—mastery over himself and others—known only to those who are doing what they were born to do.

Of course, at every stage of his career—and never more than now, on its slippery pinnacle—he had suffered the thousand irritations inseparable from a hard-working life: the trifles which waste one's time, the fools who consume one's patience, the tricky failure of the best-laid plans, the endless labour of rolling human stupidity up the steep hill of understanding. But until lately these things had been a stimulus: it had amused him to shake off trifles, baffle bores, circumvent failure, and exercise his mental muscles in persuading stupid people to do intelligent things. There was pioneer blood in him: he was used to starting out every morning to hack his way through a fresh growth of prejudices and obstacles; and though he liked his big retaining fees he liked arguing a case even better.

Professionally, he was used to intellectual loneliness, and no longer minded it. Outside of his profession he had a brain above the average, but a general education hardly up to it; and the discrepancy between what he would have been capable of enjoying had his mind been prepared for it, and what it could actually take in, made him modest and almost shy in what he considered cultivated society. He had long believed his wife to be cultivated because she had fits of book-buying and there was an expensively bound library in the New York house. In his raw youth, in the old Delos days, he had got together a little library of his own in which Robert Ingersoll's lectures represented science, the sermons of the Reverend Frank Gunsaulus of Chicago, theology, John Burroughs, natural history, and Jared Sparks and Bancroft almost the whole of history.

He had gradually discovered the inadequacy of these guides, but without ever having done much to replace them. Now and then, when he was not too tired, and had the rare chance of a quiet evening, he picked up a book from Pauline's table; but the works she acquired were so heterogeneous, and of such unequal value, that he rarely found one worth reading. Mrs. Tallentyre's "Voltaire" had been a revelation: he discovered, to his surprise, that he had never really known who Voltaire was, or what sort of a world he had lived in, and why his name had survived it. After that, Manford decided to start in on a course of European history, and got as far as taking the first volume of Macaulay up to bed. But he was tired at night, and found Macaulay's periods too long (though their eloquence appealed to his forensic instinct): and there had never been time for that course of history.

In his early wedded days, before he knew much of his wife's world, he had dreamed of quiet evenings at home, when Pauline would read instructive books aloud while he sat by the fire and turned over his briefs in some quiet inner chamber of his mind. But Pauline had never known any one who wanted to be read aloud to except children getting over infantile complaints. She regarded the desire almost as a symptom of illness, and decided that Dexter needed "rousing," and that she must do more to amuse him. As soon as she was able after Nona's birth she girt herself up for this new duty; and from that day Manford's life, out of office hours, had been one of almost incessant social activity. At first the endless going out had bewildered, then for a while amused and flattered him, then gradually grown to be a soothing routine, a sort of mild drug-taking after the high pressure of professional hours; but of late it had become simply a bore, a duty to be persisted in because—as he had at last discovered—Pauline could not live without it. After twenty years of marriage he was only just beginning to exercise his intellectual acumen on his wife.

The thought of Pauline made him glance at his clock: she would be coming in a moment. He unhooked the receiver again, and named, impatiently, the same number as before. "Out, you say? Still?" (The same stupid voice making the same stupid answer!) "Oh, no; no matter. I say *it's no matter*," he almost shouted, replacing the receiver. Of all idiotic servants—!

Miss Vollard, the susceptible type-writer, shot a shingled head around the door, said "*All* right" with an envious sigh to some one outside, and effaced herself before the brisk entrance of her employer's wife. Manford got to his feet.

"Well, my dear—" He pushed an armchair near the fire, solicitous, still a little awed by her presence—the beautiful Mrs. Wyant who had deigned to marry him. Pauline, throwing back her furs, cast a quick house-keeping glance about her. The scent she used always reminded him of a superior disinfectant; and in another moment, he knew, she would find some pretext for assuring herself, by the application of a gloved finger-tip, that there was no dust on desk or mantelpiece. She had very nearly obliged him, when he moved into his new office, to have concave surbases, as in a hospital ward or a hygienic nursery. She had adopted with enthusiasm the idea of the concave tiling fitted to every cove and angle, so that there were no corners anywhere to catch the dust. People's lives ought to be like that: with no corners in them. She wanted to de-microbe life.

But, in the case of his own office, Manford had resisted; and now, he understood, the fad had gone to the scrap-heap—with how many others!

"Not too near the fire." Pauline pushed her armchair back and glanced up to see if the ceiling ventilators were working. "You *do* renew the air at regular intervals? I'm sure everything depends on that; that and thought-direction. What the Mahatma calls mental deep-breathing." She smiled persuasively. "You look tired, Dexter . . . tired and drawn."

"Oh, rot!—A cigarette?"

She shook her small resolute head. "You forget that he's cured me of that too—the Mahatma. Dexter," she exclaimed suddenly, "I'm sure it's this silly business of the Grant Lindons' that's worrying you. I want to talk to you about it—to clear it up with you. It's out of the question that you should be mixed up in it."

Manford had gone back to his desk-chair. Habit made him feel more at home there, in fuller possession of himself; Pauline, in the seat facing him, the light full on her, seemed no more than a client to be advised, or an opponent to be talked over. He knew she felt the difference too. So far he had managed to preserve his professional privacy and his professional authority. What he did "at the office" was clouded over, for his family, by the vague word "business," which meant that a man didn't want to be bothered. Pauline had never really distinguished between practising the law and manufacturing motors; nor had Manford encouraged her to. But today he suspected that she meant her interference to go to the extreme limit which her well-known "tact" would permit.

"You must not be mixed up in this investigation. Why not hand it over to somebody else? Alfred Cosby, or that new Jew who's so clever? The Lindons would accept any one you recommended; unless, of course," she continued, "you could persuade them to drop it, which would be so much better. I'm sure you could, Dexter; you always know what to say—and your opinion carries such weight. Besides, what is it they complain of? Some nonsense of Bee's, I've no doubt—she took a rest-cure at the School. If they'd brought the girl up properly there'd have been no trouble. Look at Nona!"

"Oh—Nona!" Manford gave a laugh of pride. Nona was the one warm rich spot in his life: the corner on which the sun always shone. Fancy comparing that degenerate fool of a Bee Lindon to his Nona, and imagining that "bringing-up" made the difference! Still, he had to admit that Pauline—always admirable—had been especially so as a mother. Yet she too was bitten with this theosophical virus!

He lounged back, hands in pockets, one leg swinging, instinctively seeking an easier attitude as his moral ease diminished.

"My dear, it's always been understood, hasn't it, that what goes on in this office is between me and my clients, and not—"

"Oh, nonsense, Dexter!" She seldom took that tone: he saw that she was losing her self-control. "Look here: I make it a rule never to interfere; you've just said so. Well—if I interfere now, it's because I've a right to—because it's a duty! The Lindons are my son's cousins: Fanny Lindon was a Wyant. Isn't that reason enough?"

"It was one of the Lindons' reasons. They appealed to me on that very ground."

Pauline gave an irritated laugh. "How like Fanny! Always pushing in and claiming things. I wonder such an argument took you in. Do consider, Dexter! I won't for a minute admit that there *can* be anything wrong about the Mahatma; but supposing there were . . ." She drew herself up, her lips tightening.

"I hope I know how to respect professional secrecy, and I don't ask you to repeat their nasty insinuations; in fact, as you know, I always take particular pains to avoid hearing anything painful or offensive. But, supposing there were any ground for what they say; do they realize how the publicity is going to affect Bee's reputation? And how shall you feel if you set the police at work and find them publishing the name of a girl who is Jim's cousin, and a friend of your own daughter's?"

Manford moved restlessly in his chair, and in so doing caught his reflexion in the mirror, and saw that his jaw had lost its stern professional cast. He made an attempt to recover it, but unsuccessfully.

"But all this is too absurd," Pauline continued on a smoother note. "The Mahatma and his friends have nothing to fear. Whose judgment would you sooner trust: mine, or poor Fanny's? What really bothers me is your allowing the Lindons to drag you into an affair which is going to discredit them, and not the Mahatma." She smiled her bright frosty smile. "You know how proud I am of your professional prestige: I should hate to have you associated with a failure." She paused, and he saw that she meant to rest on that.

"This is a pretty bad business. The Lindons have got their proofs all right," he said.

Pauline reddened, and her face lost its look of undaunted serenity. "How can you believe such rubbish, Dexter? If you're going to take Fanny Lindon's word against mine—"

"It's not a question of your word or hers. Lindon is fully documented: he didn't come to me till he was. I'm sorry, Pauline; but you've been deceived. This man has got to be shown up, and the Lindons have had the pluck to do what everybody else has shirked."

Pauline's angry colour had faded. She got up and stood before her husband, distressed and uncertain; then, with a visible effort at self-command, she seated herself again, and locked her hands about her gold-mounted bag.

"Then you'd rather the scandal, if there is one, should be paraded before the world? Who will gain by that except the newspaper reporters, and the people who want to drag down society? And how shall you feel if Nona is called as a witness—or Lita?"

"Oh, nonsense—" He stopped abruptly, and got up too. The discussion was lasting longer than he had intended, and he could not find the word to end it. His mind felt suddenly empty—empty of arguments and formulas. "I don't know why you persist in bringing in Nona—or Lita—"

"I don't; it's you. You will, that is, if you take this case. Bee and Nona have been intimate since they were babies, and Bee is always at Lita's. Don't you suppose the Mahatma's lawyers will make use of that if you *oblige* him to fight? You may say you're prepared for it; and I admire your courage—but I can't share it. The idea that our children may be involved simply sickens me."

"Neither Nona nor Lita has ever had anything to do with this charlatan and his humbug, as far as I know," said Manford irritably.

"Nona has attended his eurythmic classes at our house, and gone to his lectures with me: at one time they interested her intensely." Pauline paused. "About Lita I don't know: I know so little about Lita's life before her marriage."

"It was presumably that of any of Nona's other girl friends."

"Presumably. Kitty Landish might enlighten us. But of course, if it *was*—" he noted her faintly sceptical emphasis—"I don't admit that that would preclude Lita's having known the Mahatma, or believed in him. And you must remember, Dexter, that I should be the most deeply involved of all! I mean to take a rest-cure at Dawnside in March." She gave the little playful laugh with which she had been used, in old times, to ridicule the naughtiness of her children.

Manford drummed on his blotting-pad. "Look here, suppose we drop this for the present—"

She glanced at her wrist-watch. "If you can spare the time—"

"Spare the time?"

She answered softly: "I'm not going away till you've promised."

Manford could remember the day when that tone—so feminine under its firmness—would have had the power to shake him. Pauline, in her wifely dealings, so seldom invoked the prerogative of her grace, her competence, her persuasiveness, that when she did he had once found it hard to resist. But that day was past. Under his admiration for her brains, and his esteem for her character, he had felt, of late, a stealing boredom.

She was too clever, too efficient, too uniformly sagacious and serene. Perhaps his own growing sense of power—professional and social—had secretly undermined his awe of hers, made him feel himself first her equal, then ever so little her superior. He began to detect something obtuse in that unfaltering competence. And as his professional authority grew he had become more jealous of interference with it. His wife ought at least to have understood that! If her famous tact were going to fail her, what would be left, he asked himself?

"Look here, Pauline, you know all this is useless. In professional matters no one else can judge for me. I'm busy this afternoon; I'm sure you are too—"

She settled more deeply into her armchair. "Never too busy for you, Dexter."

"Thank you, dear. But the time I ask you to give me is outside of business hours," he rejoined with a slight smile.

"Then I'm dismissed?" She smiled back. "I understand; you needn't ring!" She rose with recovered serenity and laid a light hand on his shoulder. "Sorry to have bothered you; I don't often, do I? All I ask is that you should think over—"

He lifted the hand to his lips. "Of course, of course." Now that she was going he could say it.

"I'm forgiven?"

He smiled: "You're forgiven"; and from the threshold she called, almost gaily: "Don't forget tonight—Amalasuntha!"

His brow clouded as he returned to his chair; and oddly enough—he was aware of the oddness—it was clouded not by the tiresome scene he had been through, but by his wife's reminder. "Damn that dinner," he swore to himself.

He turned to the telephone, unhooked it for the third time, and called for the same number.

That evening, as he slipped the key into his front-door, Dexter Manford felt the oppression of all that lay behind it. He never entered his house without a slight consciousness of the importance of the act—never completely took for granted the resounding vestibule, the big hall with its marble staircase ascending to all the light and warmth and luxury which skill could devise, money buy, and Pauline's ingenuity combine in a harmonious whole. He had not yet forgotten the day when, after one of his first legal successes, he had installed a bathroom in his mother's house at Delos, and all the neighbours had driven in from miles around to see it.

But luxury, and above all comfort, had never weighed on him; he was too busy to think much about them, and sure enough of himself and his powers to accept them as his right. It was not the splendour of his house that oppressed him but the sense of the corporative bonds it imposed. It seemed part of an elaborate social and domestic structure, put together with the baffling ingenuity of certain bird's-nests of which he had seen the pictures. His own career, Pauline's multiple activities, the problem of poor Arthur Wyant, Nona, Jim, Lita Wyant, the Mahatma, the tiresome Grant Lindons, the perennial and inevitable Amalasuntha, for whom the house was being illuminated tonight—all were strands woven into the very pile of the carpet he trod on his way up the stairs. As he passed the dining-room he saw, through half-open doors, the glitter of glass and silver, a shirt-sleeved man placing bowls of roses down the long table, and Maisie Bruss, wan but undaunted, dealing out dinner cards to Powder, the English butler.

Chapter VI

PAULINE MANFORD sent a satisfied glance down the table. It was on such occasions that she visibly reaped her reward. No one else in New York had so accomplished a cook, such smoothly running service, a dinner-table so softly yet brightly lit, or such skill in grouping about it persons not only eminent in wealth or fashion, but likely to find pleasure in each other's society.

The intimate reunion, of the not-more-than-the-Muses kind, was not Pauline's affair. She was aware of this, and seldom made the attempt—though, when she did, she was never able to discover why it was not a success. But in the organizing and administering of a big dinner she was conscious of mastery. Not the stupid big dinner of old days, when the "crowned heads" used to be treated like a caste apart, and everlastingly invited to meet each other through a whole monotonous season: Pauline was too modern for that. She excelled in a judicious blending of Wall Street and Bohemia, and her particular art lay in her selection of the latter element. Of course there were Bohemians and Bohemians; as she had once remarked to Nona, people weren't always amusing just because they were clever, or dull just because they were rich—though at the last clause Nona had screwed up her nose incredulously . . . Well, even Nona would be satisfied tonight, Pauline thought. It wasn't everybody who would have been bold enough to ask a social reformer like Parker Greg with the very people least disposed to encourage social reform, nor a young composer like Torfried Lobb (a disciple of "The Six") with all those stolid opera-goers, nor that disturbing Tommy Ardwin, the Cubist decorator, with the owners of the most expensive "period houses" in Fifth Avenue.

Pauline was not a bit afraid of such combinations. She knew in advance that at one of her dinners everything would "go"— it always did. And her success amused and exhilarated her so much that, even tonight, though she had come down oppressed with problems, they slipped from her before she even had time to remind herself that they were nonexistent. She had only to look at the faces gathered about that subdued radiance of old silver and scattered flowers to be sure of it. There, at the other end of the table, was her husband's dark head, comely and resolute in its vigorous middle-age; on his right the Marchesa di San Fedele, the famous San Fedele pearls illuminating her inconspicuous black; on his left the handsome Mrs. Herman Toy, magnanimously placed there by Pauline because she knew that Manford was said to be "taken" by her, and she wanted him to be in good-humour that evening. To measure her own competence she had only to take in this group, already settling down to an evening's enjoyment, and then let her glance travel on to the others, the young and handsome women, the well-dressed confident-looking men. Nona, grave yet eager, was talking to Manford's legal rival, the brilliant Alfred Cosby, who was known to have said she was the cleverest girl in New York. Lita, cool and aloof, drooped her head slightly to listen to Torfried Lobb, the composer; Jim gazed across the table at Lita as if his adoration made every intervening obstacle transparent; Aggie Heuston, whose coldness certainly made her look distinguished, though people complained that she was dull, dispensed occasional monosyllables to the ponderous Herman Toy; and Stanley Heuston, leaning back with that faint dry smile which Pauline found irritating because it was so inscrutable, kept his eyes discreetly but steadily on Nona. Dear good Stan, always like a brother to Nona! People who knew him well said he wasn't as sardonic as he looked.

It was a world after Pauline's heart—a world such as she believed its Maker meant it to be. She turned to the Bishop on her right, wondering if he shared her satisfaction, and encountered a glance of understanding.

"So refreshing to be among old friends . . . This is one of the few houses left . . . Always such a pleasure to meet the dear Marchesa; I hope she has better reports of her son? Wretched business, I'm afraid. My dear Mrs. Manford, I wonder if you know how blessed you are in your children? That wise little Nona, who is going to make some man so happy one of these days—not Cosby, no? Too much difference in age? And your steady Jim and his idol . . . yes, I know it doesn't become my cloth to speak indulgently of idolatry. But happy marriages are so rare nowadays: where else could one find such examples as there are about this table? Your Jim and his Lita, and my good friend

Heuston with that saint of a wife—" The Bishop paused, as if, even on so privileged an occasion, he was put to it to prolong the list. "Well, you've given them the example . . ." He stopped again, probably remembering that his hostess's matrimonial bliss was built on the ruins of her first husband's. But in divorcing she had invoked a cause which even the Church recognizes; and the Bishop proceeded serenely: "*Her children shall rise up and call her blessed*—yes, dear friend, you must let me say it."

The words were balm to Pauline. Every syllable carried conviction: all was right with her world and the Bishop's! Why did she ever need any other spiritual guidance than that of her own creed? She felt a twinge of regret at having so involved herself with the Mahatma. Yet what did Episcopal Bishops know of "holy ecstasy"? And could any number of Church services have reduced her hips? After all, there was room for all the creeds in her easy rosy world. And the thought led her straight to her other preoccupation: the reception for the Cardinal. She resolved to secure the Bishop's approval at once. After that, of course the Chief Rabbi would have to come. And what a lesson in tolerance and good-will to the discordant world she was trying to reform!

Nona, half-way down the table, viewed its guests from another angle. She had come back depressed rather than fortified from her flying visit to her father. There were days when Manford liked to be "surprised" at the office; when he and his daughter had their little jokes together over these clandestine visits. But this one had not come off in that spirit. She had found Manford tired and slightly irritable; Nona, before he had time to tell her of her mother's visit, caught a lingering whiff of Pauline's cool hygienic scent, and wondered nervously what could have happened to make Mrs. Manford break through her tightly packed engagements, and dash down to her husband's office. It was of course to that emergency that she had sacrificed poor Exhibit A—little guessing his relief at the postponement. But what could have obliged her to see Manford so suddenly, when they were to meet at dinner that evening?

The girl had asked no questions: she knew that Manford, true to his profession, preferred putting them. And her chief object, of course, had been to get him to help her about Arthur

Wyant. That, she perceived, at first added to his irritation: was he Wyant's keeper, he wanted to know? But he broke off before the next question: "Why the devil can't his own son look after him?" She had seen that question on his very lips; but they shut down on it, and he rose from his chair with a shrug. "Poor devil—if you think I can be of any use? All right, then—I'll drop in on him tomorrow." He and Wyant, ever since the divorce, had met whenever Jim's fate was to be discussed; Wyant felt a sort of humiliated gratitude for generosity to his son. "Not the money, you know, Nona—damn the money! But taking such an interest in him; helping him to find himself: appreciating him, hang it! He understands Jim a hundred times better than your mother ever did . . ." On this basis the two men came together now and then in a spirit of tolerant understanding . . .

Nona recalled her father's face as it had been when she left him: worried, fagged, yet with that twinkle of gaiety his eyes always had when he looked at her. Now, smoothed out, smiling, slightly replete, it was hard as stone. "Like his own death-mask," the girl thought; "as if he'd done with everything, once for all.— And the way those two women bore him! Mummy put Gladys Toy next to him as a reward—for what?" She smiled at her mother's simplicity in imagining that he was having what Pauline called a "harmless flirtation" with Mrs. Herman Toy. That lady's obvious charms were no more to him, Nona suspected, than those of the florid Bathsheba in the tapestry behind his chair. But Pauline had evidently had some special reason—over and above her usual diffused benevolence—for wanting to put Manford in a good humour. "The Mahatma, probably." Nona knew how her mother hated a fuss: how vulgar and unchristian she always thought it. And it would certainly be inconvenient to give up the rest-cure at Dawnside she had planned for March, when Manford was to go off tarpon-fishing.

Nona's glance, in the intervals of talk with her neighbours, travelled farther, lit on Jim's good-humoured wistful face—Jim was always wistful at his mother's banquets—and flitted on to Aggie Heuston's precise little mask, where everything was narrow and perpendicular, like the head of a saint squeezed into a cathedral niche. But the girl's eyes did not linger, for as they rested on Aggie they abruptly met the latter's gaze. Aggie had been furtively scrutinizing her, and the discovery gave Nona a faint shock. In another instant Mrs. Heuston turned to Parker Greg, the interesting young social reformer whom Pauline had thoughtfully placed next to her, with the optimistic idea that all persons interested in improving the world must therefore be in the fullest sympathy. Nona, knowing Parker Greg's views, smiled at that too. Aggie, she was sure, would feel much safer with her other neighbour, Mr. Herman Toy, who thought, on all subjects, just what all his fellow capitalists did.

Nona caught Stan Heuston's smile, and knew he had read her thought; but from him too she turned. The last thing she wanted was that he should guess her real opinion of his wife. Something deep down and dogged in Nona always, when it came to the touch, made her avert her feet from the line of least resistance.

Manford lent an absent ear first to one neighbour, then the other. Mrs. Toy was saying, in her flat uncadenced voice, like tepid water running into a bath: "I don't see how people can *live* without lifts in their houses, do you? But perhaps it's because I've never had to. Father's house had the first electric lift at Climax. Once, in England, we went to stay with the Duke of Humber, at Humber Castle—one of those huge parties, royalties and everything—golf and polo all day, and a ball every night; and, will you believe it, *we had to walk up and down stairs*! I don't know what English people are made of. I suppose they've never been used to what we call comfort. The second day I told Herman I couldn't stand those awful slippery stairs after two rounds of golf, and dancing till four in the morning. It was simply destroying my heart—the doctor has warned me so often! I wanted to leave right away—but Herman said it would offend the Duke. The Duke's such a sweet old man. But, any way, I made Herman promise me a sapphire and emerald *plaque* from Cartier's before I'd agree to stick it out . . ."

The Marchesa's little ferret face with sharp impassioned eyes darted conversationally forward. "The Duke of Humber? I know him so *well*. Dear old man! Ah, you also stayed at Humber? So often he invites me. We are related . . . yes, through his first wife, whose mother was a Venturini of the Calabrian branch: Donna Ottaviana. Yes. Another sister, Donna Rosmunda, the beauty of the family, married the Duke of Lepanto . . . a media-tized prince . . ."

She stopped, and Manford read in her eyes the hasty inward interrogation: "Will they think that expression queer? I'm not sure myself just what 'mediatized' means. And these Americans! They stick at nothing, but they're shocked at everything." Aloud she continued: "A mediatized prince—but a man of the *very highest* character."

"Oh—" murmured Mrs. Toy, puzzled but obviously relieved.

Manford's attention, tugging at its moorings, had broken loose again and was off and away.

The how-many-eth dinner did that make this winter? And no end in sight! How could Pauline stand it? Why did she want to stand it? All those rest-cures, massages, rhythmic exercises, devised to restore the health of people who would have been as sound as bells if only they had led normal lives! Like that fool of a woman spreading her blond splendours so uselessly at his side, who couldn't walk upstairs because she had danced all night! Pauline was just like that—never walked upstairs, and then had to do gymnastics, and have osteopathy, and call in Hindu sages, to prevent her muscles from getting atrophied . . . He had a vision of his mother, out on the Minnesota farm, before they moved into Delos—saw her sowing, digging potatoes, feeding chickens; saw her kneading, baking, cooking, washing, mend-ing, catching and harnessing the half-broken colt to drive twelve miles in the snow for the doctor, one day when all the men were away, and his little sister had been so badly scalded . . . And there the old lady sat at Delos, in her nice little brick house, in her hale and hearty old age, built to outlive them all.— Wasn't that perhaps the kind of life Manford himself had been meant for? Farming on a big scale, with all the modern appliances his forbears had lacked, outdoing everybody in the county, market-ing his goods at the big centres, and cutting a swathe in state politics like his elder brother? Using his brains, muscles, the whole of him, body and soul, to do real things, bring about real results in the world, instead of all this artificial activity, this spinning around faster and faster in the void, and having to be continually rested and doctored to make up for exertions that led to nothing, nothing, nothing . . .

"Of course we all know *you* could tell us if you would. Everybody knows the Lindons have gone to you for advice." Mrs. Toy's large shallow eyes floated the question toward him on a sea-blue wave of curiosity. "Not a word of truth? Oh, of course you have to say that! But everybody has been expecting there'd be trouble soon . . ."

And, in a whisper, from the Marchesa's side: "Teasing you about that mysterious Mahatma? Foolish woman! As long as dear Pauline believes in him, I'm satisfied. That was what I was saying to Pauline before dinner: 'Whatever you and Dexter approve of, *I* approve of.' That's the reason why I'm so anxious to have my poor boy come to New York . . . my Michelangelo! If only you could see him I know you'd grow as fond of him as you are of our dear Jim: perhaps even take him into your office . . . Ah, that, dear Dexter, has always been my dream!"

. . . What sort of a life, after all, if not this one? For of course that dream of a Western farm was all rubbish. What he really wanted was a life in which professional interests as far-reaching and absorbing as his own were somehow impossibly combined with great stretches of country quiet, books, horses and children—ah, children! Boys of his own—teaching them all sorts of country things; taking them for long trudges, telling them about trees and plants and birds—watching the squirrels, feeding the robins and thrushes in winter; and coming home in the dusk to firelight, lamplight, a tea-table groaning with jolly things, all the boys and girls (girls too, more little Nonas) grouped around, hungry and tingling from their long tramp—and a woman lifting a calm face from her book: a woman who looked so absurdly young to be their mother; so—

"You're looking at Jim's wife?" The Marchesa broke in. "No wonder! *Très en beauté*, our Lita!—that dress, the very same colour as her hair, and those Indian emeralds . . . how clever of her! But a little difficult to talk to? Little too silent? No? Ah, not to *you*, perhaps—her dear father! Father-in-law, I mean—"

Silent! The word sent him off again. For in that other world, so ringing with children's laughter, children's wrangles, and all the healthy blustering noises of country life in a big family, there would somehow, underneath it all, be a great pool of silence, a reservoir on which one could always draw and flood one's soul with peace. The vision was vague and contradictory, but it all seemed to meet and mingle in the woman's eyes . . .

Pauline was signalling from her table-end. He rose and offered his arm to the Marchesa.

In the hall the strains of the famous Somaliland orchestra bumped and tossed downstairs from the ball-room to meet them. The ladies, headed by Mrs. Toy, flocked to the mirror-lined lift dissembled behind forced lilacs and Japanese plums; but Amalasuntha, on Manford's arm, set her blunt black slipper on the marble tread.

"I'm used to Roman palaces!"

Chapter VII

"A T least you'll take a turn?" Heuston said; and Nona, yielding, joined the dancers balancing with slow steps about the shining floor.

Dancing meant nothing; it was like breathing; what would one be doing if one weren't dancing? She could not refuse without seeming singular; it was simpler to acquiesce, and lose one's self among the couples absorbed in the same complicated ritual.

The floor was full, but not crowded: Pauline always saw to that. It was easy to calculate in advance, for every one she asked always accepted, and she and Maisie Bruss, in making out the list, allotted the requisite space per couple as carefully as if they had been counting cubic feet in a hospital. The ventilation was perfect too; neither draughts nor stuffiness. One had almost the sense of dancing out of doors, under some equable southern sky. Nona, aware of what it cost to produce this illusion, marvelled once more at her tireless mother.

"Isn't she wonderful?"

Mrs. Manford, fresh, erect, a faint line of diamonds in her hair, stood in the doorway, her slim foot advanced toward the dancers.

"Perennially! Ah—she's going to dance. With Cosby."

"Yes. I wish she wouldn't."

"Wouldn't with Cosby?"

"Dear, no. In general."

Nona and Heuston had seated themselves, and were watching from their corner the weaving of hallucinatory patterns by interjoined revolving feet.

"I see. You think she dances with a Purpose?"

The girl smiled. "Awfully well—like everything else she does. But as if it were something between going to church and drilling a scout brigade. Mother's too—too tidy to dance."

"Well—this is different," murmured Heuston.

The floor had cleared as if by magic before the advance of a long slim pair: Lita Wyant and Tommy Ardwin. The decorator, tall and supple, had the conventional dancer's silhouette; but he was no more than a silhouette, a shadow on the wall. All the light and music in the room had passed into the translucent creature in his arms. He seemed to Nona like some one who has gone into a spring wood and come back carrying a long branch of silver blossom.

"Good heavens! *Quelle plastique*!" piped the Marchesa over Nona's shoulder.

The two had the floor to themselves: every one else had stopped dancing. But Lita and her partner seemed unaware of it. Her sole affair was to shower radiance, his to attune his lines to hers. Her face was a small still flower on a swaying stalk; all her expression was in her body, in that long *legato* movement like a weaving of grasses under a breeze, a looping of little waves on the shore.

"Look at Jim!" Heuston laughed. Jim Wyant, from a doorway, drank the vision thirstily. "Surely," his eyes seemed to triumph, "this justifies the Cubist Cabaret, and all the rest of her crazes."

Lita, swaying near him, dropped a smile, and floated off on the bright ripples of her beauty.

Abruptly the music stopped. Nona glanced across the room and saw Mrs. Manford move away from the musicians' balcony, over which the conductor had just leaned down to speak to her.

There was a short interval; then the orchestra broke into a fox-trot and the floor filled again. Mrs. Manford swept by with a set smile—"the kind she snaps on with her tiara," Nona thought. Well, perhaps it *was* rather bad form of Lita to monopolize the floor at her mother-in-law's ball; but was it the poor girl's fault if she danced so well that all the others stopped to gaze?

Ardwin came up to Nona. "Oh, no," Heuston protested under his breath. "I wanted—"

"There's Aggie signalling."

The girl's arm was already on Ardwin's shoulder. As they circled toward the middle of the room, Nona said: "You show off Lita's dancing marvellously."

He replied, in his high-pitched confident voice: "Oh, it's only a question of giving her her head and not butting in. She and I each have our own line of self-expression: it would be stupid to mix them. If only I could get her to dance just once for Serge

Klawhammer; he's scouring the globe to find somebody to do the new 'Herodias' they're going to turn at Hollywood. People are fed up with the odalisque style, and with my help Lita could evolve something different. She's half promised to come round to my place tonight after supper and see Klawhammer. Just six or seven of the enlightened—wonder if you'd join us? He's tearing back to Hollywood tomorrow."

"Is Lita really coming?"

"Well, she said yes and no, and ended on yes."

"All right—I will." Nona hated Ardwin, his sleekness, suppleness, assurance, the group he ruled, the fashions he set, the doctrines he professed—hated them so passionately and undiscerningly that it seemed to her that at last she had her hand on her clue. That was it, of course! Ardwin and his crew were trying to persuade Lita to go into the movies; that accounted for her restlessness and irritability, her growing distaste for her humdrum life. Nona drew a breath of relief. After all, if it were only that—!

The dance over, she freed herself and slipped through the throng in quest of Jim. Should she ask him to take her to Ardwin's? No: simply tell him that she and Lita were off for a final spin at the decorator's studio, where there would be more room and less fuss than at Pauline's. Jim would laugh and approve, provided she and Lita went together; no use saying anything about Klawhammer and his absurd "Herodias."

"Jim? But, my dear, Jim went home long ago. I don't blame the poor boy," Mrs. Manford sighed, waylaid by her daughter, "because I know he has to be at the office so early; and it must be awfully boring, standing about all night and not dancing. But, darling, you must really help me to find your father. Supper's ready, and I can't imagine . . ."

The Marchesa's ferret face slipped between them as she trotted by on Mr. Toy's commodious arm.

"Dear Dexter? I saw him not five minutes ago, seeing off that wonderful Lita—"

"Lita? Lita gone too?" Nona watched the struggle between her mother's disciplined features and twitching nerves. "What impossible children I have!" A smile triumphed over her discomfiture. "I do hope there's nothing wrong with the baby?

Nona, slip down and tell your father he must come up. Oh, Stanley, dear, all my men seem to have deserted me. Do find Mrs. Toy and take her in to supper . . ."

In the hall below there was no Dexter. Nona cast about a glance for Powder, the pale resigned butler, who had followed Mrs. Manford through all her vicissitudes and triumphs, seemingly concerned about nothing but the condition of his plate and the discipline of his footmen. Powder knew everything, and had an answer to everything; but he was engaged at the moment in the vast operation of making terrapin and champagne appear simultaneously on eighty-five small tables, and was not to be found in the hall. Nona ran her eye along the line of footmen behind the piled-up furs, found one who belonged to the house, and heard that Mr. Manford had left a few minutes earlier. His motor had been waiting for him, and was now gone. Mrs. James Wyant was with him, the man thought. "He's taken her to Ardwin's, of course. Poor father! After an evening of Mrs. Toy and Amalasuntha—who can wonder? If only mother would see how her big parties bore him!" But Nona's mother would never see that.

"It's just my indestructible faith in my own genius—nothing else," Ardwin was proclaiming in his jumpy falsetto as Nona entered the high-perched studio where he gathered his group of the enlightened. These privileged persons, in the absence of chairs, had disposed themselves on the cushions and mattresses scattered about a floor painted to imitate a cunning perspective of black and white marble. Tall lamps under black domes shed their light on bare shoulders, heads sleek or tousled, and a lavish show of flesh-coloured legs and sandalled feet. Ardwin, unbosoming himself to a devotee, held up a guttering church-candle to a canvas which simulated a window open on a geometrical representation of brick walls, fire escapes and back-yards. "Sham? Oh, of course. I had the real window blocked up. It looked out on that stupid old 'night-piece' of Brooklyn Bridge and the East River. Everybody who came here said: 'A Whistler nocturne!' and I got so bored. Besides, it was *really there*: and I hate things that are really where you think they are. They're as tiresome as truthful people. Everything in art should be false.

Everything in life should be art. *Ergo*, everything in life should be false: complexions, teeth, hair, wives . . . specially wives. Oh, Miss Manford, that you? Do come in. Mislaid Lita?"

"Isn't she here?"

"*Is* she?" He pivoted about on the company. When he was not dancing he looked, with his small snaky head and too square shoulders, like a cross between a Japanese waiter and a full-page advertisement for silk underwear. "*Is* Lita here? Any of you fellows got her dissembled about your persons? Now, then, out with her! Jossie Keiler, *you*'re not Mrs. James Wyant disguised as a dryad, are you?" There was a general guffaw as Miss Jossie Keiler, the octoroon pianist, scrambled to her pudgy feet and assembled a series of sausage arms and bolster legs in a provocative pose. "Knew I'd get found out," she lisped.

A short man with a deceptively blond head, thick lips under a stubby blond moustache, and eyes like needles behind tortoiseshell-rimmed glasses, stood before the fire, bulging a glossy shirtfront and solitaire pearl toward the company. "Don't this lady dance?" he enquired, in a voice like melted butter, a few drops of which seemed to trickle down his lips and be licked back at intervals behind a thickly ringed hand.

"Miss Manford? Bet she does! Come along, Nona; shed your togs and let's show Mr. Klawhammer here present that Lita's not the only peb—"

"Gracious! Wait till I get into the saddle!" screamed Miss Keiler, tiny hands like blueish mice darting out at the keyboard from the end of her bludgeon arms.

Nona perched herself on the edge of a refectory table. "Thanks. I'm not a candidate for 'Herodias.' My sister-in-law is sure to turn up in a minute."

Even Mrs. Dexter Manford's perfectly run house was not a particularly appetizing place to return to at four o'clock on the morning after a dance. The last motor was gone, the last overcoat and opera cloak had vanished from hall and dressing-rooms, and only one hanging lamp lit the dusky tapestries and the monumental balustrade of the staircase. But empty cocktail glasses and ravaged cigar-boxes littered the hall tables, wisps of torn tulle and trampled orchids strewed the stair-carpet, and the thicket of forced lilacs and Japanese plums in front of the lift drooped mournfully in the hot air. Nona, letting herself in with her latch-key, scanned the scene with a feeling of disgust. What was it all for, and what was left when it was over? Only a huge clearing-up for Maisie and the servants, and a new list to make out for the next time . . . She remembered mild spring nights at Cedarledge, when she was a little girl, and she and Jim used to slip downstairs in stocking feet, go to the lake, loose the canoe, and drift on a silver path among islets fringed with budding dogwood. She hurried on past the desecrated shrubs.

Above, the house was dark but for a line of light under the library door. Funny—at that hour; her father must still be up. Very likely he too had just come in. She was passing on when the door opened and Manford called her.

" 'Pon my soul, Nona! That you? I supposed you were in bed long ago."

One of the green-shaded lamps lit the big writing-table. Manford's armchair was drawn up to it, an empty glass and half-consumed cigarette near by, the evening paper sprawled on the floor.

"Was that you I heard coming in? Do you know what time it is?"

"Yes; worse luck! I've been scouring the town after Lita."

"*Lita?*"

"Waiting for her for hours at Tommy Ardwin's. Such a crew! He told me she was going there to dance for Klawhammer, the Hollywood man, and I didn't want her to go alone—"

Manford's face darkened. He lit another cigarette and turned to his daughter impatiently.

"What the devil made you believe such a yarn? Klaw-hammer—!"

Nona stood facing him; their eyes met, and he turned away with a shrug to reach for a match.

"I believed it because, just afterward, the servants told me that Lita had left, and as they said you'd gone with her I supposed you'd taken her to Ardwin's, not knowing that I meant to join her there."

"Ah; I see." He lit the cigarette and puffed at it for a moment or two, deliberately. "You're quite right to think she needs looking after," he began again, in a changed tone. "Somebody's got to take on the job, since her husband seems to have washed his hands of it."

"Father! You know perfectly well that if Jim took on that job—running after Lita all night from one cabaret to another—he'd lose the other, the one that keeps them going. Nobody could carry on both."

"Hullo, spitfire! Hands off our brother!"

"Rather." She leaned against the table, her eyes still on him. "And when Ardwin told me about this Klawhammer film—didn't Lita mention it to you?"

He appeared to consider. "She did say Ardwin was bothering her about something of the kind; so when I found Jim had gone I took her home myself."

"Ah—you took her home?"

Manford, settling himself back in his armchair, met the surprise in her voice unconcernedly. "Why, of course. Did you really see me letting her make a show of herself? Sorry you think that's my way of looking after her."

Nona, perched on the arm of his chair, enclosed him in a happy hug. "You goose, you!" she sighed; but the epithet was not for her father.

She poured herself a glass of cherry brandy, dropped a kiss on his thinning hair, and ran up to her room humming Miss Jossie Keiler's jazz-tune. Perhaps after all it wasn't such a rotten world.

Chapter VIII

THE morning after a party in her own house Pauline Manford always accorded herself an extra half-hour's rest; but on this occasion she employed it in lying awake and wearily reckoning up the next day's tasks.

Disenchantment had succeeded to the night's glamour. The glamour of balls never did last: they so quickly became a matter for those domestic undertakers, the charwomen, housemaids and electricians. And in this case the taste of pleasure had soured early. When the doors were thrown open on the beflowered supper tables not one of the hostess's family was left to marshal the guests to their places! Her husband, her daughter and son, her son's wife—all had deserted her. It needed, in that chill morning vigil, all Pauline's self-control to banish the memory. Not that she wanted any of them to feel under any obligation—she was all for personal freedom, self-expression, or whatever they called it nowadays—but still, a ball was a ball, a host was a host. It was too bad of Dexter, really; and of Jim too. On Lita of course no one could count: that was part of the pose people found so fascinating. But Jim—Jim and Nona to forsake her! What a ridiculous position it had put her in—but no, she mustn't think of that now, or those nasty little wrinkles would creep back about her eyes. The masseuse had warned her . . . Gracious! At what time was the masseuse due? She stretched out her hand, turned on the light by the bed (for the windows were still closely darkened), and reached for what Maisie Bruss called the night-list: an upright porcelain tablet on which the secretary recorded, for nocturnal study, the principal "fixtures" of the coming day.

Today they were so numerous that Miss Bruss's tight script had hardly contrived to squeeze them in. Foremost, of course, poor Exhibit A, moved on from yesterday; then a mysterious appointment with Amalasuntha, just before lunch: something urgent, she had hinted. Today of all days! Amalasuntha was so tactless at times. And then that Mahatma business: since Dexter was inflexible, his wife had made up her mind to appeal to the Lindons. It would be awkward, undoubtedly—and she did so hate things that were awkward. Any form of untidiness, moral or material, was unpleasant to her; but something must be done, and at once. She herself hardly knew why she felt so apprehensive, so determined that the matter should have no sequel; except that, if anything *did* go wrong, it would upset all her plans for a rest-cure, for new exercises, for all sorts of promised ways of prolonging youth, activity and slenderness, and would oblige her to find a new Messiah who would tell her she was psychic.

But the most pressing item on her list was her address that very afternoon to the National Mothers' Day Association—or, no; wasn't it the Birth Control League? Nonsense! That was her speech at the banquet next week: a big affair at the St. Regis for a group of International Birth-controllers. Wakeful as she felt, she must be half asleep to have muddled up her engagements like that! She extinguished the lamp and sank hopefully to her pillow—perhaps now sleep would really come. But her bed-lamp seemed to have a double switch, and putting it out in the room only turned it on in her head.

Well, she would try reciting scraps of her Mothers' Day address: she seldom spoke in public, but when she did she took the affair seriously, and tried to be at once winning and impressive. She and Maisie had gone carefully over the typed copy; and she was sure it was all right; but she liked getting the more effective passages by heart—it brought her nearer to her audience to lean forward and speak intimately, without having to revert every few minutes to the text.

"Was there ever a hearth or a heart—a mother's heart—that wasn't big enough for all the babies God wants it to hold? Of course there are days when the mother is so fagged out that she thinks she'd give the world if there were nothing at all to do in the nursery, and she could just sit still with folded hands. But the only time when there's nothing at all for a mother to do in the nursery is when there's a little coffin there. It's all quiet enough *then* . . . as some of us here know . . ." (Pause, and a few tears in the audience.) "Not that we want the modern mother to wear herself out: no indeed! The babies themselves haven't any use for worn-out mothers! And the first thing to be considered is what the babies want, isn't it?" (Pause—smiles in the audience) . . .

What on earth was Amalasuntha coming to bother her about? More money, of course—but she really couldn't pay all that wretched Michelangelo's debts. There would soon be debts nearer home if Lita went on dressing so extravagantly, and perpetually having her jewellery reset. It cost almost as much nowadays to reset jewels as to buy new ones, and those emeralds . . .

At that hour of the morning things did tend to look ash-coloured; and she felt that her optimism had never been so sorely strained since the year when she had had to read Proust, learn a new dance-step, master Oriental philosophy, and decide whether she should really bob her hair, or only do it to look so. She had come victoriously through those ordeals; but what if worse lay ahead?

Amalasuntha, in one of Mrs. Manford's least successfully made-over dresses, came in looking shabby and humble—always a bad sign. And of course it was Michelangelo's debts. Racing, baccara, and a woman . . . a Russian princess; oh, my dear, *authentic*, quite! Wouldn't Pauline like to see her picture from the "Prattler"? She and Michelangelo had been snapped together in bathing tights at the Lido.

No—Pauline wouldn't. She turned from the proffered effigy with a disgust evidently surprising to the Marchesa, whose own prejudices were different, and who could grasp other people's only piece-meal, one at a time, like a lesson in mnemonics.

"Oh, my boy doesn't do things by halves," the Marchesa averred, still feeling that the occasion was one for boasting.

Pauline leaned back wearily. "I'm as sorry for you as I can be, Amalasuntha; but Michelangelo is not a baby, and if he can't be made to understand that a poor man who wants to spend money must first earn it—"

"Oh, but he does, darling! Venturino and I have always dinned it into him. And last year he tried his best to marry that one-eyed Miss Oxbaum from Oregon, he really did."

"I said *earn*," Pauline interposed. "We don't consider that marrying for money is earning it—"

"Oh, mercy—don't you? Not sometimes?" breathed the Marchesa.

"What I mean by earning is going into an office—is—"

"Ah, just so! It was what I said to Dexter last night. It is what Venturino and I most long for: that Dexter should take Michelangelo into his office. That would solve every difficulty. And once Michelangelo is here I'm sure he will succeed. No one is more clever, you know: only, in Rome, young men are in greater danger—there are more temptations—"

Pauline pursed her lips. "I suppose there are." But, since temptations are the privilege of metropolises, she thought it rather impertinent of Amalasuntha to suggest that there were more in a one-horse little place like Rome than in New York; though in a different mood she would have been the first to pronounce the Italian capital a sink of iniquity, and New York the model and prototype of the pure American city. All these contradictions, which usually sat lightly on her, made her head ache today, and she continued, nervously: "Take Michelangelo into his office! But what preparations has he had, what training? Has he ever studied for the law?"

"No; I don't think he has, darling; but he *would*; I can promise you he would," the Marchesa declared, in the tone of one saying: "In such straits, he would become a street-cleaner."

Pauline smiled faintly. "I don't think you understand. The law is a *profession*." (Dexter had told her that.) "It requires years of training, of preparation. Michelangelo would have to take a degree at Harvard or Columbia first. But perhaps"—a glance at her wrist-watch told her that her next engagement impended—"perhaps Dexter could suggest some other kind of employment. I don't know, of course . . . I can't promise . . . But meanwhile . . ." She turned to her writing-table, and a cheque passed between them, too small to make a perceptible impression on Michelangelo's deficit, but large enough for Amalasuntha to murmur: "How you do spoil me, darling! Well—for the boy's sake I accept in all simplicity. And about the reception for the Cardinal—I'm sure a cable to Venturino will arrange it. Would that kind Maisie send it off, and sign my name?"

It was well after three o'clock when Pauline came down the Lindons' door-step and said to her chauffeur: "To Mr. Wyant's." And she had still to crowd in her eurythmic exercises (put off from the morning), and be ready at half-past four, bathed, waved and apparelled, for the Mothers' Day Meeting, which was to take place in her own ball-room, with a giant tea to follow.

Certainly, no amount of "mental deep-breathing," and all the other exercises in serenity, could combat the nervous apprehension produced by this breathless New York life. Today she really felt it to be too much for her: she leaned back and closed her lids with a sigh. But she was jerked back to consciousness by the traffic-control signal, which had immobilized the motor just when every moment was so precious. The result of every one's being in such a hurry to get everywhere was that nobody could get anywhere. She looked across the triple row of motors in line with hers, and saw in each (as if in a vista of mirrors) an expensively dressed woman like herself, leaning forward in the same attitude of repressed impatience, the same nervous frown of hurry on her brow.

Oh, if only she could remember to relax!

But how could one, with everything going wrong as it was today? The visit to Fanny Lindon had been an utter failure. Pauline had apparently over-estimated her influence on the Lindons, and that discovery in itself was rather mortifying. To be told that the Mahatma business was "a family affair"—and thus be given to understand that she was no longer of the family! Pauline, in her own mind, had never completely ceased to be a Wyant. She thought herself still entitled to such shadowy prerogatives as the name afforded, and was surprised that the Wyants should not think so too. After all, she kept Amalasuntha for them—no slight charge!

But Mrs. Lindon had merely said it was "all too painful"—and had ended, surprisingly: "Dexter himself has specially asked us not to say anything."

The implication was: "If you want to find out, go to him!"—when of course Fanny knew well enough that lawyers' and doctors' wives are the last people to get at their clients' secrets.

Pauline rose to her feet, offended, and not averse from showing it. "Well, my dear, I can only say that if it's so awful that you can't tell *me*, I rather wonder at your wanting to tell Tom, Dick and Harry. Have you thought of that?"

Oh, yes, she had, Mrs. Lindon wailed. "But Grant says it's a duty . . . and so does Dexter . . ."

Pauline permitted herself a faint smile. "Dexter naturally takes the lawyer's view: that's *his* duty."

Mrs. Lindon's mind was not alert for innuendos. "Yes; he says we *ought* to," she merely repeated.

A sudden lassitude overcame Pauline. "At least send Grant to me first—let me talk to him."

But to herself she said: "My only hope now is to get at them through Arthur." And she looked anxiously out of the motor, watching for the signal to shift.

Everything at Arthur Wyant's was swept and garnished for her approach. One felt that cousin Eleanor, whisking the stray cigarette-ends into the fire, and giving the sofa cushions a last shake, had slipped out of the back door as Mrs. Manford entered by the front.

Wyant greeted her with his usual rather overdone cordiality. He had never quite acquired the note on which discarded husbands should welcome condescending wives. In this respect Pauline was his superior. She had found the exact blend of gravity with sisterly friendliness; and the need of having to ask about his health always helped her over the first moments.

"Oh, you see—still mummified." He pointed to the leg stretched out in front of him. "Couldn't even see Amalasuntha to the door—"

"Amalasuntha? Has she been here?"

"Yes. Asked herself to lunch. Rather a to-do for me; I'm not used to entertaining distinguished foreigners, especially when they have to picnic on a tray at my elbow. But she took it all very good-naturedly."

"I should think so," Pauline murmured; adding inwardly: "Trust Amalasuntha not to pay for her own lunch."

"Yes; she's in great feather. Said you'd been so kind to her—as usual."

Pauline sounded the proper deprecation.

"She's awfully pleased at your having promised that Manford would give Michelangelo a leg up if he comes out to try his luck in New York."

"Promised? Well—not quite. But I did say Dexter would do what he could. It seems the only way left of disposing of Michelangelo."

Wyant leaned back, a smile twitching under his moustache. "Yes—that young man's a scourge. And I begin to see why. Did you see his picture in bathing tights with the latest lady?"

Pauline waved away the suggestion. How like Arthur not to realize, even yet, that such things disgusted her!

"Well, he's the best looking piece of human sculpture I've seen since I last went through the Vatican galleries. Regular Apollo. Funny, the Albany Wyants having a hand in turning out a heathen divinity. I was showing the picture to Manford just now, and telling him the fond mother's comment."

Pauline looked up quickly. "Has Dexter been here too?"

"Yes; trying to give *me* a leg up." He glanced at his bandages. "Rather more difficult, that. I must get it down first—to the floor. But Manford's awfully kind too—it's catching. He wants me to go off with Jim, down to that island of his, and get a fortnight's real sunshine. Says he can get Jim off by a little wirepulling, some time just before Easter, he thinks. It's tempting—"

Pauline smiled: she was always pleased when the two men spoke of each other in that tone; and certainly it *was* kind of Dexter to offer the hospitality of his southern island to poor Arthur . . . She thought how easy life would be if only every one were kind and simple.

"But about Michelangelo: I was going to tell you what is worrying Amalasuntha. Of course what she means by Michelangelo's going into business in America is marrying an heiress—"

"Oh, of course. And I daresay he will."

"Exactly. She's got her eye on one already. You haven't guessed? Nona!"

Pauline's sense of humour was not unfailing, but this relaxed her taut nerves, and she laughed. "Poor Michelangelo!"

"I thought it wouldn't worry you. But what is worrying Amalasuntha is that he won't be *let*—"

"Be let?"

"By Lita. Her theory is that Lita will fall madly in love with Michelangelo as soon as she lays eyes on him—and that when they've had one dance together she'll be lost. And Amalasuntha, for that reason—though she daren't tell you so—thinks it might really be cheaper in the end to pay Michelangelo's debts than to import him. As she says, it's for the family to decide, now she's warned them."

Their laughter mingled. It was the first time, perhaps, since they had been young together; as a rule, their encounters were untinged with levity.

But Pauline dismissed the laugh hurriedly for the Grant Lindons. At the name Wyant's eyes lit up: it was as if she had placed an appetizing morsel before a listless convalescent.

"But you're the very person to tell me all about it—or, no, you can't, of course, if Manford's going to take it up. But no matter—after all, it's public property by this time. Seen this morning's 'Looker-on'—with pictures? Here, where—" In the stack of illustrated papers always at his elbow he could never find the one he wanted, and now began to toss over "Prattlers," "Listeners" and others with helpless hand. How that little symptom of inefficiency took her back to the old days, when his perpetual disorder, and his persistent belief that he could always put his hand on everything, used to be such a strain on her nerves!

"Pictures?" she gasped.

"Rather. The nigger himself, in turban and ritual togs; and a lot of mixed nudes doing leg-work round a *patio*. The place looks like a Palm Beach Hotel. Fanny Lindon's in a stew because she's recognized Bee in the picture. She says she's going to have the man in jail if they spend their last penny on it. Hullo—here it is, after all."

Pauline shrank back. Would people never stop trying to show her disgusting photographs? She articulated: "You haven't seen Fanny Lindon too?"

"Haven't I? She spent the morning here. She told Amalasuntha everything."

Pauline, with a great effort, controlled her rising anger. "How idiotic! Now it *will* be spread to all the winds!" She saw Fanny and Amalasuntha gloatingly exchanging the images of their progenies' dishonour. It was too indecent . . . and the old New Yorker was as shameless as the demoralized foreigner.

"I didn't know Fanny had been here before me. I've just left her. I've been trying to persuade her to stop; to hush up the whole business before it's too late. I suppose you gave her the same advice?"

Wyant's face clouded: he looked perplexedly at his former wife, and she saw he had lost all sense of the impropriety and folly of the affair in his famished enjoyment of its spicy details.

"I don't know—I understood it *was* too late; and that Manford was urging them to do it."

Pauline made a slight movement of impatience. "Dexter—of course! When he sees a 'case'! I suppose lawyers are all alike. At any rate, I can't make him understand . . ." She broke off, suddenly aware that the rôles were reversed, and that for the first time she was disparaging her second husband to her first. "Besides," she hurried on, "it's no affair of Dexter's if the Lindons choose to dishonour their child publicly. They're not *his* relations; Bee is not *his* cousin's daughter. But you and I—how can we help feeling differently? Bee and Nona and Jim were all brought up together. You must help me to stop this scandal! You must send for Grant Lindon at once. He's sure to listen to you . . . you've always had a great influence on Grant . . ."

She found herself, in her extremity, using the very arguments she had addressed to Manford, and she saw at once that in this case they were more effective. Wyant drew himself up stiffly with a faint smile of satisfaction. Involuntarily he ran a thin gouty hand through his hair, and tried for a glimpse of himself in the mirror.

"Think so—really? Of course when Grant was a boy he used to consider me a great fellow. But now . . . who remembers me in my dingy corner?"

Pauline rose with her clear wintry smile. "A good many of us, it seems. You tell me I'm the third lady to call on you today! You know well enough, Arthur—" she brushed the name in lightly, on the extreme tip of her smile—"that the opinion of people like you still counts in New York, even in these times. Imagine what your mother would have felt at the idea of Fanny and Bee figuring in all the daily headlines, with reporters and photographers in a queue on the doorstep! I'm glad she hasn't lived to see it."

She knew that Wyant's facile irony always melted before an emotional appeal, especially if made in his mother's name. He blinked unsteadily, and flung away the "Looker-on."

"You're dead right: they're a pack of fools. There are no standards left. I'll do what I can; I'll telephone to Grant to look in on his way home this evening . . . I say, Pauline: what's the truth of it all, anyhow? If I'm to give him a talking to I ought to know." His eyes again lit up with curiosity.

"Truth of it? There isn't any—it's the silliest mare's-nest! Why, I'm going to Dawnside for a rest-cure next month, while Dexter's tarpon-fishing. The Mahatma is worlds above all this tattle—it's for the Lindons I'm anxious, not him."

The paper thrown aside by Wyant had dropped to the floor, face upward at a full-page picture—*the* picture. Pauline, on her way out, mechanically yielded to her instinct for universal tidying, and bent to pick it up; bent and looked. Her eyes were still keen; passing over the noxious caption "Dawnside Co-Eds," they immediately singled out Bee Lindon from the capering round; then travelled on, amazed, to another denuded nymph . . . whose face, whose movements . . . Incredible! . . . For a second Pauline refused to accept what her eyes reported. Sick and unnerved, she folded the picture away and laid the magazine on a table.

"Oh, don't bother about picking up that paper. Sorry there's no one to show you out!" she heard Wyant calling. She went downstairs, blind, unbelieving, hardly knowing how she got into her motor.

Barely time to get home, change, and be in the Chair, her address before her, when the Mothers arrived in their multitude . . .

Chapter IX

WELL, perhaps Dexter would understand *now* the need of hushing up the Grant Lindons . . . The picture might be a libel, of course—such things, Pauline knew, could be patched up out of quite unrelated photographs. The dancing circle might have been skilfully fitted into the Dawnside *patio*, and goodness knew what shameless creatures have supplied the bodies of the dancers. Dexter had often told her that it was a common blackmailing trick.

Even if the photograph were genuine, Pauline could understand and make allowances. She had never seen anything of the kind herself at Dawnside—heaven forbid!—but whenever she had gone there for a lecture, or a new course of exercises, she had suspected that the bare whitewashed room, with its throned Buddha, which received her and other like-minded ladies of her age, all active, earnest and eager for self-improvement, had not let them very far into the mystery. Beyond, perhaps, were other rites, other settings: why not? Wasn't everybody talking about "the return to Nature," and ridiculing the American prudery in which the minds and bodies of her generation had been swaddled? The Mahatma was one of the leaders of the new movement: the Return to Purity, he called it. He was always celebrating the nobility of the human body, and praising the ease of the loose Oriental dress compared with the constricting western garb: but Pauline had supposed the draperies he advocated to be longer and less transparent; above all, she had not expected familiar faces above those insufficient scarves . . .

But here she was at her own door. There was just time to be ready for the Mothers; none in which to telephone to Dexter, or buy up the whole edition of the "Looker-on" (fantastic vision!), or try and get hold of its editor, who had once dined with her, and was rather a friend of Lita's. All these possibilities and impossibilities raced through her brain to the maddening tune of "too late" while she slipped off her street-dress and sat twitching with impatience under the maid's readjustment of her ruffled head. The gown prepared for the meeting, rich, matronly and just the least bit old-fashioned—very different from the one designed for the Birth Control committee—lay spread out beside the copy of her speech, and Maisie Bruss, who had been hovering within call, dashed back breathless from a peep over the stairs.

"They're arriving—"

"Oh, Maisie, rush down! Say I'm telephoning—"

Her incurable sincerity made her unhook the receiver and call out Manford's office number. Almost instantly she heard him. "Dexter, this Mahatma investigation must be stopped! Don't ask me why—there isn't time. Only promise—"

She heard his impatient laugh.

"No?"

"Impossible," came back.

She supposed she had hung up the receiver, fastened on her jewelled "Motherhood" badge, slipped on rings and bracelets as usual. But she remembered nothing clearly until she found herself on the platform at the end of the packed ball-room, looking across rows and rows of earnest confiding faces, with lips and eyes prepared for the admiring reception of her "message." She was considered a very good speaker: she knew how to reach the type of woman represented by this imposing assemblage— delegates from small towns all over the country, united by a common faith in the infinite extent of human benevolence and the incalculable resources of American hygiene. Something of the moral simplicity of her own bringing-up brought her close to these women, who had flocked to the great perfidious city serenely unaware of its being anything more, or other, than the gigantic setting of a Mothers' Meeting. Pauline, at such times, saw the world through their eyes, and was animated by a genuine ardour for the cause of motherhood and domesticity.

As she turned toward her audience a factitious serenity descended on her. She felt in control of herself and of the situation. She spoke.

"Personality—first and last, and at all costs. I've begun my talk to you with that one word because it seems to me to sum up our whole case. Personality—room to develop in: not only elbow-room but body-room and soul-room, and plenty of both. That's what every human being has a right to. No more effaced wives, no more drudging mothers, no more human slaves crushed by the eternal round of house-keeping and child-bearing—"

She stopped, drew a quick breath, met Nona's astonished gaze over rows of bewildered eye-glasses, and felt herself plunging into an abyss. But she caught at the edge, and saved herself from the plunge—

"That's what our antagonists say—the women who are afraid to be mothers, ashamed to be mothers, the women who put their enjoyment and their convenience and what they call their happiness before the mysterious heaven-sent joy, the glorious privilege, of bringing children into the world—"

A round of applause from the reassured mothers. She had done it! She had pulled off her effect from the very jaws of disaster. Only the swift instinct of recovery had enabled her, before it was too late, to pass off the first sentences of her other address, her Birth Control speech, as the bold exordium of her hymn to motherhood! She paused a moment, still inwardly breathless, yet already sure enough of herself to smile back at Nona across her unsuspecting audience—sure enough to note that her paradoxical opening had had a much greater effect than she could have hoped to produce by the phrases with which she had meant to begin.

A hint for future oratory—

Only—the inward nervousness subsisted. The discovery that she could lose not only her self-control but her memory, the very sense of what she was saying, was like a hand of ice pointing to an undecipherable warning.

Nervousness, fatigue, brain-exhaustion . . . had her fight against them been vain? What was the use of all the months and years of patient Taylorized effort against the natural human fate: against anxiety, sorrow, old age—if their menace was to reappear whenever events slipped from her control?

The address ended in applause and admiring exclamations. She had won her way straight to those trustful hearts, still full of personal memories of a rude laborious life, or in which its stout tradition lingered on in spite of motors, money and the final word in plumbing.

Pauline, after the dispersal of the Mothers, had gone up to her room still dazed by the narrowness of her escape. Thank heaven she had a free hour! She threw herself on her lounge and turned her gaze inward upon herself: an exercise for which she seldom had the leisure.

Now that she knew she was safe, and had done nothing to discredit herself or the cause, she could penetrate an inch or two farther into the motive power of her activities; and what she saw there frightened her. To be Chairman of the Mothers' Day Association, and a speaker at the Birth Control banquet! It did not need her daughter's derisive chuckle to give her the measure of her inconsequence. Yet to reconcile these contradictions had seemed as simple as to invite the Chief Rabbi and the Bishop of New York to meet Amalasuntha's Cardinal. Did not the Mahatma teach that, to the initiated, all discords were resolved into a higher harmony? When her hurried attention had been turned for a moment on the seeming inconsistency of encouraging natality and teaching how to restrict it, she had felt it was sufficient answer to say that the two categories of people appealed to were entirely different, and could not be "reached" in the same way. In ethics, as in advertising, the main thing was to get at your public. Hitherto this argument had satisfied her. Feeling there was much to be said on both sides, she had thrown herself with equal zeal into the propagation of both doctrines; but now, surveying her attempt with a chastened eye, she doubted its expediency.

Maisie Bruss, appearing with notes and telephone messages, seemed to reflect this doubt in her small buttoned-up face.

"Oh, Maisie! Is there anything important? I'm dead tired." It was an admission she did not often make.

"Nothing much. Three or four papers have 'phoned for copies of your address. It was a great success."

A faint glow of satisfaction wavered through Pauline's perplexities. She did not pretend to eloquence; she knew her children smiled at her syntax. Yet she had reached the hearts of her audience, and who could deny that that was success?

"Oh, Maisie—I don't think it's good enough to appear in print . . ."

The secretary smiled, made a short-hand memorandum, and went on: "The Marchesa telephoned that her son is sailing on Wednesday—and I've sent off her cable about the Cardinal, answer paid."

"Sailing on Wednesday? But it can't be—the day after tomorrow!" Pauline raised herself on an anxious elbow. She had warned her husband, and he wouldn't listen. "Telephone downstairs, please, Maisie—find out if Mr. Manford has come in." But she knew well enough what the answer would be. Nowadays, whenever there was anything serious to be talked over, Dexter found some excuse for avoiding her. She lay back, her lids dropped over her tired eyes, and waited for the answer: "Mr. Manford isn't in yet."

Something had come over Dexter lately: no closing of her eyes would shut that out! She supposed it was over-work—the usual reason. Rich men's doctors always said they were over-worked when they became cross and trying at home.

"Dinner at the Toys' at 8.30." Miss Bruss continued her recital; and Pauline drew in her lips on a faintly bitter smile. At the Toys'—he wouldn't forget that! Whenever there was a woman who attracted him . . . why, Lita even . . . she'd seen him in a flutter once when he was going to the cinema with Lita, and thought she had forgotten to call for him! He had stamped up and down, watch in hand . . . Well, she supposed it was one of the symptoms of middle age: a passing phase. She could afford to be generous, after twenty years of his devotion; and she meant to be. Men didn't grow old as gracefully as women—she knew enough not to nag him about his little flirtations, and was really rather grateful to that silly Gladys Toy for making a fuss over him.

But when it came to serious matters, like this of the Mahatma, it was different, Dexter owed it to her to treat her opinions with more consideration—a woman whose oratory was sought for by a dozen newspapers! And that tiresome business of Michelangelo; another problem he had obstinately shirked. Discouragement closed in on Pauline. Of what use were eurythmics, cold douches, mental deep-breathings and all the other panaceas?

If things went on like this she would have to have her face lifted.

Chapter X

I T was exasperating, the way the Vollard girl lurked and ogled . . . Undoubtedly she was their best typist: mechanically perfect, with a smattering of French and Italian useful in linguistic emergencies. There could be no question of replacing her. But, apart from her job, what a poor Poll! And always—there was no denying it, the office smiled over it—always finding excuses to intrude on Manford's privacy: a hurry trunk-call, a signature forgotten, a final question to ask, a message from one of the other members of the firm . . . she seized her pretexts cleverly . . . And when she left him nowadays, he always got up, squared his shoulders, studied himself critically in the mirror over the mantelpiece, and hated her the more for having caused him to do anything so silly.

This afternoon her excuse had been flimsier than usual: a new point to be noted against her. "One of the gentlemen left it on his desk. There's a picture in it that'll amuse you. Oh, you don't mind my bringing it in?" she gasped.

Manford was just leaving; overcoat on, hat and stick in hand. He muttered: "Oh, thanks," and took the "Looker-on" in order to cut short her effusions. A picture that might amuse him! The simpleton . . . Probably some of those elaborate "artistic" studies of the Cedarledge gardens. He remembered that his wife had allowed the "Looker-on" photographers to take them last summer. She thought it a duty: it might help to spread the love of gardening (another of her hobbies); and besides it was undemocratic to refuse to share one's private privileges with the multitude. He knew all her catch-words and had reached the point of wondering how much she would have valued her privileges had the multitude not been there to share them.

He thrust the magazine under his arm, and threw it down, half an hour later, in Lita Wyant's boudoir. It was so quiet and shadowy there that he was almost glad Lita was not in, though sometimes her unpunctuality annoyed him. This evening, after the rush and confusion of the day, he found it soothing to await her in this half-lit room, with its heaped-up cushions still showing where she had leaned, and the veiled light on two arums in a dark bowl. Wherever Lita was, there were some of those smooth sculptural arums.

When she came, the stillness would hardly be disturbed. She had a way of deepening it by her presence: noise and hurry died on her threshold. And this evening all the house was quiet. Manford, as usual, had tiptoed up to take a look at the baby, in the night nursery where there were such cool silver-coloured walls, and white hyacinths in pots of silvery lustre. The baby slept, a round pink Hercules with defiant rosy curls, his pink hands clenched on the coverlet. Even the nurse by the lamp sat quiet and silver-coloured as a brooding pigeon.

A house without fixed hours, engagements, obligations . . . where none of the clocks went, and nobody was late, because there was no particular time for anything to happen. Absurd, of course, maddeningly unpractical—but how restful after a crowded day! And what a miracle to have achieved, in the tight pattern of New York's tasks and pleasures—in the very place which seemed doomed to collapse and vanish if ever its clocks should stop!

These late visits had begun by Manford's dropping in on the way home for a look at the baby. He liked babies in their cribs, and especially this fat rascal of Jim's. Next to Nona, there was no one he cared for as much as Jim; and seeing Jim happily married, doing well at his bank, and with that funny little chap upstairs, stirred in the older man all his old regrets that he had no son.

Jim seldom got back early enough to assist at these visits; and Lita too, at first, was generally out. But in the last few months Manford had more often found her—or at least, having fallen into the habit of lingering over a cigarette in her boudoir, had managed to get a glimpse of her before going on to that other house where all the clocks struck simultaneously, and the week's engagements, in Maisie Bruss's hand, jumped out at him as he entered his study.

This evening he felt more than usually tired—of his day, his work, his life, himself—oh, especially himself; so tired that, the deep armchair aiding, he slipped into a half-doze in which the quietness crept up round him like a tide.

He woke with a start, imagining that Lita had entered, and feeling the elderly man's discomfiture when beauty finds him

napping . . . But the room was empty: a movement of his own
had merely knocked Miss Vollard's magazine to the floor. He
remembered having brought it in to show Lita the photographs
of Cedarledge which he supposed it to contain. Would there be
time? He consulted his watch—an anachronism in that house—
lit another cigarette, and leaned back contentedly. He knew that
as soon as he got home Pauline, who had telephoned again that
afternoon about the Mahatma, would contrive to corner him
and reopen the tiresome question, together with another, which
threatened to be almost equally tiresome, about paying that
rotten Michelangelo's debts. "If we don't, we shall have him
here on our hands: Amalasuntha is convinced you'll take him
into the firm. You'd better come home in time to talk things
over—." Always talking over, interfering, adjusting! He had
enough of that in his profession. Pity Pauline wasn't a lawyer:
she might have worked off her steam in office hours. He would
sit quietly where he was, taking care to reach his house only just
in time to dress and join her in the motor. They were dining
out, he couldn't remember where.

For a moment his wife's figure stood out before him in brilliant stony relief, like a photograph seen through a stereopticon;
then it vanished in the mist of his well-being, the indolence
engendered by waiting there alone and undisturbed for Lita.
Queer creature, Lita! His lips twitched into a reminiscent smile.
One day she had come up noiselessly behind him and surprised
him by a light kiss on his hair. He had thought it was Nona . . .
Since then he had sometimes feigned to doze while he waited;
but she had never kissed him again . . .

What sort of a life did she really lead, he wondered? And what
did she make of Jim, now the novelty was over? He could think
of no two people who seemed less made for each other. But you
never could tell with a woman. Jim was young and adoring; and
there was that red-headed boy . . .

Luckily Lita liked Nona, and the two were a good deal
together. Nona was as safe as a bank—and as jolly as a cricket.
Everything was sure to be right when she was there. But there
were all the other hours, intervals that Manford had no way of
accounting for; and Pauline always said the girl had had a queer
bringing-up, as indeed any girl must have had at the hands of
Mrs. Percy Landish. Pauline had objected to the marriage on

that ground, though the modern mother's respect for the independence of her children had reduced her objection to mere shadowy hints of which Jim, in his transports, took no heed.

Manford also disliked the girl at first, and deplored Jim's choice. He thought Lita positively ugly, with her high cheekbones, her too small head, her glaring clothes and conceited lackadaisical airs. Then, as time passed, and the marriage appeared after all to be turning out well, he tried to interest himself in her for Jim's sake, to see in her what Jim apparently did. But the change had not come till the boy's birth. Then, as she lay in her pillows, a new shadowiness under her golden lashes, one petal of a hand hollowed under the little red head at her side, the vision struck to his heart. The enchantment did not last; he never recaptured it; there were days when what he called her "beauty airs" exasperated him, others when he was chilled by her triviality. But she never bored him, never ceased to excite in him a sort of irritated interest. He told himself that it was because one could never be sure what she was up to; speculating on what went on behind that smooth round forehead and those elusive eyes became his most absorbing occupation.

At first he used to be glad when Nona turned up, and when Jim came in from his bank, fagged but happy, and the three young people sat talking nonsense, and letting Manford smoke and listen. But gradually he had fallen into the way of avoiding Nona's days, and of coming earlier (extricating himself with difficulty from his professional engagements), so that he might find Lita alone before Jim arrived.

Lately she had seemed restless, vaguely impatient with things; and Manford was determined to win her confidence and get at the riddle behind that smooth round brow. He could not bear the idea that Jim's marriage might turn out to be a mere unsuccessful adventure, like so many others. Lita must be made to understand what a treasure she possessed, and how easily she might lose it. Lita Cliffe—Mrs. Percy Landish's niece—to have had the luck to marry Jim Wyant, and to risk estranging him! What fools women were! If she could be got away from the pack of frauds and flatterers who surrounded her, Manford felt sure he could bring her to her senses. Sometimes, in her quiet moods, she seemed to depend on his judgment, to defer rather touchingly to what he said . . .

The thing would be to coax her from jazz and night-clubs, and the pseudo-artistic rabble of house-decorators, cinema stars and theatrical riff-raff who had invaded her life, to get her back to country joys, golf and tennis and boating, all the healthy outdoor activities. She liked them well enough when there were no others available. She had owned to Manford that she was sick of the rush and needed a rest; had half promised to come to Cedarledge with the boy for Easter. Jim would be taking his father down to the island off the Georgia coast; and Jim's being away might be a good thing. These modern young women soon tired of what they were used to; Lita would appreciate her husband all the more after a separation.

Well, only a few weeks more, and perhaps it would come true. She had never seen the Cedarledge dogwood in bud, the woods trembling into green. Manford, smiling at the vision, stooped to pick up the "Looker-on" and refresh his memory.

But it wasn't the right number: there were no gardens in it. Why had Miss Vollard given it to him? As he fluttered the pages they dropped open at: "Oriental Sage in Native Garb"—. Oh, damn the Mahatma! "Dawnside Co-Eds"—oh, damn . . .

He stood up to thrust the paper under one of the heavily-shaded lamps. At home, where Pauline and reason ruled, the lighting was disposed in such a way that one could always read without moving from one's chair; but in this ridiculous house, where no one ever opened a book, the lamps were so perversely placed, and so deeply shrouded, that one had to hold one's paper under the shade to make out anything.

He scrutinized the picture, shrugged away his disgusted recognition of Bee Lindon, looked again and straightened his eye-glasses on his nose to be doubly sure—the lawyer's instinct of accuracy prevailing over a furious inward tremor.

He walked to the door, and then turned back and stood irresolute. To study the picture he had lifted the border of the lamp-shade, and the light struck crudely on the statue above Lita's divan; the statue of which Pauline (to her children's amusement) always said a little apprehensively that she supposed it must be Cubist. Manford had hardly noticed the figure before, except to wonder why the young people admired ugliness: half lost in the shadows of the niche, it seemed a mere bundle of lumpy limbs. Now, in the glare—"Ah, you carrion, you!" He clenched his fist at it. "*That's* what they want—that's their brutish idol!" The words came stammering from him in a blur of rage. It was on Jim's account . . . the shock, the degradation . . . The paper slipped to the floor, and he dropped into his seat again.

Slowly his mind worked its way back through the disgust and confusion. Pauline had been right: what could one expect from a girl brought up in that Landish house? Very likely no one had ever thought of asking where she was, where she had been— Mrs. Landish, absorbed in her own silly affairs, would be the last person to know.

Well, what of that? The modern girl was always free, was expected to know how to use her freedom. Nona's independence had been as scrupulously respected as Jim's; she had had her full share of the perpetual modern agitations. Yet Nona was firm as a rock: a man's heart could build on her. If a woman was naturally straight, jazz and night-clubs couldn't make her crooked . . .

True, in Nona's case there had been Pauline's influence: Pauline who, whatever her faults, was always good-humoured and usually wise with her children. The proof was that, while they laughed at her, they adored her: he had to do her that justice. At the thought of Pauline a breath of freshness and honesty swept through him. He had been unfair to her lately, critical, irritable. He had been absorbing a slow poison, the poison emanating from this dusky self-conscious room, with all its pernicious implications. His first impression of Lita, when he had thought her ugly and pretentious, rushed back on him, dissipating the enchantment.

"Oh, I'm glad you waited—" She was there before him, her little heart-shaped face deep in its furs, like a bird on the nest. "I wanted to see you today; I *willed* you to wait." She stood there, her head slightly on one side, distilling her gaze through half-parted lids like some rare golden liquid.

Manford stared back. Her entrance had tangled up the words in his throat: he stood before her choked with denunciation and invective. And then it occurred to him how much easier it was just to say nothing—and to go. Of course he meant to go. It was no business of his: Jim Wyant was not his son. Thank God he could wash his hands of the whole affair.

He mumbled: "Dining out. Can't wait."

"Oh, but you must!" Her hand was on his arm, as light as a petal. "I want you." He could just see the twinkle of small round teeth as her upper lip lifted . . . "Can't . . . can't." He tried to disengage his voice, as if that too were tangled up in her.

He moved away toward the door. The "Looker-on" lay on the floor between them. So much the better; she would find it when he was gone! She would understand then why he hadn't waited. And no fear of Jim's getting hold of the paper; trust her to make it disappear!

"Why, what's that?" She bent her supple height to pick it up and moved to the lamp, her face alight.

"You darling, you—did you bring me this? What luck! I've been all over the place hunting for a copy—the whole edition's sold out. I had the original photograph somewhere, but couldn't put my hand on it."

She had reached the fatal page; she was spreading it open. Her smile caressed it; her mouth looked like a pink pod bursting on a row of pearly seeds. She turned to Manford almost tenderly. "After you prevented my going to Ardwin's I had to swear to send this to Klawhammer, to show that I really *can* dance. Tommy telephoned at daylight that Klawhammer was off to Hollywood, and that when I chucked last night they all said it was because I knew I couldn't come up to the scratch." She held out the picture with an air of pride. "Doesn't look much like it, does it? . . . Why, what are you staring at? Didn't you know I was going in for the movies? Immobility was never my strong point . . ." She threw the paper down, and began to undo her furs with a lazy smile, sketching a dance step as she did so. "Why do you look so shocked? If I don't do that I shall run away with Michelangelo. I suppose you know that Amalasuntha's importing him? I can't stick this sort of thing much longer . . . Besides, we've all got a right to self-expression, haven't we?"

Manford continued to look at her. He hardly heard what she was saying, in the sickness of realizing what she was. Those were the thoughts, the dreams, behind those temples on which the light laid such pearly circles!

He said slowly: "This picture—it's true, then? You've been there?"

"Dawnside? Bless you—where'd you suppose I learnt to dance? Aunt Kitty used to plant me out there whenever she wanted to go off on her own—which was pretty frequently." She had tossed off her hat, slipped out of her furs, and lowered the flounce of the lamp-shade; and there she stood before him in her scant slim dress, her arms, bare to the shoulder, lifted in an amphora-gesture to her little head.

"Oh, children—but I'm bored!" she yawned.

BOOK II

Chapter XI

P AULINE MANFORD was losing faith in herself; she felt the need of a new moral tonic. Could she still obtain it from the old sources?

The morning after the Toys' dinner, considering the advisability of repairing to that small bare room at Dawnside where the Mahatma gave his private audiences, she felt a chill of doubt. She would have preferred, just then, not to be confronted with the sage; in going to him she risked her husband's anger, and prudence warned her to keep out of the coming struggle. If the Mahatma should ask her to intervene she could only answer that she had already done so unsuccessfully; and such admissions, while generally useless, are always painful. Yet guidance she must have: no Papist in quest of "direction" (wasn't that what Amalasuntha called it?) could have felt the need more acutely. Certainly the sacrament of confession, from which Pauline's ingrained Protestantism recoiled in horror, must have its uses at such moments. But to whom, if not to the Mahatma, could she confess?

Dexter had gone down town without asking to see her; she had been sure he would, after their drive to and from the Toys' the evening before. When he was in one of his moods of clenched silence—they were becoming more frequent, she had remarked—she knew the uselessness of interfering. Echoes of the Freudian doctrine, perhaps rather confusedly apprehended, had strengthened her faith in the salutariness of "talking things over," and she longed to urge this remedy again on Dexter; but the last time she had done so he had wounded her by replying that he preferred an aperient. And in his present mood of stony inaccessibility he might say something even coarser.

She sat in her boudoir, painfully oppressed by an hour of unexpected leisure. The facial-massage artist had the grippe, and had notified her only at the last moment. To be sure, she

had skipped her "Silent Meditation" that morning; but she did
not feel in the mood for it now. And besides, an hour is too long
for meditation—an hour is too long for anything. Now that she
had one to herself, for the first time in years, she didn't in the
least know what to do with it. That was something which no
one had ever thought of teaching her; and the sense of being
surrounded by a sudden void, into which she could reach out on
all sides without touching an engagement or an obligation, produced in her a sort of mental dizziness. She had taken plenty of
rest-cures, of course; all one's friends did. But during a rest-cure
one was always busy resting; every minute was crammed with
passive activities; one never had this queer sense of inoccupa-
tion, never had to face an absolutely featureless expanse of time.
It made her feel as if the world had rushed by and forgotten her.
An hour—why, there was no way of measuring the length of
an empty hour! It stretched away into infinity like the endless
road in a nightmare; it gaped before her like the slippery sides
of an abyss. Nervously she began to wonder what she could do
to fill it—if there were not some new picture show or dressmak-
ers' opening or hygienic exhibition that she might cram into
it before the minute hand switched round to her next engagement. She took up her list to see what that engagement was.

"11.45 Mrs. Swoffer."

Oh, to be sure . . . Mrs. Swoffer. Maisie had reminded her
that morning. The relief was instantaneous. Only, who *was*
Mrs. Swoffer? Was she the President of the Militant Pacifists'
League, or the Heroes' Day delegate, or the exponent of the
New Religion of Hope, or the woman who had discovered a
wonderful trick for taking the wrinkles out of the corners of
your eyes? Maisie was out on an urgent commission, and could
not be consulted; but whatever Mrs. Swoffer's errand was, her
arrival would be welcome—especially if she came before her
hour. And she did.

She was a small plump woman of indefinite age, with faded
blond hair and rambling features held together by a pair of
urgent eye-glasses. She asked if she might hold Pauline's hand
just a moment while she looked at her and reverenced her—
and Pauline, on learning that this was the result of reading
her Mothers' Day speech in the morning papers, acceded not
unwillingly.

Not that that was what Mrs. Swoffer had come for; she said it was just a flower she wanted to gather on the way. A rose with the dew on it—she took off her glasses and wiped them, as if to show where the dew had come from. "You speak for so *many* of us," she breathed, and recovered Pauline's hand for another pressure.

But she *had* come for the children, all the same; and that was really coming for the mothers, wasn't it? Only she wanted to reach the mothers through the children—reversing the usual process. Mrs. Swoffer said she believed in reversing almost everything. Standing on your head was one of the most restorative physical exercises, and she believed it was the same mentally and morally. It was a good thing to stand one's *soul* upside down. And so she'd come about the children . . .

The point was to form a League—a huge International League of Mothers—against the dreadful old practice of telling children they were naughty. Had Mrs. Manford ever stopped to think what an abominable thing it was to suggest to a pure innocent child that there was such a thing in the world as Being Naughty? What did it open the door to? Why, to the idea of Wickedness, the most awful idea in the whole world.

Of course Mrs. Manford would see at once what getting rid of the idea of Wickedness would lead to. How could there be bad men if there were no bad children? And how could there be bad children if children were never allowed to know that such a thing as badness existed? There was a splendid woman—Orba Clapp; no doubt Mrs. Manford had heard of her?—who was getting up a gigantic world-wide movement to boycott the manufacturers and sellers of all military toys, tin soldiers, cannon, toy rifles, water-pistols and so on. It was a grand beginning, and several governments had joined the movement already: the Philippines, Mrs. Swoffer thought, and possibly Montenegro. But that seemed to her only a beginning: much as she loved and revered Orba Clapp, she couldn't honestly say that she thought the scheme went deep enough. She, Mrs. Swoffer, wanted to go right down to the soul: the collective soul of all the little children. The great Teacher, Alvah Loft—she supposed Mrs. Manford knew about *him*? No? She was surprised that a woman like Mrs. Manford—"one of our beacon-lights"—hadn't heard of Alvah Loft. She herself owed everything to him. No one had helped her as he had: he had pulled her out of the very depths of scepticism. But didn't Mrs. Manford know his books, even: "Spiritual Vacuum-Cleaning" and "Beyond God"?

Pauline had grown a little listless while the children were to the fore. She would help, of course; lend her name; subscribe. But that string had been so often twanged that it gave out rather a deadened note: whereas the name of a new Messiah immediately roused her. "Beyond God" was a tremendous title; she would get Maisie to telephone for the books at once. But what exactly did Alvah Loft teach?

Mrs. Swoffer's eye-glasses flashed with inspiration. "He doesn't teach: he absolutely refuses to be regarded as a *teacher*. He says there are too many already. He's an Inspirational Healer. What he does is to *act* on you—on your spirit. He simply relieves you of your frustrations."

Frustrations! Pauline was fascinated by the word. Not that it was new to her. Her vocabulary was fairly large, far more so, indeed, than that of her daughter's friends, whose range was strictly limited to sport and dancing; but whenever she heard a familiar word used as if it had some unsuspected and occult significance it fascinated her like a phial containing a new remedy.

Mrs. Swoffer's glasses were following Pauline's thoughts as they formed. "Will you let me speak to you as I would to an old friend? The moment I took your hand I *knew* you were suffering from frustrations. To any disciple of Alvah Loft's the symptoms are unmistakeable. Sometimes I almost wish I didn't see it all so clearly . . . it gives one such a longing to help . . ."

Pauline murmured: "I *do* want help."

"Of course you do," Mrs. Swoffer purred, "and you want *his* help. Don't you know those wonderful shoe-shops where they stock every size and shape the human foot can require? I tell Alvah Loft he's like that; he's got a cure for everybody's frustrations. Of course," she added, "there isn't time for everybody; he has to choose. But he would take *you* at once." She drew back, and her glasses seemed to suck Pauline down as if they had been quicksands. "You're psychic," she softly pronounced.

"I believe I am," Pauline acknowledged. "But—"

"Yes; I know; those frustrations! All the things you think you ought to do, *and can't*; that's it, isn't it?" Mrs. Swoffer stood up. "Dear friend, come with me. Don't look at your watch. Just come!"

An hour later Pauline, refreshed and invigorated, descended the Inspirational Healer's brown-stone doorstep with a springing step. It had been worth while breaking three or four engagements to regain that feeling of moral freedom. Why had she never heard of Alvah Loft before? His method was so much simpler than the Mahatma's: no eurythmics, gymnastics, community life, no mental deep-breathing, or long words to remember. Alvah Loft simply took out your frustrations as if they'd been adenoids; it didn't last ten minutes, and was perfectly painless. Pauline had always felt that the Messiah who should reduce his message to tabloid form would outdistance all the others; and Alvah Loft had done it. He just received you in a boarding-house back-parlour, with bunches of pampas-grass on the mantelpiece, while rows of patients sat in the front room waiting their turn. You told him what was bothering you, and he said it was just a frustration, and he could relieve you of it, and make it so that it didn't exist, by five minutes of silent communion. And he sat and held you by the wrist, very lightly, as if he were taking your temperature, and told you to keep your eyes on the Ella Wheeler Wilcox line-a-day on the wall over his head. After it was over he said: "You're a good subject. The frustrations are all out. Go home, and you'll hear something good before dinner. Twenty-five dollars." And a pasty-faced young man with pale hair, who was waiting in the passage, added: "Pass on, please," and steered Pauline out by the elbow.

Of course she wasn't naturally credulous; she prided herself on always testing everything by reason. But it *was* marvellous, how light she felt as she went down the steps! The buoyancy persisted all day, perhaps strengthened by an attentive study of the reports of the Mothers' Day Meeting, laid out by the vigilant Maisie for perusal. Alvah Loft had told her that she would hear of something good before dinner, and when, late in the afternoon, she went up to her boudoir, she glanced expectantly at the writing-table, as if revelation might be there. It was, in the shape of a telephone message.

"Mr. Manford will be at home by seven. He would like to see you for a few minutes before dinner."

It was nearly seven, and Pauline settled herself by the fire and unfolded the evening paper. She seldom had time for its perusal, but today there might be some reference to the Mothers' Day Meeting; and her newly-regained serenity made it actually pleasant to be sitting there undisturbed, waiting for her husband.

"Dexter—how tired you look!" she exclaimed when he came in. It occurred to her at once that she might possibly insinuate an allusion to the new healer; but wisdom counselled a waiting policy, and she laid down her paper and smiled expectantly.

Manford gave his shoulders their usual impatient shake. "Everybody looks tired at the end of a New York day; I suppose it's what New York is for." He sat down in the armchair facing hers, and stared at the fire.

"I wanted to see you to talk about plans—a rearrangement," he began. "It's so hard to find a quiet minute."

"Yes; but there's no hurry now. The Delavans don't dine till half-past eight."

"Oh, are we dining there?" He reached for a cigarette.

She couldn't help saying: "I'm sure you smoke too much, Dexter. The irritation produced by the paper—"

"Yes; I know. But what I wanted to say is: I should like you to ask Lita and the boy to Cedarledge while Jim and Wyant are at the island."

This was a surprise; but she met it with unmoved composure. "Of course, if you like. But do you think Lita'll go, all alone? You'll be off tarpon-fishing, Nona is going to Asheville for a fortnight's change, and I had intended—" She pulled up suddenly. She had meant, of course, to take her rest-cure at Dawnside.

Manford sat frowning and studying the fire. "Why shouldn't we all go to Cedarledge instead?" he began. "Somebody ought to look after Lita while Jim's away; in fact, I don't believe he'll go with Wyant if we don't. She's dead-beat, and doesn't know it, and with all the fools she has about her the only way to ensure her getting a real rest is to carry her off to the country with the boy."

Pauline's face lit up with a blissful incredulity. "Oh, Dexter—would you really come to Cedarledge for Easter? How splendid! Of course I'll give up my rest-cure. As you say, there's no place like the country."

She was already raising an inward hymn to Alvah Loft. An Easter holiday in the country, all together—how long it was since that had happened! She had always thought it her duty to urge Dexter to get away from the family when he had the chance; to travel or shoot or fish, and not feel himself chained to her side. And here at last was her reward—of his own accord he was proposing that they should all be together for a quiet fortnight. A softness came about her heart: the stiff armour of her self-constraint seemed loosened, and she saw the fire through a luminous blur. "It will be lovely," she murmured.

Manford lit another cigarette, and sat puffing it in silence. It seemed as though a weight had been lifted from him too; yet his face was still heavy and preoccupied. Perhaps before their talk was over she might be able to say a word about Alvah Loft; she was so sure that Dexter would see everything differently if only he could be relieved of his frustrations.

At length he said: "I don't see why this should interfere with your arrangements, though. Hadn't you meant to go somewhere for a rest-cure?"

He had thought of that too! She felt a fresh tremor of gratitude. How wicked she had been ever to doubt the designs of Providence, and the resolving of all discords in the Higher Harmony!

"Oh, my rest-cure doesn't matter; being with you all at Cedarledge will be the best kind of rest."

His obvious solicitude for her was more soothing than any medicine, more magical even than Alvah Loft's silent communion. Perhaps the one thing she had lacked, in all these years, was to feel that some one was worrying about her as she worried about the universe.

"It's awfully unselfish of you, Pauline. But running a big house is never restful. Nona will give up Asheville and come to Cedarledge to look after us; you mustn't change your plans."

She smiled a little. "But I *must*, dear; because I'd meant to go to Dawnside, and now, of course, in any case—"

Manford stood up and went and leaned against the chimney-piece. "Well, that will be all right," he said.

"All right?"

He was absently turning about in his hand a little bronze statuette. "Yes. If you think the fellow does you good. I've been thinking over what you said the other day; and I've decided to advise the Lindons not to act . . . too precipitately . . ." He coughed and put the statuette back on the mantelshelf. "They've abandoned the idea . . ."

"Oh, Dexter—" She started to her feet, her eyes brimming. He had actually thought over what she had said to him—when, at the time, he had seemed so obdurate and sneering! Her heart trembled with a happy wonder in which love and satisfied vanity were subtly mingled. Perhaps, after all, what her life had really needed was something much simpler than all the complicated things she had put into it.

"I'm so glad," she murmured, not knowing what else to say. She wanted to hold out her arms, to win from him some answering gesture. But he was already glancing at his watch. "That's all right. Jove, though—we'll be late for dinner . . . Opera afterward, isn't there?"

The door closed on him. For a moment or two she stood still, awed by the sense of some strange presence in the room, something as fresh and strong as a spring gale. It must be happiness, she thought.

Chapter XII

"YES; this morning I think you *can* see her. She seems ever so much better; not in such a fearful hurry, I mean."

Pauline, from her dressing-room, overheard Maisie Bruss. She smiled at the description of herself, sent a thought of gratitude to Alvah Loft, and called out: "Is that Nona? I'll be there in a minute. Just finishing my exercises . . ."

She appeared, fresh and tingling, draped in a restful dove-coloured wrapper, and offered Nona a smooth cheek. Miss Bruss had vanished, and mother and daughter had to themselves the sunny room, full of flowers and the scent of a wood-fire.

"How wonderful you look, mother! All made over. Have you been trying some new exercises?"

Pauline smiled and pulled up the soft eiderdown coverlet at the foot of her lounge. She sank comfortably back among her cushions.

"No, dear: it's just—understanding a little better, I think."

"Understanding?"

"Yes; that things *always* come out right if one just keeps on being brave and trustful."

"Oh—." She fancied she caught a note of disappointment in Nona's voice. Poor Nona—her mother had long been aware that she had no enthusiasm, no transports of faith. She took after her father. How tired and sallow she looked in the morning light, perched on the arm of a chair, her long legs dangling!

"You really ought to try to believe that yourself, darling," said Pauline brightly.

Nona gave one of her father's shrugs. "Perhaps I will when I have more time."

"But one can always *make* time, dear." ("Just as I do," the smile suggested.) "You look thoroughly fagged out, Nona. I do wish you'd go to the wonderful new man I've just—"

"All right, mother. Only, this morning I haven't come to talk about myself. It's Lita."

"Lita?"

"I've been wanting to speak to you about her for a long time. Haven't you noticed anything?"

Pauline still wore her alert and sympathizing smile. "Tell me what, dear—let's talk it all over."

Nona's brows were drawn in a troubled frown. "I'm afraid Jim's not happy," she said.

"Jim? But, darling, he's been so dreadfully over-worked—that's the trouble. Your father spoke to me about it the other day. He's sending Jim and Arthur down to the island next month for a good long rest."

"Yes; it's awfully nice of father. But it's not that—it's Lita," Nona doggedly repeated.

A faint shadow brushed Pauline's cloudless horizon; but she resolutely turned her eyes from it. "Tell me what you think is wrong."

"Why, that she's bored stiff—says she's going to chuck the whole thing. She says the life she's leading prevents her expressing her personality."

"Good gracious—she dares?" Pauline sat bolt upright, the torn garment of her serenity fluttering away like a wisp of vapour. Was there never to be any peace for her, she wondered? She had a movement of passionate rebellion—then a terror lest it should imperil Alvah Loft's mental surgery. After a physical operation the patient's repose was always carefully guarded—but no one thought of sparing *her*, though she had just been subjected to so radical an extirpation. She looked almost irritably at Nona.

"Don't you think you sometimes imagine things, my pet? Of course, the more we yield to suggestions of pain and distress the more—"

"Yes; I know. But this isn't a suggestion, it's a fact. Lita says she's got to express her personality, or she'll do something dreadful. And if she does it will break Jim's heart."

Pauline leaned back, vaguely fortified by so definite a menace. It was laughable to think of Lita Cliffe's threatening to do something dreadful to a Wyant!

"Don't you think she's just over-excited, perhaps? She leads such a crazy sort of life—all you children do. And she hasn't been very strong since the baby's birth. I believe she needs a good rest as much as Jim does. And you know your father has been so wise about that; he's going to persuade her to go to Cedarledge for two or three weeks while Jim's in Georgia."

Nona remained unimpressed. "Lita won't go to Cedarledge alone—you know she won't."

"She won't have to, dear. Your father has thought of that too; he finds time to think of everything."

"Who's going, then?"

"We *all* are. At least, your father hopes you will; and he's giving up his tarpon-fishing on purpose to join us."

"Father is?" Nona stood up, her gaze suddenly fixed on her mother.

"Your father's wonderful," Pauline triumphed.

"Yes, I know." The girl's voice flagged again. "But all this is weeks away. And meanwhile I'm afraid—I'm afraid."

"Little girls mustn't be afraid. If you are, send Lita to *me*. I'm sure it's just a case of frustration—"

"Frustration?"

"Yes; the new psychological thing. I'll take her with me to see Alvah Loft. He's the great Inspirational Healer. I've only had three treatments, and it's miraculous. It doesn't take ten minutes, and all one's burdens are lifted." Pauline threw back her head with a sigh which seemed to luxuriate in the remembrance of her own release. "I wish I could take you *all* to him!" she said.

"Well, perhaps you'd better begin with Lita." Nona was half-smiling too, but it was what her mother secretly called her disintegrating smile. "I wish the poor child were more constructive—but I suppose she's inherited her father's legal mind," Pauline thought.

Nona stood before her irresolutely. "You know, mother, if things do go wrong Jim will never get over it."

"There you are again—jumping at the conclusion that things will go wrong! As for Lita, to me it's a clear case of frustration. She says she wants to express her personality? Well, every one has the right to do that—I should think it wrong of me to interfere. That wouldn't be the way to make Jim happy. What Lita needs is to have her frustrations removed. That will open her eyes to her happiness, and make her see what a perfect home she has. I wonder where my engagement-list is? Maisie! . . . Oh, here . . ." She ran her eyes rapidly over the tablet. "I'll see Lita tomorrow—I'll make a point of it. We'll have a friendly simple talk—perfectly frank and affectionate. Let me see: at what time should I be likely to find her? . . . And, no, of course not, darling; I wouldn't think of saying a word to Jim. But your father—surely I may speak to your father?"

Nona hesitated. "I think father knows about it—as much as he need," she answered, her hand on the door.

"Ah, your father always knows everything," Pauline placidly acquiesced.

The prospect of the talk with her daughter-in-law barely ruffled her new-found peace. It was a pity Lita was restless; but nowadays all the young people were restless. Perhaps it would be as well to say a word to Kitty Landish; flighty and inconsequent as she was, it might open her eyes to find that she was likely to have her niece back on her hands. Mrs. Percy Landish's hands were always full to overflowing with her own difficulties. A succession of ingenious theories of life, and the relentless pursuit of originality, had landed her in a state of chronic embarrassment, pecuniary, social and sentimental. The announcement that Lita was tired of Jim, and threatened to leave him, would fall like a bombshell on that precarious roof which figured in the New York Directory as somewhere in the East Hundreds, but was recorded in the "Social Register" as No. 1 Viking Court. Mrs. Landish's last fad had been to establish herself on the banks of the East River, which she and a group of friends had adorned with a cluster of reinforced-cement bungalows, first christened El Patio, but altered to Viking Court after Mrs. Landish had read in an illustrated weekly that the Vikings, who had discovered America ages before Columbus, had not, as previously supposed, effected their first landing at Vineyard Haven, but at a spot not far from the site of her dwelling. Cement, at an early stage, is malleable, and the Alhambra *motifs* had hastily given way to others from the prows of Nordic ships, from silver torques and Runic inscriptions, the latter easily contrived out of Arabic *sourats* from the Koran. Before these new ornaments were dry, Mrs. Landish and her friends were camping on the historic spot; and after four years of occupancy they were camping still, in Mrs. Manford's sense of the word.

A hurried telephone call had assured Pauline that she could see Mrs. Landish directly after lunch; and at two o'clock her motor drove up to Viking Court, which opened on a dilapidated

river-front and was cynically overlooked by tall tenement houses
with an underpinning of delicatessen stores.

Mrs. Landish was nowhere to be found. She had had to go
out to lunch, a melancholy maid-servant said, because the cook
had just given notice; but she would doubtless soon be back.
With gingerly steps Pauline entered the "living-room," so called
(as visitors were unfailingly reminded) because Mrs. Landish
ate, painted, modelled in clay, sculptured in wood, and received
her friends there. The Vikings, she added, had lived in that way.
But today all traces of these varied activities had disappeared,
and the room was austerely empty. Mrs. Landish's last hobby
was for what she called "purism," and her chief desire to make
everything in her surroundings conform to the habits and
industries of a mythical past. Ever since she had created Viking
Court she had been trying to obtain rushes for the floor: but
as the Eastern States of America did not produce the particular
variety of rush which the Vikings were said to have used she had
at last decided to have rugs woven on handlooms in Abyssinia,
some one having assured her that an inscription referring to
trade-relations between the Vikings and the kingdom of Prester
John had been discovered in the ruins of Petra.

The difficulty of having these rugs made according to designs
of the period caused the cement floor of Mrs. Landish's living-
room to remain permanently bare, and most of the furniture
having now been removed, the room had all the appearance of
a garage, the more so as Mrs. Landish's latest protégé, a young
cabaret-artist who performed on a motor-siren, had been suffered to stable his cycle in one corner.

In addition to this vehicle, the room contained only a few
relentless-looking oak chairs, a long table bearing an hour-
glass (for clocks would have been an anachronism), and a scrap
of dusty velvet nailed on the cement wall, as to which Mrs.
Landish explained that it was a bit of a sixth century Coptic
vestment, and that the nuns of a Basilian convent in Thessaly
were reproducing it for eventual curtains and chair-cushions.
"It may take fifty years." Mrs. Landish always added, "but I
would rather go without it than live with anything less perfect."

The void into which Pauline advanced gave prominence to
the figure of a man who stood with his back to her, looking

through the window at what was to be a garden when Viking horticulture was revived. Meanwhile it was fully occupied by neighbouring cats and by swirls of wind-borne rubbish.

The visitor, duskily blocked against a sullen March sky, was at first not recognizable; but half way toward him Pauline exclaimed: "Dexter!" He turned, and his surprise met hers.

"I never dreamed of its being you!" she said.

He faced her with a certain defiant jauntiness. "Why not?"

"Because I never saw you here before. I've tried often enough to get you to come—"

"Oh, to lunch or dine!" He sent a grimace about the room. "I never thought that was among my duties."

She did not take this up, and a moment's silence hung between them. Finally Manford said: "I came about Lita."

Pauline felt a rush of relief. Her husband's voice had been harsh and impatient: she saw that her arrival had mysteriously put him out. But if anxiety about Lita were the cause of his visit it not only explained his perturbation but showed his revived solicitude for herself. She sent back another benediction to the Inspirational Healer, so sweet it was to find that she and Dexter were once more moved by the same impulses.

"It's awfully kind of you, dear. How funny that we should meet on the same errand!"

He stared: "Why, have you—?"

"Come about Lita? Well, yes. She's been getting rather out of hand, hasn't she? Of course a divorce would kill poor Jim—otherwise I shouldn't so much mind—"

"A divorce?"

"Nona tells me it's Lita's idea. Foolish child! I'm to have a talk with her this afternoon. I came here first to see if Kitty's influence—"

"Oh: Kitty's influence!"

"Yes; I know." She broke off, and glanced quickly at Manford. "But if you don't believe in her influence, why did you come here yourself?"

The question seemed to take her husband by surprise, and he met it by a somewhat rigid smile. How old he looked in the hard slaty light! The crisp hair was almost as thin on his temples as higher up. If only he would try that wonderful new "Radio-scalp"! "And he used to be so handsome!" his wife said to herself, with the rush of vitality she always felt when she noted the marks of fatigue or age in her contemporaries. Manford and Nona, she reflected, had the same way of turning sallow and heavy-cheeked when they were under any physical or moral strain.

Manford said: "I came to ask Mrs. Landish to help us get Lita away for Easter. I thought she might put in a word—"

It was Pauline's turn to smile. "Perhaps she might. What I came for was to say that if Lita doesn't quiet down and behave reasonably she may find herself thrown on her aunt's hands again. I think that will produce an effect on Kitty. I shall make it perfectly clear that they are not to count on me financially if Lita leaves Jim." She glanced brightly at Manford, instinctively awaiting his approval.

But the expected response did not come. His face grew blurred and uncertain, and for a moment he said nothing. Then he muttered: "It's all very unfortunate . . . a stupid muddle . . ."

Pauline caught the change in his tone. It suggested that her last remark, instead of pleasing him, had raised between them one of those invisible barriers against which she had so often bruised her perceptions. And just as she had thought that he and she were really in touch again!

"We mustn't be hard on her . . . we mustn't judge her without hearing both sides . . ." he went on.

"But of course not." It was just the sort of thing she wanted him to say, but not in the voice in which he said it. The voice was full of hesitation and embarrassment. Could it be her presence which embarrassed him? With Manford one could never tell. She suggested, almost timidly: "But why shouldn't I leave you to see Kitty alone? Perhaps we needn't both . . ."

His look of relief was unconcealable; but her bright resolution rose above the shock. "You'll do it so much better," she encouraged him.

"Oh, I don't know. But perhaps two of us . . . looks rather like the Third Degree, doesn't it?"

She assented nervously: "All I want is to smooth things over . . ."

He gave an acquiescent nod, and followed her as she moved toward the door. "Perhaps, though—look here, Pauline . . ."

She sparkled with responsiveness.

"Hadn't you better wait before sending for Lita? It may not be necessary, if—"

Her first impulse was to agree; but she thought of the Inspirational Healer. "You can trust me to behave with tact, dear; but I'm sure it will help Lita to talk things out, and perhaps I shall know better than Kitty how to get at her . . . Lita and I have always been good friends, and there's a wonderful new man I want to persuade her to see . . . some one really psychic . . ."

Manford's lips narrowed in a smile; again she had a confused sense of new deserts widening between them. Why had he again become suddenly sardonic and remote? She had no time to consider, for the new gospel of frustrations was surging to her lips.

"*Not* a teacher; he repudiates all doctrines, and simply *acts* on you. He—"

"Pauline darling! Dexter! Have you been waiting long? Oh, dear—my hour-glass seems to be quite empty!"

Mrs. Percy Landish was there, slipping toward them with a sort of aerial shuffle, as if she had blown in on a March gust. Her tall swaying figure produced, at a distance, an effect of stateliness which vanished as she approached, as if she had suddenly got out of focus. Her face was like an unfinished sketch, to which the artist had given heaps of fair hair, a lovely nose, expressive eyes and no mouth. She laid down some vague parcels and shook the hour-glass irritably, as if it had been at fault.

"How dear of you!" she said to her visitors. "I don't often get you together in my eyrie."

The expression puzzled Pauline, who knew that in poetry an eyrie was an eagle's nest, and wondered how this term could be applied to a cement bungalow in the East Hundreds . . . But there was no time to pursue such speculations.

Mrs. Landish was looking helplessly about her. "It's cold—you're both freezing, I'm afraid?" Her eyes rested tragically on the empty hearth. "The fact is, I can't have a fire because my andirons are *wrong*."

"Not high enough? The chimney doesn't draw, you mean?" Pauline in such emergencies was in her element; she would have risen from her deathbed to show a new housemaid how to build a fire. But Mrs. Landish shook her head with the look of a woman who never expects to be understood by other women.

"No, dear; I mean they were not of the period. I always suspected it, and Dr. Ygrid Bjornsted, the great authority on Nordic art, who was here the other day, told me that the only existing pair is in the Museum at Christiania. So I have sent an order to have them copied. But you *are* cold, Pauline! Shall we go and sit in the kitchen? We shall be quite by ourselves, because the cook has just given notice."

Pauline drew her furs around her in silent protest at this new insanity. "We shall be very well here, Kitty. I suppose you know it's about Lita—"

Mrs. Landish seemed to drift back to them from incalculable distances. "Lita? Has Klawhammer really engaged her? It was for his 'Herodias,' wasn't it?" She was all enthusiasm and participation.

Pauline's heart sank. She had caught the irritated jut of Manford's brows. No—it was useless to try to make Kitty understand; and foolish to risk her husband's displeasure by staying in this icy room for such a purpose. She wrapped herself in sweetness as in her sables. "It's something much more serious than that cinema nonsense. But I'm going to leave it to Dexter to explain. He will do it ever so much better than I could . . . Yes, Kitty dear, I remember there's a step missing in the vestibule. Please don't bother to see me out—you know Dexter's minutes are precious." She thrust Mrs. Landish softly back into the room, and made her way unattended across the hall. As she did so, the living-room door, the lock of which had responded reluctantly to her handling, swung open again, and she heard Manford ask, in his dry cross-examining voice: "Will you please tell me exactly when and for how long Lita was at Dawnside, Mrs. Landish?"

Chapter XIII

"I BELIEVE it's the first time in a month that I've heard Nona laugh," Stanley Heuston said with a touch of irony—or was it simply envy?

Nona was still in the whirlpool of her laugh. She struggled to its edge only to be caught back, with retrospective sobs and gasps, into its central coil. "It was too screamingly funny," she flung at them out of the vortex.

She was perched sideways, as her way was, on the arm of the big chintz sofa in Arthur Wyant's sitting-room. Wyant was stretched out in his usual armchair, behind a crumby messy tea-table, on the other side of which sat his son and Stanley Heuston.

"She didn't hesitate for more than half a second—just long enough to catch my eye—then round she jerked, grabbed hold of her last word and fitted it into a beautiful new appeal to the Mothers. Oh—oh—oh! If you could have seen them!"

"I can." Jim's face suddenly became broad, mild and earnestly peering. He caught up a pair of his father's eye-glasses, adjusted them to his blunt nose, and murmured in a soft feminine drawl: "Mrs. Manford is one of our deepest-souled women. She has a vital message for all Mothers."

Wyant leaned back and laughed. His laugh was a contagious chuckle, easily provoked and spreading in circles like a full spring. Jim gave a large shout at his own mimicry, and Heuston joined the chorus on a dry note that neither spread nor echoed, but seemed suddenly to set bounds to their mirth. Nona felt a momentary resentment of his tone. Was he implying that they were ridiculing their mother? They weren't, they were only admiring her in their own way, which had always been humorous and half-parental. Stan ought to have understood by this time—and have guessed why Nona, at this moment, caught at any pretext to make Jim laugh, to make everything in their joint lives appear to him normal and jolly. But Stanley always seemed to see beyond a joke, even when he was in the very middle of it. He was like that about everything in life; forever walking around things, weighing and measuring them, and making his disenchanted calculations. Poor fellow—well, no wonder!

Jim got up, the glasses still clinging to his blunt nose. He gathered an imaginary cloak about him, picked up inexistent gloves and vanity-bag, and tapped his head as if he were settling a feathered hat. The laughter waxed again, and Wyant chuckled: "I wish you young fools would come oftener. It would cure me a lot quicker than being shipped off to Georgia." He turned half-apologetically to Nona. "Not that I'm not awfully glad of the chance—"

"I know, Exhibit dear. It'll be jolly enough when you get down there, you and Jim."

"Yes; I only wish you were coming too. Why don't you?"

Jim's features returned to their normal cast, and he removed the eye-glasses. "Because mother and Manford have planned to carry off Lita and the kid to Cedarledge at the same time. Good scheme, isn't it? I wish I could be in both places at once. We're all of us fed up with New York."

His father glanced at him. "Look here, my boy, there's no difficulty about your being in the same place as your wife. I can take my old bones down to Georgia without your help, since Manford's kind enough to invite me."

"Thanks a lot, dad; but part of Lita's holiday is getting away from domestic cares, and I'm the principal one. She has to order dinner for me. And I don't say I shan't like my holiday too . . . sand and sun, any amount of 'em. That's my size at present. No more superhuman efforts." He stretched his arms over his head with a yawn.

"But I thought Manford was off to the south too—to his tarpon? Isn't this Cedarledge idea new?"

"It's part of his general kindness. He wanted me to go with an easy mind, so he's chucked his fishing and mobilized the whole group to go and lead the simple life at Cedarledge with Lita."

Wyant's sallow cheek-bones reddened slightly. "It's awfully kind, as you say; but if my going south is to result in upsetting everybody else's arrangements—"

"Oh, rot, father." Jim spoke with sudden irritability. "Manford would hate it if you chucked now; wouldn't he, Nona? And I do want Lita to get away somewhere, and I'd rather it was to

Cedarledge than anywhere." The clock struck, and he pulled himself out of his chair. Nona noticed with a pang how slack and half-hearted all his movements were. "Jove—I must jump!" he said. "We're due at some cabaret show that begins early; and I believe we dine at Ardwin's first, with a bunch of freaks. By-bye, Nona . . . Stan . . . Goodbye, father. Only a fortnight now before we cut it all!"

The door shut after him on a silence. Wyant reached for his pipe and filled it. Heuston stared at the tea-table. Suddenly Wyant questioned: "Look here—why is Jim being shipped off to the island with me when his wife's going to Cedarledge?"

Nona dropped from her sofa-arm and settled into an armchair. "Simply for the reasons he told you. They both want a holiday from each other."

"I don't believe Jim really wants one from Lita."

"Well, so much the worse for Jim. Lita's temporarily tired of dancing and domesticity, and the doctor says she ought to go off for a while by herself."

Wyant was slowly drawing at his pipe. At length he said: "Your mother's doctor told her that once; and she never came back."

Nona's colour rose through her pale cheeks to her very forehead. The motions of her blood were not impetuous, and she now felt herself blushing for having blushed. It was unlike Wyant to say that—unlike his tradition of reticence and decency, which had always joined with Pauline's breezy optimism in relegating to silence and non-existence whatever it was painful or even awkward to discuss. For years the dual family had lived on the assumption that they were all the best friends in the world, and the vocabulary of that convention had become their natural idiom.

Stanley Heuston seemed to catch the constraint in the air. He got up as if to go. "I suppose we're dining somewhere too—." He pronounced the "we" without conviction, for every one knew that he and his wife seldom went out together.

Wyant raised a detaining hand. "Don't go, Stan. Nona and I have no secrets—if we had, you should share them. Why do you look so savage, Nona? I suppose I've said something stupid . . . Fact is, I'm old-fashioned; and this idea of people who've chosen to live together having perpetually to get away from each other . . . When I remember my father and mother, for sixty-odd years . . . New York in winter, Hudson in summer . . . Staple topics: snow for six months, mosquitoes the other. I suppose that's the reason your generation have got the fidgets!"

Nona laughed. "It's a good enough reason; and anyhow there's nothing to be done about it."

Wyant frowned. "Nothing to be done about it—in Lita's case? I hope you don't mean that. My son—God, if ever a man has slaved for a woman, made himself a fool for her . . ."

Heuston's dry voice cut the diatribe. "Well, sir, you wouldn't deprive him of man's peculiar privilege: the right to make a fool of himself?"

Wyant sank back grumbling among his cushions. "I don't understand you, any of you," he said, as if secretly relieved by the admission.

"Well, Exhibit dear, strictly speaking you don't have to. We're old enough to run the show for ourselves, and all you've got to do is to look on from the front row and admire us," said Nona, bending to him with a caress.

In the street she found herself walking silently at Heuston's side. These weekly meetings with him at Wyant's were becoming a tacit arrangement: the one thing in her life that gave it meaning. She thought with a smile of her mother's affirmation that everything always came out right if only one kept on being brave and trustful, and wondered where, under that formula, her relation to Stanley Heuston could be fitted in. It was anything but brave—letting herself drift into these continual meetings, and refusing to accept their consequences. Yet every nerve in her told her that these moments were the best thing in life, the one thing she couldn't do without: just to be near him, to hear his cold voice, to say something to provoke his disenchanted laugh; or, better still, to walk by him as now without talking, with a furtive glance now and then at his profile, ironic, dissatisfied, defiant—yes, and so weak under the defiance . . . The fact that she judged and still loved showed that her malady was mortal.

"Oh, well—it won't last; nothing lasts for our lot," she murmured to herself without conviction. "Or at the worst it will only last as long as I do; and that's a date I can fix as I choose."

What nonsense, though, to talk like that, when all those others needed her: Jim and his silly Lita, her father, yes, even her proud self-confident father, and poor old Exhibit A and her mother who was so sure that nothing would ever go wrong again, now she had found a new Healer! Yes; they all needed help, though they didn't know it, and Fate seemed to have put her, Nona, at the very point where all their lives intersected, as a First-Aid station is put at the dangerous turn of a race-course, or a pointsman at the shunting point of a big junction.

"Look here, Nona: my dinner-engagement was a fable. Would the heavens fall if you and I went and dined somewhere by ourselves, just as we are?"

"Oh, Stan—" Her heart gave a leap of joy. In these free days, when the young came and went as they chose, who would have believed that these two had never yet given themselves a stolen evening? Perhaps it was just because it was so easy. Only difficult things tempted Nona, and the difficult thing was always to say "No."

Yet was it? She stole a glance at Heuston's profile, as a street-lamp touched it, saw the set lips already preparing a taunt at her refusal, and wondered if saying no to everything required as much courage as she liked to think. What if moral cowardice were the core of her boasted superiority? She didn't want to be "like the others"—but was there anything to be proud of in that? Perhaps her disinterestedness was only a subtler vanity, not unrelated, say, to Lita's refusal to let a friend copy her new dresses, or Bee Lindon's perpetual craving to scandalize a world sated with scandals. Exhibitionists, one and all of them, as the psycho-analysts said—and, in her present mood, moral exhibitionism seemed to her the meanest form of the display.

"How mid-Victorian, Stan!" she laughed. "As if there were any heavens to fall! Where shall we go? It will be the greatest fun. Isn't there rather a good little Italian restaurant somewhere near here? And afterward there's that nigger dancing at the Housetop."

"Come along, then!"

She felt as little and light as a wisp of straw carried out into the rushing darkness of a sea splashed with millions of stars. Just the thought of a friendly evening, an evening of simple comradeship, could do that; could give her back her youth, yes, and the courage to persevere. She put her hand through his arm, and knew by his silence that he was thinking her thoughts. That was the final touch of magic.

"You really want to go to the Housetop?" he questioned, leaning back to light his cigar with a leisurely air, as if there need never again be any hurrying about anything. Their dinner at the little Italian restaurant was nearly over. They had conscientiously explored the *pasto*, the *frutte di mare*, the *fritture* and the cheese-and-tomato mixtures, and were ending up with a foaming *sabaione*. The room was low-ceilinged, hot, and crowded with jolly noisy people, mostly Italians, over whom, at unnoticed intervals, an olive-tinted musician with blue-white eyeballs showered trills and twangings. His music did not interrupt the conversation, but merely obliged the diners to shout a little louder; a pretext of which they joyfully availed themselves. Nona, at first, had found the noise a delicious shelter for her talk with Heuston; but now it was beginning to stifle her. "Let's get some fresh air first," she said.

"All right. We'll walk for a while."

They pushed back their chairs, wormed a way through the packed tables, got into their wraps, and stepped out of the swinging doors into long streamers of watery lamplight. The douche of a cold rain received them.

"Oh, dear—the Housetop, then!" Nona grumbled. How sweet the rain would have been under the budding trees of Cedarledge! But here, in these degraded streets . . .

Heuston caught a passing taxi. "A turn, first—just round the Park?"

"No; the Housetop."

He leaned back and lit a cigarette. "You know I'm going to get myself divorced: it's all settled," he announced.

"Settled—with Aggie?"

"No: not yet. But with the lady I'm going off with. My word of honour. I am; next week."

Nona gave an incredulous laugh. "So this is good-bye?"

"Very nearly."

"Poor Stan!"

"Nona . . . listen . . . look here . . ."

She took his hand. "Stan, hang next week!"

"Nona—?"

She shook her head, but let her hand lie in his.

"No questions—no plans. Just being together," she pleaded.

He held her in silence and their lips met. "Then why not—?"

"No: the Housetop—the Housetop!" she cried, pulling herself out of his arms.

"Why, you're crying!"

"I'm not! It's the rain. It's—"

"Nona!"

"Stan, you know it's no earthly use."

"Life's so rotten—"

"Not like this."

"This? This—what?"

She struggled out of another enfolding, put her head out of the window, and cried: "The Housetop!"

They found a corner at the back of the crowded floor. Nona blinked a little in the dazzle of light-garlands, the fumes of smoke, the clash of noise and colours. But there he and she sat, close together, hidden in their irresistible happiness, and though his lips had their moody twist she knew the same softness was in his veins as in hers, isolating them from the crowd as completely as if they had still been in the darkness of the taxi. That was the way she must take her life, she supposed; piece-meal, a tiny scrap of sweetness at a time, and never more than a scrap—never once! Well—it would be worse still if there were no moments like this, short and cruel as they seemed when they came.

The Housetop was packed. The low balcony crammed with fashionable people overhung them like a wreath of ripe fruits, peachy and white and golden, made of painted faces, bare arms, jewels, brocades and fantastic furs. It was the music-hall of the moment.

The curtain shot up, and the little auditorium was plunged in shadow. Nona could leave her hand in Heuston's. On the stage—a New Orleans cotton-market—black dancers tossed and capered. They were like ripe fruits too, black figs flung about in hot sunshine, falling to earth with crimson bursts of laughter splitting open on white teeth, and bounding up again into golden clouds of cotton-dust. It was all warm and jolly and inconsequent. The audience forgot to smoke and chatter: little murmurs of enjoyment rippled over it.

The curtain descended, the light-garlands blossomed out, and once more floor and balcony were all sound and movement.

"Why, there's Lita up there in the balcony," Nona exclaimed, "just above the stage. Don't you see—with Ardwin, and Jack Staley, and Bee Lindon, and that awful Keiler woman?"

She had drawn her hand away at the sight of the box full. "I don't see Jim with them after all. Oh, how I hate that crowd!" All the ugly and disquieting realities she had put from her swept back with a rush. If only she could have had her one evening away from them! "I didn't think we should find them here—I thought Lita had been last week."

"Well, don't that crowd always keep on going to the same shows over and over again? There's nothing they hate as much as novelty—they're so fed up with it! And besides, what on earth do you care? They won't bother us."

She wavered a moment, and then said: "You see, Lita always bothers me."

"Why? Anything new?"

"She says she's tired of everything, Jim included, and is going to chuck it, and go in for the cinema."

"Oh, that—?" He manifested no surprise. "Well, isn't it where she belongs?"

"Perhaps—but Jim!"

"Poor Jim. We've all got to swallow our dose one day or another."

"Yes; but I can't bear it. Not for Jim. Look here, Stan—I'm going up there to join them," she suddenly declared.

"Oh, nonsense, Nona; they don't want you. And besides I hate that crowd as much as you do . . . I don't want you mixed up with it. That cad Staley, and the Keiler woman . . ."

She gave a dry laugh. "Afraid they'll compromise me?"

"Oh, rot! But what's the use of their even knowing you're here? They'll hate your butting in, Lita worst of all."

"Stan, I'm going up to them."

"Oh, damn it. You always—"

She had got up and was pushing away the little table in front of them. But suddenly she stopped and sat down again. For a moment or two she did not speak, nor look at Heuston. She had seen the massive outline of a familiar figure rising from a seat near the front and planting itself there for a slow gaze about the audience.

"Hallo—your father? I didn't know he patronized this kind of show," Heuston said.

Nona groped for a careless voice, and found it. "Father? So it is! Oh, he's really very frivolous—my influence, I'm afraid." The voice sounded sharp and rattling in her own ears. "How funny, though! You don't happen to see mother and Amalasuntha anywhere? That would make the family party complete."

She could not take her eyes from her father. How queer he looked—how different! Strained and vigilant; she didn't know how else to put it. And yet tired, inexpressibly tired, as if with some profound inner fatigue which made him straighten himself a little too rigidly, and throw back his head with a masterful young-mannish air as he scanned the balcony just above him. He stood there for a few moments, letting the lights and the eyes concentrate on him, as if lending himself to the display with a certain distant tolerance; then he began to move toward one of the exits. But half way he stopped, turned with his dogged jerk of the shoulders, and made for a gangway leading up to the balcony.

"Hullo," Heuston exclaimed. "Is he going up to Lita?"

Nona gave a little laugh. "I might have known it! How like father—when he undertakes anything!"

"Undertakes what?"

"Why, looking after Lita. He probably found out at the last minute that Jim couldn't come, and made up his mind to replace him. Isn't it splendid, how he's helping us? I know he loathes this sort of place—and the people she's with. But he told me we oughtn't to lose our influence on her, we ought to keep tight hold of her—"

"I see."

Nona had risen again and was beginning to move toward the passageway. Heuston followed her, and she smiled back at him over her shoulder. She felt as if she must cram every cranny in their talk with more words. The silence which had enclosed them as in a crystal globe had been splintered to atoms, and had left them stammering and exposed.

"Well, I needn't go up to Lita after all; she really doesn't require two dragons. Thank goodness, father has replaced me, and I don't have to be with that crew . . . just this evening," she whispered, slipping her arm through Heuston's. "I should have hated to have it end in that way." By this time they were out in the street.

On the wet pavement he detained her. "Nona, how *is* it going to end?"

"Why, by your driving me home, I hope. It's too wet to walk, worse luck."

He gave a resigned shrug, called a taxi, wavered a moment, and jumped in after her. "I don't know why I come," he grumbled.

She kept a bright hold on herself, lit a cigarette at his lighter, and chattered resolutely of the show till the motor turned the corner of her street.

"Well, my child, it's really good-bye now. I'm off next week with the other lady," Heuston said as they stopped before the Manford door. He paid the taxi and helped her out, and she stood in the rain in front of him. "I don't come back till Aggie divorces me, you understand," he continued.

"She won't!"

"She'll have to."

"It's hideous—doing it in that way."

"Not as hideous as the kind of life I'm leading."

She made no answer, and he followed her silently up the doorstep while she fumbled for her latchkey. She was trembling now with weariness and disappointment, and a feverish thirst for the one more kiss she was resolved he should not take.

"Other people get their freedom. I don't see why I shouldn't have mine," he insisted.

"Not in that way, Stan! You mustn't. It's too horrible."

"That way? You know there's no other."

She turned the latchkey, and the ponderous vestibule door swung inward. "If you do, don't imagine I'll ever marry you!" she cried out as she crossed the threshold; and he flung back furiously: "Wait till I ask you!" and plunged away into the rain.

Chapter XIV

PAULINE MANFORD left Mrs. Landish's door with the uncomfortable sense of having swallowed a new frustration. In this crowded life of hers they were as difficult to avoid as germs—and there was not always time to have them extirpated!

Manford had evidently found out about Lita's Dawnside frequentations; found it out, no doubt, as Pauline had, by seeing her photograph in that loathsome dancing group in the "Looker-on." Well, perhaps it was best that he should know; it would certainly confirm his resolve to stop any action against the Mahatma.

Only—if he had induced the Lindons to drop the investigation, why was he still preoccupied by it? Why had he gone to Mrs. Landish to make that particular inquiry about Lita? Pauline would have liked to shake off the memory of his voice, and of the barely disguised impatience with which he had waited for her to go before putting his question. Confronted by this new riddle (when there were already so many others in her path) she felt a reasonless exasperation against the broken doorknob which had let her into the secret. If only Kitty Landish, instead of dreaming about Mesopotamian embroideries, would send for a locksmith and keep her house in repair!

All day Pauline was oppressed by the nervous apprehension that Manford might have changed his mind about dropping the investigation. If there had been time she would have gone to Alvah Loft for relief; she had managed so far to squeeze in a daily *séance*, and had come to depend on it as "addicts" do on their morphia. The very brevity of the treatment, and the blunt negative face and indifferent monosyllables of the Healer, were subtly stimulating after the verbiage and flummery of his predecessors. Such stern economy of means impressed Pauline in much the same way as a new labour-saving device; she liked everything the better for being a short-cut to something else, and even spiritual communion for resembling an improved form of stenography. As Mrs. Swoffer said, Alvah Loft was really the Busy Man's Christ.

But that afternoon there was literally not time for a treatment. Manford's decision to spend the Easter holidays at Cedarledge necessitated one of those campaigns of intensive preparation in which his wife and Maisie Bruss excelled. Leading the simple life at Cedarledge involved despatching there a part of the New York domestic staff at least ten days in advance, testing and lighting three complicated heating systems, going over all the bells and electric wiring, and making sure that the elaborate sanitary arrangements were in irreproachable order.

Nor was this all. Pauline, who prided herself on the perfect organization of every detail of both her establishments, had lately been studying the estimate for a new and singularly complete system of burglar-alarm at Cedarledge, and also going over the bills for the picturesque engine-house and up-to-date fire-engine with which she had just endowed the village patriarchally clustered below the Cedarledge hill. All these matters called for deep thought and swift decision; and the fact gave her a sudden stimulus. No rest-cure in the world was as refreshing to her as a hurried demand on her practical activity; she thrilled to it like a war-horse to a trumpet, and compelled the fagged Maisie to thrill in unison.

In this case their energy was redoubled by the hope that, if Manford found everything to his liking at Cedarledge, he might take a fancy to spending more time there. Pauline's passionate interest in plumbing and electric wiring was suffused with a romantic glow at the thought that they might lure her husband back to domestic intimacy. "The heating of the new swimming-pool must be finished too, and the workmen all out of the way—you'll have to go there next week, Maisie, and impress on everybody that there must not be a workman visible anywhere when we arrive."

Breathless, exultant, Pauline hurried home for a late cup of tea in her boudoir, and settled down, pencil in hand, with plans and estimates, as eagerly as her husband, in the early days of his legal career, used to study the documents of a new case.

Maisie, responding as she always did to the least touch of the spur, yet lifted a perplexed brow to murmur: "All right. But I don't see how I can very well leave before the Birth Control dinner. You know you haven't yet rewritten the opening passage that you used by mistake at the—"

Pauline's colour rose. Maisie's way of putting it was tactless; but the fact remained that the opening of that unlucky speech had to be rewritten, and that Pauline was never very sure of her syntax unless Maisie's reinforced it. She had always meant to be cultivated—she still thought she was when she looked at her bookshelves. But when she had to compose a speech, though words never failed her, the mysterious relations between them sometimes did. Wealth and extensive social activities were obviously incompatible with a complete mastery of grammar, and secretaries were made for such emergencies. Yes; Maisie, fagged as she looked, could certainly not be spared till the speech was remodelled.

The telephone, ringing from downstairs, announced that the Marchesa was on her way up to the boudoir. Pauline's pencil fell from her hand. On her way up! It was really too inconsiderate . . . Amalasuntha must be made to understand . . . But there was the undaunted lady.

"The footman swore you were out, dear; but I knew from his manner that I should find you. (With Powder, now, I never can tell.) And I simply *had* to rush in long enough to give you a good hug." The Marchesa glanced at Maisie, and the secretary effaced herself after another glance, this time from her employer, which plainly warned her: "Wait in the next room; I won't let her stay."

To her visitor Pauline murmured somewhat coldly: "I left word that I was out because I'm desperately busy over the new plumbing and burglar-alarm systems at Cedarledge. Dexter wants to go there for Easter, and of course everything must be in order before we arrive . . ."

The Marchesa's eyes widened. "Ah, this marvellous American plumbing! I believe you all treat yourselves to a new set of bathrooms every year. There's only one bath at San Fedele, and my dear parents-in-law had it covered with a wooden lid so that it could be used to do the boots on. It's really rather convenient—and out of family feeling Venturino has always reserved it for that purpose. But that's not what I came to talk about. What I want is to find words for my gratitude . . ."

Pauline leaned back, gazing wearily at Amalasuntha's small sharp face, which seemed to glitter with a new and mysterious varnish of prosperity. "For what? You've thanked me already more than my little present deserved."

The Marchesa gave her a look of puzzled retrospection. "Oh—that lovely cheque the other day? Of course my thanks include that too. But I'm entirely overwhelmed by your new munificence."

"My new munificence?" Pauline echoed between narrowed lips. Could this be an adroit way of prefacing a fresh appeal? With the huge Cedarledge estimates at her elbow she stiffened herself for refusal. Amalasuntha must really be taught moderation.

"Well, Dexter's munificence, then—his royal promise! I left him only an hour ago," the Marchesa cried with rising exultation.

"You mean he's found a job for Michelangelo? I'm very glad," said Pauline, still without enthusiasm.

"No, no; something ever so much better than that. At least," the Marchesa hastily corrected herself, "something more immediately helpful. His debts, dear, my silly boy's debts! Dexter has promised . . . has authorized me to cable that he need not sail, as everything will be paid. It's more, far more, than I could have hoped!" The happy mother possessed herself of Mrs. Manford's unresponsive hand.

Pauline freed the hand abruptly. She felt the need of assimilating and interpreting this news as rapidly as possible, without betraying undue astonishment and yet without engaging her responsibility; but the effort was beyond her, and she could only sit and stare. Dexter had promised to pay Michelangelo's debts—but with whose money? And why?

"I'm sure Dexter wants to do all he can to help you about Michelangelo—we both do. But—"

Pauline's brain was whirling; she found it impossible to go on. She knew by heart the extent of Michelangelo's debts. Amalasuntha took care that everyone did. She seemed to feel a sort of fatuous pride in their enormity, and was always dinning it into her cousin's ears. Dexter, if he had really made such a promise, must have made it in his wife's name; and to do so

without consulting her was so unlike him that the idea deepened her bewilderment.

"Are you sure? I'm sorry, Amalasuntha—but this comes as a
surprise . . . Dexter and I were to talk the matter over . . . to see
what could be done . . ."

"Darling, it's so like you to belittle your own generosity—
you always do! And so does Dexter. But in this case—well, the
cable's gone; so why deny it?" triumphed the Marchesa.

When Maisie Bruss returned, Pauline was still sitting with
an idle pencil before the pile of bills and estimates. She fixed an
unseeing eye on her secretary. "These things will have to wait.
I'm dreadfully tired, I don't know why. But I'll go over them all
early tomorrow, before you come; and—Maisie—I hate to ask
it; but do you think you could get here by eight o'clock instead
of nine? There's so much to be done; and I want to get you off
to Cedarledge as soon as possible."

Maisie, a little paler and more drawn than usual, declared that
of course she would turn up at eight.

Even after she had gone Pauline did not move, or give another
glance to the papers. For the first time in her life she had an
obscure sense of moving among incomprehensible and over-
powering forces. She could not, to herself, have put it even as
clearly as that—she just dimly felt that, between her and her
usual firm mastery of facts, something nebulous and impenetrable was closing in . . . Nona—what if she were to consult
Nona? The girl sometimes struck her as having an uncanny gift
of divination, as getting at certain mysteries of mood and character more quickly and clearly than her mother . . . "Though,
when it comes to practical things, poor child, she's not much
more use than Jim . . ."

Jim! His name called up the other associated with it. Lita was
now another source of worry. Whichever way Pauline looked,
the same choking obscurity enveloped her. Even about Jim and
Lita it clung in a dense fog, darkening and distorting what,
only a short time ago, had seemed a daylight case of domestic
harmony. Money, health, good looks, a beautiful baby . . . and
now all this fuss about having to express one's own personality.
Yes; Lita's attitude was just as confusing as Dexter's. Was Dexter
trying to express his own personality too? If only they would

all talk things out with her—help her to understand, instead of moving about her in the obscurity, like so many burglars with dark lanterns! This image jerked her attention back to the Cedarledge estimates, and wearily she adjusted her eye-glasses and took up her pencil . . .

Her maid rapped. "What dress, please, madam?" To be sure—they were dining that evening with the Walter Rivingtons. It was the first time they had invited Pauline since her divorce from Wyant; Mrs. Rivington's was the only house left in which the waning traditions of old New York still obstinately held out, and divorce was regarded as a social disadvantage. But they had taken Manford's advice successfully in a difficult case, and were too punctilious not to reward him in the one way he would care about. The Rivingtons were the last step of the Manford ladder.

"The silver moiré, and my pearls." That would be distinguished and exclusive-looking. Pauline was thankful Dexter had definitely promised to go with her—he was getting so restive nowadays about what he had taken to calling her dull dinners . . .

The telephone again—this time Dexter's voice. Pauline listened apprehensively, wondering if it would do to speak to him now about Amalasuntha's extraordinary announcement, or whether it might be more tactful to wait. He was so likely to be nervous and irritable at the end of the day. Yes; it was in his eleventh-hour voice that he was speaking.

"Pauline—look here; I shall be kept at the office rather late. Please put off dinner, will you? I'd like a quiet evening alone with you—"

"A quiet . . . But, Dexter, we're dining at the Rivingtons'. Shall I telephone to say you may be late?"

"The Rivingtons?" His voice became remote and utterly indifferent. "No; telephone we won't come. Chuck them . . . I want a talk with you alone . . . can't we dine together quietly at home?" He repeated the phrases slowly, as if he thought she had not understood him.

Chuck the Rivingtons? It seemed like being asked to stand up in church and deny her God. She sat speechless and let the fatal words go on vibrating on the wire.

"Don't you hear me, Pauline? Why don't you answer? Is there something wrong with the line?"

"No, Dexter. There's nothing wrong with the line."

"Well, then . . . You can explain to them . . . say anything you like."

Through the dressing-room door she saw the maid laying out the silver moiré, the chinchilla cloak, the pearls . . .

Explain to the Rivingtons!

"Very well, dear. What time shall I order dinner here?" she questioned heroically.

She heard him ring off, and sat again staring into the fog, which his words had only made more impenetrable.

Chapter XV

MANFORD, the day after his daughter had caught sight of him at the Housetop, started out early for one of his long tramps around the Park. He was not due at his office till ten, and he wanted first to walk himself tired.

For some years after his marriage he had kept a horse in town, and taken his morning constitutional in the saddle; but the daily canter over the same bridle paths was too much like the circuit of his wife's flower-garden. He took to his feet to make it last longer, and when there was no time to walk had in a *masseur* who prepared him, in the same way as everybody else, for the long hours of sedentary hurry known as "business." The New York routine had closed in on him, and he sometimes felt that, for intrinsic interest, there was little to choose between Pauline's hurry and his own. They seemed, all of them—lawyers, bankers, brokers, railway-directors and the rest—to be cheating their inner emptiness with activities as futile as those of the women they went home to.

It was all wrong—something about it was fundamentally wrong. They all had these colossal plans for acquiring power, and then, when it was acquired, what came of it but bigger houses, more food, more motors, more pearls, and a more self-righteous philanthropy?

The philanthropy was what he most hated: all these expensive plans for moral forcible feeding, for compelling everybody to be cleaner, stronger, healthier and happier than they would have been by the unaided light of Nature. The longing to get away into a world where men and women sinned and begot, lived and died, as they chose, without the perpetual intervention of optimistic millionaires, had become so strong that he sometimes felt the chain of habit would snap with his first jerk.

That was what had secretly drawn him to Jim's wife. She was the one person in his group to whom its catchwords meant absolutely nothing. The others, whatever their private omissions or indulgences, dressed up their selfish cravings in the same wordy altruism. It used to be one's duty to one's neighbour; now it had become one's duty to one's self. Duty, duty—always duty! But when you spoke of duty to Lita she just widened her eyes and said: "Is that out of the Marriage Service? 'Love, honour and obey'—such a funny combination! Who do you suppose invented it? I believe it must have been Pauline." One could never fix her attention on any subject beyond her own immediate satisfaction, and that animal sincerity seemed to Manford her greatest charm. Too great a charm . . . a terrible danger. He saw it now. He thought he had gone to her for relaxation, change—and he had just managed to pull himself up on the edge of a precipice. But for the sickening scene of the other evening, when he had shown her the photograph, he might, old fool that he was, have let himself slip into sentiment; and God knows where that tumble would have landed him. Now a passionate pity had replaced his fatuous emotion, the baleful siren was only a misguided child, and he was to help and save her for Jim's sake and her own.

It was queer that such a mood of calm lucidity had come out of the fury of hate with which he rushed from her house. If it had not, he would have gone mad—smashed something, done something irretrievable. And instead here he was, calmly contemplating his own folly and hers! He must go on seeing her, of course; there was more reason than ever for seeing her; but there would be no danger in it now, only help for her—and perhaps healing for him. To this new mood he clung as to an inviolable refuge. The turmoil and torment of the last months could never reach him again: he had found a way out, an escape. The relief of being quiet, of avoiding a conflict, of settling everything without effusion of blood, stole over him like the spell of the drug-taker's syringe. Poor little Lita . . . never again to be adored (thank heaven), but, oh, so much the more to be helped and pitied . . .

This deceptive serenity had come to him during his call on Mrs. Landish—come from her very insensibility to any of the standards he lived by. He had gone there—he saw it now—moved by the cruel masculine desire to know the worst about a fallen idol. What he called the determination to "face things"—what was it but the savage longing to accumulate all the evidence against poor Lita? Give up the Mahatma investigation? Never! All the more reason now for going on with it; for exposing the whole blackguardly business, opening poor

Jim's eyes to his wife's past (better now than later), and helping him to get on his feet again, start fresh, and recover his
faith in life and happiness. For of course poor Jim would be
the chief sufferer . . . Damn the woman! She wanted to get rid
of Jim, did she? Well, here was her chance—only it would be
the other way round. The tables would be turned on her. She'd
see—! This in his first blind outbreak of rage; but by the time he
reached Mrs. Landish's door the old legal shrewdness had come
to his rescue, and he had understood that a public scandal was
unnecessary, and therefore to be avoided. Easy enough to get
rid of Lita without that. With such evidence as he would soon
possess they could make any conditions they chose. Jim would
keep the boy, and the whole thing be settled quietly—but on
their terms, not hers! She would be only too thankful to clear
out bag and baggage—clean out of all their lives. Faugh—to
think he had delegated his own Nona to look after her . . . the
thought sickened him.

And then, in the end, it had all come out so differently. He
needed his hard tramp around the Park to see just why.

It was Mrs. Landish's own attitude—her silly rambling
irresponsibility, so like an elderly parody of Lita's youthful
carelessness. Mrs. Landish had met Manford's stern interroga-
tions by the vague reply that he mustn't ever come to *her* for
dates and figures and statistics: that facts meant nothing to
her, that the only thing she cared for was Inspiration, Genius,
the Divine Fire, or whatever he chose to call it. Perhaps she'd
done wrong, but she had sacrificed everything, all her life, to
her worship of genius. She was always hunting for it everywhere, and it was because, from the first, she had felt a touch
of it in Lita that she had been so devoted to the child. Didn't
Manford feel it in Lita too? Of course she, Mrs. Landish, had
dreamed of another sort of marriage for her niece . . . Oh, but
Manford mustn't misunderstand! Jim was perfect—*too* perfect.
That was the trouble. Manford surely guessed the meaning of
that "too"? Such absolute reliability, such complete devotion,
were sometimes more of a strain to the artistic temperament
than scenes and infidelities. And Lita was first and foremost an
artist, born to live in the world of art—in quite other values—a
fourth-dimensional world, as it were. It wasn't fair to judge her
in her present surroundings, ideal as they were in one way—a

way that unfortunately didn't happen to be hers! Mrs. Landish persisted in assuming Manford's complete comprehension . . . "If Jim could only be made to understand as you do; to see that ordinary standards don't apply to these rare natures . . . Why, has the child told you what Klawhammer has offered her to turn *one film* for him, before even having seen her dance, just on the strength of what Jack Staley and Ardwin had told him?"

Ah—there it was! The truth was out. Mrs. Landish, always in debt, and always full of crazy schemes for wasting more money, had seen a gold mine in the exploitation of her niece's gifts. The divorce, instead of frightening her, delighted her. Manford smiled as he thought how little she would be moved by Pauline's threat to cut off the young couple. Pauline sometimes forgot that, even in her own family, her authority was not absolute. She could certainly not compete financially with Hollywood, and Mrs. Landish's eyes were on Hollywood.

"Dear Mr. Manford—but you look shocked! Absolutely shocked! Does the screen really frighten you? How funny!" Mrs. Landish, drawing her rambling eyebrows together, seemed trying to picture the inner darkness of such a state. "But surely you know the smartest people are going in for it? Why, the Marchesa di San Fedele was showing me the other day a photograph of that beautiful son of hers—one of those really *Greek* beings in bathing tights—and telling me that Klawhammer, who had seen it, had authorized her to cable him to come out to Hollywood on trial, all expenses paid. It seems they can almost always recognize the eurythmic people at a glance. Funny, wouldn't it be, if Michelangelo and Lita turned out to be the future Valentino and—"

He didn't remember the rest of the rigmarole. He could only recall shouting out, with futile vehemence: "My wife and I will do everything to prevent a divorce—" and leaving his astonished hostess on a threat of which he knew the uselessness as well as she did.

That was the air in which Lita had grown up, those were the gods of Viking Court! Yet Manford had stormed instead of pitying, been furious instead of tolerant, risked disaster for Lita and Jim instead of taking calm control of the situation. The vision of Lita Wyant and Michelangelo as future film stars, "featured" jointly on every hoarding from Maine to California, had sent the blood to his head. Through a mist of rage he had seen the monstrous pictures and conjectured the loathsome letter-press. And no one would do more than look and laugh! At the thought, he felt the destructive ire of the man who finds his private desires pitted against the tendencies of his age. Well, they would see, that was all: he would show them!

The resolve to act brought relief to his straining imagination. Once again he felt himself seated at his office desk, all his professional authority between him and his helpless interlocutors, and impressive words and skilful arguments ordering themselves automatically in his mind. After all, he was the head of his family—in some degree even of Wyant's family.

Chapter XVI

PAULINE'S nervousness had gradually subsided. About the Rivingtons—why, after all, it wasn't such a bad idea to show them that, with a man of Manford's importance, one must take one's chance of getting him, and make the best of it if he failed one at the last. "Professional engagement; oh, yes, entirely unexpected; extremely important; so dreadfully sorry, but you know lawyers are not their own masters . . ." It had been rather pleasant to say that to a flustered Mrs. Rivington, stammering: "Oh, but *couldn't* he . . . ? But we'll wait . . . we'll dine at half-past nine . . ." Pleasant also to add: "He must reserve his whole evening, I'm afraid," and then hang up, and lean back at leisure, while Mrs. Rivington (how Pauline pictured it!) dashed down in her dressing-gown and crimping pins to re-arrange a table to which as much thought had been given as if a feudal aristocracy were to sit at it.

To Pauline the fact that Manford wanted to be alone with her made even such renunciations easy. How many years had passed since he had expressed such a wish? And did she owe his tardy return to the Mahatma and reduced hips, or the Inspirational Healer and renewed optimism? If only a woman could guess what inclined a man's heart to her, what withdrew it! Pauline, if she had had the standardizing of life, would have begun with human hearts, and had them turned out in series, all alike, rather than let them come into being haphazard, cranky ama-teurish things that you couldn't count on, or start up again if anything went wrong . . .

Just a touch of rouge? Well, perhaps her maid was right. She *did* look rather pale and drawn. Mrs. Herman Toy put it on with a trowel . . . apparently that was what men liked . . . Pau-line shed a faint bloom on her cheeks and ran her clever fingers through her prettily waved hair, wondering again, as she did so, if it wouldn't be better to bob it. Then the mauve tea-gown, the Chinese amethysts, and those silver sandals that made her feet so slender. She looked at herself with a sigh of pleasure. Dinner was to be served in the boudoir.

Manford was very late; it was ten o'clock before coffee and liqueurs were put on the low stand by the fire, and the little dinner-table was noiselessly removed. The fire glowed invitingly, and he sank into the armchair his wife pushed forward with a sound like a murmur of content.

"Such a day—" he said, passing his hand across his forehead as if to brush away a tangle of legal problems.

"You do too much, Dexter; you really do. I know how wonderfully young you are for your age, but still—." She broke off, dimly perceiving that, in spite of the flattering exordium, this allusion to his age was not quite welcome.

"Nothing to do with age," he growled. "Everybody who does anything at all does too much." (Did he mean to imply that she did nothing?)

"The nervous strain—" she began, once more wondering if this were not the moment to slip in a word of Alvah Loft. But though Manford had wished to be with her he had apparently no desire to listen to her. It was all her own fault, she felt. If only she had known how to reveal the secret tremors that were rippling through her! There were women not half as clever and tactful—not younger, either, nor even as good-looking—who would have known at once what to say, or how to spell the mute syllables of soul-telegraphy. If her husband had wanted facts—a good confidential talk about the new burglar-alarm, or a clear and careful analysis of the engine-house bills, or the heating system for the swimming pool—she could have found just the confidential and tender accent for such topics. Intimacy, to her, meant the tireless discussion of facts, not necessarily of a domestic order, but definite and palpable facts. For her part she was ready for anything, from Birth Control to neo-impressionism: she flattered herself that few women had a wider range. In confidential moments she preferred the homelier themes, and would have enjoyed best of all being tender and gay about the coal cellar, or reticent and brave about the leak in the boiler; but she was ready to deal with anything as long as it was a fact, something with substance and outline, as to which one could have an opinion and a line of conduct. What paralyzed her was the sense that, apart from his profession, her husband didn't care for facts, and that nothing was less likely to rouse his interest than burglar-alarm wiring, or the last new thing in electric ranges. Obviously, one must take men as they were, wilful, moody and mysterious; but she would have given the world to be told (since for all her application she had never discovered) what those other women said who could talk to a man about nothing.

Manford lit a cigar and stared into the fire. "It's about that fool Amalasuntha," he began at length, addressing his words to the logs.

The name jerked Pauline back to reality. Here was a fact—hard, knobby and uncomfortable! And she had actually forgotten it in the confused pleasure of their tête-à-tête! So he had only come home to talk to her about Amalasuntha. She tried to keep the flatness out of her: "Yes, dear?"

He continued, still fixed on the fire: "You may not know that we've had a narrow escape."

"A narrow escape?"

"That damned Michelangelo—his mother was importing him this very week. The cable had gone. If I hadn't put a stop to it we'd have been saddled with him for life."

Pauline's breath failed her. She listened with straining ears.

"You haven't seen her, then—she hasn't told you?" Manford continued. "She was getting him out on her own responsibility to turn a film for Klawhammer. Simply that! By the mercy of heaven I headed her off—but we hadn't a minute to lose."

In her bewilderment at this outburst, and at what it revealed, Pauline continued to sit speechless. "Michelangelo—Klawhammer? I didn't know! But wouldn't it have been the best solution, perhaps?"

"Solution—of what? Don't you think one member of the family on the screen's enough at a time? Or would it have looked prettier to see him and Lita featured together on every hoarding in the country? My God—I thought I'd done the right thing in acting for you . . . there was no time to consult you . . . but if *you* don't care, why should I? He's none of *my* family . . . and she isn't either, for that matter."

He had swung round from the hearth, and faced her for the first time, his brows contracted, the veins swelling on his temples, his hands grasping his knees as if to constrain himself not to start up in righteous indignation. He was evidently deeply disturbed, yet his anger, she felt, was only the unconscious mask of another emotion—an emotion she could not divine. His vehemence, and the sense of moving in complete obscurity, had an intimidating effect on her.

"I don't quite understand, Dexter. Amalasuntha was here today. She said nothing about films, or Klawhammer; but she did say that you'd made it unnecessary for Michelangelo to come to America."

"Didn't she say how?"

"She said something about—paying his debts."

Manford stood up and went to lean against the mantelpiece. He looked down on his wife, who in her turn kept her eyes on the embers.

"Well—you didn't suppose I made that offer till I saw we were up against it, did you?"

His voice rose again angrily, but a cautious glance at his face showed her that its tormented lines were damp with perspiration. Her immediate thought was that he must be ill, that she ought to take his temperature—she always responded by first-aid impulses to any contact with human distress. But no, after all, it was not that: he was unhappy, that was it, he was desperately unhappy. But why? Was it because he feared he had exceeded his rights in pledging her to such an extent, in acting for her when there was no time to consult her? Apparently the idea of the discord between Lita and Jim, and Lita's thirst for scenic notoriety, had shocked him deeply—much more, in reality, than they had Pauline. If so, his impulse had been a natural one, and eminently in keeping with those Wyant traditions with which (at suitable moments) she continued to identify herself. Yes: she began to understand his thinking it would be odious to her to see the names of her son's wife and this worthless Italian cousin emblazoned over every Picture Palace in the land. She felt moved by his regard for her feelings. After all, as he said, Lita and Michelangelo were no relations of his; he could easily have washed his hands of the whole affair.

"I'm sure what you've done must be right, Dexter; you know I always trust your judgment. Only—I wish you'd explain . . ."

"Explain what?" Her mild reply seemed to provoke a new wave of exasperation. "The only way to stop his coming was to pay his debts. They're very heavy. I had no right to commit you; I acknowledge it."

She took a deep breath, the figure of Michelangelo's liabilities blazing out before her as on a giant blackboard. Then: "You had every right, Dexter," she said. "I'm glad you did it."

He stood silent, his head bent, twisting between his fingers the cigar he had forgotten to relight. It was as if he had been startled out of speech by the promptness of her acquiescence, and would have found it easier to go on arguing and justifying himself.

"That's—very handsome of you, Pauline," he said at length.

"Oh, no—why? You did it out of regard for me, I know. Only—perhaps you won't mind our talking things over a little. About ways and means . . ." she added, seeing his forehead gloom again.

"Ways and means—oh, certainly. But please understand that I don't expect you to shoulder the whole sum. I've had two big fees lately; I've already arranged—"

She interrupted him quickly. "It's not your affair, Dexter. You're awfully generous, always; but I couldn't think of letting you—"

"It *is* my affair; it's all of our affair. I don't want this nasty notoriety any more than you do . . . and Jim's happiness wrecked into the bargain . . ."

"You're awfully generous," she repeated.

"It's first of all a question of helping Jim and Lita. If that young ass came over here with a contract from Klawhammer in his pocket there'd be no holding her. And once that gang get hold of a woman . . ." He spoke with a kind of breathless irritation, as though it were incredible that Pauline should still not understand.

"It's very fine of you, dear," she could only murmur.

A pause followed, during which, for the first time, she could assemble her thoughts and try to take in the situation. Dexter had bought off Michelangelo to keep one more disturbing element out of the family complication; perhaps also to relieve himself of the bother of having on his hands, at close quarters, an idle and mischief-making young man. That was comprehensible. But if his first object had been the securing of Jim's peace of mind, might not the same end have been achieved, more satisfactorily to every one but Michelangelo, by his uniting with Pauline to increase Jim's allowance, and thus giving

Lita the amusement and distraction of having a lot more money to spend? Even at such a moment, Pauline's practical sense of values made it hard for her to accept the idea of putting so many good thousands into the pockets of Michelangelo's creditors. She was naturally generous; but no matter how she disposed of her fortune, she could never forget that it had been money—and how much money it had been—before it became something else. For her it was never transmuted, but only exchanged.

"You're not satisfied—you don't think I did right?" Manford began again.

"I don't say that, Dexter. I'm only wondering—. Supposing we'd given the money to Jim instead? Lita could have done her house over . . . or built a bungalow in Florida . . . or bought jewels with it . . . She's so easily amused."

"Easily amused!" He broke into a hard laugh. "Why, that amount of money wouldn't amuse her for a week!" His face took on a look of grim introspection. "She wants the universe—or her idea of it. A woman with an offer from Klawhammer dangling in front of her! Mrs. Landish told me the figure—those people could buy us all out and not know it."

Pauline's heart sank. Apparently he knew things about Lita of which she was still ignorant. "I hadn't heard the offer had actually been made. But if it has, and she wants to accept, how can we stop her?"

Manford had thrown himself down into his armchair. He got up again, relit his cigar, and walked across the room and back before answering. "I don't know that we can. And I don't know how we can. But I want to try . . . I want *time* to try . . . Don't you see, Pauline? The child—we mustn't be hard on her. Her beginnings were damnable . . . Perhaps you know—yes? That cursèd Mahatma place?" Pauline winced, and looked away from him. He had seen the photograph, then! And heaven knows what more he had discovered in the course of his investigations for the Lindons . . . A sudden light glared out at her. It was for Jim's sake and Lita's that he had dropped the case—sacrificed his convictions, his sense of the duty of exposing a social evil! She faltered: "I do know . . . a little . . ."

"Well, a little's enough. Swine—! And that's the rotten atmosphere she was brought up in. But she's not bad, Pauline . . . there's something still to be done with her . . . give me time . . .

time . . ." He stopped abruptly, as if the "me" had slipped out
by mistake. "We must all stand shoulder to shoulder to put up
this fight for her," he corrected himself with a touch of forensic
emphasis.

"Of course, dear, of course," Pauline murmured.

"When we get her to ourselves at Cedarledge, you and Nona
and I . . . It's just as well Jim's going off, by the way. He's got
her nerves on edge; Jim's a trifle dense at times, you know . . .
And, above all, this whole business, Klawhammer and all, must
be kept from him. We'll all hold our tongues till the thing blows
over, eh?"

"Of course," she again assented. "But supposing Lita asks to
speak to me?"

"Well, let her speak—listen to what she has to say . . ." He
stopped, and then added, in a rough unsteady voice: "Only
don't be hard on her. You won't, will you? No matter what rot
she talks. The child's never had half a chance."

"How could you think I should, Dexter?"

"No; no; I don't." He stood up, and sent a slow unseeing gaze
about the room. The gaze took in his wife, and rested on her
long enough to make her feel that she was no more to him—
mauve tea-gown, Chinese amethysts, touch of rouge and silver
sandals—than a sheet of glass through which he was staring:
staring at what? She had never before felt so inexistent.

"Well—I'm dog-tired—down and out," he said with one of
his sudden jerks, shaking his shoulders and turning toward
the door. He did not remember to say goodnight to her: how
should he have, when she was no longer there for him?

After the door had closed, Pauline in her turn looked slowly
about the room. It was as if she were taking stock of the havoc
wrought by an earthquake; but nothing about her showed any
sign of disorder except the armchair her husband had pushed
back, the rug his movement had displaced.

With instinctive precision she straightened the rug, and rolled
the armchair back into its proper corner. Then she went up to a
mirror and attentively scrutinized herself. The light was unbecoming, perhaps . . . the shade of the adjacent wall-candle had
slipped out of place. She readjusted it . . . yes, that was better!
But of course, at nearly midnight—and after such a day!—a

woman was bound to look a little drawn. Automatically her lips shaped the familiar: "Pauline, don't worry: there's nothing in the world to worry about." But the rouge had vanished from the lips, their thin line looked blue and arid. She turned from the unpleasing sight, putting out one light after another on the way to her dressing-room.

As she bent to extinguish the last lamp its light struck a tall framed photograph: Lita's latest portrait. Lita had the gift of posing—the lines she fell into always had an unconscious eloquence. And that little round face, as sleek as the inside of a shell; the slanting eyes, the budding mouth . . . men, no doubt, would think it all enchanting.

Pauline, with slow steps, went on into the big shining dressing-room, and to the bathroom beyond, all ablaze with white tiling and silvered taps and tubes. It was the hour of her evening uplift exercises, the final relaxing of body and soul before she slept. Sternly she addressed herself to relaxation.

Chapter XVII

W HAT was the sense of it all?

Nona, sitting up in bed two days after her nocturnal visit to the Housetop, swept the interval with a desolate eye.

She had made her great, her final, refusal. She had sacrificed herself, sacrificed Heuston, to the stupid ideal of an obstinate woman who managed to impress people by dressing up her egotism in formulas of philanthropy and piety. Because Aggie was forever going to church, and bossing the committees of Old Women's Homes and Rest-cures for Consumptives, she was allowed a license of cruelty which would have damned the frivolous.

Destroying two lives to preserve her own ideal of purity! It was like the horrible ailing old men in history books, who used to bathe in human blood to restore their vitality. Every one agreed that there was nothing such a clever sensitive fellow as Stanley Heuston mightn't have made of his life if he'd married a different kind of woman. As it was, he had just drifted: tried the law, dabbled in literary reviewing, taken a turn at municipal politics, another at scientific farming, and dropped one experiment after another to sink, at thirty-five, into a disillusioned idler who killed time with cards and drink and motor-speeding. She didn't believe he ever opened a book nowadays: he was living on the dwindling capital of his early enthusiasms. But, as for what people called his "fastness," she knew it was merely the inevitable opposition to Aggie's virtues. And it wasn't as if there had been children. Nona always ached for the bewildered progeny suddenly bundled from one home to another when their parents embarked on a new conjugal experiment; she could never have bought her happiness by a massacre of innocents. But to be sacrificed to a sterile union—as sterile spiritually as physically—to miss youth and love because of Agnes Heuston's notion of her duty to the elderly clergyman she called God!

That woman he said he was going off with . . . Nona had pretended she didn't know, had opened incredulous eyes at the announcement. But of course she knew; everybody knew; it was

Cleo Merrick. She had been "after him" for the last two years, she hadn't a rag of reputation to lose, and would jump at the idea of a few jolly weeks with a man like Heuston, even if he got away from her afterward. But he wouldn't—of course he never would! Poor Stan—Cleo Merrick's noise, her cheek, her vulgarity: how warm and life-giving they would seem as a change from the frigidarium he called home! She would hold him by her very cheapness: her recklessness would seem like generosity, her glitter like heat. Ah—how Nona could have shown him the difference! She shut her eyes and felt his lips on her lids; and her lids became lips. Wherever he touched her, a mouth blossomed . . . Did he know that? Had he never guessed?

She jumped out of bed, ran into her dressing-room, began to bathe and dress with feverish haste. She wouldn't telephone him—Aggie had long ears. She wouldn't send a "special delivery"—Aggie had sharp eyes. She would just summon him by a telegram: a safe anonymous telegram. She would dash out of the house and get it off herself, without even waiting for her cup of coffee to be brought.

"Come and see me any time today. I was too stupid the other night." Yes; he would understand that. She needn't even sign it . . .

On the threshold of her room, the telegram crumpled in her hand, the telephone bell arrested her. Stanley, surely; he must have felt the same need that she had! She fumbled uncertainly with the receiver; the tears were running down her cheeks. She had waited too long; she had exacted the impossible of herself. "Yes—yes? It's you, darling?" She laughed it out through her weeping.

"What's that? It's Jim. That you, Nona?" a quiet voice came back. When had Jim's voice ever been anything but quiet?

"Oh, Jim, dear!" She gulped down tears and laughter. "Yes—what is it? How awfully early you are!"

"Hope I didn't wake you? Can I drop in on my way down town?"

"Of course. When? How soon?"

"Now. In two minutes. I've got to be at the office before nine."

"All right. In two minutes. Come straight up."

She hung up the receiver, and thrust the telegram aside. No time to rush out with it now. She would see Jim first, and send off her message when he left. Now that her decision was taken she felt tranquil and able to wait. But anxiety about Jim rose and swelled in her again. She reproached herself for having given him so little thought for the last two days. Since her parting from Stan on the doorstep in the rainy night everything but her fate and his had grown remote and almost indifferent to her. Well; it was natural enough—only perhaps she had better not be so glib about Aggie Heuston's selfishness! Of course everybody who was in love was selfish; and Aggie, according to her lights, was in love. Her love was bleak and cramped, like everything about her; a sort of fleshless bony affair, like the repulsive plates in anatomical manuals. But in reality those barren arms were stretched toward Stanley, though she imagined they were lifted to God . . . What a hideous mystery life was! And yet Pauline and her friends persisted in regarding it as a Sunday school picnic, with lemonade and sponge cake as its supreme rewards . . .

Here was Jim at her sitting-room door. Nona held out her arms, and slanted a glance at him as he bent his cheek to her kiss. Was the cheek rather sallower than usual? Well, that didn't mean much: he and she were always a yellow pair when they were worried!

"What's up, old man? No—this armchair's more comfortable. Had your coffee?"

He let her change the armchair, but declined the coffee. He had breakfasted before starting, he said—but she knew Lita's household, and didn't believe him.

"Anything wrong with Exhibit A?"

"Wrong? No. That is . . ." She had put the question at random, in the vague hope of gaining time before Lita's name was introduced; and now she had the sense of having unwittingly touched on another problem.

"That is—well, he's nervous and fidgety again: you've noticed?"

"I've noticed."

"Imagining things—. What a complicated world our ancestors lived in, didn't they?"

"Well, I don't know. Mother's world always seems to me alarmingly simple."

He considered. "Yes—that's pioneering and motor-building, I suppose. It's the old New York blood that's so clogged with taboos. Poor father always wants me to behave like a Knight of the Round Table."

Nona lifted her eyebrows with an effort of memory. "How did they behave?"

"They were always hitting some other fellow over the head."

She felt a little catch in her throat. "Who—particularly—does he want you to hit over the head?"

"Oh, we haven't got as far as that yet. It's just the general principle. Anybody who looks too hard at Lita."

"You *would* have to be hitting about! Everybody looks hard at Lita. How in the world can she help it?"

"That's what I tell him. But he says I haven't got the feelings of a gentleman. Guts, he means, I suppose." He leaned back, crossing his arms wearily behind his back, his sallow face with heavy-lidded eyes tilted to the ceiling. "Do you suppose Lita feels that too?" he suddenly flung at his sister.

"That you ought to break people's heads for her? She'd be the first to laugh at you!"

"So I told him. But he says women despise a man who isn't jealous."

Nona sat silent, instinctively turning her eyes from his troubled face. "Why should you be jealous?" she asked at length.

He shifted his position, stretched his arms along his knees, and brought his eyes down to a level with hers. There was something pathetic, she thought, in such youthful blueness blurred with uncomprehended pain.

"I suppose it's never got much to do with reasons," he said, very low.

"No; that's why it's so silly—and ungenerous."

"It doesn't matter what it is. She doesn't care a hang if I'm jealous or if I'm not. She doesn't care anything about me. I've simply ceased to exist for her."

"Well, then you can't be in her way."

"It seems I am, though. Because I *do* exist, for the world; and as the boy's father. And the mere idea gets on her nerves."

Nona laughed a little bitterly. "She wants a good deal of elbow-room, doesn't she? And how does she propose to eliminate you?"

"Oh, that's easy. Divorce."

There was a silence between the two. This was how it sounded—that simple reasonable request—on the lips of the other partner, the partner who still had a stake in the affair! Lately she seemed to have forgotten that side of the question; but how hideously it grimaced at her now, behind the lines of this boyish face wrung with a man's misery!

"Old Jim—it hurts such a lot?"

He jerked away from her outstretched hand. "Hurt? A fellow can stand being hurt. It can't hurt more than feeling her chained to me. But if she goes—what does she go to?"

Ah—that was it! Through the scorch and cloud of his own suffering he had seen it, it was the centre of his pain. Nona glanced down absently at her slim young hands—so helpless and inexperienced looking. All these tangled cross-threads of life, inextricably and fatally interwoven; how were a girl's hands to unravel them?

"I suppose she's talked to you—told you her ideas?" he asked. Nona nodded.

"Well, what's to be done: can you tell me?"

"She mustn't go—we mustn't let her."

"But if she stays—stays hating me?"

"Oh, Jim, not *hating*—!"

"You know well enough that she gets to hate anything that doesn't amuse her."

"But there's the baby. The baby still amuses her."

He looked at her, surprised. "Ah, that's what father says: he calls the baby, poor old chap, my hostage. What rot! As if I'd take her baby from her—and just because she cares for it. If I don't know how to keep her, I don't see that I've got any right to keep her child."

That was the new idea of marriage, the view of Nona's contemporaries; it had been her own a few hours since. Now, seeing it in operation, she wondered if it still were. It was one thing to theorize on the detachability of human beings, another to watch them torn apart by the bleeding roots. This botanist who had recently discovered that plants were susceptible to pain, and that transplanting was a major operation—might he not, if he turned attention to modern men and women, find the same thing to be still true of a few of them?

"Oh Jim, how I wish you didn't care so!" The words slipped out unawares: they were the last she had meant to speak aloud.

Her brother turned to her; the ghost of his old smile drew up his lip. "Good old girl!" he mocked her—then his face dropped into his hands, and he sat huddled against the armchair, his shaken shoulder-blades warding off her touch.

It didn't last more than a minute; but it was the real, the only answer. He *did* care so; nothing could alter it. She looked on stupidly, admitted for the first time to this world-old anguish rooted under all the restless moods of man.

Jim got up, shook back his rumpled hair, and reached for a cigarette. "That's *that*. And now, my child, what can I do? What I'd honestly like, if she wants her freedom, is to give it to her, and yet be able to go on looking after her. But I don't see how that can be worked out. Father says it's madness. He says I'm a morbid coward and talk like the people in the Russian novels. He wants to speak to her himself—"

"Oh, no! He and she don't talk the same language . . ."

Jim paused, pulling absently at his cigarette, and measuring the room with uncertain steps. "That's what I feel. But there's *your* father: he's been so awfully good to us; and his ideas are less archaic . . ."

Nona had turned away and was looking unseeingly out of the window. She moved back hastily. "No!"

He looked surprised. "You think he wouldn't understand either?"

"I don't mean that . . . But, after all, it's not his job . . . Have you spoken to mother?"

"Mother? Oh, she always thinks everything's all right. She'd give me a cheque, and tell me to buy Lita a new motor or to let her do over the drawing-room."

Nona pondered this answer, which was no more than the echo of her own thoughts. "All the same, Jim: mother's mother. She's always been awfully good to both of us, and you can't let this go on without her knowing, without consulting her. She has a right to your confidence—she has a right to hear what Lita has to say."

He remained silent, as if indifferent. His mother's glittering optimism was a hard surface for grief and failure to fling themselves on. "What's the use?" he grumbled.

"Let me consult her, then: at least let me see how she takes it."

He threw away his cigarette and looked at his watch. "I've got to run; it's nearly nine." He laid a hand on his sister's shoulder. "Whatever you like, old girl. But don't imagine it's going to be any use."

She put her arms about him, and he submitted to her kiss. "Give me time," she said, not knowing what else to answer.

After he had gone she sat motionless, weighed down with half-comprehended misery. This business of living—how right she had been to feel, in her ignorance, what a tortured tangle it was! Where, for instance, did one's own self end and one's neighbour's begin? And how tell the locked tendrils apart in the delicate process of disentanglement? Her precocious half-knowledge of the human dilemma was combined with a youthful belief that the duration of pain was proportioned to its intensity. And at that moment she would have hated any one who had tried to persuade her of the contrary. The only honourable thing about suffering was that it should not abdicate before indifference.

She got up, and her glance fell on the telegram which she had pushed aside when her brother entered. She still had her hat on, her feet were turned toward the door. But the door seemed to open into a gray unpeopled world suddenly shorn of its magic. She moved back into the room and tore up the telegram.

Chapter XVIII

"LITA? But of course I'll talk to Lita—"

Mrs. Manford, resting one elbow on her littered desk, smiled up encouragingly at her daughter. On the desk lay the final version of the Birth Control speech, mastered and canalized by the skilful Maisie. The result was so pleasing that Pauline would have liked to read it aloud to Nona, had the latter not worn her look of concentrated care. It was a pity, Pauline thought, that Nona should let herself go at her age to these moods of anxiety and discouragement.

Pauline herself, fortified by her morning exercises, and by a "double treatment" ($50) from Alvah Loft, had soared once more above her own perplexities. She had not had time for a word alone with her husband since their strange talk of the previous evening; but already the doubts and uncertainties produced by that talk had been dispelled. Of course Dexter had been moody and irritable: wasn't her family always piling up one worry on him after another? He had always loved Jim as much as he did Nona; and now this menace to Jim's happiness, and the unpleasantness about Lita, combined with Amalasuntha's barefaced demands, and the threatened arrival of the troublesome Michelangelo—such a weight of domestic problems was enough to unnerve a man already overburdened with professional cares.

"But of course I'll talk to Lita, dear; I always meant to. The silly goose! I've waited only because your father—"

Nona's heavy eyebrows ran together like Manford's. "Father?"

"Oh, he's helping us so splendidly about it. And he asked me to wait; to do nothing in a hurry . . ."

Nona seemed to turn this over. "All the same—I think you ought to hear what Lita has to say. She's trying to persuade Jim to let her divorce him; and he thinks he ought to, if he can't make her happy."

"But he *must* make her happy! I'll talk to Jim too," cried Pauline with a gay determination.

"I'd try Lita first, mother. Ask her to postpone her decision. If we can get her to come to Cedarledge for a few weeks' rest—"

"Yes; that's what your father says."

"But I don't think father ought to give up his fishing to join us. Haven't you noticed how tired he looks? He ought to get away from all of us for a few weeks. Why shouldn't you and I look after Lita?"

Pauline's enthusiasm drooped. It was really no business of Nona's to give her mother advice about the management of her father. These modern girls—pity Nona didn't marry, and try managing a husband of her own!

"Your father loves Cedarledge. It's quite his own idea to go there. He thinks Easter in the country with us all will be more restful than California. I haven't influenced him in the least to give up his fishing."

"Oh, I didn't suppose you had." Nona seemed to lose interest in the discussion, and her mother took advantage of the fact to add, with a gentle side-glance at her watch: "Is there anything else, dear? Because I've got to go over my Birth Control speech, and at eleven there's a delegation from—"

Nona's eyes had followed her glance to the scattered pages on the desk. "Are you really going to preside at that Birth Control dinner, mother?"

"Preside? Why not? I happen to be chairman," Pauline answered with a faint touch of acerbity.

"I know. Only—the other day you were preaching unlimited families. Don't the two speeches come rather close together? You might expose yourself to some newspaper chaff if any one put you in parallel columns."

Pauline felt herself turning pale. Her lips tightened, and for a moment she was conscious of a sort of blur in her brain. This girl . . . it was preposterous that she shouldn't understand! And always wanting reasons and explanations at a moment's notice! To be subjected, under one's own roof, to such a perpetual inquisition . . . There was nothing she disliked so much as questions to which she had not had time to prepare the answers.

"I don't think you always grasp things, Nona." The words were feeble, but they were the first that came.

"I'm afraid I don't, mother."

"Then, perhaps—I just suggest it—you oughtn't to be quite so ready to criticize. You seem to imagine there is a contradiction in my belonging to these two groups of . . . of thought . . ."

"They do seem to contradict each other."

"Not in reality. The principles are different, of course; but, you see, they are meant to apply to—to different categories of people. It's all a little difficult to explain to any one as young as you are . . . a girl naturally can't be expected to know . . ."

"Oh, what we girls don't know, mother!"

"Well, dear, I've always approved of outspokenness on such matters. The real nastiness is in covering things up. But all the same, age and experience *do* teach one . . . You children mustn't hope to get at all your elders' reasons . . ." That sounded firm yet friendly, and as she spoke she felt herself on safer ground. "I wish there were time to go into it all with you now; but if I'm to keep up with today's engagements, and crowd in a talk with Lita besides—Maisie! Will you call up Mrs. Jim?"

Maisie answered from the other room: "The delegation of the League For Discovering Genius is waiting downstairs, Mrs. Manford—"

"Oh, to be sure! This is rather an important movement, Nona; a new thing. I do believe there's something helpful to be done for genius. They're just organizing their first drive: I heard of it through that wonderful Mrs. Swoffer. You wouldn't care to come down and see the delegation with me? No . . . I sometimes think you'd be happier if you interested yourself a little more in other people . . . in all the big humanitarian movements that make one so proud to be an American. Don't you think it's glorious to belong to the only country where everybody is absolutely free, and yet we're all made to do exactly what is best for us? I say that somewhere in my speech . . . Well, I promise to have my talk with Lita before dinner; whatever happens, I'll squeeze her in. And you and Jim needn't be afraid of my saying anything to set her against us. Your father has impressed that on me already. After all, I've always preached the respect of every one's personality; only Lita must begin by respecting Jim's."

Fresh from a stimulating encounter with Mrs. Swoffer and the encouragers of genius, Pauline was able to face with a smiling composure her meeting with her daughter-in-law. Every contact with the humanitarian movements distinguishing her native country from the selfish *laissez faire* and cynical indifference of Europe filled her with a new optimism, and shed a reassuring light on all her private cares. America really seemed to have an immediate answer for everything, from the treatment of the mentally deficient to the elucidation of the profoundest religious mysteries. In such an atmosphere of universal simplification, how could one's personal problems not be solved? "The great thing is to believe that they *will* be," as Mrs. Swoffer said, à propos of the finding of funds for the new League For Discovering Genius. The remark was so stimulating to Pauline that she immediately drew a large cheque, and accepted the chairmanship of the committee; and it was on the favouring breeze of the League's applause that she sailed, at the tea-hour, into Lita's boudoir.

"It seems simpler just to ask her for a cup of tea—as if I were dropping in to see the baby," Pauline had reflected; and as Lita was not yet at home, there was time to turn her pretext into a reality. Upstairs, in the blue and silver nursery, her sharp eye detected many small negligences under the artistic surface: soiled towels lying about, a half-empty glass of milk with a drowned fly in it, dead and decaying flowers in the æsthetic flower-pots, and not a single ventilator open in the upper window-panes. She made a mental note of these items, but resolved not to touch on them in her talk with Lita. At Cedarledge, where the nurse would be under her own eye, nursery hygiene could be more tactfully imparted . . .

The black boudoir was still empty when Pauline returned to it, but she was armed with patience, and sat down to wait. The armchairs were much too low to be comfortable and she hated the semi-obscurity of the veiled lamps. How could one possibly occupy one's time in a pitch-dark room with seats that one had to sprawl in as if they were deck-chairs? She thought the room so ugly and dreary that she could hardly blame Lita for wanting to do it over. "I'll give her a cheque for it at once," she reflected indulgently. "All young people begin by making mistakes of this kind." She remembered with a little shiver the set of imitation tapestry armchairs that she had insisted on buying for her drawing-room when she had married Wyant. Perhaps it would be a good move to greet Lita with the offer of the cheque . . .

Somehow Lita's appearance, when she at length arrived, made the idea seem less happy. Lita had a way of looking as if she didn't much care what one did to please her; for a young woman who spent so much money she made very little effort to cajole it out of her benefactors. "Hullo," she said; "I didn't know you were here. Am I late, I wonder?"

Pauline greeted her with a light kiss. "How can you ever tell if you are? I don't believe there's a clock in the house."

"Yes, there is; in the nursery," said Lita.

"Well, my dear, that one's stopped," rejoined her mother-in-law, smiling.

"You've been seeing the boy? Oh, then you haven't missed me," Lita smiled back as she loosened her furs and tossed off her hat. She ran her hands through her goldfish-coloured hair, and flung herself down on a pile of cushions. "Tea's coming sooner or later, I suppose. Unless—a cocktail? No? Wouldn't you be more comfortable on the floor?" she suggested to her mother-in-law.

Every whalebone in Pauline's perfectly fitting elastic girdle contracted apprehensively. "Thank you; I'm very well here." She assumed as willowy an attitude as the treacherous seat permitted, and added: "I'm so glad to have the chance of a little talk. In this rushing life we all tend to lose sight of each other, don't we? But I hear about you so constantly from Nona that I feel we're very close even when we don't meet. Nona's devoted to you—we all are."

"That's awfully sweet of you," said Lita with her air of radiant indifference.

"Well, my dear, we hope you reciprocate," Pauline sparkled, stretching a maternal hand to the young shoulder at her knee.

Lita slanted her head backward with a slight laugh. Mrs. Manford had never thought her pretty, but today the mere freshness of her parted lips, their rosy lining, the unspoilt curves of her cheek and long white throat, stung the older woman to reluctant admiration.

"Am I expected to be devoted to you *all*?" Lita questioned.

"No, dear; only to Jim."

"Oh—" said Jim's wife, her smile contracting to a faint grimace.

Pauline leaned forward earnestly. "I won't pretend not to know something of what's been happening. I came here today to talk things over with you, quietly and affectionately—like an older sister. Try not to think of me as a mother-in-law!"

Lita's slim eyebrows went up ironically. "Oh, I'm not afraid of mothers-in-law; they're not as permanent as they used to be."

Pauline took a quick breath; she caught the impertinence under the banter, but she called her famous tact to the rescue.

"I'm glad you're not afraid of me, because I want you to tell me perfectly frankly what it is that's bothering you . . . you and Jim . . ."

"Nothing is bothering me particularly; but I suppose I'm bothering Jim," said Lita lightly.

"You're doing more than that, dear; you're making him desperately unhappy. This talk of wanting to separate—"

Lita rose on her elbow among the cushions, and levelled her eyes on Mrs. Manford. They looked as clear and shallow as the most expensive topazes.

"Separations are idiotic. What I want is a hundred per cent New York divorce. And he could let me have it just as easily . . ."

"Lita! You don't know how wretched it makes me to hear you say such things."

"Does it? Sorry! But it's Jim's own fault. Heaps of other girls would jump at him if he was free. And if I'm bored, what's the use of trying to keep me? What on earth can we do about it, either of us? You can't take out an insurance against boredom."

"But why should you be bored? With everything on earth . . ." Pauline waved a hand at the circumjacent luxuries.

"Well; that's it, I suppose. Always the same old everything!"

The mother-in-law softened her voice to murmur temptingly: "Of course, if it's this house you're tired of . . . Nona told me something about your wanting to redecorate some of the rooms; and I can understand, for instance, that this one . . ."

"Oh, this is the only one I don't utterly loathe. But I'm not divorcing Jim on account of the house," Lita answered, with a faint smile which seemed perverse to Pauline.

"Then what is the reason? I don't understand."

"I'm not much good at reasons. I want a new deal, that's all."

Pauline struggled against her rising indignation. To sit and hear this chit of a Cliffe girl speak of husband and home as if it were a matter of course to discard them like last year's fashions! But she was determined not to allow her feelings to master her.

"If you had only yourself to think of, what should you do?" she asked.

"Do? Be myself, I suppose! I can't be, here. I'm a sort of all-round fake. I—"

"We none of us want you to be that—Jim least of all. He wants you to feel perfectly free to express your personality."

"Here—in this house?" Her contemptuous gesture seemed to tumble it down like a pack of cards. "And looking at him across the dinner-table every night of my life?"

Pauline paused; then she said gently: "And can you face giving up your baby?"

"Baby? Why should I? You don't suppose I'd ever give up my baby?"

"Then you mean to ask Jim to give up his wife and child, and to assume all the blame as well?"

"Oh, dear, no. Where's the blame? I don't see any! All I want is a new deal," repeated Lita doggedly.

"My dear, I'm sure you don't know what you're saying. Your husband has the misfortune to be passionately in love with you. The divorce you talk of so lightly would nearly kill him. Even if he doesn't interest you any longer, he did once. Oughtn't you to take that into account?"

Lita seemed to ponder. Then she said: "But oughtn't he to take into account that he doesn't interest me any longer?"

Pauline made a final effort at self-control. "Yes, dear; if it's really so. But if he goes away for a time . . . You know he's to have a long holiday soon, and my husband has arranged to have him go down with Mr. Wyant to the island. All I ask is that you shouldn't decide anything till he comes back. See how you feel about him when he's been away for two or three weeks. Perhaps you've been too much together—perhaps New York has got too much on both your nerves. At any rate, do let him go off on his holiday without the heartbreak of feeling it's good-bye . . . My husband begs you to do this. You know he loves Jim as if he were his son—"

Lita was still leaning on her elbow. "Well—isn't he?" she said in her cool silvery voice, with innocently widened eyes.

For an instant the significance of the retort escaped Pauline. When it reached her she felt as humiliated as if she had been caught concealing a guilty secret. She opened her lips, but no sound came from them. She sat wordless, torn between the desire to box her daughter-in-law's ears, and to rush in tears from the house.

"Lita . . ." she gasped . . . "this insult . . ."

Lita sat up, her eyes full of a slightly humorous compunction. "Oh, no! An insult! Why? I've always thought it would be so wonderful to have a love-child. I supposed that was why you both worshipped Jim. And now he isn't even that!" She shrugged her slim shoulders, and held her hands out penitently. "I *am* sorry to have said the wrong thing—honestly I am! But it just shows we can never understand each other. For me the real wickedness is to go on living with a man you don't love. And now I've offended you by supposing you once felt in the same way yourself . . ."

Pauline slowly rose to her feet: she felt stiff and shrunken. "You haven't offended me—I'm not going to allow myself to be offended. I'd rather think we don't understand each other, as you say. But surely it's not too late to try. I don't want to discuss things with you; I don't want to nag or argue; I only want you to wait, to come with the baby to Cedarledge, and spend a few quiet weeks with us. Nona will be there, and my husband . . . there'll be no reproaches, no questions . . . but we'll do our best to make you happy . . ."

Lita, with her funny twisted smile, moved toward her mother-in-law. "Why, you're actually crying! I don't believe you do that often, do you?" She bent forward and put a light kiss on Pauline's shrinking cheek. "All right—I'll come to Cedarledge. I *am* dead-beat and fed-up, and I daresay it'll do me a lot of good to lie up for a while . . ."

Pauline, for a moment, made no answer: she merely laid her lips on the girl's cheek, a little timidly, as if it had been made of something excessively thin and brittle.

"We shall all be very glad," she said.

On the doorstep, in the motor, she continued to move in the resonance of the outrageous question: "*Well—isn't he?*" The violence of her recoil left her wondering what use there was in trying to patch up a bond founded on such a notion of marriage. Would not Jim, as his wife so lightly suggested, run more chance of happiness if he could choose again? Surely there must still be some decent right-minded girls brought up in the old way . . . like Aggie Heuston, say! But Pauline's imagination shivered away from that too . . . Perhaps, after all, her own principles were really obsolete to her children. Only, what was to take their place? Human nature had not changed as fast as social usage, and if Jim's wife left him nothing could prevent his suffering in the same old way.

It was all very baffling and disturbing, and Pauline did not feel as sure as she usually did that the question could be disposed of by ignoring it. Still, on the drive home her thoughts cleared as she reflected that she had gained her main point—for the time, at any rate. Manford had enjoined her not to estrange or frighten Lita, and the two women had parted with a kiss. Manford had insisted that Lita should be induced to take no final decision till after her stay at Cedarledge; and to this also she had acquiesced. Pauline, on looking back, began to be struck by the promptness of Lita's surrender, and correspondingly impressed by her own skill in manœuvring. There *was* something, after all, in these exercises of the will, these smiling resolves to ignore or dominate whatever was obstructive or unpleasant! She had gained with an almost startling ease the point which Jim and Manford and Nona had vainly struggled for. And perhaps Lita's horrid insinuation had not been a voluntary impertinence, but merely the unconscious avowal of new standards. The young people nowadays, for all their long words and scientific realism, were really more like children than ever . . .

In Pauline's boudoir, Nona, curled up on the hearth, her chin in her hands, raised her head at her mother's approach. To Pauline the knowledge that she was awaited, and that she brought with her the secret of defeat or victory, gave back the healing sense of authority.

"It's all right, darling," she announced; "just a little summer shower; I always told you there was nothing to worry about." And she added with a smile: "You see, Nona, some people *do* still listen when your old mother talks to them."

Chapter XIX

I F only Aggie Heuston had changed those sour-apple curtains in the front drawing-room, Nona thought—if she
had substituted deep upholstered armchairs for the hostile gilt
seats, and put books in the marqueterie cabinets in place of blue
china dogs and Dresden shepherdesses, everything in three lives
might have been different . . .

But Aggie had probably never noticed the colour of the curtains or the angularity of the furniture. She had certainly never
missed the books. She had accepted the house as it came to her
from her parents, who in turn had taken it over, in all its dreary
frivolity, from their father and mother. It embodied the New
York luxury of the 'seventies in every ponderous detail, from the
huge cabbage roses of the Aubusson carpet to the triple layer of
curtains designed to protect the aristocracy of the brown-stone
age from the plebeian intrusion of light and air.

"Funny," Nona thought again—"that all this ugliness should
prick me like nettles, and matter no more to Aggie than if it were
in the next street. She's a saint, I know. But what I want to find
is a saint who hates ugly furniture, and yet lives among it with
a smile. What's the merit, if you never see it?" She addressed
herself to a closer inspection of one of the cabinets, in which
Aggie's filial piety had preserved her mother's velvet and silver
spectacle-case, and her father's ivory opera-glasses, in combination with an alabaster Leaning Tower and a miniature copy of
Carlo Dolci's Magdalen.

Queer dead rubbish—but queerer still that, at that moment
and in that house, Nona's uncanny detachment should permit
her to smile at it! Where indeed—she wondered again—did one's
own personality end, and that of others, of people, landscapes,
chairs or spectacle-cases, begin? Ever since she had received,
the night before, Aggie's stiff and agonized little note, which
might have been composed by a child with a tooth-ache, Nona
had been apprehensively asking herself if her personality didn't
even include certain shreds and fibres of Aggie. It was all such
an inextricable tangle . . .

Here she came. Nona heard the dry click of her steps on the stairs and across the polished bareness of the hall. She had written: "If you could make it perfectly convenient to call—" Aggie's nearest approach to a friendly summons! And as she opened the door, and advanced over the cabbage roses, Nona saw that her narrow face, with the eyes too close together, and the large pale pink mouth with straight edges, was sharpened by a new distress.

"It's very kind of you to come, Nona—" she began in her clear painstaking voice.

"Oh, nonsense, Aggie! Do drop all that. Of course I know what it's about."

Aggie turned noticeably paler; but her training as a hostess prevailing over her emotion, she pushed forward a gilt chair. "Do sit down." She placed herself in an adjoining sofa corner. Overhead, Aggie's grandmother, in a voluted gilt frame, held a Brussels lace handkerchief in her hand, and leaned one ruffled elbow on a velvet table-cover fringed with knobby tassels.

"You say you know—" Aggie began.

"Of course."

"Stanley—he's told you?"

Nona's nerves were beginning to jump and squirm like a bundle of young vipers. Was she going to be able to stand much more of these paralyzing preliminaries?

"Oh, yes: he's told me."

Aggie dropped her lids and stared down at her narrow white hands. Then a premonitory twitch ran along her lips and drew her forehead into little wrinkles of perplexity.

"I don't want you to think I've any cause of complaint against Stanley—none whatever. There has never been a single unkind word . . . We've always lived together on the most perfect terms . . ."

Feeling that some form of response was required of her, Nona emitted a vague murmur.

"Only now—he's—he's left me," Aggie concluded, the words wrung out of her in laboured syllables. She raised one hand and smoothed back a flat strand of hair which had strayed across her forehead.

Nona was silent. She sat with her eyes fixed on that small twitching mask—real face it could hardly be called, since it had probably never before been suffered to express any emotion that was radically and peculiarly Aggie's.

"You knew that too?" Aggie continued, in a studiously objective tone.

Nona made a sign of assent.

"He has nothing to reproach me with—nothing whatever. He expressly told me so."

"Yes; I know. That's the worst of it."

"The worst of it?"

"Why, if he had, you might have had a good row that would have cleared the air."

Suddenly Nona felt Aggie's eyes fixed on her with a hungry penetrating stare. "Did you and he use to have good rows, as you call it?"

"Oh, by the hour—whenever we met!" Nona, for the life of her, could not subdue the mocking triumph in her voice.

Aggie's lips narrowed. "You've been very great friends, I know; he's often told me so. But if you were always quarrelling how could you continue to respect each other?"

"I don't know that we did. At any rate, there was no time to think about it; because there was always the making-up, you see."

"The making-up?"

"Aggie," Nona burst out abruptly, "have you never known what it was to have a man give you a jolly good hug, and feel full enough of happiness to scent a whole garden with it?"

Aggie lifted her lids on a glance which was almost one of terror. The image Nona had used seemed to convey nothing to her, but the question evidently struck her with a deadly force.

"A man—what man?"

Nona laughed. "Well, for the sake of argument—Stanley!"

"I can't imagine why you ask such queer questions, Nona. How could we make up when we never quarrelled?"

"Is it queer to ask you if you ever loved your husband?"

"It's queer of you to ask it," said the wife simply. Nona's swift retort died unspoken, and she felt one of her slow secret blushes creeping up to the roots of her hair.

"I'm sorry, Aggie. I'm horribly nervous—and I suppose you are. Hadn't we better start fresh? What was it you wanted to see me about?"

Aggie was silent for a moment, as if gathering up all her strength; then she answered: "To tell you that if he wants to marry you I shan't oppose a divorce any longer."

"Aggie!"

The two sat silent, opposite each other, as if they had reached a point beyond which words could not carry their communion. Nona's mind, racing forward, touched the extreme limit of human bliss, and then crawled back from it bowed and broken-winged.

"But *only* on that condition," Aggie began again, with deliberate emphasis.

"On condition—that he marries me?"

Aggie made a motion of assent. "I have a right to impose my conditions. And what I want is"—she faltered suddenly—"what I want is that you should save him from Cleo Merrick . . ." Her level voice broke and two tears forced their way through her lashes and fell slowly down her cheeks.

"Save him from Cleo Merrick?" Nona fancied she heard herself laugh. Her thoughts seemed to drag after her words as if she were labouring up hill through a ploughed field. "Isn't it rather late in the day to make that attempt? You say he's already gone off with her."

"He's joined her somewhere—I don't know where. He wrote from his club before leaving. But I know they don't sail till the day after tomorrow; and you must get him back, Nona, you must save him. It's too awful. He can't marry her; she has a husband somewhere who refuses to divorce her."

"Like you and Stanley!"

Aggie drew back as if she had been struck. "Oh, no, no!" She looked despairingly at Nona. "When I tell you I don't refuse now . . ."

"Well, perhaps Cleo Merrick's husband may not, either."

"It's different. He's a Catholic, and his church won't let him divorce. And it can't be annulled. Stanley's just going to live with her . . . openly . . . and she'll go everywhere with him . . . exactly as if they were husband and wife . . . and everybody will know that they're not."

Nona sat silent, considering with set lips and ironic mind the picture thus pitilessly evoked. "Well, if she loves him . . ."

"Loves him? A woman like that!"

"She's been willing to make a sacrifice for him, at any rate. That's where she has a pull over both of us."

"But don't you see how awful it is for them to be living together in that way?"

"I see it's the best thing that could happen to Stanley to have found a woman plucky enough to give him the thing he wanted—the thing you and I both refused him."

She saw Aggie's lifeless cheek redden. "I don't know what you mean by . . . refusing . . ."

"I mean his happiness—that's all! You refused to divorce him, didn't you? And I refused to do—what Cleo Merrick's doing. And here we both are, sitting on the ruins; and that's the end of it, as far as you and I are concerned."

"But it's not the end—it's not too late. I tell you it's not too late! He'll leave her even now if you ask him to . . . I know he will!"

Nona stood up with a dry laugh. "Thank you, Aggie. Perhaps he would—only we shall never find out."

"Never find out? When I keep telling you—"

"Because even if I've been a coward that's no reason why I should be a cad." Nona was buttoning her coat and clasping her fur about her neck with quick precise movements, as if wrapping herself close against the treacherous sweetness that was beginning to creep into her veins. Suddenly she felt she could not remain a moment longer in that stifling room, face to face with that stifling misery.

"The better woman's got him—let her keep him," she said.

She put out her hand, and for a moment Aggie's cold damp fingers lay in hers. Then they were pulled away, and Aggie caught Nona by the sleeve. "But Nona, listen! I don't understand you. Isn't it what you've always wanted?"

"Oh, more than anything in life!" the girl cried, turning breathlessly away.

The outer door swung shut on her, and on the steps she stood still and looked back at the ruins on which she had pictured herself sitting with Aggie Heuston.

"I do believe," she murmured to herself, "I know most of the new ways of being rotten; I only wish I was sure I knew the best new way of being decent . . ."

BOOK III

Chapter XX

A T the gates of Cedarledge Pauline lifted her head from a
last hurried study of the letters and papers Maisie Bruss
had thrust into the motor.

The departure from town had been tumultuous. Up to the
last minute there had been the usual rush and trepidation,
Maisie hanging on the footboard, Powder and the maid hurrying down with final messages and recommendations.

"Here's another batch of bills passed by the architect, Mrs.
Manford. And he asks if you'd mind—"

"Yes, yes; draw another cheque for five thousand, Maisie, and
send it to me with the others to be signed."

"And the estimates for the new orchid-house. The contractor
says building-materials are going up again next week, and he
can't guarantee, unless you telephone at once—"

"Has madame the jewel-box? I put it under the rug myself,
with madame's motor-bag."

"Thank you, Cécile. Yes, it's here."

"And is the Maison Herminie to deliver the green and gold
teagown here or—"

"Here are the proofs of the Birth Control speech, Mrs. Manford. If you could just glance over them in the motor, and let
me have them back tonight—"

"The Marchesa, madam, has called up to ask if you and Mr.
Manford can receive her at Cedarledge for the next week-end—"

"No, Powder; say no. I'm dreadfully sorry . . ."

"Very good, madam. I understand it was to bring a favourable answer from the Cardinal—"

"Oh; very well. I'll see. I'll telephone from Cedarledge."

"Please, madam, Mr. Wyant's just telephoned—"

"Mr. Wyant, Powder?"

"Mr. Arthur Wyant, madam. To ask—"

"But Mr. Wyant and Mr. James were to have started for Georgia last night."

"Yes, madam; but Mr. James was detained by business, and now Mr. Arthur Wyant asks if you'll please ring up before they leave tonight."

"Very well. (What can have happened, Nona? You don't know?) Say I've started for Cedarledge, Powder; I'll ring up from there. Yes; that's all."

"Mrs. Manford, wait! Here are two more telegrams, and a special—"

"Take care, Maisie; you'll slip and break your leg . . ."

"Yes; but Mrs. Manford! The special is from Mrs. Swoffer. She says the committee have just discovered a new genius, and they're calling an emergency meeting for tomorrow afternoon at three, and couldn't you possibly—"

"No, no, Maisie—I can't! Say I've *left*—"

The waves of agitation were slow in subsiding. A glimpse, down a side street, of the Marchesa's cheap boarding-house-hotel, revived them; and so did the flash past the inscrutable "Dawnside," aloof on its height above the Hudson. But as the motor slid over the wide suburban Boulevards, and out into the budding country, with the roar and menace of the city fading harmlessly away on the horizon, Pauline's serenity gradually stole back.

Nona, at her side, sat silent; and the mother was grateful for that silence. She had noticed that the girl had looked pale and drawn for the last fortnight; but that was just another proof of how much they all needed the quiet of Cedarledge.

"You don't know why Jim and his father have put off starting, Nona?"

"No idea, mother. Probably business of Jim's, as Powder said."

"Do you know why his father wants to telephone me?"

"Not a bit. Probably it's not important. I'll call up this evening."

"Oh, if you would, dear! I'm really tired."

There was a pause, and then Nona questioned: "Have you noticed Maisie, mother? She's pretty tired too."

"Yes; poor Maisie! Preparing Cedarledge has been rather a rush for her, I'm afraid—"

"It's not only that. She's just been told that her mother has a cancer."

"Oh, poor child! How dreadful! She never said a word to me—"

"No, she wouldn't."

"But, Nona, have you told her to see Disterman *at once*? Perhaps an immediate operation . . . you must call her up as soon as we arrive. Tell her, of course, that I'll bear all the expenses—"

After that they both relapsed into silence.

These domestic tragedies happened now and then. One would have given the world to avert them; but when one couldn't one was always ready to foot the bill . . . Pauline wished that she had known . . . had had time to say a kindly word to poor Maisie . . . Perhaps she would have to give her a week off; or at least a couple of days, while she settled her mother in the hospital. At least, if Disterman advised an operation . . .

It was dreadful, how rushed one always was. Pauline would have liked to go and see poor Mrs. Bruss herself. But there were Dexter and Lita and the baby all arriving the day after tomorrow, and only just time to put the last touches to Cedarledge before they came. And Pauline herself was desperately tired, though she had taken a "triple treatment" from Alvah Loft ($100) that very morning.

She always meant to be kind to every one dependent on her; it was only time that lacked—always time! Dependents and all, they were swept away with her in the same ceaseless rush. When now and then one of them dropped by the way she was sorry, and sent back first aid, and did all she could; but the rush never stopped; it couldn't stop; when one did a kindness one could only fling it at its object and whirl by.

The blessèd peace of the country! Pauline drew a deep breath of content. Never before had she approached Cedarledge with so complete a sense of possessorship. The place was really of her own making, for though the house had been built and the grounds laid out years before she had acquired the property, she had stamped her will and her wealth on every feature. Pauline was persuaded that she was fond of the country—but what she was really fond of was doing things to the country, and owning, with this object, as many acres of it as possible. And so it had come about that every year the Cedarledge estate had pushed the encircling landscape farther back, and substituted for its miles of golden-rod and birch and maple more acres of glossy lawn, and more specimen limes and oaks and cut-leaved beeches, domed over more and more windings of expensive shrubbery.

From the farthest gate it was now a drive of two miles to the house, and Pauline found even this too short for her minutely detailed appreciation of what lay between her and her threshold. In the village, the glint of the gilt weathercock on the new half-timbered engine-house; under a rich slope of pasture-land the recently enlarged dairy-farm; then woods of hemlock and dogwood; acres of rhododendron, azalea and mountain laurel acclimatized about a hidden lake; a glimpse of Japanese water-gardens fringed with cherry bloom and catkins; open lawns, spreading trees, the long brick house-front and its terraces, and through a sculptured archway the Dutch garden with dwarf topiary work and endless files of bulbs about the commander's *baton* of a stately sundial.

To Pauline each tree, shrub, water-course, herbaceous border, meant not only itself, but the surveying of grades, transporting of soil, tunnelling for drainage, conducting of water, the business correspondence and paying of bills, which had preceded its existence; and she would have cared for it far less—perhaps not at all—had it sprung into being unassisted, like the random shadbushes and wild cherry trees beyond the gates.

The faint spring loveliness reached her somehow, in long washes of pale green, and the blurred mauve of budding vegetation; but her eyes could not linger on any particular beauty without its dissolving into soil, manure, nurserymen's catalogues, and bills again—bills. It had all cost a terrible lot of money; but she was proud of that too—to her it was part of the beauty, part of the exquisite order and suitability which reigned as much in the simulated wildness of the rhododendron glen as in the geometrical lines of the Dutch garden.

"Seventy-five thousand bulbs this year!" she thought, as the motor swept by the sculptured gateway, just giving and withdrawing a flash of turf sheeted with amber and lilac, in a setting of twisted and scalloped evergreens.

Twenty-five thousand more bulbs than last year . . . that was how she liked it to be. It was exhilarating to spend more money each year, to be always enlarging and improving, in small ways as well as great, to face unexpected demands with promptness and energy, beat down exorbitant charges, struggle through difficult moments, and come out at the end of the year tired but victorious, with improvements made, bills paid, and a reassuring balance in the bank. To Pauline that was "life."

And how her expenditure at Cedarledge was justifying itself! Her husband, drawn by its fresh loveliness, had voluntarily given up his annual trip to California, the excitement of tarpon-fishing, the independence of bachelorhood—all to spend a quiet month in the country with his wife and children. Pauline felt that even the twenty-five thousand additional bulbs had had a part in shaping his decision. And what would he say when he saw the new bathrooms, assisted at the village fire-drill, and plunged into the artificially warmed waters of the new swimming pool? A mist of happiness rose to her eyes as she looked out on the spring-misted landscape.

Nona had not followed her mother into the house. Her dogs at her heels, she plunged down hill to the woods and lake. She knew nothing of what Cedarledge had cost, but little of the labour of its making. It was simply the world of her childhood, and she could see it from no other angle, nor imagine it as ever having been different. To her it had always worn the same enchantment, stretched to the same remote distances. At nineteen it was almost the last illusion she had left.

In the path by the lake she felt herself drawn back under the old spell. Those budding branches, the smell of black peaty soil quivering with life, the woodlands faintly starred with dogwood, all were the setting of childish adventures, old games with Jim, Indian camps on the willow-fringed island, and innocent descents among the rhododendrons to boat or bathe by moonlight.

The old skiff had escaped Mrs. Manford's annual "doing-up" and still leaked through the same rusty seams. Pushing out upon the lake, Nona leaned on the oars and let the great mockery of the spring dilate her heart . . .

Manford questioned: "All right, eh? Warm enough? Not going too fast? The air's still sharp up here in the hills"; and

Lita settled down beside him into one of the deep silences that enfolded her as softly as her furs. By turning his head a little he could just see the tip of her nose and the curve of her upper lip between hat-brim and silver fox; and the sense of her, so close and so still, sunk in that warm animal hush which he always found so restful, dispelled his last uneasiness, and made her presence at his side seem as safe and natural as his own daughter's.

"Just as well you sent the boy by train, though—I foresaw I'd get off too late to suit the young gentleman's hours."

She curled down more deeply at his side, with a contented laugh.

Manford, intent on the steering wheel, restrained the impulse to lay a hand over hers, and kept his profile steadily turned to her. It was wonderful, how successfully his plan was working out . . . how reasonable she'd been about it in the end. Poor child! No doubt she would always be reasonable with people who knew how to treat her. And he flattered himself that he did. It hadn't been easy, just at first—but now he'd struck the right note and meant to hold it. Not paternal, exactly: she would have been the first to laugh at anything as old-fashioned as that. Heavy fathers had gone out with the rest of the *tremolo* effects. No; but elder brotherly. That was it. The same free and friendly relation which existed, say, between Jim and Nona. Why, he had actually tried chaffing Lita, and she hadn't minded—he had made fun of that ridiculous Ardwin, and she had just laughed and shrugged. That little shrug—when her white shoulder, as the dress slipped from it, seemed to be pushing up into a wing! There was something birdlike and floating in all her motions . . . Poor child, poor little girl . . . He really felt like her elder brother; and his looking-glass told him that he didn't look much too old for the part . . .

The sense of having just grazed something dark and lurid, which had threatened to submerge them, gave him an added feeling of security, a holiday feeling, as if life stretched before him as safe and open as his coming fortnight at Cedarledge. How glad he was that he had given his tarpon-fishing, managed to pack Jim and Wyant off to Georgia, and secured this peaceful interval in which to look about him and take stock of things before the grind began again!

The day before yesterday—just after Pauline's departure—it had seemed as if all their plans would be wrecked by one of Wyant's fits of crankiness. Wyant always enjoyed changing his mind after every one else's was made up; and at the last moment he had telephoned to say that he wasn't well enough to go south. He had rung up Pauline first, and being told that she had left had communicated with Jim; and Jim, distracted, had appealed to Manford. It was one of his father's usual attacks of "nervousness"; cousin Eleanor had seen it coming, and tried to cut down the whiskies-and-sodas; finally Jim begged Manford to drop in and reason with his predecessor.

These visits always produced a profound impression on Wyant; Manford himself, for all his professional acuteness, couldn't quite measure the degree or guess the nature of the effect, but he felt his power, and preserved it by seeing Wyant as seldom as possible. This time, however, it seemed as if things might not go as smoothly as usual. Wyant, who looked gaunt and excited, tried to carry off the encounter with the jauntiness he always assumed in Manford's presence. "My dear fellow! Sit down, do. Cigar? Always delighted to see my successor. Any little hints I can give about the management of the concern—"

It was his usual note, but exaggerated, over-emphasized, lacking the Wyant touch—and he had gone on: "Though why the man who has failed should offer advice to the man who has succeeded, I don't know. Well, in this case it's about Jim . . . Yes, you're as fond of Jim as I am, I know . . . Still, he's *my* son, eh? Well, I'm not satisfied that it's a good thing to take him away from his wife at this particular moment. Know I'm old-fashioned, of course . . . all the musty old traditions have been superseded. You and your set have seen to that—introduced the breezy code of the prairies . . . But my son's my son; he wasn't brought up in the new way, and, damn it all, Manford, you understand; well, no—I suppose there are some things you never *will* understand, no matter how devilish clever you are, and how many millions you've made."

The apple-cart had been near upsetting; but if Manford didn't understand poor Wyant's social code he did know how to keep his temper when it was worth while, and how to talk to a weak over-excited man who had been drinking too hard, and who took no exercise.

"Worried about Jim, eh? Yes—I don't wonder. I am too. Fact is, Jim's worked himself to a standstill, and I feel partly responsible for it, for I put him onto that job at the bank, and he's been doing it too well—overdoing it. That's the whole trouble, and that's why I feel responsible to you all for getting him away as soon as possible, and letting him have a complete holiday . . . Jim's young—a fortnight off will straighten him out. But you're the only person who can get him away from his wife and baby, and wherever Lita is there'll be jazz and nonsense, and bills and bothers; that's why his mother and I have offered to take the lady on for a while, and give him his chance. As man to man, Wyant, I think we two ought to stand together and see this thing through. If we do, I guarantee everything will come out right. Do you good too—being off like that with your boy, in a good climate, loafing on the beach and watching Jim recuperate. Wish I could run down and join you—and I don't say I won't make a dash for it, just for a week-end, if I can break away from the family. A-1 fishing at the island—and I know you used to be a great fisherman. As for Lita, she'll be safe enough with Pauline and Nona."

The trick was done.

But why think of it as a trick, when at the time he had meant every word he spoke? Jim *was* dead-beat—*did* need a change— and yet could only have been got away on the pretext of having to take his father south. Queer, how in some inner fold of one's conscience a collection of truths could suddenly seem to look like a tissue of lies! . . . Lord, but what morbid rubbish! Manford was on his honour to make the whole thing turn out as true as it sounded, and he was going to. And there was an end of it. And here was Cedarledge. The drive hadn't lasted a minute . . .

How lovely the place looked in the twilight, a haze of tender tints melting into shadow, the long dark house-front already gemmed with orange panes!

"You'll like it, won't you, Lita?" A purr of content at his elbow.

If only Pauline would have the sense to leave him alone, let him enjoy it all in Lita's lazy inarticulate way, not cram him with statistics and achievements, with expenditures and results. He was so tired of her perpetual stock-taking, her perpetual rendering of accounts and reckoning up of interest. He admired it all, of course—he admired Pauline herself more than ever. But he longed to let himself sink into the spring sweetness as a man might sink on a woman's breast, and just feel her quiet hands in his hair.

"There's the dogwood! Look! Never seen it in bloom here before, have you? It's one of our sights." He had counted a good deal on the effect of the dogwood. "Well, here we are—Jove, but it's good to be here! Why, child, I believe you've been asleep . . ." He lifted her, still half-drowsing, from the motor—

And now, the illuminated threshold, Powder, the footmen, the inevitable stack of letters—and Pauline.

But outside the spring dusk was secretly weaving its velvet spell. He said to himself: "Shouldn't wonder if I slept ten hours at a stretch tonight."

Chapter XXI

THE last day before her husband's arrival had been exhausting to Pauline; but she could not deny that the results were worth the effort. When had she ever before heard Dexter say on such a full note of satisfaction: "Jove, but it's good to be back! What have you done to make the place look so jolly?", or seen his smiling glance travel so observantly about the big hall with its lamps and flowers and blazing hearth? "Well, Lita, this is better than town, eh? You didn't know what a good place Cedarledge could be! Don't rush off upstairs—they're bringing the baby down. Come over to the fire and warm up; it's nipping here in the hills. Hullo, Nona, you quiet mouse—didn't even see you, curled up there in your corner . . ."

Yes; the arrival had been perfect. Even Lita's kiss had seemed spontaneous. And Dexter had praised everything, noticed all the improvements; had voluntarily announced that he meant to inspect the new heating system and the model chicken hatchery the next morning. "Wonderful, what a way you have of making things a hundred per cent better when they seemed all right before! I suppose even the eggs at breakfast tomorrow will be twice their normal size."

One such comment paid his wife for all she had done, and roused her inventive faculty to fresh endeavour. Wasn't there something else she could devise to provoke his praise? And the beauty of it was that it all looked as if it had been done so easily. The casual observer would never have suspected that the simple life at Cedarledge gave its smiling organizer more trouble than a season of New York balls.

That also was part of Pauline's satisfaction. She even succeeded in persuading herself, as she passed through the hall with its piled-up golf clubs and tennis rackets, its motor coats and capes and scarves stacked on the long table, and the muddy terriers comfortably rolled up on chintz-cushioned settles, that it was really all as primitive and impromptu as it looked, and that she herself had always shared her husband's passion for stamping about in the mud in tweed and homespun.

"One of these days," she thought, "we'll give up New York altogether, and live here all the year round, like an old-fashioned couple, and Dexter can farm while I run the poultry-yard and dairy." Instantly her practical imagination outlined the plan of an up-to-date chicken-farm on a big scale, and calculated the revenues to be drawn from really scientific methods of cheese and butter-making. Spring broilers, she knew, were in ever-increasing demand, and there was a great call in restaurants and hotels for the little foreign-looking cream-cheeses in silver paper . . .

"The Marchesa has rung up again, madam," Powder reminded her, the second morning at breakfast. Everybody came down to breakfast at Cedarledge; it was part of the simple life. But it generally ended in Pauline's throning alone behind the tea-urn, for her husband and daughter revelled in unpunctuality when they were on a holiday, and Lita's inability to appear before luncheon was tacitly taken for granted.

"The Marchesa?" Pauline was roused from the placid enjoyment of her new-laid egg and dewy butter. Why was it that one could never completely protect one's self against bores and bothers? They had done everything they could for Amalasuntha, and were now discovering that gratitude may take more troublesome forms than neglect.

"The Marchesa would like to consult you about the date of the Cardinal's reception."

Ah, then it was a fact—it was really settled! A glow of satisfaction swept away Pauline's indifference, and her sense of fairness obliged her to admit that, for such a service, Amalasuntha had a right to a Sunday at Cedarledge. "It will bore her to death to spend two days here alone with the family; but she will like to be invited, and in the course of time she'll imagine it was a big house-party," Pauline reflected.

"Very well, Powder. Please telephone that I shall expect the Marchesa next Saturday."

That gave them, at any rate, the inside of a week to themselves. After six days alone with his women-kind perhaps even Dexter would not be sorry for a little society; and if so, Pauline, with the Marchesa as a bait, could easily drum up a country-neighbour dinner. The Toys, she happened to remember, were to be at the Greystock Country Club over Easter. She smiled at the thought that this might have made Dexter decide to give up California for Cedarledge. She was not afraid of Mrs. Toy any longer, and even recognized that her presence in the neighbourhood might be useful. Pauline could never wholly believe—at least not for many hours together—that people could be happy in the country without all sorts of social alleviations; and six days of quiet seemed to her measurable only in terms of prehistoric eras. When had her mind ever had such a perspective to range over? Knowing it could be shortened at will she sighed contentedly, and decided to devote the morning to the study of a new refrigerating system she had recently seen advertised.

Dexter had not yet made his tour of inspection with her; but that was hardly surprising. The first morning he had slept late, and lounged about on the terrace in the balmy sunshine. In the afternoon they had all motored to Greystock for a round of golf; and today, on coming down to breakfast, Pauline had learned with surprise that her husband, Nona and Lita were already off for an early canter, leaving word that they would breakfast on the road. She did not know whether to marvel most at Lita's having been coaxed out of bed before breakfast, or at Dexter's taking to the saddle after so many years. Certainly the Cedarledge air was wonderfully bracing and rejuvenating; she herself was feeling its effects. And though she would have liked to show her husband all the improvements she felt no impatience, but only a quiet satisfaction in the success of her plans. If they could give Jim back a contented Lita the object of their holiday would be attained; and in a glow of optimism she sat down at her writing-table and dashed off a joyful letter to her son.

"Dexter is wonderful; he has already coaxed Lita out for a ride before breakfast . . . Isn't that a triumph? When you get back you won't know her . . . I shouldn't have a worry left if I didn't think Nona is looking too pale and drawn. I shall persuade her to take a course of Inspirational treatment as soon as we get back to town. By the way," her pen ran on, "have you heard the news about Stan Heuston? People say he's gone to Europe with that dreadful Merrick woman, and that now Aggie will really have to divorce him . . .Nona, who has always been such a friend of Stan's, has of course heard the report, but doesn't seem to know any more than the rest of us . . ."

Nothing amused Arthur Wyant more than to be supplied with such tit-bits of scandal before they became common property. Pauline couldn't help feeling that father and son must find the evenings long in their island bungalow; and in the overflow of her own satisfaction she wanted to do what she could to cheer them.

In spite of her manifold occupations the day seemed long. She had visited the baby, seen the cook, consulted with Powder about the working of the new burglar-alarm, gone over the gardens, catalogues in hand, with the head-gardener, walked down to the dairy and the poultry yard to say that Mr. Manford would certainly inspect them both the next day, and called up Maisie Bruss to ask news of her mother, and tell her to prepare a careful list for the reception to the Cardinal; yet an astonishing amount of time still remained. It was delightful to be in the country, to study the working-out of her improvements, and do her daily exercises with windows open on the fresh hill breezes; but already her real self was projected forward into complicated plans for the Cardinal's entertainment. She wondered if it would not be wise to run up to town the next morning and consult Amalasuntha; and reluctantly decided that a talk on the telephone would do.

The talk was long, and on the whole satisfactory; but if Maisie had been within reach the arrangements for the party would have made more progress. It was most unlucky that the doctors thought Maisie ought to stay with her mother till the latter could get a private room at the hospital. ("A *room*, of course, Maisie dear; I won't have her in a ward. Not for the world! Just put it down on your account, please. So glad to do it!") She really was glad to do all she could; but it was unfortunate (and no one would feel it more than Maisie) that Mrs. Bruss should have been taken ill just then. To fill the time, Pauline decided to go for a walk with the dogs.

When she returned she found Nona, still in her riding-habit, settled in a sofa-corner in the library, and deep in a book.

"Why, child, where did you drop from? I didn't know you were back."

"The others are not. Lita suddenly took it into her head that it would be fun to motor over to Greenwich and dine at the Country Club, and so father got a motor at Greystock and telephoned for one of the grooms to fetch the horses. It sounded rather jolly, but I was tired, so I came home. It's nearly full moon, and they'll have a glorious run back." Nona smiled up at her mother, as if to say that the moon made all the difference.

"Oh, but that means dancing, and getting home at all hours! And I promised Jim to see that Lita kept quiet, and went to bed early. What's the use of our having persuaded her to come here? Your father ought to have refused to go."

"If he had, there were plenty of people lunching at Greystock who would have taken her on. You know—the cocktail crowd. That's why father sacrificed himself."

Pauline reflected. "I see. Your father always has to sacrifice himself. I suppose there's no use trying to make Lita listen to reason."

"Not unless one humours her a little. Father sees that. We mustn't let her get bored here—she won't stay if we do."

Pauline felt a sudden weariness in all her bones. It was as if the laboriously built-up edifice of the simple life at Cedarledge had already crumbled into dust at a kick of Lita's little foot. The engine-house, the poultry yard, the new burglar-alarm and the heating of the swimming pool—when would Dexter ever have time to inspect and admire them, if he was to waste his precious holiday in scouring the country after Lita?

"Then I suppose you and I dine alone," Pauline said, turning a pinched little smile on her daughter.

Chapter XXII

WHAT a time of year it was—the freed earth suddenly breaking into life from every frozen seam! Manford wondered if he had ever before had time to feel the impetuous loveliness of the American spring.

In spite of his drive home in the small hours he had started out early the next morning for a long tramp. Sleep—how could a man sleep with that April moonlight in his veins? The moon that was everywhere—caught in pearly puffs on the shadbush branches, scattered in ivory drifts of wild plum bloom, tipping the grasses of the wayside with pale pencillings, sheeting the recesses of the woodland with pools of icy silver. A freezing burning magic, into which a man plunged, and came out cold and aglow, to find everything about him as unreal and incredible as himself . . .

After the blatant club restaurant, noise, jazz, revolving couples, Japanese lanterns, screaming laughter, tumultuous good-byes, this white silence, the long road unwinding and twisting itself up again, blind faces of shuttered farmhouses, black forests, misty lakes—a cut through a world in sleep, all dumb and moon-bemused . . .

The contrast was beautiful, intolerable . . .

Sleep? He hadn't even gone to bed. Just plunged into a bath, and stretched out on his lounge to see the dawn come. A mysterious sight that, too; the cold fingers of the light remaking a new world, while men slept, unheeding, and imagined they would wake to some familiar yesterday. Fools!

He breakfasted—ravenously—before his wife was down, and swung off with a couple of dogs on a long tramp, he didn't care where.

Even the daylight world seemed unimaginably strange: as if he had never really looked at it before. He walked on slowly for three or four miles, vaguely directing himself toward Greystock. His long tramps as a boy, in his farming days, had given him the habit of deliberate steady walking, and the unwonted movement refreshed rather than tired him—or at least, while it tired his muscles, it seemed to invigorate his brain. Excited? No—just pleasantly stimulated . . .

He stretched himself out under a walnut tree on a sunny slope, lit his pipe and gazed abroad over fields and woods. All the land was hazy with incipient life. The dogs hunted and burrowed, and then came back to doze at his feet with pleasant dreamings. The sun on his face felt warm and human, and gradually life began to settle back into its old ruts—a comfortable routine, diversified by pleasant episodes. Could it ever be more, to a man past fifty?

But after a while a chill sank on his spirit. He began to feel cold and hungry, and set out to walk again.

Presently he found it was half-past eleven—time to be heading for home. Home; and the lunch-table; Pauline; and Nona; and Lita. Oh, God, no—not yet . . . He trudged on, slowly and sullenly, deciding to pick up a mouthful of lunch somewhere by the way.

At a turn of the road he caught sight of a woman's figure strolling across a green slope above him. Strong and erect in her trim golfing skirt, she came down in his direction swinging a club in her hand. Why, sure enough, he was actually on the edge of the Greystock course! The woman was alone, without companions or caddies—going around for a trial spin, or perhaps simply taking a stroll, as he was, drinking in the intoxicating air . . .

"Hul*lo*!" she called, and he found himself advancing toward Gladys Toy.

Was this active erect woman in her nut-brown sweater and plaited skirt the same as the bejewelled and redundant beauty of so many wearisome dinners? Something of his old interest—the short-lived fancy of a week or two—revived in him as she swung along, treading firmly but lightly on her broad easy shoes.

"Hul*lo*!" he responded. "Didn't know you were here."

"I wasn't. I only came last night. Isn't it glorious?" Even her slow-dripping voice moved faster and had a livelier ring. Decidedly, he admired a well-made woman, a woman with curves and volume—all the more after the stripped skeletons he had dined among the night before. Mrs. Toy had height enough to carry off her pounds, and didn't look ashamed of them, either.

"Glorious? Yes, *you* are!" he said.

"Oh, *me?*"

"What else did you mean, then?"

"Don't be silly! How did you get here?"

"On my feet."

"Gracious! From Cedarledge? You must be dead."

"Don't you believe it. I walked over to lunch with you."

"You've just said you didn't know I was here."

"You mustn't believe everything I say."

"All right. Then I won't believe you walked over to lunch with me."

"Will you believe me when I tell you you're awfully beautiful?"

"Yes!" she challenged him.

"And that I want to kiss you?"

She smiled with the eyes of a tired swimmer, and he saw that her slender stock of repartee was exhausted. "Herman'll be here tonight," she said.

"Then let's make the most of today."

"But I've asked some people to lunch at the club."

"Then you'll chuck them, and come off and lunch with me somewhere else."

"Oh, will I—shall I?" She laughed, and he saw her breast rise on her shortened breath. He caught her to him and planted a kiss in the middle of her laughter.

"Now will you?"

She was a rich armful, and he remembered how splendid he had thought plump rosy women in his youth, before money and fashion imposed their artificial standards.

When he reëntered the doors of Cedarledge the cold spring sunset was slanting in through the library windows on the tea-table at which his wife and Nona sat. Of Lita there was no sign; Manford heard with indolent amusement that she was reported to be just getting up. His sentiment about Lita had settled into fatherly indulgence; he no longer thought the epithet inappropriate. But underneath the superficial kindliness he felt for her, as for all the world, he was aware of a fundamental indifference to most things but his own comfort and convenience. Such was the salutary result of fresh air and recovered leisure. How absurd to work one's self into a state of fluster about this or that—money or business or women! Especially women. As he looked back on the last weeks he saw what a fever of fatigue he must have been in to take such an exaggerated view of his own emotions. After three days at Cedarledge serenity had descended on him like a benediction. Gladys Toy's cheeks were as smooth as nectarines; and the keen morning light had shown him that she wasn't in the least made up. He recalled the fact with a certain pleasure, and then dismissed her from his mind—or rather she dropped out of herself. He wasn't in the humour to think long about anybody or anything . . . he revelled in his own laziness and indifference.

"Tea? Yes; and a buttered muffin by all means. Several of them. I'm as hungry as the devil. Went for a long tramp this morning before any of you were up. Mrs. Toy ran across me, and brought me back in her new two-seater. A regular beauty—the car, I mean—you'll have to have one like it, Nona . . . Jove, how good the fire feels . . . and what is it that smells so sweet? Carnations—why, they're giants! We must go over the green-houses tomorrow, Pauline; and all the rest of it. I want to take stock of all your innovations."

At that moment he felt able to face even the tour of inspection, and all the facts and calculations it would evoke. Everything seemed easy now that he had found he could shake off his moonlight obsession by spending a few hours with a pretty woman who didn't mind being kissed. He was to meet Mrs. Toy again the day after tomorrow; and in the interval she would suffice to occupy his mind when he had nothing more interesting to think of.

As he was putting a match to his pipe Lita came into the room with her long glide. Her boy was perched on her shoulder, and she looked like one of Crivelli's enigmatic Madonnas carrying a little red-haired Jesus.

"Gracious! Is this breakfast or tea? I seem to have overslept myself after our joy-ride," she said, addressing a lazy smile to Manford.

She dropped to her knees before the fire and held up the boy to Pauline. "Kiss his granny," she commanded in her faintly derisive voice.

It was very pretty, very cleverly staged; but Manford said to himself that she was too self-conscious, and that her lips were too much painted. Besides, he had always hated women with prominent cheekbones and hollows under them. He settled back comfortably into the afternoon's reminiscences.

Chapter XXIII

DECIDEDLY, there was a different time-measure for life in town and in the country.

The dinner for Amalasuntha organized (and the Toys secured for it), there were still two days left in that endless inside of a week which was to have passed so rapidly. Yet everything had gone according to Pauline's wishes. Dexter had really made the promised round of house and grounds, and had extended his inspection to dairy, poultry yard and engine-house. And he had approved of everything—approved almost too promptly and uncritically. Was it because he had not been sufficiently interested to note defects, or at any rate to point them out? The suspicion, which stirred in his wife when she observed that he walked through the cow-stables without making any comment on the defective working of the new ventilating system, became a certainty when, on their return to the house, she suggested their going over the accounts together. "Oh, as long as the architect has o.k'd them! Besides, it's too late now to do anything, isn't it? And your results are so splendid that I don't see how they could be overpaid. Everything seems to be perfect—"

"Not the ventilating system in the Alderneys' stable, Dexter."

"Oh, well; can't that be arranged? If it can't, put it down to profit and loss. I never enjoyed anything more than my swim this morning in the pool. You've managed to get the water warmed to exactly the right temperature."

He slipped out to join Nona on the putting green below the terrace.

Yes; everything was all right; he was evidently determined that everything should be. It had been the same about Michelangelo's debts. At first he had resisted his wife's suggestion that they should help to pay them off, in order to escape the young man's presence in New York; then he had suddenly promised the Marchesa to settle the whole amount, without so much as a word to Pauline. It was as if he were engrossed in some deep and secret purpose, and resolved to clear away whatever threatened to block his obstinate advance. She had seen him thus absorbed when a "big case" possessed him. But there were no signs now of professional preoccupation; no telephoning, wiring, hurried arrivals of junior members or confidential clerks. He seemed to have shaken off "the office" with all his other cares. There was something about his serene good humour that obscurely frightened her.

Once she might have ascribed it to an interest—an exaggerated interest—in his step-son's wife. That idea had already crossed Pauline's mind: she remembered its cold brush on the evening when her husband had come home unexpectedly to see her, and had talked so earnestly and sensibly about bringing Lita and her boy to Cedarledge. The mere flit of a doubt—no more; and even then Pauline had felt its preposterousness, and banished it in disgust and fear.

Now she smiled at the fear. Her husband's manner to Lita was perfect—easy, good humoured but slightly ironic. At the time of Jim's marriage Dexter had had that same smile. He had thought the bride silly and pretentious, he had even questioned her good looks. And now the first week at Cedarledge showed that, if his attitude had grown kindlier, it was for Jim's sake, not Lita's. Nona and Lita were together all day long; when Manford joined them he treated both in the same way, as a man treats two indulged and amusing daughters.

What was he thinking of, then? Gladys Toy again, perhaps? Pauline had imagined that was over. Even if it were not, it no longer worried her. Dexter had had similar "flare-ups" before, and they hadn't lasted. Besides, Pauline had gradually acquired a certain wifely philosophy, and was prepared to be more lenient to her second husband than to the first. As wives grew older they had to realize that husbands didn't always keep pace with them . . .

Not that she felt herself too old for Manford's love; all her early illusions had rushed back to her the night he had made her give up the Rivington dinner. But her dream had not survived that evening. She had understood then that he meant they should be "only friends"; that was all the future was to hold for her. Well; for a grandmother it ought to be enough. She had no patience with the silly old women who expected "that sort of nonsense" to last. Still, she meant, on her return to town, to

consult a new Russian who had invented a radium treatment
which absolutely wiped out wrinkles. He called himself a Scientific Initiate . . . the name fascinated her.

From these perplexities she was luckily distracted by the urgent
business of the Cardinal's reception. Even without Maisie she
could do a good deal of preparatory writing and telephoning;
but she was mortified to find how much her handwriting had
suffered from the long habit of dictation. She never wrote a note
in her own hand nowadays—except to distinguished foreigners,
since Amalasuntha had explained that they thought typed communications ill-bred. And her unpractised script was so stiff and
yet slovenly that she decided she must have her hands "treated"
as she did her other unemployed muscles. But how find time
for this new and indispensable cure? Her spirits rose with the
invigorating sense of being once more in a hurry.

Nona sat on the south terrace in the sun. The Cedarledge
experiment had lasted eight days now, and she had to own that
it had turned out better than she would have thought possible.

Lita was giving them wonderfully little trouble. After the
first flight to Greenwich she had shown no desire for cabarets
and night-clubs, but had plunged into the alternative excitement of violent outdoor sports; relapsing, after hours of hard
exercise, into a dreamy lassitude unruffled by outward events.
She never spoke of her husband, and Nona did not know if
Jim's frequent—too frequent—letters were answered, or even
read. Lita smiled vaguely when he was mentioned, and merely
remarked, when her mother-in-law once risked an allusion to
the future: "I thought we were here to be cured of plans." And
Pauline effaced her blunder with a smile.

Nona herself felt more and more like one of the trench-watch-
ers pictured in the war-time papers. There she sat in the darkness on her narrow perch, her eyes glued to the observation-slit
which looked out over seeming emptiness. She had often wondered what those men thought about during the endless hours
of watching, the days and weeks when nothing happened, when
no faintest shadow of a skulking enemy crossed their span of
no-man's land. What kept them from falling asleep, or from
losing themselves in waking dreams, and failing to give warning when the attack impended? She could imagine a man led out

to be shot in the Flanders mud because, at such a moment, he had believed himself to be dozing on a daisy bank at home . . .

Since her talk with Aggie Heuston a sort of *curare* had entered into her veins. She was sharply aware of everything that was going on about her, but she felt unable to rouse herself. Even if anything that mattered ever did happen again, she questioned if she would be able to shake off the weight of her indifference. Was it really ten days now since that talk with Aggie? And had everything of which she had then been warned fulfilled itself without her lifting a finger? She dimly remembered having acted in what seemed a mood of heroic self-denial; now she felt only as if she had been numb. What was the use of fine motives if, once the ardour fallen, even they left one in the lurch?

She thought: "I feel like the oldest person in the world, and yet with the longest life ahead of me . . ." and a shiver of loneliness ran over her.

Should she go and hunt up the others? What difference would that make? She might offer to write notes for her mother, who was upstairs plunged in her visiting-list; or look in on Lita, who was probably asleep after her hard gallop of the morning; or find her father, and suggest going for a walk. She had not seen her father since lunch; but she seemed to remember that he had ordered his new Buick brought round. Off again—he was as restless as the others. All of them were restless nowadays. Had he taken Lita with him, perhaps? Well—why not? Wasn't he here to look after Lita? A sudden twitch of curiosity drew Nona to her feet, and sent her slowly upstairs to her sister-in-law's room. Why did she have to drag one foot after the other, as if some hidden influence held her back, signalled a mute warning not to go? What nonsense! Better make a clean breast of it to herself once for all, and admit—

"I beg pardon, Miss." It was the ubiquitous Powder at her heels. "If you're going up to Mrs. Manford's sitting-room would you kindly tell her that Mr. Manford has telephoned he won't be back from Greystock till late, and she's please not to wait dinner?" Powder looked a little as if he would rather not give that particular message himself.

"Greystock? Oh, all right. I'll tell her."

Golf again—golf and Gladys Toy. Nona gave her clinging preoccupations a last shake. This was really a lesson to her! To be imagining horrible morbid things about her father while he was engaged in a perfectly normal elderly man's flirtation with a stupid woman he would forget as soon as he got back to town! A real Easter holiday diversion. "After all, he gave up his tarpon-fishing to come here, and Gladys isn't a bad substitute—as far as weight goes. But a good deal less exciting as sport." A dreary gleam of amusement crossed her mind.

Softly she pushed open the door of one of the perfectly appointed spare-rooms: a room so studiously equipped with every practical convenience—from the smoothly-hung window-ventilators to the jointed dressing-table lights, from the little portable telephone, and the bed-table with folding legs, to the tall threefold mirror which lost no curve of the beauty it reflected—that even Lita's careless ways seemed subdued to the prevailing order.

Lita was on the lounge, one long arm drooping, the other folded behind her in the immemorial attitude of sleeping beauty. Sleep lay on her lightly, as it does on those who summon it at will. It was her habitual escape from the boredom between thrills, and in such intervals of existence as she was now travers-ing she plunged back into it after every bout of outdoor activity.

Nona tiptoed forward and looked down on her. Who said that sleep revealed people's true natures? It only made them the more enigmatic by the added veil of its own mystery. Lita's head was nested in the angle of a thin arm, her lids rounded heavily above the sharp cheek-bones just swept by their golden fringe, the pale bow of the mouth relaxed, the slight steel-strong body half shown in the parting of a flowered dressing-gown. Thus exposed, with gaze extinct and loosened muscles, she seemed a mere bundle of contradictory whims tied together by a frail thread of beauty. The hand of the downward arm hung open, palm up. In its little hollow lay the fate of three lives. What would she do with them? How could one conceive of her know-ing, or planning, or imagining—conceive of her in any sort of durable human relations to any one or anything?

Her eyes opened and a languid curiosity floated up through them.

"That you? I must have fallen asleep. I was trying to count up the number of months we've been here, and numbers always make me go to sleep."

Nona laughed and sat down at the foot of the lounge. "Dear me—just as I thought you were beginning to be happy!"

"Well, isn't this what you call being happy—in the country?"

"Lying on your back, and wondering how many months there are in a week?"

"A week? Is it only a week? How on earth can you be sure, when one day's so exactly like another?"

"Tomorrow won't be. There's the blow-out for Amalasuntha, and dancing afterward. Mother's idea of the simple life."

"Well, all your mother's ideas *are* simple." Lita yawned, her pale pink mouth drooping like a faded flower. "Besides, it's ages till tomorrow. Where's your father? He was going to take me for a spin in the new Buick."

"He's broken his promise, then. Deserted us all and sneaked off to Greystock on his lone."

A faint redness rose to Lita's cheek-bones. "Greystock and Gladys Toy? Is that *his* idea of the simple life? About on a par with your mother's . . . Did you ever notice the Toy ankles?"

Nona smiled. "They're not unnoticeable. But you forget that father's getting to be an old gentleman . . . Fathers mustn't be choosers . . ."

Lita made a slight grimace. "Oh, he could do better than that. There's old Cosby, who looks heaps older—didn't he want to marry you? . . . Nona, you darling, let's take the Ford and run over to Greenwich for dinner. Would your mother so very much mind? Does she want us here the whole blessed time?"

"I'll go and ask her. But on a Friday night the Country Club will be as dead as the moon. Only a few old ladies playing bridge."

"Well, then we'll have the floor to ourselves. I want a good practice, and it's a ripping floor. We can dance with the waiters. It'll be fun to shock the old ladies. I noticed one of the waiters the other day—must be an Italian—built rather like Tommy Ardwin . . . I'm sure he dances . . ."

That was all life meant to Lita—would ever mean. Good floors to practise new dance-steps on, men—any men—to dance with and be flattered by, women—any women—to stare and envy one, dull people to startle, stupid people to shock—but never any one, Nona questioned, whom one wanted neither to startle nor shock, neither to be envied nor flattered by, but just to lose one's self in for good and all? Lita lose herself—? Why, all she wanted was to keep on finding herself, immeasurably magnified, in every pair of eyes she met!

And here were Nona and her father and mother fighting to preserve this brittle plaything for Jim, when somewhere in the world there might be a real human woman for him . . . What was the sense of it all?

Chapter XXIV

THE Marchesa di San Fedele's ideas about the country were perfectly simple; in fact she had only one. She regarded it as a place in which there was more time to play bridge than in town. Thank God for that!—and the rest one simply bore with . . . Of course there was the obligatory going the rounds with host or hostess: gardens, glass, dairy, chicken-hatchery, and heaven knew what besides (stables, thank goodness, were out of fashion—even if people rode they no longer, unless they kept hounds, dragged one between those dreary rows of box stalls, or made one admire the lustrous steel and leather of the harness room, or the monograms stencilled in blue and red on the coach-house floor).

The Marchesa's life had always been made up of doing things as dull as going over model dairies in order to get the chance, or the money, to do others as thrilling to her as dancing was to Lita. It was part of the game: one had to pay for what one got: the thing was to try and get a great deal more than the strict equivalent.

"Not that I don't marvel at your results, Pauline; we all do. But they make me feel so useless and incapable. All this wonderful creation—baths and swimming-pools and hatcheries and fire-engines, and everything so perfect, indoors and out! Sometimes I'm glad you've never been to our poor old San Fedele. But of course bathrooms will have to be put in at San Fedele if Michelangelo finds an American bride when he comes over . . ."

Pauline laid down the pen she had taken up to record the exact terms in which she was to address the Cardinal's secretary. ("A *personal* note, dear; yes, in your own writing; they don't yet understand your new American ways at the Vatican . . .")

"When Michelangelo comes over?" Pauline echoed.

The Marchesa's face was sharper than a knife. "It's my little surprise. I didn't mean you or Dexter to know till the contract was signed . . ."

"What contract?"

"My boy's to do Cæsar Borgia in the new film. Klawhammer cabled a definite offer the day you left for the country. And of course I insisted on Michelangelo's sailing instantly, though he'd planned to spend the spring in Paris and was rather cross at having to give it up. But as I told him, now is the moment to secure a lovely American bride. We all know what your rich papas-in-law over here always ask: 'What debts? What prospects? What other women?' The woman matter can generally be arranged. The debts *are*, in this case—thanks to your generosity. But the prospects—what were *they*, I ask you? Months of green mould at San Fedele for a fortnight's splash in Rome . . . oh, I don't disguise it! And what American bride would accept *that*? The San Fedele pearls, yes—but where is the San Fedele plumbing? But now, my dear, Michelangelo presents himself as an equal . . . superior, I might say, if I weren't afraid of being partial. Cæsar Borgia in a Klawhammer film—no one knows how many millions it may mean! And of course Michelangelo is the very type . . ."

"*To do me the favour to transmit to his Eminence* . . . Yes; this really is a surprise, Amalasuntha." Inwardly Pauline was saying: "After all, why not? If his own mother doesn't mind seeing him all over the place on film posters. And perhaps now he may pay us back—in common decency he'll have to!"

She saw no serious reason for displeasure, once she had dropped her carefully cultivated Wyant attitude. "If only it doesn't upset Lita again, and make her restless!" But they really couldn't hope to keep all Lita's friends and relations off the screen.

"Arthur was amazed—and awfully pleased, after the first recoil. Dear Arthur, you know, always recoils at first," the Marchesa continued, with her shrewd deprecating smile, which insinuated that Pauline of course wouldn't. (It was odd, Pauline reflected; the Marchesa always looked like a peasant when she was talking business.)

"Arthur? You've already written to him about it?"

"No, dear. I ran across him yesterday in town. You didn't know Arthur'd come back? I thought he said he'd telephoned to Nona, or somebody. A touch of gout—got fidgety because he couldn't see his doctor. But he looked remarkably well, I thought—so handsome still, in his *élancé* Wyant way; only a little too flushed, perhaps. Yes . . . poor Eleanor . . . Oh, no; he said Jim was still on the island. Perfectly contented fishing. Jim's the only person

I know who's always perfectly contented . . . such a lesson . . ." The Marchesa's sigh seemed to add: "Very restful—but how I should despise him if he were my Michelangelo!"

Pauline could hear—oh, how distinctly!—all that her former husband would have to say about Michelangelo's projects. They would be food for an afternoon's irony. But that did not greatly trouble her—nor did Wyant's unexpected return. He was always miserable out of reach of his doctor. And the fact that Jim hadn't come back proved that there was nothing seriously wrong. Pauline thought: "I'll write to Jim again, and tell him how perfect Dexter has been about Lita and the baby, and that will convince him there's no need to hurry back."

Complacency returned to her. How should it not, with the list for the Cardinal's reception nearly complete, and the telephonic assurance of the Bishop of New York and the Chief Rabbi that both these dignitaries would be present? Socially also, though the season was over, the occasion promised to be brilliant. Lots of people were coming back just to see how a Cardinal was received. Even the Rivingtons were coming—she had it from the Bishop. Yes, the Rivingtons had certainly been more cordial since she and Manford had thrown them over at the last minute. That was the way to treat people who thought themselves so awfully superior. What wouldn't the Rivingtons have given to capture the Cardinal? But he was sailing for Italy the day after Pauline's reception—that was the beauty of it! No one else could possibly have him. Amalasuntha had stage-managed the whole business very cleverly. She had even overcome the Cardinal's scruples when he heard that Mrs. Manford was chairman of the Birth Control committee . . . And tonight, at the dinner, how pleasant everybody's congratulations would be! Pauline gloried in her achievement for Manford's sake. Despite his assurance to the contrary she could never imagine, for more than a moment at a time, that such successes were really indifferent to him.

Lita appeared in the drawing-room after almost everybody had arrived. She was always among the last; and in the country, as she said, there was no way of knowing what time it was. Even at Cedarledge, where all the clocks agreed to a second, one could never believe them, and always suspected they must have stopped together, twelve hours before.

"Besides, what's the use of knowing what time it is in the country? Time for *what*?"

She came in quietly, almost unnoticeably, with the feathered gait that was half-way between drifting and floating; and at once, in spite of the twenty people assembled, had the shining parquet and all the mirrors to herself. That was her way: that knack of clearing the floor no matter how quietly she entered. And tonight—!

Well; perhaps, Manford thought, all the other women *were* a little overdressed. Women always had a tendency to overdress when they dined with the Manfords; to wear too many jewels, and put on clothes that glistened. Even at Cedarledge Pauline's parties had a New York atmosphere. And Lita, in her straight white slip, slim and unadorned as a Primitive angel, with that close coif of goldfish-coloured hair, and not a spangle, a jewel, a pearl even, made the other women's clothes look like upholstery.

Manford, by the hearth, slightly bored in anticipation, yet bound to admit that, like all his wife's shows, it was effectively done—Manford received the shock of that quiet entrance, that shimmer widening into light, and then turned to Mrs. Herman Toy. Full noon there; the usual Rubensy redundance flushed by golfing in a high wind, by a last cocktail before dressing, by the hurried wriggle into one of those elastic sheaths the women—the redundant women—wore. Well; he liked ripeness in a fruit to be eaten as soon as plucked. And Gladys' corn-yellow hair was almost as springy and full of coloured shadows as the other's red. But the voice, the dress, the jewels, the blatant jewels! A Cartier show-case spilt over a strawberry *mousse* . . . And the quick possessive look, so clumsily done—brazen, yet half-abashed! When a woman's first business was to make up her mind which it was to be . . . Chances were the man didn't care, as long as her ogling didn't make him ridiculous . . . Why couldn't some women always be in golf clothes—if any? Gala get-up wasn't in everybody's line . . . There was Lita speaking to Gladys now—with auburn eyebrows lifted just a thread. The contrast—! And Gladys purpler and more self-conscious—God, why did she have her clothes so tight? And that drawing-room drawl! Why couldn't she just sing out: "Hul*lo*!" as she did in the open?

The Marchesa—how many times more was he to hear Pauline say: "Amalasuntha on your right, dear." Oh, to get away to a world where nobody gave dinners, and there were no Marchesas on one's right! He knew by heart the very look of the little cheese soufflés, light as cherubs' feathers, that were being handed around before the soup on silver-gilt dishes with coats-of-arms. Everything at Cedarledge was silver-gilt. Pauline, as usual, had managed to transplant the party to New York, when all he wanted was to be quiet, smoke his pipe, and ride or tramp with Nona and Lita. Why couldn't she see it? Her vigilant eye sought his—was it for approval or admonition? What was she saying? "The Cardinal? Oh, yes. It's all settled. So sweet of him! Of course you must all promise to come. But I've got another little surprise for you after dinner. No; not a word beforehand; not if you were to put me on the rack." What on earth did she mean?

"A surprise? Is this a surprise party?" It was Amalasuntha now. "Then I must produce mine. But I daresay Pauline's told you. About Michelangelo and Klawhammer . . . Cæsar Borgia . . . such a sum that I don't dare to mention it—you'd think I was mixing up the figures. But I've got them down in black and white. Of course, as the producers say, Michelangelo's so supremely the type—it's more than they ever could have hoped for." What was the woman raving about? "He sails tomorrow," she said. Sailing again—was that damned Michelangelo always sailing? Hadn't his debts been paid on the express condition—? But no; there's been nothing, as the Marchesa called it, "in black and white." The transaction had been based on the implicit understanding that nothing but dire necessity would induce Michelangelo to waste his charms on New York. Dire necessity—or the chance to put himself permanently beyond it! A fortune from a Klawhammer film. As Amalasuntha said, it was incalculable . . .

"It's the type, you see: between ourselves, there's always been a rumour of Borgia blood on the San Fedele side. A naughty ancestress! Perhaps you've noticed the likeness? You remember that wonderful profile portrait of Cæsar Borgia in black velvet? What gallery *is* it in? Oh, I know—it came out in 'Vogue'!" Amalasuntha visibly bridled at her proficiency. She was aware that envious people said the Italians knew nothing of their own artistic inheritance. "I remember being so struck by it at the time—I said to Venturino: 'But it's the image of our boy!' Though Michelangelo will have to grow a beard, which makes him furious . . . But then the millions!"

Manford, looking up, caught a double gaze bent in his direction. Gladys Toy's vast blue eyes had always been like searchlights; but tonight they seemed actually to be writing her private history over his head, like an advertising aeroplane. The fool! But was the other look also meant for him? That half-shaded glint of Lita's—was it not rather attached to the Marchesa, strung like a telephone wire to her lips? Klawhammer . . . Michelangelo . . . a Borgia film . . . Those listening eyes missed not a syllable.

"The offers those fellows make—right and left—nobody takes much account of them. Wait till I see your contract, as you call it . . . If you really think it's a job for a gentleman," Manford growled.

"But, my friend, gentlemen can't be choosers! Who are the real working-class today? Our old aristocracies, alas! And besides, is it ever degrading to create a work of art? I thought in America you made so much of creativeness—constructiveness—what do you call it? Is it less creative to turn a film than to manufacture bathtubs? Can there be a nobler mission than to teach history to the millions by means of beautiful pictures? . . . Yes! I see Lita listening, and I know she agrees with me . . . Lita! What a Lucrezia for his Cæsar! But why look shocked, dear Dexter? Of course you know that Lucrezia Borgia has been entirely rehabilitated? I saw that also in 'Vogue.' She was a perfectly pure woman—and her hair was exactly the colour of Lita's."

They were finishing coffee in the drawing-room, the doors standing open into the tall library where the men always smoked—the library which (as Stanley Heuston had once remarked) Pauline's incorruptible honesty had actually caused her to fill with books.

"Oh, what *is* it? Not a fire? . . . A chimney in the house? . . . But it's actually here . . . Not a . . ."

The women, a-flutter at the sudden siren-shriek, the hooting, rushing and clattering up the drive, surged across the parquet, flowed with startled little cries out into the hall, and saw the unsurprisable Powder signalling to two perfectly matched footmen to throw open the double doors.

"A fire? The engine . . . the . . . oh, it's a *fire-drill*! . . . A *parade*! How realistic! How lovely of you! What a beauty the engine is!"

Pauline stood smiling, watch in hand, as the hook-and-ladder motor clattered up the drive and ranged itself behind the engine. The big lantern over the front door illuminated fresh scarlet paint and super-polished brasses, the firemen's agitated helmets and perspiring faces, the flashing hoods of the lamps.

"Just five minutes to the second! Wonderful!" She was shaking hands with each member of the amateur brigade in turn. "I can't tell you how I congratulate you—every one of you! Such an achievement . . . you really manœuvre like professionals. No one would have believed it was the first time! Dexter, will you tell them a hot supper has been prepared downstairs!" To the guests she was explaining in a triumphant undertone: "I wanted to give them the chance to show off their new toy . . . Yes, I believe it's absolutely the most perfected thing in fire-engines. Dexter and I thought it was time the village was properly equipped. It's really more on account of the farmers—such a sense of safety for the neighbourhood . . . Oh, Mr. Motts, I think you're simply wonderful, all of you. Mr. Manford and my daughter are going to show you the way to supper . . . Yes, yes, you *must*! Just a sandwich and something hot."

She dominated them all, grave and glittering as a goddess of Velocity. "She enjoys it as much as other women do love-making," Manford muttered to himself.

Chapter XXV

MANFORD didn't know what first gave him the sense that Lita had slipped out among the departing guests; slipped out, and not come back. When the idea occurred to him it was already lodged in his mind, hard and definite as a verified fact. She had vanished from among them into the darkness.

But only a moment ago; there was still time to dash round to the shed in the service court, where motors were sometimes left for the night, and where he had dropped his Buick just in time to rush in and dress for dinner. He would have no trouble in overtaking her.

The Buick was gone.

Hatless and coatless in the soft night air, he rushed down the drive on its track. No moon tonight, but a deceptive velvet mildness, such as sometimes comes in spring before the wind hauls round to a frosty quarter. He hurried on, out of the open gate, along the road toward the village; and there, at the turn of the New York turnpike—just the road he had expected her to take—stood his Buick, a figure stooping over it in the lamp-glare. A furious stab of jealousy shot through him—"There's a man with her; who?" But the man was only his own overcoat, which he had left on the seat of the car when he dashed home for dinner, and which was now drawn over Lita's shoulders. It was she who stood in the night, bent over the mysteries of the car's insides.

She looked up and called out: "Oh, look here—give me a hand, will you? The thing's stuck." Manford moved around within lamp-range, and she stared a moment, her little face springing out at him uncannily from the darkness. Then she broke into a laugh. "You?"

"Were you asking a total stranger to repair your motor? Rather risky, on a country road in the middle of the night."

She shrugged and smiled. "Not as risky as doing it myself. The chances are that even a total stranger would know more about the inside of this car than I do."

"Lita, you're mad! Damn the car. What are you doing here anyhow?"

She paused, one hand on the bonnet, while with the other she pushed back a tossed lock from her round forehead. "Running away," she said simply.

Manford took a quick breath. The thing was, he admonished himself, to take this lightly, as nearly as possible in her own key—above all to avoid protesting and exclaiming. But his heart was beating like a trip-hammer. She was more of a fool than he had thought.

"Running away from that dinner? I don't blame you. But it's over. Still, if you want to wash out the memory of it, get into the motor and we'll go for a good spin—like that one when we came back from Greenwich."

Her lips parted in a faint smile. "Oh, but that ended up at Cedarledge."

"Well—?"

"Bless you; I'm not going back."

"Where *are* you going?"

"To New York first—after that I don't know . . . Perhaps my aunt's . . . Perhaps Hollywood . . ."

The rage in him exploded. "Perhaps Dawnside—eh? Own up!"

She laughed and shrugged again. "Own up? Why not? Anywhere where I can dance and laugh and be hopelessly low-lived and irresponsible."

"And get that blackguard crew about you again, all those—. Lita! Listen to me. Listen. You've got to."

"Got to?" She rounded on him in a quick flare of anger. "I wonder who you think you're talking to? I'm not Gladys Toy."

The unexpectedness of the challenge struck him dumb. For challenge it was, unmistakably. He felt a rush of mingled strength and fear—fear at this inconceivable thing, and the strength her self-betrayal gave him. He returned with equal violence: "No—you're not. You're something so utterly different . . ."

"Oh," she burst in, "don't tell me I'm too sacred, and all that. I'm fed up with the sanctities—that's the trouble with me. Just own up you like 'em artificially fattened. Why, that woman's ankles are half a yard round. Can't you *see* it? Or is that really the way you admire 'em? I thought you wanted to be with me . . . I thought that was why you were here . . . Do you suppose I'd have come all this way just to be taught to love fresh air and family life? The hypocrisy—!"

Her little face was flashing on him furiously, red lips parted on a glitter of bright teeth. "She must have a sausage-machine, to cram her into that tube she had on tonight. No human maid could do it . . . 'Utterly different'? I should hope so! I'd like to see *her* get a job with Klawhammer—unless he means to do a 'Barnum,' and wants a Fat Woman . . . I . . ."

"*Lita*!"

"You're *stupid* . . . you're stupider than anything on God's earth!"

"Lita—" He put his hand over hers. Let the whole world crash, after this . . .

Pauline sat in her upstairs sitting-room, full of that sense of repose which comes of duties performed and rewards laid up. How could it be otherwise, at the close of a day so rich in moral satisfactions? She scanned it again, from the vantage of her midnight vigil in the sleeping house, and saw that all was well in the little world she had created.

Yes; all was well, from the fire-drill which had given a rather languishing dinner its requisite wind-up of excitement to the arrangements for the Cardinal's reception, Amalasuntha's skilful turning of that Birth Control obstacle, and the fact that Jim was philosophically remaining in the south in spite of his father's unexpected return. The only shadow on the horizon was Michelangelo's— Dexter would certainly be angry about that. But she was not going to let Michelangelo darken her holiday, when everything else in life was so smooth and sunshiny.

She remembered her resolve to write to Jim, and took up her pen with a smile.

"I can guess what heavenly weather you must be having from the delicious taste of spring we're having here. The baby is out in the sunshine all day: he's gained nearly a pound, and is getting almost as brown as if it were summer. Lita looks ever so much better too, though she'd never forgive my suggesting that she had put on even an ounce. But I don't believe she has, for she and Nona and Dexter are riding or golfing or racing over the country from morning to night like a pack of children. You can't think how jolly and hungry and sleepy they all are when they get home for tea. It was a wonderful invention of Dexter's to bring Lita and the baby here while you were having your holiday, and you'll agree that it has worked miracles when you see them.

"Amalasuntha tells me your father is back. I expected to hear that he had got restless away from his own quarters; but she says he's looking very well. Nona will go in and see him next week, and report. Meanwhile I'm so glad you're staying on and making the most of your holiday. Do get all the rest and sunshine you can, and trust your treasures a little longer to your loving old

"MOTHER."

There—that would certainly reassure him. It had reassured her merely to write it: given her the feeling, to which she always secretly inclined, that a thing was so if one said it was, and doubly so if one wrote it down.

She sealed the letter, pushed back her chair, and glanced at the little clock on her writing-table. A quarter to two! She had a right to feel sleepy, and even to curtail her relaxing exercises. The country stillness was so deep and soothing that she hardly needed them . . .

She opened the window, and stood drinking in the hush. The spring night was full of an underlying rustle and murmur that was a part of the silence. But suddenly a sharp sound broke on her—the sound of a motor coming up the drive. In the stillness she caught it a long way off, probably just after the car turned in at the gate. The sound was so unnatural, breaking in on the deep nocturnal dumbness of dim trees and starlit sky, that she drew back startled. She was not a nervous woman, but she thought irritably of a servants' escapade—something that the chauffeur would have to be spoken to about the next day. Queer, though—the motor did not turn off toward the garage. Standing in the window she followed its continued approach; then heard it slow down and stop—somewhere near the service court, she conjectured.

Could it be that Lita and Nona had been off on one of their crazy trips since the guests had left? She must really protest at such imprudence . . . She felt angry, nervous, uncertain. It was uncanny, hearing that invisible motor come so near the house and stop . . . She hesitated a moment, and then crossed to her own room, opened the door of the little anteroom beyond, and stood listening at her husband's bedroom door. It was ajar, all dark within. She hesitated to speak, half fearing to wake him; but at length she said in a low voice: "Dexter—."

No answer. She pronounced his name again, a little louder, and then cautiously crossed the threshold and switched on the light. The room was empty, the bed undisturbed. It was evident that Manford had not been up to his room since their guests had left. It was he, then, who had come back in the motor . . . She extinguished the light and turned back into her own room. On her dressing-table stood the little telephone which communicated with the servants' quarters, with Maisie Bruss's office, and with Nona's room. She stood wavering before the instrument. Why shouldn't she call up Nona, and ask—? Ask what? If the girls had been off on a lark they would be sure to tell her in the morning. And if it was Dexter alone, then—

She turned from the telephone, and slowly began to undress. Presently she heard steps in the hall, then in the anteroom; then her husband moving softly about in his own room, and the unmistakable sounds of his undressing . . . She drew a long breath, as if trying to free her lungs of some vague oppression . . . It was Dexter—well, yes, only Dexter . . . and he hadn't cared to leave the motor at the garage at that hour . . . Naturally . . . How glad she was that she hadn't rung up Nona! Suppose her doing so had startled Lita or the baby . . .

After all, perhaps she'd better do her relaxing exercises. She felt suddenly staring wide awake. But she was glad she'd written that reassuring letter to Jim—she was glad, because it was *true* . . .

Chapter XXVI

WHEN Nona told her mother that she wanted to go to town the next day to see Mrs. Bruss and Maisie, Mrs. Manford said: "It's only what I expected of you, darling," and added after a moment: "Do you think I ought—?"

"No, of course not. It would simply worry Maisie."

Nona knew it was the answer that her mother awaited. She knew that nothing frightened and disorganized Pauline as much as direct contact with physical or moral suffering—especially physical. Her whole life (if one chose to look at it from a certain angle) had been a long uninterrupted struggle against the encroachment of every form of pain. The first step, always, was to conjure it, bribe it away, by every possible expenditure—except of one's self. Cheques, surgeons, nurses, private rooms in hospitals, X-rays, radium, whatever was most costly and up-to-date in the dreadful art of healing—that was her first and strongest line of protection; behind it came such lesser works as rest-cures, change of air, a seaside holiday, a whole new set of teeth, pink silk bedspreads, lace cushions, stacks of picture papers, and hot-house grapes and long-stemmed roses from Cedarledge. Behind these again were the final, the verbal defenses, made of such phrases as: "If I thought I could do the least good"— "If I didn't feel it might simply upset her"— "*Some* doctors still consider it contagious"—with the inevitable summing-up: "The fewer people she sees the better . . ."

Nona knew that this attitude was not caused by lack of physical courage. Had Pauline been a pioneer's wife, and seen her family stricken down by disease in the wilderness, she would have nursed them fearlessly; but all her life she had been used to buying off suffering with money, or denying its existence with words, and her moral muscles had become so atrophied that only some great shock would restore their natural strength . . .

"Great shock! People like mother never have great shocks," Nona mused, looking at the dauntless profile, the crisply waving hair, reflected in the toilet-mirror. "Unless I were to give her one . . ." she added with an inward smile.

Mrs. Manford restored her powder-puff to its crystal box. "Do you know, darling, I believe I'll go to town with you tomorrow. It was very brave of Maisie to make the effort of coming here the other day, but of course, I didn't like to burden her with too many details at such a time (when's the operation—tomorrow?), and there are things I could perfectly well attend to myself, without bothering her; without her even knowing. Yes; I'll motor up with you early."

"She'll always delegate her anxieties," Nona mused, not unenviously, as Cécile slipped Mrs. Manford's spangled teagown over her firm white shoulders. Pauline turned a tender smile on her daughter. "It's so like you, Nona, to want to be with Maisie for the operation—so *fine*, dear."

Voice and smile were full of praise; yet behind the praise (Nona also knew) lurked the unformulated apprehension: "All this running after sick people and unhappy people—is it going to turn into a vocation?" Nothing could have been more distasteful to Mrs. Manford than the idea that her only daughter should be not only good, but *merely* good: like poor Aggie Heuston, say . . . Nona could hear her mother murmuring: "I can't imagine where on earth she got it from," as if alluding to some physical defect unaccountable in the offspring of two superbly sound progenitors.

They started early, for forty-eight hours of accumulated leisure had reinforced Pauline's natural activity. Amalasuntha, mysteriously smiling and head-shaking over the incommunicable figures of Klawhammer's offer, had bustled back to town early on Monday, leaving the family to themselves—and a certain feeling of flatness had ensued. Dexter, his wife thought, seemed secretly irritated, but determined to conceal his irritation from her. It was about Michelangelo, no doubt. Lita was silent and sleepy. No one seemed to have anything particular to do. Even in town Mondays were always insipid. But in the afternoon Manford "took Lita off their hands," as his wife put it, by carrying her away for the long-deferred spin in the Buick; and Pauline plunged back restfully into visiting-lists and other domestic preoccupations. She certainly had nothing to worry about, and much to rejoice in, yet she felt languid and vaguely apprehensive. She began to wonder if Alvah Loft's treatment were of the lasting sort, or if it lost its efficacy, like an uncorked drug. Perhaps the Scientific Initiate she had been told about would have a new panacea for the mind as well as for the epiderm. She would telephone and make an appointment; it always stimulated her to look forward to seeing a new healer. As Mrs. Swoffer said, one ought never to neglect a spiritual opportunity; and one never knew on whom the Spirit might have alighted. Mrs. Swoffer's conversation was always soothing and yet invigorating, and Pauline determined to see her too. And there was Arthur—poor Exhibit A!—on Jim's account it would be kind to look him up if there were time; unless Nona could manage that too, in the intervals of solacing Maisie. It was so depressing—and so useless—to sit in a hospital parlour, looking at old numbers of picture papers, while those awful white-sleeved rites went on in the secret sanctuary of tiles and nickel-plating. It would do Nona good to have an excuse for slipping away.

Pauline's list of things-to-be-done had risen like a spring tide as soon as she decided to go to town for the day. There was hair-waving, manicuring, dressmaking—her dress for the Cardinal's reception. How was she ever to get through half the engagements on her list? And of course she must call at the hospital with a big basket of grapes and flowers . . .

On the steps of the hospital Nona paused and looked about her. The operation was over—everything had "gone beautifully," as beautifully as it almost always does on these occasions. Maisie had been immensely grateful for her coming, and as surprised as if an angel from the seventh heaven had alighted to help her through. The two girls had sat together, making jerky attempts at talk, till the nurse came and said: "All right—she's back in bed again"; and then Maisie, after a burst of relieving tears, had tiptoed off to sit in a corner of her mother's darkened room and await the first sign of returning consciousness. There was nothing more for Nona to do, and she went out into the April freshness with the sense of relief that the healthy feel when they escape back to life after a glimpse of death.

On the hospital steps she ran into Arthur Wyant.

"Exhibit, dear! What are you doing here?"

"Coming to inquire for poor Mrs. Bruss. I heard from Amalasuntha . . ."

"That's kind of you. Maisie'll be so pleased."

She gave him the surgeon's report, saw that his card was entrusted to the right hands, and turned back into the street with him. He looked better than when he had left for the south; his leg was less stiff, and he carried his tall carefully dressed figure with a rigid jauntiness. But his face seemed sharper yet higher in colour. Fever or cocktails? She wondered. It was lucky that their meeting would save her going to the other end of the town to see him.

"Just like you, Exhibit, to remember poor Maisie . . ."

He raised ironic eyebrows. "Is inquiring about ill people obsolete? I see you still keep up the tradition."

"Oh, I've been seeing it through with Maisie. Some one had to."

"Exactly. And your mother held aloof, but financed the whole business?"

"Splendidly. She always does."

He frowned, and stood hesitating, and tapping his long boot-tip with his stick. "I rather want to have a talk with your mother."

"With mother?" Nona was on the point of saying: "She's in town today—" then, remembering Pauline's crowded list, she checked the impulse.

"Won't I do as a proxy? I was going to suggest your carrying me off to lunch."

"No, my dear, you won't—as a proxy. But I'll carry you off to lunch."

The choice of a restaurant would have been laborious—for Wyant, when taken out of his rut, became a mass of manias, prejudices and inhibitions—but Nona luckily remembered a new Bachelor Girls' Club ("The Singleton") which she had lately joined, and packed him into a taxi still protesting.

They found a quiet corner in a sociable low-studded dining-room, and she leaned back, listening to his disconnected monologue and smoking one cigarette after another in the nervous inability to eat.

The ten days on the island? Oh, glorious, of course—hot sunshine—a good baking for his old joints. Awfully kind of her father to invite him . . . he'd appreciated it immensely . . . was going to write a line of thanks . . . Jim, too, had appreciated his father's being included . . . Only, no, really; he couldn't stay; in the circumstances he couldn't . . .

"What circumstances, Exhibit? Getting the morning papers twenty-four hours late?"

Wyant frowned, looked at her sharply, and then laughed an uneasy wrinkled laugh. "Impertinent chit!"

"Own up, now; you were bored stiff. Communion with Nature was too much for you. You couldn't stick it. Few can."

"I don't say I'm as passive as Jim."

"Jim's just loving it down there, isn't he? I'm so glad you persuaded him to stay."

Wyant frowned again, and stared past her at some invisible antagonist. "It was about the only thing I *could* persuade him to do."

Nona's hand hung back from the lighting of another cigarette. "What else did you try to?"

"What else? Why to *act*, damn it . . . take a line . . . face things . . . face the music." He stopped in a splutter of metaphors, and dipped his bristling moustache toward his coffee.

"What things?"

"Why: is he going to keep his wife, or isn't he?"

"He thinks that's for Lita to decide."

"For Lita to decide! A pretext for his damned sentimental inertness. A *man*—my son! God, what's happened to the young men? Sit by and see . . . see . . . Nona, couldn't I manage to have a talk with your mother?"

"You're having one with me. Isn't that enough for the moment?"

He gave another vague laugh, and took a light from her extended cigarette. She knew that, though he found her mother's visits oppressive, he kept a careful record of their number, and dimly resented any appearance of being "crowded out" by Pauline's other engagements. "I suppose she comes up to town sometimes, doesn't she?"

"Sometimes—but in such a rush! And we'll be back soon now. She's got to get ready for the Cardinal's reception."

"Great doings, I hear. Amalasuntha dropped in on me yesterday. She says Lita's all agog again since that rotten Michelangelo's got a film contract, and your father's in an awful state about it. Is he?"

"The family are not used yet to figuring on the posters. Of course it's only a question of time."

"I don't mean in a state about Michelangelo, but about Lita."

"Father's been a perfect brick about Lita."

"Oh, he has, has he? Very magnanimous— Thanks; no—no cigar . . . Of course, if anybody's got to be a brick about Lita, I don't see why it's not her husband's job; but then I suppose you'll tell me . . ."

"Yes; I shall; please consider yourself told, won't you? Because I've got to get back to the hospital."

"The modern husband's job is a purely passive one, eh? That's your idea too? If you go to him and say: 'How about that damned scoundrel and your wife'—"

"What damned scoundrel?"

"Oh, I don't say . . . anybody in particular . . . and he answers: 'Well, what am I going to do about it?' and you say: 'Well, and your honour, man; what about your honour?' and he says: 'What's my honour got to do with it if my wife's sick of me?' and you say: 'God! But *the other man* . . . aren't you going to break his bones for him?' and he sits and looks at you and says: 'Get up a prize-fight for her?' . . . God! I give it up. My own son! We don't speak the same language, that's all."

He leaned back, his long legs stretched under the table, his tall shambling body disjointed with the effort at a military tautness, a kind of muscular demonstration of what his son's moral attitude ought to be.

"Damn it—there was a good deal to be said for duelling."

"And to whom do you want Jim to send his seconds? Michelangelo or Klawhammer?"

He stared, and echoed her laugh. "Ha! Ha! That's good. Klawhammer! Dirty Jew . . . the kind we used to horsewhip . . . Well, I don't understand the new code."

"Why do you want to, Exhibit? Come along. You've got me to look after in the meantime. If you want to be chivalrous, tuck me under your arm and see me back to the hospital."

"A prize-fight—get up a prize-fight for her! God—I should understand even that better than lying on the beach smoking a pipe and saying: 'What can a fellow do about it?' *Do!*"

Act—act—act! How funny it was, Nona reflected, as she remounted the hospital steps: the people who talked most of acting seldom did more than talk. Her father, for instance, so resolute and purposeful, never discoursed about action, but quietly went about what had to be done. Whereas poor Exhibit, perpetually inconsequent and hesitating, was never tired of formulating the most truculent plans of action for others. "Poor Exhibit indeed—incorrigible amateur!" she thought, understanding how such wordy dilettantism must have bewildered and irritated the young and energetic Pauline, fresh from the buzzing motor works at Exploit.

Nona felt a sudden exasperation against Wyant for trying to poison Jim's holiday by absurd insinuations and silly swagger. It was lucky that he had got bored and come back, leaving the poor boy to bask on the sands with his pipe and his philosophy. After all, it was to be supposed that Jim knew what he wanted, and how to take care of it, now he had it.

"At all events," Nona concluded, "I'm glad he didn't get hold of mother and bother her with his foolish talk." She shot up in the lift to the white carbolic-breathing passage where, with a heavy whiff of ether, Mrs. Bruss's door opened to receive her.

Chapter XXVII

THE restorative effect of a day away from the country was visible in Pauline's face and manner when she dawned on the breakfast-table the next morning.

The mere tone in which she murmured: "How lovely it is to get back!" showed how lovely it had been to get away—and she lingered over the new-laid eggs, the golden cream, all the country freshnesses and succulences, with the sense of having richly earned them by a long day spent in arduous and agreeable labours.

"When there are tiresome things to be done the great thing is to do them at once," she announced to Nona across the whole-wheat toast and scrambled eggs. "I simply hated to leave all this loveliness yesterday; but how much more I'm going to enjoy it today because I did!"

Her day in town had in truth been exceptionally satisfactory. All had gone well, from her encounter, at Amalasuntha's, with one of the Cardinal's secretaries, to the belated glimpse of Maisie Bruss, haggard but hopeful on the hospital steps, receiving the hamper of fruit and flowers with grateful exclamations, and assurances that the surgeon was "perfectly satisfied," and that there was "no reason why the dreadful thing should ever reappear." In a wave of sympathetic emotion Pauline had leaned from the motor to kiss her and say: "Your mother must have a good rest at Atlantic City as soon as she can be moved—I'll arrange it. Sea air is such a tonic . . ." and Maisie had thanked and wept again . . . It was pleasant to be able, in a few words, to make any one so happy . . .

She had found Mrs. Swoffer too; found her in a super-terrestrial mood, beaming through inspired eye-glasses, and pouring out new torrents of stimulation.

Yes: Alvah Loft was a great man, Mrs. Swoffer said. She, for her part, had never denied it for a moment. How could Pauline have imagined that her faith in Alvah Loft had failed her? No—but there were periods of spiritual aridity which the brightest souls had to traverse, and she had lately had reason to suspect, from her own experience and from Pauline's, that perhaps Alvah Loft was at present engaged in such a desert. Certainly to charge a hundred dollars for a "triple treatment" (which was only three minutes longer than the plain one), and then produce no more lasting results—well, Mrs. Swoffer preferred not to say anything uncharitable . . . Then again, she sometimes suspected that Alvah Loft's doctrine might be only for beginners. That was what Sacha Gobine, the new Russian Initiate, plainly intimated. Of course there were innumerable degrees in the spiritual life, and it might be that sometimes Alvah Loft's patients got beyond his level—got above it—without his being aware of the fact. Frankly, that was what Gobine thought (from Mrs. Swoffer's report) must have happened in the case of Pauline. "I believe your friend has reached a higher plane"—that was the way the Initiate put it. "She's been at the gate" (he called the Mahatma and Alvah Loft "gatekeepers"), "and now the gate has opened, and she has entered in—entered into . . ." But Mrs. Swoffer said she'd rather not try to quote him because she couldn't put it as beautifully as he did, and she wanted Pauline to hear it in his own mystical language. "It's eternal rejuvenation just to sit and listen to him," she breathed, laying an electric touch on her visitor's hand.

Rejuvenation! The word dashed itself like cool spray against Pauline's strained nerves and parched complexion. She could never hear it without longing to plunge deep into its healing waters. Between manicure and hair-waver she was determined to squeeze in a moment with Gobine.

And the encounter, as she told Nona, had been like "a religious experience"—apparently forgetful of the fact that every other meeting with a new prophet had presented itself to her in identical terms.

"You see, my dear, it's something so entirely new, so completely different . . . so emotional; yes, emotional; that's the word. The Russians, of course, *are* emotional; it's their peculiar quality. Alvah Loft—and you understand that I don't in the least suggest any loss of faith in him; but Alvah Loft has a mind which speaks to the *mind*; there is no appeal to the feelings. Whereas in Gobine's teaching there is a mystic strain, a kind of Immediacy, as Mrs. Swoffer calls it . . . Immediacy . . ." Pauline lingered on the term. It captivated her, as any word did when she first heard it used in a new connection. "I don't know how one could define the sensation better. 'Soul-unveiling' is Gobine's expression . . . But he insists on time, on plenty of time . . . He says we are all parching our souls by too much hurry. Of course I always felt that with Alvah Loft. I felt like one of those cash-boxes they shoot along over your head in the department stores. Number one, number two, and so on—always somebody treading on your heels. Whereas Gobine absolutely refuses to be hurried. Sometimes he sees only one patient a day. When I left him he told me he thought he would not see any one else till the next morning. 'I don't want to mingle your soul with any other.' Rather beautiful, wasn't it? And he does give one a wonderful dreamy sense of rest . . ."

She closed her eyes and leaned back, evoking the gaunt bearded face and heavy-lidded eyes of the new prophet, and the moist adhesive palm he had laid in benediction on her forehead. How different from the thick-lipped oily Mahatma, and from the thin dry Alvah Loft, who seemed more like an implement in a laboratory than a human being! "Perhaps one needs them all in turn," Pauline murmured half-aloud, with the self-indulgence of the woman who has never had to do over an out-of-fashion garment.

"One ought to be able to pass on last year's healers to one's poor relations, oughtn't one, mother?" Nona softly mocked; but her mother disarmed her with an unresentful smile.

"Darling! I know you don't understand these things yet— only, child, I do want you to be a little on your guard against becoming *bitter*, won't you? There—you don't mind your old mother's just suggesting it?"

Really Nona worried her at times—or would, if Gobine hadn't shed over her this perfumed veil of Peace. Yes—Peace: that was what she had always needed. Perfect confidence that everything would always come right in the end. Of course the other healers had taught that too; some people might say that Gobine's evangel was only the Mahatma's doctrine of the Higher Harmony. But the resemblance was merely superficial, as the Scientific Initiate had been careful to explain to her. Her previous guides had not been Initiates, and had no scientific training; they could only guess, whereas he *knew*. That was the meaning of Immediacy: direct contact with the Soul of the Invisible. How clear and beautiful he made it all! How all the little daily problems shrivelled up and vanished like a puff of smoke to eyes cleared by that initiation! And he had seen at once that Pauline was one of the few who *could* be initiated; who were worthy to be drawn out of the senseless modern rush and taken in Beyond the Veil. She closed her eyes again, and felt herself there with him . . . "Of course he treats hardly anybody," Mrs. Swoffer had assured her; "not one in a hundred. He says he'd rather starve than waste his time on the unmystical. (He saw at once that you were mystical.) Because he takes time—he must have it . . . Days, weeks, if necessary. Our crowded engagements mean nothing to him. He won't have a clock in the house. And he doesn't care whether he's paid or not; he says he's paid in soul-growth. Marvellous, isn't it?"

Marvellous indeed! And how different from Alvah Loft's Taylorized treatments, his rapidly rising scale of charges, and the unbroken stream of patients succeeding each other under his bony touch! And how one came back from communion with the Invisible longing to help others, to draw all one's dear ones with one Beyond the Veil. Pauline had gone to town with an unavowed burden on her mind. Jim, Lita, her husband, that blundering Amalasuntha, that everlasting Michelangelo; and Nona, too—Nona, who looked thinner and more drawn every day, and whose tongue seemed to grow sharper and more derisive; who seemed—at barely twenty—to be turning from a gay mocking girl into a pinched fault-finding old maid . . .

All these things had weighed on Pauline more than she cared to acknowledge; but now she felt strong enough to lift them, or rather they had become as light as air. "If only you Americans would persuade yourselves of the utter unimportance of the Actual—of the total non-existence of the Real." That was what Gobine had said, and the words had thrilled her like a revelation. Her eyes continued to rest with an absent smile on her daughter's ironic face, but what she was really thinking of was: "How on earth can I possibly induce him to come to the Cardinal's reception?"

That was one of the things that Nona would never understand her caring about. She would credit—didn't Pauline know!—her mother with the fatuous ambition to use her united celebrities for a social "draw," as a selfish child might gather all its toys into one heap; she would never see how important it was to bring together the representatives of the conflicting creeds, the bearers of the multiple messages, in the hope of drawing from their contact the flash of revelation for which the whole creation groaned. "If only the Cardinal could have a quiet talk with Gobine," Pauline thought; and, immediately dramatizing the possibility, saw herself steering his Eminence toward the innermost recess of her long suite of drawing-rooms, where the Scientific Initiate, shaggy but inspired, would suddenly stand before the Prince of the Church while she guarded the threshold from intruders. What new life it might put into the ossified Roman dogmas if the Cardinal could be made to understand that beautiful new doctrine of Immediacy! But how could she ever persuade Gobine to kiss the ring?

"And Mrs. Bruss—any news? I thought Maisie seemed really hopeful."

"Yes; the night wasn't bad. The doctors think she'll go on all right—for the present."

Pauline frowned; it was distasteful to have the suggestion of suffering and decay obtruded upon her beatific mood. She was living in a world where such things were not, and it seemed cruel—and unnecessary—to suggest to her that perhaps all Mrs. Bruss had already endured might not avail to spare her future misery.

"I'm sure we ought to try to resist looking ahead, and creating imaginary suffering for ourselves or others. Why should the doctors say 'for the present'? They can't possibly tell if the disease will ever come back."

"No; but they know it generally does."

"Can't you see, Nona, that that's just what *makes* it? Being prepared to suffer is really the way to create suffering. And creating suffering is creating sin, because sin and suffering are really one. We ought to refuse ourselves to pain. All the great Healers have taught us that."

Nona lifted her eyebrows in the slightly disturbing way she had. "Did Christ?"

Pauline felt her colour rise. This habit of irrelevant and rather impertinent retort was growing on Nona. The idea of stirring up the troublesome mysteries of Christian dogma at the breakfast-table! Pauline had no intention of attacking any religion. But Nona was really getting as querulous as a teething child.

Perhaps that was what she was, morally; perhaps some new experience was forcing its way through the tender flesh of her soul. The suggestion was disturbing to all Pauline's theories; yet confronted with her daughter's face and voice she could only take refuge in the idea that Nona, unable to attain the Higher Harmony, was struggling in a crepuscular wretchedness from which she refused to be freed.

"If you'd only come to Gobine with me, dear, these problems would never trouble you any more."

"They don't now—not an atom. What troubles me is the plain human tangle, as it remains after we've done our best to straighten it out. Look at Mrs. Bruss!"

"But the doctors say there's every chance—"

"Did you ever know them not to, after a first operation for cancer?"

"Of course, Nona, if you take sorrow and suffering for granted—"

"I don't, mother; but, apparently, Somebody does, judging from their diffusion and persistency, as the natural history books say."

Pauline felt her smooth brows gather in an unwelcome frown. The child had succeeded in spoiling her breakfast and in unsettling the happy equilibrium which she had imparted to her world. She didn't know what ailed Nona, unless she was fretting over Stan Heuston's disgraceful behaviour; but if so, it was better that she should learn in time what he was, and face her disillusionment. She might actually have ended by falling in love with him, Pauline reflected, and that would have been very disagreeable on account of Aggie. "What she needs is to marry," Pauline said to herself, struggling back to serenity.

She glanced at her watch, wondered if it were worth while to wait any longer for her husband, and decided to instruct Powder to keep his breakfast hot, and produce fresh coffee and rice-cakes when he rang.

Dexter, the day before, had taken Lita off on another long excursion. They had turned up so late that dinner had to be postponed for them, and had been so silent and remote all the evening that Pauline had ventured a jest on the soporific effects of country air, and suggested that every one should go to bed early. This morning, though it was past ten o'clock, neither of the two had appeared; and Nona declared herself ignorant of their plans for the day.

"It's a mercy Lita is so satisfied here," Pauline sighed, resigning herself to another dull day at the thought of the miracle Manford was accomplishing. She had felt rather nervous when Amalasuntha had appeared with her incredible film stories, and her braggings about the irresistible Michelangelo; but Lita did not seem to have been unsettled by them.

"Jim will have a good deal to be grateful for when he gets home," Pauline smiled to her daughter. "I do hope he'll appreciate what your father has done. His staying on the island seems to show that he does. By the way," she added, with another smile, "I didn't tell you, did I, that I ran across Arthur yesterday?"

Nona hesitated a moment. "So did I."

"Oh, did you? He didn't mention it. He looks better, don't you think so? But I found him excited and restless—almost as if another attack of gout were coming on. He was annoyed because I wouldn't go and see him then and there, though it was after six, and I should have had to dine in town."

"It's just as well you didn't, after such a tiring day."

"He was so persistent—you know how he is at times. He insisted that he must have a talk with me, though he wouldn't tell me about what."

"I don't believe he knows. As you say, he's always nervous when he has an attack coming on."

"But he seemed so hurt at my refusing. He wanted me to promise to go back today. And when I told him I couldn't he said that if I didn't he'd come out here."

Nona gave an impatient shrug. "How absurd! But of course he won't. I don't exactly see dear old Exhibit walking up to the front door of Cedarledge."

Pauline's colour rose again; she too had pictured the same possibility, only to reject it. Wyant had always refused to cross her threshold in New York, though she lived in a house bought after her second marriage; surely he would be still more reluctant to enter Cedarledge, where he and she had spent their early life together, and their son had been born. There were certain things, as he was always saying, that a man didn't do: that was all.

Nona was still pondering. "I wouldn't go to town to see him, mother; why should you? He was excited, and rather cross, yesterday, but he really hadn't anything to say. He just wanted to hear himself talk. As long as we're here he'll never come, and when this mood passes off he won't even remember what it was about. If you like I'll write and tell him that you'll see him as soon as we get back."

"Thank you, dear. I wish you would."

How sensible the child could be when she chose! Her answer chimed exactly with her mother's secret inclination, and the latter, rising from the breakfast-table, decided to slip away to a final revision of the Cardinal's list. It was pleasant, for once, to have time to give so important a matter all the attention it deserved.

Chapter XXVIII

WHEN Nona came down the next morning it was raining—a cold blustery rain, lashing the branches about and driving the startled spring back into its secret recesses.

It was the first rain since their arrival at Cedarledge, and it seemed to thrust them back also—back into the wintry world of town, of dripping streets, early lamplight and crowded places of amusement.

Mrs. Manford had already breakfasted and left the dining-room, but her husband's plate was still untouched. He came in as Nona was finishing, and after an absent-minded nod and smile dropped silently into his place. He sat opposite the tall rain-striped windows, and as he stared out into the grayness it seemed as if some of it, penetrating into the room in spite of the red sparkle of the fire, had tinged his face and hair. Lately Nona had been struck by his ruddiness, and the vigour of the dark waves crisping about his yellow-brown temples; but now he had turned sallow and autumnal. "What people call looking one's age, I suppose—as if we didn't have a dozen or a hundred ages, all of us!"

Her father had withdrawn his stare from the outer world and turned it toward the morning paper on the book-stand beside his plate. With lids lowered and fixed lips he looked strangely different again—rather like his own memorial bust in bronze. She shivered a little . . .

"Father! Your coffee's getting cold."

He pushed aside the paper, glanced at the letters piled by his plate, and lifted his eyes to Nona's. The twinkle she always wore seemed to struggle up to her from a long way off.

"I missed my early tramp and don't feel particularly enthusiastic about breakfast."

"It's not enthusiastic weather."

"No." He had grown absent-minded again. "Pity; when we've so few days left."

"It may clear, though."

What stupid things they were saying! Much either he or she cared about the weather, when they were in the country and had the prospect of a good tramp or a hard gallop together. Not that they had had many such lately; but then she had been busy with her mother, trying to make up for Maisie's absence; and there had been the interruption caused by the week-end party; and he had been helping to keep Lita amused—with success, apparently.

"Yes . . . I shouldn't wonder if it cleared." He frowned out toward the sky again. "Round about midday." He paused, and added: "I thought of running Lita over to Greystock."

She nodded. They would no doubt stay and dine, and Lita would get her dance. Probably Mrs. Manford wouldn't mind, though she was beginning to show signs of wearying of tête-à-tête dinners with her daughter. But they could go over the reception list again; and Pauline could talk about her new Messiah.

Nona glanced down at her own letters. She often forgot to look at them till the day was nearly over, now that she knew the one writing her eyes thirsted for would not be on any of the envelopes. Stanley Heuston had made no sign since they had parted that night on the doorstep . . .

The door opened, and Lita came in. It was the first time since their arrival that she had appeared at breakfast. She faced Manford as she entered, and Nona saw her father's expression change. It was like those funny old portraits in the picture-restorers' windows, with a veil of age and dust removed from one half to show the real surface underneath. Lita's entrance did not make him look either younger or happier; it simply removed from his face the soul-disguising veil which life inter-poses between a man's daily world and himself. He looked stripped—exposed . . . exposed . . . that was it. Nona glanced at Lita, not to surprise her off her guard, but simply to look away from her father.

Lita's face was what it always was: something so complete and accomplished that one could not imagine its being altered by any interior disturbance. It was like a delicate porcelain vase, or a smooth heavy flower, that a shifting of light might affect, but nothing from within would alter. She smiled in her round-eyed unseeing way, as a little gold-and-ivory goddess might smile down on her worshippers, and said: "I got up early because there wasn't any need to."

The reason was one completely satisfying to herself, but its effect on her hearers was perhaps disappointing. Nona made no comment, and Manford merely laughed—a vague laugh addressed, one could see, less to her words, which he appeared not to have noticed, than to the mere luminous fact of her presence; the kind of laugh evoked by the sight of a dazzling fringed fish or flower suddenly offered to one's admiration.

"I think the rain will hold off before lunch," he said, communicating the fact impartially to the room.

"Oh, what a pity—I wanted to get my hair thoroughly drenched. It's beginning to uncurl with the long drought," Lita said, her hand wavering uncertainly between the dishes Powder had placed in front of her. "Grape-fruit, I think—though it's so awfully ocean-voyagy. Promise me, Nona—!" She turned to her sister-in-law.

"Promise you what?"

"Not to send me a basket of grape-fruit when I sail."

Manford looked up at her impenetrable porcelain face. His lips half parted on an unspoken word; then he pushed back his chair and got up.

"I'll order the car at eleven," he said, in a tone of aimless severity.

Lita was scooping a spoonful of juice out of the golden bowl of the grape-fruit. She seemed neither to heed nor to hear. Manford laid down his napkin and walked out of the room.

Lita threw back her head to let the liquid slip slowly down between her lips. Her gold-fringed lids fluttered a little, as if the fruit-juice were a kiss.

"When are you sailing?" Nona asked, reaching for the cigarette-lighter.

"Don't know. Next week, I shouldn't wonder."

"For any particular part of the globe?"

Lita's head descended, and she turned her chestnut-coloured eyes softly on her sister-in-law. "Yes; but I can't remember what it's called."

Nona was looking at her in silence. It was simply that she was so beautiful. A vase? No—a lamp now: there *was* a glow from the interior. As if her red corpuscles had turned into millions of fairy lamps . . .

Her glance left Nona's and returned to her plate. "Letters. What a bore! Why on earth don't people telephone?"

She did not often receive letters, her congenital inability to answer them having gradually cooled the zeal of her correspondents; of all, that is, excepting her husband. Almost every day Nona saw one of Jim's gray-blue envelopes on the hall table. That particular colour had come to symbolize to her a state of patient expectancy.

Lita was turning over some impersonal looking bills and advertisements. From beneath them the faithful gray-blue envelope emerged. Nona thought: "If only he wouldn't—!" and her eyes filled.

Lita looked pensively at the post-mark and then laid the envelope down unopened.

"Aren't you going to read your letter?"

She raised her brows. "Jim's? I did—yesterday. One just like it."

"Lita! You're—you're perfectly beastly!"

Lita's languid mouth rounded into a smile. "Not to you, darling. Do you want me to read it?" She slipped a polished finger-tip under the flap.

"Oh, no; no! Don't—not like that!" It made Nona wince. "I wish she *hated* Jim—I wish she wanted to kill him! I could bear it better than this," the girl stormed inwardly. She got up and turned toward the door.

"Nona—wait! What's the matter? Don't you really want to hear what he says?" Lita stood up also, her eyes still on the open letter. "He—oh . . ." She turned toward her sister-in-law a face from which the inner glow had vanished.

"What is it? Is he ill? What's wrong?"

"He's coming home. He wants me to go back the day after tomorrow." She stood staring in front of her, her eyes fixed on something invisible to Nona, and beyond her.

"Does he say why?"

"He doesn't say anything but that."

"When did you expect him?"

"I don't know. Not for ages. I never can remember about dates. But I thought he liked it down there. And your father said he'd arranged—"

"Arranged what?" Nona interrupted.

Lita seemed to become aware of her again, and turned on her a smooth inaccessible face. "I don't know: arranged with the bank, I suppose."

"To keep him there?"

"To let him have a good long holiday. You all thought he needed it so awfully, didn't you?"

Nona stood motionless, staring out of the window. She saw her father drive up in the Buick. The rain had diminished to a silver drizzle shot with bursts of sun, and through the open window she heard him call: "It's going to clear after all. We'd better start."

Lita went out of the door, humming a tune.

"Lita!" Nona called out, moved by some impulse to arrest, to warn—she didn't know what. But the door had closed, and Lita was already out of hearing.

All through the day it kept on raining at uncomfortable intervals. Uncomfortable, that is, for Pauline and Nona. Whenever they tried to get out for a walk a deluge descended; then, as soon as they had splashed back to the house with the dripping dogs, the clouds broke and mocked them with a blaze of sunshine. But by that time they were either revising the list again, or had settled down to Mah-jongg in the library.

"Really, I can't go up and change into my walking shoes *again*!" Pauline remonstrated to the weather; and a few minutes later the streaming window-panes had justified her.

"April showers," she remarked with a slightly rigid smile. She looked deprecatingly at her daughter. "It was selfish of me to keep you here, dear. You ought to have gone with your father and Lita."

"But there were all those notes to do, mother. And really I'm rather fed-up with Greystock."

Pauline executed a repetition of her smile. "Well, I fancy we shall have them back for tea. No golf this afternoon, I'm afraid," she said, glancing with a certain furtive satisfaction at the increasing downpour.

"No; but Lita may want to stay and dance."

Pauline made no comment, but once more addressed her disciplined attention to the game.

The fire, punctually replenished, continued to crackle and drowse. The warmth drew out the strong scent of the carnations and rose-geraniums, and made the room as languid as a summer garden. Dusk fell from the cloud-laden skies, and in due course the hand which tended the fire drew the curtains on their noiseless rings and lit the lamps. Lastly Powder appeared, heading the processional entrance of the tea-table.

Pauline roused herself from a languishing Mah-jongg to take her expected part in the performance. She and Nona grouped themselves about the hearth, and Pauline lifted the lids of the little covered dishes with a critical air.

"I ordered those muffins your father likes so much," she said, in a tone of unwonted wistfulness. "Perhaps we'd better send them out to be kept hot."

Nona agreed that it would be better; but as she had her hand on the bell the sound of an approaching motor checked her. The dogs woke with a happy growling and bustled out. "There they are after all!" Pauline said.

There was a minute or two of silence, unmarked by the usual yaps of welcome; then a sound like the depositing of wraps and an umbrella; then Powder on the threshold, for once embarrassed and at a loss.

"Mr. Wyant, madam."

"Mr. Wyant?"

"Mr. Arthur Wyant. He seemed to think you were probably expecting him," Powder continued, as if lengthening the communication in order to give her time.

Mrs. Manford, seizing it, rose to the occasion with one of her heroic wing-beats. "Yes—I *was*. Please show him in," she said, without risking a glance at her daughter.

Arthur Wyant came in, tall and stooping in his shabby well-cut clothes, a nervous flush on his cheekbones. He paused, and sent a half-bewildered stare about the room—a look which seemed to say that when he had made up his mind that he must see Pauline he had failed to allow for the familiarity of the setting in which he was to find her.

"You've hardly changed anything here," he said abruptly, in the far-off tone of a man slowly coming back to consciousness.

"How are you, Arthur? I'm sorry you've had such a rainy day for your trip," Mrs. Manford responded, with an easy intonation intended to reach the retreating Powder.

Her former husband took no notice. His eyes continued to travel about the room in the same uncertain searching way.

"Hardly anything," he repeated, still seemingly unaware of any presence in the room but his own. "That Raeburn, though—yes. That used to be in the dining-room, didn't it?" He passed his hand over his forehead, as if to brush away some haze of oblivion, and walked up to the picture.

"Wait a bit. It's in the place where the Sargent of Jim as a youngster used to hang—Jim on his pony. Just over my writing-table, so that I saw it whenever I looked up . . ." He turned to Pauline. "Jolly picture. What have you done with it? Why did you take it away?"

Pauline coloured, but a smile of conciliation rode gallantly over her blush. "I didn't. That is—Dexter wanted it. It's in his room; it's been there for years." She paused, and then added: "You know how devoted Dexter is to Jim."

Wyant had turned abruptly from the contemplation of the Raeburn. The colour in Pauline's cheek was faintly reflected in his own. "Stupid of me . . . of course . . . Fact is, I was rather rattled when I came in, seeing everything so much the same . . . You must excuse my turning up in this way; I had to see you about something important . . . Hullo, Nona—"

"Of course I excuse you, Arthur. Do sit down—here by the fire. You must be cold after your wet journey . . . so unseasonable, after the weather we've been having. Nona will ring for tea," Pauline said, with her accent of indomitable hospitality.

Chapter XXIX

NONA, that night, in her mother's doorway, wavered a moment and then turned back.

"Well, then—goodnight, mother."

"Goodnight, child."

But Mrs. Manford seemed to waver too. She stood there in her rich dusky draperies, and absently lifted a hand to detach one after the other of her long earrings. It was one of Mrs. Manford's rules never to keep up her maid to undress her.

"Can I unfasten you, mother?"

"Thanks, dear, no; this teagown slips off so easily. You must be tired . . ."

"No; I'm not tired. But you . . ."

"I'm not either." They stood irresolute on the threshold of the warm shadowy room lit only by a waning sparkle from the hearth. Pauline switched on the lamps.

"Come in then, dear." Her strained smile relaxed, and she laid a hand on her daughter's shoulder. "Well, it's over," she said, in the weary yet satisfied tone in which Nona had sometimes heard her pronounce the epitaph of a difficult but successful dinner.

Nona followed her, and Pauline sank down in an armchair near the fire. In the shaded lamplight, with the glint of the fire playing across her face, and her small head erect on still comely shoulders, she had a sweet dignity of aspect which moved her daughter incongruously.

"I'm so thankful you've never bobbed your hair, mother."

Mrs. Manford stared at this irrelevancy; her stare seemed to say that she was resigned to her daughter's verbal leaps, but had long since renounced the attempt to keep up with them.

"You're so handsome just as you are," Nona continued. "I can understand dear old Exhibit's being upset when he saw you here, in the same surroundings, and looking, after all, so much as you must have in his day . . . And when he himself is so changed . . ."

Pauline lowered her lids over the vision. "Yes. Poor Arthur!" Had she ever, for the last fifteen years, pronounced her former husband's name without adding that depreciatory epithet?

Somehow pity—an indulgent pity—was always the final feeling he evoked. She leaned back against the cushions, and added: "It was certainly unfortunate, his taking it into his head to come out here. I didn't suppose he would have remembered so clearly how everything looked . . . The Sargent of Jim on the pony . . . Do you think he minded?"

"Its having been moved to father's room? Yes; I think he did."

"But, Nona, he's always been so grateful to your father for what he's done for Jim—and for Lita. He *admires* your father. He's often told me so."

"Yes."

"At any rate, once he was here, I couldn't do less than ask him to stay to dine."

"No; you couldn't. Especially as there was no train back till after dinner."

"And, after all, I don't, to this minute, know what he came for!"

Nona lifted her eyes from an absorbed contemplation of the fire. "You don't?"

"Oh, of course, in a vague way, to talk about Jim and Lita. The same old things we've heard so many times. But I quieted him very soon about that. I told him Lita had been perfectly happy here—that the experiment had been a complete success. He seemed surprised that she had given up all her notions about Hollywood and Klawhammer . . . apparently Amalasuntha has been talking a lot of nonsense to him . . . but when I said that Lita had never once spoken of Hollywood, and that she was going home the day after tomorrow to join her husband, it seemed to tranquillize him completely. Didn't he seem to you much quieter when he drove off?"

"Yes; he was certainly quieter. But he seemed to want particularly to see Lita."

Pauline drew a quick breath. "Yes. On the whole I was glad she wasn't here. Lita has never known how to manage Arthur, and her manner is sometimes so irritating. She might have said something that would have upset him again. It was really a relief when your father telephoned that they had decided to dine at Greystock—though I could see that Arthur thought that funny too. His ideas have never progressed an inch; he's always remained as old-fashioned as his mother." She paused a moment, and then went on: "I saw you were a little startled when I asked him if he wouldn't like to spend the night. But I didn't want to appear inhospitable."

"No; not in this house," Nona agreed with her quick smile. "And of course one knew he wouldn't—"

Pauline sighed. "Poor Arthur! He's always so punctilious."

"It wasn't only that. He was suffering horribly."

"About Lita? So foolish! As if he couldn't trust her to us—"

"Not only about Lita. But just from the fact of being here—of having all his old life thrust back on him. He seemed utterly unprepared for it—as if he'd really succeeded in not thinking about it at all for years. And suddenly there it was: like the drowning man's vision. A drowning man—that's what he was like."

Pauline straightened herself slightly, and Nona saw her brows gather in a faint frown. "What dreadful ideas you have! I thought I'd never seen him looking better; and certainly he didn't take too much wine at dinner."

"No; he was careful about that."

"And I was careful too. I managed to give a hint to Powder." Her frown relaxed, and she leaned back with another sigh, this time of appeasement. After all, her look seemed to say, she was not going to let herself be unsettled by Nona's mortuary images, now that the whole business was over, and she had every reason to congratulate herself on her own share in it.

Nona (but it was her habit!) appeared less sure. She hung back a moment, and then said: "I haven't told you yet. On the way down to dinner . . ."

"What, dear?"

"I met him on the upper landing. He asked to see the baby . . . that was natural . . ."

Pauline drew her lips in nervously. She had thought she had all the wires in her hands; and here was one— She agreed with an effort: "Perfectly natural."

"The baby was asleep, looking red and jolly. He stood over the crib a long time. Luckily it wasn't the old nursery."

"Really, Nona! He could hardly expect—"

"No; of course not. Then, just as we were going downstairs, he said: 'Funny, how like Jim the child is growing. Reminds me of that old portrait.' And he jerked out at me: 'Could I see it?'"

"What—the Sargent?"

Nona nodded. "Could I refuse him?"

"I suppose that was natural too."

"So I took him into father's study. He seemed to remember every step of the way. He stood and looked and looked at the picture. He didn't say anything . . . didn't answer when I spoke . . . I saw that it went through and through him."

"Well, Nona, byegones are byegones. But people do bring things upon themselves, sometimes—"

"Oh, I know, mother."

"Some people might think it peculiar, his rambling about the house like that—his coming here at all, with his ideas of delicacy! But I don't blame him; and I don't want you to," Pauline continued firmly. "After all, it's just as well he came. He may have been a little upset at the moment; but I managed to calm him down; and I certainly proved to him that everything's all right, and that Dexter and I can be trusted to know what's best for Lita." She paused, and then added: "Do you know, I'm rather inclined not to mention his visit to your father—or to Lita. Now it's over, why should they be bothered?"

"No reason at all." Nona rose from her crouching attitude by the fire, and stretched her arms above her head. "I'll see that Powder doesn't say anything. And besides, he wouldn't. He always seems to know what needs explaining and what doesn't. He ought to be kept to avert cataclysms, like those fire-extinguishers in the passages . . . Goodnight, mother—I'm beginning to be sleepy."

Yes; it was all over and done with; and Pauline felt that she had a right to congratulate herself. She had not told Nona how "difficult" Wyant had been for the first few minutes, when the girl had slipped out of the library after tea and left them alone. What was the use of going into all that? Pauline had been a little nervous at first—worried, for instance, as to what might happen if Dexter and Lita should walk in while Arthur was in that queer excited state, stamping up and down the library floor, and muttering, half to himself and half to her: "Damn it, am I in my own house or another man's? Can anybody answer me that?"

But they had not walked in, and the phase of excitability had soon been over. Pauline had only had to answer: "You're

in *my* house, Arthur, where, as Jim's father, you're always welcome . . ." That had put a stop to his ravings, shamed him a
little, and so brought him back to his sense of what was due to
the occasion, and to his own dignity.

"My dear—you must excuse me. I'm only an intruder here,
I know—"

And when she had added: "Never in my house, Arthur. Sit
down, please, and tell me what you want to see me about—"
why, at that question, quietly and reasonably put, all his bluster
had dropped, and he had sat down as she bade him, and begun,
in his ordinary tone, to rehearse the old rigmarole about Jim
and Lita, and Jim's supineness, and Lita's philanderings, and
what would the end of it be, and did she realize that the woman
was making a laughing-stock of their son—yes, that they were
talking about it at the clubs?

After that she had had no trouble. It had been easy to throw a
little gentle ridicule over his apprehensions, and then to reassure
him by her report of her own talk with Lita (though she winced
even now at its conclusion), and the affirmation that the Cedarledge experiment had been entirely successful. Then, luckily,
just as his questions began to be pressing again—as he began to
hint at some particular man, she didn't know who—Powder had
come in to show him up to one of the spare-rooms to prepare
for dinner; and soon after dinner the motor was at the door, and
Powder (again acting for Providence) had ventured to suggest,
sir, that in view of the slippery state of the roads it would be well
to get off as promptly as possible. And Nona had taken over the
seeing-off, and with a long sigh of relief Pauline had turned back
into the library, where Wyant's empty whisky-and-soda glass
and ash-tray stood, so uncannily, on the table by her husband's
armchair. Yes; she had been thankful when it was over . . .

And now she was thankful that it had happened. The encounter had fortified her confidence in her own methods and given
her a new proof of her power to surmount obstacles by smiling
them away. She had literally smiled Arthur out of the house,
when some women, in a similar emergency, would have made a
scene, or stood on their dignity. Dignity! Hers consisted, more
than ever, in believing the best of every one, in persuading
herself and others that to impute evil was to create it, and to
disbelieve it was to prevent its coming into being. Those were

the Scientific Initiate's very words: "We manufacture sorrow as we do all the other toxins." How grateful she was to him for that formula! And how light and happy it made her feel to know that she had borne it in mind, and proved its truth, at so crucial a moment! She looked back with pity at her own past moods of distrust, her wretched impulses of jealousy and suspicion, the moments when even those nearest her had not been proof against her morbid apprehensions . . .

How absurd and far away it all seemed now! Jim was coming back the day after tomorrow. Lita and the baby were going home to him. And the day after that they would all be going back to town; and then the last touches would be put to the ceremonial of the Cardinal's reception. Oh, she and Powder would have their hands full! All of the big silver-gilt service would have to be got out of the safety vaults and gone over . . . Luckily the last reports of Mrs. Bruss's state were favourable, and no doubt Maisie would be back as usual . . . Yes, life was really falling into its usual busy and pleasurable routine. Rest in the country was all very well; but rest, if overdone, became fatiguing . . .

She found herself in bed, the lights turned off, and sleep descending on her softly.

Before it held her, she caught, through misty distances, the sound of her husband's footfall, the opening and shutting of his door, and the muffled noises of his undressing. Well . . . so he was back . . . and Lita . . . silly Lita . . . no harm, really . . . Just as well they hadn't met poor Arthur . . . Everything was all right . . . the Cardinal . . .

Chapter XXX

PAULINE sat up suddenly in bed. It was as if an invisible hand had touched a spring in her spinal column, and set her upright in the darkness before she was aware of any reason for it.

No doubt she had heard something through her sleep; but what? She listened for a repetition of the sound.

All was silence. She stretched out her hand to an onyx knob on the table by her bed, and instantly the face of a miniature clock was illuminated, and the hour chimed softly; two strokes followed by one. Half-past two—the silentest hour of the night; and in the vernal hush of Cedarledge! Yet certainly there had been a sound—a sharp explosive sound . . . Again! There it was: a revolver shot . . . somewhere in the house . . .

Burglars?

Her feet were in her slippers, her hand on the electric light switch. All the while she continued to listen intently. Dead silence everywhere . . .

But how had burglars got in without starting the alarm? Ah—she remembered! Powder had orders never to set it while any one was out of the house; it was Dexter who should have seen that it was connected when he got back from Greystock with Lita. And naturally he had forgotten to.

Pauline was on her feet, her hair smoothed back under her fillet-shaped cap of silver lace, her "rest-gown" of silvery silk slipped over her night-dress. This emergency garb always lay at her bedside in case of nocturnal alarms, and she was equipped in an instant, and had already reconnected the burglar-alarm, and sounded the general summons for Powder, the footmen, the gardeners and chauffeurs. Her hand played irresolutely over the complicated knobs of the glittering switchboard which filled a panel of her dressing-room; then she pressed the button marked "Engine-house." Why not? There had been a series of bad suburban burglaries lately, and one never knew . . . It was just as well to rouse the neighbourhood . . . Dexter was so careless. Very likely he had left the front door open.

Silence still—profounder than ever. Not a sound since that second shot, if shot it was. Very softly she opened her door and paused in the anteroom between her room and her husband's. "Dexter!" she called.

No answer; no responding flash of light. Men slept so heavily. She opened, lighted—"Dexter!"

The room was empty, her husband's bed unslept in. But then—what? Those sounds of his return? Had she been dreaming when she thought she heard them? Or was it the burglars she had heard, looting his room, a few feet off from where she lay? In spite of her physical courage a shiver ran over her . . .

But if Dexter and Lita were not yet back, whence had the sound of the shot come, and who had fired it? She trembled at the thought of Nona—Nona and the baby! They were alone with the baby's nurse on the farther side of the house. And the house seemed suddenly so immense, so resonant, so empty . . .

In the shadowy corridor outside her room she paused again for a second, straining her ears for a guiding sound; then she sped on, pushing back the swinging door which divided the farther wing from hers, turning on the lights with a flying hand as she ran . . . On the deeply carpeted floors her foot-fall made no sound, and she had the sense of skimming over the ground inaudibly, like something ghostly, disembodied, which had no power to break the hush and make itself heard . . .

Half way down the passage she was startled to see the door of Lita's bedroom open. Sounds at last—sounds low, confused and terrified—issued from it. What kind of sounds? Pauline could not tell; they were rushing together in a vortex in her brain. She heard herself scream "Help!" with the strangled voice of a nightmare, and was comforted to feel the rush of other feet behind her: Powder, the men-servants, the maids. Thank God the system worked! Whatever she was coming to, at least they would be there to help . . .

She reached the door, pushed it—and it unexpectedly resisted. Some one was clinging to it on the inner side, struggling to hold it shut, to prevent her entering. She threw herself against it with all her strength, and saw her husband's arm and hand in the gap. "Dexter!"

"Oh, God." He fell back, and the door with him. Pauline went in.

All the lights were on—the room was a glare. Another man stood shivering and staring in a corner, but Pauline hardly noticed him, for before her on the floor lay Lita's long body, in a loose spangled robe, flung sobbing over another body.

"Nona—Nona!" the mother screamed, rushing forward to where they lay.

She swept past her husband, dragged Lita back, was on her knees on the floor, her child pressed to her, Nona's fallen head against her breast, Nona's blood spattering the silvery folds of the rest-gown, destroying it forever as a symbol of safety and repose.

"Nona—child! What's happened? Are you hurt? Dexter—for pity's sake! Nona, look at me! It's mother, darling, mother—"

Nona's eyes opened with a flutter. Her face was ashen-white, and empty as a baby's. Slowly she met her mother's agonized stare. "All right . . . only winged me." Her gaze wavered about the disordered room, lifting and dropping in a butterfly's bewildered flight. Lita lay huddled on the couch in her spangles, twisted and emptied, like a festal garment flung off by its wearer. Manford stood between, his face a ruin. In the corner stood that other man, shrinking, motionless. Pauline's eyes, following her child's, travelled on to him.

"Arthur!" she gasped out, and felt Nona's feeble pressure on her arm.

"Don't . . . don't . . . It was an accident. Father—an accident! *Father*!"

The door of the room was wide now, and Powder stood there, unnaturally thin and gaunt in his improvised collarless garb, marshalling the gaping footmen, with gardeners, chauffeurs and maids crowding the corridor behind them. It was really marvellous, how Pauline's system had worked.

Manford turned to Arthur Wyant, his stony face white with revenge. Wyant still stood motionless, his arms hanging down, his body emptied of all its strength, a broken word that sounded like "honour" stumbling from his bedraggled lips.

"*Father*!" At Nona's faint cry Manford's arm fell to his side also, and he stood there as powerless and motionless as the other.

"All an accident . . ." breathed from the white lips against Pauline.

Powder had stepped forward. His staccato orders rang back over his shoulder. "Ring up the doctor. Have a car ready. Scour the gardens . . . One of the women here! Madam's maid!"

Manford suddenly roused himself and swung about with dazed eyes on the disheveled group in the doorway. "Damn you, what are you doing here, all of you? Get out—get out, the lot of you! Get out, I say! Can't you hear me?"

Powder bent a respectful but controlling eye on his employer. "Yes, sir; certainly, sir. I only wish to state that the burglar's mode of entrance has already been discovered." Manford met this with an unseeing stare, but the butler continued imperturbably: "Thanks to the rain, sir. He got in through the pantry window; the latch was forced, and there's muddy footprints on my linoleum, sir. A tramp was noticed hanging about this afternoon. I can give evidence—"

He darted swiftly between the two men, bent to the floor, and picked up something which he slipped quickly and secretly into his pocket. A moment later he had cleared his underlings from the threshold, and the door was shut on them and him.

"Dexter," Pauline cried, "help me to lift her to the bed."

Outside, through the watchful hush of the night, a rattle and roar came up the drive. It filled the silence with an unnatural clamour, immense, mysterious and menacing. It was the Cedarledge fire-brigade, arriving double quick in answer to their benefactress's summons.

Pauline, bending over her daughter's face, fancied she caught a wan smile on it . . .

Chapter XXXI

N ONA MANFORD'S room was full of spring flowers. They had poured in, sent by sympathizing friends, ever since she had been brought back to town from Cedarledge.

That was two weeks ago. It was full spring now, and her windows stood wide to the May sunset slanting across the room, and giving back to the tall branches of blossoming plum and cherry something of their native scent and freshness.

The reminder of Cedarledge would once have doubled their beauty; now it made her shut her eyes sharply, in the inner recoil from all the name brought back.

She was still confined to her room, for the shot which had fractured her arm near the shoulder had also grazed her lung, and her temperature remained obstinately high. Shock, the doctors said, chiefly . . . the appalling sight of a masked burglar in her sister-in-law's bedroom; and being twice fired at—twice!

Lita corroborated the story. She had been asleep when her door was softly opened, and she had started up to see a man in a mask, with a dark lantern . . . Yes; she was almost sure he had a mask; at any rate she couldn't see his face; the police had found the track of muddy feet on the pantry linoleum, and up the back stairs.

Lita had screamed, and Nona had dashed to the rescue; yes, and Mr. Manford—Lita thought Mr. Manford had perhaps got there before Nona. But then again, she wasn't sure . . . The fact was that Lita had been shattered by the night's experience, and her evidence, if not self-contradictory, was at least incoherent.

The only really lucid witnesses were Powder, the butler, and Nona Manford herself. Their statements agreed exactly, or at least dovetailed into each other with perfect precision, the one completing the other. Nona had been first on the scene: she had seen the man in the room—she too thought that he was masked—and he had turned on her and fired. At that moment her father, hearing the shots, had rushed in, half-dressed; and as he did so the burglar fled. Some one professed to have seen him running away through the rain and darkness; but no one had seen his face, and there was no way of identifying him. The only positive proof of his presence—except for the shot—was the discovery by Powder, of those carefully guarded footprints on the pantry floor; and these, of course, might eventually help to trace the criminal. As for the revolver, that also had disappeared; and the bullets, one of which had been found lodged in the door, the other in the panelling of the room, were of ordinary army calibre, and offered no clue. Altogether it was an interesting problem for the police, who were reported to be actively at work on it, though so far without visible results.

Then, after three days of flaming headlines and journalistic conjectures, another sensation crowded out the Cedarledge burglary. The newspaper public, bored with the inability of the police to provide fresh fuel for their curiosity, ceased to speculate on the affair, and interest in it faded out as quickly as it had flared up.

During the last few days Nona's temperature had gradually dropped, and she had been allowed to see visitors; first one in the day, then two or three, then four or five—so that by this time her jaws were beginning to feel a little stiff with the continual rehearsal of her story, embellished (at the visitors' request) with an analysis of her own emotions. She always repeated her narrative in exactly the same terms, and presented the incidents in exactly the same order; by now she had even learned to pause at the precise point where she knew her sympathizing auditors would say: "But, my dear, how perfectly awful—what *did* it feel like?"

"Like being shot in the arm."

"Oh, Nona, you're so cynical! But before that—when you *saw the man*—weren't you absolutely sick with terror?"

"He didn't give me time to be sick with anything but the pain in my shoulder."

"You'll never get her to confess that she was frightened!"

And so the dialogue went on. Did her listeners notice that she recited her tale with the unvarying precision of a lesson learned by heart? Probably not; if they did, they made no sign. The papers had all been full of the burglary at Cedarledge: a masked burglar—and of the shooting of Miss Manford, and the would-be murderer's escape. The account, blood-curdling and definite, had imposed itself on the public credulity with all the authority of heavy headlines and continual repetition. Within twenty-four hours the Cedarledge burglary was an established fact, and suburban millionaires were doubling the number of their night watchmen, and looking into the newest thing in burglar-alarms. Nona, leaning back wearily on her couch, wondered how soon she would be allowed to travel and get away from it all.

The others were all going to travel. Her mother and father were off that very evening to the Rocky Mountains and Vancouver. From there they were going to Japan and, in the early autumn, to Ceylon and India. Pauline already had letters to all the foremost Native Princes, and was regretting that there was not likely to be a Durbar during their visit. The Manfords did not expect to be back till January or February; Manford's professional labours had become so exhausting that the doctors, fearing his accumulated fatigue might lead to a nervous breakdown, had ordered a complete change and prolonged absence from affairs. Pauline hoped that Nona would meet them in Egypt on their way home. A sunny Christmas together in Cairo would be so lovely . . .

Arthur Wyant had gone also—to Canada, it was said, with cousin Eleanor in attendance. Some insinuated that a private inebriate asylum in Maine was the goal of his journey; but no one really knew, and few cared. His remaining cronies, when they heard that he had been ill, and was to travel for a change, shrugged or smiled, and said: "Poor old Arthur—been going it too strong again," and then forgot about him. He had long since lost his place in the scheme of things.

Even Lita and Jim Wyant were on a journey. They had sailed the previous week for Paris, where they would arrive in time for the late spring season, and Lita would see the Grand Prix, the new fashions and the new plays. Jim's holiday had been extended to the end of August: Manford, ever solicitous for his stepson, had arranged the matter with the bank. It was natural, every one agreed, that Jim should have been dreadfully upset by the ghastly episode at Cedarledge, in which his wife might have been a victim as well as Nona; and his intimates knew how much he had worried about his father's growing intemperance. Altogether, both Wyants and Manfords had been subjected to an unusual strain; and when rich people's nerves are out of gear the pleasant remedy of travel is the first prescribed.

Nona turned her head uneasily on the cushions. She felt incurably weary, and unable to rebound to the spring radiance which usually set her blood in motion. Her immobility had begun to wear on her. At first it had been a relief to be quiescent, to be out of things, to be offered up as the passive victim and the accepted evidence of the Cedarledge burglary. But now she was sick to nausea of the part, and envious of the others who could escape by flight—by perpetual evasion.

Not that she really wanted to be one of them; she was not sure that she wanted to go away at all—at least in the body. Spiritual escape was what she craved; but by what means, and whither? Perhaps it could best be attained by staying just where she was, by sticking fast to her few square feet of obligations and responsibilities. But even this idea made no special appeal. Her obligations, her responsibilities—what were they? Negative, at best, like everything else in her life. She had thought that renunciation would mean freedom—would mean at least escape. But today it seemed to mean only a closer self-imprisonment. She was tired, no doubt . . .

There was a tap on the door, and her mother entered. Nona raised her listless eyes curiously. She always looked at her mother with curiosity now: curiosity not so much as to what had changed in her, but as to what had remained the same. And it was extraordinary how Pauline, the old Pauline, was coming to the surface again through the new one, the haggard and stricken apparition of the Cedarledge midnight . . .

"My broken arm saved her," Nona thought, remembering, with a sort of ironical admiration, how that dishevelled spectre had become Pauline Manford again, in command of herself and the situation, as soon as she could seize on its immediate, its practical, sides; could grasp those handles of reality to which she always clung.

Now even that stern and disciplined figure had vanished, giving way, as the days passed and reassurance grew, to the usual, the everyday Pauline, smilingly confident in herself and in the general security of things. Had that dreadful night at Cedarledge ever been a reality to her? If it had, Nona was sure, it had already faded into the realms of fable, since its one visible result had been her daughter's injury, and that was on the way to healing. Everything else connected with it had happened out of sight and under ground, and for that reason was now as if it had never existed for Pauline, who was more than ever resolutely two-dimensional.

Physically, at least, the only difference Nona could detect was that a skilful make-up had filled in the lines which, in spite of all the arts of the face-restorers, were weaving their permanent web about her mother's lips and eyes. Under this delicate mask Pauline's face looked younger and fresher than ever, and as smooth and empty as if she had just been born again— "And she *has*, after all," Nona concluded.

She sat down by the couch, and laid a light hand caressingly on her daughter's.

"Darling! Had your tea? You feel really better, don't you? The doctor says the massage is to begin tomorrow. By the way—" she tossed a handful of newspaper cuttings onto the coverlet— "perhaps some of these things about the reception may amuse you. Maisie's been saving them to show you. Of course most of the foreign names are wrong; but the description of the room is rather good. I believe Tommy Ardwin wrote the article for the 'Looker-on.' Amalasuntha says the Cardinal will like it. It seems he was delighted with the idea of the flash-light photographs. Altogether he was very much pleased."

"Then you ought to be, mother." Nona forced her pale lips into a smile.

"I *am*, dear. If I do a thing at all I like to do it well. That's always been my theory, you know: the best or nothing. And I do believe it was a success. But perhaps I'm tiring you—." Pauline stood up irresolutely. She had never been good at bed-sides unless she could play some active and masterful part there. Nona was aware that her mother's moments alone with her had become increasingly difficult as her strength had returned, and there was nothing more to be done for her. It was as well that the Manfords were starting on their journey that evening.

"Don't stay, mother; I'm all right, really. It's only that things still tire me a little—"

Pauline lingered, looking down on the girl with an expression of anxiety struggling through her smooth rejuvenation.

"I wish I felt happier about leaving you, darling. I know you're all right, of course; but the idea of your staying in this house all by yourself—"

"It's just what I shall like. And on father's account you ought to get away."

"It's what I feel," Pauline assented, brightening.

"You must be awfully busy with all the last things to be done. I'm as comfortable as possible; I wish you'd just go off and forget about me."

"Well, Maisie *is* clamouring for me," Pauline confessed from the threshold.

The door shut, and Nona closed her eyes with a sigh. Tomorrow—tomorrow she would be alone! And in a week, perhaps, she would get back to Cedarledge, and lie on the terrace with the dogs about her, and no one to ask questions, to hint and sympathize, or be discreet and evasive . . . Yes, in spite of everything, the idea of returning to Cedarledge now seemed more bearable than any other . . .

In a restless attempt to ease her position she stretched her hand out, and it came in contact with the bundle of newspaper cuttings. She shrank back with a little grimace; then she smiled. After the night at Cedarledge every one had supposed—even Maisie and Powder had—that the Cardinal's reception would have to be given up, since, owing to his Eminence's impending departure, it could not be deferred. But it had come off on the appointed day—only the fourth after the burglary—and Pauline had made it a success. The girl really admired her mother for that. Something in her own composition responded to the energy with which the older woman could meet an emergency when there was no way of turning it. The party had been not only brilliant but entertaining. Every one had been there, all the official and ecclesiastical dignitaries, including the Bishop of New York and the Chief Rabbi—yes, even the Scientific Initiate, looking colossal and Siberian in some half-priestly dress that added its note to the general picturesqueness; and yet there had been no crush, no confusion, nothing to detract from the dignity and amenity of the evening. Nona suspected her mother of longing to invite the Mahatma, whose Oriental garb would have been so effective, and who would have been so flattered, poor man! But she had not risked it, and her chief lion, after the great ecclesiastics, had turned out to be Michelangelo, the newly arrived, with the film-glamour enhancing his noble Roman beauty, and his mother at his side, explaining and parading him.

"The pity is that dear Jim and Lita have sailed," the Marchesa declared to all who would give ear. "That's really a great disappointment. I did hope Lita would have been here tonight. She and my Michelangelo would have made such a glorious couple: the Old World and the New. Or as Antony and Cleopatra—only fancy! My boy tells me that Klawhammer is looking for a Cleopatra. But dear Lita will be back before long—." And she mingled her hopes and regrets with Mrs. Percy Landish's.

Chapter XXXII

NONA shut her eyes again. Ever since that intolerable night she had ached with the incessant weariness of not being able to sleep, and of trying to hide from those about her how brief her intervals of oblivion had been. During the hours of darkness she seemed to be forever toiling down perspectives of noise and glare, like a wanderer in the labyrinth of an unknown city. Even her snatches of sleep were so crowded with light and noise, so dazzled with the sense of exposure, that she was not conscious of the respite till it was over. It was only by day, alone in her room, that her lids, in closing, sometimes shut things out . . .

Such a respite came to her now; and she started up out of nothingness to find her father at her side. She had not expected to see him alone before they parted. She had fancied that her parents would contrive to postpone their joint farewells till after dinner, just before driving off to their train. For a moment she lay and looked up at Manford without being clearly conscious that he was there, and without knowing what to say if he were.

It appeared that he did not know either. Perhaps he had been led to her side, almost in spite of himself, by a vague craving to be alone with her just once before they parted; or perhaps he had come because he suspected she might think he was afraid to. He sat down without speaking in the chair which Pauline had left.

Dusk had fallen, and Nona was aware of the presence at her side only as a shadowy bulk. After a while her father put out his hand and laid it on hers.

"Why, it's nearly dark," she said. "You'll be off in an hour or so now."

"Yes. Your mother and I are dining early."

She wound her fingers into his, and they sat silent again. She liked to have him near her in this way, but she was glad, for his sake and her own, that the twilight made his face indistinct. She hoped their silence might be unbroken. As long as she neither saw nor heard him there was an unaccountable comfort in feeling him near—as if the living warmth he imparted were something they shared indissolubly.

"In a couple of hours now—" he began, with an attempt at briskness. She was silent, and he went on: "I wanted to be with you alone for a minute like this. I wanted to say—"

"Father—."

He turned suddenly in his chair, and bending down over her pressed his forehead against the coverlet. She freed her hand and passed it through the thin hair on his temples.

"Don't. There's nothing to say."

She felt a tremor of his shoulders as they pressed against her, and the tremor ran through her own body and seemed to loosen the fibres of her heart.

"Old dad."

"Nona."

After that they remained again without speaking till a clock chimed out from somewhere in the shadows. Manford got up. He gave himself one of his impatient shakes, and stooped to kiss his daughter on the forehead.

"I don't believe I'll come up again before we go."

"No."

"It's no use—"

"No."

"I'll look after your mother—do all I can . . . Goodbye, dear."

"Goodbye, father."

He groped for her forehead again, and went out of the room; and she closed her eyes and lay in the darkness, her heart folded like two hands around the thought of him.

"Nona, darling!" There were still the goodbyes to her mother to be gone through. Well, that would be comparatively easy; and in a lighted room too, with Pauline on the threshold, slim, erect and consciously equipped for travel—complete and wonderful! Yes; it would be almost easy.

"Child, it's time; we're off in a few minutes. But I think I've left everything in order. Maisie's downstairs; she has all my directions, and the list of stations to which she's to wire how you are while we're crossing the continent."

"But, mother, I'm all right; it's not a bit necessary—"

"Dear! You can't help my wanting to hear about you."

"No; I know. I only meant you're not to worry."

"Of course I won't worry; I wouldn't *let* myself worry. You know how I feel about all that. And besides," added Mrs. Manford victoriously, "what in the world is there to worry about?"

"Nothing," Nona acquiesced with a smile.

Pauline bent down and placed a lingering kiss where Manford's lips had just brushed his daughter's forehead. Pauline played her part better—and made it correspondingly easier for her fellow-actors to play theirs.

"Goodbye, mother dear. Have all sorts of a good time, won't you?"

"It will be a very interesting trip—with a man as clever and cultivated as your father . . . If only you could have come with us! But you'll promise to join us in Egypt?"

"Don't ask me to promise anything yet, mother."

Pauline raised herself to her full height and stood looking down intently at her daughter. Under her smooth new face Nona again seemed to see the flicker of anxiety pass back and forward, like a light moving from window to window in a long-uninhabited house. The glimpse startled the girl and caught her by the heart. Suddenly something within her broke up. Her lips tightened like a child's, and she felt the tears running down her cheeks.

"Nona! You're not crying?" Pauline was kneeling at her side.

"It's nothing, mother—nothing. Go! Please go!"

"Darling—if I could only see you happy one of these days."

"Happy?"

"Well, I mean like other people. Married—" the mother hastily ventured.

Nona had brushed away her tears. She raised her head and looked straight at Pauline.

"Married? Do you suppose being married would make me happy? I wonder why you should! I don't want to marry—there's nobody in the world I would marry." She continued to stare up at her mother with hard unwavering eyes. "Marry! I'd a thousand times rather go into a convent and have done with it," she exclaimed.

"A convent—Nona! Not *a convent*?"

Pauline had got to her feet and stood before her daughter with distress and amazement breaking through every fissure of her paint. "I never heard anything so horrible," she said.

Deeper than all her eclectic religiosity, deeper than her pride in receiving the Cardinal, deeper than the superficial contradictions and accommodations of a conscience grown elastic from too much use, Nona watched, with a faint smile, the old Puritan terror of gliding priests and incense and idolatry rise to the surface of her mother's face. Perhaps that terror was the only solid fibre left in her.

"I sometimes think you want to break my heart, Nona. To tell me this now! . . . Go into a convent . . ." the mother groaned.

The girl let her head drop back among the cushions.

"Oh, but I mean a convent where nobody believes in anything," she said.

THE END

THE CHILDREN

TO

MY PATIENT LISTENERS

AT

SAINTE-CLAIRE

BOOK I

Chapter I

As the big liner hung over the tugs swarming about her in the bay of Algiers, Martin Boyne looked down from the promenade deck on the troop of first-class passengers struggling up the gangway, their faces all unconsciously lifted to his inspection.

"Not a soul I shall want to speak to—as usual!"

Some men's luck in travelling was inconceivable. They had only to get into a train or on board a boat to run across an old friend; or, what was more exciting, make a new one. They were always finding themselves in the same compartment, or in the same cabin, with some wandering celebrity, with the owner of a famous house, of a noted collection, or of an odd and amusing personality—the latter case being, of course, the rarest as it was the most rewarding.

There was, for instance, Martin Boyne's own Great-Uncle Edward. Uncle Edward's travel-adventures were famed in the family. At home in America, amid the solemn upholstery of his Boston house, Uncle Edward was the model of complacent dulness; yet whenever he got on board a steamer, or into a train (or a *diligence*, in his distant youth), he was singled out by fate as the hero of some delightful encounter. It would be Rachel during her ill-starred tour of the States; Ruskin on the lake of Geneva; the Dean of Canterbury as Uncle Edward, with all the appropriate emotions, was gazing on the tomb of the Black Prince; or the Duke of Devonshire of his day, as Uncle Edward put a courteous (but probably pointless) question to the housekeeper showing him over Chatsworth. And instantly he would receive a proscenium box from Rachel for her legendary first night in Boston, or be entreated by Ruskin to join him for a month in Venice; or the Dean would invite him to stay at the Deanery, the Duke at Chatsworth; and the net result of these experiences would be that Uncle Edward, if questioned, would reply with his sweet frosty smile: "Yes, Rachel had talent but no beauty"; or: "No one could be more simple and friendly than the Duke"; or: "Ruskin really had all the appearances of a gentleman." Such were the impressions produced on Uncle Edward by his unparalleled success in the great social scenes through which, for a period of over sixty years, he moved with benignant blindness.

Far different was the case of his great-nephew. No tremor of thought or emotion would, in similar situations, have escaped Martin Boyne: he would have burst all the grapes against his palate. But though he was given to travel, and though he had travelled much, and his profession as a civil engineer had taken him to interesting and out-of-the-way parts of the world, and though he was always on the alert for agreeable encounters, it was never at such times that they came to him. He would have loved adventure, but adventure worthy of the name perpetually eluded him; and when it has eluded a man till he is over forty it is not likely to seek him out later.

"I believe it's something about the shape of my nose," he had said to himself that very morning as he shaved in his spacious cabin on the upper deck of the big Mediterranean cruising-steamer.

The nose in question was undoubtedly not adventurous in shape; it did not thrust itself far forward into other people's affairs; and the eyes above, wide apart, deep-set, and narrowed for closer observation, were of a guarded twilight gray which gave the nose no encouragement whatever.

"Nobody worth bothering about—*as usual*," he grumbled. For the day was so lovely, the harbour of Algiers so glittering with light and heat, his own mood so full of holiday enterprise—it was his first vacation after a good many months on a hard exhausting job—that he could hardly believe he really looked to the rest of the world as he had seen himself that morning: a critical cautious man of forty-six, whom nobody could possibly associate with the romantic or the unexpected.

"Usual luck; best I can hope for is to keep my cabin to myself for the rest of the cruise," he pondered philosophically, hugging himself at the prospect of another fortnight of sea-solitude before—well, before the fateful uncertainty of what awaited him just beyond the voyage . . .

"And I haven't even *seen* her for five years!" he reflected, with that feeling of hollowness about the belt which prolonged apprehension gives.

Passengers were still climbing the ship's side, and he leaned and looked again, this time with contracted eyes and a slight widening of his cautious nostrils. His attention had been drawn to a young woman—a slip of a girl, rather—with a round flushed baby on her shoulder, a baby much too heavy for her slender frame, but on whose sleepy countenance her own was bent with a gaze of solicitude which wrung a murmur of admiration from Boyne.

"Jove—if a fellow was younger!"

Men of forty-six do not gasp as frequently at the sight of a charming face as they did at twenty; but when the sight strikes them it hits harder. Boyne had not been looking for pretty faces but for interesting ones, and it rather disturbed him to be put off his quest by anything so out of his present way as excessive youth and a rather pathetic grace.

"Lord—the child's ever so much too heavy for her. Must have been married out of the nursery: damned cad, not to—"

The young face mounting toward him continued to bend over the baby, the girl's frail shoulders to droop increasingly under their burden, as the congestion ahead of her forced the young lady to maintain her slanting position halfway up the liner's flank.

A nurse in correct bonnet and veil touched her shoulder, as if offering to relieve her; but she only tightened her arm about the child. Whereupon the nurse, bending, lifted in her own arms a carrot-headed little girl of four or five in a gaudy gipsy-like frock.

"What—another? Why, it's barbarous; it ought to be against the law! The poor little thing—"

Here Boyne's attention was distracted by the passage of a deck-steward asking where he wished his chair placed. He turned to attend to this matter, and saw, on the chair next to his, a tag bearing the name: "Mrs. Cliffe Wheater."

Cliffe Wheater—Cliffe Wheater! What an absurd name . . . and somehow he remembered to have smiled over it in the same way years before . . . But, good Lord, of *course*! How long he must have lived out of the world, on his engineering jobs, first in the Argentine, then in Australia, and since the war in Egypt—how out of step he must have become with the old social dance of New York, not to situate Cliffe Wheater at once as the big red-faced Chicagoan who was at Harvard with him, and who had since become one of the showiest of New York millionaires. Cliffe Wheater, of course—the kind of fellow who was spoken of, respectfully, as having "interests" everywhere: Boyne recalled having run across Wheater "interests" even in the Argentine. But the man himself, at any rate since his marriage, was reputed to be mainly interested in Ritz Hotels and powerful motorcars. Hadn't he a steam-yacht too? He had a wife, at any rate—it was all coming back to Boyne: he had married, it must be sixteen or seventeen years ago, that good-looking Mervin girl, of New York—Joyce Mervin—whom Boyne himself had danced and flirted with through a remote winter not long after Harvard. Joyce Mervin: she had written to him to announce her engagement, had enclosed a little snap-shot of herself with "Goodbye, Martin," scrawled across it. Had she rather fancied Boyne—Boyne wondered? He had been too poor to try to find out . . . And now he and she were going to be deck-neighbours for a fortnight on the magic seas between Algiers and Venice! He remembered the face he had contemplated that morning in his shaving-glass, and thought: "Very likely she hasn't changed a bit; smart women last so wonderfully; but she won't know *me*." The idea was half depressing and half reassuring. After all, it would enable him to take his observations—and to have his deck-chair moved, should the result be disappointing.

The ship had shaken her insect-like flock of tugs and sailing-boats off her quivering flanks; and now the great blue level spread before her as she headed away toward the morning. Boyne got a book, pulled his hat over his nose, and stretched out in his deck-chair, awaiting Mrs. Wheater . . .

"This will do—yes, I think this will do," said a fluty imma-ture voice, a girl's voice, at his elbow. Boyne tilted his head back, and saw, a few steps off, the slim girl who had carried the heavy baby up the gangway.

The girl paused, glanced along the line of seats in his direction, nodded to a deck-steward, and disappeared into the doorway of a "luxe" *suite* farther forward. In the moment of her pause Boyne caught a small pale face with anxiously wrinkled brows above brown eyes of tragic width, and round red lips which, at the least provocation, might bubble with healthy laughter. It did not occur to him now to ask if the face were pretty or not—there were too many things going on in it for that.

As she entered her cabin he heard her say, in her firm quick voice, to some one within: "Nanny, has Chip had his Benger? Who's got the cabin with Terry?"

"What a mother!" Boyne thought, still wondering if it were not much too soon for that maternal frown to have shadowed her young forehead.

"Beg pardon, sir—there's a new passenger booked for your cabin." The steward was passing with a couple of good-looking suit-cases and a bundle of rugs.

"Oh, damn—well, it had to happen!" Boyne, with a groan, stood up and followed the steward. "Who is it, do you know?"

"Couldn't say, sir. Wheater—Wheater's the name."

Well, at last a coincidence! Mrs. Cliffe Wheater's chair was next to his own, and his old Harvard class-mate was to share his cabin with him. Boyne, if not wholly pleased, was at least faintly excited and interested by this unexpected combination of circumstances.

He turned, and saw a little boy standing in the door of the cabin, mustering him with a dispassionate eye.

"All right—this will do," said the boy quietly. He spoke in a slightly high-pitched voice, neither querulous nor effeminate, but simply thin and a little tired, like his slender person. Boyne guessed him to be about eleven years old, and too tall and reasonable for his age—another evidence of the physical frailty betrayed by his voice. He was neatly dressed in English school-boy clothes, but he did not look English, he looked cosmopolitan: as if he had been sharpened and worn down by contact with too many different civilizations—or perhaps merely with too many different hotels.

He continued to examine Boyne, critically but amicably; then he remarked: "I'm in here, you know."

"You are? I thought it was to be your father!"

"Oh, did you? That's funny. Do you know my father?"

"I used to. In fact, I think we were at Harvard together."

Young master Wheater looked but faintly interested. "Would you mind telling me your name?" he asked, as if acquitting himself of a recognized social duty.

"My name's Boyne: Martin Boyne. But it's so long since your father and I met that he wouldn't have been likely to speak of me."

Mr. Wheater's son reflected. "Well, I shouldn't have been likely to be there if he did. We're not so awfully much with father," he added, with a seeming desire for accuracy.

A little girl of his own age and size, but whose pale fairness had a warmer glow, had advanced a step or two into the cabin, and now slipped an arm through his.

"I've been hunting for you everywhere," she said. "Judith sent me."

"Well, here's where I am: with this gentleman."

The little girl lifted her deeply fringed lids and bent on Boyne the full gaze of two large and accomplished gray eyes. Then she pursed up her poppy-red lips and looked at her brother. "For a whole fortnight—Terry, can you *bear* it?"

The boy flushed and pulled away his arm. "Shut up, you ass!" he admonished her.

"Do let me ask Judith to tip the steward—"

He swung about on her angrily. "*Will* you shut up when I tell you to? This gentleman's a friend of father's."

"Oh—" the little girl murmured; and then added, after another fringed flash at Boyne: "He doesn't look it."

"Blanca—will you please get out of here?"

She wavered, her bright lips trembled, and she turned in confusion and ran down the deck. "She doesn't know anything—she's only my twin," said Terry Wheater apologetically.

He completed his scrutiny of the cabin, looked a little wistfully at Boyne, and then turned and sauntered away after the delinquent.

Boyne returned to the deck and his book; but though the latter interested him, it did not prevent his keeping watch, out of the tail of his eye, on the empty chair which bore Mrs. Wheater's name. His curiosity to see her had grown immensely since his encounter with her son and daughter—in the latter of whom he discovered, as the past grew clearer to him, a likeness to her mother at once close and remote. Joyce Mervin—yes, she had had those same poppy-red lips in a face of translucent pallor, and that slow skilful way of manœuvring her big eyes; but her daughter seemed made of a finer frailer stuff, as if a good deal of Mrs. Wheater's substance had been left out of her, and a drop of some rarer essence added. "Perhaps it's because the child is only half a person—there was always too much of her mother," Boyne thought, remembering Joyce Mervin as being rather aimlessly abundant. "In such cases, it's probably enough to be a twin," he decided.

But how puzzling it all was! Terry was much less like Cliffe Wheater than his twin was like their mother. There too—even more so in the boy's case—quality seemed to have replaced quantity. Boyne felt, he hardly knew why, that something obvious and almost vulgar might lurk under Blanca's fastidiousness; but her brother could never be anything but distinguished. What a pity such a charming lad should look so ill!

Suddenly, from the forward *suite*, the young lady with the baby emerged. She had her sleepy cherub by the hand and was guiding him with motherly care along the deck. She sank into the chair next to Boyne's, pulled the baby up on her knee, and signalled to a steward to draw a rug over her feet. Then she leaned back with a sigh of satisfaction.

"This is something like, eh, Chip?" she said, in her gay fluty voice.

Chip laughed a genial well-fed laugh and fingered the brim of her hat appreciatively. It was evident that the two had the very highest opinion of each other.

Chapter II

IT was none of Boyne's business to tell his new neighbour that the chair she had chosen was Mrs. Cliffe Wheater's; the less so as she might (he decided on closer inspection) turn out to be a governess or other dependent of that lady's. But no (after another look); she was too young for the part, even if she had looked or acted it—and she didn't. Her tone in addressing her invisible companions was that of command, not subservience: they were the nurses and governesses, not she. Probably she had taken Mrs. Wheater's chair because it was one of the few empty ones left, and was well aware that she might presently be asked to evacuate it. That was just what Boyne would have liked to spare her; he didn't see Joyce Wheater—the Joyce he had known—yielding her seat without a battle.

"I beg your pardon; but in case somebody should claim this chair, I might find another for you before the whole front row is taken up."

The phrase sounded long and clumsy, but it was out before he had time to polish it. He had to hear her voice again, and also to get her to turn her eyes his way. She did so now, with perfect composure. Evidently she was not surprised at his addressing her, but only at the fact he imparted.

"Isn't this my chair?" She reached for the label and examined it. "Yes; I thought it was."

"Oh, I'm sorry—"

"That's all right. They *are* filling up, aren't they?"

Her brown eyes, under deep lashes like Blanca's, rested on him in polite acknowledgment of his good will; but he was too bewildered to see anything but a starry blur.

Mrs. Cliffe Wheater, then—this child? Well, after all, why not? His Mrs. Cliffe Wheater she obviously could not be; but in these days of transient partnerships there was no reason for expecting it. The Wheaters *he* knew must have been married nearly twenty years ago; and Cliffe Wheater, in the interval, had made money enough to treat himself to half-a-dozen divorces and remarriages, with all the attendant outlay. "No more to him than doing over a new house—good deal less than running a steam-yacht," Boyne half enviously reflected.

Yes; his neighbour was obviously a later—was the latest—Mrs. Wheater; probably two or three removes from poor Joyce. Though why he should think of her as poor Joyce, when in all probability she had moved off across the matrimonial chess-board at the same rate of progression as her first husband . . . Well, at any rate, if this was a new Mrs. Cliffe Wheater, Boyne might insinuate himself into her field of vision as an old friend of her husband's; a sufficient plea, he argued, between passengers on a pleasure-cruise. Only, remembering Terry's cool reception of his father's name, he hesitated. These modern matrimonial tangles were full of peril to the absentee . . .

The question was answered by the appearance of Blanca, who came dancing toward them like a butterfly waltzing over a bed of thyme.

As she approached, the young lady at Boyne's side said severely: "Child! Why haven't you got on your coat? Go and ask Scopy for it at once. The wind is cold."

Blanca leaned against her with a caressing gesture. "All right." But instead of moving she slanted her gaze again toward Boyne. "He says he used to know father," she imparted.

The young lady turned her head also, and Boyne felt the mysterious weight of her eyes upon his face. "How funny!" was her simple comment. It seemed to strike all the group with equal wonder that Martin Boyne should be on speaking terms with its chief. "Not smart enough, I suppose; no Bond Street suit-cases," he grumbled to himself, remembering the freight of costly pig-skin which had followed his neighbour up the gangway.

The latter's attention had already turned from him. "Blanca! I tell you to go and put on your coat. And see that Terry has his . . . Don't lean on me like that, child. Can't you see that Chip's asleep?"

She spoke a little wearily, almost irritably, Boyne thought; but as she bent over the child her little profile softened, melting into something puerile and appealing. "Hush!" she signalled; and Blanca, obedient, tiptoed off.

Boyne, at this, invoking Uncle Edward, patron saint of the adventurous, risked a playful comment. "You've got them wonderfully well in hand."

She smiled. "Oh, they're very good children; all except . . . *Zinnie*—!" she screamed; and Boyne, following her horrified glance, saw a stark naked little figure with a shock of orange-coloured hair and a string of amber beads capering toward them to the wonder and delight of the double row of spectators in the deck-chairs.

In a flash the young lady was on her feet, and Boyne was pressing a soap-scented bundle to his breast. "Hold Chip!" she commanded. "Oh, that little red devil!" She sped down the deck and catching up the orange-headed child gave her a violent shaking. "*You*'ll be catching cold next, you wretch," she admonished her, as if this were the head and front of the child's offending; and having pushed the culprit into the arms of a pursuing nurse she regained her seat.

"How nicely you've held him! He's still asleep." She received back the hot baby, all relaxed and slumber-scented, and the eyes she turned on Boyne were now full of a friendly intimacy—and much younger, he thought, than Blanca's. "Did you ever mind a baby before?" she asked.

"Yes; but not such a good one—nor so heavy."

She shone with pride. "Isn't he an armful? He's nearly two pounds heavier than most children of two. When Beechy was his age she weighed only . . ."

"Beechy?" Boyne interrupted. "I thought you called her Zinnie."

"Zinnie? Oh, but she's not the same as Beechy." She laughed with something of a child's amusement at the ignorance of the grown up. "Beechy's a step—but you haven't seen the other steps," she reminded herself. "I wonder where on earth they are?"

"The steps?" he echoed, in deeper bewilderment.

"Bun and Beechy. They only half belong to us, and so does Zinnie. They're all three step-children. But we're just as devoted to them as if they were altogether ours; except when Bun is naughty. Bun is my only naughty child—oh, do hold Chip again!" she exclaimed, and once more Boyne became the repository of that heap of rosy slumber.

"There's Bun now—and I never trust him when he's by himself! I *can't*," she wailed, as a sturdy little brown boy in a scarlet jumper came crawling down the deck on all fours, emitting strange animal barks and crowings. "He's going to do his menagerie-tricks. Oh, dear— And he can't, with the ship rolling like this. His mother was a lion-tamer. But he'll hurt himself, I know he will—oh, Scopy! Yes; do take him . . ."

A gaunt narrow-chested lady with a face hewn into lines of kindly resolution, and a faded straw hat cocked sideways on her blown gray hair, had appeared in Bun's wake and set him on his feet as firmly as the rolling deck permitted. His face, dusky with wrath, squared itself for a howl; but at that moment a very small brown girl, with immense agate-coloured eyes and a thicket of dark curls, dashed out of a state-room, and hurried to him with outstretched arms. Instantly the offender's wrath turned to weeping, and the two little creatures fell dramatically on each other's bosoms, while the governess, unmoved by this display of feeling, steered them sternly back to their quarters.

The young lady at Boyne's side leaned back with a laugh. "Isn't Scopy funny? She can't bear it when Bun falls on Beechy's neck like that. She calls it 'so foreign and unmanly.' And of course they *are* foreign . . . they're Italian . . . but I'm too thankful that Beechy has such an influence over Bun. If it weren't for her we should have our hands full with him." She hugged the sleep-drunk Chip to her bosom.

"You must have your hands rather full as it is—I mean even without Bun?" Boyne ventured, consumed by the desire to see farther into this nursery tangle, and follow its various threads back to the young creature at his side. "Travelling with them all like this—and without Wheater to help you out," he pushed on.

At this she shrugged a little. "Oh, he's not much at helping out; he loathes to travel with us," she said, slightingly yet not unkindly. Boyne was beginning to think that her detached view of human weaknesses was perhaps the most striking thing about her.

"But Terry helps—most wonderfully," she added, a smile of maternal tenderness lighting her small changeful face, in which so many things were always happening that Boyne had not yet had time to decide if it were pretty or just curiously loveable.

"My cabin-mate," Boyne smiled. "Yes; a big boy like that must be a comfort." He dared not say "a big son like that," for he could not believe that the girl at his side could be the mother of a tall lad of Terry's age. Yet she had distinctly not classed him among the "steps"! In his perplexity he ventured: "A chap of that age is always so proud of his mother."

She seemed to think that this needed consideration. "Well, I don't know that Terry's proud of Joyce, exactly—but he admires her, of course; we all do. She's so awfully handsome. I don't believe even Blanca is going to come up to her."

Joyce! Boyne caught at the familiar name as at a life-belt. Evidently his old friend Joyce Mervin was still situated somewhere within the Wheater labyrinth. But where? And who was this young thing who gave her her Christian name so easily? Everything that seemed at first to enlighten him ended only by deepening his perplexity.

"Do you know that Joyce, as you call her, used to be a great friend of mine years ago?" There could be no harm, at least, in risking that.

"Oh, was she? How jolly! She says she looked exactly like Blanca then. Did she? Of course she's a little thick now—but not nearly as much so as she imagines. She does so fret about it. It's her great unhappiness."

Boyne laughed. "You mean she hasn't any worse ones?"

"Oh, no. Not now. They've been on a new honeymoon since Chip . . . haven't they, old Chippo?"

"They . . . ?" On a new honeymoon? Since Chip? Then the sleeping cherub was not the property of the girl at his side, but of Joyce Mervin . . . Joyce Wheater . . . Joyce Somebody . . . Oh, how he longed to ask: "Joyce *who*?"

This last step forward seemed really to have landed him in the heart of the labyrinth; the difficulty now was to find his way out again.

But the young lady's confidences seemed to invite his own. Or was it just that she had the new easy way with people? Very likely. Still, an old fogey out of the wilderness might be excused for taking it as something more—a sign of sympathy, almost an invitation to meet her fresh allusions with fresh questions.

"Yes; we were friends—really great friends for a winter . . ."

("That's long, for Joyce," said his neighbour parenthetically.)

" . . . such good friends that I should like to tell you my name: Martin Boyne—and to ask what your—"

"Oh—*oh*!!!" She shrilled it out so precipitately that it cut his last word in two. At first he could not guess the cause of this new disturbance; but in a moment he discovered the young Bun walking with bare feet and a cat-like agility along the backs of the outer row of deck-chairs, while their occupants ducked out of his way and laughed their approval of his skill.

"She was also a tight-rope dancer—his mother was," the girl flung back, leaping in Bun's direction. Having caught and cuffed him, and cuffed him again in answer to his furious squeals, she dragged him away to the firm dishevelled lady who had previously dealt with him. When she returned to her seat, pale and a little breathless, she looked as if her domestic cares sometimes weighed on her too heavily. She dropped down by Boyne with a sigh. "If ever you marry," she enjoined him ("And how does she know I never have?" he wondered), "don't you have any children—that's all I say! Do you wonder mother and father don't care to travel with the lot of us?"

Chapter III

THE luncheon-signal crashed in on this interrogation, and Boyne was left alone to make what he could of it. At the first sound of the gong his neighbour was on her feet, hardly heeding his suggestion that, if she had not already chosen her seat, they might meet at a table for two in the restaurant.

"Thanks a lot; but of course I lunch with my children." And he remembered with regret that their ocean-palace had a separate dining-room for youthful passengers.

"Dash it—I should have liked a few minutes' quiet talk with her."

Instead, he drifted back to his usual place at a table of waifs and strays like himself: an earnest lady in spectacles who was "preparing" Sicily; an elderly man who announced every morning: "I always say the bacon on these big liners is better than anything I can get at home"; and a pale clergyman whose parishioners had sent him on a holiday tour, and whose only definite idea was to refuse to visit catacombs. "I do so want to lead a pagan life just for once," he confided to Boyne, with an ascetic smile which showed, between racking coughs, his worn teeth and anæmic gums.

Luncheon over, Boyne hurried back to his corner, hoping to find the seat at his side already occupied; but it was empty, and empty it remained as the long blue day curved down imperceptibly toward evening.

"Father and mother don't care to travel with the lot of us," the girl had said.

"Father and mother"? That, as far as Boyne could make out, could mean only the Cliffe Wheaters, his old original Cliffe Wheaters, in their before-the-letter state, as it were. In that case the thin eager girl at his side would be their daughter, their eldest daughter, born probably soon after a marriage which, some thirteen or fourteen years later, had produced the sturdy and abundant Chip.

"Very unmodern, all that." It gave Boyne a more encouraging view of the conjugal state than he had lately held, and made him look forward with a lighter mind to meeting the lady who awaited him in the Dolomites—the lady he had not seen for five years. It must certainly be pleasant to be the parent of a large reliable baby like Chip . . .

But no sooner did he imagine that he had solved the puzzle of the Cliffe Wheaters than the image of the enigmatic trio, Zinnie, Bun and Beechy, disarranged his neat equation. The "steps"—who on earth were the "steps," and how and where did they fit into the family group which seemed, with Judith (hadn't they called her that?) at one end, and Chip at the other, to form its own unbroken circle? Miss Wheater, he remembered, had tossed him a few details about the two brown children, Bun and Beechy. "They're foreigners . . . Italians . . ." But if so, they belonged neither to Cliffe Wheater nor to his wife; certainly not to his wife, since Judith had added, in speaking of Bun: "His mother was a lion-tamer . . ." not as if using the term metaphorically, but as stating a plain social fact.

As for Zinnie, the little red devil, she remained wholly unaccounted for, and there was nothing in her clever impudent face, with its turned-up nose and freckled skin under the shock of orange hair, to suggest any blood-relationship to the small Italians. Zinnie appeared to be sharply and completely American— as American as Beechy and Bun were Italian, and much more so than the three elder Wheaters, who were all so rubbed down by cosmopolitan contacts. The "steps," in fact, had the definiteness of what the botanists call species, whereas Judith, Blanca and Terry were like exquisite garden hybrids. The harder Boyne stared into the problem the more obscure it became.

Even the least eventful sea-voyages lend themselves to favourable propinquities, and in the course of the afternoon the gray-haired lady whom the young Wheaters addressed as "Scopy" reappeared on deck, this time alone, and seemingly in quest of a seat. Boyne instantly pointed out the one next to his, and the lady, saying with an austere smile: "I believe ours are on the other side, but I can take this while Judith's resting," settled herself at his side in an attitude of angular precision.

As she did so she gave him a look of shy benevolence, and added: "I understand from Judith that you're a friend of her people."

Boyne eagerly acquiesced, and she went on to say what a comfort it was, when they were on one of these long treks with the children, to come across anybody who was a friend of their parents, and could be appealed to in an emergency. "Not that there's any particular reason at present; but it's a good deal of a responsibility for Judith to transport the whole party from Biskra to Venice, and we're always rather troubled about Terry. Even after four months at Biskra he hasn't picked up as we'd hoped . . . Always a little temperature in the evenings . . ." She sighed, and turned away her sturdy weather-beaten face, which looked like a cliff on whose top a hermit had built a precarious refuge—her hat.

"You're anxious about Terry? He does look a little drawn." Boyne hoped that if he adopted an easy old-friend tone she might be lured on from one confidence to another.

"Anxious? I don't like the word; and Judith wouldn't admit it. But we always have our eye on him, the dear boy—and our minds." She sighed again, and he saw that she had averted her head because her eyes were filling.

"It is, as you say, a tremendous responsibility for any one as young as Miss Wheater." He hesitated, and then added: "I can very nearly guess her age, for I used to see a good deal of both her parents before they were married."

It was a consolation to his self-esteem that the lady called "Scopy" took this with less flippancy than her young charges. It seemed distinctly interesting to her, and even reassuring, that Boyne should have been a friend of the Cliffe Wheaters at any stage in their career. "I only wish you'd gone on seeing them since," she said, with another of her sighs.

"Oh, our paths have been pretty widely divided; so much so that at first I didn't know whether . . . not till I saw Chip . . ."

"Ah, poor little Chipstone: he's our hope, our consolation." She looked down, and a faint brick-red blush crossed her face like sunset on granite. "You see, Terry being so delicate—as twins often are—Mr. Wheater was always anxious for another boy."

"Well, Chip looks like a pretty solid foundation to build one's hopes on."

She smiled a little bleakly, and murmured: "He's never given us a minute's trouble."

All this was deeply interesting to her hearer, but it left the three "steps" still unaccounted for; the "steps" of whom Judith had said that they were as much beloved as if they had been "altogether ours."

"Not a minute's trouble—I wish I could say as much of the others," his neighbour went on, yielding, as he had hoped she would, to the rare chance of airing her grievances.

"The others? You mean—"

"Yes: those foreign children, with their scenes and their screams and their play-acting. I shall never get used to them—never!"

"But Zinnie: Zinnie's surely not foreign?" Boyne lured her on.

"Foreign to *our* ways, certainly; really more so than the two others, who, on the father's side . . ." She lowered her voice, and cast a prudent eye about her, before adding: "You've heard of Zinnia Lacrosse, the film star, I suppose?"

Boyne racked his mind, which was meagrely peopled with film stars, and finally thought he had. "Didn't she marry some racing man the other day—Lord Somebody?"

"I don't know what her last enormity has been. One of them was marrying Mr. Wheater—and having Zinnie . . ."

Marrying Wheater—Zinnia Lacrosse had married Cliffe Wheater? But then—but then—who on earth was Chipstone's mother? Boyne felt like crying out: "Don't pile up any more puzzles! Give me time—give me time!" but his neighbour was now so far launched in the way of avowal that she went on, hardly heeding him more than if his face had been the narrow grating through which she was pouring her woes: "It's inconceivable, but it's so. Mr. Wheater married Zinnia Lacrosse. And Zinnie is their child. The truth is, he wasn't altogether to blame; I've always stood up for Mr. Wheater. What with his feeling so low after Mrs. Wheater left him, and his wanting another boy so dreadfully . . . with all those millions to inherit . . ."

But Boyne held up a drowning hand. Mrs. Wheater had left Wheater? But when—but how—but why? He implored the merciless narrator to tell him one thing at a time—only one; all these sudden appearances of new people and new children were so perplexing to a man who'd lived for years and years in the wilderness . . .

"The wilderness? The real wilderness is the world *we* live in; packing up our tents every few weeks for another move . . . And the marriages just like tents—folded up and thrown away when you've done with them." But she saw, at least, that to gain his sympathy she must have his understanding, and after another cautious glance up and down the deck she settled down to elucidate the mystery and fill in the gaps. Of course, she began, Judith having told her that he—Mr. Boyne was the name? Thanks. Hers was Miss Scope, Horatia Scope (she knew the children called her "Horror Scope" behind her back, but she didn't mind)—well, Judith having told her that Mr. Boyne was a friend of her parents, Miss Scope had inferred that he had kept up with the successive episodes of the couple's agitated history; but now that she saw he didn't know, she would try to make it clear to him—if one could use the word in speaking of such a muddled business. It took a great deal of explaining—as he would see—but if any one could enlighten him *she* could, for she'd come to the Wheaters' as Judith's governess before Blanca and Terry were born: before the first, no, the second serious quarrel, she added, as if saying: "Before the Hittite invasion."

Quarrels, it seemed, there had been many since; she had lost count, she confessed; but the bad, the fatal, one had happened when Mrs. Wheater had met her Prince, the wicked Buondelmonte who was the father of Bun and Beechy: Beatrice and Astorre Buondelmonte, as the children were really named.

Here Boyne, submerged, had to hold up his hand again. But if Zinnie was Wheater's child, he interrupted, were Bun and Beechy Mrs. Wheater's? And whose, in the name of pity, was Chipstone? Well . . . Miss Scope said she understood his wonder, his perplexity; it did him credit, she declared, to be too high-minded to take in the whole painful truth at a glance. No; Bun and Beechy, thank heaven, were *not* Mrs. Wheater's children; they were the offspring of the unscrupulous Prince Buondelmonte and a vile woman—a circus performer, she believed—whom he had married and deserted before poor Mrs. Wheater became infatuated with him. ("Infatuated" was a horrid word, she knew; but Mrs. Wheater used it herself in speaking of that unhappy time.)

Well—Mrs. Wheater, in her madness, had insisted on leaving her husband in order to marry Prince Buondelmonte. Mr. Wheater, though she had behaved so badly, was very chivalrous about it, and "put himself in the wrong" (Boyne rejoiced at the phrase) so that his wife might divorce him; but he insisted on his right to keep Terry with him, and on an annual visit of four months from Judith and Blanca; and as there was a big fight over the alimony Mrs. Wheater had to give in about the children—and that was when Judith's heart-break began. Even as a little thing, Miss Scope explained, Judith couldn't bear it when her parents quarrelled. She had had to get used to that, alas; but what she couldn't get used to was, after the divorce and the two remarriages, being separated from Terry, and bundled up every year with Blanca, and sent from pillar to post, first to one Palace Hotel and then to another, wherever one parent or the other happened to be . . . It was that, Miss Scope thought, which had given the grown-up look to her eyes . . .

Luckily Mrs. Wheater's delusion didn't last long; the Prince hadn't let it. Before they'd been married a year he'd taken care to show her what he was. Poor Judith, who was alone with her mother during the last dreadful months, knew something of *that*. But Miss Scope realised that she mustn't digress, but just stick to the outline of her story till it became a little clearer to Mr. Boyne . . .

Well—when Mrs. Wheater's eyes were opened, and the final separation from the Prince took place, she (Mrs. Wheater) was so sorry for Beatrice and Astorre—there was really nobody kinder than Mrs. Wheater—that she kept the poor little things with her, and had gone on keeping them ever since. Their father had of course been only too thankful to have them taken off his hands—and their miserable mother too. Here Miss Scope paused for breath, and hoped that Mr. Boyne was beginning to grasp—

"Yes; beginning; but—Chipstone?" he patiently insisted.

"Oh, Chip; dear Chip's a Wheater all right! The very image of his father, don't you think? But I see that I haven't yet given you all the threads; there are so many . . . Where was I? Oh, about Mrs. Wheater's separation. You know there's no divorce in Italy, and she thought she was tied to the Prince for life. But luckily her lawyers found out that he had been legally married—in some Italian consulate at the other end of the world—to the mother of Bun and Beechy; and as the woman was still alive, the Prince's marriage with Mrs. Wheater had been bigamous, and was immediately annulled, and she became Mrs. Wheater again—"

"And then?"

"Then she was dreadfully miserable about it all, and Mr. Wheater was miserable too, because in the meanwhile he'd found out about the horror he'd married, and was already suing for a divorce. And Judith, who was thirteen by that time, and as wise and grown up as she is now, begged and entreated her father and mother to meet and talk things over, and see if they couldn't come together again, so that the children would never have to be separated, and sent backward and forward like bundles—"

"She did that? That child?"

"Judith's never been a child—there was no time. So she got Mr. and Mrs. Wheater together, and they were both sore and unhappy over their blunders, and realised what a mess they'd made—and finally they decided to try again, and they were remarried about three years ago; and then Chip was born, and of course that has made everything all right again—for the present."

"The present?" Boyne gasped; and the governess smoothed back her blown hair, and turned the worn integrity of her face on his.

"If I respect the truth, how can I say more than 'the present'? But really I put it that way only for fear . . . for fear of the Fates overhearing me . . . Everything's going as smoothly as can be; and we should all be perfectly happy if it weren't for poor Terry, whose health never seems to be what it should . . . Mr. and Mrs. Wheater adore Chip, and are very fond of the other children; and Judith is almost sure it will last this time."

Miss Scope broke off, and looked away again from Boyne. Her "almost" wrung his heart, and he wanted to put his hand out, and clasp the large gray cotton glove clenched on her knee. But instead he only said: "If anything can make it last, you and Judith will"; and the governess answered: "Oh, it's all Judith. And she has all the children behind her. They say they refuse to be separated again. Even the little ones say so. They're much more attached to each other than you'd think, to hear them bickering and wrangling. And they all worship Judith. Even the two foreigners do."

Chapter IV

T HE children, at first, had been unanimously and immovably opposed to going to Monreale.

Long before the steamer headed for Palermo the question was debated by them with a searching thoroughness. Judith, who had never been to Sicily, had consulted Boyne as to the most profitable way of employing the one day allotted to them, and after inclining to Segesta, Boyne, on finding that everybody, including Chip, was to be of the party, suggested Monreale as more accessible.

"And awfully beautiful too?" Judith was looking at him with hungry ignorant eyes.

"One of the most beautiful things in the world. The mosaics alone . . ."

She clasped ecstatic hands. "We must go there! I've seen so little—"

"Why, I thought you'd travelled from one end of Europe to the other."

"That doesn't show you anything but sleeping-cars and Palace Hotels, does it? Mother and father never even have a guide-book; they just ask the hall-porter where to go. And then something always seems to prevent their going. You must show me everything, everything."

"Well, we'll begin with Monreale."

But the children took a different view. Miss Scope, unluckily, had found an old Baedeker on the steamer, and refreshing her mind with hazy reminiscences gleaned from former pupils, had rediscovered the name of a wonderful ducal garden containing ever so many acres of orange-trees always full of flowers and fruit. Her old pupils had gone there, she recalled, and been allowed by the gardeners to pick up from the ground as many oranges as they could carry away.

At this the children, a close self-governing body, instantly voted as one man for the Giardino Aumale. Boyne had already observed that, in spite of Judith's strong influence, there were moments when she became helpless against their serried opposition, and in the present case argument and persuasion entirely

757

failed. At length Terry, evidently wishing, as the man of the party, to set the example of reasonableness, remarked that Judith, who had all the bother of looking after them, ought to go wherever she chose. Bun hereupon squared his mouth for a howl, and Blanca observed tartly that by always pretending to give up you generally got what you wanted. "Well, you'd better try then," Terry retorted severely, and the blood rose under his sister's delicate skin as if he had struck her.

"Terry! What a beast you are! I didn't mean—"

Meanwhile Beechy, melting into tears at the sight of Bun's distress, was hugging his tumbled head against her breast with murmurs of: "*Zitto, zitto, carissimo! Cuor mio!*" and glaring angrily at Judith and Terry.

"Well, I want to go where there's zoranges to eat," said Zinnie, in her sharp metallic American voice, with which she might almost have peeled the fruit. "—'r if I don't, I want something a lot better'nstead, n' I mean to have it!"

Boyne laughed, and Judith murmured despairingly: "We'd better go to their orange-garden."

"Look here," Terry interposed, "the little ones are mad to hear the end of that story of the old old times, about the two children who'd never seen a motor. They're all so fed up with airships and machinery and X rays and wireless; and you know you promised to go on with that story some day. Why couldn't we go to the place you want to see, and you'll promise and swear to finish the story there, and to have chocolates for tea?"

"Oh—and oranges; I'll supply the oranges," Boyne interposed. "There's a jolly garden next to the cloister, and I'll persuade the guardian to let us in, and we'll have a picnic tea there."

"An'masses of zoranges?" Zinnie stipulated, with a calculating air, while Beechy surreptitiously dried Bun's tears on her crumpled pinafore, and Bun, heartlessly forsaking her to turn handsprings on the deck, shrieked out: "Noranges! Noranges! NORANGES!"

"Oh, very well; I knew—" Blanca murmured, shooting her gray glance toward Boyne; and Judith, lifting up Chip, triumphantly declared: "He says he wants to go to Monreale."

"That settles it, of course," said Blanca, with resigned eyelids.

A wordy wrangle having arisen between Zinnie, Beechy and Bun as to whether the fruit for which they clamoured should be called zoranges or noranges, Judith and Miss Scope took advantage of the diversion to settle the details of the expedition with Boyne, and the next morning, when the steamer lay to off Palermo, the little party, equipped and eager, headed the line of passengers for the tug.

Boyne, stretched out at length on a stone bench in the sun, lay listening with half-closed eyes to Judith's eager plaintive voice. He had bribed the custodian to let them pass out of the cloister into the lavender-scented cathedral garden drowsing on its warm terrace above the orange-orchards. Far off across the plain the mountains descended in faint sapphire gradations to the denser sapphire of the sea, along which the domed and towered city gleamed uncertainly. And here, close by, sat Judith Wheater in the sun, the children heaped at her knee, and Scopy and Nanny, at a discreet distance, knitting, and nursing the tea-basket. Judith's voice went on: "But when Polycarp and Lullaby drove home in the victoria with the white horse to their mamma's palace they found that the zebra door-mat had got up and was eating all the flowers in the drawing-room vases, and the big yellow birds on the wall-paper were all flying about, and making the most dreadful mess scattering seeds about the rooms. But the most wonderful thing was that the cuckoo from the nursery clock was gone too, so that the nurses couldn't tell what time it was, and when the children ought to be put to bed and to get up again . . ."

"Oh, how perfectly lovely," chanted Bun, and Beechy chorused: "Lovely, lovely . . ."

"Not at all," said Judith severely. "It was the worst thing that had happened to them yet, for the cook didn't know what time it was either, and nobody in the house could tell her, so there was no breakfast ready; and the cook just went off for a ride on the zebra, because she had no carriage of her own, and she said there was nothing else to do."

"Why didn't they tell their father'n'mother?" Zinnie queried in a practical tone.

"Because they'd got new ones, who didn't know about the cuckoo either, I guess," said Bun with authority.

"Then why didn't the children go with their old fathers an' mothers?" Zinnie inserted.

"Because their old mother's friend, Sally Money, wasn't big enough . . . big enough . . . big enough . . . for her to take them all with her . . ." Bun broke off, visibly puzzled as to what was likely to follow.

"Big enough to take them all on her back and carry them away with her. But I daresay the new father and mother would have been all right," Judith pursued, "if only the children had been patient and known how to treat them; only just at first they didn't; and besides, at the time I am telling you about, they happened to be away travelling—"

"Then why didn't the children telephone to them to come back?"

"Because there weren't any telephones in those days."

"No telephones? Does it say so in the hist'ry books?" snapped Zinnie, sceptical.

"Course it does, you silly. Why, when Scopy was little," Terry reminded them, "she lived in a house where there wasn't any telephone."

Beechy, ever tender-hearted, immediately prepared to cry at the thought of Scopy's privation; but Scopy interpolated severely: "Now, Beatrice, don't be *foreign*—" and the story-teller went on: "So there was no way whatever for them to get any breakfast, and—"

"Oh, I know, I know! They starved to death, *poverini*!" Beechy lamented, promptly transferring her grief to another object, and flinging her little brown arms heavenward in an agony of participation.

"Not just yet. For they met on the edge of the wood—"

("What wood? There wasn't any wood before," said Zinnie sharply.)

"No, but there was one now; for all the trees and flowers from the wall-papers had come off the wall, and gone out into the garden to grow, so that the big yellow birds should have a wood to build their nests in, and the zebras should—"

"Zebras! There was only one zebra." This, sardonically, from a grown-up looking, indifferent Blanca.

"Stupid! He'd been married already and had a lot of perfectly lovely norphans and three dear little steps like us, and Mrs. Zebra she had a big family too, no, she had two big families,"

Zinnie announced, enumerating the successive groups on her small dimpled fingers.

"Oh, how lovely for the zebra! Then all the little zebras stayed together always afterward—f'rever and ever. Say they did—oh, Judith, *say* it!" Beechy clamoured.

"Of course they did. (Zinnie, you mustn't call Blanca stupid.) But all this time Polycarp and Lullaby were starving, because the clock had stopped and the cook had gone out on the zebra . . ."

"And they were starving—slowly starving to death . . ." Zinnie gloated.

"Yes; but on the edge of the wood whom did they meet but a great big tall gentleman with a mot—no, I mean a pony-carriage . . ."

"What's a pony?"

"A little horse about as big as Bun—"

("Oh, oh—I'm a pony!" shouted Bun, kicking and neighing.)

"And the pony-carriage was full—absolutely brim full of—what do you think?" Judith concluded, her question drowned in a general cry of "Oranges! No, noranges—zoranges!!!" from the leaping scrambling group before whom, at the dramatic moment, Boyne had obligingly uncorded his golden bales, while Miss Scope and Nanny murmured: "Now, children, children—now—"

"And this is our chance," said Boyne, "to make a dash for the cathedral."

He slipped his hand through Judith's arm, and drew her across the cloister and into the great echoing basilica. At first, after their long session on the sun-drenched terrace, the place seemed veiled in an impenetrable twilight. But gradually the tremendous walls and spandrils began to glow with their own supernatural radiance, the solid sunlight of gold and umber and flame-coloured mosaics, against which figures of saints, prophets, kings and sages stood out in pale solemn hues. Boyne led the girl toward one of the shafts of the nave, and they sat down on its projecting base.

"Now from here you can see—"

But he presently perceived that she could see nothing. Her little profile was studiously addressed to the direction in which he pointed, and her head thrown back so that her lips were parted, and her long lashes drew an upward curve against her pale skin; but nothing was happening in the face which was usually the theatre of such varied emotions.

She sat thus for a long time, and he did not move or speak again. Finally she turned to him, and said in a shy voice (it was the first time he had noticed any shyness in her): "I suppose I'm much more ignorant than you could possibly have imagined."

"You mean that you don't particularly care for all this?"

She lowered her voice to answer: "I believe all those big people up there frighten me a little." And she added: "I'm glad I didn't bring Chip."

"Child!" He let his hand fall on hers with a faint laugh. What a child she became as soon as she was away from the other children!

"But I do want to admire it, you know," she went on earnestly, "because you do, and Scopy says you know such a lot about everything."

"It's not a question of knowing—" he began; and then broke off. For wasn't it, after all, exactly that? How many thousand threads of association, strung with stored images of the eye and brain, memories of books, of pictures, of great names and deeds, ran between him and those superhuman images, tracing a way from his world to theirs? Yes; it had been stupid of him to expect that a child of fifteen or sixteen, brought up in complete ignorance of the past, and with no more comprehension than a savage of the subtle and allusive symbolism of art, should feel anything in Monreale but the oppression of its awful unreality. And yet he was disappointed, for he was already busy at the masculine task of endowing the woman of the moment with every quality which made life interesting to himself.

"Woman—but she's not a woman! She's a child." His thinking of her as anything else was the crowning absurdity of the whole business. Obscurely irritated with himself and her, he stood up, turning his back impatiently on the golden abyss of the apse. "Come along; it's chilly here after our sun-bath. Gardens are best, after all."

In the doorway she paused a moment and sent her gaze a little wistfully down the mighty perspective they were leaving. "Some day, I know, I shall want to come back here," she said.

"Oh, well, we'll come back together," he replied perfunctorily. But outside in the sunlight, with the children leaping about her, and guiding her with joyful cries toward the outspread tea-things, she was instantly woman again—gay, competent, composed, and wholly mistress of the situation . . .

Yes; decidedly, the more Boyne saw of her the more she perplexed him, the more difficult he found it to situate her in time and space. He did not even know how old she was—somewhere between fifteen and seventeen, he conjectured—nor had he as yet made up his mind if she were pretty. In the cathedral, just now, he had thought her almost plain, with the dull droop of her mouth, her pale complexion which looked dead when unlit by gaiety, her thick brown hair, just thick and just brown, without the magic which makes some women's hair as alive as their lips, and her small impersonal nose, a nose neither perfectly drawn like Blanca's nor impudently droll like Zinnie's. The act of thus cataloguing her seemed to reduce her to a bundle of negatives; yet here in the sunshine, her hat thrown off her rumpled hair, and all the children scrambling over her, her mouth became a flame, her eyes fountains of laughter, her thin frail body a quiver of light—he didn't know how else to put it. Whatever she was, she was only intermittently; as if her body were the mere vehicle of her moods, the projection of successive fears, hopes, ardours, with hardly any material identity of its own. Strange, he mused, that such an imponderable and elusive creature should be the offspring of the two solid facts he recalled the Cliffe Wheaters as being. For a reminder of Joyce Mervin as he had known her, tall, vigorous and substantial, one must turn to Blanca, not Judith. If Blanca had not had to spare a part of herself for the making of Terry she would have been the reproduction of her mother. But Judith was like a thought, a vision, an aspiration—all attributes to which Mrs. Cliffe Wheater could never have laid claim. And Boyne, when the tired and sleepy party were piled once more into the motor, had not yet decided what Judith looked like, and still less if he really thought her pretty.

He fell asleep that night composing a letter to the lady in the Dolomites. ". . . what you would think. A strange little creature who changes every hour, hardly seems to have any personality of her own except when she's mothering her flock. Then she's extraordinary: playmate, mother and governess all in one; and the best of each in its way. As for her very self, when she's not with them, you grope for her identity and find an instrument the wind plays on, a looking-glass that reflects the clouds, a queer little sensitive plate, very little and very sensitive—" and with a last flash of caution, just as sleep overcame him, he added: "Unluckily not in the least pretty."

Chapter V

"I'M so much interested in your picturesque description of the little-girl-mother (sounds almost as nauseating as 'child-wife,' doesn't it?) who is conducting that heterogeneous family across Europe, while the parents are jazzing at Venice. What an instance of modern manners; no, not manners—there are none left—but customs! I'm sure if I saw the little creature I should fall in love with her—as you are obviously doing. Luckily you'll be parting soon, or I should expect to see you arrive here with the girl-bride of the movies and a tribe of six (or is it seven?) adopted children. Don't imagine, though, that in that case I should accept the post of governess." And then, p.s: "Of course she's awfully pretty, or you wouldn't have taken so much pains to say that she's not."

One of Rose Sellars's jolly letters: clever, understanding and humorous. Why did Boyne feel a sudden flatness in it? Something just a trifle mincing, self-conscious—prepared? Yes; if Mrs. Sellars excelled in one special art it was undoubtedly that of preparation. She led up to things—the simplest things—with the skill of a clever rider putting a horse at a five-barred gate. All her life had been a series of adaptations, arrangements, shifting of lights, lowering of veils, pulling about of screens and curtains. No one could arrange a room half so well; and she had arranged herself and her life just as skilfully. The material she had had to deal with was poor enough; in every way unworthy of her; but, as her clever hands could twist a scarf into a divan-cover, and ruffle a bit of paper into a lamp-shade, so she had managed, out of mediocre means, a mediocre husband, an ugly New York house, and a dull New York set, to make something distinguished, personal, almost exciting—so that, in her little world, people were accustomed to say "Rose Sellars" as a synonym for cleverness and originality.

Yes; she had had the art to do that, and to do it quietly, unobtrusively, by a touch here, a hint there, without ever reaching out beyond her domestic and social frame-work. Her originality, in the present day, lay in this consistency and continuity. It was what had drawn Boyne to her in the days of his big wanderings, when, returning from an arduous engineering job in Rumania or Brazil or Australia, he would find, in his ever-shifting New York, the one fixed pole of Mrs. Sellars's front door, always the same front door at the same number of the same street, with the same Whistler etchings and Sargent water-colours on the drawing-room walls, and the same quiet welcome to the same fireside.

In his homeless years that sense of her stability had appealed to him peculiarly: the way, each time he returned, she had simply added a little more to herself, like a rose unfurling another petal. A rose in full sun would have burst into quicker bloom; it was part of Mrs. Sellars's case that she had always, as Heine put it, been like a canary in a window facing north. Not due north, however, but a few points north by west; so that she caught, not the sun's first glow, but its rich decline. He could never think of her as having been really young, immaturely young, like this girl about whom they were exchanging humorous letters, and who, in certain other ways, had a precocity of experience so far beyond Mrs. Sellars's. But the question of a woman's age was almost always beside the point. When a man loved a woman she was always the age he wanted her to be; when he had ceased to, she was either too old for witchery or too young for technique. "And five years is too long a time," he summed it up again, with a faint return of the apprehension he always felt when he thought of his next meeting with Mrs. Sellars.

Five years was too long; and these five, in particular, had transformed the situation, and perhaps its heroine. It was a new Rose Sellars whom he was to meet. When they had parted she was still a wife—resigned, exemplary, and faithful in spite of his pleadings; now she was a widow. The word was full of disturbing implications, and Boyne had already begun to wonder how much of her attraction had been due to the fact that she was unattainable. It was all very well to say that he "wasn't that kind of man"—the kind to tire of a woman as soon as she could be had. That was all just words; in matters of sex and sentiment, as he knew, a man was a different kind of man in every case that presented itself. Only by going to the Dolomites to see her could he really discover what it was that he had found so haunting in Rose Sellars. So he was going.

"Mr. Boyne—could we have a quiet talk, do you think?"

Boyne, driven from the deck by the heat and glare, and the activities of the other passengers, was lying on his bed, book in hand, in a state of after-luncheon apathy. His small visitor leaned in the doorway, slender and gray-clad: Terry Wheater, with the faint pinkness on his cheek-bones, the brilliance in his long-lashed eyes, that made his honest boy's face at times so painfully beautiful.

"Why, of course, old man. Come in. You'll be better off here than on deck till it gets cooler."

Terry tossed aside his cap and dropped into the chair at Boyne's bedside. They had shared a cabin for nearly a fortnight, and reached the state of intimacy induced by such nearness when it does not result in hate; but Boyne had had very few chances to talk with the boy. Terry was always asleep when the older man turned in, and Boyne himself was up and out long before Terry, kept in bed by the vigilant Miss Scope, had begun his leisurely toilet. Boyne, by now, had formed a fairly clear idea of the characteristics of the various young Wheaters, but Terry was perhaps the one with whom he had spent the least time; and the boy's rather solemn tone, and grown-up phraseology, made him lay aside his book with a touch of curiosity.

"What can I do for you, Terry?"

"Persuade them that I ought to have a tutor."

"Them?"

"I mean the Wheaters—father and mother," Terry corrected himself. The children, Boyne knew, frequently referred to their parents by their surname. The habit of doing so, Miss Scope had explained, rose from the fact that, in the case of most of the playmates of their wandering life, the names "father" and "mother" had to be applied, successively or simultaneously, to so many different persons; indeed one surprising little girl with black curls and large pearl earrings, whom they had met the year before at Biarritz, had the habit of handing to each new playmate a typed table of her parents' various marriages and her own successive adoptions. "So they all do it now; that is, speak of their different sets of parents by their names. And my children have picked up the habit from the others, though in their own case, luckily, it's no longer necessary, now that their papa and mamma have come together again."

"I mean father and mother," Terry repeated. "Make them understand that I must be educated. There's no time to lose. And *you* could." His eyes were fixed feverishly—alas, too feverishly—on Boyne's, and his face had the air of precocious anxiety which sometimes made Judith look so uncannily mature.

"My dear chap—of course I'll do anything I can for you. But I don't believe I shall be seeing your people this time. I'm going to jump into the train the minute we get to Venice."

The boy's face fell. "You are? I'm sorry. And Judy will be awfully sold."

"That's very good of her—and of you. But you see—"

"Oh, I can see that a solid fortnight of the lot of us is a good deal for anybody," Terry acquiesced. "All the same, Judy and I did hope you'd stay in Venice for a day or two. We thought, you see, there were a good many things you could do for us."

Boyne continued to consider him thoughtfully. "I should be very glad if I could. But I'm afraid you overrate my influence. I haven't seen your parents for years. They'd hardly remember me."

"That's just it: you'd be a novelty," said Terry astutely.

"Well—if that's an inducement . . . Anyhow, you may be sure I'll do what I can . . . if I find I can alter my plans . . ."

"Oh, if you could! You see I've really never had anybody to speak for me. Scopy cuts no ice with them, and of course they think Judy's too young to know about education—specially as she's never had any herself. She can't even spell, you know. She writes stomach with a *k*. And they've let me go on like this, just with nurses and nursery-governesses (that's really all Scopy is), as if I wasn't any older than Bun, when I'm at an age when most fellows are leaving their preparatory schools." The boy's face coloured with the passion of his appeal, and the flush remained in two sharp patches on his cheeks.

"Of course," he went on, "Judy says I'm not fair to them— that I don't remember what a lot they've had to spend for me on doctors and climate, and all that. And they did send me to school once, and I had to be taken away because of my beastly temperature . . . I know all that. But it *was* a sell, when I left school, just to come back again to Scopy and Nanny, and nobody a fellow could put a question to, or get a tip from about what other fellows are learning. Last summer, at St. Moritz, I met a boy not much older than I am who was rather delicate too, and he'd just got a new father who was a great reader, and who had helped him no end, and got a tutor for him; and he'd started Cæsar, and was getting up his Greek verbs—with a temperature every evening too. And I said to Judy: 'Now, look at that.' And she said, yes, it would be splendid for me to have a tutor. And for two weeks the other fellow's father let me work a little with him. But then we had to go away—one of our troubles," Terry interrupted himself, "is that we're so everlastingly going away. But I suppose it's always so with children—isn't it?—with all the different parents they're divided up among, and all the parents living in different places, and fighting so about when the children are to go to which, and the lawyers always changing things just as you think they're arranged . . . Of course a chap must expect to be moving about when he's young. But Scopy says that later parents settle down." He added this on a note of interrogation, and Boyne, feeling that an answer was expected, declared with conviction: "Oh, but they do—by Jove, they do!"

Inwardly he was recalling the warm cocoon of habit in which his own nursery and school years had been enveloped, giving time for a screen of familiar scenes and faces to form itself about him before he was thrust upon the world. What had struck Boyne first about the little tribe generically known as the Wheaters was that they were so exposed, so bared to the blast—as if they had missed some stage of hidden growth for which Palace Hotels and Riviera Expresses afforded no sufficient shelter. He found his gaze unable to bear the too-eager questioning of the boy's, and understood why Miss Scope looked away when she talked of Terry.

"Settle down? Rather! People naturally tend to as they get older. Aren't your own parents proving it already? Haven't you all got together again, so to speak?" Boyne winced at his own exaggerated tone of optimism. It was a delicate matter, in such cases, to catch exactly the right note.

"Yes," Terry assented. "You'd think so. But I know children who've thought so too, and been jolly well sold. The trouble is you can never be sure when parents will really begin to feel old. Especially with all these new ways the doctors have of making them young again. But anyhow," he went on more hopefully, "if you would put in a word I'm sure it would count a lot. And Judy is sure it would too."

"Then of course I will. I'll stop over a day or two, and do all I can," Boyne assured him, casting plans and dates to the winds.

He was not certain that the appeal had not anticipated a secret yearning of his own; a yearning not so much to postpone his arrival at Cortina (to that he would not confess) as to defer the parting from his new friends, and especially from Judith. The Monreale picnic had been successfully repeated in several other scenes of classic association, and during the gay and clamorous expeditions ashore, and the long blue days on deck, he had been gradually penetrated by the warm animal life which proceeds from a troop of happy healthy children. Everything about the little Wheaters and their "steps" excited his interest and sympathy, and not least the frailness of the tie uniting them, and their determination that it should not be broken. There was something tragic, to Boyne, in the mere fact of this determination—it implied a range of experience and a power of forethought so far beyond a child's natural imagining. To the ordinary child, Boyne's memories told him, separation means something too vague to fret about beforehand, and too pleasantly tempered, when it comes, by the excitement of novelty, and the joy of release from routine, to be anything but a jolly adventure. Boyne could not recall that he had ever minded being sent from home (to the seashore, to a summer camp, or to an aunt's, when a new baby was expected) as long as he was allowed to take his mechanical toys with him. Any place that had a floor on which you could build cranes and bridges and railways was all right: if there was a beach with sand that could be trenched and tunnelled, and water that could be dammed, then it was heaven, even if the porridge wasn't as good as it was at home, and there was no mother to read stories aloud after supper.

He could only conjecture that what he called change would have seemed permanence to the little Wheaters, and that what change signified to them was something as radical and soul-destroying as it would have been to Boyne to see his mechanical toys smashed, or his white mice left to die of hunger. That it should imply a lasting separation from the warm cluster of people, pets and things called home, would have been no more thinkable to the infant Boyne than permanence was to the infant Wheaters.

Judith had explained that almost all their little friends (usually acquaintances made in the world of Palace Hotels) were in the same case as themselves. As Terry had put it, when you were young you couldn't expect not to move about; and when Judith proceeded to give Boyne some of the reasons which had leagued her little tribe against the recurrence of such moves he had the sick feeling with which a powerless looker-on sees the torture of an animal. The case of poor Doll Westway, for instance, who was barely a year older than Judith, and whom they had played with for a summer at Deauville; and now—!

Well, it was all a damned rotten business—that was what it was. And Judith's resolve that her children should never again be exposed to these hazards thrilled Boyne like the gesture of a Joan of Arc. As the character of each became more definite to him, as he measured the distance between Blanca's cool self-absorption, tempered only by a nervous craving for her twin brother's approval, and the prodigal self-abandonment of Beechy, as he compared the detached and downright Zinnie to the sinuous and selfish Bun, and watched the interplay of all these youthful characters, he marvelled that the bond of Judith Wheater's love for them should be stronger than the sum of such heredities. But so it was. He had seen how they could hang together against their sister when some childish whim united them, and now he could imagine what an impenetrable front they would present under her leadership. Of course the Cliffe Wheaters would stay together if their children were determined that they should; and of course they would give Terry a tutor if he wanted one. How was it possible for any one to look at Terry and not give him what he wanted, Boyne wondered? At any rate, he, Boyne, meant to accompany the party to Venice and see the meeting. Incidentally, he was beginning to be curious about seeing the Wheaters themselves.

Chapter VI

THERE was no doubt about the Wheaters' welcome. When Boyne entered the big hall of their hotel on the Grand Canal he instantly recognized Cliffe Wheater in the florid figure which seemed to fill the half-empty resonant place with its own exuberance. Cliffe Wheater had been just like that at Harvard. The only difference was that he and his cigar had both grown bigger. And he seemed to have as little difficulty in identifying Boyne.

"Hullo!" he shouted, so that the hall rocked with his greeting, and the extremely slim young lady in a Quaker gray frock and endless pearls to whom he was talking turned her head toward the newcomer with a little pout of disdain. The pout lingered as her eyes rested on Boyne, but he perceived that it was not personally addressed to him. She had a smooth egg-shaped face as sweetly vacuous as that of the wooden bust on which Boyne's grandmother's caps used to be done up, with carmine lips of the same glossy texture, and blue-gray eyes with long lashes that curved backward (like the bust's) as though they were painted on her lids; and Boyne had the impression that her extreme repose of manner was due to the fear of disturbing this facial harmony.

"Why, Martin dear!" she presently breathed in a low level voice, putting out a hand heavy with rings; and Boyne understood that he was in the presence of the once-redundant Joyce Wheater, and that in her new fashion she was as glad to see him as ever.

"I've grown so old that you didn't recognise me; but I should have known *you* anywhere!" she reproached him in the same smooth silvery voice.

"Old—you?" he found himself stammering; but the insipidities she evidently awaited were interrupted by her husband.

"Know him? I should say so! Not an ounce more flesh on him than there used to be, after all these years: how d'yer do it, I wonder? Great old times we used to have in the groves of John Harvard, eh, Martin, my boy? 'Member that Cambridge girl you used to read poetry to? *Poetry*! She was a looker, too!

'Come into the garden, Maud' . . . *Garden* they used to call it in those days! And now I hear you're a pal of my son's . . . Well, no, I don't mean Chipstone—" he smiled largely— "but poor old Terry . . . Hullo, why here's the caravan! Joyce, I say—you've told them they're to be parked out at the *Pension Grimani*? All but Chip, that is. Can't part with Chipstone, can we? Here they all come, Judy in the lead as usual. Hullo, Judy girl! Chippo, old man, how goes it? Give us your fist, my son." He caught his last-born out of Judith's arms, and the others had to wait, a little crestfallen, yet obviously unsurprised, till the proud father had filled his eyes with the beauty of his last achievement. "Catch on to him, will you, Joyce? Look at old man Chippo! Must have put on another five pounds since our last meeting—I swear he has . . . you just feel this calf of his! Hard as a tennis ball, it is . . . Does you no end of credit, Judy. Here, pass him on to the room next to your mother's . . . Wish you'd develop that kind of calf, Terry boy . . ."

"Look at *my* calfs, too! I can show them upside down!" shouted Bun, bursting in with a handspring upon these endearments; while Blanca, wide-eyed and silent, fastened her absorbed gaze on the golden thatch of her mother's intricately rippled head, and Joyce clasped the children, one after another, to her pearls.

Give Terry a tutor? Boy's own idea, was it? Good old chap— always poking around with books. Wheater would have thought that Terry knew enough to be his own tutor by this time . . . Funny, wasn't it, for a son of *his*? Cut out to be a Doctor of Divinity; or President of a University, maybe! Talk of heredity—for him and Joyce to have turned out such a phenomenon! Hoped Chipstone wouldn't turn into a Doctor of Divinity too. But of course they'd give Terry a tutor—wouldn't they, Joyce? The boy was dead right; he couldn't be loafing about any longer with the women . . . Did Boyne happen to know of a tutor, by any chance? Wheater'd never before had anything of the sort to bother about. Right up on schools, of course—always meant to send Terry to Groton; but his rotten temperature had knocked that out, so now . . .

The three were sitting after dinner on the balcony of the Wheaters' apartment, watching the Grand Canal, gondola-laden, lamp-flecked, furrowed with darting motor-boats, drift beneath them in rich coils and glassy volutes. There was nothing doing in Venice, Wheater had explained, so early in the season; it was as dead as the grave. Just a handy place to meet the children in, and look them over before they were packed off to the Engadine or Leysin. And besides, the Wheaters had come there to pick up their new steam-yacht; the "Fancy Girl," a real beauty. They were going on a short cruise in her before they left for Cowes, and Venice was a handy place to try her out. By-and-by, if Boyne liked, he and Joyce and Wheater might drift out to the Piazza, and take an ice at Florian's, and a turn on the Canal—not very exciting, but the best Wheater could suggest in the circumstances. But Boyne said: why not stay where they were? And Joyce, with a shrug that just sufficiently displaced the jet strap attaching her dress to her white shoulder, remarked that Cliffe never *could* stay where he was, but that nobody objected to his painting Venice red if he wanted to . . .

"Where'd I get the paint, at this time of year? Nobody here but guys with guide-books, and old maids being photo'd feeding the pigeons . . . Hotels cram full of 'em . . . Well, look here; about that tutor? You haven't come across anybody on your travels that would do, Martin? University chap, and that sort of thing?"

Martin didn't believe he had; but Mrs. Wheater, lifting a white arm to flick her cigarette into the Canal, said: "*I* know a tutor."

"Hell—you *do*?" her husband laughed incredulously. " 'Nother cigar, old chap? These Coronas ain't bad—specially made for me." He loosed the golden sheathings from a cigar and held his lighter to it.

"I know a tutor," Mrs. Wheater repeated. "Exactly the right person, if only we can persuade him to take the job."

"Well—I'll be blowed! Where'd you excavate him?"

She was silent for a moment; then she said: "I've been going to the galleries with him. It's the first time I've ever *seen* Venice. Fanny Tradeschi got him out from England to tutor her boys, and then she was bored here, and rushed back to Paris, and left him stranded. His name is Ormerod—Gerald Ormerod. It would be the greatest privilege for Terry if he could be persuaded . . ."

"Oh, I guess I can persuade him all right. I don't believe Fanny remembered to settle with him before she left."

"No, she didn't; but he's awfully proud. You'd better not take that tone with him, Cliffe."

"What; the tone of asking him what his screw is?"

"Shouting like that at the top of your lungs—as if everybody less rich than yourself was deaf," said his wife, with a slight steel edge in her silver voice.

"Hul*lo*! That the size of it? Well, fix it up with him any old way you like. I'm off for a round of the town . . . Not coming along, Martin? Well, so long . . . Can't for the life of me see why you've stuck yourself down at that frowsy *pension* with the children; I'm sure I could have bullied the manager here into giving you a room . . . Have it your own way, though. And you and Joyce can map out a tour for to-morrow: only no galleries for me, thank you! Look here—d'ye think I'd disturb Chipstone Wheater Esqre if I was just to poke my head in and take a look at him on my way out? Listen—my shoes don't creak the least bit . . . Oh, hang it, I don't care, I'm going to, anyway . . ."

Of the Joyce Mervin of Boyne's youth, the young Joyce Wheater of her early married days, nothing, apparently, was left in the slim figure leaning over the balcony at Boyne's elbow. Then she had been large, firm and rosy, with a core of artless sensibility; now she seemed to have gone through some process of dematerialization (no doubt there were specialists for this too) which had left a translucent and imponderable body about a hard little kernel of spirit.

"It's impossible to make Cliffe feel *nuances*," she murmured to her cigarette after Wheater had gone; then, turning to Boyne: "But now we can have a good talk—just like old times, can't we?" She settled down in her armchair, and exchanged her measured syllables for a sort of steely volubility which rattled about Boyne's head like a hail of *confetti*. She was awfully glad to see him, really she was, she declared; he *did* believe her when she said that, didn't he? He'd always been such a perfect friend, in the silly old days when she herself was just a stupid baby, years younger in experience than Judy was now . . . What did Martin think of Judy, by the way? Did he appreciate what a miracle the child was? Positively, she was older and wiser than any of them;

and the only human being who had any influence whatever with Cliffe . . .

Oh, well: Cliffe . . . yes . . . It was awfully dear and sweet of Martin to say that he was glad she and Cliffe had come together again, and she was glad too, and she was ever so proud of Chip, and she *did* recognize poor Cliffe's qualities, she always had, even when things were at their worst . . . but, there, it was no use pretending with Martin, it never had been; and there was no denying that Cliffe had got into dreadfully bad hands when she left him . . . utterly demoralized and cowed by that beastly Lacrosse woman . . . and the money pouring out like water . . . Yes, she, Joyce, had seen it was her duty to take him back; and so she had. Because she still believed in the sanctity of marriage, in spite of everything. She hoped Martin did too? For if you didn't, what was there left to hold society together? But all the same, if one came to feel that by living with a man, even if he *was* one's husband, one was denying one's Ideal: that was awful too, wasn't it? Didn't Martin think it was awful?

Yes, Martin supposed it was; but he rather thought a bunch of jolly children were a pretty good substitute for any old Ideal he'd ever met. Mrs. Wheater laughed, with somewhat more of the old resonance, and said she thought so too, and that was what Judy had argued—no, Martin would never know how wonderful Judy had been during the ghastly days when Buondelmonte was dragging her, Joyce, through the mire, literally through the mire! "Why, there were things I couldn't tell even *you*, Martin—"

Martin felt his gorge rise. "Things I hope that Judy wasn't told, then?"

Mrs. Wheater's shoulder again slipped its light trammels in a careless shrug. "Bless you, you don't have to tell the modern child things! They seem to be born knowing them. Haven't you found that out, you dear old Rip van Winkle? Why, Judy's like a mother to me, I assure you."

"She's got a pretty big family to mother, hasn't she?" Boyne rejoined, and Mrs. Wheater sighed contentedly: "Oh, but she loves it, you know! It's her hobby. Why, she tried to be a mother to Zinnia Lacrosse . . . Fancy a child of Judy's age attempting to keep a movie star straight! She used to give good advice to Buondelmonte . . . But that nightmare's over now, and we're all together again, and there's only Terry, poor darling, to worry about. I *do* worry about him, you know, Martin. And isn't it sweet of him to want to be properly educated? For Cliffe, of course, education has always just been college sports and racing-motors. That's one reason why I've missed so much . . . but I am determined that Terry shall have all the opportunities I haven't had. This tutor I was speaking about, Gerald Ormerod—I wonder if you'd see him for me to-morrow, Martin? It's no use asking Cliffe—he'd just shout and brag, and spoil the whole thing. Gerald—I've got to calling him Gerald because Fanny Tradeschi always did—he comes of very good people, you see, and he's almost too sensitive . . . too much of an idealist . . . I can't tell you what it's been to me, these last weeks, to see Venice through the eyes of some one who really cares for beauty . . . You'll have a talk with him about Terry, Martin dear? I'm sure Cliffe would give any salary you advise—and it would be the saving of our poor Terry to be with some one really sensitive and cultivated . . . and Bun, too . . . he might put some sort of reason into Bun, who's beginning to get quite out of hand with Scopy . . . And, Martin, don't forget: you can fix the salary as high as you like."

Chapter VII

Two days later Boyne sat taking his morning coffee with Judith Wheater at a rickety iron table in the mouldy garden of the *Pension Grimani*. He had bribed a maid to carry out their breakfast, so that they might escape the stuffiness of the low-ceilinged dining-room, full of yesterday's dinner smells, of subdued groups of old maids and giggling bands of school-girls, and of the too-pervasive clatter of the corner table about which Scopy and Nanny had gathered their flock. It was Boyne's last day in Venice, and he wanted a clear hour of it with Judith. Presently the family would surge up like a spring tide, every one of them—from Mr. and Mrs. Wheater, with the "Fancy Girl" lying idle off San Giorgio, and a string of unemployed motors at Fusina, to Beechy and Zinnie squabbling over their new necklaces from the Merceria, and Miss Scope with a fresh set of problems for the summer—all wanting Boyne's advice or sympathy or consolation, or at least his passive presence at their debates. All this was rather trying, and the eager proximity of the little Wheaters made privacy impossible. Yet Boyne was more than ever glad that he had resisted the persuasions of their parents, and carried his luggage to the *Pension Grimani* instead of to the Palace Hotel. The mere existence of Palace Hotels was an open wound to him. Not that he was indifferent to the material advantages they offered. Nobody appreciated hot baths and white tiles, electric bed-lamps and prompt service, more than he whose lot was usually cast in places so remote from them. He loved Palace Hotels; but he loathed the mere thought of the people who frequented them.

Judy, he discovered, was of the same mind. Boyne had felt a little resentful of the fact that only the Wheaters' youngest-born was to share the luxury of their hotel; it seemed rather beastly to banish the others to frowsy lodgings around the corner. At the moment he had avoided Judy's eye, fearing to catch in it the reflection of his thought: most of Judy's feelings were beginning to reverberate in him. But now, in the leisure of their first talk since landing, he learned that no such feeling had marred the meeting of the little Wheaters with their parents.

Blanca, Judith owned, probably had minded a little, just at first. Silly Blanca—she was always rather jealous of the fuss that Joyce and father made about Chip. Besides, she loved smartness, and picking up new ideas about clothes from the *chic* women in hotel restaurants; and she liked to be seen about with Joyce, who was so smart herself, and to have other smart ladies say: "Is this your dear little girl? We should have known her anywhere from the likeness."

But it was precisely because of Blanca that Judith most disliked going to "Palaces." "Ever since she got engaged to the lift-boy at Biarritz . . ."

"Engaged?" Boyne gasped. "But, Judy . . . but Blanca's barely eleven . . ."

"Oh, I was engaged myself at Blanca's age—to a page at a skating-rink." Judith's small face, as she made the admission, had the wistful air of middle-age looking back on the sweet follies of youth. "But that was different. He was a very nice little Swiss boy; and I only gave him one of my hair-ribbons, and he gave me one of his livery buttons; and when he went home for his holiday he sent me dried edelweiss, and forget-me-nots pasted on cards. But these modern children are different. Blanca's boy wanted a ring with a real stone in it; and he was a horrid big thing with a fat nose that wriggled. Terry and I could hardly bear it. And when Scopy found out about it she made an awful row, and threatened to write to mother . . . so altogether we're better off here. In fact I wrote to father that we'd better put up at a place like this, where the children can rush about and make a noise, and nobody bothers. I think it's rather jolly here, don't you, Martin?"

She had called him Martin, as a matter of course, since the second day out from Algiers; and he could never hear his name in her fresh young trill without a stir of pleasure.

He said he thought the *Pension Grimani* awfully jolly, and was glad it suited the rest of them as well as it did him. Then she asked if it was all right about Terry's tutor, and what he thought of the young man. The answer to this was more difficult. Boyne was not sure what he thought. He had had an interview with Mr. Ormerod on the previous day; an interview somewhat halting and embarrassed on his own part, perfectly firm and self-possessed on the tutor's. Mr. Ormerod was a good-looking young Englishman with the University stamp upon him. He had very fair hair, somewhat long and rumpled, lazy ironic gray eyes, and a discontented mouth. He looked clever, moody and uncertain; but he was cultivated and intelligent, and it seemed certain that Terry would learn more, and be more usefully occupied, in his care than in Miss Scope's. Boyne's embarrassment proceeded not only from the sense of his unfitness to choose a tutor for anybody, but from the absurdity of having to do so with the pupil's parents on the spot. Mr. Ormerod, however, seemed neither surprised nor disturbed. He had seen Terry, and was sure he was an awfully good little chap; his only hesitation was as to the salary. Boyne, who had fixed it to the best of his judgment, saw at once that, though it exceeded the usual terms, it was below Mr. Ormerod's mark. The young man explained that the Princess Tradeschi had let him down rather badly, and that it was a beastly nuisance, but he really couldn't give in about his screw. Boyne remembered Mrs. Wheater's parting injunction, and to get over the difficulty suggested throwing in Bun. "There's the little Buondelmonte boy—a sort of step-son; he's rather a handful for the governess, and perhaps you would take him on for part of the time. In that case—"

This closed the transaction to Mr. Ormerod's advantage, and enabled Boyne to report to the Wheaters that their eldest son's education would begin the next day. And now he had to answer Judith's question.

"He strikes me as clever; but I don't know how hard he'll make Terry work."

"Oh, Terry will make *him* work. And as long as Joyce wants it I'm glad it's settled. If she hadn't, father might have kicked at the price. Not that he isn't awfully generous to us; but he can't see why people should want to be educated when they don't have to. What does it ever *lead* to, he says." She wrinkled her young brows pensively. "I don't know; do you? I can't explain. But if Terry wants it I'm sure it's right. You've read a lot yourself, haven't you? I don't suppose I shall ever care much about reading . . . but what's the use of bothering, when I should never have a minute's time, no matter how much I cared to do it?"

He reminded her that she might have time later, and added that, now that her parents were in an educational mood, he wondered she didn't take advantage of it to get herself sent to a good school, if only to be able to keep up with Terry. At this she smiled a little wistfully; it was the same shy doubtful smile with which she had looked about her in the cathedral at Monreale, trying to puzzle out what he saw in it. But her frown of responsibility returned. "Go to school? Me? But when, I'd like to know? There'll always be some of the children left to look after. Why, I shall be too old for school before Chip is anywhere near Terry's age. And besides, I never mean to leave the children—*never*!" She brought the word out with the shrill emphasis he had already heard in her voice when her flock had to be protected or reproved. "We've all sworn that," she added. "We took an awful oath one day at Biskra that we'd never be separated again, no matter what happened. Even Chip had to hold up his fist and say: 'I swear.' We did it on Scopy's 'Cyclopædia of Nursery Remedies.' And if things went wrong again, and I was off at one of your schools, who'd see to it that the oath was kept?"

"But now that all the children are safely with your own people, couldn't you let the oath take care of itself, and think a little of what's best for you?"

She raised her eyes with a puzzled stare which made them seem as young as Zinnie's. "You'd like me to go to school?"

He returned the look with one of equal gravity. "Most awfully."

Her colour rose a little. "Then I should like to."

"Well, then—"

She shook her head and her flush faded. "I don't suppose you'll ever understand—you or anybody. How could I leave the children now? I've got to get them off to Switzerland in another fortnight; this is no place for Terry. And suppose Mr. Ormerod decides he won't come with us—"

"Won't come with you? But it's precisely what he's been engaged to do!"

She gave an impatient shrug like her mother's, and turned on Boyne a little face sharp with interrogation. "Well, then, suppose it was mother who didn't want him to?"

"Your mother? Why, child, it was she who found him. She knows all about him; she—"

"She jolly well likes doing Venice with him," Judy completed his sentence with a hideous promptness. It was Boyne's turn to redden. He averted his eyes from her with one of Miss Scope's abrupt twists, and pushed his chair back as if to get up. Judy leant across the table and touched his sleeve timidly.

"I've said something you don't like, Martin?"

"You've said something exceedingly silly. Something I should hate to hear if you were grown up. But at your age it's merely silly, and doesn't matter."

She was on her feet in a flash, quivering with anger. "My age? My age? What do you know about my age? I'm as old as your grandmother. I'm as old as the hills. I suppose you think I oughtn't to say things like that about mother—but what am I to do, when they're true, and there's no one but you that I can say them to?"

He never quite knew, when she took that tone, if he was most moved or offended by it. There were moments when she frightened him; when he would have given the world to believe either that she was five years older than she said, or else that she did not know the meaning of the words she used. At such moments it was always the vision of Rose Sellars which took possession of him, and he found himself breathlessly explaining this strange child to her, and feeling that what was so clear to him would become incomprehensible as soon as he tried to make it clear to others, and especially to Mrs. Sellars. "There's nothing to be done about it," he thought despairingly. Aloud he remarked, in an impatient tone: "You're very foolish not to go to school."

She made no reply, but simply said, with a return of her wistful look: "Perhaps if you were going to stay here you'd lend me some books."

"But I'm not going to stay here; I'm off to-morrow morning," he answered angrily, keeping his head turned away with an irritated sense that if he should meet her eyes he would see tears in them.

Her own anger had dropped—he knew it without looking at her, and he had the sense that she was standing near him, very small and pale. "Martin, if you'd only stay! There are so many things left undecided . . . Father and mother can't make up their minds where to go next, and it's always when they've got nothing particular to do that they quarrel. They can't get anybody to go on the yacht with them—not till Cowes. And if they have to chuck the cruise father wants to go to Paris, and mother wants to go motoring in the hill-towns of Italy (where are they, do you know?). And if they get wrangling again what in the world is to become of us children?"

He turned back then, and put his hand on her arm. There was an old bench, as shaky as the table, under a sort of ragged sounding-board of oleanders. "Sit down, my dear." He sat beside her, smiling a little, lighting a cigarette to prove his ease and impartiality. "You're taking all this much too hard, you know. You've too much on your shoulders, and you're over-tired: that's all. I've been with your father and mother for two days now, and I see no signs of anything going wrong. The only trouble with them is that they're too rich. That makes them fretful: it's like teething. Every time your father hears he's made another million it's like cutting a new tooth. They hurt to bite on when one has so many. But he'll find people soon to go off for a cruise with him, and then he'll have to decide about your summer. Your people must see that this place is not bracing enough for Terry; and they'll want him to settle down somewhere in the mountains, and get to work as soon as possible."

The tone of his voice seemed to quiet her, though he suspected that at first she was too agitated to follow what he said. "But what sort of people?" she brought out at length, disconsolately.

"What sort of people?"

"To go on the yacht. That's another thing. When mother is away from father, and I'm with her, it's easier in some ways— except that then I fret about the other children. When Joyce and father are together they do all sorts of crazy things, just to be in opposition to each other. Take up with horrid people, I mean, people who drink and have rows. And then they get squabbling again, as they did when Buondelmonte sent father the bill for his Rolls-Royce . . ."

"Buondelmonte?"

"Yes; but Joyce said we were never to talk about that—she forbade us all."

"She was quite right."

"Yes; only it's true. And they do get into all sorts of rows and muddles about the people they pick up—"

At this moment Boyne, hearing a shuffle on the gravel, looked around and saw the maid approaching with a card. The maid glanced doubtfully at the two, and finally handed the card to

Boyne, as the person most likely to represent law and order in the effervescent party to which he seemed to belong. It was a very large and stiff piece of paste-board, bearing the name: *Marchioness of Wrench*, and underneath, in a sprawling untaught hand: "To see my daughter Zinnie Wheater," the "my" being scratched out and "her" substituted for it. Boyne, after staring at this document perplexedly, passed it on to Judith, who sprang up with an astonished exclamation.

"Why, it must be Zinnia Lacrosse! Why, she's married again! It's true, then, what Blanca saw in the papers . . ." She looked inquiringly at Boyne. "Do you suppose she's really here?"

"Of course I'm here!" cried a sharp gay voice from the doorway; and through the unkempt shrubbery an apparition sparkling with youth and paint and jewels swept toward them on a wave of perfume.

"Hullo, Judy—why, it's *you!*" But the newcomer was not looking at Judith. She stood still and scrutinised Boyne with great eyes set like jewels in a raying-out of enamelled lashes. She had a perfectly oval face, a small exquisitely curved mouth, and an air of innocent corruption which gave Boyne a slightly squeamish feeling as she turned and flung her arms about Judy.

"Well, old Judy, I'm glad to see you again . . . Who's your friend?" she added, darting a glance at Boyne through slanting lids. All her gestures had something smooth and automatic, and a little larger than life.

"He's Mr. Boyne. He's father's friend too. This is Zinnia Lacrosse, Martin."

"No, it isn't, either! It's the Marchioness of Wrench. Only I'm just called Lady Wrench, except on visiting-cards, and when they put me in the newspapers, or I talk to the servants. And of course you'll call me Zinnia just the same, Judy. How d'ye do, Mr. Boyne?" murmured the star, with an accession of elegance and a languidly extended hand. But she had already mustered Boyne, and was looking over his shoulder as she addressed him. "What I'm after is Zinnie, you know," she smiled. "Wrenny's waiting in the gondola—Wrenny's my husband—and I've promised to take her out and show her to him."

She cast an ingratiating glance at Judith, but the latter, quietly facing her, seemed to Boyne to have grown suddenly tall and authoritative, as she did when she had to cope with a nursery mutiny.

"Now, Zinnia," she began, in the shrill voice which always gave Boyne a sense of uneasiness, "you know perfectly well—"

"Know what?"

"You know what the agreement is; and you know Scopy and I aren't going to listen to anything—"

"Fudge, child! What d'you suppose I'd want to break the agreement for? Not that I care such an awful lot for Cliffe's old alimony, you know. It don't hardly keep me in silk stockings. If I wanted to carry Zinnie off, that wouldn't stop me half a second. But I only want to show Wrenny that I can have a baby if I choose. Men are so funny about such things; he doesn't believe I've ever had one. And of course I can see he's got to have an heir. Look here, Judy, ain't I always dealt with you white? Let me see her right away, won't you? I've got a lovely present for her here, and one for you too—a real beauty . . . Can't you understand a mother's feelings?"

Judy still kept her adamantine erectness. Her lips, colourless and pressed together, barely parted to reply to the film star, whose last advance she appeared not to have noticed.

"Of course you can see Zinnie. You needn't get excited about that. Only you'll see her here, with me and Mr. Boyne. All your husband has got to do is to get out of the gondola and come into the house."

"If you'd been brought up like a lady you'd call him Lord Wrench, Judy."

Judith burst out laughing. "Mercy! Then you'd better call me Miss Wheater. But if you want to see Zinnie you haven't got any time to lose, because father's going to send for the children in a minute or two, and take them all off on the yacht."

"Oh, Judy—but he can't prevent my seeing Zinnie!"

"Nobody wants to prevent you, if you'll do what I say."

The Marchioness of Wrench pondered this ultimatum for a moment, staring down at her highly polished oval nails. Then she said sullenly: "I'll try; but I don't believe he'll get out of the gondola. He's dead lazy. And we wanted to take Zinnie for a row." Judith made no reply, and finally Lady Wrench moved back toward the vestibule door with a reluctant step.

"I'll go and fetch Zinnie," Judith announced to Boyne, advancing to the house by another path; but as she did so a small figure, bedizened and glass-beaded, hurled itself across the garden and into her arms.

"Judy! That was Zinnia, wasn't it? I saw her from my window! Nanny said it wasn't, but I knew it was. She hasn't gone away without seeing her own little Zinnie, has she? I'll never forgive you if she has. Did she bring a present for me? She always does. Blanca's crazy to come down and see her clothes, but Scopy won't let her. She's locked her up."

Judith gave one of her contemptuous shrugs. "Oh, Scopy needn't have done that. It won't hurt Blanca to see your mother. There, stop pinching me, Zinnie, and don't worry. Your mother's coming back. She's only gone to get her husband to introduce him to you."

"Her new husband? What's his name? Nobody ever told me she had a new husband. 'Cos they always say: 'You're too little to understand.' Zif I wasn't Zinnia's own little daughter! Judy, hasn't she got a present for me, don't you think? If it's nothing but choc'lates, course I'll divvy with the others; but if it's jewelry I needn't, need I?" Zinnie's ruddy curls spiralled upward and her face flamed with cupidity and eagerness. With a flash of her dimpled fists she snatched the new Merceria beads from her neck and thrust them into the pocket of her frock. "There's no use her seeing I've had presents already—you don't mind, Martin, do you?" she queried over her shoulder, addressing Boyne, who had given her the necklace that morning. He burst out laughing; but Judith, before he could intervene, caught hold of the delinquent and gave her a wrathful shake. "You nasty false ungrateful little viper you—"

"Oo-oo-oo," wailed Zinnie, hunching up her shoulders in a burst of sobs.

"There—now, Wrenny, you just look at that. I wish I had my lawyers here! That's the way those Wheater people treat my child—" Lady Wrench stood in the garden door and pointed with a denunciatory arm toward her weeping infant. Over her shoulder appeared the fair hair and puzzled eyes of a very tall young man with a sickly cast of countenance, a wide tremulous mouth and a bald forehead. "Oh, Lord, my dear," he said.

Chapter VIII

LADY WRENCH had snatched up her daughter and stood, in an approved film attitude, pressing Zinnie's damp cheek against her own, while the child's orange-coloured curls mixed with the red gold of hers. "What's that nasty beast been doing to momma's darling?" she demanded, glaring over Zinnie's head at Judith. "Whipping you for wanting to see your own mother, I suppose? You just tell momma what it was and she'll . . ."

But Zinnie's face had cleared, and she was obviously far too much absorbed in her mother's appearance to heed the unimportant questions which were being put to her. She slid her fat fingers through the pearls flowing in cataracts down Lady Wrench's bosom. "Oh, Zinnia, are they real? Blanca says they can't be—she knows they can't, 'cos they're twice as big as Joyce's."

"Blanca? Why, is Blanca here? Where is she?"

"Scopy's got her locked up, so's she can't come down and stare at you, but she found Martin's op'ra glasses in his room'n she's looking at you through them'n she says they're so pow'ful she can count the pearls, and can't she come down, please, Zinnia, 'cos she wants to see f'you've got the same Callot model's Joyce's jess ordered, 'cos it'll make Joyce wild'n she'll want to get another one instead as quick as she can. Please, Zinnia!"

Lady Wrench's brow had cleared as quickly as her daughter's. She burst out laughing and pressed her lips to Zinnie's cheek. "There, Wrenny, what d'you think of that, I'd like to know? Isn't she my really truly little girl?"

Lord Wrench had shambled slowly forward in her wake. He stood, lax-jointed, irresolute, in his light loose flannels, a faded Homburg hat tilted back from his perplexed brow, gazing down on the group from the immense height to which his long limbs and endless neck uplifted him.

"Yes, I'll take my oath she's that," he replied, in a voice which seemed to come from somewhere even higher than his hat; and he gave a cackle that rose and overreached his voice, and went tinkling away to the housetops.

His wife's laugh joined and outsoared his, and she dropped down on the bench, still hugging Zinnie. "Judy thought we wanted to *steal* her, Wrenny—think of that! Oh, I forgot you didn't know each other—Lord Wrench, Judy Wheater. And this is Mr. Boyne, a friend of Cliffe's—aren't you a friend of Cliffe's, Mr. Boyne? My present husband, the Marqu—no; that's wrong, I know—just my husband. But where's Blanca, Judy? Do let her come down, and Terry too; that's a darling! After all, I'm their step-mother, ain't I? Or I was, anyhow . . . Is Blanca as much of a beauty as ever, Mr. Boyne? If that girl had more pep I wouldn't wonder but what I could do something with her on the screen. Judy, now, would never be any good to us—would she, Wrenny? Too much of a lady, I always used to tell her . . ."

"Shut up: here she is," Lord Wrench interpolated. As he spoke Judith reappeared with her younger sister. Blanca's eyes were stretched to their widest at the sight of her former step-mother, though her erect spine and measured tread betrayed nothing of her eagerness to appraise Lady Wrench's dress and jewels. Behind them walked Miss Scope, helmeted as if for a fray, her hands mailed in gray cotton, and clutching her umbrella like a spear.

"Well, Blanca! How are you? How you've grown! And what a looker you're going to be! Only you're so fearfully grand—always was, wasn't she, Judy? You're a lady yourself, but you ain't *such* a lady. Well, Blanca, shake hands, and let me introduce you to my new husband. Wrenny, this is Blanca, who used to come and stay, with Terry and Judy, when Cliffe and me were married. Where's Terry, Blanca? Why didn't he come down too? I'd love to see him."

"Terry's with his tutor at present," said Blanca distantly, though her eyes never for a second detached themselves from Lady Wrench's luminous presence.

"But he said he wouldn't have come down even if he hadn't of been," chimed in Zinnie, peering up maliciously into her mother's face. "He says he isn't 'quisitive like Blanca, and he can't be bothered every time somebody comes round to see the steps."

Lord Wrench, at this, joined Boyne in a fresh burst of laughter, but his bride looked distinctly displeased. "Well, I see Terry's tutor hasn't taught him manners anyhow," she snapped, while

Miss Scope admonished her youngest charge: "*In*quisitive, Zinnie; you're really old enough to begin to speak correctly."

"No, I'm not, 'less Bun and Beechy do too," Zinnie retorted.

"Beatrice and Astorre are foreigners," Miss Scope rejoined severely.

"Well, so are you, you old flamingo! You're not a real true Merrican like us!"

"Zinnie," cried Blanca, intervening in her brother's behalf in her grandest manner, "Terry never said any such thing"; but Zinnie, secure in her mother's embrace, laughed scorn at her rebukers, until Judith remarked: "I'm very sorry, but children who are rude are not to be taken on the yacht today. Father particularly told me to tell you so. Zinnie, if you don't apologise at once to Miss Scope I'm afraid you'll have to stay behind alone with Nanny."

"No, she won't, either, my Zinnie pet won't! She'll go out in the gond'la with her own momma and her new father," Lady Wrench triumphantly declared. But Zinnie's expressive countenance had undergone a sudden change. She detached herself from the maternal embrace, and sliding to the ground slipped across to Miss Scope and endearingly caught her by a gray cotton hand. "Scopy, I'm not a really naughty Zinnie, say I'm not—'cos I don't want to go out in a bally old gond'la, I want to go'n father's steam-yacht, I do!"

Fresh squeals of approval from Lord Wrench greeted this hasty retraction. "Jove—she's jolly well right, the kid is! No doubt about her being yours, Zinnia," he declared; whereat the lady rejoined, with an effort at lightness: "Zif I couldn't have a yacht of my own any day I like that'd steam all round that old hulk of Cliffe's! And I will too—you'll see," she added, sweeping a circular glance about the company.

"Righto. Come along now, and we'll pick one out," her husband suggested with amiable irony.

"Well, maybe I will," she menaced, rising to her feet with the air of throwing back an ermine train. But Blanca had advanced and was lifting shy eyes to hers. "Your dress is so perfectly lovely, Zinnia; I think it's the prettiest one I ever saw you in. Isn't it from that Russian place mother's always talking about, where it's so hard to get them to take new customers?"

The star cast a mollified smile upon her. "You bright child, you! Well, yes; it is. But even if your mother could persuade them to take her on she wouldn't be able to get this model, because the Grand Duke Anastase designed it expressly for me, and I've got a signed paper saying it's the only one of the kind they'll ever make. See the way it's cut across the shoulders?"

Blanca contemplated this detail with ecstatic appreciation, and Lady Wrench, gathering up her sable scarf, glanced victoriously about her. "I guess anybody that wants to can buy a steam-yacht; but you can count on one hand with two fingers missing the women that Anastase'll take the trouble to design a dress for."

"Oh, I say, come on, old girl," her husband protested, shifting his weight wearily from one long leg to another; and Lady Wrench turned to follow him.

"Well, goodbye, Zinnie child. Next time I'll call for you on my two thousand ton oil-burner. Oh, look here—seen my bag, Wrenny? I believe I brought some caramels for the child—" She turned back, and began to fumble in a bejewelled bag, while the two little girls' faces fell at the mention of caramels. But presently a gold chain strung with small but lustrous pearls emerged from a tangle of cigarettes and bank-notes. "Here, Zinnie, you put that on, and ask Blanca to look at the pearls under the microscope, and then tell you if they're false, like your momma's."

Blanca paled at the allusion. "Oh, Zinnia, I never said yours were false! Is that what that little brute told you? I only said, I couldn't be sure they weren't, at that distance—"

Lady Wrench laughed imperturbably. "Well, I should think you'd have been sure they *were*, being so accustomed to your mother's. But movie queens don't have to wear fake pearls, my pet, 'cos if the real ones get stolen they can always replace 'em. You tell that to Mrs. Cliffe Wheater number three. And you needn't look so scared—I bear no malice." She drew a small packet from the bag. "See, here's a ring I brought you: I guess that'll bear testing too," she added, flinging the little box into Blanca's hand.

Blanca, white with excitement, snapped open the lid, which revealed to her swift appraising eye a little ruby set in brilliants.

She drew it forth with a rapturous "Oh, Zinnia," and slipped it onto her hand, hastily thrusting the box into a fold of her jumper.

"When I give presents I don't go to the ten-cent store for them," remarked Lady Wrench, with a farewell wave of her hand. "So long, everybody! Shouldn't wonder if we met again soon by the sad sea waves. Wrenny and I are honeymooning out at the Lido, and maybe you'll all be over for the bathing. It's getting to be as gay as it is in August. All the smart people are snapping up the bathing tents. The Duke of Mendip's got the one next to ours. He's Wrenny's best friend, you know. By-bye, Judy. Mr. Boyne, hope you'll dine with us some night at the Lido Palace to meet the Duke. Ask for the Marchioness of Wrench—you'll remember?"

She vanished in a dazzle of pearls and laughter, leaving Blanca and Zinnie in absorbed contemplation of their trinkets till Miss Scope marshalled them into the house to prepare for the arrival of the "Fancy Girl" 's launch.

After the children were gone, Judy lingered for a moment in the garden with Boyne. Her features, so tense and grown-up looking during the film star's visit, had melted into the small round face of a pouting child.

"Well—that's over," Boyne said, flinging away his cigarette as though the gesture symbolised the act of casting out the Wrenches.

"Yes," she assented, in a tone of indifference. "Zinnia doesn't really matter, you know," she added, as if noticing his surprise. "She screams a lot; but she doesn't mean anything by it."

"Well, I should think you'd be glad she didn't, for whatever she meant would be insufferable."

Judith raised her eyebrows with a faint smile. "We're more used to fusses than you are. When there are seven children, and a lot of parents, there's always somebody fighting about something. But Zinnia's nothing like as bad as she looks." She paused a moment, and then, irrepressibly, as if to rid her heart of an intolerable weight: "But Blanca got away with my present. Did you see that? I knew she would! That's what she came down for—to wangle it out of Zinnia. Pretending she thought that old Callot model was one of Anastase's! There's nothing mean enough for Blanca!" Her eyes had filled with large childish tears, and one of them rolled down her cheek before she had time to throw back her head and add proudly: "Not that I care a straw, of course. I'm too grown up to mind about such rubbish. But I know Blanca must have noticed my 'nitials on the box. Didn't you see how quick she was about hiding it?"

BOOK II

Chapter IX

THE next day, during the journey through the hot Veneto and up into the mountains, the Wheater children and their problems were still so present to Boyne that he was hardly conscious of where he was going, or why.

His last hours with his friends had ended on a note of happiness and security. The new yacht, filled and animated by that troop of irrepressible children, whom it took all Miss Scope's energy and ubiquity to keep from falling overboard or clambering to the mast-head, seemed suddenly to have acquired a reason for existing. Cliffe Wheater, in his speckless yachting cap and blue serge, moved about among his family like a beneficent giant, and Mrs. Wheater, looking younger than ever in her white yachting skirt and jersey, with her golden thatch tossed by the breeze, fell into the prettiest maternal poses as her own progeny and the "steps" scrambled over her in the course of a rough-and-tumble game organised by Boyne and the young tutor.

The excursion had not begun auspiciously. Before the start from the *pension*, Bun and Beechy, imprisoned above stairs during Lady Wrench's irruption, had managed to inflict condign punishment on Zinnie for not having them fetched down with Blanca, and thus making them miss an exciting visit and probable presents. Terry's indifference to the whole affair produced no effect on the irascible Italians; and as Zinnie, when roused, was a fighter, and now had a gold necklace with real pearls to defend, all Judith's influence, and some cuffing into the bargain, were needed to reduce the trio to order; after which Boyne had to plead that they should not be deprived of their holiday. But once on the deck of the "Fancy Girl" all disagreements were forgotten. It was a day of wind and sparkle, with a lagoon full of racing waves which made the yacht appear to be actually moving; and after Beechy had drenched her new frock with tears of joy at being reunited to Chipstone, and Blanca and Zinnie had shown Lady Wrench's presents to every one, from the captain to the youngest cook-boy, harmony once more reigned among the little Wheaters.

Mr. Ormerod, with whom Terry was already at ease, soon broke down the reserve of the others. He proved unexpectedly good at games which involved scampering, hiding and pouncing, especially when Joyce and Judith took part, and could be caught and wrestled with; and Cliffe Wheater, parading the deck with Chip, whom he had adorned with a miniature yachting cap with "Fancy Girl" on the ribbon, was the model of a happy father. He pressed Boyne to chuck his other engagements and come off down the Adriatic as far as Corfu and Athens; and Boyne, lounging there in the bright air, the children's laughter encircling him, and Judith perched on the arm of his chair, asked himself why he didn't, and what better life could have to offer. "Uncle Edward would certainly have accepted," he thought, while his host, pouring himself another cocktail from the deck-table at his elbow, went on persuasively: "We'll round up a jolly crowd for you, see if we don't. Somebody's sure to turn up who'll jump at the chance. Judy, can't we hustle around and find him a girl?"

"Here's all the girl I want," Boyne laughed, laying his hand on hers; and a blush of pleasure rose to her face. "Oh, Martin—if you would—oh, can't you?" But even that he had resisted—even the ebb of her colour when he shook his head. The wandering man's determination to stick to his decisions was strong in him. Too many impulses had solicited him in too many lands: it was because, despite a lively imagination, he had so often managed to resist them, that a successful professional career lay behind him, and ahead—he hoped—comparative leisure, and the haven he wanted.

He had tried to find a farewell present for Judith—some little thing which, in quality if not costliness, should make up for her disappointment at being done out of Lady Wrench's. Judith's frank avowal of that disappointment had been a shock to him; but he reflected again what a child she was, and called himself a prig for expecting her standards to be other than those of the world she lived in. After all he had had no time to search for anything rare, and could only push into her hand, at the last moment, a commonplace trinket from the Merceria; but her childish joy in it, and her way of showing that she valued it doubly because it came from him, made the parting from her harder. And now, alone in the dusty train, he was asking himself why he had not stayed in Venice.

As a matter of fact there were several reasons; among them the old-fashioned one that, months before, he had promised to meet Mrs. Sellars in the Dolomites. In a world grown clockless and conscienceless, Boyne was still punctual and conscientious; and in this case he had schooled himself to think that what he most wanted was to see Rose Sellars again. Deep within him he knew it was not so; at least, not certainly so. Life had since given him hints of other things he might want equally, want even more; his reluctance to leave Venice and his newly-acquired friends showed that his inclinations were divided. But he belonged to a generation which could not bear to admit that naught may abide but mutability. He wanted the moral support of believing that the woman who had once seemed to fill his needs could do so still. She belonged to a world so much nearer to his than the Wheaters and their flock that he could not imagine how he could waver between the two. Rose Sellars's world had always been the pole-star of his whirling skies, the fixed point on which his need for permanence could build. He could only conclude, now, that he combined with the wanderer's desire for rest the wanderer's dread of immobility. "Hang it all, you can't have it both ways," he rebuked himself; but secretly he knew that that was how the heart of man had always craved it . . .

Had all that happened only forty-eight hours ago? Now, as he sat on the balcony of the *châlet*, over against the mighty silver and crimson flanks of the Cristallo group, the episode had grown incredibly remote, and Boyne saw his problems float away from him like a last curl of mist swallowed up in the blue behind the peaks.

Simply change of air, he wondered? The sudden rise into this pure ether that was like a shouting of silver trumpets? Partly, perhaps—and all that had chanced to go with it, in this wonderful resurrection of a life he had secretly thought dead.

"Bethesda is what you ought to call this," he murmured to himself. It was so like Rose Sellars, the live Rose Sellars who had already replaced his delicately embalmed mummy of her, to have found this *châlet* on the slope above the big hotels, a place so isolated and hidden that he and she were alone in it with each other and the mountains. How could he have so underrated his old friend's sense of the wonder of the place, and of what she owed to it, as to suppose that, even for two or three weeks, she would consent to be a number in a red-carpeted passage, and feed with the rest of the numbers in a blare of jazz and electricity? The *châlet* was only just big enough for herself and her maid, and the cook who prepared their rustic meals; had there been a corner for Boyne, she assured him that he should have had it. But perhaps it added to the mystery and enchantment that to see her he had to climb from the dull promiscuity of his hotel into a clear green solitude alive with the tremor of water under meadow-grasses, and guarded by the great wings of the mountains.

"You do really like it?" she had asked, as they sat, the first evening, on the balcony smelling of fir-wood, and watched the cliffs across the valley slowly decompose from flame to ashes.

"I like it most of all for being so like you," he answered.

She laughed, and turned an amused ironic face on him—a face more than ever like one of those light three-crayon drawings of which she had always reminded him. "Like me? Which—the *châlet* or the Cristallo group?"

"Well, both; that's the funny part of it."

"It must make me seem a trifle out of drawing."

"No; first aloof and aloft, and then again small and sunny and near."

She sighed faintly, and then smiled. "Well, I prefer the last part of the picture. I'd a good deal rather be a sunny balcony than a crystal peak. But I enjoy looking out on the peak."

"There you are—that's what I meant! It's the view from *you* that I've missed so, all these years."

She received this in a silence softened by another little laugh. The silence seemed to say: "That will do for our first evening," the laugh: "But I like it, you know!"

Aloud she remarked: "I'm glad you came up here after Venice and the millionaires. It's all to the good for the mountains—and for me."

Their first direct talk about themselves had ended there, drifting away afterward into reminiscences, questions, allusions, the picking up of threads—a gradual leisurely reconstruction of their five years apart. Now, on this second evening, he felt that he had situated her once more in his own life, and established himself in hers. So far he had made no allusion to his unsatisfied passion. In the past, by her own choice, her sternly imposed will, their relation had been maintained in the strict limits of friendship, and for the present he found it easier, more natural, to continue on the same lines. It was neither doubt nor pride that held him back, nor any uncertainty as to her feeling; but simply his sense of the well-being of things as they were. In the course of his life so much easy love had come his way, he had grown so weary of nights without a morrow, that he needed to feel there was one woman in the world whom he was half-afraid to make love to. Rose Sellars had chosen that he should know her only as the perfect friend; just at first, he thought, he would not disturb that carefully built-up picture. If he had suspected a rival influence he would not have tolerated delay; but as they travelled together over her past he grew more and more sure that it was for him the cold empty years of her marriage had kept her. Manlike, he was calmed rather than stimulated by this, though he would have repudiated more indignantly than ever the idea that she was less desirable because she was to be had. As a matter of fact, he found her prettier and younger than when they had parted. Every change in her was to her advantage, and he had instantly discarded his sentimental remembrance of her—dense coils of silvery-auburn hair, and draperies falling to the ankles—in favour of the new woman which her hair, dressed to look short, and her brief skirts, had made of her. Freedom of spirit and of body had mysteriously rejuvenated her, and he found her far more intelligent and adaptable than he had guessed when their relation had been obscured by his passion and her resistance. Now there was no resistance—and his passion lay with folded wings. It was perfect.

Every day they went off on an excursion. Sometimes they hired a motor, leaving it, far afield, for a long climb; but neither could afford such luxuries often, nor did they much care for them. Usually they started on foot, with stick and rucksack, getting back only as the great cliffs hung their last lustre above the valley. Mrs. Sellars was a tireless walker, proud of her light foot and firm muscles. She loved all the delicate detail revealed only to walkers: the thrust of orchis or colchicum through pine-needles, the stir of brooks, the uncurling of perfumed fronds, the whirr of wings in the path, and that continual pulsation of water and wind and grasses which is the heart-beat of the forest. Boyne, always alive to great landscape, had hitherto been too busy or preoccupied to note its particulars. It was years since he had rambled among mountains without having to look at them with an engineering eye, and calculate their relation to a projected railway or aqueduct; and these walks opened his eyes to unheeded beauties. It was like being led through the flowered borders of an illuminated missal of which he had hitherto noticed only the central pictures.

Better still were the evenings. When he first came a full moon held them late on the balcony, listening and musing, and sent him down dizzy with beauty through the black fir-shadows to his hotel. When the moon had waned, and the nights were fresh or cloudy, they sat by the fire, and talked and talked, or turned over new books and reviews. Boyne, with his bones and his brain so full of hard journeys and restless memories, thought he would have liked to look forward to an eternity of such evenings, in just such a hushed lamplit room, with a little sparkle of fire, reviews and papers everywhere, and that quiet silvery-auburn head with its mass of closely woven braids bending over a book across the hearth. Rose Sellars's way of being silently occupied without seeming absorbed was deeply restful. And then her books! She always managed to have just the ones he wanted to get hold of—to a homeless wandering man it was not the least of her attractions. Once, taking up a volume they had been talking of, Boyne recalled Judith Wheater's wistful: "Perhaps you might lend me some books." From what fold of memory had the question—and the very sound of the girl's voice—come back to him? He was abruptly reminded that it was a long time since he had given a thought to the little Wheaters.

There had been so many years to cover in the exchange of reminiscences that he had not yet touched on his encounter with them; and Mrs. Sellars seemed to have forgotten the description of the little band which had amused her in his letters. But now he was reminded, with a pang, of the contrast between her ordered and harmonious life (she always reminded him of Milton's "How charming is divine philosophy!") and the chaotic experiences of the poor little girl who for a moment had displaced her image. Inconceivably vulgar and tawdry, sordid and inarticulate, under all the shouting and the tinsel, seemed that other life and those who led it. Boyne would have brushed the vision away with contempt but for the voice which had called to him out of the blur. With a sigh he put down the book he had opened. Mrs. Sellars, who sat at the table writing, looked up, and their eyes met. "What were you thinking of?"

He had a start of distrust—the first since he had been with her. Would she understand if he tried to explain; if she did, would she sympathize? He shrank from the risk, and evaded it. "Seeing you so hard at work reminds me of all the letters I haven't written since I've been here."

She arched her eyebrows interrogatively, and he was sure she was thinking: "Why doesn't he tell me that he's no one to write to when he's with me?" Aloud she said: "You know I'm burdened with any number of fond relations who are consumed with the desire to know how I'm spending my first holiday."

"You're a wonderful correspondent."

As if scenting irony she rejoined: "So are you."

"I haven't been since I came here."

"Well, come and share the inkpot." She made the gesture of pushing it over to him, but he shook his head and stood up. "The night's too lovely. Put on your cloak and come out on the balcony."

She held her pen suspended, her eyes following his. "On the balcony? But there's no moon—"

"*Because* there's no moon," he insisted, smiling.

At that, smiling too, she drifted out to him.

Chapter X

"DARLING MARTIN,

"It's lovely here and very warm. Weve been baithing at the Lido and weve been out on the yaht again. Buondelmontes wife the lion taimer is dead and he has maried a rich American airess and Beechy and Bun are very much exited they think theyle get lots of presents now like Zinnie got from her mother and the one I was to get but Blanca took it, but I do like yours a hundred times better Martin dear, because you gave it to me and besides its much more orriginal.

"Ime worried because Buondelmonte mite want Bun back now hese rich and it would kill Beechy if Bun went away but I made him sware again on Scopys book he wont go whatever hapens.

"Mother and father had a grate big row because Mother wanted Zinnia and Lord Rench invited on the yatch and father said he woudnt it was too low, so she said why did he mind when she didnt. She wants to know the Duke of Mendip whose with them and Zinnia invites Gerald every day to lunch and dine and that makes Joyce fureaous. You will say I ought not to tell you this dear Martin then what can I do if there is a Row between them about Gerald Terry will loose his tutor and its too bad so I want to get away with the children as quick as we can.

"Terry said he must see this before I send it to you because I spell so badly but I wont let him because hed stop me sending it.

"Please Martin dear I do imploar you write and tell father to send us off quickly. Terry's temprature has gone up and Ime worried about everything. How I wish you were here then theyde do what you say.

"Your Judith who misses you."
"P.S. Please dont tell the Wheaters that Ive written."

Boyne's first thought, as he put the letter down, was that he was glad it had come after what had happened that very evening on the balcony. There had happened, simply, that the barriers created by a long habit of reticence had fallen, and he had taken Rose Sellars into his arms. It was a quiet embrace, the hushed surface of something deep and still. She had not spoken; he thanked his gods for that. Almost any word might have marred the moment, tied a tag to it, and fitted it with others into some dusty pigeon-hole of memory. She had known how to be different—and that was exquisite. Their quiet communion had silently flowered, and she had let it. There was neither haste nor reluctance in her, but an acquiescence so complete that what was deepest in both of them had flowed together through their hands and lips.

"It will be so much easier now to consult her—she'll understand so much better."

He didn't quite know why he felt that; perhaps because the merging of their two selves seemed to include every claim that others could have on either of them. Only yesterday he might have felt a doubt as to how Mrs. Sellars would view the Wheater problem, what she could possibly have in common with any of the Wheaters, or their world; now it was enough that she had him in common, and must share the burden because it was his.

He went over Judith's letter again slowly, imagining how Mrs. Sellars's beautiful eyes would deepen as she read it. The very spelling was enough to wring her heart. He would take the letter to her the next day . . . But the next day was here already. He pushed back his window, and leaned out. In the cold colourless air a few stars were slowly whitening, while behind the blackness of the hillside facing him the interstellar pallor flowed imperceptibly into morning gold. His happiness, he thought, was like that passing of colourless radiance into glow. It was joy enough to lean there and watch the transmutation. Was it a sign of middle-age, he wondered, to take beatitude so quietly? Well, Rose, for all her buoyancy, was middle-aged too. Then he remembered their kiss, and laughed the word away as the sun rushed up over the mountains.

All that day there was too much to do and to say; there were too many plans to make; too many memories to retrace. Boyne did not forget Judith Wheater's letter; her problem lay like a vague oppression in the background of his thoughts; but he found no way of fitting it into the new pattern of his life. Just yet—

It was decided that he and Mrs. Sellars should linger on in
the mountains for another month—a month of mighty rambles,
long hours of summer sunlight, and nights illuminated by a
waxing moon. After that, Boyne's idea had been that they
should push on at once to Paris, and there be married as quickly
as legal formalities allowed. It was at this hint of an immediate marriage that he first noticed, in Mrs. Sellars, the recoil of
the orderly deliberate woman whose life has been too vacant
for hurry, too hopeless for impatience. Theoretically, she told
him with a smile, she hated delay and fuss as much as he did—
and how could he question her eagerness to begin their new
life? But practically, she reminded him, there were difficulties,
there might even be obstacles. Oh, not real ones, of course!
She laughed that away, remarking with a happy blush that she
was of age, and her own mistress. ("Well, then—?" he interjected.) Well, there were people who had to be considered; who
might be offended by too great haste: her husband's family, for
instance. She had never hit it off with them particularly well,
as Boyne knew; but that was the very reason, she insisted, why
she must do nothing that might give them cause . . . ("Cause
for what?") Well, to say unpleasant things. She couldn't possibly
marry within a year of her husband's death without seriously
offending them—and latterly, she had to admit, they had been
very decent, especially about straightening out Charles's will,
which had been difficult to interpret, Mr. Dobree said.

"Mr. Dobree?"

"He's been such a friend to me through everything, you
know," she reminded him, a shade reproachfully; and he
remembered then that Mr. Dobree was the New York lawyer
who had unravelled, as much as possible to her advantage, the
tangle of Charles Sellars's will—the will of a snubbed secretive
man whose only vindictiveness had been posthumous. Mr.
Dobree had figured a good deal of late in Mrs. Sellars's letters, and she had given Boyne to understand that it was he who
had brought the Sellars family to terms about the will. Boyne
vaguely remembered him as a shy self-important man with dark-
gray clothes that were always too new and too well-cut—the
kind of man whose Christian name one never knew, but had to
look up in the "Social Register," and then was amused to find
it was Jason or Junius, only to forget it again at once—so fatally

did Mr. Dobree tend always to become Mr. Dobree once more. A man, in short, who would have been called common in the New York of Boyne's youth, but now figured as "a gentleman of the old school," and conscientiously lived, and dressed, up to the character. Boyne suspected him of being in love with Mrs. Sellars, and Mrs. Sellars of feeling, though she could not return the sentiment, that it was not ungratifying to have inspired it. But Boyne's mind lingered on Mr. Dobree only long enough to smile at him as the rejected suitor, and then came back to his own grievances.

"You don't mean to say you expect me to wait a whole year from now?"

She laughed again. "You goose. A year from Charles's death. It's only seven months since he died."

"What of that? You were notoriously unhappy—"

"Oh, *notoriously*—"

He met her protest with a smile. "I admit the term is inappropriate. But I don't suppose anybody thinks your marriage was unmitigated bliss."

"Don't you see, dear? That's the very reason."

"Oh, hang reasons—especially unreasonable ones! Why have you got to be unhappy now because you were unhappy then?"

"I'm not unhappy now. I don't think I could be, ever again, if I tried."

"Dear!" he rejoined. She excelled at saying nice things like that (and was aware of it); but her doing so now was like putting kickshaws before a hungry man. "It's awfully sweet of you," he continued; "but I shall be miserable if you insist on things dragging on for another five months. To begin with, I'm naturally anxious to get home and settle my plans. I want some sort of a job as soon as I can get it; and I want *you*," he concluded, putting his arm about her.

Obviously, what struck her first in this appeal was not his allusion to wanting her but to the need of settling his plans. All her idle married years, he knew, had been packed with settling things, adjusting things, adapting things, disguising things. She did see his point, she agreed at once, and she wanted as much as he did to fix a date; but why shouldn't it be a later one? There were her own aunts too, who had always been so kind. Aunt Julia, in particular, would be as horrified as the Sellarses at her marrying before her year of mourning was over; and she particularly wanted to consider Aunt Julia.

"Why do you particularly want to consider Aunt Julia? I seem to remember her as a peculiarly stupid old lady."

"Yes, dear," she agreed. "But it's just because she *is* peculiarly stupid—"

"If you call that a sufficient reason, we shall never get married. In a family as large as yours there'll always be somebody stupid left to consider."

"Thanks for your estimate of my family. But it's not the only reason." Her colour rose a little. "You see, I'm supposed to be Aunt Julia's heir. I found it out because, as it happens, Mr. Dobree drew up her will; and the doctors say any one of these attacks of gout—"

"Oh—."

He couldn't keep the disenchanted note out of his voice. The announcement acted like a cold douche. It ought, in reason, to have sent a pleasant glow through him, for he knew that, in spite of Mr. Dobree's efforts, Mrs. Sellars had been left with unexpectedly small means, and the earnings of his own twenty years of hard work in hard climates had been partly lost in unlucky investments. The kind of post he meant to try for in New York—as consulting engineer to some large firm of contractors—was not likely to bring in as much as his big jobs in the past; and the appearance of a gouty aunt with benevolent testamentary designs ought to have been an unmixed satisfaction. But trimming his course to suit the whims of rich relations had never been his way—perhaps because he had never had any rich relations. Anyhow, he was not going to be dictated to by his wife's; and it gave him a feeling of manliness to tell her so.

"Of course, if it's a case of choosing between Aunt Julia and me—" he began severely.

She raised her eyebrows with that soft mockery he enjoyed so much when it was not turned against himself. "In that case, dear, I should almost certainly choose you."

"Well, then, pack up, and let's go straight off to Paris and get married."

"Martin, you ought to understand. I can't be married before my year of mourning's out. For my own sake I can't; and for yours."

"Damn mine!"

"Very well; I have my personal reasons that I must stick to even if I can't make you understand them." Her eyes filled, and she looked incredibly young and wistful. "I don't suppose I ought to expect you to," she added.

"You ought to expect me to understand anything that's even remotely reasonable."

"I had hoped so."

"Oh, dash it—" he began; and then broke off. With a secret dismay he felt their lovers' talk degenerating for the first time into a sort of domestic squabble; if indeed so ungraceful a term could be applied to anything as sweetly resilient as Rose's way of gaining her end. Was marriage always like that? Was the haven Boyne had finally made to be only a stagnant backwater, like other people's? Or was it because he had been wandering and homeless for so long that the least restraint chafed him, and arguments based on social considerations made him fume? He was certainly in no position to quarrel with Mrs. Sellars for wishing to better her fortunes, and the discussion ended by his lifting her hand to his lips and saying: "You know I want only what you want." The coward's way out—and he knew it. But since he had parted with the substance of his independence, why cling to the form? He felt her eyes following his inner debate, and knew that the sweetness of her smile was distilled out of satisfaction at his defeat. "Damn it," he thought, "what cannibals marriage makes of people." He suddenly felt as if they were already married—as if they had been married a long time . . .

During their first fortnight not a cloud had shadowed their comradeship; but now that love and marriage had intervened the cloud was there, no bigger than the Scriptural one, but menacing as that proverbial vapour. She was kinder than ever because she had gained her point; and he knew it was because she had gained her point. But was it not his fault if he had begun thus early to distinguish among her different qualities as if they belonged to different vintage years, and to speculate whether the quality of her friendship might not prove more exquisite than her love could ever be? He was willing to assume the blame, since the joy of holding her fast, of plunging into her enchanted eyes, and finding his own enchantment there, was still stronger than any disappointment. If love couldn't be friendship too, as he had once dreamed it might, the only thing to do was to make the most of what it was . . .

Judith Wheater's letter had been for over a week in Boyne's pocket when he pulled it out, crumpled and smelling of tobacco.

He and Mrs. Sellars were reclining at ease on a high red ledge of rock, with a view plunging down by pine-clad precipices, pastures and forests to illimitable distances of blue Dolomite. The air sang with light, the smell of crushed herbs rose like incense, and the hearts of the lovers were glad with sun and wind, and the glow of a long climb followed by such food as only a rucksack can provide.

"And now for a pipe," Boyne said, in sleepy beatitude, stretching himself out on the turf at Mrs. Sellars's elbow. He fumbled for his tobacco pouch, and drew out with it the forgotten letter.

"Oh, dash it—"

"What?"

"Poor little thing! I forgot this; I meant to show it to you days ago."

"Who's the poor little thing?"

For a moment he wavered. His old dread of her misunderstanding returned; and he felt he could not bear to have her misunderstand that letter. What was the use of showing it, after all? But she was holding out her hand, and he had no alternative. She raised herself on her elbow, and bent her lustrous head above the page. From where he lay he watched her profile, and the subtle curves of the line from ear to throat. "How lovely she still is," he thought.

She read attentively, frowning a little in the attempt to decipher Judith's spelling, and her mouth melting into amusement or compassion. Then she handed back the letter. "I suppose it's from the little Wheater girl you wrote about? Poor little thing indeed! It's too dreadful. I didn't know there really *were* such people. But who are the Wheaters she speaks of in the postscript, who are not to be told?"

Boyne replied that those were her parents.

"Her parents? Why does she speak of them in that way?"

He explained that in the Wheater circles it was the custom among the children to do so, the cross-tangle of divorces having usually given them so many parents that it was more convenient to differentiate the latter by their surnames.

"Oh, Martin, it's too horrible! Are you serious? Did the poor child really tell you that?"

"The governess did—as a matter of course."

She made a little grimace. "The sort of governesses they must have, in a world where the parents are like that!"

"Well, this particular one is a regular old Puritan brick. She and Judith keep the whole show together." And he told her about the juvenile oath on Scopy's "Cyclopædia of Nursery Remedies."

"She doesn't appear to have grounded her pupils very thoroughly in spelling," Mrs. Sellars commented; but her eyes were soft, and she took the letter back, and began to read it over again.

"There's a lot I don't begin to understand. Who are these people that Mrs. Wheater wants to invite on the yacht because they know a Duke, and Mr. Wheater won't because it's too low?"

"They're Lord and Lady Wrench. Wasn't there a lot in the papers a month or two ago about Lord Wrench's marrying a movie star? He has a racing-stable; I believe he's very rich. Her name was Zinnia Lacrosse."

"A perfect name. But why, in the Wheater world, are movie stars regarded as too low? Too low for what—or for whom?" Her mouth narrowed disdainfully on the question.

"Well, this one happens to have been Wheater's wife—for a time."

"His *wife*?"

"Not for long, though. They've been divorced for much longer than they were married. So I suppose Mrs. Wheater doesn't see the use of making a retrospective fuss about it."

"Practical woman! And who's the Gerald that she and the other lady are fighting for?"

"Oh, he's the boy's tutor; Terry's tutor. Or was to have been. I'm afraid he's a rotter too. But Terry, poor chap, is the best fellow you ever saw. I back him and Judith and Scopy to keep the ship on her course, whatever happens. If only Terry's health holds out."

"And they get him another tutor."

"As things go, he's lucky if he has any."

Mrs. Sellars again sighed out her contempt and amazement, and let the letter fall. For a long time she sat without moving, her chin on her hand, looking out over the great billowing landscape which rolled away at their feet as if driven on an invisible gale. When she turned to Boyne he saw that her eyes were full of a puzzled sadness. "Don't the Wheaters *care* in the least about their children?"

In old days, in their melancholy inconclusive talks, she had often confessed her grief at being childless; and now he heard in her voice the lonely woman's indignation at the unworthiness of those who had been given what she was denied. "Don't they *care?*" she repeated.

"Oddly enough, I believe they do. I'm afraid that's going to be our difficulty. Why should they have taken on the steps if they hadn't cared? They certainly seem very fond of the children, whenever they're with them. But it's one thing to be fond of children, and another to know how to look after them. My impression is that they realised their incapacity long ago, and that's why they dumped the whole problem on Judy."

"Long ago? But how old is Judy? This is the writing of a child of ten."

"She's had no time to learn any other, with six children to look after. But I suppose she's fifteen or sixteen."

"Fifteen or sixteen!" Mrs. Sellars gave a little sigh. "Young enough to be my daughter."

It was on the tip of his tongue to say: "I wish she had been!" But he had an idea it might sound queerly; and instead he stretched out his hand and took back the letter. The gesture seemed to rouse her to a practical view of the question. "What are you going to do about it, dearest?"

"That's what I want you to tell me."

This stimulated her to action, as he had known it would. He was glad that he had consulted her: she had been full of sympathy, and might now be of good counsel. How stupid it was ever to mistrust her!

"Of course you must write to her father."

"Well—perhaps. But doing that won't get us much forrarder."

"Not if you appeal to him—point out that the children oughtn't to be kept in Venice any longer? Didn't you say he knew the climate was bad for the boy?"

"Yes; and Wheater will respond at once—in words! He'll say: 'Damn it, Joyce, Boyne's right. What are the children doing here? We'll pack them off to the Engadine to-morrow.' Then he'll cram my letter into his pocket, and no one will ever see it again, except the valet when he brushes his coat."

"But the mother—Joyce, or whatever her name is? If he tells *her*—"

"Well, there's the hitch."

"What hitch?"

"Supposing she wants to keep the children in Venice on account of Gerald?"

"Gerald? Oh, the tutor! Oh, Martin—" A shiver of disgust ran over her. "And you dare to tell me she's fond of her children!"

"So she is; awfully fond. But everything rushes past her in a whirl. Life's a perpetual film to those people. You can't get up out of your seat in the audience and change the current of a film."

"What *can* you do about it?"

He lay back on the grass, frowning up into the heavens. "Can't think. Unless I were to drop down to Venice for a day or two, and try talking to them." To his surprise, he found that the idea opened out before him rather pleasantly. "Writing to that kind of people's never any sort of good," he concluded.

Mrs. Sellars was sitting erect beside him, her eyes bent on his. They had darkened a little, and the delicate bend of her lips narrowed as it had when she asked what there could be in the Wheater world that movie stars were too low for.

"Go back to Venice?" He felt the edge of resistance in her voice. "I don't see of what use that would be. It's a good deal to ask you to take that stifling journey again. And if you don't know what to write, how would you know any better what to say?"

"Perhaps I shouldn't. But at any rate I could feel my way. And I might comfort Judith a little."

"Poor child! I wish you could." She was all sweetness again. "But I should try writing first. Don't you think so? Write to her too, of course. Whatever you decide, you'd better begin by feeling your way. It's always awkward to interfere in family matters, and if you turned up again suddenly the Wheaters might think it rather odd."

He was inclined to tell her that nothing would seem odd to the Wheaters except what seemed inevitable and fore-ordained to her. But he felt an irritated weariness of the whole subject. "I daresay you're right," he agreed, pocketing his pipe and getting to his feet. It was not his idea of a holiday that it should be interfered with by other people's bothers, and he put Judith's letter back into his pocket with an impatient thrust. After all, what business was it of his? He would write the child a nice letter, of course; but Rose was right—the idea of going down to Venice was absurd. Besides, Judith's letter was more than a week old, and ten to one the party had scattered by this time, and the children were safe somewhere in the mountains. "Poor little thing, she's always rather overwrought, and very likely she just had a passing panic when she wrote. Hang it, I wish she hadn't written," he concluded, relieved to find a distant object for his irritation.

Arm in arm, he and his love wandered down the mountain.

Chapter XI

"OF course I've written to her—I wrote last night," Boyne assured Mrs. Sellars the next evening. He was conscious of a vague annoyance at being called to account in the matter—as if he couldn't deal with his own correspondence without such reminders. But Mrs. Sellars's next word disarmed him. "I'm so glad, dear. I should have hated to feel that our being so happy here had made you neglect your little friend."

That was generous, he thought—and like her. He adored her when she said things like that. It proved that, in spite of her little air of staidness, she was essentially human and comprehending. He had persuaded her that night—for fun, for a change, after her months of seclusion—to come down and dine with him, not at his own modest hotel, but at the towering "Palace" among the pines below the *châlet*, where he thought the crowd and gaiety of the big restaurant might amuse her, and would at any rate make their evenings at the *châlet* more delicious by contrast.

They had finished dining, and were seated over their coffee in a corner of the big panelled hall to which the other diners were slowly drifting back. Boyne, seeing Mrs. Sellars, for the first time since his arrival, in the company of women as graceful and well-dressed as herself, noted with satisfaction that not one of them had exactly her quality. But the groups about the other tables were amusing to study and speculate about, and he sat listening to her concise and faintly ironic comments with an enjoyment mellowed by the flavour of the excellent cigar he had acquired from the head-waiter.

"The girl in peach-colour, over there by the column—lovely, isn't she? Only one has seen her a thousand times, in all the 'Vogues' and 'Tatlers.' Oh, Martin, won't it be too awful if beauty ends by being standardised too?"

Boyne rather thought it had been already, in the new generation, and secretly reflected that Mrs. Sellars's deepest attraction lay in her belonging to a day when women still wore their charm with a difference.

"I'm sure if I owned one of these new beauties I shouldn't always be able to pick her out in a crowd," he agreed.

She laughed her satisfaction, and then, sweeping the hall with lifted eye-glass: "That one you would . . ."

"A new beauty? Where?"

"Beauty—no. Hardly pretty . . . but different. The girl who's just come in. Where's she vanished to? Oh, she's speaking to the porter. Now she's looking this way—but you can't see her from where you're sitting. She's hardly more than a child; but the face is interesting."

He barely caught the last words. The porter had come up with a message. "Young lady asking for you, sir." Boyne got to his feet, staring in the direction indicated. He had not been mistaken. It was Judith Wheater who stood there, frail and straight in her scant travelling dress, her hat pulled down over her anxious eyes, so small and dun-coloured that she was hardly visible among those showy bare-armed women. Yet Mrs. Sellars had picked her out at once! Yes, there was something undeniably "different"; just as there was about Mrs. Sellars herself. But this was no time for such considerations. Where on earth had the child come from, and what on earth had brought her?

"Wait a minute, will you? It's some one I know." He followed the porter between the tables to where Judith stood in the shadow of the stairway.

"Child! Where in the world have you dropped from?"

"Oh, Martin, Martin! I was so afraid you'd gone!"

He caught her by both hands, and she lifted a drawn little face to his. Well, why not? He had kissed her goodbye in Venice; now he touched his lips to her cheek. "Judy, how in the world did you get here? Have the heads of the clan come too?"

"Oh, Martin, Martin!" She kept fast hold of him, and he felt that she was trembling. She paid no attention to his question, but turned and glanced about her. "Isn't there a writing-room somewhere that we could go to? There's never anybody in them after dinner."

He guided her, still clinging to him, to one of the handsomely appointed rooms opening off the corridor beyond the hall. As she had predicted, its desks were deserted, its divans unoccupied. She dropped down by Boyne, and threw her arms about his neck.

"Oh, Martin, say you're glad! I must hear you say it!"

"Glad, child? Of course I'm glad." Very gently he released himself. "But you look dead-beat, Judy. What's the matter? Has anything gone wrong? Are your people here?"

She drew back a little and turned full on him her most undaunted face. "If you mean father and mother, they're in Venice. They don't know we're here. You mustn't be angry, Martin: we've run away."

"Run away? Who's run away?"

"All of us; with Scopy and Nanny. I always said we'd have to, some day. Scopy and Terry and I managed it. We're at the *Pension Rosenglüh*, down the hill. Father and mother will never guess we're here. They think we've gone to America on the Cunarder that touched at Venice yesterday. I left a letter to say we had. Terry was splendid; he invented it all. We hired motors at Padua to come here. But I'm afraid he's dreadfully done up. This air will put him right though, won't it?" She poured it all out in the same tone of eager but impartial narrative, as if no one statement in her tale were more surprising or important than the others—except, of course, the matter of Terry's health. "The air here is something wonderful, Martin, isn't it?" she pleaded; and he found himself answering with conviction: "There's simply nothing like it."

Her face instantly grew less agitated. "I knew I was right to come," she sighed in a tired voice; and he felt as if she were indeed an overwrought child, and the next moment might fall asleep on his shoulder.

"Judy, you're dreadfully done up yourself, and you look famished. It's after ten. Have you had anything to eat since you got here?"

"I don't believe I have. There wasn't time. I had to see the children settled first, and then make sure you were here."

"Of course I'm here. But before we do any more talking you've got to be fed."

"Well, it would be nice to have a bite," she confessed, recovering her usual confident tone.

"Wait here, and I'll go and forage." Boyne walked down the corridor and back into the hall, where people were beginning to group themselves about the bridge-tables. The fact of finding himself there roused him to the recollection of having left

Mrs. Sellars alone with his empty coffee-cup. Till that moment he had forgotten her existence. He made his way back to their corner, but it was deserted. In the so-called "salon," against a background of sham tapestries and gilt wall-lights, other parties were forming about more bridge-tables; but there also there was no sign of Mrs. Sellars.

"Oh, well, she's got bored and gone home," he thought, a little irritably. Surely it would have been simpler and more friendly to wait . . . but that was just a part of her ceremoniousness. Probably she had thought it more tactful to disappear. Damn tact! That was all he had to say . . . The important thing now was to give Judy something to eat, and get her back to her *pension*. After that he would run up to the *châlet* and explain.

He found a waiter, learned that it was too late to resuscitate dinner, and ordered ham sandwiches and cocktails to be brought at once to the writing-room. On the whole, he found it simplified things to have Mrs. Sellars out of the way. Perhaps there was something to be said for tact after all.

The first sip of her cocktail brought the glow back to Judith's eyes and lips, the next made her preternaturally vivid and alert. She must eat, he told her—eat at once, before she began to talk; and he pushed his own sandwiches on to her plate, and watched her devouring them, and emptying first her glass and then his. She sparkled at him across its brim, but kept silence, obediently; then she asked for a cigarette, and leaned back at ease against the cushions.

"Well, we're all here," she declared with satisfaction.

"Not Chip?" he questioned, incredulous.

"Chip? I should think so! Do you suppose I'd have stirred an inch without Chip?"

"But what the deuce is it all about, child? Have you gone crazy, all of you?"

"Father and mother have. They do, you know. I warned father we'd run away if it happened again."

"What happened?"

"Why, what I told you would. But I don't suppose you ever got my letter? I was sure you'd have answered it if you had." She turned her eyes on him with a look of such unshaken trust that he stammered uncomfortably: "Tell me all about it now."

"Well, everything went to smash. I knew it would. And then all the old shouting began—about detectives, and lawyers, and mother's alimony. You know that's what the children mean when they talk about mother's old friend Sally Money. They've heard about her ever since they can remember. They think mother sends for her whenever anything goes wrong . . ."

"And things have gone thoroughly wrong?"

"Worse than ever. They were dividing us up already. Bun and Beechy back to Buondelmonte, because he's married a rich American. And Zinnia is ready to take Zinnie. Lord Wrench thinks she's so awfully funny. And father would have had Chip, of course, and we three older ones would have begun to be sent back and forth again as we used to be, like the shabby old books Scopy used to get out of the lending library at Biarritz. You could keep the stupid ones as long as you liked, but the jolly ones only a week." She turned her burning face to his. "Now, Martin, didn't I *have* to get them all away from it?"

The food and wine had sent such a flame through her that he began to wonder if she had fever, or if it were only the glow of fatigue. He took her hand and it was burning, like her face.

"Child, you're too tired. All the rest will keep till to-morrow. Put on your hat now, and I'll take you down the hill to your *pension*."

"But, Martin, you'll promise and swear to see us through?"

"Through everything, bless you. On Scopy's book. And now come along, or you'll fall asleep in your tracks."

In reality he had never seen her so acutely wakeful; but she submitted in silence to being bundled into her hat and coat, and linked her arm confidingly in his as they threaded their way among the bridge-players and out into the great emptiness of the night. The moon hung low above the western peaks, and the village clock below them in the valley chimed out the three quarters after eleven as they walked down the road between blanched fields and sleeping houses. On the edge of the village a few lights still twinkled; but the *Pension Rosenglüh*, demurely withdrawn behind its white palings, showed a shuttered front to the moon. Boyne opened the garden gate, and started to go up the doorstep ahead of Judith. "Oh, you needn't ring, Martin. It would wake everybody. I don't believe the door's locked. I told

Scopy to see that I wasn't shut out." She tried the door-knob, which yielded hospitably, and then turned and flung her arms about her companion.

"Martin, darling, I don't believe I'd ever have dared if I hadn't known you'd see us through," she declared with a resounding kiss.

"The devil you wouldn't!" he murmured; but he pushed her gently in, thinking: "I ought never to have given her that second cocktail." From the threshold he whispered: "Go upstairs as quietly as you can. I'll be down in the morning to see how you're all getting on." Then he shut the door on her, and slipped out of the gate.

Midnight from the village clock! What would his friend say if he knocked up the *châlet* at that hour? Half way to the hotel he left the road and branched upward through the fir-wood, by a path he knew. But there were no lights in the *châlet*.

Chapter XII

B EFORE mounting to Mrs. Sellars's the next morning Boyne went down to the *Pension Rosengliih* to gather what farther details he could of the strange flight of the little Wheaters.

As he reached the *pension* gate he was met by Miss Scope, looking more than commonly gaunt and ravaged, but as brightly resolute as her fellow-conspirator. Her gray cotton glove enfolded Boyne's hand in an unflinching grasp, and she exclaimed at once how providential it was that they should have caught him still at Cortina. She added that she had been on the look-out for him, as both Judith and Terry were still asleep, and she was sure he'd agree that they had better not be disturbed, after all they'd been through; especially as Terry was still fever-ish. The other children, he gathered, had already breakfasted, and been shepherded out by Nanny and the nursemaid to the downs above the valley; and meanwhile perhaps Mr. Boyne would come in and have a chat.

The word seemed light for the heavy news he was prepared to hear; but he suspected that Miss Scope, like the Witch of Atlas, was used to racing on the platforms of the wind, and laughed to hear the fire-balls roar behind. At any rate, her sturdy composure restored his own balance, and made him glad of the opportunity to hear her version of the adventure before his next encounter with Judith.

Miss Scope was composed, as she always was—he was soon to learn—in real emergencies. She had been through so many that they seemed to her as natural and inevitable as thunder-storms or chicken-pox—as troublesome, but no more to be fussed about. Nevertheless, she did not underrate the gravity of the situation: to do so, he suspected, would have robbed it of its savour. There had been cataclysms before—times when Judy had threatened to go off and disappear with all the children—but till now she had never even attempted to put her threats into execution. "And now she's carried it off with a master hand," Miss Scope declared in a tone of grim triumph.

But carried it where to? That was the question Boyne could not help putting. He was sure Judith had been masterly—but

where was it all going to lead? Had any of them taken that into
account, he asked?

Well, Miss Scope had to own that their departure had been
too precipitate for much taking into account. It had to be then
or never—she had seen that as clearly as Judy and Terry. The fact
that Terry was with them showed how desperate the situation
was—

"Desperate? Really desperate?"

"Oh, Mr. Boyne! If you'd been through it twice before, as my
poor children have . . ."

Listening to the details of her story, he agreed that it must
indeed have been awful, and ended by declaring that he did
not question Judith's reasons; but now that the first step in the
mutiny was taken, how did Miss Scope imagine that they were
going to keep it up? In short, what did they mean to do when
they were found out?

"I think Judith counts very much on your intervention.
That's the reason she was so anxious to find you still here. And
of course she hopes there'll be time—time to consider, to choose
a course of action. She believes it will be some days before we're
found out, as you put it. I daresay she's told you that she left
a letter . . . Mr. Boyne," said Miss Scope, interrupting herself
with her sternest accent, "I hope you don't think that, in ordinary circumstances, I should ever condone the least deceit. The
children will tell you that on that point I'm inexorable. But
these were not ordinary circumstances." She cleared her throat,
and brought out: "Judith said in the letter that we'd sailed for
America. She thinks her father will hurry there to find them,
and in that way we shall gain a little time, for the steamer they're
supposed to be on is not due in New York for ten days."

The plan seemed puerile, even for so immature a mind as
Judith's; but Boyne did not raise that point. He merely said: "I
hope so. But meanwhile what are you all going to live on? It
costs something to feed such an army."

Miss Scope's countenance turned from sallow to white. Her
eyes forsook his face, as they did when she talked of Terry,
and she brought out, hesitatingly: "Judith, I understand, has
means . . ."

"Poor woman!" Boyne thought. "I believe she's plumped in
all her savings.—I see," he said. He was filled with a sudden

be introduced, if Joyce and Wheater both marry again, as I've no doubt they will, in no time."

Mrs. Sellars, her chin resting on her hand, sat listening in a silence still visibly compounded of bewilderment and disgust. For a minute after Boyne had ceased speaking she did not move or look up. At last she said, in a low voice: "It's all too vile for belief."

"Exactly," he agreed. "And it's all true."

"The horrors those children must know about—"

"It's to save them from more horrors that Judith has carried them away."

"I see—I see. Poor child!" Her face melted into pity. "Just at first it was all too new to me. But now I'm beginning to understand. And I suppose she came here hoping you would help her?"

"I suppose she didn't have much time to think or choose, but vaguely remembered I was here, as her letter showed."

"But the money? Where in the world did they get the money? You can't transport a nursery-full of children from one place to another without paying for it."

Boyne hesitated a moment; but he felt he must not betray Miss Scope, and merely answered that he hadn't had time to go into all that yet, supposed that in an easy-going extravagant household like the Wheaters' there were always some funds available, the more so as preparations were already being made to send the children off to the mountains.

"Well, it's all hideous and touching and crazy. Where are the poor little things—at your hotel?" Mrs. Sellars had gone indoors, and was picking up her hat and sunshade. "I should like you to take me down at once to see them."

Boyne was touched by the suggestion, but secretly alarmed at what might happen if Mrs. Sellars were exposed unprepared to the simultaneous assault of all the little Wheaters. He explained that Judith had taken her flock to an inexpensive *pension* in the village, and that the younger children, when he had called there, were already away on the downs, and Judith and Terry still sleeping off their emotions. Should he go down again, he asked, and bring Judith back alone to the *châlet*? "You'd better see her first without the others. You might find the seven of them rather overwhelming."

Seven? Mrs. Sellars confessed she hadn't realised that there were actually seven. She agreed that it would be perhaps better that she should first see Judith without her brothers and sisters, and proposed that Boyne should invite her to come back with him to the *châlet* to lunch. "If you think she won't be too frightened of a strange old woman?" The idea of Judith's being frightened of anything or anybody amused Boyne, but he thought it charming of Mrs. Sellars to suggest it, and was glad, after all, that she was there to support and advise him. When she had had a quiet talk with Judith he felt sure she would be on the children's side; and perhaps her practical vision might penetrate farther than his into the riddle of what was to be done for them.

"If only," he said to himself, "Judith doesn't begin by saying something that will startle her"; and he thought of warning Mrs. Sellars not to expect a too great ingenuousness in his young friend. Then he reflected that such a warning might unconsciously prejudice her against the girl, and decided that it would be wiser to trust to Judith's natural charm to overcome anything odd in her conversation. If there were hints to be given, he concluded, there would be less risk in giving them to Judith.

But the utility of giving hints in that quarter became equally dubious at first sight of her. Refreshed and radiant after her night's rest, and unusually pretty in her light linen frock, and a spreading hat with a rosy lining, Judith received him at the gate of the *pension* in an embrace which sent her hat flying among the currant-bushes, and exposed her rumpled head and laughing eyes to his close inspection. "You look like a pansy this morning," he said, struck by the resemblance of her short pointed oval and velvet-brown eyes to the eager inquisitive face of the mountain flower. But Judith was no gardener, and rejected the comparison with a grimace. "How horrid of you! Nasty wired things in wreaths at funerals! I don't feel a bit as if I were at a funeral. It's so jolly to be here, and to have found you. You've come to say you'll lunch with us, haven't you? The children will be mad with joy. It was partly because I promised them we'd find you here that they agreed to come. Blanca and Zinnie unsettled them at first—they're always afraid of missing some excitement if they have a row with mother. But I told them we'd have lots more excitement with you." She was hanging on his arm, and drawing him up the path to the house.

"I must tell the landlady you're coming to lunch. Scopy's upstairs with Terry, and she told me to be sure not to forget, so that the cook could give us something extra." By this time they were in the little sitting-room, which smelt of varnish and dried edelweiss, and had a stuffed eagle perched above the stove. Judith sat down on the slippery sofa, and dragged Boyne to a seat at her side. "And first, I was to ask you what pudding you'd particularly like."

"Oh, bless you, any pudding. But about lunch—"

She drew herself up, and tossed him an arch smile. "Or perhaps you're here incog., with a lady, and would rather not come? I told Scopy I shouldn't wonder—"

"Nonsense, Judith; how absurd—"

"Why absurd? Why shouldn't you be here with a lady? *Vous êtes encore très bien, mon cher* . . ." She drew her deep lids half shut, and slanted an insinuating glance at him.

"Don't talk like a manicure, child. As a matter of fact, I have an old friend here who wants very much to see you, and who kindly suggested—"

"An old lady-friend?"

"Yes."

"As old as Scopy?"

"No; probably not as old as your mother, even. I only meant—"

"But if she's younger than mother, how can you say she's old? Is she prettier, too?" Judith broke in searchingly.

"I don't know, really; I haven't thought—"

"Well, I don't believe she's as well-dressed. Unless, perhaps, you think Joyce's clothes are sometimes just a shade *too*—"

"I haven't thought about that either. What I mean by 'old' is that Mrs. Sellars and I have been friends for years. She's living in a *châlet* on the hill above the hotels; and she wants me to bring you up to lunch with her today."

"Me—only me?" Judith questioned, visibly surprised.

Boyne smiled. "Well, my dear, I'm sure she would have liked to invite you all, Chip included; but her house is tiny and couldn't possibly take in the whole party. So, to avoid invidious distinctions, why not come by yourself and make her acquaintance? I want you awfully to know her, for no one can give you better advice than she can."

Judith drew herself up stiffly and her face became a blank. "I don't want anybody's advice but yours, Martin. But of course I'll go if you want me to."

"It's not a question of what I want. But you may be sure if my advice is any good it will be because I've consulted Mrs. Sellars. Two's not too many to get you out of this predicament. I sometimes think you don't realise what an awful row you're all in for."

"If she's not as old as mother, and you've never noticed how she's dressed, you must be in love with her," Judith went on, as if his last words had not made the least impression on her.

"I don't see what difference it makes if I am or not," he retorted, beginning to lose his temper. "The point is that she happens to be one of the kindest and most sensible women I know—"

"That's what men always think," said Judith thoughtfully. She drew back to study him again through half-closed lids. "It's a wonderful thing to be in love," she murmured; and then continued with a teasing smile: "Blanca's ever so much sharper than I am. She said: 'Why's Martin in such an awful hurry to rush away from Venice, if he isn't slipping off on the quiet to meet a friend?' I suppose," she added, with a fall in her voice, and a corresponding droop of the lips, "it was awfully stupid of me to blunder in on you like this, and you're racking your brains to think how you can get rid of us all, and keep out of a row with father and mother."

Boyne, half-exasperated and half-touched, as he so often was in his talks with her, and especially when he knew she wished to give him pain, laid his hand reproachfully on hers. "Look here, Judith, I could shake you when you talk such drivel. The only thing I'm racking my brains about is how to help you to get what you want. To keep you all together, as you are now, and yet not let your father and mother think that I've had anything to do with this performance. You're quite right; I do want to stay on good terms with them, because if I do I may succeed in persuading them that, whatever happens, they've no right to separate you children again. If I do that I shall have done my best for you. But I don't see my way to it yet, and that's why I want you to come and make friends with Mrs. Sellars."

To his surprise she listened in an attentive silence, and, when he had ended, lifted to his the face of an obedient child. "Of course I'll do what you want, Martin. But don't you think your friend would perhaps understand better if I had Nanny bring up Chip to see her after lunch?"

"Bless you—of course she would," he agreed enthusiastically; and she thereupon proposed that before they started he should come upstairs and see Terry.

Chapter XIII

SEEING Terry, Boyne had to admit, was the surest way of attaching one, body and soul, to the cause of the little Wheaters. Whatever Mrs. Sellars thought of Judith—a question of obvious uncertainty—there could be no doubt as to what she would think of Terry.

There had been moments during the morning when Boyne did not see how any good will on either part could bridge the distance between Mrs. Sellars's conception of life, and Judith Wheater's experience of it; but between Mrs. Sellars and Terry there would be nothing to explain or bridge over. Their minds would meet as soon as their eyes did. "I'll bring her down to see him after lunch," Boyne decided.

There was no hope of Terry's being up that day. The excitement of the flight, and the heat and fatigue of the journey, had used up his small surplus of strength, and he could only lie staring at Boyne with eager eyes, and protest that he knew the air of Cortina would put him all right before long. Scopy had already had the doctor in, and administered suitable remedies, and the patient's temperature had dropped to nearly normal. "If only father and mother will let us stay here I'm sure I shall be patched up this time. And you'll be here for a bit to look after the children, won't you, Martin?"

Boyne said he would stay as long as he could, and at any rate not leave till the little Wheaters' difficulty with their parents was on the way to adjustment. He pointed out that negotiations would no doubt be necessary, and Terry promptly rejoined: "That's just why Judy and I decided to come here. We knew that if we could get hold of you, you'd back us up, and help us to make some kind of terms with father and mother." His eyes fixed his friend's with a passionate insistence. "You see, Martin, it won't do, separating us again—it really won't. We're not going to get any sort of education at this rate. And as for manners! The children have all been completely demoralised since Zinnia's visit. Now they've heard of Buondelmonte's marriage, and the steps have gone off their base too; and as for Blanca she thinks of nothing but dressing-up and flirtation . . . As soon as things go wrong between father and mother the children seem to feel it in the air; even before the actual fighting begins, they all get out of hand. Zinnie gave Bun a black eye the other day because he said he was going to be a Prince again, and live in his father's palace in Rome, and have his own Rolls . . . a child who hardly knows his letters!" Terry concluded with a gesture of contempt.

"I know, old man. It's all wrong," Boyne agreed, "and something's got to be done, and done soon. That's what I'm going to try to make your father and mother see. Meanwhile you must make the most of this respite to get a good rest. I promise I'll do what I can when the time comes."

"Oh, you needn't promise," Terry said, letting his head sink back contentedly on the pillows.

On the way up the hill with Judith, Boyne was able to gather some of the details she had been too tired and excited to impart the night before. Miss Scope's confidences were always in the nature of sombre generalizations. When it came to particulars, she retreated behind professional secrecy; and Boyne had not liked to force her defences. Besides, he knew that no such scruples would hamper Judith, who saw life only in particulars. But, after all, there was nothing very unexpected in Judith's story. As she said, it was always the same old row over again. As soon as Zinnia Lacrosse had cast a covetous eye on Gerald Ormerod, Joyce had decided that she could not live without him. The thought of his dining every night at the Lido with the Wrenches and the Duke of Mendip, while she and Wheater sat alone on the deck of the "Fancy Girl," or made the most of such mediocre guests as they could collect, was too much for a high-spirited woman; and Joyce had suddenly requested her husband to sack the tutor. Wheater, surprised, had protested that Terry liked him (and Terry did—he was very jolly, and a good teacher, Judith impartially admitted); whereupon Joyce had declared that if Ormerod wasn't sent away at once she intended to divorce Wheater and marry him. Wheater, of course, was furious, and there had been, in Judith's language, an all-round circus, complicated by the fact that what Gerald really wanted was to marry *her*—

"What—what? Marry *you*? Have you all of you gone crazy?" Boyne found himself indignantly repeating.

Judith smiled. "I'm not crazy. And I'm nearly sixteen. And I suppose I'm a nairess." (She pronounced the word as she wrote it.) "But you don't imagine I'd leave the children, do you? Besides, Terry says it would be ridiculous to marry till I can learn how to spell."

"My God—I should say it would," cried Boyne furiously. What on earth would come of it, he asked himself, if she opened the conversation with Mrs. Sellars on this note? "Judith, look here—."

"But I don't know, after all," she went on, in a reflective tone. "Gerald says some of the greatest people never *could* spell. Napoleon couldn't—or Madame de Sévigné—and Shakespeare signed his name differently every time."

"I see you've taken a course in history since I left," Boyne sneered; to which she responded with simplicity: "No; but he told me that one day when he found me crying because of my awful spelling."

"Well, you're quite right to cry about your spelling. And Terry's quite right to say that the first thing you want is to have some sort of an education, all of you."

"Perhaps, then, it would have been better for me to marry Gerald," she rejoined, with a return of her uncanny impartiality. "But no," she interrupted herself; "I never could have kept the children if I had; so what's the use?"

"Well, here we are," Boyne broke in nervously.

"Why, you poor child, how young you are, after all!" Mrs. Sellars exclaimed, swaying forward to drop an impulsive kiss on Judith's cheek. Boyne's first thought was, how young she looked herself, in her thin black dress, her auburn head bent like an elder sister's above Judith's; then how much too young Judith was to be conciliated by that form of greeting.

Judith looked at her hostess with a smile. "Young for what?" she asked, with an ominous simplicity.

"Why—for all your responsibilities," the other answered, checked in her premeditated spontaneity.

Judith was still smiling: a small quiet smile from which the watchful Boyne augured no good.

"I suppose I ought to be flattered," she said. "I know that at your age and mother's it's thought awfully flattering to be called young. But, you see, I'm not sixteen yet, so it's nothing extraordinary to me."

"Your being so young makes it extraordinarily kind of you to come and see an old lady like me," Mrs. Sellars smiled back, taking nervous refuge in platitudes.

Judith considered her with calm velvety eyes. "Oh, but I wanted to come. Martin says you'll be a friend; and we need friends badly."

Mrs. Sellars's eyes at once softened. "Martin's quite right. I'll be as good a friend as you'll let me. I'm so glad you've come to share my picnic lunch. And Martin will have told you how sorry I was not to have room for the whole party in this tiny house."

"Well," said Judith, "he thought you'd find us rather over-whelming—"; but Mrs. Sellars laughed this away as an unauthorized impertinence of her old friend's.

On the whole, things were beginning better than the old friend had expected. He only hoped Rose wouldn't mind Judith's chucking down her hat on the sitting-room sofa, and turning to the glass above the mantelpiece to run her fingers through her tossed hair. Once at table, Mrs. Sellars led the talk to the subject of the little Wheaters, whose names she had cleverly managed to master, and whose acquaintance she expressed the wish to make at the earliest opportunity, "steps" and all. "For I assure you," she added, "I'm not as easily overwhelmed as Martin seems to think."

Judith was always at her best when she was talking of the children, and especially of Terry, whose name Mrs. Sellars had spoken with a sympathy which brought a glow to the girl's cheek. "Oh, Terry's far and away the best of us; you'll love Terry. If only he could have half a chance. I don't mean about his health; father and mother have really done all they could about that. But he's never had any proper education, and he isn't strong enough yet to go to school." She went on, forgetting herself and her habit of being on the defensive, carried away by the need to explain Terry, to put him in the handsomest possible light before this friend of Martin's, who was so evidently a person of standards and principles—like Terry himself. It was just another bit of poor Terry's bad luck, she pursued; for ever so long he'd been begging and imploring their parents to let him have a good tutor, like other boys of his age who weren't strong enough for school; and finally they had understood, and agreed that he couldn't be left any longer to Scopy and the nurses; and then, when the tutor was finally found, and everything working so well, Joyce had to take it into her head to marry him. Didn't Mrs. Sellars agree that it was a particularly rotten piece of luck?

Yes; Mrs. Sellars did agree. Only, Boyne saw from the curve of her lips, "luck" was not precisely the noun she would have used, nor "rotten" the adjective.

"But surely it's just a passing whim of—of your mother's. When it comes to the point, she won't break up everything in order to marry this young man."

Judith's eyes widened. "Well, what can mother do—if she's in love with him?"

Mrs. Sellars lowered her lids softly, as if she were closing the eyes of a dead self. "Why, she could . . . she could . . . think of all of you, my dear."

"Oh, she'll do that," Judith rejoined. "She has already. She and father are fighting over us now. That's why we bolted. Hasn't Martin told you?"

"I think Martin felt he'd rather have you tell me about it yourself—that is, as much as you care to," said Mrs. Sellars, with tactful evasiveness.

Judith pondered, her brows gathering in a puzzled frown. "I don't know that there's anything more to tell. I brought the children away so that we shouldn't be separated again. If children don't look after each other, who's going to do it for them? You can't expect parents to, when they don't know how to look after themselves."

"Ah, my dear," murmured Mrs. Sellars. With an impulsive movement she put her hand on Judith's. "Just say that to your mother as you've said it to me, and she'll never give you up for anybody."

Judith's frown relaxed, and her eyebrows ran up incredulously. "She has before, you know. What are you to do when you fall in love? That's one thing I never mean to do," she announced, in a decisive tone. "Besides, you know," she went on, "one does get used to children. I suppose you've never had any, have you?" Mrs. Sellars made a faint sign of negation. "Oh, well," Judith continued encouragingly, "I daresay it's not too late. But if you'd had all of us on your hands, and the three steps besides, you'd probably take us for granted by this time. Not that mother isn't fond of us—only she has these heart-storms. That's what poor Doll Westway used to call them. And *she* knew—"

Mrs. Sellars laid down the spoon with which she was absently stirring her coffee. "Doll Westway—?"

Judith's face lit up. "You knew her?"

"No," said Mrs. Sellars, in a tone of rejection acutely familiar to Boyne, but obviously unremarked by the girl.

"She was my very best friend," Judith went on. "You never saw anybody so lovely to look at. In tea-rose bathing tights—"

"My dear," Mrs. Sellars interrupted, "don't you think it seems a pity to sit indoors in such weather? If you've finished your coffee, shall we move out on the balcony? Martin, do find the cigarettes." Her sweetness suffused them like a silvery icing. Judith, obviously puzzled, rose to follow her, and Boyne distributed cigarettes with a savage energy. Oh, damn it, what had gone wrong again now?

But whatever had gone wrong was, for the moment at any rate, set right by the appearance of a blue-veiled nurse who was conducting a rosy little boy up the slope beneath the balcony. "Hullo! This way—here I am!" Judith joyously signalled to the pair; and Mrs. Sellars, leaning over the railing at her side, instantly declared: "Here's somebody too beautiful not to be the celebrated Chip."

Yes; it was clever of Judith to have arranged that Chipstone should appear at that moment. To a childless woman the sight of that armful of health and good humour must be at once a pang and a balm. Mrs. Sellars's eyes met Boyne's, smiling, trembling, and his signalled back: "Damn Aunt Julia." Chipstone had already filled the air with his immovable serenity. They had gone back into the sitting-room to greet him, and he settled himself Buddha-like on Mrs. Sellars's knee, and laughed with satisfaction at the sight of Judy and Martin and Nanny grouped admiringly before him. Whatever came Chip's way seemed to turn into something as fresh as new milk with the bubbles on it.

"Oh, Chip's a good enough fellow," said Judith, fondly disparaging. "But wait till you see Terry . . ."

"Terry couldn't come; but the rest of us have," announced a sharp little voice outside the door.

"Good gracious! If it isn't Zinnie!" Judith jumped up in a rush of indignation; but before she could reach the door it had opened on the self-possessed figure of her little step-sister, behind whose fiery mop appeared the dark bobbing heads of Bun and Beechy.

"Well, if ever—I never did! Susan swore to me she'd never let 'em out of her sight while we was away," Nanny ejaculated, paling under Judith's wrathful glance.

"She never did, neither," said Zinnie composedly. "She watched us almost all the way; but we could run faster than her, 'cos she's got a shoe't hurts her, 'n' so after a while she had to give up chasing us. Didn't she?" This was flung back to the "steps" for corroboration.

But a masterly somersault had already introduced Bun to the centre front, where he remained head down, bare legs and sandal-soles in air; and Beechy had rushed up to Mrs. Sellars and flung her passionate arms about Chipstone. "Oh, my Cheepo, we thought we'd losted you, and you were dead," she joyfully wailed; and Chip received her pæan with a rosy grin.

"Yes, 'n' Judy hadn't ought to of sneaked away and left us all like that, 'n' not said anything 'bout coming here, but only 'ranged for Chip to come and see you, when he's the youngest of the bunch—ought she of?" Zinnie appealed indignantly to Mrs. Sellars; who replied that it evidently didn't seem fair, but she must take the blame to herself for living in such a small house that she hadn't been able to invite them all to lunch because the dining-room wouldn't have held them. "And I suppose," she concluded diplomatically, "Chipstone was chosen to represent you because he takes up the least room."

"No, he doesn't, either; I do!" shouted Bun, swiftly reversing himself and facing Mrs. Sellars in a challenging attitude. "I can crawl through a croky hoop, and I can—"

"You can't hold your tongue, and Chip can, and that's why I brought him, and not the rest of you," cried Judith, administering a shake to Bun, while Nanny seized upon Beechy to stifle her incipient howl of sympathy.

"Oh, these dreadful children—." It was another voice at the door, this time so discreetly pitched, so sweetly deprecating, that Mrs. Sellars instinctively rose to receive a visitor who seemed as little used as herself to noisy company.

"I *am* so sorry—." Blanca was in the room now, slim, white-frocked, imperturbable, with an air of mundane maturity which made Judith seem like her younger sister.

"Poor Susan told me they'd run away from her when they found Nanny was coming here with Chip, and I rushed after them, but couldn't catch them. I'm sorry, but it wasn't my fault." Prettily breathless, she excused herself to Judith; but her long lashes were busy drawing Mrs. Sellars and Boyne into their net. "Darling Martin!" She bestowed on him one of her mother's most studied intonations. "I'm Terry's twin," she explained to Mrs. Sellars.

The latter, at ease with graces so like her own, replied with a smile that, since Terry could not come, she appreciated his sending such a charming delegate. Judith shot a grimace at Boyne, but Blanca, with a sudden rush of sincerity, declared: "Oh, but when you've seen Terry you won't care for any of the rest of us."

"Yes, she will; she'll care for Beechy and me because we're Roman Princes!" Bun shouted, threatening another handspring which a gesture from Judith curtailed.

Zinnie pushed him aside and planted herself firmly in front of their hostess. "My mother could buy 'em all out if she wanted to, 'cos she's a movie star," she affirmed in her thin penetrating voice. "But I'd never let her, 'cos we all love each other very much, 'n' Judy's made us all swear on Scopy's book we'd stay together till we got married. I'm probably going to marry Bun."

At this announcement signs of damp despair revealed themselves on Beechy's features; but Bun, regardless of the emotions he excited, interposed to say: "My *real* mother was a lion-tamer; but that don't matter, 'cos she's dead."

Mrs. Sellars had risen to the occasion on one of her quick wing-beats. Games, tea and more games had been improvised with the promptness and skill which always distinguished her in social emergencies; and the afternoon was nearly over when a band of replete and sleepy children took their way home to the *Pension Rosenglüh*. On the threshold of the *châlet* Zinnie paused to call up to the balcony: "I s'pose 'f you'd known we were coming you'd have had some presents ready for us—." A cuff from Judith nipped the suggestion, and the flock was hurried off down the hill, but not too quickly to catch Mrs. Sellars's response: "Come up to-morrow and you'll see!"

Mrs. Sellars, however, did not wait till the next day to return the little Wheaters' visit. Soon after their departure she gathered up an armful of books, selected for Terry's special delectation, and walked down to the *pension* with Boyne. The younger children were by this time at supper; but the visitor was introduced to Miss Scope, and conducted by her to Terry's bedside. Neither Judith nor Boyne accompanied her, since the doctor did not want his patient to see many people till he had recovered from his fatigue. Mrs. Sellars, for this reason, remained only for a few minutes with the little boy, and when she rejoined Boyne, who was waiting for her at the gate, she said simply: "I'm glad I came." Boyne liked her for knowing that he would guess the rest. He had never had any doubts about this meeting.

When he got back to his hotel he found the telegram which he had been expecting since the morning. "For God's sake wire at once if children with you and Chipstone all right worried to death cannot understand insane performance police traced them to Padua where they hired motors for Botzen please ship them all back immediately will wire you funds. Wheater."

"Damn it—well, I'll have to go and see him myself," Boyne muttered, crumpling up the paper and jamming it into his pocket. The message had shattered his dream-paradise of a day, and now the sooner the business ahead of him was over the better for everybody. But with a certain satisfaction he concluded, after a glance at the clock: "Too late to wire tonight, anyhow."

Chapter XIV

"HERE—how was I to answer this?" Boyne challenged Mrs. Sellars that evening, pushing the telegram across the dinner-table, where they had lingered over their wood-strawberries and cream.

She had been charming about the Wheater children after their departure; appreciative of Judith—with a shade of reserve—discerning and tender about Terry, and warmly motherly about the others. It was heart-breaking, the whole business . . . and so touching, the way they all turned to Martin for help . . . regarding him apparently as their only friend (how well she understood that!) . . . But what on earth was he going to do about it? What possible issue did he see?

All through dinner they went in and out of the question, till Boyne, feeling that, thanks to Terry, her sympathy was permanently secured, drew the Wheater telegram from his pocket. Mrs. Sellars scrutinised it thoughtfully.

"When did this come?"

"Just now. I found it when I went back to the hotel."

She sighed. "Of course the Wheaters were bound to find out within twenty-four hours where they'd gone. Poor little conspirators! I wish we could have kept them a day or two longer . . . especially with that boy so overdone . . ."

"Well, perhaps we can."

Her eyebrows queried: "How?" But instead of taking this up he said: "You haven't told me yet what I'm to answer."

Her mobile brow sketched another query. "What *can* you answer? Their father'll come and fetch them if you don't send them back."

"I certainly shan't do that."

"Shan't—? Then what?" Her eyes darkened, and she took up the telegram and studied it again; then she lifted a faintly mocking smile to Boyne. "I confess I'm curious to hear your alternative."

He considered this with a frown of perplexity. "Why should I answer at all?"

"If you don't, Wheater has only to telephone to your hotel, and find out if you're still here, and if you've been seen about with a party of children."

"I shan't be here. I'll pack off at once—to Pieve di Cadore, or somewhere."

"And the children?"

"I'll take them with me."

"Are you serious?"

"Absolutely."

She received this with a little silken laugh. "Then you're a child yourself, dear. How long do you suppose it will be before you're run down? You'll only be making things worse for the children—and for yourself."

"Hang myself! But for them—." He frowned and pondered again. "Well, damn it; perhaps. But what have you got to suggest?"

"That you should persuade Judith to take them straight back, of course. I'm awfully sorry for them all—and Terry especially. But as far as I can see there's nothing else to do."

He stood up and began to pace the floor. "I'll never do that."

She leaned her white arms on the table and her smile followed his impatient pacings. "Then what?"

"I don't know. Not yet. Anyhow, I've got the night to think it over."

"All the thinking in the world won't get you any farther."

He met her smile with a grin which was almost antagonistic. "I've got out of one or two tighter places in my life before now."

"I've no doubt you have," she returned in her tone of slightly humorous admiration.

There they had dropped the discussion, both too experienced in debate not to feel its uselessness. And the next morning had, after all, told Boyne, without any one's help, what he intended to do. He decided that his first step was to see Judith; and he was down at the *pension* before the shutters of her room were unlatched. Miss Scope was summoned to the sitting-room, and he told her that Judith must come down immediately to see him.

"Bad news, Mr. Boyne—oh, I hope not?"

"Well, you didn't seriously suppose it was going to take Wheater much longer than this to run you down, did you?"

Miss Scope whitened. "Are the police after us?"

"The police?" He burst out laughing. "To arrest you for abduction? If they do, it shall be over my dead body."

She turned to go, and then paused to face him from the threshold. "Whatever Judith did was done with my knowledge and consent—consent; I don't say approval," she declared in an emphatic whisper.

"Of course, of course. But send her down at once, will you please?"

A moment later Judith was there, huddled into a scant poppy-coloured dressing-gown, her hair tumbling thickly over childish eyes still misty with sleep. "What is it, Martin? The police?"

He laughed again, this time more impatiently. "Don't be ridiculous, child. You're as bad as Scopy. You didn't really believe your father would have you arrested, did you?"

She met this with another question. "What *is* he going to do?"

Boyne handed her the telegram, and she flashed back: "You haven't answered it?"

"Not yet."

"Well, we'll have to start at once, I suppose."

Boyne stared at her, so unprepared for this prompt abdication that the feeling uppermost in him was a sudden sense of flatness. He had come there ready to put up a fight, valiant if unresourceful, and now—

"Couldn't we catch a steamer at Trieste?" she continued, apparently pursuing some inward train of thought. The unexpected question jerked him back out of his supineness.

"Trieste? Why Trieste?" He stared at her, puzzled. "Where to?"

"Oh, almost anywhere where they can't reach us too quickly." As if unconscious of his presence, she continued to brood upon her problem. "Perhaps, do you know, after all, we'd better go to America. Don't you think so? There's Grandma Mervin—Joyce's mother. We might go to her. And meanwhile you can make the Wheaters think we're still here, and so they won't be worried, and we shall have time to slip away."

In spite of himself, Boyne's first feeling was one of relief that she meant to keep up the struggle. To begin with, it was more like her; and he had reached the point of wanting her at all costs to be like herself. But he kept his wits sufficiently to reply on a note of sarcasm: "Thank you for the part for which I'm cast. But, my poor child, even if you could get away to America without your parents' knowing it, such journeys cost money, and I don't suppose—"

"Oh, I've oceans of money," she answered with a startling composure.

"What do you call oceans of money? Scopy's savings?" he taunted her.

Judith flushed up. "She told you?"

"She told me nothing. I guessed."

Her head drooped for a moment; then she raised it with a confident smile. "Well, of course I shall pay her back. She's sure of that. She knows I'm a nairess."

"Heroic woman! But how far do you expect to go on what she's contributed?"

This also Judith faced with composure. "Not very—poor dear Scopy! But, you see, I've got a lot besides."

"A lot of money?"

She leaned her rumpled head back against the hard sofa, apparently determined to enjoy his bewilderment for a moment longer before enlightening him. "Don't you call five thousand dollars a lot of money?" she asked.

Boyne gave a whistle of astonishment, and she nodded softly in corroboration.

"You had five thousand dollars—of your own?"

"No. But I knew where father had them."

Boyne jumped to his feet, and stood glaring down at her incredulously. "You knew—?"

"Don't gape at me, Martin. If you like to call it so, I stole the money. He always has a lot about, because it bores him so to write cheques."

"And you helped yourself—to what you wanted?"

"It was awfully easy. I knew where the key was." She seemed anxious to disclaim any undeserved credit in the matter. "And, anyhow, I knew part of it was intended for our expenses in the Engadine this summer. So it really wasn't exactly like stealing—was it?"

Boyne sat down again, this time in a chair on the farther side of the room. There seemed to be something almost maleficent in the proximity of the small scarlet figure with rumpled hair and sleep-misted eyes, curled up defiantly in the sofa corner. "You told your father this, I suppose, in the letter you left for him?"

"Told him I'd taken the money?" She laughed. "If I had, there wouldn't have been much use in taking it—would there?"

He groaned, and sat silent, his eyes fixed on the carefully scrubbed boards of the floor. For a while he concentrated his whole attention on one of their resinous knots; then, with limbs of lead, he slowly stood up again. "Well, I wash my hands of you—all of you."

Judith rose also, and went quickly up to him. "Martin," she said in a frightened voice, "what are you going to do?"

"Do? Nothing. You'd better answer that telegram yourself," he retorted roughly, shaking off the hand she had put out. He walked across the room, blinked unseeingly at his hat and stick, which he had thrown down on the table, and turned to go out of the door without remembering to pick them up. On the threshold he was checked by Judith's passionate clutch on his arm. Her lifted face was wet and frightened. "Martin—why don't you say you think I'm a thief, and have done with it?"

He swung round on her. "I think you're an unutterable fool. I think the average Andaman islander has a more highly developed moral sense than you."

"I don't know who they are. But Doll Westway always used to—"

"Used to what?"

"Go to her mother's drawer. There wasn't any other way. They all hate the bother of paying bills—parents do." She clung to him, her lips still trembling.

"Miss Scope knows about this, I suppose?"

She nodded. "I persuaded her. She hated it awfully—but she saw there was no other way. She's saved so little herself—because she has a brother who drinks . . ."

"And Terry? Does Terry know?"

"Oh, Martin! Terry? How could you think it? But you don't really, do you? You just said that to frighten me. Oh, Martin . . . you'll never tell Terry, will you? I shall die if you do. It doesn't matter about anybody else . . ."

He stood silent, suffering her clasp of desperate entreaty, as if a numbness had crept into the arm she held, and yet as if every nerve in it were fire. Something of the same duality was in his brain as he listened. It struck him dumb with the sense of his incapacity. All the forces of pity—and of something closer to the soul than pity—were fighting in him for her. But opposed to them was the old habit of relentless unconditional probity; the working man's faith in a standard to be kept up, and imposed on others, at no matter what cost of individual suffering. "I can't let her drift," was as near as he could come to it . . .

"Martin, tell me what you want me to do," she whispered, her lips trembling. His own hardened.

"Sit down at that table and write to your father that you took the money—and why you took it."

For a while she considered this painfully. "If I don't," she finally brought out, "shall you tell Terry?"

He gave her an indignant look. "Of course I shan't tell Terry!"

"Very well. Then I will."

Boyne flushed with the suddenness of his triumph, and most of all at the reason for it. "That's my Judy!"

She coloured too, as if surprised, but her face remained drawn and joyless. "But if I do, the game's up—isn't it?"

"The game's up anyhow, my dear."

Her colour faded. "You mean you're really going to give us away?"

He paused, and then said with deliberation: "I'm going to Venice at once to see your father."

"To tell him we're here?"

"Of course."

Her hand fell from his arm, and she stood drooping before him, all the youth drained out of her face. He was frightened at the effect of his words. Her boundless capacity for suffering struck him as the strangest element in her tragic plight.

"Then you give us up altogether? You don't care any longer what becomes of us?"

He paused a moment, and then turned back into the room, and took her two cold hands in his.

"Judith, look at me." She obeyed.

"Can't you understand that I care for only one thing at this moment? That you should realise what you've done—"

"About the money?" she breathed.

"Of course. About the money."

"You really think that matters more than anything else?"

The unexpectedness of the question suddenly cut him adrift from his argument. It seemed to come out of some other plane of experience, to be thrust at him from depths of pain and disillusionment that he had not yet begun to sound.

"You see," she pressed on, snatching at her opportunity, "if we could only get to Grandma Mervin's, I believe she'd keep us. At any rate, she'd try to make mother see that we mustn't be separated. I know she would, because in her letters to mother she always calls us 'those poor children.' She's awfully old-fashioned, Grandma Mervin . . . And the money, Martin—father won't find out for ever so long that it's gone. There was a lot more where I took it from. He always has such heaps with him; and he never knows how much he's spent. Once he had a valet who stole a lot, and he didn't discover it for months . . . And without that money we can't possibly get to America . . ."

Boyne pulled himself together with an effort, averting his eyes from the perilous mirage. "And you're gambling on being as lucky as the other thief?" There—saying that had cleared his conscience, and he could go on more humanely: "Don't you see, child, that this business of the money spoils the whole thing? You've got to give it back to me; and I've got to take it to your father. Then I'll put up the best fight I can for you."

Of this appeal she seemed to hear only the last words. "You will—oh, Martin, darling, you really will?"

In an instant her arms were about his neck, her wet face pressed against his lips. ("Now . . . now . . . now . . ." he grumbled.) "I knew it, Martin! I knew in my soul you'd never chuck us," she exulted in the sudden ecstasy of her relief. Waves of buoyancy seemed to be springing beneath her feet. "Martin, I know you'll know just what to say to them," she chanted.

"Go upstairs, Judith, and get that money," he admonished her severely.

She turned and left the room. While she was gone he stood gazing out of the window. Of all the world of light and freedom before him, its spreading mountain slopes, its spires of granite reared into a cloud-pillared sky, and the giant blue shadows racing each other across the valleys, he saw nothing but the narrow thread of railway winding down to Venice and the Wheaters. He had still to make Judith write the letter to her father. He had still to deliver her—this child who trusted him—bound and helpless into the hands of the enemy.

Chapter XV

"D AMN—damn, damn—oh, *damn!*" It seemed to be the
only expletive at Cliffe Wheater's command, and Boyne
felt that he had used it so often that it was as worn out as an old
elastic band, and no longer held his scattered ideas together.

He plunged down into an armchair of the Lido Palace
lounge—the Wheaters had moved out to the Lido—and sat
there, embraced by a cluster of huge leather bolsters, his good-
humoured lips tinged with an uneasy purple, the veins in his
blond temples swollen with a helpless exasperation. "Damn!"
he ejaculated again.

The place was empty. It was the hour of the afternoon sun-
bath on the sands below the hotel, and no one shared with them
the cool twilight of the hall but a knot of white-jacketed boys
languishing near the lift, and a gold-braided porter dozing
behind his desk.

Boyne sat opposite to Wheater, in another vast slippery armchair to which only a continual muscular effort could anchor
his spare frame. He sat and watched Cliffe Wheater with the
narrow-lipped attention he might have given to the last stages
of a debate with a native potentate on whom he was trying to
impose some big engineering scheme which would necessitate
crossing the ruler's territory.

But with the potentate it would have been only a question of
matching values; of convincing him of the material worth of
what was offered. In such negotiations the language spoken,
when interpreted, usually turned out to be the same. But in his
talk with Wheater, Boyne had the sense of using an idiom for
which the other had no equivalents. Superficially their vocabularies were the same; below the surface each lost its meaning
for the other. Wheater continued to toss uneasily on a sea of
incomprehension.

"What in hell can I do about it?" he demanded.

It was almost unintelligible that anything should have happened to him against which his wealth and his health could
not prevail. His first idea seemed to be that it must be all a
mistake—or somebody else's damned negligence. As if they had

forgotten to set the burglar alarm, or to order the motor, or to pay the fire-insurance, or to choke off a bore at the telephone, or, by some other unstopped fissure in the tight armour of his wellbeing, had suddenly let tribulation in on him. If he could get at the offender—if he only could! But it was the crux of his misery that apparently he couldn't—

"Not that I blame the child," he said suddenly, looking down with an interrogative stare at his heavy blond-haired hands, with their glossy nails and one broad gold ring with an uncut sapphire. He raised his eyes and examined Boyne, who instantly felt himself leaping to the guard of his own face.

"That business of the money—you understand, Judith didn't in the least realise . . ." Boyne began.

"Oh, damn the money." That question was swept away with a brush of the hand: Boyne had noticed that the poor little letter of confession he had extracted from Judith had received hardly a glance from her father, who had pocketed the bank-notes as carelessly as if they were a gambling debt. Evidently the Lido Palace values were different. It was the hideous inconvenience of it all that was gnawing at Wheater—and also, to be fair to him, a vague muddled distress about his children. "I didn't know the poor little chaps cared so much," was all this emotion wrung from him; none the less, Boyne felt, it was sincere.

"They care most awfully for each other—and very much for you and Joyce. What they need beyond everything is a home: a home with you two at its head."

"Oh, damn," Wheater groaned again. It was as if Boyne had proposed to him to ascend the throne of England. What was the use of dealing in impossibles? There were things which even his money couldn't buy—and when you stripped him of the sense of its omnipotence he squirmed like a snail out of its shell.

"Why can't there not be rows?" he began again, perspiring with the oppression of his helplessness.

"There wouldn't be, if you and Joyce would only come to an understanding."

The aggrieved husband met this derisively. "Joyce—and an understanding!"

"Well—she's awfully fond of the children; and so are you. And they're devoted to both of you, all of them. Why can't you and she agree to bury your differences, and arrange your lives so that you can keep the children together, and give them something that looks like a home, while you both . . . well, do whatever you like . . . privately . . ." Boyne felt his lips drying as they framed this arid proposal.

Wheater leaned his elbows on his knees and gazed at the picture presented. "Joyce doesn't care to do what she likes privately," he replied, without irony.

"But the children—I'm sure she doesn't want to part with them."

"No; and no more do I. And what's more, I won't!" He brought down a clenched fist on the leather protuberance at his elbow. It sank in soggily, as if the Lido armchair had been the symbol of Joyce's sullen opposition. "By God, I can dictate my terms," Wheater pursued, sonorously but without conviction.

Boyne stood up with a sense of weariness. His bones felt as stiff as if he had been trying to hang on to a jagged rock above a precipice; his mind participated in their ache.

"Look here, Cliffe, what's the use of threats? Of course you're all-powerful. Between you, Joyce and you can easily destroy these children's lives . . . "

"Oh, see here!" Wheater protested.

"Destroy their lives. Look at that poor Doll Westway, who was kicked about from pillar to post . . . Judith told me her miserable story . . ."

"I don't see the resemblance. And what's more I strongly object to being classed with a down-and-outer like Charlie Westway. Why, man, no law-court in the world would have given a blackguard like that the custody of his children. Whereas mine will always be perfectly safe in my hands, and Joyce knows it; and so do her lawyers."

"I daresay; but the trouble is that the children need Joyce at least as much as they do you. And they need something that neither one of you can give them separately. They need you and Joyce together: that's what a home is made of—togetherness . . . the mysterious atmosphere . . ." Boyne broke off, nervously swallowing his own eloquence.

Wheater gave him a helpless look. "Have a drink?" he suggested. He waved his hand to the white-coated guardians of the lift. Far off across the empty reaches of the hall a waiter appeared with napkin and tray—sail and raft of a desert ocean.

"Hi!" Wheater called out feverishly. Boyne wondered that he did not brandish his handkerchief at the end of a stick. The two men drank in a desperate silence.

Capturing Joyce's attention was less easy. It was difficult even to secure her presence. Not that she avoided her husband—on the contrary, she devoted all the time she could spare to arguing with him about their future arrangements. And she had flung herself on Boyne in an agony of apprehension about the children. But once assured of their safety she remarked that their going off like that had served Cliffe right, and she hoped it would be a lesson to him; and thereupon hurried away to a pressing engagement on the beach, promising Boyne to see him when she came up to dress for dinner—anywhere between eight and nine. She supposed Cliffe would look after him in the interval?

It was nearer nine than eight when Boyne finally waylaid her in an upper corridor, on the way back to her room. She relegated him to her sitting-room while she got out of her bathing tights, and presently reappeared swathed in perfumed draperies, with vivid eyes, tossed hair as young as Judith's, and the animating glow imparted by a new love-affair. Boyne remembered Terry's phrase: "With all the new ways the doctors have of making parents young again," and reflected that this oldest one of all was still the most effective. She threw herself down on a lounge, clasped her arms behind her head, and declared: "It was too clever of Judith to give her father that scare. Now perhaps he'll come to his senses." Yes, Boyne thought—she was going to be more difficult to convince than Wheater.

"What do you call coming to his senses?"

"Why, giving all the children to me, of course—to me and Gerald." Her lids closed softly on the name. Boyne was frightened by a reminder of Judith's way of caressing certain thoughts and images with her lashes. He hated anything in the mother that recalled what he most loved in her daughter . . .

"The trouble is, Joyce, that what they want—what they need—is not you and . . . and anybody else . . . but just you and Cliffe: their parents."

"Me and Cliffe! An edifying spectacle!"

"Oh, well, they've discounted all that—at least Judith and Terry have. And they're incurably fond of you both. What the younger ones require, of course, is just the even warmth of a home—like any other young animals."

She considered her shining nails, as if glassing her indolent beauty in them.

"You see," Boyne pressed on, "it's all these changes of temperature that are killing them."

"What changes of temperature?"

"Well, every time there's a new deal—I mean a new step-parent—there's necessarily a new atmosphere, isn't there? Young things, you know, need sameness—it's their vital element."

Joyce, at this point, surprised him by abounding in his own sense. It was never she who wanted to change, she assured him. Hadn't she come back of her own accord to Cliffe, and loyally made the attempt all over again—just on account of the children? And what had been the result, as far as they were concerned? Simply their being compelled to assist, with older and more enlightened eyes, at the same old rows and scandals (for Cliffe *was* scandalous) which had already edified their infancy. Could Boyne possibly advise the renewal of such conditions as a "vital element" in their welfare, the poor darlings? It would be the most disastrous experiment that could be made with them. Whereas, if they would just firmly declare their determination to remain with Joyce, and only with Joyce, Cliffe would soon come to his senses—and, anyhow, as soon as another woman got hold of him, he wouldn't know what to do with the children, and would be only too thankful to know they were in safe hands. And had Boyne considered what a boon it would be to dear Terry to have Gerald always with him, not as a salaried tutor, but, better still, as friend, companion, guardian—as everything his own father had failed to be? Boyne must have seen what a fancy Terry had taken to Gerald. And Gerald simply loved the boy. That consideration, Joyce owned, had influenced her not a little in her determination to break with Wheater.

Joyce was much more articulate than her husband, and, para-doxical as it seemed, proportionately harder to deal with. She swept away all Boyne's arguments on a torrent of sentimental verbiage; and she had the immense advantage over Wheater of believing that the children would be perfectly happy with her, whereas Wheater merely believed in his right to keep them, whether his doing so made them happy or not.

But these considerations were interrupted by Joyce's abrupt exclamation that it was past nine already, and the Wrenches and the Duke of Mendip were waiting for her . . . of course dear Martin would join them at dinner? . . . No; Martin thought he wouldn't, thanks; in fact, he'd already promised Cliffe . . .

"But Cliffe's coming too. Oh, you didn't know? My dear, he's infatuated with Sybil Lullmer. She came here to try and catch Mendip, and failing that she's quietly annexed Cliffe instead. Rather funny, isn't it? But of course that kind of woman sticks at nothing. With her record, why should she? And Cliffe has had to make up with Zinnia Wrench because it was the easiest way of being with Sybil . . . So you will dine with us, Martin, won't you? And do tell me—you're sure Chip's perfectly contented? And you think Cortina will do Terry good?"

Half an hour later, Boyne, who had sternly told himself that this also was part of the game, sat at a table in the crowded Lido Palace restaurant, overhanging the starlit whisper of the Adriatic. His seat was between Zinnia Lacrosse and Joyce Wheater, and opposite him was a small sleek creature, who reminded him, when she first entered, of Judith—who had the same puzzled craving eyes, the same soft shadowy look amid the surrounding glare. But when he faced her across the table, saw her smile, heard her voice, he was furious with himself for the comparison.

"Do you mean to say you don't know Syb Lullmer?" Joyce whispered to him under cover of the saxophones. "But you must have heard of her as Mrs. Charlie Westway? She always manages to be in the spot-light. Her daughter Doll committed suicide last year at Deauville. It was all pretty beastly. Syb herself is always chock full of drugs. Doesn't look it, does she? She might be Judy's age . . . in this light. What do you think of her?"

"I think she's hideous."

Mrs. Wheater stared. "Well, the dress-makers don't. They dress her for nothing. Look at her ogling Gerald! That's what makes Cliffe so frantic," Cliffe's wife smilingly noted. After a moment she added: "A nice step-mother for my children! Do you wonder I'm putting up a fight to keep them?"

From across the table Mrs. Lullmer was speaking in a low piercing whine. When she spoke her large eyes became as empty as a medium's, and her lips moved just enough to let out a flat knife-edge of voice. "I told Anastase I'd never speak to him again, or set foot in his place, if ever I caught him selling one of the dresses he'd designed for me to a respectable woman; and he said: 'Why, I never saw one in my establishment: did you?' And I said to him: 'Now you've insulted me, and I'll sue you for libel if you don't take fifty per cent off my bill.' I'm poor, you see," Mrs. Lullmer concluded plaintively, sweeping the table with her disarming gaze. The Duke, Zinnia, Lord Wrench and Cliffe Wheater received the anecdote with uproarious approval. Gerald Ormerod looked at the ceiling, and Joyce looked tenderly at Gerald. "I got off twenty-five per cent anyhow," Mrs. Lullmer whined, spreading her fluid gaze over Boyne . . .

All about them, at other tables exactly like theirs, sat other men exactly like Lord Wrench and Wheater, the Duke of Mendip and Gerald Ormerod, other women exactly like Joyce and Zinnia and Mrs. Lullmer. Boyne remembered Mrs. Sellars's wail at the approach of a standardised beauty. Here it was, in all its mechanical terror—endless and meaningless as the repetitions of a nightmare. Every one of the women in the vast crowded restaurant seemed to be of the same age, to be dressed by the same dress-makers, loved by the same lovers, adorned by the same jewellers, and massaged and manipulated by the same Beauty doctors. The only difference was that the few whose greater age was no longer disguisable had shorter skirts, and exposed a wider expanse of shoulder-blade. A double jazz-band drowned their conversation, but from the movement of their lips, and the accompanying gestures, Boyne surmised that they were all saying exactly the same things as Joyce and Zinnie and Mrs. Lullmer. It would have been unfashionable to be different; and once more Boyne marvelled at the incurable simplicity of the corrupt. "Blessed are the pure in heart," he thought, "for they have so many more things to talk about . . ."

Out in the offing the lights of the "Fancy Girl" drew an unheeded triangle of stars, cruising up and down against the dusk. A breeze, rising as darkness fell, carried the reflection toward the shore on a multitude of little waves; but the sea no longer interested the diners, for it was not the hour when they used it.

"I say—why shouldn't we go and finish our cigars on board?" Cliffe Wheater proposed, yearning, as always, to have his new toy noticed. The night was languid, the guests were weary of their usual routine of amusements, and the party, following the line of least resistance, drifted down to the pier, where the "Fancy Girl"'s launch lay mingling the glitter of its brasses with the glow of constellations in the ripples.

"To-morrow morning, old man," Wheater said, his arm in Boyne's, "we'll have it all out about the children . . ."

Chapter XVI

B OYNE knew that "morning," in the vocabulary of the Lido, could not possibly be construed as meaning anything earlier than the languid interval between cocktails and lunch, or the still more torpid stretch of time separating the process of digestion from the first afternoon bath. All his energies were bent on getting the Wheaters to fix on one or the other of these parentheses as the most suitable in which to examine the question of their children's future; and he accounted himself lucky when they finally agreed to meet him in a quiet corner of the hotel lounge before luncheon.

Unfortunately for this plan, no corner of the lounge—or of its adjacent terraces—could be described as quiet at that particular hour. The whole population of the "Palace" was thronging back through its portals in quest of food and drink. Hardly had Boyne settled Mr. and Mrs. Wheater in their fathomless armchairs (his only hope of keeping them there lay in the difficulty of getting up in a hurry) when Lady Wrench drifted by, polishing her nails with a small tortoiseshell implement, and humming a Negro Spiritual in her hoarse falsetto.

"Goodness—what you people doing over here, plotting together in a corner? Look as if you were rehearsing for a film . . ." She stopped, wide-eyed, impudent, fundamentally indifferent to everything less successful than her own success.

"I don't know what we *are* doing," Joyce returned with a touch of irritability. "Martin seems to think he ought to tell us how to bring up the children." It obviously seemed preposterous to her that Zinnia Wrench should be idling about, polishing her nails and humming tunes, while this severe mental effort was exacted of one who, the night before, had been up as late, and danced as hard, as the other.

"Something's *got* to be decided," Wheater growled uncertainly.

"Oh, well—so long," smiled Lady Wrench. "I'm off to see Mendip's new tent; the one he's just got over from: where is it? Morocco, I guess he said. But isn't that a sort of leather?

Somewhere in South Africa, anyhow . . . They're just rigging it up. It's a wonder."

"A new tent?" Joyce's face lit up with curiosity, and the scattered desire to participate in everything that was going.

"Yes; absolutely different from anything you've ever seen. The very last thing. Sort of black Cubist designs on it. Might give Anastase ideas for a bath-wrap. Hullo, Gerald—that you? I've been looking for you everywhere; thought you'd got drowned. Come along and see Mendip's tent."

Joyce raised a detaining hand. "Gerald—Mr. Ormerod! Please. I want you to stay here. We're discussing something about which I may need your advice."

"Oh, look here, Joyce, I say—" her husband interrupted.

His wife gave him a glance of aggrieved dignity. "You don't want me to be without advice, I suppose? You've got Martin's."

Wheater groaned: "This isn't going to be a prize fight, is it?"

"I don't know. It might. Sit down, please, Gerald." Mrs. Wheater indicated an armchair beside her own, and Ormerod reluctantly buried his long limbs in it. "In this heat—" he murmured.

"Oh, well, s'long," cried Lady Wrench, evaporating.

"Joyce—Cliffe! Look here: have you seen Mendip's new tent?" Mrs. Lullmer, exquisite, fadeless, her scant bathing tights inadequately supplemented by a transparent orange scarf, paused in a plastic attitude before the besieged couple. "Do let's rush down and take a look at it before cocktails. Come on, Cliffe."

Mrs. Wheater drew her lips together, and a slow wave of crimson rose to her husband's perspiring temples.

"See here, Syb; we're talking business."

"Business?" Instantly Mrs. Lullmer's vaporous face became as sharp-edged as a cameo, and her eyes narrowed into two observation-slits. "Been put on to something good, have you? I'm everlastingly broke. For God's sake tell me!" she implored.

Wheater laughed. "No. We're only trying to settle about the children."

"The children? Do you mean to say you're talking about them still? That reminds me—where's my own child? Pixie, pet! Ah, there she is. Darling, nip up to my room, will you, and get mummy one of those new lipsticks: no, not *Baiser Défendu*, sweet, but *Nouveau Péché*—you know, the one that fits into the gold bag the Duke gave me yesterday."

An ethereal sprite, with a pre-Raphaelite bush of fair hair, and a tiny sunburnt body, detached herself from a romp with a lift-boy to spring away at her mother's behest.

"Pixie's such a darling—always does just as I tell her. If only my poor Doll had listened to me!" Mrs. Lullmer observed to Boyne, with a retrospective sigh which implied that the unhappy fate of her eldest daughter had been the direct result of resistance to the maternal counsels.

"Well—as I was saying—" Boyne began again, nervously . . .

But a fresh stream of bathers, reinforced by a troop of arrivals from Venice who had steamed over to the Lido for lunch, closed in vociferously about the Wheaters, and at the same instant the big clock on the wall rang out the stroke of one.

"See here, old Martin—this is no time for business, is it? I believe Joyce has asked half of these people to lunch," Wheater confessed to his friend with a shame-faced shrug. "But afterward—"

"All right. Afterward."

Lunch was over; the Duke's tent had been visited; and one by one the crowd in restaurant and grill-room had dispersed for bathing or bridge.

"Why not here?" Boyne suggested patiently to Mrs. Wheater.

"Here?" She paused under the lifted flap of the stately Moroccan tent, her astonishingly youthful figure outlined against the glitter of the sands.

"Why not?" Boyne persisted. "It's cool and quiet, and nobody is likely to bother us. Why shouldn't you and Cliffe go into this question with me now?"

She wavered, irresolute. "Where's Cliffe, to begin with? Oh, out there—under Syb's umbrella, of course. *I'm* perfectly willing, naturally—"

"Very well; I'll go and recruit him."

Boyne threaded his way between the prone groups on the beach to where Mrs. Lullmer lay, under the shadow of a huge orange-coloured umbrella, with Cliffe Wheater outspread beside her like a raised map of a mountainous country.

"I say, Cliffe, Joyce is waiting for you in the Duke's tent—for our talk."

Wheater raised a portion of his great bulk on a languid elbow. "What talk? . . . Oh, all right." His tone implied that, at the moment, it was distinctly all wrong; but he got slowly to his feet, gave himself a shake, lit a cigarette, and shambled away after Boyne. At the tent door Mrs. Lullmer swiftly overtook them. "I suppose you don't mind—" she smiled at Joyce; and Wheater muttered, half to his wife and half to Boyne: "She's had so much experience with children."

"All I want is what is best for mine," said Mrs. Wheater coldly; adding, as they re-entered the tent: "Martin, you'll find Gerald somewhere about. Won't you please tell him to come?"

Wheater gave an angry shrug, and then settled down resignedly on one of the heaps of embroidered Moroccan cushions disposed about the interior of the tent. Boyne's first inclination was to come back empty-handed from a simulated quest for Ormerod; but, reflecting that if he did so Joyce would seize on this as another pretext for postponement, he presently returned accompanied by the tutor, in whose wake Lady Wrench trailed her perfumed elegance. "See here, folks, I guess if anybody's got a right to be here I have," she announced with a regal suavity. "That is, if you're proposing to make plans about my child."

This argument seemed—even to Boyne—incontrovertible; and Lady Wrench sank down upon her cushions with a smile of triumph.

"Pity Buondelmonte's not here," Wheater growled under his breath to Boyne; and Lady Wrench, catching the name, instantly exclaimed: "But Wrenny is—I left him this minute at the bar; and I don't see why I shouldn't have my own husband's advice about my own child."

It was finally conceded that the benefit of Lord Wrench's judgment could not properly be denied to his wife; and, as Lord Wrench and the Duke of Mendip were too inseparable to be detached from one another on so trivial a pretext, and as the conference was taking place in the shelter of the Duke's own tent, it surprised no one—not even Boyne—when the two gentlemen strolled in together, and accommodated themselves on another pile of cushions. "Mendip wants to see how these things are done in America," Lord Wrench explained, before composing himself into a repose which seemed suspiciously like slumber; while the small dry-lipped Duke mumbled under his brief moustache: "Might come in useful—you never know."

"I'm sure *I* don't know exactly what we're supposed to be talking about," Joyce Wheater began. "I've said a hundred times that all I care for is what's best for the children. Everybody knows I've sacrificed everything for that once before. And what earthly use has it been?"

"Ah, that's what I say," Lady Wrench agreed with sudden sympathy. "You might cut yourself in pieces for a man, and his dirty lawyers would come and take your child away from you the next day, and haggle over every cent of alimony. But if it comes to money, I'll spend as much as anybody—"

"Oh, shut up, Zinnia," her husband softly intervened, and redisposed himself to rest.

"I don't think you ought any of you to look at the matter from a legal stand-point," Boyne interrupted. "My friends here are awfully fond of their children, and we all know they want what's best for them. The only question is how that best is to be arrived at. It seems to me perfectly simple—"

("Solomon," said the Duke, with his dry smile.)

"No. Exactly the reverse. Division is what I'm here to fight against—no; not fight but plead." Boyne turned to Cliffe Wheater. "For God's sake, old man, let the lot of them stay together."

"Why, they *were* together; they would have been, as long as they'd stayed with me," Wheater grumbled helplessly.

His wife reared her golden crest with a toss of defiance. "You don't suppose for a minute I'm going to abandon my children to the kind of future Cliffe Wheater's likely to provide for them? Gerald and I are prepared—"

"So are Cliffe and I," murmured Mrs. Lullmer, with a glance at the Duke under her studied lashes. The Duke threw back his head, and became lost in an inspection of the roof of the tent. "Cliffe and I," repeated Mrs. Lullmer, more incisively.

"Well, and what about me and Wrenny, I'd like to know?" Lady Wrench broke in. "I guess I can afford the best lawyers in the country—"

"I don't see that the law concerns these children," Boyne intervened. "What they need is not to be fought over, but just to be left alone. Judith and Terry understand that perfectly. They know there is probably going to be another change in their parents' lives, but they want to remain together, and not be affected by that change. I'm not here to theorise or criticise— I'm simply here as the children's spokesman. They're devoted to each other, and they want to stay together. Between you all, can't it be managed somehow—for a time, at any rate?"

"But my Pixie would be such a perfect little companion for Terry and Blanca. She knows all the very nicest children everywhere. That's one of the great advantages of hotel life, isn't it? And, after all, Judith may be marrying soon, and then what will become of the others?" Mrs. Lullmer turned a meaning smile on Boyne. "Haven't *you* perhaps thought of Judith's marrying soon, Mr. Boyne?"

Boyne curtly replied that he hadn't; and Lady Wrench intervened: "I want my Zinnie to have a lovely simple home life, out on our ranch in California. This kicking about in hotels is too horribly demoralising for children." She bent her great eyes gently on Mrs. Lullmer. "You know something about that, Mrs. Lullmer."

Mrs. Lullmer returned a look as gentle. "Oh, no; my children were never on a ranch at Hollywood," she said.

"Hollywood—Hollywood!" gasped Lady Wrench, paling with rage.

Mrs. Lullmer arched her delicate brows interrogatively. "Isn't Hollywood in California? Stupid of me! I was never in the West myself."

Joyce Wheater raised herself on her elbow. "I'm sure I don't see the use of this. Four of the children are mine and Cliffe's. I've always tried to make them all happy. I've treated Zinnie, and Buondelmonte's children, exactly like my own; and this is all the thanks I get for it! No one could be more competent than Gerald to direct Terry's education; which is something his father never happens to have thought of. But of course everybody here is trying to put me in the wrong . . ."

Mrs. Lullmer looked her soft surprise. "Oh, no. Don't say that, Joyce. All I feel is that perhaps the poor babies haven't been quite loved enough. You don't mind my suggesting it, do you? If they were mine, I don't think I should care so awfully much about making them into high-brows. What I should want would be just to see them all healthy and rosy and happy, and romping about all day like my little Pixie . . ."

"With lift-boys and barmen. Yes; I guess that *is* about the best preparation for life in the smart set," said Lady Wrench parenthetically.

Mrs. Lullmer smiled. "Yes; Pixie's little friends are all in what I believe you call the 'smart set.' I confess I think that even more important for a child than learning that Morocco is not in South Africa."

"Not in South Africa? Where is it, then, I'd like to know? Wrenny, you told me—"

"Well," said the Duke, getting up, "I'm off for a swim."

This announcement instantly disorganised the whole group. Nothing—as Boyne had already had occasion to remark—chilled their interest in whatever they were doing as rapidly as the discovery that one of the party had had enough of it, and was moving on to the next item of the day's programme. And no one could dislocate a social assemblage as quickly as the Duke of Mendip. The shared sense that wherever he was, there the greatest amount of excitement was obtainable, dominated any divergence of view among his companions. Even Lord Wrench roused himself from his slumbers and gathered up his long limbs for instant departure, and his wife and Mrs. Lullmer followed his example.

"Mercy, what time is it? Why, there's that diving match off Ella Muncy's raft!" Lady Wrench exclaimed. "I've got fifty pounds on the Grand Duke; and directly afterward there's the mannequin show for the smartest bathing-dresses; I've given a prize for that myself."

Mrs. Lullmer had taken a stick of rouge from her mesh-bag, and was critically redecorating her small pensive face. "Coming, Cliffe?" she negligently asked. "You're one of the judges of the diving match, aren't you?"

Cliffe Wheater had scrambled heavily to his feet, and stood casting perplexed glances about him. "I did say I'd be, I believe. Damn it all—I'd no idea it was so late . . ."

"It's always late in this place. I don't see how we any of us stand it," murmured Mrs. Lullmer. "I always say we're the real labouring classes."

Joyce Wheater still sat negligently reclined. "Very well, then; I suppose we may consider the matter settled."

"Settled—settled? Why, what do you mean?" Wheater stammered uneasily from the threshold.

"We came here to decide about the children, I believe. I assume that you agree that I'm to keep my own."

"Keep them? Keep them? I agree to no such thing. Martin, here, knows what my conditions are. I've never agreed to any others, and never shall—"

"Ormerod! Ormerod! Where the deuce is Gerald Ormerod? He's next on the diving programme, and Mrs. Muncy's just sent word to say that everything's being held up—oh, here you are, Gerald! Come along, for God's sake, or I shall catch it . . ."

A bronzed young amphibian, dripping and sputtering from the sea, had snatched back the tent flap, singled out Gerald Ormerod, still supine in his corner, and dragged him to his feet. "Dash it, wake up, old man, or there'll be no end of a rumpus."

Joyce Wheater sprang into sudden activity. "Gerald, Gerald— but of course you mustn't miss your turn! Cliffe, is the launch there to take us out to the raft? How can I have forgotten all about it?" She addressed herself plaintively to Boyne. "That's what always happens—whenever there's any question of the children, I forget about everything else . . ."

Wheater laid a persuasive hand on Boyne's shoulder. "You see how it is, old man. In this hell of a place there's never any time for anything. See here—come along with us to this diving match, won't you? The sea's so calm I've had the launch lying to out there ever since lunch; we'll be out at the raft in no time . . . No? You won't? Well—sorry . . . it's a pretty sight. To-morrow then . . . Oh, you're really off to-morrow morning, are you? Can't see why you don't stay on a day or two, now you're here. Of course the children are all right where they are for the present—we all know that. And if you stayed on for a day or two we could go into the whole thing quietly . . . No? Well, then—why, yes, tonight, of course. Tell you what, old man: you and Joyce and I will go out to the 'Fancy Girl' after dinner, and talk the whole thing out by ourselves. That suit you?"

BOOK III

Chapter XVII

O N the afternoon of the fourth day Boyne stood again in the sitting-room of the *châlet* facing the Cristallo group.

He had wired to Judith Wheater: "All right, don't worry"; but to Mrs. Sellars he had made no sign. He knew she did not wholly approve of his journey, though she had made no unfavourable comment, and had even offered of her own accord to keep an eye on the *Pension Rosenglüh* in his absence. It was not necessary for Rose Sellars to formulate objections; they were latent everywhere in her delicate person, in the movements of her slim apprehensive fingers, the guarded stir of her lashes. But the sense of their lurking there, vigilant guardians of the threshold, gave a peculiar quality to every token of her approval. Boyne told himself that she was not a denier, but that rarer being, a chooser; and he was almost certain where her choice would lie when all the facts were before her.

She was out when he reached the *châlet*, and his conviction strengthened as he sat awaiting her. It drew its strength from the very atmosphere of the place—its self-sufficing harmony. "*Willkommen, suesser Daemmerschein!*" His apostrophe took in the mighty landscape which overhung him; the sense of peace flowed in on him from those great fastnesses of sun and solitude, with which the little low-ceilinged room, its books and flowers, the bit of needle-work in the armchair, the half-written letter on the desk, had the humble kinship of quietness and continuity. "I'd forgotten that anything had any meaning," he thought to himself as he let the spell of the place weave its noiseless net about him.

"Martin—but how tired you look!" She was on the threshold, their hands and lips together. He remembered that kiss afterward . . . She lingered close, her arms on his shoulders. "I didn't even know you'd got back." There was the faintest shadow of reproach in her tone.

"I didn't know till the last minute when I could get away—I just jumped into the first train," he explained. He was conscious of the weariness in his voice. He passed his hand over his eyes as though to see if it would brush away her image, or if there were still women like her in the world, all made of light and reason. "Dear!" he said, more to himself than her.

"You've failed?" Her eyes were full of an unmixed sympathy; there was nothing in them to remind him that they had foreseen his failure.

"No," he exclaimed, "I've succeeded!"

"Oh—." He fancied he detected a hint of flatness in the rejoinder; there are occasions, he knew, when one has to resign oneself to the hearing of good news. But no; he was unfair. It was not that, it was only the echo of his own fatigue. For, as she said, he was tired—thoroughly tired . . .

She continued, with a faint smile: "You don't look like somebody who has succeeded."

"I daresay not. I feel rather like one of the fellows they let down into a disused well, and haul up half-asphyxiated . . ."

"It was—asphyxiating?"

"Some of it; most of it. But I'm coming to. And I've got what I wanted." He returned her smile, and sat down beside her.

"How wonderful! You mean to say you've reconciled the Wheaters?"

"I've reconciled them to the idea of not separating the children—for the present, at any rate."

"Oh, Martin—splendid!" She was really warming to the subject now. Her face glowed with a delicate appreciation. "It will do Terry more good than all the Alps and Dolomites piled on top of one another."

"Yes; and Judith too, incidentally." He had no intention of not including Judith in his victory.

"Of course; but Judith's a young lady who is eminently capable of fighting her own battles," Mrs. Sellars smoothly rejoined.

"She ought to be—she's had to fight everybody else's."

He leaned his head against the back of his armchair, and wondered what had become of the glow with which he had entered the room. It had vanished instantly under the cool touch of Mrs. Sellars's allusion to Judith. He had succeeded, it was true: there could be no doubt that he had succeeded. The mere fact of gaining time was nine tenths of the battle; and that he had already achieved. But already, too, he was beginning to wonder how he was to fit Rose Sellars into the picture of his success. It was curious: when they were apart it was always her courage and her ardour that he felt; as soon as they came together again she seemed hemmed in by little restrictions and inhibitions.

"Do tell me just what happened," she said.

"Well—at the very last minute they decided to make me, informally, into the children's guardian: a sort of trial-guardian, you might call it."

"A trial-guardian?" Her intonation, and the laugh that followed it, lifted the term into the region of the absurd. "What a jolly thing to be a trial-guardian!"

"Well, I'm not so sure." Boyne faced her irritably. "It's not a joke, you know."

"I shan't know what it is till you explain."

Explain—explain! Yes; he knew now that the explaining was just what he was dodging away from. To Judith and Terry no explanations would be necessary. He would only have to say: "It's all right," and be smothered in hugs and jubilations. Those two would never think of asking for reasons—life had not accustomed them to expect any. But here sat lovely Logic, her long hands clasped attentively—

"Oh, by Jove!" Boyne exclaimed, clapping his own hands first on one pocket, then on another. "Here's something I got for you in Venice."

He drew forth a small parcel, stringless and shapeless, as parcels generally seemed to be when they emerged from his pockets, unwrapped the paper, and pressed the catch of a morocco box. The lid flew open, and revealed a curious crystal pendant in a network of worn enamel.

"Oh, the lovely thing! For me?"

"Oh, no; not that," he stammered. He jerked the trinket back, wrapped the box up, and pushed it into his pocket with the exasperated sense of blushing like a boy over his blunder.

"But, Martin—"

"Here—." He delved deeper, pulled out another parcel, in wrappings equally untidy, and took up one of the long hands lying on her knee. "This is for you." He slipped on her fourth finger a sapphire set in diamonds. She lowered her lids on it in gentle admiration. "It's much too beautiful," her lips protested. Then her mockery sparkled up at him. "Only, you've put it on the wrong hand—at least, if it's meant for our engagement."

"Looks as if it were, doesn't it?" he bantered back; but inwardly he was thinking: "Yes, that's just the trouble—it looks like the engagement ring any other fellow would have given to any other woman. Nothing in the world to do with her and me." Aloud he said: "I hadn't time to find what I wanted—" and then realised that this was hardly a way of bettering his case. "I wanted something so awfully different for you," he blundered on.

"Well, your wanting that makes it different—to me," she said; and added, more tepidly: "Besides, it's lovely." She held out her left hand, and he slipped the jewel on the proper finger. "It's rotten," he grumbled. The ring had cost him more than he could afford, it had failed to please her, he saw himself that it was utterly commonplace—and saw also that she would never forgive him for pocketing the trinket he had first produced, which was nothing in itself, but had struck her fancy as soon as she knew it was not meant for her. Should he pull it out again, and ask her to accept it? No; after what had passed that was impossible. Judith Wheater, if he had been trying an engagement ring on her finger (preposterous fancy!) would have blurted out at once that she preferred the trinket he had shoved back into his pocket. But such tactlessness was unthinkable in Mrs. Sellars. Not for the world, he knew, would she have let him guess that she had given the other ornament a thought.

She sat turning her hand from side to side and diligently admiring the ring. "And now—do tell me just what happened."

"Well—first, of course, a lot of talk."

He settled himself in his chair, and tried to take up the narrative. But wherever he grasped it, the awkward thing seemed to tumble out of his hold, as if, in that respect too, he were always taking the wrong parcel out of his pocket. To begin with, it was so difficult to explain to Mrs. Sellars that, after the Wheaters had been reassured as to the safety and wellbeing of the children, the negotiations had been carried on piecemeal, desultorily, parenthetically, between swims and sun-baths, cocktails and fox-trots, poker and baccara—and, as a rule, in the presence of all the conflicting interests.

To make Mrs. Sellars understand that Lady Wrench, her husband and Gerald Ormerod had assisted at the debates as a matter of course was in itself a laborious business; to convey to her that Mrs. Lullmer—still notorious as the former Mrs. Westway—had likewise been called upon to participate, as Joyce's possible successor, was to place too heavy a strain on her imagination. Her exquisite aloofness had kept her in genuine ignorance of the compromises and promiscuities of modern life, and left on her hands the picture of a vanished world wherein you didn't speak to people who were discredited, or admit rivals or enemies to your confidence; and she punctuated Boyne's narrative with murmurs of dismay and incredulity.

"But in that crowd," Boyne explained, "no man is another man's enemy for more than a few minutes, and no woman is any other woman's rival. Either they forget they've quarrelled, or some social necessity—usually a party that none of them can bear to miss—forces them together, and makes it easier to bury their differences. But generally it's a simple case of forgetting. Their memories are as short as a savage's, and the feuds that savages remember have dropped out. They recall only the other primitive needs—food, finery, dancing. I suppose we *are* relapsing into a kind of bloodless savagery," Boyne concluded.

Besides, he went on, in the Wheater set they could deal with things only collectively; alone, they became helpless and inarticulate. They lived so perpetually in the lime-light that they required an audience—an audience made up of their own kind. Before each other they shouted and struck attitudes; again like savages. But the chief point was that nobody could stay angry—not however much they tried. It was too much trouble, and might involve too many inconveniences, interfere with too many social arrangements. When all was said and done, all they asked was not to be bothered—and it was by gambling on that requirement that he had finally gained his point.

"And your point is, exactly—"

Well, as he got closer to it, Boyne was not even sure that it could be defined as a point. It was too shapeless and undecided; but he hoped it would serve for a time—and time was everything; especially for Terry . . .

"They've agreed to leave the children together, and to leave them here, for the next three or four months. The longest to bring round was Lady Wrench. Her husband has taken a fancy to Zinnie, and he's so mortally bored by life in general that his wife clutches at anything that may amuse him. Luckily, according to the terms of the divorce—"

"Which divorce?" Mrs. Sellars interpolated, as though genuinely anxious to keep her hand on all the clues.

"Wheater *versus* Zinnia Lacrosse. It was Wheater who got the divorce from the present Lady Wrench. Legally he has the final say about Zinnie, so the mother had to give in, though she has a right to see the child at stated intervals. But of course my battle royal was over Chipstone; if the Wheaters had insisted on keeping Chipstone till their own affairs were settled in court the whole combination would have been broken up."

"And how did you contrive to rescue Chipstone?"

Boyne sank down more deeply into his armchair, and looked up at the low ceiling. Then he straightened himself, and brought his gaze to the level of Mrs. Sellars's. "By promising to stay here and keep an eye on the children myself. That's my trial-guardianship." He gave a slight laugh, which she failed to echo.

"Martin!"

His eyes continued to challenge hers. "Well—?"

She turned the sapphire hesitatingly on her finger. "But these children—you'd never even heard of them till you met them on board your steamer a few weeks ago . . ."

"No; that's true."

"You've taken over a pretty big responsibility."

"I like responsibilities."

Mrs. Sellars was still brooding over her newly imprisoned finger. "It's very generous of you to assume this one in such a hurry. Usually one doesn't have to go out of one's way to find rather more of them than one can manage. But in this case, I wonder—"

"You wonder?"

"Well, I had understood from Terry—and also from your friend Judith—that what all the children really want is to go to America: to Mrs. Wheater's mother, isn't it?"

"Yes; that's it; and I hope they'll pull it off by-and-by. But at present the Wheaters won't hear of it. I never for a moment supposed they'd consent to putting the ocean between themselves and Chip. My only chance was to persuade them that, now

Terry's in the mountains, they'd better leave him here, and the others with him, till the hot weather's over. With those people it's always a question of the least resistance—of temporizing and postponing. My plan saved everybody a certain amount of mental effort; so they all ended by agreeing to it. But of course it's merely provisional."

"Happily," Mrs. Sellars smiled; and added, as if to correct the slight acerbity of the comment: "For you must see, dear, that you're taking a considerable risk for the future—"

"What future?"

"Why—suppose anything goes wrong during these next few months? You'll be answerable for whatever may happen. With seven children—and one of them already grown up!"

Boyne frowned, and stirred uneasily in his chair. "If you mean Judith, in some ways she's as much of a child as the youngest of them."

Mrs. Sellars smiled confidentially at her ring. "So a man would think, I suppose. But you forget that I've had four days alone with her . . . She's a young lady with very definite views."

"I should hope so!"

"I agree with you that it makes her more interesting—but conceivably it might lead to complications."

"What sort of complications?"

"You ought to know better than I do—since you tell me you've been frequenting the late Mrs. Westway at the Lido. Judith doesn't pretend to hide the fact that she lived for a summer in the bosom of that edifying family . . ."

"She doesn't know it's anything to hide. That's what's so touching—"

"And so terrifying. But I won't sit here preaching prudence; you'd only hate me for it. And all this time those poor infants are waiting." She stood up with one of her sudden changes of look and tone; as if a cloud had parted, shedding a ray of her lost youth on her. He noticed for the first time that she was all in white, a rose on her breast, and a shady hat hanging from her arm. "Do go down and see them at once, dear. It's getting late. I'll walk with you to the foot of the hill; then I must come back and write some letters . . ." He smiled at the familiar formula, and she took up his smile. "Yes; really important letters—one of them to Aunt Julia," she bantered back. "And besides, the children will want to have you all to themselves." Magnanimously she added: "I must say they all behaved beautifully while you were away. They seemed to feel that they must do you credit. And as for Terry—I wish he were mine! When the break-up comes, as of course it will, why shouldn't you and I adopt him?"

She put on her hat, and linked her arm in Boyne's for the walk down the hill; but at the fringe of the wood, where the path dipped to the high road, she left him.

"You'll come back and dine? I've got some news for you too," she said as he turned down to the village.

Chapter XVIII

Recent memories of Armistice Day—remote ones of Mafeking Night, which he had chanced to experience in London—paled for Boyne in the uproar raised by the little Wheaters when, entering their *pension* dining-room, he told them that everything was all right.

He had not imagined that seven could be so many. The miracle of the loaves and fishes seemed as nothing to the sudden multiplication of arms, legs and lungs about that rural supper-table. At one end of the expanse of coarse linen and stout crockery, Miss Scope, rigid and spectacled, sat dispensing jam without fear or favour; at the other Judith was cutting bread and butter in complete unawareness of her immortal model. Between the two surged a sea of small heads, dusky, ruddy, silver-pale, all tossing and mixing about the golden crest of Chipstone, throned in his umpire's chair. For a moment, as usual, Bun and Zinnie dominated the scene; then Terry, still pale, but with new life in his eyes, caught his cap from the rack with a call for three cheers to which the others improvised a piercing echo. ("Luckily we're the only boarders just now," Miss Scope remarked to Boyne as he pressed her hand.)

In this wonderful world nobody asked any questions; nobody seemed to care for any particulars; their one thought was to bestow on their ambassador the readiest token of their gratitude, from Blanca's cool kiss to the damp and strangulating endearments of Beechy. To Boyne it was literally like a dip into a quick sea, with waves that burnt his eyes, choked his throat and ears, but stung him, body and brain, to fresh activity. "And now let's kiss him all over again—and it's my turn first!" Zinnie rapturously proposed; and as he abandoned himself once more to the battering of the breakers he caught a small voice piping: "We suppose you've brought some presents for us, Martin."

The law which makes men progressively repeople the world with persons of their own age and experience had led Boyne, as he grew older, to regard human relations as more and more ruled by reason; but whenever he dipped into the universe of the infant Wheaters, where all perspective ceased, and it was far more urgent to know what presents he had brought than what fate had been meted out to them by their respective parents, he felt the joy of plunging back into reality.

The presents were there, and nobody had been forgotten, as the rapid unpacking of a small suit-case showed—nobody, that is, but Judith, who stood slightly apart, affecting an air of grown-up amusement, while Blanca and the little girls were hung with trinkets, and Bun made jubilant by an electric lamp. Even Miss Scope had an appropriate reticule, Nanny a lavishly garnished needle-case; and the bottom of the box was crammed with books for Terry.

The distributing took so long, and the ensuing disputes and counter-claims were so difficult of adjustment, that twilight was slipping down the valley when Boyne said to Judith: "Come and take a turn, and I'll tell you all about it."

They walked along the road to a path which led up the hillside opposite to the hotels, and from there began to mount slowly toward the receding sunlight. Judith, unasked, had slipped her arm through Boyne's, and the nearness of her light young body was like wings to him. "What a pity it's getting dark—I believe I could climb to one of those ruby peaks!" he said, throwing his head back with a deep breath; and she instantly rejoined: "Let's run back and get Bun's lamp; then we could."

Boyne laughed, and went on, in a voice of leisurely satisfaction: "Oh, Bun wouldn't part with that lamp—not yet. Besides, we're very well as we are; and there'll be lots of other opportunities."

"There will? Oh, Martin—they're really going to let us stay?" Her strong young hands imprisoned him in a passionate grasp.

"Well, for a time. I made them see it was Terry's best chance."

"Of course it is! And, Martin—they'll leave us all together? Chip and all?"

"Every man of you—for the summer, at any rate." They had stopped in the fern-fringed path, and he stood above her, smiling down into her blissful incredulous eyes. "There's one condition, though—" Her gaze darkened, and he added: "You're all to be accountable to me. I've promised your people to keep an eye on you."

"You mean you're going to stay here with us?" Her lips trembled with the tears she was struggling to keep back, and he thought to himself: "It's too much for a child's face to express—." Aloud he said: "Let's sit down and watch the sunset. This tree-trunk is a pretty good proscenium box."

They sat down, and he set forth at length the history of his negotiations. Complicated as the narrative was, it was easier to relate to his present hearer than to Mrs. Sellars, not only because fewer elucidations were necessary, but because none of the details he gave shocked or astonished Judith. The tale he told evidently seemed to her a mere bald statement of a matter-of-course affair, and she was too much occupied with its practical results to give a thought to its remoter bearings. She listened attentively to Boyne's report of the final agreement, and when he had ended, said only: "I suppose father's made some arrangement about paying our bills?"

"Your father's opened an account for me: Miss Scope and I are to be your ministers of finance."

She received this in silence; for the first time since his return he felt that the news he brought was still overshadowed for her. At last she asked: "Was father awfully angry . . . you know . . . about that money?"

The question roused Boyne with a start. He perceived that in his struggle to adjust conflicting interests he too had lost sight of the moral issue. And how confess to Judith that, as for her father, he had hardly been aware of it? He felt that it was a moment for prevarication. "Of course your father was angry—thoroughly angry—about the whole thing. Anybody would have been."

She lowered her voice to insist: "But I mean about my taking his money?"

"Well, he's forgiven you for that, at any rate."

"Has he—really and truly?" Her voice lifted again joyfully. "Terry was sure he never would."

Boyne turned about on her in surprise. "Terry—then you told him after all?"

She made a mute sign of assent. "I had to."

"Well, I understand that." He gave her hand a little squeeze. "I'm glad you did."

"He was frightfully upset, you know. And furious with me. I was afraid I'd made him more ill. He wouldn't believe me at first. He said if I had no more moral sense than that, the first thing I knew I'd land in prison."

"Oh—." Boyne could not restrain a faint laugh.

"That didn't worry me very much, though," Judith confessed in a more cheerful tone, "because I've seen a good deal more of life than Terry, and I've known other girls who've done what I did, and none of them ever went to prison."

This did not seem as reassuring to Boyne as it did to the speaker; but the hour for severity was over, the words of rebuke died on his lips. At last he said: "The worst of it was hurting Terry, wasn't it?" and she nodded: "Yes."

For a while after that they sat without speaking, till she asked him if he thought the Wheaters had already started divorce proceedings. To this he could only answer that it looked so, but he still hoped they might calm down and think better of it. She received this with a gesture of incredulity, and merely remarked: "There might have been a chance if Syb Lullmer hadn't been mixed up in it."

"I do wish you wouldn't call that woman by her Christian name," Boyne interrupted.

Judith looked at him with a gentle wonder. "She wouldn't mind. Everybody else does." She clearly assumed that he was reproving her for failing in respect to Mrs. Lullmer.

"That's not what I meant. But she's such a beast."

"Oh, well—." Judith's shrug implied that the epithet was too familiar to her to have kept more than a tinge of obloquy. "I rather hope she won't marry father, though."

"I hope to God she won't. What I'm gambling on is that he and your mother will get so homesick for you children that they'll patch things up on your account."

Her smile kept its soft incredulity. "They don't often, you know; parents don't."

"Well, anyhow, you've got a reprieve, and you must make the most of it."

"I wish you'd say 'we,' not 'you,' Martin."

"Why of course it's 'we,' my dear—that is, as long as you all behave yourselves."

They both laughed at this, and then fell silent, facing the sunset, and immersed, in their different ways, in the overwhelming glory of the spectacle. Judith, Boyne knew, did not feel sunsets as Rose Sellars did—they appealed to a different order of associations, and she would probably have been put to it to distinguish the quality of their splendour from that of fireworks at the Lido, or a brilliant *finale* at the Russian ballet. But something of the celestial radiance seemed to reach her, remote yet enfolding as a guardian wing. "It's lovely here," she breathed, her hand in Boyne's.

He remembered, at a similar moment, Rose Sellars's quoting:

> *All the peaks soar, but one the rest excels;*
> *Clouds overcome it;*
> *No, yonder sparkle is the citadel's*
> *Circling its summit—*

and he murmured the words half aloud.

Judith's pressure tightened ardently on his hand. "Oh, Martin, how beautifully you do describe things! The words you find are not like anybody else's. Terry says you ought to be a writer."

"Well, in this case, unluckily, somebody found the words before me."

"Oh—." Her enthusiasm flagged. She hazarded: "Mrs. Sellars?"

He gave a little chuckle at her sharpness. "In a way, yes—but, as a matter of fact, Robert Browning got ahead of both of us."

This seemed to give her a certain satisfaction. "Then she just cribbed it from him? Is he another friend of hers?"

"Yes; and will be of yours some day, I hope. He died long before you were born; but you'll find some of the best of him in one of the books I brought to Terry."

"Oh, he's just an author, you mean," she murmured, as if the state were a strictly posthumous one. Her attention always had a tendency to wander at the mention of books, and he thought she was probably a little vexed at having been betrayed into a conversational slip; but presently, with a return of her habitual buoyancy: "I'd rather hear you talk than anybody who's dead," she declared.

"All right; I'll make it a rule to give you only my own vintage," he agreed, gazing out past her into the light. They continued to sit there in silence, the sea of night creeping softly up to them, till at length they were caught in its chill touch. Boyne got reluctantly to his feet. "Come along, child. Time to go down," he said.

"Oh, not down yet—up, up, up!" She caught his arm again, pulling him with all her young strength along the pine-scented steep to where the mystery of the forest drew down to meet them. "I want to climb and climb—don't you? I want to stay up all night, as if we were coming home at sunrise from a ball. It's like a great ballroom over there, isn't it," she cried, pointing to the west, "with the lights pouring out of a million windows?"

Boyne laughed, and suffered himself to be led onward. The air on that height was as fresh as youth, and all about them were the secret scents that dew and twilight waken into life. He knew that he and Judith ought to be turning homeward; but, even if she had released his captive arm, it was growing too dark to consult his watch. Besides, the wandering man in him, the man used to mountains, to long lonely tramps, to the hush and mystery of nights in the open, felt himself in the toils of the old magic. It was no longer Judith drawing him on, but the night itself beckoning him to fresh heights. The child at his side had travelled with him into the beauty as far as she could go, and now he needed nothing from her but the warmth of her nearness. His highest moments had always been solitary . . .

She seemed to guess that there was nothing else to say, and they continued to mount the hill in silence. As they rose the air turned colder, the fires faded, and above them arched a steel-blue heaven starred with ruddy points which grew keen and white as darkness deepened. It was not till they passed out of the fringes of the forest to an open crag above the valley, and saw the village lights sprinkling the black fields far below, that Boyne unwillingly woke to the sense of time and place.

"Oh, by Jove—you must come!" he exclaimed, swinging round to guide his companion down the ledge.

She made no answer, but turned and followed him along the descending path. He could feel that she was too tired and peaceful for reluctance. She moved beside him like a sleepy child bringing back an apronful of flowers from a happy holiday; and the fact of having reassured her so quickly awed Boyne a little, as if he had meddled with destiny. But it was pleasant, for once, to play the god, and he let himself drift away into visions of a vague millennium where all the grown people knew what they wanted, and if ever it happened that they didn't, the children had the casting vote.

By the time they reached the *pension*, and Judith had loosed her hold of Boyne's arm, he was afraid to look at his watch, but pushed her through the gate with a quick goodnight—and then, a moment later, called to her in an imperious whisper. "Judith!" She hurried back to the summons.

"Did you really think I hadn't brought you any present?"

She gave an excited little laugh. "N—no; I really thought perhaps you had; only—"

"Only what?"

"I thought you'd forgotten some one else's, and had imagined I shouldn't much mind your taking mine, because I'm so much older than the others . . ."

"Well, of course I should have imagined that; but here it is."

He pulled out the parcel he had inadvertently produced in Mrs. Sellars's sitting-room, and Judith caught it to her with a gasp of pleasure.

"Oh, Martin—"

"There; own up that you'd have been fearfully sold if I'd forgotten you."

She answered solemnly: "If you'd forgotten me I should have died of it."

"Well—run off with you; we're hours late," he admonished her.

"Mayn't I look at it before you go?"

"You baby, how could you see in the dark? Besides, I tell you there's no time."

"Not even time to kiss you for it, Martin?"

"No," he cried, slamming the gate shut, and starting up the hill toward his hotel at a run.

When they started on their walk nothing had been farther from Boyne's mind than this disposal of the crystal pendant, though it was for Judith that the trinket had been chosen. Since Mrs. Sellars, owing to his blunder, had seen and coveted it, he felt a certain awkwardness about letting it appear on Judith's neck, and decided that his little friend must again be left out in the general distribution of presents. But during their walk in the mountain dusk, while she hung on his arm, pressed close by the intruding fir-branches, he needed more and more to think of her as a child, and, thinking thus, to treat her as one. He knew how the child in her must have ached at being left out when he unpacked his gifts; and when the time came to say goodnight it was irresistible to heal that ache. There was no way of doing it but to take the pendant from his pocket—the pendant which he had meant for her, and which it had taken so long to unearth at the Venetian antiquary's that there was no time for much thought of Mrs. Sellars's—the pendant which was Judith's by right because, like her, it was odd and exquisite and unaccountable.

"If only she doesn't parade it up at the *châlet*!" the coward in him thought, as he climbed the hill. But all the while he knew it was exactly what she would do.

"Oh, well, damn—after all, I chose it for her," he grumbled, as if that justified them both.

In the *châlet* sitting-room Mrs. Sellars, in her cool evening dress, looked up the table at which she sat, not writing a letter but reading one. She laid it down thoughtfully as he entered.

"I'm afraid it's awfully late—I hadn't time to go to the hotel and brush up; you don't mind?" he said, blinking a little in the lamplight, and passing his hand through his rumpled hair. As he bent to kiss her his glance fell on the admonishing needles of the little travelling clock at her elbow. "You don't mean to say it's after nine?"

"What does it matter? As a matter of fact, it's after half-past. I was only afraid something had gone wrong about the children."

He tossed his hat down with a laugh. "Bless you, no! Everything's as right as right. But I had to get the Lido out of my lungs; and a long tramp was the only way."

Her smile told him how much she loved him for hating the Lido. "And what do you think my news is? You know I said I had something to tell you. Mr. Dobree is coming here to see me—he arrives next week." She announced the fact as if it were not only important, but even exciting.

"Oh, damn Mr. Dobree!" Boyne rejoined with a careless benevolence. The door had opened on the candlelight of their little dinner-table, on its sparkle of white wine and smell of wild strawberries and village bread. "Well, this is good enough for me," Boyne said, as he dropped into the seat opposite Mrs. Sellars with a sense of proprietorship which made Mr. Dobree's movements seem wholly negligible.

Chapter XIX

THE next day there occurred, with a fatal punctuality, exactly what Boyne had foreseen. Mrs. Sellars had invited Judith, Terry and Blanca to lunch; and when they appeared Mrs. Sellars's eye instantly lit on the crystal pendant, Judith's on the sapphire ring. The mutual reconnaissance was swift and silent as the crossing of search-lights in a night sky. Judith said nothing; but Blanca, as Mrs. Sellars bent to kiss her, raised her hostess's hand with an admiring exclamation. "A new ring! What a beauty! I never saw you wear it before."

Mrs. Sellars smiled, and tapped Blanca's cheek with her free hand. "What sharp eyes! But everybody seems to have had a present from Venice—so why shouldn't I?"

Blanca returned the smile, lifting her own wrist to display a hoop of pink crystal. "Isn't mine sweet? Nobody finds presents like Martin."

"So I thought when he showed me Judith's last night."

Mrs. Sellars turned to the older girl, but not to kiss her. She reserved her endearments for the younger children, and merely laid a friendly touch on Judith's shoulder. "Such a wonder, that pendant—I never saw one like it. Decidedly, not Venetian; seventeenth century Spanish, perhaps? It's a puzzle. You're lucky, my dear, to have a *connaisseur* to choose your presents."

That was all—and then a jolly lunch, simple, easy, full of chaff and laughter, Mrs. Sellars, always a perfect hostess, was at her best with Terry and Blanca. The boy touched and interested her, the little girl (Boyne divined) subtly flattered her by a wide-eyed but tactful admiration. Boyne wondered if Mrs. Sellars had noticed how Blanca's clear gray eyes darkened with envy at the praise of the crystal pendant. What a fool he had been not to give the crystal to Blanca, and the tuppenny bracelet to Judith, who would have liked it best because it came from him! Decidedly, he was doomed to blunder in his dealings with women, even when they were no more than little girls. Meanwhile Terry was telling Mrs. Sellars about the books Boyne had brought him, and how he and Judith had already hunted down Boyne's quotation from "The Grammarian's Funeral"—"You know, that splendid one he told Judith yesterday, about 'all the peaks soar'; she came home last night saying it over and over for fear she'd forget it, and woke me up to hunt for it before she went to bed."

"It was so splendid, hearing it up there on the mountain, in the dark, with the stars coming out," Judith glowed, taking up the tale, while Blanca ingenuously added: "It was so late when Judy got home that we were all asleep, and Scopy had to go down and let her in. Did you see Scopy in her crimping-pins, Martin; or had you gone when she opened the door?"

"Yes—the coming of twilight up on the heights is something to remember," Mrs. Sellars intervened, letting her eyes rest attentively on Boyne's before she turned them again to Terry. "But there are better things than that in Browning, you know. Bring me your book to-morrow, and I'll show you . . ."

It all went off perfectly—and Boyne, when he started the children homeward after lunch, was wondering whether tact were as soothing as a summer breeze, or as terrible as an army with banners.

He was to drop the young Wheaters at their *pension*, and afterward meet Mrs. Sellars at the post-office for a climb in the direction of Misurina. At the corner of the highroad descending to Cortina he signalled the hotel omnibus, packed in the twins, and walked on with Judith. At the moment he would rather have escaped from the whole party; but Judith had declared her intention of walking, and he could not do otherwise than go with her. They waited under the trees for the omnibus to sweep on with its load of dust and passengers, and almost at once Judith said: "I suppose you're engaged to Mrs. Sellars, aren't you, Martin?"

The suddenness of the question struck him like a blow, and he realised for the first time that he had never spoken to Rose Sellars about making their engagement known. He had never even asked her if she had broken the news to her formidable aunt, or to the galaxy of minor relatives with whom she maintained her incessant exchange of letters. Her insistence that their marriage should be put off for nearly half a year seemed to make the whole question too remote for immediate decisions. "I suppose I ought to have asked her if she wanted it announced," he thought, reflecting remorsefully that his long exile had made him too careless of the social observances. He turned an irritated eye on Judith. "What in the world put such an idea into your head?"

"Why, your bringing her a ring from Venice, and her putting it on the finger where engagement rings are worn," Judith replied with a smiling promptness.

"Oh, that's the finger, is it?" Boyne said, temporising; and then, with an abrupt clutch at simplification: "Yes; I am engaged to Mrs. Sellars. But I don't think she wants it spoken of at present."

He turned his gaze away to the long white road glinting through the trees under which he and Judith were withdrawn. Things happened so suddenly and overwhelmingly in Judith's face that he did not feel equal to what might be going on there till he had steadied his gaze by a protracted study of the landscape. When he looked at her again he received the shock of smiling lips and eyes, and two arms thrown filially about him.

"You darling old Martin, I'm so glad! At least I am if you are—really and truly?"

Her hug was almost as suffocating as Zinnie's, and given—he divined it instantly—with the same whole-hearted candour. "So Blanca was right after all! How lovely it must be to be in love! For I suppose that's the reason why you're marrying? I know you're awfully romantic, though you sometimes put on such a gruff manner; I'm sure you wouldn't marry just for position, or for money, or to regularise an old *liaison*; would you?"

"An old *liaison*?" Boyne laughed, but with a touch of vexation. "The ideas you've picked up—and the lingo! You absurd child—why, 'regularise' isn't even English . . . And can't you see, can't you imagine, that a man's first need is to—to respect the woman he hopes to marry?"

Judith received this with a puzzled frown. "Oh, I can *see* it; I have, often—in books, and at the movies. But I can't imagine it, exactly. I should have thought wanting to give her a good hug came before anything."

Boyne shrugged impatiently. Things that seemed funny, and utterly guileless, when she said them to others, shocked him when she commented on his private concerns in the vocabulary of her tribe. "What's the use? You're only a baby, and you repeat things like a parrot, as all children do. Mrs. Sellars is the most perfect, the most exquisite . . ." He broke off, feeling that such asseverations led nowhere in particular, and continued at a tangent: "I can tell you one thing—I should never have dared to take on the job of looking after you children if she hadn't been here—"

Judith's face fell. "Oh, is she going to stay all summer, then?"

"I devoutly hope so! Being with somebody like her is so exactly what . . ." This, again, seemed to land him in a sort of rhetorical blind alley, and he stepped down from it into the dust of the highroad. "Come along; we mustn't dawdle. I'm due at the post-office." He was aware that a settled anger was possessing him, he hardly knew why. Hardly—yet just under the surface of his mind there stirred the uneasy sense that he was perhaps disappointed by Judith's prompt congratulations. Half an hour earlier, he would have said that her approval would add the final touch to his happiness; that there was nothing he wanted more than to have her show herself in fact the child he was perpetually calling her. "The youngest of them all"—that was how he had described her to Mrs. Sellars. Was it possible he had not meant what he said?

He was roused by Judith's squeeze on his arm. "I don't know why you're so cross with me, old Martin. I do really want anything you want . . ."

"That's a good Judy . . . and what rot, dear, thinking I'm cross. Only, remember, it's your secret and mine, and not another soul's." After all, he tried to tell himself, Judith's knowing of his engagement was already a relief. It would do away with no end of hedging and prevaricating. And he was sure he could trust to Judith's discretion; sure of it without her added pressure on his arm, and the solemn: "On Scopy's book!" which had become the tribal oath of the little Wheaters. Boyne had sometimes winced at Judith's precocious discretion, as another proof of what she had been exposed to; now he hailed in it a guaranty of peace. "Perhaps there's something to be said for not keeping children in cotton wool—for she *is* only a child!" he repeated to himself, insistently.

That very evening, while he and Mrs. Sellars were talking over the likelihood of picking up some kind of a tutor for Terry, she asked irrelevantly: "By the way, do the children know of our engagement?"

Contradictory answers rose to Boyne's lips, and he gulped them down to mumble: "I didn't suppose I was authorized to tell anybody."

"But hasn't anybody guessed?"

"Well—as a matter of fact, Judith has. Today. I can't imagine—"

Mrs. Sellars smiled. "My ring, of course. Trust Blanca, too! It was stupid of me not to think of it. But perhaps it's better—"

"Much better."

She pondered. "Only I'd rather no one else knew—at least for the present. Out of regard for Aunt Julia—till I've heard from her." Boyne, relieved, expressed his complete agreement. "Besides," she continued, "I like it's being our secret, don't you? We won't even tell Mr. Dobree."

"Oh, particularly not Mr. Dobree," Boyne replied emphatically.

Two days later Mr. Dobree arrived; and Boyne learned that an event which seems negligible before it happens may fill the picture when it becomes a fact. The prospect of Mr. Dobree's arrival had now become the fact of Mr. Dobree's presence; and Mr. Dobree, though still spare and nimble for a man approaching sixty (he was ready, and glad, to tell you to what exercises he owed it), took up a surprising amount of room. He was like somebody who travels with a lot of unwieldy luggage—his luggage being, as it were, the very absence of it, being his tact, his self-effacingness, his general neatness and compactness. Wherever you turned, you were in the aura of Mr. Dobree's retractility, his earnest and insistent dodging out of your way, which seemed to leave behind it a presence more oppressive than any mere physical bulk—so that a dull fat man rooted in your best armchair might have been less in the way than the slim and disappearing Mr. Dobree. Mr. Dobree's tact seemed to Boyne like a parody of Mrs. Sellars's; like one of those monstrous blooms into which hybridizers transform a delicate flower. It was a "show" tact, a huge, unique, disbudded tact grown under glass, and destined to be labelled, exhibited, given a prize and a name, and a page to itself in the florists' catalogues. Such at least was Boyne's distorted vision of the new guest at the *châlet*.

Mr. Dobree (as became a man with such impedimenta) was lodged, not at Boyne's inn, but at the "Palace" where Boyne and Mrs. Sellars had once dined. From there a brisk five minutes carried him to the *châlet*; except when his urgent hospitality drew Mrs. Sellars and Boyne to the big hotel. The prompt returning of invitations was a fundamental part of Mr. Dobree's code. He seemed to think that hospitality was something a gentleman might borrow, like money, but never, in any circumstances, receive as a gift; and this obliged Mrs. Sellars to accept his repeated invitations, before, in the battle of their tacts, hers came off victorious, and she made him see that it may be more blessed to receive than to be invited out. The sapphire had vanished from her finger before Mr. Dobree's arrival; and this precaution, for which Boyne blessed her, made him, for Mr. Dobree, simply an old friend, a guest of the Sellars's in New York days, whom one could be suitably pleased to meet again.

Boyne was less pleased to meet Mr. Dobree. His coming was natural enough; and so was Mrs. Sellars's pleasure at seeing him, since he brought not only the latest news of Aunt Julia but papers which settled satisfactorily the matter of Mr. Sellars's will. Boyne had resented what promised to be a tiresome interruption of pleasant habits; but before long he discovered that Mr. Dobree's presence left him free to spend much more time with his young friends of the *Pension Rosenglüh*. This made him aware that during the last weeks he had forfeited a certain amount of his liberty, and he found himself perilously pleased to recover it. He assured Mrs. Sellars that it would look very odd to Mr. Dobree, who had come to discuss family matters with his client, if a third person were present at these discussions; and armed with this argument he proceeded to dispose of his time as he pleased.

His liberation gave a new savour to the hours spent with the little Wheaters; and as for Mr. Dobree (with whom the children had had only one brief and awe-inspiring encounter), he came in very handily as the theme of the games they were always calling on Boyne to invent. To ascertain Mr. Dobree's Christian name (Boyne told them) had long been his secret ambition; but hitherto he had not even been able to learn its first letter. A chance glimpse of Mr. Dobree's glossy suit-cases showed his initials to be A.D., and the letter A was one calculated, as Boyne said, to give them a good gallop. Indeed, he found the puzzle so absorbing that one day, when Judith remarked on his unusual absent-mindedness, he had to own that he had not been listening to what she said because all his faculties were still absorbed in the task of guessing Mr. Dobree's Christian name.

"But Mrs. Sellars must know—why don't you ask her?"

"Must know? Do you think so? I doubt it."

"But she talks of him as an old friend—as old as you."

"Even that doesn't convince me. I doubt if anybody knows Mr. Dobree's Christian name. How should they? Can you imagine anybody's ever having called him by it, or dared to ask him what it was?"

"Well, you might ask her," suggested Judith, from whose make-up a taste for abstract speculation was absent.

"Ask her? Not for the world! Suppose she did know? All our fun would be over."

"Of course it would," cried Terry, plunging into the sport. "If she knows, she mustn't be asked till we've exhausted every other possibility; must she, Martin?"

"Certainly not. I see you grasp the rules of the game. And now let's proceed by elimination. Abel—Abel's the first name in A, isn't it, Terry?"

"No! There's a Prince Aage of Denmark, or something; I saw him in 'The Tatler,' " exulted Terry.

"All right. Let's begin with Aage. Do any of you *see* Mr. Dobree as Aage?" This was dismissed with a general shout of incredulity.

"Well, then: as Abel—Abel Dobree? Don't be in a hurry: try to deal with this thing in a mood of deliberateness and impartiality."

"No, no, no—not Abel!" the assistance chorused.

"Oh, I'm going to sleep," Judith grumbled, stretching out at full length on the sunburnt grass-bank on which the party were encamped.

"Let her—for all the use she is!" Boyne jeered. "Now then—Adam?"

"Adam's a Polish name, isn't it? Who *was* Adam?" Judith opened her eyes to ask.

"A national hero, I think," said Blanca, with a diligent frown.

Miss Scope, perched higher up the bank, cut through these conjectures with a groan. "Children—children! One would think I'd brought you up like savages. Adam—"

"Oh, Scopy means the Adam in the Bible: but Mr. Dobree's parents wouldn't have called him after anybody as far away as that," Blanca shrugged; while Zinnie interposed: "Who was already dead, and couldn't have given him a lovely cup for his christening." Beechy, her face wrinkling up in sympathy at such a privation, wailed out: "Oh, poor little Mr. Dobree—"; and Boyne, recognizing the difficulty, pursued: "Aeneas, then; but he's almost as far away as Adam, I'm afraid."

This drew him into a discussion with Terry regarding the relative seniority of the Biblical and Virgilian heroes, in the intervals of which Miss Scope continued to demand despairingly: "But what in the world are you all arguing about, when we know that Adam was the First Man?"

Judith lifted her head again from its grassy pillow. With half-closed eyes she murmured to the sky: "I don't believe Mr. Dobree would care a bit if his godfather was Adam or not. He could buy himself any christening cup he liked. I believe he's a very rich man."

"Oh, then, do you think he'll give us all some lovely presents when he goes?" Zinnie promptly inferred.

"What makes you think he'll ever go?" Judith retorted, closing her eyes.

"Annibal—Annibal! Annibal begins with an A! I know because he was a Prince, my ancestor," shouted Bun, leaping back into the game.

Chapter XX

M RS. SELLARS'S social discipline was too perfect to permit her, even in emergencies, to neglect one obligation for another; and after Mr. Dobree had been for a week at Cortina she said one day to Boyne: "But I've seen nothing lately of the little Wheaters. What's become of them?"

He assured her that they were all right, but had probably been too shy to present themselves at the *châlet* since Mr. Dobree's arrival; to which Mrs. Sellars replied, with the faintest hint of tartness, that she had never had occasion to suspect the little Wheaters of being shy, and that, furthermore, Mr. Dobree did not happen to be staying at the *châlet*.

Boyne smiled. "No; but they know he's with you a good deal, and he's a more impressive figure than they're used to."

He saw that she scented irony in this, and was not wholly pleased with it. "I don't know what you mean by impressive; I didn't know anything in the world could impress the modern hotel child. But Mr. Dobree is very sorry for them, poor dears, and I'm sure it would interest him to see something of them. Why shouldn't we take them all on a picnic to-morrow? I know Mr. Dobree would like to invite them."

Boyne felt that, for all the parties concerned, the undertaking might prove formidable. He pointed out that, if Zinnie and the two Buondelmonte children were included in an all-day expedition, Miss Scope's presence would be necessary, since otherwise all Judith's energies would be absorbed in keeping the party in order; and Mrs. Sellars acquiesced: "Yes, the poor little things are dreadfully spoilt."

Boyne was secretly beginning to be of the same mind; but Mrs. Sellars could no longer criticise his young friends without rousing his instinctive opposition. "They certainly haven't had much opportunity to become little Lord Fauntleroys, if that's what you mean," he said impatiently; and his betrothed rejoined: "What I mean is that Mr. Dobree feels sorry for them because of the kind of opportunity they have had. You see, he was one of the lawyers in the Westway divorce."

Boyne gave her a quick look, in which he was conscious that his resentment flamed. "I'm hanged if I see what there can be in Mr. Dobree's mind to make him connect the Westway divorce with the Wheater children."

"Why, simply his knowledge of Judith's intimacy with that wretched drug-soaked Doll Westway, and his familiarity with the horrible details that led up to the girl's suicide. She and Judith were together at Deauville the very summer that she killed herself. Both their mothers had gone off heaven knows where. Judith proclaims the fact to every one, as you know."

Boyne had removed his eyes from Mrs. Sellars's face, and was staring out at the familiar outline of the great crimson mountains beyond the balcony. A phrase of Stevenson's about "the lovely and detested scene" (from "The Ebb-tide," he thought?) strayed through his mind as he gazed. It was hateful to him to think that he might hereafter come to associate those archangelic summits with Mrs. Lullmer's smooth impervious face, and Mr. Dobree's knowledge of the inner history of the Westway divorce.

He turned back to Mrs. Sellars. "Aren't you getting rather sick of this place?" he asked abruptly.

She gave back his irritated stare with one of genuine surprise. "Sick of what? You mean of Cortina?"

"Of the whole show." His sweeping gesture gathered up in one contemptuous handful the vast panorama of mountain, vale and forest. "I always feel that when scenery gets mixed up with our personal bothers all the virtue goes out of it—as if our worries were so many locusts, eating everything bare."

Mrs. Sellars was silent for a moment; then her hand fell on his. "I've always been afraid, dear, that this queer responsibility you've assumed was going to end by getting on your nerves—"

Boyne jumped up, drawing abruptly away from her. "Responsibility? What responsibility?" He walked across the room, turned back, and awkwardly laid an answering caress on her hair. "Gammon! It's Mr. Dobree who gets on my nerves—just a little." ("Hypocrite!" he cursed himself inwardly.) "Fact is, I liked Cortina a damned sight better when you and I and the children had it all to ourselves." He saw the light of reassurance in her averted cheek. "Just my beastly selfishness, I know—I needn't tell you that men *are* beastly selfish, need I?" He laughed, and her faint laugh echoed his.

"Mr. Dobree is going soon, I believe," she volunteered.

Boyne pulled himself together. "Well, that makes it a good deal easier to be unselfish while he's here, and I take it upon myself to accept his picnic for to-morrow. I'll drop down and announce it to the children." He flattered himself that his simulation of buoyancy had produced the desired effect, and that his parting from Mrs. Sellars was unclouded. But half way down the hill he stood suddenly still in the path, and exclaimed aloud: "But after he's gone; what then?"

The picnic was beautifully successful—one of those smooth creaseless well-oiled successes as to which one feels that at any moment it may slip from one's hold and reveal the face of failure. A very Janus of a picnic, Boyne thought . . .

To the chief actors, however, it presented no such duality, but was the perfect image of what constitutes A Good Time For The Young People, when made out of the happy union of tact and money. To Mr. Dobree it was certainly that, and he was justified in feeling that if you order the two roomiest and most balloon-tired motors obtainable, and fill enough hampers with the most succulent delicacies of a "Palace" restaurant, and are actuated throughout by the kindliest desire to give pleasure, happiness will automatically follow.

As regards the younger members of the party, it undoubtedly did. Terry was strong enough to enjoy the long day on the heights without fear of Miss Scope's thermometer; Blanca was impressed by the lavish fare which replaced their habitual bread and chocolate; and the small children were in the state of effervescence induced by freedom from lessons and the sense of being the central figures of the day.

And Judith—?

After lunch the younger members of the party trailed away with Miss Scope to hunt for wild strawberries while the others sat pillowed in moss beside a silver waterfall. Boyne, supine against his boulder, studied the scene and meditated from behind a screen of pipe smoke. Judith, a little way off, leaned luxuriously against her mossy cushion, her hat tossed aside, her head resting in the curve of an immature arm. Her profile looked small and clear against the auburn tremor of bracken turned inward by the rush of the water. A live rose burned in her cheeks, darkening her eyebrows and lashes, and putting a velvet shadow under her closed lids. She had fallen asleep, and sleep surrendered her unguarded to her watchers.

"She looks almost grown up—she looks kissable. Why should she, all of a sudden?" Boyne asked himself, suddenly disturbed, not by her increased prettiness (the measure of that varied from hour to hour) but by some new quality in it. He turned his eyes away, and they fell on Mr. Dobree, who sat facing him in the studied *abandon* of a picnicker unused to picnics. Mr. Dobree's inexhaustible wardrobe had supplied him with just the slightly shabby homespun suit and slightly faded hat adapted to the occasion; and Boyne wondered whether it were this change of dress which made him also seem different. But no: the difference was deeper. Despite his country clothes, Mr. Dobree did not look easier or less urban; he merely looked more excited and off his guard. His clear cautious eyes had grown blurred and furtive; one could almost see a faint line stretching from them to the recumbent Judith. Along that line it was manifest that Mr. Dobree's thoughts were racing; and Boyne knew they were the same thoughts as his own. The discovery shocked him indescribably. But he remembered that the levelling tendencies of modern life have levelled differences of age with the rest; and that Mr. Dobree was, to all intents and purposes, but little older than himself. Moreover, he was still brisk and muscular; his glance was habitually alert; in spite of his silver hair there seemed no reason why he should not share with Boyne the contemplation of Judith's defenceless beauty.

But if this was Boyne's conclusion it was apparently not Mr. Dobree's. As Boyne continued to observe him, Mr. Dobree's habitual pinkness turned to a red which suffused even his temples and eyelids, so that his carefully brushed white hair looked like a sunlit cloud against an angry sky. But with whom was Mr. Dobree angry? Why, with himself, manifestly. His eyes still rested on the dreaming Judith; but the rest of his face looked as if every muscle were tightened in the effort to pull the eyes away. "He's frightened—he's frightened at himself," Boyne thought, calling to mind—with a faint recoil from the reminder—that he also, once or twice, had been vaguely afraid of himself when he had looked too long at Judith. Had his eyes been like that, he wondered? And the muscles of his face been stretched in the effort to detach the eyes? The thing was not pleasant to visualise; and he disliked Mr. Dobree the more for serving as his mirror . . .

But suddenly Mr. Dobree was on his feet, his whole attention given to Mrs. Sellars. Again Boyne followed his change of direction with a start. Mrs. Sellars—but then she had been there all the time! Shadowed by her spreading hat, her light body bedded in the turf, she looked almost as young and sylvan as Judith. But somehow she had been merged in the landscape, all broken up into a dapple of sun and shade, of murmurs and soughings: her way of fitting into things sometimes had this effect of effacing her. She lifted her head, and in the shade of the hat-brim Boyne caught a delicate watchfulness of brows and lips, as of tiny live things under a protecting leaf.

Mr. Dobree was challenging her jauntily. "Do you see why those young cannibals should monopolise all the wild strawberries? Suppose we leave Mr. Boyne to mount guard over the sleeping beauty, and try to bag our share before it's too late?"

The words said clearly enough: "Take me away—it's high time," and Mrs. Sellars's gay little answer: "Come on—I'll show you a patch they'll never find," seemed to declare as clearly: "I know; but I'll see that you don't come to any mischief."

She was on her feet before his hands could help her up; something light and bounding in her seemed to spring to his call. "This way, this way," she cried, starting ahead of him up the boulder-strewn way. Boyne heard their voices mounting the streamside, mingling with the noise of the water, fading and flashing out again like the glimpses of her dress through the beech-leaves. He lay without moving, watching the smoke of his pipe rise in wavering spirals, twisted out of shape by puffs of air from the waterfall. With Mr. Dobree's withdrawal the ideas suggested by his presence had gone too; Judith Wheater seemed once more a little girl. Though perplexities and uncertainties still lingered on the verge of Boyne's mind his central self was anchored in a deep circle of peace. Every fibre of him was alive to the exquisite moment; but he had no need to fly from it, no fear of its flying from him. Judith's sleep was a calm pool in which he rested.

He fancied he must have been watching her for a long time, his thoughts enclosing her in a sort of calm fraternal vigilance, when she opened her eyes and turned them on him, still dewy with sleep.

"Martin!" she hailed him drowsily; then, fully awake, she sat up and exclaimed: "Darling, when are you going to be married? I've positively got to know at once."

She was always startling Boyne, but she had perhaps never startled him more than by this question; for even as she spoke he had been half unconsciously putting it to himself. He remembered, as something already far off, picturesque and unreal as a youthful folly, his resentment of Mrs. Sellars's delay in fixing a date for their marriage. Was it only two or three weeks ago that he had sent her, with a basket of gentians picked on a lofty upland, a quotation from Marvell's "Coy Mistress"? Now all that seemed an undergraduate's impatience. She had taught him that they were very well as they were, and if he still asked himself when they were to be married, the question had imperceptibly taken another form. "What in God's name will become of the children after we're married?" was the way he now instinctively put it.

He too sat up, and gazed into Judith's sleepy eyes. As he did so he was aware that an uncomfortable redness (which did not, he hoped, resemble Mr. Dobree's) was creeping up to his temples.

"When I'm going to be married? Why? What's the odds? I don't know that it's anybody's business, anyhow," he grumbled in an ill-assured voice.

Judith brushed the rebuff aside. "Oh, but it is—it's mine. For a very particular reason," she continued, as if affectionately resolved to break down the barrier of his reserve.

"A reason? Nonsense! What has a chit like you got to do with reasons?"

"You mean I'm so unreasonable?" A quick shadow crossed her face. "You didn't really mean that?"

"I didn't mean anything at all—any more than you do. I only meant: why aren't we very well as we are?"

Her eyes grew wide at this, and continued to fix him with a half mocking gravity, while her lips rounded into a smile. "Oh, but, Martin dear, it's Mrs. Sellars who ought to say that—not you!"

Boyne burst out laughing. How could one ever keep serious for two minutes with any of these preposterous children? And once more he told himself that Judith was as preposterous, and as much of a child, as the youngest of them.

"You know, darling, you ought to be *empressé*, impatient, passionate," she adjured him, as if his very life depended on his following her advice.

He leaned on his elbow and examined her with deliberation. "Well, of all the cheek—!"

She shook her head, still smiling. "I'm not cheeky; I'm really not, Martin. But sometimes you strike me as having so little experience—"

("Thank you," Boyne interjected.)

"Oh, I mean in those sorts of ways. As if you'd lived all your life so far away from the world."

"From your world? So I have, thank heaven." After a moment he added with severity: "So has Mrs. Sellars—thank heaven too."

The girl stood up, and crossing the mossy space between them, dropped down beside him and laid her hand on his arm. "Now I've offended you. Doll Westway always said I had no tact. And all I wanted was to explain why I have to know as soon as possible when you're to be married."

"Well, you certainly haven't explained that," Boyne answered, turning away from her to relight his pipe.

"No; but I'm going to. And you'll be pleased. It's because we've all clubbed together—even the steps and Scopy have—to give you a really jolly wedding present; and I think you'll like what we've found. We unearthed it the other day at Toblach, at the *antiquaire*'s. And we want to know exactly the right moment to give it to you. You do love presents, don't you, Martin?" she urged, as if straining her utmost to reach some human chord in him. He met the question with another laugh.

"Love presents? I should think I did! Almost as much as you do." She coloured a little at the insinuation; and perceiving this, he hastened on: "It's awfully dear of you all, and I'm ever so grateful. But there was no need to be in such a devil of a hurry."

Her face became all sympathy and interrogation. "Oh, Martin, you don't mean—things haven't gone wrong, have they?" Her look and intonation showed that she would have been genuinely distressed if they had. A pang like neuralgia shot through Boyne—yet a pang that was not all bitter. He took her hand, and laid what she had once called a "grown up kiss" on it. "Of course not, dear. And thank you—thank you for everything . . . Whatever you've all chosen for me, I shall love . . . Only, you know, there's really no sort of hurry."

She met this in silence, as something manifestly final. Folding her arms behind her, she let her head droop back on them, and her gaze wandered lazily skyward through the flicker of boughs.

Boyne had got his pipe going again. Gradually the tumult in his mind subsided. He sank back lazily at her side, tilting his hat over his brows, and saying to himself: "What on earth's the use of thinking ahead, anyhow?"

Directly in the line of his vision, Judith's sandalled feet lay in a bed of bracken, crossed like a resting Mercury's. He could almost see the little tufted wings at the heels. For the moment his imagination was imprisoned in a circle close about them.

Chapter XXI

THAT evening, when the children, weary but still jubilant, had been dropped at the *Pension Rosenglüh*, and Boyne had joined Mrs. Sellars for a late dinner at the *châlet*, the first thing that struck him was that his sapphire had reappeared on her hand.

He wondered afterward how it was that he, in general so unobservant of such details, had noticed that she had resumed the modest stone; and concluded that it was because of Judith's ridiculous cross-examination about the date of his marriage. He almost suspected that, baffled by his evasiveness, the pertinacious child had ended by addressing herself to Mrs. Sellars, and that the latter, thus challenged, had put on her ring. But no—though Judith was sometimes lacking in tact (as she herself acknowledged) this indiscretion could not be imputed to her, for the reason that Mrs. Sellars—Boyne remembered it only now—had not reappeared on the scene till it was time to pack the sleepy picnickers into the motors. She and Mr. Dobree had been a long time away. They had apparently prolonged their walk, and, incidentally, had failed to find the promised strawberries—or else had consumed them on the spot. And on the way home Judith and Mrs. Sellars had not been in the same car. Why, then, had Mrs. Sellars suddenly put on her ring? Boyne would only suppose that she had decided, for reasons unknown to him, to announce their engagement that night to Mr. Dobree, who was no doubt going to join them at dinner.

The idea obscurely irritated Boyne; he felt bored in advance by the neat and obvious things Mr. Dobree would consider it becoming to say. Boyne's whole view of Mrs. Sellars's friend had been changed by his sudden glimpse of the man who had looked out of Mr. Dobree's eyes at Judith. Before that, Boyne had pigeon-holed him as the successful lawyer, able in his profession, third-rate in other capacities, with a methodically planned existence of which professional affairs filled the larger part, and the rest was divided up like a carefully-weighed vitamin diet (Mr. Dobree was strong on vitamins) between exercise, society, philanthropy and travel. Now, a long way off down this fair perspective, a small, an almost invisible Dobree, lurked and prowled, staring as he had stared at Judith. A sudden irritation filled Boyne at the thought of what, unknown to Mrs. Sellars, peered and grimaced behind her legal counsellor. It was as if Mr. Dobree had unconsciously evoked for him some tragic allegory of Judith's future . . .

"Where's your friend? Are we waiting for him?" Boyne's question sounded abrupt in his own ears, but was received by Mrs. Sellars with her usual equanimity.

"Mr. Dobree? No, we're not waiting for him. He's not coming."

Boyne felt relieved, yet vaguely baffled. If Dobree wasn't coming (he immediately thought), why the devil wasn't he? And what was he up to instead?

"Chucked you for a party at the 'Palace,' I suppose? I'm glad he didn't drag you up there to dine with him."

"No; I don't think he's giving a party—or going to one. He had letters to write; and he said he was tired."

This seemed to dispose of the matter, and Boyne, still faintly disturbed, followed his betrothed to the dining-table, at which of late he had so seldom sat alone with her.

"Don't you like it better like this?" she asked, smiling at him across the bowl of wild roses which stood between them.

It was indeed uncommonly pleasant to be alone with her again. She gratified him, at the outset, by praising the behaviour of the children on the picnic; and as they talked he began to think that his growing irritability, and his odd reluctance to look forward to their future together, had been caused only by the intrusion of irrelevant problems and people. "When we're alone together everything's always all right," he thought, reassured.

Dinner over, they drifted out onto the balcony in the old way, and he lit his cigar, and yielded to the sense of immediate well-being. He saw that Rose Sellars knew he was glad to be alone with her, and that the knowledge put her at her ease, and made her want to say and do whatever would maintain that mood in him. There was something pathetic in the proud creature's eagerness to be exactly what he wished her to be.

"Judith was looking her very prettiest today, wasn't she? Mr. Dobree was so much struck by her," she said softly, after a silence.

It was as if she had flung a boulder into the very middle of the garden-plot she had just been at such pains to lay out. Boyne met the remark with an exasperated laugh.

"I should say he *was* struck. That was fairly obvious."

"Well—she is striking, at times," Mrs. Sellars conceded, still more gently.

"As any lovely child is. That's what she is—a lovely child. Dobree looks at her like a dog licking his jaws over a bone."

"Martin—!"

"Sorry. I never could stand your elderly men who look at little girls. If your friend is so dotty about Judith, he'd better ask her to marry him. He's rich, isn't he? His money might be an inducement—who knows?"

"Marry her? Marry Judith? Mr. Dobree?" Mrs. Sellars gave way to a mild mirth. His words certainly sounded absurd enough when she echoed them; but Boyne, for the moment, was beyond heeding anything but the tumult in his own veins.

"Why not?" he continued. "As the poor child is situated, money is a big consideration. What's the use of being a hypocrite about it? If she's to fight her parents, and keep the children together, she'll need cash, and a big pile of it; and a clever lawyer to manœuvre for her, too. I call it an ideal arrangement."

Mrs. Sellars waited a little before answering; then she said: "I don't see how the biggest fortune, and the cleverest lawyer in the world, could keep the Wheaters from ordering their children home the day they choose to. But I'm sure that if Judith wanted help and advice no one would be more happy to give it to her than Mr. Dobree."

"Ah, there you're right," Boyne agreed with an ironic shrug.

"Well, and don't you think perhaps it might be a good thing if she did consult him—or at least if you did, for her?"

"If I intervened in any way between Dobree and Judith I don't think he'd thank you for putting me up to it."

"Why—what do you mean?"

"If you don't know what I mean I can only suppose you didn't notice how he was looking at the child this afternoon, before you carried him off for a walk."

Mrs. Sellars fell silent again. He saw the faint lines of perplexity weaving their net over her face, and reflected that when a woman is no longer young she can preserve her air of freshness only in the intervals of feeling. "It's too bad," he thought, vexed with himself for having upset the delicate balance of her serenity. But now she was smiling again, a little painfully.

"Looking at her—looking at her how?"

"Well—as I've told you."

The smile persisted. "I certainly didn't see anything like that. And neither did I carry him off for a walk; as it happens, it was he who carried *me*—"

"Oh, well," Boyne murmured at this touch of feminine vanity.

Mrs. Sellars continued: "And I don't think he's thinking of Judith in the way you imagine—or that he can have looked at her in that way. I hope he didn't; because, as it happens, he took me off on that walk to ask me to marry him."

The words dropped from her with a serene detachment, as if they had been her luminous little smile made audible. "I don't know that it's quite fair to him to tell you," she added, with one of her old-fashioned impulses of reserve.

It was Boyne's turn to find no answer. For some time he sat gazing into the summer darkness without speaking. "Marry him? Marry Dobree—you?"

"You see you were right: he does want to get married," she softly bantered. "It was what he came for—to ask me. I'd no idea . . . And now he's going away . . . he leaves to-morrow," she added, with a faint sigh in which deprecation and satisfaction were perceptibly mingled. If it was her little triumph she took it meekly, even generously—but nevertheless, he saw, with a complete consciousness of what it meant.

Boyne laughed again, this time at himself.

"I don't know what you see in it that is so absurd," Mrs. Sellars murmured, a faint note of vexation in her voice. Again he found no reply, and she continued, with the distant air she assumed when echoing axioms current in her youth: "After all, it's the highest honour a man can—"

"Oh, quite," Boyne agreed good-humouredly. He rubbed his hand across his forehead, as if to brush away some inner confusion. But it was no use; he couldn't straighten his thoughts out. He couldn't shake off the fact that his surprise and derision had not concerned Rose Sellars at all—that his laugh had simply mocked his own power of self-deception, and uttered his relief at finding himself so deceived. "So *that* was all!" The words escaped him unawares. In the dusk he felt the shadowy figure at his side stiffen and withdraw from him.

"Shall we go in? It's getting chilly," said Mrs. Sellars, turning back toward the lamplight.

Boyne, still in the bewilderment of his own thoughts, followed her into the room. He noticed that she had grown unusually pale. She sat down beside the table, and began turning over the letters and papers which the evening post had brought. Boyne stood in front of the fireplace, his hands in his pockets, watching her movements as one letter after another slipped through her fingers. But all he could see was the sapphire ring, re-established, enthroned, proclaiming his own destiny to all concerned and unconcerned.

"So you told him you were already engaged?"

She looked up at him. "It was only fair, wasn't it?"

"Certainly—that is, if being engaged was the only obstacle."

"The only obstacle?"

"If you were prepared to marry Dobree, supposing you'd still been free."

She weighed this, and then laughed a little, but without much gaiety. "How do I know what I should have done if I'd been free?"

He continued to look at her. "Do you want to try?"

The colour rose to her forehead. She dropped the letters, and composed her hands on them as if in the effort to control a secret agitation. "Is this a way of telling me you're vexed because I announced our engagement to Mr. Dobree?"

He hesitated, feeling (and now he hated himself for feeling) that it was a moment for going warily. "Not vexed; that's not the word. Only I did agree with you that, as long as—as nothing about our future was definitely settled—it was ever so much pleasanter keeping our private affairs to ourselves. It was your own idea, you know; you proposed it," he reminded her, as she remained silent.

"Yes; it was my idea." She pondered. "But you needn't be afraid that Mr. Dobree will betray us."

"It's not a question of betraying. It's just the feeling—"

"The feeling that some one else is in our secret? But all the Wheater children have been—for a long time." She spoke the words ever so lightly, as if she had barely pencilled them on a smooth page.

Boyne was startled. He could see no analogy, but did not know how to explain that there was none. "Oh, the children; but the children don't count. Besides, that wasn't my fault. Judith guessed." He smiled a little at the reminiscence. "But perhaps Mr. Dobree guessed," he added, with a return of ease. After all, he was carrying it off very well, he thought—though what he meant by "it" he would have been put to it to say.

Mrs. Sellars gave another little laugh. "Oh, no; Mr. Dobree didn't guess. I had to dot the *i*'s for him. The fact is"—she paused a moment—"he was convinced that you were in love with Judith Wheater."

Instantly all the resentments and suspicions which Boyne had dismissed rushed back on him. He had been right, then—he had not mistaken the signs and portents. As if they were ever mistakable! "How rotten," he said in a low voice.

Mrs. Sellars dropped one of the letters which she had absently taken up again.

"Martin—"

"Rotten. The mere thinking of such a thing—much less insinuating it to any one else. But it just shows—" He broke off, and then began again, on a fresh wave of indignation: "Shows what kind of a mind he must have. Thinking in that way about a child—a mere child—and about any man, any *decent* man; regarding it as possible, perhaps as natural . . . worst of all, suggesting it of some one standing in my position toward these children; as if I might take advantage of my opportunities to—to fall in love with a child in the schoolroom!"

Boyne's words sounded in his own ears as if they were being megaphoned at him across the width of the room. He dropped down into the nearest chair, hot, angry, ashamed, with a throat as dry as if he had been haranguing an open-air meeting on a dusty day.

Opposite him, Mrs. Sellars remained with her hands suspended above the letters. The sapphire burned at him across the interval. "Martin . . . but you *are* in love with her!" she exclaimed. She paused a moment, and then added in a quieter voice: "I believe I've always known it." They sat and looked at each other without speaking.

At length Boyne rose, and started to move around the table to where she was sitting.

"This is ridiculous—" he began.

She held up her hand, and the gesture, though evidently meant only to check the words on his lips, had the effect also of arresting his advance. He felt self-conscious and clumsy, and dimly resented her making him feel so. He was sure it was she who had been ridiculous, not he; yet, curiously enough, the conviction brought him no solace. Again they faced each other, guardedly, apprehensively, as if something fragile and precious, which they had been carrying together, had slipped between their fingers and been broken. He felt that, if he glanced at the floor, he might see the glittering fragments . . .

Mrs. Sellars was the first to recover her self-possession. She rose in her turn, and going up to Boyne laid her hand on his arm.

"I wonder why we're trying to hurt each other?" She looked at him through moist lashes, and he felt himself a brute for not instantly taking her in his arms and obliterating their discussion with a kiss. But there lay the glittering fragments, and he could not seem to reach to her across them.

"Now I know what she thinks of Judith," he reflected savagely.

"It's all my fault, Martin; I know I'm nervous and stupid." She was clasping his arm, pleading with lifted eyes and lips. Her self-abasement humiliated him. "If she really thinks what she says, why doesn't she kick me out?" he wondered.

"I suppose I walked too far today, and got over-tired; and what Mr. Dobree said startled me, upset me . . ."

He smiled. "His asking you to marry him?"

She smiled back a little wearily. "No. But what he said about—about your interest in Judith. You must understand, dear, that sometimes your attitude about those children is a little surprising to people who don't know all the circumstances."

Boyne felt himself hardening again. "What business is it of people who don't know all the circumstances? *You* do; that's enough."

She seized at this with a distressing humility. "Of course I do, dearest; of course it is. And you'll try to forget my stupid nerves, won't you? Try to think of me as I am when there's nobody in the world but you and me?" Her arms stole up to his shoulders, her hands met behind his neck, and she drew his head down softly. "If only it could always be like that!"

As their lips touched he shut his eyes, and tried, with a violent effort of the will, to recall what her kiss would have meant to him on the far-off day when the news of Sellars's death had overtaken him somewhere in the Nubian desert, and in the middle of the night he had started awake, still clutching the letter, and crying out to himself: "At last . . ."

Chapter XXII

NEXT day, when Boyne thought over the scene of the previous night, he found for it all the excuses which occur to a sensible man in the glow of his morning bath.

It was all the result of idling and lack of hard exercise; when a working man has had too long a holiday, and resting has become dawdling, Satan proverbially intervenes. But though at first Boyne assumed all the blame, by the time he began to shave he had handed over a part to Mrs. Sellars. After all, it was because of her old-fashioned scruples, her unwillingness to marry him at once, and let him get back to work, that they were still loitering in the Dolomites. It probably wasn't safe for middle-aged people to have too much leisure in which to weigh each other's faults and merits.

But then, again, suddenly he thought: "If we'd been married, and gone home when I wanted to, what would have become of the children?" It was undoubtedly because Mrs. Sellars had insisted on prolonging their engagement that Boyne had become involved in the Wheater problem; but when he reached this point in his retrospect he found he could not preserve his impartiality. It was impossible to face the thought of what might have happened to the little Wheaters if chance had not put him in their way . . .

After all, then, everything was for the best. All he had to do was to persuade Mrs. Sellars of it (which ought not to be difficult, since it was a "best" of her own devising), and to banish from his mind the disturbing figure of Mr. Dobree. Perhaps—on second thoughts—his irritability of the previous evening had been partly due to the suspicion that Mrs. Sellars, for all her affected indifference, was flattered by Mr. Dobree's proposal. "You never can tell—" Boyne concluded, and shrugged that possibility away too. The thought that he might have had to desert his young friends in their hour of distress, and had been able, instead, to stay and help them, effaced all other considerations. So successfully did he talk himself over to this view that only one cloud remained on his horizon. Mrs. Sellars had said: "I don't see how the biggest fortune, and the cleverest lawyer in the world, could keep the Wheaters from ordering their children home the day they choose to"; and in saying it she had put her finger on Boyne's inmost apprehension. He had told himself the same thing a hundred times; but to hear it from any one else made the danger seem more pressing. It reminded him that the little Wheaters' hold on him was not half as frail as his own on them, and that it was folly to indulge the illusion that he could really direct or control their fate.

And meanwhile—?

Well, he could only mark time; thank heaven it was still his to mark! The Lido season had not yet reached its climax, and till it declined and fell he was free to suppose that its devotees would linger on, hypnotized. As between taking steps for an immediate divorce, and figuring to the last in the daily round of entertainment, Boyne felt sure that not one of the persons concerned would hesitate. They could settle questions of business afterward; and it was purely as business that they regarded a matter in which the extent of the alimony was always the chief point of debate. And what could replace the excitement of a Longhi ball at the Fenice, or of a Marriage of the Doge to the Adriatic, mimed in a reconstituted Bucentaur by the rank and fashion of half Europe? No one would be leaving Venice yet.

But, all the same, the days were flying. The increasing number of arrivals at Cortina, the growing throng of motors on all the mountain ways, showed that before long fashion would be moving from the seashore to the mountains; and when the Lido broke up, what might not break up with it? Boyne felt that the question must at last be faced; that he must have a talk about it that very day with Judith.

It was more than a month since Judith and her flock had appeared at Cortina; and the various parents concerned had promised Boyne that the children should be left in the Dolomites till the summer was over. But what was such a promise worth, and what did the phrase mean on lips so regardless of the seasons? Nothing—Boyne knew it. He was conscious now that, during the last four weeks, he had never gone down to the *Pension Rosenglüh* without expecting to be told that a summons or a command had come from the Lido. But so far there had been none. The children were protected by the fact that there was no telephone at the *pension*, and that none of their parents was capable—except under the most extreme pressure—of writing a letter.

When it was impossible to telephone they could, indeed, telegraph; but even the inditing of a telegram required a concentration of mind which, Boyne knew, would become increasingly difficult as the Lido season culminated. Telegrams did, of course, come, especially in the first days, both to Boyne and to Judith: long messages from Joyce about clothes and diet, rambling communications from Lady Wrench, setting forth her rights and grievances in terms which, by the time they had passed through two Italian telegraph-offices, were as confused as the thoughts in her own mind; and lastly, a curt wire from Cliffe Wheater to Boyne: "Wish it definitely understood relinquish no rights whatever how is Chipstone reply paid."

To all these communications Boyne returned a comprehensive "All right," and, acting on his advice, Judith did the same, merely adding particulars as to the children's health and happiness. "On the whole, you know," she explained to Boyne, "it's a relief to them all, now the thing's settled—I always knew it would be." She and Terry still cherished the hope that in the autumn she would be permitted to take the children out to Grandma Mervin, in America; or that, failing permission, she would be encouraged by Boyne to carry them off secretly. With this in view, she and Miss Scope saved up every penny they could of the allowance which Cliffe Wheater had agreed to make, and which Boyne dealt out to them once a week. But all these arrangements were so precarious, so dependent on the moods of unreasonable and uncertain people, that it seemed a miracle that the little party at the *Pension Rosenglüh* was still undisturbed. Certainly, if it had been possible to reach them by telephone they would have been scattered long ago. "As soon as they break up at the Lido they'll be after you," Boyne had warned Judith from the first; but she had always answered hopefully: "Oh, no: not till after Cowes, if they still go there; and if they don't, after Venice there's Biarritz. You'll see. And before Biarritz there's a fortnight in Paris for autumn clothes."

Cowes, in due course, had been relinquished, the Lido exerting too strong a counter-attraction; but after a few more weeks that show also would be packed away in the lumber-room of spent follies.

The fact of having these questions always on his mind kept Boyne from being unduly disturbed by his discussion of the previous evening with Mrs. Sellars. In the wholesome light of morning a sentimental flurry between two sensible people who were deeply attached to each other seemed as nothing compared to the ugly reality perpetually hanging over the little Wheaters; and he felt sure that Mrs. Sellars would take the same view.

She did not disappoint him. When he presented himself at the luncheon hour the very air of the little sitting-room breathed a new serenity; it was as if she had been out early to fill it with flowers. Boyne was not used to delicate readjustments in his sentimental relations. For so many years now his feeling for Rose Sellars had been something apart, like a beautiful picture on the wall of a quiet room; and his other amorous episodes had been too brief and simple for any great amount of manœuvring. He was therefore completely reassured by the gaiety and simplicity of her welcome, and thought to himself once again that there was everything to be said in favour of a long social acquiescence. "A stupid woman, now, would insist on going over the whole thing again, like a bluebottle that starts in banging about the room after you're sure you've driven it out of the window."

There was nothing of the blue-bottle about Mrs. Sellars; and she was timorously anxious that Boyne should know it. But her timidity was not base; if she submitted, she submitted proudly. The only sign she gave of a latent embarrassment was in her too great ease, her too blithe determination to deny it. But even this was minimised by the happy fact that she had a piece of news for him.

She did not tell him what it was till lunch was over, and they were finishing their coffee in the sitting-room: she knew the importance of not disturbing a man's train of thought—even agreeably—while he is in the act of enjoying good food. Boyne had lit his cigar, and was meditating on the uniform excellence of the coffee she managed to give him, when she said, with a little laugh: "Only imagine—Aunt Julia's on the Atlantic! I had a radio this morning. She says she's coming over to Paris to see you."

Boyne had pictured Aunt Julia—when he could spare the time for such an evocation—as something solid, ponderous, essentially immovable. She represented for him the obstinate stability of old New York in the flux of new experiments. It was like being told that Trinity Church, for instance, was taking a Loretto-flight across the Atlantic to see him.

Mrs. Sellars laughed at his incredulous stare. "Are you surprised? I'm not. You see, Aunt Julia was always the delicate sister, the one who had to be nursed. Aunt Gertrude, the strong one, who did the nursing, died last winter—and since then Aunt Julia's been perfectly well."

They agreed that such resurrections were not uncommon, and Mrs. Sellars went so far as to declare that, if she didn't get to Paris in time to meet Aunt Julia, she was prepared to have the latter charter an aeroplane and descend on Cortina. "Indeed we're only protected by the fact that I don't believe there's any landing-field in the Dolomites."

She went on to say that she would have to leave in a day or two, as Aunt Julia, who was accustomed to having her path smoothed for her, had requested that hotel rooms fulfilling all her somewhat complicated requirements should be made ready for her arrival, a six-cylinder motor with balloon tires and an irreproachable chauffeur engaged to meet her at the station, and a doctor and a masseuse be found in attendance when she arrived—as a result of which precautions she hoped, after an interval of repose, to be well enough to occupy herself with her niece's plans.

Boyne gasped. "Good Lord—what that cable must have cost her!"

"Oh, it's not the cost that ever bothers Aunt Julia," said Aunt Julia's niece with a certain deference.

Boyne laughed, and agreed that Mrs. Sellars could not prudently refuse such a summons. Somehow it no longer offended him that she should obey it from motives so obviously interested. He could not have said why, but it now seemed to him natural enough that she should hold herself at the disposal of a rich old aunt. He wondered whether it was because her departure would serve to relieve a passing tension; but he dismissed this as a bit of idle casuistry. "The point is that she's going—and that she and I will probably be awfully glad to see each other when she gets back."

Mrs. Sellars cast a wistful look about her. After a pause she said: "You don't know how I hate to think that our good evenings in this dear little room are so nearly over," in a tone suggesting that she had rather expected Boyne to say it for her, and that he had somehow missed a cue.

"But why over? Not for more than a week, I hope? You're not going to let yourself be permanently annexed by Aunt Julia?"

She smiled a little perplexedly: evidently other plans were in her mind, plans she had pictured him as instinctively divining. "Not permanently; but I don't quite know when I shall be able to leave her—"

"Oh, I say, my dear!"

The perplexity lifted from her smile: it seemed to reach out to him like a promise. "But then I expect you to join me very soon. As soon as Aunt Julia's blood-pressure has been taken, and the doctor and the masseuse and the chauffeur have been tested and passed upon."

Boyne listened in astonishment. It had never seriously occurred to him that he was to be involved in the ceremony of establishing Aunt Julia on European soil. "Oh, but look here— what earthly use should I be? Why should I be butchered to make Aunt Julia's holiday?"

"You won't be. It will be—almost the other way round. I'm going to do everything I possibly can for Aunt Julia; everything to start her successfully on her European adventure. And then I'm going to present the bill."

"The bill?"

She nodded gaily. "You're the bill. I'm going to present you, and say: 'Now you've seen him, can you wonder that I mean to marry him at once, whether you like it or not?' "

The words fell on a silence which Boyne, for the moment, found it impossible to break. Mrs. Sellars stood by her writing-table, her slender body leaning to him, her face lit with one of those gleams of lost youth which he had once found so exquisite and poignant. He found it so now, but with another poignancy.

"You mean—you mean—you've changed your mind about the date?" He broke off, the words "of our marriage" choking on his lips. Through a mist of bewilderment he saw the tender mockery of her smile, and knew how much courage it disguised. ("I stand here like a stock—what a brute she'll think me!")

"Did you imagine I was one of the dreadful women who never change their minds?" She came close, clasped her hands about his arm, lifted her delicate face, still alight with expectation. The face said: "Here I am: to be cherished or shattered—" and he thought again of the glittering fragments he had seen at his feet the night before. He detached her hands, and lifted them, one after another, to his kiss. If only some word—if only the right word—would come to him!

"Martin—don't you *want* me to change my mind?" she suddenly challenged him. He held her hands against his breast, caressing them.

"Dear, first of all, I don't want to be the cause of you doing anything that might offend your aunt . . . that might interfere . . . in any way . . . with her views . . ." No; he couldn't go on; the words strangled him. He was too sure that she was aware they did not express what he was thinking, were spoken only to gain time.

But with a gentle tenacity she pursued: "It's awfully generous of you to think of that. But don't you suppose, dear, I've been miserable at asking you to linger on here when I've always known that what you wanted was to be married at once, and get back to work? I've been imprisoned in my past—I see it now; I had become the slave of all those years of conformity you used to reproach me with. For a long time I couldn't get out of their shadow. But you've opened my eyes—you've set me free. How monstrous to have waited so long for happiness, and then to be afraid to seize it when it comes!" Her arms stole up and drew him. "I'm not afraid now, Martin. You've taught me not to be. Henceforth I mean to think of you first, not of Aunt Julia. I mean to marry you as soon as it can be done. I don't suppose the formalities take very long in Paris, do they? Then, as soon as we're married, we'll sail for home."

He listened in a kind of stupor, saying inwardly: "It's not that I love her less; it can't be that I love her less. It's only that everything that happens between us always seems to happen at the wrong time."

The silence prolonged itself, on her side stretched and straining, on his built up like a wall, opaque, impenetrable. From beyond it came her little far-off laugh. "Dear, I'm utterly in your hands, you see!"

Evidently there had to be an answer to that. "Rose—" he began. Pretty as her name was, he hardly ever called her by it; he had always felt her too close to him to need a name. She looked up in surprise.

He made a fresh start. "But you see, darling, how things are—"

A little tremor ran across her face. "What things?"

"You know that, after you'd refused to consider the possibility of our getting married at once, I pledged myself . . ."

The tremor ceased, and her face once more became smooth and impenetrable. He found himself repeating to vacancy: "I pledged myself . . ."

She drew quietly away, and sat down at a little distance from him. "You're talking about your odd experiment with the Wheater children?"

"It's more than an experiment. When I saw the parents in Venice I told them, as you know, that I'd be responsible for the welfare of the children as long as they were left with me."

"As long as they were left with you! For life, perhaps, then?" She leaned forward, her face drawn with the valiant effort of her smile. "Martin! Is all this serious? It can't be! You can't really be asking me to understand that all our plans—our whole future, yours and mine—are to depend, for an indefinite length of time, on the whim of two or three chance acquaintances of yours who are too heartless and self-engrossed to look after their own children!"

Boyne paused a moment; then he said: "We had no plans—I mean, no immediate plans—when I entered into the arrangement. It was by your own choice that—"

"My own choice! Well, then, my own choice, now, is that we should have plans, immediately." She stood up, trembling a little. She was very pale, and her thin eyebrows drew a straight black bar across her forehead. "Martin—I ask you to come with me at once to Paris."

"At once? But just now you said in a week or two—"

"And now I say at once: to-morrow."

He stood leaning against the chimney, as far from her as the little room allowed. A tide of resistance rose in him. "I can't come to-morrow."

He was conscious that she was making an intense effort to steady her quivering nerves. "Martin . . . I don't want to be unreasonable . . ."

"You're never unreasonable," he said patiently.

"You mean it might have been better if I were!" she flashed back, crimsoning.

"Don't be—now," he pleaded.

"No." She paused. "Very well. Come to Paris in a few days, then."

"Look here, dear—all this is of no use. No earthly use. I can't come in a few days, any more than I can come to-morrow. I can't desert these children till their future is settled in one way or another. I've said I'd stick to them, and I mean to. If I turned my back on them now they'd lose their last chance of being able to stay together."

She received this with bent head and hands clasped stiffly across her knee; but suddenly her self-control broke down. "But, Martin, are you mad? What business is it of yours, anyhow, what becomes of these children?"

"I don't know," he said simply.

"You don't know—you don't know?"

"No; I only feel it's got to be. I'm pledged. I can't get round it."

"You can't get round it because you don't want to. You're pledged because you want to be. You want to be because Mr. Dobree was right . . . because . . ."

"Rose, take care," he interrupted, very low.

"Take care? At this hour? Of what? For whom? All I care for is to know the truth . . ."

"I'm telling you the truth."

"You may think you are. But the truth is something very different—something you're not conscious of yourself, perhaps . . . not clearly . . ."

"I believe I'm telling you the whole truth."

"That when I ask you to choose between me and the Wheater children, you choose the Wheater children—out of philanthropy?"

"I didn't say out of philanthropy. I said I didn't know . . ."

"If you don't know, I do. You're in love with Judith Wheater, and you're trying to persuade yourself that you're still in love with me."

He lifted his hands to his face, and covered his eyes, as if from some intolerable vision she had summoned to them. "Don't Rose, for the Lord's sake . . . Don't let's say stupid things—"

"But, dear, I must." She got up and came close to him again; he felt her hands on his arm. "Listen, Martin. I love you too much not to want to help you. Try to feel that about me, won't you? Then everything will be so much easier."

"Yes."

"Try to understand your own feelings—that's the best way of sparing mine. I want the truth, that's all. Try to see the truth, and face it with me—it's all I ask."

He dropped his hands, and turned his discouraged eyes on her. But he could only feel that he and she were farther apart than when he had last looked at her; all the rest was confusion and obscurity.

"I don't know what the truth, as you call it, is; I swear I don't; but I know it's not what you think. Judith's as much a child to me as the others—that I swear to you."

"Then, dear—"

"Then, I've got to stick to them all the same," he repeated doggedly.

For a time the two continued to stand in silence, with eyes averted, like people straining to catch some far-off sound which will signal relief from a pressing peril. Then, slowly, Boyne turned to Mrs. Sellars. His eyes rested on her profile, so thin, drawn, bloodless, that a fresh pang shot through him. He had often mocked at himself as a man who, in spite of all his wanderings, had never had a real adventure; but now he saw that he himself had been one, had been Rose Sellars's Great Adventure, the risk and the enchantment of her life. While she had continued, during the weary years of her marriage, to be blameless, exemplary, patient and heroically gay, the thought of Boyne was storing up treasures for her which she would one day put out her hand and take—no matter how long she might have to wait. Her patience, Boyne knew, was endless—it was as long as her hair. She had trained herself to go on waiting for happiness, day after day, month after month, year after year, with the same air of bright unruffled vigilance, like a tireless animal waiting for its prey. One day her prey, her happiness, would appear, and she would snap it up; and on that day there would be no escape from her . . .

It was terrible, it was hideous, to be picturing her distress as something grasping and predatory; it was more painful still to be entering so acutely into her feelings while a central numbness paralysed his own. All around this numbness there was a great margin of pity and of comprehension; but he knew this was not the region by way of which he could reach her. She who had always lived the life of reason would never forgive him if he called upon her reason now . . .

"Rose—" he appealed to her.

She turned and he saw her face, composed, remodelled, suffused with a brilliancy like winter starlight. Her lips formed a smiling: "Dear?"

"Rose—"

She took his hand with the lightest pressure. "Dearest, what utter nonsense we've both been talking! Of course I don't mean that you're to desert the Wheater children for me—and of course you don't mean that you're to desert me for them; do you? I believe I understand all you feel; all your fondness for the poor little things. I should shiver at you if you hadn't grown to love them! But you and I have managed to get each other all on edge, I don't know how. Don't you feel what a mistake it would be to go in and out of this question any longer? I have an idea I could find a solution almost at once, if only I weren't trying to so hard. And so could you, no doubt." She paused, a little breathlessly, and then resumed her eager monologue. "Let's say goodbye till to-morrow, shall we?—and produce our respective plans of action when we meet again. And don't forget that the problem may solve itself without regard to us, and at any minute."

She had caught at the last splinter of the rock of Reason still visible above the flood; and there she clung, dauntless, unbeaten, uttering the right, the impartial word with lips that pined and withered for his kiss . . .

"Oh, my dear," he murmured.

"To-morrow?"

"Yes—to-morrow."

Before he could take her in his arms she had slipped out of reach, and softly, adroitly closed the door on him. Alone on the landing he was left with the sense that that deft gesture had shut him up with her forever.

Chapter XXIII

IT was growing more and more evident to Boyne that he could recover his old vision of Mrs. Sellars only when they were apart. He began to think this must be due to his having loved her so long from a distance, having somehow, in consequence of their separation, established with her an ideal relation to which her slightest misapprehension, her least failure to say just what he expected, was a recurring menace.

At first the surprise of finding her, after his long absence, so much younger and more vivid than his remembrance, the glow of long-imagined caresses, the whole enchanting harmony of her presence, had hushed the inner discord. But though she was dearer to him than ever, all free communication seemed to have ceased between them—he could regain it only during those imaginary conversations in which it was he who sustained both sides of the dialogue.

This was what happened when he had walked off the pain and bewilderment of their last talk. For two hours he tramped the heights, unhappy, confused, struggling between the sense of her unreasonableness and of his own predicament; then gradually there stole back on him the serenity always associated with the silent sessions of his thought and hers. On what seemed to him the fundamental issues—questions of fairness, kindness, human charity in the widest meaning—when had she ever failed him in these wordless talks? His position with regard to the Wheater children (hadn't he admitted it to her?) was unreasonable, indefensible, was whatever else she chose to call it; yes, but it was also human, and that would touch her in the end. He had no doubt that when they met the next day she would have her little solution ready, and be prepared to smile with him over their needless perturbation.

The thought of her deep submissive passion, which contrasted so sharply with his own uneasy self-assertiveness, was the only anxiety that remained with him. He knew now how much she loved him—but did he know how much he loved her? Supposing, for instance, that on getting back to his hotel, now, this very evening, he should find a line telling him that she had decided for both their sakes to break their engagement: well, could he honestly say that it would darken earth and heaven for him? Mortified, hurt, at a loose end—all this he would be; already the tender flesh of his vanity was shrinking, and under it he felt the thrust of wounded affection. But that was all—in the balance how little!

He got back late to the hotel, and walked unheedingly past the letter-rack toward which, at that hour, it was usual to glance for the evening mail. The porter called to him, waving a letter. The envelope bore the New York post-mark, and in the upper corner Boyne recognised the name of the big firm of contracting engineers to whom he had owed some of his most important jobs. They still wrote now and then to consult him: no doubt this letter, which had been forwarded by his London bankers, was of that nature. He pushed it into his pocket, deciding to read it after he had dined. And then he proceeded to dine, alone in a corner of the unfashionable restaurant of his hotel, of which the tables with their thick crockery and clumsy water-carafes seemed like homely fragments of a recently-disjoined *table d'hôte*, the long old-fashioned hotel table at which travellers used to be seated in his parents' day. A coarse roll lay by his plate, the table bore a bunch of half-faded purply-pink cosmos in an opaque blue vase: everything about him was ugly and impersonal, yet he hugged himself for not being at the *châlet* table, with its air of exquisite rusticity, its bowl of cunningly-disposed wild flowers, the shaded candles, the amusing food. Yes; and he was glad, too, not to be sharing the little Wheaters' pudding at the *Pension Rosenglüh*; he was suddenly aware of an intense unexpected satisfaction in being for once alone, his own master, with no one that he need be on his guard against or at his best before; no one to be tormented or enchanted by, no one to listen to and answer. "Decidedly, I'm a savage," he thought, emptying his plateful of savourless soup with an appetite he was almost ashamed of. The moral of it, obviously, was that he had been idle too long, that what he was thirsting for at this very moment was not more rest but more work, and that the idea of giving up his life of rough and toilsome activity for the security of an office in New York, as he had aspired to do a few short months ago, now seemed intolerable. Too old for the fatigue and hardships of an engineer's life? Why, it was the fatigues and the hardships which, physically speaking, had given the work its zest, just as the delicate mathematical calculations had provided its intellectual stimulus. The combination of two such sources of interest, so rare in other professions, was apparently what he needed to keep him straight, curb his excitable imagination, discipline his nerves, and make him wake up every morning to a steady imperturbable view of life. After dinner, sitting in the dreary little lounge, as he lit his pipe and pulled the letter from his pocket he thought: "I wish to God it was an order to start for Tierra del Fuego!"

It was nothing of the sort, of course: merely an inquiry for the address of a young engineer who had been Boyne's assistant a few years earlier, and whom the firm in question had lost sight of. They had been struck with Boyne's estimate of the young man's ability, and thought they might have an interesting piece of work for him, if he happened to be available, and was not scared by hardships and responsibility. Boyne put the letter into his pocket, leaned back in his chair, and thought: "God! I wish I was his age and just starting—for anywhere."

His mind turned round and round this thought for the rest of the evening. Perhaps he could make Mrs. Sellars understand that, after all, he had made a mistake in supposing he had reached the age for sedentary labours. Once they were married she would surely see that, for his soul's sake, and until the remainder of his youth was used up, she must let him go off on these remote exciting expeditions which seemed the only cure for—for what? Well, for the creeping grayness of age, no doubt. The fear of that must be what ailed him. At any rate he must get away; he must. As soon as the fate of the little Wheaters was decided, and he and Rose were married, and he had established her in New York, he must get back into the glorious soul-releasing world of girders and abutments, of working stresses, curvatures and grades.

She had talked of having her little plan ready for him the next day. Well, he would have one for her, at any rate; this big comprehensive one. First, the Wheater tribe transplanted (he didn't yet see how) to the safe shelter of Grandma Mervin's wing; then his own marriage; then—flight! He worked himself into a glow of eloquence, as he always did in these one-sided talks, which never failed to end in convincing Mrs. Sellars because he unconsciously eliminated from them all the objections she might possibly have raised . . . He went to bed with a sense of fresh air in his soul, as if the mere vision of escape had freed him . . .

Mrs. Sellars had not said at what hour she expected him the next day; so he decided to wait till lunch, and drop in on her then, as his habit was when they had no particular expedition in view. In the morning he usually strolled down to see how the *Rosenglüh* refugees were getting on; but on this occasion he left them to themselves, and did not go out till he made for the *châlet*. As he approached it he was startled by a queer sense of something impending. Oh, not another "scene"; Rose was much too intelligent for that. What he felt was just an uneasy qualm, as if the new air in his soul's lungs were being gradually pumped out of them again. He glanced up at the balcony, lifting his hand to signal to her; but she was not there. He pushed open the hall door and ran up the short flight of stairs. The little sitting-room was empty: it looked speckless and orderly as a tomb. He noticed at once that the littered writing-table was swept and garnished, and that no scent of viands greeted him through the dining-room door.

She had gone—he became suddenly sure that she had gone. But why? But when? Above all, why without a word? It was so unlike her to do anything abrupt and unaccountable that his vague sense of apprehension returned.

He sat down in the armchair he always occupied, as if the familiar act must re-evoke her, call her back into the seat opposite, in the spirit if not in the flesh. But the room remained disconcertingly, remained even spiritually empty. He had the sense that she had gone indeed, and had taken her soul with her; and the discovery made a queer unexpected void in him. "This is—absurd!" he heard himself exclaiming.

"Rose!" he called out; there was no answer. He stood up, and his wandering eye travelled from the table to the mantelpiece. On its shelf he saw a letter addressed to himself. He seized it and tore it open; and all at once the accents of the writer's reasonableness floated out into the jangled air of the little room.

"Dearest—After you left yesterday I had a radio from Aunt Julia, asking me to get to Paris as soon as I could, so I decided to motor over to Padua this morning, and catch the Orient Express. And I mean to slip off like this, without seeing you, or even letting you know that I'm going, because, on second thoughts, I believe my little plan (you know I promised you one) will be all the better for a day or two more of quiet thought; so I'll simply write it to you from Paris instead of talking it to you hurriedly this morning.

"Besides (I'll confess) I want to keep the picture of our happiness here intact, not frayed and rubbed by more discussion, even the friendliest. You'll understand, I know. This being together has been something so complete, so exquisite, that I want to carry it away with me in its perfection . . . I'll write in a few days. Till then, if you can, think of me as I think of you. No heart could ask more of another. Rose."

He sat down again, and read the letter over two or three times. It was sweet and reasonable—but it was also desperately sad. Yes; she had understood that for a time it was best for both that they should be apart. And this was her way of putting it to him. His eyes filled, and he wondered how he could have thought, the night before, that if he suddenly heard she was leaving it would be a relief . . .

But presently he began to visualise what the day would have been if he had found her there, and they had now been sitting over the lunch-table, "fraying and rubbing" their happiness, as she had put it, by more discussion—useless discussion. How intelligent of her to go—how merciful! Yes; he would think of her as she thought of him; he could now, without a shadow of reserve. He would bless her in all honesty for this respite . . .

He took a fading mountain-pink from one of the vases on the mantelpiece, put it in his pocket-book with her letter, and started to walk down to the village to send her a telegram. As he walked, he composed it, affectionately, lingeringly. He moved fast through the brisk air, and by the time he had reached the foot of the hill a pang of wholesome hunger reminded him that he had not lunched. Straight ahead, the *Pension Rosenglüh* lay in his path, and he knew that, even if the little Wheaters had finished their midday meal, Miss Scope would persuade the cook to conjure up an omelette for him . . .

Instantly he felt a sort of boyish excitement at the idea of surprising the party; and finding the front door unlatched, he crossed the hall and entered the private dining-room which had been assigned to them since the arrival of adult boarders less partial than himself to what Judith called the children's "dinner-roar."

His appearance was welcomed with a vocal vigour which must have made the crockery dance even in the grown-up *Speisesaal* across the hall. "Have the wild animals left a morsel for me?" he asked, and gaily wedged himself in between Judith and Blanca.

Chapter XXIV

U NINTERRUPTED communion with the little Wheaters
always gave Boyne the same feeling of liberation. It was
like getting back from a constrained bodily position into a natural one. This sense of being himself, being simply and utterly
at his ease, which the children's companionship had given him
during the Mediterranean voyage, but which he had enjoyed
only in uncertain snatches since their arrival at Cortina, came
back to him as soon as he had slipped his chair between Judith's
and Blanca's at the lunch-table. He would not ascribe it to her
having gone, but preferred to think it was because her going left
him free to dispose of himself as he chose. And what he chose
was, on the spot, to resume his half-fatherly attitude toward the
group, and devote every moment of his time to them.

Being with them again was like getting home after a long and
precarious journey during which he had been without news of
the people he loved. A great many things must have happened
in the interval, and not a moment must be lost in gathering up
the threads. There were, in fact, many threads to be gathered.
He got a general outline of the situation that very evening from
Miss Scope—learned that Terry's health was steadily improving, that the young Swiss tutor whom Boyne had unearthed at
Botzen was conscientious and kind, and got on well with Terry,
but found Bun hopelessly unmanageable ("And nothing new
in that," Miss Scope commented); that on the whole the three
little girls, Blanca, Zinnie and Beechy, though trying at times,
were behaving better than could have been hoped, considering
the unusual length of their holiday; and lastly that Chipstone,
even in the process of cutting a new tooth, retained his rosy
serenity, and had added a pound or more to his weight.

All this was as absorbing to Boyne as if every one concerned
had been of the highest interest and consequence. He had a long
talk with the tutor, went carefully into the question of Terry's
studies, suggested a few changes, and encouraged and counselled the young man. As to luring or coercing Bun up the steep
way of knowledge, a stronger hand would be needed; and while

Bun ranged unchecked there was not much to be done with the little girls. Even Blanca, though she felt herself so superior in age and culture, found the company of her juniors tolerable, and their bad example irresistible, when there was nothing better going. But, as against these drawbacks, there was the happy fact that the high air, which had done all the children good, had transformed Terry from a partial invalid into a joyous active boy who laughed at temperatures and clamoured for second helpings. And so far the Lido had refrained from interfering. On the whole, therefore, as the weeks passed, Boyne had more and more reason to be satisfied with his achievement. To give the children a couple of months of security, with the growing hope of keeping them all together under old Mrs. Mervin's roof, had assuredly been worth trying for. The evening after Mrs. Sellars's departure he wrote a long letter to Grandma Mervin.

Boyne, once more alone with the children, found that his confused feeling about Judith had given way to the frank elder-brotherly affection he had felt for her on the cruise. Perhaps because she herself had become natural and simple, now that there were no older people to put her on the defensive, she seemed again the buoyant child who had first captivated him. Or perhaps his thinking so was just a part of his satisfaction at being with his flock again, unobserved and uncriticised by the grown up. He and they understood each other; he suspected that, even had their plight not roused his pity, his own rest-lessness and impulsiveness would have fraternized with theirs. "The fact is, we're none of us grown up," he reflected, hugging himself for being on the children's side of the eternal barrier.

His talks with Judith turned, as usual, on the future of the children. He sometimes tried to draw from her the expression of a personal preference; but she seemed to want nothing for herself; she could not detach herself, even in imagination, from the others. For them she had fabulous dreams and ambitions. If only they could keep together till they were grown up! She had a quaint vision of their all living in a house somewhere in the country (perhaps her father would buy them one when she came of age); a house which should be always full of pets and birds; and leading there a life in which the amusements of the nurs-ery were delightfully combined with grown up pursuits. And for each of the children she had thought out a definite career. Blanca, of course, was to be "lovely": to Judith loveliness was a vocation. Terry was to be a great scholar, the guide and counsellor of the others—she had a savage reverence for the wisdom and authority to be acquired from books. Bun was manifestly meant to drive racing-motors, and carry off championships in games and athletics; Beechy would marry and have heaps of children, yet somehow be always able to look after Bun; and Zinnie— well, Zinnie was undoubtedly predestined to be "clever"; a fate of dubious import. But Judith hoped it would not be with the sharp cunning of little Pixie Lullmer, who seemed so childish and simple, and was really an abyss of precocious knowledge, initiated into all the secrets of hotel life; a toad of a child, Judith summed it up, whereas her poor half-sister, Doll Westway, had hated it all so much that she had taken the shortest way out by shooting herself . . .

Ah—and Chipstone! Well, there was no hurry about Chipstone, was there? But he was so large and calm, and so certain to get what he wanted, that Judith thought perhaps he would be a banker—and own a big yacht, and take them all on wonderful cruises. And Nanny and Susan would of course always stay with them, to look after Beechy's children . . .

Boyne had decided to write to old Mrs. Mervin without mentioning the fact to Judith. He had meant to consult her, had even intended to have a talk with her on the day when Mrs. Sellars's abrupt departure had momentarily unsettled his plans; but when the idea recurred to him Judith was already re-established in his mind as the blithe creature of their first encounter, and he had a superstitious dread of doing anything to change the harmony of their relation. After all, he could plead the children's cause with their grandmother as well as Judith could; and if his appeal were doomed to failure she need never know it had been made. He found himself insisting rather elaborately, in his own mind, on the childishness he was fond of ascribing to her when he talked of her to others; and now he feared lest anything should break through that necessary illusion. In his letter to Mrs. Mervin he tried to combine the maximum of conciseness and of eloquence, and ended by reminding her that the various parents might intervene at any moment, and begging her to cable at once if, as he earnestly hoped, she could give her assent to the plan. The sending off of the letter was like handing in an essay at school; with its completion he seemed entering with the children on a new holiday. "Two or three weeks' respite, anyhow; and then," he thought, "who knows? I may be able to carry them all back to New York with me." Incredible as it was, he clung to the hope with a faith as childish as Judith's.

Mrs. Sellars had said that she would write in a few days. Instead, she telegraphed to announce her arrival in Paris, and again, a little later, to inform Boyne of Aunt Julia's. To each message she added a few words of tender greeting; but ten days or more elapsed before the telegrams were followed by a letter.

Boyne found it one evening, on his return from a long expedition with the children. He had ceased, after a day or two, to speculate on Mrs. Sellars's silence, had gradually, as the days passed, become unconscious of their flight, and was almost surprised, when he saw her handwriting, that a letter from Paris should have reached Cortina so quickly. He waited till after dinner to read it, secretly wishing to keep the flavour of the present on his lips. Then, when the task could no longer be postponed, he withdrew to the melancholy lounge, and settled himself in the same slippery chair in which he had sat when he read the letter of the engineers asking if he could trace the whereabouts of the young man to whom they wanted to offer a job. "It's to say she's coming back," he muttered to himself as he broke the seal. But Mrs. Sellars did not say that.

The letter was one of her best—tender, gay and amusing. The description of Aunt Julia's arrival was a little masterpiece. The writer dwelt at length on the arts she had exercised—was still exercising—to persuade the family tyrant that he, Boyne, was justified in wishing for an immediate marriage, and she added, on a note of modest triumph, that success was already in sight. "But even if it were not, dear," the letter pursued, "I shouldn't allow that to alter my plans—our plans—and I'm prepared to have you carry me off under Aunt Julia's nose (formidable though that feature is), if she should refuse her sanction. But she won't; and the important question is what we intend to do, and not what she may think about it."

At this stage Boyne laid the letter aside, took out a cigar, cut it, and put it down without remembering to light it. He took up the letter again.

"But it's more important still that we should come to a clear understanding about our future—isn't it, dearest? I feel that I made such an understanding impossible the other day by my unreasonableness, my impatience, my apparent inability to see your point of view. But I did see it, even then; and I see it much more clearly now that I have studied the question at a sufficient distance to focus it properly. Of course we both know that, whatever decision we reach, some of the numerous papas and mammas of your little friends may upset it at a moment's notice; but meanwhile I have a plan to propose. What you want—isn't it?—is to guard these poor children as long as possible from the unsettling and demoralising influence of continual change. I quite see your idea; and it seems to me that those most exposed to such risks are the ones we ought to try to help. By your own showing, Mr. Wheater will never give up Chipstone for long; Zinnie, and Prince Buondelmonte's funny little pair, are bound to be claimed by their respective parents now that they have settled down to wealth and domesticity. As for the enchanting Judith, though you persist in not seeing it, she will be grown up and married in a year or two; and meanwhile, if the Wheaters do divorce, she will probably choose to remain with her mother, as she did before. The twins, in fact, seem to me the chief victims. They are old enough to understand what is going on, and not old enough to make themselves lives of their own; and above all they are at an age when disintegrating influences are likely to do the most harm. You have often told me that poor Terry's health has been an obstacle between him and his father (what a horrible idea that it should be so!), and that the bouncing Chip has cut him out. Terry needs care and sympathy more than any of them; and I am sure you will feel, as I do, that it would be unthinkable to separate dear little Blanca from the brother she adores. What I propose, then, is that you should ask Mr. and Mrs. Wheater to give up the twins—regarding us in any capacity you like, either as their friends, or as their legal guardians, if that is better—till they come of age. I will gladly take a share in looking after them, and I believe that between us we can turn them into happy useful members of society. If you agree, I am ready to—"

Boyne stopped reading, folded up the letter and thrust it into his pocket. There rushed over him a wave of disappointment and disgust. "Dear little Blanca indeed!" he muttered furiously. "Useful members of society!" That Mrs. Sellars should calmly propose to separate the children was bad enough; but that, of the lot, she should choose to foist on him the only one he could feel no affection for, and hardly any interest in—that to the woman he was going to marry Blanca should alone seem worthy of compassion among the four little girls who had been cast upon his mercy, this was to Boyne hatefully significant of the side of Mrs. Sellars's character to which, from the moment of their reunion, he had been trying to close his eyes. "She chooses her because she knows she need never be jealous of her," was his inmost thought.

Well, and supposing it were so—how womanly, how human, after all! Loving Boyne as she did, was it not natural that she should prefer to have under her roof the two children least likely to come between herself and him, to interfere in any way with their happiness? Yes—but was that loving him at all? If she had really loved him would she not have entered into his feeling about the little group, and recognised the cruelty of separating them? He paused a moment over this, and tried conscientiously to imagine what, in a similar case, his love for her would have inspired him to do. Would it, for instance, ever induce him to live with Aunt Julia as a dependent nephew-in-law? A million times no! But why propound such useless riddles? No one could pretend that the cases were similar. Rose Sellars would simply be asking him to gratify a whim; what he was asking of her was vital, inevitable. She knew that it lay with him, and with no one else, to save these children; she knew that, little by little, his whole heart had gone into the task. Yet coolly, deliberately, with that infernal air she had of thinking away whatever it was inconvenient to admit, she had affected to sympathise with his purpose while in reality her proposal ignored it. Send back the younger children to their parents—to such parents as Zinnia Lacrosse and Buondelmonte!—return Judith to her mother, to a mother about to marry Gerald Ormerod, who, by Judith's own showing, would have preferred herself? Boyne recoiled from the thought as from the sight of some physical cruelty he could not prevent. He got up, threw away his cigar, and went out hatless, indignant, into the night.

The air was warm, the sky full of clouds tunnelled by shifting vistas of a remote blue sprinkled with stars. Boyne groped his way down the obscure wood-path from his hotel, and walked across the fields to the slopes which Judith and he had climbed on the day of his return from the Lido. It was from that day— he recalled it now—that Rose Sellars's jealousy of Judith had dated; he had seen it flash across her fixed attentive face when, the next morning, Judith had blurted out an allusion to their ramble. Boyne—he also remembered—had given Mrs. Sellars to understand that on that occasion he had gone off for a walk by himself, "to get the Lido out of his lungs"; very likely his prevarication had first excited her suspicion. For why should he dissemble the fact that he had been with Judith, if Judith was only a child to him, as he said? Why indeed? It seemed as though, in concealing so significant a fact, he had simply, unconsciously, been on his guard against this long-suspected jealousy; as if he had always guessed that the most passionate and irrational of sentiments lurked under Mrs. Sellars's calm and reasonable exterior. If it were so, it certainly made her more interesting—but also less easy to deal with. For jealousy, to excite sympathy, must be felt by some one who also inspires it. Shared, it was a part of love; unshared, it made love impossible. And Boyne, in his fatuous security, could not imagine feeling jealous of Mrs. Sellars. "Though of course I should hate it like anything, I suppose . . ." But the problem was one that he could only apprehend intellectually.

He tramped on through the summer night, his mind full of tormented thoughts; and as he groped upward among the pines he remembered that other night, not many weeks since, when he had climbed the same path, and his feet had seemed winged, and the air elixir, because a girl's shoulder brushed his own, and he listened to unpremeditated laughter.

It was so late when he got back to the hotel that the porter, unwillingly roused, looked at him with a sulky astonishment.

"There was a lady here—she left a parcel for you."

"A lady? Where's the parcel?"

"Up in your room. I had to help her to carry it up. It was awkward getting it round the turn of the stairs. She left a letter for you too."

Awkward round the turn of the stairs? What on earth could the object be, and who the lady? Boyne, without farther questions, sprang up to his room. Rose had come back—there could be no doubt of it. She had decided, adroitly enough, to follow up her letter by the persuasion of her presence. At the thought he felt flurried, unsettled, as if she had come too soon, before he had set his mind in order to receive her.

And what could she possibly have brought him that had to be manœuvred up the hotel stairs? Whatever it was, he could not, try as he would, figure her labouring up to his room with it, even with the assistance of the porter. Why, she had never even been to his room, the room with every chair and table of which Judith and the other children were so carelessly familiar! It was utterly unlike Rose—and yet Rose of course it must be . . .

He flung open his door, and saw a large shrouded object in the middle of the floor; an object of odd uncertain shape, imperfectly wrapped in torn newspapers tied with string. The wrappings yielded to a pull, and an ancient walnut cradle with primitive carven ornaments revealed itself to his petrified gaze. A cradle! He threw himself into a chair and stared at it incredulously, as if he knew it must be an hallucination. At length he remembered the porter's having mentioned a letter, and his glance strayed to his chest of drawers. There, perched on the pincushion, was an envelope addressed in a precise familiar hand—the hand of Terry Wheater, always the scribe of the other children when their letters were to be subjected to grown up criticism. Boyne tore the envelope open and read:

"Darling Martin,

"We are all of us sending you this lovely cradle for your wedding present because we suppose you are going to be married very soon, as we think Mrs. Sellars has gone to Paris to order her trousseau. And because you have been like a father to us we hope and pray you will soon be a real father to a lot of lovely little children of your own, and they will all sleep in this cradle, and then you will think of

Your loving Judith, Terry, Blanca—"

Under the last of the rudimentary signatures, Chipstone had scrawled his mark; and below it was a scribbled postscript from Judith: "Darling, I open this while Terry's not looking to say he said we oughternt to call the craidle lovely, but it is lovely and we wanted you to know it was. Judith."

In the midnight silence Boyne sat and laughed and laughed until a nervous spinster in the next room banged on the wall and called out venomously: "I can hear every word you're both saying."

BOOK IV

Chapter XXV

B OYNE had been wrong in imagining that Mrs. Sellars might
come back unannounced to assure herself of the effect of
her letter. She did not do so; and after two days he decided that
he could no longer put off sending some kind of answer.

Only, what could he say?

Being with the children all day and every day, sharing their
meals, their games and scrambles, had gradually detached his
thoughts from Mrs. Sellars, reducing her once more to the
lovely shadow she had so long been; with the difference that
she was now a shadow irrevocably, whereas before he had always
believed she might become substantial. Finally he girt himself
to the task; and at once his irritation, his impatience, seemed
to materialise her again, as if she were fated to grow real only
when she thwarted or opposed him. He wondered if that were
another of the peculiarities of being in love. "People get too
close to each other—they can't see each other for the nearness, I suppose," he reflected, not altogether satisfied with this
explanation. He wrote: "And as to what you propose about the
children, do please believe that I don't mean to be unreasonable—but, unless I'm a little mad, your suggestion apparently
amounts to this: that I should shove them straight back into
the hell I've temporarily got them out of. For them that hell,
at least the worst of it, is being separated from each other; and
you ask me to separate them, when to keep them together is
the one thing that they and I have been fighting for. I make
no comment on your proposal to hand over the younger ones
to Lady Wrench and Buondelmonte; women like you are what
they are at the price of not being able even to picture such people
as those two. But I know what they are, and never, as long as I
can help it, will I be a party to giving back into such hands these
children who have trusted me. And when you say that Judith,
thanks to whom the younger ones have developed a sense of

927

solidarity and mutual trust in a world which is the very negation of such feelings—that Judith should be asked to see her work deliberately wrecked, and all the feelings she has cultivated in the others trampled on—" He broke off, flung down the pen, and sat hopelessly staring at what he had written. "Oh, hell—that's no use," he groaned.

The truth was that, even in his most rebellious moments, he could not trick himself into the idea that he had a grievance against Mrs. Sellars. In reality it was the other way round. When he had gone to Venice to negotiate with the Wheaters about the future of their mutinous family he had gone as an affianced man. In pledging himself to his strange guardianship he had virtually pledged Mrs. Sellars also, and without even making his promise depend on her consent. He had simply assumed that because she loved him she would approve of whatever he did, would accept any situation he chose to put her in. He had behaved, in short, like a romantic boy betrothed to a dreamer of his own age. All this was true, and it was true also that Mrs. Sellars had never reproached him with it. The sense of her magnanimity deprived his argument of all its force, and benumbed his angry pen. He pushed away the letter, pulled out another sheet, and scrawled on it: "Awfully sorry but cannot undo what I have done do try to understand me dearest."

Yes, a telegram was better: easier to write, at any rate . . . He tore up the letter, put on his hat, and walked down to the post-office with his message.

For its answer he had only twenty-four hours to wait; and when Mrs. Sellars's telegram came it merely said: "I do understand you letter follows . . ." Well, that was not unsatisfactory, as far as it went; but when two days more had elapsed, it was not a letter but a small registered packet which the postman put into Boyne's hands. Even in the act of signing the receipt, at his very first glance, he had guessed what the packet contained. He went up to his room, a little dizzy with the abruptness of the event, and angrily ripped off seal and string, revealing the morocco box he had expected to find there. For a minute or two he sat looking at the box, almost as unconscious of what he was feeling as a man in the first minute or two after being stabbed or shot. "So that's that," he said aloud. But what "that" was going to be he had as yet no notion. It was a wound, of course—but was it mortal? He didn't know. Suddenly, with a mumbled curse at his own plight, he snapped the box open and saw a thin slip of paper twisted about the sapphire ring. On the paper he read: "I shall always remember; I shall never resent; and that is why I want you to give this to some woman who can make you as happy as you have made me." He pitched the box and the paper aside, and hid his face in his hands. After all he must have loved her, he supposed—or at least the vision of her which their long separation had created . . .

He was roused by a knock, and looking up with dazed eyes saw Judith Wheater standing doubtfully on the threshold.

"Oh, Martin dear—were you asleep, or have you got one of those beastly headaches?" She came in and closed the door without waiting for his answer. "Have I disturbed you most awfully?" she questioned, passing her cool hand softly over his hair.

"Yes—no." He wondered whether her sharp eyes had already detected the open ring-box, and the paper signed with Rose's name. But to try to conceal them would only attract her attention. He put up his hand and pressed hers. "Yes—I believe I have got a beastly headache," he said.

"Then I'd better be off, perhaps?" she interrupted reluctantly. She was bending over him with the look she had when one of the children fell and scraped a knee, and Boyne could not help smiling up into her anxious eyes. "That depends on what you came for. What's up? Anything wrong at *Rosenglüh?*"

"Not particularly. But, you know, dear, we haven't seen you for two whole days . . ."

"You haven't?" In the struggle which had been going on in his mind since he had received Mrs. Sellars's letter he had completely forgotten the passage of time. "No more you have," he exclaimed. "I didn't realise I'd neglected you all so shamefully. Fact is, I've been tied up to a boring piece of business that I had to get off my chest. Sit down and have a cigarette." He fumbled for a box, and shoved it across the table to Judith, who had settled down comfortably into his only armchair. "Oh, Martin, how lovely to be here all alone with you!"

"Well, I don't believe you'll find me particularly good company," he rejoined, suddenly conscious of the ears of the acrimonious spinster next door, and wondering if he ought not to propose to Judith to finish her visit in the garden.

"Oh, yes, I shall, if you'll let me talk to you," she declared with her rich candour; and Boyne laughed in spite of himself.

"I've never been able to prevent your talking when you wanted to," he remarked, lighting a cigarette; and Judith thrust her thin shoulder-blades into the chair-back, crossed her legs, and sighed contentedly: "Few can."

"Well, then—what's your news?"

"A letter from mother, this morning."

The laugh died on Boyne's lips. The expected menace—here it was! He knew Joyce never wrote unless she had news of overwhelming importance, and usually of a disagreeable nature, to impart. "What does she say?" he asked apprehensively.

"Not much. I can't quite make out. She just says she's given up Gerald, and that she realises for the first time what a rotten rubbishy life she's been leading, and wants us all to forgive her for it."

"She *does*? But then—?"

Judith shrugged away his anticipations with a faint smile. "Oh, that's not particularly new. Mother always realises about the rottenness of her life when she's going to make a change."

"A change? What sort of a change?"

"Getting engaged to somebody else, generally."

"Oh, come, my dear! Why shouldn't it mean, this time, just what I've always hoped: that your father and mother see they can't get on without you—all of you—and that they're going to patch it up for good and all?"

Judith scanned him half-humorously through the veil of her cigarette-smoke. "Like in the nicer kind of movies?"

"You young sceptic, you! Why not? Your mother's too intelligent not to be fed up with jazz some day—"

"That's what she says. She says she's met somebody who's opened her eyes to how wrong it all is—and that always means she's going to get engaged again." Boyne was silent, and Judith added: "Anyhow, she's leaving at once for Paris to start divorce proceedings, because she says it's too wicked to live any longer with a man like father."

The load dropped from Boyne's heart. If Mrs. Wheater was leaving for Paris without suggesting that the children should join her, it was at least a respite—how long a one he couldn't guess, but at any rate enough to provide an excuse for deferring action. That was as far as his hopes dared venture. But he met Judith's eyes, and was surprised at their untroubled serenity. "Aren't you afraid—?" he began; and she rejoined immediately: "With you here? Why should we be?"

Immediately the sense of his responsibility descended on him with a redoubled weight. To have taken the risks he had for these children was mad enough; but to find that his doing so had deified him in their imagination, made them regard him as a sort of human sanctuary, turned his apprehensions to dismay.

"But, my child—look here. We've been awfully lucky so far; but we mustn't forget that, any day, this arrangement of ours may go to smash. How can I prevent it?"

She gave him all her confidence in a radiant look. "You have till now, haven't you? And if there's another row, couldn't we all nip over quietly to America with you?" She paused, and then began again, with a shade of hesitation that was new in her: "I suppose you'll be married very soon now, won't you, Martin? And when I got mother's letter this morning we wondered—Terry and I wondered—whether, if Grandma Mervin is afraid to take us in, we couldn't all go and live with you in New York, if we children paid a part of the rent? You see, father and mother couldn't possibly object to that, and I know you and Mrs. Sellars are fond of Chip and the steps, and we big ones really wouldn't be any trouble. Scopy and I have saved up such a lot out of father's allowance that I daresay you could afford to take a biggish house; and we'd all be awfully decent in the morning about not keeping the bath a minute longer than we had a right to."

The abruptness of Judith's transitions from embittered shrewdness to nursery simplicity was always disconcerting. When ways and means had to be considered, the disenchanted maiden for whom life seemed to have no surprises became once more the helpless little girl in the hands of nurses and governesses. At such moments, Boyne thought, she was like a young Daphne, half emerging into reality, half caught in the foliage of fairyland.

"My dear child—"

She always responded to every change in his intonation; and as he spoke he saw the shadow in her eyes before it reached her lips. Trying to keep a smile on them, she interrupted: "Now I've said something stupid again."

"You've said something unexpected—that's all. Give me a little time—"

She sprang up, and moved toward him with one of her impulsive darts. "Martin! When people ask for time, it's always for time to say no. Yes has one more letter in it, but it doesn't take half as long to say. And now you'll hate me for asking you something that you've got to take time to answer."

"Not a bit of it. I want time because I've got several answers. And the first is: how do you know your Grandma Mervin won't take you all in?"

She shook her head. "Because I wrote to her a month ago, and she's taking time before she answers. And besides—really and truly—I've always known that if Grandma Mervin did take us in, she'd give us up again the minute father shouted loud enough. You see," Judith added, with a sudden spring back to her wistful maturity, "grandma gets a big allowance from father."

"All right; that brings me to my second answer. How do you know your father won't order you back at once to the Lido—or wherever he is—if your mother has definitely decided to leave him?"

"Because father's gone off to Constantinople on the yacht with Syb—Mrs. Lullmer, I mean—and a whole crowd of people."

In spite of himself, Boyne again drew a breath of relief. If Wheater was off on the "Fancy Girl" with a band of cronies, and his wife rushing to Paris to start divorce proceedings, there might indeed be no need for an immediate decision. Never had procrastination seemed so sweet.

"Well, my dear, in that case it would appear that they're both going to let you alone—for a while, at any rate. So why jump unnecessary ditches?"

Judith responded with a joyful laugh. "Who wants to, darling? I don't! As long as you're with us I always feel safe." Again a little shiver of apprehension ran over Boyne; but he dissembled it by joining in her laugh. The more precarious was the tie between himself and the little Wheaters, the more precious seemed the days he could still hope to spend with them; he would not cloud another with vain fears. "Right you are. Suppose we go and do something desperate to celebrate the occasion? What about a good tramp for you and me, and then supper with the little Wheaters?"

She stood looking at him with her happiest eyes. "Hurrah, Martin! I haven't seen you so jolly for days. Terry was afraid you were moping because Mrs. Sellars had gone—he thought that was why you hadn't been to see us, and we decided that I'd better come up and find out."

"Trust you to find out," he grinned; and added sardonically: "I'm bearing up, as you see. But come along. Don't let's waste any more sunshine."

She moved obediently toward the door, but stopped short half-way with an exclamation of surprise. Boyne, who was rummaging in a corner for his stick, turned about to see her standing before the ancient cradle.

"Oh, Martin, you—you keep your boots in it!" A reproachful flush rose to her face, and was momentarily reflected in his own. Hang it—why was he always such an untidy fellow? And why was a cradle so uncommonly handy to hold boots? "Jove—how stupid! Must have been that confounded chambermaid—" But he broke off in confusion as he caught Judith's incredulous eye. "Well, hang it, you know—I've nothing else to put in it just at present," he cried defiantly.

Her face softened, and she met his banter with the wistful tentative gaze that he called her Monreale look. "But very soon you will have, won't you? A baby of your own, I mean," she explained. "I suppose you and Mrs. Sellars are going to be married as soon as she gets back with her trousseau, aren't you? Blanca and I were wondering if perhaps she'd ask us to be bridesmaids . . ."

Boyne was flinging the boots out of the cradle with an angry hand, and made no answer to this suggestion. Judith stood and watched him for a few moments; then she went to his side and slipped her arm through his. "Why, Martin—I believe you're very unhappy!" she exclaimed.

"Unhappy? Unhappy?" He swung around on her, exasperated. "Well, yes; I suppose I am unhappy. It's a way people have, you know. But, for the Lord's sake, can't you ever let things be? Can't you ever keep from treading on people's toes? I—oh, damn it, Judy; look here, for God's sake don't cry! I didn't mean to say anything to hurt you . . . I swear I didn't . . . Only sometimes . . ."

"Oh, I know, I know—you mean I have no tact!" she wailed.

"Damn tact! I'm thankful you haven't. There's nothing I hate as much as tact. But here—don't look so scared, child. There's no harm done . . . only don't try meddling with grown up things. It'll just wreck everything if you do . . ."

"But how can I not meddle when I love you so, and when I see that things are going wrong for you? Martin," she flung out breathlessly, "you don't mean to say you're not going to be married after all?"

Temptation suddenly twitched through him. It was as if saying "Yes" to her question might be the magic formula of freedom. After all, there lay the ring; he *was* free, technically—had only to utter the words to make them true. But he thrust his hands into his pockets and stood sullenly planted before the corner of the table on which he had tossed the open ring-box. "Not in this way," he thought. Aloud he said: "I mean that I don't yet know when I'm going to be married. That's all."

"Positively all?" He nodded.

"Ah," she sighed, relieved. It was evident that she identified herself whole-heartedly with his sentimental troubles, of whatever nature and by whomsoever they were caused.

She was still looking up at him, her face full of compunction and perplexity, and suddenly he put his arm about her and bent his head to her lips. They looked round and glowing, as they did in laughter or emotion; they drew his irresistibly. But he turned his head aside, and his kiss fell harmlessly on her cheek, near the tear-hung lashes. "That's my old Judy. Come, cheerio. On with your hat, and we'll go up the mountain." He saw that she was still trembling, and took her by the arm in the old brotherly way. "Come," he repeated, "let's go out."

In the doorway she paused and flung a last tragic glance at the cradle. "You poor old Martin, you! I suppose it's because you're so unhappy that you put your boots in it?" she sighed.

Chapter XXVI

To Boyne the calm of the next day brought no reassurance. Too many uncertainties hung close. After a night of pondering he had sent back the ring to Mrs. Sellars, with a brief line saying that she was of course free if she chose to be, but that he could not so regard himself till they had had a talk, and she had convinced him that she would be happier if their engagement ended.

He knew that he was merely using an old formula, the accepted one in such cases, and he longed to get away from it, to be spontaneous, honest, himself. But as he wrote it became clear to him that he was terribly sorry for Rose Sellars, terribly sorry for having disappointed her; and that such phrases—the kind he had been brought up on—were the devices of decent people who hated to give pain, and were even capable of self-sacrifice to avoid it. "After all, they were a lot better than we are," he thought; and the thought softened the close of his letter, and impelled him to add: "Do be patient with me, dear. As soon as I can get away I'll come."

This done, the whole problem vanished to the background of his mind. He was hardly aware that he was no longer thinking of it. His life of practical activities and swift decisions had given him the habit of easily dismissing matters once dealt with. He flattered himself that he could thus dispose of sentimental cares as easily as of professional problems; and to a certain extent it was true. Behind the close-knit foreground of his daily life there had hung for years the mirage of Rose Sellars; but that mirage was now the phantom of a phantom, and he averted his eyes lest he should find that it had faded into nothing.

After Mrs. Wheater's letter to Judith there came no more alarms to the *Pension Rosenglüh*; and the days slipped by in a security which seemed satisfying to Judith, and even to Miss Scope. But summer was waning in the high valleys of the Dolomites; tourists were scattering, the big hotels preparing to close. By-and-by a cold sparkle began to fill the air in the early mornings, and at night the temperature fell to freezing. On the lower slopes the larches were turning to pale gold, and the bare cliffs burned with an intenser fire against a sky as hard as metal. The very magic of the hastening days warned Boyne that they could not last, and that the change in the landscape symbolized another, as imminent, in the fortunes of his party.

Mrs. Sellars had written again—sweetly and reasonably—saying that she intended to remain for the present with Aunt Julia, who was settled in Paris for two or three months. If Boyne really wished for another talk, she added, she hoped he would be able to come before long; but in any case he could count on her affectionate understanding. She closed her letter with a friendly message to the children.

Boyne had been afraid that Judith would revert again to the subject of his private anxieties; but she contrived, by a visible effort which made him feel for the first time that she was really growing up, to keep off the forbidden topic. His own return to a more equable mood no doubt helped her; and so did the presence of the younger children and their preceptors. Boyne half-unconsciously avoided being alone with Judith; and the shortening days and freshening temperature curtailed their expeditions, and gave more time for games and romps around the cheerful stove in the children's dining-room.

It was there that, one rainy afternoon, he found himself sitting with the younger children. Judith had gone with Miss Scope and Nanny to Toblach, to fit out the family with autumn underclothes, Terry was upstairs, working with his tutor, Chip asleep in Susan's care; and Blanca, in the corner nearest the stove, was brooding over a torn copy of "The Tatler" with the passionate frown she always bent on the study of fashion-plates. "Skirts *are* going to be fuller," she said. "I've been telling Judy so for a month . . ."

Zinnie lifted her head from the rapt contemplation of an electric engine which Bun was putting together under Boyne's directions. "The lady that was here today had her skirt longer; a lot longer than Judy's," she remarked.

Beechy, whose attention was also riveted on the motions of Bun's agile fingers, interrupted indignantly: "She wasn't pretty like our Judy."

"The lady? What lady?" Boyne interposed, vaguely apprehensive. "Have you got a new lodger here?"

Blanca re-entered the conversation with a sniff. "You wouldn't have taken her for one if you'd seen her. She's not the *Rosenglüh* kind. She would certainly have been at the 'Palace' if it hadn't been closed. Not exactly smart, you know—smartness has been so overdone, hasn't it? She was—what's that funny old word that Scopy loves?—distinguished. At least, I *think* that's what distinguished means . . . the way that lady looked. Her clothes awfully plain; but not the least 'sports.' Rather governessy, really . . . like Scopy young, if Chanel could have dressed her . . ." Blanca paused, reduced to silence by the hopelessness of the attempt to fit her words to her meaning.

Boyne looked up from the engine. "Perhaps when you've finished with her clothes you'll tell me what she came for."

"To see you—you—*you*!" cried Zinnie, executing a double handspring she had lately learned from Bun, to the despair of Beechy, who was so fat that she invariably collapsed midway of the same attempt. "I could have told you that," Zinnie added, "for I spoke to her."

"You did? What impertinence!" cried Blanca, bounding from her seat. Bun, flat on his stomach, his legs in the air, his curls mixed with the engine, chanted over his shoulder: "Girls are always butting in—butting in . . ."

"Nasty rotters, girls are!" sympathised Beechy, always ready to champion her brother, and not as yet very clear as to her own sex.

Zinnie's reprisals were checked by the discovery that the landlady's gold-fish aquarium, which usually stood in the larger and colder public dining-room, had been brought in and placed on a stand before the window. She tiptoed off to inspect this forbidden Paradise while Boyne got to his feet and picked up the electric wire. "Where's the battery? Are your rails straight? Now, then, Bun, are you ready?" He turned to Zinnie. "To see *me*, did you say? What on earth for? Did she tell you?"

"Tell Zinnie! So likely!" ejaculated Blanca with a shrug. She turned to Boyne, drawing her lids together with her pretty cat-like smile. "*Félicitations, cher ami. Elle était plutôt bien, la dame, vous savez.*"

"Oh, shucks—zif we didn't all of us talk French!" commented Zinnie, still watchfully circling about the aquarium.

The door opened, and a maid came in with a card which she handed hesitatingly to Boyne. The name on it was: *Princess Buondelmonte*, and underneath was written: "begs Mr. Boyne to see her on important business." Boyne crammed the card into his pocket without speaking, conscious that the eyes of all the children were upon him.

"It's the lady, it's the lady, I know it is!" Zinnie piped. "I heard her say she was coming back to see Martin. She's come all the way from Rome to see him."

Blanca, at his side, had slid an insinuating hand in his. "From Rome? Oh, Martin, who is it? Mayn't I come with you, at any rate as far as the door? I do want to see if her dress is made of kasha or crepella . . . just to be able to tell Judy . . ."

Boyne checked her firmly. "You've got to stay here and mind the infants. It's nothing important—I'll be back in a few minutes." He thanked his stars that the lady had sent in her card instead of confiding her name to the maid. He could not imagine what his noble visitor wanted of him, but the very sight of the name had let loose all his fears. As he left the room he turned and sent a last glance toward the group sprawling around the engine, which had after all refused to start—orange curls mixed with brown and dusky, sunburnt legs kicking high, voices mixed in breathless controversy. How healthy and jolly they all looked! And how good they smelt, with that mixed smell of woollen garments, and soap, and the fruity fragrance of young bodies tumbled about together. As Boyne looked back at them he thought how funny and dear they were, and how different the world might have been if Rose Sellars had freed herself when he and she were still young . . .

A lady with a slim straight back was standing in the sitting-room, attentively examining the stuffed eagle above the stove. She turned at Boyne's entrance and revealed a small oval face, somewhat pale, with excessively earnest gray eyes, and a well-modelled nose and brow. It puzzled him to discover why an assemblage of such agreeable features did not produce an effect of beauty; but a second glance suggested that it was because their owner had never thought about being beautiful. That she had graver preoccupations was immediately evident from the tone of her slow and carefully-modulated speech. "Mr. Boyne?"

she asked, as though she feared he might deny his identity, and was immediately prepared, if he did, to disprove the denial; and on his saying that he was, she continued, with a touch of nervousness: "I have come all the way from Rome to see my children."

"Your children—?" Boyne echoed in astonishment; and she corrected herself with a slight blush. "I should say the Prince's. Or my step-children. But I hate the word, for I feel about them already as if they were my own."

Boyne pushed an armchair forward, and she sat down, crossing her feet neatly, and satisfying herself that the skirt which Zinnie described as long was so adjusted as not to reveal too much of the pretty legs above her slender ankles. "They *are* here—Astorre and Beatrice?"

Boyne heard her with dismay, but kept up a brave exterior. "Here? Oh, yes—certainly. Mr. and Mrs. Wheater sent all the children here a few weeks ago—for the climate."

Princess Buondelmonte met this with a smile of faint incredulity. "In your charge, I understand? Yes. But of course you must know that Mr. and Mrs. Wheater have really no business whatever to send my husband's children here, or anywhere else." She paused a moment, and added: "And I have come to take them home."

"Oh, Princess—" Boyne exclaimed.

She raised her handsome eyebrows slightly, and said: "You seem surprised."

"Well—yes. At any rate, I'm awfully sorry."

"Sorry? Don't you think that children ought to be in their own home, with their own parents?"

"Well, that depends."

"Depends! How can it ever—?" She crimsoned suddenly, and then grew even paler than before. "I don't suppose you intend to insinuate—?" She broke off, and he saw that her eyes had filled with tears. "For, of course, that I won't tolerate for a single instant," she added a little breathlessly, as though throwing herself on his mercy in a conflict she felt to be unequal if it should turn on Prince Buondelmonte's merits as a father.

Boyne felt so sorry for her that he answered: "I wasn't thinking of insinuating anything. I only meant that this little group of children have always been together, and it has made them so fond of each other that they really regard themselves as one family. It seems a pity, it seems cruel . . ."

"Cruel?" she interrupted. "The real cruelty has been to deprive the poor little things for so long of a father's influence, to take advantage of . . . of Prince Buondelmonte's misfortunes, his undeserved misfortunes, to keep his children without a real home, without family associations, without . . . without any guiding principle . . ." She leaned forward, her grave almost terrified eyes on Boyne. "What guidance have they had? What moral training? What religious education? Have you or your friends ever thought that? It's a big responsibility you've assumed. Have you never thought you might some day be asked to account for the use you've made of it?"

Boyne heard her with a growing wonder. She spoke slowly but fluently, not as if repeating a lesson learned by rote, but as though she were sustaining a thesis with the ease of a practised orator. There was something didactic—perhaps forensic, rather—in her glib command of her subject. He saw that she was trembling with nervousness, yet that her nerves would never control her; and his heart sank.

"I'm afraid I can't answer all your questions," he said, "I've only been with the children for a few weeks. Mr. and Mrs. Wheater asked me to keep an eye on them during the . . . the settling of certain family matters; but I can assure you that since I've known them they've always been in an atmosphere of the greatest kindness and affection; and I'm inclined to think that's the most important thing of all."

Princess Buondelmonte listened attentively, her brows drawn together in a cautious frown. "Of course I'm not prepared to admit that unreservedly. I mean, the kindness of salaried assistants or . . . or of inexperienced persons may do as much harm as good. To any one who has gone at all deeply into the difficult and absorbing subject of child-psychology—" she paused, and added with an air of modest dignity: "I ought perhaps to explain that I took my degree *cum laude*, in Eugenics and Infant Psychology, at Lohengrin College, Texas. You may have heard that my grandfather, Dr. Judson Tring, was the founder of the college, and also its first President." She stopped again, glanced half proudly, half shyly at Boyne, as though to see how much this glimpse of her genealogy had impressed him, and then pursued: "Can you give me, for instance, any sort of assurance that Astorre and Beatrice have ever been properly psychoanalyzed, and that their studies and games have been selected with a view to their particular moral, alimentary, dental and glandular heredity? Games, for instance, should be quite as carefully supervised as studies . . . but I know how little importance Europe still attaches to these supremely vital questions." No adequate answer occurred to Boyne, and she rose from her seat with an impatient gesture. "I don't know that there is any use in continuing a discussion which would not, in any case, affect my final decision, or Prince Buondelmonte's—"

"Oh, don't say that!" Boyne exclaimed.

"Don't—?"

"Not if it means you won't listen to any plea—won't first consider what it's going to be to these children to be suddenly uprooted . . ."

She interrupted: "It was not Prince Buondelmonte who first uprooted them. It was through circumstances of which he was himself the victim—I may say, Mr. Boyne, the *chivalrous* victim—that he found himself obliged (or thought himself obliged) to trust Astorre and Beatrice for a while to Mrs. Wheater. He did it simply in order that no breath of calumny should touch her." The Princess paused, and added, with a genuine tremor in her voice: "Though Mrs. Wheater was not his children's mother my husband always remembers that for a time she bore his name."

If the Princess's aim had been to reduce her interlocutor to silence, she had at last succeeded. Boyne sat speechless, wondering how much the granddaughter of Dr. Judson Tring believed of what she was saying, and to what extent her astounding version of the case was the result of patient schooling on her husband's part. He concluded that she was incapable of deliberate deception, and fully convinced of the truth of her assertions; and he knew this would make it all the harder to reason with her. For a few moments the two faced each other without speaking; then Boyne said: "But surely the fact that Prince Buondelmonte did leave his children with Mrs. Wheater ought to be considered. If he was willing to have her keep them he must have thought she knew how to take care of them."

The Princess again interrupted him. "My husband left his children with Mrs. Wheater for the reasons I've told you; but also because, owing to unfortunate circumstances, he had at the time no home to give them, and they had no mother to care for them. Now all that is changed. Since our marriage we have fortunately been able to buy back the Buondelmonte palace in Rome, and I am as anxious as he is that his children should come and live with us there."

Boyne stood up impatiently. The talk was assuming more and more the tone of a legal debate; conducted on such lines there seemed no reason for its ever ending. If one accepted the Princess's premises—and Boyne had no way of disproving them—it was difficult to question her conclusions. All he could do was to plead his lack of authority. He reminded his visitor that Mrs. Wheater, to whom, for whatever reason, their father had confided Bun and Beechy, had, in her turn, passed them over to their present guardians, who were therefore answerable to her, and her only. The Princess's lips parted nervously on the first syllable of a new protest; but Boyne interrupted: "Princess! It's really so simple—I mean the legal part. If your husband has a right to his children, no one can prevent his getting them. The real issue seems to me quite different. It concerns only the children themselves. They're so desperately anxious not to be separated; they're so happy together. Of course none of that is my doing. It's their eldest step-sister—or whatever you like to call her—Mrs. Wheater's eldest daughter, Judith, who has kept the six of them together through all the ups and downs of their parents' matrimonial troubles. Before you decide—"

The Princess lifted an imperative hand. "Mr. Boyne—I'm sorry. I can see that you're very fond of the children. But fondness is not everything . . . it may even be a source of moral danger. I'm afraid we shouldn't altogether agree as to the choice of the persons Mrs. Wheater has left in charge of them—not even as to her own daughter. The soul of a child—"

"Yes," Boyne acquiesced; "that's the very thing I'm pleading for. If you could see them together . . ."

"Oh, but I intend to," she responded briskly.

Her promptness took him aback. "Now, you mean?"

She gave a smiling nod. "Certainly. You don't suppose I came from Rome for any other reason? But you needn't be afraid of my kidnapping them." Her eyes became severe again. "I hope it won't have to come to that; but of course I intend to see my husband's children."

"Oh, all right," Boyne agreed. He was beginning to divine, under her hard mechanical manner, something young and untried, something one might still reach and appeal to; and he reflected that the sight of the children would perhaps prove to be the simplest way of reaching it. "The children are playing in the other room," he said. "Shall I go and get Bun and Beechy, or do you prefer to see them first with the others?"

The Princess said, yes, she thought she would like to see them all together at their games. "Games have such a profound psychological significance," she explained with a smile.

"Well, I'm glad you're going to take them by surprise. It's always the best way with children. You'll see what jolly little beggars they are; how they all understand each other; how well they get on together . . . I'm counting on the sight to plead our cause."

He led her down the passage and threw open the door of the children's dining-room.

On the threshold they were met by a burst of angry voices. Everything in the room was noise and confusion, and the opening of the door remained unheeded. In all his experience of the little Wheaters, Boyne had never before seen them engaged in so fierce a conflict: it seemed incredible that the participants should be only four. Some were screaming, some vituperating, some doing both, and butting at each other, head down, at the same time. The floor was strewn with the wreckage of battle, but the agitated movements of the combatants made the origin of the dispute hard to discover. "God," Boyne ejaculated, stepping back.

Zinnie's voice rose furiously above the others. "It wasn't me't upset the 'quarium, I swear it wasn't, Blanca—and those two wops know it just as well as I do . . ."

Bun squealed back: "It was you that tried to bathe Chip's rabbit in it, you dirty little lying sneak, you!"

"No, I didn't, neither; but Nanny don't never give him enough to drink, 'n so I just ran up and brought him down while Chip was asleep, 'n if Beechy hadn't gone and butted in—"

"You rotten little liar, you, you know you were trying to find out if rabbits can swim."

"No, I wasn't, either. And it was Beechy pushed me 'gainst the 'quarium, and you know it was . . ."

" 'Cos the rabbit was drownding, and Judy'd have killed you if you'd of let it," Beechy wailed.

"She'll kill you anyhow if you call us wops again," roared Bun.

Blanca, reluctantly torn from her study of "The Tatler," had risen from the stove-corner and was distributing slaps and shakes with a practised hand. As she turned to the door, and saw Boyne and his visitor on the threshold, her arms dropped to her sides, and she swept the shrieking children into a corner behind her. "Oh, Martin, I'm so sorry! Did you ever see such a pack of savages? They were playing some silly game, and I didn't realise . . ." She addressed herself to Boyne, but, as usual, it was the newcomer who fixed her attention. "What will your friend think?" she murmured with a deprecating glance.

Princess Buondelmonte, pale and erect, stood in the doorway and returned her gaze. "I shall think just what I expected to," she said coldly. She turned to Boyne, and continued in a trembling voice: "It is just as I was saying: nothing in a child's education should be left to chance. Games have to be directed even more carefully than studies . . . Telling a child that an older person will kill it seems to me so unspeakably wicked . . . This perpetuating of the old militarist instinct . . . 'Kill' is one of the words we have entirely eliminated at Lohengrin . . ." Still nervously, she addressed herself again to Blanca. "I do hope," she said, "that the particular little savage who made that threat doesn't happen to be mine—to be Prince Buondelmonte's, I mean?"

Blanca was looking at her with a captivated stare. "You don't mean to say you're his new wife? Are you the Princess Buondelmonte, really?"

"Yes, I'm the Princess Buondelmonte," the visitor assented, with a smile of girlish gratification which made her appear almost as young as Blanca. It was manifest that, however heavily the higher responsibilities weighed on her, she still enjoyed the sound of her new title.

But Bun, brushing aside the little girls, had flung himself impetuously upon her. "Are you really and truly my father's new wife? Then you must tell him he's got to send me a gun at once, to shoot everybody who calls me and Beechy a wop."

The visitor stooped down, laying a timid yet resolute hand on his dark head. "What I shall do, my dear, is to carry you off at once, you and little Beatrice, to your own home—to your own dear father, who's pining for you—to a place where nobody ever talks about shooting and killing . . ."

Bun's face fell perceptibly. "Won't my father give me a gun, don't you suppose? Then I don't believe Beechy 'n me 'd care such a lot about going."

The Princess's lips narrowed with the same air of resolution which had informed her hand. "Oh, but I'm afraid you've got to, Astorre. This is not your real home, you know, and I'm going to take you both away to the loveliest house . . . and your father'll give you lots of other things you'll like ever so much better . . ."

"Not than a gun, I won't," said Bun immovably.

Chapter XXVII

"Take away my children? Take them away from me?" Judith Wheater had pushed open the door, and stood there, small and pale, in her dripping mackintosh and bedraggled hat. She gave a little laugh, and her gray eyes measured the stranger with a deliberate and freezing scrutiny. "I don't in the least know who you are," she said, "but I know you don't know what you're talking about . . ." She glanced away to the ravaged scene, and the frightened excited faces of the children. "Heavens! What an unholy mess! What on earth has been happening? Oh, the poor drenched rabbit . . . Here, wrap it up in my scarf . . . Nanny, take the children upstairs, and send Susan at once to tidy up. Yes, Blanca; you must go too. If you can't keep the little ones in order you've got to be treated like one of them." She turned to the bewildered visitor. "I'm Miss Wheater. If you want to see me, will you please come into the sitting-room?" Her eye fell on Boyne, who had drawn back into the dusk of the passage, as if disclaiming any part in the impending drama. "Martin," she challenged him, "was it you who brought this lady here?"

"It's the Princess Buondelmonte, Judith."

Judith again scanned her with unrelenting eyes. "I'm afraid that won't make any difference," she said. The Princess stood drooping her high crest a little, as if unused to receiving instructions from one so much smaller and younger than herself. Boyne remembered how Judith had awed and baffled Mrs. Sellars on their first meeting, and his heart swelled with irrational hopes. "Judith," he cautioned her, below his breath.

"This way. You'll come too, please, Martin." She led them down the passage, and into the sitting-room. After she had closed the door she pushed forward a chair for the Princess Buondelmonte, and said with emphasis: "Perhaps you don't know that Mr. Boyne has been appointed the guardian of the children."

The Princess did not seat herself. She leaned on the back of the chair, and smiled down at the champion of the little Wheaters. "They seem to have a great many guardians. I hear you're one of them too."

"Me?" Judith's eyes widened in astonishment. "I'm only their eldest sister. All I do is just to try to look after them."

Something in her accent seemed to touch the Princess, who seated herself in the chair on which she had been leaning, made sure that her skirts did not expose more than a decent extent of ankle, and began to speak in a friendlier tone. "I'm sure you're perfectly devoted to them—that all you want is what's best for them."

Judith paused a moment. "That depends on what you mean by best. All I want is for us all to stay together."

The Princess made a sign of comprehension. "Yes . . . But supposing it was not what's best for the children?"

"Oh, but it is," said Judith decisively. The other hesitated, and she pressed on: "Because nobody can possibly love them as much as Martin and Miss Scope and me."

"I see. But you seem to have forgotten that they have parents . . ."

"No. It's the parents who've forgotten," Judith flashed back.

"Not all of them. Since I'm here," the Princess smiled.

"What? Because you've just married Prince Buondelmonte, and probably think he ought to have remembered to look after Bun and Beechy? Well, I think so too. Only he didn't, you see; not when they were little, and had to be wiped and changed and fed, and walked up and down when they were cutting their teeth. And now that they're big enough to cut up their own food and be good company, I suppose you and he think it would be fun to come and carry them off, the way you'd pick out a pair of Pekes at a dog-show . . . only you forget that in the meantime they've grown to love *us* and not you, and that they're devoted to all the other children, and that it would half kill them to be separated from each other . . ."

"Oh—devoted?" the Princess protested with her dry smile.

"Of course they are. Why do you ask? Because they were having a scrap when you came in? Did that tussle about a gold-fish frighten you? Have you never seen children bite and scratch before?" Judith gave a contemptuous shrug. "I pity you," she said, "the first time you try to give Bun castor-oil . . ."

Was it victory or defeat? Boyne and Judith sat late in the little sitting-room, asking themselves that, after the Princess

Buondelmonte had gone. It had been Boyne's idea—and almost his only contribution to the fiery dialogue between the two—that the Princess should be invited to return in the evening and share the children's supper. The proposal, seconded by Judith after a swift glance at Boyne, seemed to surprise their visitor, and to disarm her growing hostility. The encounter with Judith had not tended to soften her feelings, and for a moment it looked as if things were taking a dangerous turn; but Boyne had intervened with the suggestion that the Princess, having seen the children at their worst, should be given a chance to meet them in pleasanter circumstances. He added that he would be glad of another talk with her; and as she did not leave till the next day, and was staying at an hotel near his own, he asked if he might walk back there with her, and fetch her down again for supper. She accepted both suggestions, and after a mollified farewell to Judith, started up the hill with Boyne. He saw that she was still inwardly agitated, and clutching desperately at what remained of her resolution; and he put in a pacifying word in excuse of Judith's irritability, and assured the Princess that the Wheaters would make no difficulty in recognising the Prince's legal right to his children. The real question, he went on, was surely quite different; was one of delicacy, of good taste, if you chose to call it so. Mrs. Wheater had taken in Beechy and Bun when their father was not able to; she had given them the same advantages as her own children (the Princess, at this, sounded an ironic murmur), and had shown them the same affection; though all she had done, Boyne hastened to add, was as nothing to the patient unflagging devotion of their step-sister—who technically wasn't even a step-sister. On that theme Boyne did not have to choose his words. They poured out with a vehemence surprising even to himself. The Princess, he supposed—whatever her educational theories were—would agree that the first thing young children needed was to be loved enough; above all, children exposed as they were in the Wheater world, where every new divorce and remarriage thrust them again into unfamiliar surroundings. Through all these changes, Boyne pointed out, Judith had clung to her little flock, loving them, and teaching them to love each other; she had even inspired governesses and nurses with her own passionate fidelity, so that in a welter of change the group had remained together, protected and happy. If only, Boyne pleaded, they could be left as they were for a few years longer; perhaps if they could it would be found, when they finally rejoined their respective families, that under Judith's care they had been better prepared for life than if their parents had insisted on separating them.

The Princess listened attentively to his arguments, but said little in reply; Boyne suspected that she had been taught not to commit herself unless she was on familiar ground, and apparently she was unfamiliar with the kind of plea he made. The sentiments he appealed to seemed to have a sort of romantic interest for her, as feudal ruins might have for an intelligent traveller; but he saw that there were no words for them in her vocabulary.

When they went back to the *Pension Rosenglüh* for supper the children, headed by Terry and Blanca, presented a picture of such roseate harmony that the Princess was evidently struck. To complete the impression, Chip, who was always brought down at this hour to say goodnight, walked in led by Nanny, placed a confiding palm in the strange lady's, said "Howoodoo," and wound his fingers in her hair, which he pronounced to be "ike Oody's"—for Chip was beginning to generalise and to co-ordinate, though his educators could not have put a name to the process, any more than the Princess could to the instinctive motions of the heart.

Supper, on the whole, was a success. The children were unusually well-behaved; even Zinnie subdued herself to the prevailing tone. Bun and Beechy, seated one on each side of their new step-mother, and visibly awed by her proximity, demeaned themselves with a restraint which the Princess made several timid attempts to break down. It was evident that what she had said about the prohibition of fire-arms still rankled in Bun, and both children were prim and non-committal, as they always were—to a degree unknown to the others—once their distrust was aroused. The Princess, to conceal her embarrassment, discoursed volubly about the historic interest of the ancestral palace which her husband had succeeded in repurchasing, and promised Bun that one of its spacious apartments should be fitted up as a modern playroom, in which he would learn to replace his artless antics by the newest feats in scientific gymnastics. Bun's eyes glittered; but after a reflective silence he shook his head. "We couldn't," he said, "not 'f we wanted to the most awful way; 'cos we've all sworen a noath on Scopy's book that we wouldn't."

This solemn self-reminder caused Beechy's eyes to fill, and Zinnie to cry out: "We'd be damned black-hearted villains if we did!"

The Princess looked distressed. "What do you mean by swearing an oath, Astorre?" she asked, pronouncing the words as if they were explosives and must be handled with caution.

"I mean a nawful oath," Bun explained, with an effort at greater accuracy.

"But I can't bear to hear children talk about swearing—or about villains either," his step-mother continued, turning with a reproachful smile to Zinnie, who promptly rejoined: "Then you'd better not ever have any of your own"; which caused the Princess to blush and lower her grave eyes.

To hide her constraint she addressed a question to the company in general. "What is this book that you children speak of as Miss Scope's? The choice of books is so imp—"

None of the younger children could pronounce the name of the book, and they therefore preserved a respectful silence; but Terry interrupted with a laugh: "Oh, it's the book that Scopy cures us all out of. It's called the 'Cyclopædia of Nursery Remedies'."

The Princess received this with a dubious frown. "I don't remember a book of that name being used in our courses at Lohengrin; is it a recent publication?"

Miss Scope sat rigid and majestic at the opposite table-end. Thus directly challenged, she replied reassuringly: "Dear me, no; it's been thoroughly tested. My mother and all my aunts used it in their families. I believe even my grandmother—"

"Even your grandmother? But then the book must be completely obsolete—and probably very dangerous."

Miss Scope smiled undauntedly. "Oh, I think not. My mother always found it most reliable. We were fourteen in the family, ten miles from the railway, in Lancashire, and she brought us through all our illnesses on it. In a family of that size one couldn't always be sending for the doctor . . ."

This gave her interlocutor's dismay a new turn. "Fourteen in your family? You don't mean to say your mother had fourteen children?"

Miss Scope replied with undisguised pride that that was what she did mean; and the Princess laid down her fork with the air of one about to spring up and do battle against such deplorable abuses. "It's incredible . . ." she began; then broke off to add in a lower tone: "But I suppose that at that time—" her glance at Miss Scope's white head seemed to say that the whole business was an old unhappy far-off thing, and she resumed more hopefully: "In the United States such matters will soon be regulated by legislation . . ."

She met Miss Scope's horrified stare, and glanced nervously about the table, as if realising that the subject, even at Lohengrin, might hardly be considered suitable for juvenile ears. To relieve her embarrassment she leaned across Bun and addressed herself once more to Zinnie.

"You must be Lady Wrench's little girl, aren't you, my dear? Only think, I saw your mother the other day in Venice," she said, in an affable attempt to change the conversation.

Zinnie's face sparkled with curiosity. "Oh, did you see her, truly? What did she have on, do you remember?"

"Have on—?" The Princess hesitated, with a puzzled look, and Judith intervened: "Zinnie has a passion for pretty clothes."

"I think *yours* are awfully pretty," Zinnie insidiously put in, addressing the Princess; and added: "Are you sure my mother didn't give you any presents to give us?"

"Zinnie!" came reprovingly from Miss Scope.

The Princess shook her head. "No; she didn't give me any presents. Perhaps she thinks you ought to come and get them. But she gave me a message for you when she heard that I was coming here—she told me to tell you how dreadfully she wanted to see her little girl again."

Zinnie grew scarlet with excitement and gratification; such notice lifted her at once above the other children. But an afterthought soon damped her pride. "If she really feels like that I'd of thought she'd of sent me a present," she objected doubtfully.

"Presents aren't everything. And it's not very nice to associate the people you love with the thought of what they may be going to give you. Besides," continued the Princess illogically, "if your mother is so generous, think how many presents you'd get if you were always with her."

This seemed to plunge Zinnie into fresh perplexity. "Always with her? How could I be? She doesn't want to 'dopt the lot of us, does she? 'Cos you see we've all sweared—"

"You mustn't say swear," said the Princess.

"Swore," Zinnie corrected herself.

"I mean, not use such words," the Princess explained.

"But we *did*," said Zinnie, "on Scopy's book; so she'd have to 'dopt us all, with Judy. Do you s'pose she would?"

"I don't know about that; perhaps it might be difficult. But why shouldn't she want to have her own little daughter with her?" The Princess again leaned over, and laid a persuasive hand on Zinnie's. "Don't you want me to take you back to Venice, to your own real mother, when I go to-morrow?"

There was a pause of suspense. Boyne signed to Judith to keep silent, and the children, taking the cue, remained with spoons above their pudding, and eyes agape, while this perfidious proposal was submitted. Zinnie, from crimson, had grown almost pale; the orange spirals of her bushy head seemed to droop with her drooping lips. Her head sank on her neck, and she twisted about in its crease of plumpness the necklace her mother had given her. "What kind of presents 'd you s'pose they'd be?" she questioned back with caution.

"Oh, I don't know, dear. But you oughtn't to think about that. You ought to think only of your mother, and her wanting so much to have you. You must give me an answer to take back to her. Shan't I tell her you want to go to her, Zinnie?"

Zinnie hung her head still lower. If it had been possible for a Wheater child to be shy, she would have appeared so; but in reality she was only struggling with a problem beyond her powers. At last she raised her head, and looked firmly at the Princess. "I should like to consult my lawyer first," she said.

Boyne burst out laughing, and the Princess nervously joined him, perhaps to cover the appearance of defeat.

Having so obviously failed to inspire the children with confidence, she once more addressed herself to Miss Scope. "I should be so much interested in talking over your educational system with you. I suppose you've entirely eliminated enforced obedience, as we have at Lohengrin?"

"Enforced—?" Miss Scope gave an incredulous gasp, and her charges, evidently struck by the question, again remained with suspended spoons, and eyes eagerly fixed on the Princess. Miss Scope gave a curt laugh. "I've never known children to obey unless they were forced to. If you know a way to make them, I shall be glad to learn it," she said drily.

This seemed to cause the Princess more disappointment than surprise. "Ah, that's just what we won't do; *make them*. We leave them as free as air, and simply suggest to them to co-operate. At Lohengrin co-operation has superseded every other method. We teach even our little two-year-olds voluntary co-operation. We think the idea of obedience is debasing." She turned with a smile to her step-son. "When Astorre and Beatrice come to live with me the first thing I shall do is to make them both co-operate."

Bun received this unsmilingly, and Beechy burst into passionate weeping and flung her arms jealously about her brother. "No—no, you bad wicked woman, you mustn't! You shan't operate on Bun, only on me—if you *must*!" she added in a final wail, her desperate eyes entreating her step-mother.

"But, my dear, I don't understand," the Princess murmured; and Judith hurriedly explained that Blanca had been operated upon for appendicitis the previous year, and that the use of the word in connection with her illness had had an intimidating effect on the younger children, and especially on Beechy.

"But this is all wrong . . . dreadfully wrong . . ." the Princess said with a baffled sigh. No one found an answer, and supper being over, Judith proposed that they should return to the sitting-room. The children followed, marshalled by Miss Scope, and the Princess again tried to engage them in talk; but she could not break down the barrier of mistrust which had been set up. Finally she suggested that they should all play a game together—a quiet writing game she thought would be interesting. A table was cleared, and paper and pencils found with some difficulty, and distributed among the children, the youngest of whom were lifted up onto sofa-cushions to make their seats high enough for collaboration. The Princess explained that the game they were going to play was called "Ambition," and that it had been introduced into the Vocational Department of Juvenile Psychology at Lohengrin in order to direct children's minds as early as possible to the choice of a career. First of all, she continued, each was to write down what he or she would most like to be or to do; then they were to fold the papers, and Mr. Boyne was to shake them up in his hat, and read them out in turn, and as he read the children were to try to guess who had made each choice.

The game did not start with as much *élan* as its organiser had perhaps hoped. The children were still oppressed by her presence, and all of them but Terry hated writing, and were unused to abstract speculations on the future; moreover, they probably felt that if they were to state with sincerity what they wanted to be their aspirations would be received with the friendly ridicule which grown ups manifest when children express their real views.

All this made for delay and hesitation, and it was only Terry's persuasion, and the fear of disobeying the tall authoritative lady who had suddenly invaded their lives, which finally set their pencils going. Boyne received the papers, shook them up conscientiously, and began to read them out.

"Al If Boy—oh, a *lift-boy*; yes—." Zinnie's burning blush revealed her as the author of this ambition, and Boyne read on: "An Ambassadoress"—Blanca, of course; and the added vowel certainly gave the word a new stateliness. "A great Poet, or the best Writer of Detective Stories," in Terry's concise hand, showed him torn between a first plunge into Conan Doyle, and rapturous communion with "The Oxford Book of English Verse."

Boyne read on: "Never brush meye tethe," laboriously printed out by Beechy; "A Crow Bat"—an aspiration obviously to be ascribed to Bun: "A noble character" (bless Scopy! As if she wasn't one already—); and lastly, in Judith's rambling script: "An exploarer." At the reading of that, something darted through Boyne like a whirr of wings.

The ambitions expressed did not long serve to disguise the choosers, and there was a prompt chorus of attributions as Boyne read out one slip after the other. The Princess had apparently hoped that something more striking would result. She said the game usually promoted discussion, and she hoped the next stage in it would lead to freer self-expression. The children, she explained, were now to say in turn why—that is, on what grounds—they wanted to be this or that. But an awestruck silence met her invitation to debate, and Beechy again began to show signs of emotion. The Princess seemed much distressed, but was assured by Miss Scope that this breach of manners was due only to over-excitement, and the strain of sitting up later than usual—she hoped the Princess would excuse her, but really the children had better go to bed. At this suggestion all the faces round the table lit up except Zinnie's, which was clouded by a pout. She slipped down from her cushions with the others, but when her turn came to file by the Princess for goodnight, she held up the march-past to ask: "N'arn't there going to be any prizes after that game?"

She was swept off in Miss Scope's clutch, and the Princess, after a timid attempt at endearment, imperfectly responded to, when Bun and Beechy took leave, sat down for a talk with Boyne and Judith. Much as she had evidently seen to disapprove of in the bringing-up of the little Wheaters she was in a less aggressive mood than in the afternoon; something she had been unprepared for, and had only half understood, in the relation of the children to each other and to their elders, seemed imperceptibly to have shaken her convictions. Though she continued to repeat the same phrases, it was with less emphasis; and she listened more patiently to Boyne's arguments, and to Judith's entreaties.

Judith was presently called away to say goodnight to the children, and as soon as the Princess and Boyne were alone, the former began abruptly: "But you must listen to me, Mr. Boyne; you must understand me. It's not only that I cannot conscientiously approve of the way in which Beatrice and Astorre are being brought up: it is that I need them myself—I need them for my husband." She coloured at the avowal, and went on hastily: "If he is to begin a new life—and he *has* begun it already—his first step ought to be to take back his children. You must see that . . . You must see how I am situated . . ." Her voice broke, and Boyne suddenly felt the same pity for her as when she had shown her fear that he might be hinting a criticism of Prince Buondelmonte's past.

"I'll do what I can—only trust me," he stammered.

Judith came back, and the Princess, still a little rigid from the effort at self-control, began at once to thank her for her kindness, and to say that she was afraid it was time to go. She would tell Prince Buondelmonte, she added, with an effort at cordiality, that the children seemed very well ("*physically* well," she explained), and she would give him the assurance—she hoped she might?—that some sort of understanding as to their future would soon be reached.

Victory or defeat? Judith and Boyne, sitting late, asked each other which it was, but found no answer.

Chapter *XXVIII*

ALL the next day the rain continued. It was one of those steady business-like rains which seem, in mountain places, not so much a caprice of the weather as the drop-curtain punctually let down by Nature between one season and the next. Behind its closely woven screen one had the sense of some tremendous annual scene-shifting, the upheaval and overturning of everything in sight, from the clouds bursting in snow on the cliff-tops to the mattresses and blankets being beaten and aired in the hotel windows.

These images were doubtless born of Boyne's own mood. When he opened his shutters on the morning after the Princess Buondelmonte's apparition it seemed to him as if she herself had hung that cold gray mist before the window. He was afraid of everything now—of what the post might bring, of what his own common-sense might dictate to him, above all, of seeing Judith again, and having his apprehensions doubled by hers.

The worst of it was that, even should all their tormentors agree to leave them in peace, they could not—more particularly on Terry's account—delay on that height through the coming weeks of storm and rain. Moreover, all the hotels and *pensions*, which would reopen later for the season of winter sports, were preparing to close for their yearly cleaning and renovating. After the middle of October there would be no demand for accommodation till the arrival of the Christmas lugers and ski-ers. If it proved possible to keep the little Wheaters together any longer the best plan would probably be to transport them to Riva or Meran till winter and fine weather were established together in the mountains.

Boyne turned over these things with the nervous minuteness with which one makes plans for some one who is dying, and will never survive to see them carried out. It seemed to give him faith in the future, a sense of factitious security, as it sometimes does, beside a deathbed, to think: "To-morrow I'll see what the doctor says about a warmer climate."

Judith and Miss Scope shared his idea about Meran or Riva, and for some time had been talking vaguely of going down to look for rooms. But the ever-recurring difficulty of persuading a boarding-house keeper to lodge seven children made them decide that it would be best to try to hire an inexpensive villa. The episode of the goldfish and the rabbit had not endeared them to their present landlady, and they felt the hopelessness of trying to ingratiate themselves with another, in a place where they were unknown, and where the autumn season would be at its height. It had therefore been decided that Judith, Miss Scope and Boyne should motor to Meran that very week to look over the ground. But on reflection Boyne hesitated to leave the children alone with their nurses, even for so short an absence. With Joyce in Paris, once more reorganising her life, and the Princess Buondelmonte returning to Rome unsatisfied, danger threatened on all sides. Any one of these cross-blasts might dash to earth the frail nest which had resisted the summer's breezes; and Boyne, heavy-hearted, set out to call another council at the *Pension Rosenglüh.*

As he left the hotel a telegram was handed to him. He glanced first at the signature—Sarah Mervin—then read what went before. "I will gladly receive own dear grandchildren subject to parents' final settlement of affairs fear cannot assume responsibility step-children letter follows" . . . "A lawyer's cable," Boyne growled as he pocketed it. "That's the reason it's taken so long to compose."

Fresh bitterness filled him as he saw one more prop withdrawn from under the crazy structure of his hopes. "These people," he reflected, "all act on impulse where their own wants are concerned, and call in a lawyer when it's a question of anybody else's." But in his heart he was not much surprised. Mrs. Mervin was no longer young, and it is natural for ageing people to shrink from responsibilities. Besides, she might well plead that it was no business of hers to take in children she had never seen, and whose parents were eager, and financially able, to care for them. On second thoughts, it really did not need Judith's bald hint as to the allowance her grandmother received from Cliffe Wheater to account for the poor lady's attitude. "I don't see what else she could have done," the impartial Boyne was obliged to admit in the course of his interminable argument with the other, the passionate and unreasonable one.

What a Utopia he and Judith had been dreaming! He wondered now how he could have lent himself to such pure folly . . . Well, the dream was over, and his was the grim business of making her see it . . . Heavily he went down the hill through the rain.

At the *pension* Judith was watching for him from the window. She opened the door and led him into the sitting-room, where a sulky fire smouldered, puffing out acrid smoke. The landlady said it was always like that—the stove always smoked on the first day of the autumn rains, unless there was a little wind to make a draught. And there was not a breath today; the only way was to leave a window open, Judith explained as she turned to Boyne. Her face was colourless and anxious; he could see that she had been treading the wheel of the same problems as himself. The sight made him resolve to try and hide his own apprehensions a little longer.

"Well, old Judy—here we are, after all; and not a breach in the walls yet!"

"You mean she's gone—the Princess?"

He nodded. "I saw her off to Rome an hour ago."

Her eyes brightened, as they always did at his challenge; but it was only a passing animation. "And you haven't had any telegram?" she questioned.

The question took him unprepared. "I—why, have you?"

"Yes. From mother. Here." She produced the paper and thrust it feverishly into his hand. Boyne's anger rose—evidently, he thought, old Mrs. Mervin had waited to communicate with her daughter before answering him. What cowardice, what treachery! He pictured all these grown up powers and principalities leagued together against the handful of babes he commanded, and the bitterness of surrender entered into him. It was not that any of these parents really wanted their children. If they had, the break-up of Judith's dream, though tragic, would have been too natural to struggle against. But it was simply that the poor little things had become a bone of contention, that the taking or keeping possession of them was a matter of pride or of expediency, like fighting for a goal in some exciting game, or clinging to all one's points in an acrimoniously-disputed law-suit. Boyne unfolded Mrs. Wheater's telegram, and read: "You must come to Paris immediately bringing Chip I must see you at once do not disobey me stop telegraph Hotel Nouveau Luxe Mother."

The vague phrasing made it impossible to guess whether the message were the result of a cable from Mrs. Mervin, or simply embodied a new whim of Joyce's. Boyne, on the whole, inclined to the latter view, and felt half ready to exonerate Mrs. Mervin. After all, perhaps she had kept faith with him, and her message was only the result of her own scruples.

He tossed the telegram onto the table with a shrug. "Is that all? You've heard nothing else?"

Yes; it appeared she had. Nanny, the day before, had received a letter from Mrs. Wheater's maid Marguerite, an experienced person who wielded a facile but rambling pen. This letter Judith had coaxed from Nanny, unknown to Miss Scope; for Miss Scope, even in the extremest emergencies, would not admit the possibility of her charges using, as a means of information, what the Princess would have called "salaried assistants."

Marguerite's news, if vague, was ample. It appeared that Mrs. Wheater had met in Venice a gentleman a good deal older than herself, whose name the maid could not even approximately spell, but who was quite different from any of the other gentlemen in her mistress's circle.

"Different—different how?"

"She says he's made a different woman of mother," Judith explained. "He's made her chuck Gerald, to begin with."

"But, for God's sake, why? I thought she was chucking your father on account of Gerald."

Judith went into this with the lucid impartiality she always applied to the analysis of her parents' foibles. She reminded Boyne that Joyce never stuck long to one thing, and that she had decided to marry Gerald chiefly in order to annoy her husband, and to have an excuse for detaining the young tutor at the Lido when the children left. "He's rather a Lido man, Gerald is," Judith commented, "and it made all the other women so furious. That's always rather fun, you know."

But, after all, she pursued, her mother had much more sense than her poor father, who was always the prey of women like Zinnia Lacrosse or Sybil Lullmer. "She does pull herself together sometimes—especially since that awful time with Buondelmonte. And so, when she met this other gentleman, who is so much older, and very religious, and enormously rich, and who only wants to influence her for good, Marguerite says it made her feel how dreadfully she'd wasted her life, and what a different woman she might have been if she'd known him years before. You see, he doesn't want to marry her, but only to be her friend and adviser. He thinks she's been married often enough. And so, in order not to leave Gerald at a loose end, she's kept him on as secretary till he can get another job, and she and Gerald and the other gentleman have gone to Paris together to see what had better be done. And the gentleman says she ought to have us all with her; and he feels awfully fond of us already, and knows mother will be ever so much happier if we're with her . . ."

"Oh, my God—then it's all up with us," Boyne groaned.

Judith made no answer, and he went on: "It only remains now to hear from Lady Wrench and the Princess!"

"Or Grandma Mervin—there's still grandma," Judith rejoined, half hopefully.

Boyne hesitated a moment; then he said to himself that there was no use in any farther postponement. "No; I've heard from her," he said.

Judith's eyes were again illuminated. "You have? Oh, Martin! If she'd only take us all, perhaps it would satisfy mother and the new gentleman. Oh, Martin, she doesn't say no?"

Silently—for no words came to him—he gave her the cable, and walked away to the window to be out of sight of her face. For a while he stood watching the gray curtain of failure that hung there between him and his golden weeks; then he pulled himself together and turned back.

"Judy—"

She handed him the cable.

"After all, you expected it, didn't you?" he said.

She nodded. "It doesn't make so much difference, anyhow," he continued, in an unconvinced voice, "if Bun and Beechy have to go . . ."

She pondered on this for a few moments without answering. Then, with one of her sudden changes of tone: "Martin," she broke out impetuously, "do you suppose she was right, after all—I mean the Princess—about our being so dreadfully behind the times? Do you suppose, if we did all the things she suggested: if we got new teachers and new books, and some-body for Bun's gymnastics, it would make any difference—do you think it would?" Every line of her face, from lifted eyebrows to parted lips, was a passionate demand for his assent. "After all, you know—perhaps she was right about some things: that stupid old book of Scopy's, for instance. Of course we all know poor darling Scopy's a back number. And about Bun's gymnas-tics too. Do you suppose if we took a villa at Meran we could afford to fit up a room like the one she described, and get an instructor—didn't she call him an instructor? And then there's fencing and riding—I dare say she was right about that too! But after all—" she paused, and her eyes looked as the rain did when the sun was trying to break through it. "After all, Martin," she began again, "the main thing is that the children are so well, isn't it? Look at our record—see what the summer has done! You wouldn't know Terry, would you, if you were to see him now for the first time after meeting us on the boat at Algiers? And Chip—isn't Chip a miracle? Every one stops Nanny in the street to admire him, and they always think he must be three years old. He was just beginning to walk alone when he came here—now he runs like a hare! Nanny gets worn out chasing him. And the tricks he's learnt to do! He can imitate everybody; I believe he's going to be a movie star. Have you seen him do the lion, with Bun as lion-tamer? Or the old man at the market, all doubled up with sciatica, who leans on a stick, and holds one hand behind his back? But it's a wonder! Oh, Martin, wait, and I'll fetch him down now to do the old man for you—shall I?"

Once again her grown up cares had vanished in the childish pride of recounting Chip's achievements. Would it always be like this, Boyne wondered, or would life gradually close the gates of the fairyland which was still so close to her? He would have given most of his chances of happiness to help her keep open that communication with her childhood. And what if he were the one being who could do it? The question wound itself through his thoughts like a persuasive hand insinuating itself into his. This heart-break of separation that was upon her—what if he alone had the power to ease it? He stood looking down at her perplexedly.

"Judy—Chip's a great man, and I'd love to see him do the old gentleman with the sciatica. But first . . ."

"Yes—first?" she palpitated. But under his gaze her radiance gradually faded, and her lips began to tremble a little. "Ah, then you don't think . . . there's any hope for us?"

"I think you've got to go to Paris and see your mother."

"And take Chip? I'll never take Chip! I won't!"

"But listen, dear—." He sat down, and drew her to the sofa beside him, speaking as he might have to a child on a holiday who was fighting the summons back to school.

"Listen, Judy. We've done our best; we all have. But the children are not yours or mine. They belong to their parents, after all." How dry and flat his phrases sounded, compared with the words he longed to say to her!

She drew back into the corner of the sofa. "That Buondelmonte woman's got at you—she's talked you over! I knew she would." She was grown up again now, measuring him with angry suspicious eyes, and flinging out her accusations in her mother's shrillest voice.

"Why, child, what nonsense! You said just now that perhaps the Princess was right . . ."

"I never did! I said, perhaps we ought to get a new Cyclopædia for Scopy, and have Bun taught scientific gymnastics; and now you say . . ."

"I say that fate's too much for us. It didn't need the Princess Buondelmonte to teach me that."

She made no answer, and they sat in silence in their respective corners of the sofa, each gazing desperately into a future of which nothing could be divined except that it was the end of their hopes. Suddenly Judith flung herself face down against the knobby cushions and broke into weeping. Boyne, for a few minutes, remained numb and helpless; then he moved closer, and bending over drew her into his arms. She seemed hardly aware of his nearness; she simply went on crying, with hard uneven sobs, pressing her face against his shoulder as if it were the sofa-cushion. He held her in silence, not venturing to speak, or even to brush back her tumbled hair, while he pictured, with the acuity of his older and less articulate grief, what must be passing before her as the fibres of her heart were torn away. "It's too cruel—it's too beastly cruel," he thought, wincing at the ugly details which must enter into her vision of the future, details he could only guess at, while she saw them with all the precision of experience. Yes, it was too cruel; but what could he or she do? He continued to hold her in silence, listening to the beat of the rain on the half-open window, and smelling the cold grave-yard smell of the autumn earth, while her sobs ran through him in shocks of anguish.

Gradually her weeping subsided, and Boyne took courage to lift his hand and pass it once or twice over her hair. She lay in his hold as quietly as a frightened bird, and presently he bent his head and whispered: "Judy—." Why not? he thought; his heart was beating with reckless bounds. He was free, after all, if it came to that; free to chuck his life away on any madness; and madness this was, he knew. Well, he'd had enough of reason for the rest of his days; and a man is only as old as he feels . . . He bent so close that his lips brushed her ear. "Judy, darling, listen . . . Perhaps after all there's a way—"

In a flash she was out of his arms, and ecstatically facing him. "A way—a way of keeping us all together?" Ah, how hard her questions were to answer!

Boyne drew her down again beside him. Crying was a laborious and disfiguring business to her, and her face was so drawn and tear-stained that she looked almost old; but its misery was shot through with hope. If he could have kept her there, not speaking, only answering her with endearments, how easy, how exquisite it would have been! But her face was tense with expectation, and he had to find words, for he knew that his silence would have no meaning for her.

"Judith—" he began; but she interrupted: "Call me Judy, or I shall think it's more bad news." He made no answer, and she flung herself against him with a cry of alarm. "Martin! Martin! You're not going to desert us too?"

He held her hands, but his own had begun to tremble. "Darling, I'll never desert you; I'll stay with you always if you'll have me; if things go wrong I'll always be there to look after you and defend you; no matter what happens, we'll never be separated any more . . ." He broke off, his voice failing before the sudden sunrise in her eyes.

"Oh, Martin—" She lifted his hands one by one to her wet cheeks, and held them there in silent bliss. "Then you don't belong any longer to Mrs. Sellars?"

"I don't belong to any one but you—for as long as ever you'll have me . . ."

Her eyes still bathed him in their radiance. "My darling, my darling." She leaned close as she said it, and he dared not move, in his new awe of her nearness—so subtly had she changed from the child of his familiar endearments to the woman he passionately longed for . . . "Darling," she said again; then, with a face in which the bridal light seemed already kindled, "Oh, Martin, do you really mean you're going to adopt us all, and we're all going to stay with you forever?"

Chapter XXIX

BOYNE felt like a man who has blundered along in the dark to the edge of a precipice. He trembled inwardly with the effort of recovery, and the shock of finding himself flung back into his old world. Judith, in a rush of gratitude, had thrown her arms about him; and he shrank from her touch, from the warm smell of her hair, from everything about her which he had to think back into terms of childhood and comradeship, while every vein in his body still ached for her. There was nothing he would have dreaded as much as her detecting the least trace of what he was feeling. His first care must be to hide the break in their perfect communion—the fact that for a moment she had been for him the woman she would some day be for another man, in a future he could never share. He undid her hands and walked away to the window.

When he turned to her again he had struggled back to some sort of composure. "Judy, child, I wish you wouldn't take such terrible life-leases on the future." He tried to smile as he said it. "I'm always afraid it will bring us bad luck. We'd much better live from hand to mouth. I'm ready to promise all that a reasonable man can—that I'll put up another big fight for you, and that I don't despair of winning it. At any rate, I'll be there; I'll stand by you; I won't desert you . . ." He broke off, reading in her unsatisfied eyes the hopelessness of piling up vague assurances . . .

"Yes," she assented, in a voice grown as small and colourless as her face.

He stood before her miserably. "You do understand, dear, don't you?"

"I'm not sure . . ." She hesitated. "A little while ago I thought I did."

His nerves began to twitch again. Could he bear to go into the question with her once more—and what would be the use if he did? The immediate future must somehow or other be dealt with; but the last few minutes had deprived him of all will and energy. He had the desolate sense of her knowing that he had failed her, and yet not being able to guess why.

"Of course I'll do what I can," he repeated.

She remained silent, constrained by his constraint; and he saw the disappointment in her eyes.

"You don't believe me?"

Still she looked at him perplexedly. "But you said . . . I thought you said just now that you'd found a way of keeping us all together. No matter what happened; you had a plan, you said."

His senseless irritation grew upon him. Could such total simplicity be unfeigned? Could she have such a power of awaking passion without any inkling of its meaning? He hated himself for doubting it. In time—a short time, perhaps—her rich nature would come to its ripeness; but as yet the only full-grown faculties in it were her love for her brothers and sisters, and her faith in the few people who had shown her kindness in a world unkindly.

"I'm sorry," she continued, after pausing for an answer which did not come. "I must have misunderstood you, I suppose."

Boyne gave a nervous laugh. "You did, most thoroughly."

"And—you won't tell me what you really meant?"

He stood motionless, his hands in his pockets, staring down at the knots in the wooden floor, as he had stared at them on the day when she had owned to having taken her father's money—but in a mental perturbation how much deeper! A few minutes before, it had seemed like profanation to brush her with the thought of his love; now, faced by her despair, by her sense of being left alone to fight her battles, he asked himself whether it might not be fairer, even kinder, to speak. At the thought his heart again began to beat excitedly. Perhaps he had been too impetuous, too inarticulate. What if, after all, a word from him could wake the sleeping music?

The difficulty was to find a beginning. What would have been so simple if kisses could have told it, seemed tortuous or brutal when put in words. He shrank not so much from the possibility of hurting her as from the sudden fear of her hurting him beyond endurance.

"Judith," he began, "how old are you?"

"I shall be sixteen in three months—no, in five months, really," she said, with an obvious effort at truthfulness.

"As near as that! Well, sixteen is an age," he laughed.

She continued to fix her bewildered eyes on him, as if seeking a clue. "But I look a lot older, don't I?" she added hopefully.

"Older? There are times when you look so old that you frighten me." He remembered then that she had spoken to him with perfect simplicity of Gerald Ormerod's desire to marry her, as of the most natural thing in the world; and his own scruples began to seem absurd. "I'm always forgetting what a liberal education she's had," he thought with a touch of self-derision.

He cleared his throat, and continued: "So grown up that I suppose you'll soon be thinking of getting married."

The word was out now; it went sounding on and on inside of his head while he awaited her answer. When she spoke it was with an air of indifference and disappointment.

"What's the use of saying that? How can I ever marry, with all the children to look after?" It was clear that she regarded the subject as irrelevant; her tone seemed to remind him that he and she had long since dealt with and disposed of it. "You might as well tell me that I ought to be educated," she grumbled.

He pressed on: "But it might turn out . . . you might find . . ." He had to pause to steady his voice. "If we can't prevent the children being taken away from you, you'll be awfully lonely . . ."

"Taken away from me?" At the word her listlessness vanished. "Do you suppose I'll let them be taken like that? Without fighting to the very last minute? Let Syb Lullmer get hold of Chip— and Bun and Beechy go to that Buondelmonte man?"

"I know. It's hateful. But supposing the very worst happens— oughtn't you to face that now?" He cleared his throat again. "If things went wrong, and you were very lonely, and a fellow asked you to marry him—"

"Who asked me?"

He laughed again. "If I did."

For a moment she looked at him perplexedly; then her eyes cleared, and for the first time she joined in his laugh. Hers seemed to bubble up, fresh and limpid, from the very depths of her little girlhood. "Well, that would be funny!" she said.

There was a bottomless silence.

"Yes—wouldn't it?" Boyne grinned. He stared at her without speaking; then, like a blind man feeling his way, he picked up his hat and mackintosh, said: "Where's my umbrella? Oh, outside—" and walked out stiffly into the passage. On the doorstep, still aware of her nearness, he added a little dizzily: "No, please—I want a long tramp alone first . . . I'll come in again this afternoon to settle what we'd better do about Paris . . ."

He felt her little disconsolate figure standing alone behind him in the rain, and hurried away as if to put himself out of its reach forever.

Chapter XXX

IT was still raining when the Wheater colony left Cortina; it was raining when the train in which Boyne and Judith were travelling reached Paris. During the days intervening between the receipt of Mrs. Wheater's telegram and the clattering halt of the express in the gare de Lyon, Boyne could not remember that the rain had ever stopped.

But he had not had time to do much remembering—not even of the havoc within himself. After the struggle necessary to convince Judith that she must go to Paris and take Chip with her—since disobedience to her mother's summons might put them irretrievably in the wrong—he had first had to help her decide what should be done with the other children. Once brought round to his view, she had immediately risen to the emergency, as she always did when practical matters were at stake. She and Boyne were agreed that it would be imprudent to leave the children at Cortina, where the Princess, or even Lady Wrench, might take advantage of their absence to effect a raid on the *pension*. It took a three days' hunt to find a villa in a remote suburb of Riva where they could be temporarily installed without much risk of being run down by an outraged parent. Boyne put the *Rosenglüh* landlady off the scent by giving her the address of Mrs. Wheater's Paris banker, and letting it be understood that Judith was off to Paris to prepare for the children's arrival; and Blanca and Terry, still deep in Conan Doyle, gleefully contributed misleading details.

The excitement of departure, and the business of establishing the little Wheaters in their new quarters, left no time, between Boyne and Judith, for less pressing questions; and Boyne saw that, once their plan was settled, Judith was almost as much amused as the twins by its secret and adventurous side. "It will take a Dr. Watson to nose them out, won't it?" she chuckled, as she and Boyne, with Chip and Susan, scrambled into the Paris express at Verona. It was not till they were in the train that Boyne saw the cloud of apprehension descend on her again. But then fatigue intervened, and she fell asleep against his shoulder as peacefully as Chip, who was curled up opposite with his head in Susan's lap. As they sat there, Boyne remembered how, on the day of Mr. Dobree's picnic, he had watched her sleeping by the waterfall, a red glow in her cheeks, velvet shadows under her lashes. Now her face was pinched and sallow, the lids were swollen with goodbye tears; she seemed farther from him than she had ever been, yet more in need of him; and at the thought something new and tranquillizing entered into him. He had caught a glimpse of a joy he would never reach, and he knew that his eyes would always dazzle with it; but the obligation of giving Judith the help she needed kept his pain in that deep part of the soul where the great renunciations lie.

In Paris he left his companions at the door of the *Nouveau Luxe*, where Mrs. Wheater was established, drove to his own modest hotel on the left bank, and turned in for a hard tussle of thinking. He could no longer put off dealing with his own case, for Mrs. Sellars was still in Paris. He had not meant to let her know of his arrival till the next day; he needed the interval to get the fatigue and confusion out of his brain. But meanwhile he must map out some kind of a working plan; must clear up his own mind, and consider how to make it clear to her. And after an unprofitable attempt at rest and sleep, and a weary tramp in the rain through the dusky glittering streets, he suddenly decided on immediate action, and turned into a telephone booth to call up Mrs. Sellars. She was at home and answered immediately. Aunt Julia was resting, she said; if he would come at once they could talk without fear of interruption.

He caught the tremor of joy in her voice when he spoke her name—but how like her, how perfect of her, to ask no questions, to waste no time in exclamations; just quietly and simply to say "Come"! The healing touch of her reasonableness again came to his rescue.

He would have liked to find her close at hand, on the very threshold of the telephone booth; at the rate at which his thoughts were spinning he knew he would have to go over the whole affair again in his transit to her hotel. But there was no remedy for that; he could only trust to her lucidity to help him out.

Aunt Julia's apartment was in a hotel of the rue de Rivoli, with a row of windows overhanging the silvery reaches of the

Tuileries gardens and the vista of domes and towers beyond. The room was large, airy, full of flowers. A fire burned on the hearth; Rose Sellars's touch was everywhere. And a moment later she stood there before him, incredibly slim and young-looking in her dark dress and close little hat. Slightly paler, perhaps, and thinner—but as she moved forward with her easy step the impression vanished. He felt only her mastery of life and of herself, and thought how much less she needed him than did the dishevelled child he had just left. The thought widened the distance between them, and brought Judith abruptly closer.

"Well, here I am," he said—"and I've failed!"

He had prepared a dozen opening phrases—but the sudden intrusion of Judith's face dashed them all from his lips. He was returning to ask forgiveness of the woman to whom he still considered himself engaged, and his first word, after an absence prolonged and unaccountable, was to remind her of the cause of their breach. He saw the narrowing of her lips, and then her victorious smile.

"Dear! Tell me about it—I want to hear everything," she said, holding out her hand.

But he was still struggling in the coil of his blunder. "Oh, never mind—all that's really got nothing to do with it," he stammered.

She freed her hand, and turned on the electric switch of the nearest lamp. As she bent to it he saw that the locks escaping on each temple were streaked with gray. The sight seemed to lengthen the days of their separation into months and years. He felt like a stranger coming back to her. "You've forgiven me?" he began.

She looked at him gravely. "What is it I have to forgive?"

"A lot—you must think," he said confusedly.

She shook her head. "You're free, you know. We're just two old friends talking. Sit down over there—so." She pointed to an armchair, sat down herself, and took off her hat. In the lamp-light, under the graying temples, her face looked changed and aged, like her hair. But it was varnished over by her undaunted smile.

"Let us go back to where you began. I want to hear all about the children." She leaned her head thoughtfully on her hand, in the attitude he had loved in the little sitting-room at Cortina.

"I feel like a ghost—" he said.

"No; for I should be a little afraid of you if you were a ghost; and now—"

"Well—now . . ." He looked about the pleasant firelit room, saw her work-basket in its usual place near the hearth, her books heaped up on a table, and a familiar litter of papers on a desk in the window. "A ghost," he repeated.

She waited a moment, and then said: "I wish you'd tell me exactly what's been happening."

"Oh, everything's collapsed. It was bound to. And now I—"

He got up, walked across the room, glanced half-curiously at the titles of some of the books, and came back and leaned against the mantelpiece. She sat looking up at him. "Yes?"

"No. I can't."

"You can't—what?"

"Account for anything. Explain anything—" He dropped back into his chair and threw his head back, staring at the ceiling. "I've been a fool—and I'm tired; tired."

"Then we'll drop explanations. Tell me only what you want," she said.

What he really wanted was not to tell her anything, but to get up again, and resume his inarticulate wanderings about the room. With an effort of the will he remained seated, and turned his eyes to hers. "You've been perfect—and I do want to tell you . . . to make you understand . . ." But no; that sort of talk was useless. He had better try to do what she had asked him. "About the children—well, the break-up was bound to come. You were right about it, of course. But I was so sorry for the poor little devils that I tried to blind myself . . . "

His tongue was loosened, and he found it easier to go on. After all, Mrs. Sellars was right; the story of the children must be disposed of first. After that he might see more clearly into his own case and hers. He went on with his halting narrative, and she listened in silence—that rare silence of hers which was all alertness and sympathy. She smiled a little over the Princess Buondelmonte's invasion, and sighed and frowned when he mentioned that Lady Wrench was also impending. When he came to Mrs. Wheater's summons, and his own insistence that Judith and Chip should immediately obey it, she lifted her eyes, and said approvingly: "But of course you were perfectly right."

"Was I? I don't know. When I left them just now at the door of that Moloch of a hotel—"

She gave a little smile of reassurance. "No; I don't think you need fear even the *Nouveau Luxe*. I understand what you're feeling; but I think I can give you some encouragement."

"Encouragement—?"

"About the future, I mean. Perhaps Mrs. Wheater's news about herself is not altogether misleading. At any rate, I know she's taken the best legal advice; and I hear she may be able to keep all the children—her own, that is. For of course the poor little steps—"

Boyne listened with a sudden start of attention. He felt like some one shaken out of a lethargy. "You've seen her, then? I didn't know you knew her."

"No; I've not seen her, and I don't know her. But a friend of mine does. The fact is, she ran across Mr. Dobree at the Lido after he left Cortina—"

"*Dobree?*" He stared, incredulous, as if he must have heard the wrong name.

"Yes; hasn't she mentioned it to the children? Ah, no—I remember she never writes. Well, she had the good sense to ask him to take charge of things for her, and though he doesn't often accept new cases nowadays he was so sorry for the children—and for her too, he says—that he agreed to look after her interests. And he tells me that if she follows his advice, and keeps out of new entanglements, he thinks she can divorce Mr. Wheater on her own terms, and in that case of course the courts will give her all the children. Isn't that the very best news I could give you?"

He tried to answer, but again found himself benumbed. Her eyes continued to challenge him. "It's more than you hoped?" she smiled.

"It's not in the least what I expected."

She waited for him to continue, but he was silent again, and she questioned suddenly: "What *did* you expect?"

He looked at her with a confused stare, as if her face had become that of a stranger, as familiar faces do in a dream. "Dobree," he said—"this Dobree . . ."

She kindled. "You're very unfair to Mr. Dobree, Martin; you always have been. He's not only a great lawyer, whose advice

Mrs. Wheater is lucky to have, but a kind and wise friend . . .
and a good man," she added.

"Yes," he said, hardly hearing her. All the torture of his hour
of madness about Mr. Dobree had returned to him. He would
have liked to leap up on the instant, and go and find him, and
fight it out with his fists . . .

"I can't think," she continued nervously, "what more you
could have hoped . . . "

He made a weary gesture. "God knows! But what does it
matter?"

"Matter? Doesn't it matter to you that the children should
be safe—be provided for? That in this new crash they should
remain with their mother, and not be tossed about again from
pillar to post? If you didn't want that, what did you want?"

"I wanted—somehow—to get them all out of this hell."

"I believe you exaggerate. It's not going to be a hell if their
mother keeps them, as Mr. Dobree thinks she'll be able to. You
say yourself that she's fond of them."

"Yes; intermittently."

"And, after all, if the step-children are taken back by their
own parents, that's only natural. You say the new Princess
Buondelmonte seems well-meaning, and kind in her way; and
as for Zinnie—I suppose Zinnie is the one of the party the best
able to take care of herself."

"I suppose so," he acceded.

"Well, then—." She paused, and then repeated, with a sharper
stress: "I don't yet see what you want."

He looked about him with the same estranged stare with
which his eyes had rested on her face. Something clear and
impenetrable as a pane of crystal seemed to cut him off from
her, and from all that surrounded her. He had been to the country from which travellers return with another soul.

"What I want . . . ?" Ah, he knew that well enough! What
he wanted, at the moment, was just some opiate to dull the
dogged ache of body and soul—to close his ears against that
laugh of Judith's, and all his senses to her nearness. He was
caught body and soul—that was it; and real loving was not the
delicate distraction, the food for dreams, he had imagined it
when he thought himself in love with Rose Sellars; it was this
perpetual obsession, this clinging nearness, this breaking on

the rack of every bone, and tearing apart of every fibre. And his apprenticeship to it was just beginning . . .

Well, there was one thing certain; it was that he must get away, as soon as he could, from the friendly room and Rose's forgiving presence. He tried to blunder into some sort of explanation. "I don't suppose I've any business to be here," he began abruptly.

Mrs. Sellars was silent; but it was not one of her speaking silences. It was like a great emptiness slowly widening between them. For a moment he thought she meant to force on him the task of bridging it over; then he saw that she was struggling with a pain as benumbing as his own. She could not think of anything to say any more than he could, and her helplessness moved him, and brought her nearer. "She wants to end it decently, as I do," he thought; but his pity for her did not help him to find words.

At length he got up and held out his hand. "You're the best friend I've ever had—and the dearest. But I'm going off on a big job somewhere; I must. At the other end of the world. For a time—"

"Yes," she assented, very low. She did not take the hand he held out—perhaps did not even see it. When two people part who have loved each other it is as if what happens between them befell in a great emptiness—as if the tearing asunder of the flesh must turn at last into a disembodied anguish.

"You've forgotten your umbrella," she said, as he reached the door. He gave a little laugh as he came back to get it.

Chapter XXXI

T HE next day Boyne lunched at the *Nouveau Luxe* alone with Mrs. Wheater and Judith. He had wondered if it would occur to Joyce that it might be preferable to lunch upstairs, in her own rooms; but it had not; and his mind was too dulled with pain for him to care much for his surroundings. No crowd could make him feel farther away from Judith than the unseeing look in her own eyes.

Mrs. Wheater was dressed with a Quaker-like austerity which made her look younger and handsomer than when he had last seen her, in the rakish apparel of the Lido. She had acquired another new voice, as she did with each new phase; this time it was subdued and somewhat melancholy, but less studied than the fluty tones she had affected in Venice. Altogether, Boyne had to admit that she had improved—that Mr. Dobree's influence had achieved what others had failed to do. After lunch they went upstairs, and Joyce proposed to Judith that, as the rain had stopped, she should take Chipstone and Susan to the Bois de Boulogne. She herself wanted to have a quiet talk with dear Martin—Judith could send the motor back to pick her up at four; no, at half-past three. She had promised to go to a wonderful loan exhibition of Incunabula with Mr. Dobree . . . Judith nodded and disappeared, with a faint smile at Boyne.

Mr. Dobree had opened her eyes to so many marvels, Joyce continued when they were alone. Incunabula, for instance— would Boyne believe that she had never before heard of their existence? Mr. Dobree had thought she must be joking when she asked him what they were. But Martin knew how much chance she had had of cultivating herself in Cliffe's society . . . Yes, and she was beginning to collect books—first editions—and to form a real library. Didn't he think it would be a splendid thing for the children—especially for Terry? She blushed to think that while the family travelled over Europe in steam-yachts and Blue Trains and Rolls-Royces, poor Terry had had to feed on the rubbish Scopy could pick up for him in hotel libraries, or the *cabinets de lecture* of frowsy watering-places. Mr. Dobree had been horrified when he found that Cliffe, with all his millions, had never owned a library! But then he didn't know Cliffe.

Joyce went on to unfold her plans for the future. She spoke, as usual, as if they were fixed and immutable in every detail. She had decided to buy a place in the country—near either Paris or Dinard, she wasn't sure which. Probably Dinard on account of Terry's health. The climate was mild; and it was said that there were educational advantages. If the sea was too strong for him she could find a house somewhere inland. But they must be near a town on account of the children's education, and yet not in it because of the demoralising influences, and the lack of good air. In a few days she was going down to look about her at Dinard . . .

Boyne knew, she supposed, that she had begun divorce proceedings? Of course she ought to have done it long ago—but in that *milieu* one's moral sense got absolutely blunted. Evidence—? Heavens! She already had more than enough to make her own terms. Horrors and horrors . . . There was no doubt, Mr. Dobree said, that the courts would give her the custody of all the children. And from now on they would be the sole object of her life. Didn't Boyne agree that, at her age, there couldn't be a more perfect conclusion? Oh, yes, she knew—she looked younger than she really was . . . but there were gray streaks in her hair already; hadn't he noticed? And she wasn't going to dye it; not she! She was going to let herself turn frankly into an *old woman*. She didn't mind the idea a bit. Middle-age was so full of duties and interests of its own; she had a perfect horror of the women who are always dyeing and drugging themselves, in the hopeless attempt to keep young—like that pitiable Syb Lullmer, for instance. She had learned, thank heaven, that there were other things in life. And her first object, of course, was to get the children away from hotels and hotel contacts—from all the *Nouveaux Luxes* and the "Palaces." She was counting the minutes till she could create a real home for them, and make them so happy that they would never want to leave it . . . She knew Boyne would approve . . . The monologue ended by her expressing her gratitude for all he had done for the children, and her delight at being reunited to Judith and Chip—Chip, oh, he was a wonder, so fat and tall, and walking and talking like a boy of four. And Judith told her it was all thanks to Boyne . . .

Mrs. Wheater seemed genuinely sorry to think that Bun and Beechy would probably have to return to their father. But perhaps, she added, if the new Princess Buondelmonte was so full of good intentions, and so determined to have her own way, the two children might get a fairly decent bringing-up. Buondelmonte wasn't as young as he had been, and might be glad to settle down, if his wife made him comfortable, and let him have enough money to gamble at his club. And as for Zinnie—Joyce shrugged, and doubted if either her mother or Cliffe would really take Zinnie on, when it came to the point. She was rather a handful, Zinnie was; no one but Judy could control her. Still, grieved as Joyce would be to give up the "steps," poor little souls, she was too much used to human ingratitude not to foresee that they might be taken from her at any moment. But her own children—no! Never again. Of that Boyne might be assured. She had learned her lesson, her eyes had been opened to her own folly and imprudence; and Mr. Dobree had absolutely promised her—oh, by the way, wasn't Martin going to stay and see Mr. Dobree, who would be turning up at any minute now to take her to see the Incunabula? She thought he and Martin had met at Cortina, hadn't they? Yes, she remembered; Mr. Dobree had been so struck by Martin's devotion to the children. She hoped so much they might meet again and make friends . . . Boyne thanked her, and thought perhaps another time . . . but he was leaving Paris, probably; he couldn't wait then . . . He got himself out of the room in a confusion of excuses . . .

All day he wandered through the streets, inconsolably. His will-power seemed paralysed. He was determined to get away from Paris at once, to go to New York first, in quest of a job, and then to whatever end of the world the job should call him. There was no object in his lingering where he was for another hour. He and Rose Sellars had said their last word to each other—and to Judith herself what more had he to say? Yet he could not submit his mind to the idea that his happy unreal life of the last weeks was over; that he would never again enter the *pension* at Cortina, and see the little Wheaters flocking about him in a tumult of welcome, begging for a romp, a game, a story, clamouring to have their quarrels arbitrated, demanding to be taken on a picnic—with Judith serene above the tumult, or laughing and twittering with the rest . . . When he grew too tired to walk farther he turned in at a post-office, and wrote a cable which he had been revolving for some hours. It was addressed to the New York contractors who had written to ask if he could trace the young engineer who had been his assistant. Luckily he had not been able to, and he cabled: "Should like for myself the job you wrote about. Can I have it? Can start at once. Cable bankers."

This message despatched, he turned to the telephone booth, rang up the *Nouveau Luxe*, and asked to speak to Miss Wheater. Interminable minutes passed after he had put in his call; Mrs. Wheater's maid was found first, who didn't know where Judith was, or how to find her; then Susan, who said Judith had come back, and gone out again, and that all she knew was that the ladies were going to dine out that evening with Mr. Dobree, and go to the theatre. Then, just as Boyne was turning away discouraged, Judith's own voice: "Hullo, Martin! Where are you? When can I see you?"

"Now, if you can come. I'm off tonight—to London." He suddenly found he had decided that without knowing it.

She exclaimed in astonishment, and asked where she was to meet him; and he acquiesced in her suggestion that it should be at a tea-room near her hotel, as it was so late that she would soon have to hurry back for dinner. He jumped into a taxi, secured a table in a remote corner of the tea-room, and met her on the threshold a moment later. It was already long after six, and the rooms were emptying; in a few minutes they would have the place to themselves.

Judith, a little flushed with the haste of her arrival, looked gracefully grown up in her dark coat edged with fur, a pretty antelope bag in her gloved hand. The bare-headed girl of the Dolomites, in sports' frock and russet shoes, had been replaced by a demure young woman who seemed to Boyne almost a stranger.

"Martin! You're not really going away tonight?" she began at once, not noticing his request that she should choose between tea-cakes and *éclairs*.

He said he was, for a few days at any rate; the mere sound of her voice, the look in her eyes, had nearly dissolved his plans again, and his own voice was unsteady.

The fact that it was only for a few days seemed to reassure Judith. He'd be back by the end of the week, she hoped, wouldn't he? Yes—oh, yes, he said—very probably.

"Because, you know, the children'll be here by that time," she announced; and, turning her attention to the trays presented: "Oh, both, I think—yes, I'll take both."

"The children?"

"Yes; mother's just settled it. Mr. Dobree wrote the wire for her. If Nanny gets it in time they're to start to-morrow. Mr. Dobree thinks we may be able to keep the steps too—he's going to write himself to Buondelmonte. And he doesn't believe the Wrenches will ever bother us about Zinnie . . . at least not at present. He's found out a lot of things about Lord Wrench, and he thinks Zinnia'll have her hands full with him, without tackling Zinnie too."

She spoke serenely, almost lightly, as if all her anxieties had been dispelled. Could it be that the mere change of scene, the few hours spent with her mother, had so completely reassured her? She, who had always measured Joyce with such precocious insight, was it possible that she was deluded by her now? Or had she too succumbed to Mr. Dobree's mysterious influence? Boyne looked at her careless face and wondered.

"But this Dobree—you didn't fancy him much at Cortina? What makes you believe in him now?"

She seemed a little puzzled, and wrinkled her brows in the effort to find a reason. "I don't know. He's funny looking, of course; and rather pompous. And I do like you heaps better, Martin. But he's been most awfully good about the children, and he can make mother do whatever he tells her. And she says he's a great lawyer, and his clients almost always win their cases. Oh, Martin, wouldn't it be heavenly if he could really keep us together, steps and all? He's sworn to me that he will." She turned her radiant eyes on Boyne. "Anyhow, the children will be here the day after to-morrow, and that will be splendid, won't it? You must get back from London as soon as ever you can, and take us all off somewhere for the day, just as if we were still at Cortina."

Yes, of course he would, Boyne said; on Scopy's book he would. She lit up at that, asking where they'd better go, and finally settling that, if the rain ever held up, a day at Versailles would be jollier than anything . . . But it must be soon, she reminded him; because in a few days Mrs. Wheater was going to carry them all off to Dinard.

Yes, she pursued, she really did feel that Mr. Dobree, just in a few weeks, had gained more influence over her mother than any one else ever had. Judith had had a long talk with him that morning, and he had told her frankly that he was doing it all out of interest in the children, and because he wanted to help her—wasn't that dear of him? Anyhow, they were all going to stand together, grown ups and children, and put up a last big fight. ("On Scopy's book," Boyne interpolated with a strained smile.) And they were to have a big house in the country, with lots of dogs and horses, she continued. And the children were never to go to hotels any more. And Terry was to have a really first-rate tutor, and be sent to school in Switzerland as soon as he was strong enough; in another year, perhaps.

Boyne sat watching her with insatiable eyes. She looked so efficient, so experienced—yet what could be surer proof of her childishness than this suddenly revived faith in the future? He saw that whoever would promise to keep the children together would gain a momentary hold over her—as he once had, alas! And he saw also that the mere change of scene, the excitement of the flight from Cortina, the encouragement which her mother's new attitude gave her, were so many balloons lifting her up into the blue . . . "It will be Versailles, don't you think so?" she began again. "Or, if it rains deluges, what about the circus, and a big tea afterward, somewhere where Chip and Nanny could come too?" She looked at him with her hesitating smile. "I thought, perhaps, if you didn't mind—but, no, darling," she broke off decisively, "we won't ask Mr. Dobree!"

"Lord—I should hope not; not if I'm giving the party." He found the voice and laugh she expected, gave her back her banter, discussed and fixed with her the day and hour of the party. And all the while there echoed in his ears, more insistently than anything she was saying, a line or two from the chorus of Lemures, in "Faust," which Rose had read aloud one evening at Cortina.

> *Who made the room so mean and bare—*
> *Where are the chairs, the tables where?*
> *It was lent for a moment only—*

A moment only: not a bad title for the history of his last few months! A moment only; and he had always known it. "An episode," he thought, "it's been only an episode. One of those things that come up out of the sea, on a full-moon night, playing the harp . . . Yes; but sometimes the episodes last, and the things one thought eternal wither like grass—and only the gods know which it will be . . . if *they* do . . .

"*L'addition, mademoiselle*? Good Lord, child; four *éclairs*? And a Dobree dinner in the offing! Ah, thrice-happy infancy, as the poet said . . . Yes, here's your umbrella. Take my arm, and we'll nip round on foot to the back door of the *Luxe*. You've eaten so much that I haven't got enough left to pay for a taxi . . ."

From the threshold of the hotel she called to him, rosy under her shining umbrella: "Thursday morning, then, you'll fetch us all at ten?" And he called back: "On Scopy's book, I will!" as the rain engulfed him.

On the day fixed for the children's picnic Boyne lay half asleep on the deck of a South American liner. It was better so—a lot better. The morning after he had parted from Judith at the door of the *Nouveau Luxe* the summons had come: "Job yours please sail immediately for Rio particulars on arrival"; and he had just had time to pitch his things into his portmanteaux, catch the first train for London, and scramble on board his boat at Liverpool.

A lot better so . . . The busy man's way of liquidating hopeless situations. It reminded him of the old times when, at the receipt of such a summons, cares and complications fell from him like dust from a shaken garment. It would not be so now; his elasticity was gone. Yet already, after four days at sea, he was beginning to feel a vague solace in the empty present, and in the future packed with duties. No hesitating, speculating, wavering to and fro—he was to be caught as soon as he landed, and thrust into the stiff harness of his work. And meanwhile, more and more miles of sea were slipping in between him and the last months, making them already seem remote and vapoury compared with the firm outline of the future.

The day was mild, with a last touch of summer on the lazy waves over which they were gliding . . . He closed his eyes and slept . . .

At Versailles too it was mild; there were yellow leaves still on the beeches of the long walks; they formed golden tunnels, with hazy blueish vistas where the park melted into the blur of the forest. But the gardens were almost deserted; it was too late in the season for the children chasing their hoops and balls down the alleys, the groups of nurses knitting and gossiping on wooden chairs under the great stone Dianas and Apollos.

Funny—he and the little Wheaters seemed to have the lordly pleasure-grounds to themselves. The clipped walls of beech and hornbeam echoed with their shouts and laughter. What a handful the little Wheaters were getting to be! Terry, now, could run and jump with the rest; and as for Chip, rounder than ever in a white fur coat and tasselled cap, his waddle was turning into a scamper . . .

In the sun, under a high protecting hedge, Miss Scope and Nanny sat and beamed upon their children; and Susan flew down the vistas after Chip . . .

Boyne and Judith were alone. They had wandered away into one of the *bosquets*: solitary even in summer, with vacant-faced divinities niched in green, broken arcades, toy temples deserted of their gods. On this November day, when mist was everywhere, mist trailing through the half-bare trees, lying in a faint bloom on the lichened statues, oozing up from the layers of leaves underfoot, the place seemed the ghostly setting of dead days. Boyne looked down at Judith, and even her face was ghostly . . . "Come," he said with a shiver, "let's get back into the sun—." Outside of the *bosquet*, down the alley, the children came storming toward them, shouting, laughing and wrangling. Boyne, laughing too, caught up the furry Chip, and swung him high in air. Bun, to attract his attention, turned a new somersault at his feet, and Zinnie and Beechy squealed: "Martin, now's the time for presents!" For, since the Princess Buondelmonte had been so shocked by their cupidity, it had become a joke with the children to be always petitioning for presents.

"Little devils—as if I could ever leave them!" Boyne thought.

"Tea, sir?" said the steward. "Ham sandwiches?"

Chapter XXXII

BOYNE was coming back from Brazil. His steamer was approaching Bordeaux, moving up the estuary of the Gironde under a September sky as mild as the one which had roofed his sleep when, nearly three years earlier, he had dreamt he was at Versailles with the little Wheaters.

Three years of work and accomplishment lay behind him. And the job was not over; that was the best of it. A touch of fever had disabled him, and he was to take a few weeks' holiday in Europe, and then return to his task. His first idea had been to put in this interval of convalescence in America; to take the opportunity to look up his people, and see a few old friends in New York. But he was sure to find Rose Sellars in New York, or near it; he could hardly go there without being obliged to see her. And the time for that had not yet come—if it ever would. He looked at his grizzled head, his sallow features with brown fever-blotches under the skin, and put away the idea with a grimace. The tropics seemed fairly to have burnt him out . . .

Rose Sellars had been kind; she had been perfect, as he had foreseen she would be. He knew that, after a winter on the Nile with Aunt Julia, she had returned to her own house in New York; for, once re-established there, she had begun to write to him again. From her letters—which were free from all recriminations, all returning to the past—he learned that she had taken up her old life again: the reading, the social round, the small preoccupations. But he saw her going through the old routine with transparent hands and empty eyes, as he could picture the ghosts of good women doing in the world of shadows.

His own case was more fortunate. His eyes were full of visions of work to be, his hands of the strength of work done. Yet at times he too felt tenuous and disembodied. Since the fever, particularly—it was always disastrous to him to have to interrupt his work. And this flat soft shore that gave him welcome—so safe, so familiar—how it frightened him! He didn't want to come in contact with life again, and life always wooed him when he was not at work.

It was odd, how little, of late, he had thought of the Wheaters. At first the memory of them had been a torture, an obsession. But luckily he had not given his address to Judith, and so she had not been able to write; and Mrs. Sellars had never once alluded to the children. His work in Brazil lay up country, far from towns and post-offices; but bundles of American newspapers straggled in at uncertain intervals, and from one he had learned that the Wheater divorce had been pronounced in Mrs. Wheater's favour, from another, about a year later, that Cliffe had married Mrs. Lullmer. There had been an end of the story . . . and Boyne had lived long enough to know that abrupt endings were best.

As his steamer pushed her way up the estuary he was still asking himself how he should employ his holiday. All his thoughts were with his interrupted work, with the man who had temporarily replaced him, and of whose judgment and temper he was not quite sure. He could not as yet bring himself to consider his own plans for the coming weeks, because, till he could get back to Brazil, everything that might happen to him seemed equally uninteresting and negligible.

At dinner that evening, at the famous *Chapeau Rouge* of Bordeaux, the fresh truffles cooked in white wine, and washed down with a bottle of Château Margaux, insensibly altered his mood. He had forgotten what good food could be like. His view of life was softened, and even the faces of the people at the other tables, commonplace as they were, gradually began to interest him. At the steamer landing the walls were plastered over with flamboyant advertisements of the watering-places of the Basque coast: Cibour, Hendaye, St. Jean de Luz, Biarritz. A band of gay bathers on a white beach, under striped umbrellas, was labelled Hendaye; another, of slim ladies silhouetted on a terrace against a cobalt sea, while their partners absorbed cocktails at little tables, stood for Biarritz. The scene recalled to Boyne similar spectacles all the world over: casinos, dancing, gambling, the monotonous rattle and glare of cosmopolitan pleasure. And suddenly he felt that to be in such a crowd was what he wanted—a crowd of idle insignificant people, not one of whom he would ever care to see again. He fancied the idea of bands playing, dancers undulating over polished floors, expensive food served on flowery terraces, high play in crowded over-heated gaming-rooms. It was the lonely man's flight from himself, the common impulse of hard workers on first coming out of the wilderness. He took the train for Biarritz . . .

The place was in full season; but he found a room in a cheap hotel far from the sea, and forthwith began to mix with the crowd. At first his deep inner loneliness cut him off from them; that people should be leading such lives seemed too absurd and inconsequent. But gradually the glitter took him, as it often had before after a long bout of hard work and isolation; he enjoyed the feeling of being lost in the throng, alone and unnoticed, with no likelihood of being singled out, like Uncle Edward, for some agreeable adventure.

Adventure! He had come to hate the very word. His one taste of the thing had been too bitter. All he wanted now was to be amused; and he hugged his anonymity. For three days he wandered about, in cafés, on terraces above the sea, and in the gaming-rooms. He even made an excursion across the Spanish border; but he came back from it tired and dispirited. Solitude and scenery were not what he wanted; he plunged into the Medley again.

On the fourth day he saw the announcement: "Gala Dinner and Dance tonight at the *Mirasol*." The *Mirasol* was the newest and most fashionable hotel in Biarritz—the "Palace" of the moment. The idea of assisting at the gala dinner took Boyne's fancy, and in the afternoon he strolled up to the hotel to engage a table. But they were all bespoken, and he sat down in the hall to glance over some illustrated papers. The place, at that hour, was nearly empty; but presently he heard a pipe of childish laughter coming from the corner where the lift was caged. Several liveried lift-boys were hanging about in idleness, and among them was a little girl with long legs, incredibly short skirts and a fiery bush of hair. Boyne laid down his paper and looked at her; but her back was turned to him. She was wrestling with the smallest of the lift-boys, while the others looked on and grinned. Presently a stout lady descended from a magnificent motor, entered the hotel and walked across the hall to the lift. Instantly the boys stood to attention, and the red-haired child, quiet as a mouse, slipped into the lift after the stout lady, and shot up out of sight. When the lift came down again, she sprang out, and instantly resumed her romp with the boys. This time her face was turned toward Boyne, and he saw that she was Zinnie Wheater. He got up from his chair to go toward her, but another passenger was getting into the lift, and Zinnie followed, and disappeared again. The next time it came down, two or three people were waiting for it; Zinnie slipped in among them, flattening herself into a corner. Boyne sat and watched her appearing and disappearing in this way for nearly an hour—it was evidently her way of spending the afternoon. And not for the first time, presumably; for several of the passengers recognised her, and greeted her with a nod or a joke. One fat old gentleman in spats produced a bag of sweets, and pinched her bare arm as he gave it to her; and a lady in black with a little girl drew the latter close to her, and looked past Zinnie as if she had not been there . . .

At last there came a lull in the traffic, the attendants relapsed into lassitude, and Zinnie, after circling aimlessly about the hall, slipped behind the porter's desk, inspected the letters in the mahogany pigeon-holes against the wall, and began to turn over the papers on the desk. Then she caught sight of the porter approaching from a distance, slid out from behind the desk, waltzed down the length of the hall and back, and stopped with a yawn just in front of Boyne. For a moment she did not seem to notice him; but presently she sidled up, leaned over his shoulder, and said persuasively: "May I look at the pictures with you?"

He laid the paper aside and glanced up at her. She stared a moment or two, perplexedly, and then flushed to the roots of her hair. "Martin—why, I believe it's old Martin!"

"Yes, it's old Martin—but you're a new Zinnie, aren't you?" he rejoined.

Her eyes were riveted on him; he saw that she was half shy, half eager to talk. She perched on the arm of his chair and took his neck in her embrace, as Judith used to.

"Well, it's a long time since I saw you. I'm lots older—and you are too," she added reflectively. "I don't believe you'd have known me if I hadn't spoken to you, would you?"

"Not if you hadn't had that burning bush," he said, touching her hair. His voice was trembling; he could hardly see her for the blur in his eyes. If he closed his lids he might almost imagine that the thin arm about his neck was Judith's . . .

"Well, how's everybody?" he asked, a little hoarsely.

"Oh, awfully well," said Zinnie. "But you don't look very well yourself," she added, turning a sidelong glance on him.

"Never mind about me. Are you here together, all of you—or have the others stayed at Dinard?"

"Dinard?" She seemed to be puzzled by the question.

"Wasn't your mother going to buy a house in the country near Dinard?"

"Was she? I dunno. We've never had a house of our own," said Zinnie.

"Never anywhere?"

"No. I guess it would only bother mother to have a house. She likes hotels better. She's married again, you know; and she's getting fat."

"Married?"

"Didn't you know about that either? How funny! She's married to Mr. Dobree," said Zinnie, swinging her legs against Boyne's chair.

Boyne sat silent, and she continued, her eyes wandering over him critically: "I guess you've had a fever, haven't you—or else something bad with your liver?"

"Nothing of the sort. I was never better. But you're all here, then, I suppose?" His heart stood still as he made a dash at the question.

"Yes; we're all here," said Zinnie indifferently. "At least Terry's at school in Switzerland, you see; and Blanca's at a convent in Paris, 'cos she got engaged again to a lift-boy who was a worse rotter than the first; and Bun and Beechy are in Rome, in their father's palace. They hate writing, so we don't actually know how they are."

"Ah—" Boyne commented. He looked away from her, staring across the deserted hall. "But Chip's here?" he asked.

Zinnie shook her red curls gravely. "No, he isn't here either." She hesitated a moment, swinging her legs. "He's buried," she said.

"Buried—?"

"Didn't you know that either? You've been ever so far away, I suppose. Chip got menin—meningitis, isn't it? We were at Chamonix, for Terry. The doctors couldn't do anything. It was last winter—no, the winter before. We all cried awfully; we wore black for three months. And so after that mother decided she'd better marry Mr. Dobree; because she was too lonely, she said."

"Ah, lonely—"

"Yes; and so after a while we came to Paris and she was married. It must have been two years ago, because the steps were with us still; and Beechy and I wore little pink dresses at the wedding, and Bun was page. I wonder you didn't see our photographs in the 'Herald.' Don't you ever read the 'Herald'?"

"Not often," Boyne had to admit.

Zinnie continued to swing her legs against the side of his chair. "And it's then we found out what Mr. Dobree's Christian name is," she rambled on. "We had work doing it; but Terry managed to see the papers he had to sign the day of the wedding, and so we found out. His name's Azariah. We never thought of that, did we? It's the name of a man who made millions in mines; so I s'pose when he died he left all his money to Mr. Dobree."

"Made millions in mines?"

"Well, that's what Scopy said. She said: 'Not know that? You little heathens! Why, of course, Azariah was a minor prophet.'"

"Oh, of course; naturally," Boyne murmured, swept magically back to the world of joyous incongruities in which he had lived enchanted with the little Wheaters.

"So we think that's why he's so rich, and why mother married him," Zinnie concluded, with a final kick on the side of the chair; then she slid down, put her hands on her hips, pirouetted in front of Boyne, and held out the bag of pink glazed paper which the old gentleman who wore spats had given her. "Have a chocolate? The ones in gold paper have got liqueur in 'em," she said. Boyne shook his head, and she continued to look at him attentively. At last: "Martin, darling, aren't those *Abdullahs* you're smoking? Will you let me have one?" she said in a coaxing voice.

"Let you have one? You don't mean to say you smoke?"

"No; but I have a friend who does." Boyne held out his cigarette-case with a shrug, and she drew out a small handful, and flitted away to the lift. When she came back her face was radiant. "It's awfully sweet of you," she said. "You always were an old darling. Don't you want to come upstairs and see mother? She was a little tired after lunch, so I don't believe she's gone out yet."

Boyne got to his feet with a gesture of negation. "Sorry, my dear; but I'm afraid I can't. I—fact is, I'm just here for a few hours . . . taking the train back to Bordeaux presently," he stammered.

"Oh, are you? That's too bad. Mother will be awfully sorry—and so will Judy."

Boyne cleared his throat, and brought out abruptly: "Ah, she's here too—Judy?"

Zinnie stared at the question. "Course she is. Only just today she's off on an excursion with some P'ruvians. They've got an awfully long name—I can't remember it. They have two Rolls-Royces. She won't be back not till just before dinner. She'll have to be back then, because she's got a new dress for the dance tonight. It's a pity you can't come back and see her in it."

"Yes—it's a pity. But I can't." He held out his hand, and she put her little bony claw into it. "Goodbye, child," he said; then, abruptly, he bent down to her. "Kiss me, Zinnie." She held up her merry face, and he laid his lips on her cheek. "Goodbye," he repeated.

He had really meant, while he talked with her, to go back to his hotel and pack up, and catch the next train for anywhere. The place was like a tomb to him now; under all the noise and glitter his past was buried. He walked away with hurried strides from the *Mirasol*; but when he got back to his own hotel he sat down in his room and stared about him without making any effort to pack. He sat there for a long time—for all the rest of the afternoon—without moving. Once he caught himself saying aloud: "She's got a new dress for the dance." He laughed a little at the thought, and became immersed in his memories . . .

Boyne dined at a restaurant—he didn't remember where—turned in at a cinema for an hour, and then got into his evening clothes, and walked up through the warm dark night to the *Mirasol*. The great building, shining with lights, loomed above a tranquil sea; music drifted out from it, and on the side toward the sea its wide terrace was thronged with ladies in bright dresses, and their partners. Boyne walked up among them; but as he reached the terrace a drizzling rain began to fall, and laughing and crying out the dancers all hurried back into the hotel. He stood alone on the damp flagging, and paced up and down slowly before the uncurtained windows. The dinner was over—the restaurant was empty, and through the windows he saw the waiters preparing the tables again for supper. Farther on, he passed other tall windows, giving on a richly upholstered drawing-room where groups of elderly people, at tables with shaded lamps, were playing bridge and poker. Among them he noticed a stout lady in a low-necked black dress. Her much-exposed back was turned to him, and he recognised the shape of her head, the thatch of rippled hair, silver-white now (she had kept her resolve of not dyeing it), and the turn of her white arms as she handled her cards. Opposite her sat her partner, also white-headed, in a perfectly cut dinner-jacket; the lamp-light seemed to linger appreciatively on his lustrous pearl studs and sleeve-links. It was Mr. Dobree, grown stouter too, with a reddish fold of flesh above his immaculate collar. The couple looked placid, well fed, and perfectly satisfied with life and with each other.

Boyne continued his walk, and turning an angle of the building, found himself facing the windows of the ballroom. The terrace on that side, being away from the sea, was but faintly lit, and the spectacle within seemed therefore more brilliantly illuminated.

At first he saw only a blur of light and colour; couples revolving slowly under the spreading chandeliers, others streaming in and out of the doorways, or grouped about the floor in splashes of brightness. The music rose and fell in palpitating rhythms, paused awhile, and began again in obedience to a rattle of hand-clapping. The floor was already crowded, but Boyne's eyes roved in vain from one slender bare-armed shape to another; then he said to himself: "But it's nearly three years since I saw her. She's grown up now—perhaps I'm looking at her without knowing her . . ."

The thought that one of those swaying figures might be Judith's, that at that very instant she might be gazing out at him with unknown eyes, sent such a pang through him that he moved away again into the darkness. The rain had almost ceased, but a faint wind from the sea drove the wet air against his face; he might almost have fancied he was crying. The pain of not seeing her was unendurable. It seemed to empty his world . . .

He heard voices and steps approaching behind him on the terrace, and to avoid being scrutinised he mechanically turned back to the window. And there she was, close to him on the other side of the pane, moving across the long reflections of the floor. And he had imagined that he might not know her!

She had just stopped dancing; the arm of a very tall young man with a head as glossy as his shirt-front detached itself from her waist. She was facing Boyne now—she was joining a group near his window. Two or three young girls greeted her gaily as she passed them. The centre of the room was being cleared for a pair of professional dancers, and Judith, waving away a gilt ballroom chair which somebody proffered, remained standing, clustered about by other slender and glossy young men. Boyne, from without, continued to gaze at her.

He had not even asked himself if she had changed—if she had grown up. He had totally forgotten his fear that he might not recognise her. He knew now that if she had appeared to him as a bent old woman he would have known her . . . He watched her with a passionate attentiveness. Her silk dress was of that peculiar carnation-pink which takes a silver glaze like the bloom on a nectarine. The rich stuff stood out from her in a double tier of flounces, on which, as she stood motionless, her hands seemed to float like birds on little sunlit waves. Her hair was moulded to her head in close curves like the ripples of a brown stream. Instead of being cut short in the nape it had been allowed to grow, and was twisted into a figure eight, through which was thrust an old-fashioned diamond arrow. Her throat and neck were bare, and so were her thin arms; but a band of black velvet encircled one of her wrists, relieving the tender rose-and-amber of her dress and complexion. Her eyes seemed to Boyne to have grown larger and more remote, but her mouth was round and red, as it always was when she was amused or happy. While he watched her one of the young men behind her bent over to say something. As she listened she lifted a big black fan to her lips, and her lids closed for a second, as they did when she wanted to hold something sweet between them. But when she furled the fan her expression changed, and her face suddenly became as sad as an autumn twilight.

"*Judith*!" Boyne thought; as if her being Judith, her being herself, were impossible to believe, yet too sweet for anything else in the world to be true . . . It was one of her moments of beauty—that fitful beauty which is so much more enchanting and perilous than the kind that gets up and lies down every day with its wearer. This might be—Boyne said to himself—literally the only day, the only hour, in which the queer quarrelling elements that composed her would ever join hands in a celestial harmony. It did not matter what had brought the miracle about. Perhaps she was in love with the young man who had bent over her, and was going to marry him. Or perhaps she was still a child, pleased at her new dress, and half proud, half frightened in the waking consciousness of her beauty, and the power it exercised . . . Whichever it was, Boyne knew he would never know. He drew back into an unlit corner of the terrace, and sat there a long time in the dark, his head thrown back and his hands locked behind it. Then he got up and walked away into the night.

Two days afterward, the ship which had brought him to Europe started on her voyage back to Brazil. On her deck stood Boyne, a lonely man.

THE END

CHRONOLOGY

NOTE ON THE TEXTS

NOTES

Chronology

1862   Born January 24 at 14 West 23rd Street, New York City, and baptized Edith Newbold Jones on Easter Sunday, April 20, at Grace Church on Broadway and 11th Street; third and last child of George Frederic Jones and Lucretia Stevens Rhinelander (brothers are Frederic, b. 1846, and Henry, b. 1850). Parents belong to long-established, socially prominent New York families. (Phrase "keeping up with the Joneses" is alleged to have been coined in reference to two of father's aunts.) Father's income based on Manhattan landholdings. Rumors persist as to whether Edith is the daughter of Jones, or of her brother's English tutor, or else of Lord Brougham, an elderly Scottish peer.

1865   Receives gift of spitz puppy, Foxy, beginning a lifelong passion for small dogs.

1866   Post–Civil War depression in real estate market causes family to move to Europe for prolonged residence in attempt to economize. Sails to England in November with parents, nurse Hannah Doyle ("Doyley"), and brother Henry, who begins law studies at Trinity Hall College, Cambridge.

1867   Family spends year in Rome. Befriends Margaret ("Daisy") and Arthur Terry, children of American painter Luther Terry and niece and nephew of Julia Ward Howe. Daisy, later Daisy Chanler, will be lifelong friend.

1868   Family travels through Spain and settles in Paris. Taught to read by father; recites Tennyson for visiting maternal grandmother. Begins "making up," inventing stories using parents and their friends as characters. Is allowed to read Louisa May Alcott, *The Water Babies*, and *Alice in Wonderland*, but not Mark Twain, Bret Harte, or "Uncle Remus."

1870–71   Stays at Wildbad, a spa in Württemberg, while mother takes water cure. Studies New Testament in German, takes walks in Black Forest. Suffers severe attack of

typhoid fever (later remembers convalescence as beginning of recurrent apprehension of "some dark undefinable
menace forever dogging my steps, lurking and threatening"). Family settles in Florence at end of 1870.

1872–75   Family returns to the United States, dividing year between
three-story brownstone on West 23rd Street, New York,
and Pencraig, their summer home in Newport, Rhode
Island. At Pencraig rides pony, swims in cove, watches
archery contests, visits neighboring family of astronomer
Lewis Rutherfurd. Studies French, medieval and romantic German poetry with Rutherfurd family governess,
Anna Bahlmann (who later becomes her governess, and,
in the 1890s, a regular correspondent), but parents believe
that formal education would be too much of a strain after
her convalescence for typhoid fever. Attempts, at age
eleven, to write first novel, which begins, "'Oh, how do
you do, Mrs. Brown?' said Mrs. Tompkins. 'If only I had
known you were going to call I should have tidied up the
drawing-room.'" Shows draft to mother, who comments,
"Drawing-rooms are always tidy." Begins lifelong friendship with sister-in-law Mary ("Minnie") Cadwalader
Jones, wife (later divorced) of brother Frederic. In father's
eight-hundred-volume New York library finds histories
(including Plutarch, Macaulay, Carlyle, Parkman), diaries
and correspondence (Pepys, Cowper, Madame de Sévigné), criticism (Sainte-Beuve), art history and archaeol-
ogy (Ruskin, Schliemann), poetry (Homer and Dante
in translation, most English poets, some French), and a
few novels (Scott, Irving). Mother forbids the reading of
contemporary fiction until marriage. Later remembers
reading as "a secret ecstasy of communion." Summer 1875,
forms close friendship with Emelyn, daughter of Edward
Abiel Washburn, rector of Calvary Church, New York.
(Emelyn forms a romantic attachment to Edith, which
Wharton later characterizes as "degenerate.")

1876–77   Begins *Fast and Loose*, 30,000-word novella about trials
of ill-starred young lovers, autumn 1876. Keeps enterprise
secret from everyone except Emelyn Washburn. Finished
January 1877, manuscript includes mock-hostile reviews
("every character is a failure, the plot a vacuum"). Her
first published work is translation of "Was die Steine
Erzählen" ("What the Stones Tell") by Heinrich Karl

Brugsch in *Saturday* magazine, completed with the assistance and published under the initials of the Reverend Washburn.

1878–79   *Verses*, volume of twenty-nine poems, printed in Newport, arranged and paid for by one of her parents. Poem "Only a Child" appears in the New York *World*. Summer 1879, Newport neighbor Allen Thorndike Rice, editor of the *North American Review*, shows some of her poems to Henry Wadsworth Longfellow, who then sends them to William Dean Howells. Howells accepts five for publication in March and April 1880 issues of *Atlantic Monthly*. Makes social debut a year early, at age seventeen, perhaps due to father's ill health.

1880–81   Courted in New York, Newport, and Bar Harbor, Maine, by Henry Leyden Stevens, twenty-one-year-old son of socially ambitious widow Mrs. Paran Stevens. November 1880, goes to southern France with mother and ailing father. Henry Stevens joins them September 1881.

1882   Father, age sixty-one, dies in Cannes in March. Inherits over $20,000 in trust fund and a share of father's estate. Taken up by social set of brother Henry, men fifteen to twenty years older than her. In August, engagement to Henry Stevens announced in Newport, with marriage scheduled for October. Engagement is broken off in October, apparently at insistence of Mrs. Stevens, who found Edith to be too much of "an ambitious authoress." Travels with mother to Paris.

1883   Spends summer at Bar Harbor. Meets Walter Van Rensselaer Berry, twenty-four-year-old Harvard graduate studying for admission to the District of Columbia bar. In August, Edward Robbins ("Teddy") Wharton, friend of brother Henry, arrives in Bar Harbor and begins courtship. A thirty-three-year-old Harvard graduate interested mainly in camping, hunting, fishing, and riding, he lives with his family in Boston and receives a $2,000 annuity from them.

1884   In October, hires Catherine Gross, Alsatian immigrant, as personal attendant (she will be Wharton's companion and housekeeper for over four decades).

1885–88   Marries Edward Wharton April 29, 1885, at Trinity Chapel, New York City. Claims later in life not to have known "what being married was like" until several weeks after her marriage. Henry Stevens dies of tuberculosis, July 18, 1885. Whartons move into Pencraig Cottage, small house on mother's Newport estate, leaving every February for four months of European travel, mostly in Italy. Introduced by Egerton Winthrop, wealthy New York art collector and their occasional traveling companion, to contemporary French literature and works of Darwin, Huxley, Spencer, Haeckel, and other writers on evolution. Meets Henry James in Paris, 1887, but is too shy to speak to him. Whartons spend a year's income (about $10,000) on four-month Aegean cruise, 1888. Learns in Athens that she has inherited $120,000 from reclusive New York cousin Joshua Jones. Begins to suffer from periodic asthma, exhaustion, and anemia. Rents small house on Madison Avenue, New York City.

1889   Four poems accepted for publication by *Scribner's Magazine*, *Harper's Monthly*, and *Century Illustrated Monthly Magazine*. Rents narrow house on Fourth Avenue near 78th Street (eventually 884 Park Avenue), later purchasing it for $19,670 in November 1891.

1890–92   Father-in-law William Craig Wharton commits suicide, May 1891. Short story, "Mrs. Manstey's View," accepted by *Scribner's* May 1890, published July 1891. Rents out Park Avenue house for $1,300 a year until 1896. Sister-in-law Minnie Jones separates from brother Frederic after discovering his infidelity in 1887 with Elsie West (whom he will later marry). Works on long short story, "Bunner Sisters." It is rejected by *Scribner's*, December 1892.

1893   Buys Land's End, Newport estate overlooking the Atlantic, for $80,000 in March. Works with Boston architect Ogden Codman on decoration of its interior. French novelist Paul Bourget and his wife are guests. Three stories, "That Good May Come," "The Fulness of Life," and "The Lamp of Psyche," accepted by *Scribner's*, whose editor, Edward Burlingame, proposes a short-story volume for Charles Scribner's Sons. Wharton agrees, suggesting inclusion of "Bunner Sisters." Sails for Europe in December.

1894–95   Burlingame rejects "Something Exquisite" (later revised and published as "Friends"). Writes to him from Florence, expressing gratitude for his criticism and doubt about her abilities. Travels through Tuscany. Visits Violet Paget ("Vernon Lee"), English novelist and historian of eighteenth-century Italy. After research at monastery of San Vivaldo and in Florence museums, identifies group of terracotta sculptures, previously thought to date from the seventeenth century, as work of the late fifteenth- to early sixteenth-century school of the Robbias. Writes article for *Scribner's* on her findings and surrounding Tuscan landscape. Notifies Burlingame in July 1894 that short-story volume will need another six months to prepare. Suffering from intense exhaustion and nausea, breaks off correspondence with Burlingame for sixteen months. Writes "The Valley of Childish Things, and Other Emblems," collection of ten short fables, and sends it in December 1895 to Burlingame, who rejects it.

1896–97   Writes, with architect Ogden Codman, *The Decoration of Houses*, study of interior arrangements and furnishings in upper-class city homes. Shows incomplete manuscript to Burlingame, who gives it to William Brownell, senior editor at Scribner's. Manuscript rejected by English publisher Macmillan. Minnie and Frederic Jones divorce. Summer 1897, resumes friendship with Walter Berry, who stays for a month at Land's End, assisting Wharton in the revision of *The Decoration of Houses*. Wharton persuades Brownell to increase the number of halftone plates and makes extensive recommendations concerning the book's design. Published by Scribner's December 1897; sales are unexpectedly good. In 1897 or 1898, mother moves to Paris (brothers Frederic and Henry both live in Europe); meetings and correspondence with her become infrequent.

1898   Writes and revises seven stories from March to July, despite recurring illness. In letter to Burlingame, discusses her earliest stories: "I regard them as the excesses of youth. They were all written 'at the top of my voice,' & The Fulness of Life is one long shriek—I may not write any better, but at least I hope that I write in a lower key." Takes out $50,000 mortgage on Land's End to purchase 882 Park Avenue, adjoining 884 Park, for household staff to live in. Goes to Philadelphia in October; suffers from depression and illness, while also continuing to write.

1899 January, settles with Edward for four-month stay in house at 1329 K Street in Washington, found for them by Walter Berry, who becomes close literary adviser and supporter. *The Greater Inclination*, long-delayed collection of short stories, published by Scribner's in March to enthusiastic reviews; sales exceed 3,000 copies. Protests to Scribner's that book has been insufficiently advertised. Begins extensive correspondence with Sara ("Sally") Norton, daughter of Harvard professor Charles Eliot Norton. Summer, travels in Europe, where mother is terminally ill in Paris; joined by the Bourgets in Switzerland; tours northern Italy with them, through Bergamo and Val Camonica. Returns to Land's End in September. Seeking escape from Newport climate, visits Lenox, Massachusetts, in fall.

1900 Novella *The Touchstone* (in England, *A Gift from the Grave*) appears in the March and April *Scribner's*; published by Scribner's in April, selling 5,000 copies by year's end. Travels in England, Paris, and northern Italy, again accompanied by the Bourgets. Spends summer and fall at rented house, The Poplars, in Lenox while Edward goes on yachting trip. Begins work on novel *The Valley of Decision*. Makes notes for "A Moment's Ornament," which eventually becomes *The House of Mirth*. Sends Henry James copy of "The Line of Least Resistance"; he responds with praise and detailed criticism, encouraging further effort. Wharton removes story from volume being prepared.

1901 February to June, negotiates purchase for $40,600 of 113-acre Lenox property extending into the village of Lee. After breaking with Codman, hires architect Francis V. L. Hoppin to design house modeled on Christopher Wren's Belton House in Lincolnshire, England. Oversees landscaping and gardening. *Crucial Instances*, second volume of stories, published by Scribner's in April. Mother dies in Paris, age seventy-six, on June 1. Her will leaves large sums outright to Frederic and Henry but creates a trust fund for Wharton's share of the remainder of the estate, which will revert to brother Frederic upon Wharton's death. Trust eventually amounts to $92,000, of which Wharton may only draw on the estate rental income; total annual income from parents' and Joshua Jones's trusts is about $22,000. Wharton visits London and Paris and persuades her brothers to make husband Edward co-trustee with brother Henry. Works on play *The Man of Genius* (never finished) and on dramatization of Prosper Mérimée's *Manon Lescaut* (never produced).

1902   *The Valley of Decision*, historical novel set in eighteenth-century Italy, published by Scribner's in February in two volumes. Wharton criticizes its design while it is being prepared. Suffers from nausea, depression, fatigue after publication. Reviews are generally enthusiastic and sales are good, about 25,000 copies in the first six months. Begins *Disintegration*, novel set in contemporary New York society, but does not finish it, and considers (but never begins) a sequel to *The Valley of Decision*. Writes travel articles, poetry, theatrical reviews, and literary criticism, including essays on Gabriele D'Annunzio and George Eliot. Translates Hermann Sudermann's play *Es Lebe das Leben* as *The Joy of Living* (it runs briefly on Broadway and in London and sells in book form for a number of years). Henry James writes Wharton in August that *The Valley of Decision* is "accomplished, pondered, saturated," and "brilliant and interesting from a literary point of view," but urges her to abandon historical subject matter "in favour of the American subject. . . . *Do New York!* The 1st-hand account is precious." Rehires Codman as decorator for Lenox house. Meets Theodore Roosevelt in Newport at christening of his godchild, son of Wharton's friends Daisy and Winthrop Chanler, beginning a long friendship. Moves into Lenox house, named "The Mount" after Long Island home of Revolutionary War ancestor Ebenezer Stevens, in September. Edward is ill in summer.

1903   January, sails for Italy with ailing husband. Travels slowly north from Rome through Tuscany, the Veneto, and Lombardy, inspecting estates for series of articles commissioned by R. W. Gilder for *Century*. Enjoys her first automobile ride. Visits Violet Paget at Villa Pomerino outside of Florence. Meets art expert Bernhard

Berenson, who strongly dislikes her. (They later become close friends.) Goes to Salsomaggiore, west of Parma, for treatment of her asthma, the first of many regular visits. Spends summer and fall at The Mount, with interval at Newport. Sells Land's End for $122,500, June 13. Begins work on *The House of Mirth*. Writes Sally Norton in August that Edward seems to be having "a sort of nervous collapse." Novella *Sanctuary* published by Scribner's in October. Sails for England, early December. Henry James visits London, from Rye, in mid-December.

1904   Edward purchases their first automobile, a Panhard-Levassor. With Edward driving, travels south to Hyères for a stay with the Bourgets, then to Cannes and Monte Carlo and back across France. In England, visits Henry James in Rye and tours Sussex with him. Returns to Lenox in late spring. Enthusiastic about motor travel, hires Charles Cook as a permanent chauffeur (he retains this position until 1921, when he suffers a stroke). *The Descent of Man*, collection of stories, published by Scribner's in April. After reading reviews, writes Brownell that "the continued cry that I am an echo of Mr. James (whose books of the last ten years I can't read, much as I delight in the man) . . . makes me feel rather hopeless." Hires Anna Bahlmann as secretary and literary assistant. Agrees with Burlingame in August to begin serialization of *The House of Mirth* in January 1905 *Scribner's*; undertakes schedule of intense work (usually writing in the morning) to meet deadline. (Finishes in March 1905; serialized January–November.) House guests at The Mount include Brooks Adams and his wife, George Cabot Lodge (son of Senator Henry Cabot Lodge), Walter Berry, and Gaillard Lapsley, American-born don of medieval history at Trinity College, Cambridge. Henry James arrives in October with his friend Howard Sturgis, whom Wharton calls "the kindest and strangest of men." *Italian Villas and Their Gardens*, based on magazine articles written the previous year, published by The Century Company in November and spurs a revived interest in classic Italian gardens. Returns to New York just before Christmas.

1905   Henry James visits at 884 Park Avenue for a few days in January. Whartons dine at the White House with President Roosevelt in March. *Italian Backgrounds*, sketches written since 1894, published by Scribner's in April. After European trip in spring, including visit to Salsomaggiore for asthma treatment, returns to The Mount. House guests include printer Berkeley Updike, illustrator Moncure Robinson, publisher Walter Maynard, Robert Grant, novelist and judge of the probate court in Boston, and Henry James. Visits Sally and Charles Eliot Norton. *The House of Mirth* published by Scribner's, October 14, in first printing of 40,000; 140,000 copies in print by the end of the year, "the most rapid sale of any book ever published by Scribner," according to Brownell. Literary earnings for year exceed $20,000. Reviews generally favorable. Begins novel *Justine Brent* (later retitled *The Fruit of the Tree*). December, undertakes collaboration on stage version of *The House of Mirth* with playwright Clyde Fitch.

1906   Sails for France, March 10. Through Paul Bourget, enters intellectual and social circles of Paris, especially those of the Faubourg St. Germain. Among new acquaintances are poet Comtesse Anna de Noailles, historian Gustave Schlumberger, and his close friend, Comtesse Charlotte de Cossé-Brissac. Goes to England at the end of April. Whartons and Henry James make short motor tour of England. Visits Queen's Acre, Howard Sturgis's home in Windsor, for the first time (it soon becomes the center of her English social life). Meets Percy Lubbock, young writer and disciple of Henry James. Returns to France and takes motor tour with brother Henry, visiting cathedrals at Amiens and Beauvais, and Nohant, home of George Sand. Returns to Lenox in June and continues working on *Justine Brent*. Novella *Madame de Treymes* appears in the August *Scribner's* (published by Scribner's in March 1907). September, goes to Detroit with Edward and Walter Berry to see first performance of stage version of *The House of Mirth*. October opening in New York is a critical and commercial failure; Wharton calls the experience "instructive." Edward is away from Lenox, hunting and fishing, during much of the fall. Literary earnings for the year total almost $32,000.

1907   Returns to Paris in January and rents the apartment of the George Vanderbilts at 58 Rue de Varenne, in the heart of the Faubourg St. Germain. *The Fruit of the Tree* serialized in *Scribner's*, January–November. March, takes a "motor-flight" through France with Edward and Henry James, visiting Nohant and touring southern France. Invites James to stay for another month, and takes a short automobile trip with James and Gaillard Lapsley. Engages instructor to teach her contemporary French; for a lesson exercise, writes a precursor sketch of *Ethan Frome*. April, sees much of William Morton Fullerton, forty-two-year-old Paris correspondent for the London *Times*, former student of Charles Eliot Norton, and friend of Henry James. Spends summer at The Mount. Sales of *The Fruit of the Tree*, published by Scribner's in October, reach 60,000. Reviews are good. Fullerton arrives at The Mount in October for a two-day visit. Wharton begins a journal addressed to him. Returns to Paris in December. *The House of Mirth* appears as *Chez les Heureux du Monde* in the *Revue de Paris*, translated by Charles du Bos, a young follower of Bourget.

1908   January–February, Edward afflicted by "nervous depression." Wharton leads active social life, seeing linguist Vicomte Robert d'Humières, American ambassador Henry White, watercolorist Walter Gay and his wife, Matilda, James Van Alen, Fullerton, Comtesse Rosa de Fitz-James, Bourget, playwright Paul Hervieu, Charles du Bos, and others. February, spends time with Fullerton while Edward is away, and begins an affair with him in March. Edward, suffering from depression and pervasive pain, leaves for spa at Hot Springs, Arkansas, March 21. Wharton writes Brownell that Edward's illness has prevented her from making much progress on new novel, *The Custom of the Country*, and doubts that it will be ready for serial publication by January 1909. April, moves to brother Henry's townhouse on Place des États-Unis when he goes to America on business. Egerton Winthrop visits. When Henry James visits, arranges to have Jacques Émile Blanche paint portrait that she considers the best ever done of him. May, has first significant meetings with Henry Adams. Meditates in her journal on her affair with Fullerton; writes series of love sonnets. May 22, gives Fullerton journal addressed to him; he returns it the following day as she leaves for America. On fifth day of crossing, writes story "The Choice"; resumes work on *The Custom of the Country*. In Lenox, has difficulty breathing for six weeks; tells Sally Norton she has hay fever. Scribner's publishes *The Hermit and the Wild Woman*, fourth collection of stories, in September, *A Motor-Flight Through France*, travel account, in October. Writes poetry, enjoys reading Nietzsche's *Jenseits von Gut und Böse (Beyond Good and Evil)*. Leaves for Europe, October 30. Introduced by Henry James to aging George Meredith at Box Hill, near London; meets Somerset Maugham; goes with James Barrie to see performance of his play *What Every Woman Knows*. At Stanway, Gloucestershire home of Lady Mary Elcho, meets two young Englishmen who become close friends: Robert Norton, a landscape painter, and John Hugh Smith, a banker expert in Anglo-Russian financial affairs. Sees much of Henry James, who soon professes exhaustion from her visits, referring to her as "the Angel of Devastation." Crosses to France with Howard Sturgis for Christmas. Literary earnings for year are about $15,000.

1909   January, Edward arrives in Paris, suffering from insomnia and inexplicable pain in his face and limbs. Work on *The Custom of the Country* again interrupted. Continues to write poetry, including "Ogrin the Hermit," long narrative based on a portion of the Tristan and Iseult legend. When lease on 58 Rue de Varenne expires, moves to large suite in Hotel Crillon, Place de la Concorde, March. Edward returns to Lenox in mid-April. *Artemis to Actaeon*, book of poetry, published by Scribner's in late April. French short-story collection, *Les Metteurs en Scène*, published in May. Involves Henry James and Frederick Macmillan, Fullerton's publisher, in complicated scheme to conceal gift of money to Fullerton to meet blackmail demands of an ex-mistress. June, goes to London with Fullerton; they spend the night at the Charing Cross Hotel. After Fullerton leaves for America, writes "Terminus," fifty-two-line love poem. Stays in England until mid-July, visiting with Sturgis, Lapsley, and James. When Fullerton returns, they spend night in Rye at James's Lamb House. September, Henry Adams arranges another meeting between Wharton and Bernhard Berenson. Friendship develops. Edward arrives in Paris with his sister Nancy in October; soon confesses to Wharton that during the summer he sold some of her holdings, bought property in Boston, and lived there with his mistress.

Edward returns to Boston. Later admits to embezzling $50,000 from Wharton's trust funds; makes restitution by drawing upon $67,000 recently inherited from his mother, who died in August.

1910   Moves into apartment at 53 Rue de Varenne, January. Writes stories "The Eyes" and "The Triumph of Night." Sells New York houses. Edward returns to Paris in February, agrees to enter Swiss sanatorium for treatment of his depression. Goes to England in March to see Henry James, who is recovering from a "nervous breakdown." Begins short novel *Ethan Frome*. Walter Berry moves to Paris, stays in Whartons' guest suite for several months. July 3, sees Nijinsky dance in *L'Oiseau de Feu*. Affair with Fullerton ends. Visits Henry and William James at Lamb House in August. Sails in September to New York with Edward. October, Edward departs on trip around the world; Wharton returns to Paris, ill and exhausted. *Tales of Men and Ghosts* published by Scribner's in October; sells about 4,000 copies.

1911   January, confesses to Hugh Smith that "my writing tires and preoccupies me more than it used to." Tries unsuccessfully with William Dean Howells and Edmund Gosse to secure the Nobel Prize for Henry James. Edward returns to Paris in April. May, at Salsomaggiore for hay fever; resumes concerted work on *The Custom of the Country*. Returns to Lenox at beginning of July. Has Henry James, Hugh Smith, and Lapsley as guests. Wharton and Edward agree to formal separation in late July, then reverse decision. Returns to Europe in September after entrusting Edward with power to sell The Mount. *Ethan Frome* serialized in *Scribner's* from August through October, published by Scribner's in September. Reviewers in America and England call it one of her finest achievements. Disappointed with Scribner's reports of sales (4,200 copies by mid-November), Wharton protests lack of advertising, poor distribution, and bad typesetting. With Berry, tours central Italy and visits Berenson for the first time at his home, Villa I Tatti, near Florence, in October. Puts *The Custom of the Country* aside in November to work on novel *The Reef.* Visits England, November–December.

1912   Edward arrives in February at Rue de Varenne and stays
        until May. Relations remain distant and strained. Visits
        Spain with Rosa and Jean Du Breuil; and La Verna,
        monastery in Tuscany mountains, with Berry; their car
        must be lowered by ropes for them to return. Sale of The
        Mount for undisclosed sum completed in June. Offers
        to live with Edward in United States, but he refuses.
        Summer, sees much of Henry James during visits to
        England. Arranges with Charles Scribner for $8,000 of
        her royalties to be given to James under the guise of an
        advance for his novel-in-progress, *The Ivory Tower*. (James
        receives $3,600 in 1913; the novel is never completed.) *The
        Reef* published by D. Appleton and Company, which had
        given her $15,000 advance. Reviews are relatively poor;
        sales reach 7,000. Resumes work on *The Custom of the
        Country*. In November, meets with brother Frederic, who
        has had a stroke.

1913   *The Custom of the Country* appears in *Scribner's*, Janu-
        ary–November. Receives unexpected letter from brother
        Henry denouncing her for coldness toward Countess
        Tecla, his mistress and intended wife. Sues Edward for
        divorce on grounds of adultery; Paris tribunal grants
        decree, April 16. Helps to initiate effort to raise gift of
        $5,000 for Henry James's seventieth birthday; effort aban-
        doned when James discovers and angrily rejects it. Drives
        across Sicily with Berry in April. Friendship develops with
        Geoffrey Scott, author of *The Architecture of Humanism*,
        with whom she travels through northern Italy. Favorably
        impressed by premiere of Igor Stravinsky's ballet *Le Sacre
        du Printemps* in Paris, May 29. Considers buying house
        outside of London, but eventually decides against it.
        August, finishes *The Custom of the Country*. Travels with
        Berenson through Luxembourg and Germany, stopping
        at Cologne, Dresden, and Berlin. Begins autobiographi-
        cal novel *Literature*, never completed. *The Custom of the
        Country* published by Scribner's in October; sales reach
        nearly 60,000. December, sails to New York with Berry
        for wedding of niece, landscape gardener Beatrix Jones
        (daughter of brother Frederic and Mary Cadwalader),
        and Yale historian Max Farrand. Delayed when she
        contracts influenza, misses ceremony but arrives in time
        for reception. Finds New York "queer, rootless" and
        "overwhelming."

1914   Returns to Paris in January. Sends Henry James copy of
        Marcel Proust's recently published *Du Côté de chez Swann*.
        March, sails from Marseilles to Algiers with Percy Lub-
        bock. Drives through northern Algeria and Tunisia, "an
        unexpurgated page of the Arabian Nights!" Frightened in
        Timgad, Algeria, by attack from intruder in her room, but
        breaks away from him and screams; he flees. July, tours
        Spain with Berry for three weeks, viewing cave paintings
        at Altamira. Returns to Paris July 31, three days before
        outbreak of war between France and Germany. August,
        establishes workroom near Rue de Varenne for seam-
        stresses and other women thrown out of work by the eco-
        nomic disruption of general mobilization. Collects funds,
        selects supervisory staff, arranges for supply of work
        orders, free lunches, and coal allotments. Late August,
        goes to Stocks, English country house rented from novel-
        ist Mrs. Humphry Ward, a trip planned before the war.
        Sees Henry James at Rye. After learning of battle of the
        Marne, makes arrangements, with difficulty, to return to
        Paris; succeeds by end of September. November, estab-
        lishes and directs American Hostels for Refugees. Selects
        Elisina Tyler, friend since 1912, as administrative deputy;
        raises $100,000 in first twelve months. (Hostels assists
        9,330 refugees by end of 1915, providing free or low-cost
        food, clothing, coal, housing, medical and child care, and
        assistance in finding work.)

1915   February, visits the front in the Argonne and at Verdun
        with Berry. Tours hospitals, investigating need for blan-
        kets and clothing; watches French assault on village of
        Vauquois. Makes four more visits to front with Berry
        in next six months, including tour of frontline trenches
        in the Vosges; describes them in articles for *Scribner's*
        (collected in *Fighting France, from Dunkerque to Belfort*,
        published by Scribner's in November). April, organizes
        Children of Flanders Rescue Committee with Tyler,
        establishing six homes between Paris and the Normandy
        coast. Committee sets up classes in lacemaking for girls,
        industrial training for boys, French for Flemish speakers.
        Nearly 750 Flemish children, many of them tubercular,
        cared for in 1915. Increasingly concentrates on fund-
        raising and creation of sponsoring committees in France
        and the United States, delegating daily administration
        to Tyler. Arranges benefit concerts and an art exhibition.

Edits *The Book of the Homeless* (published by Scribner's in January 1916), with introductions by Marshal Joffre and Theodore Roosevelt. Contributors of poetry, essays, art, fiction, and musical scores include Cocteau, Conrad, Howells, Anna de Noailles, Hardy, Sargent, Santayana, Yeats, Eleanora Duse, Sarah Bernhardt, Henry James, Max Beerbohm, Paul Claudel, Edmond Rostand, Monet, Renoir, Leon Bakst, and Stravinsky. Wharton does most of the translations. Proceeds (approximately $2,500 from the book, $7,000 from the sale of art and manuscripts) go to Hostels and Rescue Committee. Friendship develops with André Gide, who serves on a Hostels committee. October, makes short visit to England to visit ailing Henry James. Learns in December that James is dying; writes Lapsley: "His friendship has been the pride & honour of my life."

1916   Henry James dies February 28. Spring, helps establish treatment program for tubercular French soldiers. Made Chevalier of the Legion of Honor, March. Mourns deaths of Egerton Winthrop (tells Berenson that Winthrop and Henry James "made up the sum of the best I have known in human nature") and secretary Anna Bahlmann. Informs Charles Scribner that she is working on novel *The Glimpses of the Moon* and a work "of the dimensions of *Ethan Frome*. It deals with the same kind of life in a midsummer landscape." Offers the latter for serial publication, but Charles Scribner declines, having already scheduled her 1892 "Bunner Sisters" for fall; accepts offer from Appleton for book and from *McClure's* for serial. Feels financial pressure due to expense of refugee work, reduced literary earnings, and effects of American income tax. *Xingu and Other Stories* (all except one story written before the war) published in October by Scribner's.

1917   *Summer*, companion piece to *Ethan Frome*, serialized in *McClure's* for $7,000, February–August; published by Appleton July 2. Makes two final visits to war zones in April and October. Grows fond of Ronald Simmons, young American officer and painter. After tuberculosis treatment centers are taken over by the Red Cross, establishes four convalescent homes for tubercular civilians. September–October, makes month-long tour of French Morocco with Walter Berry. Witnesses self-lacerative ritual dances and visits harem, noting its air of "somewhat melancholy respectability."

1918   February, gives lecture on American life at the Société des Conférences, and April, gives talk to American soldiers that becomes first chapter of *French Ways and Their Meaning*. After long negotiation, purchases Jean-Marie, house in village of St. Brice-sous-Forêt, outside of Paris in March for 90,000 francs (will restore its original name, Pavillon Colombe). Summer, begins novels *The Marne* and *A Son at the Front*. May–July, has three minor heart attacks. June, brother Frederic dies; Wharton, long estranged from him, writes sadly of her brother Henry's failure to contact her. Deeply grieved by death from Spanish flu of Ronald Simmons, August 12. *The Marne* published by Appleton in December.

1919   Rising expenses, support of financially troubled Mary Cadwalader Jones, establishment of trust fund for three Belgian children, together with changing New York real estate market and effects of American income tax, create financial pressure. Accepts offer of $18,000 from *The Pictorial Review* for serial rights to her next novel. Unable to finish *The Glimpses of the Moon*, suggests *A Son at the Front*, but editors cable her: "War Books Dead in America." Proposes novel *Old New York* (later retitled *The Age of Innocence*), set in 1875. Magazine accepts, and Appleton advances $15,000 against royalties. Leases Ste.-Claire-du-Vieux-Château in Hyères, overlooking Mediterranean. Moves into Pavillon Colombe in July. Starts to create gardens for both houses, with advice from garden-designers Lawrence Johnston and niece Beatrix Farrand. *French Ways and Their Meaning*, collection of magazine articles, published by Appleton. "Beatrice Palmato" outline and fragment, explicit treatment of father-daughter incest, probably written at this time (the story is never finished). Made Chevalier of the Order of Leopold by King Albert of Belgium.

1920   Howard Sturgis dies in January; end of Queen's Acre gatherings. *In Morocco*, travel account, published by Scribner's in October after serialization the previous year. *The Age of Innocence*, serialized in *The Pictorial Review* July–October, published by Appleton in October, sells 66,000 copies in six months (by 1922 it earns Wharton $50,000).

November, given the Prix de Vertú from the Académie française. December, moves to Hyères for several months.

1921   Resumes work on *The Glimpses of the Moon*. Writes *The Old Maid*, novella about out-of-wedlock birth (rejected by *Ladies' Home Journal* for being "a bit too vigorous for us"). Begins long friendship with Philomène de Lévis-Mirepoix (later Philomène de la Forest-Divonne, who will write journalism and novels under the name Claude Sylve). *The Age of Innocence* awarded Pulitzer Prize in May. Later learns that the jury had originally voted for Sinclair Lewis's *Main Street*, but had been overruled by the trustees of Columbia University, who thought it too controversial. Writes to Lewis in August of her "disgust" at the action and invites him to St. Brice (he makes the first of several visits in October). *The Old Maid* bought by *RedBook* for $2,250 (serialized February–April 1922). September, finishes *The Glimpses of the Moon*. Goes to Hyères in mid-December.

1922   At Hyères until late May; June to mid-December at St. Brice. Summer, longtime friend and correspondent Sally Norton dies. When estranged brother Henry dies in August Wharton writes Berenson that "he was the dearest of brothers to all my youth." *The Glimpses of the Moon* serialized in *The Pictorial Review*; published by Appleton in July, sells more than 100,000 copies in America and Britain in six months, earning her $60,000 from various rights and royalties. Reads William Gerhardi's *Futility* and begins correspondence with him.

1923   Film version of *The Glimpses of the Moon*, with dialogue titles by F. Scott Fitzgerald, released in April. (Six other films were made from Wharton's works from 1918 to 1934; she had no involvement in any of the productions.) In May, invited by Yale University to receive honorary Doctor of Letters degree. Although reluctant to attend, decides she needs to see United States if she is to continue writing about it. Accepts degree (the first to be awarded to a woman by Yale) at commencement in New Haven, June 20. Returns to France after eleven-day visit (during which she meets playwright Edward Sheldon), her first since 1913 and her last. Novel *A Son at the Front* published by Scribner's in September, fulfilling promise made a decade earlier to give Scribner's another novel after *The Custom of the Country*; sales are poor. Works on novel *The Mother's Recompense*. Promoted to Officier of the Legion of Honor. Meets Lytton Strachey during visit to Pontigny.

1924   January, Gerhardi visits Ste.-Claire, and becomes a regular visitor. *Old New York*, collection of four novellas, published by Appleton in May in boxed sets of four volumes. Titles are *False Dawn (The 'Forties), The Old Maid (The 'Fifties), The Spark (The 'Sixties), New Year's Day (The 'Seventies)*. About 26,000 sets sold in six months, with another 3,000 volumes sold individually. Declines election as honorary vice-president of the Authors' League of America. Begins keeping diary sporadically as notes for a future autobiography.

1925   Becomes first woman to be awarded Gold Medal for "distinguished service" by National Institute of Arts and Letters. *The Mother's Recompense* published by Appleton in April after serialization in *The Pictorial Review* October 1924–March 1925. Sales are good, earning her $55,000 in the first few months. June, receives inscribed copy of *The Great Gatsby* from Fitzgerald. July, Fitzgerald visits St. Brice; the encounter is strained and awkward. *The Writing of Fiction*, collection of five essays, including long appreciation of Proust, published by Scribner's in the late summer. In September, travels to Spain with Berry.

1926   Charters 360-ton steam yacht *Osprey* for ten-week cruise with guests, including Robert Norton and Daisy Chanler, through the Mediterranean and Aegean, March–June. *Here and Beyond*, collection of short stories, published by Appleton in summer. *Twelve Poems* published in London by The Medici Society. Elected to the National Institute of Arts and Letters. September, travels with Berry through northern Italy. Finishes novel *Twilight Sleep* in November. Buys Ste.-Claire, Hyères home, for $40,000.

1927   January, Berry suffers mild stroke; convalesces at Hyères for five weeks, depressed and irritable. *The Pictorial Review* pays $40,000 for serial rights to novel *The Children* after *Delineator* offers $42,000; promises *Delineator* the novel *The Keys of Heaven*, based on famous 1847 murder of the Duchesse de Choiseul. *Twilight Sleep* published by Appleton in May; sells well. Walter Berry suffers second stroke in Paris, October 2. Wharton visits him on his deathbed;

he dies October 12. Writes Lapsley: "No words can tell of my desolation. He had been to me in turn all that one being can be to another, in love, in friendship, in under-standing." Mildred and Robert Bliss nominate Wharton for the Nobel Prize, repeating their efforts, with no suc-cess, in 1928 and 1929. November, assembles packet of documents, mostly concerning Edward's illness, labelled "For my biographer."

1928   Edward Wharton dies in New York, February 7. *The Children* is serialized in *The Pictorial Review* April–July, published by Appleton in September; earns $120,000 from sales and film rights. May, travels to Spain with Daisy Chanler, and spends summer in England, meet-ing Evelyn Waugh. Begins novel *Hudson River Bracketed*, with material from earlier unfinished novel *Literature*, after abandoning *The Keys of Heaven*. Friendship devel-ops with Desmond MacCarthy, British writer and editor. December, *The Age of Innocence*, dramatized by Margaret Ayer Barnes, opens on Broadway, runs until June 1929, then tours for four months, earning Wharton $23,500.

1929   January, severe winter storms devastate Ste.-Claire gar-dens; describes effect as "torture." February, learns that *Delineator* began serialization of *Hudson River Bracketed* in September 1928, six months ahead of schedule. Severely ill in March with myocarditis and an irregular heartbeat. Recovers by midsummer. Saddened by death of Geoffrey Scott in August. Finishes *Hudson River Bracketed* (pub-lished by Appleton in November) and begins restoration of Ste.-Claire gardens. Awarded Gold Medal for "special distinction in literature" by American Academy of Arts and Letters. Elected to the Royal Society of Literature in Britain. Begins friendship with museum curators Eric Maclagan, Louis Metman, and Louis Gillet.

1930   Elected to the American Academy of Arts and Letters. *Certain People*, collection of short stories, published by Appleton in summer. Begins novel *The Gods Arrive*, sequel to *Hudson River Bracketed*. Autumn, friendship develops with art critic and historian Kenneth Clark while travel-ing in Tuscany. December, meets Aldous Huxley, who introduces her to anthropologist Bronislaw Malinowski. Turns down honorary doctorate from Columbia Univer-sity on grounds of health (it is offered and refused again the following year and in 1934). After stock market crash, royalties for year total only $5,000, compared to $95,000 in 1929.

1931 Fullerton visits twice, in June and September. Visits England in July and sees H. G. Wells, Harold Nicolson, and Osbert, Sacheverell, and Dame Edith Sitwell. Attends several Roman Catholic services during visit to Rome in November.

1932 January, finishes *The Gods Arrive*. Rejected for serial publication by *The Saturday Evening Post*, *Liberty*, and *Collier's* because it features an unmarried couple living together. Sold to *Delineator* for $50,000 despite Wharton's anger over handling of *Hudson River Bracketed*, appearing February–August. Published by Appleton later in year, it sells poorly. Begins autobiography *A Backward Glance*. Visits Rome in May. Becomes godmother to Kenneth Clark's son Colin.

1933 Catherine Gross, Wharton's companion since 1884, falls into paranoid dementia in April, dies in October. Elise Duvlenck, her personal maid since 1914, dies May 29. *Human Nature*, collection of short stories, published by Appleton. By threat of legal action, forces *Ladies' Home Journal* to honor pre-Depression agreement to pay $25,000 for her autobiography; installments appear October 1933–March 1934. June, vacations in England with Gaillard Lapsley, visits Wales for the first time; August, goes to Salzburg for a week and October, visits Holland. Begins novel *The Buccaneers* (never finished, but published by Appleton-Century in 1938 with Wharton's long outline of the remainder of the story and an afterword by Lapsley).

1934 Tours England and Scotland. Guided through National Gallery in London by Kenneth Clark. *A Backward Glance* published by Appleton-Century. Breaks with Appleton editor Rutger Jewett, who had acted as her agent without commission for over a decade, blaming him for decreased literary earnings; engages James Pinker as new agent.

1935 *The Old Maid*, dramatized by Zoë Akins, opens in New York for successful run. April, suffers mild stroke, with temporary loss of sight in left eye. September 22, Mary Cadwalader Jones dies.

1936   *Ethan Frome*, dramatized by Owen and Donald Davis,
        tours United States after successful New York run. Income
        from both plays is about $130,000, ending financial worry.
        Visits England in the summer. *The World Over*, collection
        of short stories, published by Appleton-Century.

1937   Sends last completed short story, "All Souls'," to her agent,
        February. Health declines; suffers heart attack, June 1,
        while visiting Ogden Codman to discuss new edition
        of *The Decoration of Houses*. Has stroke on August 7 and
        dies at St. Brice on the evening of August 11. Buried near
        Walter Berry in the Cimetière des Gonards, Versailles,
        August 14. Last story collection, *Ghosts*, published post-
        humously in September.

Note on the Texts

This volume contains four novels by Edith Wharton: *The Glimpses of the Moon* (1922), *A Son at the Front* (1923), *Twilight Sleep* (1927), and *The Children* (1928).

Most of Wharton's novels, including the four novels in this volume, were published first in periodicals and then in book form, the serialization often beginning before Wharton had finished writing the final chapters, and the book sometimes appearing shortly before the serialization ended. Because of this situation, Wharton sent her American book publishers revised proofs showing her latest alterations. This volume therefore uses the first American edition as its text for each of these four novels.

Wharton began writing *The Glimpses of the Moon* in 1916. By 1919 her work on it had stalled, and she did not pick it up again until 1921, at which time she wrote to her friend Bernard Berenson that the novel "tries to picture the adventures of a young couple who believe themselves to be completely affranchis & up-to-date, but are continually tripped up by obsolete sensibilities, & discarded ideals.—A difficult subject, which of course seemed the easiest in the world when I began it." She finished it in September 1921, and it was serialized in the *Pictorial Review* from May to August 1922 and published in New York by D. Appleton and Company in July 1922. An identical British edition was published by Appleton in September 1922.

A Son at the Front was begun in summer 1918, around the time of the death on August 12 of Ronald Simmons, on whom she based the character of Boylston. (She considered printing "In Memory of Boylston" on the title page.) In July 1919, she offered the novel to Appleton to be serialized and then published in book form, but Rutger B. Jewett, Wharton's editor at Appleton, cabled her: "War Books Dead in America." Appleton serialized *The Age of Innocence* instead. *A Son at the Front* was serialized in *Scribner's Magazine* from December 1922 to September 1923 and published by Charles Scribner's Sons in September 1923. A British edition was published by Macmillan in September 1923, using different plates but identical in text to the American first edition.

Wharton proposed to her editor at Appleton in May 1925 "another novel of ultra-modern New York life," which became *Twilight Sleep*. She finished the novel in November 1926. It was serialized in the *Pictorial Review* from February to May 1927 and published by Appleton in

May 1927. An identical British edition was published by Appleton in June 1927.

Wharton's work on *The Children* began in February 1927 and was finished in January 1928. Serialized in the *Pictorial Review* from April to July 1928, it was published by Appleton in September 1928. Copies of the first edition exist in two states. *The Children* was selected for the September 1928 offering of the Book-of-the-Month Club, and thus a larger print run was needed. The plates were duplicated, and the Book-of-the-Month Club set was altered to differentiate it by adding "*First Printing, September, 1928*" to the copyright page, and an arabic "(1)" replaced a roman "(I)" for the printing code number on the last page. However, when the plates were machined, one set was damaged on pages 122 and 135, requiring those pages to be reset. This resetting introduced variant line breaks at 122.23 ("when . . . racking" instead of "you . . . my") and an error at 135.14: "moters" for "motors." Then, as the books were bound, sheets from the two printings were intermixed, so that copies with the error on page 135 can have either "(1)" or "(I)" on the last page. This volume uses a copy of the first edition in which "motors" appears at 135.14, and 122.23 begins "you" and ends "my." A British edition was simultaneously published by Appleton using the book-club plates ("when . . . racking" and "moters").

This volume presents the texts of the original printings chosen for inclusion here, but it does not attempt to reproduce features of their typographic design. The texts are presented without change, except for the correction of typographical errors. Spelling, punctuation, and capitalization are often expressive features, and they are not altered, even when inconsistent or irregular. The following is a list of typographical errors corrected, cited by page and line number: 44.12, agglutinative; 61.29, we've; 62.6, Vanerlyn; 74.16, grasped; 120.26, place.; 126.26, she I; 146.15, monuths; 178.35, Buttles'; 203.26, keenly "Ah,"; 220.20–21, pleaded. "Two; 250.30, threatres,; 268.25, we was; 274.31, Frankfort; 276.20, Fortin-Luscluze; 296.19, 'Of; 301.34, "No."; 326.3, from a; 361.24, farther; 386.33, lips; 393.3, happened?'; 449.15, the the; 483.12, different.—; 588.2, knew; 674.25, letters,; 706.28, woke; 789.26, retractation; 812.11, tarring; 904.11, prepare; 924.16, childred; 938.25, fragance; 961.29, back."; 984.10, hornbean.

Notes

In the notes below, the reference numbers denote page and line of this volume (the line count includes headings). No note is given for material included in standard desk-reference books. Biblical quotations are keyed to the King James Version. For references to other studies and further information than is included in the Chronology, see Hermione Lee, *Edith Wharton* (New York: Alfred A. Knopf, 2007); and Sarah Bird Wright, *Edith Wharton A to Z* (New York: Checkmark Books, 1998).

THE GLIMPSES OF THE MOON

1.1–2 THE GLIMPSES OF THE MOON] Wharton explained in a November 1919 letter to Marcel Prévost, the editor of the *Revue de France*, which published the book in translation, that "la lune en question est la lune de miel qui re-apparait entre les épais nuages d'un mariage très agité et très 'modern style'": The moon in question is the honeymoon that reappears between the thick clouds of a very agitated and very 'modern style' marriage.

33.24 *Le Rire?*] French satirical magazine published from 1894 to 1959. In 1915, they published a caricature of Wharton by Abel Faivre on their cover.

33.27 *Marius*] *Marius the Epicurean: His Sensations and Ideas*, an 1885 novel by English writer Walter Pater.

38.32 Aquileia] Ancient Roman city about seventy miles up the coast of Italy from Venice.

42.20 *Wilhelm Meister*] *Wilhelm Meister's Apprenticeship*, novel by German writer Johann Wolfgang von Goethe published in 1795–96.

54.19 Browning's "Toccata,"] "A Toccata of Galuppi's," a favorite of Wharton's, is an 1855 poem by English poet Robert Browning.

55.30 *"What of soul was left, I wonder—?"*] See note 54.19. The next line is, "when the kissing had to stop?"

59.25 Tiepolo's great vault] Giovanni Battista Tiepolo (1696–1770), Wharton's favorite painter, created a major fresco in the nave of the Church of the Scalzi in Venice in 1743–45. The fresco was destroyed in 1915 by Austrian aerial bombing.

84.11 atropine] Drug made from the belladonna plant that dilates the pupils, originally used as a cosmetic (thus the name "belladonna," Italian for "beautiful woman").

97.34   Nouveau Luxe] Wharton's name in her novels for the Ritz, which she disliked; to her it represented vulgar, nouveau-riche American tourists.

117.20   Apex City] The same fictional midwestern hometown Wharton gave to ruthless social climber Undine Spragg in *The Custom of the Country*.

144.13   *boîte*] A small restaurant or nightclub.

185.21   *bonne*] French: children's nurse.

195.31–32   Nessus-shirt] In Greek mythology, Hercules was killed by a poison shirt that had been painted with the blood of the centaur Nessus.

A SON AT THE FRONT

229.2–3   *Something veil'd . . . beings.*] From "Spiritual Characters among the Soldiers" in *Specimen Days* (1882), by Walt Whitman.

230.3   Ronald Simmons] Simmons (1885–1918) was born in Providence, Rhode Island, the son of the president of a coal company. He graduated from Yale in 1907, studied architecture at the Massachusetts Institute of Technology for three years, and then moved to Paris, where he continued architectural studies before turning to painting. After World War I began, Simmons helped organize the the the Comité des Étudiants Américains de L'École des Beaux-Arts, which supported former students of the school serving at the front. In 1916 he befriended Wharton and helped run the convalescent centers she had established for tubercular French soldiers. When the United States entered the war in 1917, Simmons served as a civilian member of the American Military Commission before being commissioned as an officer in the U.S. Army. Unfit for front-line duty because of short-sightedness and a weak heart, he served as an intelligence officer with the Inter-Allied Bureau in Paris and then with the supply service in Bordeaux. In August 1918 Simmons fell victim to the Spanish flu epidemic and died at Marseilles. Wharton based the character of Boylston in *A Son at the Front* on him.

246.3   Bois] The Bois de Boulogne, a large park at the edge of the 16th arrondissement of Paris and a popular promenade destination for the upper class.

247.19   a first edition of Lavengro] *Lavengro: The Scholar, the Gypsy, the Priest* (1851), an autobiographical novel by English author George Borrow.

248.14   the Engadine] A valley in the Swiss Alps famous as a health resort because of its sunny climate.

255.15   diligence journey] A diligence was a type of stagecoach drawn by four or more horses that could hold about fifteen passengers.

258.28   Tauchnitz] Inexpensive paperback editions of British, American, and German authors, precursors to modern mass-market paperbacks, produced by German publishing firm Bernhard Tauchnitz starting in 1841.

261.13–14   *maréchal des logis*] Sergeant.

271.20   India-rubber plant] *Ficus elastica*, an ornamental houseplant. It produces a milky white latex that was once used to make rubber.

275.32   'The Golden Bough'] *The Golden Bough: A Study in Comparative Religion* (1890) by Scottish anthropologist Sir James George Frazer. It was first read by Wharton in the 1890s.

278.17   '*Nous l'avons eu, votre Rhin allemand,*'] French: We had it once, your German Rhine. From "Le Rhin allemand" (1841) by Alfred de Musset, a literary reply to Nikolaus Becker's popular "Rheinlied" (1840). Both poems were written in response to the Rhine crisis that began in the summer of 1840 when the Thiers ministry called for reestablishing the eastern border of France on the Rhine. In October 1840 Louis-Phillippe dismissed Thiers, ending the crisis.

278.18   Hock] German white wine, sometimes specifically from the Rhine region.

280.6   *Kriegsgefahrzustand*] German declaration of "threatening danger of war."

283.3–4   it's up to him . . . American slang] From poker terminology; newly in common use at the start of World War I.

286.25   crossing of Luxembourg and the invasion of Belgium] The German army occupied Luxembourg on August 2, 1914, and invaded the neutral country of Belgium on August 4 in an attempt to outflank the French forces positioned on the German border. The violation of Belgian neutrality caused Great Britain to declare war on Germany on August 4.

287.4   Channel tunnel] The idea of creating a Channel Tunnel between England and France had first been suggested in 1802 and first attempted in 1881–82, but was abandoned because of concerns for national defense. Construction did not begin on the current Channel Tunnel until 1988; it was completed in 1994.

287.6–7   Belgium had announced her intention of resisting] On August 3, 1914, the Belgian government informed the German government of its intention "to repel, by all means in their power, every attack upon their rights." German troops invaded Belgium the following morning.

287.23   Saverne] Protests began in the Alsatian town of Saverne (Zabern) after the press reported on November 6, 1913, that a young Prussian officer in the local garrison, Lieutenant Günther von Forstner, had made insulting and provocative remarks about the local population. On November 28 troops from the garrison illegally arrested and imprisoned more than two dozen townspeople, and on December 2 von Forstner severely beat a disabled shoemaker who had publicly mocked him. A military court sentenced him to forty-three days' imprisonment, but the sentence was overturned in January 1914 on the grounds that Forstner had been defending the honor of the army. The Saverne incidents resulted in widespread protests throughout Germany against military independence from civil authority.

288.18   the Rosenkavalier] *Der Rosenkavalier*, 1911 opera by German composer Richard Strauss.

291.2   *On les aura, pas, mon vieux?*] French: We'll get them, no, my old man?

292.28   *laiterie?*] A small restaurant or café where milk-based drinks are served.

293.28   "sad dog,"] Slang: a wicked or debauched man.

294.21   *Chasseurs Alpins*] Elite mountain infantry of the French army, created in the late nineteenth century.

294.31   Nancy . . . German occupation] Nancy was occupied by German troops in 1870–71 during the Franco-Prussian War, but remained in France under the terms of the peace treaty.

300.32   the burning of Louvain] Alarmed by rumors of partisan snipers, German troops killed more than two hundred civilians in the Belgian city of Louvain, August 25–30, 1914, and burned much of the town, including the university library.

300.33   the bombardment of Rheims.] The Germans began shelling Reims on September 12, 1914, and caused severe damage to its cathedral on September 19.

304.40   crape] Mourning cloth.

308.26   "Kommandantur"] German: headquarters.

309.36–37   Raffet . . . interpreted Napoleon's campaigns] Auguste Raffet (1804–1860), French illustrator famous for his lithographs depicting Napoleonic campaigns.

314.12   "p.t.o."] Abbreviation: please turn over.

314.13–14   Nouveau Luxe] See note 97.34.

321.23–24   Juan de Borgoña's pictures of the Inquisition, in the Prado.] Borgoña (c. 1470–1536), born in the Duchy of Burgundy, is credited with introducing the High Renaissance style of painting to Spain.

326.3   Umbrian triptych] The Umbrian School, an Italian Renaissance school of painting, which included Perugino and Raphael.

326.12   *Infirmière-Major*] Matron, or senior nurse.

328.15   "dolman" and "mantle"] The dolman mantle, a women's outer garment fashionable in the 1870s and '80s, with large cape-like sleeves; and dolman sleeves, popular during the Civil War, which were created by sewing the sleeve into a low armhole to give the appearance of sloping shoulders.

328.17   play "Caste."] Comedy (1867) concerning distinctions of class and rank, by English dramatist Thomas William Robertson.

328.30   *cabinet particulier*] A private dining room at a restaurant.

334.12   Ford runabout] An early style of car body, with no windshield, top, or doors, and two seats. Ford's Model A and Model T automobiles were runabouts until about 1915.

334.13   *papier timbré*] Stamped paper for official documents or correspondence.

345.4   *embusqués*] Shirkers, or soldiers not at the front.

347.33   porte-cochère] A covered portico or archway next to a building's entrance through which a carriage or automobile could drive.

348.3   *entresol*] A mezzanine or intermediate floor.

348.29   *Postes de Secours*] Emergency medical centers at the front; literally rescue posts.

358.19   *pâtes tendres*] Bone china.

360.26   Barye *cire-perdue*] A lost-wax cast replica of a sculpture by Antoine-Louis Barye (1796–1875), famous for his sculptures of animals.

361.4–5   Neuve Chapelle] Town in the Artois region, site of a British offensive, March 10–13, 1915.

368.12   *On se fait une raison*] French: It is a reason.

370.4   *cafés chantants*] Outdoor cafés with live music.

371.2   *Chasseurs à Pied*] French light infantry.

380.11   *Allons donc!*] French: Surely not! or Come now!

381.10–11   *"une femme exquise"* or *"une bonne vieille"*] French: "an exquisite woman"; "a good old woman."

387.13   Agnus Dei] In the Roman Catholic Church, a wax disc impressed with the figure of a lamb bearing a cross and blessed by the Pope; often worn on a chain as a necklace.

393.6   *Lusitania*] The British ocean liner RMS *Lusitania*, en route from New York to Liverpool, was torpedoed and sunk without warning off the coast of Ireland by a German U-boat on May 7, 1915, with the loss of 1,198 lives, including 128 U.S. citizens. The Germans justified the sinking on the grounds that the ship had carried munitions in its cargo. After an exchange of diplomatic messages, President Woodrow Wilson obtained on September 1 a pledge from the German government that its submarines would no longer attack passenger liners without warning.

393.6   the writing on the wall.] Cf. Daniel 5.

393.23 *Maine*] USS *Maine*, an American armored cruiser, blew up and sank in Havana harbor on February 15, 1898, with the loss of 262 of its crew. A U.S. board of inquiry determined in March 1898 that the explosion was caused by an underwater mine, and its conclusion was reaffirmed by a second investigation in 1911. (An unofficial investigation in 1976 attributed the explosion to a coal bunker fire on board the ship.) The destruction of the *Maine* was widely attributed in the United States to the Spanish, and the event contributed to the American declaration of war on Spain on April 25.

394.27–30 Russia retreating . . . Suvla.] German and Austro-Hungarian forces broke through the Russian lines in Galicia at Gorlice-Tarnow on May 2, 1915, and began crossing the San River on May 16. Italy declared war on Austria-Hungary on May 23, 1915, and began the first of many unsuccessful offensives along the Isonzo River on June 23. Allied troops landed on the Gallipoli peninsula on April 25, 1915, at several locations, including Anzac Cove (named after the Australian and New Zealand Army Corps). On August 6, 1915, the forces at Anzac began attacking inland as British troops staged a new landing further north at Suvla Bay.

395.6–11 "If thou ascend . . . thee?"] Cf. Psalm 139.

400.23 Mangle!] A clothes press, to wring water from laundry.

401.15 *Chasseur Alpin*] See note 294.21.

401.18 *laiterie*] See note 292.28.

423.15 Mater Dolorosa] Latin: Mother of Sorrows. A name for the Virgin Mary.

423.40 Scarlet Woman] The Whore of Babylon from the Book of Revelation in the Bible; after the Reformation it was often used in Protestant churches to refer to the Roman Catholic Church.

429.2 Preparedness!] The call for enhanced military preparedness was led by Wharton's friend, former U.S. president Theodore Roosevelt.

429.34 Plattsburg] A camp designed to provide the rigors of military training, with a view to preparing a pool of potential junior officers, was established in 1915 in Plattsburgh, New York, by General Leonard Wood (1860–1927), a former chief of staff of the U.S. Army. Some 16,000 men had undergone training at Plattsburgh and similar camps by the time America entered the war in April 1917.

432.21 *Déjeuner du jour*] French: Lunch of the day.

449.23–24 the old song . . . more.] Cf. "To Lucasta, Going to the Warres," by English poet Richard Lovelace.

462.16 The Germans had attacked at Verdun] The Germans began their offensive at Verdun on February 21, 1916. The battle lasted until December 18, by which time the French had regained much of the ground they had earlier lost.

468.23   *Chasseur Alpin*] See note 294.21.

468.29   *dot*] French: dowry.

471.18   *paperasserie*] French: waste paper.

478.23   *Dulce et decorum*] Cf. Horace's Odes III.ii.13: "Dulce et decorum est pro patria mori." It is sweet and honorable to die for your country.

479.2   Verdun] See note 462.16.

479.8   the Somme] In the battle of the Somme (July–November 1916), the British, French, and German armies lost a combined total of more than a million men killed, wounded, and missing.

481.24   Plattsburg] See note 429.34.

484.3   Bernstorff!] Johann Heinrich von Bernstorff (1862–1939), German ambassador to the U.S., 1908–17.

487.19   "America has declared war on Germany."] President Woodrow Wilson requested a declaration of war against Germany on April 2, 1917; it was passed by the Senate on April 4 and by the House of Representatives on April 6.

487.34–35   first brown battalions . . . Concorde] The first troops of the American Expeditionary Force (AEF) arrived in France in June 1917.

TWILIGHT SLEEP

503.2–6   FAUST . . . Ort.] From Johann Wolfgang von Goethe's play *Faust: The Second Part of the Tragedy*, Act 5 (1832). Faust: And you, who then are you? / Care: I am your guest. / Faust: Be gone! / Care: I am here, in my proper place.

505.20–21   Eurythmic exercises.] May refer either to a pseudoscientific system of therapeutic medicine in which the subject performs expressive movements in response to music that was developed in the early 1920s by Austrian philosophers Rudolf Steiner and Marie von Sivers or to "sacred dances," also called Gurdjieff movements, developed by George I. Gurdjieff at his Institute for the Harmonious Development of Man at Fontainebleau, near Paris, which opened in 1922. Gurdjieff taught that most people spend their lives in "waking sleep"; his teachings promised to allow one to ascend to a higher state of consciousness.

507.35 Mahatma exercises] See note 505.20–21 for Gurdjieff movements.

509.33–34   Sealyham's] Sealyham terriers are rare small Welsh terriers popular during World War I and associated with Hollywood stars and the British Royal Family.

510.7   the last of the Capetians] The Capetian dynasty is one of the largest and oldest of European royal houses, and ruled France from 987 to 1328. Members of the dynasty still hold many titles in Europe.

512.6   "Twilight Sleep"] Also called the Freiburg method, an anesthesia and amnesiac used for childbirth in the early twentieth century consisting of scopolamine and morphine. It was abandoned in part because it depressed infants' central nervous systems, producing poor breathing capacity, and also because of the emotional effects on mothers who had no memory of childbirth.

515.26   "Mahatma"] Based on Paramahansa Yogananda (1893–1952), a Hindu yogi who led a popular Self-Realisation Fellowship in the 1920s and whose book *The Science of Religion* (1920) espoused the unity of all religions and that the purpose of life was avoidance of pain; and Pierre Bernard (1875–1955), alias "Oom the Omnipotent," who instructed wealthy New Yorkers on breathing exercises and whose "Mystic Order of the Tantriks of India" at Clarkstown Country Club became the center of a number of sex scandals. See also note 505.20–21 for George I. Gurdjieff.

515.39–40   Self-Annihilation, Anterior Existence, and Astral Affinities] Occult ideas. Self-annihilation: effacing the individual soul to become one with God or the universe. Anterior existence: past lives. Astral affinities: the attraction of the soul to certain animals or people, causing the soul to take on characteristics of the affinity.

516.11   Marcel-waving] Popular hairstyle of the 1920s, similar to a finger wave but produced with hot curling irons.

521.25   kakemono] Japanese ornamental scroll.

521.27   Sung vase] A *meiping* vase from the Chinese Song dynasty (960–1279) traditionally used to display plum blossoms.

528.5   Brewster] Brewster & Co. produced town cars until 1925 and was also the U.S. sales agent and body supplier for Rolls-Royce.

531.34   the 'Looker-on'] Based on the *Cheltenham Looker-On*, a social periodical published in Cheltenham, England, from 1833 to 1920, widely quoted for its gossip.

533.1   Iphigenia] In Greek mythology, the daughter of Agamemnon and Clytemnestra, whom Agamemnon sacrifices to appease the goddess Artemis so that his ships can sail to war against Troy.

546.9   not-more-than-the-Muses] A frequently repeated guideline for nineteenth-century dinner parties stipulated that the party should be not less than the number of the Graces (three), and not more than the number of the Muses (nine).

551.1–2   mediatized prince] A prince who has been dispossessed of his authority, usually through annexation by another monarchy, yet retains his title.

555.6   *Quelle plastique!*] French: What a figure!

573.30   Taylor-ized effort] I.e., scientifically managed. Taylorism analyzes workflows to improve productivity in manufacturing, and is named for

American mechanical engineer Frederick Winslow Taylor (1856–1915), author of *The Principles of Scientific Management* (1911).

576.6   a poor Poll!] Poll: parrot.

589.22   Ella Wheeler Wilcox] American author and poet (1850–1919) whose works supported the positive thinking or New Thought movement, which taught that "right thinking" would produce healing.

606.32–33   the Housetop] Wharton's parody of cabarets and nightclubs such as the Jardin de Danse on the rooftop of the New York Theater, where the foxtrot originated in 1914.

607.7–9   the *pasto*, the *frutte di mare*, the *fritture . . . sabaione*.] Italian: pasta, seafood, fries, custard.

617.15   moiré] Fabric with a wavy or watered appearance, usually silk.

622.40   hoarding] Billboard.

648.6   Dresden shepherdesses] Porcelain figurines of idealized shepherdesses manufactured in Meissen near Dresden, Germany, which were especially popular in the mid-eighteenth century.

648.14   Aubusson carpet] Large handwoven carpets from the villages of Aubusson and Felletin in Creuse, France, made especially for the French nobility.

648.26   Carlo Dolci's Magdalen] Carlo Dolci (1616–1686), Italian painter known for his religious figures.

656.16   Dutch garden] Rectangular garden enclosed with hedges or walls, with symmetrical geometric arrangements of dense plant groupings.

670.32   Crivelli's enigmatic Madonnas] Carlo Crivelli (c. 1430–1495), Italian Renaissance painter who produced many *Madonna and Child* paintings.

675.3   *curare*] A muscle-relaxing drug.

680.38   *élancé*] French: slim.

THE CHILDREN

737.4   Martin Boyne] Inspired by Wharton's friend Léon Bélugou (1865–1934), a civil engineer with a very young wife who was a critic of Alfred Binet's educational theories, based on psychological testing.

737.22   *diligence*] See note 255.15.

737.23   Rachel] Elisabeth Rachel Félix (1821–1858), French stage actress known as Mademoiselle Rachel. She toured the United States in 1855.

737.24   Ruskin] John Ruskin (1819–1900), English writer on art, architecture, and society.

741.8   Benger?] Benger's Food, a powder that could be mixed with milk to make infant formula or with other foods for invalids or the elderly.

757.26   Baedeker] Popular travel guidebooks produced by German publisher Verlag Karl Baedeker since 1827.

758.12   *"Zitto, zitto, carissimo! Cuor mio!"*] Italian: "Hush, hush, dear! My heart!"

759.17   the victoria] An elegant open horse-drawn carriage.

760.24   *poverini!*] Italian: poor people!

781.14–15   'Cyclopædia of Nursery Remedies.'] Probably based on *Cyclopedia of Diseases of Children: Medical and Surgical*, 2 vols., edited by John M. Keating (1889).

817.19–20   the Witch of Atlas] Cf. *The Witch of Atlas* (1824) by English poet Percy Bysshe Shelley.

823.16–17   *Vous êtes encore très bien, mon cher . . .*] French: You are still very nice, my dear . . .

839.22   Andaman islander] Aboriginal pygmy people living in a group of islands in the Bay of Bengal, India, whose first contact with outsiders occurred in the late eighteenth century.

852.40–853.1   *Baiser Défendu . . . Nouveau Péché*] French: *Forbidden Kiss . . . New Sin.*

859.21   *Willkommen, suesser Daemmerschein!*] German: Welcome, sweet Twilight! From Johann Wolfgang von Goethe's play *Faust: The First Part of the Tragedy* (1808).

862.39   baccara] Baccarat, a card game.

867.3   Mafeking Night] May 17, 1900, when public celebration broke out across Britain over the relief of the Siege of Mafeking, or Mahikeng, South Africa, a decisive British victory during the Second Boer War.

871.12–15   *All the peaks soar, . . . summit—*] From Robert Browning's 1855 poem "A Grammarian's Funeral."

876.40   "The Grammarian's Funeral"] See note 871.12–15.

882.24   Prince Aage of Denmark] Prince Aage, Count of Rosenborg (1887–1940).

882.25   'The Tatler,'] British society magazine founded in 1901.

885.13–15   phrase of Stevenson's . . . Ebb-tide,"] From *The Ebb-Tide* (1894) by Scottish novelist Robert Louis Stevenson and his stepson Lloyd Osbourne.

885.35   Gammon!] Rubbish, or nonsense.

888.12   soughings] Rushing sounds.

889.15   Marvell's "Coy Mistress"] "To His Coy Mistress," poem by English poet Andrew Marvell (1621–1678).

901.20   Longhi ball at the Fenice] A period-costume ball at the La Fenice opera house in Venice, a famous theater built in 1792.

901.20–21   Marriage of the Doge . . . Bucentaur] Every year the Doge of Venice celebrated the symbolic marriage of Venice to the sea by casting a ring from the state barge, called the Bucentaur, into the Adriatic Sea.

916.8–9   *Speise-saal*] German: dining room.

937.9   Chanel] French haute couture fashion house founded by Coco Chanel (1883–1971) in 1909.

937.36–37   *Félicitations, . . . vous savez.*] French: Congratulations, dear friend. She was pretty nice, the lady, you know.

938.13   kasha or crepella] Kasha: wool fabric in a diagonal twill weave, made from the coat of the vicuña, an endangered relative of the llama. Crepella: high-quality wool fabric in a plain weave.

940.37   Lohengrin College, Texas.] Named for Richard Wagner's opera *Lohengrin* (1850). Wagner supported theories of master race ideology.

960.2   Nouveau Luxe] See note 97.34.

974.2   Moloch] An ancient Ammonite god associated with child sacrifice.

977.22   Incunabula] The earliest examples of printed books, pamphlets, and broadsides, printed before 1501.

982.35–39   the chorus of Lemures, . . . *only*—] From Johann Wolfgang von Goethe's play *Faust: The Second Part of the Tragedy*, Act 5 (1832).

983.8   *L'addition, mademoiselle?*] French: The bill, miss?

984.19   *bosquets*] A grouping of identical trees planted in lines in a formal French garden and traditionally paved with gravel.

*This book is set in 10 point ITC Galliard, a
face designed for digital composition by Matthew Carter
and based on the sixteenth-century face Granjon. The paper
is acid-free lightweight opaque and meets the requirements for
permanence of the American National Standards Institute.
The binding material is Brillianta, a woven rayon cloth
made by Van Heek–Scholco Textielfabrieken, Holland.
Composition by Publishers' Design and Production Services, Inc.
Printing and binding by Edwards Brothers Malloy, Ann Arbor.
Designed by Bruce Campbell.*